Andrew Greeley

THREE COMPLETE NOVELS

The Passover Trilogy

ABOUT THE AUTHOR

ANDREW GREELEY is a priest of the Archdiocese of Chicago, a Professor of Sociology at the University of Arizona, a Research Associate at the National Opinion Research Center, a syndicated columnist, and the author of ten best-selling novels that have been translated into many foreign languages.

Andrew Greeley

THREE COMPLETE NOVELS

The Passover Trilogy

Thy Brother's Wife

Ascent into Hell

Lord of the Dance

A BERNARD GEIS ASSOCIATES BOOK

Avenel Books • New York

This 1987 edition is published by Avenel Books, distributed by Crown Publishers, Inc., 225 Park Avenue South, New York, New York 10003 by arrangement with Warner Books.

Printed and Bound in the United States of America

Library of Congress Cataloging-in-Publication Data

Greeley, Andrew M., 1928–
The Passover trilogy.

Contents: Thy brother's wife—Ascent into hell—
Lord of the dance.
I. Title.
PS3557.R358P28   1987   813'.54   87-989
ISBN 0-517-63170-9

h g f e d c b

CONTENTS

INTRODUCTION

As soon as humankind began to suspect that there might be a Power lurking behind the goodness it intermittently experienced as enveloping human life, it began to wonder what this Power was like. How could one deal with this (sometimes) gracious Power unless one knew what or who the Power was?

So humankind turned to metaphor: the Power was like something that humans experienced in their ordinary life. From these initial attempts at metaphor there rose all the myths and mythologies—noble and base, beautiful and savage, enlightened and degraded—that even in our time strive to explain the meaning of human life and the relationship between the human person and the Power that overshadows it.

One of the oldest—possibly *the* oldest—metaphors is fertility. Just as the reproductive energies of the various observable species give life to plants and animals and humans, so God gives life to all things. God is like fertility—perhaps, even, God is fertility. The fertility cult is perhaps the primordial human religion. Not only was God like fertility, but God must be beseeched so that the fertility of the flocks and the fields and the tribe continues. The God who gave life must sustain it.

Fertility rituals stirred deep resonance in humankind's psyche precisely because its own reproductive urges were so demanding, so devastating, so delightful, and, on occasion, so demonic. The fertility festivals, which came especially at the times of planting and harvest, often degenerated into frenzied orgies, rituals of sacred prostitution, and even rites of human sacrifice. The gods and goddesses of life frequently became devouring monsters.

Even in the early years of this century in some places in Europe, men and women made love in the fields at the time of the planting of the crops, hoping to influence the mysterious forces of nature of which they were a part.

Yahweh, the God of Prophetic Judaism, was the Lord and Master of all, utterly independent of human processes and disdainful of human attempts to force His hand through rituals. He was not merely the God of fertility, but the God who gave all life and all fertility. Hence Passover, the spring festival of the Jews, honored not the processes of fertility but God's gift of life and freedom to His people. It recalled their escape from the slavery of Egypt and their experience of Him in the desert of Sinai that forged them into a people—His people. The God of the Passover indeed ruled over the natural processes as their master and creator, but He had also entered into a personal covenant with His people.

Nonetheless, the rituals of the Passover absorbed earlier benign semitic fertility customs. The ritual of the Passover lamb can be traced back to the spring festivals of a pastoral people who offered a lamb in gratitude to its god for the fertility of the flocks. And the ritual of the unleavened bread was rooted in the later customs of an agricultural people celebrating the first harvest of the fields. The raw materials were the same, but a new overlay of meaning was attached to them, focusing the attention of the worshipers away from an earthly process as a source of life and toward a transcendent origin of all life.

In most languages the Christian spring festival and the Jewish spring festival have the same name (*Pascha, Pasch, Pasque*) and theoretically even the same date (disparities exist about when the Lunar month of Nisan begins). Jesus ate his last Passover meal (his last supper) with his followers the night before he died. He is the unleavened bread of the new covenant, the new paschal lamb. He is the new Moses leading the people out of slavery into a new life of freedom.

Again the raw materials are the same; another new overlay of meaning was added; it did not destroy that which came before but redirected it. For the early Christian Yahwehist, the new life and the new freedom are for the whole race, not just one people; for the individual person, not just the collective nation; and for the human spirit, not just the human body (themes that had been anticipated in the Judaism of the centuries immediately before the common era but which the early Christians believed had been fused into a new synthesis in their experience of the Risen Jesus).

A curious transformation of its Jewish heritage took place in Christianity in the early centuries of the Christian era, a transformation that affected the later shape of the Christian Passover. The other world religions, at least in their official and purest forms, rejected paganism, the worldly and corrupt. There was no room in Prophetic Judaism for sacred groves and sacred statues and earthly rituals. But early Catholicism, filled with the optimism it experienced in its encounter with Jesus-yet-alive and convinced that in the enfleshing of Jesus all of material creation was sanctified, experienced little difficulty in absorbing from paganism everything that seemed good, true, and beautiful—art, music, philosophy, ritual, ceremony, custom. All were, in the brave words of Saint Ignatius of Antioch, "naturally Christian."

Early Catholicism was not afraid that its Passover would be corrupted by absorbing into its ceremonies pagan spring fertility rituals. Judaism had wrested the feast of the paschal lamb and the feast of the unleavened bread away from pagans and eliminated from the rituals of these now united festivals explicit reference to plant, animal, and human fertility because it feared that the purity and transcendence of Yahweh would be corrupted by such associations. Primitive Catholicism reversed the process. Nothing could corrupt the transcendence of God, the early Catholics argued, so they reassimilated the explicit fertility references of Passover as spring festival (and Christmas as mid-winter festival) and reinterpreted these symbols in terms of their experience with the Jesus-still-alive.

The first manifestation of this new attitude in the celebration of the Christian Passover was the addition in the fourth century of the rite of fire and water. While there was justification in the Exodus story for such a change (the pillar of fire hovered over the waters of the sea), in fact the rite was a Roman spring fertility rite: the fire represented the male organ, as it does in most nature religions and in the depths of the human unconscious; and the water, the female organ. The union of the two, in a symbolism patent to anyone familiar with the ancient religious symbols of humankind, represents sexual intercourse. Moreover, the words spoken as the candle was plunged into the water left little doubt about the meaning intended: "May this candle fructify these waters." (In the new Catholic rite of the Easter vigil, the ceremony has been bowdlerized: the priest *may* plunge the candle into the waters and the text is deprived of all sexual implication. For fear of shocking the laity, the liturgical reformers have cut the heart out of a ceremony that is fifteen hundred years old.)

The meaning attached to this addition to the Christian Passover reflected the Catholic conviction (never rejected but always feared in the course of Catholic history) that human sexual passion is a mirror—in the words of the liturgy of the wedding Mass—of God's love for us. Human passion is then a pale imitation of divine passion. When Jesus returned from the dead, the preachers of early Catholic Rome told their congregants, he consummated his marriage with his bride, the Church. Those who are baptized with the candle-impregnated water are the first fruits of this loving passion.

So, to the previous overlays, Catholicism added both a new interpretation of God-as-giver-of-life in the terms of its Jesus experience and a rapproachement with pagan fertility symbols now explained in light of Jesus' description of God's passionate love for humanity.

Yet another overlay was to come in many countries as local pagan customs were assimilated, most notably in the Anglo-Saxon countries in which some of the symbols of the Teutonic spring festival were added, including the very name "Easter," which is the title of the feast of the Anglo-Saxon goddess of Dawn and Spring—"Easterne." The "east" is the region of the dawn and under the rule of the goddess of dawn, whose Roman cognate was Aurora and whose Irish cognate was Brigid (both sun goddesses), the latter promptly converted with her sun cross into a Christian saint.

Three of the fertility symbols associated with the goddess Easterne were rabbits, lilies, and eggs, symbols of the superabundance of life over death that were easily coopted for the celebration of the Christian Passover.

All four layers of symbols—lamb, bread, fire and water, and dawn—are essentially pagan. Judaism absorbed the first two explicitly (and the latter two less explicitly) and gave them a new level of meaning: Yahweh was the transcendent source of all life. Catholicism added yet another meaning: the transcendent God, by His own admission, is involved in a love affair with us for which human fertility experiences, symbols, and stories are valid metaphors.

In the Catholic Passover, Holy Thursday emphasizes the feast of the unleavened bread; Good Friday, the festival of the paschal lamb; and the Easter Vigil (on Holy Saturday evening), the celebration of the rising sun and the mixing of fire and water to produce new life.

I conceived of *The Passover Trilogy* as a meditation in story form on these three different themes of the Catholic Passover. The feast of the unleavened bread is a feast of commitment, of covenant—between God and people, and among the people to God and to one another. *Thy Brother's Wife* is a story of commitment, of a covenant renewed in the Holy Thursday liturgy between God and people, between priests and God, and between priests and people.

The feast of the paschal lamb is a feast of sacrifice, of one creature taking on the sins of the whole community. My Good Friday meditation, *Ascent into Hell*, is the story of a man who spent much of his life in the misguided crucifixion of himself, a man who discovers at last that the Lord of the Passover is not a God of rules but a God of love, a God whose forgiveness cannot be earned since it is already given. Holy Saturday, the festival of fire and water, is a feast of rebirth, of coming back from the dead, of beginning once again, themes found in *Lord of the Dance*. "Resurrection," to quote Noele Marie Brigid Farrell, the novel's heroine, "isn't supposed to be easy."

The quotes from St. John's Gospel in *Thy Brother's Wife* are taken from the "last supper" discourse of Jesus to his followers, his final covenant-making meal with his followers. The quotes in *Ascent into Hell* are from the *Tre Ore,* the three-hour Good Friday service of the pre-Vatican-Council Church.

It should be noted that in each of the stories a passionately pursuing, implacably tender woman represents God's maternal love in the Catholic spring festival of rebirth. Nora Cronin in *Thy Brother's Wife* not only experiences God laughing at her the way she laughs at her teenage daughter, but also represents God's womanly love for the men in her life. Maria McLean in *Ascent into Hell* testifies to God's love, which is not earned but given and never revoked. And the irrepressible Noele Farrell (who also symbolizes the Church) stands for a love that never quits, is never turned away, never grows weary, and never gives up.

The image of the motherhood of God is part of the Catholic tradition even if it is not always emphasized. Jesus describes himself in the seventh chapter of St. John's Gospel as a nursing mother. Catholic theologians and mystics of the Middle Ages (notably St. Anselm, St. Bernard, and Blessed Juianna) speak of God as our loving mother or urge us to drink the milk of grace from the breasts of Christ, our loving mother. Cardinal Nicholas of Cusa formalized this tradition in the early modern era when he wrote about the "coming together of opposites" in God: God, he suggested, is androgynous, combining those traits that we attribute to men and those we attribute to women. Pope John Paul I, in one of his audience talks during his brief September pontificate, said we should picture God not only as our loving father but also as our loving mother. Thirty-two percent of Americans picture God equally as mother and father or even more mother than father. As a woman once remarked to me, "If you've ever held a baby in your arms and nursed him, you know that God must love us something like the way you love the baby."

Professor Ingrid Schafer in her study of my fiction, *Eros and the Womanliness of God,* sees this theme of the womanliness of God as the fundamental "myth" (religious story) of all my novels. I believe her analysis is correct. I also believe, on the basis of mail I've received and systematic research about the readers of my novels, that, while some critics and many of my fellow priests are immune to these symbols in my stories, the ordinary reader as well as the serious scholar has no trouble understanding either the myth of human passion as a metaphor for divine passion or the myth of the motherhood of God.

All Saints, 1986   *Andrew Greeley*

Thy Brother's Wife

To the Memory

of

JAMES F. ANDREWS

DISCLAIMER

THOSE READERS WHO insist, contrary to a writer's protests, that they "know" the persons on whom the characters in a novel are based cannot be prevented, I suppose, from playing their guessing games, even when they are told that they are inevitably going to be wrong. Nonetheless, they are wrong about the characters in this book, all of whom are the products of my imagination.

In particular, Chicago has never been blessed by an Archbishop as wise as Eamon McCarthy. Moreover, the courage of Sean Cronin, however bizarre his motivations, is far greater than that of any American hierarch of whom I am aware.

—*Andrew Greeley*

Ubi caritas et amor, ibi Deus est.

"Where there is charity and love, God is always present."
(Hymn sung at the Washing of the Feet on Holy Thursday)

BOOK ONE

*I pray for them . . . for those whom thou hast given me . . .
protect them by the power of thy name that they may be one as we
are one . . . I pray thee not to take them out of the world but to
keep them from evil.*

—JOHN 17:9, 12, 15

Chapter One
1951

AFTER SUPPER ON Holy Thursday evening, Father McCabe motioned Sean Cronin
away from the black line of seminarians filing in silence out of the house chapel.
"Mistah Cronin," he snapped, "go to my office."

Sean walked down the dimly lit corridor and waited at the door of the disciplinarian's office, his heart beating rapidly. What would his father say if he were
sent home in disgrace? As far as he could remember, he hadn't violated any
rules, but in the atmosphere of suspicion and distrust that permeated Mundelein
a sudden and final decision to expel a student could be made arbitrarily on the
basis of very little evidence.

When the last of the seminarians finished reporting minor infractions of the
rules to Father McCabe—being late for class; not turning out lights at 9:45;
violating the "great silence" between lights out and the end of morning mass,
McCabe shuffled out of his office, a tall lean shaggy dog of a man, and, almost
without looking at Sean, beckoned him inside.

"Your father called earlier this afternoon," he said abruptly. "Your brother
has been reported missing in action. He led a night patrol on Heartbreak Ridge.
They ran into a Chinese outpost. He didn't come back."

Time stood still for Sean. Abstractedly he noticed the rancid cigar smoke that
filled the room, the disarray of papers and books tossed about on desks and
chairs. Fighting nausea, he groped desperately for control of his voice. "May I
phone my father?" Why had they waited hours to tell him about Paul?

"I see no point in that," said Father McCabe. "Missing isn't dead."

"On Heartbreak Ridge it probably is." Sean felt as though life were ebbing
out of his body, just as it must have from his brother's. "May I go to my room?"

"Don't pamper yourself." Father McCabe's voice took on the machine-gun
quality that was a sign of his impatience with a seminarian. "You may go to the
chapel for five minutes and then join your classmates at recreation. Others
besides the Cronin family have suffered loss in this world."

"Yes, Father," Sean said meekly, controlling his desire to smash his fists
against the five-o'clock shadow on McCabe's jaw.

In the chapel, Sean was numb. Paul Martin Cronin, the bright, brash Medal of
Honor winner who was supposed to become president of the United States one

5

day, either a prisoner or dead. What was his father feeling now? And Aunt Jane? The favorite of her two nephews gone; what light would be left in her life?

And Nora. . . . What happens to a sixteen-year-old when the man she has always known she would marry vanishes in fog and the snowdrifts of Korea?

A dry sob burst from Sean's chest. "Oh, my God! Why Paul?"

The five minutes allotted by Father McCabe were quickly spent. Sean blessed himself with holy water and left the chapel. He descended to the first floor of the building and walked down the dark hallway into the twilight of the half-hour evening smoking period.

The knot of his classmates standing on the porch of the red brick colonial style building opened to make room for him. Most of his classmates liked and even admired Sean—despite his family's wealth, his father's obvious ecclesiastical ambitions for him, and his own careful observance of the rules. They kidded him about being a "model seminarian," yet they always seemed pleased when he joined a group of them.

"What did the Moose want?" Jimmy McGuire, Sean's closest friend, used the nickname given to McCabe in recognition of his shambling walk and unkempt appearance.

Sean could not bring himself to share his grief. "He wanted to make sure that my sister is coming visiting Sunday." Sean tried to grin suggestively.

Nora was indeed the principal attraction of visiting Sundays. The seminary only grudgingly recognized the existence of family. Seminarians were not permitted to go home at Christmastime, and even on the day of their ordination their families were packed off back to Chicago while the young priests ate dinner with the faculty and the other clergy. It was the way Cardinal Mundelein wanted it; even though Cardinal Mundelein had been dead for more than a decade, it was the way things were still done.

Visiting Sunday, then, was a privilege conceded reluctantly three times each semester. The seminarian and his family—limited to three members—were permitted to visit for two hours in a classroom building with disciplinarians like McCabe watching with beady eyes to see that no contraband food or affection was exchanged.

In such an edgy and resentful environment, Nora was a sturdy spring flower who caused every male and most of the female heads to turn when she entered the large lecture hall. She was just a bit over five feet nine inches tall, with the lithe body of a woman athlete. Her flawless complexion was framed by rich auburn hair that fell halfway to a willowy waist. Nora was dazzling.

Joe Cleary, the class mimic, reenacted the now-famous scene between Sean and Father McCabe that had taken place earlier in the year, with perfect imitation of both their voices:

"Mistah Cronin, who was that *woman* who visited you today?"

"That was my Aunt Jane, Father. She's my father's sister and housekeeper."

"I don't mean her, boy; I mean the younger one. Who was that younger woman, Mistah Cronin?"

"My sister, Nora, Father. She's been here every visiting Sunday."

"That young woman has never been here before, Mistah Cronin."

"Sure she has, Father. She's just—uh, er, I mean she's grown up some since last year."

The cluster on the porch howled at Cleary's imitation of Sean.

"Is she your *blood* sister?"

"No, Father, she's my foster sister, but she's lived with us since she was a little girl."

"Then she may not visit you, Mistah Cronin. Only blood sisters are permitted. No foster sisters."

"Yes, Father. I didn't know that was one of the rules."

"Mistah Cronin, we make up the rules as we go along."

More laughter from the class. The last line, however true to character, had not really been spoken by Father McCabe.

"It's a good thing for all of us, Sean," said Jimmy McGuire, "that your father leaned on the Cardinal. What would visiting Sunday be without Nora?"

Roger Fitzgibbon, a smoothly handsome young man with black hair, pale white skin, and infinite charm, said, "I thought Nora was your adopted sister."

"Not really. My father never did get around to the formalities of adoption." Sean did not add that, as a foster daughter, Nora Riley was far more dependent on Michael James Arthur Cronin than any adopted daughter would ever be. Mike Cronin liked to keep his women dependent, however much he loved them.

At seven thirty the bell rang the end of the smoking period. Jimmy McGuire caught his eye, and Sean lagged behind the others to talk to him.

"Is it Paul?" Jimmy's freckled face was anxious in the fading twilight, the cheery leprechaun changing into the solemn good friend.

Sean nodded.

"Dead?" Jimmy asked incredulously.

Sean shook his head. "No, missing."

"While there's life there's hope, Sean. You know that," Jimmy said.

"Do I? I guess so. I'm too numb right now to know much of anything."

"Women are lucky," Jimmy said. "They can cry and get some of the pain out."

"Nora isn't crying," Sean said as they entered the building. "She's not that kind."

"A real Cronin!" said Jimmy with a soft laugh. He patted Sean on the back, expressing more sympathy with that gesture than any words could possibly have.

"A real Cronin," agreed Sean sadly, thus breaking the rule against talking in the building, a violation he decided he would not report to Father McCabe.

In his room Sean took off his cassock and hung it carefully in the closet. They did not strictly insist that you wear a cassock in your room, although it was praised as a sign of virtue if you wore it all the time. He closed one of the windows; the late March evening was turning cool. He looked out on the courtyard across the neatly landscaped grass and shrubbery, toward the gymnasium and the dark night sky beyond it. The last thing he wanted to do was turn to his desk and see the picture of Paul.

Finally he forced himself to sit on the hard wooden chair and confront his brother's handsome face, with its devil-may-care grin and mischief-filled eyes: a black Irish warrior with the looks of a movie star. "Goddamn reckless fool," he said. "Paul Martin Cronin, you won one Medal of Honor up at the Reservoir. Why did you have to be a hero a second time?"

He laid his head on his arm and began to sob. It had all come so quickly. Only nine months ago Paul had graduated from Notre Dame with a diploma he had just barely earned and a commission in the Marine Corps that was awarded only because the NROTC commanding officer chose to ignore a couple of drinking episodes. The summer had been devoted not to water skiing and girls at their Oakland Beach home but to advanced officers' training at Quantico. Then, just as Sean returned to the seminary, Paul was fighting toward the Yalu River with the Tenth Corps, commanding a platoon of Marines who were even younger than he was. Five months later he was the recipient of a Congressional Medal of Honor from Douglas MacArthur himself.

Sean raised his head from the desk. Thank God no one had seen him cry. Especially his father. Michael Cronin had set rigid standards for his sons. He had mapped out their futures with a precision rarely seen outside of a war council room. There was no allowance in his plan for any sign of weakness, in his sons or in himself. He was a man of enormous energy and charm, the kind of person people turned to watch as he walked down the street, although he was only five feet nine inches tall and already balding. His body radiated vitality, his green eyes sparkled with rapidly changing emotions. His finely shaped jaw, tilted ever so slightly in the air, promised a fight or an evening of fun, or possibly both. Women, as Sean had learned all too well, found Michael Cronin irresistible, and men delighted in his quick wit and intelligence.

Unfortunately for his children, Michael Cronin firmly believed that you raised two motherless sons by the same kind of quick, intuitive thrusts with which you assaulted an enemy position, courted a woman, or sank hundreds of thousands of dollars into pork belly futures.

Sean wondered what his father would be doing now. Calling the Pentagon for news? Cursing Truman and the Marine Corps? Damning the "Communist conspiracy" that had sent his son on "police action" in Korea?

Would Martha, the latest of his father's chic socialite friends, be around? Probably not. In times of rage and grief, Michael Cronin disdained the company of his always very discreet companions. He would doubtless be furious with the seminary for not letting him talk to Sean on the phone. On the other hand, his position had always been that seminary discipline was a good thing for someone like Sean; it would make a man out of him. So he would not push either Father McCabe or Monsignor Flaherty, the rector, to bend the rules—as he had forced them to bend the rules to permit Nora to come on visiting Sundays.

"Missing isn't dead," Sean told himself. The Moose was right about that at least. If he had any faith at all, he would resign himself to God's will and hope for the best.

Reluctantly he reached for the battered brown spiral notebook in which he was keeping a journal—an idea he had not shared with his spiritual director, who would strongly disapprove, especially since he would guess quite correctly that Sean was doing it in imitation of Thomas Merton's *Seven Storey Mountain,* a book upon which Father Meisterhorst frowned. Sean began to write.

Holy Thursday. The Last Supper. The First Mass. The beginning of the Priesthood. The night Jesus washed the feet of his disciples to show what authority meant. The night he called us not servants but friends. The night that he prayed to the Heavenly Father to protect his friends from evil. Dammit, Lord, you didn't protect Paul from evil. What will I do without him? Sometimes I don't understand him, but I love him and I don't want to lose him. I would give up the priesthood, give up anything, if he were still alive.

Why am I writing these lines? Are you out there listening, out there in the night sky with the half moon coming up over the lake?

He hesitated, his pen poised over the page.

Life seems to be nothing but heartbreaks. Mother dead. Aunt Jane the way she is. Now Paul probably gone. This Holy Thursday evening, I don't think I believe in you at all.

He tossed the pen aside and slammed the notebook closed. He must get back to work. McCabe was right. He ought not to pamper himself. He reached for the green-covered Latin philosophy textbook. He would memorize the pages he needed to know for tomorrow's recitation. He opened the philosophy book and flipped to the appropriate page. It was not required that you understood what Carolus Boyer was saying. It was only necessary that you be able to repeat it verbatim to the professor.

Suddenly he put the philosophy text aside and opened the notebook again. In large, bold print he scrawled three words: *MISSING ISN'T DEAD!*

A week later, on the visiting Sunday after Easter, Sean paid little attention to the solemn vespers in the main chapel. That afternoon he had had a conversation with his father that left him badly shaken.

It had never occurred to him that, with Mike Cronin's obsession about the family, it would be Sean's obligation to keep the Cronin name alive if anything ever happened to Paul. But after visiting hours, as Mike was getting into his limousine, he had turned to his son and said, "So it's understood that if Paul doesn't come back, you'll leave the seminary?"

Sean had been stunned. "Paul will come back," he said, hoping he sounded confident. "We have to believe that."

"Well, if he doesn't come back, we have to keep the family going."

That was the way it was with Michael Cronin. Decisions were made as though there had been discussion and consultation and agreement from everyone, but in fact the decisions were his and there was no appeal. Sean had always been aware that it was only luck that his desire to become a priest had corresponded with his father's wishes.

Later, at the Benediction after the vespers, the thought came to Sean that if Paul were dead he would also have to marry Nora. She had been brought into the Cronin family after the war, not only because her father, Edward Riley, had been General Cronin's aide on Leyte Island, but because the Rileys were a family with "good blood." She had been selected to bear the children who would keep the Cronin line alive. If Paul were dead, those children would be Sean's.

As the four hundred male voices sang enthusiastically "Holy God, we praise thy name," at the end of Benediction, Sean decided that the thought of Nora Riley as his wife and the mother of his children was disconcerting perhaps but not entirely unpleasant.

Chapter Two
1938–1950

IT WAS DURING the summer of 1938 that Michael Cronin decided that his elder son, Paul, was to become president of the United States and that his younger son, Sean, was to become a priest and "probably a cardinal." The decision was made spontaneously, without reflection. Nonetheless, it was permanent and irrevocable.

Their mother, whom Sean could remember only as a cloud of golden gentleness, had died four years before in an auto accident. Aunt Jane, his father's maiden elder sister who now lived with them, was watching the seven- and nine-year-old boys as they played in the sand in front of their Oakland Beach home. The sprawling house was rooted in concrete high above the lakeshore. Michael Cronin had built it for his bride at the time of their marriage, in 1928, just when he was beginning to take his money out of the stock market because "there were too many poor people owning stock." The house was called "Glendore," after the home of his ancestors in West Cork, and, although the house on Glenwood Drive in Chicago was his official residence, Michael Cronin considered Glendore his real home.

Bob Elson had finished describing another victory for the Cubs in the late-season pennant drive sparked by their new manager, Gabby Hartnett. The radio on the sundeck just above the beach was playing "You Must've Been a Beautiful Baby," while Mike and two of his business associates, Ed Connaire and Marty Hoffman, discussed the possibility of purchasing land where they were certain real-estate development would shortly begin. "If there's a war," Mike said, "the people who own the land around Chicago are going to become rich overnight."

"Is the idea of a war to defend the country or help your business?" Joan Gordon asked with a grin. She was a "friend" of Mike's from New York, a pretty woman who looked dainty in a swimsuit that had never been touched by water. The three men laughed hoarsely, and there was the sound of popping beer bottles as Mike opened another round.

It was at that moment that Paul, who had been watching the white breakers rushing up on the beach, made an impulsive dash into the lake. Sean trailed after him. Each wave was bigger than its predecessor, and one knocked Paul off his feet. The undertow, surprisingly strong for the lake, pulled him out into the churning waves.

With no awareness of what he was doing, Sean plunged into the lake after his brother. Paul lashed out at him frantically, terrified by the strength of the waves and unable to catch his breath before the next surge of water filled his mouth. One of Paul's flailing blows landed on Sean's jaw. Dazed and confused, he too slipped under the water and into the overpowering clutch of the undertow. A wall of white crashed around his head.

Sean remembered the words of his swimming instructor and permitted the water to pull him off the sand bottom. He floated free of the undertow, broke the surface of the lake, and searched desperately for his brother.

Paul was only a few feet away, screaming with fear. Back on the beach, no one, including Aunt Jane, seemed to notice the drama being enacted by the two boys. Still sputtering and choking, Sean dove back into the waves, broke water once, then plunged again toward his brother, who had sunk under the surface and was now rapidly drifting out beyond the protective sandbar.

Sean thought he had lost Paul. He was tempted to turn away to save his own life when, miraculously, it seemed, he caught sight of a frantically kicking leg. He dived once again, grabbed his brother around the chest, and pulled him toward shore just as the swimming instructor had recommended. This time Paul came peacefully enough.

They had almost made it to the beach when a gigantic breaker smashed against their backs, tumbling both of them into the waves again. Sean hit his head against the bottom, twirled over once, then struggled to his feet. Terrified and unable to move, Paul clung to him.

"Help," he whispered, almost breathless. "Help me, Sean." Sean was able to keep his balance and pull Paul back toward the shore. Choked with water, his feet slipping in the undertow, he struggled, still dragging his brother, until they were safe on the hot sand.

When Aunt Jane reached them, she pulled Paul, always her favorite, out of Sean's grasp and hugged him protectively.

"Paul, you brave, brave little thing," she wailed. "You risked your life to save that foolish child."

Sean never did know whether his father believed Aunt Jane's version of the story, although Mrs. Gordon, who enveloped him in her arms and pressed him against her soft, sweet-smelling body, whispered in his ear, "I saw what really happened."

He nestled against her, still breathing heavily. "Please don't tell," he begged. He knew instinctively that it was important to his brother to be considered heroic.

After dinner that night, before the two boys were sent to bed, Ed Connaire's wife, Margie, asked them, "What were you thinking about out there in the water?"

"I was praying to God to help me," said Sean, who had made his First Communion a few months before.

"I wasn't thinking anything. I was trying to get out of the water," said Paul.

"It sounds like you have a religious leader and a political leader here," said Marty Hoffman, rubbing the perspiration off his bald head as he sipped yet another beer.

"A president and a cardinal!" Michael Cronin exclaimed.

And that was that.

Joan Gordon, naked from her shower, peered through the drapes covering the French windows. The sun had set and there was a thin gray haze lingering over the lake.

She made certain that the latch on the window to the balcony was open. Surely Mike would come tonight, despite his sister's disapproval. It was time, past time. He had not brought her from Chicago merely to sit on the beach and listen to his strange, crude friends talk of money.

In the brief years of her widowhood she had not lacked for wealthy suitors; none, however, were so fascinating as Mike. She was both attracted to and frightened by his intense vitality and his dancing green eyes. She sighed and released the drape. Was he expecting her to come to him? He was a difficult man to understand.

She removed the featherweight rose gown from the bed and slid it over her shoulders. Then she slipped on the thin matching robe and knotted it loosely.

As she brushed her short blond hair with indifferent vigor, she noted again how much the face in the mirror looked like that of his late wife's, whose portrait hung over the fireplace. Never mentioned, Mary Eileen Morrisey Cronin was still a palpable presence in this lakeside mansion, and not merely in the face of her younger son, the gentle little boy with the soft brown eyes who had begged her to hide his heroism.

The French window opened and Mike entered, wearing a blue silk robe and carrying a bottle of champagne and two glasses. Uneasy, but preserving her outward calm, Joan Gordon continued to brush her hair. "You were joking about your sons this afternoon, weren't you?"

He was struggling with the cork on the champagne bottle. "About one being cardinal and the other president? No, I think it's a good idea. A word here, a word there, at this time in the boys' lives, will plant the seed. Get them competing with each other to see who moves up faster. Good for them." The cork popped, and a little bit of the bubbly drink flowed out of the bottle. Deftly Mike caught it in one of the champagne glasses.

"Your family is important to you, isn't it?"

"Yes, it is." He handed her the glass.

"And if Sean doesn't want to be a priest and Paul doesn't want to be a politician?"

He shrugged. "Children become what their parents want them to become. Sean and Paul will do what I want them to do. They'll have to work hard, of course, and do their part"—he poured a glass for himself—"but I'll buy their way around any obstacles."

"Money can buy anything?" She was alarmed by the cold gleam in his eye.

"Just about." Dismissing his sons abruptly, he said, "I only drink champagne with naked women." He took the glass from her hands and covered her lips with a long, searching kiss. Then, while she tried to recover her breath, he brushed aside her robe and gently pulled the gown from her shoulders. His hands were strong, yet sensitive. "Now you're really worth toasting." He drained the glass and began to kiss her again. He led her to the bed. She was paralyzed by desire as his mouth moved against her flesh. Then his teeth began to rip at her. She moaned, not with pain, since he was not hurting her.

Just as he entered her, he said in triumph, "You're mine, you know."

She knew it was true.

Mike, complacent in his male power, had watched the sun come up from Joan Gordon's balcony overlooking the lake. Then he returned to his room to dress for breakfast. Pansy, the cook, was delighted by his order for orange juice, bacon and eggs, and toast. Normally he drank only coffee in the morning.

He drained his second glass of orange juice and dug into the bacon. It had been a good night. Joan Gordon was an excellent sexual partner, infinitely more responsive than Mary Eileen had ever been. He frowned at the thought of his wife. Why did she come to his mind so often after a night of lovemaking?

Jane entered the room, her lean face grimmer than ever. She sat down at the table across from him. Her plate contained one poached egg, all she ever allowed herself for breakfast. "You were in that woman's bedroom last night," she accused him.

"Jane, how can you be so deadly dull at this hour on a lovely summer morning?"

"I will not have you carrying on in this house. We must maintain standards. If you insist on bringing your women here, I demand that you at least behave with common decency."

Mike suddenly realized how much Jane had changed in the four years since she had come to care for the boys. What little spark there had been in her had been replaced by a sour, unbending old maid. "And if I don't?"

Ignoring the threat in his voice, Jane replied, "I'll tell Jane Gordon why you can never marry her or any other woman. Your precious secret will be out in the open, and your sons will be exposed for what they are—especially Sean."

Mike felt his heart sink. The bloom had quickly worn off the day. "What do you know about that?"

"Do you think you solved everything when you pensioned off your chauffeur and sent him back to Ireland? He told me everything before he left. And you won't be able to pension me."

"You're skating on thin ice, Jane," he warned her.

She laughed, an empty, contemptuous sound. "You always were a blowhard, Mickey. I'm not afraid of you."

Mike knew that Jane was not afraid of him. But he also knew that she would never do anything to jeopardize the security of the life he offered her. Without his family, she had no one. And where else could she go to indulge her habit of secret drinking? "I think we have a standoff, Jane," he said.

He picked up his fork and piled it high with scrambled eggs. Perhaps it would be a good day after all.

On a cold Easter Sunday in 1942, after the family had gone to Easter mass in tiny Notre Dame Church in Oakland Beach, and after the noon meal, Aunt Jane was instructed to take the two boys to a movie at the Marquette Theater in Michigan City. She pretended to be offended by the carryings-on of the Marx Brothers, but Sean noted with satisfaction that she laughed as loudly as anyone else in the theater.

Sean had almost not been allowed to go to the movies because he had ripped his trousers in a fight the day before. Three boys from Michigan City had taunted him about his elegant clothing while he waited patiently for the Cronin Packard to turn the corner onto Lake View Drive. Sean had refused to fight them until two of them grabbed his arms and the third hit him in the stomach. Although they were bigger than he was, he broke free, chose the weakest of the attackers, and began to pummel the boy. Just then Paul arrived on the scene. When Sean and Paul were through, the three assailants went home weeping, cursing and promising vengeance.

"Not bad, kid," Paul said, ruffling his brother's hair. "For an eleven-year-old, you do pretty well."

"We ought to fight other kids more often instead of fighting each other," Sean agreed.

"Why not do both?" Paul laughed.

Although he was only eighteen months older, Paul was already half a head taller and two grades ahead of Sean in school—next year he would graduate from St. Titus and enroll, like his father before him, at Mt. Carmel. Paul did not permit Sean to forget for a moment that he was the older and the bigger and the more advanced of the two, although his manner of lording it over "little brother" was always genial.

When they returned from the movie, the reason their father wanted them out of the house became clear. While they were immersed in the Marx Brothers' antics, Michael Cronin had been readying himself for overseas duty.

The sky was a grim and brutal gray as Mike, resplendent in his colonel's uniform, told his sons that his unit had been called to active duty and bid them an emotional farewell. ''In case I don't come back, I want you to remember how important your family is,'' Mike said. ''Since your great-grandfather migrated here as a penniless farm worker, we have fought to establish the Cronin name. We were here in Chicago before Marshall Field or Potter Palmer. When my father lost his fortune in 1917, I had to leave school and forget my dream of Notre Dame and go to work. I remember hearing a man say in back of St. Bernard's Church on a Sunday morning, 'We watched 'em go up and now we watch 'em go down.' '' There was rare pain in Mike's damp green eyes. ''By the time I was twenty-five I had earned back the money my father lost—I showed them all that quality pays off. Do you understand that, Paul and Sean? There's nothing more important than family.''

Both boys nodded.

''If I don't come back,'' Mike continued, ''Paul, you're going into politics, and Sean, you're going into the Church.''

''You bet, Dad,'' Paul said absently, not paying any more attention to his father's personal catechism than he usually did.

''Well, then, men,'' Mike said, ''you have your orders and you know what has to be done.''

Sean was certain that his father wanted to embrace them but didn't know how. The farewell ended with Mike saying, ''Get along now and eat your dinner before it gets cold. I'll have Jeremy drive me back to Chicago.''

After Sean cried himself to sleep that night, he dreamed of his mother as he often did, a soft golden radiance. When he awoke, he was not sure for a moment whether she was alive or dead. Then, fully awake, he realized sadly that she was indeed dead.

Nora Riley was an unhappy, terrified ten-year-old when Michael Cronin visited her at Angel Guardian orphanage in the autumn of 1945. Nine years of her life had been warm and peaceful: affectionate parents, a sweet young brother, a gaily decorated apartment in the Brainard district on the South Side of Chicago. Then a telegram from the War Department telling of her father's death on Leyte, followed a month later by a fire from a lighted cigarette in the apartment next door that took the lives of her mother and baby brother, and Nora Riley was a numb, grief-stricken orphan.

The doctors at the orphanage talked to her, shook their heads, and told the nuns that eventually the ''poor thing'' would be all right. Nora knew that too. However, ''eventually'' seemed a long time away, and now she was lonely and frightened.

''You look like your mother. Her eyes,'' said General Cronin when he met Nora. His own hard eyes watched her carefully. Her father had served with General Cronin. His last letter home, which her mother read and reread through grief-stricken tears, had praised General Cronin's bravery and goodness.

''Yes, sir,'' she said. But Mother had been pretty, and Nora knew that she was too tall and too thin.

''Do you like it here?''

"No, sir," she replied honestly. "I don't."

General Cronin considered for a moment. "Would you like to come and live with my family?" he asked.

Nora decided that nothing could be worse than the orphanage. "All right, sir."

"Don't call me sir," he ordered. "Call me Uncle Mike."

"Yes, sir." She found herself grinning. "Yes, sir, Uncle Mike."

General Cronin laughed and kissed her.

The Cronin house on Glenwood Drive seemed like a castle on a hill, filled with friendly servants, a room of her own, and neighborhood kids who welcomed her enthusiastically. There was much less enthusiasm from Aunt Jane.

"Why did you bring her here, Michael?" Jane demanded on Nora's first day in her new home. "We have enough trouble keeping Paul and Sean out of mischief."

"I brought her home because she's Edward and Kathy's daughter, and because I wanted to," the General said calmly.

"I don't want another woman in my house," Aunt Jane said petulantly.

"She's a child, not a woman," he replied. "And she's here to stay."

Aunt Jane was silent for a moment. Then, as though admitting defeat, she said, "The child has bad teeth. We'll have to get her to an orthodontist at once."

Paul Cronin, a sixteen-year-old football star at St. Ignatius for whom Nora instantly developed a worshipful crush, hardly acknowledged her existence. His younger brother, Sean, a freshman at Quigley Seminary, who had the kindest smile Nora had ever seen, took her under his wing and explained to her who all the servants were and how to behave with them. He introduced her to the neighbors. He even walked her over to St. Titus and talked about her to the Mother Superior, a cheerful woman in black and white Dominican habit.

"Thank you, Sean," Nora said when they walked back down the drive, lined with enormous oak trees turning red and gold in the autumn sunlight. "Are you my brother now?" A little bit of warmth had slipped through the tundra in Nora Riley's young soul.

"Kind of half brother, half friend. Is that all right?"

"Great," she assented. "Perfect."

The war between Aunt Jane and Nora raged on whenever Mike was not present. It reached fever pitch by Christmas. Sean's attempts at making peace were ignored by both combatants. Aunt Jane harassed Nora about everything from the hem length on her school uniform to her table manners. Nora responded with stubborn silence. If she cried over the persecution, it was in the privacy of her room.

Christmas-tree decoration time brought the contest to a head. Normally, Sean decorated the tree with the assistance of Pansy and Erithea, the cook and the maid. It was always a huge tree, filling the front of their parlor, because his father remembered the days "before the war"—he meant the first war—when his family could afford only a tabletop tree.

After Aunt Jane discovered that Nora was going to help with the decorations, she insisted on participating for the first time that Sean could remember. Despite the Christmas music playing on their large console Philco radio, Aunt Jane had little of the Christmas spirit. Every ornament that Nora put on the tree, every string of tinsel she draped across a branch had to be changed, usually with a protest about clumsiness that must have been inherited from her parents.

Sean was fascinated by the bony little waif who had transformed their house by her slow smile and piercing blue eyes. He had learned her moods as he learned the moods of everyone he was close to, instinctively and without paying conscious attention to the process. He saw the thunderclouds building up in her eyes. Nervously, he suggested, "Maybe we ought to stop for the day. I have to go over to Titus for Midnight Mass practice. Father—"

Jane was not listening. "Can't you see that's the wrong place for the angel?" She pulled the ornament out of Nora's hand. "Put it here." The angel, a prize Michael Cronin had brought home from France, fell from Jane's hand and crashed on the floor. "You clumsy little fool!" She slapped Nora's face. "You've broken my brother's angel!"

Lightning leaped from Nora's eyes, but she said nothing.

"That's enough, Aunt Jane." Sean grabbed her wrist. He almost felt sorry for his poor lonely aunt and her silent drinking. He could smell the bourbon on her breath.

"Neither one of you have any right to be in this house," Jane hissed and fled from the parlor.

Nora, her foot on the staircase, whirled. Hands on her thin little hips, she opened her mouth as if to say something. She hesitated, then ran up the stairs.

Later, Sean knocked on the door of her room. She was huddled over the desk, weeping silently. "So you do cry."

She nodded but did not move from the desk.

He sat beside her and touched her shoulder reassuringly. "It's all right, Nora. Aunt Jane does that to everyone."

"What did she mean about neither one of us belonging here?"

"I'm not sure. She says crazy things. It's the drinking. Some sort of batty notion that I'm my mother's son and Paul is my father's son."

"That *is* odd." Nora's tearstained face turned toward him. "Whatever could she mean by that?"

"Probably that I look so much like my mother. It doesn't matter." Yet it did matter. Deep down inside, Jane's mysterious comment troubled Sean greatly.

After Michael Cronin returned from the war in 1945 with a Distinguished Service Cross, two Purple Hearts, and a matching pair of Silver Stars, he had hurled himself back into Cronin Enterprises as though he were trying to make up for the lost years. His office continued to be located in a small suite in the Field Building, with four associates and a handful of clerks and secretaries providing all the staff needed for his mysterious local, national, and international deals.

Over the next few years his sons saw him only a little more than they had when he was in the Philippines, sometimes at Oakland Beach in the company of one of the beautifully turned-out women friends who still visited him there, and sometimes at the house on Glenwood Drive, where the friends were never admitted.

One evening, when Sean had finished his third year at Quigley Seminary and Paul his freshman year at Notre Dame, the family was gathered in the parlor at Glendore. The French windows were opened and the curtains stirred in the light breeze that came off the lake. Sean was reading and Paul was shocking Aunt Jane with his description of the movie *The Lost Weekend,* which he had seen the night before with his current girl friend, a certain Caroline Flaherty, whom his father had dismissed as "not being from a good family."

Mike, hands jammed in the pockets of his white flannel trousers, paced the balcony like a captain on the bridge of his ship. He seemed tired and older than his forty-eight years. There were lines in his face that had not been there the year before, and his eyes had lost some of their vitality.

"Where's Nora?" he asked, as though only then realizing she was not at home.

"Taking a golf lesson," Sean said. "The pro at Long Beach Country Club says she may break a hundred before the summer is over."

"The kid has good blood, but she's a mess. Too tall, too thin. In a couple of years I'll have to send her to modeling school. Maybe they can teach her to stand up straight. You can't marry a girl with bad posture, can you, Paul?"

Sean was startled. This was the first he had heard of a marriage between Nora and Paul. Like all his father's other decisions, it was proclaimed as something that had already been discussed and settled.

"Certainly not," said Paul, with his customary good humor. "Make her stand up straight."

Paul didn't think his father was serious. Sean was not so sure. "She has pretty eyes," he commented.

"You're supposed to be a seminarian. You shouldn't be looking at girls' eyes." Mike, who adored his foster child, chuckled at the compliment.

"I don't think they're pretty at all." Aunt Jane entered the discussion with a predictably unflattering remark, but Mike paid no attention to it. Indeed, it often seemed he had not heard anything that Aunt Jane said in the last five years.

In the background there was the sound of a slamming door and footsteps running up the stairs.

"Hi!" Nora Riley, the subject of their conversation, entered the parlor. She was still tall and skinny, but she had deep penetrating blue eyes that demanded your attention and the beginnings of what might one day be a pretty face.

"What did you shoot, punk?" Sean asked her.

"Ninety-eight," she said. "Next summer I'll beat you." There was a faint trace of a grin.

"No more golf lessons for you, young lady. It's not dignified. I don't want to see you with those clubs again." The command was harsh but the tone was affectionate, almost caressing.

"My mother played golf, Uncle Mike," Nora said softly.

Michael Cronin grunted in disapproval. Nonetheless, the golf lessons continued.

The summer of 1948 was the best summer yet for Sean Cronin. His relationship with Paul had changed. The rivalry and competitiveness were there, but now Paul viewed him as an ally and even as a friend. They were tennis and golf partners and an enthusiastic, if as yet inexperienced, sailing crew. Paul was generous in his praise of Sean's skills, though usually the praise cast Sean in the role of the dutiful second-in-command.

Being second-in-command on the *Mary Eileen* or the tennis court didn't bother Sean. To be respected by his handsome, popular brother, and to be admitted to his circle of friends, was more than enough.

One day Sean returned in the early afternoon to the house overlooking the lake. He had been thoroughly drubbed by Nora in their eighteen-hole golf match and, after a six and five defeat, he was not ready to risk himself in another eighteen holes.

He moved to the deck chair on the balcony, nodding over a copy of *A Bell for Adano*. It was one of those humid summer days on the shore of Lake Michigan, with big thunderheads building up in the sky.

He was stirred from his sleeplike reverie by the sound of a woman pleading. "No. Please don't. Oh, no . . . don't!"

Who was the woman? he asked himself. Aunt Jane had gone to Chicago on one of her shopping expeditions. Nora was still at the club. The Packard was in the driveway, which meant that his father was in the house—alone, Sean had thought. He stirred in his chair. The French window next to him led into his father's study. The window was open and the drapes were not completely drawn. The scent of the roses that decorated the study teased his nostrils. Still in his reverie, Sean glanced lazily into the study.

His father was in the den with Mrs. Conway, a friend from Baltimore who had come to visit him frequently that summer. Mike was none too gently pulling off her clothing, despite what seemed to Sean to be her adamant resistance.

Sean watched, fascinated. He knew he shouldn't be there, but he couldn't pull himself away. Anyway, if he attempted to move, his father might hear him and that would be even worse.

"Take off your slip, woman," his father ordered, though in a pleasant tone of voice. "I can't do everything myself."

Mrs. Conway quickly obeyed. A pretty platinum blonde in her late thirties, she was breathtaking with her clothes off. Mike took off his own clothes. Then he pulled her to him and bent her over backward. He assaulted the front of her body with lingering, hungry kisses.

Mike seemed harsh, even brutal with her, but at the same time delicate and gentle. Her cries and moans turned from protest to pleasure. She pleaded with him at first to stop, then to continue, and finally to finish.

To Sean's transfixed eyes, the scene was horrifying, frightening, compelling, and beautiful. So that's what it was like. . . .

Most beautiful of all was the tenderness with which his father and Mrs. Conway caressed each other after their passions had found fulfillment.

At dinner that night, Mrs. Conway glowed with pleasure. No wonder she comes to Oakland Beach so often, thought Sean. His father seemed both self-satisfied and sad.

"There's a different set of rules for men like Dad," Paul said. He was floating on his back above the sandbar, fifty yards off the beach. "If he needs a woman after he's worked himself into exhaustion for a month to bring off a deal, why shouldn't he have one? He's discreet about it and tasteful in his choice of women. What's wrong with it?"

"How important do you have to be to get a dispensation from the moral law?"

"That stuff's fine for the seminary"—Paul sniffed contemptuously—"but it doesn't apply in the real world."

"He seems so straitlaced about everything else." Sean's toes just barely touched the sandbar six feet beneath the placid surface of the lake.

"Women are meant to be enjoyed," Paul said confidently. "Unless, of course, you're going to be a priest. Besides, you take him too seriously. He's a great man, but half of what he says is bullshit. . . . Come on, let's swim back to the beach. That mist drifting down the shore will fog everything in.''

Paul rarely worried about danger and certainly not about ground fog on the beach. He obviously didn't want to discuss the subject.

They swam ashore; Sean with ease and Paul heavily, at the end, because of too much beer and too many cigarettes. As they were drying themselves, shivering in the chill mist, Sean pushed the point. ''What do you mean, not take Dad seriously?''

''Oh, hell, Sean.'' Paul was impatient. ''I don't pay attention to ninety percent of what he says. Nora doesn't take him seriously either. Even Aunt Jane doesn't, half the time. You're the only one who believes all his bullshit. Hell, I bet you really expect to be archbishop of Chicago.'' There was an edge of contempt in Paul's voice.

Sean felt his face grow warm. ''It wouldn't be right to deliberately seek it,'' he said firmly. ''But the Church needs good leadership, and I'll try to do the best job I can. I'm probably never going to be a cardinal, but I wouldn't turn it down.''

''Come on, little brother, let's get back to the house; I need a beer.'' Paul patted him patronizingly on the head. ''You should be the favorite, not me. You're the only one in the family who's like him. I wouldn't be surprised if you become a cardinal long before I'm even a United States senator.'' Now Paul's laughter was self-mocking. ''Can you imagine that—Senator Paul Martin Cronin!''

Chapter Three
1951

SEAN CRONIN SLUMPED over the wheel of his car, too weak for the moment to drag himself out of the battered 1948 Chevy and then climb the stairs to Glendore. Working at the Maryville Orphanage for most of the summer had been a disaster. Nagging worry about Paul was never far from his mind. The pressure from his father to leave the seminary weighed heavily on him. And he did not look forward to spending two weeks on the shores of Lake Michigan. During the past week Aunt Jane had been even more frequently ''under the weather,'' and Nora's giddy teenage crowd rasped on his nerves.

His father's business trips to the Middle East produced mixed feelings in Sean. For all his peculiarities Sean missed Mike Cronin. On the other hand, the Fourth of July weekend this year had been a disaster. Not only was there tension between his father and Mrs. Conway, a tension that his father never before permitted in his friendships, but the strain of long hours of work, compulsive business travel, and reckless living were taking their toll, though he was only fifty-one years old. When he was in full flush of energy and enthusiasm, he seemed ten years younger; yet on the few occasions when he was in temporary repose, he looked ten years older.

If Mary Eileen Cronin had lived, perhaps she could have warned her husband that the martinis and the Scotch were exacting a terrible toll. For a moment, Sean thought of his mother. He could only picture her as a young woman a few years older than he now was. He still had dreams in which she was alive, dreams which were so powerful that it took him several minutes of wakefulness to dismiss them as a childhood wish. He had read somewhere in a psychology book that such dreams about a dead parent could last all one's life. He hoped they would; they were wonderful dreams.

With a sigh, Sean pushed open the car door and walked up the steps to the main level of the house.

Nora was in the parlor with Maggie Martin, watching Milton Berle on the television set. Both were dressed in their summer uniforms, Bermuda shorts and cotton shirts. Nora's shirt was her usual unspectacular white, Maggie's an eye-stopping pink. A half foot shorter than Nora, Maggie was a pretty sixteen-year-old with long blond hair and a tendency to giggle.

"Hi, Sean," she said. "Nice to see you again." She fluttered her eyelids.

"Good evening, Maggie," he replied flatly and retreated to a corner of the room, far from the two teenagers. He turned on the reading light and buried himself in a chair with Graham Greene's *The End of the Affair*. Over the top edge of the book he saw a brief wry smile from Nora.

Berle's string of witticisms eventually ended and, even more blessedly, Maggie bounced out of the house in a crescendo of giggles.

"She's really okay," Nora said in defense of her friend. "She just doesn't know how to act when you're around."

"Hmmmmm."

"Mind if I sit down and read with you?"

"If you want," said Sean, thinking how improbable was the "affair" about which Graham Greene was writing. Nora curled up on the sofa opposite him and took a book off the coffee table. *From Here to Eternity*. Aunt Jane certainly was slipping if Nora was permitted to read such "trash."

"How's Aunt Jane?"

Nora did not look up. "Very much under the weather."

Nora's auburn hair was tied behind her head in a long ponytail, revealing the flawless bones of her face and head. Her eyes caught his watching her and he quickly turned away.

"And when will Dad be home again?" Sean asked after a pause.

"Labor Day weekend, if he finishes his business with the sheikhs."

"And Mrs. Conway?"

"That's over. They had a terrible row. She wanted marriage. Uncle Mike is only buying oil this year, not wives."

"She seemed like a nice woman. Too bad."

Nora closed her book, a finger between the pages, and regarded him coolly, almost dispassionately. "You look gray, Sean."

"The orphanage was a bad experience," he said, feeling the emotion seeping out of him. "They're not really orphans, of course, mostly kids from broken homes. Lonely, desperate for attention and love. They cling to you almost as though they're afraid you're going to let them down the way their parents did." He sighed in frustration. "I worked so hard with those kids that I was too tired to sleep at night, and none of it did a damn bit of good. In the end, I had to leave them the way everyone always has."

"Are we all that different, Sean?" she asked. "We're as hungry for love as they are, maybe more so. The only reason we don't cling is—well, how do you cling to people like Uncle Mike or Aunt Jane? When Mrs. Conway was here, I wanted to be with her all the time. That's the same thing as clinging."

Sean sighed. "You're a very remarkable sixteen-year-old, Nora," he said. "No, I don't like the way that sounds. You're a very remarkable woman."

Nora leaned forward and touched his face with amazingly tender fingers. Time stood still. For a moment it seemed that the peace would never end. Then she broke the spell of the magic moment and said, with a laugh, "*Young* woman!"

Sean was confused by his reaction to her nearness. You're a seminarian, he told himself. You're going to be a priest. You shouldn't feel this way about a girl. He retrieved *The End of the Affair*. He did not want to see the light in her eyes.

Jimmy McGuire and Sean Cronin sat on the edge of the raft watching the sun sink toward the horizon through the haze of Chicago.

"Sets earlier every day, doesn't it?" said Sean.

"They call that the changing of the seasons," replied Jimmy. "We morose Irish can make of it whatever we want, so long as we remember that after Christmas the days get longer again."

Sean's slim red-haired friend from the seminary was at Oakland Beach for a long weekend. His visit provided a welcome interlude, breaking the routine.

"Your golf game left a lot to be desired today," Sean said accusingly.

Jimmy kicked at the waters of the lake. "My God, how could anyone play a good game of golf with Nora around? I'm sorry, I know she's your sister, but a body like hers ought to be barred from the golf course."

Sean laughed. "She's not really my sister. And I'll make her wear a very loose shirt tomorrow."

"Don't you dare!" Jimmy exclaimed.

"Then don't blame me if she beats you tomorrow as badly as she beat you today."

"Losing to Nora"—Jimmy grinned mischievously—"is more fun than beating anyone else. And I know she's not your real sister, but if she isn't a sister, what is she to you?"

Such shifts from the facetious to the dead serious were characteristic of Jimmy McGuire.

"I don't really know," Sean said slowly.

"Don't you think you ought to find out?"

"I guess I'm trying to," Sean said. He was alarmed that the intensity of his feeling for Nora was so obvious.

"You're in very deep waters, Sean. If you're not careful, you and Nora are going to get hurt."

"I'll never hurt Nora," he said stubbornly. "Never."

"Excuse my skepticism," said Jimmy. "I don't see how you can possibly avoid hurting her."

Nora rested her head on the leather car upholstery as they watched *An American in Paris* on the drive-in movie screen. In the back seat of the Chevy there were smothered sighs from Maggie Martin and Tom Shields. Nora couldn't understand how Maggie could neck with so many different boys. Poor Maggie. Everyone liked her, she was the life of the parties at which Nora stood shyly on the fringes. Yet Maggie did not like herself and would turn unpredictably petulant just when she had everyone's attention and affection.

Her date, Tom Shields, was a tall thin young man with limp brown hair, destined to become a doctor like his father, Roy, the Cronin family doctor and longtime friend. Tom was too serious for fun-loving Maggie. He had gone to Quigley Seminary with Sean and would graduate from Notre Dame next year. He was as interested in conversation as necking, but Maggie didn't think she was smart enough to talk seriously. So they necked instead.

Nora was not greatly concerned about the electricity that seemed to be leaping back and forth between her and Sean. The summer would soon be over and Sean would return to the seminary. Confident that Paul was still alive, she did not take seriously Uncle Mike's plan that Sean should leave the seminary and, in a few years, marry her. She had to admit to herself, though, that the thought of being Sean's wife was an interesting one.

Nora looked at Sean out of the corner of her eye. The movie was ending and he was removing the sound box from the car door. He was not strikingly handsome like Paul, but at six feet one, with a strong trim body, soft warm eyes, neat blond hair, and a cleanly carved face, Sean was more than merely good-looking— and when he looked sad your heart ached and you would do absolutely anything to bring back the magic smile. It occurred to Nora that she was glad she would never have to make a choice between the two brothers.

They dropped Maggie and Tom at Maggie's house and returned home. It was an unusually hot night, and Sean proposed a walk on the beach. Nora was delighted.

"I think Tom's hooked," Sean said as they arrived at the bottom of the stairs on the sundeck. "He's always been sweet on that little baggage, and she lets him do whatever he wants."

"Baggage is not a nice word," said Nora, kicking off her loafers. "And he does the things she wants him to do. They're both hooked." She felt the warm sand seep around her toes.

Then, they were in each other's arms, kissing, at first awkwardly, hesitantly, and then fiercely.

"Sweeter than wine?" Nora asked after a few minutes, quoting one of the hit songs of the summer to cover her confusion.

"Sweeter than the finest German *Eiswein*," Sean said hoarsely. He stroked the firm muscles of her back.

"Too warm for this clinging to each other," she said into his chest.

"I guess so." He felt as though they would stand there, holding each other, ankle deep in the sand of Oakland Beach, for the rest of eternity.

He tilted her chin up and brought his lips down to meet hers. His kisses became more demanding. His hands followed the contours of her body.

"Very, very nice, Sean," she murmured through the haze into which she was sinking. "Too nice, I think."

"Too nice," Sean agreed heavily, pulling back from her. "I . . . I hope you're not angry?"

"Of course I'm not angry," she said, trying to sound relaxed. "It's summer and we're young, so we must cling to each other while we still can."

Nora Riley considered the young woman opposite her in the mirror, as she applied her eye makeup exactly the way she had been taught in modeling school. Not bad, she told herself.

When her instructor had told her that she had the body of a Greek goddess and the face of a Titian madonna, Nora had laughed. Then she had gone home and looked at herself in the mirror. She was astonished to find that the description was not altogether inaccurate. She had never expected to be anything more than plain.

"Getting ready for the country club dance?" Uncle Mike burst into her room, smiling cheerfully. "I don't approve of all that makeup."

"Then you wasted your money sending me to modeling school," she said, "because I'm doing exactly what they taught me."

"Sean has to leave the seminary," he said, in his direct manner. "Now that Paul's gone, he has to assume responsibility of the second-in-command."

"I keep telling you"—Nora tried to keep the hand with her makeup brush steady—"that Paul isn't dead."

"Sure he's dead," said Mike harshly. "Sean is only kidding himself by going back to the seminary this year. I can tell that he's sweet on you, and you can keep him from going back to the seminary if you want." His voice was ingratiating. Nora adored Uncle Mike, despite all his faults. She wanted him to be happy. If marrying Sean would make him happy . . . but that was ridiculous.

"Sean is never in his life going to do for someone else," she said decisively, "something that he has not already made up his own mind to do."

Father McCabe looked up at Sean, an ominous anger showing on his lank, unshaven face. "Mistah Cronin, will you ever learn that there is not a special set of rules for the Cronin family simply because your father is a rich man?"

"I do my best to keep all the rules, Father," Sean said, trying to control himself.

"Oh, you keep all the small rules." Father McCabe scratched his bristly chin. "It's the big ones you violate. You know you are not supposed to receive mail from young women, yet such letters still come to you. How do you expect us to recommend you for ordination when you have such involvements?"

Nora again, he thought helplessly. Her letters were utterly harmless, not the slightest reference to the passions of last summer. "I'm not aware of receiving anything in the mail, Father," he said uneasily, watching heavy snow flurries falling outside of the disciplinarian's window.

"What do you call this, then?" Father McCabe triumphantly displayed a blue envelope and two pages of notepaper.

"I told you many times, Father, that Nora Riley is my foster sister. She writes to me once a month."

"Sisters don't write letters like this," insisted McCabe, holding the letter between thumb and forefinger as though he were afraid it was contaminated with infectious germs.

"Nora is an innocent child," Sean said. "I'm sure, Father, that you can't find a single inappropriate phrase in her entire letter."

"Oh?" said McCabe triumphantly. "What about the way she ends the letter?"

Sean sighed with momentary relief. As he had hoped, Nora was too discreet to say anything incriminating. "Father, she's ended her letters to me for the three years I've been here at Mundelein with the words, 'All my love.' They don't mean anything more than such words would mean from anyone's sister."

Father McCabe ignored his argument, demonstrating that it was effective.

"You may write to her tonight and tell her that she is never to write you again as long as you are at this seminary. Is that clear?"

"Yes, Father." Sean could hardly contain his anger. "May I have the letter so I can reply to it?"

"You certainly may not," McCabe said brusquely. With three quick twists of his thick fingers, he tore up the fragile paper into tiny pieces and threw them in the wastebasket. "Now go to your room."

Sean, his fists clenched in violent rage, pounded the desk in his room. That goddamned bastard. Why would anyone want to be a priest when a vicious fool like that had power? What right did he have to read Sean's mail, to tear it up, to forbid Nora to write him?

Abruptly he grabbed his journal, gripped his pen in rage, and began to scratch angry words on its pages. Then, slowly, he calmed down.

> *I'm as bad as McCabe. Nora's letters are innocent enough and so, for that matter, is Nora. But my feelings for her aren't innocent. Not a day, not an hour, has passed over the last five months that I have not thought about her or felt the sensation of her lips pressed against mine. I'm hungry for her like a starving man is hungry for food, and I can't persuade myself that my feelings are sinful. I suppose I ought to leave the seminary and marry her now, before Paul comes back and takes her away from me. I'll tell McCabe after dinner that I'm leaving.*

He pondered the words he had written. At the end of the seven-fifteen recreation period, he would corner McCabe and tell him what he could do with his seminary. Then he wrote a brief appendix to his decision.

> *We're not supposed to ask for signs from you, and I'm not asking for a sign. I've made up my own mind. If you want to change it, that's up to you. You'll have to do it by 7:15 tonight.*

Sean and Jimmy McGuire took a walk during the recreation period after dinner.

"I'm going to see the Moose at seven fifteen, Jimmy," Sean said. "I'm leaving."

"Don't be a fool. Of course you're not leaving."

"Dad wants me to. I have to replace Paul."

"I won't discuss it," Jimmy said. "You're the only good seminarian in this whole miserable place. You keep the rules because you believe that they really are the will of God."

"I've never told anyone, Jim, but I'm plagued by doubts all the time. Hardly a day goes by that I don't need a sign that He's out there and that He cares about me."

"Shit." Jimmy was unimpressed. "You think you're an archangel or something? Everyone has doubts. You know as well as I do that doubt and faith are compatible. Hell, I heard you say that in class last week."

"How can I go through life as a priest and not believe in God?"

"If you mean"—Jimmy was losing his patience—"how can you go through life as a priest plagued with doubts, the answer is, Why should you be different from anyone else? I'll tell you what your problem is, Cronin: you're mad at God because he took your mother away from you. Me, I wish I had a strong enough sense of God to be mad at him.''

"Maybe you're right," Sean conceded. "But I'm still leaving."

"I won't bet on it, because I don't want to take your money away from you.'' Jimmy sounded like a professor ending a difficult lecture to which the class had paid little attention.

Sean strode into his room at seven sixteen and threw the heavy pseudo–West Point overcoat that he was required to wear onto his bed. The last time he would have to put on that goddamned thing. Just before he stormed out of the room down to McCabe's office, he noticed a tiny sheet of paper that had been slipped under his door—the carefully cut quarter size of typing paper that McCabe used for his notes. Sean picked it up impatiently.

> *Your father called this afternoon to say that the Defense Depart-*
> *ment has confirmed that your brother Paul is alive and a prisoner*
> *of war in North Korea.*

BOOK TWO

Jesus, fully aware that he had come from God and was going to God, rose from the meal and took off his cloak. He picked up a towel and tied it around himself. Then he poured water into a basin and began to wash his disciples' feet and dry them with the towel he had around him.

—JOHN 13:3–5

Chapter Four
1953

"YOU CAN'T BE brainwashed unless you have a brain." Paul Cronin grinned engagingly. "They tried but gave up when they found they had nothing to work with."

The group of young women around him, dressed in their Sunday morning summer dresses, giggled their approval.

Paul tilted his head and stuffed his hands in his trousers pockets. "They weren't exactly pleasant folks, to tell you the truth," he said soberly. "I'm glad it's all over. . . . Come on, Sean, we'd better get home for breakfast before Aunt Jane has a fit."

The gaggle of worshipers, eyes still shining, scattered. Sean got into Paul's new Corvette, wondering at how little his brother had changed. A year of combat and a year and a half in a POW camp seemed to have touched him only lightly. There was perhaps a bit more strain around the eyes and a little more restlessness. Otherwise he was the same genial, gregarious Paul.

"What's next for you, Paul?" Sean asked as the car turned down the lake drive. A thin haze hung over the lake already. It would be another humid windless day.

"I guess it will be politics, like Dad wants. I learned to make decisions and issue orders in the Marines. I'm good at it."

There was a hint of seriousness in Paul's gray eyes. Beneath the charm and the laughter there was ambition. Not, perhaps, a ruthless, compelling urge for power, but rather a relaxed low-key delight in the joys of victory.

"Law school, then?"

"Sure, why not?" Paul shrugged and turned the car into the long driveway. "But first I want to take a year off, see the country."

"Dad won't like it," Sean said.

Paul turned off the ignition. "Speaking of Dad, he seems to have changed since I left."

"Sometimes I think he's like a rubber band that is stretching and stretching and—"

"Does he really expect me to marry that overgrown tomboy?" Paul interrupted.

26

"You'd better ask him." Sean climbed out of the Corvette.

"Nothing against her," Paul continued, smiling cheerfully and tossing the car keys into the air. "She just isn't my kind of woman, if you know what I mean."

"Not quite," said Sean. "Anyway, Nora has a mind of her own."

"I don't think he means it." Paul pocketed his keys. "He won't insist."

"Don't bet on that, big brother."

Paul Cronin enjoyed being a war hero. It kept his father off his back, and ever since he had come home from Korea, Paul had enjoyed more girls with less effort than all the rest of the years of his life put together. Maggie Martin was only one of his conquests.

They were in her parents' house at Oakland Beach while the rest of her family was in Chicago. "Jambalaya" was playing somewhere in the background.

"Why don't you get me another beer?" he asked, giving her his most winsome boyish smile.

"Sure, Paul," she said. "Anything you want."

Outside the window, a jagged lightning flash raced madly across the sky, briefly illuminating the restless waters of the lake. Then there was a roar of thunder.

"Here's your beer, Paul," she said, pathetically eager to please him.

"I'd like more than a beer, Maggie," he said, rising from the couch and pulling her to him. He kissed her expertly, his hands caressing her back.

When it became clear that Paul would not be satisfied with only necking, Maggie at first tried to pull back. But the lure of Paul Cronin was too strong, and she finally gave in.

Later, soothing her sweat-drenched body, Paul realized that Maggie Martin, for all her wide-eyed blond innocence, was the most sensual virgin he had ever possessed. In fact, she was just about perfect—eager to learn and unbelievably hungry. There were more good times to be enjoyed with her, he thought, as he drifted to sleep, but he would have to make certain that she understood that there would never be anything more between them than just a good time. . . .

A Chinese bugle slashed the cool night air. Paul rolled over in confusion, trying desperately to clear his head of the effects of the beer he had drunk before his bout with Maggie. At first, the nightmare duplicated reality. Where was Makuch? Where the hell was that damn Polack? He twisted around in his foxhole, just as a flare exploded above him, then dropped with agonizing slowness into the smooth waters of the reservoir. Oh, my God. . . . Chinks, thousands of them, swarming up the side of the hill. Automatic weapon in one hand, hand grenades still attached to his belt, Paul squirmed out of the foxhole and began to run. The enemy was coming toward him. To hell with Makuch. To hell with the rest of the outfit. He ran in a crouch along the ridge. He had to get away. Then he tripped on a pile of loose rocks and plunged headlong down the side of the ridge. He had stumbled into a deserted .50-caliber machine-gun position. He rolled over in time to see a half dozen Chinks running toward him with bayonets in ready position. There were more coming. He grabbed at the gun, pulled the trigger, and watched as the Chinks collapsed in front of him bellowing with pain. The machine gun jammed. He fired his automatic. Then the nightmare took over. Maggie Martin, naked and screaming, was the first of the Chinks whose heads exploded in front of him. . . .

He awakened, unsure whether it was his own screams he had heard. He was soaking wet, as he always was after such dreams. They had haunted him now for two years, ever since that terrifying night by Chosun Reservoir. It was the first time he had ever killed anyone, and he must have killed scores that night. His body trembled at the memory.

He sat on the edge of the couch and automatically lit a cigarette, wondering if the nightmares would ever stop.

Makuch *knew*. He was the only one in the outfit who knew. The look of contempt in his eyes revealed that the Polack from Pittsburgh had seen his platoon commander panic and desert his command. He knew that Paul wasn't entitled to his Medal of Honor. He had seen him stumble into the machine-gun nest as he was trying to flee.

Paul stubbed out his cigarette and explained to Maggie that it had been an ordinary nightmare. Then he quickly made his excuses, kissed her good night, and left.

Sean Cronin reached for his journal impatiently. He had made no entries in it since his impetuous decision to leave the seminary, a decision that God had canceled out very quickly. Lightning was dancing across the lake. Sean watched the show with hypnotized fascination.

> *Your thunderstorms are much better than the human dramas for which you write the scripts,* he wrote slowly. *Paul is back, as cheerful and carefree as ever, unmarked, it seems, by a year and a half in a prisoner-of-war camp. When he laughs, everybody in the room laughs. When he smiles, everybody feels happy. When he suggests that the crowd do something—like going off to a movie—we all go along.*
>
> *Paul wants to spend a year wandering around the country— getting to know America better, he said. Dad won't like it. Before the summer is over, Paul's going to have to agree to go to law school and marry Nora when she gets out of college in three years. I wonder if she'll agree, too.*
>
> *I don't feel any sadness now over Paul and Nora. They're made for each other; they just don't know it yet. They're both handsome and intelligent. His laughter and her depth will balance each other perfectly.*
>
> *Six months ago, I was in love with her. I've never quite said it that way to myself, but there isn't any doubt. I was head over heels in love with Nora Riley. I'm over it now, I think, but still I wonder if I would change places with Paul if I could. But you don't permit things like that, do you?*
>
> *Ah, YOU, that's the question! How can anyone want to be a priest as much as I want to, and still doubt you? I want . . . I want . . . what do I want?*

Mike Cronin sighed in contented satisfaction and looked down at the woman sleeping next to him. Lorna Mahoney was proving herself an apt pupil. It was amazing how quickly these stiff prudish women could discover their own sexuality when he trapped them in a mixture of adoration and fear. Mike delighted in women, especially when he was able to transform them into the kind of responsive instrument of pleasure to which he felt a man such as himself was entitled.

There was no joy in buying a woman. The trick was to pursue them, slowly, lovingly, implacably, until they were eager to give themselves over to you.

Nor did he become disinterested after a successful conquest. Reeducation was as important as victory—MacArthur had proven that in Japan. It was mostly a matter of kindness and attention, with a bit of aloofness thrown in to keep them anxious and docile. When he was finished with his reeducation program, a woman was as good as a Japanese geisha at giving pleasure—which was, after all, what she was there for.

He continued to enjoy a woman until she began to hint at marriage. Then Mike ended the relationship. Some of them complained, but they usually stopped when they saw the size of his farewell check. None of them had any trouble finding husbands, and presumably the lucky man benefited from the skills their wives had learned from Mike. So it all worked out.

He lit a cigarette and puffed on it complacently. You had to control them, of course, keep them under your thumb. That was the only way to deal with women. That was how it was with everyone. Life was a jungle. You controlled the other beasts or they controlled you.

The only serious mistake he had ever made with a woman was his marriage to Mary Eileen. He frowned. That had been a disaster. Thank heavens, he had been able to protect his sons from the knowledge of the possibility of a bad inheritance from that side of the family. Hardly a day passed when he did not worry about the weakness showing up.

He decided that he should stop thinking about his wife and pay more attention to the delectable dessert he had in bed with him. Lorna was still sound asleep, her body spread luxuriously next to him. He eased the sheet away from her so he could savor her body in the bursts of lightning that now seemed to be just outside her bedroom window. She was less spectacularly developed than some of his other companions but made up for it by her intensity. His women were older now, in their early forties instead of their middle thirties. One must maintain a sense of proportion about these things. Lorna had started to talk of marriage sooner than most of the others; one of the problems of companions who were older was that they thought of marriage a lot sooner. For a moment he permitted himself to be tempted with the thought of marriage. No, it was impossible for him.

He would have to see Paul settled down before the summer was over. He would pull strings to get him into Northwestern Law School despite his college grades. Then Paul would marry Nora when she graduated from St. Mary's. Sean would be a priest by then, and he could officiate at the ceremony.

The marriage would be a great event: Paul safely married and Sean a priest. Both would be well on their way in the careers for which they were so brilliantly fitted by family and training.

Lightning seemed to explode, bathing Lorna in an eerie blue light. Mike put his sons from his mind and pulled the sheet the rest of the way off her body.

Nora put a candle in front of her Madonna and ignited the tiny lump of incense in the blue glass dish in front of the statue. Her piety was a jealously preserved secret, unknown even to her closest friend at school, where Nora was thought of as both an athlete and an exceptional student. In the privacy of her room, Nora would kneel on bare knees, entranced by the smell of incense, the glow of the candle, and an awareness of a Presence that pervaded the atmosphere.

Ever since she had escaped from the fire that had killed her mother and her baby brother, Nora Riley knew with absolute certainty that she was supposed to do something special in life. It appeared that the something "special" was Paul Cronin, with whom she had fallen in love, even though the two of them kept a wary distance from each other. Life with Paul would be exciting. She would be the wife and mother, working in the background, guiding his life and soothing his hurts, as he walked the road to the White House.

Paul would be the first Catholic president of the United States and she would be his first lady. That was important enough, wasn't it?

The Presence, enveloping her as gently as the faint aroma of incense, did not disagree. Yet Nora realized with vague unease, as she drifted off to the hills and meadows of this special love, that it didn't agree either.

"It's time we had a serious talk." Mike Cronin stared at the neat rows of Chicago streets that extended westward from the Field Building toward the burgeoning suburbs springing up beyond the west side of the city.

"Okay, if you say so," Paul agreed. "I've only been back for a couple of months, though. I think I'm entitled—"

"You're goddamned not entitled to anything," his father barked. "Your Medal of Honor doesn't entitle you to be thrown out of every tavern of northern Indiana and to screw everything that moves in Oakland Beach. I saw more combat than you did, and I came home and settled down to business."

"You weren't in a Korean prison camp; it's different," Paul sputtered.

"If you think I'm going to support you for the rest of your life, you're wrong." The top of Mike's bald head was flaming red, a very bad sign indeed.

"Okay, okay," Paul said nervously. "I'll go up to Northwestern tomorrow and see if they'll take me."

"You'll go up there today," Mike corrected him. "And, officer in the Marine Corps or not, you'll stay away from Maggie Martin. Her parents are too powerful to offend. Find your women somewhere else besides Oakland Beach and the neighborhood. And remember—after Nora's graduation you're going to marry her, just as everyone's agreed." His father hovered over him like an angry red-faced avenging angel.

"I don't object to that," Paul said, trying to placate his father. "But I'm not sure she'll go along." He reached for his cigarettes.

"She's got no choice but to go along. You're going to be the first Catholic president of this country, and Nora's going to be the First Lady—whether she wants to or not."

"I think I may be able to win her over," Paul said. He sensed that a display of confidence would soothe his father's ruffled feathers. Then, in a burst of candor, he added, "You don't have to worry about me, Dad. I found out in the Marines that if you smile at people the right way they'll do almost anything for you."

"Well, that's settled then." Mike's mind was obviously turning to something else. It was time for Paul to get out of his office. Paul was suddenly aware that life could get very difficult in the years ahead if he weren't careful. And maybe even if he were.

Chapter Five
····································· **1954** ·····································

"Two more years," Roger Fitzgibbon said as he and Sean Cronin labored on the weeds in the tennis court behind the theology hall at the seminary. "Just watch. When we're ordained, they'll blacktop this court."

"I suppose so," Sean replied. He was barely listening to his friend. He knew he was in trouble with the seminary authorities. His conference with the rector in preparation for minor orders had been postponed, a sure sign that there was a debate raging behind the scenes about whether to ordain him. At best the outcome could be a "clip": he would not be ordained to the lesser orders of acolyte and reader but rather would be kept in limbo until the following year. Not expelled exactly—although no one would be unhappy if he solved their problem for them by leaving—but not approved either. To make matters worse, Sean had no idea why he was under a cloud.

"Thinking about Motherwell?" Roger asked sympathetically as he tossed a handful of weeds into the battered bushel basket next to the net. "Are you sure you passed your STB exam?"

"Joey Jim told me that I'd passed the exam, and he wanted to see me about something else." Sean wiped the perspiration off his face. "Have you ever heard of him talking about anything besides exams?"

Roger shook his head. "Nope, not once. I thought all this business about a clip was silly talk until I heard that he wanted to see you. No matter how you look at it, it can't be good."

"That's what I think too," Sean agreed.

The seminary held one principle of priestly training absolutely sacred: no one ought to be too good at anything, much less successful at a number of things. Athletic ability was tolerated, so long as it did not include every sport or accompany "too much" intellectual curiosity. High grades were viewed with suspicion, especially when combined with a propensity to read too many books. Intellectualism was taken to be almost a sure sign of pride. Affluence, especially the rumored great wealth of the Cronin family, was also a grave danger to a priestly vocation, because it made a young man think he might be independent of Church authority.

Sean accepted the basic theory. Seminarians were in training to be curates for most of their lives, cogs in the ecclesiastical machine, neat pieces of salami, sliced off with precision by a machine that made each slice almost identical to the previous one. Pastors in the archdiocese did not need or want curates who did not fit the mold. Too much "singularity" interfered with service to the Church.

Yet, try as he might, Sean could not quite conform. He kept all the rules, he did his work, he asked few difficult questions in the classroom, he fit in smoothly with his classmates. Yet lurking in the background always was the flamboyant image of his father. The rector and many of the faculty were terrified at the possibility that after ordination Sean might turn into a clerical Mike Cronin. Almost any excuse to "cut him down to size" would be eagerly seized as a pretext, not for expelling him, but for making his life so unpleasant that he would leave—quite possibly, as the rector once suggested to him, for another diocese. "We'll give you a strong recommendation, son," the old man had said in a conspiratorial tone.

Sean wondered what his father's reaction would be to a postponement of ordination. Probably try to buy the minor orders for him. Sean grimaced. That would only make matters worse.

Roy Shields carefully packed his stethoscope into the jacket of his white suit. "Are you ever going to slow down, Mike?" he asked. There was reproach in his voice.

"Not if I can help it." Mike Cronin buttoned his tailor-made white shirt. "Why rust out when you can burn out?"

"I'd like you to come into Little Company of Mary for a couple of days. For a full range of tests."

"There's nothing wrong?" Mike tried to sound confident.

"Nothing specific," Roy assured him. "I'd just feel better if I could run some tests."

"Your job, Major"—Mike was talking to one of his staff surgeons again—"is to make me feel better, not to make yourself feel better."

"You drink too much, you smoke too much, you're carrying ten pounds more than you should, you never relax, you drive yourself from one end of the year to the other, there's no peace or stability in your life." The normally placid Dr. Shields ticked off his litany of charges almost as though he were angry. "What's the point in it, Mike? You don't need the money. Why don't you take time off and enjoy life?"

"Goddamn it, Roy, I *do* enjoy life." Mike knotted his tie. "And I intend to continue to enjoy it until my sons are established in their careers."

The doctor sighed. "Take it just a little slower."

Mike laughed. "Okay, Roy, if it will make you happy, I'll cut down on everything." He winked. "Well, almost everything."

In his limousine, Mike admitted to himself that Roy had scared him. Maybe he ought to cut down on the drinking and smoking . . . go to Glendore for a week and enjoy the coming of spring. There was no point in burning himself out. Give up smoking and drinking altogether. He had the willpower to do it if he wanted to. Maybe even settle down with Jenny Warren. He frowned. Jane wouldn't like that, would she?

He turned that unpleasant thought off and virtuously rubbed out his cigar. Give up smoking and drinking, but not Jenny. That seemed a fair enough trade. Roy hadn't said there was anything wrong with sex. And with Jenny, sex was something special indeed. He smiled in self-satisfaction. A cool, elegant New England aristocrat, reserved to the point of iciness until she took off her clothes, Jenny Warren was the best woman he had bedded in a long time, a challenge to his ingenuity.

He thought of the things she could do with her prim and proper Bostonian mouth. "Jeremy, I want to make a call," he told his chauffeur as he reached for the phone. He dialed Jenny's number.

When she picked up the phone in her apartment, he said, "There's a flight from Midway to Frankfurt on Thursday afternoon. Let's find a castle on the Rhine and drink wine all weekend."

She agreed enthusiastically. Mike relaxed on the soft cushions of his limousine, his imagination playing with a slightly tipsy Jenny, spread-eagled beneath him on a castle bed. That was the way to stay young.

He opened the door to the bar and mixed himself a stiff Scotch as Jeremy turned the Caddy down 55th Street.

He lit a cigar and puffed on it complacently. Better to burn out than rust out. He drained the Scotch and poured himself another drink.

Paul Cronin sipped his beer thoughtfully. The Dive was a crumby, dank Rush Street bar, but it was the place where most of the law school students gathered. It was therefore also the place for Paul to be with his unlimited money and his ready laugh, doing favors, collecting friends, amassing influence. It was all pathetically easy, and a great deal more fun than studying for tests.

He had discovered that law school was like everything else in his life. He could succeed with very little effort. As an experiment, he had barely studied for the midyear exams—there was a cool delicious joy in the defiance of such a gesture, a bold toss of the dice. He had not led his class, but he had been in the middle, enough to please his father and earn him a new sports car that Nora loved to drive.

Nora . . . he paused to consider that problem. She was a knockout. Not his kind of woman, like Maggie Martin, whom he still occasionally saw for the hell of it, but the kind of girl who would make a very presentable wife. The old man was often right: Nora probably was a good idea, or at least, all things considered, not a bad one.

"You been studying hard?" Jack Coles asked him.

Paul didn't particularly like Jack, who was handsome in a dark, white-teeth-grin sort of way. But Paul was friendly toward him, as he was toward everyone.

"Not too hard," Paul said cheerfully. "Have a beer."

"Thanks. . . . Say, wouldn't it be nice to know what the questions for the finals are going to be?"

Paul suppressed a yawn. "I suppose so."

Jack sipped his beer while Paul slipped a dollar bill to the bartender.

"It can be done," Jack said softly. "It will cost a few dollars, but it can be done."

Paul's interest was aroused. "You can get the exams?"

Jack looked around nervously. "With a few dollars, maybe five hundred."

"Sounds great," Paul assented. "You want to stop by my house this evening?"

"Sure," said Jack with feigned unconcern. "I might just do that."

After Jack left, Paul wondered why he had become involved in such a crackpot scheme. It was fun to outwit the faculty, most of whom were pompous frustrated federal judges. But he wasn't going to study very hard anyway, so what difference did it make if he knew what the questions were? Besides, even senile Dean Weaver could smell something fishy if Paul Cronin did better than his gentleman's C.

Paul didn't often question his own motives. He simply wanted to be a leader of other men, to be recognized when he walked down Michigan Avenue the way he was recognized in the corridors of the law school. It seemed to him to be a perfectly legitimate ambition. And he had all the talent necessary for the task. What the hell, why not aim as high as you could? Paul felt a headache coming on, as almost always happened when he thought too much about himself. He ordered another beer. How much did he really want to "settle down" with Nora and enter politics? He knew there was a lot of work to be done, crime to be fought, racial justice to be pursued, the Russians to be watched—all the things Jack Kennedy was talking about.

The Kennedys did not bother trying to analyze themselves. Why should he?

Halfway through his beer, the headache disappeared. So, too, had all qualms about paying for the theft of the final exams.

"Sit down, young man," said Joseph James Motherwell, S.J. "You're in big trouble." His eyes widened and his lips pursed as if in wonder at the size of Sean's trouble. "I want to talk to you about it."

Joey Jim was a New Deal Democrat from downstate Illinois, a pixielike seventy-year-old who talked with a nasal twang and clipped words as though he were a cowboy. A superb teacher with impeccable academic standards, his childlike face beamed with pleasure whenever he caught a student unprepared. His thin white hair and rimless spectacles made him look like an innocent angel, one that the seminarians had learned could be very dangerous if you hadn't studied the night before.

"I guess I'm going to be clipped," Sean said.

"Clipped?" Motherwell beamed with pleasure. "Why, young man, most of the faculty want to expel you."

"What have I done?" Sean asked. He wondered why he wanted to stay.

"You've made a serious mistake, young man." Motherwell readjusted the sash of his tattered old "Jesuit" cassock. "You've been born the son of a rich father who has high ambitions for you."

"Father Motherwell, Dad is a man of taste and refinement. However, there are a few things that obsess him. One of them is his desire that I become a priest. It may be crazy, but he's my father and I won't apologize for him."

"I don't think it's a crazy idea at all," Motherwell said. "You're one of the most gifted seminarians to come through this place in the last twenty-five years. You keep the rules, you're devout, you have great influence on others, you work hard, you have vision and imagination. Perhaps you're a little too cautious and conservative, but that's a good way to begin."

Joey Jim almost never paid compliments. Sean was thunderstruck. "But—"

"But nothing, young man. Not everyone is as envious as the Rector or your classmate Mr. Fitzgibbon."

"Roger? He's one of my best friends."

"Well, now, I don't know about that." Motherwell's eyes were hard. "He was the one who told them about the tailor-made suits your father sends you. They found them in your closet."

"I'm being clipped for tailor-made suits?" Sean was astonished.

Motherwell tilted his head and became even more of a pixie. "Don't you think that's a good reason to clip someone, young man?"

"I don't wear the suits."

"They think"—Motherwell pointed a finger at Sean—"that when your father finds out you've been clipped, he'll try to buy ordination for you. Then they'll persuade the Cardinal to dismiss you. So you'd better not tell your dad, eh?"

"Did you block the expulsion?" Sean asked.

"I wasn't the only one, young man." He pursed his lips knowingly. "A group of us said we'd go to the Cardinal and protest."

Sean stood up. "Why, Father? Why go to all that trouble for me?"

"Well, young man, let's just say that I like to keep the Rector on his toes."

■ ■ ■

The Second City playhouse was cramped, uncomfortable, and unbearably hot; the drinks were expensive and not very good; and the wit of two young comics named Alan Arkin and Severn Darden was quite beyond Paul Cronin's comprehension. Yet, when one of his Jewish classmates, Tony Swartz, proposed that they take their dates to the fashionable new comedy review, Paul had quickly assented. Swartz was a class leader and destined for one of the prestigious downtown law firms. Paul was cautious with Jews; he had not known any when he was growing up, but they seemed to fit his father's stereotype—industrious, bright, and different.

To his surprise Nora seemed to enjoy the Second City wit and to be especially amused by a skit about football returning to the University of Chicago. Nor was she put off by Tony's slightly bitchy intellectual date, a slender, dark-skinned woman named Muriel. Muriel had made a few disparaging remarks about Catholic virgins when Nora mentioned she was a student at St. Mary's College but backed off when Nora ignored her in her most aristocratic manner.

Tony had been frankly admiring Nora's cool beauty. Paul was not sure whether to be proud or offended. He was even more uncertain when Nora banned all talk about Senator Joseph McCarthy, a favorite whipping boy of the law school students: "Let's not ruin the evening with that man. The Democrats will win a majority in the Senate next autumn and he'll be finished."

"Dad wouldn't like to hear you say that," he said cautiously.

"Uncle Mike is not likely to hear me say that," she replied, ending the discussion.

"Did they call you in on the exam theft?" Tony asked Paul as they were returning from a trip to the men's room.

"Yes, but the Dean admitted that no one who had the questions beforehand could have done so poorly with the answers." Paul laughed. "I think Jack would have carried it off if he hadn't been so hungry."

"I feel badly about Jack being expelled, but he sure messed up the curve." Tony shook his head.

Paul was glad when they reached the table and the conversation ended. He did not want to remember how, in his panic, he had hinted to the Dean that Jack Coles might have been the source of the advance information.

On the whole, Nora was more of a success with his friends than he had expected. And his good-night kiss did not catch her off guard. Her lips and tongue responded eagerly and her body pressed tightly against his. Catholic virgin she might be, but she was not bashful about necking.

"You're not a bad kisser, Paul Cronin," she said appreciatively, her fingers lightly touching his neck.

"I could get to like this too," he agreed.

"We'll have to try it again." She brushed his lips quickly this time and disappeared through the door of the house on Glenwood Drive. The Old Man apparently was off in Paris or Berlin or somewhere.

A nice girl, all right, with a great build and a fierce, prickly temper. Why, he wondered, as he drove back to his apartment near Lincoln Park, was he so wary of her? Probably because she seemed in such complete control of everything, including her passions.

. . .

Outside, the birds were singing and the blue sky seemed to be smiling contentedly down on the Rhine River.

"More wine?" Jenny Warren filled Mike Cronin's glass and returned to the delicate kisses with which she had been teasing and rewarding him. Thank God he was still capable of responding to such a woman, even if she was fifteen years younger.

"I love you, Michael," she said simply. "I don't understand you, but I love you and I'd do anything for you."

"I'll probably think of something before tonight." He laughed, trying to hide his wavering emotions.

"I only wish . . ." The kisses stopped and she leaned back, her fingers tracing a light design on his chest.

"What do you only wish?"

"I only wish I knew what haunts you so I could help make it go away."

He almost told her.

"This will make a man out of you, son," said the Rector, a fat foolish man with long flowing hair. "It will teach you the danger of vanity."

Vanity was the reason being given for the delay of his ordination to minor orders. Motherwell had won a point, though. The Rector promised Sean that if he stayed out of trouble during the summer, he would catch up with his classmates in the fall. It also seemed that Jimmy McGuire had done the unheard of—defended him to the Rector in the name of his classmates.

"Vanity is a bad thing," Sean temporized, refusing to admit his guilt to a charge that had been so obscurely made. In the course of the Rector's rambling explanation, his sin seemed to be virtually nonexistent.

"We all have to be humble, son." The Rector folded his hands piously on his massive oak desk, inherited from the Cardinal Mundelein era.

"Humility is a good thing." Sean wondered why he was taking such crap from a seminary at which he did not want to stay. Why was he making such foolish sacrifices when he was not even sure that he really wanted to be a priest? Was it his vocation or his father's? If they had only thrown him out, the decision to leave would not have been his.

"Some of your teachers had very glowering things to say about you," the Rector assured him. He meant glowing.

"That was very kind of them," Sean agreed. Damn you, Motherwell. If it hadn't been for you, I might be out of here and doing what I want to do.

And what do I want to do?

I want to take Nora away from Paul. That's what I want to do.

Chapter Six
1954

SEAN CRONIN GLARED at the brown spires of St. Mary's College. He could hardly wait to see Nora, yet at the same time he was resentful that he had been given the job of bringing her home at the end of the school year. It was Jeremy's day off and Paul was busy with the last details for his summer clerkship in a law office.

"This place is worse than a convent," Sean muttered to Tom Shields, who was waiting to pick up Maggie Martin.

"Academically it's excellent, Sean," the thin studious young medical student replied. "The Christian Culture program that Nora is in provides a first-class education. Much better than the one I received at Notre Dame."

"All they need is a course in cooking and diaper washing," Sean sneered.

"Come on, Sean. You don't mean that. You're proud of Nora's intelligence, just as I'm proud of Maggie's."

"I'd be even more proud of them if they'd get their asses out here so we could escape from this creepy place." Sean was still angry from the injustice and the humiliation of the clip, but he was unable to release his pent-up emotions by speaking about it, lest his father hear and make matters even worse.

Finally, the two young women appeared, both clad in the Bermuda shorts that they were strictly forbidden to wear during the school year. Nora's long auburn hair flowed loosely in the spring breeze. Maggie made a soft, cuddly counterpoint to her tall, austere friend.

Sean packed Nora's suitcases in the trunk of the Cadillac and quickly drove to the crowded streets of South Bend and then the hot concrete of Highway 20 with its gas-belching trucks and flat northern Indiana farmland. A road to hell, he often told himself, paved with bad intentions.

Finally, he broke his silence. "How can you put up with that cruddy place? Pious nuns simpering around. Rules from the late Middle Ages. Irrelevant education and phony liberal crap."

Nora had been humming "Three Coins in the Fountain," as it played on the car radio. "Maybe it is a bit old-fashioned. Yet when Sister Madeleva reads her poetry, I see something to be said for the tradition. It needs to be modernized, but I don't want it to be lost."

"Women writing poetry, the acme of irrelevance."

Nora slammed the radio dial. "What's going on? You haven't said a friendly thing since I came out of the dorm. You didn't kiss me; you didn't say it was good to see me; you've sulked, complained, and sneered. If you're trying to pick a fight with me, you've damn well succeeded. What's eating you?"

"Nothing," he snarled. "Not a goddamn thing."

"All right." She moved as far as she could from him in the copious front seat of the Cadillac. "I can sulk as long as you can . . . longer. Until judgment day if I have to. We're supposed to be friends, and I can wait till you treat me like one again and tell me what those bastards at the seminary have done to you now."

Nora's unerring instincts shocked him even more than her language, words he had never heard from her before.

"I'm sure you can outsulk me, Nora," he said sheepishly. And out poured the story.

She was sympathetic and supportive. "I won't tell Uncle Mike," she promised.

"I know you won't."

They were quiet for a time, sharing the powerful emotions of their friendship. Nora made him turn off U.S. 20 and drive toward La Porte. It was a different world: trees, shade, old, old homes, front porches, quiet side streets.

"What a lovely little town," he said.

"It means the Gate, of course," she said. "It's the northern end of what was once the Great American Forest. People traveled through here for hundreds of years because it was the gateway to the prairies. Dunes on the north and forests to the south. And what's more, Mr. Smart-ass Sophisticate Sean Cronin, it's older than Chicago and fifteen minutes from Oakland Beach. You're such a terrible conservative you've never bothered to come down here and see it."

Sean laughed. It was good to be with Nora again.

They ate hamburgers at a tiny lunch stand overlooking a small azure lake on which kids were water skiing. Nora boasted that she had learned how to ski in Fort Lauderdale at Easter and offered to teach him. He told her that he had learned the summer before at the villa—a northern Wisconsin prison of sorts to which seminarians were sent during the summer to keep them separate from the laity to whom in a few years they would be ministering—and that he would gladly beat her at a competition.

They both laughed happily.

"They *will* ordain you a priest, won't they?" Nora asked after they had ordered ice-cream sodas for dessert.

"Sure, if I want to put up with their bullshit. I half wish they'd thrown me out. Then I wouldn't have to make my own decision."

Nora was baffled. "You want to be a priest, don't you, Sean? You always have."

"I don't know." He was admitting his doubts to her for the first time, indeed the first time to anyone. "I'm not sure. Sometimes yes, sometimes no. I wonder if it's not Dad's vocation instead of mine."

"Couldn't Uncle Mike be supporting the right thing for the wrong reason?"

"Maybe so. I'm so confused I don't know. If they'd thrown me out, I would have had a sign from God."

"God doesn't work that way." She dismissed his heresy decisively. "Anyway, what would you do if you were thrown out and cheated of making your own choice?"

"Probably take you away from Paul," he said impulsively.

Nora almost choked on her soda. "Oh, Sean, I'm not Paul's. I'm not anyone's. No one is going to take me away from anybody. Besides, if you should ever marry, you don't deserve to be stuck with somebody like me. You would need someone a lot better." She grinned impishly and went back to her soda.

You declare your love for a woman and she thinks it's a joke. Serves you right, Sean thought to himself. "You *are* going to marry Paul, though?"

"He's lots of fun and he's a good kisser." She grinned again. "And he's sweet to me, and it will make Uncle Mike happy . . . and I think I love him. Don't worry, Sean, I'll make up my own mind."

Sean kept his fingers firmly on the wheel of the Caddy all the way back to Chicago. He was afraid that if he freed even one arm he would embrace Nora, kiss her, and then try to hold her in his arms for the rest of his life. It was an excellent idea. Unfortunately, he had offered to marry her and she had not even heard. It was also against what the spiritual director would have called "God's Holy Will."

. . .

The enormous front lawn of the Cronin house on Glenwood Drive was perfect for a garden party. Long green canopies were hung, tables filled with filets and lobsters and ham and corned beef were arranged around the lawn, three bars were in constant operation, serving the best wine and whiskey that money could buy. A five-piece string orchestra played Viennese and Irish music, while waiters in formal dress passed through the crowd, politely offering their trays of delicacies. God cooperated with a glorious Saturday afternoon in June.

All this was in honor of Senator Joseph R. McCarthy, the man of the hour for most Irish Catholics. Everyone in the neighborhood, as well as hordes of Mike's business associates, had been invited. They all came, no matter what they thought of "Tail Gunner Joe," because they did not want to risk offending Michael Cronin. The only exceptions were a few local Democratic politicians, who did not know whether it was safe to risk the disapproval of their new chairman, County Clerk Richard J. Daley, an unknown factor thus far in Chicago political life.

Sean was introduced to the Senator, whom he instantly sized up as a lush who needed a shave. How could his father see political greatness in the man? Paul, who was sticking like glue to the Senator, seemed unperturbed by the guest of honor's bleary eyes and slurred voice.

Jenny Warren hugged Sean vigorously and told him how well he looked. Most of his father's "friends" were fond of Sean, and he had become sufficiently tolerant to admit they were nice women. He wished his father would marry Jenny; she was a sweet and lovely lady who might bring some order and calm into Mike's life.

Sean joined Roger Fitzgibbon and Jimmy McGuire at the fringe of the party.

"Vanity of vanities, all is vanity," cracked Jimmy.

"At least Nora isn't part of the vanity." Sean needled Jimmy whenever he could about his longtime crush on Nora.

"She and Maggie certainly divert attention from the Tail Gunner," Jimmy agreed. In sheath dresses with short sleeves and matching shoes, the two young women were indeed images of contrasting youthful loveliness.

"I can see your brother's point," Roger said. Roger wore French cuffs and a vest and what was surely a tailor-made suit.

"It's a long way to go before he and Nora are a definite thing." Sean realized he didn't even like to hear a hint of eventual marriage.

"Nora?" Roger raised an elegant eyebrow. "I thought it was Maggie. Remember the night last winter when we bumped into them at that bar near Loyola, Jimmy? When we were on vacation?"

"I think they're just friends," Jimmy said. His red face turned even redder.

"They looked like more than friends," Roger said.

Later, when Roger had slipped away, Sean said to Jimmy, "I want the truth about that night, and I don't mean about why you two were breaking rules."

"You and the rules," Jimmy said impatiently. "Well, they were very, very affectionate before they saw us. Didn't bother her. Paul was kind of embarrassed. They left right after they talked to us."

"How affectionate?" Sean insisted.

Jimmy gulped. "I'll give it to you straight. I wouldn't be surprised if they spent part of the night in bed."

"That's straight enough." Sean was chilled to the marrow despite the June warmth.

Jenny Warren, smelling as lovely as she looked, interrupted them. "There's a bit of a problem with your Aunt Jane. I'm afraid I'd make things worse."

"Okay," said Sean. It was not okay, but at least he had something else to think about. "Get Ed Connaire and tell him. I'll see what I can do."

Jane, in an out-of-date burgundy spring dress, was in back of the house, shouting drunken orders at the cook. Jane Cronin was no longer a secret drinker.

Nora arrived at the same time as Sean, in time to see Jane stumble over an evergreen bush and onto the grass in front of a case of wine bottles.

"Miserable bastards," Jane said, as they helped her to her feet. "Trash."

"Easy, Aunt Jane. We'll get you into the house for a nap."

"Don't want to nap." Jane swayed dangerously.

Sean held her firmly and breathed a sigh of relief as Ed Connaire joined them.

"Easy, Jane," said the burly red-haired construction contractor. "It's going to be all right."

"It would be better if we'd let her kill her little bastard." She waved a drunken hand at Sean. "She and her priest friend . . . bastards . . . they're all worthless."

"It's all right, Jane. It's all right." Ed circled her with his muscular arms. He whispered to Sean, "I'll take care of it from now on, son."

He led the still-muttering Jane toward the back stairs of the house. Erithea was waiting patiently at the door. Jane was tottering uncertainly.

"We're going to wait for Ed," Nora said, her jaw firmly set, "and ask him what all that means. I'm not going to have you worrying about her nasty cracks any more."

Sean felt cold. He wanted to hide in the basement.

Ed Connaire looked dubious at first when Sean and Nora cornered him; then he nodded his head thoughtfully, and the three walked silently down the hill to the sidewalk on Glenwood Drive.

"It's not as bad as it sounds, Sean. It was all so long ago. I suppose you have a right to know, although I wish it could be forgotten. It doesn't make any difference—"

"Maybe I should be the judge of that," Sean said.

Ed cracked his massive knuckles. "Sure, Sean, only please try to understand that some things happen for which no one is really to blame."

"Sean understands," Nora said. "He still needs to know."

Ed smiled appreciatively. "All right Nora, you win. Sean, your father and mother were very different kinds of people. They both tried, but the first years of marriage are always hard, and—well, your father was traveling so much. Mike pretends now that their marriage was perfect, but your mother was never really happy at the house at Oakland Beach. Even though Mike had Glendore built because he thought it was what she wanted, she was discontented. She became depressed, especially after Paul was born . . . that often happens, you know."

"I know. Please go on, Ed."

"Your mother turned to religion, and your father, with the best intentions in the world, wouldn't let her continue to see the priests she had started to bring around. He was afraid it was becoming an obsession. Then, when you came along, Mary Eileen became even more depressed. One day, when Mike was in Europe on business, your mother took the car out and had the accident. No one could ever prove that she had done it on purpose, but it was a terrible sad wake, Sean. She was so young and so lovely. And they couldn't even open the casket.

Some people were mad at your father because the wake was only one night. But he was right. It was too terrible for everyone. Doc Shields said it was a blessing, because she might have been crippled for the rest of her life.''

"I wonder if she thought it was a blessing," said Sean bitterly.

"Drop it, Sean," Nora said. "Ed is right. It was long ago and it was tragic and it was no one's fault."

Sean regained his self-control. "Of course. Thank you, Ed. I did have to know, and now that I do I'll forget about it."

"I sure hope I did right in telling you." Ed rubbed his hands together.

"You did, Ed," said Nora. "Now it can all be buried and left in God's hands."

"He's not telling the whole story, Nora," Sean said softly as the old giant slowly climbed the steps back to the lawn party.

"Don't torment yourself. It won't do any good."

"Our lives could have been different," Sean said.

Nora drew his face down to hers and kissed him. "That's for being Sean, the most decent person I know."

That night Nora knelt at the side of her bed, wrapped in a large bath towel. "You know what I have to say. Help him to be a good priest, help me to take care of him, help me to love him the way I should love him."

There were no answers. There never were.

As she fell asleep that night, she felt a little guilty. She had kept her love for Sean in a tightly sealed compartment of her heart, a compartment that had almost exploded open when he had awkwardly hinted at marriage in the car coming home from St. Mary's. He had been angry at the seminary and hoping that she could be a substitute for his priestly vocation. Nora had known better.

She drifted off to sleep. Tonight there would only be peace, even on the subject of Sean Cronin.

Chapter Seven
1956

SEAN COULD NOT sleep the night before ordination. He tossed and turned on the stiff mattress in his room in the Sacred Orders building at Mundelein, knowing that many of his classmates were doing exactly the same thing. Outside the window, the smell of May flowers hung in the air, sweet, gentle, young. This was the day he had worked for since entering Quigley as a freshman twelve years before. It would be the happiest day of his life, everyone assured him. Yet he did not feel happy. He was no more certain of his vocation now than he had been through the twelve long years. His faith was as thin as a communion wafer. While he was eager to work in his first parish assignment, he now found it harder to pray than ever before.

He struggled out of bed, sat at his desk, and turned on the lamp. No lights-out rule the night before ordination. He looked at the shelf at the side of his desk, at the seven brown-covered ring-binder notebooks that were his diary for the seven years at Mundelein. He slid one off the shelf. Its cover felt reassuringly smooth beneath his fingers. He slowly flipped its pages. Yes, he would be ordained tomorrow. It was too late to turn back now. He had become a subdeacon the year before and a deacon last fall. He was now committed to a life of celibacy; he might just as well be a priest.

Briefly, he thought of Nora, a nostalgic love out of a forgotten past. She and Paul would probably break the news of their engagement to him after his first Mass, with characteristic tact trying not to upstage him during the day.

He sat at his desk for a long time, hardly noticing the hours pass. The first light of day creased the eastern sky behind the red-brick auditorium. Then the sun slowly eased its way over the horizon, turning the early morning a faintly glowing rose. With a start, he noticed the clock staring at him disapprovingly from his desk. He was already late for the preliminaries in the basement of the main chapel.

Five minutes later he rushed down the steps into the noisy crowd of his classmates. Father Roache, the genial majordomo of ordination ceremonies, whose principal job was to calm the jumpy nerves of the priests-to-be, cracked into the microphone, "Okay, guys, relax; Sean's going to go through with it after all."

The laughter was inappropriately loud, but it settled a lot of nerves, Sean's not included.

"Hey, you had me worried," Jimmy McGuire whispered, already dressed in his white alb with a deacon's stole over his shoulder and the priest's chasuble over one arm. "Last-minute cold feet?"

"Do I have feet?" Sean asked innocently.

The high point of the ordination ceremony came when the newly ordained priests, wearing the chasubles they had carried into the sanctuary, stood in ordered ranks in front of the altar in the colonial-style chapel, their hands annointed with the oil of ordination. Each priest attending the ceremony marched up and down the rows imposing his hands on the hands of the new priests and then joining old Cardinal McNulty on the platform of the main altar. The older priests then raised their right hands in the air as though in solemn benediction. It was the moment that many said was the most inspiring and most awesome part of the three-hour-long ritual.

Sean, however, felt nothing at all, just sore knees, an aching back, and a bad headache. Was God punishing him for his lack of faith?

Then, in a tottering voice, with frequent corrections as Father Roache whispered the right words into his ear, Cardinal McNulty chanted the form of the Sacrament of Ordination to the Priesthood over the newly ordained priests:

> *"Almighty Father, grant to these servants of yours the dignity of the priesthood. Renew within them the spirit of holiness. May they be faithful to the ministry they receive from you, Lord God, and be to others models of right conduct . . . so that the words of the Gospel be preached to the ends of the earth and the family of nations, made one in Christ, may become God's one Holy People."*

Later, at the first blessing ceremony held on the steps and lawn surrounding the main chapel, clusters of families and friends in bright dresses and summer suits circled around the young priests, who were trim and self-conscious in their brand new cassocks. Mike Cronin, uncharacteristically giving way to Irish emotion, wept as Sean, for the first time, said, "May the blessing of almighty God, Father, Son, and Holy Spirit, descend upon you and remain with you always."

Paul embraced Sean enthusiastically after his blessing and after he had kissed the hands on which the oil of ordination had not yet dried. "You already look like a cardinal, Sean, and you sure say the blessing like one."

And then it was Nora's turn: Nora, glowing with fresh full beauty in her virginal sleeveless white dress. After Nora kissed Sean's hands, they embraced tenderly.

"I'm so proud of you, Sean," she said through her tears.

"And I'm proud to have you as a sister," he replied, wondering as he said it whether they were the right words.

A First Mass banquet for Sean was held in the sun-filled dining room of the Beverly Country Club. The only awkward moment came when Mike Cronin proposed a toast to his son, "the future cardinal," embarrassing Sean and offending most of the old and new priests who were there.

As the banquet broke up, Nora and Paul walked up to Sean. "We have something to tell you," Paul said, grinning.

"I can't imagine what it is." Sean grinned back.

"You tell him," Paul said.

"He's *your* brother, *you* tell him," said Nora.

"Well"—Paul's embarrassment, amazingly enough, seemed genuine—"Nora claims that sometime in August she wants to make an honest man out of me."

"Nonsense," said Nora. "When he was trying to find a toast for the newly ordained Father Cronin, he discovered a couple of wedding toasts and remembered what weddings were for."

"You'll officiate?"

"I'd have my lawyers sue if you asked anyone else."

As Paul and Nora walked away, hand in hand, a tall, glorious, handsome young couple, it occurred to Father Sean Cronin that Michael Cronin's plans for his family were well under way.

Too bad Mary Eileen could not have been there yesterday to see her son become a priest. It was working out, in spite of all the things that might have gone wrong, Mike Cronin thought, as he tightened the belt on his robe and poured himself another glass of orange juice.

Despite a bad beginning, the night had been rewarding. Jenny Warren had been reluctant to make love when they returned to the empty house on Glenwood Drive after the First Mass banquet. Mike, bristling with enthusiasm over the ordination of one son and the impending marriage of the other, had enthusiastically won her over. It would be a shame to have to give her up, but none of his women seemed to understand that marriage could never be part of the arrangement.

He dismissed Jenny from his mind and returned to thinking about Sean. The boy was a strange one; he read too much poetry, but he had the mark of greatness on him. A discreet visit to the Cardinal in a week, and a large check folded in two and placed on his desk, would doubtless guarantee Sean an excellent assignment and would be the first step in his career. After that, in a couple of years, another check would mean graduate school in Rome and a place on old McNulty's staff. It would be a lot easier, he was convinced, to buy a career for Sean in the Church than to get that damn fool Paul through his bar exam.

Jenny entered the dining room, her round pretty face soft with pleasurable memories, her thin pink negligee loose enough to hint that she would like more to remember.

"Hey, Jenny," he said softly, "do you think my boy is going to be a cardinal?"

Instead of studying for his bar exam, Paul was daydreaming over the latest issue of *Playboy,* linking in his imagination the auburn-haired centerfold with Nora. After two years of heavy necking and petting, he wanted her badly. Not because his sex life was frustrated, but because she fascinated him. Paul's taste ran usually to soft, compliant women. Nora was mysterious, aloof, and seemingly unassailable.

His near North Side "pad," just off Lake Shore Drive, was carefully furnished with pillows, cushions, low soft chairs, and throw rugs. It had all the elegance and comfort necessary to make it *the* place for his law school classmates to come with their dates.

Paul sighed happily. He had not wasted the three years in law school. He had carefully chosen as friends the young men who would be useful in the years ahead: lawyers, politicians, bankers, an occasional journalist. Flattery, fun, pleasure—these were the techniques for attracting them. It was all informal and casual, yet he could tell when he glanced around his apartment during a party that everyone in the room was calculating how they could use everyone else.

That was the way it ought to be. So much the better for him that his calculations were never revealed by his amiable, smiling eyes.

Paul knew that it was time to turn domestic and raise a family. Nora would be a stabilizing influence in his life, and he probably needed that. He would stop the screwing around, too. Political success would come easy. He was a winner, of that there was no doubt. He wanted also to be a man of substance. Nora would help give him depth.

"Are you really going to marry him?" Maggie Martin Shields shook her head in disbelief. "I mean, he's great-looking, and I know you've been dating, but you're so serious and he—well, he seems to enjoy his fun."

They were sitting on the beach, luxuriating in the feel of the mid-July sun on their smooth young skin. Nora was careful in her answer. She knew that Maggie had once had a crush on Paul, and there were signs that her three-month-old marriage to Tom Shields had not settled down yet. Maggie seemed as restless as ever.

"I'm mad about him, Maggie, and I'm impressed by how much he's grown up in the last couple of years. He's thoughtful and attentive and he's studied so hard for the bar exam. I can't think of anybody I'd rather marry than Paul Cronin."

"Not even Sean?" Maggie arched her bare shoulders suggestively.

"Sean's a priest," Nora said firmly.

"Men are men," said Maggie. "I don't care whether they're priests or not." Maggie rolled over on her stomach. "You're naive, Nora. You're going to be in for a terrible surprise. Men don't really care about women. They want a woman's body and nothing more."

"Paul's a gentleman. I'm not afraid of him," Nora insisted, knowing that she was very much afraid of being alone in a bedroom with her husband-to-be, despite all the reading she had done about sex. "In any event," Nora said, "he may be a little surprised too."

Chapter Eight
1956

JIMMY MCGUIRE, HAPPY in his assignment in Oak Lawn and proud of the parish car his pastor had purchased for him—since young priests could not own cars for their first five years—stopped late one evening to talk with Sean at St. Jadwiga rectory. Sean answered the doorbell himself—housekeepers, cooks, and maids at St. Jadwiga's were irregular—and led Jimmy up the shaky staircase to his tiny room on the back of the second floor.

"Does Dudon ever come out of his room?" Jimmy jerked his thumb in the direction of the pastor's elaborate suite at the front of the house.

"Not really, save to take care of his Chihuahuas and to say the first Mass on Sunday." Sean slumped in the battered old chair that was one of the two pieces of furniture in his study.

"Chihuahuas?"

"Yes. He raises full breeds or pedigrees or whatever they call prizewinning Chihuahuas. He had a big crisis last Sunday when one of the bitches—it's not a pejorative term if you're a dog—gave birth just before the six-thirty Mass."

"How crazy is he?" Jimmy asked, now quite serious.

"Oh, I don't suppose he's any more crazy than any other unmarried man of fifty-five who has nothing except dogs to live for. Remember, Jimmy, that this was a nice little Bohemian parish where everybody loved him and he didn't have to work. It became part of the black ghetto overnight. So he just sits up in his room trying to pretend it didn't happen and hoping that the chancery office will remember him."

"While you do all the work?"

"Well, that's what we're ordained for, isn't it?"

"Do you think your father—"

"Yes, I think my father went to see the Cardinal, offered to make a contribution, and almost got away with it. Then the Cardinal dug out a file card on me from Mundelein that warned him against me. So he pocketed Dad's check and sent me here to St. Jadwiga's. But I'm glad I'm here. If we don't like working in poor parishes we don't belong in the priesthood."

"You should at least take a day off," Jimmy said.

Sean relaxed a bit. "I know I should, Jimmy," he said. "And I appreciate the concern. I'll see you guys next Thursday."

"And I'll believe that when I see you on the first tee." Jimmy paused. "Is Nora really going to marry Paul?"

Sean felt his spirits lift. "That's what they both tell me."

"You always said I had a soft spot for Nora," McGuire said awkwardly, "and you were right. I just wonder. They're such different personalities."

Sean tried to consider Jimmy's observation objectively. Jimmy was a good judge of human nature. "I know what you mean, Jimmy. I used to think the same thing myself, and I know they're going to have some tough adjustments. In a way, it will be harder on Paul. Nora has all the willpower."

Jimmy was unimpressed. "Look, do me a favor, for old times' sake and all of that. Make sure Nora knows what she's doing. Tell her about Paul and Maggie."

There was a long pause while nameless emotions struggled in Sean's heart.

"Sure," he said finally.

Nora and Sean sat in the Berghoff Restaurant on Monroe Street surrounded by frantic businessmen and lawyers, enjoying, as they always did, each other's company. His telephone call had been mysterious, and Nora, only a few days away from her wedding, was uncharacteristically falling behind schedule. Nevertheless, a call from Sean proposing lunch took precedence, and she postponed her scheduled task of arranging the seating chart for the reception.

When he saw the tall, lovely young woman wave to him and then walk gracefully across the dining room, Sean had realized again how dishonest had been his defense to the seminary that Nora was "almost a sister." There was no doubt that brothers did not react to their sisters the way he reacted to Nora. Reluctantly, he banished his fantasies to a dark corner of his imagination.

"I'm glad you were able to come," he said.

"I'll have lunch with you, Sean, any time you'd like," she said. "How's it going at St. Joshua?"

"Jadwiga." He emphasized the word and then, noting her amused smile, said sheepishly, "You know, you really are an impish little bitch."

She sank her teeth into a juicy mixture of cheese, sauerkraut, and ham. "I don't think the word 'little' is appropriate, and that doesn't answer my question. Uncle Mike is furious about your assignment."

Sean pushed his plate aside. "It's all right, Nora, it really is. I'm happy. I'm doing the work I've always wanted. Anyhow, it's you, not me, who's on the agenda for this lunch."

"Oh?" Nora wondered why her heart seemed to be sinking.

"Look." He stumbled a bit. "Well, you know how it is with me and Paul. We're competitors, we're fighters, difficult, contentious people. . . ."

"Well, you are, anyhow."

"You also know how much I love him. I know all his faults, I guess, yet I still worship him and have for as long as I can remember. Sometimes he's superficial, and sometimes he's unreliable, and sometimes he seems only interested in his own pleasures. When you know him as well as I do, you know that he has the capability of being very deep and very serious and very responsive."

Nora felt a rush of affection swelling up inside her. "Oh, Sean." She reached across the table to touch his hand. "I know Paul's failings. We all were raised in the same house, remember? I do love him and he does love me, and he's grown up so much in the past few years. Bobby Kennedy told me after the Democratic convention that Paul was the best floor leader they had, and if there were more like him it would be Stevenson and Kennedy instead of Stevenson and Kefauver this November. He'll be all right, wait and see. And I'll be all right too. Please, don't worry about us." She tightened her grip on his hand.

Sean was flustered. "I don't suppose it will be any more difficult for you and Paul than it is for other young married people." He hesitated. "It may be a little different, that's all." He could not bring himself to tell her about Paul and Maggie.

Nora released her hold on his long, tense fingers. Maybe it was a sin to touch a priest's hand that way. "Don't worry, please don't. I know what I'm doing. I'm going into this marriage with both eyes open."

Chapter Nine
······························*1956*································

MICHAEL CRONIN WAS afraid. He was afraid of death.

His son Sean considered that conclusion carefully. Early in life Sean had realized that his father was not like the fathers of his friends, that he was different. Now, at the age of twenty-five, the disturbing truth hit Sean with terrible clarity. Much of his father's frantic activity was a desperate rush to escape from death. As he grew older he was losing the race. His ideas became more fixed, his gestures more nervous, his eyes more icy. The old charm and wit were still there, but they were gradually slipping away.

"Do you understand all that I've told you?" Mike's cold green eyes peered up at Sean, who was sitting across from him at the littered desk in the dark, heavily paneled study of their home on Glenwood Drive, a home which his father refused to leave, even though his vast wealth could purchase an entire neighborhood far better than Beverly.

Sean tried to concentrate. "Most of it, Dad. Counting the land and the stock portfolio and the oil interests and everything else, you're worth more than half a billion dollars. I'm afraid I don't understand all the companies and the partnerships. I'd need a diagram for that."

His father laughed. "The IRS would love to have one too."

"Well, I think I understand most of it, even without the diagram," Sean said carefully. He knew this was important to his father.

Mike sighed and relaxed in his large red leather chair. "I want you to know all these things before Paul's marriage. Paul will run the business, of course, at least until he's elected to something. But there will be a group of trustees, like my old buddies Marty Hoffman and Ed Connaire, to watch him until he's forty. You'll be too busy being a priest"—Mike was still terribly dissatisfied with Sean's calm acceptance of the St. Jadwiga's assignment—"so the trust will simply pay you a check every month for the rest of your life. They'll have the right to increase the size of the check, and if you need money for something special, for yourself, not for the Church, then you can apply to them. I'll instruct them and their successors to be generous. Do you understand?"

Sean understood very well. His father intended to keep him firmly under control for all of Michael Cronin's life and then, through the trustees, under equally firm control after he died. It didn't make any difference to Sean. "I understand."

"Mind you, any time you need anything while I'm still alive, no matter how much it is, just come and ask and I'll take care of it—no questions asked, no strings attached."

Not much, thought Sean. "And what do you do with all the money you make every year, Dad?" he asked.

The long and detailed answer left Sean flabbergasted. His father gave a great deal of money away, much of it secretly. While there were Cronin Halls being built at Fordham, Notre Dame, Boston College, and Northwestern, the typical Cronin gift was anonymous.

"You're very generous," Sean said with genuine respect.

"All you have to do is say the word and I'll build a new church and a new school and a new rectory for St. Jagoff, or whatever the hell the name is. Just say the word."

"That will be the day," Sean said softly to himself.

Sean found it difficult to deliver the sermon before the wedding ceremony. He was distracted by the glitter and brass of the military wedding—Mike had insisted that Paul be married as befitting a major in the United States Marine Corps—and by the bride's beauty in her loosely flowing old-fashioned wedding gown. Nora might have been his bride, his wife. He might have shared his life with her, enjoying her beauty and delighting in her wit and intelligence. It was God's will that he give her up, God's will that she marry his brother. Yet, as he tried to concentrate on his carefully prepared sermon, disturbing images of Nora lying next to him on their marriage bed raced through his mind.

"It is our prayer today for Paul and Nora in their married life together," Sean read, "with all its joys and sorrows, that they find not only each other but also the One whose love for His people is both unending and an extension. We want to tell them today that even in their most lonely and difficult moment God's love will be with them, and so will the support of the Church and of all their family and friends. And so . . .''

He stumbled through the exchange of vows and the blessings of the rings with almost as much nervousness as did the bride and groom. He was careful not to look long at Nora's ecstatic face and volcanic blue eyes. By the time he came to the nuptial blessing after the Pater Noster, he had better self-control, yet his hand trembled as he gave them Holy Communion. He was relieved when it came time for the final blessing.

> *May the Lord Jesus, who was a guest at the wedding in Cana,*
>   *bless you and your families and friends.*
>   *Amen.*
> *May Jesus, who loved his Church to the end,*
>   *always fill your hearts with love.*
>   *Amen.*
> *May he grant that, as you believe in his resurrection,*
>   *so you may wait for him in joy and hope.*
>   *Amen.*
> *And may almighty God bless you all,*
>   *the Father, and the Son, and the Holy Spirit.*
>   *Amen.*
> *May almighty God, with his Word of blessing, unite*
>   *your hearts in the never-ending bond of pure love.*
>   *Amen.*
> *May your children bring you happiness, and may your generous*
>   *love for them be returned to you, many times over.*
>   *Amen.*

Nora was not like the other virgins Paul had deflowered. She did not try to turn off the light or scurry into the bathroom. Rather, as soon as they were inside the bridal suite of the Drake, she calmly drew the drapes on the parlor windows and with a natural poise undressed before him.

Paul's confidence evaporated. His new wife was spectacularly inviting, yet he was untouched by desire.

Their first union was a near disaster. The masculine potency of which he was so proud deserted him. His bride was utterly unaffected by their coupling, save for one soft cry of pain. His satisfaction was trivial.

Afterward, Nora cried quietly next to him on the bed. "I'm sorry, I'll try to be better next time," she murmured.

So she blamed herself? Paul sighed with relief and patted her head reassuringly. "Don't worry about it, Nora. Everything will work out fine. All we had to do today was begin." He cradled her in his arms, muttering soothing words about how beautiful she was. That seemed to calm her down. His new wife would be very easy to satisfy.

Later that night the dream about Chosun returned. Joe Makuch dressed in a Chink uniform led the charge. His face changed into Nora's as he plunged the bayonet deep into Paul Cronin's belly.

Paul woke up screaming and grabbing at his stomach. His new wife embraced him, rested his head against her chest, and crooned a soft lullaby into his ear.

Thus comforted on his wedding night, Paul Martin Cronin fell back to sleep.

Joe Makuch turned up in Paul's office a week after he returned from his honeymoon. Once a trim, tough professional master sergeant, Joe was now fat, bald, and greasy, an overweight goblin of a man who had the Midas touch in reverse—everything he did turned to rock.

"I need a favor, Major," Makuch said, nervously revolving his grimy fedora in his hands. "I wouldn't bother you if I had anyone else to turn to. But this is an emergency. They built a new highway on the other side of town, one of them freeway things, and my gas station fell flat on its face. Made ten thousand bucks last year and only a couple hundred this year. I got a chance to pick up another station near an interchange on the other side of town. It won't cost me much at all . . . and it's right off the freeway interchange, a real gold mine."

Paul sighed. Given Joe's luck, they would close the interchange next year. The problem wasn't paying a few thousand dollars of blackmail now to shut him up about the Chosun Reservoir. The problem was that the drain could keep on forever and get bigger every year.

"Sure, I understand how it is, Joe. You saved my life a couple of times, so what the hell." He grinned reassuringly. "You name it, and if I've got it, I'll give it to you."

Joe Makuch named fifteen thousand dollars, and Paul wrote him a check. He would find an explanation for his father somehow, when he had to.

BOOK THREE

He came to Simon Peter, who said to him, "Lord, are you going to wash my feet?"

Jesus answered, "At the moment you do not know what I am doing, but later you will understand."

"Never!" said Peter. "You shall never wash my feet."

Jesus replied, "If I do not wash you, you could have nothing in common with me."

"Then, Lord," said Simon Peter, "not only my feet, but my hands and my head as well."

—JOHN 13:6–9

Chapter Ten
1962

NORA CRONIN WAS not pleased with the phone call she received in Washington from Maggie Shields, who still lived in Chicago. Eileen, Nora's five-year-old daughter, was in nursery school, and three-year-old Mary was taking one of her rare naps. For Nora it meant an hour and a half of peace, during which she could finish Katherine Anne Porter's *Ship of Fools*. Then the jangling telephone and Maggie's peace-shattering news.

Maggie had always needed attention, and now she was complaining about Tom's preoccupation with his growing OB practice. Indeed, Maggie seemed to be jealous of every one of Tom's patients. There was little in life that made Maggie feel important. Nora sighed. She had reluctantly given up trying to persuade Maggie that she was worthwhile. Twenty years of being told by her parents that she was cute but empty-headed could not be undone.

"And I think it's just terrible about Sean." The subject of Maggie's conversation changed abruptly.

Nora put aside the book in which her finger, until then, had kept the place. "What's the matter with Sean?"

"Well, when did you see him last?"

Nora felt guilty. Sean had been absent from her mind, it seemed, for months. There were enough other things to preoccupy her. "Only for a few days, at Oakland Beach. He didn't take much of a vacation last year."

"He never takes vacations. It's just work, work, work with those Negroes who don't appreciate him. Tom says he thinks he's killing himself. Why doesn't he ask the new Archbishop to transfer him out of that hellhole?"

"Sean says the old Cardinal sent him to St. Jadwiga's to prove that a rich man's son couldn't last in a poor parish, and that if he asks out the Cardinal will win, even if he's dead."

"That sounds like Sean, all right," Maggie said.

"Is Tom really worried about his health?"

"Tom said he thinks Sean will end up in the hospital if he doesn't stop."

After she got rid of Maggie, Nora walked to the bay window of their old Georgetown house and looked out onto the narrow street. The leaves turned red and gold in Washington later than in Chicago. It was November, the week after the election. The falling leaves had carpeted the lawn in front of their house. She had once been in love with Sean—now from the safety of retrospect she could admit that—and she had almost forgotten about him.

Nora had been only moderately happy in her marriage. She had realized within a few months that her husband was spoiled, petulant, and self-indulgent, although charming and intelligent. He might grow up someday, but she feared it wasn't very likely.

In six years of living with Paul, she had also discovered with gratification that she could put up with a marriage that was less than satisfactory and not lose her sense of self in it the way Maggie had. Despite the fact that she was as much a mother as a wife to Paul, her life was not unhappy. Her two little girls were pure joy. She had her books, her music, and her involvement in the social and cultural life of the glittering Kennedy administration.

Anyway, there was no point in being angry at Paul. It had little effect. He was contrite, humble, apologetic, and then promptly forgot everything he said. Their sex life was low-key, mildly satisfying if not exciting. Nora suspected that she was undersexed. She also suspected that there were other women. Everyone in Washington seemed to have another woman or another man. The Kennedys set the tone there, as well as in so many other things these days. While she found their infidelities distasteful, she could not resist their charm any more than could anyone else in Washington. And especially the charm of the Attorney General.

The Kennedys were a lot like Paul: likable, at times brilliant, but they used everyone. Paul was only a high-grade errand boy, despite his title of Special Assistant to the Attorney General. If he should ever become unproductive, they would drop him in a minute. Everyone in the administration knew that was the way the Kennedys were. Still, they were all willing to take their chances, wear their PT-boat tie clasps, and hope they were among those who were admired and respected and were not being used.

Nora returned to her chair and retrieved *Ship of Fools,* but she did not open it. It would be as easy for her to have a lover as it was for Paul to have other women. Easier, perhaps. Heaven knows, there was no lack of offers. Naive, South Side Irish girl that she was, it had taken her several months to recognize the propositions for what they were. She routinely turned them down. She was simply not interested.

There were more pluses than minuses in her life, the little girls especially. Perhaps she was too objective, too dispassionate. Nora considered that possibility very carefully. Lord knew, the Kennedys liked her because they thought she was a fighter. Perhaps she was a fighter, yet now didn't seem to be the time to fight.

She had played touch ball with them the previous summer at the beach in Hyannis. Her height and speed made her a strong competitor. In sweat shirt and cutoff jeans, she intercepted pass after pass, twice taking the ball out of the outstretched hands of the Attorney General of the United States and once running the interception for a touchdown. Bobby hadn't liked that at all.

"It's not fair, Nora"—he pronounced it as though her name was "Norar"— "a woman as beautiful as you shouldn't be so fast."

"I'm not fast at all, Mr. Attorney General," she had taunted him. "I'm a virtuous housewife."

Bobby thought that was very funny, but the next time she reached over his shoulder for an interception, she found herself flying through the air and landing on the beach just as an enormous wave arrived at the same place as she.

Soaking wet and furious, she stormed out of the water and shouted, "I don't give a goddamn if you are a Kennedy, I'll get even with you!"

The touch-ball game ended then in laughter and she had become a Kennedy favorite, with the phrase, "I don't give a goddamn if you are a Kennedy," being recalled whenever she was present—much to Nora's embarrassment.

At the White House for dinner, a week before the Cuban Missile Crisis, the Attorney General had needled her. "I'm still waiting for your revenge, Nora."

"That's part of the fun," she said. "I'll get you at a time when you're least ready."

"You're a great fighter," the Attorney General had said.

Much later, or so it seemed, Eileen bounded in from school, and the nanny brought a sleepy-eyed Mary down from the nursery.

The little girls were so beautiful, much more Riley than Cronin. She sighed. Uncle Mike had not forgiven her for her failure to produce a male child. Paul's disappointment was obvious too. Her reproductive apparatus was not as healthy as the rest of her. Both births had been difficult, and Mary's dangerous. Tom Shields, who had delivered both of the little girls, had shaken his head discouragingly. "No more for a while, Nora; wait at least a couple of years."

Nora had not hesitated to use the birth control pill. Priests like Sean Cronin, who vigorously denounced it as unnatural, simply didn't understand what sex meant to a husband and wife, even the placid sex between herself and Paul. Three years was long enough, though, and she felt she ought to try again.

While she was absentmindedly mediating a quarrel at the dinner table between her blond vivacious younger daughter and her raven-haired serious older daughter, Nora thought again of Maggie's call. She decided to tell Paul about her phone conversation with Maggie and suggest that he go to Chicago to see if things were really so bad with Sean, even though Sean had discouraged such visits in the past.

The sun was shining very brightly on Paul Cronin's life. Still in his early thirties, he was an important man in Washington. He had stood at Nicholas Katzenbach's side through the integration crises at the University of Alabama and the University of Mississippi. While he had not actually been with the Attorney General in the situation room during the missile crisis, he had been waiting with a few others when Robert Kennedy returned to his office at the Justice Department.

Paul had built up a network of contacts and friends, far more powerful than the Chicago crew he still carefully tended from a distance. Paul was a Kennedy man, all right, yet there was no point in being only a Kennedy man—especially when you were in a position to do important favors for people who would still be powerful in Washington long after the Kennedys had gone.

His quiet dinner parties, presided over with classic charm by Nora, were events where some of the brightest men and women in Washington could share ideas and hopes. They were just large enough so that the Kennedys would know about them and be impressed, but not so large that they would feel threatened.

In the second Kennedy administration, he would probably begin as an undersecretary somewhere and then work his way up to being a full cabinet member before returning to Chicago to run for the Senate. He had a beautiful, gifted, and much-admired wife, two gorgeous little girls, and a life ahead of him filled with promise and possibilities. Moreover, the next time he took Christine Waverly out for an early evening cocktail, he was sure he could score. A smooth, honey-haired blonde with a trim, compact body, just a few years out of Bennington, Chris Waverly was already one of the most powerful women reporters in Washington.

Paul felt no particular guilt about calling from the office to tell his wife that he would be delayed in a conference with the Attorney General when, in fact, he would be continuing his pursuit of Chris Waverly. There was the sex that you had with your wife, which was pleasant enough, and then there was the exciting pursuit of challenging women. A man, or at least a man like him, was entitled to both. He had remained faithful to Nora through her first pregnancy, although it had driven him almost mad. Then he had fallen during the delay while she recovered. After that, he didn't try, contenting himself with being faithful most of the time. He figured that made him better than most men his age in Washington.

For Nora, he had enormous respect and even admiration. She was smart, shrewd in her evaluation of people, and extremely attractive. Paul was intrigued and fascinated by her composure and by the aura of mystery that surrounded her. Nora was always surprising, except in bed, and Paul preferred her that way.

The only real problem, he told himself as he parked his Ferrari in their driveway, was that they had no son. And Tom Shields had been blunt: "If you love your wife, no more children for a while."

Paul Cronin loved his wife, or at least he was proud of her, but he wanted a son. He could not force Nora to take another chance, but she seemed ready now.

She was reading in the parlor, wearing a beige silk robe. "You didn't have to wait up for me," he said as he entered the room and tossed a heavy briefcase on one of the easy chairs.

She closed her book and embraced him. "No problem, darling. I have a sandwich in the refrigerator for you if you're hungry."

"Wonderful," he said, patting her bottom appreciatively. After his foreplay with Chris, he would certainly need her tonight. "I don't deserve this attention. You're the only wife I know of who is sympathetic and understanding."

"Better say tolerant," she said, leaving for the kitchen.

While he munched on a roast beef sandwich, Nora perched on the side of the sofa.

"Maggie Shields called today," she said.

"What did she want?" he said, feeling some pleasure from memories of his affair with Maggie.

"Tom's worried about Sean. He thinks he's ruining his health at St. Jadwiga's. I think Sean's trying to show your father, and the priests, and the dead Cardinal, and everyone else that he can handle one of the toughest assignments in the city."

Paul paused. The sandwich did not seem quite so tasty any more. The one person in the world he really worried about, aside from himself, was his little brother. "Do you think Maggie's exaggerating?"

Nora's face tightened in a thoughtful frown. "I don't usually take Maggie all that seriously. But she's not likely to misquote Tom, and if he says that Sean is running himself into the ground, I think there's a problem."

Paul began to eat his sandwich again, slowly and thoughtfully. "There are ways we can get him out of there, I suppose, although the old man is too stubborn to eat a little bit of crow. I guess I'll have to do it."

"Why don't you go to Chicago first and see how bad Sean really is?" she said.

Paul sipped from his beer glass. "I'd like to do that, but I don't think I can get away for a few weeks."

"Sean may not have a few weeks to spare. If we wait until Christmas, he could end up in a hospital."

"No, not a hospital. Not Sean." Paul suddenly saw a way to look after Sean without inconveniencing himself. "Why don't you go? Anna can take care of the kids. You'd only be gone for a few days. Besides, Sean would have a hard time admitting to me that he's worn out."

Nora hesitated. "I will if you want me to, Paul. I don't like to leave you alone in Washington, though."

He winked at her. "Don't worry about that. Bob Kennedy works us so hard that I don't even notice women any more."

"I bet." She laughed.

Amused, he thought, but not suspicious. "Speaking of Bob, by the way, he said I should give you his best and tell you that he's still waiting for your vengeance."

Nora laughed. "And it's going to come very soon. Just tell him that!"

Later that night, Paul pretended to himself that Nora was Chris Waverly; often he could make love to his wife only if he pretended that she was someone else.

His desire for Chris pushed him into stirring depths in Nora of which he was afraid. As they lay exhausted in each other's arms, she kissed him affectionately and said, "That was very nice. Thank you."

"Do you think we ought to try for a son one of these days?" he said, sensing her vulnerability.

"I've been thinking the same thing," she said softly. "As soon as I get back from Chicago. . . ."

She was soon asleep. Paul remained awake, feeling worthless as he always did after he made love to his wife. He would never be good enough for her. He had known that from the beginning. He would be a political success, but that was not enough. Nora deserved better. Someone like Sean.

Chapter Eleven

1962

THE MEETING IN the Attorney General's office was inconclusive. The union leader they were after was certainly a thief, yet they had no evidence, even though they knew there were records of payoffs in the office of George Sandler, the Washington lobbyist for the union. The records were Sandler's own insurance against ending up in Chesapeake Bay if power changed hands in the union; he was not likely to tell the truth to the grand jury unless there was incriminating information against him.

When the meeting was over, Paul walked back to his office with Bud O'Hara, who was supervising the investigation.

"Can't the Bureau get into Sandler's office?" he asked softly.

O'Hara eyed him with his cold Texas eyes. "That's against the law, Paul." He spoke with equal softness.

"Come on." Paul laughed. "You were the one who was talking about functional justice the other day."

The Texan shrugged. "Truth is, we don't want to try it. You know how touchy the Director is. He only breaks the law when it's his idea. Some of us think that he's in bed—figuratively, although you never can tell about the Director—with the union president."

They stopped at the door of O'Hara's office. "Any objection if we find the evidence some other way?" Paul asked lightly.

The Texan didn't hesitate. "None whatever."

Lawrence called for Michael Cronin at the door of Little Company of Mary Hospital in the new Mercedes limousine. New chauffeur, new limousine. Mike sighed. Everyone was growing old. It didn't seem the same with Jeremy gone.

Jane was surviving, though. Seventy years old and a chronic alcoholic, she refused to die. She had just pulled through another heart attack, causing the doctors to marvel.

He no longer believed that Jane would ever reveal his secret. Even if she tried, he could shut her up. That had always been true. Why had he lost his nerve? He should have married Jenny Warren; she was a spectacular woman. Should have said to hell with Jane after the ordination and married Jenny.

Too late now. She was married to a damn fiddle player. Did she do the same things to him that had so delighted Mike? The fiddle player was seven years younger than Mike, still in his middle fifties.

Mike sighed. After Jenny he had lost interest in women, other than an occasional fling here and there.

He bid Lawrence good night and mixed himself a final drink in his lonely house. It was too big for one man, but he had to keep it as a place for the kids to come home to from Washington. And for Sean on his day off, even if he never came home on his day off.

Mike sipped his drink slowly. He worried endlessly about Sean. He seemed more like Mary Eileen with every passing day—idealistic, unreal. He wondered if Jane might be right about him. There was no way of ever knowing for sure.

The headache which had bothered him for the last couple of weeks returned. He decided to mix himself another drink. If Sean would come to his senses and get the hell out of that nigger parish . . . but it was essential not to give in to him. He had to realize his mistakes. Giving in to Mary Eileen had been a disaster. He should have been firm with her much earlier.

Then the lights went out on him. It was as though someone had clubbed him on the back of his head. The next thing he knew, the clock said three in the morning. He must have fallen asleep, he told himself. Too much to drink. He staggered upstairs to bed, wavering uncertainly as he climbed the staircase.

In the morning he told himself that nothing unusual had happened. The feeling of falling through space was merely part of a hangover.
After two drinks.

St. Jadwiga's was worse than Nora could ever have dreamed. Even the parkway in front of the battered old red and brown brick apartment buildings on Douglas Boulevard seemed decrepit and worn. The stone church, with its wooden bell tower, seemed ready to fall apart. The school next door to it badly needed tuck-pointing, and the two-story wooden rectory almost surely was a fire hazard. Worst of all was the dirt. Everything—windows, doors, gutters, sidewalks, the concrete schoolyard—was filthy. Paper, beer cans, and whiskey bottles littered the ground in front of the rectory, which once long ago may have been a lawn. No wonder Sean had forbidden them to visit his parish.

She parked her rented Chevrolet in front of the rectory. As she turned off the ignition, Nora steeled herself for her encounter with Sean. Every time she was with him her heart beat faster and her throat tightened. Realistic as always, Nora knew that a part of her wanted to go to bed with him. She smiled faintly to herself. If she had recognized those emotions the day he had blunderingly offered to leave the seminary for her, she might have taken him up on the offer.

She squared her shoulders and got out of the car. Her passion for Sean was controllable and would be controlled. After all, he was her brother-in-law, and almost her brother. She gingerly walked up the decaying wooden steps and pushed the old-fashioned bell on the door front. She heard no bell ring inside. She waited and pushed it again, and then once more. Still there was no answer. Perhaps Sean was at the school.

She walked down the steps and through the passageway between the church and the school. At the back of the rectory there was a small alleyway surrounded by high fences. On the left hand was a door that led to the church and on the right hand a stairwell descending to what seemed to be a boiler room. The church door was locked. A pounding sound seemed to be coming from downstairs. Nora turned up her coat collar against the chill November winds and picked her way through the litter down into the boiler room.

There was half a foot of water on the floor of the room, and in darkness broken only by a single dim light bulb, a man was on top of the boiler with a wrench, wrestling with the pipe fitting.

"Pardon me," she said politely. "Can you tell me where Father Cronin is?"

"He's on top of the boiler putting the finishing touches on repairs," said a weary voice. "Don't worry, Sister. Tell the principal that we'll have the heat on in another half hour. Thank God it isn't the middle of January."

"It's not *a* sister, Sean," she said, trying to hide her dismay. "It's *your* sister."

The figure on the boiler turned toward her. "Nora? Just give me another second here. . . . Ugh, this thing is hard to twist. There, that does it." He climbed down off the boiler, oblivious to the water swishing around his legs, and flipped the button at the side of the rusty old turbine. There was a cranking and groaning sound within it and then a recalcitrant and dubious hum.

"Well, it seems to be working again. Come on back to the rectory. I'll make you a cup of coffee." Sean was wearing black trousers and a black shirt with a Roman collar. He was thin and worn, at least fifteen pounds underweight.

The rectory kitchen was a mess. Dirty dishes were piled up in the sink, and the cupboards and shelves were littered with empty cans and containers. "Georgetown or Hyannisport it is not," said Sean, with a pale reflection of his once-magic smile.

"You do the cooking, the housekeeping, and the janitoring, as well as the priesting?" Nora asked incredulously. "Here, give me that. I'll make the coffee—and I'll wash the coffee cups before we use them. I'm not going to bring some infectious Douglas Boulevard disease back to my kids."

A bit more light now appeared in Sean's eyes. "Same old Nora. Move in and take charge. Yes, I do everything around here; that is, everything except teach at the school. The pastor comes for Mass on Sunday morning and then goes back to his mother's house. Otherwise, it's all mine."

"You can't afford any help?" She searched for detergent to wash the dishes.

"Every penny we have goes for heat and electricity, and food for the nuns, and salaries for the lay teachers. The chancery office"—he frowned—"is not going to provide any subsidy to a parish in which the assistant is a wealthy man. That is precisely what the late Cardinal told me. So we make do."

"Why keep the parish open then?" Nora asked, cleaning the coffee cups.

"Because we educate four hundred kids a year and give them a lot better education than the public schools. Because we salvage a couple of dozen juvenile delinquents every year. Because there are a few hundred Catholics, most of them converts, who come to Mass here every Sunday. And because somebody has to visit the people of the neighborhood when they're in the hospital or in jail."

Nora took a deep breath. "You became a priest, Sean, to do these things?"

He slumped at the chipped porcelain-top kitchen counter with a weariness that tore at her heart. "I can't imagine anything I could do that would be more priestly. Come on, after we've had the coffee, I'll take you through our school."

The school was as decrepit as the rectory and the church. The corridors and the classrooms desperately needed a coat of paint. The windows were filthy. But inside the classrooms it was no different from the St. Titus grammar school that Nora Riley had attended fifteen years before. The faces of the students might be black, but the order, the discipline, the demanding presence of "S'ter," and the vigorous pursuit of learning were all the same. The children stood respectfully when Sean entered the classroom, with the traditional "Good Morning, Father" slow singsong. He introduced her as Nora, and they replied, "Good morn-ing, No-ra."

"Good morning, boys and girls," said Nora, remembering the greeting.

In the corridor after the tour of the classrooms, Sean leaned against the wall. "We have four hundred and twenty-nine kids in this school, Nora," he said proudly. "All of them will go to high school, and two thirds of them will go to college, and I don't think the Catholic Church has ever done a better thing."

"At the cost of your life?" she said hotly.

"It's a good cause to die in, Nora," Sean said, his body sagging against the wall.

Nora had decided to plead with Uncle Mike to salvage St. Jadwiga and Sean. Mike greeted her at the door of his new office with an embrace.

"You're looking as beautiful as ever, Nora," he said.

Nora thought Uncle Mike looked older, weaker. There was a tremor in his hand and already, at one thirty in the afternoon, there was the smell of whiskey on his breath.

"What brings you to Chicago?" he asked. Outside his window the Chicago skyline, a veritable museum of architectural splendor, was set sharply against the gray November sky. To the south were the railroad tracks, the drive, and a midget airfield on the island off the lake shore. No views like that in Washington.

"We had a phone call from Maggie Shields," Nora said. "Tom is worried about Sean. Paul is busy seeing that justice survives in the nation, so he sent me here to find out whether Maggie is exaggerating. She's not. Sean is sick and tired and worn out, and he must have help."

"If he wants money, he can ask me," Mike said. "I'll give him whatever he needs to take care of that slum of his."

"You know he'll never ask, Uncle Mike. He's as stubborn as you are. And while the two of you are busy being stubborn, Sean's ruining his health and probably his life."

"He's wasting his time out there, the damned fool," Mike said.

"No, he's not," Nora flared at him. "He's doing wonderful work, but he's doing it all by himself and he's done it for too long. You give money to dozens of charities. Why can't you give some to your own son?"

"I won't give him a goddamn cent. He's old enough to take care of himself and that's final, young woman. I won't hear another word about it."

Nora's temper snapped. "You're a hateful old man." She picked up her coat, yanked open the door of the apartment, slammed it in his face as he hurried after her, and ducked into a waiting elevator just as the door opened. She wept as she rode down, as much for the look of pain on Michael Cronin's face as for the plight of Father Sean Cronin.

Paul Cronin considered the "tools" he had obtained from a contact at the CIA: a tiny camera, keys, a small flashlight, gloves, tape to secure the door, a device for searching out alarm systems. He had visited George Sandler the day before. The lobbyist was a sleek little man with ferretlike eyes and nervous hands who had glanced anxiously at a file cabinet behind his desk when Paul warned that they might subpoena his records.

"You don't have enough evidence to warrant that, Mr. Cronin," Sandler said cautiously.

Paul didn't want to frighten him into destroying the files before he had a chance to steal them. "You're right, I guess—so far. We're going to get the whole lot of you, though. There's no reason for you to go to jail. We'd provide you with a new life and protection."

"For how long?" the other man asked bitterly. "I don't trust Bob Kennedy any more than I trust Carmine da Silva."

"You should have thought of that," Paul had replied, "before you got mixed up with his union."

Paul left after that exchange, confident that he could find his way around the office at night. Sandler thought he was safe. He would be surprised to find that, in the Kennedy administration, you fought fire with fire.

Access to the building was easy. The guard at the door was sound asleep. Paul didn't have to pretend that he was a telephone repairman. He could let himself out the back door into the alley behind K Street when he was finished. He didn't need the dark glasses and the cap which were part of his repairman's disguise. He'd be careful just the same. No point in being recognized.

The keys were not much help in opening the office door, especially since in the dim corridor light he couldn't see distinctly. You would think the CIA would have better technology.

Then he saw the light above the elevator door go on. My God, someone coming up.

For the first time he thought of the consequences if he was caught. Terror gripped at his stomach. He wanted to run. The elevator light was like the flares above the Reservoir.

At the last minute he saw a door that looked as if it might be a restroom. He ran down the corridor and pushed the door open. The door swung shut after him. Paul leaned against it, breathing heavily. He was so frightened that he broke out in a heavy sweat. What would happen if they found him? He gulped for air.

After the panic came dizziness and, after the dizziness, nausea. Paul stumbled around the men's room, found a urinal, and vomited into it. After he had emptied his dinner he felt better. He had to pull himself together and make his escape. Down the back stairs. Why the hell had he tried such a stupid trick anyway? Dumb recklessness.

When he was sure he could walk steadily, he eased open the door. No sign of anyone, no sound.

He slipped into the corridor, hesitated, and then, unexpectedly, turned not toward the exit but back down the corridor to Sandler's office.

From then on, it was astonishingly easy. The first key he tried opened the door. He had no trouble finding the file case; the second key fit that lock. Then with the thin, powerful beam of the penlight splitting the darkness, he rapidly thumbed through the contents of the cabinet until he found the incriminating financial records. O'Hara had been sure they would be there.

His heart pounding and his head light with excitement, Paul rapidly shot two rolls of film—thirty-two pictures in all. Enough to put several corrupt union leaders behind bars for a long time to come.

In the alley afterward, Paul was triumphant. He had mastered his fear. He deserved a reward. Tomorrow night he would have it. No more fooling around with Chris Waverly. Even if he had to rape her.

Nora was shopping in Marshall Field's, buying sheets, blankets, dishes, and even clothing for Sean. Paul would have to come to Chicago to see the new Archbishop. Sean should either be transferred from St. Jadwiga's or the diocese must help him out financially. Paul was persuasive enough to be able to talk to the Archbishop, who was reportedly a decent and kindly man, into forgetting the past.

She saw a familiar face on the escalator. "Jenny," she exclaimed. "Jenny Warren!"

Michael Cronin's former companion was as pretty as she had been at Nora's wedding, if perhaps a little more subdued.

Jenny hesitated, as though she did not want to recognize Nora, but then, presumably against her better judgment, she waited at the bottom of the escalator. "Jenny Marsh now, Nora. It's good to see you."

"Let's have lunch and talk about old times."

Again Jenny hesitated. "I ought not to. . . . Will you swear that you won't tell your Uncle Mike?"

"Sure," said Nora.

Over lunch they exchanged histories of the past six years. Jenny had married the first cellist with the New York Philharmonic. Her husband was in Chicago for a concert. They were very happy. Both his children and both her children were married, and they lived a pleasant, peaceful life, organized around his music.

"I really hoped back in 1956 that you'd be my stepmother," said Nora, after an awkward lull in the conversation.

Jenny's pretty face became sad. She sipped her tea. "I thought I would be. Mike . . . he didn't exactly promise, but he certainly led me to believe . . . of course. I should have known. He was so kind and so tender and so gentle to begin with, and such a marvelous lover. Well, I deceived myself about some things and pretended other things that weren't so. And then he changed. At first I didn't even notice it—maybe because I didn't want to notice it."

"What was it like?" Nora asked gently.

"He became cool and distant. Then one morning I was told by my landlord that the lease on my apartment had been canceled. I was literally out on the street."

"He dumped you without a word?"

Jenny nodded her head. "Yes. I went to stay at my sister's in New Jersey. Two weeks later a messenger delivered an envelope with fifty thousand-dollar bills." Jenny began to cry. "As though that could blot out the pain!"

For the first time in her life, Nora realized that she didn't really know Michael Cronin. She wondered if anyone did.

Clad in jeans and a black sweat shirt, Nora was standing on a rickety step-ladder, painting the walls of Sean's study. Before she went back to Washington, she would fix up his room and the kitchen, stock the refrigerator and the shelves with food, and feed him a couple of solid meals.

Outside, two lanky Negro teenagers were playing basketball in the chill November sunlight. Nora wondered why they weren't in school. Were they delinquents of the sort that Sean seemed to attract to the rectory?

She took a few minutes off from her painting and went to the head of the stairway leading down into the basement. Standing there, she could hear Sean instructing potential converts in the basement classroom.

"It's hard to believe that God loves you when you're poor and hungry, when there isn't enough heat in your apartment, and when you're not sure whether you'll have a job next week. You wonder how God lets things like that happen, when other people seem to be doing okay. You wonder if there even is a God. I can't prove to you the existence of God. Nobody can prove that. All I can say is that whenever you experience love, you experience God. And God is as present on Douglas Boulevard as he is everywhere else in the world. He loves us, and some day he's going to make everything right and we're all going to be happy with him. In the meantime, you have to get ready for God by trying to love one another with all the power you have so that there may be more of God's love in the world."

Nora fled back to her brush and her bucket of paint, tears streaming down her face. Who were she and Paul to decide that Sean shouldn't be doing what he was doing, shouldn't be talking to those poor people with so much love and affection and dedication in his voice?

Still, as she painted the wall, she told herself that she and Paul loved Sean and that God could not possibly want them to stand by idly while he worked himself to death.

"Why are you doing that?" Sean said, leaning against the doorway of his study. "I mean, we could probably hire somebody to do it."

She threw the wet paintbrush at him. "Because I love you, you damn fool. Do you think you're the only one in the family that can make sacrifices for other human beings?"

He showed the first bright Sean Cronin smile she had seen since she had come to St. Jadwiga's as he picked up the brush, walked over to the ladder, and very gently put it back into the bucket. His face averted so that she couldn't see it, he said, "Some of us are just born lucky, I guess. I'm lucky that I have you for a sister."

Later that afternoon she called Paul at his office. "Just a brief progress report. It's worse than Maggie thought. I'm cleaning up the place where he lives and giving him a few good meals, but we've got to get him out of here. Mike won't help."

"Damn!" Paul said.

"I'll stay in touch, but I think you'd better practice for an interview with the new Archbishop."

"Okay . . . I've got to run now. Oh, by the way, the kids are fine, but we all miss you."

"Do you really?" Nora asked the dead telephone.

Chapter Twelve
1962

SEAN CRONIN LOOKED at his face carefully in the mirror as he combed his long blonde hair. He needed a haircut. He needed a new suit. He needed a rest, a long rest. No wonder Nora looked so anxious. I scare even myself. One vacation in six years.

Two years before, Jimmy McGuire had dragged him off to Vail, insisting that Sean had an obligation to learn how to ski. The instructor assigned to him, Sandra Walker, was a woman in her mid-twenties with long honey-blonde hair and a superb body. She was spontaneous, direct, and bubbling with laughter. She even was able to make fun of Sean's initial awkwardness on skis without hurting his feelings. He did not tell her that he was a priest, and he watched with fear and pleasure the affection that grew in her lively gray eyes.

Then, one day, a substitute instructor replaced her. Sean was disappointed but asked no questions. The next day Sandra was back, subdued and snappish. Again he asked no questions and, after his lesson, trudged halfway down the slope toward his ski lodge. Then he paused and walked back to the instructor's office.

Sandra was hunched over her desk, sobbing. As naturally as though she were his daughter, he put his arms around her and drew her head to his chest. The whole story poured out. High school sweethearts who rediscovered each other in San Francisco six months before. He a Navy pilot. At first, letters every week, then every day, neither of them quite ready to say the word marriage. Then news of a crash on a carrier.

"Thanks for listening," she said as she and Sean walked back into town. "You're a nice shoulder to cry on." A little bit of bubble was back.

Sean did a lot of listening during the next week—on the ski slopes, in the dining room of the lodge, in the swimming pool. Sandra had crowded a lot of life into twenty-six years.

Then she invited him to her apartment for dinner. Sean knew he should not accept, and yet he did. Wine, fondue, cool jazz on the phonograph. A textbook seduction scene.

After dinner they sat in front of the blazing hearth. "Do you like me, Sean?"

He gathered her into his arms and caressed her back. "You know that I do, Sandra. But you deserve better than a quick grab because you're on the rebound from a tragedy." He had wanted to accept the invitation in her voice, but something held him back.

"You've been wonderful. . . . I might have killed myself."

"No, you wouldn't. And whatever help I've been would be undone if I went to bed with you. So stay in my arms for a few minutes, and then we'll say good-bye."

Jimmy McGuire was waiting for him when Sean returned to the room at the lodge. A compulsive postcard writer, Jimmy did not even look up from the stack of cards on which he was working. "Did you go to bed with her?" he asked.

"It would have been unfair to take advantage of her."

"And you're the one who thinks you don't have any faith."

Sean shook the memories from his mind. He could hear the sounds of Nora preparing dinner for him downstairs. The first woman to prepare dinner for him since Sandra Walker.

Sean studied Nora, seated across the dinner table. Even in a sweat shirt and jeans, she was beautiful. In addition to the beauty, there were now also poise and sophistication.

"Is there something wrong with me, Sean?" she asked. "You're staring."

"I was just thinking that with candlelight and wine you ought to be wearing black lace instead of a black sweat shirt."

Nora laughed. "That's a terrible thing for a priest to say!"

"Probably," he conceded. "I do appreciate what you're doing, though, Nora. And it's all right for you to give me the lecture that you've very carefully prepared."

Her forehead tightened almost imperceptibly. "I'm not going to try to persuade you that your talents are being wasted at St. Jadwiga, Sean. Your father and Paul might think so, but I don't. I've had a chance to watch you work around here for the last couple of days, and I think you're good at it. I also think you're only a couple of steps away from being Mistah Kurtz."

"Joseph Conrad's hero gone native? I suppose you're right, Nora, I have been here too long."

She pushed the roast beef platter at him, and he helped himself to another slice. "You must know that if you continue this way, your life might not be a very long one."

"Maybe. But as long as the Archbishop wants me to be here, it's God's will and I'm staying . . . and all your persuasive charms won't change my mind on that.''

"It seems to me a silly way for the Church to treat a priest." She looked at him over the rim of a water glass filled with burgundy.

"There's a tremendous amount of envy in the priesthood, probably worse than in any other occupation. There aren't many rewards. Some priests resent me because they think I'm rich. Some of them because I'm getting a reputation for being good at my work. It's a heads-I-lose tails-they-win situation. If I fail here, they say, I told you so, a rich man's son can't hack it. And if I succeed, it's because of my father's money.''

"Can't you do anything?''

"No. That's the way it is. The Church is not going to change.''

"The Church will change, Sean," she argued. "Will because it has to.''

"We disagree,'' he said, shrugging off her comment. He noticed that there was now a bit of fire in her eyes.

"How many of your parishioners understand Latin?'' she said. "I suppose you think it sinful for married people to enjoy sex with one another? And that priests shouldn't have any friends among the laity? And that everything a pope or bishop or pastor says is God's word?''

"My parishioners like the mystery of Latin. I don't think it's sinful for married people to enjoy sex; they probably ought to enjoy it more than they do—as long as the main purpose is procreation. Priests ought to be men apart, men unlike other human beings. And yes, of course, the pope and the bishops and the pastors do represent God.''

"And what happens to couples who have five or six kids? Should they stop sleeping with each other if they can't afford any more?'' Her frown was now deep.

He didn't want to fight. "Look, I know it's tough. We have to be very gentle and sympathetic with them in confession. In time, someone will develop a rhythm method of birth control that will be as effective as any other. Until then, we have to resist the contraceptive mentality . . . the mentality that leads people to not want children. That's the real problem.''

Nora pounded the table and almost upset the wine bottle. "Will it shock you to know, Sean Cronin, God's chosen spokesman, that I've been using the birth-control pill for a couple of years because the doctor said it would be better if I waited a while between children? Would you rather I throw Paul out of the bedroom—or do I push my luck? Do you want to see me in Holy Sepulcher Cemetery before I'm thirty? Is that God's will? Does the pope tell you that?''

Sean swallowed hard. "I can't help what I believe. Maybe I'm so rigid because I'm afraid that if I relax any of my beliefs the whole ball of wax will come apart.'' He buried his head in his hands. "I don't want to fight with you.''

She reached across the table and took his hand. "How much do you pray, Sean?'' she asked.

That question surprised him. "Not very much, I guess. Too busy. . . .''

She squeezed his hand hard. "What kind of a priest is it who doesn't pray?'' It was not a judgment or an accusation but a statement of compassion.

"I don't know anything any more, Nora. Sure, I should pray. There's no time.

No time to think. No time for anything. You have more faith than I do. That's why you can take chances and why I keep all the rules."

His head sagged on the linen tablecloth that she had purchased that day at Marshall Field's. She continued to hold his hand tightly.

Paul's office phone buzzed. Bud O'Hara would see him now. He replaced the phone with a gesture of impatient annoyance: 8:30 P.M. The Kennedy administration had to show its dedication by working impossible hours. No wonder so many of the marriages were in trouble.

O'Hara had Paul's collection of photographs spread out on the desk in front of him. "Where did you find these?" he asked.

"A lucky break—from an informant." Paul gave the formal reply that was expected in such circumstances.

"Lucky for all of us. This will be the end of Carmine da Silva," the Texan said. "You'll question our friend on K Street again tomorrow? I imagine he'll turn into a cooperative witness after a few hints about what we have."

"I'll be happy to take care of it. I think he'll be ready to begin a new life at government expense."

"Fine work," O'Hara said. "We should have more breaks like this."

Paul was thoroughly pleased with himself.

Sean helped Nora on with her coat. "You're going back to Washington on Monday?"

"Yes. I guess I'll have to tell Paul that I failed at my mission. He'll worry about you, Sean." She fastened the buckle on her coat and turned up the collar. "He does care about you. Sometimes I think you're the only one in the world he really cares about."

"Don't be ridiculous," Sean said. "I'm grateful for the house cleaning and the food and the sermon and . . . and the love too."

She patted his cheek affectionately. "It was fun. Somehow it's all going to work out."

Sean wished he could believe her. "I'll walk you down to the car," he said. "These streets aren't exactly safe at night."

He opened the rectory door to discover that not even the steps of the rectory were safe. Two men with stocking caps over their faces, dressed in shabby clothes, pushed their way in. One jammed a gun in Sean's stomach. The other pointed a knife at Nora's throat. "Now, you just turn around, Father, and go back into the office," said the man with the gun. "Neither you nor your lady friend here are gonna get hurt."

Sean was frightened. Two kids, probably high on dope, both with dangerous weapons. "Be careful with those things," he pleaded. "We'll do whatever you want." His whole body was trembling.

"That's right, man, you gonna do exactly what we tell ya, and the first thing you gonna do is open that safe." The young Negro gestured the priest toward the battered iron box in the middle of the rectory office. "You gonna open that safe and give us every penny that's inside."

Sean had never bothered to lock the safe. There was very little money in it, and it had become a storehouse for parish records. With shaking fingers he pulled back the iron handle and yanked the ponderous door of the safe open.

"Now, real slow, get out the money in there and put in on the desk. Nice and easy." The thief gestured with his gun.

There was twenty-five dollars and forty-seven cents in the safe. Sean laid it on the desk.

"Hey, man, you gotta have more money than that!"

"We don't, though," said Sean. "What little we take in on Sunday goes to the bank on Monday morning."

"Man, you're rich. Everybody in the neighborhood knows that. You gotta have more money. Let me see your wallet."

Sean could not shake his terror. Nora's face was drawn, her eyes closed, the point of the knife at her neck. He removed the wallet from his black trousers and placed it on the desk. Still pointing the gun with his right hand, the thief shook four one-dollar bills out of the wallet.

"Man, you gotta do better than this, or you and your lady friend are gonna be in real trouble. Oscar, what's she got in her purse?"

Nora yielded her purse silently and without resistance. Oscar—now Sean knew who they were—opened the purse. "Shut your mouth, ya damn fool," he said. "Now this whitey priest knows who we are, and that ain't good. . . . This cunt don't have nothing except a coupla bucks, credit cards, and some traveler's checks."

The other man hefted his gun lightly in his hand. "Well now, Father. We seem to have a real problem here. There's more money in this house than we've got and you're gonna have to give us all of it, or my friend over there is gonna want to carve some fancy things on your lady friend's face."

"There isn't any more money," Sean said. Her wondered if he and Nora would have to die, now that he knew who they were. "This is a poor parish and we don't have any money."

"Well, now, that sure is a shame. Oscar, why don't you just set to work."

Oscar poked Nora's neck with the knife. A little stream of red dripped down the blade. "You're gonna be real cooperative, Father," Oscar said, "or I'm gonna have to do some mean things with this little knife of mine."

Nora's face was white. "Please, there's nothing more here." Her voice sounded small and terrified.

He jabbed at her throat again, and there was another trickle of blood.

Fury was building inside of Sean, cold, murderous hate. Something turned loose inside of him. He hurled himself on the man with the gun and knocked the gun arm aside. The gun went off, filling the room with smoke and gunpowder. Sean kicked his surprised opponent in the groin and then hit him in the face, knocking him back against the safe, where he slid to the floor, dazed. Oscar, the man with the knife, was coming toward Sean. "You asked for it, priest," Oscar said, his left arm out wide, his right arm extended. He bore down on Sean and then struck quickly with the gleaming six-inch blade.

But not quickly enough. Sean grasped the parish seal from the desktop and smashed it against Oscar's arm. The force of the blow spoiled Oscar's aim, and the knife, instead of piercing Sean's stomach, slashed against Sean's left arm. Then the knife slipped out of Oscar's fingers as he grasped his broken forearm. Sean picked up the chair behind the rectory desk and smashed it over Oscar's head. When Sean grabbed the gun lying in front of him on the floor, Oscar hobbled toward the hallway, joined by his friend, who had recovered. "Let's get out of here, man. Fuckin' priest's gonna waste us."

The invaders fled, Sean pursuing them to the door of the rectory. Only as he stood at the doorway and pointed the gun at the fugitives, disappearing into the raw November night, did he realize that he could not kill them.

He lowered the weapon and walked slowly back to the rectory. For the first time he was conscious of a sharp jabbing pain.

"Your arm!" Nora exclaimed.

He looked at the blood dripping down his arm, over his hand, and on to the rectory floor. "Just a small cut," he said. A few more inches and it might have been an artery.

Nora huddled in her coat. "Those were the boys who were playing basketball outside this afternoon, weren't they?"

"That's right," said Sean. "They graduated from our grammar school three years ago. Sister Alicia always said they were troublemakers."

While they waited for the police to arrive, Sean kept his good arm around Nora's shoulder. "I'm all right, Sean, I'm all right," she repeated, over and over again as she strove to recover her calm before the police arrived.

"Of course you're all right, Nora. I should have listened to Sister. They were troublemakers."

It was a good thing that the police arrived quickly. Father Sean Cronin, his pulses still racing from the encounter, was filled with desire for his foster sister as he held her close and comforted her.

Chris Waverly was even better than Paul had anticipated. The drink at her apartment had turned into seduction, but she did more of the seducing than he, murmuring as she unbuttoned his shirt, "I thought you'd never give me a chance to get at you."

Paul was accustomed to passive, yielding women like Maggie Martin, and to a wife whose sexual depths he carefully avoided arousing. He had never before encountered a woman with such polished sexual skills and imperious hunger. Chris overwhelmed him. Her sleek body was a well coordinated and irresistible instrument of excitement. She aroused him, taunted him, teased him, drove him to the point of madness, and then, when he thought he could stand no more, she would begin again.

Afterward, they lay in the rumpled sheets of her bed, smoking, she coolly and he distracted and exhausted.

"You're an interesting man, Paul Cronin," she said. "A few things to learn, maybe, but worth teaching. I think you'll keep coming back for more schooling."

"It was fantastic," he said, still unable to organize his thoughts.

"No, it wasn't, not really. It was only a fair beginning. But that's all right. Come on, let's see if we can make a little more progress in today's lesson." Her hands began to explore his body.

After their second roller-coaster tumble, Paul fell asleep. The Chinese infantry attacked once again in his dream. This time a naked and deadly Chris Waverly jammed the bayonet into his belly. He woke screaming.

"Hey," she said. "I'm not that bad, am I? You're the first one who's ever awakened screaming after a tussle with me."

"It's not you," he gasped. "It's a dream I have about a night attack in Korea. It comes and goes."

"Poor Paul," she said gently. "Relax now and let mother Chris calm you down."

Chris was tender and affectionate. The terrors of the dream slowly ebbed. For a moment, Paul thought that he was in the life-preserver arms of his wife.

Joe Makuch was waiting the next day in the outer office at the Justice Department. It had been six years since Paul had seen him.

Paul mentioned a ten o'clock conference with the Attorney General, but he nonetheless had to listen to the sad tale of the decline of Joe Makuch: the bankruptcy of his gas station, his move to Los Angeles, the inevitable divorce, the children who didn't care to see their father. Now he had a marvelous opportunity to start life over with a new woman and a new auto dealership specializing in English sports cars.

"Well, I certainly hope the new dealership works out for you," Paul said nervously, glancing at his watch. "Foreign cars are going to be big in the years ahead."

"I can't purchase the place unless I come up with twenty-five thousand dollars." Joe Makuch could not meet Paul's eyes. "I thought you might lend it to me—you know, for old times' sake."

"Life here in Washington is expensive, Joe. But I'll see what I can do—for old times' sake."

"Sure. I know that things are tough all over," Makuch agreed. "But I thought you might be able to scare up the change for me. Maybe your father would be interested in investing in one of your old Marine buddies. After all, that business at the Reservoir was messy—it wouldn't look so good in the newspapers." Makuch was being much more explicit about the blackmail than he had been in the past.

"Dad has always believed that one should be loyal to the men with whom one has shared combat," Paul said. "I imagine we'll find a way to work things out. I'll be in touch with you in a few days with the details. Now I'd better get down to the Attorney General's office before I find myself out of a job."

As he walked down the wide corridor, honeycombed with offices on either side, Paul's hands were covered with sweat. He dried them off, before he entered the Attorney General's office, and fixed his face into a casual grin, although inside he was feeling rage—and the beginnings of a desire for revenge.

Chapter Thirteen
1962

EILEEN AND MARY Cronin started to shriek with joy as soon as they saw their mother walk down the steps from the United Airlines jet at National Airport. Paul sighed with relief. It would be good to have Nora back. He missed her as he would miss a close friend. His affair with Chris had become a never-ending series of paroxysms of delight. Indeed, he had visited her apartment that morning before breakfast and returned in due time to collect his daughters for the trip to the airport. He smiled briefly at the recollection of one or two of her more ingenious tricks. Nevertheless, she could not make the Korean dreams go away, and Nora could.

Nora knelt down and hugged her two gloriously happy daughters. Then she and Paul embraced each other enthusiastically. Nora cocked a quizzical eye at him. "You must have missed me." She pressed hard against him.

Paul felt the warm security of his life preserver. "How could I help missing a wife like you?" he said, squeezing her again. "After I heard about the close call you had in Chicago . . ."

She disengaged herself. "I'm sure the newspapers here exaggerated. Nobody pushes a Cronin around."

"But it didn't melt the old man's heart?"

Nora lifted Mary into her arms and tugged at Eileen's hand. "Made him even worse. He chewed me out on the phone for ten minutes. I shouldn't have taken such chances, and Sean was responsible for risking the life of the mother of his grandchildren. I finally hung up on him."

Paul led his family toward the parking lot. In the car, riding back to Georgetown, he said, "Do you have any idea of how we can handle this Sean thing?"

"I talked with Jimmy McGuire, and he said the new Archbishop is a reasonable man, not vindictive or resentful like McNulty was. He thinks that if someone like you—well, that if you would see the Cardinal and fill him in on the background, he'd wipe the slate clean."

"I'm sure Bobby will give me a day or two off if I explain why to him. . . ." His voice trailed off.

"He goddamn well better," Nora said with uncharacteristic profanity.

"Mommy," said Eileen from the back seat, "you should *never* talk like that!"

"That's right, darling. I know I shouldn't. Mommy's just tired from the long airplane ride."

"Oh," said Eileen, granting absolution. "That's different."

Robert Kennedy frowned. "I suppose that officially we don't know how Cronin obtained these records."

"No, sir," said Bud O'Hara.

"Functional justice again?" asked the Attorney General.

"Cronin is a good man." O'Hara wanted no part of responsibility for Cronin's violation of the law.

"I know he is. But he's also a reckless gambler." He grinned. "A Kennedy can't object to that, I suppose. Yet we *could* have nailed da Silva some other way. This wasn't necessary."

"It saved us a lot of time," O'Hara replied.

"We ought to put a letter in Cronin's file commending him for progress in the investigation."

"Yes, sir," said the Texan, who never called the Attorney General by his first name.

"And perhaps we ought to reconsider his value to the administration here in Washington." He hesitated and shook his head. "We'll miss Nora."

The difference between Paul Cronin and the Attorney General was that Bob Kennedy would need a cause before he broke into the office of a citizen. Paul Cronin would break into the same office purely for the hell of it.

■   ■   ■

Cardinal Eamon McCarthy was a short, slight man of sixty-two, with salt-and-pepper hair and shrewd brown eyes peering through thick horn-rimmed glasses. "I'm very happy you came to see me, Mr. Cronin," he said. "I must say I was impressed by the newspaper account of your brother's behavior during that robbery attempt. It would seem"—he smiled briefly—"that you are not the only one in the family with heroic proclivities."

"I may have the medal, Your Excellency," said Paul smoothly, "but Sean has about four times as much courage as I do."

"Indeed?" The Archbishop's voice was mild and reedy. He seemed to be a timid, diffident sort of man. "Some of the people on my staff have tried to persuade me it was scandalous for a woman to be having supper at St. Jadwiga's rectory, even though she was a member of Father Cronin's family. It seemed to me that they were drawing a bit of a long bow."

Paul leaped at the opportunity. "Nora came to Chicago because we were advised that Sean is in failing health. I was stuck at the Justice Department, so I asked Nora to investigate. I can't imagine anyone seeing something wrong."

The Archbishop tapped his finger lightly on the manila folder that was in front of him. "As far as I've been able to gather, your brother has done remarkable work there under extraordinary conditions. I wouldn't be at all surprised if, as you say, his health is in danger." He flipped open the file. "Your brother's record at the seminary was excellent, at the top of his class most of the time. He apparently is also a man of strong commitment and dedication to the priesthood. Indeed, there is a note here in the file from one of his seminary teachers." The Archbishop held up a single-spaced letter, typed on both sides of a sheet of seminary stationery. "It recommends him for graduate study. Without making any judgments about my predecessor's decisions"—again the Archbishop smiled—"I should think that Father Cronin ought to be encouraged in such work, don't you?"

The Archbishop was making it very easy indeed. Paul would not even have to raise the question of the renewed flow of Michael Cronin's generosity to the Archdiocese of Chicago if his son was sent to graduate school. "Sean has always been a fine student. I think he would enjoy graduate school enormously."

"Yes, indeed." The Archbishop closed the file. "Very well, then," he said. "The matter is settled."

"By the way, Your Excellency, I wonder if I may make a request of you. I would just as soon Sean didn't know that I—"

The Archbishop smiled. "I understand perfectly, Mr. Cronin," he said. "I, too, have a brother."

After he left the Victorian gray pile of stone on Wabash Avenue that was the Chicago chancery office, Paul consulted his watch. He still had some time before his return trip to Washington. He could surprise Maggie Shields at her Lincoln Park West apartment. After his victory with the Archbishop, he deserved a prize. On second thought, he decided Maggie was a trivial piece of candy compared to Chris. He could wait until he reached Washington.

Maggie Shields poured herself a second gin and tonic, insisting mentally that two drinks in the afternoon were not a serious sign unless you needed them. She was not turning into one of those quietly drinking frustrated doctors' wives. She had a lot to live for. She was twenty-seven years old, her figure was in better shape than it had ever been since her marriage, her children were attractive, even if they were a nuisance when they were not out at the playground with their nurse, and her life was still ahead of her.

Only she was bored silly—with her serious husband, for whom delivering babies into the world was more important than his own sex life; with her difficult eldest daughter, Nicole; with the confines of their apartment overlooking the park; with herself. Her friends were all married and talked about nothing but teeth and toilet training. The free-floating intellectuals in the neighborhood were too highbrow. She did not like to read, and the soap operas on television held her attention for only a few hours each day. The infrequent vacations she took with Tom were no help. He tried to become amorous, and that bored her worse than anything.

She had thought about divorce, but she couldn't face being alone. Maybe she ought to open a shop somewhere, sell expensive dresses to wealthy women. She would be good at that. Her taste in clothes was excellent. The slacks and blouse she was wearing cost three hundred dollars and made her look ravishing. It might be worth trying. Tom would go along.

The telephone rang. It was Paul. He wouldn't be able to stop by after all. The Attorney General needed him back in Washington. It had been months since Paul had come to see her. She did not know how long she could stand not being with him. He was the only thing in her life that made her feel alive.

She poured herself another drink. Maybe she could invent an excuse to go to Washington.

Paul Cronin arrived late at the Kennedys' home in Virginia. The garden behind the house was illuminated by hundreds of twinkling lights. The end of the November Indian summer had lingered long enough for the Kennedys to have one of their outdoor parties.

Pleading a delay at the airport and a need to stop by his office, Paul had telephoned Nora and told her to take the Mercedes off to Virginia and he would join her in the Ferrari later.

"What about your wife?" Chris had asked when they were finished making love. She was lying casually on top of him, her flesh pressed against his.

"What do you mean, 'What about her'?" he replied. He knew that he should leave for Virginia any minute, and that he would not.

"Do you love her?"

"Does it make any difference?"

"Not especially. I just like to know where I stand." She kissed him provocatively.

"Yes, I do love her. It's not like—"

"Not very good in the sack, huh? That's her problem, I guess. I like you a lot, Paul." Her kisses were now becoming insistent. "I intend to keep you around a long time. If I make up my mind that I want you permanently, I'll do my best to take you away from your gorgeous Nora. I just thought it fair to warn you."

"I'm warned." He tried to sound casual, but under the circumstances it was impossible to make any serious response to Chris.

Now, as he searched for Nora among the crowd in the Attorney General's garden, he told himself that neither Chris nor anybody else could possibly take him away from Nora.

"There you are. I thought you would never come." This time it was Nora who initiated the passionate embrace. "You told me the news was good on the phone," she said, releasing him. "What are the details?"

"Sean is being sent to Rome to study Church history."

"Marvelous!" Nora exclaimed, embracing him again. "I knew you could charm the Archbishop."

Paul was at the bar later when the Attorney General of the United States, fully dressed, toppled into his swimming pool. When Paul heard the splash and the mixed cries of horror and delight, he pushed his way through the throng to the edge of the pool. The other Kennedys and members of the staff were there first and were helping the bedraggled but laughing Attorney General out of the pool.

"Who did it? Who did it?" The words were forming on everyone's lips.

Bob Kennedy made his way through the crowd to Nora Riley Cronin. "We're even now, Nora, I guess," he said with his most infectious grin.

"Who, me?" said Nora innocently.

The Attorney General laughed and turned to Paul. "Do you ever win any fights, Paul?"

"I have sense enough not to try," Paul said.

As the Attorney General started for the house and a dry set of clothing, he turned once more to Paul. "By the way, I'd like to see you for a few minutes tomorrow—if you have the time."

Paul could not help but notice that the Attorney General was no longer smiling.

Sean Cronin waited in the long, elaborately carpeted corridor of the chancery office that led to the Archbishop's suite. On both of the walls of the corridor were pictures from the career of George William Mundelein, the first Cardinal of Chicago. "Do you know what it's about?" Sean asked Roger Fitzgibbon, who was now acting as assistant chancellor before going to Rome to study canon law.

Fitzgibbon had been busy, rushing up and down the corridor delivering documents to the offices of the vicar general, the chancellor, and the vice-chancellor. "I don't know for sure," he said brusquely, indicating by tone and manner that he didn't have much time to talk. "I suppose, though, that there's been some complaint about Nora being in your rectory when it was robbed."

"Nora?" Sean said, incredulously.

"Not very prudent, Sean. Not very prudent at all," said Fitzgibbon, shaking his head disapprovingly.

Sean had an urge to smash Fitzgibbon's pious face, just as he had smashed the faces of the robbers at St. Jadwiga's.

When he was finally shown into the Archbishop's office, the Archbishop came immediately to the point. "Sit down, Father Cronin. First of all, let me congratulate you on the—er—well, I suppose the right word would be 'efficient' way in which you handled the attempted robbery at St. Jadwiga's."

"Thank you, Your Excellency," Sean said, trying to read the shrewd little Archbishop.

"I was wondering, Father Cronin, whether you would be willing to apply the same efficiency to a small task I have in mind?"

"Of course, Archbishop."

"You say yes before you even know what it is? Well, I certainly cannot criticize enthusiasm. My task, however, may take some time. I need a Church historian, a well-trained and competent one. I propose to send you to Rome to study history at the Gregorian University, and I would ask you to concentrate especially on the history of the Church's teaching and practice in regard to the sacrament of matrimony. I would be relieved to have someone with such competence on my personal staff both at the Vatican Council and afterward. Are you still enthusiastic about my task, Father?''

"Even more so," said Sean. He was scarcely able to believe what he had heard.

"Excellent," said the Archbishop. "We're going to see many changes in the Church in the years ahead, Father Cronin. I'm inclined to agree with the late Archbishop of Paris that the crises will be crises of growth and not of decline. I feel the American Church will suffer badly for its lack of proper scholarship. The change may be disconcerting."

"The Church won't change," Sean said. "It won't change because it can't change."

The Archbishop tapped his pencil lightly on his blotter. "I'm afraid I must disagree, Father." And then, echoing what Nora had said the week before, the Archbishop of Chicago added, "The Church will change because it has to change."

"Paul, I need help," Bobby Kennedy said, running his fingers nervously through his thick hair.

"Anything wrong?" Paul asked. There were warning gongs sounding inside his head.

Kennedy grinned his charming grin. "It's a rough assignment, but an important one. You know as well as I do, maybe better than I do, that Chicago is the center of organized crime and that our Crime Task Force in Chicago is a mess. Too damn much hanging out in bars, if you ask me. Can't tell the good guys from the bad guys any more. You've been so good here—well, I thought we might send you to Chicago. You're young for the job, although that doesn't bother me, of all people." Again the charming grin. "It's a great challenge."

Paul knew that he had no real choice. He was being dismissed from the Attorney General's staff in the nicest way possible. He was being kicked upstairs.

"We'll miss Nora, God knows," Kennedy said. Then he added, somewhat lamely, "You too, of course."

BOOK FOUR

*This is my commandment. Love one another as I have loved you.
A man can have no greater love than to lay down his life for his
friends. You are my friends if you do what I command you. I shall
not call you servants any more, because a servant does not know
his master's business. I call you friends.*

—JOHN 15:11–15

Chapter Fourteen
1963

SEAN CRONIN WALKED through the Piazza Farnese with quick steps. Although
concerned that he would be late for dinner, he smiled cheerfully and said *buona
sera* to a young couple walking in the opposite direction. They responded with
solemn silence. Sean had learned enough history to know why the Roman people
hated the clergy; the citizens of Rome had neither forgiven nor forgotten the
absolutism of the papal state and the repeated crushing of their attempts to
achieve democratic self-government. Yet, raised as he was on the South Side of
Chicago where priests were greeted routinely and greeted in return, Sean could
not adjust to the hostility of the young people.

It was one of the few things he did not like about Rome. Everything else—the
catacombs, St. Peter's, the Vatican gardens, the Via Veneto, the baroque churches
and palaces, the street urchins, and the noise—he enjoyed enormously.

The months had been busy: learning Italian and entering Gregorian University
in the middle of the year; taking courses in the history of Christian attitudes and
practices on marriage that the Archbishop wanted him to study; learning his way
around Rome; meeting new friends. It had been an exciting and challenging six
months that quickly blotted out the nightmare years at St. Jadwiga's. Then, a few
weeks before, the death of John XXIII and the election and installation of a new
pope. Sean's mind was still jammed with the sights and sounds as he stood in the
Piazza of St. Peter's and saw the white smoke go up and heard the first blessing
"to the city and to the world" of Giovanni Battisti Montini, Pope Paul VI. How
could anyone want to change a church that had so much grace and beauty in its
ceremonies?

He continued across the Piazza Farnese toward Chicago House, trying not to
notice the dirty looks his cassock and clerical hat earned him. Already some of
his classmates at the Greg were abandoning clerical garb, behavior that Sean felt
was dangerously close to apostasy.

The small sixteenth-century palazzo at the end of the narrow street that Sean
had just left belonged to his friends the Alessandrinis—Angèlica and Francésco—
members of the black, or papal, nobility who had chosen Pope Pius IX over
Victor Emmanuel in 1870. The *Principio,* a thin handsome man, and the

Principessa, who was lovely in a delicate, ethereal way, were people his own age. They now lived in only one fourth of that ancient family palace but did not seem to lack money, although it was not clear if either of them had ever worked a day in their lives. Sean had met them at a cocktail party at the American embassy, and they had promptly taken him under their wing.

Their "little party" this afternoon had included an assortment of curial bureaucrats and the great wise old Cardinal Menelli, who had dropped a few hints about what had happened at the conclave. Sean had felt vaguely uneasy. He had cheered enthusiastically for the new Pope, and it did not seem right to hear him discussed by Menelli in such a cynical manner. Moreover, while Sean was deeply opposed to changes that might impinge on the timeless serenity of the Church, and horrified by the translation of the Mass into English, his sense of fairness was affronted by the trickery and deceit that seemed to be a matter of course in Vatican politics. It had been much more pleasant to watch Angèlica's delicate fingers dance up and down the keyboard as she played "a little Vivaldi concerto" than it was to try to understand Rome.

At Chicago House, in the Via Sardegna, just off the Via Veneto, Eamon McCarthy, the Cardinal Archbishop of Chicago, shook his head unhappily. "It isn't like the first session, Father Cronin, not like it at all. The new Pope is a brilliant man. He understands what is happening in the Church intellectually, far better than did his predecessor." The Cardinal's hair was now almost entirely white and his normally serene brown eyes were troubled. "But I believe he is making a grave mistake. The forces of change have been unleashed. They should be guided, but they cannot be slowed down. I fear that he does not trust his fellow bishops. There will be deep trouble if that is the case."

Each evening at the dinner table at Chicago House, the Cardinal would discuss the events of the Aula of St. Peter's that day. The Chicago students who also lived in the elaborate palazzo that Cardinal Mundelein had purchased—to show that an American Cardinal could live as elaborately in Rome as an Italian Cardinal—listened intently to Eamon McCarthy's analysis. Sean found that he was the only one at the table who thought the Church was changing too rapidly. Jimmy McGuire, who had come to Rome in the fall to study canon law, had become more radical with each passing year. He even wore a black turtleneck at the dinner table instead of a cassock. Unaccountably, the Cardinal did not seem to mind.

"As you know, Father Cronin," the Cardinal said, directing the discussion to Sean, "I've asked you to specialize in the history of marriage and sexuality in Catholic teaching because I am convinced that that is the most corrosive issue we face. The other things we do at the Council are important, but mostly for scholars and priests. Sexuality is important to all our lay people."

Sean sensed that he was on the spot, as he frequently was in such discussions. It seemed to him that he was being tested every night. "In an age when sex has become a pleasure unto itself, Eminence, we have to remind our people that sex is basically for procreation."

Jimmy, who had remained Sean's closest friend despite their theological differences, spoke up abruptly. "Most married men and women will tell you that that's not why they sleep with one another at night."

"The pill doesn't change anything, Jimmy," Sean said. He knew from previous arguments that Jimmy thought the pill might be a legitimate Catholic form of birth control. "And I'm sure the bishops of the world have no intention of making exceptions for the pill."

"Oh, Father Cronin, are you sure of that?" The Cardinal smiled his quick little smile. "If there were a secret ballot, and if it was clear that the Pope had not prescribed beforehand the outcome of that ballot, I tell you this, Father Cronin: the bishops of the world for reasons of the pastoral good of our married people would vote for a change on birth control."

"I can't believe that, your Eminence," Sean said.

"Ah, come now, Father Cronin. You are such an idealist. A bishop, much less a cardinal archbishop, cannot afford to be that kind of an idealist. We may not understand the theology, we may not have insight into history, but if we are listening to our priests and to our people we know that *something* has to be done on the birth-control question."

"If you say so, it must be true," Sean conceded.

"Oh, it's true all right, Father," the Cardinal said quietly. "A number of us are going to try to see the Pope next week and persuade him to open up the Council for discussion of the problem. I suppose"—he sighed—"he will not listen to us."

"And what will that mean, Eminence?"

"That will mean, my dear Father Cronin," the Cardinal said in his gentle voice, "that sometime before this decade is over the Church will be confronted by disaster."

Paul Cronin realized that he was not going to eliminate organized crime in Chicago. The proper strategy was some fast and easy victories, a lot of public acclaim, and then an escape from the quicksand. He had already been successful in putting a number of small-time hoods behind bars, and he was now gearing up to uncover mob infiltration of a local labor union. Tony Swartz, who had joined him as his assistant, believed in what they were doing, with an idealism born of the Kennedy years. He seemed unaware that Paul cared little about the effects of the Chicago Strike Force, except as a stepping-stone for his own ambitions for political office and as an excuse to go to Washington frequently to see Chris Waverly.

She was now waiting for him in the Sans Souci restaurant, a block away from the White House. Paul had selected the Sans Souci because it was no longer an "in" restaurant, and there was less chance that he would run into anyone who knew Nora. A year ago, all the bright young men from the White House had gone there for lunch, usually to sit admiringly at the feet of the tall, black-haired Pat Moynihan, who was the closest thing to a house intellectual that the Kennedys had. Then the second-raters discovered that the Sans Souci was the place to be, and the White House staff found other places to eat.

Chris lit a cigarette and sampled her martini. Paul would be late. The Kennedys cared about no one's time but their own. Yet, still riding the crest of their Cuban missile crisis triumph, they were the toast of the nation. It would not last, of that Chris was sure.

Paul would be filled with his most recent triumphs in Chicago—putting some cheap hood behind bars. He might have illusions as to why he had been sent to Chicago; she had none. The Kennedys had decided he was dangerous to have around. He had been shipped out.

Chris had not made up her mind about Paul. He was fine in bed, if perhaps not the great lover he imagined himself to be. He was pleasant, attractive, and charming, and he was filthy rich. He was the kind of man Chris wanted—a nice sort with some conscience but not too much. The news business was becoming tiresome. She had never intended to stay in it after thirty, and she had been searching for a man who would be tolerable as a mate and whom she could mold into a major political power. Paul seemed to fill the bill. He had natural political skills and instincts. He was ambitious but not excessively so. Above all, he had the knack of saying exactly the right thing in exactly the right way when the red light of the television camera blinked on.

For all her cynicism, Chris felt a knot in her throat when Paul finally burst into the Sans Souci, brimming with energy and enthusiasm. Watch it, she told herself, you may be turning into a romantic.

His greeting, as he slid into the booth next to her, was a quick peck on the cheek. Chris guided his chin toward her mouth and responded with a long, lingering kiss. "When are you going to come back to Washington and make an honest woman of me?" she purred, releasing him only after she was sure that he had been thoroughly shaken.

"What do you mean?" His broad smile was briefly hesitant.

"You and I are a lot alike. Both of us want to see you go places in Washington. And both of us were behind the door when consciences were passed out. . . . Your Nora probably needs a man with a very stern conscience."

"Someone like my brother Sean?"

"A priest?"

He signaled the waiter for his drink order. "I'm only joking. Sean hardly knows that women exist."

Nora Cronin could not concentrate on the book she was reading. Her husband was in Washington at a meeting concerning the Chicago Strike Force. He would be coming home soon. Nora missed him more than she usually did when he was away. Although she had waited for Tom Shields to give her the go-ahead to become pregnant, this pregnancy was much more difficult than the other two had been.

She closed the book and rested it on what was left of her lap. Three more weeks. It was absurd to think that she would die, yet the thought kept stealing into her mind. She was only twenty-eight years old and the picture of health, save for a womb that didn't seem to want to function properly, particularly when a child was leaving it. She had learned from her mother and from the nuns at school that everything was part of God's plan. Perhaps God was punishing her. But she didn't know why.

She yearned to be at Oakland Beach, basking in the sunlight in the morning, swinging a golf club in the afternoon, and chatting with the neighbors over cocktails in the evening. Glendore seemed so far away, and she had almost forgotten what a golf club felt like.

She grabbed the edge of the table to help keep her balance as she stood. If she got much bigger, she thought, they would have to devise a pulley system to raise and lower her from a sitting position.

The first pain came. It was not like the pains of her previous labor; rather it felt as if the baby inside her was trying to tear her apart.

Luckily, Mary and Eileen, who were utterly delighted at the prospect of having a baby brother, were asleep upstairs. Somehow they had all gotten into the habit of thinking of this new baby as a boy. Undoubtedly, Mike Cronin's influence at work.

Another even more stabbing pain ripped through her. She screamed for the housekeeper. "Anna, come quickly. Something is terribly wrong!"

I'm going to die after all, she thought, as she fell to the floor, unconscious.

Sean stared in stunned disbelief at the cablegram. He was as numb as he had been when Father McCabe told him that his brother was missing in action in Korea. NORA CRITICAL. RETURN IF YOU CAN. PAUL.

Oh, God. No. Don't take her, please don't.

He went down the steps from his attic room in Chicago House to the floor below where the Cardinal lived. Eamon McCarthy was sitting at his desk in suspenders and a white collarless shirt. The new red robes of his cardinalship were hanging behind him. He was poring over a stack of papers, the flimsy sheets that came from the *typis polygattis vaticanis*.

"Your Eminence. . . ." Sean hesitated in the doorway.

The kindly man peered over his glasses. "Yes, Sean? You look troubled." It was the first time he had called Sean anything but Father Cronin.

Hardly able to speak, Sean showed him the cablegram.

"Of course you must go home at once," said the Cardinal. "Your family needs you more than I do just now."

"Thank you, Your Eminence. I'm sure Nora will be all right—"

"It's all in God's hands. In any event, catch the first plane in the morning and stay as long as necessary."

"I'll return as soon as Nora is out of danger."

"I will pray for her, Father Cronin. I shall pray very hard indeed. I'm sure that she will recover."

Sean's stomach was twisted with fear. "It's all in God's hands." Sean echoed the Cardinal's words, searching in the depths of his being for enough faith in God to believe what he was saying. He found nothing.

Nora knew that death had retreated when the hospital smells began to bother her again: the antiseptic odor at first, then overcooked food, and then human sickness. The terrible, terrible cold leaked slowly out of her veins and she found herself yearning for the warmth of the sunlight.

She had just finished giving her yet unnamed daughter her bottle. The little girl was lying next to her on the bed, tiny but alert, intrigued, it seemed, by the world into which she had been plunged so abruptly and unceremoniously. Tears of sadness flowed down Nora's cheeks.

"Why so many tears?" It was Sean. Had he been there all along? She had fallen into the habit of drifting in and out of sleep, as much a result of the depression that had taken control of her as of the medication or any actual physical exhaustion.

"She's a perfectly presentable little girl, isn't she?" she said after a long while.

"More than presentable," he said, poking his finger at his niece, who poked back with her own tiny finger. "I don't know much about babies, but this one is the most beautiful I've ever seen. The spitting image of her mother."

"No one wants her." Nora began sobbing. "Not her grandfather, or her father, or her mother. We're all angry at her because she's not a little boy."

"I've just watched you with her. I don't think you're angry at her any more," Sean said. "You just haven't had a chance to get used to the idea of another little Cronin girl. What's her name, by the way?"

"She doesn't have a name. We didn't have any girls' names ready, we were so sure it would be a boy. I've thought about Michele—"

"No," Sean said, "she's not a Michele. I know what she is. She's a Noreen. A little Nora."

Despite her weakness and her pain, Nora Riley Cronin sat up in bed and smiled. "You're right. She *is* a Noreen."

Sean baptized his new niece in the grim nondenominational chapel of the hospital on the morning of November 22.

"Noreen Marie Cronin"—Sean poured liberal amounts of water on her tiny bald head—"I baptize you in the name of the Father and of the Son and of the Holy Spirit."

Noreen Marie Cronin marked her entry among God's people not by wailing in protest at the cold water cascading over her face but rather by gurgling happily and trying to swallow some of the water.

On the way to the airport that afternoon, Sean studied his brother carefully. They had spent little time together in the last ten years. Who was Paul Cronin now? As far as appearances went, he was a tall, handsome New Frontiersman, his dark wavy hair cut in the Kennedy style, his PT-boat tie clip a discreet but impressive badge. A very successful and very important young politician.

"It doesn't make Dad happy now that we're both doing what he wanted us to do, does it, Paul?"

Paul glanced at him quickly. "Did you call him yesterday?"

"All I got was a stream of orders to pass on to the Pope, who Dad thinks is a weak-kneed sniveler."

"Probably like the orders I get to pass on to the President, who Dad calls a lightweight poseur."

They laughed together, and Sean felt a brief sensation of the old camaraderie that had been greatest in the past when they won a tennis match or a sailboat race together.

"He was disappointed, I suppose, that Noreen isn't a boy?" Sean said tentatively.

"Furious. Chewed Nora out, I'm afraid, while she was still having blood pumped into her. As though it were her fault. And then he invented some 'urgent business' so that he could miss the baptism."

"Sounds like Dad. Won't even give in to genetics," Sean said.

"God, I was so frightened that we were going to lose Nora. I don't know what I'd do without her, Sean. My life would fall apart."

A niggling voice in the back of Sean's brain told him that, while he ought not to doubt Paul's sincerity, the sentiment of his little speech sounded disturbingly artificial. Sean realized that he knew little about the man who was his brother, and even less about the quality of his marriage.

Paul drove the Mercedes into the parking lot at O'Hare. "I'll park here and walk with you. The Strike Force can spare me for another hour or so, I'm sure."

Something seemed to be amiss as they walked through the parking lot under the gray November sky. Little knots of people were gathered in intense conversation, and there seemed to be no one waiting for taxis or racing to the terminal building.

Paul's words echoed Sean's thoughts. "Something strange is going on here. Do you feel it too?"

At the edge of the parking lot, just across from the terminal, a stewardess in a United Airlines uniform was crying into a fragile lace handkerchief.

"Excuse me, miss." Paul turned on his considerable charm. "Can you tell me what has happened?"

The girl looked up from her handkerchief, her face red and puffy. "They've shot the President!"

Chapter Fifteen
····························· *1963–1964* ·····························

PAUL CRONIN WAITED nervously in the Mayor's outer office. The interview was important, and he needed all his cool to carry it off. At least three very important friends had interceded with the Mayor for him. He had all the right credentials: Notre Dame graduate, war hero, Kennedy aide, the Strike Force, good family. He would make an ideal "blue ribbon" candidate for state senator. He also had his father's money behind him for the campaign. If the Cook County Committee would slate him at their meeting in December, there would be no primary contest; the only other announced candidates were obvious hacks.

"I know your father well; we grew up together," the short red-faced Mayor said, pumping his hand. "And your poor mother, God rest her soul. A great Chicago family, the Cronins. And you've got a great future in politics in this city. And in the country, with your wonderful work for President Kennedy, God be good to him. . . ."

The nonstop monologue continued, with Paul being permitted only an occasional word. Finally the Mayor came to the point. "I'm glad to see you're thinking of elective office in this county. We need more fine young men like you in politics. It's a great vocation—like your brother's, though not as holy. I'm sure the slating committee will be very interested in your presentation."

It sounded like an endorsement to Paul. "Your support will be very important, Your Honor."

"The slating committee's gotta make its own decisions." The Mayor rushed on. "They have to consider *all* the candidates and choose the one they think has the best chance of being the best senator from your district. And, of course, the man who has the best chance of winning."

"I hope that I win their support, Mr. Mayor, because I'm in the race till Election Day."

"That's the kind of spunk I admire. This city of Chicago needs your kind of young man in politics," the Mayor said. He stood and held out his hand.

Paul knew when he walked out of the office that he had the nomination in the bag. It didn't have to be a very big bag, because state senator was not an important job. Springfield was dullsville, and members of the Illinois General Assembly had very little clout unless they were willing to stay in Springfield for a lot longer than he intended. But in four years the veteran Congressman from the

third district would probably retire. A presentable record in Springfield would be
the first step to Congress, then to the Senate, then to . . . well, any place.

Paul wondered whether Dick Daley was baffled by such a forceful application
for such a small job. Probably not. The Mayor had a reputation for being able to
read the cards before they were dealt.

Elizabeth Hanover, the woman who was serving as chairman of the Gallery
Committee, was not Mike's kind of woman. She was tall and slender and
black-haired. Moreover, she displayed none of the shy modesty that Mike usually found appealing.

Mike had been persuaded to lend his name to a civic group that would fund an
impressionist gallery on the North Side. He meant to attend the first meeting and
then quietly disappear. If it were not for his hope that Paul would be slated to run
for the State Senate, he might not have even bothered to show up at the first
meeting.

However, his kind of woman or not, Elizabeth was stunning: about ten years
younger than he, smoldering black eyes, a throaty voice, and a figure that stirred
welcome feelings in Mike. He wasn't over the hill yet.

Elizabeth accepted his invitation to lunch at the Mid-America Club on the top
floor of the new Prudential Building. As they watched the snowflakes gently
cover the brown squares of Grant Park and the ugly railroad tracks that bisected
it, they talked first of Monet, then of Mike's plans for Paul's election campaign.

By the time they were finished with lunch, there was no one left in the dining
room save the two of them and the always polite waiters. There was a brief
silence. Elizabeth ground out her cigarette.

"Isn't your apartment on Outer Drive East?" She gestured toward the lake,
now hidden by the snow.

"Great view of the lake," he said. He felt like a tongue-tied sixteen-year-old.

"Then perhaps we ought to go there and make love." She picked up her
purse. "Find out whether we like each other in bed and get that out of the way."

Mike's expression never changed, although he was startled by her candor.

They held hands as they walked against the stinging lake wind and the thick
blanket of snow. "Do you belong to the health club?" She pointed toward the
bubble-top swimming pool at the base of the tall fog-shrouded skyscraper. "I'll
bring my swimming suit the next time."

"Are you so certain there will be a next time?" he asked.

"Oh, yes," she said confidently.

She was right.

Michael Cronin was admitted to the Mayor's office promptly at the scheduled
time of his appointment. There was the usual preliminary small talk. Then they
got down to business. Mike was smooth and relaxed, confident that Richard
Daley was no different from the Chicago politicians he had known before the
war.

"I've lost touch with Chicago politics over the years," he said. "I've been out
of town so much that things kind of slipped away from me until Paul came home
from Washington."

"You're doing an important job in the international economic community,
Mike." The Mayor spoke like a defense attorney.

"I suppose some people would think it's just selfishness that I've become interested again, now that Paul is seeking public office."

"If a man doesn't support his own son, who will he support?" The Mayor's round face was bright with admiration.

"Of course, we'll provide most of the money for Paul's campaign. . . ." He hesitated, trying to make his offer as indirect as possible. "And after that, Dick, you can be sure that my contributions to anything the party thinks important will be substantial."

The Mayor stared at Mike, his face unreadable. Mike felt his own smile fade.

"Election contributions are funny things, Mike." Daley's tone turned nostalgic. "I remember when I was running for sheriff, a man came from our friends on the West Side and offered me two hundred and fifty thousand dollars. That was a lot of money in those days. I told him I didn't want his money, and he turned around and went down the street and gave it to my opponent, Elmer Walsh, and Elmer won. So the next time when I was running for county clerk he came again and offered me fifty thousand and I took it. Then, on Election Day, I called him and gave it back. He said, 'Why did you take it if you weren't going to use it?' and I said, 'That way, you can't give it to my opponent.' "

Mike wondered if he should laugh or be angry. So he laughed and Daley laughed with him. Then the Mayor heaved himself out of his massive chair briskly, shook hands with him, and told Mike that he was sure the slating committee would listen "with deep emphasis to what Paul has to say to us."

As he walked out into the subzero gloom of Washington Boulevard, Mike decided that Richard Daley was considerably different from the politicians he had known in the 1930s.

That afternoon Elizabeth made him forget about politics. She was a firm believer in love in the afternoon, especially after a swim in the pool.

She stood above him, hands complacently on her bare hips. "You know, Michael, I can't imagine anyone more different from me in background or taste, but I'm quite besotted with you. I think I'll keep you for a while." She grinned in amusement.

Under her urging he had given up smoking, swam in the pool every day, was losing weight under a doctor's guidance, and felt twenty years younger. "I hope you do." He laughed. "You've taken all the joys out of my life. All but one."

She cocked her head. "And that one?"

"Makes everything else shine as brightly as that blue sky out there."

"Oh, Michael, you are a dear." She bent over him and teased his lips with hers, her breasts brushing against his chest. "I'm going to keep you around for a long, long time."

No woman ever had such power over him. Yet he loved it. If only Jane were not in the way.

Paul was sure to win the election. Tony Swartz had designed a superlative campaign. There was plenty of money for television advertising, Paul had routed the incumbent, Roy Flanagan, in their television debate, and the two Chicago papers had endorsed him, one dismissing Flanagan as one of the worst of the hacks. Paul had crossed and recrossed the district while Flanagan had made almost no public appearances, silenced by campaign managers who suspected that Flanagan lost votes every time he opened his mouth.

The enthusiastic cheers of the audiences were strong wine for Paul. He understood how Jack Kennedy must have felt when he set an audience on fire. Even if Paul had only the vaguest idea of how the problems of Chicago could be solved, and even if he could actually do little toward solving them, he really believed that he was the better candidate. One paper spoke enthusiastically of his "patent sincerity," a line that Nora had read aloud with some amusement in almost the same tone of voice with which Chris Waverly read it over the telephone when she had seen the endorsement on the AP wire.

The polls the day before the election showed a close race; Paul lagged a few points behind Flanagan, but there was a large undecided vote. If the weather was favorable on Election Day and the turnout in the black wards was heavy, Tony predicted they would win 58 percent of the vote.

Paul sat in their suite at the Palmer House and watched the early returns on television, preparing his acceptance speech.

Tony came into the room, his hand clutching tally sheets. "We've cracked the black wards, Paul. We're going to beat them. Not by much, but we're going to win!"

Nora's arms were instantly around him. Paul kissed her then, and slipped away from her. He strode to the window. Outside, the El train creaked slowly down Wabash Avenue. This was it. This was the start of what he had been working toward his entire life.

Flanagan's phone call conceding the election was almost anticlimactic. It was the challenge, playing the odds, that excited Paul.

Then Richard Daley was on the television screen. "I want to congratulate young Paul Cronin for the fine race he ran. We need more men like him in Cook County politics. He'll do the Democratic Party proud in Springfield."

"I'm coming home with you," Elizabeth said as they left the ballroom of the Palmer House and walked out into the clear Chicago evening.

"I don't know that I'm up to it tonight, Elizabeth," Mike Cronin said. "This campaign's damn near drained me."

"At our age, Michael, there ought to be times when it's enough for two people just to huddle in each other's arms."

So they held each other in his king-size bed and watched the full moon turn the buildings on Michigan Avenue silver.

"I'll give it to you straight, Michael," she said, her fingers cool and soothing on his face.

"When haven't you?" He searched for a laugh and couldn't find one.

"I want to marry you. I'm not saying I'll dump you if you don't marry me. I'll come around as long as you want. Yet I think you'd better marry me. I'll keep you alive for a long time and make every day of it worthwhile." She snuggled closer to him. "Without me I don't think you're going to make it for long."

A deep groan welled up within him. She was right. Yet there was no way.

"And you've got to stop worrying about those sons of yours. Leave them alone. Let them live their own lives. Forget about Paul's political career. He's a sure success, even though he's not half the man you are. I don't know Sean, but I'm sure he can take care of himself. Forget them."

"I live for them," he pleaded.

"Live for me."

She was right. "You make it sound tempting, Elizabeth. I'll have to think."

"I'll be waiting." She sounded disappointed but by no means defeated.

Chapter Sixteen
1964

THE FIRST COMMITTEE meeting of the Birth Control Commission, established by Pope John and expanded by Pope Paul, was in May of 1964. Among the new members added for this session were Thomas Shields, a Chicago gynecologist and a specialist in fertility, and Father Sean Cronin, who was finishing his doctoral work on the history of marriage at Pontifical Gregorian University. It was a bizarre crowd of people gathered in the plain, high-ceilinged room. Sunlight streamed through the large window, turning the slightly dull plaster that seemed to mark all Vatican buildings into a glowing yellow. Seated around the brown conference table were bishops from Africa, theologians from Western Europe, a demographer from the Philippines, an English cardinal, and some frankly bored curial staff members, including the Alessandrinis' friend, Umberto Menelli.

Everyone spoke in his own language, and there was no simultaneous translation. Sean could get along passably well in Italian and was struggling with French, but German was completely beyond him. The meeting which should have been exciting was ponderous and dull. Moreover, much to Sean's astonishment, the committee seemed to have decided that the entire birth-control doctrine was now under question. And even more to his astonishment and dismay, the weight of opinion around the table seemed to favor the possibility of change.

After the meeting, at which little was accomplished, Tom Shields and Sean shook hands warmly. Tom had arrived a few days before, but there had been no chance to meet and talk.

"Everyone's fine." Tom's face wrinkled in a broad grin. "Nora's already hitting golf balls around the country club. Noreen's trying to walk—a little dynamo if I ever saw one. Everyone is still thrilled by Paul's victory, especially Maggie. She worked her tail off for Paul during the campaign."

Poor Maggie, Sean thought to himself, the moth flying too closely to the Cronin flame.

"My father is satisfied, I suppose?"

"You know your father. Absolutely jubilant about Paul's winning the nomination one night, and calm and serene at a board meeting the next day."

They were interrupted by a French theologian who had been hostile to Sean throughout the meeting. He was a bald-headed mean-looking man with sunken dark eyes. After a few minutes of polite conversation, the theologian said to Sean, "Monsignor wishes promotion in the Church. No?"

"Not in particular," Sean said.

"But Monsignor wears a cassock as only the curialists do, and he supports their position, does he not?" In addition to a sneer, the Frenchman had bad teeth.

"I am not a monsignor." Sean's tone was icy. "I wore a cassock today because this is my first meeting and I did not know what the proper attire would be. I support no one's position but my own." He turned his back on the Frenchman, who shrugged his shoulders and glided away.

"Pleasant cuss," Tom said.

"At the risk of sounding like my father, how the hell was I supposed to know that even the goddamned English Cardinal would wear a sport shirt?"

A continent away, Paul Cronin ambled down the street toward the Shields' Oakland Beach house. Tom Shields was in Rome, the children were at play school, and Nora was on the golf course. When he wanted to see Maggie, as he did now, he merely had to walk down Lake Shore Drive to the Shields' Dutch colonial house. It was a beautiful replica of the past, protected by a huge concrete seawall, against which the silver waves were beating on this windy Thursday of the Fourth of July weekend.

He slipped around to the side entrance of the house. No point in letting anyone see him go in. Maggie was a useful sexual resource. Nora was recovered now and they had resumed their uneventful sex life, but Paul needed other women.

Maggie was waiting for him in her frilly fourposter bed. She had been notified fifteen minutes earlier to prepare for his arrival. She held a wineglass to her mouth, although it was only ten o'clock in the morning. The Beatles were playing on the phonograph, and she wore only lace panties as a token of her residual modesty.

She kissed him, a hungry, longing kiss. "Am I better than Nora?" she asked. It was the first time she had ever mentioned Nora in these circumstances.

Paul was startled. "God, yes," he said.

"I knew I was!" She said it triumphantly and took a long sip of her wine. "Why don't you divorce her and marry me?"

Paul started to undress. "You know that kind of talk is off limits," he said cautiously. "It would be the end of my career, Nora and Tom would be destroyed, the children . . ." He sat down and drew her into his arms.

His kisses became demanding. He could sense that her sexual need had driven all other thoughts from her mind. A pleasant way to put an end to a dangerous conversation.

They were too involved in their lovemaking to hear the doorbell ring, but not so much so to miss Nora's voice at the foot of the stairs.

"Hey, Maggie. Are you up there?"

There was a rattle of golf clubs as Nora, who disdained a caddy cart, dropped her clubs somewhere in the Shields' parlor.

"Oh, my God," gasped Maggie. She slipped out from under Paul, pulled on a robe, brushed a few unruly strands of her curly blonde hair away from her ashen face, and raced down the stairs.

"I went back to bed after the kids ate their breakfast. . . ." Maggie was stammering.

Oh, good God, woman, Paul pleaded mentally. Cool it. Don't let her think you've got something to hide.

"I stopped by to see if you want to come to the club with me and then have lunch—"

"Oh, no . . . no, no," Maggie said.

"Suit yourself." Nora sounded puzzled but not upset.

When Maggie returned to the bedroom, Paul was hungry for her. The danger had turned him on like a powerful aphrodisiac.

Yet he told himself, as she responded to his fervor, that something had to be done about Maggie. She was becoming too demanding.

On the morning of Noreen Marie Cronin's first birthday party, her mother opened a letter from the Collegio Santa Maria dell'Lago, Via Sardegna 44, Roma. Sean's infrequent letters were eagerly awaited, and Paul did not mind if she opened them before he came home. Her one-year-old, a vigorous, even-tempered little comedian, clung to her mother's legs as she collected the morning mail and resolutely resisted her progress back to the parlor. "Let go, Noreen," her mother pleaded absentmindedly. "I have a letter from Uncle Sean."

Noreen did not let go; mommies, after all, were for hugging. So Nora dragged her to the chair and began to read Sean's letter.

Dear Paul and Nora,

The third session of the Vatican Council is almost over, and I'm even more confused than before about the state of the Church. I've slowly come around to the view that we need profound and systematic changes. Nora is right when she says that the Church has lost touch with the problems and needs of contemporary human beings. Yet I don't like the change that's going on here. It's too abrupt, too European, and, if you want to know what I really think, too intellectual. There is no serious attempt to maintain continuity with the traditions of the past. Paul VI makes matters worse by his nervous hand-wringing. I find that I'm against everything. I don't like the Pope. I don't like the Roman Curia, who are a bunch of cheap political fixers. I don't like the European theologians, who are arrogant, and I don't like many of the bishops, who pretend to know everything when they don't know anything.

The Cardinal is a shining light among them, a man with taste, respect for the past, and a strong sense of the problems of the present. He's right when he says that the Church has to change, and he also has the pragmatic sense to realize that if the change gets out of hand we're going to have chaos. But the change is already out of hand. The melancholy complaints of the Pope, the wild ideas of the theologians, the endless maneuvering of the Curia, and the stupidity of the bishops are all creating one monumental catastrophe. And the parish priests are going to have to be the ones to pick up the pieces.

I'm appalled at the grimness and depression of what I have written. I've been here too long. Some days I almost think St. Jadwiga's was better. I'll be eager to get home after Christmas and begin my new work.

And that brings me to something I don't quite know how to tell you. Archbishop McCarthy has made me a vice-chancellor. Jimmy McGuire also. He is to be responsible for administration and I for personnel. It will probably be announced a few days after you get

*this letter. I told the Cardinal that I was far more conservative
than he and therefore unqualified for the position.*

*He paid no attention. He said it was good to balance his lib-
eralism with my conservatism and then smiled that quick smile of
his. I'm never quite sure what it means.*

*Anyway, I'll be back soon to a job that may make St. Jadwiga's
look easy. And Happy Birthday, of course, to Noreen.*

God bless.

                                                              Sean.

Nora put the letter on the coffee table in front of her, tears in her eyes.
"Noreen, your Uncle Sean is a stupid sonofabitch. Unqualified, indeed."
Noreen responded with a bright one-year-old giggle.

The night before he was to return to the United States, Sean had supper with
the Alessandrinis, or rather with the *Principessa,* since Francésco was unaccountably absent. No particular explanation for his absence was offered. The
Principessa received him in a black minidress with a deep V-neck and a tightly
fitting bodice. Warning bells clanged in Sean's head as soon as she opened the
door. He ought to run.

He did not run, however.

The meal was a long, leisurely affair. The *Principessa* flirted outrageously
with Sean as she always did. It was eleven o'clock before the espresso was
served in the parlor. The lights were dim and Sean's head was reeling from the
excellent wine.

"So," she said, "you go home tomorrow to America to be 'Vice-Chancellor
for Personnel,' whatever that means in your foolish, capitalistic Church. You
have no concern for leaving Angèlica brokenhearted in Rome."

"I doubt that you will be brokenhearted for long," he said, trying to clear his
head. "Anyway, I'll be back for meetings of the Birth Control Commission, and
I suspect the Cardinal is going to use me as an envoy."

She took his hand in hers. Her fingers began to caress his arm.

"It's nice to have you all alone," she said, leaving no doubt as to her meaning. She leaned against him, available, inviting.

He put one arm around her and felt the expansion and contraction of the back
of her rib cage beneath his hand. "You're a beautiful woman, Angèlica. You've
been a bright spot in two rather dismal years. I hope you don't mind if I say
thanks, but no thanks." He kissed her forehead lightly and rose unsteadily to his
feet.

Much to his surprise, she did not seem offended. "My Francésco will be so
unhappy to have missed you tonight. I will absolutely insist that his fool work at
the Vatican does not keep him from dinner the next time you come." Her smile
glittered briefly. "It has been a marvelous evening, *caro mio.* And I will miss
you." She hastily pecked his cheek.

As he walked rather uncertainly across the dark and deserted Piazza Farnese,
Sean wondered what would have happened to him if he had turned down an
American woman who had made herself so vulnerable. Say, an Irish-American
woman from Chicago. He would be on the floor, wounded and bleeding.

It was only when he had returned to the Via Sardegna, however, that it occurred to him that he was probably neither the first nor the last priest to be caught in the *Principessa* Alessandrini's web. The thought disappointed him.

In February, Sean sat in the tiny office on the second floor of the Chicago chancery, stiff and uncertain in his new role as Vice-Chancellor for Personnel. There was a foot of snow on the streets of Chicago and the temperature was well below zero. Across from him sat his classmate, Peter Flynn. Either Peter wanted to transfer from the affluent parish in Lake Forest to which he was assigned or he was about to leave the priesthood. Sean's heart sank. Transfers he could handle easily. Defections from the priesthood shocked and horrified him.

They talked a bit about the seminary, about Rome, and about Lake Forest. Then there was an anxious pause.

Peter broke the silence. "I'm going to leave the priesthood and marry. There's a woman in the parish. She's a widow with four children. We love each other. If I could marry her and stay in the priesthood, I would. The life is too lonely. There is no one who will love me if I remain a priest, and Martha . . . well, Martha has made me want to live again."

"What about your promise to the Church?" Sean asked bluntly.

"I want to keep my promise to the Church." Peter had tears in his eyes. "The Church won't let me. If I could be a married priest, I'd stay on in the priesthood."

"I don't think you would, Peter." Sean's voice was cold. "You've had two of the best assignments in the archdiocese. Good people. Good pastors. Good fellow priests. You're unhappy in the priesthood because of something deep inside yourself. Now this woman comes along and provides you with an excuse—"

"Don't call Martha 'this woman,' " Flynn said.

"You're going to bed with her, I suppose?"

"Is that a question I have to answer to apply for a dispensation?"

"No, it's a question you have to answer if you don't want to be suspended from your parish at this moment for causing a scandal among the laity. Do you think you could carry on an illicit love affair with one of your parishioners and not shock the rest of the parish?" Sean had no evidence that there was scandal in the parish, but he was willing to wager that there was, and Flynn did not deny the charge.

"You're a vindictive bastard!"

"Because I believe that priests should keep their promise and not screw the first available woman parishioner who comes along?"

White and tense with anger, Peter Flynn rose from his chair. "Fuck your dispensation!"

Sean stared at the open doorway through which Flynn had stormed. He had handled things even worse than he feared he would.

He walked down the corridor to Jimmy McGuire's office.

"Congratulations," said that cheerful cleric as Sean slipped into the chair across from him.

"For what?"

"The boss has just made us monsignors. His secretary tells me the documents have come through from Rome. You'll look gorgeous in purple buttons, my boy. Your father will celebrate, and Nora's eyes will widen with admiration."

"Leave Nora out of it," said Sean.

"What happened?"

"Peter Flynn."

"Oh, yeah." Jimmy dropped a stack of files into a drawer of his desk. "I heard he was thinking of leaving. Chew him out?"

"I made him so angry that he didn't even apply for a dispensation."

Jimmy shrugged philosophically. "No point in chewing them out once they've made up their minds. In fact, no point in chewing them out, no matter what the circumstances."

"He seemed so damned self-righteous, so proud of himself because he'd been able to get a woman into bed with him."

"If you always doubted that you could, maybe that's something to be proud about."

"I don't know what's going wrong with the world and the Church, Jimmy. Drugs, violence, student protests, barbaric music, kids sleeping around, priests saying Mass with cocktails and hors d'oeuvres, nuns and priests shacking up during summer institutes, half-naked dancing on the altar during services . . . the world's going crazy."

Jimmy sighed. "The world has always been crazy. Go easy on people like Peter. There, but for the grace of God, and that sort of thing."

"I'd never do anything like that," Sean insisted. "Maybe I'm old-fashioned, Jimmy. When I make a commitment, I keep it."

Chapter Seventeen
1965

ON A STICKY, humid, partially overcast Thursday afternoon in late July, Paul Cronin walked impatiently back and forth in front of the broken-down South Shore railroad station in the downtown slums of Michigan City, Indiana. The escalating war in Vietnam seemed far away, as did the race riots in the nation's big cities.

Down the street, with considerable huffing and puffing, the battered old orange trolley train turned the corner and chugged to a weary stop in front of the station. Chris Waverly stepped off uneasily, her light green dress wilted and her blond hair rumpled. "So that's what it was like fifty years ago!" she said. "I'm sorry about those articles I've written in favor of mass transportation. Give me the auto and the airplane any time. Hi, lover boy." Her kiss was lingering and inviting. "See how much I'm willing to suffer just to spend a few hours with you?"

Paul looked anxiously around to make sure that none of his neighbors were at the train stop. He had pleaded with Chris to rent a car, but she assured him that she would lose her way in the wilderness of northern Indiana. "I'm sorry I couldn't come to Chicago. I didn't know that you'd be in town, and Nora left me in charge of the girls."

"Have I complained? I've always wanted to see your summer hideaway."

On the lakeshore the haze was lifting and the overcast blowing away. The winds were changing as promised, and the humidity would be gone in a few hours. Paul pushed the accelerator of his Porsche hard, and the car swept down the drive at sixty-five miles an hour.

"You're going a bit fast, aren't you?" Chris asked, clinging to his arm.

"Slow down. I'll keep. Besides, these dunes and lake of yours are kind of pretty."

Paul reduced the speed slightly. He loved the thrill of reckless driving just as he loved the thrill of a reckless love affair carried on while his wife was in Chicago. The excitement of the risk he was taking was almost as good as the excitement of making love to Chris again.

At the Michianna Beach Inn, a few miles down the lake from his home, a room had been reserved for "Mr. and Mrs. Waverly." Fortunately, Paul had never been at the sleek new luxury motel. The Oakland Beach Irish preferred their own homes and the old familiar restaurants.

It was a bad day for Chris to show up with little notice. Nora had impulsively driven to Chicago to "do something" about Mary's persistent cough. It was both the housekeeper's and the baby-sitter's day off. Only at the last minute had Paul been able to draft the fifteen-year-old Hanrahan girl to watch the children. He felt rushed and anxious.

Chris was in no mood to be hurried. Their lovemaking was leisurely and fulfilling.

When Paul got up from the bed to get dressed, Chris said, "Sneaking around like this is exciting, isn't it, Paul?" He could not resist the arms stretched out to him like a hungry child's. Instantly he was back in her arms and back in bed once again.

With careful solemnity, Noreen Cronin began to negotiate the stairs from her house down to the beach, one step at a time, both feet securely on each step before she tried the next one. She kept her balance with her sand shovel, waving it in the air like a royal scepter.

Noreen knew that she was not supposed to go to the beach by herself. She was being a bad girl. Yet today everyone was being bad. Even Marcie Hanrahan's mother was bad. She had come along the beach shouting that Marcie had to go home and help with the supper, and she should "this very instant bring those little brats up to their father."

Noreen didn't like being called a little brat. She didn't like being left alone in the house with her sister Eileen, who was so busy with her friend Nicole that she wouldn't play even one game with Noreen.

If Eileen was being bad, then she could be bad too. Anyway, she had to finish her sand castle before Daddy came home. Daddy would like the castle.

She continued her careful descent.

"It's a nice area." Chris was carefully arranging her makeup as Paul rushed her back to the South Shore depot. "I think I'm going to enjoy living here."

Paul was baffled by Chris's assumption that he was going to divorce Nora and make her his wife. He had never given her any reason to think so. "Nora would never give up the house," he said, trying to make a joke of it. "And even if she did, we wouldn't dare live there."

"How terribly provincial, but then this is the provinces, isn't it? I suppose you and I don't belong in the provinces anyway." She put away her compact and squeezed his leg. "But we do belong together, don't we, Paul?"

Paul groaned inwardly. Maybe they did belong together, but he could not possibly marry her.

When Paul returned home, Eileen and Nicole Shields were in the recreation room listening to records. "Everything okay? Where's the baby-sitter?"

"Her mother came and made her go home," Eileen said, with manifest disinterest. "So we came up to the house."

"Smart girl." Paul pecked at her approvingly. "The baby in her room?"

"I suppose so."

Paul mixed himself a gin and tonic as a reward for the tensions that had accompanied the pleasures of the afternoon. Chris worried him. She had seemed a little bit too flaky today. She couldn't really believe that he would give up his family for her.

He went to his room and put on a swimsuit. A little dip in the lake would do very nicely. First he would make sure about Noreen.

Gin and tonic in hand, he pushed open the door of Noreen's room. She wasn't there. He checked the rest of the house. No Noreen.

He rushed back to the rec room. "Where is she? Where's the baby?" he shouted at Eileen.

"I have to go home now." Nicole scurried quickly out the door and down the steps.

Eileen's face turned ashen. "Isn't she in her room?"

"You little fool. You've lost the baby!"

"You lost her," Eileen shouted back. "You went away when Mommy said you should watch us."

He slapped her and pushed her across the room. Then he raced out of the house.

He cut a furious path through the sun worshipers on the beach. Everyone had seen Noreen. The lifeguard thought she had walked up the beach. Two mothers thought she had walked down the beach. Some teenagers swore that they had seen some men take her on a boat. A younger child was certain that Noreen was somewhere building sand castles near the house.

Martin O'Riordan, an ancient Oakland Beach patriarch, announced pompously to the crowd that was gathering around Paul, "We'll organize a search party to find her."

"You goddamn fool!" Paul yelled. He was becoming irrational. "If you'd been watching her in the first place, she wouldn't be lost." He turned and ran, paying little attention to the murmurs of astonishment that trailed after him.

Halfway down the beach he lost his wind and sank into the sand, breathing heavily. Oh, God, please help me find her. Nora will never forgive me.

Then he trudged slowly back to the house. Must get hold of yourself . . . call the police . . . get professional help . . . can't crack up. . . .

Three teenagers were sitting at the foot of the stairs to the Cronin house. They stood up as he approached them.

"Hi, Mr. Cronin," one of the boys said, a tall slender lad whose name Paul remembered was Bob.

"Have you seen my baby?" he asked desperately.

"Sure. We found her sleeping on the dunes. She said she wanted to come home, so Michelle carried her here."

"Where is she?" Paul exploded.

"We brought her up to the house and Eileen put her to bed," Michelle said. Paul dashed up the steps and into the house.

"You could at least say thank you," Michelle hollered after him, with all the Irish-woman's rage at injustice. "We saved her."

The next afternoon Paul was relaxing on the balcony with the Sunday papers, thanking all the saints in heaven that he had calmed down before Nora returned. Tom and Maggie had come for dinner the night before and not a word had been said about the disaster of the afternoon.

Nora came up from the beach from her daily swim, a towel around her shoulders.

"You made a real ass out of yourself yesterday, didn't you?" she began without any preliminaries. "You hurt Eileen, ranted at your neighbors, insulted that old fool O'Riordan, and acted like an insensitive bastard in front of the teenagers who saved your daughter. Don't look surprised. You should know you can't keep anything secret in a resort community."

"It was all a misunderstanding. . . ." He searched desperately for an excuse.

"It sure was. I want to know the name of the misunderstanding. Don't bother lying to me. I can tell by the look on your face that you were with another woman."

Paul was intimidated by her deadly composed voice.

"Well—er—now, Nora, it really isn't a very important—I mean, that is—"

"Who is she?" Nora demanded.

To his amazement, Paul found himself blurting out the name. "Chris Waverly." He reached for the empty beer can on the end table next to him and then put it down nervously. "It's not an important relationship, Nora. I mean, it isn't serious. You shouldn't—"

"Which one of us leaves?"

"Which one of us leaves where?"

"This house, this minute. Either you get out or I do."

Paul stood up awkwardly. "I guess I can move back to Glenwood Drive." He hesitated.

"Back to a hotel room in Chicago. I don't want you in this house, and I don't want you on Glenwood Drive either."

"Now, Nora, this isn't the end of everything. I'm sure we can work it out. There's no reason—"

"Get out!" She lost her composure and began to scream at him. "Get out and stay out!"

There was a stack of problems on Sean Cronin's desk that Monday morning. Two more applications for dispensations from the priesthood; three letters, two of them signed, accusing priests and nuns of fornication; a signed petition of complaint against the principal of a Catholic school in a north-western suburb, claiming that she had ridiculed the doctrine of the Assumption to a group of children on August 15; and a complaint from a pastor that his curate was telling people in the confessional that birth control was not a sin.

Sean tore up the anonymous letter and threw it in the wastebasket. One of the priests who was accused of having a lover, he noted, was fifty-seven years old.

"No fool like an old fool," he muttered to himself. Then he felt ashamed of his snap judgment. Signed or not, a complaint was a form of character assassination that he ought not to believe until he had more evidence.

The telephone on the desk next to him jangled. He picked it up and heard the unmistakable voice of his father: "What the hell is Nora doing throwing Paul out of the house? She won't even speak to him. All she would say to me was that he can have his whores."

"I haven't heard anything. But I think we can assume that if Nora's thrown Paul out, he must have given her good reason."

"That's not the point. The point is you should fix it up. They'll both listen to you." The phone line went dead. Sean eased his phone back on its cradle and it rang almost at once.

"Cronin here," he said, knowing full well that it was a Cronin on the other end of the line too: Paul Cronin, this time.

Sean saw his brother in the office in the cathedral rectory rather than in the chancery. If Paul felt any strain, he did not show it. Indeed, he spent ten minutes discussing the National League pennant race and the St. Louis Cardinals. Finally, almost as an afterthought, he said, "I suppose Nora has talked to you?"

"No," said Sean. "She has not."

"We have a problem. She knows that I've been seeing another woman. She's thrown me out."

"Oh?"

"It's one of those things that happens. You know what I mean. Not a big deal at all. A reporter from Washington."

Sean could hardly believe his brother would be so casual about his infidelity. "I presume it's not a serious relationship?"

"Just a passing thing. Nora's a wonderful wife, but sometimes marriage and sex are just not the same thing."

"Well, what do you want me to do about it?" The dull, dark office with its heavy old furniture perfectly reflected Sean's mood at the moment.

"She won't talk to me. . . . I thought you might be able to persuade her to give me another chance."

"What makes you think Nora will listen to me?"

Paul seemed surprised at the question. "You're a priest, aren't you? Of course she'll listen to you. Aren't priests supposed to help people put their marriages back together again?"

Sean sighed. "I'll see what I can do."

It was a crisp, sunny August morning in the middle 70s, with a light breeze blowing off the lake and a faint touch of autumn in the air. Mary and Eileen were playing on the beach. Nora and Noreen were building sand castles. Sean watched them silently for some time from the bottom of the stairs. There was no doubt that Noreen was the foreman on this construction job.

"Uncle!" She gestured with her small shovel.

Nora, a sweat shirt over her bikini, glanced up. "I suppose I should have expected you."

Sean joined her by the sand castle. "Run along and play with Mary and Eileen," Nora instructed Noreen. "Uncle Sean is going to preach me a sermon."

Sean sat next to her on the beach towel. She drew her long, elegant legs up beneath her chin and said calmly, "Okay, let's have it."

"I'm not going to preach a sermon, Nora. You have every right to be furious."

"Your brother is a spoiled, self-indulgent little boy. The fool can't even understand why I'm angry." Her voice was flat and hard.

"There are times in every marriage when things are difficult—"

"Now comes the part in the sermon about the importance of commitment. You always were very good, Sean, in lecturing about commitments."

"I believe in them," said Sean. "Human life is impossible unless we keep our commitments. Paul needs you. He says he'll fall apart without you, and I'm sure that's true."

"Of course it's true," she snapped. "Right now I'd like to see him fall apart."

"Don't you love him?"

Nora dug at the sand with a tiny twig. "Love him? What's love? I've produced three children that are his. I have some feelings of affection for him. I suppose I'll take him back when I calm down. You're the expert on love, Sean. Does all that add up to love? Or does it merely add up to making the best of a bad bargain?"

Sean felt enormous tenderness for her. He wanted to put his arm around her shoulder and reassure her. Instead, he said, "That's just the way it appears now, Nora. It will get better."

"The hell it will."

"Paul says there won't be any more—"

"He probably means that promise. Maybe he'll even keep it for a few weeks."

Sean took a deep breath. "Nora, there's no way I can say this delicately, so I'm not going to try. Is the relationship sexually fulfilling to you?"

Her eyes turned hard. "None of your goddamn business."

"I know it's none of my business, but I'm making it my business."

"You want me to turn into a sex kitten and compete with his women?"

"You're a passionate woman, Nora. Your life will be desperately unfulfilling if you don't find an outlet for those passions."

"Listen to the priest turn sex expert." Her words dripped with sarcasm. "Do you want me to use Paul for sexual kicks the way he uses me? Is that what you want? Very smart of you, because then I'll be cemented to him so strongly that the Cronin family won't have to worry about a scandal. Sex as cement, that's what you have in mind, isn't it?"

"Sex as love," said Sean hesitantly.

"Love doesn't enter into it at all," she said sadly. "Go away, Sean. You preached your sermon. You invaded my privacy, undressed me, and made me look at myself so that I don't like what I see. I hope your brother and your father are happy with the results."

Sean stood up and brushed the sand off his slacks. "I didn't do it for them, Nora."

"Go away," she said. "I'll take him back when I calm down. Maybe she'd be better for him than I am. I don't know. Anyway, I made a commitment, and I'll stand by it till he walks out on me. Now go away and leave me alone."

. . .

That night, Sean found in the bottom of the drawer in his desk in the cathedral rectory a battered brown notebook that had once been his spiritual diary. It was a long time since he had made an entry.

> *In the middle course of life, as Dante said—well, maybe not quite the middle course yet—I do not like what I see. My father is becoming a difficult old man, demanding, unpredictable. My brother, whom I worshiped most of my life, has been well de- scribed by his wife as a spoiled, self-indulgent little boy. Nora is locked into a life of unhappiness and frustration, and I'm making a mess out of my job. I'm no more confident that you're out there listening than I've ever been, probably a little less confident. Not believing in you, I tried to believe in the Church; and now the Church I believed in is collapsing all around me. Not able to make a commitment to you, I made a commitment to the priest- hood; and the priesthood is crumbling. I wonder if I ought not to leave like everyone else? I wonder if commitments—any commit- ment and every commitment—are not tragic mistakes.*

During a lull on the Sunday of the Labor Day weekend, while Nora was on the golf course and his daughters were firmly supervised by Maggie and Tom Shields on the beach, Paul managed to sneak a phone call to Chris Waverly at her Martha's Vineyard holiday retreat.

"Hi," she said. "Where have you been hiding?"

Paul started making excuses, but Chris cut him off. "Which of us is it going to be?" she said. "You've got to choose."

"She's my wife and the mother of my children, Chris. I can't leave her."

"You will sooner or later," Chris said. "We're two of a kind, Paul. You can't do without me, and I can't do without you."

As Paul talked to Chris on the phone, there was a strong pull in her direction. He knew that when the phone conversation was over, however, the opposite tug would be irresistible again. "She'll never let me go," he said defensively.

"You mean you're too much of a coward to try to break away."

"I'm sorry you feel that way, Chris." He tried to sound reasonable and adult.

"Have it your own way, Paul, but don't think you're going to get away from me so easily."

"What do you mean?" Paul sensed the Chinese bayonet in his gut once again.

"I mean that you can't discard me like yesterday's news. It's not a nice feeling. Sooner or later, I'm going to make you sorry for what you've done to me."

Chapter Eighteen
1965

In August, Sean received a phone call from Elizabeth Hanover, who wanted to talk with him. He proposed lunch or the cathedral rectory. She responded by suggesting that they meet on neutral ground—the Lincoln Park lagoon.

She wore dark brown slacks and a beige silk shirt. She showed faint signs of nervousness, unusual in such a normally cool woman.

They sat down on an old bench at the edge of a small green meadow. A few yards from them toddlers were playing under the careful eyes of young mothers in shorts and halters. "Are you on my side, or are you against me?" she asked bluntly.

"I'm on your side, of course. And priests don't bite, Elizabeth."

She laughed and relaxed. "Sorry. I've never talked to a priest before."

"What happens when you have one for a stepson?"

A faint tinge of color appeared in her cheeks. "I'm committed to your father, Sean. Does that offend you, a mistress committed to a man?"

"I want Dad to be happy. I've never seen him as happy as he is with you."

"Does it offend you that I'm your father's mistress?" She was testing him, poking at him to make sure he was human.

"You couldn't possibly offend me, Elizabeth."

"I think I'd like to have you for a stepson. If only I could get Jane out of the way."

"You think she's an obstacle?" Sean was surprised.

Elizabeth frowned. "I don't know how or why, but she has a strange hold on Michael."

"Perhaps we Cronins are more trouble than we're worth."

"No. From the first moment Michael came into that committee meeting, he owned me. Chemistry? Love at first sight? I don't know and I don't care."

Lucky Dad, Sean thought with a touch of envy. "He's mellowing, it seems to me."

"I met him at the right time. He doesn't have to dominate women any more, and I think he's giving up trying to run his sons' careers. He's letting go of things that are good to let go of. So he can live longer."

"With you to love him," Sean agreed.

Elizabeth Hanover's tears were like everything else about her—direct and straightforward. Sean put his arm around her until the tears were over.

"I've never been hugged by a priest before." She wiped away the last traces of her weeping.

"If you have a priest stepson, you'd better get used to it."

That night Sean dreamed about Mary Eileen. He awoke and groggily wondered if he had had this same dream every night. No, this one was different. His mother was still alive, but now his mother was Elizabeth. Then his father took her away from him, just as he had taken away Mary Eileen.

That couldn't have been in the dream before.

Sean did not go back to sleep.

Jane Cronin was buried at the time the Watts riots were taking place in Los Angeles and there was concern that the same sort of thing might occur on the South Side of Chicago.

At her instructions, the Mass was said at St. Ann's Church on Garfield Boulevard, now renamed after St. Charles Luwanga, an African martyr, a fact of which Jane was probably unaware or she would have changed her will.

There was some unease as the little group of mourners filed into the old church, even though the young pastor insisted that the neighborhood would never be another Watts. Nora wondered how the dilapidated old building could possibly ever have been an elegant church for the well-to-do lace-curtain Irish of the turn of the century. According to Sean, one of the pastors was quite mad and had not opened the parish hall to parishioners for twenty years. Now the black members of the parish were enjoying it immensely. God's ways were sometimes ironic.

Paul, Marty Hoffman, Ed Connaire, and Tom Shields were pallbearers. A badly shaken Mike Cronin leaned on Nora for support as they walked down the aisle of the church, with Eileen and Mary trailing behind them.

Sean's face was an unreadable mask, as though he were trying to find some meaning in his aunt's long, unhappy life.

To the bitter end, Jane had persisted in her animosity toward Nora, despite Nora's daily visits to Little Company of Mary Hospital. Nora was certain that Aunt Jane knew a secret from the family past, something that could hurt Sean badly. There were angry and knowing hints the last days in the hospital. In fact, a few hours before she died, Jane emerged from her half coma and said, "Things are never what they seem, Nora, never what they seem. Don't forget that. You'll all die like I'm dying, lonely and afraid." It sounded like a curse.

"What do you mean, Aunt Jane?" Nora felt a hand of ice momentarily touch her heart.

"I'm the only one who knows everything. Ed Connaire thinks he knows, but he doesn't know everything. It will all come out some day, and then we'll see how proud and mighty your priest really is."

Recalling the words, Nora shuddered as the body of Jane Cronin was committed to the earth from which she came. She resolved that she would corner Ed and find out what he was holding back.

After the final prayer, she told the two girls to talk to Uncle Sean and darted back into the group of mourners to find Ed Connaire. She had hesitated at first because of the occasion, but then she steeled herself and drew him away from the open grave.

"There were a lot of mysterious remarks in the last few days at the hospital," she began without preliminaries. "I know you haven't told us everything. I want to hear it all now."

The stocky contractor's hair was white, but his eyes were lively and his face almost unlined. "I've told you almost everything, Nora," he said.

"I want to know what's not covered by the 'almost.' I've got to know."

"Let sleeping dogs lie."

She shook her head. "If she's said those terrible things to me, she's said them to Sean. You know *he* won't let sleeping dogs lie. I should be prepared."

Connaire nodded. "You're right, I suppose. It was such a long time ago. No one meant anything bad."

"Ed," she said. There was a warning note in her voice.

"All right, Nora. There never was saying 'no' to you. . . . You see, Mary Eileen was a very sick woman after Paul was born. Always misty and vague. Well, one of the priests from New Albany stopped in often to see her at Oakland Beach when your father was away. They became good friends, very close. Too close, to hear Jane tell it. Then Mary Eileen became pregnant with Sean. No one was ever sure—"

"My God," Nora said in dismay.

"Personally, I think he's Mike's son, and Mike would never tolerate any other suggestion. Anyway, Mike had the young priest transferred to the other end of the state of Michigan."

"There couldn't have been anything." Nora leaned against a large burial monument.

Connaire cracked his massive knuckles. "Poor Mary Eileen thought there was. She was even more—er—depressed after Sean's birth. She tried to smother him in his crib one night. Mike stopped her just in time. She said Sean was a child of sin and God wanted him destroyed. . . . Nora, I swear that's all there is. She died in the car crash not long after that. I hope you won't tell Sean."

"Of course not." She was numb. "I hope he never finds out. I'll be ready if he does, though. Thanks, Ed."

Her daughters bounced over to her then, fascinated by the dramas written out on the headstones. Absently Nora listened to their babble, while she studied the inscription on a discreetly expensive monument at the edge of the Cronin plot:

MARY EILEEN MORRISEY CRONIN
1908–1934

Beloved Wife and Mother
She Left Us Too Soon

Twenty-six years old, four years younger than I am, Nora thought. She would be only in her middle fifties today.

Elizabeth Hanover's elegant dark head disappeared into one of the limousines. Nora thought, What would Mary Eileen think of you?

And of me?

Mike Cronin poured his second drink. Elizabeth would not approve, but she was not around tonight to approve or disapprove. He had told her he wanted to be alone with his grief, and she had quietly agreed. The two years with her had been the best since Mary Eileen. No, the best since his mother died. So much peace and warmth. Now he was free to marry her. Jane was dead and no one else would stop him. Tomorrow he would ask her. Sean would do the honors. Sean and Elizabeth got along famously.

Deep down in the darkest corner of his soul was a voice that told him that, Jane or not, he could never marry Elizabeth. He groaned aloud. Goddamn it, it wasn't fair.

Still, it was the way things were. He would call her tomorrow and tell her that they had better not see each other for a few weeks. Ease out gradually.

Maybe it had all been a mistake. Maybe he should have never listened to Jane. God, how can a man know what to do? At the time it had seemed the right thing to do, the only thing to do. Now he was no longer certain of anything.

BOOK FIVE

Do not let your hearts be troubled. Trust in God still, and trust in me. There are many rooms in my Father's house; if there were not, I would not have told you. I'm going now to prepare a place for you; after I've gone and prepared your place, I shall return to take you with me, so that where I am you may be too.

—JOHN 14:1–3

Chapter Nineteen
1966

NORA CRONIN CELEBRATED her tenth wedding anniversary with her three daughters at Oakland Beach. She played golf in the morning, and in the afternoon, keeping one eye on the three little girls frolicking on the beach, she read Masters and Johnson's *Human Sexual Response*. She decided with some dissatisfaction that her own responses were distinctly below normal.

The thought was interrupted by the ringing of the telephone which she had installed on the sundeck. It was Sean, calling to wish her a happy anniversary from O'Hare Airport.

"Well, thanks for remembering," she said.

"Has Paul called?" he asked.

"Oh, sure. He called from London. London doesn't count on your tenth anniversary. Everybody's deserted me. You're going to Rome. Tom's already over there with Maggie. And my husband is on a junket in London. I'm relegated to the backwaters of southern Michigan. Serves me right, I guess."

"You don't sound brokenhearted," Sean said.

"Of course not. Anyway, thanks for calling. I'll be looking forward to seeing you in Rome week after next."

"I wanted to ask you about that. I'm not so sure that dragging me along is a good idea. Maybe you and Paul can use the time alone—"

"Don't be silly, Sean. You'll make a good tour guide, and Paul has his heart set on the old threesome being together again."

The truth was, Nora thought as she hung up, she was as ambivalent as Sean about the trip to Europe. She wanted to see Italy. Uncle Mike had forbidden her to tour Europe when she was in college: "too dangerous for a young girl." Then she had not wanted to leave the children alone when they were young. But Paul's desire for the "old threesome" to travel through Italy together worried her. As she and Paul drifted further and further apart, the outside walls of the tightly sealed house in her brain labeled "Sean Cronin" had started crumbling. She was not so much afraid of Sean as she was afraid of herself with him. Perhaps it was the result of having passed her thirtieth birthday.

She pulled off her shirt, made sure the straps on her swimsuit were properly adjusted, told the baby-sitter to keep a close eye on the girls, and plunged into the lake for her half-mile swim.

Paul had been an instant success in the state legislature, winning high marks from both the Daley Democrats and the independents for his energy and enthusiasm. Nora was surprised and impressed by how much he loved the rough-and-tumble of legislative politics: the whispered cloakroom conversations, the long barroom sessions, the late-night phone calls in which the work of politics was really accomplished. He was good at it, all right.

She had been impressed, too, by his liberalism and compassion. It was not what she had expected from the man she married. She was sorry to see it slipping away now that the Mayor was dangling a big plum in front of him.

The week before, the *Sun-Times* had called editorially for a new aviation commissioner to "straighten out the mess at O'Hare." Then the paper went on to recommend that the Mayor appoint someone of "proven ability," such as State Senator Paul Cronin. It praised Paul's war record, his service in the Kennedy administration, his legislative ability, and his "proven compassion," none of which even to his wife seemed grounds for turning over the city's airports to his supervision.

Paul was horrified and promptly called a friend in City Hall to pass the word to the Mayor that he was not behind the article. The word came back that the Mayor knew that he wasn't, but would Paul be interested in the job?

"It would be a great challenge," Paul had replied.

Nora agreed that it would be an important step in his career, yet she hated to see his newfound concern for the poor and the oppressed disappear so quickly.

Later, after her swim and after the children were properly showered, she opened a bottle of champagne to drink a toast to her anniversary. Would the next ten years be like the last ten years? Soon Noreen would be in school and Nora would have time on her hands. She had better find something to do, or she would turn into a bored old bitch.

She felt a slight shudder of fear as she sipped the gaily bubbling liquid.

Paul Cronin celebrated his tenth wedding anniversary by making love to Maggie Shields in her room at the George V in Paris.

Flying back to London late that evening to continue his study of local government in England, he decided that he would end the relationship. The pleasure of their sex had been marred for him by Maggie's plea that he leave Nora for her.

Even worse, Maggie had insisted on taking some pills before they made love. She had purchased them from a drug dealer on the Left Bank. Marijuana was one thing. This was something else. Paul sensed that Maggie was tottering on the brink of some kind of spectacular action. He didn't want to be near her when it happened.

Why, he wondered, did he always return to Maggie despite his resolutions to stop seeing her? It wasn't the sex. It was good, but he had had better.

Now there was a look of hopelessness in her eyes. He did not want to be even partly responsible for that hopelessness. He would finish the affair for good this time. Cut it off before it got totally out of hand.

A vague thought passed through his mind. How long had that emptiness lurked

in her moody brown eyes? He exorcised the thought by smiling at the pretty Air
France cabin attendant and ordering a second drink.

Tom Shields waited for Sean at a sidewalk café on the Via della Conciliazione,
the Tiber on his right and the great silver dome of St. Peter's on his left. He had
picked up Sean, battered and worn from a delayed Alitalia trip, at Fiumicino
airport the previous afternoon. He had taken the priest to Chicago House on the
Via Sardegna, told him to get a good night's sleep, and promised to meet him
whenever he awakened the following morning. Tom was staying at the Columbus Hotel, next to the sidewalk café, because it was close to the committee
meeting place. When Maggie came down from Paris in a few days they would
move to the more luxurious Hassler. The trip through Europe with Maggie had
been something less than a total success. She had complained about the incon-
venience of travel and the inadequacies of even deluxe hotel accommodations,
and she was unimpressed by the museums and monuments that fascinated him,
although she did enjoy the night life and the expensive department stores.

Tom drained his cup of espresso and signaled the waiter for a refill as a light
blue Lancia pulled up by one of the elaborate lampposts on the outer sidewalk of
the Conciliazione. Sean, dressed in a light gray suit and a navy blue turtleneck,
emerged from the car, turned around, and kissed—or, more precisely, was
kissed by—a very pretty woman. Tom Shields was stunned.

Sean, grinning broadly, slipped between two elderly couples and joined Tom
at the tiny table.

"Who was that?" Tom asked.

"Oh, just a princess I happen to know—the Principessa Alessandrini, as a
matter of fact." Sean waved his hand as though he were kissed by a princess
every day.

Actually, he knew that he should stay away from Angèlica. She was becoming
an obsession with him, proof of how badly his years in Rome had affected his
self-discipline. His fantasies about possessing her were vivid and explicit. She
had even found her way into his dreams, often becoming confused with his
mother. When he awoke he had to sort them out, to insist to himself that one
woman was very much alive and one was dead.

"I'm not sure about you, Sean," Tom said. "I suspect that woman may be
trying to seduce you."

Sean sat next to him at the table. "May be? She's very definitely trying to
seduce me—quite obvious about it." He grinned. "Don't worry. I'm immune to
that sort of thing."

Yes, if ever there was a man immune to womanly charm, Tom Shields thought,
it was Sean Cronin.

"How's Maggie?" Sean asked.

Tom had never discussed his problem with anyone, but Sean was so warm and
seemed so genuinely interested. "Up and down, to tell you the truth. Maggie
gets depressed a lot. We had a suicide attempt a few months ago. Worries the
hell out of me, and I don't know what to do about it."

"Maggie?" Sean asked incredulously.

"We've tried therapy but nothing seems to work. There's a strong strain of
depression in it all, though the doctors tell me the suicide attempt was mostly an
effort to gain attention. I'm afraid she might push her luck too far some day and
not gain the attention quickly enough to save her."

"What's she depressed about?" Sean asked, putting his hand on Tom's arm.

"I think mostly it's the demands that life makes on her to grow up. At least that's what one of the doctors said, and it seems to me to be true. Maggie has been pouting since our wedding day. I've tried paying no attention to it, and I've tried giving it all my attention. No matter what I do, or the kids do, or what the doctors do, she's still fundamentally dissatisfied with her life. The suicide attempt, they tell me, was a protest against the injustices that have been done to her—only most of the injustices are in her mind."

"God!" exclaimed Sean, tightening the grip on Tom's arm. "How do you stand it?"

"I struggle on. I blame myself when I'm away from home, but then when I'm home it doesn't seem to make any difference. I brought her with me to Europe for this meeting, thinking a vacation together would help. Then she decided to stay in Paris, even though her big complaint about these meetings before has been that I left her alone too much. I don't know what to do. I sometimes think there's nothing I *can* do."

Sean wished that, like a magician pulling a rabbit out of a hat, he could offer an insight that would be of help to Tom. But he wasn't a magician. "There are some things we can't do anything about, Tom. We just have to let happen what's going to happen."

For no apparent reason, a picture of Nora flashed through his mind.

Roger Fitzgibbon had become more Roman than the Romans, wearing not only a cassock but a clerical hat and light overcoat even though it was the middle of a heat wave.

Roger had engineered an appointment in the Secretariat of State when Cardinal McCarthy had passed him over to make Jimmy McGuire vice-chancellor. Sean knew that this must have galled his ambitious classmate, but there was never a sign of resentment when they crossed paths in the streets around the Vatican. Never offend a potential ally.

"Good to see you, Sean." Roger smiled his toothy grin. "Hear you're knocking them dead at the Birth Control Commission."

They were across the street from the gate to the Vatican Holy Office. The gray building looked down upon them as if with aloof disapproval.

"I hear you met my colleague, Martin Spalding Quinlan, at the Alessandrinis the other night," Roger continued. "You really are in high company, Sean. The Prince is one of the most influential of the black nobility."

"Is it true that Marty added the Spalding to his name because it sounds so Episcopal?"

Roger laughed easily. "I wouldn't know about that. But he's certainly going to be a bishop very soon. Somewhere in the West, I gather. The first step up. There are those in the Secretariat who think he may succeed our beloved Eamon some day."

"Deliver us from a faggot bishop," Sean said fervently.

Roger raised an eyebrow. "Oh, come now, Sean. That's not fair. Martin's taste is impeccable, of course, and he has a wonderful eye for line and texture, but you're sophisticated enough to know that doesn't mean anything."

Sean wondered whether or not Roger's remark meant that he agreed that Quinlan was homosexual. Regardless, Sean was certain that the man who might be his next archbishop would hear a detailed account of the conversation. Well, at least the Principessa Angèlica would never make a play for Martin Spalding Quinlan.

Back in his room at Chicago House on Via Sardegna, Sean recalled the final vote at the Birth Control Commission. Even the four or five bishops from Africa and Asia, about whom he was uncertain, went with the majority and voted for change. There were only seven votes for the minority, including the chairman's. A five-to-one landslide for those who thought change was possible. Paul VI had his lifeline if he wanted it.

"You do not vote, Monsignor Cronin?" the chairman had asked, his surprise evident.

"I can accept neither position." Sean weighed each word carefully. "You can show me as abstaining."

"Abstaining? What does that mean?" asked the chairman.

"It means not eating meat on Friday," joked Sir Hubert, the Aussie anthropologist.

Everyone in the room tittered.

"Just note that I was present and didn't vote," said Sean.

As the meeting was breaking up and handshakes and farewells were being exchanged, the greasy French theologian accosted him. "You try to please everyone, Monsignor Cronin, and you succeed in pleasing no one. That is the fate of ambitious men." He turned and walked away.

"Bastard," whispered Tom Shields.

"Maybe that fellow's right, Tom," Sean said, staring after the retreating Frenchman. "Maybe I *am* trying to please everyone."

"That's not what the young clergy in Chicago say about you. The young priest in our parish says that all his classmates have a tremendous amount of respect for your integrity. They say that even when you're wrong, you're wrong for the right reasons."

Sean was astonished. "The next thing you'll try to tell me is that I'm popular with the junior clergy."

"I won't try to tell you that because you're a sufficiently morose Irishman not to want to believe it. It's still true. Popular and, if the young clergy are typical, getting more popular."

If they found out about his birth control vote, Sean told himself in his room, his popularity would soon begin to wane. He looked up. Cardinal McCarthy was standing in his doorway.

"Good evening, Monsignor." The little man's voice was as mild and self-effacing as ever. The enormous responsibility of being Cardinal Archbishop of Chicago was taking its toll on him, but nothing seemed to shatter his serenity. "Need I say that everyone in the Curia is talking about your vote this morning. The cardinals I met with at the Sacred Congregation this evening were very much impressed."

"I didn't do it to impress anybody, Your Eminence," he said wearily.

"I'm sure you did not, Monsignor. Nonetheless, that was what you accomplished. Rome does not often value independence, much less integrity. Sometimes and on some issues, however, a man of independence and integrity has a uniquely powerful position."

Sean couldn't help but grin. "Your Eminence, what in the hell am I supposed to do with this unique power I've earned today?"

The Cardinal's smile lasted longer this time. "One of the things you're going to do, Monsignor Cronin, is come to Castel Gandolfo with me later on in the month, after your vacation. Macchi himself—the Pope's secretary—called me a little while ago and said the Pope very much wanted to have a personal talk with you. I trust you don't mind discussing the reasons for your vote with His Holiness?" Eamon McCarthy fingered the plain gold band on his right hand, as he always did when he was afraid he might be pushing one of his priests too hard.

"The Pope's the boss, Your Eminence. Of course I'll see him."

"I'm not sure that he's the boss any more, Monsignor Cronin. However, he still believes that he is. I will send word to Monsignor Macchi tomorrow to make the proper arrangements."

Only after the Cardinal left did Sean realize that he had refused to commit Sean to the meeting without asking him first.

Sean arranged for a dinner party when Nora arrived in Rome. He watched the interaction between Nora and the Principessa Angèlica as the full moon illuminated the late medieval church across from Sabatini's restaurant. The setting was perfect: pure white tablecloths, fine red wine, and the obvious admiration of the other people in the outdoor dining area. Francésco was being attentive to Paul, while Angèlica had clearly decided that there was little point in competing with Nora and chose, rather, to play the role of the gracious papal noblewoman. In turn, Nora entertained the party with stories of touch football games and swimming pool escapades with the Kennedy clan.

Both women ignored Maggie Shields, Angèlica from the very beginning and Nora after one or two unsuccessful attempts to bring her into the conversation. Maggie looked lovely. With her pretty eyes and even prettier smile, she could have been part of the entertainment. Instead, she remained distant.

By the time Nora had reached the point in her story where she had "clipped" Bob Kennedy, the other two women had faded into the background of Sean's imagination. So, too, had the other guests, and the piazza, and the moonlight, and the Tiber and the city of Rome and the world. Hard work at the Birth Control Commission meetings, weariness from his unwanted job at the Chicago chancery, disillusionment with the stupidity and venality of the Church bureaucracy, his lingering flirtation with the Principessa—all were taking their toll on his faith and his commitment. He knew now what he wanted. He wanted Nora. The trip through Italy with her would be a joy and a terror. With the courage that comes from despair, he didn't care what happened.

The rest of the world gradually faded back in, creating a halo around Nora's strong facial bones and radiant auburn hair. Everyone was laughing, even Angèlica, who had no idea what American football was about.

Sean felt the muddy waters of damnation swirl around him. What would happen, would happen.

Chapter Twenty
1966

DESPITE ITS UNQUESTIONED elegance, the Royal Danieli Hotel on the Grand Canal in Venice served croissants that were something less than totally fresh, Nora Cronin decided. Nora hated the stingy continental breakfasts and thought that they were very little improved by the addition, as a concession to American tourists, of orange juice—at an extra charge, of course. For a woman who never had breakfast without bacon, this European custom was a profound affront.

Outside the window of her room, a fine gray mist hung over Venice, a city that was considerably less than she had expected.

She pushed aside her breakfast tray and climbed out of bed. Paul, who could not stand eating breakfast in his room, was downstairs, doubtless with Sean, who thought that breakfast in bed was too much a concession to human frailty.

Nora tugged off her badly rumpled gown and walked to the bathroom. A morning like this in Venice required a leisurely bath instead of a brisk shower.

Nora was uneasy about traveling with her two brothers—only they weren't really brothers; she had married one and was in love with the other. The trip was pleasurable but, in a deeply melancholy way, foreboding. It was absurd to think anything was going to happen . . . yet. . . .

She slipped into the soothing waters of the tub. Every woman has a built-in antenna that tells her when a man is undressing her in his imagination, Nora thought. She may be offended, frightened, or flattered, depending on who the man is. Nora was enormously flattered by the intensity in Sean's eyes when they occasionally flicked in her direction. She wanted to be undressed before him as much as he wanted her that way.

Normal human reaction, she told herself. Nothing unusual about it. Sean would never make a pass, especially not at his brother's wife. And anyway, he was a priest.

The door of the bathroom opened and Paul entered. He stood silently over the tub, regarding her with a mixture of awe and desire, a little boy in need of his mother's soothing affection. Filled with guilt at her adulterous thoughts of Sean, she reached out of the tub, unbuckled his belt, and slowly pulled down the zipper on his trousers.

They were having a late lunch in a quaint, charming fifteen-room hotel on the cliff just outside the town of Amalfi with its glittering little cathedral. On the western horizon the sun was setting fire to the deep blue waters of the Mediterranean. The remaining ten days of their vacation were going to be spent near Naples, relaxing and resting, as Sean had insisted, in small hotels and on mostly deserted beaches.

"Capri is out there in that direction." Sean pointed in the distance. "The sunsets are spectacular. You'll see why old Tiberius Caesar moved his headquarters from Rome to Capri."

"The Hyannis of his administration," Nora joked.

"Or the Johnson City," said Paul cynically. "I hope he had more comfortable beds in those days than we do in our rooms here."

"Signor Cronin?" The *proprietario* of the hotel leaned discreetly over their table. "A telephone call from America."

Paul scrambled up, as though eager to get away from the table, and quickly walked out of the dining room. He had been jumpy the past few days, barely able to hide his desire for the vacation to be over.

Sean looked at his brother's back uneasily. "I wonder who could be calling?" He would not meet Nora's eyes, afraid even to look at her while they were alone together.

Paul was back in a few moments, his eyes and his face glowing with happiness. "It was the Mayor's office. Daley's offering me the job of aviation commissioner."

Sean shook Paul's hand enthusiastically and Nora hugged him. Paul ordered a bottle of Nebbiolo, a sparkling Italian red wine. He accepted their toast with a smile.

"I don't want this to be the end of the vacation for you two," he said. "Daley only wants me home for a press conference. I'm sure I'll be able to fly right back. Do you think you can take care of Nora while I'm gone, Sean?"

"I'm sure she can take care of herself," Sean said. "I'll stay around until you get back, though."

"Wonderful!" Paul drained the Nebbiolo in his glass and filled it again. "It's a tremendously important job—three airports, one of them the busiest in the world. His Honor wants to expand operations at Midway again and thinks we may need a fourth airport. It's a terrific challenge."

Nora knew that she should protest. She ought to be at her husband's side at the press conference. The European vacation should come to an end. She should not stay at the Bay of Naples with Sean. Instead, she said, "You have to promise to hurry back." She felt like a hypocrite.

Nora had not been surprised when Paul called that morning to tell her that he would not be able to rejoin her, after all.

"I'm afraid I've got some bad news." Paul hadn't sounded as if he felt it was bad news. "The Mayor wants me to start tomorrow. He promised me a vacation afterward. He said he hoped you wouldn't be too angry."

Nora, barely able to hide the disappointment in her voice, told him that she would catch the first plane into O'Hare. To her relief, he insisted that she and Sean continue on without him.

Now she walked over to the vanity table and considered the woman in the mirror. Her thoughts were clinical. "You know what you're doing," she said to her reflection. "You know exactly what's going to happen, and you want it to happen."

She removed a container of pills from her travel case and flipped open the lid. The pills seemed to be watching her, each one in its carefully appointed daily place. This was the time each day when she took one out and swallowed it.

She shrugged her shoulders, flipped the lid closed, and tossed the container in the trash basket underneath the washbasin.

She unbuttoned her blouse and slowly removed it, then untied her hair and let it cascade over her shoulders. The day had been difficult. The electricity between her and Sean was crackling back and forth just as it had that summer when Paul had been reported missing in action. Sean had kept up the pretense of being a tour guide, lecturing on the history of the Amalfi, the reason why a small town like

Amalfi had a cathedral, the religious difficulties that Catholicism had faced in Italy.

She had listened dutifully and sympathized with the problems of the Italian Church. Yet in the back of her mind she was aware of what she knew was going to happen. Even if Sean did not yet know.

She made sure the door between their two suites was unlocked on her side. She willed him to come through it. She waited on the bench in front of the vanity table.

Sean wrapped the soft robe around his wet body. The shower had not helped either his headache or his tension. The vacation had been hellish. Paul's well-meaning cheerfulness and Nora's paralyzing attractiveness were driving him out of his mind. Now he was alone with her.

He would not permit anything to happen. She was his brother's wife, his childhood sister. She was lonely and frustrated in an unsatisfying marriage.

But he wanted her. He wanted her laughter and her wit, her quick intelligence and her cool self-possession, her astonishing blue eyes and her mobile, generous smile. He wanted every inch of her superb body. This . . . this need for Nora was something very different from the desire he had felt for Sandra in Vail.

He shook his head to drive out the rationalizations. He would not succumb. He sat firmly in the chair by the window and opened a doctoral dissertation on sixth-century marriage customs. If he could only last until morning, there would be no problem. Anyway, he was an inexperienced virgin. He knew nothing about lovemaking. He would make a fool of himself. He would not be able to satisfy her.

He probably wouldn't do any worse than Paul.

He turned a page of the Latin text. Paul is her husband, you damn fool, and you're not, he said to himself.

Fifteen minutes later he threw the book aside and walked across the room. He opened the connecting door and entered Nora's room, his robe pulled tight around his long, hard body.

Nora stood up, uncertainty showing on her face as he approached her. He stopped, when their two bodies were almost touching, and stroked her cheek, his fingers light and gentle. He could feel her relax. She wanted to be his.

His hands traced the outline of her face, her shoulders, her arms, her body; slowly, as if he was unveiling a statue, he undressed her until she stood naked before him. He lifted her long auburn hair back over her shoulders so that nothing hid her from him. Again, his fingers gently outlined her body.

He untied the belt on his robe, pushed it off his shoulders, and let it fall to the floor.

Then they came together in the overwhelming love they had felt for each other since she had come into the Cronin family long ago, a lonely, frightened orphan.

As the first light creased the black waters of the Mediterranean, they were still clinging to each other, their bodies sweat-soaked. "You're a wonderful lover, Sean," she said.

"A rank amateur, I'm afraid."

"That doesn't matter. You're more concerned about me than you are about yourself."

"Who else would I be concerned about?" Sean asked. He was surprised that the tenderness of his passion would be thought remarkable. There was so much he had to learn.

They were on a beach at Capri, having walked a mile from the hotel and around several headlands to a sheltered cove. Nora spread the blanket on the beach. As she finished, she felt Sean's arms around her waist. He could not look at her, touch her, caress her enough. His fingers undid the straps of her halter.

"Sean, not in public," she said.

"Nonsense." He laughed. "This beach is reserved for nude bathing. By custom, anyhow. It's just our luck to be here this morning by ourselves."

The bottom of her suit joined the top in the sand.

They lay on the blanket holding hands. They shared a sense of freedom enhanced by the soft sea breezes and the warm sun penetrating their bodies.

Nora felt Sean turn on his side. She opened her eyes and met his stare. She could not remember a time in her life when she was happier than she was at this moment.

He brought his face down to hers. "Will this be the first time a man has ever made love to you on a beach?" he whispered against her ear.

It was naive perhaps, Nora knew, but it meant a great deal to Sean that their lovemaking have a purity about it. If Nora could not be a virgin in fact, then this would have to substitute.

They made love slowly, exploring every secret of each other's bodies. Later, they swam in the Mediterranean. Nora did most of her half mile before she returned to the beach. Walking out of the water naked and dripping wet, her feet crunching in the sand, she looked at Sean, lying on the blanket, and she was filled with joy. He was so handsome. She did not give him a chance to take the first step in renewing their lovemaking. This time it was her turn.

On their last night together, Sean's groans of pleasure turned into sobs. "Oh, God, what have we been doing, Nora? What terrible things have we been doing?"

"Don't go turning guilty on me now," she commanded. "I refuse to think that any of this is wrong. We're not committing sin, and I won't have you stirring up your goddamned conscience."

"We both have commitments. Solid ones."

She covered herself with the sheet as if protecting herself from his weakness. "Neither one of us is going to give up our commitments, Sean. I'm going back to Paul. You're going back to your Church. This is just an interlude. Paul doesn't own my body, and the Church doesn't own you."

"But we made promises—"

"Promises that we are going to keep. It's not our fault that we couldn't go through life without showing our love for each other. I'm sure God doesn't think it's wrong. You know that yourself, Sean. It's just your clerical conscience that won't let you admit it."

"Are you saying that there are special rules for us?"

She wrapped more of the sheet around her. "No, I'm not saying anything about rules. This has been a time when the rules don't apply. They'll start applying again as soon as I leave for Chicago. This has been a good thing for both of us and I won't let you say otherwise.''

"I wish to God I could believe that.''

He would have a hard time afterward, Nora knew, on the one hand proud of his successful conquest, and on the other, burdened with guilt because of a love that he thought was sinful.

"You know I'm right,'' she said soothingly. "Otherwise neither one of us would have done it.''

"I don't know, I just don't know. I'm too confused to figure it out.''

"Then stop trying and enjoy the time we have left,'' she said.

And to emphasize the command, she reasserted her control over his body with her fingers and then with her lips.

Chapter Twenty-one
1966–1967

SEAN CRONIN AND Eamon McCarthy were shown into the summer office of Castel Gandolfo in the cool hills south of Rome. Outside the window of the tall uncomfortable old room there was a garden of flowers. The aroma, soothing and tantalizing, reminded Sean of Nora's scent. He tried to banish her from his mind. He was about to have an interview with the leader of more than 700 million Catholics. He must concentrate on other things besides a woman's body.

The Pope was even shorter than he appeared in his public audiences, a frail old man in white, with nervous hands and glowing eyes. He was relaxed and calm, a compassionate and sensitive man.

"So, Monsignor Cronin,'' he said, "you dissented from both sides. It seemed important to listen to your position, too.'' The Pope gestured tentatively and smiled disarmingly, almost diffidently.

Sean took a deep breath. "I dissented, *Santità*, because I think both sides are wrong. Any public reaffirmation of the old teaching is bound, after all these years of delay, to offend the married laity who already think we do not understand their position. On the other hand, I do not believe the Church is ready for change. We have not developed a theory of human sexuality or human nature that provides a context for such change. A decision either way will simply postpone indefinitely the development of such a theory. Either way the Church loses.''

"This is very interesting, Monsignor Cronin,'' the Pope said thoughtfully. "However, I am the Vicar of Christ and it is my duty to defend the teachings of Christ. I do not have many years left to live, and I do not know how I would explain to my God if I failed in my responsibilities. The Catholic people all over the world live in uncertainty. Does it not seem to you that as Vicar of Christ I must end their doubt?''

"With all respect, *Santità*,'' Sean said, "I think most of them have very little doubt any more. You will simply create new doubt about the papacy if you decide with the minority. And if you decide with the majority, without a fully developed theory to support such a decision, you will create chaos.''

"Will there not be more chaos if I postpone a decision indefinitely?'' The Pope was literally wringing his hands.

"I sympathize with your problem, for you must steer a middle ground between going too fast and too slow."

"If we change, many of the simple laity will be frightened."

"I disagree, Holiness," Sean insisted. "The simple laity like the new Church; they like it, in fact, I think more than I do. Hence, my recommendation to get a few steps ahead by developing a new Catholic theory of sexuality—rooted in the past, of course. *Before* the laity are ready for it, not after."

The Pope smiled. "Ah, Monsignor Cronin, perhaps you are right. You are a perceptive young priest. And I'm an old man, perhaps pope at the wrong time. I do not know what should be done. I promise you, however, I will remember very seriously the things you have said."

Then there were medals and pictures and the usual ceremony at the end of a papal audience.

As Sean and Eamon McCarthy were walking from the entrance of the old castle to the Cardinal's Oldsmobile, Eamon shook his head. "You are a constant source of amazement to me, Sean; I think of you as a conservative, yet you have a private audience with the Vicar of Christ and read him a stern lecture about his failing as a leader of the Church, something that not even the most radical of liberals would dream of doing."

"I'm sure I didn't do that."

"Moreover, not only did you do it and get away with it, you actually earned the Pope's admiration. There are not too many men whom Giovanni Battista Montini admires."

Sean opened the door for the Cardinal and then walked around to the driver's seat. After he was inside, he said, "The Pope would make a very grave mistake if he admired me."

The bored priest who heard Sean's confession in St. Peter's muttered only a few words about stern discipline and then gave him a disgracefully light penance—two rosaries—and a hasty absolution. Such quick mechanical absolution did not even begin to reach the depths of Sean's pain. Worst of all, even though he was ashamed, he did not feel guilt. He was both confused and dismayed, but he could not escape from a sense of enormous satisfaction and complacency.

Angèlica seemed to be the only one to turn to for understanding. She listened intently as he poured out the story, occasionally nodding her head sympathetically.

She sipped her espresso at a corner table at the sidewalk café just off the Piazza del Populo where they had met. "For once in my life I will be absolutely serious. I think it is surely a good thing for you. You have loved her all your life and she has loved you. What could be more natural than that you express your love for each other? For an Italian priest, it would not be sinful at all."

"You mean that a romp in the hay is occasionally useful for a priest?" he asked skeptically.

Angèlica made a face over her espresso. "Bah, you Americans are such terrible prudes. A romp in the hay, indeed! No. I mean, it is good for Sean Cronin to learn that he does not control himself completely. You cannot escape being a man, Sean, simply because you are intelligent and have an answer for everything and a rule or a principle or a theory to apply to every situation. Welcome into the human race.''

This was a very different Angèlica from the casual temptress of the Palazzo Alessandrini. Sean felt grateful to her. ''Maybe you're right, Angèlica. This morning, out at Castel Gandolfo, I told off the Pope. I would not ever have thought of doing that three weeks ago.''

''Did he mind?'' She raised a delicate eyebrow.

''No, as a matter of fact, he seemed to like it.''

Nora gave birth to Michael Paul Cronin, the long-awaited Cronin heir, in May. He was baptized by his Uncle Sean in early July of 1967 in St. Titus Church. Mayor Richard J. Daley was the godfather, and his wife, Eleanor, was godmother. Michael Cronin, the proud grandfather, glowed happily. The baby's three sisters watched the ceremony as their uncle performed it with awe and wonder, although the youngest of the three, Noreen, was concerned about whether her little brother would cry when the water was poured on him. She had been assured that she herself had not uttered a single wail of protest.

Paul Cronin seemed pleased to have a son at last. Dr. Thomas Shields, who brought Mickey into the world, smiled contentedly as the ceremony progressed. Maggie Martin Shields, as usual, seemed distracted and sad.

Mickey was the picture of health, a golden child cut from the same cloth as his sister Noreen and his Uncle Sean. He accepted all the attention as though it was his as a matter of right.

However, the one who was most serene during the baptismal ceremony was Mickey's mother. Nora was still pale and thin two months after the difficult birth of her son, and sat through the ceremony instead of standing. But the glint was still in her eyes. No one in St. Titus Church had any doubt that in a month or two her golf handicap would be back where it ought to be.

At the end of the ceremony, Sean poured the water over the infant's head, saying the time-honored words: ''Michael Paul, I baptize you in the name of the Father, and of the Son, and of the Holy Spirit.''

Noreen Cronin was greatly disappointed. Her little brother not only did not cry, but he licked the water with his tongue, just as legend said she had done.

At the party afterward at Glenwood Drive, Sean had a moment alone with Nora. ''Whose is he?'' he asked her bluntly, after months of avoiding the question.

''I don't know, Sean, I don't know. There's no way I will ever know. He's a Cronin, isn't that enough?''

''Whose do you wish he was?'' He could have chopped off his tongue as soon as the words were out.

''I don't want to think about that,'' she said. ''Do you?''

''I guess not. He's a Cronin. I suppose that's all that matters.''

''Yes, look at him,'' she said, her face shining with a mother's love. ''He certainly is a Cronin, isn't he?''

Sean knew that in his heart he would never be satisfied with that answer, even though, short of paradise, that would be the only answer he would ever have.

BOOK SIX

I leave to you my own peace, I give you a peace the world cannot give; this is my gift to you.

—JOHN 14:27

Chapter Twenty-two
1968

"IF I WERE a thirty-seven-year-old black man instead of a thirty-seven-year-old white man," said congressional candidate Paul Cronin, "I would be angry tonight. Martin Luther King was one of the greatest leaders ever produced in this country. Now he is dead, killed by a racist. Oh, yes, if I were a black man I would be terrified, outraged, and I would feel very destructive."

The mostly white crowd in the small park next to the Rock Island commuter station stirred uneasily. Commissioner Cronin was speaking to them from a red, white, and blue platform, decorated with CRONIN FOR CONGRESS banners. The Commissioner was popular, especially in this end of the district. With the organization's vote, he was thought to be a shoo-in for election. Yet the speech he was giving was more appropriate for the black end of the district than the white. How come Paul Cronin was taking *their* side?

"If I were a thirty-seven-year-old black storekeeper in Chicago tonight," the Commissioner continued, "I would be even more angry and more frightened, for I would not know when a Molotov cocktail would come through the window of my store. I would be furious that the violent murder of a good man, who opposed violence, would be used as an excuse for more violence and more murder and, quite possibly, for my own murder. And I would be very grateful indeed if the Mayor's influence with the President was such that one phone call could send the protection of the Hundred and First Airborne—to return order to my street, my neighborhood, my city. I would mourn Martin Luther King. I would be angry at the senseless violence, whether it be carried on by whites or blacks, and I would thank God for Richard J. Daley and Lyndon Baines Johnson."

The candidate ended his speech in a tone of ringing triumph. Paul Cronin had charmed them again. The audience cheered enthusiastically. Even the small group of well-to-do blacks who stood off on one side applauded. They had more experience with the gangs of teenage looters in the neighborhood than did the whites in the crowd.

"Just the right note," said Monsignor Sean Cronin, chancellor of the Roman Catholic Archdiocese of Chicago, to Nora Cronin, who was seated next to him. Sean suspected that she provided many of the core ideas for Paul's campaign speeches.

"No matter what happens," said Nora, "Paul is going to get elected. He's in a sweet position. He can ride on Bob Kennedy's coattails."

The candidate, boyishly handsome with his hair long, but not too long, joined them for a moment before being drawn away by a reporter. "What did you think, little brother?" He grinned. "Not bad for a district where you have to keep both whites and blacks happy."

"You're a superb politician," Sean agreed.

It was true enough, he thought, as he drove through the forest preserve toward 87th Street and the Dan Ryan Expressway. Paul was Chicago's fair-haired boy. He could do no wrong as far as the public was concerned. Even his private life was leveling out. The birth of Mickey seemed to have introduced a new element in the relationship between Paul and Nora. Sean couldn't quite put his finger on it. It was as though both Paul and Nora had come to an agreement that Nora, having produced a son, had fulfilled her family duties.

The fateful interlude in Italy had had a profound effect, even though neither of them talked about it. Nora was now more self-confident and self-possessed. Sean had become almost as reckless as his now politically cautious brother used to be. And, of course, there was Mickey, the magic, happy little boy whose father would never be known for sure and who was the result, one way or the other, of what had happened that week at the Bay of Naples.

Sean parked his car in the cathedral parking lot, but instead of going to his room he walked down the street to the new chancery building and rode up in the elevator. The light was on in Jimmy McGuire's office, next to his own.

"Hi, Sean," said the always cheerful Jimmy. "Do the paratroopers have any roadblocks on the Ryan?"

"The city's quiet," Sean said. "There's still smoke, but the fires are burning out, and the radio says there's some looting on the West Side. But the worst is over. Maybe we didn't need the troops after all."

"Me, I'm glad they're here. It will make everybody think twice. . . . You're not planning on working at this hour of the night, are you?"

"I want to go over that financial problem at St. Fintan's. No one can figure out how many different bank accounts the late pastor had and which ones reflect his money and which ones reflect the parish's money."

"You can bet on it that all of it was parish money, and by the time the lawyers are finished, we'll only get half," Jimmy said. "The boss is off confirming at St. Andrew's tonight, isn't he?"

Sean wanted to get to his own office and begin work, yet Jimmy's good humor was seductive—an endless temptation to idle away time. "I don't know how he stands it. Confirmations, graduations, parish anniversaries, meetings in Rome or in Washington, half the kooks in the city of Chicago wanting to see him, the telephone ringing from one end of the day to the other, conflicts between pastors and people and people and curates, women wanting to be ordained, priests wanting to marry . . . the old man is going to work himself into an early grave. He's the most conscientious man I've ever met."

Jimmy eyed him levelly. "The second most conscientious man I know."

Sean ignored the remark and went to his own office, where he began to pore over the complex financial machinations of Father Michael John O'Brien and the parochial funds of St. Fintan the Hermit Parish. Try as he might, however, he could not drive pictures of Nora from his mind. Sheer physical hunger for her had abated, but every time he saw her the light in her incredible blue eyes, the quick explosion of her smile, and the curves of her flawless body hit him with sledgehammer force. Nothing would ever happen between them again, he promised himself. But the guilt, the torment, and the self-contempt he now felt because of their experience, would never go away, it seemed, nor would the shattering memories of its pleasures. "Oh, God!" he sobbed, burying his head in his hands. "What have I done?"

The day after the assassination of Martin Luther King, Michael Cronin was rushed from his apartment at the new John Hancock Center to the emergency room of Passavant Hospital. The doctors diagnosed the attack as a brain "spasm," something like a small stroke, the sort of trauma Eisenhower had suffered during his first term.

"The President served four more years and is still alive at seventy-eight," the softspoken brown-skinned neurologist from India commented reassuringly.

Yet it seemed to Sean that the touch of death was on his father's face in the hospital bed. He seemed so frail.

While Sean stood at his bedside, Elizabeth Hanover slipped quietly into the room. She took Mike's hand, oblivious of the needles in his veins. The sick man's eyes came alive.

Good God, Sean thought, he's in love with her. Like I am with Nora. How can it be that he's never married her?

"The offer still stands, Michael." She spoke with characteristic directness.

His father seemed to begin to say yes; then the life died from his eyes, and he pulled his hand away. . . .

"I'll keep up my visits, Sean, indefinitely, if you don't mind," Elizabeth said later when she and Sean were in the corridor outside Mike's room.

That stalwart, timeless woman seemed suddenly to be showing her age. Her face was lined, her normal parade-ground back a little bent.

"Be your realistic self, Elizabeth, and find someone else. This game is over."

"You're being the sensible WASP and I'm being the sentimental Irishman." She leaned her head against his shoulder.

"We're not sentimental about death," Sean said. "Not even lingering death."

Paul Cronin walked briskly up Michigan Avenue under a brooding November sky. Despite his self-confident stride and the quick smile with which he greeted passersby who recognized his face from television news conferences, he was worried about Sean's reaction to the suggestion he was about to make. It was the only possible solution, but Sean was so unpredictable these days that Paul could not count on his being sensible.

Paul glanced up at the towering walls of the Magnificent Mile. The top of the Hancock Tower was shrouded in fog. Planes would be stacked up at O'Hare. Before he had become Aviation Commissioner he had paid no attention to such things. Now that he knew all that could go wrong at the world's busiest airport, his hands turned sweaty when the weather was bad. He couldn't talk to the Mayor any more about a new airport. "Them protestors come out every time we mention it, Paul. Haven't we got enough of them protestors as it is? Besides, you run for Congress and let me worry about O'Hara."

The Mayor always called it "O'Hara." He liked Paul, thought he had done a good job taking the heat about airport expansion, and wanted to reward him with a return to Washington.

Paul was happy about going back to Capitol Hill; now the only complication was his father's stroke. Paul did not like having to go to the hospital. The old man was getting better, all right, but now he *looked* like an old man. Paul shuddered. He didn't want to think about his father's death.

Makuch had called him to offer sympathies and brag about his own success in the business world. Paul could tell he was still a loser. Always had been a loser. Paul had been afraid that the call was a prelude to a demand for more money, but Makuch merely wanted to pretend that he was an old friend anxious about Mike Cronin's health. He congratulated Paul on his campaign for Congress. There was an ominous note in his voice when he said, "It will be nice to have one of us in Congress."

Would he ever be rid of Makuch?

The newspapers in the lobby of Passavant Hospital had headlines about the peace demonstrators at the Pentagon. Damn fool war. How could they make the Korean mistake all over again? He was glad that his "key post" in the city government provided an excuse not to ask to have his commission activated.

His stomach jumped at the thought of huddling in a foxhole while mortars thudded all around. He had not slept for almost a week after watching the siege of Khesanh on television. Even Nora could not exorcise the thump of the explosions and the screams of the wounded at Chosun Reservoir.

"Took you long enough," said Sean. His face looked like that of a stern novice master.

"I had a rough session with Connaire and Hoffman," Paul pleaded. "More troubles."

Sean melted, as he always did, when Paul offered an excuse. He patted his brother's shoulder affectionately. "What are those two old gombeen men up to now?"

They sat on a couch in the lobby. Snow flurries danced against the dirty windowpanes. "The IRS has been hassling the Cronin Fund for more than a year. First I've heard of it. Ed and Marty had it out with Dad. . . ." Paul was glad to find an excuse not to face his father's frail, wounded body, to postpone his visit, if only for a short time.

"How bad is it?" Sean asked. He sounded as if he were spoiling for a chance to take on the IRS.

"Bad enough. Someone has to go in and straighten out the mess, someone Dad trusts and who's smart enough to figure where all the bones are buried. And it has to be done now."

Sean raised an eyebrow. "Who? Not you. A politician can't afford to be caught in such a mess. Me?"

"No way." These brief conversations with Sean about family problems brought back the comaradery of the old days. How had they lost it?

"Then who? A politician can't, a churchman shouldn't . . . who? Who does Dad trust to put his complicated generosity into the order that would satisfy the IRS?"

Paul hesitated, fearing his brother's anger. "Nora," he said tentatively.

To his surprise Sean approved enthusiastically. "Who else? Of course, she's perfect." He paused. "Wonderful idea, Paul. Who else but Nora?"

Nora tried to concentrate on *The Confessions of Nat Turner,* though her mind wandered frequently to the conversation that lay ahead of her. Something terribly important, Paul had said. What could Uncle Mike want of her that was terribly important?

"He's ready to see you now, Mrs. Cronin," said the matronly black nurse with the smile of relief she always reserved for Nora, the only visitor who could calm down Mike Cronin.

He looked much better. In a few weeks he would be able to fly to Florida to complete his rehabilitation. "Well, tough guy"—she kissed him—"when are you going to stop this goldbricking and get back to work?"

Mike laughed. "I fooled them all, didn't I? None of them thought I'd be able to head for Florida after Christmas. Give me a few months and I'll be back in the swing of things."

"Better believe it," she said admiringly. "Now, what's this about an important conversation? Every conversation with me is important, Michael Cronin, and don't you dare think otherwise."

Mike grinned. "Stirred up your curiosity, did I? It's nothing too important. . . . I just want you to take over the Fund for a few months till I come back from Florida. I'll be busy enough running Paul's campaign for Congress from down there without having to fight off the IRS vultures too."

"Why me?" she said, after a pause to gather her thoughts.

"Why not you? One son running for Congress, another running for auxiliary bishop; who else do I have besides my daughter?"

"Uncle Mike, I'm flattered. I appreciate the vote of confidence. I don't know whether I can do it. . . ."

"Don't blubber like a damn fool, woman." He seemed remarkably happy for a man giving up a prized possession. "Of course you can do it. I wouldn't ask you if you couldn't. Anyway, it will only be for a few months."

Nora knew that she should feel hesitant over the responsibility and sad for Uncle Mike's loss. Yet her mind sang for joy. Yes, certainly she could do it. Better than anyone else.

Chapter Twenty-three
1968

THE LIMOUSINE PICKED Nora up every morning promptly at nine thirty. By then the three girls were in school and Mickey had been fed breakfast. Nora arrived at her office at the Cronin Foundation at ten o'clock and worked straight through until three o'clock—five hours every day of the week. She was home by three thirty to supervise the girls when they stormed in from St. Titus School to play with the endlessly enjoyable Mickey. She would also preside over dinner.

Nora felt tremendous guilt over her new occupational responsibilities. She was the mother of a child still a long way from school years and she was playing in the big league of business and finance. She knew that many of the other mothers at St. Titus were muttering about her, although she spent no more time at the office than they did shopping and playing golf. Such an argument, however, assuaged neither her conscience nor the criticisms of her neighbors. To make Nora's problems worse, she reveled in the excitement of the Cronin Foundation. She enjoyed every moment in the office, as well as the forty minutes of work each day in the back of her plush Cadillac limousine.

At first, the men who worked for her, many of them older than she was, were inclined to patronize her. However, no one ever did that twice. Nor did anyone make a second pass.

Nora frowned. She did not know quite what to make of her relationship with her husband. They had made love the night before: mechanical, but still good sex. They both were now competent at satisfying each other. Yet they were drifting even further apart. Paul had his politics and she had the business. Both were more or less oblivious of the other's concerns, although Paul was only too happy to take her political advice. He seemed to respect and admire her. Was that what marriage was about after almost twelve years? Maybe they were better off than most.

Her thoughts returned to the Cronin Foundation. One day, when she was sitting behind the vast oak desk in what used to be Mike Cronin's office, Nora had come across a stack of bills she couldn't make any sense of. "Mr. Conley," she asked one of the few remaining clerks from the early days of the business, "I can't seem to place this bill for eighteen thousand dollars for St. Helena's Nursing Home up in Lake County. It merely says 'Services rendered. Mary.' Do you know why we pay this bill every six months?"

The little old man with the red nose and a few streaks of snow-white hair became agitated. He reached for the bills. "I'm afraid Mr. Cronin told me not to bother you with these. They shouldn't have been sent through. I've been paying that bill every six months, doing it for a long time, more than thirty years, as far as I can remember."

"Back to 1938?" Nora asked incredulously.

"Is this 1968? Well, then, it's more than thirty years. I've been paying that bill since 1934. Do you want me to stop?"

"No." She gave the bill back to the old man. "If Mr. Cronin wants the bill paid, then of course keep on paying it."

She made a note on the pad inside of her compact notebook with its hand-tooled leather cover: *Check St. Helena's.*

Sean Cronin's phone rang. It was the Archbishop. "Monsignor Cronin, could you spare me a few minutes?"

"Of course, Eminence." Sean collected the information on St. Fintan the Hermit and walked down the corridor. He smiled at the elderly woman who was Eamon McCarthy's secretary and walked into the office of the Cardinal Archbishop of Chicago.

The Cardinal looked pale. "Bad trip to Rome, Eminence?" Sean asked with genuine concern.

"About the same, Monsignor." The inevitable smile. "The Roman Curia has not changed, nor has my body clock."

"You ought to take some time off, Eminence. Get away somewhere and rest."

"I believe, Monsignor, that that is a case of the pot calling the kettle black. In any event, I see from the stack of papers you brought in that you anticipated my question. You have solved the problem of St. Fintan the Hermit?" The Archbishop folded his hands in his lap, as though waiting to hear a lecture.

"It's a complex matter, Eminence. Every one of the five bank accounts, each with approximately fifty thousand dollars in it, is almost certainly made up of money siphoned off the Sunday collections through the late pastor's long years in the parish. There is no evidence that he had appreciable income of his own, or that there was money from his family. Moreover, it appears from various checks drawn on each of these accounts that the pastor considered all these funds to be parish funds. For example, he has paid the salaries of secretaries from it, the construction of new basketball backboards in the gym, annual contracts for snow removal from the parking lots. He even reimbursed the parish for payments of the seminary tax to us here at the chancery. I'm convinced that the pastor created these accounts with no intent to embezzle money from the archdiocese, but rather with the intent of hiding from us the large reserve his parish had amassed. He must have been fearful that we would confiscate some of it or force him to buy Catholic bishop bonds with it, or perhaps lower the annual assessments of his parish. Unfortunately, he died without leaving any records to confirm that these accounts were not his own."

"As a quick estimate, Monsignor," the Cardinal asked, "how common would you say that this practice is in the archdiocese?"

Sean hesitated. Better to err on the side of being conservative. "I would suggest, Eminence"—he moved his chair closer to the Cardinal's desk—"that perhaps a third of the parishes engage in practices like this, though usually not with such extensive funds or with such sloppy records."

The Cardinal looked tired for a moment. "We would need a certified accountant in every parish to prevent this sort of thing, wouldn't we, Monsignor?"

"Yes, Eminence."

"Well, I suppose we could engage in legal combat with his heirs at the cost of considerable fees to lawyers and even more considerable scandal. Therefore, we will settle with the heirs, giving them somewhere between a fifth and a quarter of the funds that rightly belong to the Catholic bishops of Chicago and to the people of God in St. Fintan the Hermit Parish. I presume that is what you would recommend?"

"I see no other option, Eminence."

"Very well, Monsignor. See that it is done. . . . There is another matter on which I ought to remark. I learned in Rome that sometime this summer we will have a papal encyclical on the birth-control issue."

Sean's heart sank. "Oh, no," he murmured.

"Oh, yes, Monsignor. And, as you can imagine, it will be the worst kind of encyclical. The only question in Rome now is whether the Pope will choose to make it an 'infallible' encyclical. Those who know him best say that the word 'infallible' will go into the text and that he will cross it out at the last minute. I am told that the encyclical will come sometime in July. I assure you, Monsignor Cronin, I will be visiting our mission in Guatemala at that time."

"It will be an absolute disaster," Sean said hoarsely.

"A position that I myself took five years ago, if you remember, Monsignor. I'm glad you've come around to my way of thinking. For weal or woe"—the Cardinal's eyes twinkled briefly—"the Catholic laity and especially the Catholic clergy have available the majority position that some imprudent commission member released to the press."

"I can't imagine who would have done that, Eminence," Sean said softly.

"Nor can I. In any event, Monsignor, I would advise you to prepare some carefully worded thoughts on the subject. Our friends in the press will surely want your comments when the encyclical is issued . . . especially"—again the quick smile and the quicker twinkle—"since it is well known that you voted neither for the minority nor for the majority position."

"Maybe they'll put that on my gravestone," said Sean Cronin.

At fourteen months, Mickey Cronin was a skilled walker, babbler, arranger of building blocks, and charmer of women, especially his sisters.

Eileen, Mary, and Noreen bounced into Nora's study. "We want to play with Mickey."

With a show of great reluctance, Nora handed her son over to the three girls, for whom he was a fascinating live doll.

"Unfaithful punk," she murmured as Mickey eagerly extended his arms to Eileen.

Mickey would cavort with anyone. His face and his coloring were pure Cronin, and his disposition was a carbon copy of Noreen's, save for the fact that, unlike his active sister, he slept soundly through the night, every night.

As Nora watched him crawl from sister to sister, delighted by the dilemma of having to choose between three enthusiastic surrogate mothers, she murmured, "You kids will spoil the little so-and-so rotten."

That was not true. Mickey was such a happy even-tempered child that nothing ever seemed to spoil him.

Yet Nora's happiness with her son was well on the way to being spoiled. She had been slow to reflect on what had happened between her and Sean. Sickness during pregnancy, the long recovery after Mickey's birth, and her involvement at the Cronin Foundation had been excuses not to think about it. It was a subject which she had been walling away in its own separate compartment.

It would not stay within its walls, however. Nora's reactions were not the reckless guilt of Sean but rather an aloof self-disdain. She, who had so prized her own fidelity to commitments, had blithely violated the central commitment in her life and led another to do so too. That Mickey was probably the result of such a shattered commitment did not change the facts. Self-possessed and self-controlled Nora Riley Cronin was as much a victim of the fires of irrational passion as were her husband, and Uncle Mike, and Mary Eileen and Maggie Shields.

Welcome into the human race, she told herself bitterly.

Sorry? She didn't know. Given another chance, she might do the same thing again and once more drive away the loving Presence that had been with her so long and which was now gone, perhaps forever.

There would be punishments, of that Nora felt certain. She waited for them calmly, knowing that the costs would have to be met. In the meantime, the Foundation provided an outlet for those dangerous energies within her.

"He loves you more than us." Noreen broke into her mother's reverie.

Mickey had crawled to his mother's feet and was looking up expectantly, not so much demanding affection and attention as patiently and brightly waiting for what was his due.

"Poor Mickey," she said, lifting him off the floor, not altogether sure why she should say that.

Chapter Twenty-four
1968

WHEN PAUL CRONIN arrived in Los Angeles, there was a note waiting for him at the hotel that said *Maggie called*. Paul sighed. Maggie had worked like a trooper during the primary battle. Paul had avoided her carefully, both because his desire for her had cooled and because Maggie was becoming irrational. He could not afford to be mixed up with someone like that, especially when he was running for the Congress of the United States. Besides, the last-minute Kennedy campaign, shaken badly in Wisconsin, had involved a considerable number of young women, mostly graduate students, for whom sex, power, and opposition to the rules meant virtually the same thing. They were outspokenly liberated and ready for almost any sexual experimentation. Indeed, there were three of them, roommates, who were undoubtedly eagerly waiting for him in their room on the ninth floor.

He noted that there was an additional single-word message on the pink slip with Maggie's phone number. *"Urgent."* He crumpled the piece of paper and dropped it in the cigarette receptacle by the elevator door.

Maggie was waiting for Paul in front of the hotel the next morning. She was wearing a soft blue dress and looked more appealing than ever. She told Paul that Tom was tied up at a conference. She wanted only to talk to Paul for a few minutes. He was uneasy, but she brought back too many pleasant memories from the past for him to refuse.

They had barely left the hotel before she was pressing against him as though they were in a bedroom instead of a car.

"Maggie, please don't do this," he pleaded. "I thought we agreed that my father's sickness—"

"What does he have to do with it?" she said, more pathetic than sullen.

"We can't take the risks," he said. "A scandal would kill him. I . . . I can't live with that on my conscience." It was as good an excuse as any. He didn't want to hurt her. It had to stop. Yet he felt himself slipping. She was so soft and warm and ready.

"You don't care about me any more." Her voice was so low he could barely hear her. "No one does. I might as well be dead."

The mention of death calmed his desire. "That's a foolish thing to say, Mag. You have everything going for you. You don't need me to be happy."

"Yes, I do," she insisted, but she drew back toward the other side of the car. "You're the only one who ever cared."

"That's just not so," he argued. "Everyone likes you."

She was sniffling softly. "No one has ever liked me."

Maggie needed help, but Paul knew that he wasn't the one to help her. He thought about talking to Tom. No, that would never work. The best thing he could do was to stay away from her.

$\bullet \quad \bullet \quad \bullet$

Nora joined Paul in Los Angeles the night of the California primary. The energies of Camelot had slowed. Many of the familiar faces were older, and the younger faces, particularly those of the women, were much harder. Nora wondered, without too much concern, how many of them had been in bed with her husband.

There was an uncomfortable hush in the ballroom of the hotel as everyone watched the early tabulations on the huge blackboard behind the stage. Gene McCarthy was obviously doing better than anyone had expected. McCarthy was the spoiler. He had spoiled Johnson's chances for reelection, and he might well spoil Bobby's chances for the nomination, throwing the primary to his bitter rival, Hubert Humphrey. And that, Nora realized, would mean Richard Nixon in the White House. She shuddered. She had met Nixon once at a party in Washington, a strange man whose eyes and gestures were unconnected with his words.

"Glad to see you, Nora." The candidate walked over and embraced her briskly.

Nora pecked at his cheek. "I hear they have some swimming pools outside," she said.

"I like you, Nora, because you're still a fighter, but I think I'll stay away from those swimming pools." Bobby smiled. The strange mixture of diffident charm and ruthlessness had its usual effect on Nora, depriving her of her usual reserved aloofness.

"How well are we going to do tonight?"

Robert Kennedy grimaced. "We're going to win and we're going to claim a big victory, but we're not going to win by much. So nothing's going to be decided. I hope you can persuade your friend Mayor Daley to support us. By the way, I hear you're doing great with the business."

"Yes—I'm getting along swimmingly."

Bobby Kennedy laughed, squeezed her hand, and walked toward the platform. Paul joined her a few moments later. "Did you see Bobby?"

"He just walked up to the platform and then disappeared—back to the Kennedy suite, I suppose."

"We're going to win big," said Paul. "California will finish off Clean Gene."

Much later in the evening it was clear that Clean Gene had been beaten, but only by a few percentage points. Robert Kennedy's victory statement was hollow and tired, and the enthusiasm of the supporters forced. Paul and Nora were standing near the platform, and as the Senator climbed down from the stage, he signaled them to follow him.

They crowded after him into a corridor just off the main ballroom. Nora wondered how anyone could stand to be a politician with the enormous pressure of campaigning and endless media attention.

There were two quick, sharp explosions just ahead of them. People shoved forward, shouting and screaming. Someone was being wrestled to the ground. Without thinking, Nora moved ahead and then stopped in unbelieving horror.

On the floor, with part of his head blown away, was Senator Robert F. Kennedy, the second of the Kennedy brothers to fall to an assassin's bullet. The crowd swirled and pushed around Nora. Pale, worn, shattered, but very much in charge, Ethel Kennedy was giving instructions. The Senator was carried down the corridor and out of the building. Nora, still immobile, leaned against the wall, reciting over and over to herself, mechanically and automatically, the words of the Act of Contrition:

"Oh, my God, I am heartily sorry for having offended thee because I dread the loss of heaven and the pains of hell. But most of all because I have offended thee, my God, who art all good and deserving of all my love. . . ."

In August of 1968, while Paul was discreetly moving into the Hubert Humphrey camp, opposing the war but also opposing the McCarthy-McGovern peace forces converging on Chicago for the Democratic Convention, Sean was interviewed by an Associated Press reporter who was doing an article on the recent birth-control encyclical.

He was on the spot. It was the spot of his own making and his own choosing, and he might just as well pay the price. He didn't much care. The birth-control encyclical was a catastrophe for the Church and would appall, insult, and infuriate American Catholics. Yet as a churchman he had to loyally honor it. To be a good churchman meant that you be a good hypocrite.

"Is it accidental that the Archbishop is in Guatemala, Monsignor?" asked the reporter.

"Quite accidental. The Cardinal's trip to Guatemala has been planned for months."

"Is your statement official?"

"I'm not making any statement. Bishop Conway's statement is the official stand of the Archdiocese. We welcome the Pope's decision and we will commend it to the Catholic faithful for their attention and their obedience."

"You were one of the few who voted with the minority in favor of the encyclical, weren't you, Monsignor?"

"No, I didn't vote with either the minority or the majority."

"Then are you in favor of or against the encyclical?"

"The encyclical is the official though not infallible teaching of the Church. I support the teaching of the Church, while I regret the fact that it was issued before the subject of sexuality in the Church was given an opportunity to achieve greater maturity."

"Does that mean, Monsignor, that you think the Pope may have made a mistake in issuing this encyclical, *Humanae Vitae*?"

"As regards to the timing, he may well have made a mistake." Again, more furious scribbling. To hell with the reporter. To hell with the Pope. To hell with everybody.

"Do you expect American Catholics to obey the encyclical?"

"I am sure that many of them will continue their present practices," he said flatly.

"Do you think the Church will ever change on birth control, Monsignor?"

Sean stared glumly at the floor. "No one claims that this encyclical is infallible. And in the words of Harry Truman, 'Never say never, 'cause never is a helluva long time.' "

The journalist laughed. "One final question, Monsignor. If you had to do it over again, how would you have voted?"

Sean hesitated. He wasn't certain of anything any more. God, church, priesthood, doctrine—all were confusion. "I think I might very well have voted with the majority."

. . .

The Cardinal Archbishop of Chicago was exhausted upon his return from Guatemala. Even after two days resting at the house at 1555 North State Parkway, he still looked drawn and withered when his chancellor joined him in his office. "You look tired, Eminence."

"I am tired, Monsignor Cronin, very tired." He nervously fingered the press clippings on the desk in front of him. "Someday, Sean, I'm going to understand you. Six years ago you were one of the most conservative clergymen of your generation. Now you are a blunt and outspoken radical. You must know that somebody's going to send these clippings to Rome."

"Let them," Sean said.

The Cardinal sighed. "I have given your name, Sean, to the Congregation for the Making of Bishops, as my top recommendation for a new auxiliary bishop. Do you realize that your statement on the encyclical may affect the possibility of Rome's acquiescing to my recommendation?"

"To hell with them, Eminence. I don't want to be an auxiliary bishop. If you'd asked me, I would have told you no."

"That, Monsignor Cronin, is precisely why I didn't ask you."

Chapter Twenty-five
1968

NORA CRONIN, STILL badly shaken by the memories of the awful scene in Los Angeles, had warned her husband to stay away from the Conrad Hilton Hotel during the Chicago Democratic Convention. Even if Nixon should be elected, Paul's seat was relatively safe. He should avoid the hippies and the police and the National Guard, oppose the war, support Mayor Daley, and vote for Hubert Humphrey, who had the nomination locked up.

Nora tried to follow her own advice. She worked late at the office, since the children were at Oakland Beach with the housekeeper, but she made certain that the limousine was waiting to drive her home.

One night, however, as they made their way out of the city, she saw police, National Guard troops, and screaming kids rushing up and down Wabash Avenue. At the corner of Harrison and Michigan, a car careened by and a paper bag thrown from it exploded against the Cadillac, spilling human excrement down the side of the car door. Appalled, Nora did her best to ignore the nightmare around her: police on one side; foul-mouthed kids on the other, shouting obscenities at National Guardsmen who were, if anything, even younger than the protestors. Bullhorns bellowed, blue lights swirled, police and protestors dashed back and forth across the street. Tear-gas canisters were fired, sounding like exploding shells. Nora felt for a moment as if she were plunging into Dante's Inferno. Then the driver turned the limousine off Michigan Avenue and away from the debacle. Not until they were well away from the city did she feel the tension leave her body.

Nora had remained at her office after the others had left because she was increasingly called upon to make decisions for Cronin Enterprises. These offices were located across the corridor in the Field Building from the Cronin Foundation and were as disorderly and confused as her operation was neat and disciplined. She was becoming the *de facto* head of the enterprises. Mike always went along with her suggestions nowadays, without even consulting Marty Hoffman or Ed Connaire.

Yet it was not only the pressure of extra work that had kept her in her office. For perhaps the hundredth time, she studied carefully the file on St. Helena's. What could it mean? Ed Connaire had been vague about the priest who was perhaps Mary Eileen's lover. Could he still be alive and living at the nursing home—for some reason Mike Cronin's responsibility? Nora did not want to know. She wanted to bury the past with all its shame. Yet she had contributed her own shame to the history of the Cronins. Maybe . . .

Nora didn't know what came after maybe. There would be no real peace, however, until she rolled back the rock from the tomb that had been sealed for over thirty years and found the truth that was buried at St. Helena's.

The day after his election, Paul, realizing that his first two terms in Congress would be served under a Republican president, pondered his future. He had won handsomely in the third district: indeed, by the biggest margin a Democratic candidate had ever received. He would have to serve three or four terms in the Congress before he could think of running for the United States Senate. In 1976 he would be forty-six years old, a bit older than he had hoped to be when he got into the Senate but certainly not too old in 1980, when he could make the run for the roses. Not the Old Man's game plan, but not bad either.

Thumbing through a stack of congratulatory telegrams and messages on his desk in the City Center, he pulled out a message from Maggie Shields. Again there was the single word, *Urgent*. He crumpled the note as he had crumpled all messages from Maggie through the summer and tossed it in the wastebasket.

There would be plenty of opportunities for replacing Maggie in Washington. Nora would stay in Chicago, at least for a while, because it was awkward to change the children's schools at the present. Besides, she was now the only one who could keep Cronin Enterprises going.

Paul was not upset by his wife's success in business. It would mean that their marriage would consist of trips by her to Washington and by him to Chicago— together one or two nights a week at the most, and sometimes not that often. He could have most of the advantages of being a bachelor in Washington and none of the disadvantages. He would merely have to be careful and make sure that Nora never again caught him.

He would miss the kids. They adored him, although Eileen, the oldest, was now frequently contemptuous of him for reasons he did not at all understand.

He would phone Nora dutifully every day. Appearances must be maintained. Besides, she had sound instincts of judgment about people, and as an occasional bed partner she had certain good qualities.

The next half dozen years in his life, then, seemed to hold remarkable promise.

The Cardinal studied Sean thoughtfully. "Someday, Monsignor Cronin, you are going to have to explain your magic to me. It would be most useful to understand it during the few remaining years I have left to deal with the Vatican."

"Beg pardon, Eminence?"

"I have just had a phone message from the Apostolic Delegate," said the Cardinal. "He's informed me that the Pope, with the recommendation from the Congregation for the Creation of Bishops, has named you Titular Bishop of some

city in Asia Minor, which I believe is substantially below the level of the Aegean
Sea, and Auxiliary Bishop of Chicago. I would, under normal circumstances,
congratulate one who has received such an important appointment. However, as
I understand it, this is an appointment that you have not desired, did not want,
and would be tempted not to accept. I will content myself with telling you,
Bishop Cronin, that you are certainly going to accept that appointment, if I have
to constrain you at the point of a gun." Eamon McCarthy permitted himself the
luxury of a broad, self-satisfied smile.

"Shit," said the new Auxiliary Bishop of Chicago.

Jimmy McGuire dreaded the dinner at the Mid-America Club, now in its new
quarters atop the slender white marble pillar of the Standard Oil Building. "The
fifth largest in the world," Sean told the three visiting bishops. "We also have
Number One and Number Four."

The Mid-America, Sean had assured Jimmy, would be the best place to go.
Any of the more exclusive eating clubs would be a waste of money. "The
Episcopal palate, James," Sean said, "is almost as undeveloped as the Episcopal
conscience."

Jimmy didn't mind the guests. Martin Spalding Quinlan from Boise was
indeed a pompous dullard, a neat little altar boy with precise French cuffs and
carefully tinted hair. Harold Wheaton, an auxiliary from Washington, was all
right; discreet, cautious, but basically a rubicund political realist. Modesto Gomez
from the Southwest said very little because, if one were to believe Sean Cronin,
he had very little to say.

A dinner with such men on the last day of the meeting of the national hierarchy
in Chicago could be pleasant, or at worst harmless, if it were not almost certainly
to be the occasion for one of Sean's reckless diatribes against his brother bishops.
You had to take the good with the bad, Jimmy supposed. Something had happened to Sean around the time of the last meeting of the Birth Control Commission that had made him one of the most courageous and progressive churchmen
in America. It also had made him restless, angry, and foolhardy. None of the
Cronins, Jimmy mused, seemed very good at balance.

Jimmy's worst fears were realized during the main course.

Sean had ordered Château Lafite-Rothschild to follow the white Châteauneuf-
du-Pape with which the meal had begun, mostly, Jimmy was certain, for the
raised eyebrows such an extravagance would produce. Marty Quinlan was commending the recent document from the Holy Office on human sexuality and
arguing that the bishops should have taken up his proposal to send a positive
reply to Rome, thanking the Pope for such an insightful reaffirmation of the
tradition. These were words, Jimmy thought, not unlike those which could have
been heard from Sean during his first half-dozen years in the priesthood.

"Bullshit," Sean said. He filled his wine-glass for the second time.

"It's so hard for us to know what proposals to act upon." Harold Wheaton
tactfully changed the subject. "I think we ought to develop a program of in-
service training for the bishops, so they can learn how to budget their time and
their energies. Otherwise we spread ourselves too thin."

Sean made a grand gesture with his glass. "The most important course in such
a program, Harry, would be a course in lying. You can't be a good bishop unless
you're an accomplished liar. We lie to Rome about how enthusiastically we
receive their bullshit; we lie to the priests and the laity about how they should

enforce such rulings; we lie to the press about what we really think. We even lie to ourselves, although we know that we won't be able to sleep at night because of what that goddamn encyclical is doing in our dioceses. Some of us are ready-made psychopathic liars. The rest of us are the do-it-yourself variety.''

"You don't mean that, Sean," Modesto Gomez protested mildly.

Jimmy protested much less mildly as he and Sean walked back to the cathedral rectory after leaving their guests at the Palmer House. "Cronin, you're an ass. Every word of what you said tonight will go to the delegation tomorrow morning. You know the only hope we have of continuing Eamon's policies here is for you to be the next cardinal. Do you want to give Chicago to Marty Quinlan on a silver platter?"

"Do you want a cardinal who is guilty of incest and adultery?" Sean exploded.

Jimmy was stunned. So that was it. He had better say the right thing now. "Sean, are you going to revel in guilt for the rest of your life? The truth is, you damn fool, that what bothers you is not the sin, which God forgives, but the mark on your stainless white record. Sean Cronin isn't perfect. He's a sinner like the rest of humankind. So he's excused from keeping his big mouth shut, even when it endangers the entire archdiocese?"

"You're fun when you get mad, Jimmy," Sean said through clenched teeth.

"You and Nora work it out between each other?" Jimmy softened his tone.

"Not really. How can we work it out? It happened, and that's that."

"A fine Christian you are, Bishop. You both have a long time to live, a family to share, and you love each other. You can't go around forever in a paralysis of guilt. Have you ever read the Gospel about forgiveness?" His voice rose. "No, I forgot. God forgives sinners but Sean Cronin doesn't, not when the sinner is himself."

"I don't know how to handle it," Sean said wearily. "It haunts me every day."

"It made you a brave and honest churchman and Nora a successful businesswoman, didn't it?" Jimmy was guessing, but he had no choice but to play for high stakes here on Wabash Avenue at midnight. "Isn't that the crooked lines of God, drawing good from evil?"

"*A felix culpa?*" Sean said. "I don't buy the 'happy fall' theology. Never did."

"Heretic," Jimmy mumbled. He knew that he had planted questions and doubts. He hoped his friend would ponder them, perhaps constructively.

"I'm sorry I lost my temper and told you," Sean said after they had walked another block in dead silence. "I don't want to destroy your respect for Nora."

"You really are an ass," Jimmy said. He was genuinely angry for one of the few times in his life.

Chapter Twenty-six
1968–1969

THE NUN IN charge of St. Helena's, Sister Margarita, was not much older than Nora and obviously intimidated by Nora's impressive presence in her smartly tailored suit. "I hope there's nothing out of order, Mrs. Cronin," she said.

"Not at all, Sister Margarita." Nora tried to sound reassuring yet not patronizing. "There's no question but that we will continue to pay for the care of Mary, but as the person responsible now for the Cronin Foundation, I'm obliged to familiarize myself with the various expenses of the fund. Do I understand that Mary has been here since 1934?" Nora felt a terrible wrenching pain in her stomach. "And you have no idea of what her last name is?"

"None at all, Mrs. Cronin. Mr. Cronin assured the nun who was in charge in those days—there have been eight other heads of St. Helena's between her and myself—that he had all the records carefully filed in the bank, and that it was absolutely essential, as a work of Christian charity, to take care of this poor woman." She hesitated and then went on uncertainly. "Of course, I reviewed the matter when I assumed responsibility the year before last. My training in hospital administration, needless to say, made me very uneasy about such a practice, but it didn't seem possible after all these years to review the case. . . . I would ask you to believe that I made this decision quite independently of the contributions Mr. Cronin regularly makes to our institution."

"Look, Sister Margarita," Nora said, "I'm newer at my job than you are at yours. I'm not going to make any trouble. I just want to know more about Mary."

The nun was visibly relieved. "She came here, as you seem to be aware, in late 1934, diagnosed as incurably psychotic. She was then, as far as we can tell, in her late twenties, which would make her now about sixty. There has been little change in her condition since then. She is mostly, though not entirely, withdrawn from the world. Yet she is patient and cooperative and almost always pleasant. You're the first visitor she's had that anyone can remember. A resident psychiatrist says that long ago all hope of progress was lost. He does think, however, that back in the late 1930s a serious effort might have been successful . . . with some remission of the problem. Of course, in the late 1930s Catholic institutions did not have available the psychiatric facilities and skills that we now have." The nun sighed. "A lot of things have changed, Mrs. Cronin."

"Indeed they have, Sister. Do you think it will do any harm if I see Mary?"

"Oh, not at all, Mrs. Cronin, but I must tell you that neither will it do any good."

On her way home from the institution, as her driver skirted the city on the tri-state toll road, Nora was too shaken even to glance at her briefcase filled with work. There was no doubt who Mary was. Her features were like those of Nora's own daughter Mary: fifty years older, perhaps, but the same. And her eyes were Sean's eyes—fragile, hurt, and yet tender. More to the point, she had suddenly become attentive when the nun introduced her as Nora Cronin. Mary's aimless chatter had ceased and she became lucid for a moment. "Nora Cronin?" she said. "Why, my name is Cronin too. I had almost forgotten."

Nora decided that she would never tell Paul, if only because she did not want to take the risk of discovering that her husband already knew about the mysterious Mary. Should she tell Sean?

Nora drew a deep breath. Sean thought his faith was weak, that he didn't believe in God, at least not strongly enough. He did, of course. He played a childish game with himself, looking for "signs" from God all the time. Nora shook her head in disapproval. As though God didn't give signs every day. Sean would think his mother some kind of sign. And he would be furious at Uncle

Mike. None of it would help anyone, not Mary Eileen, not Sean, not Uncle Mike.

She examined her reactions. Was she angry at Uncle Mike? She should be, but she was not. Poor man. He was wrong, but she was certain he had done what he thought best.

She gathered up her gloves and her purse. I guess you're elected to carry the burden of the secret, Nora, she said to herself. Who else?

Eleven-year-old Nicole Shields discovered her mother's body on her parents' bed when she returned home from school. It was a month after the 1968 Presidential election. Her mother was dressed in a pale blue dress, the one she had worn on the previous Easter Sunday. She seemed to be quietly sleeping. Nicole, who frequently fought with her mother, murmured an unenthusiastic greeting as she walked down the hall to her own room. Then, puzzled by why her mother would be sleeping with her Easter dress on, she walked back to the bedroom.

Her mother's chest did not seem to be moving.

Nicole felt a sudden chill. Reluctantly she walked toward the bed, telling herself that her mother was only asleep. She stood at the side of the bed. No, it couldn't be . . . her mother had had too much to drink. She touched her mother's face. It was cool. She picked up her hand. It was cold too. Then it seemed to close on her own, like a claw pulling her down.

Nicole jumped away, dropping the hand back on the bed. Screaming hysterically, she ran from the room. It was a long time before she calmed down enough to call her father.

Like a man in a dream, Tom Shields called one of his neighbors who was a specialist in internal medicine and summoned an ambulance from the emergency room at Little Company of Mary Hospital. Maggie had finally pushed her luck too far. She had signaled her need for attention and affection, time had run out before anyone had heard her signal. Sitting on the bed next to the lifeless body of the woman he had always loved but never understood, Tom Shields wondered, as he had so often during their marriage, what more he could have done that he had not. He was certain that the failure was his, but he could never put his finger on what the failure was. Idly, he reached for the note on the table next to the bed. Maggie's final message. She was always leaving "final messages."

He opened the envelope and began to read:

> *I can't stand it anymore. I'm sick of pretending. I hate it. You're the only one I've ever loved. And after all the good times we've had, and all the things we've done together, you don't want me any more. There's no point in going on. Love, Maggie.*

Tom Shields glanced at the envelope. It was not addressed to him, as he had first assumed, but rather to Congressman Paul Cronin.

All feeling drained out of him. He put the final note from his wife in the pocket of his jacket. There was no point in letting anyone else see it.

. . .

Congressman-elect Paul Cronin was so pleased with himself that he left his office at the City Center early and took the four o'clock Rock Island train home. He whistled "Hail to the Chief" softly as he sprang up the stairs of his house and opened the door. Nora was sitting in the parlor, her hair tied severely behind her head, a handkerchief held in one hand.

"What's the matter, Nora?" He knew his wife's moods well enough to understand that something terrible had happened.

"Maggie finally did it," said Nora, her voice hoarse. "She tried to kill herself. This time she succeeded."

"Good God," Paul said. He remembered with a feeling of relief the crumpled telephone messages.

Chris Waverly eyed Paul skeptically. "You haven't changed much, Congressman," she said. Her tone was bitter. "Coming back to Washington, huh?"

Chris's figure was as crisp and trim as ever, but her face was thin and the lines on it made her look hard. She looked at least a decade older than Nora.

"I hope we can be friends, Chris," Paul said.

"Not a chance." She snubbed out her cigarette. "By the way, I heard your old flame Maggie—you know, the one you used to bed when neither Nora nor I was available—I heard she killed herself. Any chance it was because of you? It would make an interesting story, wouldn't it? I can see the headlines, 'Mistress commits suicide after Congressman spurns her.' "

Paul's heart sank. He had been a fool to tell Chris about his longtime affair with Maggie. It seemed amusing to brag about it in those days. Damn Chris and her memory. Even worse, Maggie's daughter, Nicole, had told his daughter Eileen that Maggie had left a note addressed to Congressman Cronin but that her father had taken it. So Shields probably knew about the affair. If Chris implicated Paul in Maggie's suicide, his seat in Congress would be worthless. Daley wouldn't even slate him in 1970.

But there would be no way that Chris could know about the note. "Good hunting, Chris," he said brazenly. "You just try to involve me in this tragedy."

"Believe me, lover boy, I intend to."

Sean was surprised but delighted when his secretary told him that Congressman Cronin had come to see him, but the dull look in his brother's eyes and the lifeless tone in his voice suggested that Paul was in trouble. "What's wrong, Paul? Can I help?"

"As a matter of fact, that's what I wanted to talk about. I think you may be able to be a big help. You see—well, I don't know quite how to put it. Maggie Shields had a crush on me for a long time; you remember the way she was back when she was a teenager. Well, whatever her problems, she got the idea that she was in love with me. . . . As God is my witness, Sean, there hadn't been anything between us—it was all in her imagination—but she left a suicide note addressed to me. There's a reporter in Washington . . . if she ever gets her hands on that note, if Tom Shields should be angry and give her the note. . . . You know what Daley thinks about that sort of thing."

"You want me to go to Tom Shields and ask him to destroy the note?" Sean asked.

"You've always been close to Tom. He trusts you. You can explain that there never was anything between me and Maggie—"

"Of course, I'll try," Sean said. He couldn't refuse Paul, even though he knew that it might mean the end of his friendship with Tom Shields.

They were sitting in Tom Shields's house early on a Wednesday afternoon. The first snow of the year had dusted the barren backyard of the house. Tom was thin, pale, haggard, still painfully mourning.

"How did he know about the letter?" he asked Sean.

"Apparently Nicole saw it on the bedstand."

"Damn, I thought she might have. I've been afraid to ask her. . . . Do you want to see it?"

"If you want to show it to me, Tom," he said gently.

Tom Shields riffled a notebook on his desk and pulled out a piece of light blue feminine stationery. He jabbed it at Sean.

Sean unfolded the note, read it quickly, and folded it up again. "Paul says that there was never anything between them, that it was all part of Maggie's problem."

"Your brother was very much part of her problem." Tom Shields was icy cold. "He's lying, Sean. He's been carrying on with her for years, God knows how many years. Maggie was a confused, unhappy, superficial woman, God rest her. I did everything I could, but none of it was good enough. Still, everything I tried to do was canceled out by that lousy bastard—" Tom's voice turned into a sob.

"I don't know what to say, Tom. I'm broken up over Maggie's death too."

"But not so broken up that you won't try to take that note away from me to save your brother from scandal. . . . I suppose you know that a reporter has already called to interview me about Maggie and her relationship with Paul? And so you've come to save his hide?"

"It's up to you, Tom," Sean said. He held out the folded paper.

Tom threw a matchbook at Sean. "Burn the goddamn thing. Only don't say another word to me as long as you live."

Sean felt a momentary pang of compassion for his brother as Paul strode briskly across the lobby of the Illinois Athletic Club toward the couch where Sean was waiting for him. Paul shook hands with two men, smiled genially at another, and waved at two more men during the quick twenty-yard walk. Trim and fit in a perfectly fitting pinstriped suit, the Congressman displayed his quick wit and easy charm even though fear must have been gnawing at him.

"Did you get it?" Paul's voice cracked.

"I did."

"Where is it? I can't risk anyone making a copy." Once the smile vanished, the pallor on Paul's face was evident.

"I burned it."

"Are you sure?"

"I'm sure. How long was your affair with Maggie going on? Since you came back from Korea?"

"Not really. Like I told you, it was mostly in her mind. Poor Maggie was not very well. Come on, let's have lunch.'' Paul tried to recapture some of his usual nonchalance.

Sean did not believe his brother. Paul was a pathetic liar. "I've got to get back to the office. There's a lot of work to do.''

Paul's face registered his disappointment. "I was counting on it.''

"Can't be helped.''

So many things had changed since they were boys. Paul had been the bigger and older and more successful son then. Now, for all his political success, he didn't have the feel of a winner.

Sean's compassion turned to triumph. Then the triumph turned to guilt.

That night Sean sat in his room in the cathedral rectory, the old brown spiral notebook in front of him, the page empty. His pen was in his hands, but no words would come. Angrily, he put the pen aside. There was a knock at the door and Father Kane entered, one of the young priests on the cathedral staff.

"Hi, Terry,'' he said. Whatever the problem, he had to smile cheerfully at the other clergy lest they be afraid they were in trouble with him. "What is it?''

"Nora Cronin called when you were on the phone about twenty minutes ago.'' He extended a note to Sean. "I told her you were talking to the Apostolic Delegation, and she said I shouldn't interrupt you.''

One of the many disadvantages of being a bishop was that you had to put up with tedious calls from supercilious Italian junior staff members of the Delegate. "Thanks, Terry, I'll call her right back.''

Nora had been worried about Mickey. He didn't seem to be bouncing back from the cold he had had several weeks before. She had taken him to the hospital for tests. Sean had been so shattered by the terrible meeting with Tom Shields that he had not thought to call her to find out how the little boy was doing.

He dialed the number and a child's voice said, "Congressman Cronin's residence. This is Noreen Cronin speaking.''

"Hi, Noreen, it's Uncle Sean. Is your mother home?''

"Oh, hi. Sure, Mom's home. Just a minute, I'll get her.''

"Hello, Sean.'' Nora sounded like a stranger.

Sean knew that something was terribly, terribly wrong. "What's the matter with him, Nora?''

"He has leukemia.''

Mickey Cronin died just before Christmas of 1969. He was two and a half years old. He had been a happy, golden little boy until the very end, laughing, playing, enjoying life, teasing his mother and sisters, unperturbed by his stay in the hospital and the various treatments the doctors gave him in a futile attempt to save his life. Death came quickly on the nineteenth of December. A mild cold had turned into a sudden high fever. His mother rushed him to the hospital. Then, the next morning, while Nora and the three solemn little girls stood around the bed, the life on this earth of Michael Paul Cronin came to an end. The girls, the older two imitating their mother, were solemn and self-possessed. The weeping Noreen insisted that her mother and sisters pray for Mickey. By the time Bishop Cronin arrived, Noreen had stopped crying. "Oh, Uncle Sean,'' she exclaimed enthusiastically, "Jesus and Mary came and took Mickey home to heaven with them.''

Congressman Cronin arrived only after the body of little Mickey had been taken to Donnellan's funeral home. He had not understood from what his wife had told him the night before that Mickey's condition was as critical as it turned out to be. And so, because of an important subcommittee meeting that he had to attend before the Christmas recess, he had taken a late plane.

Nora rejected a wake. She wanted to have a simple funeral the next morning, for only the family. The wonderful little boy's body must be quickly and discreetly put in the ground without any time for either grief or consolation. Paul agreed, and his tight-lipped brother offered no objections. But Mickey's sisters would not hear of it. Their little brother was to be sent on a long journey to Heaven, and they wanted a spectacular farewell. So the funeral was delayed a day, and the classmates of each of the girls filed into the church just before the Mass of the Resurrection began.

Most of the rest of St. Titus parish was there, and much of the Chicago political establishment. The poinsettias were already on the altar for Christmas, and young Eileen Cronin would not permit their removal. In fact, Eileen, not her mother, took charge of the funeral arrangements, even to the extent of selecting the reading for her uncle, the story of Jesus and Mary and Joseph fleeing into Egypt. The Mayor and Mrs. Daley knelt right behind the family. Michael Cronin wept through much of the Mass. Paul was stony-faced and grave through the entire service.

Sean told them that they must no longer think of Mickey as a little boy, but now as a full-fledged man, whose power of knowledge and love were only slightly less than that of an angel. Mickey now knew more things than all the people in the church put together and loved more powerfully than any of them could possibly love in this life. There were few dry eyes in the church when the Bishop's sermon was over. At the grave site, Noreen said to her uncle, "I always knew Mickey would be smarter than I am."

BOOK SEVEN

*I am the way, the truth, and the light. No one can come to the
Father except through me. If you know me, you know my father
too. From this moment you know him and have seen him.*

—JOHN 14:6–7

Chapter Twenty-seven
1970

SEAN CRONIN TOSSED aside the *Chicago Tribune* sports section. Broadway Joe
Namath was telling the world how he personally would wipe out the Baltimore
Colts. Sean felt a strong affinity for Broadway Joe. Tell off the world so you
won't hear your own demons.

He had an appointment with Nora. It was the first time she had ever called for
an appointment. At the quiet family Christmas party she had been sad but
dry-eyed. When he left, she said firmly, "There's something I want to talk to
you about after the first of the year."

She was waiting for him in Jimmy McGuire's office. Nora and Jimmy were
joking as they had for so many years. But she was pale and shaken, the memories
of her lost child haunting her.

"Come to see me or Jimmy?" Sean asked, rather more abruptly than he had
intended.

"Jimmy. He smiles and laughs and you don't."

"Come on down to my office anyway." She followed him down the twisting
stairway.

"Are you going to get to the lake at all?" Sean asked, fumbling with the
materials to make coffee on the sideboard behind his desk. It was impossible for
him to see Nora and not imagine her pain at losing her son—his son.

"Forget the coffee, for the love of Heaven, Sean," she said with unaccustomed brusqueness. "There's something I have to tell you."

Sean sat down as he was ordered. "Okay, Nora, let's have it."

Her blue eyes filled with tears. "Sean, your mother is still alive."

Sister Margarita was very deferential. Bishops did not often visit obscure
nursing homes in Lake County. Moreover, her elaborate respect suggested that
Bishop Cronin deserved special honor. The damn woman was probably a feminist beneath her formal mask and looked on him as a hero for his reckless,
spur-of-the-moment endorsement of the ordination of women, Sean thought.

"Your Excellency must understand," she said soothingly, "that our patient is
not lucid for more than a few moments at a time and that there is no continuity
between lucid intervals. Sometimes she thinks Mrs. Cronin is her mother, and

other times she thinks that she is her own daughter. It is all very sad, although fortunately there does not seem to be any mental pain.''

''I understand,'' Sean said automatically as they followed the nun to his mother's room.

He had steeled himself during the ride there in Nora's Mercedes—she had refused to let him drive. Yet the first sight in over thirty-five years of the woman who had brought him into the world was like a savage blow to his chest. The soft face, the vague, kind eyes, the faded golden hair—he had seen them all many times in his dreams; age and suffering had changed her gentle beauty, not destroying it but ravaging it so that one could appreciate what she once must have been.

She did not seem to realize Sean was in the room.

''Connie Crawford,'' she exclaimed to Nora. ''I haven't seen you in ages. Where have you been? When are you going to marry that nice O'Reilly boy?''

''I brought another guest,'' Nora said softly, gesturing with a hesitant hand toward Sean.

Mary Eileen peered at Sean as though she were seeing him through a thick fog. ''Terry.'' She choked. ''Terry . . . oh, my God, Terry . . . where have you been? They told me I'd never see you again . . . dear wonderful Terry . . . I knew you'd come back.''

She embraced Sean and sobbed against his chest. ''Who's Terry?'' he whispered to Nora.

''I think he's the priest she knew when she was sick. Your Roman collar must bring back his memory. . . . Maybe—maybe you look like him too.''

''It will be all right now, Mary Eileen, everything will be all right now.'' He tried to sound reassuring. ''We'll take care of you.'' He stroked her long, carefully combed gold and silver hair until the sobbing stopped.

She pulled back. ''I'm fine, Father.'' She was stiff and formal again. ''It was good of you to come. I suppose you know Father O'Connor from New Albany. He's a very good friend of mine.''

''Terry O'Connor?'' said Sean cautiously.

''Of course. He's such a marvelous priest. He has a deep devotion to the Mother of Sorrows. He was a wonderful help to me when I was sick. I believe I've already introduced you to my daughter, Jane Cronin. She's named after her aunt, you know.'' Mary Eileen giggled. ''Although she's much prettier than her aunt, don't you think?''

''As pretty as you are, Mary Eileen,'' said Sean.

''Don't call me that.'' She was briefly petulant. ''Mary Eileen died a long time ago. She was so sick she tried to kill the baby. . . .'' The anger passed like a brief spring shower. ''Will you dance with me, Mike? It's been so long since we danced together.''

Sean Cronin held his mother in his arms as tears streamed down his face. He would be many different people for Mary Eileen in future visits, he knew, but he would never be her son.

Nora slipped the Mercedes into the no-parking zone in front of the Holy Name Cathedral. The police would not give a ticket to a car with Bishop Cronin in it.

''I think I'd better have the whole story, Nora,'' he said, breaking a somber silence that had lasted since they left St. Helena's.

Nora told him everything, from the conversation with Ed Connaire at Jane's funeral through her discovery of the check to the first visit to Mary Eileen and, finally, her decision to tell him when Mickey died. "I had no right to protect you. I'm sorry."

"Protect me from what?" His voice was thick with suppressed anger.

"God, Sean, don't talk to me that way. Protect you from anger toward your father, from guilt when that anger is over, from all the bitterness and frustration that is pent up inside you, from the self-destruction that's waiting to explode. . . ."

"Shouldn't that have been my choice?" His voice was unnaturally quiet.

"I had a choice to make too," she said simply.

"That miserable vile old man. He locked up his wife for thirty-five years because he was ashamed of a nervous breakdown he probably caused."

"That's not fair, Sean. She was unstable. She would have been in a home for thirty-five years in any case."

"And the goddamn family reputation? Can't let the rumor get around that the Cronin genes are defective."

"Sean," she pleaded.

"Who is my father, Nora?" His anger seemed momentarily spent. "I have found a mother. Have I lost a father?"

"You're Sean Cronin, and I'll always love you."

"That doesn't solve the problem, does it?"

"Don't tell Uncle Mike that you know about Mary." It was the wrong time and the wrong way to say it, but she had to.

He turned to her and examined her face as though she were a stranger. "Why the hell not?"

"It will kill him."

"He deserves to be killed."

"My God, Sean, who are you to judge that? How can anyone—"

"He deprived me of my mother for thirty-five years," he shouted. "*I* can judge that!"

"If you have any love for me, Sean, leave him alone." She had played her last card, knowing in the moment she laid it down that it was not high enough.

"You care that much about him?"

"I care about him, yes. I care more about you. After you've had the satisfaction of hurting him, you'll suffer more than he does. Don't you have enough guilt already?" She clutched at his arm, as if to physically restrain him.

Sean wrenched away from her. "You're a whore, Nora. You're as bad as he is." He jumped out of the car and ran off down Wabash Avenue in the bitter cold January twilight, his black coat flapping in the harsh winter wind.

Sean towered over his father, his fists balled into knots.

"Something wrong, Sean?" the old man asked. The perennial Christmas tree of Chicago's famous Loop glowed through one window of Mike's apartment, and the neat orderly lines of streetlights twinkled through another.

"How did you and Jane do it, Dad? How many people did you bribe? How many cops and doctors and undertakers did you have to pay off?"

Mike Cronin was shaken by every word spoken by his son. "It was easy," he said, his voice weak. "There actually was an auto accident. You were in the car. It was the third time she had tried to . . . to kill you. Our doctor, Roy Shields, was a good friend—he thought it was the best way out. We crossed state lines to confuse the police and the undertakers, had a closed casket wake. Only Jane and Roy and the chauffeur and I knew. . . .''

"Jane took me away from her."

"She had to, Sean. Mary Eileen tried to kill you. I had to bring Jane into the house to watch you. There was no one else I could trust." Mike was begging for sympathy.

"And you never visited her, not once since 1934."

"That's not true, Sean." Mike pressed knotted fingers against his forehead. "I went many times in the first years, even the day I left to go overseas in 1942. She never knew me, thought I was her father. It didn't do her any good, and it hurt me terribly. Can't you believe that I hurt too?"

"You miserable bastard!" Sean pulled his father out of the easy chair in which he had been sitting and shook him as though he were a rag doll. "I hope to hell I'm not your son!"

He threw his father back into the chair and stomped out of the apartment.

A few minutes later, when the sub-zero cold on Delaware Place stung at his face, Sean began to feel the guilt that Nora had predicted. He found a dime in his pocket and went into a phone booth to call his brother.

Sean waited for Paul in the vast Red Carpet Room above the United Airlines gates at O'Hare. Paul had told him on the telephone that this half hour before his flight back to Washington was the only time he could see him.

Sean glanced around at the executives who swarmed into the room, like sleek bees to a honeycomb of gold.

Paul arrived late, rushing breathlessly up the escalator, although not so quickly as to miss the opportunity to scan the room for possible constituents or cronies.

"Nora seems to be bouncing back pretty well," Paul said, toasting his brother with a vodka and tonic. "It's been a lot worse on her than on me. She'd been with Mickey all the time. I hardly got to know the poor little fellow."

"Our mother is still alive, Paul."

The vodka and tonic rested a moment at Paul's lips, and his darting gray eyes froze. "What? You'd better tell me all about it," he said softly and lowered the glass.

Sean told him all about it, except for the part about Nora's discovering "Mary" and then hiding her discovery for over a year. And he did not mention Father Terry O'Connor. When he finished, Paul's face was slack and pale. His fingers drummed convulsively on the arm of the plush beige sofa on which he was sitting. "My God," he said.

Sean waited, sensing that his brother was groping for an appropriate reaction. Outside, a huge 747 nosed into a jetway, its wide body gleaming silver.

"From what you say, she would have been in a home all this time anyway," Paul said. "Still, why did the old man . . . ?"

"The disgrace, damn it!" Sean snapped. "The disgrace of the mother of his sons being mad."

Paul shook his head. "Yeah, but . . . you know, he really believes that stuff about bad blood."

"Sure he does. And how could he make one son president and the other a cardinal if the world knew they had a mother who's mad? Hell, they probably would have thrown me out of the seminary if they thought there was insanity in the family."

Paul moved his empty glass around the surface of the coffee table. "Still, it's a damn fool stupid thing to do."

Sean's anger came flooding back. "Worse than stupid. He's the one that's the lunatic."

"I suppose so," Paul agreed. "He meant well. . . ."

"Do I have to tell you what the streets of Hell are paved with?" Sean retorted.

"I don't know what to say, Sean. I've got to sleep on this, figure it out, put some meaning to it. You aren't going to go public with it, are you?"

"No point in that, is there? Not now."

"No." Paul's relief was obvious. "I guess not." He reached for his hand-tooled leather attaché case and struggled out of the sofa. "I've got to catch that plane now. You don't mind?"

"You'll visit her the next time you're home? She won't know you, but—"

"Sure I will. It will take some getting used to, though." Paul seized on the promise. "Next time I'm in town."

As he watched his handsome brother walk out of the lounge, Sean knew that Paul would never set eyes on Mary Eileen Cronin.

For hours, Mike huddled in his chair, watching the lights of the city, unable to react to what had happened. Sean had discovered his secret. How didn't matter. Mike always knew that he would one day, one way or another.

He was still shaking from the terror of the confrontation. Good God, a man tried, he made mistakes, he did his best. No one ever understood, they never tried to understand. What the hell was he supposed to do? Let her kill the little kid? Even if he wasn't my son—and I suppose that he wasn't—I had to protect him. No gratitude, none at all. He doesn't realize how much I gave up.

Maybe I ought to call Elizabeth. She's the only one who came close. . . . No, I can't call her. She's married now. I gave that up too.

The lights of the Loop flickered on and off. A sharp stab of pain cut through Mike Cronin's head.

Then the lights of the Loop went out completely.

Chapter Twenty-eight
1973

"Play it again, Sam," Bishop Sean Cronin ordered Monsignor James McGuire.

Jimmy managed an unusually wan smile. "I hadn't noticed your resemblance to Bogart until now, boss, but there *is* a similarity—around the mouth and teeth, if you get what I mean."

"Play it." Sean was in an unusually good mood, in part because he had found something that upset his normally unflappable second-in-command. Jimmy pushed the button on the tape player. The television screen came alive and Sean saw himself, calm and cool, with a touch of gray at his temples. His pale hair was too long, his suit was rumpled, and if one looked closely one could see that his shoes weren't polished. "Lovemaking between a man and woman," the person on the screen was saying, "can mean many different things. Through lovemaking, lovers forgive one another, show their gratitude to one another, declare their love, renew their vows, chase their anxieties and their anger, reestablish communication, make life livable for one another, challenge, stimulate, excite, and reassure one another. Also, of course, it is the means for continuing the human race."

The pious Jesuit who shared the panel with Sean was outraged. "Even if you are a bishop, I must be frank, Your Excellency. Those are tasteless, vulgar words."

"Really, Father? It had been my understanding that it's precisely all those complex dimensions of marriage and love that led St. Paul to call it a great sacrament."

"You're a celibate, aren't you?" the Jesuit asked with a hint of a smirk. "How would a celibate know these things?"

"I try to keep my vows, yes." A slight frown marred the Vicar General's handsome face. "I do counseling every evening in the cathedral rectory, I hear confessions on weekends, I have friends and family, and I *am* a male member of the human race with the usual male reactions . . . that's how I know."

The Jesuit exploded. "Bishop, those are scandalous things you're saying!"

"Scandalous for a bishop to be a member of the human race?"

Jimmy pushed the stop button on the video recorder.

"So that's what all the cardinals in the United States, except for Eamon, want to censure me for? Jimmy, they're full of baloney."

"My information is that they won't go after you by name. They'll simply pass a general resolution recommending that bishops not talk about intimate human relationships on radio or television programs. It's a way of getting at you and, of course, getting at Eamon too. They know he won't be at the November meeting because he's still recuperating from his heart attack. You've got to fight for his sake as well as your own."

"Don't be ridiculous, Jimmy." Sean was as relaxed as he had been on the television screen. "Eamon's quite capable of conspiring against them himself, if he wants to, and he thinks he knows better than to try to save me from my own folly. Forget it. It doesn't make a damn bit of difference."

"Sean, it will destroy you. You'll be finished in the American Church."

Sean shrugged and rose from his chair in the chancellor's office. "How many times do I have to tell you, Jimmy, I don't care about my future in the American Church?"

"What do you care about, Sean? You work here all day and then half the night at the cathedral rectory. You hear confessions Saturday afternoon and evening. You say two Masses on Sunday. You don't take a day off. You're in Washington or Rome at least once a month. You don't even see your brother or Nora and the kids. What *do* you care about?"

Sean put his hands in his pockets. "I'm not sure, Jimmy. If I ever find out I'll let you know. In the meantime, I've got to go deal with Father Camillo of the Soldiers of Christ. I'll at least have a little fun bouncing that so-and-so from the diocese."

"If I had a sister like Nora, I'd visit her," Jimmy said firmly.

"I'm sure you would, Jimmy, I'm sure you would."

. . .

Father Camillo had the manner and voice of a Spanish aristocrat and the looks to match, a face out of El Greco, tan skin, liquid brown eyes. Moreover, he had the worldwide power of the Soldiers of Christ behind him, a secret international Catholic society made up of priests and laity, modeled to some extent after the Communist Party with small cells and a strategy of infiltrating elite groups in critical social positions. He had begun the conversation in Sean's office by trying to intimidate the Vicar General of the Archdiocese of Chicago, as though the latter were something of a peasant.

He didn't get very far. Sean cut him off and flipped open a manila folder. "Let's see, Father Camillo, we have three reports of your group infiltrating young people's organizations in parishes of the archdiocese. One of the priests whose group was infiltrated sent a young woman who could speak Spanish to a meeting where you and your colleagues were present. She overheard some very interesting conversations, Father, the sort of things that one would expect from a Communist infiltrating a union, but hardly from a priest in an organization concerned about spiritual values and guidance."

Camillo raised his hand in protest. "But I am sure she exaggerated—"

"And then we have protests from five husbands whose wives joined your organization. Apparently they won't sleep with their men without permission from their spiritual guide, who, in a number of cases, seems to be you, Father Camillo."

"Slander!"

"Perhaps, Father, perhaps. Then there are a number of women who have also protested because, once their husbands became part of your group, they insisted that the wife kneel and ask for their blessing before she left the house. They also claimed the right to make all decisions of the family. That doesn't work with Irishwomen, Father. A cultural difference between them and the Spanish, I suppose."

"The husband is the head of the home," Camillo insisted.

"Just barely, especially if he's Irish. Now let's see. Oh, yes. We have records of four young women who ended up in the hospital because they had scourged themselves rather too severely at the recommendation of their spiritual guide. Then there are parents who report their children are spying on them, pastors who find that their curates have hidden tape recorders in their offices and listened to their conversations, and faculty members at a Catholic university here who think they were denied tenure because of your group's conniving. We also have several copies of your confidential magazine, which, in effect, repudiates the Second Vatican Council. All in all, a very interesting dossier, Father Camillo."

The Spaniard's thin lips were white with rage. "You have no right to sit in judgment on what we do, Monsignor."

"Now, there you are wrong, Father Camillo. I am the Vicar General of this archdiocese, and I have the right to revoke your permission to continue to work in this archdiocese. And I am doing so. Here is a copy of a letter; the original will be put in the mail this afternoon, and you will note that I am sending a copy to the Apostolic Delegate and to the Sacred Congregation of the Clergy in Rome. I'm sure you may appeal if you want, but to tell you the truth, I doubt that it will work because if you persist in your appeal these materials may be leaked to the press with very considerable negative effect on your work around the country."

"I demand to see the Cardinal."

"No one is going to see the Cardinal for several weeks, Father Camillo. He is recovering from his heart attack, but he is not receiving visitors. I can assure you that His Eminence has given his full approval to this decision.''

"You yourself are also subject to judgment," snarled the Soldier of Christ.

"Ah, yes, indeed. And I wouldn't be surprised to learn that you and your friends have something to do with the kangaroo court that's going to sit in judgment on me in November. To tell you the truth, Father Camillo, I don't care what you or they say. Whenever the Cardinal Archbishop wants my resignation, he can have it, as he well knows. Nonetheless, as long as I am his Vicar General, I will carry out his wishes. And I assure you, Father Camillo, it is his wish that you and your community leave this diocese within the month. If you have not departed then, we will be forced to take canonical action. And, incidentally, there are also ways to make things difficult for you civilly. We do have a holdover from Old Spain, you know. The civil authorities occasionally cooperate with us. I bet that place of yours in Hyde Park is violating all kinds of zoning regulations.''

The Spaniard was trembling with rage as he stood up. "You will regret this, Monsignor. You will regret this as long as you live.''

"Get out," Sean said. He slammed the folder shut and stood his full six feet one inch. "Get out before I lose my patience.''

Father Camillo got out.

Sean checked his calendar to see what other appointments were written in. He was weary and depressed, a weariness that sleep could not cure and a depression that nothing exorcised. He was going through the motions, doing what a priest should do, trying to be what a bishop should be. His self-esteem and self-confidence were shattered, his faith still weak, and his hope, at best, paper thin.

Where was the Holy Spirit in his life?

The following Saturday, after Mass and before confessions, Sean went to visit the sick. First of all, a visit to the Cardinal at his house on North State Parkway.

Eamon McCarthy, thinner, paler, and old, was relaxing on the couch on the second floor, studying the overseas edition of *L'Osservatore Romano.* "You look much better than you did a week ago, Eminence.'' Sean wondered if the magnificent old man would ever look himself again.

"Very good of you to say so, Bishop Cronin. I'm feeling much better. If it were not for the doctor's instructions, I would come down Monday and relieve you of your many administrative burdens.'' The smile, quick and mocking, had not changed a bit.

"You'd have a hard time finding the chancery office, Eminence. We've moved it across the street. But I'm sure Monsignor McGuire would be happy to let you use his office.''

"Yes, of course. I knew I could count on you to leave me at least a cubbyhole somewhere or other. Any serious problems this week . . . the kind you could tell me about without violating the doctor's orders to protect me from my own sense of responsibility?''

"Just two, Eminence.'' Sean hesitated, then continued. "I ordered the Soldiers of Christ out. Father Camillo was something less than cooperative. I assume he will appeal to the Apostolic Delegate, who, as you know, is no friend of yours.''

"Nor a friend of yours, I might add, Bishop Cronin. But then we both know the Apostolic Delegate would not dare to overrule a Cardinal. No, I'm afraid that Father Camillo will have to take his white Freemasons somewhere else and the

Archdiocese of Chicago will be spared them in the future. And I can tell from the look on your face that there is something else and you are debating whether you should tell it to me or not. You'd better tell me, Bishop.''

"Jimmy has learned from one of his canon law friends that there's a movement under way to censure me at the bishops' meeting in November. The resolution will be introduced by all the cardinals—all but yourself, of course—and will not mention me explicitly but will rather lament the fact that certain bishops have said imprudent things about marital intimacy on television and urge that such things do not happen again.''

Eamon McCarthy smoothed the few strands of hair still left on the top of his head. "And it is, of course," the Cardinal said thoughtfully, "a way of punishing me for tolerating you.''

"As to that, Eminence, it is a punishment richly deserved.''

"Doubtless. And I presume, being who you are, you intend to ignore the whole thing until after it's over, at which time you will tell the gentlemen of the press that you would say exactly the same thing on television all over again if the circumstances permitted?''

"You know me very well, don't you, Eminence?''

"Too well, Bishop Cronin, too well. Certainly so well that I will not attempt to dissuade you from your course of action. In truth, I would be somewhat disappointed if you told me you were going to do anything else, given the fact that every new foolish thing you do brings you one step closer to becoming my successor. I would imagine this particular incident will absolutely guarantee that you will be the next Cardinal Archbishop of Chicago.''

"My father would be happy to hear that, Eminence.''

"Yes, doubtless. Well, Bishop Cronin, you need not trouble yourself on my account. I will follow my doctor's orders and refuse to worry about your fate next month at the bishops' meeting.''

But of course he would. There was not the slightest doubt in Sean's mind about that.

Michael Cronin's suite in the John Hancock Center was equipped as a sort of half-way hospital, with a nurse in attendance as well as a housekeeper. Sean visited his father every week, a ritual that left him emotionally exhausted. The doctors assured him that his father's crippling stroke had been inevitable, but Sean knew that their quarrel about Mary Eileen had been the catalyst.

When the hospital first called to tell him of the stroke he had still been so angry that he had refused to go to see his father. Then the rage faded. Who was he to sit in judgment of another human being? Nora had been right again.

The old man sat in his room and either watched television or stared at Lake Michigan. He could walk a few feet by himself and with one hand operate the television remote control. Sometimes he would scratch a few words on a pad of paper attached to the side of his wheelchair. Often, when Sean left their brief meeting, he wondered if the magical science that had saved his father's life and now kept him alive was a blessing or not.

"I think Agnew got off lucky." Sean went through the political events of the previous week. "And I can't imagine anything funnier than Gerald Ford as vice-president. You know, they say that he can't walk and chew gum at the same time.''

There was a faint grimace on Mike's face.

"And Paul is calling for Nixon's impeachment for the Watergate cover-up. He's taking some heat from his constituents, but I bet by next summer Paul will get so much credit for being one of the first to call for impeachment procedures that the Mayor will be happy to slate him for the Senate in '76. What do you think?"

The cramped hand scrawled two illegible words on the note pad. Sean, who had learned with practice to understand most of his father's scrawling, peered over his shoulder and deciphered *Nixon-bum.*

"You better believe he's a bum," Sean agreed. "Too bad Paul isn't going to be able to run against him. There wouldn't be an easier man to beat for the presidency in '76."

His father's response was to turn on the television to the Notre Dame game. The Fighting Irish, everyone agreed, were destined to be national champions this year. His father's apartment in the Hancock Center was sufficiently high for the signals from the South Bend television station to get through clearly.

Sean watched the first quarter and then excused himself. It was time to get back to the cathedral to hear confession.

His father made no sign that he heard him say good-bye or that he noticed he had left the room.

After he heard confessions, Sean went to his room and tossed his cassock on the battered old ottoman. Then he hurried down the stairs for dinner. As he went by the office at the entrance of the cathedral, the telephone operator handed him a note. *Sister Margarita from St. Helena's Home asked you to call at once. Important.*

Sean returned the call quickly, nervously jabbing at the telephone dial. "Bishop Cronin here, Sister," he said at Sister Margarita's infinitely courteous "Good evening."

"Oh, yes, Bishop. I'm glad you called. Mary seems to be slipping. I don't think she can last too much longer."

Chapter Twenty-nine
1973

MOST DAYS IN Washington for Congressman Paul Cronin were good days. A rising power in Congress, chairman of a subcommittee of the Judiciary Committee, admired and respected by his colleagues, and a favorite of the press, the forty-four-year-old Congressman from Illinois was marked by everyone as a man with a very promising future. He had managed to combine the Cook County organization and the support of Richard J. Daley with liberal stands on race, women's rights, and, especially, the war in Vietnam. His wit and charm and good looks made him a favorite of Washington hostesses and a popular escort for many of the unattached young women of Washington.

But this particular November day had been a disaster. First of all, a delegation from home had called upon him to express grave reservations about his resolution calling for the impeachment of President Nixon. They were not important people from the district, but blacks and whites from the East End. They had come to Washington to press for release of loan funds to stabilize their community. Paul expected their visit to him to be a gesture of gratitude for his success in prying the monies loose. It turned out, however, that they were less interested in his clout with HUD than his failure to support "Our President" against the odious John Dean.

As he sat in the bar at the Statler Hotel, waiting for Stan Carruthers, a colleague from upstate, to join him for an evening on the town, Paul remembered his response.

"As a congressman of the United States, I am sworn to uphold the Constitution. As a member of the House Judiciary Committee, it is my most solemn obligation to consider whether a president—any president—is guilty of high crimes or misdemeanors in office. There is sufficient evidence, it seems to me, to warrant further investigation by my committee. I would be derelict in my constitutional obligations if I did not demand that investigation. I would like very much to have your support, but in the absence of your support, I will go ahead with my sworn obligation. I can do nothing else."

There was some applause, but Paul was well aware that there were many who were not applauding either his opposition to the war or his enthusiasm for impeaching Nixon.

Then Makuch had appeared in his office. He had decided that the twenty-thousand-dollar-a-year subsidy he was getting from Paul was not enough.

"I must say, Paul, that I'm dismayed by your opposition to the President." He flipped the envelope with the twenty thousand-dollar bills into his pocket as though it were a payment for an electric light bill.

"I have a constitutional responsibility—"

"Fuck constitutional responsibility," Makuch said. "He's our president and you'd better leave him alone, or some people are gonna find out about the Reservoir. I imagine that there are people over at the White House who would be interested in that information."

Paul felt his face flame and his fists clench. He choked back the impulse to say that Makuch had grown moderately wealthy with Cronin money, and he would be cutting off a source of regular income. Maybe Makuch didn't need the money any more. "We'll have to see what the investigations turn up," he said instead.

"Fuck the investigations," Makuch said. "You'd better think about what I'm saying. You're skating on thin ice."

After Makuch left, Paul drummed his fingers thoughtfully on his desk. Blackmail was bad enough, but now Makuch was demanding more than money. He was demanding political power, cracking the whip to see if Paul would jump. He almost certainly knew that Paul was destined for the Senate and possibly the White House. If he enjoyed throwing his weight around politically, he would revel in the years ahead. The bind would get worse for Paul. If he waffled on the impeachment now, it would certainly be held against him when he was up for reelection next year and when he was running for the Senate. He could probably survive, but it would be awkward, very awkward. Unless he completely misread the signs, Nixon would be terribly unpopular by summer, and a liberal Democrat who voted in favor of him would look like a hypocrite. Of course Makuch might change his mind before summer. But what if he didn't?

And the bind would get worse as the years went on.

Paul nursed his drink thoughtfully. He was really not up to a night with Carruthers. It would be much better to go to Sally Grant's apartment. She was half expecting him anyway.

Carruthers finally arrived, apologizing for his tardiness. His wife and children had arrived unexpectedly from home for the weekend, and hence he was unavailable for the evening. But they might at least have a drink before he went home, he said.

"I'm taking a lot of heat," Paul said. "People from back home are leaning on me. Some fellow is even digging around in my war record trying to find something dirty."

Carruthers, a thin, sallow man with a high hairline and long black sideburns, shook his head sympathetically. "It's a rough one. The crowd over at the White House are not going to get more pleasant if the walls begin to crumble around them. Anyway, your war record is all right. You're a Medal of Honor winner, aren't you? And a POW? I mean, isn't the big line on you that a Medal of Honor winner was opposing the war in Vietnam?"

"I'm okay," responded Paul. "But it's hard to prove that charges are false once they're made. All I need with the senatorial race coming up in '76 are unsubstantiated charges like that drifting around."

Carruthers stirred his vodka martini thoughtfully. "Is this an individual or a group of people?"

"Just one guy."

"There are ways things like that can be taken care of. People can be leaned on a little bit, if you know what I mean. Nothing really messy, of course. It's usually pretty effective."

"Oh?" said Paul. "I might be interested in something like that."

Carruthers scribbled something on a napkin and passed it across the table. "They're a very discreet bunch, Paul. You can trust them."

Paul stuffed the napkin into the pocket of his jacket without looking at it. "I hear Tip O'Neill is just about ready to send the signal to the party regulars. We're not going to be alone much longer."

"I think we already have enough on the bastard to impeach him four times over."

After Carruthers left, Paul had another drink and then walked down Massachusetts Avenue to Dupont Plaza. Under a streetlight, he took out the napkin from his pocket. On it there was the name "Eric" and a phone number. He memorized the phone number and tore the napkin into tiny pieces.

Sally Grant lived in an elegant apartment just off Dupont Plaza. A lush redhead, she was an analyst at the Securities and Exchange Commission. She had a simple, uncomplicated animal hunger. Indeed, when she opened the door of her apartment, she was dressed in thin black lace, more than ready for Paul's arrival. "God, Paul, I thought you'd never come." She hugged him ferociously and half dragged him into the bedroom

His dreams after they made love were restless and troubled. He was back at the Reservoir, flares exploding over him in the dark. The hordes of screaming, bayonet-wielding Chinese burst out of the darkness and stabbed at his gut.

"What the hell's the matter with you?" Sally demanded, as he woke up in the middle of a scream.

"Nightmares from the war days," he said sluggishly. "They come and they go."

"The trouble with you, Paul Cronin," Sally said, "is that you're too goddamned reckless."

She scurried out of the bedroom and came back with a tumbler full of Scotch. He drained it in a single gulp.

"What do you mean, I'm too reckless?" he asked.

She sat on the edge of the bed, clutching her frilly nightgown at her throat. "I don't quite know what I mean. I guess I think you get off on taking chances, running risks, courting danger. You're a married congressman from a district where your wife is as popular as you are, if not more so, and you've got at least three different women—that I know of—in this city, and if I'm able to find out about the other two without any trouble, just about everyone in Washington must know about them too. What if you get caught? What if your wife catches you? What if the press catches you? What if the White House goes after you to stop you from pushing this impeachment?"

"I don't intend to get caught," Paul said.

"Do you know what people say on the Hill about you? They say you're smart, you work hard, you're charming, and that you're a Mississippi riverboat gambler. You lucked out on opposition to the war. You're probably going to luck out on impeachment. But one of these days you're going to draw for the high card and lose. Mississippi riverboat gamblers, they say on the Hill, never become committee chairmen, much less presidents."

Paul rubbed his eyes. "And what does all this have to do with my dreams?"

"I don't know how it figures, Paul. I have the feeling that you did something reckless a long time ago, and it comes back and haunts you in your sleep."

Paul slid out of bed and began to dress. "I am what I am, Sally," he said. "Take me or leave me." He wasn't sure which option he wanted Sally to take. She was getting too serious. She was beginning to remind him of Maggie Shields.

The next day in the kitchen of his home in Georgetown, Paul was pouring over his staff's memo on impeachment. He had called "Eric" an hour before and had arranged to meet him in a bar around the corner from the Shoreham Hotel. The voice at the other end of the line had been smooth and cultivated. It asked no questions; indeed, it did not even seem particularly interested in Paul's name.

The doorbell rang and Paul, who was fending for himself since his housekeeper had Saturday off, answered it. It was his daughter Eileen and her friend, Nicole Shields. They were both high school seniors and had come to Washington for the weekend to investigate colleges for the following year. The trip was a lark for Eileen, a slightly shorter version of her mother who was certainly going to St. Mary's of Notre Dame. Nicole, an introverted but sexy-looking girl, was just as certainly not going to Notre Dame.

Tom Shields had remarried two years previously. His second wife was a black-haired nurse from Ireland with a gorgeous figure and a mind that matched Tom's. All the kids except Nicole seemed to get along well with their stepmother, but the tempestuous older daughter of Maggie Shields treated Fiona with silent contempt.

"Too bad Notre Dame isn't on national TV." Eileen hugged him dutifully. "I can't stand to listen to games on the radio. They make me so nervous."

"I think football is ridiculous," said Nicole, staring at Paul with bold appraisal.

"I'm afraid I won't even be able to listen to the game," he said. He remembered for the first time that he was supposed to take the two girls to dinner. "If

I'm going to show off you beautiful young girls at the Lion d'Or tonight, I've got to finish these memos about getting rid of Mr. Nixon.''

"Getting rid of Mr. Nixon?" Nicole said. "That would be a lot of fun."

Paul suspected that if Eileen were not with them her friend would almost certainly make a pass at him. It had been a long time since he had had one that young. He would bet that she was anything but inexperienced.

"We won't keep you," said Eileen with characteristic efficiency. "Just stopped by to say hello. We have to get over to Trinity College. We'll probably listen to the game there."

"I wish you were staying here tonight," he said. He was actually rather pleased with the fact that they were not. "But I know how young people like to hang around college dorms."

"It's where the action is," said Eileen brightly. She was a typical high school senior: bright, attractive, happy, her whole life stretching out ahead of her in promise. Nicole, on the other hand, with her angry, dangerous eyes, seemed doomed already. Why did Eileen hang around with her? Concern or family loyalty, he supposed. And why did Nicole hang around with Eileen? Maybe she sensed there was some chance of survival in the radiance of his eldest daughter.

"Your mother called from Panama night before last, Eileen. She was going out to San Miguelito to see about the housing project there." What did his daughters think of their parents' intermittent marriage? Indeed, what did they think of him? Lively Eileen, quiet Mary, and madcap Noreen seemed utterly unperturbed by anything their parents did. Self-possessed like their mother. Did they make the same sharp, keen judgments that Nora made?

"Is she going to stop here on the way home?" Eileen asked.

"No, she's going home for a board meeting; then she's coming here."

"Mother's just amazing," Eileen said. "I don't know how she does it, much less make it seem so easy . . . I mean, you're a marvel too, Dad, but mother's a woman."

"That she surely is, Eileen."

After the two girls left, Paul went back to his memo, although he did turn on the radio to listen to the Notre Dame–Georgia Tech game. Nora *was* an amazing woman. Eileen was right about that. His respect for her increased each year. He was now talking the feminist line in his public speeches and was thankful that his wife was a feminist role model. He could point to the proof that he practiced what he preached.

Their interludes together were cordial. Living apart some of the time, he supposed, was good for the marriage. That way he could imagine to himself that Nora was one of his mistresses. It was easier for him to deal with Nora as a part-time mistress than as a full-time wife.

Eric was a tall, handsome Nordic blond, hardly the mafioso that Paul had expected. Rather, he was a smooth businessman in impeccably tailored clothes. He had a faint Swedish accent.

"We have a full range of services, sir." He never called Paul by name. "We guarantee full satisfaction, total discretion, and we accept payment only after our task is accomplished." He hesitated for a moment. "Normally we make a minimal response to the problem. It's just as well, however, that you do not ask too many specific questions about the exact technique we will use, since it might be disruptive for you to know. I can assure you that in a case like the one you have described, it will be very likely that quite simple preventive measures will be more than adequate. Our charge, by the way, will be twenty-five thousand dollars.''

"You're sure there won't be any trouble afterward?'' Paul asked.

Eric gestured suavely over his glass of soda water. "None at all. There are certain kinds of pain which, when professionally administered, dissuade even the bravest men from doing anything that would risk a repetition.''

Paul was horrified by the Swede's cruel businesslike attitude, yet he knew of no other way to deal with the problem of Joe Makuch. "Remarkable,'' he muttered softly.

"Now, if you will provide me with some more details about this Mr. Makuch, we'll be able to activate our program against him.''

"You're sure it will work?''

"You may rely on us, sir. We guarantee satisfaction.''

Chapter Thirty
1973

NORA CONSIDERED THE remaining half of her gin and tonic. She must make it last for another half hour, the time she had assigned herself to sunbathe in the comforting tropic warmth on the balcony of her hotel. In the distance, the blue of the ocean and the blue of the sky merged into a single gentle background. Nora sighed. Why couldn't the weather be like this in Chicago in November?

No more than one gin and tonic a day when she was on the road, and no drinks at all at home, save for an occasional glass of wine with dinner. Nora did not entirely accept the judgments made by her friends, that at thirty-eight she was more beautiful than ever. Nonetheless, she was not going to permit herself to go to seed, and drinking was a quick way to do just that.

The phone jangled in her hotel room. She wrapped her wrinkle-free travel robe around herself and struggled out of the lounge chair. It was the first secretary from the embassy.

"Mr. Thornton said that you had a fine time out at San Miguelito this afternoon. I'm delighted to hear it.''

"It's a South Side Chicago Irish parish in the middle of the tropics,'' she responded enthusiastically. "Father Leo has that district organized like the most efficient ward in Chicago. The liturgy was beautiful, the little kids were wonderful, and the housing project seemed to be perfect. And Leo didn't give me a hard time, as so many of the clergy do, about my requirement that the Cronin Foundation make a small profit. He says his people don't want gifts or charity. They want the chance to do something for themselves. That's the reason the Foundation exists, you know.''

"I understand, though it's an unusual approach in this part of the world. People get used to government loans they know they don't have to pay back, or to church gifts. Private businesses making loans with small interest are unusual.''

Nora tightened the belt on her gown. "Leo says that both the other ways deprive people of their self-respect.''

"Well, maybe they do. . . . Thornton said you seemed a little tired at the end of the day. I hope that doesn't mean you'll turn down a dinner invitation for this evening?''

"Oh, no," Nora replied cheerily. "A mile swim in the ocean and a half hour basking in the sunlight, and I'd very much appreciate dinner. Thanks for the invitation." The first secretary would make the usual pass halfway through dinner. She would reject it briskly, and the rest of the evening would be pleasant.

"I'll be by about seven thirty then."

"Fine, just fine."

Nora had had two affairs since Mickey's death, one in Paris and one in Chicago. Both brief, intense, and utterly unsatisfying. They provided neither the sweet unbearable ecstasy of her two weeks with Sean nor the routine affection of her sex life with Paul. Illicit sex had been consigned to the same ash can of rejected escapes as had gin and tonics.

Her experience with Sean convinced her that she was not undersexed and that she would be much better off with passion as a regular part of her life. Since illicit sex didn't work, she decided, she would have to make licit sex work. If affection for a charming little-boy husband wasn't much to build passion on, it was better than nothing.

Her own cold-bloodedness shocked her; as always, however, Nora was interested in discovering more about herself. Paul was a thoroughly presentable, if shallow, male, more attractive than most of the men who made passes at her. Occasional sex with a husband you don't love but don't hate either—one could do much worse.

She went back to the balcony, stretched out on the lounge, and unfastened her robe.

Part of Nora was dead. She presumed it would remain dead, killed by the poison of guilt, pain, and regret. Nora accepted the verdict. The part of her that still lived would pass out its years, doing its best, lamenting that which had been lost but refusing to quit. She would continue to be a wife, a mother, and a businesswoman until the comedy was finished.

She tasted the gin and tonic carefully. Either she would have to drink it more quickly or stir out of her comfortable position and get ice cubes from the refrigerator in her room. She rolled over on her stomach. She was rich, successful, and even becoming famous. Yet part of her, the important part, the part that mattered, was numb and cold and would, it seemed, remain that way forever.

If that was the way it was to be, then so be it.

Even the businesswoman-philanthropist role was losing some of its attractiveness. She was good at it now, very good indeed, but the fun was going out of that too. Somehow, some way, she had to find greater challenges.

When Nora arrived home at eleven o'clock the following night, exhausted from the plane trip and worn out by the long wait for a cab at O'Hare, she found the parlor of the old house on Glenwood Drive decorated with streamers and a banner proclaiming *¡Bien Venidos Mama!* Her three daughters were playing samba music on their flutes, enthusiastically if not altogether precisely.

Later, when they were all laughing and exhausted, sitting closely around the coffee table in the parlor, Nora asked Eileen, "How was Dad when you saw him in Washington? I talked to him from the airport in Miami, but we only had a few minutes.''

"He looked tired. And he was working hard on the impeachment. But otherwise he was fine. I wasn't able to spend much time with him because I was busy keeping Nicole out of trouble.''

"I don't see how you put up with her," Nora said. "She drives Tom and Fiona crazy. It's good of you to take care of her."

"Taking care of people runs in the family." Eileen grinned. "Anyway, I like her . . . well, some of the time."

Mary and Noreen disappeared to their rooms, after much hugging and many good-night kisses. Eileen hung around. "Speaking of taking care of people. . . ." She slouched into the couch. "Did you hear the Murrays are getting a divorce? An annulment from the Church too."

"I'm not surprised," Nora said. She sensed a heart-to-heart talk, probably long overdue. A pang of guilt assailed her.

"Why haven't you ever divorced Dad?" Sixteen-year-olds can be disconcertingly direct.

"Dad, to begin with, is not an alcoholic and he doesn't beat me—"

Eileen made an annoyed face. "Oh, I know *that*. But, Mom, you're so distant from each other. Doesn't it become boring?"

"All relationships are boring some of the time; there's more between me and Dad now than there ever has been." She had to choose her words very carefully. There would be no hiding from Eileen.

"I know *that* too, but Mom, he's so *shallow* and you're so deep, so much more like Uncle Sean. Why do you stay with Dad?"

"There are many kinds of love, Eileen. All loves are different and they all have their own commitments. You keep the commitments until they become absolutely impossible."

"Why? Why should you be stuck with a commitment you made a long time ago?"

Nora felt lightheaded and wished she had a cool gin and tonic. "Because if people don't keep their commitments, no one can trust anyone else."

Eileen's face was locked in a deep frown. "Will I make the same kind of mistakes?"

"You've had a much better childhood than I, Eileen. More confidence in yourself. I don't think you'll make many serious mistakes. Just so long as you don't think I'm lonely or frustrated or miserable in keeping my promises."

"Keeping promises is a good thing," Eileen agreed. "Otherwise, where would I be?" She brightened considerably, returned to being a happy teenager, and hugged her mother.

I guess I did all right, thought Nora. At least I'll be more ready for the next one.

Noreen dashed into the room. "Oh, I forgot. Uncle Sean called at dinnertime and said you were to call him at his private number no matter how late you got in. He sounded kind of worried."

Was it Uncle Mike? Nora walked across the room and looked up in her private phone book Sean's number at the cathedral. It had been a long time since she had used it. She punched the numbers on the phone. Sean answered at the first ring.

"Cronin," he said, sounding like a man who had not slept for a month.

"My name too," she said.

"Nora, thanks for calling. I hate to disturb you. Mary died this morning. I'm going to be saying the Funeral Mass at the home tomorrow at eleven thirty. Sister and I will be the only ones there. Paul says he can't get away. I thought you might—''

"I'll be there, Sean. Of course, I'll be there."

For the gospel of the Mass in the little pseudo-baroque chapel, Sean chose the story of the resurrection of Lazarus from St. John's Gospel. His homily was brief. "It may seem today that Mary's life was a foolish waste. She lived sixty-five years, and the last forty of those years she did not know who she was, did not recollect anything of her childhood, of her girlhood, of her young adult years, did not remember her family or her friends or those who loved her. She was not, as far as we could tell, lonely, but she was surely alone, a lost soul. And yet, we know that God loved Mary, and that now all the joys of life are part of a bright, glowing joy that will never go pale, never be dimmed, never end for all eternity. There is only one thing we can understand today. God loves Mary, and he loves all of us."

Sean went on with the Mass, lifting the bread and then the wine in offering. The young nun discreetly wiped her eyes. For Nora there were no tears.

Then, suddenly, the Presence, gone for so long, returned. There was no forgiveness, no blame, no lifting of burdens of guilt, no message that at last she was forgiven. Rather, the love that surrounded Nora behaved as though it had never left, chided her gently for not noticing its presence, and enveloped her in caressing and tender warmth. Embraced by such love, Nora realized how irrelevant was forgiveness, how foolish was anger, and how ridiculous was guilt. The part of her that had been numb and dead was alive again, so vital and so happy; the numbness seemed only to have been a very minor part of a faintly disturbing dream she had had long ago.

When Sean put the sacred host in her hands at communion time with the words, "Nora, the Body of Christ," tears finally came, tears of joy for Sean and for herself.

Later, Nora and Sean stopped for lunch in a quiet little restaurant just outside of Libertyville, not far from the seminary at Mundelein. As soon as they had ordered their meal, she said, "Sean, if you can find it in your heart to forgive me, I want to be friends again. I've been a fool these last couple of years, blaming myself for Mickey's death and blaming you . . . well, blaming you for everything. It's ridiculous, and I promise it won't happen again."

"I'd much sooner have you as a friend than as an enemy, Nora. Besides, I'm the one who should be on his knees begging for forgiveness."

She felt her face grow warm. "I want to talk about Italy. . . . I—I loved you then, Sean, and I always will. The terrible physical hunger is gone. I'm sure it won't come back—"

He looked into her eyes. "I'm never going to be so sure of myself again, Nora. So I won't make any promises." His face was transformed by a smile. "But I think you're reasonably safe from me so long as we never go on vacation together again."

They both laughed, the tension eased, and they were happy and even young again.

. . .

Paul felt his fingers tremble as he read the small newspaper clipping that Eric had presented him with in the bar near the Shoreham. "I'm sorry, sir, about this regrettable incident. These things do happen occasionally, and while we assume full responsibility for them, they still cause us a great deal of concern."

The clipping said that Joseph Makuch had been found early that morning dead in his car on Interstate 98, the victim of a heart attack. Mr. Makuch had apparently felt the first pains of the attack, driven his car off to the side of the road, and then died from a massive blockage of the heart artery before he was able to get out of the car and seek help. He was forty-five years old, survived by his widow, Carolyn, and two sons, Arnold and Joseph.

Paul returned the clipping to Eric. "What happened?" he asked.

"The man had a heart condition, sir." Eric frowned. "Apparently an autopsy was done and the pathologist reported that Makuch could have died almost any time within the past year. The usual causes, I'm afraid. Overindulgences in food and drink, too many cigarettes, no exercise . . . a bad way to live."

"And your—er—uh, I mean, your operatives—"

"Merely forced his car to the side of the road and disembarked from their own car. Even in the legal sense, I'm sure they would not be held responsible. Of course there will be no charge, and I can promise you that if in the future you require our services, we will make sure that this does not happen again."

On the way back to his house in Georgetown, Paul wondered what Eric and his "associates" would have done if they had known about Joe Makuch's bad heart. He was shocked by the death of the man who had blackmailed him and exhilarated by the feeling of freedom that the death brought—the first freedom from the fear of exposure that he had experienced in all that time. Too bad Makuch had to die, of course, but Paul felt no guilt over his death. After all, the man had a bad heart. He should have taken better care of himself.

Chapter Thirty-one
1973

IF MIKE CRONIN was surprised that Sean had come to visit him in the morning on the wrong day of the week, he did not show it. Rather, he turned away from the television set and looked at his son blankly.

"Turn it off," Sean said.

One of his father's twisted fingers pushed the button. The picture and the sound died.

"I'll be only a few moments, Mrs. Calloway," he said to the smiling, even-tempered black nurse, who took the hint and left the room.

He turned again to his father. "We buried Mary Eileen yesterday."

A strange, wild light flowed momentarily in his father's eyes. The crippled hand scrawled on the note pad. *"Where?"*

"At the home. She won't be at your side in death any more than she was in life." He turned and walked to the door, fearful that his turbulent emotions would spill out and he would say more than he wanted to say. It was not up to him to punish his father. He had done enough of that already.

As he left the room, he heard the television set click on.

Paul placed the breakfast tray next to Nora on the bed. "Orange juice, bacon, pancakes, coffee . . . you worked up a big appetite last night."

"And you've become quite the cook! The hotcakes look good."

"Out of a package." Paul kissed her forehead.

Nora drew the sheet closer to her throat. For a few moments last night, drugged by wine and loneliness, they had been lovers. It was a deception. It could never work between them. Paul was too much a child. Still, her body was satisfied and Paul was obviously pleased.

"It was wonderful last night." She felt that she owed him a compliment.

He kissed her again. "Maybe we should do it a little more often. I'd like that. . . . Did you see Sean and Dad in Chicago?"

"Only Sean. He absolutely refuses to fight this censure thing."

"Censure?" Paul frowned.

"Hasn't he told you? Some bizarre Spanish order has persuaded a group of cardinals to introduce a censure motion at the bishops' meeting—about his television interview last year."

"He doesn't deserve that!" Paul's voice took on a tone that Nora recognized from their childhood. It was the voice of the older brother ready to defend his younger sibling.

"Can you stop them?"

"I sure as hell can try," he said.

"Best restaurant in Washington." Paul gestured at the dining room of the Lion d'Or. "At this moment I can see two Senators, three other Congressmen, and one Cabinet member . . . some of them are even with their wives."

Sean, feeling pleasantly relaxed after two Irish whiskeys, smiled along with his brother. "And no other bishops, with or without wives."

"I suspect they wouldn't know about the Lion d'Or."

"Oh, some of them would, but they just wouldn't want the others to know they know about it." They laughed again. Then Paul became serious, or rather adopted the facial expression and tilt of his head that, for him, passed for seriousness.

"How's the old man? Every time I come home I mean to go see him, but there's so much of a rush with Nora and the kids and all. . . ."

Sean played with his butter knife. "About the same. I guess he slips a little bit each time I see him, but that's been going on for years now, and I think he has a long way more to slip before he hits bottom. I have no idea what he thinks, what he feels, how he manages to survive."

"It's a shame. I hope nothing like that happens to me."

"I suppose you've heard about my troubles with the cardinals?"

Paul was quickly disposing of his salad. "Yes, I read about it." He was trying to sound casual. "You can't let those bastards do it to you, Sean. Hell, what motivation am I going to have to run for Senator if you're not already Archbishop of Chicago?"

Sean's laugh was hollow. "I'm not going to be Archbishop of Chicago, Paul.

I hereby proclaim the competition over. I'm not going to fight. It's not worth it. I probably deserve censure for a lot more things than that one televison program. Let them do whatever they want.''

"You *have* to fight them, Sean.'' Paul put down his salad fork. "You simply *have* to fight them.''

"I'm not going to fight them. And what's more, I insist that you don't try to fight them for me. Understand?''

Paul swallowed half of his glass of wine in a single gulp, as though it were water to quench his thirst. "Sure, Sean. If you say that I shouldn't fight them, then I won't fight them.''

"So good of you to come to visit me, Congressman,'' said Alfonse Cardinal Michaels. "You understand how very little time we have in Washington, although of course I appreciate your invitation to lunch.''

"Always happy to oblige a Prince of the Church,'' Paul said. The Prince of the Church's suite in the Statler was not especially princely, but it was big, appropriate enough for Michaels, who was a tall, stocky man with iron-gray hair and thick glasses. He was alleged to have one of the lowest golf handicaps in the hierarchy.

"If you're ever in Chicago, Your Eminence,'' Paul said, "I'd like to play golf with you. Perhaps we could persuade my wife to accompany us. She was a junior champion as a young woman. Her handicap is still four, and that's without working on it.''

The Cardinal laughed. "I'm afraid I wouldn't stand a chance against such skill, Congressman, but I might take you up on it sometime. Your brother the Bishop doesn't play golf, does he?''

The first mention of Sean. "He used to play, but he's been so busy being a bishop, with Cardinal McCarthy's illness, you know, that he hasn't played in a number of years.''

"Yes, it's certainly a shame about poor Eamon. He's never had very strong health. He was a couple of years ahead of me at the North American, you know.''

"I certainly hope''—Paul moved quickly now—"that nothing comes of this ridiculous censure motion that's aimed at Sean.''

"Oh, now,'' said the Cardinal, "it really isn't aimed at him.''

"Most people think it is, Your Eminence, and it will put me in a very awkward position.''

"Oh? I don't see why you should be embarrassed.''

"Sean's extremely popular in my district. If the Church censures him, the people in my district are going to demand that I take a stand. I've got enough trouble with this Watergate thing as it is, and I certainly wouldn't want to get into a fight with the hierarchy. But my district wouldn't give me any choice.''

"Is that so?'' The Cardinal seemed interested and sympathetic.

Paul was creating his story out of whole cloth. Sean was indeed popular, but there would be little constituent pressure to denounce the hierarchy for going after him. "I could possibly be put in a position where my people would expect me to take a vigorous stand against everything the Church wanted, from help for Catholic schools to tax exemptions for Church property—that sort of thing. You know, Your Eminence. I'd certainly hate to change my position, especially since my membership on the judiciary committee is so crucial for such issues, but our neighborhood is the kind of place where you stand up for your own or you get out.''

"Are you trying to blackmail me?'' The Cardinal's voice turned cold.

"Yes, Your Eminence,'' Paul said. "That's precisely what I'm trying to do. I'm telling you to leave my brother alone. He doesn't know I'm doing this. Indeed, he explicitly told me not to do anything. He's still my brother, however, and I'm not going to let a bunch of bullies pick on him. Leave him alone, or you'll regret it.''

There was a long pause while the Cardinal's shrewd blue eyes probed into Paul Cronin's soul. Finally the great man spoke. "I've always admired family loyalty, Congressman. I've always admired it very much.''

On the last day of the bishops' meeting, Paul invited Sean to the Monocle Restaurant, a sleek, plush bistro on D Street, around the corner from the Capitol.

"Order the Crab Imperial; they know how to do it here,'' Paul said.

Sean, however, ordered bay scallops and declined the bottle of wine Paul offered. His brother looked disappointed but quickly masked his feelings behind bluff enthusiasm.

"No censure vote after all?''

Sean shrugged indifferently. "I suspect Eamon made a few phone calls.''

"I'm glad it worked out. And sorry you can't stay here until the weekend. Nora's going to be in town, and it would be nice for the three of us to be together again.''

"You two certainly have a peripatetic marriage.''

A tinge of sadness touched Paul's eyes. "It works out well enough. Maybe after the next election she'll be able to shift her base from Chicago to Washington. We have good times when we're together. It takes a long time to be friends, Sean. A long time.'' The last sentence escaped in a burst of candor.

"I'm sure it does.'' Sean felt guilt and anguish. How could Paul and Nora ever be close when Nora carried with her the memories of Amalfi?

"You should have married her.''

"What?'' Sean wished he had accepted the wine.

Paul drained his gin and tonic. "I'm not up to her. She's a woman of substance and depth. She deserves a husband more like you. You should be a politican too. The old man made a big mistake.''

Sean struggled to regain his composure. "I don't know what you're talking about, Paul. You were the star athlete, the war hero, the charmer. I couldn't win a race for precinct captain.''

"It takes more than those things.'' Paul signaled for another drink. "I don't know what to call it—character? Anyway, you'd make a good president, and I might not. You would love Nora the way she ought to be loved, and I can't.'' He waved a hand vaguely. "It's too late to change anything. I'm her husband and I might just end up in the White House. With any luck''—he grinned—''I won't be any worse a president than I am a husband.''

. . .

The Cronins were together at Paul and Nora's home on Christmas Day, all except Mike Cronin, who refused to leave his apartment even to celebrate Christmas. For Nora, it was the best Christmas in years. She and Sean were friends again. Her daughters were safely on their way to young womanhood. And her marriage had settled into an easy and relaxed pattern.

"The daughters" arranged one of their usual performances before the Christmas meal: flute music, Christmas carols, crazy little skits, including a dialogue among the "three old Cronins," with Eileen playing her father, Mary playing a very solemn "Bishop Uncle" and Noreen, of course, playing her mother. Noreen had about half the lines in the miniature drama because she had written the skit.

After the entertainment was finished, Noreen bustled around the room, filling glasses with sparkling burgundy for the six of them. "Now, Mother, a few extra drinks on Christmas aren't going to affect your good looks at all." She giggled, as bubbling herself as the burgundy.

Eileen offered the toast. "To the old Cronins, it's good to have them here with us on Christmas Day. They're really not all that bad, not when you consider how old they are!"

The burgundy was downed with much laughter. It warmed Nora's throat and stomach. She was close to tears. She wished she could preserve the precious moment forever. From now on, she hoped and prayed, everything would go well for the "old Cronins."

Sean Cronin could not sleep. The excitement of Christmas Eve and Christmas Day at the cathedral, the brilliant liturgy, the superb choir, and the fun of Christmas afternoon with his family ought to have left him at peace. Yet for Sean there was no peace. There would never be peace. He tried to make an entry into his journal, but the words would not come.

He closed the notebook and went back to bed. Eileen's toast tormented him. Things *were* very good this day for the three "old Cronins," better than they'd been for a long time. But his mother was in a stranger's grave, and his father was alone, unloving and unloved. Was aloneness, then, the destiny of all the Cronins?

Sean shivered. The interlude of happiness this afternoon was a deception, a trick. For Paul and Nora and himself, he sensed the worst was yet to come.

BOOK EIGHT

Lord, God, you make use of the ministry of priests for regenerating your people. Make us persevere in serving your will that in our days by the gift of your grace the people concentrated to you may increase in merit and numbers through Jesus Christ our Lord. Amen.

PRAYER OF PRIESTLY RECOMMITMENT
HOLY THURSDAY LITURGY

When he had washed their feet and put on his clothes again, he went back to the table. "Do you understand," he said, "what I have done to you? You call me master and lord and rightly so I am. If I, then, the lord and master have washed your feet, you should wash each other's feet. I have given you an example so you may copy what I have done to you."

—JOHN 13:12–15

Chapter Thirty-two
1976

MARCH WAS A wonderful time in Rome. Spring had survived its tentative beginnings and the occasional rains washed away the sour smells of the decrepit, phony old city. Sean didn't even mind the hideously dull meeting of the Commisssion on the Revision of the Code of Canon Law. In fact, he rather enjoyed jousting with Cardinal Pèricle Felici, who was grimly determined to use every trick at his command—and they were many and clever—to undo the entire Vatican Council. From Felici's viewpoint, Sean was a dangerous combination of historical knowledge and pastoral experience. Furthermore, he spoke Latin too well, although not, of course, as well as did the Cardinal, who wrote sonnets in Latin.

In such a fine mood was Sean Cronin that he invited Roger Fitzgibbon to dinner at the Tre Scalini on the Piazza Navona. They drank a toast to their twentieth anniversary in the priesthood, which was only two months away. Roger's carefully groomed hair had vanished, he had put on weight, and the assignment as a delegate, or nuncio, for which he had been hoping had not yet appeared. He confessed, however, that the *Sostitúto,* the famous Under Secretary of State, Archbishop Benelli, had hinted broadly to him that he might well be in the running for a posting to Nairobi later in the year. Sean decided that he would put in a kind word for Roger with Cardinal McCarthy.

"You know, you're on everyone's *tèrna* for Chicago when Eamon steps down." Roger flipped the *spaghetti alla bolognése* around his fork with practiced ease.

"Programmed number three, I hope." Sean sipped his wine.

"Not on Eamon's list. Not on a lot of people's. Benelli clearly likes you—"

"Maybe that's because I blew up at him once and told him he was an arrogant, narrow-minded son of a bitch. Tell you the truth, he seemed to love it. Who are the real candidates?"

"There's some mention of O'Malley from Denver—"

"Oh, my God. He's to the right of Caesar Augustus. He'd destroy Chicago."

"And your old friend Martin Spalding Quinlan." Roger's smile was sly and complacent.

"That's enough to ruin my day." Sean shoved aside his pasta.

But it wasn't Sean's problem, it was Chicago's. If the Holy See sent a despicable little neuter, it was their fault, and God's, not Sean Cronin's.

The week after he returned from Rome, Sean called to make an appointment with the Apostolic Delegate in Washington. The next morning he was among the tens of thousands of people who swarmed into O'Hare International Airport. On the way into that vast, sprawling glass and concrete barn, he encountered Tom and Fiona Shields, the latter pregnant for the second time.

"Off to celebrate mid-Lent in Florida, I bet," said the Bishop.

"From the color of yourself," said the articulate Fiona, "you should be joining us. Or is it one of the rules of your order that bishops have to look gray and haggard all the time?"

"We've been trying to help shoulder the Archbishop's load," Sean admitted.

"Ah, 'tis now that I understand it. We worry about the Cardinal's health, but not about the health of the Bishop. Shame on ye, Sean Cronin. Shame on ye."

Her mocking grin made the Florida sunlight look doubly attractive.

"Is Nicole enjoying working on my brother's campaign?"

Tom's eyes narrowed ever so slightly. The old wounds had been healed, the old angry words forgotten. Yet, as Sean had suspected, Tom clearly did not like Nicole working for her mother's lover. "She certainly seems to enjoy it," he finally said. "And it was good of Eileen to get her the job after she dropped out of college. I'm not sure a political campaign offers quite the stability that Nicole needs—"

"What Nicole needs," Fiona commented, "is a life of her own, Tom, whether you and I like it or not."

"I guess so," Tom agreed. "At least it looks as if she's working for a winning candidate, which means she has a job until next November."

Sean was sorry he had initiated the conversation. He didn't like to discuss Paul with the late Maggie Shields's husband.

Fiona Shields didn't like to either. "And how's the lovely Nora?" she asked.

"Sure, we don't see so much of her any more."

"She's spending more time in Washington now that the two older girls are in college. If Paul's elected Senator, I suppose she'll move there more or less permanently. Oh, that's my plane that's boarding over there. I'd better run." He bade the Shieldses good-bye and hurried into the boarding area for the flight to Washington. He was not happy that Nicole was working for Paul. Paul should have had more sense than to hire her.

As the plane took off, Sean jammed his *Chicago Sun-Times* into the pocket on the seat in front of him and began to struggle through *Humboldt's Gift,* more out of a sense of obligation to keep up with current literature than any enjoyment of the story. After a few pages, he closed it impatiently and reached for the latest spiral notebook in his attaché case.

He had made a momentous decision yesterday before he had phoned the Delegate. It was a decision that was inevitable. He had intended to write something in his journal the night before, but there had been a confirmation and a counseling case in the rectory, and an idiotic letter from Rome about the seminary—a letter that presumed the year was 1910—which had to be answered. When he was finished he was so tired he could barely see the pages of the notebook, so he resolved he would write something on the plane to Washington.

The words were slow in coming.

> *Holy Week is approaching again, a quarter of a century since Paul was missing in action in Korea. I have no more faith now than I did then. I plug along at my work. I have almost no faith in you and now even less in the Church and the priesthood. I have no faith in anyone or anything. What I do is mechanically routine. If only I could believe in something.*

He hesitated and then began again.

> *You refused a sign to your Judean critics who demanded to view a miracle. So I will not ask for a sign. I will rather tell you I need one, I desperately need some sign that you are there and I'm not being a fool.*

The small Beechcraft twin-engine plane dropped out of the clouds somewhere under six hundred feet, vibrated sharply in a wind gust, and then settled into its final approach to the airport. Senatorial candidate Paul Cronin shook himself fully awake. "Rockford?"

"Moline," said Tim Burns, his bright and ambitious young campaign manager. "We changed that last night, remember?"

"Oh," said Paul sleepily. "I remember. Yes."

The bump of the landing awakened the third member of the campaign party, Nicole Shields, who in some vague way was an aide to Burns. "Explain to me again," she said, "why it's necessary to cover seven of these places the week before the primary election even though the polls show us way ahead?"

Nicole was a disturbing presence on the plane. She was dark and tempestuous, the most tantalizing nineteen-year-old Paul had ever known. He wondered if she was sleeping with Burns. Probably. Paul gathered up his notes. He couldn't afford to take that risk. Too much trouble with the Shields family as it was. Besides, as a candidate for the United States Senate, he had to be careful—a girl less than half his age, the daughter of a woman whose family thought she killed herself because of him—that would be the kind of scandal that would finish him off quickly.

As Tim Burns held the umbrella over his head and a chill March wind assaulted his face, Paul helped Nicole out of the Beechcraft. She managed to press her body momentarily against his as she stumbled down the slippery stairs.

Her taunting young flesh sent a stab of sweetness through him. God, he wished he were twenty-six instead of forty-six. He also wished he had not seen Chris

Waverly with her mocking smile among the reporters covering his rally in Chicago the night before.

Congressman Cronin and his two aides huddled together under the umbrella as they walked toward the terminal. The local television crew was waiting for them. "The latest polls show you ahead of Mr. Mitchum by twelve points, Congressman," said an eager television journalist. "Do you have any comment?"

Paul started to quote Richard Daley on the polls and then realized that this was downstate and you didn't quote Daley downstate. "I'd rather have six points after the election," he said, smiling engagingly, "than twelve points before it."

He hoped that Nora did not see the Moline television tape. She might note how close to him Nicole Shields was standing.

"My decision is final, Monsieur l'Archevêque," Sean said to the Apostolic Delegate at his office in Washington. "I am well aware that the Cardinal has submitted his resignation effective on his birthday, September fifth. I also know that he has put my name at the top of the list for his recommended successor."

"But of course he has, Bishop Cronin," said the shrewd, charming French aristocrat who represented the Holy See in the United States. "It is no secret that you have been running the archdiocese and running it very well for the last few years while the Cardinal's health has been poor." The Delegate, as different as day was from night from the usual Italian careerists who came to Washington, had a marvelously effective diplomatic technique of being utterly candid at least half the time and totally secretive the other half.

"Be that as it may, Monsieur l'Archevêque, I do not wish to be considered as a successor. I assume that the Holy See has not taken such a possibility seriously. I am a native Chicagoan, I am too young and too outspoken. While I presume that I am not exactly the winterbook favorite to succeed His Eminence—"

The Gallic eyebrows shot up quizzically. "Winterbook favorite, Bishop Cronin?"

"An American racing term, Archbishop. You see, many months before the three-year-old thoroughbreds are tested in preliminary races, listings are made of their relative potential."

The Delegate made a note on a pad at the enormous desk behind which he was sitting. "Winterbook favorite, very interesting." There was a touch of green on the bushes in the Archbishop's garden. Spring came to Washington early. Spring, Easter . . . Holy Thursday, a time of rebirth, a time of renewed commitments.

"The point, Monsieur l'Archevêque, is that since the Cardinal recommended me as his successor, I feel an obligation to make it clear to you, and through you to the Holy See, if necessary, that under no circumstances will I serve. In the classic words of the American General Sherman, 'I will not run if nominated, I will not serve if elected!' "

"Of this General Sherman, I have heard," said the Archbishop. "He also said 'War is hell,' did he not?"

It was said of the Delegate that he had learned more about America in three months than his predecessors had in seven years. He probably knew more about the Church in America than did many of Sean's colleagues in the hierarchy. "He did, Monsieur l'Archevêque. I hope I have made myself clear?"

The Delegate smiled. "Oh, yes, Bishop Cronin, you have made yourself very clear. I will keep in mind what you have said. I am sure, however, that if the Holy Father should insist, you would be happy to serve."

"This is not a diplomatic visit, Monsieur l'Archevêque," Sean said. "I am not engaged in complicated Irish-American politics. I gave that up a long time ago. I leave that to my brother. You would be well advised to inform the Holy See that under no circumstances will I be Archbishop of Chicago or archbishop of anyplace else."

The Delegate nodded. "But of course I will tell them if you insist, Bishop Cronin." He made another note on his pad. "I may be able to persuade them that you really mean it. However, I must tell you that . . . oh, yes"—he glanced at his notebook again and then laughed pleasantly—"oh, yes, Bishop Cronin, you are surely the winterbook favorite."

"You what?" said Harold Wheaton, one of Washington's auxiliary bishops, that evening while they were eating dinner in the high-ceilinged dining room of the rectory at the bishop's parish, a rectory that was built when Abraham Lincoln was President of the United States.

"I told the Apostolic Delegate to take my name out of the running. I meant it, Harry. I don't want you, or your boss, or any of my friends, or any of your friends, or anybody campaigning for me. If anyone asks why, tell them 'for spiritual and personal reasons.' "

"You're not going to resign from the priesthood, are you?" Harold Wheaton was incredulous.

"No, I'm not thinking of leaving the priesthood."

"What if the choice is you or Quinlan or that old fool O'Malley or some other horse's ass?"

Sean hesitated. "My answer would still be no."

"No one ever said you were an easy man to figure out, Sean. I will pass the word that this is not the usual discreet political tactic. But you know what? I think like every other crazy thing you do in your life, this is only going to enhance your chances of becoming the angel to the Church of Chicago."

Sean sighed. Damned if he did, and damned if he didn't. "They're going to be awfully embarrassed when I turn them down."

Later that evening, in the guest room of Bishop Wheaton's rectory with the street noises of Washington barely audible outside, Sean stared once again at his journal. Nothing to add. He had said no and he meant it. That was that.

The thought of calling Nora, which had been with him since he had awakened in the morning, returned again, insistent, demanding. She was spending most of the time in Washington, having opened up an office in a building just down the street from Lafayette Park. He glanced at his watch: nine thirty.

He dialed the first six numbers of the house in Georgetown, hesitated over the seventh, and then slowly replaced the phone in its cradle.

Chapter Thirty-three
1976

NORA SIGHED IN relaxed contentment. The sun, the sound of the water, the warmth of the beach on a day in late June were the greatest tranquilizers in the world. Ever since she had been brought into the Cronin household, Glendore had been home much more than the house on Glenwood Drive. It was good to be home again. The first year in Washington had been difficult; her fortieth birthday, a husband who was a more tolerable little boy than he used to be, but still a little boy, the difficulties of opening the Washington office for Cronin Enterprises, and her trips around the country and around the world had worn her out.

"Old girl can't take it any more," she said, patting her belly and reassuring herself that it was still presentably flat.

She insisted that July was the month for the family to be at Oakland Beach. Eileen and Mary, students at Notre Dame, *not* St. Mary's—What, oh, what, is the world coming to? thought Nora—were perfectly content to put off summer employment until August. Paul, however, had managed to mess up his schedule so badly that he would only be there for part of the Fourth of July weekend.

She was angry at Paul. It was important that their far-flung family spend some time together. Paul didn't need a junket to Puerto Rico to boost his senatorial image; he was a shoo-in no matter what Jimmy Carter—the likely Democratic candidate—did or said. And subcommittee meetings in Washington in the summertime were ridiculous, especially since, even if he lost the Senate race, Paul would not return to the House of Representatives. Yet he was afraid of being accused of absenteeism, or so he said, so the most he would be in Oakland Beach was for the weekend of the Fourth and perhaps one other weekend at the end of the month.

Paul was running a remarkably intelligent and cautious campaign. Yet every once in a while he did something foolish. It had been only with grave difficulty that she had talked him out of adding South Africa to his tour. He would almost certainly say something wrong there.

Nora begain to anoint her shoulders and back with suntan lotion. Noreen was on the golf course, and the older girls were sailing on the *Mary Eileen*. Another hour of peace and quiet before the three of them came storming in.

The phone next to her on the sundeck rang. "Damn!" she protested. She dropped the suntan lotion as she picked up the phone. "Nora Cronin," she said in her best businesswoman's voice.

"I want to sell the Sears Tower and buy the Merchandise Mart, Mrs. Cronin. Do you think you can act as the broker in the deal for me?"

"Good morning, Monsignor McGuire." She smiled affectionately. "I'm sorry, I've already sold the Sears Tower to someone else. He was a little short Italian who claimed that he worked for the Institute of Religious Works."

"Then you're really in the world of high finance, Mrs. Cronin. Just hang onto your purse when the people from the IOR are around."

"Nonsense, Monsignor. The Chicago Irish are much smarter than Vatican bankers."

"Funny you should mention them, but I need a favor, Nora." Jimmy was suddenly serious. "Can you come down here and take off our hands one utterly exhausted bishop? The man's literally stumbling around, bumping into things, he's so tired. When the Archbishop's resignation is effective in September, he's going to become administrator, and we don't need an administrator who hasn't had a summer vacation."

Nora hesitated, but only for a moment. "Of course, Jimmy. I'll be down there tomorrow morning and give him his marching orders. . . . Is he going to be the next archbishop?"

"Odds-on favorite, but you know Sean. He's told Rome that he absolutely, positively, will not accept the job."

Nora retrieved the fallen suntan lotion with her feet. "And I'm sure he's convinced them he means it."

"Somebody is going to have to tell him to take the job, even if he doesn't want it."

"Who?"

"Come on, Nora Riley Cronin." Jimmy was his carefree, merry self again. "There's only one person who can get away with giving orders to Sean Cronin, and it ain't the Pope."

"See you tomorrow morning, Monsignor."

She unfastened the halter on her swimsuit and rolled over on her stomach. This was the year that she and Sean were going to have to finally sort things out. It wasn't going to be easy. Mary Eileen's death had brought them together again, but there was still an awkward, halting friendship, haunted by unexorcised demons from the past.

"Sean, you look like hell," Nora said. She was standing at the door of the Auxiliary Bishop's office in the chancery skyscraper.

"Nora, I'm busy." He looked up from the desk, frowning at her.

Oh, God, he *was* tired. She had seen faces like that on the old men at the home where Mary Eileen had lived and died.

"You shouldn't come down here without an appointment."

Nora laughed. "Would you look at who's turning into a pompous churchman. Even his own sister can't come into his sacred office without getting permission."

Nora turned to the handsome black woman working in Sean's outer office. "Mrs. Jackson, will you get Monsignor McGuire for me?"

"Yes, ma'am," said Mrs. Jackson. She was no doubt overjoyed to see somebody who would give orders to the Auxiliary Bishop.

"Nora, please. I know I'm tired . . . overworked. . . . I should have called you before, but this morning is just too much. Now if you'll let me get back to work. . . ."

"No way am I going to let you get back to work, Bishop Cronin. Ah, there you are, Monsignor McGuire. I take it the Bishop has a hectic schedule of appointments for the next three weeks even though it's summertime and there are no confirmations or anniversary celebrations?"

"Yes, indeed," said Monsignor McGuire.

"Monsignor McGuire," she said, "cancel them all. The Bishop is leaving with me after lunch to spend the Fourth of July weekend with his family. He will be permitted to return here only when we are ready to certify to you that he will not be a boorish, insufferable ogre. Is that clear, Monsignor McGuire?"

"Absolutely, Your Holiness," Jimmy said. "When they call and ask for Bishop Cronin, we will just say, 'Bishop *who?*' "

She turned to Sean. "Now is *that* clear to you, Bishop Cronin?"

Sean smiled. "Yes, ma'am."

"I'll be in front of the cathedral rectory at one thirty. You be there too. With your golf clubs. Understand?" She gave up trying to hide her maternal smile.

Sean looked younger already. "Yes, Your Holiness," he said.

"Well, am I glad that's settled," Jimmy said. "Vacation for the rest of us begins when we get rid of the boss."

Nora dusted off her hands as though chewing out an overworked bishop was a piece of cake. "Where I am, Monsignor McGuire, *I'm* the boss." To herself she said, Oh, God, Nora, this is going to be a tough one.

It took until the bicentennial weekend for Sean to relax and realize how tired he really was. It seemed that he had been tired ever since he had been ordained twenty years before. St. Jadwiga's, graduate school, the council, the Birth Control Committee, parish work at the cathedral—no time to relax, no time to think, not even much time to pray. No wonder he was a wreck. No wonder even Jimmy McGuire couldn't take him any more and had to have Nora come and drag him off.

The renewal and rededication themes of the bicentennial celebration were a powerful sermon for him. Indeed, he gave a sermon on these themes at a small Mass he said for the Cronins and some of their neighbors on the morning of July Fourth. He talked about tall ships and tall spirits and freedom and hope and recommitment and persuaded himself that it was time to revive his own spirits and renew his own life—he would not work so hard, he would take more time off, he would learn how to pray again.

A tiny voice deep inside of him expressed skepticism.

In the afternoon, while Nora was presiding over the preparation of the festival dinner, Sean and his brother relaxed at the beach. Paul had been thoroughly drubbed on the golf course once again by his youngest daughter.

"It isn't even close any more," he said. "She was twelve strokes up on me yesterday. Today she was seventeen strokes up—not because my game was worse but because the little brat shot a seventy-six."

It was hard to tell whether Paul was proud of his daughter or felt threatened by her.

"Will Nora let her go on the golf tour when she's older?" Sean asked.

"I'm sure she will. Not that it would make much difference. Noreen will do what she wants to do. But, as Nora says, that's one child we'll never have to worry about."

"Amazing how much she's like her mother at the same age," Sean said. He put aside the book he had been reading and tucked it under his beach chair. "A lot more confident, though, not a trace of awkwardness . . . maybe happier."

"Oh, yes, a lot happier," Paul agreed. "She doesn't have Dad around to hound her. You know, little brother, I sometimes think it's a good thing that the old man is out of our hair. He would have made life miserable for the kids."

For a moment Sean seethed. What a damn-fool, stupid, patronizing, unkind thing to say. They were having a spectacular Fourth of July weekend while their father was practically a prisoner in the Hancock Tower, with his nurse and his inevitable television set. Then he realized that Paul was probably right. Michael Cronin would have made his granddaughters' lives difficult. "Dad's slipping," he said. "I don't think it will be much longer now. I hope you get a chance to see him before you go to Puerto Rico."

"Oh, I will. No problem. It's just that my life is so crazy I don't know where I'm headed half the time." Paul shrugged, his shoulders hinting at the enormous burdens carried by a member of the House of Representatives.

"What does that labor convention in Puerto Rico have to do with the senatorial race in November?" Sean was curious. "Are there going to be that many delegates from Illinois?"

"Oh, 1976 doesn't have anything to do with it." Paul waved aside the question and took a swallow from his beer can. "It's '80 and '84 that I have in mind. They invited me to talk, and it's a good place to start building for the future." He blew the foam off his lips.

"You're thinking that far ahead?"

"Yes, though sometimes, to tell you the truth, I'm not sure why. I'd just as soon laze around Oakland Beach all summer with Nora and the kids. However, I'm in the game and I guess I have to play it out."

And a little prudence. The words sprang into Sean's mind, but not to his lips. Although he'd become politically cautious, his brother had, if anything, grown personally more reckless through the years. He drove faster, swung his golf club more fiercely—especially when it was clear his daughter was going to beat him. And he had plunged into the lake for a swim the day before, braving a treacherous undertow and four-foot waves. What was it in Paul that made him court danger?

"What's on your mind?" Paul said. "You suddenly turned serious on me. You thinking about Dad?"

"No. I was thinking about how difficult a politician's life must be."

Paul waved both his arms expansively. "Don't feel too much pity for us. We love the attention, the public eye. Once you're addicted to it, it beats everything, even sex. Anyway, I think I'll have a swim. The little hellcat can't beat me at that. At least not yet." He strolled toward the inviting waters of the lake.

"Be careful," Sean shouted after him, instantly wishing he had swallowed his words.

"Don't worry, I can take care of myself." Paul laughed and dove under a cresting wave.

The next senator from Illinois had put on a little weight, and his muscles were not as hard and taut as they used to be. Yet, even if he was somewhat out of condition, he was a handsome and appealing figure.

The evening before Paul was to leave for San Juan, Nora and the two men in her life dined at the Apricot Restaurant in La Porte and then returned to the balcony overlooking the lake for coffee and Irish Mist. Paul lit a cigarette, Nora put the coffeepot on a small table, humming a Sousa march. The air was humid and still, the lake a black blanket under the stars. Mosquitos and fireflies buzzed around them.

"Don't go to San Juan, Paul," Sean said suddenly. "Stay here for another week. You need the rest. We ought to spend more time together."

Nora fought to hold down her panic. For a moment it sounded like Amalfi all over again.

"Sean's right," she said. "You do look tired. You don't need that talk for your campaign. Besides, you should get a checkup."

Paul laughed. "You're beginning to sound like a worried suburban housewife. I'm fine, never better. I'll see the doc during the August recess. Besides"—he waved his cigarette—"I can't let the union leaders down."

"Don't go," Sean repeated.

"Why not?" Paul was curious.

"I don't really know why not." Sean was deadly serious. "I have a feeling about it, that's all."

Nora had never heard Sean sound so gloomy. "What kind of feeling?" she asked. He was frightening her.

Sean shrugged his shoulders. "I'm being foolish. Forgive me. Exhaustion must finally be catching up."

"Don't worry, Sean," Paul said. "If I'm not here to fight off the terrors, Nora will take care of you."

Chapter Thirty-four
1976

NICOLE SHIELDS HAD persuaded Paul—nagged him, might be a better way of putting it—to leave the hotel and drive to the beach on the west side of the island. It was terribly hot, but there was a breeze coming off the Caribbean and the beach was deserted. Nicole pulled her sweat shirt over her head, undid the bra of her bikini, and ran toward the water. Paul tagged along behind.

Nicole turned to him. "Not afraid of the ocean, are you? Or are you afraid of me?"

Without high heels, she was a small woman: short like her mother but much more slender. Her body had the piquant appeal of an early teenager, but her seductiveness was not so much in her face or figure as in an enormous sexual energy. "A little bit of both," he admitted. She grabbed his hands and drew close to him, pressing his palms against her naked breasts.

"Don't be afraid of me. I won't bite. Or, if I do, you won't mind."

Two years before, Paul would have been tempted. Instead, he said, "Let's go swimming, Nicole. Senatorial candidates don't do it on the beach."

She sulked all the way back to San Juan, puffing nervously on a joint. Ever since Nora had moved to Washington, Paul had been resolutely faithful. He felt he had straightened out his life. It was time to do so. He didn't want any lurking scandals when he made his big move. Moreover, he and Nora seemed on their way at last to becoming friends. He was not going to risk ruining a good thing. He would never understand his wife, but no doubt about it, she would make a wonderful First Lady.

Nicole wasn't worth it.

Sean lay sleepless in his bed. The luminous clock face told him it was two o'clock. He could hear the waters of the lake slapping gently at the beach just below the dark window. Two weeks at Glendore had revived him physically and psychologically. He had not thought about the Church or the priesthood or the archdiocese for more than a few minutes. He had read mystery stories and science fiction—from a seemingly inexhaustible collection that Mary had gathered—swam, water skied, sailed, played golf.

He had no desire to return to the chancery office; to the telephone, the mail, the idiotic letters from Rome, the protestors, and the charismatics; and to all the myriad right-wing and left-wing organizations that demonstrated each day. He did not want to have to attend a committee meeting with a group of bishops ever again—dry, bloodless, unfeeling old men. The rest of his life, as far as he was concerned, should be spent in the peace and undemanding affection of Oakland Beach.

His desire for Nora was as strong as ever, but somehow that no longer seemed a serious problem. Nora was a hostess and a nurse and a friend. The old savage, imperious desire that had shattered his confidence and his self-esteem in Italy, that kind of desire seemed to have died out.

"Getting old, I guess," he told himself. "But if you don't want to be in that bedroom with her down the corridor, how come you're not asleep?"

Nicole Shields carefully injected the hypodermic needle into her vein. Coke was a lot quicker and more spectacular than grass and, everybody said, not nearly as dangerous as heroin. She had been able to find a source in San Juan, recommended by one of her Chicago friends, who guaranteed that San Juan coke was "pure as the driven snow."

She injected the coke slowly, carefully. She wasn't hooked on cocaine and didn't intend to be, nor did she want her arm to be marked by scars. Life was too much fun to do yourself in that quickly. But she had something to celebrate. After his speech tonight he would come to her room, and by the next morning she would own him. And then she would destroy him, just as he had destroyed her mother. She would make her affair with him public, and he would lose everything: his wife, his kids, his seat in the Senate, his future.

Ecstasy started to flow through her veins like a tropical river at flood tide, and she forgot about her mother and Paul Cronin and everything else.

There was a knock at the door. She said blissfully, "Come in."

It was Helen Colter, another junior staff aide to the Congressman. Helen was four years older than Nicole, plain and prudent. She looked disapprovingly at the sight of Nicole spread out on the bed in her underwear. "Have you made copies of the speech?" she asked.

"There . . . on the chair." Nicole's voice was languorous. "Would you like some cocaine? There's nothing in the world like it."

"No, thank you." Helen shook her head in irritation and picked up the stack of speeches.

"Well, there's nothing like it—'cept screwing a future United States senator."

"What would you know about that?"

"By tomorrow morning, honey"—she smiled sweetly—"I'll know everything there is to know about it."

Nora was trying unsuccessfully to read *Trinity*. The air-conditioning system installed after Glendore was built had broken down. The night air was sullen and humid. She had thrown open the windows in her bedroom, but her red, white, and blue bicentennial sleep shirt—a present from her daughters—was soaked with perspiration.

She shifted uneasily on her bed and put aside her reading glasses. Something had to be done about Sean. When she had sailed so blithely into the chancery at the behest of Jimmy McGuire, she was confident that a few weeks of rest would rehabilitate him and give them both a chance to exorcise all the demons of the past. It would be easy, she thought, to straighten things out with him once and for all.

Now, after having him around the house for three weeks, it did not look simple at all. Sean obviously adored her. Her own response to the quiet pain in his eyes was every bit as powerful as it had been in Italy. She had overestimated her maturity.

Yet Nora was afraid to clear the air, afraid that if she opened the door to discussion, her weakness would lead her to an even greater surrender than Amalfi. And perhaps on a deeper level she was more afraid that her strength would rule out the possibility of any such surrender in the future.

There was a soft knock on the door. "Come in," she said, her heart thudding against her chest.

It was Sean, of course. Trim and solid in a T-shirt and swimming trunks. "I thought you'd be awake. I can't sleep either. Want to try a swim?"

She almost said yes, then realized that the beach might be even more dangerous than her bedroom. "I don't think so," she said. "Too much exercise today for an old body."

The thin drapes stirred restlessly on a draft of air.

"Presentable enough body as far as I can see," he said. "Hey . . . do you want a drink?"

She wanted one desperately. It would be a mistake. Her defenses would be shattered if she had any alcohol in her. "A martini would be wonderful," she said.

While she waited for his return she tried to banish the memories of the hotel room in Amalfi. Same thing all over again. Her body, beyond her control, began its relentless preparations for sexual union. "I can't do it," she moaned under her breath. "I won't." But the stirrings she felt made her not at all sure that she wouldn't. She ought to get out of bed, put on a robe, join Sean in the parlor.

Instead, she lay on the bed, her palms pressed against the damp sheet, as though she were paralyzed.

The pitcher contained only enough for two martinis. Sean was deceiving himself as much as she was.

He sat on the far edge of the king-size bed, the blue sheets an ocean separating them. "To the next First Lady."

"You mean to Rosalyn?" she joked.

"Do you want the job?" Sean was serious.

"I like Washington. I like being a congressman's wife. I think I'll like being a senator's wife. After that, I don't know."

Sean sipped his drink and leaned toward her. "What's in it for you, Nora?"

"There are a lot of payoffs," she said uneasily.

"And you're happy?" He leaned back on his arm, one tightly knuckled hand depressing the edge of the bed.

She wet her lips. "Yes. Sometimes more than others."

"I love you, Nora," he said, his voice gentle. "I always will."

"I love you too, Sean. Of course I do. . . ." She tried to sound matter-of-fact. It came out a sigh.

Then he came around to her side of the bed and, prying the glass from her fingers, took her in his arms. He was a natural lover, knowing by instinct what to do just as he had ten years before. Gently he slid her shirt up and began to caress and kiss her body. She felt as though she were floating on a cloud of tenderness. Another few seconds and it would be too late. Neither of them would be able to stop.

As though returning from a faraway galaxy, she pushed his hands aside. "I don't think so, Sean,'' she murmured in a voice she hardly recognized. ''If we don't stop, we'll lose each other for the rest of our lives.''

He pulled back, jolted to his senses. ''I'm sorry. I don't know what happened. . . .''

With as much modesty as she could summon, she rearranged her shirt with trembling hands. ''Come on, Sean, we both know what happened.'' She would try to get control of herself by being the efficient administrator.

''I'll leave right away,'' he said. ''Drive back to Chicago tonight.'' He was almost to the door. Running away.

''You'll do no such thing,'' she said. ''You'll sit down, and then we're going to have the talk we should have had a long time ago.''

She sat up straight, her back against the headboard. ''What happened in Amalfi was the natural consequence of all of our lives. It had to be. . . . You can handle it under your moral theology—the circumstances took control over us, robbed us of our freedom. . . .''

Sean laughed bitterly. ''Nora Riley Cronin, moral theologian. Well, I think I'll go along with your opinion, Professor Cronin.''

Nora relaxed. She was certain she would be able to handle the situation now, to establish boundaries where there were no boundaries.

''You know I'll always love you, Sean. But we both have other commitments, commitments we're not going to turn our backs on. I'll be your mother, your sister, your friend, your inspiration, but I won't be your mistress, because that would mess you up and it would mess me up, and it would mess up my family, and it would mess up your Church.''

''Maybe I really came here tonight, Nora, to hear you say those things more than to make love to you.''

''Can you live with this kind of love, Sean?''

''I'm going to have to learn to, aren't I?'' he murmured.

Both the Cronins were really little boys, she thought, each needing her. Fair enough; she would mother them both, each according to his needs, keep her fingers crossed, and leave the rest to God.

Then, without warning, the Presence was there, enveloping the two of them, caressing, encouraging, reassuring. You never told me it was to be this way, Nora silently chided the Presence.

Rarely did the Presence say anything. Rather it absorbed, bathed, and soothed her. Tonight, however, it laughed. Not a sardonic laugh; rather it laughed at her the way she often laughed at Noreen when that teenage tomboy did something particularly wonderful.

Everyone, sighed Nora, wants to be a mother. Even you.

Esteban Muñoz was the best journeyman electrician in all of San Juan. There was not an electrical problem in the entire sky-high Barrington Hotel on the beach in San Juan that Esteban could not solve before the sun had set, and it was a very bad electrical engineer who designed that hotel's wiring.

Unfortunately for Esteban's peace of mind, the chief electrician at the hotel, for whom Esteban was forced to work, a certain José Alvarez, was jealous of Esteban's greater skills, for if the management at the Barrington should ever find out that Esteban did all the work and José took all the credit, they would fire José and give Esteban the job he deserved—chief electrician at the Barrington.

Esteban took it for granted that there would be some harassment, but the harassment was especially heavy when the labor leaders were in San Juan; the hotel wished to prove that even though its workers did not belong to a union they could keep a modern hotel running efficiently.

All day Esteban ran from broken lamps to dead outlets to nonfunctioning air-conditioning units to disturbed television sets. Finally, late in the afternoon, on the very top floor, he discovered a loose wire at the end of the corridor. He was busy soldering and taping it when José came upon him and screamed many terrible curses. There were three air-conditioning units not functioning properly on the second floor. The loose electrical wire could wait; if it had not caused a fire before today, then it would not cause one today.

Esteban protested, but to no avail. He would be fired if he did not repair the air conditioners immediately. He hastily taped the dangling wire, closed the panel in the wall, and then, at the end of the corridor, flipped up the master switch for that floor.

Before he went home that night, however, Esteban stopped at the office of Señor Manuel Ramirez, the assistant general manager of the hotel, and warned him in the presence of his own good friend, Humberto García, that there were dangerous wires on the fifteenth floor that ought to be fixed.

Señor Ramirez was upset with Esteban. He told him that he knew he was only trying to obtain overtime pay for the weekend. He ordered Esteban out of the office and warned him that on Monday morning he would discuss his future at the hotel with Señor Alvarez.

Long before Monday morning, however, Esteban would thank the Madonna that he had had the presence of mind to bring Humberto García into Señor Ramirez's office when he made his complaint. It was the wisdom of the Madonna, he would tell his wife María Isabel, that protected him from perhaps going to jail and guaranteed him employment at the Barrington Hotel for as long as he wished it.

The labor leaders and their wives had been well dined and well wined. Paul Cronin realized that his role was as much entertainment as politics. He also understood that even if the labor barons and baronesses did not remember a single word he said, it was still important that he impress them as being a likable, promising, very pro-union member of the Congress of the United States.

The union leaders were not interested in practical programs. They were interested in stirring words and energetic visions, a repetition of the old rallying cries tempered by the new common sense. Paul gave them exactly what they wanted. The old Irishman who was the president of the union bellowed to the audience at the end of Paul's speech, "This is the best goddamned politician I've heard since John Kennedy talked to us in 1958."

Paul modestly disclaimed such a compliment, but he nevertheless spent forty-five minutes accepting the congratulations of the assembly. He noted how many handshakes were gnarled and rough from long years of manual labor. His father's old cliché that the labor bosses had never done an honest day's work did not seem to be true after all.

In the elevator ride to the fourteenth floor, Paul's spirits soared. He was enormously pleased with himself. The unions and the city organization would be a strong political base. Yes, indeed, it had been a very good night's work.

Estéban Muñoz had discovered the loose electrical wire on the fifteenth floor just as it became dangerous. The insulation around the wire had eroded through the years until it was little more than a live wire loose within the wall between the corridor and room 1502, a room that remained unoccupied during the convention. If Muñoz had been permitted to finish his work, there would have been no danger of fire. But he had not, and now sparks from the fire had already started to smolder in the wall.

Paul tossed his coat on the chair in the parlor of his suite, opened the small refrigerator, put some ice cubes in a tumbler, and half filled the tumbler with whiskey. He loosened his tie and took a hearty swallow of the drink. Then he noticed a piece of paper that had been slipped under the door. He picked it up and glanced at it. *I'm in room 1510 and waiting. N.*

He rolled the note into a ball and tossed it into the wastebasket. A stupid little girl, sending a note like that.

He hung his jacket in the closet and sat down on the couch. Ten thirty in San Juan, nine thirty in Chicago. Still time to call Nora.

That's what he would do, he would call Nora. He would not go up to room 1510. That would be a ridiculous thing to do. He dialed the long-distance operator and gave her the number. The line at Glendore was busy. He hung up, drummed his fingers on the telephone table, then rose, went to the closet, put on his jacket, and walked out to the corridor.

As Paul was leaving the elevator on the fifteenth floor, Helen Colter entered it. Politely he held the door for her. "Wonderful speech tonight, Senator," she said.

"Let's not anticipate the wishes of the people of the state of Illinois, Helen," he said. "But thanks for the compliment anyway."

Helen flushed slightly and then smiled in response to his engaging boyish grin, a grin that seemed to be especially effective with unattractive girls like her.

Paul hesitated. Could Helen have guessed where he was going? But what difference would that make? She was too devoted to him to blab about it. And she certainly wouldn't tell Nora.

He knocked on 1510, and a dreamy voice said, "Come in; it's open."

Nicole Shields was stretched out invitingly on the bed, her childish body available, a languid smile on her face. It was, he told himself, a face that would not be pretty for nearly as long as her mother's had been.

She was a much more intense and inventive lover than her mother, however, and the Congressman enjoyed himself thoroughly. A flaky kid with enormous energy and kinky ways. Nothing serious, just a little bit of entertainment on a hot summer evening in San Juan, Puerto Rico.

It was only after their lovemaking was finished that Paul realized how high his partner was. "What have you been taking?" he asked her, half asleep.

"A little coke, a couple of pills, that's all," she mumbled.

Then they both were asleep.

The smell of the smoke from the fire at the other end of the corridor had teased Paul's nostrils for many precious minutes before he finally struggled

awake and realized there was a fire someplace. He turned on the light. Smoke
was seeping under the door. He jumped out of bed, rushed over and felt the
door. It was hot; a fire in the corridor. Smoke inhalation was the danger: He
must soak a towel with water, wrap it around his face, and make a dash for the
exit stairway.

He pulled on his clothes and, with shoes untied, dashed into the bathroom,
soaked four towels, two for him, two for Nicole. Then he hurried back to the bed
where she lay peaceful and complacent, in the afterglow of lovemaking.
He shook her roughly. "Come on, Nicole, wake up! This damned place is on
fire!"

There was no reaction. He shook her again and yet again. Then he remembered what she had said about coke and pills.

"Oh, my God!" he exclaimed. "She's out. I'll have to carry her." He lifted
her up and was surprised at how light she was, nothing but an innocent and
bedraggled little child. He staggered toward the doorway and heard the crackle
of flames in the corridor.

Then he was in the Reservoir again and the Chinese were attacking. He heard
not the wail of the fire sirens but the screaming of the charging enemy. He saw
not the wall of the room glowing red, before it burst into flames, but the flares
breaking the night darkness above the cold waters of the Reservoir.

In his terrified imagination he saw himself running down the stairwell with a
naked drugged-out nineteen-year-old girl in his arms. It would be the end of
everything, everything he had worked for all his life.

Without any hesitation he threw the unconscious girl back on her bed, wrapped
the towels around his face, yanked open the door of room 1510 and, body bent
over, ran desperately for the stairs as the flames seemed to race along the corridor
in pursuit of him.

On the fourteenth floor, people were emerging from their rooms, frightened,
confused, uncertain what to do, and already beginning to cough from the smoke.
Congressman Cronin took charge of the fourteenth floor, since many members of
his staff were on it, and with cool efficiency organized its evacuation.

Chapter Thirty-five
1976

AT SEVEN O'CLOCK in the morning Nora was awakened in her bedroom at
Oakland Beach by the telephone. "What's wrong?" she asked when she heard
Paul's voice. She was suddenly tense.

"Everything's all right," he reassured her. "I wanted to call you before
someone else did or before you heard it on the news. There was a fire here at the
hotel last night. The upper six stories were burned out. They managed to evac-
uate everyone and there don't seem to be any fatalities—some people in the
hospital with smoke inhalation, that's all."

"You're sure everyone's all right?" Nora was shaking her head to make sure
she really was awake.

"Everyone's fine. They even think I'm a hero. The floor I was on was the one
that was in the most danger. I helped get everybody out."

"Oh, Paul, I'm so glad you're okay."

"Well, I am too," he said. "I'll call you again later and let you know how things are."

The seven-thirty news on the *Today Show* showed pictures of the upper stories of the Barrington Hotel, blazing red against the Caribbean sky. It also carried interviews with a number of guests in the hotel, most of them union leaders and their families, praising Congressman Paul Cronin for his quick thinking and his cool nerve under pressure. Thank God I wasn't there, Nora said to herself. I'm sure I would have panicked.

She was making herself a second cup of coffee when Eileen, deathly pale, joined her in the kitchen.

"Nothing to worry about, Eileen," Nora said. "Dad's all right. He just called. Everyone escaped from the hotel alive."

"Not everyone, Mom. I just heard a special report. They found Nicole's body in a room on the fifteenth floor."

The evening news showed a grief-stricken Congressman Cronin discussing the tragedy of Nicole Shields's death. "She was so young, so energetic, she had such a wonderful figure. I can't help but hold myself in some way responsible for her death."

Then the anchorman was on the television screen looking like a slightly prosperous undertaker. "Late word from San Juan indicates a probable reason why Nicole Shields did not escape from her room on the fifteenth floor. The medical examiner reports that she had taken a heavy dose of cocaine and amphetamines and was unconscious when the fire engulfed her room. The fifteenth floor of the Barrington Hotel was almost entirely unoccupied. The only other person with a room on that floor was another member of Congressman Cronin's campaign staff, who was fortunately in the coffee shop at the time of the fire."

Tears came easily to Paul at Nicole's funeral, although he did not bother to ask himself for what he was weeping. It was too bad Nicole had to die, but so far everything else had gone well. He had been the first to notice that Nicole was missing after the sun rose over the Caribbean. He had raced up to her room with one of the San Juan Police Department inspectors. Together they had discovered the body lying on what was left of the bed in the smoke-blackened room. Paul's nausea at the stench and smell were authentic enough. He had insisted on staying with the body while the police inspector went downstairs for medical personnel. This gave him time to look around the room for the one article of clothing he had forgotten the night before. He found his necktie half under the chair cushion, stuffed it into his pocket, and waited for the police to return.

The only things that unnerved him during the difficult day were the presence of Chris Waverly at the press conferences and the strange expression on Helen Colter's face. Chris had come to the convention to cover his speech. Her presence always unsettled him, and he was shaken by her whispered comment. "You're a hero again, huh, lover boy? Whenever you're a hero, other people seem to die."

Helen was harder to figure out. She seemed to be watching him uncertainly, as though wondering if he knew something more about Nicole's death. Well, she could not prove that he had ever been in Nicole's room at all, much less that he had stayed there until the fire had spread. Still, she had seen him on the fifteenth floor. If she should take a notion to talk to anyone. . . .

The grand ballroom of the Midland Hotel in Chicago was filled with a laughing, expectant crowd. It was obvious to Sean that everyone knew Congressman Paul Cronin would win an overwhelming victory. The totals on the giant blackboard on the stage showed a lead that was increasing every minute. The prediction of a 450,000-vote victory now seemed reasonable.

Sean did not want to be on the platform with the Senator-elect and his family. The suggestion of a union between Church and State in such a tableau did not seem appropriate. He was happy, nonetheless, about Paul's victory, happy especially for Nora and the kids, who had worked hard during the final six weeks of the campaign.

Nora's preoccupation with the election did not deter her from her new project of rehabilitating Sean. He grinned wryly—discreetly tailored suits ordered for him by Nora, lunch once a week, a new-style haircut about which he was given little choice.

Superficially, he felt more at ease, but his deep bafflement was not resolved. He was drifting closer to resigning from the priesthood. Yet he laughed more and slept better and found that a smile came more quickly to his lips. Not only Jimmy McGuire but the younger priests on the chancery office staff kidded him when he became moody and melancholy. "Isn't it about time you had lunch with Nora again?" one of them would say.

Sean recalled the occasion when, during his last visit to Rome for a meeting of the Ecumenical Committee to which, for some obscure reason he did not comprehend, he had been appointed, he had supped with the Alessandrinis. They were as handsome as ever with their jet-black hair, now dusted with fine white snowflakes. "Can you imagine, càro mio," protested the Principessa, "I now have two daughters in their late teens who wear jeans and T-shirts and chew gum and listen to rock and roll and talk like Americans?"

"Black nobility who talk like Americans!" said Sean. He was trying to get used once again to Campari and soda.

"You will, of course, be the next Archbishop of Chicago. Everyone in Rome says it. There is no doubt about it."

"I will not be the next Archbishop of Chicago," he said forcefully. "In fact, I'm probably going to leave the priesthood."

Francésco seemed dismayed, but Angèlica merely smiled knowingly. "You and Montini will do so on the same day, càro mio."

The thought had become more precise and more demanding in the months since that quiet evening off the Piazza Farnese. He had no idea what he would do after he left the priesthood, but resignation seemed to be the only way out of the agonizing dilemma that now beset him. Nora's kindness had opened to him the possibility of a life free from the burden that he had known since ordination. There were other things a man could do besides mediate conflicts between pastors and curates, attend insipid committee meetings, and screen stacks of complaining letters that seemed to get higher every day. Sean demanded a sign. If one didn't come quickly, he would leave the priesthood. Indeed, if they tried to force the archbishopric upon him, that would be enough of a negative sign and he would certainly leave.

There was a tumultuous ovation as Senator-elect Paul Cronin emerged on the platform with his family.

Chris Waverly listened to Paul's victory statement with wry amusement. Her resentment toward the new Senator had long since ebbed. Chris could carry a grudge for longer than most people, but living for vengeance was ridiculous. She occasionally hung around the Cronin campaign because of a vague, unspecified hunch that there was something just a little bit missing in Paul Cronin. There was no substance at the center of him. Someday he might provide a story. As the senatorial campaign progressed, however, Chris wondered if perhaps she was wrong. Paul Cronin had matured and run a careful, intelligent, neatly calculated campaign. His response to the tragedy in the Barrington Hotel had been, in fact, precisely the proper mixture of grace and sadness. Yet there was a tiny pinprick of doubt that would not go away.

"One final word," said the handsome, triumphant Senator-elect from the podium. "There is one person not here today whom we all miss and who should share the credit for our victory. I'm sure that in that land of happiness to which we all hope to go, Nicole Shields is celebrating with the rest of us."

The applause was again enthusiastic. As Chris turned to leave the ballroom, she noticed one of the young women on the Senator's staff. The girl's face was taut with a mixture of grief and anger. Tears were flowing down her cheeks.

"Something wrong, kid?" asked Chris sympathetically.

"The hypocritical sonofabitch," Helen Colter said. "He was in bed with Nicole when that fire started."

Tom Shields had agreed to see Chris Waverly only because she insisted she had something of personal importance to tell him. His hands trembled as he read the typed copy of her interview with Helen Colter that she had handed him without a word. "He killed them both," he said faintly. "He killed my wife and my daughter."

"Your wife too?"

"My wife too. He used Maggie as a convenience and broke her heart in the process. She attempted suicide more to gain his attention than anything else. The last time she left a note, not for me but for him."

Chris's head was whirling. "Do you have that note, Dr. Shields?" she asked gently.

"No." His response was bitter. "I gave it to his brother, Bishop Cronin, and he destroyed it."

"I see. How can you be sure then that they had an affair?"

Shields walked over to the wall, shoved aside the picture, spun the combination on a wall safe, and took out a leather-bound book. "She kept a diary. I found it among her things long after the funeral. Just like Maggie to forget about the diary. It records in very considerable detail her escapades with Paul Cronin."

"I see." Chris asked to see the diary.

"It's all yours," Tom Shields said. "Here, take the damn thing, do whatever you want with it."

"Are you sure, Dr. Shields? You and your wife and your other children might get hurt."

"I don't give a goddamn," Tom exploded. "I'm sick of Paul Cronin. It's time somebody exposed him for what he is."

The night he was sworn in as a member of the United States Senate, Paul Cronin woke up screaming. Nora put her arms around him and crooned softly and sweetly. Her power to exorcise Paul's terrible nightmares seemed to be waning. Now the Chinese attack at the Reservoir and the burning of the Barrington Hotel had blended into one nightmare, and the pain of the imagined Chinese bayonet in his stomach haunted him during the day as well as at night.

It took Paul a long time to calm down. And then, exhausted and breathing heavily, he finally relaxed in her embrace. "God, it's terrible, Nora," he whimpered.

"I don't understand it, Paul. Both in Korea and in San Juan you saved people's lives. Why do you have the nightmares? Maybe you ought to see someone."

"That wouldn't do any good." He laughed weakly. "There isn't all that much difference between a hero and a coward, you know. It would have been so easy to panic in both those situations."

"The dreams are an alternate scenario?" she asked.

"Something like that."

Nora was worried about Paul's dreams. If he wouldn't go for help, maybe she should.

"You're suggesting, Mr. Connors," Chris Waverly said, "that Senator Cronin may have ordered the execution of Joe Makuch?"

Chris had spent an exhausting few weeks tracking down Paul Cronin's old Marine Corps buddies. After reading Maggie's diary and interviewing Helen Colter, it was a short jump to the conclusion that the nightmares Paul used to have about Korea could be related to yet another skeleton hiding in his rapidly filling closet. It had not been hard for her to find Steven Connors in Atlanta and to check out his background and credentials.

Now, sitting in the cool, crisp, modern office of the Connors Construction Company, she knew she had hit the jackpot.

"I knew Makuch was blackmailing Paul," the handsome black man said. "He bragged to me about it. I didn't approve, mind you, but it was none of my business. Anyway, I figured that Cronin owed somebody something after running out on us at the Reservoir and then getting a Medal of Honor for it."

"That doesn't prove that he had Makuch killed. The autopsy showed that he died of a heart attack."

"I can't prove it, exactly. But Makuch called me the morning he died and said he was sure there were people following him. He said there had been a strange look in Paul's eyes the last time he paid the blackmail money to him."

"Are you willing to testify that Makuch told you that Senator Cronin had paid blackmail to him for twenty years?"

"Yes, I'm willing to say that," said Steven Connors. "I'm reluctant to do it. I don't want the publicity. But if Paul has his eye on the presidency . . . he's a coward, a phony, a hypocrite. I could not—I simply will not let him preside over a country in which my children and grandchildren must live."

"Thank you very much, Mr. Connors. You're a brave man."

"Or a coward for waiting so long. You *will* get him, Miss Waverly?"

"Oh, don't worry about that. I'll get him, all right."

Chapter Thirty-six
1977

ON A FRIDAY in the middle of Lent in 1977, Bishop Sean Cronin granted an off-the-record interview to Chris Waverly. He had no particular desire to see her. Her reputation was that of an able but acid-penned investigative reporter. Sean was afraid that she might have somehow found out about him and Nora and intended to use that information to embarrass Paul. Moreover, the tension of waiting for the appointment of a new archbishop—long delayed—was beginning to tell on his nerves and that of all the priests in the chancery and the diocese.

"Yes, Miss Waverly," he said. "How can I help you?"

Chris Waverly's hair had obviously been touched up to keep it blond. She was a hard-looking woman, yet still attractive. "I'll be blunt, Bishop. I have enough information about your brother to have him expelled from the United States Senate. Moreover, I have information that you have cooperated with him in at least one of his escapades, sufficient information, I should tell you, to frustrate any plans you might have of becoming the next Archbishop of Chicago."

"I believe that's a technique used by investigative reporters called 'intimidate them with the first question.' I don't intimidate, Miss Waverly."

"Intimidation or not, Bishop, I can destroy you."

"No, you can't. Nothing can destroy me. I am not interested in being Archbishop of Chicago. I intend to refuse the appointment if it's offered to me. If it is forced on me, I will resign from the priesthood. Now where does your intimidation get you?"

Chris Waverly regarded Sean intently. "Do you deny that you persuaded Dr. Thomas Shields to give you the farewell letter his wife wrote to your brother? Do you deny you destroyed that letter?"

"Of course I don't deny it. Why should I? It was an embarrassing letter for all concerned. Tom didn't have the heart to destroy it, so I did for him."

"Do you deny that your brother had an affair with Maggie Shields?"

"I am not privy, Miss Waverly, to my brother's sex life. I don't believe a word of what you say, but I certainly have no proof that it's not true."

"Do you deny that your brother was in bed with Nicole Shields when the fire in the Barrington Hotel started? And that he paid blackmail for twenty years to a man named Makuch who knew he had been a coward and not a hero in Korea?"

"That's absurd. Let's end this interview, Miss Waverly." Sean stood up. "I can see no useful purpose in continuing it."

"You're different from Paul, Bishop," Chris said. "You may be an honorable man and be telling the truth. I'm not sure. But your precious brother is in very

hot water, and unless you're careful you're going to be in hot water with him."
She extended a business card. "Here's my card. Please call me if you change
your mind."

"Get out," Sean said quietly. Chris Waverly shrugged and dropped the card
on the floor as she left his office.

Seething with anger, Sean picked up the card, tore it in two, and threw it in
the wastebasket. Then, after a few moments of brooding anger, he fished the
pieces out of the basket, stared at them grimly, and put them together with
Scotch tape.

"Jimmy." He buzzed the chancellor's office. "See if you can keep the world
away from me for a few hours. I have to make a trip to Washington. And, by the
way, it has nothing to do with who will be your next archbishop."

Paul paced nervously back and forth in his office in the Senate Office
Building. Outside the window, the great dome of the Capitol stood as a
reminder that this was the seat of what was surely the most powerful legislative
body in the world.

"Chris Waverly has had it in for me for years. Wanted to sleep with me a long
time ago. I turned her down, of course, and she's never forgiven me."

"She waved a diary at me, Paul. Said it was Maggie's, and that it had the
details of your love affair."

"Tom Shields wouldn't give her a book like that, even if it were true and even
if Maggie had kept such a record."

"She says that you were in bed with Nicole the night of the hotel fire." There
was steel in Sean's voice.

Paul dismissed the charge with a wave of his hand, but his eyes were dancing
randomly, nervously.

"She does know one true thing." Sean pushed on relentlessly. "She knows
that Tom gave me Maggie's farewell letter to you and that I destroyed it."

"So much the worse for you, little brother." Paul grinned crookedly. "Chris
is a bitch. She might just do a story based on that one fact and hint about a lot
of other things. It will stir up a little trouble for a day or two, and then it will be
forgotten. Anyway, you keep saying you don't want to be Archbishop of Chicago."

"Even if a quarter of what she says is true, you can imagine what it will do
to Nora and the kids."

"Oh, the hell with Nora and the kids," Paul said. "I don't need this sort of
thing just at the beginning of my career in the Senate. And I'm not going to have
it. You can count on it, little brother. Not a word of this is ever going to appear
in print."

"How are you going to stop it, Paul?"

"Just don't worry about it. I'll take care of everything."

Sean saw his brother clearly for the first time. Every charge Chris had made
against Paul was probably true. He stood up, wanting to escape from the office
as quickly as he could. There was an evil in his brother that amazed and frightened him.

.   .   .

As soon as Sean left the office, Paul punched a number into the telephone. "Eric? I wonder if we could get together this afternoon. It's similar to a matter we discussed last year."

"Of course, sir. We're always happy to oblige."

At National Airport, Sean stood staring at the bank of telephones, oblivious to the people streaming by him. Chris Waverly was a bitch. She had raked up a scandal that would destroy not only Paul but Nora and the children. Yet her charges were probably true. In any event. . . .

He walked to the telephones, waited until one was vacant, went inside the booth, and closed the glass door.

"Yes?" Chris Waverly said.

"Bishop Cronin, Miss Waverly. I must apologize for not believing you the other day. I hope you won't go ahead with the story. Too many innocent people are going to be hurt. I think I can promise you that Paul will step down after his first term in the Senate, and that he will never run for the presidency. Be that as it may, however, until you make a definite decision or until you've finished writing the story and have it in the hands of your editor, I suggest you disappear from sight and that you disappear with very effective security precautions."

"Is that a threat, Bishop?" Her voice was hostile.

"No, Miss Waverly," Sean said wearily. "It is not a threat. I don't especially like you or what you're doing, but I don't want any accident you may suffer on my conscience."

"I see." There was a pause on the other end of the conversation. "Very well, Bishop. I'll take your advice. You *are* different from your brother."

Sean staggered away from the telephone booth like a man who had been on an all-night drunk.

Paul poured himself a second drink with an unsteady hand. He had come to Chicago the day before. He felt more secure here. Would the damn telephone never ring? There would be little peace or relaxation for him until he received a confirmatory phone call from Eric. He could not imagine the reason for the delay.

Finally, the phone rang and Paul jumped at it.

"This is Eric. I'm sorry to disturb you at home."

"Goddammit, man, it's all right. What's happening? Why the delay?"

"We're doing the best we can, sir," Eric said. "We just have not been able to resolve the matter. Our team can't find the person in question. We'll continue to look, of course."

Paul felt his muscles and bones melt. It was over. The story would appear any day, and a quarter century of his efforts would have been wasted. "Keep on trying. It's a matter of life and death," he said.

"Of course, sir. Of course we will. I'll be back in touch with you, as soon as I have something to report."

Paul wished that the Chinese bayonet had really found his gut on the hillside by the Reservoir. Like a man in a dream, he walked out of the study and down the steps and away from the house.

A rainstorm accompanied him from Chicago to Oakland Beach. He drove recklessly, ignoring the speed limit and the slippery road. What difference would a speeding ticket make now? He drove by the white gate at Oakland Beach and on to the New Albany Marina. He would take out the *Mary Eileen* and sail away from all his problems.

The marina was deserted, only a few boats were in the water in early April. The *Mary Eileen* was rarely used before the kids arrived in June, but there were standing orders of twenty years' duration that it was to go into the harbor on the first day of spring.

He started the motor, backed out of the slip, and flipped on the weather radio. The prediction was for strong winds following the rainstorm.

The lake was smooth and there was almost no wind when he cleared the harbor mouth. He unfurled the jib, ran up the mainsail, and turned off the motor. The wind would be from the northeast. Why not make a straight run for Chicago? It was a strong boat, actually the fourth to bear the name, twenty-eight feet of solid fiberglass and carefully constructed rigging and masts. Comfortable, too. It could sleep six, although as far as he knew no one had ever spent the night on it.

He thought briefly of the nights he and Nora had spent together over the years. He was sorry he had not been kinder to Nora.

Then he admitted to himself that he had driven up to the lake so recklessly because he wanted to die. But wasn't that ridiculous? Why die when Eric could be calling that very minute to tell him of his success?

He brought the boat around. The wind and waves were picking up. Now was the time to return to the harbor. He hesitated, thinking of what would lie ahead if Eric failed. Scandal, disgrace, humiliation . . . the press, for so long his ally, riding him into the ground.

He headed back out into the lake, away from shore and into the storm.

The sun dove rapidly for the horizon as the *Mary Eileen* speeded on. She skipped from wave to wave as if she were rushing to join it. The halyards strained and the rigging screamed. Paul Cronin stood exultantly at his tiller. This was the way to go out, the wind blasting at your face, hair streaming in the fading light, the cold lake water washing over the prow of the boat and down the gunwales to form puddles at your feet.

The wind was soon more than twenty knots and the waves up to six feet. The *Mary Eileen* roared like a banshee as she rode up and down the waves. Paul screamed in harmony with her. The Reservoir, Heartbreak Ridge, Maggie, Nicole, Mickey—his life raced before him. All right, all right, I gave it a pretty good go. A few things went wrong, that's all. Get out while I'm still ahead.

One of the stays on the mast snapped. The mast tottered, swayed, and then crashed back toward the cockpit, barely missing Paul's head and enveloping him in billowing nylon. He struggled free.

Nora. Yes, Nora. He still wanted to live.

He ducked into the cabin and grabbed for the microphone on his radio. "Mayday, Mayday," he bellowed. "*Mary Eileen* in distress two miles off Michigan City. Mayday, Mayday. This is Senator Cronin, I have lost my mast. Do you hear me? Michigan City Coast Guard, do you hear me?"

He flipped the "Receive" button, expecting the reassuring response of the Coast Guard, located only a few miles away. There was no answer.

"Mayday, Mayday," he shouted again, this time close to panic. A terrible thought occurred to him. He switched on the cabin lights. Nothing. He flicked the switch again. No battery. Only enough to start the auxiliary motor and turn on the weather radio.

"Mayday, Mayday," he sobbed into the dead microphone.

The *Mary Eileen* wallowed drunkenly in slashing waves. Paul pulled himself out of the cabin. Cut the mainsail free and use the jib as a sea anchor. He had seen it done once in a movie. The mainsail was dragging the boat broadside into the wind.

He dodged under the fallen mast and struggled back into the cabin, a freezing wave slamming into his face. He had to get the sail cut quickly. The *Mary Eileen* was "capsize proof"—but that didn't apply to storms like this when it was hull to the wind. He slammed doors open and shut in the cabinets until he came upon a knife. Not much of a knife but it would have to do.

He pushed upward against the cockpit door to get out of the cabin. It was wedged tight by the weight of the fallen mast and would not budge. The boat had imprisoned him. It would roll over and the water would sweep in in an overwhelming tide. He pounded against the door until his fists were bleeding. Then the boat spun around under the force of another huge wave that dumped water into the cockpit and through the ventilator in the cabin door. God, the water was cold.

But the door swung open. Paul heaved himself back into the slippery cockpit.

The sun was setting now, turning the throbbing waters of the lake red and purple. Paul slashed away at the sail, ripping it frantically and trying to remember how you rigged a sea anchor with a jib.

There was one last piece of sail at the top cleat of the mast. He climbed up on the cockpit seat and leaned over the stern to slash it free.

He saw the wave coming, not much larger than the others, but at a different angle. It slammed into the stern, knocking Paul from the seat and smashing him against the mast. For a moment he seemed to hang free in the air; then his fingers clutched at the mast.

It was too slippery to hold. The boat spun again and Paul Cronin plunged into Lake Michigan. He was not wearing a life jacket.

A life preserver would not help, he told himself, as he hit the lake. He would not survive more than half an hour in water that cold.

The pain in his body from the icy purple waters was like fire. He remembered the stories about Irish fishermen who refused to learn to swim lest they prolong their death agonies.

He wished he had never learned to swim.

He thought back to the time so many years before when Sean had rescued him from the lake. What had happened to him since then? Why had everything gone so wrong?

Then the parade of faces again: the old man, Maggie, Chris, Richard Daley, his girls, Nora, and then, finally, his brother.

Chapter Thirty-seven
1977

NORA AND SEAN stood side by side over the closed casket in the moments before six United States Senators came to carry the sealed casket of the late Junior

Senator from Illinois to the hearse in which he would make his last ride down
Glenwood Drive for his final Mass at St. Titus Church.

Nora was weeping, as she had so often wept during the wake and the funeral.

"Suicide or accident, Sean?" She asked the question that they both had been
afraid to ask.

"God loves us all, Nora, no matter what." He gave the only answer he could.

After the body of Senator Paul Martin Cronin had been laid to rest in Holy
Sepulcher Cemetery and the mourners had eaten the traditional meal at the
Rosewood Inn, Sean and Nora drove Michael Cronin back to his apartment at the
Hancock Tower. It was a flawless April afternoon, a false hint of spring hovering
over the city.

The girls had held up well. Mary and Eileen were dry-eyed, although their
faces were pinched with pain. Noreen wept, but softly and quietly. She had
appointed herself custodian of "Gramps," doggedly pushing his wheelchair
down the aisle of the church.

As she grew older, Noreen seemed more like her grandmother. No wonder
Uncle Mike saved his rare smiles for her. Poor Mike, the wake and funeral had
been harder on him than on anyone else. He had cried through the Mass and then
again at the burial ceremony. He was slipping rapidly.

"I'll hold the door, Noreen," Sean said softly as the elevator on the forty-
fourth floor of the Hancock Tower opened.

"Gramps never had such a quick nurse," crowed Noreen, deftly steering
through the door.

Youth bounded back so quickly. Nora would spend a long time trying to
understand her own grief. She had loved Paul. A strange love, perhaps, but still
a true love in its way.

The three of them stood awkwardly in the parlor of Uncle Mike's apartment,
handing him over to the care of his nurse and yet not knowing how to leave.

Mike Cronin's hand scrawled an illegible word on the note pad attached to his
chair. Sean bent over the pad, gently moving the twisted fingers away from the
word. "Glendore," he said, puzzled.

"He wants us to take him up there," said Noreen. "Don't you, Gramps?"
Mike nodded his head.

"Tomorrow all right?" asked Nora. A trip to Oakland Beach would mean all
that less time to think.

Again he nodded.

As they rode down in the elevator, Noreen broke the silence. "He wants to die
up there," she said firmly.

That night Sean went to the cathedral rectory. Wabash Avenue was deserted,
cold, unfriendly. In either direction, there were only the buildings and the
streetlights. He hurried through the door of the white stone building, itself cold
and unfriendly.

In his room he poured himself one of his rare nightcaps, swallowed it quickly,
and poured another. He strove to feel grief. In a way he was responsible. If he
had not warned Chris Waverly . . .

Who was Paul Cronin? Who was this brother about whose death he could feel
numbness but no pain? Had there ever been a real Paul Cronin? Had pressure
from their father cut the core out of his brother's personality?

Sorrow would come eventually; it was still too soon. The important thing was that the sign was as clear as it could be: Paul was dead; Nora was free to marry. The mistakes he and Nora had made a quarter of a century ago could now be canceled out. They would wait a discreet amount of time and then quietly be married. There was no point in his applying for a dispensation, because Rome did not dispense bishops. About that he couldn't care less.

His phone rang.

"Cronin," he said.

"Chris Waverly, Bishop. I'm sorry about your brother's death."

Her voice was gentle.

"Thank you, Miss Waverly. I appreciate your sympathy."

"I had been sitting up here for days trying to make up my mind whether to use the story. I finally decided not to, on the condition that Paul agree to never run for the presidency. I didn't want to hurt you . . . or his family. Then I heard."

"I appreciate that decision." Sean tried to keep his voice neutral.

"Was it suicide, Bishop?"

"We'll never know, Miss Waverly. We'll never know how much moral responsibility was involved. I suspect with Paul that there never was much of that."

"I've destroyed all the documents."

"I appreciate that."

"You are very different from your brother, Bishop Cronin. I don't believe in much myself, but I do hope you're the next Archbishop of Chicago."

"I'm not going to be the next Archbishop of Chicago, but it's nice of you to say it just the same."

"I'm sure you will be," said Chris Waverly. "Good luck."

On Palm Sunday, Noreen, Sean, and Nora rode to Oakland Beach to visit Mike. The two adults were moody and preoccupied, paying little attention to the wonderful spring day. Noreen considered talking about Easter and resurrection and decided against it. She knew that teenagers didn't preach sermons to bishops.

"You haven't heard from the Delegate yet?" Nora broke the silence.

"Not since the funeral," Sean said. "Why?"

"Jimmy told me that everyone in Rome is saying that they're going to offer you Chicago. You are going to take it, aren't you?"

"No," he said.

"You will," Nora said.

"I won't," he responded stubbornly.

"I don't want an argument on such a nice day," Noreen intervened. Poor grown-ups, she thought, all their heavy decisions made them forget what life was supposed to be about.

When they arrived at Glendore, Mathilda directed them to the study. Noreen had been told by her mother that her grandfather had built Glendore when he and her grandmother were just married. It was hard to think of him as a young man with a bride.

"Hi, Uncle Mike," Nora said in a cheery voice. Then she saw that Mike was sitting in his chair, hunched over, crying.

Outside, the waters of the lake were as smooth as a sheet of thin blue ice. Noreen wondered if Gramps was angry at the lake for taking her father.

"What is it, Dad?" Sean's voice was gentle.

"He's holding something in his hand," Nora said. "It looks like a picture."

Noreen took the picture out of his hand. "It's a picture of Daddy and Uncle Sean with Gramps and Grandma when they were little boys."

Then, not quite knowing why, Noreen threw her arms around her grandfather and wept with him.

Sean glanced at his watch. Another hour before the Holy Thursday services would begin. He was physically and emotionally drained.

On Wednesday he had received a call from the Delegate.

"I must begin, Archbishop Cronin, by telling you how very, very sorry I am for the tragedy in your family."

"I appreciate that, Archbishop." Sean repeated his now familiar response to sympathy. "My sister and her children and I also appreciate your very kind telegram and the Holy Father's cablegram."

"Yes, of course," said the Delegate mechanically. "Of course. But now, unfortunately, I must talk to you about the future instead of the past."

Sean was immediately guarded. Had they chosen someone else? Oddly enough, he felt a tinge of disappointment. He expected to turn the appointment down, not to be passed over. "Of course, Your Excellency."

"It is, Archbishop, the Holy Father's wish—" That was the second time the Delegate had called him "Archbishop." The canny Frenchman could not have made the same mistake twice.

"No."

"The Holy Father expressly commands you, in virtue of your vow of obedience—"

"Henri." He called the Delegate by his first name, something he had never done before. "Tell the Holy Father to go to hell."

"Oh, Archbishop Cronin, your response will not deter him in the least. He absolutely insists. Moreover, he told me confidentially that he is planning a Consistory before Pentecost—only seven weeks away—and then I shall have to call you Cardinal Cronin."

"No, I will not do it."

"Sean, yes, you will." So the Delegate was using first names too.

"Archbishop, we can sit here and argue about this for the next hour, and my answer will still be no."

"We will not argue about it at all. I will phone you again tomorrow before the Holy Thursday services, and you will give me your formal acceptance." The line went dead.

Ten minutes later the phone rang again. "Overseas operator," said a muffled voice. Then Sean heard the usual gibberish of transatlantic confusion followed by a bewildered Italian operator wanting "Monsignor Cronin" while a nasal Bronx voice insisted that they had a "Bishop Cronin" on the line. Finally, a soft but firm voice said, "Montini *aqui*."

Sean felt an emptiness in his stomach as he had as a little boy when Mike gave him orders. "Cronin *aqui*," he said. *"Buona sera, Santità."*

"We have called"—Paul VI spoke in hesitant but precise English, just as he had at Castel Gandolfo—"to state again what *Monsieur le délégat* has told you. It is our hope that you will agree to take up the burden of serving the Church in Chicago. It is a very important city. We need you."

A gentle voice, but Sean felt the same reaction as when Mike ordered him to leave the seminary and marry Nora. Only now he was not the same Sean.

"I cannot, *Santo Padre*," he replied. He felt his chest wrench with the trauma of refusing a parent.

"We are sorry about your brother's death, Monsignor," said the Pope, ignoring his refusal. "Life is very short for all of us. That is why—"

"My conscience does not permit it, *Santo Padre*," Sean interjected.

"We hope you will at least do us the honor of praying over it for a day." The Pope sounded even more hesitant, vulnerable as he always was to the appeal of conscience.

Eager for a compromise solution, even a transitory one, Sean agreed. "Of course, *Santità*, I will pray for it."

"*Monsieur le délégat* will call you again, my son."

After the papal voice faded, Sean rushed to the bathroom and retched violently. He had said no to a parent. It was not easy, but this time he had done it. Now he had merely to stick to his decision.

Sean looked at his watch again. Nora was going to visit and the Delegate was going to call him before he would go down to the cathedral. There, in his recommitment to priestly service, he would move his lips but he would say no words.

Then Nora was at the door, beautiful in a light blue suit; skirt, jacket, and sweater impeccably tailored. The touches of age around her eyes and her mouth somehow made her more endearing.

"Do you have a few minutes?" she asked.

"Of course. Come in and sit down. I have something I want to talk about."

"Me too," she said. "I didn't wear black because I'm not going to be able to stay for Mass at the cathedral. There are a couple of things I've got to do, and I guess I never really believed in black anyway."

"It doesn't matter," Sean said automatically. "What do you want to talk about?"

"No, you first," Nora insisted. She leaned forward, hands folded.

Sean took a deep breath, gripped the edge of his desk tightly and began. "Nora, I'm going to resign from the priesthood. I want to marry you. You need a husband. I need a wife. It's time to correct all the mistakes we made twenty-five years ago."

"I can't," she said in a small voice. "I simply can't, Sean. It's impossible. Please don't ask me."

"Why is it impossible?" He was anxious, ready to explode. "Don't you love me?"

She leaned forward. "Of course I love you, Sean. I've always loved you. If you weren't a priest, I'd marry you tomorrow. But you *are* a priest." She shook her head slowly, tears forming in her clear blue eyes.

"Holding me to my commitment?"

"That's right. I've tried to honor most of my commitments, even if a lot of them were those I made because of other people. Now I'm going to start making my own commitments freely and independently for myself. I still believe in commitments, Sean."

"You won't change your mind?" He felt as though a light had gone out inside him.

"No, I won't. Anyway, how can you possibly think of turning your back on all the priests of Chicago who love you so much, and the laity for whom you've become the Church?'' She leaned forward even more intently, her face wrinkled in a frown. "How can you possibly think of letting them down?''

"Goddammit, Nora,'' he shouted. "I don't believe in any of it anymore. I never did. I have no commitments.''

"Don't be silly, Sean, of course you do. Uncle Mike was wrong about a lot of things. He was right about you. . . . Has the Apostolic Delegate called to tell you you're the next Archbishop of Chicago?''

Sean hesitated. What was the point of keeping it a secret? "Yes, both he and the Pope called, and I turned them both down.''

"Sean, call and tell them you've changed your mind. Do it before they have a chance to offer it to someone else.''

"The Delegate is going to call me back sometime in the next half hour,'' he said lamely.

"Well, I hope you come to your senses before then,'' she said. And then she smiled sweetly at him. "Oh, Sean, I do love you, and I always will love you, but I won't be your wife.''

He nodded, competing emotions struggling within him.

"What will happen to you? What will you do with your life?''

Nora straightened up, her back strong and firm. "That's what I wanted to talk to you about. The Governor has decided to appoint me to the Senate to fill out the remainder of Paul's term. I'm going to accept. The Governor has an odd notion that I'll step down two years from now and give him a clear shot at it. I've let him think that's what I'm going to do—but he's wrong.''

"In God's name, Nora, why?''

"Because I'll be good at it. I have all the right political instincts. I've known that for years as I watched Paul's successes and failures.'' Nora stood up. "Well, I'd better go now. I must buy the proper sort of dress for the announcement that I'm going to be the new Senator from Illinois.''

"I wish you happiness,'' Sean said, putting his arms around her.

For a moment they stood silently together. She was soft and sweet, an angel of love. He could feel her determination begin to melt into surrender. If he insisted now he could have her, he was sure, have a life with her in which the sweetness would never end. Images from their past love tumbled through his mind. Oakland Beach . . . Amalfi. . . . Yet surely the sweetness would be short-lived. Having her, he would lose her. Not having her, he could love her forever. Not for Jimmy McGuire, not for the Delegate, not for all the priests of Chicago, not even for the Pope, but for Nora . . . yes, for Nora . . . he would do what his damn fool Church and his damn fool God wanted him to do. He disengaged himself from the embrace. "I've got to get ready for Mass.''

Nora walked to the door of his study. Her firm shoulders sagged. She paused and turned slowly; her face was streaked with tears.

Oh, God, Nora, he thought, his heart sinking, don't blow it now.

She bit her lip. "Buy you lunch in Washington next week?''

"In the Senate dining room,'' he insisted. Waves of warmth and grace surged across the room and enveloped him.

She grinned through her tears. "Where else?'' She hesitated, then her head tilted up. "You *will* say yes to the Delegate.'' It was more an order than a question. She smiled and left the room.

Her warmth and peace lingered with Sean. He picked up a pen and a sheet of paper from his desk, since his journal was in his bedroom.

"You damn fool," he wrote. *"You missed God's sign for thirty years.''*

He crossed out the words, tore the paper into little pieces, and threw them into the wastebasket. Because he had lost his mother, God sent him Nora, the best sign of God's love he would ever have. The same father who had taken away his mother brought the shy little girl into his life so long ago. Talk about the twisted lines of God.

The phone rang. "Cronin," he said.

"I trust, Archbishop Cronin, that you have changed your mind." The Delegate was being brusque and businesslike. "I assume that now you will accede to the wishes of the Holy Father imposed upon you in solemn obedience."

"Nope, Henri," said Bishop Cronin. "I don't really take that holy obedience stuff seriously." He hesitated for just the right dramatic effect and grinned to himself and said, "But I freely decide to serve."

There was a long silence at the other end of the line as the shrewd old French ex-missionary tried to sort out the meaning of those words. "Well, then, that is so much the better, no?"

"If you say so, Henri." Sean was now beginning to enjoy himself. There were many things he was going to enjoy in the years ahead.

"Congratulations, Sean," said the Delegate. "This makes me very happy personally."

"I think you'll live to regret it, but that's your problem."

The Delegate merely chuckled.

After he hung up, the new Archbishop of Chicago donned his black cassock, buttoning up carefully each of the purple buttons. He could hear the cathedral choir practicing the Holy Thursday music. They were singing a haunting medieval hymn, *"Ubi Caritas et Amor."*

Sean Cronin walked down the steps of the rectory to go into the cathedral and repeat with his priests his vows of commitment. He sang softly the words of the hymn to himself.

> *Where charity and love prevail*
> *There God is ever found;*
> *Brought here together by Christ's love*
> *By love are we thus bound.*
>
> *With grateful joy and holy fear*
> *His charity we learn;*
> *Let us with heart and mind and soul*
> *Now love him in return.*
>
> *Forgive we now each other's faults*
> *As we our faults confess;*
> *And let us love each other well*
> *In Christian holiness.*
>
> *Let strife among us be unknown,*
> *Let all contention cease;*
> *Be his the glory that we seek,*
> *Be ours his holy peace.*
>
> *Let us recall that in our midst*
> *Dwells God's begotten Son;*

As members of his Body joined
We are in him made one.

No race nor creed can love exclude
If honored by God's Name;
Our brotherhood embraces all
Whose Father is the same.

A PERSONAL AFTERWORD

WHY WOULD A priest write a novel, particularly a secular novel, about adultery, incest, and sacrilege?

Why would Jesus tell parables about secular events like wedding banquets and ne'er-do-well sons and treasure hunters and adulterous women? Why would writers in the Jewish scriptures tell tales about passionate love affairs between unmarried young people (the Song of Songs), about adulterous kings (the David Cycle) and hateful, incestuous and murderous families (the Joseph Cycle)?

The answer is that, since the beginning of humankind, religion has been most effectively communicated in stories that appeal to the whole person instead of being communicated in doctrinal treatises aimed at the intellect alone. The purpose of the religious tale is not to edify but to shatter preconceptions, to open up to the imagination new possibilities of living in the world and relating to the Ultimate.

This particular religious story will be successful if the reader is disconcerted by a tale of commitments that are imperfectly made and imperfectly kept—but that are still kept. And by the image of a God who draws straight with crooked lines, who easily and quickly forgives, and who wants to love us with the tenderness of a mother.

A.G.

Ascent into Hell

For

DAN HERR

May he never "Stop Pushing"

NOTE

THIS IS THE story of why one man became a priest and why he left the active priesthood.

Hugh Donlon is a product of my imagination and is not based on any priest I know. I do not intend to suggest that his story is typical either of men who become priests or of men who leave the active priesthood. Nor is his wife intended to be typical of the women who marry priests who have withdrawn from the ministry. I am not writing a sociological study about marriages between priests and nuns.

Father Donlon, his family, his friends, and everyone else in the novel are creatures of my imagination. Those who love to search a novel for traces of a roman à clef or a "thinly veiled autobiography" are perfectly free to do so, of course, having paid their money and perhaps even having finished the book. A search for "real" counterparts of the characters of my story, however, tells more about the searchers than it does about the story.

Nor should it be assumed because Hugh Donlon is a priest and I am a priest that his voice is my voice. Only Maria speaks for me. Moreover, like God, I refuse to assume responsibility for the moral behavior of my creatures.

Background information about the workings of the Chicago Board of Trade was furnished by Robert Brennan and Richard Mortell. They are not responsible for any inaccuracies in my description of what might have happened at that splendid institution—but in fact did not.

April is the cruellest month, breeding
Lilacs out of the dead land . . .

T. S. ELIOT

Prologue
1933

"Woman, behold, thy son. . . . Son, behold, thy mother."

ON GOOD FRIDAY night Thomas Donlon knelt in the sacristy of the chapel at Oak Park Hospital. He had come to bargain with God.

A nun unlocked the door to the sanctuary so that he could pray for his wife in the presence of the Blessed Sacrament, hidden away until Holy Saturday morning. He turned off the single electric light and knelt on the hard wooden prie-dieu in front of the fussy old sacristy cabinet with its many little drawers and panels. The flickering red sanctuary lamp bathed the room in a bloodred glow—the blood of Jesus who had died for Thomas Donlon's sins, the blood of his wife Peggy who might die before the night was over, perhaps a punishment for his sins.

When he met her, only a year ago, Peggy was a lovely girl, dressed in white, standing next to the pergola at Twin Lakes after Mass on a Sunday morning in June, sweet, innocent, and radiantly beautiful. His father, a wealthy, dishonest, and penurious police captain, was dead. At twenty-five, Tom Donlon had inherited the family money and the string of family apartment buildings, a position in a prestigious Loop law firm, and a promise from the Organization that he would eventually be slated for a place on the Cook County Superior Court.

He had spent the previous year in Europe, at first a lonely exile wandering amid the ruins of a collapsing banking system and an eroding social order. Then in Salzburg he met a young music teacher.

But the girl would not come home with him, fearing, perhaps rightly, that she would wither in the harshness of a nation she did not know. Tom Donlon instead went to Twin Lakes looking for a wife.

And he found one, a sumptuously beautiful young woman with buttermilk skin and thick, jet-black hair—a Black Irish Venus.

It was a speedy courtship. The Curtins were delighted that such a fine young man wanted to marry their Peggy. Even if she was only eighteen, he was too good a catch to pass up, especially since it seemed that the Depression might never end. Peggy thought she was in love, but was in fact an innocent traded by her family to a lustful young man for veiled promises of political advantage and financial rewards.

He swam with her the afternoon they met, discovering that in a white swimsuit she was every bit as enticing as she was in a white dress. He kissed her in the mysterious, humid darkness of the golf course that night, after a dance at the Red Barn, held her close in his arms, and told her, honestly enough, that she was the most beautiful woman he had ever known.

She trembled when he caressed her, but her lips were firm and generous in their response to his. Dimly he realized that she was too young to marry and that her parents should delay the match for a year or two. Yet the Curtins wanted his clout, he wanted Peggy, and she wanted to be in love, even if her intended was a slight, bookish, reserved young man—except when his hands were gliding over her body.

Tom Donlon was a man of stern principle, in reaction perhaps to his father's total lack of principle. A voice in the back of his head told him softly that his courtship of Peggy was little more than an exercise in the buying of a wife and that he was violating all his principles by exploiting the Curtin greed. Yet his lust for her was so powerful that he turned off the voice the way he would turn off his Philco radio.

On their wedding night he discovered, as he should have foreseen, that she was altogether unprepared for marriage. Instead of being angry at her, Tom Donlon was furious at himself for forcing her into his bed, innocent of both reflection and freedom.

At that moment love replaced lust. He rearranged her rumpled nightgown, straightening out the white lace and the whiter limbs, patted the hand pathetically clutching a pearl rosary, and told his bride not to worry, their love would triumph. Several days later at an Ozark honeymoon hotel, Peggy had insisted they consummate their marriage and she had done her best to cooperate. Months after that, when their first child was beginning to stir in her body, his patience and sensitivity were rewarded, aided considerably by magic words he had found in a booklet called "An Examination of Conscience for Catholic Married Woman." The words were "In matters which pertain to the rendering of the marriage debt, the good Catholic wife trustingly follows the lead of her husband." The formula, repeated mysteriously and with no explanation at the Convent of the Sacred Heart, where Peggy had attended high school, sufficed to legitimate passion. Peggy discovered that she enjoyed sex, perhaps not as much as he did, but enough to admit guiltily that she liked it and to wonder if she were "abnormal." Tom suspected that eventually, with patience and love, his woman would become more of a wanton than he.

In their few months together, Tom found that his wife was not merely a pretty girl with firm breasts, long, straight legs and a promise of blossoming sexuality. Peggy was fascinating and unpredictable—the kind of woman who unveils some of her mystery and then retreats into yet deeper mystery.

Prudish in her opposition to smoking and drinking ("Not in my house, whatever Governor Roosevelt says"), Peg nevertheless was the life of the somewhat stuffy parties organized by the wives of Tom's law partners. She would sing the latest Broadway song in a clear, pretty voice after only a hint of an invitation, and after a few parties, with no invitation at all.

She was talented with a watercolor brush but afraid to show the results of her work. When Tom took a painting from her by brute force and exclaimed in surprise at its pastel loveliness, she forbade him to tell anyone that she painted, much as if it were a secret vice. Yet she clapped her hands in happiness when he insisted that she go to the Art Institute for the lessons that Maude Curtin had sternly forbidden.

Peggy was rigid in her pieties and deeply believing in her faith, afraid of God's punishing wrath, and confident of His generous love. She was absurdly modest with her own body, though it was Tom's whenever he wanted it, but almost persuaded him to take her to Sally Rand's show at the Century of Progress World's Fair.

And now she was close to death.

She had gone to bed early, pleading a faint headache. About midnight she had called for him. He was curled up in the parlor with a book of medieval history, a passion that had now taken second pace to another in his life.

"I'm scared, Tommy, I think the baby is coming."

"A week early?"

"I know . . . the pains are regular . . . and they hurt."

Dr. Walter Mohan, cheerful and indulgent, was waiting for them in the empty Emergency Room at Oak Park Hospital. One look at Peg and his demeanor changed.

Hugh Thomas Donlon was born seven hours later, a six-pound, five-ounce baby boy, healthy and screaming. Doc Mohan, a thin, red-haired man in his early forties with a trace of the brogue, was grimly serious when he discussed Peg's condition. "We have a hemorrhage problem, Tom, and I don't like the looks of it. The next twenty-four hours will be touch and go."

Her skin parchment pale, her voice weak, Peg was calm and brave. "Everything is in God's hands, darling. We'll have to pray for our own resignation to His holy will."

Desperate with fear, Tom stumbled into the bloodred sacristy of the hospital chapel.

I'd be here even if I didn't believe a thing, he admitted finally to the Deity. For hours he'd pleaded, begged, implored. Now he remembered his mother's custom of making promises to God. Captain Daniel "Dollars" Donlon of the Chicago police had had little patience with Harriet Donlon's promises; in fact he'd had little patience with anything about that vague and wistful woman, especially her attempts to teach their only child the moral principles that the captain ignored all his life. Tom had never made a "promise" before. It couldn't hurt and it might help.

What could he give?

"Look, if you want the boy to be a priest, I won't oppose that. I promise you. Leave me Peg and you can have Hugh."

A damn fool thing to say. Peg had once remarked that it would be wonderful "if God blessed us with a vocation for one of our sons." Inwardly he'd been revolted at the idea, then upset with himself. God knows the poor Church needed good priests.

"I hope your intelligence isn't insulted by such a promise." He addressed the Lord much as a good lawyer with a weak case would address a distinguished federal judge—the kind of judge Tom wanted to be someday. "It was a stupid remark. Don't blame Peg for my stupidity. If you want my son, now or later, you can have him, regardless. If you want Peg now too, you can have her. Only please don't want her.''

At some point even the most penitent offender has no recourse save to throw himself on the mercy of the court.

Finally he slipped out of the chapel and ran down the empty corridor to her room. Doc Mohan was smiling.

"I hope you were in the chapel praying for me, Tommy," she said weakly as he took her in his arms.

"I was, very hard." His breath was coming in gulps, as though he'd run many miles on a humid August day.

She seemed surprised. "That was so good of you. I was ready to die, but I asked God for more time so I could thank you for all the love. . . ." Her voice trailed off.

"Still pretty weak," said Mohan, "but out of the woods, thank heaven. So young. . . .''

'Too young,'' said Tom Donlon, turning away to hide his tears.

Several weeks later, Tom Donlon thought about the Fireside Chat he'd listened to before going to bed. He had turned off the radio as soon as Roosevelt was finished, so that it would not wake Peg, though he knew that once she was asleep a Big Bertha shell would not wake her.

They were living in a small and rather stodgy furnished apartment in one of his buildings on Austin Boulevard. He'd argued that they ought to save their money so they might eventually buy a house and furniture for it, instead of wasting money on new furniture for a small apartment. Maude Curtin was outraged, having expected that her princess would promptly move into a palace, at least what passed for a palace in North Austin.

Peggy merely laughed, refusing to take Tom's financial caution seriously. "I like living here," she insisted. "I want my husband close to me whenever he's in the house. If I get tired of it, I'll buy a house."

He did not doubt that she meant it. An obedient and docile woman she was. Yet when she soon became weary of riding the Austin and Washington boulevards bus to the Loop, she went to a Packard agency in Oak Park, wrote a check for $750, and presented him with the car as "a birthday present."

He almost read her a lecture on the value of money, thought better of it, and took his place in the plush driver's seat of the Packard. A good lawyer knows when to plead "nolo contendere."

It had been a year since he'd cast his vote, for Franklin D. Roosevelt. In the twilight between waking and sleeping he calculated that Peggy would vote in her first national election three years from now, in 1936; and it would be the off-year election of 1954 when Hugh would cast his first vote. What would the country be like then? Would the Depression last that long? What kind of world would Hugh face in his young manhood?

He'd do all right. A tough young man, putting on lots of weight, although he looked so small it was difficult to imagine him walking into a flag-decorated polling place as a member of the Democratic Party.

Tom Donlon laughed to himself. Of course, he would be a Democrat. He was a Catholic, wasn't he?

That night created wonder and mystery that would fascinate and trouble Tom Donlon for the rest of his life.

He woke suddenly from a deep sleep. Peg was nursing their son, who required but one feeding a night and then quickly went back to sleep. Tom had assumed that his wife, both prudish and fastidious, would put the baby on a bottle as quickly as she could. Again he'd underestimated her. She loved providing her own milk for the adored boy child.

His heavy eyelids closed. Go back to sleep. Then he forced them open again. There was something strange. . . .

Peg was sitting next to the bed, Hugh in her arms. A light was radiating from them, soft and misty and very bright. She had slipped the straps of her nightdress off her shoulders and the baby's skin and her own cream white body seemed to blend into one. Her eyes were afire with infatuation, possession, delight.

She saw him watching and smiled at him too, inviting him into their communion. "I saved some of my milk for you."

"What . . . ?" he stammered.

"You've wanted to taste it and were afraid to ask." She drew his head firmly to her nipple.

Her milk was sweet and warm, like Peggy herself. She was administering her sacrament to him. The light crept around him too.

"I have enough love for both of you," she said complacently.

No longer a child bride with a live doll, Peggy was age-old woman, mysterious, absorbing, life-giving, totally captivating. She put the sleeping Hugh back in his crib, patted Tom's head, turned off the light, and cuddled next to him. Father and son had both been nourished. Mother and wife could sleep.

The next morning, a Sunday—Mass at St. Lucy's, Father Coughlin and Walter Winchell on the Philco—Tom tried to tell himself it had been a dream. Yet Peg was next to him in bed, the straps off her shoulders, her nightdress hanging from her waist, her breasts strong and reassuring.

Had the light been real?

Was that kind of ardent, physical love between a mother and son dangerous?

He brushed his lips against hers and touched lightly the breast from which he'd drunk as if it were a chalice from which a priest might say Mass. She continued to sleep.

I'm not sorry I bargained with God for you.

BOOK ONE

"I thirst."

Chapter One
1954

THE GIRL WHO opened the door just as Hugh was about to put his key in the lock was so disconcertingly beautiful that he stepped back abruptly, as if to shield his eyes from a blinding light.

She seemed to be about twenty, pale burnished hair, an expressive and mobile face with a clear suggestion of barely suppressed comedy, a figure slim rather than voluptuous in bermuda shorts and print blouse, feet in sandals, both hands jammed jauntily into her pockets.

"Hi," she said, light blue eyes dancing with fun as she stood in the panel of light in the doorway.

"Hi," he said, his voice unnaturally thin. "I'm Hugh Donlon."

"Course you are." Her face crinkled.

"I live here."

"Course you do; would you like to come in . . . ?"

"You live here?" he stammered with minimum understanding.

Her head tilted to one side, her smile amused yet tolerant, she regarded him with the benign grace of a wealthy countess.

"Sure. . . . It's all right for you to come in. I'm not dangerous."

I'm staring at her and acting like a clod, Hugh told himself. But I don't care. She's gorgeous.

He stepped through the doorway into the small parlor of their summer home. "Do you have a name?" he asked.

The room was comfortably ugly with mismatched old furniture and threadbare rugs. His mother had won the argument about a Lake Geneva summer home, as she always won the mild disagreements between her and his father, but the judge had made his point that the home ought not to be ostentatious. Ezio Pinza was singing "Some Enchanted Evening" from *South Pacific* on a record player of dubious vintage.

"Doesn't everyone?" There was a flicker of intelligence as well as humor in her rapidly changing eyes. This one is smart too, he thought. She'd got me on the defensive and is going to make the most of it. That's all right, pretty lady. With you I don't mind being on the defensive.

In one graceful movement she crossed the room to turn off the record player, crumpled a bubble gum wrapper into her pocket, and hid a copy of a film magazine under a newspaper on the many-spotted coffee table.

Seminarian or not, Hugh exercised a young man's right to consider carefully what it was about a young woman that made her beautiful.

Her smile came first. Not quite a smile, really, half smile, half grin, hinting at amusement, confidence, sophistication, mischief—and assuming as a matter of course and a matter of simple justice that she saw right through him.

He felt his face grow warm.

And her eyes. Soft blue like the waters of Lake Geneva. Changing rapidly as the lake did on a windy day when small cumulus clouds raced across it trailing lights and shadows as if it were momentarily Holland instead of Wisconsin and the lake was on loan for a Rembrandt painting.

Her face was a little too thin perhaps and the nose a little too long. Yet her fair skin was flawless and her delicate facial bones promised loveliness that time would not alter. Her slender body suggested femininity rather than flaunting it; breasts small and perfectly shaped, as if a sculptor had molded them to make men clench their hands; slender waist; and pert rear end. Hugh cut off the flow of his imagination. He was, after all, studying for the priesthood.

"Do I get to learn what the name is?" he said, trying to sound cool and collected.

"If you've decided that I pass the exam." She sat on the couch and gestured toward the decrepit easy chair next to it, all confidence.

"With highest honors," he said.

"I'm Maria. In fact, I'm Maria Angelica Elizabetha Vittoria Paola Pia Emmanuela . . . almost enough for a baseball team."

And now, astonishingly, he saw a touch of vulnerability, perhaps even a little fear in her Rembrandt eyes. Why should you be afraid of me, pretty countess?

"I should know you, Maria?" he asked cautiously.

"You've known me for a long time." Shaking her head in mock displeasure, and then in a total transformation, she ceased to be a countess and became a waitress. "You want a beer . . . ? I know what you want. Don't go away."

He followed her with his eyes as she rushed from the room, then reproved himself sharply. He'd given up girls four years ago when he'd entered the seminary. Young women like Maria could make his heart pound, but they must be kept at a distance, especially after the four depressing weeks at Holy Family Orphanage. He wondered what had happened to his own family.

He was glad to be home, sitting in a warm and familiar room with its mixture of white wicker chairs, beige couches with broken springs and torn fabric from his grandparents' house on West End, and the rag rugs that were in the house when the Donlons bought it and tended to skid on the slippery wood floor. Golf clubs, tennis rackets, swimsuits, and laundry were heaped in various empty places and the light bulbs were always too dim because no one could remember to buy stronger bulbs on their trips to the store in Walworth.

The only bright colors in the room were his mother's latest watercolors, hanging by family insistence on every available wall space, including that above the rarely used fireplace.

The dominant colors were blue and gold, blue skies, gold waters on the lake, blue like that in Maria's eyes, gold like that in her hair.

"Eccolo." Maria returned. "Raspberries and cream. Your mother insisted that we must lay in a great supply of raspberries for the return of the firstborn."

"Maria who?"

She sat cross-legged on the couch. The clouds wiped out the sunlight in her eyes. The game was over and she was sad. "Maria Manfredy, who else? I'm your sister's classmate at Trinity, the daughter of the shoe repairman on Division

Street . . . you know, the handsome man with gray hair and the pretty wife who speaks hesitant English.''

Not twenty, but sixteen or seventeen. Hugh was furious at himself. Taken in by a kid and a shoemaker's daughter at that. Countess indeed. The orphanage must have been worse than he thought.

"I'm sorry, Maria," he said. "I guess I don't remember you; people change."

Her wonderful eyes could not stay cloudy for long. Sunlight flooded back in.

"I might have changed a *little*." With the return of sunlight came both mischief and intelligence.

Hugh revised his opinion again. Seventeen all right, but no ordinary seventeen. She can be any one of a number of people and she's trying to find out which one I like the most. All of them, I think.

"Don't you remember the time you carried me home?"

Now she was shy and winsome. This Maria is the most appealing of all. When her eyes plead with me that way, she owns me.

"How could I forget something like that?"

"Well. . . ." She took a long breath, like a diver before a leap into a pool. "I was a proud little girl going to St. Ursula's on a Sunday afternoon in my First Communion dress for practice of the May Crowning procession. It had just stopped raining and there was even a rainbow in the sky. Some big kids chased me and called me a little Dago and shot rubber-band guns. I fell on the curbstone and cut my knee and got my dress all muddy. Then the big kids ran away and left me there sobbing and I was sure I was going to die of disappointment and disgrace. The captain of the patrol boys came by and cleaned my dirty face, wiped away my tears, fixed the cut on my knee as best he could. Then he took me by the hand and walked to Division Street with me. So I started to cry again, because my mother and father would be so disappointed that their only child couldn't march in the May Crowning.

"Now do you remember? You had to carry me the last half block to the store, because I didn't want to go home. My father said that Judge Donlon was the best man in the parish, even if he was a politician, and my mother—not knowing what your mother would think about such a terrible thing—gave you a glass of homemade red wine and you drank most of it, without even making a face. Then you and my mother and father made me laugh and you went to see Sister Cunnegunda and even though I missed practice I was still in the May Crowning.''

Tears were streaming down her face. He wanted to wipe them away again.

He took her chin in his hand and turned her head in his direction.

She was intrigued, a little frightened, and unresisting.

I'm going to kiss her, Hugh thought. I have to kiss her.

There was a noise outside.

"Car door, your parents," Maria whispered.

He barely heard her.

"Don't," she said, pulling away from him.

His mother saw them sitting together on the couch and there was a hint of unease in her smile of greeting.

"We didn't expect you home so soon . . . we went to the movies."

His father covered his concern more skillfully. "You were right, Maria. *The Robe* is an excellent film."

"Are you here all alone?" his mother asked. "Where's Marge?"

"She's out with Joe Delaney," Maria said timidly.

"And I don't suppose Tim has showed up yet," Judge Donlon said. "Mother, father, brother, sister, all somewhere else when you come home."

"Maria was here," Hugh said.

"And you didn't have the slightest idea who I was, kind of thought I might be a glamorous thief." Before the judge and Mrs. Donlon had a chance to examine their son's face more closely, Maria took over the party.

She served up "another round of raspberries and cream on the house" and told the May Crowning story again, this time as high comedy, ending with Hugh staggering down Division Street after drinking a bottle of the "Manfredy's bathtub grapa."

Despite herself, Mrs. Donlon laughed till she cried. "You look happy and relaxed, Hugh," she said when she recovered. "The time at the orphanage must have been good for you."

"I feel fine," he said, not wanting to admit that the happiness and peace had come only when Maria appeared in the panel of light at the front door.

"I tell you what." Maria never seemed to wind down. "It's so warm and stuffy . . . why don't we poor stay-at-homes go for a moonlight swim . . . ?" Then her voice trailed off and she did wind down. Fragility and fear returned to her eyes.

Worried that she might have gone too far with the proper Donlons? Hugh thought not. You could never go too far, Maria. We're not like you but you're what we think maybe we could be, if we ever got time after our serious responsibilities are fulfilled.

His mother was the first to succumb to Maria's fading voice, his mother who had probably never gone for a midnight swim in her life.

"That's a wonderful idea, dear. I was thinking the same thing myself."

His father managed to keep a reasonably straight face.

Maria was silent, almost invisible five minutes later, as, wearing a modest black swimsuit and a sweat shirt, she walked after the elder Donlons to the edge of the pier. Hugh followed behind her, still yearning to touch her lips with his.

The humidity was so thick that it seemed to be a physical presence, like a ghost with clammy hands and hot breath, a heavy sinister spirit, lurking in the moonless sky, too elusive to be illumined by the faint glow of starlight.

Peggy dove off the pier gracefully, quite unafraid of the darkness. The judge followed her.

Maria hesitated. "I can't swim very well."

"It was your idea and now you're scared." Hugh taunted her gently.

"A woman can have second thoughts." She pulled off her sweat shirt and dropped it on the pier.

Too dark to see her shoulders, merely a pale white gash in the night.

Hugh pushed the pale white gash off the end of the pier.

He half expected that she would be furious. Instead, she popped to the surface laughing and spitting water. "It's great, fraidy cat, come on in."

Hugh dove in and swam out to the raft with his mother, while the judge kept Maria company.

"Why have we never done this before?" Peggy asked. "I think I might be able to paint the scene . . . swimmers on a moonless night."

"How was *The Robe*?" Maria asked Peggy shyly when they were all together again at the pier.

"It was very moving," Peggy replied solemnly, "to see our Lord and Savior's life portrayed on the screen, even indirectly. The movie will give me a lot to think about.''

"A tremendous number of historical inaccuracies,'' the judge commented. "For example, the legionnaires in Palestine were unquestionably Syrian, not Italian.''

"I wish I were as pretty as Jean Simmons,'' blurted Maria, definitely a teen-ager now.

"You're much prettier, dear,'' Peggy said generously, "and you'll be pretty all your life. . . . I sometimes wonder what He thinks about us. Nineteen centuries later and we're still selfish and unkind and resistant to His Holy Will.''

"I bet He's much happier with us now than He would be if we hadn't gone swimming tonight . . . hey, where's the pier?'' Maria, having floated too far away, flailed in the water. "I'm not too good at this swimming thing. . . .''

Hugh grabbed her arm in the darkness and pulled her toward the pier. She brushed against him for a delightful moment.

"I'm going to learn to swim, just you wait. I'll be as graceful as one of those cute dolphins.'' She eased out of his grasp and reached for the ladder, breathing hard as she tried to catch her breath. "Anyway, He made the lake and the moon and this night for us—He even made the pier for me to cling to—and we should be grateful.''

My countess even preaches sermons, Hugh thought. And when she brushes against me I think I'm going to die.

"And we should be grateful to Him for sending you to make us appreciate the night,'' his mother said, even though Maria's theology was foreign to her own somber vision of the Deity.

"Now you'll make me cry, Mrs. Donlon.'' Maria lost the pier again. But this time, alas, she did not need Hugh's help to find it.

And he could hardly put his arms around her, even in the dark, with his mother and father floating beside him.

Walking up the lawn to the house, Hugh and Maria fell behind his parents. In the distance lightning cut jagged lines in the night sky. Outraged crickets continued their protest against the heat. Hugh and Maria paused, in unspoken agreement, underneath the tiny light at the entrance to the gazebo that served as Peggy's studio.

Hugh tilted her chin up so he could look into her eyes, mischievous, mocking, yet so easily hurt. Wet hair glued to her head, water still on her face and shoulders, Maria was a piquant little slave, utterly his if he wanted her. In the heaviness of the summer night she seemed to promise an eternity of sweetness and life if only he would take her in his arms.

"You're an amazing person, Maria,'' he said lamely, his fingers feeling the pulse racing through her throat.

"Not bad for a high school junior, huh?'' She giggled.

Hugh knew with total clarity that he had the power at that instant to decide for or against the priesthood. To envelop Maria in his arms would be to repudiate his priestly vocation.

Why did temptations have to be so pathetic and so lovely?

And was she a temptation? Perhaps, after all . . .

Hugh decided for the priesthood. "We'd better go inside . . .'' he said, releasing her chin.

"Too many mosquitoes out here." Maria laughed. "A guy could get badly bitten."

Chapter Two
·· *1954* ··

LATER THAT NIGHT, Hugh knelt in his shorts at the side of his bed, saying his night prayers. He prayed for Tim that he would stay out of trouble, for Marge that she would be protected from harm, for his parents that they would worry less about their children, for his classmate and friend Jack Howard who was thinking of leaving the seminary.

And thank You too for sending Maria to bring us some laughter.

The sheets were clammy, the air was still, crickets were buzzing outside. Maria was in the bedroom next door, alone till Margie came home. His parents were sleeping down the corridor. A thin wall between him and the lovely Maria.

Father Meisterhorst would be horrified. The spiritual director of the seminary had harassed Hugh for three years about the girls he had necked with and petted when he was in high school. There would be bad thoughts about these "sins of the past," the old man had thundered, and powerful temptations to seek out his "partners in sin" and begin again.

Hugh was not convinced that his sins were that great, though he regretted them. He felt no inclination to seek out his high school sweethearts, some of whom were engaged, a few even married, and one a mother. He had no trouble containing his fantasies about the mild conquests of his teen-age days.

Maria was another matter. No older than the girls he'd passionately kissed in high school, but more threatening and more appealing. It was a test of his vocation he didn't need.

But he wasn't going to leave his own home to escape from her.

Life consisted of hard choices, for the love of God. There would be other attractive women who would force him to make difficult decisions.

He was at an age when a man looks for a wife, unless he is committed to something else. The juices of his body made Maria attractive. To resist her appeal was a measure of his character.

Besides, she chewed bubble gum.

Peg Donlon's hand tightened its hold on her husband's. He felt the familiar reassuring pressure of the pearl rosary beads. Twenty-two years and he loved her more than ever.

They had held hands through the film, and she'd cuddled next to him in the car coming home.

He stopped once on the highway to kiss her.

The swim inflamed them both even more. They were in each other's arms as soon as the bedroom door was closed. During the middle years of their marriage, when she was busy with the children and he with wartime cases and then learning the craft of an appellate judge, his campaign to free his bride so that she could become a wanton had languished. Then, after a retreat with the Jesuits at

Barrington, Tom realized that he had turned away from romance, a bad thing, especially for a medievalist.

After the retreat he discovered that Peg was at the height of her sexual desires, a breathtaking and head-spinning challenge.

Some retreat, he grinned ruefully.

She was, of course, still ashamed of her "animality" and doubtless pestered priests in the confessional for a reassurance that they could not give. Her shame did not, however, restrain her in their bedroom. Soon both their bodies were spent, but not satisfied.

After a long silence, she said, "Will they let him go back?"

She was thinking of Tim, their second son, a freshman at Notre Dame until he was suspended for smuggling liquor on campus.

"I think so. They usually give offenders one more chance. He did it for fun, not profit. Just an undergraduate prank."

"Why does he do such things?"

The judge sighed. He had heard too many cases in the Superior Court before being appointed to the federal bench by President Roosevelt to deceive himself about Tim. The boy needed professional help, but did not seem to want to benefit from it.

"It's not easy to have a father who's a judge," he said guardedly.

"And Marge?" Nighttime was for lovemaking and worrying about children. "I never spoke to my mother the way she speaks to me."

"Things have changed since the war," he said lamely.

"I thought Maria would be a good influence on her."

"Thank God, she has friends like Maria," he agreed, knowing that it was Maria and Hugh who most worried his wife on this humid, passionate summer night. "That little Italian girl made a simple thing like swimming a sacrament, a revelation of God's grace. Very neat, very pointed, very simple. He did make the lake and the sky and the moon and us. Sometimes we Irish need to be reminded of the sacredness of such things."

"Sicilians are morally lax."

"Now, come on, you're as fond of the girl as everyone else."

"Of course, I like her. How can you not like her? I thought the swim was wonderful. But did you see how Hugh reacted to her? God forgive me for putting his vocation in such danger."

"If Hugh can't live in a world where there are young women like Maria and not lose his vocation, it seems to me that God doesn't want him all that much."

"I'm terribly worried about our responsibility," Peg insisted.

He stroked her thick black hair, in which a few streaks of handsome white had begun to appear. "All we can do is our best. God doesn't expect anything more."

"I hope you're right," his wife murmured anxiously, and the hand with the rosary began to caress his chest. Her lips pressed down on his. "I love you so much. I don't want to fail as the mother of your children."

Hugh still could not sleep. He gave it up as a bad job, pulled on slacks and a sweat shirt, and walked softly down the hall, out of the house, and down to the pier that jutted into Lake Geneva—a long, narrow, fjordlike lake carved out of the hills of southern Wisconsin by a glacier forty thousand years ago. Only the stars shared the early morning hours with him.

It had been said of him when he turned down the scholarship to Michigan and went to the seminary that the vocation was his mother's, not his. But that did not seem fair either to his family or himself. Mom and Dad would be extremely happy, each in his own way, if he persevered to ordination. But they leaned over backward to grant him freedom in his decision. They were the ones who'd insisted that he go to Fenwick High School instead of the seminary after he had been caught necking with Flossie Mahoney in her basement. He had to "know his own mind," the judge had argued.

He could announce tomorrow that he was leaving the seminary and they would accept his decision, with a few tears from Mom, perhaps, but no recrimination.

Marry a girl like Maria? A wild thought under the starry skies.

They would accept her too. A good, sweet girl, his mother would say.

No, the vocation wasn't his mother's. Insofar as God worked through human beings, the vocation had to be attributed to the demanding religious faith in which he'd been raised, a faith that challenged him to do his best even, indeed especially, when it was difficult.

He thought of the problems when he had been in eighth grade, problems that led him to make up his mind that he had to be a priest. He had fought Marty Crawford in the schoolyard after Marty had called his mother a dirty name. The next week they'd lost to St. Kevin's in a football game because Father Shay, the priest from St. Kevin's, was also the ref and timekeeper and ended the game just before St. Ursula scored the winning touchdown. Hugh had told Father Shay that he was a cheater.

Then Marty was killed in an auto accident after he'd committed a mortal sin with a girl from the public school at Park Nine. At least everyone said they'd committed a mortal sin, and if they had, Marty went straight to hell.

Hugh felt responsible for Marty's death. If he hadn't beaten Marty so badly in the fight he would not have been reckless and stolen the car.

Then he'd kissed Flossie in the Mahoneys' basement recreation room, and was taking off her blouse when Mr. Mahoney caught them. He knew he was going to hell for all eternity, just like Marty. He was so angry at himself he didn't care.

All the problems came to a head at the retreat for the eighth-grade boys. The retreat master was Father Slawson, who used magic tricks and games as part of his instruction—dancing skeletons, exploding boxes, darkened rooms, pictures and diagrams of hell. He told the boys that they were cisterns of filth and that their dirty thoughts would lead them to an eternity of suffering in the deepest flames of hell.

"If you want to avoid hell," he said, "you must follow the call of God and become a priest. God gives everyone a call to the priesthood. He's as generous with his vocations as he is with the rain in the spring, the leaves in the fall, the snow in the winter. You can turn your back on a vocation, you can waste it, you can waste it away. But if you do, you will be consumed by the fires of hell for all eternity. If you wish to be happy forever with God and his angels and saints, you will flee this wicked world and become one of God's chosen priests."

On Friday night of the retreat week, Hugh sat in silence at the Donlons' supper table, pondering Father Slawson's grim words while Timmy, his freckled face twisted in its usual frown of complaint, protested against the fish.

"You should eat the fish even if you don't like it," Peggy told him. "Our Lord didn't want to die on the cross, but He did it anyway. The things that are hard to do are always the things that are best to do."

"Jesus didn't have to eat this fish." Tim pushed his red hair out of his eyes.

"But you do." The judge settled the matter as he would a sentence.

"Jesus could have found a lot easier way to save us from our sins." Peggy pushed her point. "He chose the terrible death of the cross to show us how much He loved us."

Hugh was puzzled. "You didn't marry Dad because it was the hardest thing to do, did you?"

The judge chuckled and Peggy blushed. "It's my purgatory on earth . . . no, seriously." She rested her hand on her husband's. "Your poor father is the one who's the saint for putting up with me. It's love that matters, the only thing that matters. When love says do something hard, then you do it. When love gives you a fine husband"—she smiled at Tom—"then you thank God for your good fortune."

"Can I have some more peas?" Margie, a pretty second grader with curly brown hair and wide brown eyes, interrupted on her favorite subject, food.

"What's for dessert?" asked Tim.

"No fish, no dessert," his mother said adamantly.

Tim looked as if he were going to cry, then remembered his mother's oft-repeated dictum "Donlons don't cry" and poked disconsolately at his fish.

That night Hugh decided he would certainly be a priest.

Older now, he knew that Father Slawson had exaggerated. Yet he also believed that to be an "alter Christus"—an Other Christ—was the most perfect thing a human being could do. It was a tough challenge. Responding to tough challenges made you a man, like his father.

So he would be a priest not because his mother and father wanted him to be a priest but because it was the most noble way of proving that he was a manly human being, brave enough and strong enough to give up appealing young women even if they set you on fire when they brushed against you in the waters of the lake.

You don't run away from them, Hugh told the skeptical stars, you resist the temptation.

Maria lay on the bed, hands clasped behind her head, listening to the crickets, the water lapping the shore, Marge's gentle breathing. Her friend had spilled out a story of passionate lovemaking after *Three Coins in the Fountain* and then quickly and easily fallen asleep. Marge would probably go all the way before the summer was over. Most likely without a twinge of guilt. How had such pious parents produced a daughter like Marge, who apparently had no morals, and a son like Tim, who was always in trouble for drinking or stealing or cheating?

And what was she doing as the guest of this convoluted Irish family, which had adopted her for the summer? She was, Peggy had insisted to Maria's mother, a good infuence on Margie. Yet Maria's parents, whom she adored and who adored her, were dismayed by the invitation, because they feared their daughter would be moving into a situation that was way beyond her. On the other hand, like everyone else in St. Ursula's, they thought the Donlons were outranked only by the archangels, so they'd agreed.

Maria did not know what to think of the stern but gentle judge, who seemed to laugh whenever she spoke, and his gorgeous wife, who sometimes seemed to like Maria more than she did her own daughter. Uncertain how to act, Maria set out to charm them by her fun-loving, carefree manner. Beneath her laughter, however, there was a shrewd, calculating Sicilian mind, one that operated by feel, hunch, and occasional leaps of insight. She was not a rationalist like her Irish friends who made up plausible though self-deceiving explanations for the crazy things they did. Maria inched her way down the street of life, in the dark, taking only the chances that her instincts said were worth taking.

Marge was her best friend and Maria earned them the reputation of being the funniest girls in the class. Yet Maria knew that she was four or five years more grown-up than Marge.

There was a lot she could learn from the Donlons, her instincts told her, and maybe a little bit she could do for them. So she hid her bubble gum and listened carefully to the way the Donlons talked. She imitated their manners, not because she expected anything from them but because it seemed sensible to adjust herself to their life as long as she was their guest.

Hugh required more than adjustment, she realized. There was a frightening power in those eyes, a fire of barely concealed desire. When other men looked at her that way she felt dirty. When Hugh considered her as a woman . . . she shivered. She felt like a woman.

Was he really going to be a priest? Could a man become a priest and still ignite electric currents inside her?

Would not such a man make a terrible mistake if he tried to do without a woman?

Maria was a realist about her future. In a year she would be out of high school, working probably at the West End Bank, whose president was a customer of her father's. In another year or two she would be married, a prospect she didn't find especially appealing. She had almost no social life, despite Marge's attempts to push her into one. None of the boys she knew from a distance appealed to her, neither the rich kids from Fenwick who occasionally danced with her at Trinity mixers or the slick, sleek young men from the old neighborhood of whom her uncles and cousins spoke approvingly. They were not the kind of men with whom she would want to share a life or, she shuddered, a bedroom.

Hugh Donlon was different. He was throat-catchingly beautiful, six-one, broad shoulders, strong muscles, and with the graceful movements of the dancers she had seen in the movies. His thick black hair and pale skin, much like his mother's, and the sad eyes and quick smile reminded her of a preternaturally masculine angel.

"Shut up, heart," she whispered under her breath. "You'll wake up everyone in the house!"

She couldn't drive him out of her thoughts. He had been the towering hero of the neighborhood through the last years of grammar school and the four years at Fenwick. It was expected that he would go to Quigley Seminary, but his parents and Monsignor "Muggsy" Brannigan said he should have a normal adolescence and attend Fenwick, like the other boys from the parish. He'd done his best to keep a low profile. He'd refused to run for class office and stayed away from football and basketball because the judge was afraid too much success too young might "turn his head" and because his mother was afraid he would be hurt on the football field.

It didn't work. In his junior year he was elected class president by acclamation against his will and dragged out to football practice. As a senior he'd led the Friars through an up and down season to the city playoff at Soldiers Field against an awesomely powerful Austin High School team—a "West Side grudge match," it was called. Fenwick was outweighed, outcoached, and outplayed. Yet they had held Austin to a 6-0 lead for three quarters, the touchdown coming on a block of one of Hugh's many punts.

Maria remembered that game as if it had been the day before yesterday. A frantic sixth grader, she and her father watched the game from behind the goalpost. Some men who were sitting near them blamed Fenwick's coach for trying to beat Austin at their own game instead of "letting Donlon throw the ball." Maria hated the Fenwick coach with all her heart.

Then at the beginning of the fourth quarter, Hugh had to punt from his own goal line again. The men said it was time for a fake kick. If he broke beyond the Austin line, there would be no one to stop him. They also said that the Fenwick coach would never let him do it.

The ball was snapped and the Austin team swarmed in on Hugh again, trying for another blocked punt. There was no time to kick the ball. As soon as he caught the snap, Hugh ran sharply to the right, dodged a massive Austin end, and took off down the sidelines. A hundred thousand people, most of them teenagers, stormed to their feet, shouting encouragement or dismay. Maria couldn't see over the heads of the big people in front of her. Her last glimpse of the field was a golden jersey closing in on Hugh's streaking black. Her father, who knew how much she adored Hugh, boosted her to his shoulder, in time for her to see the black shirt cross the goal line.

Fenwick's kicker, who had such poor eyesight he could barely see the goalpost, kicked the extra point. Hugh, who had held for the kick, walked slowly off the field as the crowd shouted its approval. Fenwick's coach seemed displeased. Maria hated him still more.

Fenwick won 7-6 and Kerry Regan, who was Hugh's steady, claimed that they went all the way that night. Maria did not believe it. Not Hugh.

He was offered athletic scholarships to Michigan and Harvard, but not to Notre Dame. Instead he went to the seminary and disappeared from sight.

But he'd never completely disappeared from Maria's thoughts. When she and Marge became close friends in their freshman year at Trinity, she bombarded her with questions about her brother who was going to be a priest. She knew other boys in the neighborhood who wanted to be priests, but they were not like Hugh. And she had never met anyone like the Donlons.

Yes, the Donlons were fascinating, passionate, and mysterious. And Hugh was the greatest of their mysteries.

Okay, do You *really* want him to be a priest?

If You don't, do You mind if I fall in love with him?

Again no answer. Maria gave up and went to sleep.

Chapter Three

1954

THE NEXT MORNING, in the clear light of another sizzling, humid day, Hugh felt foolish about his worries under the stars of the night before. Maria was, after all, a giggly teen-ager like his sister, beautiful, yes, in an understated way, but nothing to worry about. When it was decided that he was to take the two of them to the tennis courts, he did not object. At the courts Marge quickly abandoned them and sped off in Joe Delaney's Impala convertible—a plotted rendezvous,

Hugh decided in disgust at his sister's flagrant violation of family rules about going steady.

He was left with Maria, a stunning vision in white halter and tennis shorts, borrowed from Marge.

Not all that understated.

Maria was graceful and quick on her feet, but no match for him, even though he spotted her thirty points a game. Yet she managed to win two games of the first seven, taking savage delight in beating him.

The day was ferociously hot and soon the sweat was pouring off both their bodies. Hugh removed his soaking shirt.

"Not fair," Maria shouted from the other side of the court, "trying to distract me. Afraid I'll beat you?"

"You're a fine one to talk about distractions," he yelled back.

She won the first point of their eighth game by returning his best serve, in a lucky mis-hit that sent her into fits of laughter. With her two-point handicap, she led forty-love, and Hugh had to struggle for each of the next four points because Maria, driven to a frenzy by the excitement of the final game, raced around the court like a dervish, making unconscious and impossible returns.

At set point, his first serve was long and he followed with a powder puff. Maria banged it into the net.

She threw her racket into the air and caught it. "You cheat, Irish, and if you dare jump over the net, I hope you fall on your face. I'm a poor loser."

"I think you're a great sport." He walked confidently to the net to shake her hand.

"Why didn't you give me three points . . . ?"

As their hands touched, time stood still for Hugh.

He leaned over the net and kissed her, his lips brushing her cheek, and then her waiting lips.

She was inexperienced and nervous, hardly ever kissed before. He put his arms around her and drew her head to his chest, sweating young body against sweating young body. His hands felt the smooth skin of her back. Then he kissed her again, gently so as not to frighten her.

"Am I glad I didn't win!" she sighed contentedly.

You must look like an adoring little simp, Maria Angelica; you have no pride or dignity at all.

All right, I don't. I'm sorry, but he's gorgeous in his swimming trunks at the tiller of a sailing dory. On the water he seems so free and happy—not tied down to all those silly obligations that come from being a Donlon.

They had sailed for three hours in Hugh's trim little sailboat, the *Pegeen*. Maria had learned that the "sheet" was not the sail, but the rope that held the sail; that when he shouted "Ready about" she was supposed to loosen the jib sheet; and that when he shouted "Hard a lee" she was supposed to let it go and jump to the other side of the tiny craft and grab the other jib sheet, port or starboard, depending.

She knew she would never learn the difference between "port" and "starboard."

She fell over the side only once—when the boom hit her—and thoroughly soaked her black Fenwick shirt (which she wore because he liked it) and white bermudas.

Hugh dragged her back into the boat and warned her sternly about watching the boom.

She insisted he'd never told her what the boom was and she laughed at his impatience. She also laughed every time he gave an order and promptly replied "Yes, sir" or "No, sir," as if she were a midshipman in *Mutiny on the Bounty*.

Then Hugh laughed with her and seemed to revel all the more in the freedom and joy of the *Pegeen* dancing on the waves.

"Why are you looking at me so oddly?" he asked, a faint flush on his face— at least his face seemed redder than the sun had made it.

"You've been looking at me oddly since I got my clothes wet," she replied.

"That's only admiration . . ." His flush increased. "You're looking at me like . . . like a gambler, a countess in a gambling casino."

"All the Sicilian countesses are dead." She decided to tell the unvarnished truth. "I was admiring you . . . the way you seem so free and happy out here on the lake . . . kind of flowing along with the wind and the water and everything. I think right now you're the real Hugh Donlon."

He turned away, embarrassed, a second grader praised by his nun. Hugh Donlon shy and embarrassed. Wow, Maria.

"You see too much with those dancing blue eyes, young woman. You're right, though . . . the wind, the water, the sail, the tiller, my hand on the rope. . . ."

"Sheet. . . ."

"All right." He laughed delightedly. "I feel as if I'm part of God's creation out here, not pulling the world together but just fitting into place with the tiller and the sheet. You can laugh. I won't be mad."

And on shore you're trying to hold the whole world together. "I've already embarrassed you, so I won't embarrass you anymore, except by saying that you're beautiful when you're doing that."

He smiled, a gentle, modest smile, released the tiller, took her chin in his hand, kissed her gently, ran his hand lightly down her throat and over a Fenwick-covered breast, and recaptured the tiller—a smooth quick movement like that of a practiced dancer.

"Thank you, Maria." He sounded choked. "I'm glad you like me when I'm happy."

A legion of emotions raced through Maria's brain, all of them conspiring to make her light-headed. "I'll never settle for less," she said, and cursed herself for being a silly little fool. Silly lovesick little fool.

After Hugh skillfully brought the *Pegeen* into its slip on the other side of the pier from the diving board, he gave Maria a lesson in how canvas sails should be folded and packed. Hot, tired, and still light-headed, Maria was a bad pupil. The canvas slipped out of her hands and fell on the lawn.

"That's not the way to do it," he snapped. "Come on, Maria, you can do better."

Adoration turned to fury. Maria went into what her mother called the "Mount Aetna act."

"Don't you ever dare say anything like that to me again," she screamed at him. "I am not a summer camper, nor a slave girl, nor a kid in catechism class, nor a poor old nun in a sacristy, nor a housekeeper, nor an adoring Altar Society Woman. . . ."

Hugh collapsed on an old tree stump, laughing deliriously.

"What's so funny?" she demanded, hands jammed defiantly against her hips.

"Me." He grinned sheepishly. "If you're around me for long, Maria, you'll learn that I am a terrible dolt . . . the kind of dummy who spends a wonderful afternoon on a lake with a beautiful girl and then worries about the rules for folding canvas. I hope you'll forgive me. Irish conscience, I suppose. Now I've made you cry. . . ."

"You laugh at yourself often?" she said through the tears, her heart threatening to shatter for the sadness in his eyes.

"Not often enough. Why are you crying?"

"Because you're so wonderful." Maria turned away from him and ran up the lawn toward the house.

The judge stalked angrily out of the cottage as soon as Senator Joseph R. McCarthy appeared on their tiny TV screen. He could not stand the sight of the man. The Democrats would simply have to win the fall congressional elections and take away his committee chair.

He settled in a lounge chair in the shade of their huge oak tree at the foot of the pier and opened a book about late fourteenth-century French poetry. Maria, however, distracted him. Clad in a two-piece blue bathing suit, she was wrestling with Hugh at the other end of the pier. Lucky Hugh, to have such a gorgeous creature to throw into the lake. Young girls normally had little effect on Judge Donlon. Peg was more than enough woman for his life.

But it was a humid, sleepy day; he couldn't take his eyes off the little blond Sicilian, probably Norman or Germanic genes somewhere. And even if her father was a shoemaker, Manfredy was an aristocratic name. The girl had the elegance of a Dresden doll, the drive of a union organizer, and the quick intelligence of a high-priced lawyer for the defense—the kind the Mob employed.

He reproved himself for his ethnic prejudice.

Peg slipped by him, careful not to disturb his concentration on the medieval French—and also careful not to come too close. So great was the attraction between them this summer that they were afraid to touch one another in public.

The white strapless swimsuit with the broad red stripe from hip to opposite breast into which she had poured herself merited Maria's rapt appreciation.

Maria and Peg, he mused to himself, half asleep and half aroused. Such beautiful women. . . .

Hugh abandoned his combat with the little Sicilian and dragged his laughing mother toward the water.

For a moment Tom Donlon saw her nursing the boy in the apartment on Austin Boulevard. . . . He had told her of his "promise" to God after Tom Junior—or Tim, as he came to be called—was born. Peggy had not been impressed. "I dedicated Hugh to Our Lord the moment he stirred inside me," she said.

That had disturbed him. It laid a double burden on the child, and one Peg had imposed with too much innocence.

Marge (Margaret Junior) was the last of their children because there was a hysterectomy at the time of her birth, one the doctor thought necessary, although not as necessary as Tom had told his wife or the lurking Monsignor Clifton O'Meara, who thought the decision ought to be his. Three pregnancies and three miscarriages in seven years had not affected Peg's looks but had worked havoc with her uncertain reproductive system.

Tom regretted the need to deceive his wife. A Jesuit moralist from the seminary had assured him that the operation was justified. Peggy was too much of a child to be trusted with her own decisions in such crucial matters.

She was a wonderful wife, but she would never escape completely the damage done by Maude Curtin.

Hugh finally heaved her into the water, while Maria, who had withdrawn discreetly from the encounter, watched respectfully.

Would Maude Curtin's damage be visited on their own children? Tim and Marge certainly had their problems. And Hugh . . . mightn't he be better off if he left the seminary and took up with a girl like Maria?

At the edge of the pier, Hugh, tall, strong, and solidly muscled, momentarily appeared between the two women, one slender, the other voluptuous, one with short blond hair, the other with long black hair. The two women seemed to be fighting for him, one in the name of an overarching God, the other in the name of young love. Tom knew which one would win. He was not sure that she ought to win or that her victory would make her happy for very long.

There was conspiring at the end of the pier. Then the judge saw three attackers creeping toward him, a beautiful wife, a lovely girl, and his handsome son. Tom Donlon had never in his life been thrown into the lake. But, however much an affront such an attack was to the dignity of the federal judiciary, he'd come quietly.

Well, maybe a little struggle. For symbolic purposes. On a humid summer resort day, when two attractive women were tugging at you, symbols were quite important.

He carefully placed the French book under his chair. No reason to get it wet.

Maria was helping Peg set the table for supper, something she did routinely, without being asked, much to Marge's chagrin.

Marge and her mother had fought again earlier in the afternoon. Peg wondered whether it was "healthy" for Marge to see only Joe Delaney. There were so many other "nice boys" at Geneva this summer. "Can't you spend one night at home, and eat supper with us . . . ? Hugh's here for the first time this summer. And you have a guest. Don't you think you could help me prepare dinner occasionally?"

"You don't need ne," Marge snapped. "Maria does all the housewife work. She likes it."

"Leave me out of your fights," Maria said quickly.

"You can't fight with my mother," Marge sulked. "She's too pious to fight. Just like Hugh. You'd think they were both priests."

"Don't say such wicked things," Peggy pleaded. "Why can't we have a little peace in this house? Why do you fight me all the time?"

"You bring it on yourself," Marge shouted, rushing out of the house in response to Joe Delaney's imperious horn.

Marge was spoiled. She fought ceaselessly with her parents, who loved her, and with Hugh, whom she worshiped as a big brother. She seemed to be hooked on fighting the way some men were hooked on drink.

When Marge staged her explosions, Maria slipped out of sight and hummed opera tunes to herself.

"You Italians are a happy, carefree people," Peggy said, remembering the mischief of tossing a fully clad judge of the Seventh Circuit into the waters of Lake Geneva.

"Not really." Maria interrupted the aria she'd been humming. "My father says we're a morose and fate-haunted people who try to pretend we're great lovers and singers and dancers.''

"You don't pretend, Maria."

The girl had been puzzled the first day about the role of salad forks and horrified by the absence of wineglasses. She could not understand Peggy's grim opposition to "the creature." Still, she was a quick and discreet imitator. And could make fun of herself by joking about "potato forks, meat forks, vegetable forks, and, Peggy, *dessert* forks."

Peggy was "Mrs. Donlon" when others were around and "Peggy" privately. Instead of being offended, Peg was somehow flattered.

"That's because my mom and dad are really happy. We're exceptions, I think."

Back to the aria.

I like the poor thing. Why does she have to be a threat to Hugh's vocation? Why doesn't she go after Tim?

"Don't your parents want you to go to college? You're very smart; I'm sure you'd do well."

Maria considered, her expressive face in one of its rare interludes of thoughtfulness. "They'd be proud of me, I suppose, and they'd make any sacrifice. But I don't see the point. I can read books and listen to music without going to college."

Peggy had visited the shoemaker's shop to persuade Maria's mother to let her come to Lake Geneva. The mother was a very attractive but very shy woman in her midthirties who treated Peggy like royalty. It was a difficult conversation, because Paola spoke little English.

Yet she'd granted Peggy's request without the slightest loss of dignity.

"You'll probably marry quite young, then?"

Maria arranged the coffee cups. "Only if someone like the judge sweeps me off my feet."

They both laughed. "Brought it on myself," Peggy admitted.

Merciful heaven, I like her better than Marge. Such an appealing little body too. Grandchildren.

"Actually, I think I'll do what my father did and go to Italy to find myself a spouse. Someone handsome and quiet who will laugh at me all the time and do what I tell him."

"I think that few men would not want to."

Maria blushed. "Thank you," she said simply.

The girl was a threat to God's holy will.

Yet how could God object to someone so sweet?

"You look like you're angry at me." Dressed in a crisp white blouse and neatly pressed pink bermuda shorts, with a matching ribbon in her hair, Marge was leaving again with Joe Delaney, driving to Delevan for a dance. "Figure you're failing in your responsibilities to be a stabilizing influence on me?"

"You're a spoiled little bitch," Maria said bluntly.

"Okay, I've heard Hugh's lecture. Now I'll listen to yours."

"You adore Hugh, he's your wonderful big brother, that's what you've always told me."

It was dusk and the mosquitoes were beginning to bite, the fireflies to glow.

"You think I should drop Joe like the rest of them do." Her lower lip turned down in a childish pout.

"I think you should be nice to your family," Maria insisted, her own temper, normally as quiescent as a dormant volcano, sending up warning signals.

"You wouldn't if you were me. . . . Don't worry, my mother knows you're trying to stabilize me. Anyway, she likes you more than she does me."

Marge turned and ran toward the Delaney Cadillac, not permitting Maria a chance to blow.

So she walked over to the pier and cried instead . . . till the mosquitoes drove her into the house.

For a time, God, seminary, vocation, Father Meisterhorst, ceased to exist. Only Maria, Maria of the waiting lips and the submissive body. They kissed whenever they could, in the car, on the pier when no one was looking, in the water as he taught her to swim, outside the dance hall at the amusement pier in town, in the parlor of the cottage when they were alone, in the motorboat on the lake, in the back of the movie theater.

They ignored his parents and indeed everyone else in the adult world. They existed only for the sweet taste of each other's lips, the endearing touch of each other's hands, the warmth of each other's encircling arms.

The ritual dance of his high school years, in which young men and women fought a tug-of-war about where the line was to be drawn, was impossible with Maria. She drew no lines. He was the one who had to draw the line of tenderness and respect.

Then the seminary intruded itself, unannounced and unwanted.

They had watched *Three Coins in the Fountain* in rapt wonder, its sentimental romanticism matching their mood perfectly. He had caressed her leg lightly throughout the film and she had huddled in his arm as though her continued existence depended on his protection.

They had emerged from the theater into the humid night wrapped in a haze of dreamlike passion, she especially lovely in white bermuda shorts and a black Fenwick T-shirt that hung lightly against her breasts.

"Hello, Hugh." It was a chillingly familiar voice. "That wasn't the Rome I studied in, worse luck for me."

It was Father John Xavier Martin, a young professor of canon law from the seminary, one of the few diocesan priests on the mostly Jesuit faculty.

"Good evening, Father Xav." Hugh had stumbled over the words, then quickly regained his balance. "Did you throw any coins in the Fontana di Trevi?"

His arm was still around Maria. As deftly as he could, he slipped it away.

"Yeah," the young priest said disconsolately. "Hasn't worked so far."

"Uh, Father Martin, this is Maria Manfredy, a classmate of my sister, Marge."

"Hello, Maria." Father Martin pretended to notice her for the first time. "Happy to meet you. Did you go to Fenwick too?"

"I go to Trinity, Father, like Marge Donlon." The words came smoothly, just the right touch of respect for a priest in her voice, "We kind of cheer for Fenwick because there's nothing else around."

"That's the way life is." Father Martin took her in very carefully. "Nice to meet you, Maria . . . Have a good summer, Hugh."

He vanished into the summer night.

"Are you in trouble?" Maria was deadly pale in the glow of the street light.

"Nothing I can't talk my way out of if I have to," he said with more confidence than he felt.

Marge could hardly wait to get home and tell Maria about her triumph. Maria was the only one who understood her, the only one who cared, the only one who realized what a drag it was to be stuck with such dull, lifeless people as her parents.

She loved them, of course. They were wonderful people. But they lived by rules and regulations. They had no fun, no good times, no excitement. How had they managed to work up enough passion to conceive three children?

And Hugh, dear boy, was so pious, even though he didn't believe any of the stuff, not really. Tim was the only one in the family with any life and they were driving him to a head doctor.

No head doctor for Marge. She would split as soon as she could and sneak fun in the meantime.

Now that she was no longer a virgin, she thought triumphantly, there would be a lot more fun. Mom would be furious if she found out. What the hell did she think sexual organs were for?

Maria disapproved. But Maria understood. Indeed, when she was preparing to go all the way with Joe Delaney she thought of it as a kind of travelogue she could celebrate with Maria.

Actually, it wasn't much. Joe was clumsy and crude. Unbutton the blouse, pull down the shorts, rip at the underwear, fondle me, get inside me, lay all over me like I was a water float, and then scream like a maniac. There's got to be more to it than that.

She had not particularly enjoyed her deflowering and now she hurt.

Well, it was done, anyhow. Out of the way. That's what counted.

Still, she'd make a big production out of it for Maria; give the pious little frump some thrills.

"See you tomorrow night?" Joe asked hungrily as she jumped out of the car.

"Maybe," she said curtly.

Maria, dressed in shorty pajamas, was sitting up in bed reading. She turned to Marge as she charged into the room, her face anguished by anxiety and love.

Marge fell into her arms and wept bitterly.

Chapter Four
1954

HUGH'S PARENTS WERE painfully aware of the romance. He drove with them every morning to the eight o'clock Mass in the little church on the hills above Fontana and continued to receive Holy Communion, because, despite what Father Meisterhorst would say, he did not think he and Maria were sinning seriously. Then they would return to the cottage for breakfast before the two girls awoke. Dad would leave for the golf course, Mom would retreat to the gazebo converted into a studio for her watercolors, and he would sit in the parlor, read some passages from Abbott Marmion, without comprehending any of the words, and labor through a chapter of *Lord of the Flies* before the girls appeared and the day began.

The judge and Peggy had spoken of their fears only once.

The morning after their meeting with Martin, on the way home from Mass, his father began tentatively, "Maria is a very lovely young woman."

"We feel responsible . . ." his mother said.

"Nothing to feel responsible about, Mom. Maria and I are having a good time together. Neither of us thinks it's going to last. I'll go back to Mundelein and she'll go back to Trinity. We'll both have pleasant memories for years to come. That's all."

The judge tried another tack as he brought the three-hole Buick to a halt in the driveway behind the cottage. "If you should decide to leave the seminary, Maria might be an ideal young woman to, uh . . . court. She and you seem to balance each other very nicely."

"We like her very much," his mother insisted. "We don't want to interfere with your decision or with God's will."

Hugh laughed easily. "It's not going to go that far. Can't I have a short summer romance without you thinking about grandchildren?"

Peg started to say something, then stopped.

Later that morning, after the judge had left for the golf course and his mother had retreated to the gazebo, Hugh sat in the parlor, waiting for the girls to come down for breakfast. As he reread the same page from Marmion for the third time, he reprimanded himself. It was not as easy as he'd pretended to his parents. He was in love with Maria. It was a passing summer love, no doubt, but also an exhilarating and disturbing love. He was breaking seminary rules, risking heartache for himself and for her, needlessly worrying his parents. He was both reckless and irresponsible. He couldn't stop.

He didn't want to stop.

Tim was more blunt than Mom and Dad. "Hey, does that Manfredy dish put out for you? Most Guinea girls do. I bet she's terrific!"

"She doesn't and we're just friends," Hugh replied hotly. As much as he liked Tim, or thought he did, he was offended by his incorrigible cynicism. In Tim's world nothing was straight. He conned professors at Notre Dame to give him an A or a B even though the con job took more time and effort than study. He lied to girls when it was as easy to tell them the truth. He cheated in tests even though he knew the answers without cheating. That was the way life was with Tim.

"Get it while you can, brother," Tim advised as they drove from the train stop at Williams Bay.

There was no point in arguing with Tim or being angry at him. "Go easy on the booze this weekend, will you?" Hugh said, changing the subject. "You know how Mom and Dad worry."

"I know." Tim sounded genuinely sorry. "I guess I do like it a little too much. But you gotta kill the pain of school. Once I escape from the damn classroom, I'll settle down."

Tim was the smartest of the three Donlons and, when he set his mind to it, the most charming. Only he didn't set his mind to it very often. He was too busy devising some new piece of kinkiness.

Girls thought Tim Donlon was cute—a thin little redhead with a freckle-drenched face and an appealing grin, he seemed to them to be a "perfect Irish leprechaun." His good humor, quick tongue, and ready wit confirmed the leprechaun image.

So he was much more successful with girls than were other Notre Dame freshmen with better looks and more athletic ability.

Tim for his part had learned how to get the most out of a young woman with the least effort. There were ways of necking and petting that gave a girl what she wanted and left her pretty much at his disposal.

Maria obviously liked him. She bantered with him more than she did with Hughie. Since she was probably putting out for Hugh, why not for him too?

It was a risk but that made it all the more fun.

So, driving over to the grocery in Fontana, he made his move. Poor Mom, I'm doing exactly what she wants, taking the girl's mind off Hugh.

She wasn't a bad kisser, either. Hugh had warmed her up nicely.

But then she struggled to escape from his arms, tears in those warm blue eyes.

You win some and you lose some.

"I wouldn't hurt you for the world, Maria," he said apologetically.

"I didn't say it wasn't nice." She rearranged her peasant blouse.

He laughed. "I like you, Maria, I really do." And that was the honest truth.

"Why are you always in trouble, Tim"—she was good at setting up defenses too—"stealing the chalice from the sacristy, taking the money from the parish carnival, getting caught with the beer at Notre Dame? What would you do with the chalice? And you don't need the money, do you? And I bet you didn't drink any of the beer."

"Not that beer, anyway." He laughed. "I don't know. But I can tell you what the head doctor says. He says I'm a thrill-seeker."

"Head doctor?" She seemed astonished that there was such a thing.

"Sure. If a Donlon has trouble, he goes first to the priest, then to the psychiatrist. You know the Bobs at Riverview? The most dangerous ride in the park? I ride them all day when I'm there. Nothing else is any fun."

"Do you *have* to?" she asked softly.

"No, not till I get on them. Then I can't get off."

"I don't understand." She sounded as if she were trying to grasp a theorem in math class.

"Remember the time I stole the chalice from the church over in Fontana? You know what I mean. I'm sure Marge told you all about it. I mean, they left it there in the sacristy, just asking for it to be stolen. And I jimmied the window one Sunday night and took it out. They didn't even notice the marks on the windowsill. Vanished into thin air." Timmy chuckled, remembering the expression on Monsignor Schultz's face.

"You *had* to take it?"

"I wanted it so bad I dreamed about it at nights, not because I would do anything with it and not because I needed it but because it was there to be taken. I would have been all right if I hadn't had to look at it on the altar during Mass. Then one Sunday it was too much. I had to have it, like riding the Bobs."

"Oh. . . . Did you feel good after you took it?"

"Kind of proud, for being so slick. But the real fun is actually doing it . . . and laughing at comic characters like old man Schultz. I was going to give it back. . . ."

"And then you were caught, much to your mother's distress."

"That's what the head doctor says."

"What?"

Tim glanced at her, at the opposite end of the front seat of the family Buick. God damn Hugh; why did he always have to get the best? Oh, well, that's the way it always was and always would be.

"The head doctor says I do it because my mother tells me not to."

"She never tells Hugh not to, does she?"

Too damn smart.

"I don't hurt anyone," he said.

Hugh and Maria were floating aimlessly on the Donlon Chris-Craft in the middle of the lake, under a ceiling of closely crowded stars, after watching Audrey Hepburn in *Roman Holiday*. They drove in the boat to Geneva town because it was more private and more romantic than a car, even if it did cause a faint lift of his mother's eyebrow when they walked down to the pier in the purple twilight.

After the movie, they visited the dance hall where Maria had sung "Buttons and Bows" for the cheering young people, and played at the pinball machines in the arcade on the amusement pier.

Now they were relaxing in the front seat of the boat, one of his arms around her shoulders, and the other at rest on her belly over the Fenwick T-shirt, which had become a kind of uniform, washed fastidiously every night before she went to bed.

"Wouldn't it be nice to float here forever?" he said contentedly.

"Marry me," she replied.

"Huh?" Hugh sat up, surprised, his hand retreating quickly from her stomach.

"I don't mean now." She was still passive in his arm. "I mean next year when I graduate from high school."

"You're too young to marry, Maria." A frigid terror crept into his veins despite the warmth of the night.

"I'll be as old as your mother was when she married the judge."

God, help me not to hurt her. "I can't imagine a better wife. . . ."

"I'm a great cook, and I'll be good in bed once I learn how, and I'll give you lots of cute babies and I'll be beautiful when I'm old like my mother is, and I'll learn to read books, and I won't embarrass you too much, and I'll love you always and I'll make you happy every day of your life."

"There would never be an unhappy day, or a dull one either." He edged out of their embrace. "But I'm going to be a priest, Maria."

"No, you're not," she said confidently. "You like women too much."

"We don't give up women because we don't like them, Maria." He shifted uneasily in the damp leather seat.

"Some men like women and can give them up. I guess it's a good idea. . . . You're not one of them, Hugh. You like us too much. You . . . you drink me in as if I were a cool glass of lemonade on a hot day."

"I don't mean to humiliate you." He laughed nervously.

"Who's humiliated? I love it. Any woman would. And you look at every attractive woman that way. I saw you taking in that man's wife at the ice cream stand tonight. She was real old . . . at least thirty. . . . You won't be able to get along without one of us. I'll make the sacrifice." She laughed. "And be the one."

"You're wrong, Maria," he said slowly, wondering whence came her quick, sure insights.

"I'm right," she replied pleasantly. "The point is that you're in the seminary because of your family. If you had your own way, you'd be hunting for a wife."

"My family isn't forcing me." He retreated from her to the safety of the steering wheel of the Chris-Craft.

"They've persuaded you that you're free. They think you are. And you think you are. You're not, though. You know it will please the judge, especially if you're some kind of intellectual priest. And it will make Peg deliriously happy. And . . . now don't start this boat till I'm finished . . . and you'll satisfy the crazy Donlon notion that if something is hard, maybe impossible, then it has to be what God wants. And if it's something that's fun and will make you happy, then it has to be sinful."

"I have to start the motor, so we don't drift into Black Rock."

He turned over the engine and at slow speed pointed the boat back toward the middle of the lake, searching his heart for a response to her furious assault. I love you, Maria, even when you're angry. Especially when you're angry. "But if you're called to be a priest," he said finally, "you have to ask whether you dare turn down God's invitation. Happiness is irrelevant."

Maria exploded. "That's the worst thing I've ever heard in my life. I'm not as good a Catholic as you Donlons maybe, but I know God wants us to be happy. If you become a priest because you think you have to, Hugh, you're not doing what God wants."

"I am too," he snapped, trying to control his own anger.

"And it's not just the priesthood either." She jabbed his chest with an imperious finger. "Even if you weren't going to be a priest, you still wouldn't marry me. You'd be afraid I'd make you be Hugh Donlon on the sailboat, filled with joy and life . . . and love."

Hugh felt as if someone had opened a door inside him and let in a tiny sliver of light.

He slammed the door shut. "You're just being a romantic," he said, as something wonderful and terrifying faded away into the dark.

Chapter Five
1954

ONE HAS TO lose one's virginity sometime, Maria supposed. It might as well be with Hugh Donlon. He wouldn't hurt her, the way Joe Delaney had hurt poor Marge. Yet she was frightened as the red and white Buick bumped down the back road under a frowning gray sky. Clear-eyed about herself as always, Maria knew that her innocence and inexperience might make her act foolishly. She would keep her steady patter of wisecracks going till the last minute and then fall apart.

I hope you understand, God. I don't think You'll send me to hell. You do want me to love him, don't You?

The Lord had no comment.

A silly raspberry-picking expedition. "Len Mulloy has a couple of hundred acres of woods up there that they use for hunting. Even has a hunting lodge. He told us we could bootleg his raspberries."

All I want is that he love me a little longer.

And the worried look on poor Peg's face as they drove off. She knows lust when she sees it, that woman. We're rivals for you, my darling. She wants you for God and I want you for me.

Why can't I hate her?

And why do I love you so much?

There was no wind when they parked at the end of the twin ruts and hiked into the woods. But by the time their baskets were almost filled with the succulent red fruit and their fingers smeared with the juice, a stiff breeze was blowing through the tops of the trees and low clouds were scudding across the patches of sky above them. Maria shivered. It was turning cold.

"It's going to rain," she warned.

"No, it isn't, the weather forecast said the front wouldn't come through till tonight. Let's fill this last basket."

"All right, it's not going to rain. Heaven forbid that the forecast be wrong."

They plunged farther into the woods and filled the last bucket. A few raindrops were falling on their faces, then the drops turned into a torrent, quickly soaking them to the skin.

"It's not raining," she shouted over the wind. "Just a figment of my superstitious southern Italian imagination."

"Let's make a run for the hunting lodge," he shouted back in high good humor. "It's up this way, I think."

The rain fell in great billowing gray sheets; lightning darted across the sky and leaped occasionally into the woods. The wind howled through the treetops.

The rain was cold and Maria shivered as they dashed blindly about the woods, water streaming into their eyes and down their faces.

"Front's coming through tomorrow."

Breathless and battered, they stumbled into a clearing and, fruit baskets still banging against their legs, rushed across the open space to the door of the hunting lodge. Hugh fiddled with a number of keys and then threw the door open. Inside there were a couple of rustic couches and some old tables and chairs and a tattered rug thrown on the floor. The room smelled of mildew and disinfectant.

"You're soaking wet," Hugh said.

"Can't be. The front isn't coming till tonight."

He rummaged through a linen closet and found two beach towels. "Wrap this around yourself," he ordered, throwing her one. "I'll build a fire to warm us and dry out our clothes."

"Yes, master."

In the bathroom, Maria peeled off her clothes, and critically considered the young woman in the dark mirror. Almost as if you'd planned it this way, Maria Angelica. She folded the towel around herself and, appraising the short blond hair plastered down on her skull, ordered her heart to stop pounding. It refused to obey.

He's kidding himself about what will happen. I'm not.

So which one is us is worse? She took a deep breath and returned to the parlor.

A fire was already crackling in the fireplace. The room smelled of pitch and smoke, like a bonfire of autumn leaves. Clever boy scout, my man.

His towel tied at his waist, Hugh was making instant coffee on an ancient electric grill.

He handed her a cup. "I was wrong about the rain." He smiled apologetically. "At least you provided a desert island with all the comforts of home."

He was thoughtful for a moment. Then his face turned quizzical, then hard and determined. Maria was frightened.

"What . . . ?" she said.

He stood up, took the coffee out of her hand, and lifted her to her feet, examining her as if she were a work of art he was about to bid on. His fingers touched the towel knotted under her shoulder and it dropped to the floor.

She didn't move, frozen in a mixture of fear, shame, and desire. He continued to examine her gravely, respectfully.

Then his fingers began to explore her face, as if the rest of her could wait until later, carefully examining her cheeks, chin, eyes, nose, lips, wet blond hair.

Maria gave herself to him.

His hands crept down her throat and neck and his lips followed where his fingers had prepared the way. Lightly he touched her shoulders, her back, her chest, and then with infinite delicacy her breasts, first one and then the other, encircling them as if they might break under the pressure of his touch.

"Oh, God, yes," Maria moaned as his lips relentlessly followed his fingers.

"Pretty, pretty," he murmured.

A languid peace suffused her flesh. All would be well. She would not fail.

They teetered on the brink. She waited expectantly to topple over the side with him.

Then with a convulsive spasm, Hugh twisted away, fell on the rustic couch behind him, and buried his head in its pillows.

Maria stood above him, motionless as a statue, conscious of the firelight caressing the smooth contours of her body. Then she picked up the towel, wrapped it around herself once again, and sat on the edge of a chair across the room.

Hugh did not speak, did not move.

Maria waited.

"I'm sorry," he said at last in a choked voice.

"I'm not angry, nor hurt, nor humiliated, nor anything like that."

Surprisingly, she was not.

Another long wait. And Maria thought, all right, up there, You really taught me a lesson. Someday I'll thank You. But not now.

"The rainstorm we didn't have isn't here anymore," she said finally.

He didn't look up from the pillows. "Will you go down to the car and wait for me? I won't be long."

"Yes," Maria said softly. "I'll wait as long as you want."

Her clothes were still damp as she put them on in the bathroom. At the doorway of the lodge she paused. "I'm taking half the raspberries. Don't forget the rest."

Rain was still dripping from the trees as she trudged through the mud and water back down the path to the red and white Buick waiting, wet and indignant, at the end of the ruts. A typical summer storm, sudden, fierce, and over in an instant.

Hugh and his father drove Maria to the train station in Walworth on Sunday night to catch the Milwaukee Road to Chicago and the three rooms in the back of the shoemaker's shop on Division Street. Peggy was meeting with a committee planning the Lake Geneva Art Fair, Marge was having dinner at the Delaney house, and a sober Tim was at Notre Dame trying to arrange for his readmission.

Hugh was at the wheel of the lumbering Buick, his father next to him in the front seat. Maria was in the back, as vivacious as ever, entertaining them in the car with an account of a visit to the "old neighborhood"—where her life still had its emotional roots even though she lived on Division Street—by relatives from Sicily "via the University of Rome."

"My cousin Marco—he's the one from Rome—says to my uncle Geno, he says, 'Don Eugenio, what do you do for culture?'

"No one ever asks Geno this before. So he waves his hand and says, 'Marco, when you own three pizza parlors, who needs culture?' "

The judge didn't approve. "Culture's important, Maria."

"I know it is. That's why I listen to the opera every Saturday afternoon."

"What's your favorite opera, Maria?" the judge asked.

"*Rigoletto*," she said without hesitation. "It's so sad . . . but the poor girl got what she deserved, fooling around with dukes and important people like that."

They arrived at the railroad station.

The Walworth train stations on Sunday nights at the end of the summer were dismal places—husbands returning for a lonely week at the office, families sadly anticipating the end of vacation, older kids going back to jobs in the city and wondering why summers were better when they were fourteen, dust and dirt and the blinding sunlight of day's end, too much luggage, too many people, and the certainty that the train would be late, hot, and crowded.

Maria was wearing a light summer dress, two years old and a bit small. In shorts and slacks she could have passed for a countess. In a badly fitting dress she was a shoemaker's daughter.

They left the car, Hugh carrying her old-fashioned black suitcase. In it, he imagined, was the black Fenwick T-shirt.

"I want to say something to you, young woman." The judge was his most judicial.

"Yes, Your Honor?"

"I admire your loyalty to the old neighborhood and its culture, of which you make fun so lovingly. But the old neighborhood is changing, Maria. We're hiring law clerks from Taylor Street now . . . even one woman applicant this year who was better qualified than all the young men."

"Not a blonde, I hope."

The judge smiled his faint, quick smile. "It has not been my pleasure to meet the young woman. That's beside the point, Maria."

"I understand, Judge Donlon." The train whistle sounded only a few hundred yards away. "You don't want me to get lost between the old old neighborhood and the new old neighborhood . . . to say nothing of the new new neighborhood, where lots of kids growing up in the old old neighborhood will end up living . . . in River Forest." Her eyes filled with the tears she'd been fighting back during the ride.

"Precisely." The judge turned away so that he would not see them.

The yellow and green train huffed into the station and seemed to collapse with a weary sigh.

She embraced both of them, awarding each a fervent kiss on the cheek, clinging a little longer to Hugh. "Don't anyone say anything but good-bye or I'll be a weeper all the way to Chicago." Then she turned quickly and slipped into the crowd pushing toward the train.

"*Arrivederci*, Maria." The words fell softly from Hugh's lips.

On the step of the train she turned, smiled radiantly through her tears, and bid them farewell with a wave of the hand.

The countess again. The countess saying good-bye.

"For reasons I don't want to examine closely," the judge said in the Buick on the way back to Lake Geneva, "she reminds me of your mother at that age."

Chapter Six
1954

FORGETTING MARIA AFTER he returned to the seminary was much more difficult than Hugh had imagined. He raced through letters from home, hoping for news of her; he imagined the click of her heels on the empty sidewalks outside his window, although he had never seen her in high heels; he dreamed about her at night, fantasized about her through morning meditations, recalled her grin and her laughter during dull theology classes.

He would not, he could not, leave the seminary.

Sheer willpower, however, was not enough to exorcise the girl who followed him down the silent, dark corridors of the seminary residence hall.

In desperation, he turned to his friend Jack Howard. Their roles were now reversed. Hugh had helped Jack through a crisis in his vocation. Now it was Jack's turn. But the short, stocky young man was at a loss.

"It's beyond me, Hugh. Maybe you ought to leave."

"I can't do that. And I can't talk to Meisty or any of the Jebs. They'll report me to the rector and I'll be out on my buns."

"Pat Cleary talked to Xav Martin after you bailed him out of trouble last year, when the rector was going to expel him. He says that Xav is opposed to the whole system here, even if he pretends to go along. He says you can trust Xav to keep his mouth shut."

He had kept his mouth shut so far.

Hugh waited another week. At last the ghost of Maria was beginning to fade. Then he received two letters: a brisk businesslike note from the judge saying that Tim had been caught again with beer in his room and expelled, and one from Tim saying he was joining the Navy and protesting that he hadn't touched the beer but was only smuggling it into the dorm for others.

"The Navy is mostly my idea, Hughie. Mom thinks it will help. You know how the judge dislikes the military. I don't know, maybe it's a good idea to go away for a couple of years. It's not fair that I should be a problem for the rest of you."

Hugh pounded his desk in frustration. No, it wasn't a good idea at all. The

Navy wouldn't help Tim. He needed professional assistance. He should never have stopped seeing his psychiatrist.

Fine lot of help I've been to him. More concerned with my own problems than with his. And my problems are mostly imaginary.

That night Hugh made an appointment with Father Martin.

Worried and nervous, he walked on tiptoes into the canon lawyer's room the next night at the end of the after-supper smoking period.

Father Martin waved his hand negligently. He was a lean, black Irishman, a canonical Tyrone Power. "Sit down, Hugh. What's on your mind?"

"The girl you didn't meet when we didn't encounter each other at a movie in Lake Geneva. She's on my mind all the time."

"What girl?" Martin raised his trim eyebrow.

Hugh leaned forward on the edge of his chair. The heat of early September had turned into a serene golden autumn, mellowing the red brick buildings and the vast green lawns of the seminary. The grass outside Father Martin's window seemed to be the same color as Maria's hair.

"The one in the Fenwick T-shirt."

"*That* one." Martin rolled his eyes. "Yes, I remember the T-shirt. I suppose she's worth talking about. Sit down and tell me about her."

Hugh did, at great length and in elaborate detail.

Xav Martin rubbed his cheek, which looked unshaven fifteen minutes after the razor had touched it. "Sounds like you're in love with her, or think you are. . . . Some of us are like that, Hugh. We go from one steamy romance to another. We're always in love. Mostly genes and hormones. It doesn't matter whether we're married or celibate. We're romantics. But the priest romantic doesn't have to jump into bed with his parishioners and the married romantic doesn't have to commit adultery with his secretary. If you're a romantic, life is more interesting and more difficult. Maria is probably the first of many, even if you should leave and marry her. You'll get used to it."

"What should I do?" Hugh pleaded.

"Right now? Nothing. The ghost will go away. Then you can make up your mind whether you want to be a priest."

"I do want to be a priest," Hugh said firmly.

Father Martin studied him intently.

"I do," Hugh insisted.

"Then you'll have to give up Maria."

"I know. . . ."

Hugh talked to Xavier Martin every week for the rest of the semester. Slowly Maria retreated from his consciousness. He did not see her the following summer; another Trinity girl replaced her as the "good influence" on Marge. The judge and Peg did not mention her name. Even Marge had seemed to forget her, although perhaps that was only a kindly pretense.

Maria remained only a memory etched in his brain, never to be completely erased.

Chapter Seven
1956

"IT'S FOR YOU and it's a boy," Paola yelled from the store, the location of their party-line phone.

Maria leaped up with such enthusiasm that her Introductory Accounting text flew across the room.

"Boys don't call me," she said breathlessly as she dived into the store and grabbed the phone from her smiling mother's hand. "Only one."

"Hello, Maria, I hope I'm not disturbing you."

Maria's heart did several flying turns and ended up in her throat.

Hugh.

"Just going out," she lied.

Paola shook her head indulgently and slipped out of the store.

"I won't keep you a minute. . . ."

"I can spare a few." She grabbed one of her father's awls and held it up like a weapon. "How were the raspberries last summer?"

"Same old Maria." His nervous laugh suggested his heart was halfway up his throat too. Maria resolved to be nice. "I'd like to ask for some help."

Was he *leaving* the seminary? "I'll be serious," she promised.

"I'm flying to Las Vegas for part of the winter vacation. Marge is living there now, you know. I wonder if you have any ideas about how I can persuade her to go back to school. She did see you before she left San Francisco with the English dance director."

"When I saw her it was a Brazilian soccer player."

"Oh."

"My advice is don't," Maria said, rushing into the void. "Don't fly to Vegas. Don't try to persuade her to return to school. Don't do anything. She needs time away from the family. The more you folks lean on her, the longer that time will be."

"We love her, Maria."

"She loves you too; but she has to be free of that love for a while. It's the only way she'll ever grow up and leave the spoiled little girl behind."

How can I cry with you over the phone?

"That's harsh."

"Okay, it's harsh. It's also true."

"Maybe you're right. . . . How's the bank?"

"It survives."

"I'm glad to hear it. I hope you'll be able to attend my first Mass. . . ."

"Sure."

You need someone to make you laugh and make you cry, my darling Hugh. Why couldn't it be me?

She said good-bye and hung up.

Hugh tried to distract himself from the memory of Maria's voice and the song in her laughter by absorbing every detail of the scenery below on the long flight from Midway Airport to Las Vegas. Calling her had been an impulsive mistake, undoing the hard-won independence of his years-long self-denial.

He hadn't wanted her advice about Marge. Rather, he'd wanted to talk to her, to hear her laughter, to revel in her vitality again.

Now he concentrated on the profligate beauty of the Grand Canyon, which curiously made him feel as if he were in church. He tried to put Maria out of his mind. For heaven's sake, he was only a few months away from the subdeaconate and a promise of perpetual celibacy. What had he been thinking?

The elder Donlons didn't travel much. Highway 12 to Lake Geneva had been enough for his father and mother. But now Tim was touring the world in the Navy, Marge had settled in Las Vegas with a lover, and he was spending half of his two-week winter vacation on a pagan fling in Las Vegas.

A winsome stewardess flirted with him outrageously during the flight, ignoring her other passengers so she could sit on the armrest of the seat across the aisle from him and swing her lovely legs as she talked about the skiing at Vail, the shows in Vegas, and the surf at La Jolla.

A cute and lively little doll, with a neat figure and long brown hair, the sort of doll you would carry home to mother.

She broadly hinted that she would have time to see him during her two-day layover in Las Vegas.

Would she go to bed with him? Probably. She was looking for a husband. The celibate could not be sure what he was missing. What would it be like to carry this little doll into a bedroom?

After two quarters at Lone Mountain College in San Francisco, Marge had quit school and moved in with an English choreographer—the "English" calculated to be especially offensive to her parents. She refused to go home or to let her parents visit her, or even to talk more than a few minutes with them on the phone.

"I don't hate you," she wept bitterly on one occasion. "I love you terribly. That's why I can't talk to you."

The choreographer moved from San Francisco to Las Vegas, to direct a show at one of the casinos on the Strip. Marge went along as his "assistant," maintaining that she was learning to be a professional dance director, a claim her father said was so patently absurd as not to merit comment.

The judge still thought of Marge as the tousle-haired little girl who had climbed into his lap and stared worshipfully into his eyes. Angry and disgusted, he had wanted to give up on her. Peggy had rebuked him. "She's our daughter and we must stand by her. Maybe she'll change her mind. We must pray to God for her and try to understand where we failed."

Marge was torn between anger and eagerness as she waited at the airport with Larry and her friend Jean Hartmann for Hugh's plane to land.

Oddly enough, she missed Hugh the most. The big brother/little sister relationship had worked well for both of them, except when Hugh felt the urge to be pious. And even then, after delivering his sermons, he relaxed, forgot about them, and became her childhood hero again.

So she desperately wanted to see him.

On the other hand, she was furious with her parents for having sent him to lure her back, especially because she was lonely and more than a little afraid.

Damn it, why can't they leave me alone?

Larry was a dear but not terribly exciting after the first enthusiasms. There were times when he reminded her of her father.

Only he was not as good a choreographer, by a long shot, as her father was a judge. Larry was going nowhere and Marge did not intend to go nowhere with him.

"Why does your brother want to be a priest?" Jean asked.

"Beats me," Marge replied, not wanting to talk about it. "Mom's influence, I suppose; it's one way to keep your son for yourself."

Jean was a last-minute idea. She would distract Hugh from his mission and—who knows?—maybe he would fall for her. That would prevent him from wasting his life as a priest. Marge knew Jean was Hugh's kind of woman.

Like Maria.

Marge felt a pang of guilt. She'd lost touch with Maria. Had not answered any of her letters at Lone Mountain. Did not want to think about Maria's common sense. Or her love.

"Can one be a man and still be a priest?" Larry asked politely. "I should think it would be rather difficult."

"Wait and see," Marge said firmly.

The seat belt sign went on for the descent into Las Vegas. Hugh stuffed *The Man in the Gray Flannel Suit* into a duffel bag under the seat in front of him. Suburbia was another strange world—although perhaps more like the one in which he would work the year after next than Vegas would be.

All the more reason to find out what the Vegas world was like.

Or the world in which he would work if he turned down the Cardinal's offer of graduate study.

The white-haired, forgetful old man had called him into his red brick house on the lake across from the seminary on a weekend in early December. Seminary authorities, he'd said, spoke very highly of him. Most efficient sacristan in main chapel in years. Top-notch administrator. Didn't offend people. Advisers were telling him he should train a man in business administration. Didn't know whether it made much sense. Trusting in the Holy Spirit was better than newfangled planning ideas. Probably ought to give it a try. Send him to graduate school, Loyola or De Paul.

At first Hugh was exultant. He would put some order into the chaos of diocesan affairs. Then he hesitated. He wanted to be a parish priest, not a businessman in a Roman collar.

"I have to think about what such work might do to my prayer life," he'd said.

Understand the problem. Hard to pray in an office all day long.

Rumor had it that the job had been offered to Sean Cronin in the class ahead of him. Cronin was a moody, intense young man, son of a millionaire, with blond hair, hooded brown eyes. He kept his distance from most people, though he was well liked in his own class and close to Jimmy McGuire, who was one of the finest men in the seminary.

"No one told me anything about it," he'd replied curtly to Hugh's question. "Suit yourself. If you hate other human beings, it might be fun."

The "No Smoking" sign came on. Beneath him the desert was barren, like the life of a priest who was not happy.

Only one mention of Maria the last two years. On her midterm break from college—just before she'd quit—Marge had said that Maria liked her job at the bank. Hugh's heart had stood still. The sound of her name had hit him like an air hammer.

The weary Lockheed settled on the runway. His fellow passengers prepared to dash for the exit as soon as the plane stopped. In Vegas, apparently, you didn't waste a moment in your haste to get to the gaming tables.

"Have fun," the winsome cabin attendant said as he left.

"I'll try."

Tim Donlon strolled casually into the jeweler's shop. It was the most fashionable one he had yet visited, on Garden Road down the street from the Bank of China and a magnet for American and English tourists, who would marvel at how cheap Thai jade and silver were in Hong Kong.

He wore his full petty officer's uniform with radar technician's stripes and trim cap on such adventures. The cap hid his red hair. The uniform made him look honest and respectable.

The Navy was not as dull as Notre Dame. Tim enjoyed the ports his carrier visited in the Mediterranean, and later in the Pacific. But watching a radar screen for eight hours every day was a bore. The poker games when he was off duty were mildy exciting, even if his experience at the pinochle table on Mason Avenue made him so much better than most of his shipmates that there was little challenge in relieving them of their money. But not exciting enough.

He turned to theft and smuggling for excitement. The heady experience of lifting jewelry and carrying dope in the world's great ports was better than the sauce, even better than sex, although it was best when he mixed sex with it.

Some of the jewels he gave away to shipmates whose money he'd won or to women who amused him or to young American tourists on the street. Taking the forbidden article was more important than the money he might make from selling it.

The interior of the jeweler's shop was covered with thick red sound-absorbing carpet and the walls were hung with heavy orange drapes. The store was a cross between a cathouse and a funeral home.

He drifted to a glass counter where a young woman was showing jewels to an elderly American couple. Young women clerks were the easiest mark in every port in the world.

The girl was something special, classic Chinese beauty, slim, poised, with neatly coiffed hair, long lacquered nails, seductive little body, a vest-pocket dragon lady.

Her English was perfect, with a slight Irish accent—she was probably a convent-educated girl—more intelligent and sophisticated than her look-alikes in the cathouses on the other side of town.

"A present for your girl, sailor?" She smiled beguilingly.

"Something in jade and silver, miss." He talked like a redneck. "I hope it doesn't cost too much."

"We have all kinds of prices." She smiled again and removed a tray from the locked counter.

He searched for the piece he wanted to snatch—not too big; a large piece would be quickly missed. Ah, there it was, a pendant with exquisite carved jade; maybe fifteen hundred American dollars.

"How much is this, miss?" He pointed at a tasteless set of earrings. "I've only three hundred dollars to spend."

"Your girl can have a number of lovely things in that price range. May I suggest some possibilities?"

Now the trick was to wait till she was momentarily distracted, or to distract her himself.

Chapter Eight
··· *1956* ···

PEG DONLON SPENT the cold blustery afternoon painting. She had not considered winter as a subject for watercolors before. Now she saw fire in the snow and sunlight. Fire, that was what people liked in her paintings; she was not a great artist, certainly, but her works sold consistently, making more money than she'd dreamed possible when Tom ordered her to go to the Art Institute, from which Maude Curtin had barred her on the strength of rumors it offered classes in Life Drawing.

The fire in her work was something new. She'd sold a half-dozen blazing paintings before she overheard someone discuss their "sexual content."

She replenished her brush and added a little blue to her sky. Most of her work was from memory or sketch.

Why did sex have to appear in everything . . .? She hadn't even spoken the word before 1945.

She'd finally given up trying to talk to priests about her questions on sex. She used to confess impatience, distractions in prayer, unkind thoughts and words, and impure thoughts about her husband and other men and then add tentatively that she'd enjoyed too much pleasure in some of the actions involved in rendering the marriage debt. The priests would ask about birth control, then ask if the act was "completed in the proper way," then tell her that nothing else was sinful.

What if sexual relations were too intense, too pleasurable, too destructive of self-control? How did you ask a priest those things?

She tried to concentrate on her easel. Make the snow look thirsty for the sunlight.

Was she being punished for her animal pleasure by what was happening to her children? Would God punish Hugh by taking away his vocation because his mother enjoyed pleasure so much?

She put aside her paintbrush and reached for the comforting pearl rosary beads.

Marge was still angry at her brother. He was so goddamn smooth and personable. Larry, who was an atheist and prepared to dislike him intensely, was won over in two minutes. Jean Hartmann, a Missouri Synod Lutheran before she fled her Nebraska cow town, didn't want to meet him. By the time they were eating their steaks, his wide smile had thawed the Rhine Maiden too.

Marge had dished it out to Hugh as soon as he came off the plane and kissed her lightly on the forehead.

"I'm not going back, Hugh, not ever. I love all of you, but I won't live in that dull prison on North Mason. I don't believe in anything you believe in. I don't want any part of Church or God or rules. I want to be myself, to have fun, to love, to be free. Do you understand that? I won't listen to any sermons and I won't take any advice. I know what I'm doing and if you want to call it living in sin, that's your problem.''

She realized as the torrent poured out how childish she sounded.

"I've come for the warm weather.'' He laughed. "And to tell you I love you.''

The restaurant where they went for supper after he'd checked into his "respectable" motel a mile off Las Vegas Boulevard, was typical of the city—superb steaks, a juke box affirming that what Lola wants Lola gets, and slot machines clanking in the background. Beef and money, that's our Vegas.

Marge's plan was that Jean would take Hugh to the casinos after supper, show him the sights, and then end up at their show for the second performance. If Hugh objected to being turned loose with an unemployed Vegas chorus girl—available beef—he showed no sign of his displeasure.

He said with a boyish grin, "You must protect me from the cardsharps, Jean.''

"The games are all honest, Hugh,'' she replied with her slow, dental-hygiene smile. "The players have to be protected only from themselves.''

Jean was a bit too voluptuous and her hair a bit too white to be quite the all-American farmgirl. And she was too slender and too wholesome seeming to qualify as a German ice goddess. She was intelligent, lonely, and now terrified. She also couldn't get religion off her mind, though it was five years since she'd left her denominational college and run away to Vegas.

Hugh managed to take Marge aside for a few moments after they left the restaurant.

"I meant what I said about no pressure, kid, but I have to tell you I miss you.''

The tears began to form, in the back of her head, it seemed.

"And I'd love to bring you home if you want or whenever you want. It has to be your choice, though. And any time I can help . . . now or later . . . I promise"—he winked—"No I-told-you-so's.''

The tears came in torrents and she melted into his arms. He could have taken her back to the airport that moment.

But, instead, he went off with Jean to visit the casinos.

She knew she was being quite irrational. Most of her life was irrational. Nonetheless she was bitterly angry at him for not taking her back to the airport.

Hugh watched the blackjack dealer intently. The odds were a bit better than two-to-one that his down card was a nine or higher. With the eight card up he had seventeen points to Hugh's thirteen with three cards.

"Give me another,'' Hugh said in an artificially casual tone.

A three of hearts. The odds were still better than even that he would not go over twenty-one on the next card. He pushed the whole thousand dollars in chips into the center of the table. "Had a run of luck so far. May as well shoot the works.''

Jean's fingers tightened on his arm, a disturbing but pleasant pressure. She didn't quite approve.

Five of diamonds.

"Twenty-one.'' He grinned merrily as he turned over his four of spades.

The dealer winced because he knew as well as Hugh did that only high cards remained in the deck. He dealt himself a queen of hearts.

"Never trust the deadly lady,'' Hugh said lightly. "Enough for me. Take the money and run, as my mother always said.''

They cashed in their chips and left for the midnight show at Margie's casino.

"You took an awful chance,'' Jean said reprovingly, "with all that money.''

"Not really. Those are the situations you dream about, a fifty-fifty chance after a night of luck."

"How did you know it was fifty-fifty?"

"I'll show you tomorrow. Incidentally, I've seen enough of the casinos. They scare me, these pale, unsmiling people in their vast mausoleums, all tied up in knots."

"I don't know what else to show you. . . . I don't want to be in the way."

"Why don't I take you to dinner tomorrow night and then we can see a movie and pick up Larry and Marge after their show. That is, if you have nothing else to do."

"Oh, no," Jean said bitterly, "I have nothing else to do."

The show was terrible, not obscene, not even vulgar, despite the scant garments on the chorus girls. Rather, it was dull. Larry didn't have much talent, a fact that Marge, smart little wench that she was, would soon figure out.

Las Vegas fascinated and repelled Hugh—pulsating, frantic, empty, hopeful, despairing, unsmiling, youthful, ancient. Purgatory and hell all rolled into one, with perhaps a touch of the excitement of paradise.

They congratulated Larry and Marge on the show. Hugh pleaded fatigue, promised he would go out with them the next night after the show, and went to look for a cab back to his motel.

"Tell them I love them when you report home," Marge yelled after him, "and that I'm staying here."

Hugh turned around and smiled affably. "I'll make my own reports."

"Disgusted by it all?" Jean asked in the cab.

"Not exactly. More bored. It isn't very good, is it? I mean, even as shows here go?"

"No, it's not. I'm promised the next opening in the chorus line, though, and I'll take it."

He walked with her from the cab to a shabby apartment on the very fringe of the desert. Paint was peeling from the outside wall, the sidewalk was cracked, and a garbage can had fallen across the outside stairway to the second floor. There was a faint and unpleasant smell, like a blocked toilet. Romantic Vegas.

"No pool? Why don't I pick you up tomorrow afternoon? I'll have a car then. You can swim at the motel with me and I'll prove I can count the deck."

"I'd like that." She extended a hand at the door of her apartment.

He took the hand and kissed her on the forehead, just as he'd kissed Marge. "See you."

The Chinese girl was good. She kept one eye on the tray and the other on the rest of the store. She'd learned the skills of a salesperson in a port city. You didn't trust anyone.

Tim pretended to ponder two purchases, a set of earrings worth about two hundred dollars and a bracelet that cost three hundred. He would return one of them to the tray and cup the pendant with the flying dragons in his hand with the same quick movement.

"I don't want to sound like money is the only thing, ma'am," he said in a broad Georgia drawl. "I think Cindy would like the earrings better, but I feel kind of cheap spending only two hundred dollars."

The girl laughed pleasantly. "She will be so glad to have her redhaired sailor back she won't mind how much you spend." The older woman who seemed to be the manager of the shop babbled impatiently in Chinese. The salesgirl answered, also impatiently, without taking her eyes off Tim.

"You Chinese folk certainly do notice red hair." Mistake to say that, bad mistake. It would reinforce her memory.

Again the impatient babble from Mrs. Manager.

Exasperated, the clerk turned away for an instant and spoke sharply to her boss. The older woman subsided into resentful silence.

Quickly Tim returned the bracelet and snatched the pendant. Now was the moment of truth. "I'll follow your advice, miss, and take the earrings. They sure are pretty." He reached into his jacket pocket, dropped the pendant, and withdrew his wallet.

"Cindy will love her gift."

Gravely Tim handed her three fifty-dollar bills and five tens. The sales receipt was made out to CPO Marshall T. Sims of the destroyer *Evans Carlson.*

He thanked the girl for her helpfulness, complimented her on her courtesy, bowed politely to Mrs. Manager, and walked out the door and across the street, his heart pounding with suppressed excitement.

Halfway down the block toward the nineteenth-century Cathedral of St. John on Albert Road, he permitted himself the luxury of looking back.

Both the salesgirl and the manager were at the door of the shop, looking intently in his direction.

And a Hong Kong policeman was hurrying through the crowd to meet them.

Chapter Nine
1956

IN THE DARKNESS of a late winter afternoon, Tom Donlon stepped off the Austin Boulevard bus at Lemoyne Avenue with deliberate caution. The street was slippery, slush over ice. Not the time to spend a month in the hospital with a broken hip.

It was turning cold again; he shivered as he walked the short block to Mason Avenue and the oversize bungalow that Peggy had picked out just before Tim was born. She did not buy it herself, as she had bought the Packard. Yet it was clear that, even though he thought eight thousand dollars was a lot of money, Thomas Donlon had no real choice.

Many happy memories in that house. And sadness too. Tim in Asia someplace, writing rarely. Marge a rebel, living with an Englishman (he shuddered at the thought) in a gambling casino, and Hugh . . . the perhaps unwise bargain he'd made with God.

Dick Daley, the new mayor, had been blunt about it: If there was a Democratic administration in the next ten years, Tom Donlon was going to the Supreme Court. "Time we had someone from the great city of Chicago."

Tom doubted he would accept the appointment. The house on Mason Avenue was where he belonged. A house of deep love and anguished sorrows. . . .

What had they done wrong?

How many times had he asked that question?

But when he entered the house, after being careful not to slip on the steps on the front porch, he could think only of his wife.

"Peggy . . . ?"

The shower was running.

He walked rapidly to their bedroom in the rear of the house. Peg was all that remained as he faced old age and death.

And Peggy made life worth living.

"Isn't Jean gorgeous?" Marge asked, trying to avert another "it's your choice" conversation with her brother.

"Lovely girl. . . ." Hugh seemed uninterested. "Do you like Vegas?"

They were sitting in the parlor of her apartment. Hugh was properly impressed by its tasteful comfort. She prepared her own breakfast and his lunch—English muffins, fresh grapefruit, bacon, home-ground coffee. I'm a good cook too, big brother.

"What's the matter with it?" she asked defensively. Larry was still asleep. It had been a mistake not to wake him. She didn't want to face Hugh alone.

"Sinful?"

"Unhappy. Dante would revel in it. Isn't unhappiness the worst of sins? No one smiles. The gambling is grimmer than an Irish wake. The music is depressing, the shows are frantic, the people act like last-minute Christmas shoppers who don't believe in Christmas. It's a treadmill to nowhere."

"Lots of beautiful women." She tried to parry his attack by a counterattack.

"Right." He sighed. "I've seen more half-naked young women in the last twenty-four hours than I've seen in my whole life. But you know what? After the first hour it's a bore. At first I couldn't understand why the men didn't even notice the cocktail waitresses. Then I didn't notice them either. What's the point in being surrounded by voluptuous women if the place is so dismal you can hardly see them? Las Vegas is a frigid palace."

"I bet you'd like to lay Jean," Marge fired back.

Hugh laughed, stood up, and kissed her cheek. "You're wonderful, Marge," he said. "I love you."

Outside there was a cold wind and icy slush. Inside Thomas Donlon was enveloped in timeless warmth.

"I should put supper on," Peg murmured.

"It can wait." He stroked her back slowly.

"Are we abnormal, Tommy?"

"If you mean are there many men in St. Ursula who come home at five o'clock, drag their insincerely protesting spouse out of the shower, and make love before supper, the court will have to rule that we are not typical. Not abnormal though. Those other men don't have wives that are so pretty they can't keep their hands off them."

"We're emotional people." She rested her head against his chest. "Though we pretend to the world that we're not. Our children are emotional too, even Hugh. Remember Maria?"

"Speaking of Maria, I saw Mike Flaherty today on LaSalle Street, the president of West End Bank. Said they were quite pleased with her."

"Hugh was in love with her . . . so were you a little bit."

"So were we all."

"What if Hugh is too . . . too emotional to be a priest and marries someone who is not as nice as Maria. We froze her out, you know. What if it were God's will that Hugh marry Maria instead of becoming a priest?"

A typical Peggy scruple, convoluted as a Supreme Court opinion and, like many Supreme Court opinions, containing a valid point.

"We never told him we'd be happy to have her as a member of our family"— Peggy persisted in her scruple—"even if we would be happier if he became a priest. Could you have been a celibate, Tom?"

"What a time to ask a question like that, Margaret Mary Curtin Donlon. . . . Yes, I suppose I could have, if I were happy as a priest."

"I'm glad to know that," she sighed. "If you could have, then Hugh can."

Jean split the water of the motel pool with long, powerful strokes—Valkyrie as athlete. In love again, Xav Martin had predicted? Well, not exactly.

Jean climbed out of the pool, wrapped a big towel around herself, and sat in the deck chair next to Hugh, breathing heavily. "The older you become the easier it is to get out of shape."

Nothing wrong with the shape as far as he could see; in a trim white bikini she was, despite her obvious physical strength, strangely vulnerable.

"Want to see the card trick?"

"Dying to."

She shrugged out of the towel and picked up the deck of cards lying on the poolside table. "What do I do?"

"Deal out twenty-six cards. Let me see each one and then put it on the pile facedown."

"I don't believe this and I don't know whether I'll believe it even if I see it, but here goes."

"You can go more quickly," he said as she showed him the cards. "I only need a glance. . . . All right, now pick them up and turn each one over from the bottom as I identify it. The first card is the nine of clubs. . . ."

He named each of the twenty-six cards.

"Gosh." She was awed.

"Now, I'll tell you the cards you're still holding, not, alas, in any order."

He didn't miss one of those either. For the last six he gave her the odds that each new card would be higher than a six.

Jean leaned back on the deck chair wide-eyed. "Amazing, you would make millions here. And you're going to be a priest?"

"Where the odds against success in any given case are astronomical."

"I suppose so." She rubbed suntan lotion on her long legs absently. Only a year or two older than he at most and already by the standards of this terrible place a has-been. He took the tube from her hand and rubbed the lotion on her back.

On the chorus line Jean would be just one more well-built dancer, indistinguishable from the others, an easily replaceable spare part. Only when a body became a person with fears and hopes did it invade his imagination and demand sympathy, affection, and desire.

"Tell me about it, Jean," he said quietly.

"About what?" She looked up quickly, too quickly.

He finished his businesslike work with the lotion. "You are up to your eyelids with worry, you've found a near-clergyman who is different from the pastors back home and enjoys being with you. You want to tell him about it, but you're afraid." He gave her the tube. "Spill it."

First spilled the tears, accompanied by shoulder-racking sobs, such lovely shoulders. He resisted the urge to wrap his arm around them.

Then the story: honor student in high school, three years at a rigid denominational college, expelled for drinking, one drink and sick in the washroom; flight to Vegas in humiliation and rage, disowned by family, string of lovers, most of them cruel. Early success in chorus lines, aided by being in the right people's beds. Then the realization that she had little dancing and singing talent—Margie in a few years—unemployment, loneliness, chastity beause she'd been hurt enough. The next choice, if she wanted to eat, was to become a call girl or go home and accept the role of scarlet woman.

My God, what do I say next? Pretend to be confident. "Enough for one afternoon, Jeanie. Put your clothes on. We'll eat a big steak, see *Smiles of a Summer Night,* and meet here at the parsonage tomorrow."

She wiped her nose with a tissue and smiled an all-American smile. "Parsonages can be anywhere, can't they?"

"I sure hope so."

That night when he kissed her on the forehead again, she leaned against him for a fraction of a second, not so much inviting or promising sex as yearning for support.

Dear God, help me to come up with something.

When he was trying to go to sleep, Hugh realized with a twinge of guilt that he had barely thought of his sister for the last eight hours. He had come to Vegas to salvage Marge, not to become involved with a terrified chorus girl.

Tim Donlon was scared. He ought to have stayed on his ship. Instead, he'd come ashore to sell the pendant, even though he didn't need the money. He offered it to a middle-aged American couple at the Star Ferry terminal. They almost bought it for a thousand dollars, a great bargain. The man was ready, but the wife was suspicious of what a "common sailor" would be doing with such an expensive piece.

So he'd walked back toward Government House, hoping to find another such couple—prosperous but not minding a bit of crookedness.

He wandered near the shop where he'd snatched the piece. There were wealthy Americans on that street usually. And he was in dirty fatigues and looked like a different person. There was not much danger that he would be recognized.

Then he saw the pretty salesgirl only thirty yards behind him in the narrow, crowded street.

He hurried down Queen's Road, across Procession Street, and into the teeming Chinese district. His shadow kept doggedly behind him, almost running despite her spike heels. He dashed through the central marketplace and ducked into one of the tiny side lanes beyond it.

There was a razor-sharp switchblade in his back pocket, useful for threatening angry rednecks on the ship. Only twice in his adventures had it been necessary to open the blade and only one of those times had he actually cut anyone, a Corsican in an alley in Naples who was coming after him with a knife of his own—a quick slash from Tim and the surprised thug had dropped his blade and shouted in pain.

The woman was only a dozen yards behind him now, slipping through the crowd like an agile halfback. Alone, the crazy little fool.

He tried to lose her by dodging into a black passageway between two buildings; a few feet into it, the lights from the street offered only a dim glimmer. The crazy girl came after him.

He grabbed her, twisted her arm behind her back, and held the knife blade at her throat. "Make a sound and I'll kill you," he hissed.

If she'd cried out, he would have run like hell through the passageway, hoping that there was an opening at the other end.

"What's your name?" She was quaking against him. The power of life and death over her was unbearably sweet.

"Jane. Please, sailor . . . don't kill me."

He released her arm and, keeping the knife blade against her throat, fondled her gently. "Why did you chase me by yourself?"

"Manager woman blamed me, said she'd fire me. Don't kill me . . . I'll go to bed with you."

Everyone in Hong Kong had a price. He continued to caress her, reveling in his absolute control. He thought about hurting her, just a little.

"A nice offer, Jane, but I'll decline it. If you come after me again, I'll cut little pieces off your body for a couple of days, then you'll plead with me to let you die. Understand?"

He had to hold her so she wouldn't collapse. "I won't tell," she stammered.

He kissed the nape of her neck and dropped the chain of the pendant over her head. "You can figure out how to explain to the old dragon lady where you found this. If you want to be sliced up, turn your back before you're on Queen's Road."

In his bunk on the carrier, Tim savored the biggest kick yet. Restore a dead woman to life. Much more fun than screwing her.

Maybe that was how God got his kicks. You take something away, scare the hell out of them, and then give it back.

"Did you have summers like that?" Jean asked Hugh, handing him her tube of suntan cream.

He put aside *The Quiet American,* a book that deeply depressed him, and performed his cream-spreading responsibilities.

"You mean like *Smiles of a Summer Night*? Yes, one. And you?"

"Lots of them. Same guy every summer too."

"Is he married?"

"No, he claims he wants to marry me." She screwed the cover back on the tube. The cloudless desert sky was implacably blue above them.

"Henry Kincaid is his name, a classmate from the first grade on. Same church, same Sunday school, same high school and college. Nothing more than hugging and kissing, ever. We were dreadfully wholesome. Then they caught me in the washroom with liquor on my breath and he turned on me just like everyone else.

"He was a fundamentalist—we all were—but at Stanford Law School he changed. Now he's a successful lawyer in Los Angeles. Still a Jock—ski, surf, backpack, the whole thing. Visits me every six months and politely asks me to forgive him and marry him."

"Redeeming the fallen woman?" Hugh asked.

"Oh, no, Henry's finished with self-righteousness. He wants me because he thinks he loves me. He's wrong, of course, I'm not the lawful-wife type anymore."

"Twenty years from now would he throw Vegas at you in an angry quarrel?"

The corner of her lip turned up in a curious smile. "More likely the other way around. I might tell him that I married him to avoid becoming a full-fledged hooker."

"Why not marry him, Jean?"

She sighed and pushed the long blond veil away from her face. "Sometimes I'm awfully close. I wouldn't have to work for the rest of my life. I could go back to school, have children. I'm mildly happy to see him when he comes over the mountains, mildly sorry when he goes back, and then I don't think of him for the next six months, except when I'm worried about how I'm going to pay the rent."

"Thank about one thing for the next day or two. Or imagine one thing: What will it be like five years from now if you marry him?"

Her jaw tensed in Teutonic stubbornness. "I will not marry him, Hugh. . . ." Then the jaw relaxed and the half-smile returned. "I'll think about it, though, Pastor, if I can swim in your pool now."

He swam next to her, wondering about the various ways humans give themselves to each other. Because he would be a priest in another year and because she was frightened and lonely she had given him something much more intimate than her body. She had given him her trust.

Now what was he supposed to do with it?

Hugh was sipping a glass of sherry, something he'd learned to do despite Peggy's ban on drinking. Marge was gulping her second Scotch and water and Larry was at the theater fretting over his show.

"I'm surprised you found time to fit me into your schedule," she snapped irritably.

"And you'd complain as well if I was around too much," he replied bluntly. "No matter what I do, it's wrong. So this way I'm certainly not trying to deprive you of your freedom."

"You like Jean more than me. . . ."

Hugh laughed. She joined in.

"God, what a spoiled brat I am," she admitted.

"An unhappy spoiled brat. . . . Do you want to know what really annoys me about you?"

She didn't really. "I suppose so."

"Someday you're going to come home—on your own, you're too stubborn to do it any other way. Two months after that, you'll have bought back into everything you left behind and you'll never admit that there has been a change, much less that you were wrong."

"Goddamn bastard." She threw her Scotch at him, not the glass, because she didn't want to hurt him, only the precious brown liquid.

Still, they kissed affectionately when he left.

Was he right? No, of course not. She'd never go back.

Well, not for a long time.

Hugh woke up that night with imperious sexual longings. All those half-naked bodies had finally caught up with him. The licentiousness of Las Vegas had invaded his dreams, filled them with images of breasts and buttocks, and demanded that he find out what it was like to make love to a woman.

He threw on his clothes, bolted out the door of his room, and drove at seventy miles an hour across town to Jean's apartment, not altogether sure that he was not still dreaming.

Outside her door, parked in the car, and almost mindless with desire, he realized that he was awake.

He started the car, backed up to turn around, and drove slowly back to his motel.

What demons lurked in the desert darkness beyond the beam of his headlights? What beautiful, sensuous, enticing agents of hell?

How could they be so appealing and still be evil?

Such temptations would probably come often when he was a priest.

Every time a desirable woman trusted herself to him?

He licked his lips apprehensively. Not too many of them would live on the edge of the desert.

The next day Jean showed him Lake Mead and Hoover Dam. Not a word about her man in California. You can't force help on people if they don't want it.

Back at the pool she began very cautiously.

"I did the imagining I promised." She was sitting on a towel at his feet clad today in a white one-piece swimming suit, her body slumped over pathetically.

"And?"

"Henry and I would have two, maybe three, well-behaved children. I'd be taking classes in voice or something of the sort. We'd belong to a country club. We wouldn't fight much, neighter of us would be unfaithful, and we'd both be bored silly."

"You don't know that."

"There's no spark between us and never will be. He asks me to come back to California with him the way he'd ask me out for a Coke."

"Give me your hands, Jean." Punt formation on the goal line. "Both of them. Now, I'm going to presume a lot on a short friendship. You're still an innocent farmgirl, terribly guilty about her fall from grace. Your punishment will not be complete until you've degraded yourself so much that no one will want you." Her hands in his, she was like a medieval vassal, kneeling in front of a liege lord, a vassal smelling of suntan oil. "You don't want to be forgiven, Jean. That's why you won't forgive yourself."

She jerked her hands away furiously. "Leave me alone." She dashed into his room, emerged a few moments later fully clad in skirt and blouse, jumped into a cab at the door of the motel, and was gone.

Blocked kick.

Lesson for the future: Don't tell people the truth about themselves unless you're sure they're ready to hear it.

The next morning Hugh called his father. "He's not rich, Dad, and never will be. He does all right. He pays her a salary, probably more than she's worth. He's a kind man, probably better than she deserves."

A noncommittal grunt. Then, "How does she look?"

"Fine, more like Mom every day, taller and thinner maybe and with your hair, still . . ."

"I know, Hugh, I know, And the weather?"

"Dull, nothing but sun and clear blue sky."

His father chuckled, though clearly his heart wasn't in it.

After he'd hung up, Hugh considered the phone thoughtfully. Dangerous, potentially deadly instrument. He was going to meddle where he had no right to meddle. Part of being a priest. Follow your gut instincts.

He called information, then dialed the number he was given. "I'm Hugh Donlon, you've never heard of me, and you'd better listen to what I have to say."

The one at the other end listened. First astonishment, then, in rapid order, dismay, anger, outrage. At last a trace of amusement.

With a clear conscience, more or less, Hugh dove into the pool. It was up to God now.

Judge Donlon poured himself a cup of coffee and moved aside the tedious brief he'd been reviewing. Lawyers became more pedantic and obscure with each passing year. Hugh certainly sounded self-possessed. Very much in charge. Nearly twenty-four, the age of John of Austria at Lepanto, and Buckingham at Culloden Moor.

Peggy was right, even if she didn't quite comprehend the meaning of her instinct. There was no place in present-day Catholicism for any of the Donlon children. They were passionate activists who did not and could not hide their real nature as he and Peg did. The Church had found room for him and his wife because they carefully hid the violence of their love beneath a veneer of piety and convention that fooled everyone but their three children.

The veneer, the pose of angelic immunity to passion—that was what sent Tim to the Navy and Marge to Las Vegas.

What would it do to Hugh?

Could there possibly be a place in the priesthood, the dull, arid priesthood, for so turbulent a young man? How could he hide the restless energy and the relentless ambitions that even he himself did not perceive?

The judge sipped his coffee, black with no sugar. They had excluded the magic Maria too quickly. Could they bring her back? Did he and Peggy have the courage to talk to Hugh about her?

Hugh was to return to Chicago on a United DC-6 that Sunday morning. He'd left his Hertz Chevy at the in-town station. Margie picked him up there. First they would stop at the casino to see Larry and then pause at Jean's apartment. She'd called as Marge was leaving, pleading that they stop for just a minute.

He shrugged indifferently. "Plenty of time."

At Jean's house they encountered an unexpected scene. Hank Kincaid was there, not flustered as he usually was but determined. Jean was packing her clothes into two battered suitcases.

Hank was a hayseed—big, rawboned plainsman, support-your-local-sheriff-type, with bad eyes, rimless glasses, and a reedy voice.

But today his eyes were shining. He kissed Marge confidently—never did that before—and shook hands vigorously with Hugh.

"Glad to meet you, Father."

"I don't deserve the title quite yet," Hugh said modestly.

"What the hell is going on?" Marge demanded when she was able to corner Jean in the kitchen.

"He didn't ask this time. He insisted. I . . . ." Happy tears were streaming down her cheeks. "I want to go with him now . . . we made love . . . I never . . . Marge." She hugged her friend. "He was wonderful."

Marge melted, temporarily, and congratulated her. Jean was happy and her happiness must be shared, however short-lived it was likely to be.

On the way to the airport, Marge vented her fury on Hugh. "Who gave you the right to play God?"

"Huh?" His innocence was not convincing.

"Do you realize what kind of hell you've condemned them to? What do you think they're going to be suffering in ten years?"

"I'm not responsible for what they do with their chance." His confidence had been shaken by her attack. "You're angry because Jean's going back to her past, as you know you're going to do someday."

"I'll never sell out," Marge screamed at him. "You treated her just like you treated Maria. Tease them and then run. That's my brother Hugh."

She swerved onto the shoulder and then recaptured control of the car.

"Don't kill us, you little fool."

"I can drive better than you can."

"You cannot."

They quarreled like sullen children but by the time they reached the airport Margie's temper had changed.

She patted Hugh's cheek affectionately. "You're not all that bad, Hughie." She redefined what they had witnessed at Jean's apartment—without the slightest twinge of guilt over the abrupt change. "Didn't you see the stars in their eyes? You gave them the push that they needed."

"I don't know. . . ."

"They're calling your flight. . . . Hughie, promise me something. Promise me you'll never forget how to laugh at yourself."

"I'll try. . . ."

They hugged again and he was gone.

The DC-6 staggered toward Chicago. The first part of the flight was smooth, but beyond the Rockies they encountered a massive weather front. One of the cabin attendants was sick.

Hugh put aside Edmund Wilson's disturbing book on the Dead Sea Scrolls. Wilson was anti-Catholic and anti-Christian, but the discoveries at the Wadi Qumran raised problems that worried Hugh. He'd paid little attention to the new theological currents that had swept up on the American shore from Europe and no attention at all to the new studies in sacred scripture. Classes in scripture at Mundelein were a time for mending socks and writing letters.

His restless imagination turned back to the scene in Jean's apartment.

It was easy to imagine what had happened. Hank insisted she come to California. She said no again. He said he'd take her by force if he had to. Surprised and probably not altogether displeased by his show of fire, she said he wouldn't dare. So he dared. Poor man, all the years of waiting.

There were stars in their eyes, were there not? Marge was right, he had not messed up their lives.

He prayed that he had done the right thing and then returned to his fantasy.

She resisted his affection at first, then passion and love broke through the barriers of fear and resentment and pain and despair.

Just as God had intended passion and love to cooperate.

Did he really want to give up such joy?

Could he give it up?

He thought of the cabin attendant on the flight out, then of Jean again.

How could he turn his back on such delights for the rest of his life?

Maria.

. . .

It was eleven o'clock when he arrived at Mason and Lemoyne tired and depressed. He reported to his parents when he reached their house that eventually Marge would bounce back and pretend that Las Vegas had never happened.

"Isn't there the risk she'll destroy herself first?" The judge looked older than his forty-nine years.

Too shrewd. Hugh threw up his hands in a gesture of helplessness.

"Where did we go wrong, Hugh?" his mother asked sadly.

"Where God went wrong." He was irritable and too tired to care. "He created human beings with freedom. You had children, a risky business for both you and God."

For a moment it seemed that they wanted to change the subject. He waited impatiently.

"I'm dead tired."

"Of course," said his father, with obvious relief. "Get some sleep."

"Poor dear." His mother hugged him and patted his cheek.

In bed Hugh wondered what his parents had been afraid to talk about.

The next day, Hugh sat in the tired old Buick on Madison Street across from the West End Bank. Although it was only one thirty, the clouds and falling snow made it seem like dusk. The lights in the bank window shone fitfully through the snowflakes and reminded him of Christmas decorations in the State Street stores, warm, appealing, but artificially gay.

He glanced at the *Sun-Times* on the seat next to him. Israel refused to withdraw from the Gaza Strip. Winter storm warning for tonight. Las Vegas light-years away. The big gentle snowflakes were melting as they touched the street. Soon, however, the snow would pile up again.

His excuse again was to seek Maria's advice about Marge. The foolish thoughts of the plane ride had been dismissed. He was motion sick, that was all.

He had bought new ice skates in the shopping center at Harlem and Lake. He was going home. He'd parked here for a moment's respite, a dangerous exercise.

No future, no point, no sense, no reason.

He turned on the ignition, eased the car backward, shifted the gear, and hesitated. What had she said? He couldn't live without a woman. Some men could, but he couldn't.

He shifted into first, inched forward, and then turned off the ignition.

The bank was bright and businesslike, only one woman at a teller's window. Not much trade on a February afternoon. His eyes roamed the desks for a blonde. He thought he saw her. The girl turned, as if hearing his thought; pretty, but not Maria.

"Can I help you, sir?" the guard asked politely.

"Is Maria here today?"

The crusty old man's lined face dissolved into a cheerful smile. "Maria is in school this afternoon, sir. She'll be back tomorrow morning."

"I see." Tomorrow morning would never come, not till after eternity. "No, no message."

The guard unbent a little more. "I suppose you know her, sir, so you'll understand my meaning when I say that it is a much less interesting bank when she's not here."

Outside the air was dense with big dancing snowflakes; now they were sticking to the pavement of Madison Street.

BOOK TWO

"Father forgive them, for they know not what they do."

Chapter Ten
1964

"FATHER, MAY I ask you a personal question?"

A woman's cultivated voice, not from Chicago, not from Boston or New York either. Perhaps Philadelphia or Baltimore. The tone of intellectual respect sounded like what one would expect from a graduate of a Catholic women's college—Daughters of the Sacred Heart, perhaps Manhattanville.

"Surely." He was trapped in a sticky, airless confessional on a hot summer Saturday, just as he was trapped in St. Jarlath's parish and in the priesthood, which, despite the joys of ordination day, had not brought him the happiness he'd expected.

For seven years now he had fought a psychotic pastor. The battle was at best a draw. In the meantime, while he was stuck in a stagnant backwater, the Church had been going through the most dramatic change in its history.

In a way, it served him right. He had chosen the backwater. After his trip to Las Vegas, he had declined the cardinal's offer of business school training. Now the world had forgotten about him.

"It's a somewhat delicate matter. . . . I've hesitated . . . you're such a sympathetic confessor. . . ."

"I'll try to help."

"My husband and I engage in oral sex on some occasions. He says that it is not sinful—he is a devout Catholic, Father—and I don't know what to think. The sisters and priests in my college said that it was a terrible sin of perversion."

"Do you find it repellent?" Her question was asked with increasing frequency in the confessional. The sexual revolution was catching up even with well-educated, well-to-do Catholics.

"No, Father; at first, I was . . . a bit shocked, and then, frankly, found it quite enjoyable."

"The Church has always taught that a husband and wife may do anything to promote their love that is not repellent to either spouse, so long as the marriage act is properly completed. Is this a form of birth control for you and your husband?" The real sin, the only sin that mattered.

"Oh, no, Father, we have two children and we want more."

"Yet the seed is spilled when you make love this way?" Fall back on the biblical words; they're safe.

"In these matters, Father, as I'm sure you understand, the emotions are complicated. It's hard to sort out what one's intentions are. One wants to love one's husband with special intensity perhaps to make up for a cruel thing one has said. There are no conscious reflections on anything else.''

"Do you think God would be angry at you for wanting to love your husband and heal wounds you had caused?''

"No, of course not. You've been very helpful, Father.''

She was looking for the clear-cut ethical "yes" or "no" of the Moral Guidance college textbook. That he could not provide. Only she and her husband could make the moral decisions on such matters; yet they had been taught that the priest in the confessional could and indeed must make such moral choices for them.

He gave her absolution and sent her home to her husband, who probably didn't realize what a fortunate man he was.

Everything was changing, the questions people asked, the answers priests gave. Some priests were already hinting broadly in the confessional that there was a change on the way in birth control. His friend Jack Howard bluntly told his people to make up their own minds.

Hugh didn't see how there could be a change on the birth control question. Yet the spirit of change was in the air. Some priests thought that celibacy would be optional before the decade was over. Again, Hugh could not imagine that, any more than he could the altar being turned around to face the people, or the Mass being sung in English. Where would it all end?

Still, he had helped the woman and that was what a man became a priest to do. . . .

The thought brought with it one of the occasional experiences of joy that still made the priesthood worthwhile for him. They had not been so frequent lately, not as in the beginning.

The first Christmas at St. Jarlath's had been a time of exalted happiness. Sullivan was in Arizona for his "health." Kilbride was in the hospital. And Hugh was acting pastor, for all practical purposes. Pastor, his first year in the parish. He had conducted Midnight Mass with carols and flowers and bells ringing out across the snow, and felt the warmth of the people's support as he greeted them in the back of church.

That was the kind of joy of which the happiness of ordination was supposed to be a promise.

And how ecstatically happy he had been on that occasion too, the long-awaited, seemingly impossible goal finally a dazzling reality.

It had been a perfect clear blue day—filled with the resonance of possibility. When he was imparting his First Blessing, after the old cardinal ordained him, Peggy and the judge wept as they knelt in the radiant sunlight in front of the redbrick colonial-style main chapel. Even Tim briskly kissed his hand. Only Marge was absent—living in England, not even sending a note.

Three days later, on a postcard of Mount Vesuvius, he heard a voice from the past.

> *Dormant volcanoes remind me of you. Marriage a useful institu-*
> *tion. First son a naval officer like his father. Salutes me every*
> *morning before breakfast. Crazy life, but I'm happy. Be a good*
> *priest. (Don't leave the sailboat.)*
>
> *Blessings, Maria!*

"Bless me, Father, because I have sinned.'' A lisping voice no more than seven years old interrupted his reverie about Maria. "I missed my morning prayers, I was disobedient sixteen times, and I committed adultery three times.''

"You really should tell God good morning when you wake, shouldn't you?''

"Yes, Father.''

"Sixteen times is a lot to be disobedient, isn't it?''

"My little sister is disobedient a lot more than that.''

"Uh-huh. . . . Now, how did you commit adultery?''

"I called mother shit behind her back.''

"That wasn't very nice.''

"It was terrible, Father. I love Mommy, and I don't want to go to hell.''

"God loves you too much to let you go to hell. That's a bad word, especially about your mommy. But God is like your mommy; he doesn't stay angry at you.''

"Mommy would be awful mad if she knew I called her shit.''

And Mommy would die of laughter if she were listening to this. Stay a comic angel, little guy.

"Well, we just won't tell her and we won't use that word about her again, okay?''

"Yes, Father.''

Of such is the Kingdom of Heaven made? Well, sometimes.

"Father, I have a problem about my marriage.'' A man's voice this time, mature, successful, used to giving orders. What else in St. Jarlath's?

"I'll try to help.''

"My wife and I were married outside the Church eighteen years ago. We have not received the sacraments since then. We tried for an annulment on the grounds that her first husband was insane at the time of the marriage. We couldn't find good enough proof, I guess, though the man has been in an asylum for twenty years. Now my wife's priest tells her that as long as she is convinced this first marriage was not valid because of her former husband's problem it is all right for us to return to the sacraments.'' A small laugh. "I keep up pretty much on the changes in the Church, Father; but I must have missed this one. Is it something new?''

"No, it's not new, sir. It's called the Internal Forum Solution. More use of it has been made recently. In an annulment case the Church merely decides whether the evidence is strong enough to say officially that the first marriage was invalid. Often, the evidence is too weak but the party involved is absolutely convinced in good faith that she or he is free to marry again because of the invalidity of the first marriage. The Church cannot officially so decree, but a confessor or an adviser can tell the person that his or her good faith seems sincere.''

"Does that mean that my wife and I have been married all along?''

"Not in the eyes of the Church officially and publicly, but yes in the eyes of the Church privately and unofficially and, of course, in the eyes of God.''

"I'll be damned. . . .''

"No, sir, that's what won't happen, not as long as you and your wife honestly believe that you were free to marry.''

"Father, do you realize we have five kids, all in Catholic schools, and that tomorrow for the first time I'll be able to receive Communion with them?''

"Congratulations to all of you,'' Hugh said.

Some marriages worked, some didn't. Nine times out of ten a priest could tell on the wedding day whether it would work or not. It was the tenth one that threw you.

Maria has chosen well.

One radiant spring Sunday morning a year and half ago, after the nine o'clock

Mass, a naval officer had approached him in the back of the church and extended a hand. "Lieutenant Commander Steven McLain, Father. I'm staying at the Admiral's house for the weekend."

Hugh detected a soft southern accent, Atlantic seaboard perhaps. "Welcome aboard, Commander," he replied, grasping his hand.

McLain was tall, about Hugh's height, but thinner, with a clear, handsome face, short brown hair and far-seeing eyes. Judging from his wings and campaign ribbons, he was a seasoned aviator. "I told my wife I'd be coming to Mass here today. She's still in Washington, and I'm on assignment to a shore base in the Far East. Just stopping over with my retired C.O. here. Maria said she doubted you'd remember her but to extend her best wishes anyway."

"How long have you been married, Commander?" Hugh smiled.

"Six years, sir," he said, grinning complacently.

"If you've been married to that woman for six years, do you think it possible that anyone could ever forget her?"

The aviator beamed. "Actually, no, Father."

"Tell me more."

"We have two boys five and four; we've had two terms of sea duty, one on a carrier off Vietnam, and a term just ending at the Pentagon. Maria has lived in Naples, San Diego, Tokyo, Honolulu, and Arlington, Virginia, and taken a good many courses in business administration all over the world."

"And now?"

The handsome face clouded. "I'm bound for shore duty at Cam Ranh Bay. She's going to live with her parents. The bank she used to work for has offered her a good position. Maria, as I'm sure you know, Father, is more than capable of taking care of herself—and the children. And she'll be much happier with her parents than in some naval port. Or with my folks in Charleston."

"Commander." Hugh shook the young officer's hand. "Anyone who married Maria would have to have taste. When you call her, please tell her that I think with you two it was mutual."

The commander smiled, enormously pleased by the compliment. "Pray for us, Father."

"Indeed I will."

A couple of times after that meeting, Hugh had fantasized about calling Maria. Images from the raspberry lodge danced in his head. But he decided not to. There was no reason to court trouble, and, besides, he genuinely liked her man.

Hugh shifted uneasily in the confessional. In the church, children's voices were singing the hauntingly sweet Gelineau psalms, music for an empty church on a stifling summer day. He peeked through the curtain. There was no one else in line.

Monsignor Sullivan, the pastor of St. Jarlath's, refused to believe that participated worship, much less worship in English, was coming. When it arrived, he said to Hugh, "You take care of the preparations, educate the people, that sort of thing."

After the first Sunday, Sullivan withdrew completely. "Hire a Vincentian or a Jesuit to take my Masses indefinitely. I'll have to read up on these things."

Monsignor Sullivan had not read a book in thirty years. He would say private Masses from now on, in Latin. "My doctor recommends it for health reasons," he told the people.

So Hugh had had to supervise the change in liturgical patterns that had existed for fifteen hundred years. Lloyd Kilbride, the other curate, was a drunk and could not be relied on even to find the church. The only resource in the parish to help Hugh was Sister Elizabeth Ann, an innocent and eager young nun, who was a few years out of college and a liturgical authority—which meant that she had attended two courses at the Summer Institute.

Two more courses on the Christian Worship than Hugh could claim.

"They sound wonderful, Sister," he said, standing at the rear of the sanctuary, which he had entered to encourage her last-minute liturgical preparations. "Sixth-grade girls learn more quickly than anyone else in the world."

"Thank you, Father." Sister Elizabeth, genuinely pleased, was blessed with long dark eyelashes, big brown eyes, and a sweet, open face that could become very lovely on such occasions. "We were just finishing. . . . Very nice, girls; be sure to be on time tomorrow. We want to teach your parents to sing with you."

The kids disappeared quickly; it was, after all, a sweltering August afternoon, and the pastor would not permit the use of air conditioning merely for confessions and choir practice.

"Shouldn't you be on vacation?" There was a flattering concern for him in her eyes.

"Father Kilbride is under the weather. The pastor's health prevents him from hearing confessions. And the Jesuits couldn't make it." He grinned. "Someone had to be here."

"So you came back from your vacation."

He nodded. Must be careful. Young nuns are prone to crushes on priests. "How was the Summer Institute?" he asked, changing the subject.

"It was wonderful." She lowered her eyes. "We learned about Karl Rahner's influence on Church music."

The great German theologian would have been horrified to be told that he'd influenced Church music in any way. "Maybe we could use him to direct our choir."

Sister Elizabeth Ann was a farmgirl from Iowa, possessed of the body of a model and the naiveté of a fourteen-year-old child. But she had a first-rate mind, and she had taken most of the courses required for a Master's in Theology. Despite her youthfulness, she had been a delegate to the Chapter that was reforming their Order. According to the other sisters at St. Jarlath's, Sister Elizabeth Ann had been one of the most influential delegates there.

"That one will be Mother General someday," said one of the old nuns in St. Jarlath's Convent, "or whatever they'll be calling it by then."

Jack Howard, who had attended the Summer Institute with Sister Elizabeth Ann, on the other hand, took a dyspeptic view of her and similar young nuns.

"They need a rigid and authoritarian Order, to have a Mother they can both love and hate. Now they're busy destroying their Mother. They won't have anything left to love or hate and they'll leave the day after they've won their final victory over her. Then they'll find some other love/hate object—some poor dumb, horny priest, I suppose."

"Not Elizabeth Ann," Hugh protested.

"Sweet and pretty and diffident, huh, Hugh? Keep a close eye on the set of that jaw and stay away from her."

Hugh didn't believe him, but maybe Jack was right about Sister. She could be tough if properly encouraged. She'd certainly done in Augustus Ambrose Aquinas Sullivan. She'd fought him with cool and collected intelligence and she'd won.

It had all begun when the sisters discarded the habit—the vestments their Order had worn for more than a century—and donned blue skirts, white blouses, and tiny blue veils. Some of the older nuns looked much less attractive and some of the younger ones emerged as very attractive indeed.

"That Elizabeth has great knockers," said Lloyd Kilbride at supper. "The studs in eighth grade will enjoy school a lot more than they used to."

When Lloyd was sober, he was vulgar; when he was drunk, he was obscene. That night he was halfway between.

"Can't have that sort of thing going on," Monsignor Sullivan mumbled inarticulately; he too was several sheets to the wind, a more recent habit for him than for Kilbride, who had been a lush since ordination.

The pastor had no idea who Sister Elizabeth Ann was; indeed he had no idea who any of the nuns were, as he avoided them as much as he avoided the schoolchildren. Sex, however, was one of his obsessions, and he was determined to drive it from his parish, much as St. Patrick drove the snakes from Ireland. No Christian Family groups and no Cana Conferences were tolerated at St. Jarlath's. The people should have better things to do than sit around and talk about sex.

Hugh had assumed that Sullivan would forget about Sister Elizabeth Ann, as he forgot about most other things that involved the parish.

However, the next week the old pastor happened into her classroom just as she was extolling the ethics of racial justice and the courage of Martin Luther King.

The pastor stormed out of the class, called the Mother General, and demanded that the "nigger lover" be removed from his parish.

A year or two earlier the miscreant would have been deported on the first train to the Mother House in Milwaukee. Gus Sullivan was used to winning his battles with nuns, whom he considered a form of life substantially inferior to his large German shepherd (named, appropriately, Adolph, or Dolphie for short). He would have won this fight too, if Sister had been less guileful and Hugh had not intervened.

Sister Elizabeth Ann had wept hysterically in Hugh's office. Finally Hugh had given in. He was, after all, in her camp.

"What am I supposed to do?" she sniffled.

"Fight the son of a bitch. You have more clout than I do. You're a member of the Chapter of your Order. Call the Mother General and demand that she support you. Tell her you'll go public if she doesn't. Turn the story over to the *National Catholic Reporter*."

She dried her tears, crumpled up the tissue, and looked at Hugh beseechingly. "Will you support me?"

He hesitated. "I'll talk to the Mother General if you want."

The next morning, Sister Baldwina, the Mother General, was on the phone. She did not sound like a pious and diffident old nun.

"We seem to have a problem, Father."

"Don't we all, Sister?"

"Is the man quite mad?"

"Try evil. He respects power, though."

"Aha . . . that sort. I know them well. What would you suggest?"

"Tell him Elizabeth Ann stays the school year or you withdraw all the sisters next week. He'll cave in."

"And at the end of the school year?"

"He's likely to forget it. He usually does. If not, renew the threat."

"Admirable, Father, admirable . . . we have high hopes for Sister Elizabeth

. . . the kind of young woman who will see us through these troubled years. She is, however, so very young and so very fragile. I hope that we can protect Sister until she matures a little more.''

"From men like Monsignor Sullivan? I may be some help in that regard. He's probably not her most serious problem though.''

"Quite,'' said the Mother General, perhaps understanding more than Hugh meant.

Sister Elizabeth Ann listened closely to Father Donlon's homily, although not so closely as to forget about her sixth-grade class. If she took her eyes off them for a moment, the girls would squirm and giggle and perhaps offend the parishioners who were opposed to liturgical change.

Father Donlon was a good preacher, forceful and dramatic and very popular with the people. But theologically he was quite backward, and socially rather conservative. He needed a lot of "updating"—although there was nothing to criticize in this morning's homily.

"We must remember,'' he concluded, "that we do not earn God's forgiveness by our sorrow or by our reparation. God's love is a given. It's always there, waiting patiently for us. We need only turn to Him to receive it. He is pleased with our efforts but He is even more pleased with us. That's why He made us. You cannot earn God's love because He gave it to you before you started to earn it. No more than any love can be earned. Love is always given before the effort to win it or it will never be won.''

The congregation shifted uneasily as he returned to the altar. Father Donlon, they were thinking, made it too easy. He was preaching strange new doctrines. There would be more phone calls of protest.

Sister sighed to herself as she prepared the choir for the offertory psalm. Father Donlon was not a happy man. Did he believe that God loved him?

Probably not.

He needed help, poor, lonely, confused priest.

And she wanted to help him.

There were only three calls to Hugh protesting his sermon, two anonymous and one from Professor Hines, who taught optics at Loyola and fancied himself an intellectual. The point in all the calls was the same—Hugh was a Protestant. God's love could too be earned. How dare he teach false doctrine and make people think the way to heaven was an easy one?

Hines promised that he would write a letter of protest to the chancery the next day, a promise made at least two Sunday afternoons every month.

"Tell them that I am preaching that First Grace is an unearned gift,'' Hugh said tartly.

"I certainly will,'' the professor replied.

"And then read the documents of the Council of Orange.'' Hugh slammed the phone down.

Last year he had been investigated by the chancery on orders from the Apostolic Delegate because someone had written a letter to the Pope complaining about his false doctrine.

It turned out that his offense was to read a gospel from the new Confraternity of Christian Doctrine New Testament translation—approved by the American Bishops, which referred to the "man, Jesus."

"That's a doctrine propounded by the Council of Ephesus, Father," he said to the chancery office investigator.

"We must be careful not to shock the laity," the bald bureaucrat had admonished him.

"Are you ordering me to retract and tell them that Jesus does not have a human nature?" he demanded. "And to repudiate the official translation of the American hierarchy?"

The canonist backed down quickly. And Xav Martin, by then the new rector at Mundelein, went to bat for him. The doddering old cardinal forgot about the Roman inquiry.

The phone rang again. "St. Jarlath's," he snapped. "Father Donlon."

"Hugh, there's going to be a marriage in our family. Your father is at Butterfield and I can't reach him. You're the first to know."

"Tim?" He wasn't going to marry that Maguire bitch, was he?

"Marge. She wants you to officiate of course."

"Who's the groom?" he asked guardedly, conscious that his heart was beating rapidly. Dear God, protect Margie, she's still the little sister I adore.

"An English nobleman." His mother sounded as if she could hardly believe her own words.

"Oh, my God," Hugh replied. "What will Dad say?"

Chapter Eleven
1964

HIS MOTHER'S CALL reached Tim Donlon in his bachelor apartment in Old Town just as he was preparing to make love to Estelle Maguire.

Estelle pouted over the delay.

"Doesn't that woman ever leave you alone?" she whined.

"It's not every day your sister announces her engagement to an English lord," he said mildly.

"It's time for you to marry too," Estelle replied.

She assumed they were going to march down the middle aisle soon. Nor was Tim opposed. He was almost thirty and he was tired of bachelorhood.

Estelle, moreover, was not a bad catch in his view—distracting in bed, fun at parties, a good beer drinker. But he'd become involved with her mostly because her father was rich. A wealthy real estate man on the fringes of the Organization, Larry Maguire had been convicted by a federal court on mail-fraud charges, a conviction sustained two-to-one on appeal, with his father casting the deciding vote. Maguire served six months and then was released on parole, coming home with a suntan.

Both Tim's parents regarded the Maguires with abhorrence; they were loud, vulgar, and corrupt. But they were also wealthy. Estelle was an architect with her own office and clientele, and although her designs were like haunted Gothic castles in a Charles Addams cartoon, her father's money and clout kept the money pouring in.

Not that Tim needed the money, really. Fresh out of the Navy, he'd bought himself a seat on the Board of Trade for $25,000 with his poker and smuggling earnings. He soon became a successful commodities trader notwithstanding a few scrapes with some of the fogies at the Exchange.

Tim loved every second of the Exchange. If you were caught once or twice, that went with the territory. It was like working all day in a gambling casino.

He no longer worked with the kids in the inner-city parishes, which he'd tried when he came out of the service. Whites were not wanted in those parishes anymore, and far be it from him to complain. So he turned to hospitals and routinely sent large checks every four months to Oak Park, where he was born, to St. Anne's, which was near his home parish, and to Mother Cabrini because, well, because that was where Maria had come into the world.

He no more understood his charity than he understood his gambling. Maria had said he was two different people. Well, maybe he was. But there was nothing to be done about it.

Estelle was only the most recent and persistent of his women. He'd often thought he should have gone after Maria in earnest when Hugh backed out. Why had he never tried?

Damn Hugh, anyway. Every time they saw each other, Hugh urged him to go back into therapy. Wasn't it obvious he wasn't the kind therapy helped?

So, after all, it was Estelle. Estelle was trying to get herself pregnant so he'd have to marry her. She didn't need to do that. He was prepared to marry her anyway. But if that was the way she wanted it, he was happy to oblige.

"I suppose you'll be going to the wedding," she said as he returned to the bed.

"If I'm invited." He rolled her over and swatted her ample rump.

Estelle laughed lasciviously.

He hit her again. Harder.

For a fleeting moment Tim Donlon realized how alone he was.

And always would be.

Marge was more than amused to learn from her father, when he finally broke through the maze of the transatlantic phone net at one in the morning, British time, that he thought her intended was English.

Wait till they meet him, she said to herself when they'd finished talking. She laughed herself back to sleep.

Marge had traveled to London five years earlier and found herself a job at the Playboy Club in Park Lane. From there she'd graduated to a roulette table at Hugh Hefner's fashionable Clermont Club in Berkeley Square. There, in the flocked crimson, second-floor casino, and in very advanced décolletage, she had attracted almost as much attention as did the fortunes that rode on each spin of the wheel.

But she also saw that her time was running out. She finally knew how poor Jean Kincaid had felt. After a certain age, you're not much good to the Playboy empire, and there are a lot of lovely late-twenties hookers in the West End.

One night a great bear of a man appeared, a young fellow with long blond hair and a thick Irish brogue, and hung around her table, apparently enjoying more than his sizable winnings.

One of the younger girls later told Marge that he was Lord Kerry, an Anglo-Irish peer who had inherited a fortune in Dublin real estate and made a bigger one building towns in Nigeria.

Marge was surprised, because her best guess was that he was a couple of years younger than she and innocent of any wit.

He was waiting at the door when she left. She crisply told him she was not for sale and went back to her lonely apartment.

He was back the next night. "Only dinner, nothing else, solemn word."

So it was dinner and a handshake at the end—in the cabbage-smelling hallway of her second floor walk-up flat with a meter in which she inserted shillings when she wanted heat. He spoke in a rolling mumble that she barely understood: "Anglo-Irish. Church of Ireland, of course. Mother Catholic, though. Catholic myself. Bad show. Lose to everyone. Double outcast. No roots at all." Followed by a huge laugh and a giant, affectionate Irish grin.

Dinner again and another handshake. Marge decided that he was cute. And perhaps the most clever man she'd ever met.

After the third dinner she kissed him. He was flustered and unskilled.

"That won't do at all," she remonstrated. "Here, let me show you how."

He was much better after being instructed. She told him so.

"Learn quickly." He was hugely pleased with himself.

The next night he proposed. "Good Catholic gel. Good wife. Need one. Time to settle down. Hope you'll agree."

Marge was utterly astonished, and oddly moved. He was a lovely young man who had been taken in by a clever tongue and a sexy body.

"It won't work, Liam," she said at the door to her apartment. "I'm afraid I've not been a nice girl for the last couple of eons. Not exactly a hooker, mind you, but hardly the sweet Irish-American colleen you seem to think I am."

Liam Wentworth, Lord Kerry, took charge of her with a bear hug and demonstrated that he could speak perfectly grammatical English when it was necessary.

"My dear young woman, I know exactly who and what you are and even have a fairly good idea of the reasons you left your parents and acted so foolishly for several years. I intend to make you my wife regardless. I know who you are better than you do. Is that clear?"

He increased the pressure of his embrace, lifting her off the floor while his lips sought hers with vigorous determination.

Marge saw the life preserver that was being thrown. It was a comfortable, attractive, decent one, a life jacket you couldn't help but like. Instinctively she grabbed for it. And in the act of grabbing, like turned to love.

Hugh stood in the sanctuary of the nineteenth-century gray Gothic pile that was the Cathedral of His Gracious Lordship the Bishop of Kerry, as a fierce Irish rain pelted the stained-glass windows. A marriage two weeks after the engagement. His strange, fascinating brother-in-law wasted no time.

After he persuaded his mother that Kerry was in Ireland, as in the Kerry Dances ("Now, why didn't I think of that?"), and his father assured her that Liam was Norman Irish for Guillame ("Bill, my dear, nothing more than that"), Peggy was disposed to give her future son-in-law the benefit of the doubt ("If you're sure he's Catholic."). Liam won her over completely at first encounter.

"Know why the gel is so beautiful now. Doesn't hold a candle to her mother. Mind if I kiss you?"

Peggy didn't mind at all.

The transformation in Marge was breathtaking. Without the slightest admission that she'd been anything but a pious and devout Catholic all her life, she bought a white wedding dress worth a thousand dollars for the ceremony in the cathedral at Killarney.

Of course, Hugh would officiate. "Wouldn't have it any other way. Brother-in-law. Fine Yank. Cardinal can stand in the sanctuary."

Gus Sullivan had told Hugh he couldn't take time off for the wedding and Hugh had told Gus that if he wanted to complain to the administrator, now that the cardinal was dead, he could go right ahead and complain.

The Cardinal Primate of All Ireland (to be distinguished from the Archbishop of Dublin, not a cardinal and the primate only of Ireland, not All Ireland) and two visiting bishops, in addition to the Bishop of Kerry, waited in the sanctuary with Hugh, who had arrived only the night before the wedding and met only a couple of the members of the enormous wedding party.

The maid of honor was Liam's sister, a dreamy eighteen-year-old referred to as "the poet," who looked like a tragic heroine of an Abbey Players film and drank John Jameson's like a lorry driver.

The first of the bride's attendants to come down the aisle, stunning in a light green dress and long blond hair, was not a poet. She was, rather, a disguised countess.

"Maria!" Hugh exclaimed as she devoutly genuflected to the altar, and, with a hint of mockery, to him.

"Late starter," she whispered, smiling.

His hands trembled through the ceremony and not because the evident nervousness of Liam and Marge infected him.

He tried not to look at Maria during his homily.

"Forgiveness is the essence of love. To love is to forgive, to forgive is to love. Liam and Margaret will have to forgive each other often during their years together. Each time they do they will grow in love and have a deeper awareness of God's forgiving love. They will teach one another how much God loves us. They will be sacraments of God's love for each other."

"Good show," mumbled Liam.

And later he added, "That was a fine homily, Hugh; someone like you should be preaching on TV."

None of the family could figure out the pattern according to which Liam spoke, sometimes in monosyllables and sometimes in sentences. In response to Hugh's question, Marge said that it made no difference to her at all.

Hugh was seated next to Maria at the main banquet table in the Great Southern Hotel in Killarney. Foolishly he wondered whether the renewal of their acquaintance would be awkward.

Marriage, motherhood, world travel, and business school had not changed Maria. She was still the sometime countess, sometime waitress.

In five seconds they were talking as if they had seen each other every Saturday for the last ten years.

"So we were in London on the way to Steve's new assignment—do you like him, Hugh? Isn't he a dear?—and I said I must look up my friend Margie, who is probably starving to death in some attic. And we find her with this massive Viking type, halberd and all, and she claims she's going to marry him in two days and can I be in the wedding party. Well, this Viking ordered his elves to stitch my threads together—don't you think the color of the gown matches my eyes, Hugh?—and here I am."

"And you're bound for Spain?"

"That's right. So the bank gives me a leave and I find somewhere else to take my last accounting course. Have you ever had any accounting? Priests ought to study accounting. Do you want to hear how I met Steven?"

"I don't have any choice, but, yes, I do."

The Donlons had been responsible for Steven in a way. If they hadn't hassled her about college, she wouldn't have gone to night school and therefore wouldn't have been offered a blind date for a summer dance in Lake Forest.

At Loyola she'd become a coffee-drinking companion of a girl from Manhattanville named Joan Cardin. Joan pleaded with her to attend the country club dance with a "nice Catholic Navy boy, quiet but cute."

Well, the boy was cute and had pretty eyes and not much to say, which was all right with her because, awed as she was by the country club, she was into more than her usual chatter.

He'd kissed her in the garden, which she assumed was part of country club routine. He was a healthy young male animal who wanted a woman. To her surprise, she discovered she was a healthy young female animal who wanted a man.

They'd laughed most of the rest of the evening. Then Maria dismissed him from her mind. Nice boy, good kisser, but nothing more.

Then letters and long-distance calls from Norfolk, Virginia, began pouring into the shoe repair store. She was spirited off to Charleston to meet mama and grandmama and a variety of sisters, brothers, cousins, uncles, and aunts, all of them more or less outrageous.

The McLains, it turned out, were Irish and Scotch and French, and part Indian (a fact of which they all were inordinately proud), and staunchly Catholic. They'd been polite and kind to her and hid their skepticism as well as they could. She'd countered by telling outlandish stories about her relatives in the Mafia. After two days, they realized she was pulling their legs and hailed her as one of the family.

She'd gone home quite certain she would postpone any decision for at least a year.

Six weeks later they were married at St. Ursula's, with Monsignor "Muggsy" Brannigan officiating.

"And that's the whole story." She smiled through her champagne glass at Hugh. "Are you impressed?"

"I'm glad you're happy, Maria," he said.

"Nice homily today." She ignored his cliché.

"Thank you." His face felt very hot.

"And you don't believe a word of it."

"I beg pardon?"

Her eyes were cool and calculating. "You figure that God forgives everyone but Donlons. For you folks there's a different set of rules. Well, maybe he even forgives Marge and poor Tim. But not Hugh Donlon; he has to earn God's love."

And she turned to the Bishop of Kerry, who was on the other side of her, and ignored Hugh for the rest of the meal.

"Are you angry with me?" he asked her after Liam's younger brother, Brendan, had proposed a toast in Gaelic.

"Exasperated." She touched his hand. "Hugh Thomas Donlon, there's as much goodness and power and love in you as there is water in Dingle Bay . . . well, I haven't seen Dingle Bay yet . . . all the love and trust in God you talked about in that beautiful homily." There were tears in her Rembrandt eyes. "And you've buried it under a mountain of rules. . . ."

"I should break the rules?" he said irritably.

"God help us if you did. You know what I mean, and it doesn't have anything to do with rules."

"I don't," he insisted.

"Do you still sail the *Pegeen*?" Another quick touch of her hand on his, this time a sign of hope.

He slammed the door shut again.

"It was too much of an expense. I sold it and bought a new set of golf clubs."

"How like a Donlon."

She turned from him just as she had on the lawn after she'd told him how beautiful he was.

After the bride and groom left, Maria took charge of the party, learning the step dances from the Irish cousins, singing with the bishop—an interminable ballad that pleaded with a certain Paddy Reilly to return to Ballyjamesduff—pouring champagne for everyone who wanted it, and even dancing in the rain that had poured down on Killarney all day.

Steve McLain, clearly adoring, asked Hugh, "Would you believe that the bishop asked her what county in Ireland her family was from and she told him County Palermo and the bishop thought she was kidding?"

"Like you, Steve, I'd believe anything about her."

The judge joined them a minute or two later. "Hugh," he said expansively, "do you have the feeling we may just have come in on a happy ending?"

"I told you it would work out."

"You did, indeed. But you didn't promise herself there as entertainment."

Herself, blond hair plastered to her head and dress plastered to her body, kissed Hugh on the cheek as she left. "Come see us in Spain."

"Please do," Steven urged him.

"I will," he lied.

On the Aer Lingus 707 back to Chicago, Tim told Hugh that there would be another wedding soon. Estelle was pregnant.

Chapter Twelve
·· *1965* ··

IN THE YEAR after the two weddings, Sister Elizabeth Ann expanded her empire to include the teen-agers of the parish, a risky experiment, making her even more liable to Gus Sullivan's psychopathic wrath. One summer night Hugh checked in at the high club dance in the parish hall, half hoping to avert any trouble that the chief engineer could report to the vacationing monsignor.

Sister was the center of attention. There was no dancing, of course. The "high club" was in fact a drugstore corner moved inside. Lakeridge, the St. Jarlath's suburb, frowned on teen-age hangouts, so the kids who were too young to have cars hung out around the parish instead—that is, when Monsignor wasn't in town.

As they couldn't dance at the "dance," Elizabeth Ann had decided they ought to sing. At first the "nun with the guitar" had attracted only the girls, and only the freshman girls at that. But her singing was so pure and her laughter so appealing that by now everyone swarmed around her as soon as she walked into the parish hall. Even the senior boys showed up—perhaps, Hugh speculated, because they agreed with Lloyd Kilbride's appraisal of the nun's attractions.

Hugh, who enjoyed teen-agers and related well to them, felt somewhat rueful that he'd been abandoned for a pretty woman with a musical voice. But as he watched her lead the youthful chorus in "Cumbayah," he found himself fascinated to the point of transfixion by the rhythmic movements of her body, all the more compelling because she was quite unconscious of them.

A good thing Monsignor Sullivan wasn't about. Hugh thought of himself as a man almost unable to hate other human beings. Yet it was easy for him to hate Augustine Ambrose Aquinas Sullivan—Triple A to the rest of the diocese.

Gus Sullivan had been assigned to St. Jarlath's when the parish consisted of a handful of big homes along Sheridan Road facing the lake and a few blocks of servants' flats stretching toward the hinterland of northern Illinois. After the war, Lakeridge had expanded rapidly; the very wealthy on Sheridan Road were joined by the quite wealthy on the curving, treelined streets between the Northwestern tracks and the Eden's expressway: Corporation presidents were joined in church by brokers, doctors, lawyers, vice-presidents, and commodity traders.

In a few years the collections at St. Jarlath's quintupled and Gus Sullivan claimed credit for this success as a mark of his financial acumen, a judgment the Church officially validated by bestowing on him the monsignorial purple. Tireless in his scheming, even after receiving his purple, he'd expanded his network of cronies to include the most affluent people from the new neighborhoods and left the rest of the parish to his curates.

Unlike many of the old timers, who kept a careful watch on the activities of their young assistants, Sullivan didn't give a damn what Hugh did; he could have five mistresses on the side, as far as the pastor cared, so long as they didn't disturb his peace.

Monsignor Sullivan faced the world with a number of certainties.

Money was important. The church's steady income proved that he was a good pastor. Moreover, those parishioners who had the most money were the closest to God. Therefore, the pastor should be closest to them.

Authority was important. He possessed authority that he shared with the Pope and the cardinal. Therefore, he was right all the time because he could count on the Pope and the cardinal to back him up.

Sex was important—as the worst of all sins and the worst of all threats to the salvation of his people, especially those who were not as rich as his friends. Therefore, one must do all that one could to prevent any discussion of sex in the parish. "If they talk about it less, Father," he assured Hugh on one occasion, "they'll do it less."

Finally, his peace was important. Pastors had to be protected for those critical moments when they make the decisive choices that shape the future, like building a new twelve-room parochial school. That decision had been made in 1947. As far as Hugh could see, it was the last decision Sullivan had made and was about as risky as buying a dozen oranges. Nonetheless, Sullivan's peace and health had to be protected at all costs lest he be unprepared whenever another such crisis might arise.

Two conclusions followed from this final premise: first, that the pastor take as many vacations as possible to husband his resources—Palm Springs for the two months in the winter (usually during the troublesome season of Lent) and Eagle River for the two months in the summer (with his rich friends picking up the tab); and, second, that the curates do all of the work. This appealed to the pastor's sense of fairness. He did the thinking and they did the work.

Kilbride was useless, indeed worse, as Hugh had to cover up his drunkenness, an effort he felt was pointless but was still demanded by loyalty to the priesthood.

So Hugh did all the work.

Not that he minded work. He loved the work of the parish and was good at it. Sick calls early in the morning, the weary old faces smiling when he came into the bedroom; visits to grammar school classes to joke and laugh with the smart, bright-eyed kids; hospital calls to bring a little light to the anxious and depressed; counseling young people whose hopes could still be salvaged; instructing young couples before marriage and rejoicing in their discovery that the Church could be more than negative in its impact; reconciling older lovers who were tired and bored but still in love, even if they didn't know it; cheering for the grammar school football and volleyball teams and showing tall, taciturn teen-agers that he was still better at basketball than they were; instructing adults in the new, postconciliar Church, adults who were eager to understand and to act; helping business and professional men to think through the difficult ethical problems they faced in their work. Mass, sermons, anointing the dying, wakes, funerals—Hugh loved it all.

But the activity and the rewards were not enough to satisfy him. He was restless, dissatisfied, often lonely. That should not be. He was working too hard, not praying enough, not controlling his fantasy life, nor his shamefully voyeuristic eyes. The women in the parish were mostly older than he, but he found them infuriatingly attractive in their aloof, well-groomed, artfully preserved, self-confident way.

Yet he no longer considered celibacy a serious problem in his life. When all was said and done, the most painful issue was not knowing where his own fault ended and Sullivan's began. Was Sullivan the problem or was there a deeper problem, inside himself?

He was a priest for life. And the answer now was not some other assignment but the one he had, St. Jarlath's, where he did all the work, bore all the responsibility, and had not the slightest authority to meet the responsibility with.

The last created constant problems. A typical St. Jarlath's cycle was for the pastor to order him to begin a new activity, such as a grammar school varsity sports program—usually because one of his wealthy cronies had complained that the "young priests aren't doing anything for the kids"—next, for him to succeed, because the organizational and economic resources of the parish assured that these programs were almost always successful, and then, as sure as the sun rose each morning over Lake Michigan, the eastern boundary of St. Jarlath's parish, the pastor would find one of his major premises violated—the project would cost too much money, or become a threat to authority, or involve sex, or disturb his peace.

It was Hugh's task to convey these definitive and arbitrary judgments to the parishioners and defend as best he could the mad pastor's whims. He did not miss the expressions of seething contempt in their eyes. Yet the theory of loyalty to a superior, "Christ's representative over you," that he had learned in the seminary demanded that he not criticize Gus to the people of the parish.

All he could say was that perhaps next year or the year after the program would be revived.

"After my kids are out of school," said the chairman of the St. Jarlath's Varsity Club at one of those times. "You've got no balls, Father; you're a hack; you're the dummy through which the monsignor speaks. A man like you would never make it in my world."

"We all have bosses, Mr. Ryan," he said, clenching his fists.

"I don't," Ryan sneered.

Ryan was right and Hugh knew it; he was a clerk, an errand boy, a flunky, a man permitted no hormones in a community where hormones counted enormously. Not to have a woman was perhaps understandable, but not to be his own man was inexcusable.

Moreover, not only was Sullivan arbitrary and unpredictable; he was insensitive and cruel. When an Army officer from the parish was killed in Vietnam and his wife and parents requested that a grammar school classmate who taught at Boston College say the Mass, Triple A said no. It was his iron rule that only parish priests officiate at weddings, funerals, and baptisms. Jesuits might be useful for Sunday help; they could not be counted on to say the proper things at funerals.

Hugh was deputed to convey the pastor's decision to the young widow. "Father Kilbride will say the Mass."

Father Kilbride did say the Mass. He was drunk. His sermon was an unintelligible babble and the idiot didn't even have in mind the right war.

"I'll never set foot in a Catholic church again," the widow said when Hugh apologized at the gravesite.

Another of Sullivan's decrees was that there would be no more mixed marriages in the parish—especially to Jews. Hugh was forced to tell young people who had lived their entire lives in St. Jarlath's to go to other parishes, unless, that is, they happened to be part of the pastor's clique, in which case the marriage was performed without challenge no matter how problematic it might be.

Gus Sullivan was a cruel and insensitive tyrant because any other approach to the world would have revealed him as an incompetent fool, and at some level in his armadillo personality he knew it. That was why he eventually went after Sister Elizabeth Ann, because he feared if he didn't get her, she'd get him.

Most of the parishioners to whom Hugh talked complained bitterly about Gus. Some even wrote letters of protest to the chancery. Yet respect for the leader was so deeply ingrained in the Catholic people that there was not yet an organized campaign against him and no direct confrontations.

Moreover, much of the parish was quite content with old Gus. The monsignor, they would assert piously, had done such a wonderful job with St. Jarlath's, as if an orangutan could not have done as much.

"If there was a referendum," Lloyd Kilbride had said in one of his rare completely sober moments, "the bastard would win in a walk."

There were some parishioners who loyally supported Hugh, albeit Hugh was still less willing than they to do battle. Strongest in his support was Benedict Fowler, a millionaire commodities trader who had not penetrated the pastor's inner elite, although only because the pastor had not kept up on the distribution of wealth in the parish.

In his midforties, Fowler seemed the very stereotype of an Irish ward heeler—which is what his father had been. Big and gruff, with a genial grin, a gregarious tongue, and a cigar always clenched between his teeth, he worked a crowd the way Dick Daley did. When he moved laughingly into a group of people, they laughed too, unless, that is, they happened to notice that his hard brown eyes never did.

Ben had married somewhat late in life. Helen Fowler was at least ten years younger than he and, by almost unanimous agreement, was the most beautiful woman in the parish. "That ass is quite a piece of work," Father Kilbride had said appreciatively. A little less than average height, with soft honey-blond hair, a clear cream complexion, and a figure like a nineteenth-century odalisque, Helen was indeed something to look at.

Whenever she appeared at a meeting, with or without her husband, the men became attentive and the women restive. Unfortunately, "I think the young people deserve our support" was the most exalted intellectual contribution she seemed capable of making at parish committee meetings. The impassive mysterious face that hinted at secret insight appeared, in fact, to hide nothing at all. Although Ben seemed reasonably considerate and kind to her, he often acted as if he were unaware of her existence. And her daughter, Linda, a sullen but prematurely sexy and precociously intelligent child in her last year of grammar school, was quite frankly bored by her mother's interest in St. Jarlath School.

The spring after Helen first became involved, Hugh was invited to a giant garden party at the Fowlers', a sit-down dinner on a Sunday afternoon—five hundred guests under canopies, two orchestras, food from one of the finest French restaurants in Chicago. The silver sparkled, the linen gleamed, and the wine flowed. The bare-shouldered women chattered away while their mostly rotund men simply ogled.

"With what he made last week in soybeans," one guest remarked, "he won't even notice the cost of this bash."

Ben cornered Hugh after the roast beef had been served. He leaned over the table, genial grin and smelly Havana, quite at odds with the freshness of the day.

"How you doing, Padre? Glad you could come. Didn't invite the old man— don't want that so-and-so around here. How do you put up with him?"

"He's the pastor, Ben."

"Always loyal, huh? That's what I admire about you. Real Irish trooper." He coughed violently and wiped his mouth with his handkerchief. "Hey, look, this will all be over by eight o'clock. Some of the folks are coming back for a swim, about nine. Why don't you get your trunks and join us? See you then, Padre."

Ordinarily Hugh avoided intimate social gatherings with his parishioners. But he had missed his Thursday golf date with Jack Howard and Pat Cleary for two weeks running, and he needed the swim.

So he returned and found a group of four couples huddled in robes at poolside. Only Helen Fowler was in the water, gliding with quiet, careful strokes. In the water she didn't seem the slightest bit awkward. Hugh dropped his towel on a chair and enthusiastically dove in beside her.

"Good evening, Father," she said softly.

"Good evening, Helen."

The subject of the conversation at the side of the pool was, as Hugh had feared, Monsignor Augustine Ambrose Aquinas Sullivan. Al Downs, a hip-shooting Loop trial lawyer, was just finishing the prosecution's case.

"What about it, Father?" Al leaned back complacently on his lounge chair. "Do we get a conviction?"

Helen climbed out of the pool and Hugh followed her, her statuesque charms disturbingly close. "I'm not a jury, Al," he said, sitting down, "and the Church doesn't try pastors."

"How can you put up with him, Father?" demanded a redhaired woman in her late thirties, the wife of a prominent doctor, who, as far as Hugh could tell, never said anything.

"If it keeps up much longer"—Al was closing in for a kill—"we'll have to send a formal protest to the new cardinal. Would you be on our side?"

"I don't think it'll do any good," Hugh said evasively. Helen leaned over him with a tall rum and tonic. Her scent lingered after her, teasing him with its sensual delight.

"You don't think the cardinal will force pastors to retire at seventy?" Ben waved his cigar. "Some of the boys down at the Exchange have heard that rumor."

Hugh felt increasingly uncomfortable. "I hope you buy or sell soybeans on better information than that."

There was general laughter; even Helen smiled faintly through the halo of cigarette smoke around her head.

Hugh stood up. "And now, if you'll excuse me, I think I'd better go back to work on tomorrow's homily." He turned to Helen and thanked her.

"You gotta come back, Father," Ben Fowler said as he left. "The pool's here; someone else should use it besides us."

The "dance" was breaking up and Sister Elizabeth Ann and her favorites were sweeping up the debris and picking up Coke bottles when Hugh returned to the school hall.

"A question came up at the Institute I'd like to discuss with you," Sister began at once, her eyes modestly lowered. "Some of the sisters say it's unjust for us not to be permitted to call priests by their first names. Do you agree with that?"

"In theory, I might, Sister. But in this parish we have enough trouble as it is without stirring up the pastor and the old timers because of something relatively unimportant."

"In private?" she asked.

"And run the risk of slipping in public?"

"You're right, of course." She smiled warmly.

"Thank you, Sister." He laughed and she laughed. Then he went into the rectory and she went across the yard toward the convent.

In his room he turned off the air conditioner and opened the window because he disliked the feeling of being closed in. He was trapped, sunk in the quicksands of St. Jarlath's, the way America seemed to be sinking in the quicksands of Vietnam.

He turned on the radio and then turned it off. "A Hard Day's Night" on every station. There was no TV in his room. He didn't feel like walking down the corridor of the empty building to the TV room. He should, as he'd said, work on tomorrow's sermon, still only half finished.

He picked up Robin Moore's *The Green Berets*, read a few pages, and tossed it aside. No sermon ideas there.

He dialed the first five numbers of the Fowlers' phone and then hung up.

He would have to talk to someone or he'd lose his mind.

He called the convent and asked for Sister Elizabeth Ann.

"Yes, Father," said the discreet voice, although he hadn't identified himself. Much too late to make this call.

"Calling about the liturgy, Sister."

Sister Elizabeth came on.

"Hi, Liz, this is Hugh. I'm sorry about being a prig on the first-name issue."

Her warm and joyous laughter eased his pain.

"You're impossible," she said affectionately.

Chapter Thirteen
1965

HUGH AND SISTER Elizabeth Ann ate a long brunch after the ten o'clock Mass, at which the sixth graders had sung "My Soul Is Thirsting for the Lord" with such gusto the congregation had spontaneously joined in. Many parishioners complimented Hugh in the back of the church; unfortunately other and more "important" ones clearly would have complained to the pastor had he not been in Eagle River.

It was an iron law of Catholic reform: Those who approved spoke to the curates; those who opposed complained to the pastor.

However, all triumphs, even small and temporary ones, were meant to be savored. So he and Liz were savoring theirs in the rectory kitchen.

They were the only ones in the rectory. The cook and housekeeper were personal servants to Monsignor Sullivan. When he went on vacation, they were furloughed with pay. Lloyd Kilbride had returned to Guest House, a treatment center for alcoholic priests. Hugh was expected to fend for himself.

Liz made bacon and eggs and thawed coffee cake from the freezer. Hugh liberated a bottle of the pastor's best sauterne from the private wine cellar, the key to which he'd copied a few years earlier. The pastor's wine, naturally, was purchased with parish funds, so it seemed only right, Hugh opined, that it be enjoyed by the curates as well as the pastor and his friends.

"To Gelineau and the sixth-grade psalmsters," he toasted.

"May they survive another year," Liz toasted back.

She was an extremely pretty woman, he realized, no makeup, simple skirt and blouse, simple smile, simple good looks. Sweet, fragile, lovely.

"I keep telling myself this place is an excellent opportunity to liberate souls in purgatory," he said grimly.

Liz colored faintly. "Oh, Father . . . I mean Hugh . . ." Redder yet, most becomingly so. "I hate to disullusion you. The souls in purgatory are *out.*"

"Really? That's a loss. What do we tell kids in the dental chair when the drill begins . . . or people dying of cancer?"

He resented the loss of the souls in purgatory. They were useful for preaching and teaching about suffering.

"You tell both groups"—she smiled over her coffee cup—"that by spiritualizing their suffering, they do what Jesus did when he died on the cross; they purify themselves and absorb pain from others. That's sound psychological truth, you know, and it frees them from the burden of mythological stories about imaginary places like purgatory."

"Uh-huh, what about heaven?"

Liz shifted momentarily in her chair. As she did so, her breasts pressed against her freshly pressed blouse. In that instant of revelation, more devastating to Hugh than if the blouse had fallen away, he felt faith and virtue desert him.

She waved a hand and laughed. "We survive, perhaps immersed in the mind of God. That's not important. What is important is that we try to achieve as best we can the kingdom of God on earth by working for social justice."

He gulped the delicately sweet white wine, hoping it would distract him.

"Immersed in the mind of God, will I be me?" Lovely Liz and good white wine notwithstanding, Hugh was dismayed; his religion was being taken away from him.

And the wine made him more, not less, aware of her own delicate sweetness.

She smiled delightedly and filled his glass again. "Don't you think, *Father* Donlon, that that's a selfish concern? Are you willing to leave to God the way you survive?"

"I don't think so," he said somberly. "I want to be me."

Is this how a rapist feels before he assaults a woman? He quickly drained his glass and filled it again.

"I want to be what God wants," she said with the same piety that Sister Cunnegunda used to praise the devotion to the Sorrowful Mother. The substance of devout ideology might change, the style did not—simple ideas, phrased in terse phrases, and preached with intense conviction. Yet she did know more about what the Church was thinking these days than he did.

Later, in his room, Hugh decided he would have to ask Monsignor Martin, the new rector of the seminary, about Sister Elizabeth Ann's religion. What she had said had truly disturbed him, although the thought of Xav Martin mercifully had exorcised his temptation.

Xav would say, "Typical half-baked summer-school theology. Let me give you a list of books to read, Hugh, so you can immunize yourself against such drivel."

Unfortunately, there was no time at St. Jarlath's to read.

Hugh turned his attention to the two months' accumulation of mail that was piled on his desk.

The mail was like a review test of his priesthood. First, requests for First Communion records: Some damn fools in the East were so obsessive they wouldn't marry parish young folks without proof of First Communion, a requirement that went far beyond the code of canon law. Second, marriage notices to record in the baptismal records. Third, checks for Mass stipends to be recorded, and fourth, corrections in the annual statement the parish sent on of a person's financial contribution. It was all secretarial work that he would have to do sometime before the school year started. The monsignor's secretary was too busy to take care of such matters.

There were occasional surprises: an advertisement for a series of books on the abnormal psychology of adolescence; a new sermon outline series; two new sets of Sunday missals with the latest liturgical changes; a revised hymnal with Vatican Council hymns, whatever they might be.

He shoved the pile away. None of it was worth a damn. He was a failure. How many sermons, classes, lectures, instructions, programs, visits, conversations, conferences, meetings, phone calls . . . and what did he have to show for it? Marge was going to produce a child. And he had produced nothing at all except two months' worth of sacramental records.

He pounded his tiny desk and watched the pile of mail slide off.

Wearily, he picked up the paper and envelopes and piled them in a neat stack again.

There was one envelope he had not noticed. From "Kincaid" in Manhattan Beach, California. They had moved.

Dear Hugh,

I've been meaning to write you for a long time. The pictures in the papers of Marge's wedding forced me to renew my good intentions. As you must imagine, I had a good laugh and a happy one over Marge's turning respectable. I must say you predicted that long ago. I finally went over to the priest's house and asked Father Mihail, our priest, for your address. He wondered why I wanted to write to you and I told him a little bit about what you did for us. He told me that priests receive so little positive encouragement for good work they've done that I ought to thank you. I was surprised. I said I thought priests didn't get discouraged. He laughed and said I had a lot to learn about Catholicism yet, "and yourself with all that convert's zeal too."

When Laura came we decided she had to be baptized. We valued our Lutheran heritage but there didn't seem to be any way to go back to it. We went over to the priest's house and told Father Mihail that we'd never been in a priest's house before and we'd never talked to a full-fledged priest.

So he took our Laura in his arms—she's a very cute little blond, much better looking than her mother—and said he wasn't going to let her go and that if we wanted to have her back we'd have to become Catholics too and, sure, conversion nowadays meant that we would be Catholics and Lutherans at the same time.

So we became Catholics and think of ourselves as Lutherans and Catholics. We started thinking that way even before Pope John, who was a lot like Father Mihail. Laura has a little brother now and there's another one on the way, so you can see what good Catholics we've become.

All of which is a way of building up to you, Father Hugh. It didn't take me long to figure out why Hank had come across the mountains to carry me away like a captive princess. I was furious with you for about ten seconds and then I knew I'd love you for the rest of my life. It was the last chance for both of us. We never would have taken the chance unless you'd forced us to.

I was wrong about everything. Hank and I fight a lot and all my other predictions were wrong too. Well, not all of them. I do have my degree from UCLA and am in graduate school now.

Would you believe that Laura, poor thing, was born nine months to the day after Hank came over the mountains to drag me away?

Our love is not always easy. It is not supposed to be. But neither of us has any doubt about it. Nor do we doubt that we owe it all to you.

I'm sure you have better things to do than answer letters like this. But, please, do put us on your Christmas card list.

Love,
Jean

"Hey, honey, I forgot. Padre Hugh is coming over to swim in a couple of hours. Make him a sandwich and give him a beer, would you, sweetheart?"

"Of course."

She tingled with excitement. She thought Father Donlon was the most beautiful man she'd ever seen, and she was perfectly aware that he couldn't take his eyes off her. It would be nice to have him to herself for an hour or two on a sunny Sunday afternoon.

Helen was the product of a marriage that had broken up when she was three. During her grammar school and high school years she had lived at Maryville and then started to work as a typist in a Loop law office. She worked there for five interesting years and became a competent and skillful legal secretary. She routinely fended off passes from men who wanted to use her, and longed for a man to marry. Unfortunately, the men she thought she might want to marry found her dull after the first date.

She didn't think she was dull, only painfully shy. But it came to the same thing.

In recent years she had frequently looked back to the relative poverty of those working years with fondness. She knew she had been good at her work. When the partners in the firm raised her salary every six months and said she was the best legal secretary on LaSalle Street, she had glowed with happiness. She'd received few compliments in her years at Maryville and none that acknowledged her ability as well as her good looks.

Then Ben had appeared in the office and promptly asked for a date. He thought she was intelligent because she listened to him without interrupting. When he proposed, she'd asked herself, Why not?

She was fond of her husband. He was generous and kind if not always considerate. His sexual needs were minimal, which was all right with her. She kept a neat house, listened to his monologues, gave him a daughter who bitterly disliked her mother, and enjoyed the privileges and prerogatives of his wealth.

She was bored and starved for affection. Yet loyalty to her husband and a low level of sexual interest herself had made it easy for her to turn down the inevitable passes. For someone who looked like either an ex-model or a graduate of a rich girls' finishing school, propositions, usually crude, were as much part of daily life as were dawn and sunset.

When Father Hugh arrived, Helen waited for him at poolside in a new black bikini that most women her age wouldn't have dared wear even in the privacy of the bedroom. She was pleased by the quick widening of his eyes.

"Ben had to go to the airport for a sudden conference and Linda is with her friends. He said I should give you a drink and a sandwich."

Hugh swam a half mile in the pool, hardly noticing her as she waited patiently at the edge, legs curled underneath her.

Afterward he ate a roast beef sandwich and drank a bottle of Pepsi. While he ate, Helen smoked several cigarettes and watched him intently through large sunglasses. He was certainly gorgeous. What would it be like to kiss him?

What harm in finding out?

"A soybean conference?" he asked as he ate the sandwich.

She shrugged. "I suppose so. I don't understand his business very well."

They continued the small talk until at length he announced that he had to leave. He hardly looked as if he were running away.

She snubbed out her cigarette and sprayed her mouth with a tube from her purse. She kissed him on the lips as they walked through the vast sunken living room on their way to his car.

It was a long sweet kiss, longer and sweeter than she had expected.

"Good-bye, Father." She turned quickly so he could not see her face. It was all she wanted. It had been enough.

Hugh had accepted Ben's invitation because he had experienced a terrible letdown after the high created by Jean's letter. He returned to the pool a half dozen more times in August, three of them times when Helen was there alone. Finally he did not wait to be invited but called and told her he was coming.

Whenever they were alone, they kissed, and the kissing became more passionate with every visit. The last time the kiss turned into a silent embrace on deep blue sofa cushions under a Motherwell collage. They clung to each other for minutes on end, a delirious, timeless experience like drowning in a sea of honey.

Moreover, she wanted nothing more, it seemed, than affection. There was no hint that she was willing to go further and indeed a strong hint in the opposite direction. When, almost automatically, his hands had begun to explore, she had slipped gracefully away from him.

He was shaken, nevertheless, when he encountered Linda Fowler as he was leaving the house, just as he had finished wiping her mother's lipstick off his face and jamming the telltale handkerchief into his Windbreaker pocket. The child smirked. Had she been watching? Did she know?

Probably not. Linda always smirked.

Chapter Fourteen
1965

THE PEGEEN GLIDED rapidly through the water, picking up speed; soon it was touching only the tops of the waves, like the old *Yankee Clipper* taking off from Flushing Bay.

Then they were airborne, spinning through the clouds in a glorious, dancing frenzy. The wind bit into his face and his naked chest, his long hair trailed behind him, and he was singing at the top of his lungs. His heart soared even higher than the whirling boat turned airplane.

Maria was working at the jib, laughing and singing with him.

No, not Maria. Helen.

He kissed her and began to tear at her clothes. The joy of flying through space turned to terror. He tried to pull back from her but couldn't.

The boat began to plummet toward the dismal waters below. He forced his way into her just before they hit the angry waves.

He awoke soaked in sweat. He could not remember the dream the next morning. He never could. But this wasn't the first time it had become a nightmare.

In his still groggy mind, he heard Maria's words at Killarney.

If you break one rule, you'll break them all.

Passionately kissing another man's wife. Why was he doing it? It made no sense.

Hugh spent the last weekend of the summer with his parents at the lake and returned to the parish firmly resolved to meditate fifteen minutes every day, do spiritual reading for ten minutes, and some other serious reading for fifteen minutes and to say the rosary and part of the Divine Office before he went to bed every night.

And to stay away from the Fowler house.

He was thoroughly ashamed of the flirtation, had confessed it humbly, and was determined that nothing like it would ever happen again.

At the rectory, the secretary told him that the pastor had been home for the weekend but was forced to leave on Sunday night by urgent business in San Diego. He'd left word that Hugh should make sure the boiler was repaired before the school year started and bids collected for resurfacing the parking lot.

Hugh threw the notes into the wastebasket in front of the secretary, punishing her because he could not punish Monsignor Sullivan, and went upstairs to unpack.

Then he walked over to the white stone convent to ask Sister Elizabeth Ann about the Sunday liturgy.

Sister Superior was away. The old nun who was the cook answered the door.

"Oh, Father, Sister isn't with us anymore. Monsignor was very upset about the hymns at the ten o'clock Mass yesterday. He called Mother Baldwina. Mother wasn't home, so Sister Gertrudis, our vicar general . . . er, vice-president, told Sister that she would have to return to the motherhouse and stay there till Mother came back. Sister was very unhappy, but she's a good, obedient, religious person, even if she is a little modern, so she went to the motherhouse last night. Mother won't be home until tomorrow."

Hugh put his golf clubs back into the trunk of his car, called Jack Howard, and pleaded with him to meet him at the course. He took out his fury on Bobolink Country Club and beat Jack by three strokes.

"I'll say one thing and one thing only," Jack said somberly. "Even though I'm not among that young woman's fans, I'm glad for her that she's escaped that hellhole. No, I'll say another thing. You get out of there too, just as quickly as you can. There's no kindly mother general to save you."

"I can't let the people down."

"They'd let you down at the drop of a hat. Most of them think Sullivan is not only sane, but lovable. Your image says that Hugh Donlon can beat everyone the way he beat Austin High School. The difference is that Austin wasn't a madman."

"I'll beat him," Hugh insisted.

"He'll destroy you. You can't beat a psychopath."

"Is that what he is?"

That was exactly what Mother Baldwina called monsignor the next morning.

"Even if I were here, dear Father, I would have made the same decision as my vice-president. I cannot permit Sister to suffer any more at the hands of that psychopath. Do you realize that he ordered the ushers forcibly to remove her from the sanctuary where she was directing the hymns? He didn't ask her to leave. He came in, saw her directing the music, and without a word to Sister instructed the ushers to drag her out by force. Sister was nearly hysterical when she finally got home to the motherhouse."

"She's so important to the parish, Mother," he said humbly.

"I realize that, dear Father, and she is also important to us. I will not have her humiliated again. The poor child is too fragile to be subjected to such treatment. I'm sorry for St. Jarlath's but my first duty is to protect Sister."

"Certainly." He tried to sound urbane. How could he explain that he would miss her terribly?

"I am also writing a detailed letter to the cardinal describing what happened and warning him that if there is any repetition all our sisters will leave on the first Northwestern train."

"That won't make any difference."

"I hope you're wrong, Father. In any case, it is now out of your hands and mine and up to Cardinal McCarthy."

"Yes, Mother."

"You haven't asked about Sister's next assignment."

"No, Mother."

"Do you wish to know?"

Now, what in the hell was he supposed to make of that?

"I'm not about to run after her, Mother Baldwina, if that's what you think. It was not that kind of relationship."

"She admires you greatly."

"That's good of her, Mother; I repeat, it was not that kind of a relationship. I understand your concern, but you have the wrong man for that sort of thing."

The telephone was wet from his perspiring hand. He shifted it to the other.

A sigh. "My apologies, Father. These days one does not know. . . . In any event, I feel it best to send Sister back to full time university work so she can finish her degree program. She needs a vote of confidence from the Order."

"I'm glad there are some prudent religious leaders left in the Church."

"You are indeed a very clever young man with your tongue."

So the school year began without Sister Elizabeth Ann. Hugh tried to do the entire liturgy program by himself. His good intentions about reading and prayer vanished quickly. He was soon tired again. Nor were his spirits improved by the return of Lloyd Kilbride.

"Where's the nun with the big knockers?" were his first words to Hugh at supper the night he returned. "I hear she got the sack."

"The pastor raped her," snapped Hugh.

After supper there was a message that Ben Fowler had called.

Hugh returned the call.

"Padre, Al Downs is having a meeting tonight about his favorite subject. At his house. He wanted me to ask you if you were interested in coming. No obligation."

"Are you going, Ben?"

A pause. "I think I have to."

"I'll be there."

It was a council of war—twenty people, fifteen more than Hugh had expected.

"It has to stop," Downs began. "If we have any integrity left, we've got to do something about him. I take it we're all agreed that dragging that poor young nun off the altar was the final act of lunacy?"

There was already a bill of particulars itemizing the cruelties and stupidities of Monsignor Sullivan for many years: widows and children insulted at funerals, young people driven out of the Church, parishioners humiliated, students summarily expelled from the school because the pastor did not think they were dressed modestly enough—especially girls whose physical development had begun early—programs arbitrarily terminated, unresponsiveness to parishioners' requests, frequent prolonged absences from the parish, signs recently of excessive drinking.

"What do you think, Padre?" asked Ben Fowler, cigar out of his mouth and pointing at the sheet of paper.

"A lot of it won't fly." Helen was not present. Why not? "He may well be within his canonical rights in his vacations. You should not make charges of alcoholism without better proof. He is also the pastor and can terminate programs whenever he wants. If you removed pastors for being unresponsive to their parishioners or driving young people out of the Church by authoritarianism, you'd have to fire half the pastors in the archdiocese. If I were you, I'd concentrate on the cruelties, particularly at the time of death. Also the persecution of grammar school girls for their sexual development. And you could make a good deal out of the public displays. He can terminate lecture programs if he wants, but to publicly insult a visiting priest who is on the seminary faculty is a bit of a scandal. And, of course, dragging the sister off the altar was quite improper, even though regulation of the parish liturgy is well within his authority."

"Anything else, Father?" Downs hunched forward like a cat moving in on a canary.

"Well, it's hard to say how the new cardinal will react to this sort of problem. He's been away at the Council a good deal and has not reshaped the diocese in his image yet. It's said that he's quite untraditional in some respects. Nevertheless, I would be very cautious, if I were you. Protest your respect for authority. Praise Monsignor Sullivan's many accomplishments—I'm sure you can think of some—and concentrate on the terrible harm being done to souls."

"Mail him the letter?" asked Downs.

Hugh thought for a moment. "No. Call Monsignor Cronin, the vice-chancellor for personnel, and ask for an appointment. Tell him what it's about and who will be coming. Cardinal Eammon McCarthy will apparently see anyone who asks for an appointment. Be courteous and respectful. But don't leave any doubt that you are deeply concerned."

"Anything else?" said the red-haired woman whose name he could never remember.

"Yes. It is critically important that you keep this plan secret. If Monsignor Sullivan finds out, he will make you the issue, not himself. He knows how to use power to protect himself."

"Thanks, Father." Ben beamed. "Glad to have you aboard."

The others crowded around to shake his hand.

Poor people. Even a craven priest on their side was better than none.

"If there's nothing else, I probably ought to be back in the rectory. No one else covering for sick calls."

Faker. The teen-ager in charge of the door and the phone, paid with money lifted from the collection, could find him with a quick phone call.

He was afraid to be too close to treason.

. . .

Helen was standing at the door of her Mercedes. "I came to pick Ben up."
Impulsively his lips brushed hers.

She quickly pulled away. "I think Linda has been spying on us. Ben is
suspicious."

As he drove away, he thought he saw Benedict in the doorway. Might he have
seen the kiss?

Chapter Fifteen
1965

FOR THE GOOD of his soul Hugh decided to spend a few days at the retreat house
at Mundelein. He would talk to Xav Martin, who always seemed to have the
right answers in time of troubles. Hugh had avoided Monsignor Martin because
he knew Xav would force the hard decision and the confessor at the monastery
would not.

He locked the safe after Mass on Sunday, checked the Mass schedule for the
week to make sure there were Jesuits and Vincentians coming to do the work that
the parish clergy would not do, locked all the doors in the church, packed a small
suitcase, and sat down for what he hoped would be a peaceful ham sandwich and
Coke—his first meal since the cup of coffee at breakfast.

It was not to be peaceful. Sister Mariana, the new school principal, called and
insisted that he come to the convent on a matter of "the utmost urgency."

Sister Mariana was a small thin woman with hard eyes and a harder voice. In
her middle forties, she preached the new "collegiality" of power sharing in the
Church, but ran her school with all the permissiveness of a German submarine
captain on combat duty.

She did not like St. Jarlath's. The people had too much money and the children
were spoiled. Nor did she like Hugh, who as the pastor's representative could
overrule her decisions, a prerogative he rarely exercised but one that rankled
nonetheless.

"I'm leaving in five minutes for a short retreat." Hugh glanced at his watch
as he walked in the back door of the convent. "What's the problem?"

He stood in the corridor between the kitchen and the parlors, underneath ugly
portraits of St. Pius X and St. Maria Goretti, making it clear that he had not come
for a long talk.

"More trouble with your dear children from this wonderful parish of affluent
Catholics. Serious trouble."

"What kind?"

"Sex." She said the forbidden word with unconcealed relish.

Hugh was not impressed. "What kind of sex?"

"Eighth-grade sex. There was a party at the Mintons' house last night. The
Fowler child was apparently the leader. Mrs. Kennedy was on the phone to me
this morning, demanding that we take action against her and the Minton child."

"Did they have intercourse, Sister?"

Sister Mariana was shocked and offended. "I'm sure they did not. Nevertheless, they went quite far. The Fowler girl was practically naked, according to
Mrs. Kennedy."

Strip poker or some variant of it. Nothing changes. "Have you talked to anyone else?"

"All but the Fowlers. She is a very difficult child." Sister Mariana hesitated, realizing perhaps that she might be going too far.

"Sister, I'm leaving for Mundelein. I'll be back on Wednesday night. Till then you may want to discuss the matter with the pastor if he returns or with Father Kilbride. My position is that we are not in the business of policing the morals of the young people of the community when they are not on parish grounds. If Mrs. Kennedy has complaints against Linda Fowler, she should bring them to Mrs. Fowler and not to us. We cannot and will not expel children for what they do in private homes. I will have a chat with Linda and with her parents next week. Is that clear?"

"Yes, Father." The hatred in her eyes would have annihilated him if it could.

"Good, pray for me while I'm on retreat."

Fat chance.

Xav Martin, his hair turning silver and his dark eyes preoccupied by the tensions of transforming the seminary, listened patiently and sympathetically as Hugh poured out his story.

He remained silent when Hugh was finished.

"I guess I only see you when I'm in trouble." Hugh was flustered by the silence.

"No, that's all right." Xav crossed his legs and rubbed his jaw. "I'm here to help anytime you want me. . . . I can't help but wonder, Hugh"—he hesitated again—"why you have to do it all yourself. Can't God take care of a little bit of the work?"

"We're supposed to work as if everything depends on us," Hugh replied with a quote from seminary spirituality.

"Sure." Xav waved it away. "But you can't assume total responsibility for the people of St. Jarlath's. The woman is not the problem, as I'm sure you know. The problem is that you are too stubborn or too idealistic to give up a lost cause. Get out of St. Jarlath's before it destroys you."

"And Gus?"

"The new boss will retire him in a few months anyway."

"Somehow that doesn't seem . . ."

"Manly?" Xav's dark eyes flashed.

"Maybe I should make an appointment with Sean Cronin."

"Damn right you should."

Later he thought about it in the quiet of the ugly retreat house chapel.

In the last years at the seminary and the time since ordination he had kept his passions under rigid control, practicing the asceticism of denial he had been taught in the seminary. He had come to believe that sex was no longer a problem in his life. It was as if he'd built a great earthen dam to hold the torrents of sexual desire back. Then the touch of Helen's lips had excited a slight tremor; a tiny earthquake had sent a jagged crack across the face of the dam. Before he realized what had happened, the massive wall collapsed and, unwilling but powerless, he was swept along by the flood. Now the dam must be rebuilt from the ground up.

At St. Jarlath's that would be impossible.

He needed a parish with not quite so much work, more time to read and pray, and a long distance from Lakeridge and the Fowlers.

Dear God, he prayed wearily, thank You for helping me to see what I must do to continue to serve You as a priest. Forgive my pride. Help me to learn humility from the wonderful examples of that virtue You have given me in my parents. I want to be a priest. Help me to persevere. Give me the strength to see that my refusal to admit defeat is weakness rather than strength. It is weakness of the spirit that has kept me at St. Jarlath's and made me prone to the weakness of the flesh.

It all seemed very neat.

The night Hugh returned to Chicago, Ben Fowler called him. "Could the wife and I come to see you tomorrow night? About this business with Linda?"

The man's voice sounded tired and discouraged. What were the costs of being a commodity millionaire? For the first time, Hugh had a hint that they could be very high.

"How about the day after? I'm tied up tomorrow." Sister Elizabeth had insisted he come to a lecture by a young Swiss theologian. "Okay, I'll be free at nine thirty." He searched his appointment book . . . six other appointments.

"How bad is it, Padre?"

"I don't think this incident itself was too bad, Ben. It's a warning signal, however, that Linda will need more supervision."

"I suppose you're right. Attractive women need supervision, don't they?"

The next morning Hugh drafted a one-paragraph note to Monsignor Cronin requesting an interview on the subject of a change of assignment. He signed the letter, put it in a St. Jarlath's envelope, and sealed the flap.

Now, when to mail it? Before or after the letter from the parishioners?

Wait till after their letter. Let them have the first shot. His interview might give the chancery an opportunity to ask what he thought about the situation.

Am I procrastinating? Nonsense, the letter is here on my desk, signed and sealed. I've made up my mind to mail it a week from Monday.

Chapter Sixteen
1965

HUGH DELIBERATED OVER whether to wear sports clothes or priestly garb for his dinner with Liz. The latter was safer and more appropriate. On the other hand, a Roman collar would be out of place at a lecture by the famous liberal Swiss theologian Hans Küng.

He was glad he'd chosen sports clothes when Liz embraced him and kissed him with rather more fervor than he thought advisable. And he was glad he'd chosen the rendezvous he had as he directed her toward their table in the Hungarian restaurant on Wabash Avenue, a more discreet place for this supper than one of his father's clubs. A priest kissed in the Chicago Club could cause the scandal of the century.

"Tell me everything about St. Jarlath's," she pleaded when they were seated.

She was dressed in skirt, blouse, and sweater, no veil—no sign, in fact, that she was a religious woman. Her face was slightly flushed with pleasure. A night out and intellectual stimulation too. Her bright-eyed zest made Hugh feel middle-aged.

"I'll begin with the scandal first." He told her about the eighth graders.

"Do you find her attractive, the mother, I mean? I suppose most men would." Her hand paused as she was buttering her fresh French bread.

"The goulash here is great, don't miss it . . . you mean Helen? She's certainly not unattractive. I'm not sure that she's very intelligent. . . ."

"She's socially useless." Liz dismissed Helen with a wave of her knife. "What does she do with her time? One child and help at home. She's a parasite, a whore; that's why the poor daughter is confused."

There was a nasty edge to Sister Liz tonight.

"I'd kind of feel sorry for her if that were true. . . . There's other news too. A letter is probably going to the cardinal this week about the pastor. The people, or some of them, are finally determined to have a change."

"Do you think it will work?"

"Not the first time, perhaps. The Church never acts against corruption or madness early enough. But it rarely waits till the bitter end either. The chancery will do something about St. Jarlath's at just the right time to offend the maximum number of people."

She laughed gaily and dug into the goulash. "Oh . . . this is good . . . you're a terrible cynic, Hugh."

"Now tell me about graduate school."

It was all that she had hoped for and more, she said—challenging teachers, stimulating fellow students, time to read books and write papers, an opportunity for personal development and self-fulfillment.

"What are you going to write your dissertation on?"

"I'm devoting my time to learning and developing myself, instead of doing that academic Mickey Mouse stuff."

"I thought that disssertations were good training in self-discipline and skill."

She abruptly dismissed the thought. "Self-fulfillment is what matters these days, not self-discipline, Hugh; you know that." She sounded faintly disappointed in him. "Anyone can learn skills. . . . Now you tell me about yourself."

"Not much there. Well, that's not altogether true. I have a letter here in my wallet." He patted his jacket. "To the chancery, asking for a transfer from St. Jarlath's. I decided down at the Trappists' last week that I had to get out if I was going to survive. My emotions are mixed . . . guilt and relief."

A spasm of pain on her pretty face and a quick hand on his. "I know how hard that must be for you, Hugh. But it's right; I'm sure it's right. It will purify and spiritualize you."

"It will take a lot more than that to purify me," he laughed, liking and not liking her concern.

Sister Elizabeth paid little attention to Hans Küng's talk. She applauded for the charismatic young Swiss when everyone else did, and laughed and cheered when it seemed appropriate. Tonight would be considered an important and electrifying night, she was sure. It would be useful to be able to claim in the years ahead that one had been present at such a crucial historical event. But Hugh Donlon was more important to her than Hans Küng. Like most men, Hugh was insensitive and unperceptive. She supposed that it would take a long time to change that. His family was certainly a bad influence. He was also incorrigibly straight. He would not even kiss her good night at the end of the evening.

His theology was terribly old-fashioned. He thought that parishes like St. Jarlath's were important. He didn't realize that the local parishes would soon wither away in the New Church.

She sighed and joined the standing ovation for Küng in the great barn of McCormack Place.

Honesty in the Church had been Küng's subject. Hugh Donlon needed to hear a lot of honesty, she thought. He needed to be told that he was not the knight in shining armor he thought he was. He needed to come into contact with his real self, his basic humanity, as she had done in graduate school.

He needed her help more than ever.

She introduced him to her friends from the Christ Commune as they left the hall. Hugh was ill-at-ease; he didn't want to be introduced to anyone on what seemed like a "date" with a nun.

Still, she was proud of him. He would straighten out in time.

And she would take care of him.

Helen Fowler was terrified. She'd never seen Ben so mad. He was silent for several days about Linda's escapade and then erupted without warning at the supper table. It was her fault more than Linda's. She had only one child and all the money she needed. Couldn't she do anything right?

Helen was tongue-tied. "I try, Ben . . ." she stammered.

"Well, you don't try enough, you little nitwit."

Helen didn't try to defend herself. She was afraid that he would hit her.

"And you, you little tart, if you ever do anything like that again, I'll kill you, do you hear me, I'll kill you!"

Linda was terrified too. "I won't, Daddy. I won't do it again. I swear."

He slapped the girl twice across the face and she burst into hysterical sobs. "Mommy makes love with Father Donlon and you don't hit her."

Ben hit Helen's face with a closed fist, sending her sprawling against one of the lacquered Chinese cabinets in their parlor.

"Whore!" he snarled.

"I didn't do anything wrong," she implored as she tried to control her sobs.

"Yeah? Well, let that be a warning to you not to."

"Nothing wrong at all," she pleaded.

"We'll see." His anger was spent and he half-believed her.

It was easy for Hans Küng to talk about honesty. He did not have to face Ben and Helen Fowler with the guilty knowledge that he had been too familiar with Helen. The conversation would be an exercise in dishonesty from the opening shot.

Hugh's efforts with Linda that afternoon had failed completely. The girl, tall for her age and on the way to being even more elegantly blond than her mother, opted for sulkiness rather than intelligence. The scandal over the Kennedy party was a bore to her. What was all the fuss about? Joannie Kennedy should have kept her big mouth shut. They hadn't done anything really wrong. Other people did worse things.

She seemed to Hugh to be amused by him. Was she really spying on them?

Then, at the door of the rectory office, she turned to him, suddenly a frightened little girl again. "Was it a terrible sin, Father Donlon?" she asked uncertainly. "Will I go to hell for it?"

"No, Linda." He tried to smile gently. "God loves you too much for that to happen. We grown-ups worry about how young people can hurt themselves terribly without realizing what they're doing."

"Yes Father," she said docilely, as though she understood, which of course she did not.

After Linda left the rectory, Hugh was depressed. The girl had inherited her mother's beauty and her father's shrewdness. That ought to be enough to assure survival. Sadly, she had also acquired intelligence from some recessive gene, a gift that would probably push her into tragedy.

She would not only suffer, as beautiful and inexperienced young women unequipped with values must do. She would know she was suffering. And there was nothing he could do to help her.

His heart filled with love for her, the same kind of burning priestly love he had felt for the boy who'd called his mother shit. If only he could protect them all from the tragedies of life.

He sighed as he trudged up the terrazzo stairs to his room. Priestly love, like all love, was powerless to shield children from the pains of experience. Still, a priest ought to be able to do something to help a child like Linda.

"As to the facts," he told her parents that evening, "it would appear that a number of the girls, including Linda, engaged in some necking and petting and may have taken off their blouses. No more and no less. They are not the first young women their age to engage in such activities out of boredom or curiosity or the need for affection."

"Geez, Padre." Ben's cigar dangled from his fingers. "I don't know what to think. Helen here says that the kid knows the score. I can't believe she's had enough instruction. . . ."

Hugh's hands, wet with perspiration, were shaking. There had been a two-word phone conversation with Helen before they came: "He knows."

He must keep Ben on the defensive. "A girl is much more likely to listen to what her father says about men than what her mother says, especially at her age."

"Me?" Ben was astonished. "Hey, Padre, when I come home from the Board of Trade I'm really beat. You ever been there? You know what it's like? I can't handle that sort of thing. That's the wife's job."

It wouldn't do any good, but Hugh was going to try. "Two things matter for a girl like Linda—what her father says to her and the relationship between her father and her mother. If her father is close and interested and if her parents' sexual relationship is warm and not exploitive, she learns far more than she would from all the explicit sex instruction we could possibly give her."

"Great, Padre, sure appreciate the help." Ben was on his feet, eager to escape from a situation he couldn't control.

"Hey, are you going to be at the meeting at Downs's house tomorrow night?"

"I suppose so."

"Great."

"Well, honey''—Ben stood back to let Helen out the door of the rectory—
"we have to take the padre seriously. Gotta enjoy one another more, huh?"

He swatted her buttocks with his vast paw. He was deliberately hurting her in
Hugh's presence and threatening to hurt her even more.

Helen turned crimson, not in anger so much as in shame.

In another era, Hugh thought as he went to his room, I would have killed him
on the spot.

Ben said nothing to Helen on the way home. She knew he was furious. He
must have sensed the chemistry between her and Hugh. She resigned herself to
a savage beating. Maybe she even deserved it.

As soon as they were inside the house, he dragged her to their bedroom and
beat her mercilessly. His rage was cool and controlled. He didn't strike her face,
but he inflicted injuries that would hurt for many days. She wept but she didn't
scream.

When he was finished, he threw her on the bed. "The next time I'll mess up
your face and cut off your tits," he said. He was breathing heavily, choking on
his rage, and on the phlegm from those terrible cigars.

Later he returned, beat her again, and then made brutal love to her.

"I'll fix that son of a bitch Donlon," he said when he was finished.

The final meeting of the protest committee, Hugh learned on Friday morning
from Al Downs, had been stormy. Some people had lost their nerve. Two
couples walked out, insisting they couldn't protest against a poor old man in bad
health. Three others demanded a stronger letter, including a charge of faking bad
health.

"I turned into a moderate, would you believe?" Al's laugh on the phone
reminded Hugh of the sound of hyenas in western movies. "We finally decided
to go with the original letter. It'll be in the mail Monday."

Hugh was alarmed. "If those couples who walked out should to go Sullivan,
you're finished."

"They won't. Ben Fowler put the fear of God in them. We're okay; you
know, Father, it's a hell of a way to run a church."

"We're a long way from Galilee, Al. I suppose there's no way to avoid such
situations as long as the Church is made up of human beings. We spend a lot of
our time fighting one another."

"I'd hell of a lot sooner defend a murder rap than draft another letter to a
cardinal, I can tell you that."

"Well, it's over now, Al, for better or for worse."

"It can't get any worse here, can it, Father?"

"I suppose not," Hugh replied.

He was wrong, it could get a lot worse.

As he was finishing the ten o'clock Mass on Sunday morning, Monsignor
Sullivan, in full purple regalia, rochet, mozzetta, the whole works, appeared in
the sanctuary like the Avenging Angel of the Apocalypse.

He knows, Hugh thought, feeling a big hole in the pit of his stomach.

"See that young priest," the monsignor thundered. "Get a good look at him because you'll never see him on the altar of this church again. He is a Judas priest, a traitor to your pastor and your parish, which have provided him a home for the last four years. . . ."

Three years off, Hugh thought, calmly drying the chalice.

"He and a tiny group of malcontents have organized a conspiracy to replace me, your beloved pastor who has served you generously and unselfishly for more than a quarter-century. Listen to the letter they're going to send to the cardinal tomorrow."

He had the letter, the whole thing. He read it with great gusto and parenthetical remarks of his own. "Promise to continue to cooperate, do they? Well, we don't need their cooperation, any more than we need this Judas priest, do we, my beloved people? We will get rid of them all, just like I'm going to get rid of this young punk. . . ."

Hugh finished Mass and calmly walked into the sacristy. As he was taking off his vestments, he heard Sullivan's final shot. "Mr. Guinan has the copy of a petition that has been assembled by a group of loyal parishioners in defense of their beloved and saintly pastor. Anyone who wants to sign it may. No obligation, or course. I'll be there in back of church to welcome your cooperation. Let's all band together against the Judases in our midst."

Hugh waited in the cool antiseptic sacristy with its pale stained-glass windows casting the kind of light you would expect in a hospital chapel.

"I took you into this parish and shared my people with you," the pastor rampaged as he entered. "You're a nothing. You have no rights other than those I give you. And you presume to challenge me with my own people. You are an ungrateful cad, Father Donlon; my people love me and will stand by me. They will drive you out of this parish and destroy your reputation, wherever you are assigned. You ought to leave the priesthood now, because I promise you that you will never have another happy day in it.

"How dare you presume to criticize and connive against a man who is God's appointed representative over you? Answer me, young man. Don't stand there with that self-satisfied smile on your face. . . ."

"I'm not smiling," Hugh said, choking back his rage. Gus Sullivan was indeed God's duly appointed representative. Did God appoint sociopaths to rule over parishes?

Hugh strode out of the sacristy and went to his room; he collected a few clothes, put them in a bag, tore up his letter to the chancery, got into his car, and drove home to Mason Avenue. His departure from St. Jarlath's would require some explaining to his parents.

On second thought, he would not need to offer any explanation. They would be overjoyed that he was out of the place.

Tuesday Sean Cronin called from the chancery. "I thought you'd be at home, Hugh. The boss would like to see you."

"I imagine so. When?"

Late that afternoon, Hugh was sitting in Cronin's office in the old-fashioned gray chancery building, with its high ceilings, dismal maroon carpets, and grotesque paintings of white-clad popes and red-clad hierarchs.

The vice-chancellor was nervous. He fidgeted with a paperweight model of St. Peter's in Rome.

"Bad operation, Hugh. You never should have organized anything like that with such loose security. Now Sullivan has you on the defensive."

"I didn't organize it. They asked me how to write to the cardinal and I told them. I believe what we were taught at the seminary about loyalty and obedience."

Cronin rubbed his hand through thick blond hair. "Really? I didn't think anyone bought that stuff anymore. You didn't organize it? Well, I'm glad to hear that. I knew you would be much better at plotting. Still, you should have had enough sense not to trust that Fowler fellow. I hear that a lot of the other people want to boil him in oil."

"He'll keep."

Someday I'll smash that insect.

Then they were called into the cardinal's office. Hugh felt the touch of unease that high authority causes in priests. It was replaced with fury at the little sandy-haired man with the mild face and the thick glasses.

"I'll begin, Your Eminence, if you don't mind. . . ."

A quick little smile and a diffident hand gesture.

"I know that in the Church those who have authority can do no wrong and those who don't have it can do no right. So I'm fully prepared to be the scapegoat. Transfer me as you intend and retain Monsignor Sullivan as you intend. But spare me the hypocrisy. You know that the charges in the letter are mild compared to what you have in your files, and have had for years. You know that the man should have been removed long ago. Don't lecture me on the importance of loyalty or authority or respect for a sick old man."

The cardinal toyed with a ballpoint pen. "I quite agree, Father, that he should have been replaced long ago. In a month or two we will announce a retirement policy that will appeal to him, whether he wants it or not. I have been here briefly, as you know, and there are so many things. . . ." He dismissed his own problems with a minute movement of the pen. "I do not think of you as the disgraced curate and Monsignor as the betrayed pastor. . . ."

"He's still the winner and I'm the loser."

"Some will see it that way, Father. It is an unjust assessment. However, the world is unjust. Nevertheless, you are a man of great promise and abilities, Father Donlon. I would like to arrange an assignment for you that would do you honor, both because I do not want unjust judgments made about your new assignment and because I need your talents. . . ."

He paused, as though waiting for an answer.

"I need advisers with scholarly credentials, particularly in the areas that are important to the Church. I wonder if you would consider going to the university to obtain a degree in demography . . . the population issues the Church faces require expertise in this."

"I'll do it if I'm ordered to. Only if I'm ordered to."

The cardinal removed his glasses and began to polish them. "Perhaps when you're less angry."

"No!"

The cardinal sighed. "Very well. I hoped we could settle this more genially. You're . . . you have reason to be very angry, I suppose. . . . Monsignor Cronin, would you be good enough to make the arrangements?"

"I accept the order, Your Eminence." Hugh stood at the door. "I have no choice. Nevertheless, I consider the entire affair to be a violation of justice. I promise you that I will not forget it.''

"We shall have no peace in the world, Father''—the cardinal readjusted his glasses—"as long as we refuse to forget violations of justice.''

"I'm not looking for peace,'' Hugh said, then turned on his heel and walked out of the cardinal's office.

BOOK THREE

"This day thou shall be with me in paradise."

Chapter Seventeen
1968

"IS THE BOSS around?" Professor Duncan Leo, a spare, trim young man with a blond mustache and transparent blue eyes peered into Hugh's cubbyhole in the Center for Research in Uniform Demography (CRUD). As the only man who had obtained tenure when Professor Talcott Kingsley Homans was out of the country, he was distinctly unwelcome at CRUD. Homans did not like to be reminded how his own summer promotion had been slipped by the Demography Department two decades earlier.

"Gone to Indonesia this morning and left me a batch of papers to correct." Hugh looked up from his calculator.

"So what else is new?" Duncan sat on the edge of the hard wooden chair that was the only concession to luxury in the cubbyhole CRUD had provided for Hugh. "Good news from Michigan; they've seen your dissertation draft and your article on village structure and agricultural productivity. They will offer you an appointment for next fall, tenure track, assistant professor at seventeen five, which is almost what I make, no requirement that the dissertation be accepted. They know that Talcott will make you sweat it out if he possibly can."

"It's certainly an attractive offer." Hugh hesitated. "I'll have to consider it; I feel I owe the Church in Chicago—"

"—nothing. You paid your dues by grinding out problems on that machine for TKH and correcting his papers. Seriously, won't they let you go?"

"The cardinal said it was up to me."

"So, that settles it. Michigan is in no hurry. Let me know after Christmas and we'll initiate the process for a formal offer."

Duncan Leo bounced enthusiastically out of the cubbyhole.

Hugh pushed a stack of introductory demography exams under a pile of green-edged computer printouts. He was a good demographer, no doubt, with a nice fat offer from Michigan. They'd wanted him as a quarterback seventeen years ago and now they wanted him as something more important.

A first-rate demographer—and still a priest. Did it make any sense? Was he really a priest? Everyone thought he was—his family, Liz, the cardinal, the priests at St. Medard's, where he lived, the students and faculty in the department. The only one who had any doubts was he.

And he had shared those doubts with no one. Not even Liz, who was now his closest friend.

He said Mass every morning at St. Medard's, preached at two Masses on Sunday, wore clerical garb except when he was physically on the university campus (and black slacks there), went to the annual reunions of his seminary class, even played an occasional game of golf on Thursdays in the summer with Pat Cleary and Jack Howard. He would have spent his summer vacations with them too, if there had been time for summer vacations.

He was not a radical 1960s priest. He did not march on picket lines, did not sign petitions. And he'd stayed in his cubbyhole through the long summer week when Liz and the other members of the Christ Commune had confronted the Chicago police in front of the Conrad Hilton Hotel during the Democratic convention.

Liz was unhappy with his conservatism. His consciousness, he replied, laughing at her attractive anger, was unraisable.

Despite the closeness of his relationship with her, Hugh had kept some distance from the Christ Commune and its assorted group of priests, ex-priests, nuns, and ex-nuns, some of whom were married, some of whom were living together, some of whom were dating—a confusing example of Church reform run amok, he thought. He was skeptical about couples engaged in "third way" relationships, the nongenital love affairs between priests and nuns that, they said, were neither "strictly celibate nor strictly noncelibate."

What the hell did that mean?

Yet he was careful not to ridicule the Commune itself, because Liz was part of it. Indeed, the only reason for hanging around there was to keep an eye on her.

Liz was having a hard time finding herself these days, especially since her return to the university after a two-year stint of high school teaching in Montana. They were very close now, the relationship more secure than ever because he kept his fantasies and desires under strict control. She was still sweetness and laughter, a lovely fund of joy and excitement, some of the time.

Yet there was an anger in her too, which he had barely noticed at St. Jarlath's, and a snappish impulse to intellectual arrogance. Both tendencies seemed to be especially strong when she was with the communards. Hugh was caught between an obligation to protect her and an obligation to respect her freedom. Hence he tolerated the Commune and waited for the return of her contagious smile as soon as they left the apartment building that the Commune occupied.

Supper there the other night had been typical.

Theo, a fat, balding priest from the Albertin Fathers (of whom Hugh had never heard), was lecturing on celibacy to the group as they ate.

"We historians are realists; we know that celibacy was imposed against the will of the clergy to prevent ecclesiastical property from passing into the hands of the children of priests. . . ."

"Was that a serious problem?" Hugh asked innocently.

"Of course, it was," Theo said, frowning in exasperation.

"Well, then, maybe it was a good solution."

"The point is that it is not a problem today."

"Might become one." Phony intellectuals like Theo were a pushover. He'd never finish a dissertation, never be a scholar.

"Anyway," Theo went on, "the spiritual arguments in favor of celibacy can easily be refuted by Marxist analysis. We are able to see correctly today that it is merely a technique for keeping the lower clergy in a subservient role. . . ."

"Jesus and St. Paul refuted by Marxist analysis?" Hugh asked in feigned dismay.

"Hugh, please," Liz said irritably.

Hugh remained loyally silent for the rest of the meal and even joined the long grace led thereafter by Jackie, a nun or an ex-nun, he couldn't remember which. She said the words of the Consecration of the Mass over the bread as part of her grace and distributed it to the rest of them, as though it were Holy Communion.

She also prayed for the destruction of the American imperialist aggressors in Vietnam.

Hugh consumed the make-believe Communion without a twinge of guilt. He did not pray for the destruction of the Americans in Vietnam, however. He would not pray for Steven McLain's destruction.

The archdiocese viewed Hugh as a voice of reason among a multitude of well-meaning crazies.

It was an image Hugh enjoyed.

Even his relationship with Liz was discreet. It was not a "third way" liaison by any means. Hugh's only mistake was to bring her for supper one Sunday to North Mason Avenue.

From the outset, Liz was defensive and insecure. The long periods of silence at the table embarrassed her, for, although Peggy appeared to be determined to be sweet with her, Liz sensed that Peggy was hostile underneath.

When Peggy responded to Liz's question about "what she did" with a brief description of her teacher's aid work at St. Ursula, on the other hand, Liz merely nodded in polite accompaniment. Hugh knew that she thought such volunteer work was "part of the problem."

Hugh rushed in. "She's a painter too."

"Oh, Hugh. They're just pretty watercolors, not *relevant* at all." Peggy said it with more irony than Hugh had imagined her capable of.

"I'd love to see them." Liz was as determined to be polite as Peggy was. She daintily cut her Yorkshire pudding.

So after dinner everyone went on a tour of Peggy's studio in the converted sleeping porch overlooking the backyard. Peggy was in what her husband called a "Monet mood" and the porch looked like a pastel children's nursery.

"How very interesting," Liz said guardedly.

Over coffee in the parlor, Peggy struck back. "And you're doing your dissertation in educational administration, my dear?"

"Theoretically," Liz said.

"I don't understand what you mean," Peggy pressed, sensing her defensiveness.

"Actually, I'm engaged in discovering myself."

"How very interesting. . . ."

All in all, Peggy won the match—the more experienced of the female cougars squabbling over the meat.

Bad chemistry between them, Hugh thought as he and Liz escaped the house on North Mason Avenue with enormous relief.

"The married parish priest has been more typical and more common in the history of Christianity than the celibate priest," Theo said at another supper.

"Besides," Jackie interrupted, "celibacy was originally based on the belief that sex was evil. If it is grounded on a false premise, then it has to be false, doesn't it? And those of us who are witnessing against celibacy by our life-style are bearing witness to the truth, as Jesus taught we should."

"Absolutely," Theo agreed.

Hugh was on the brink of pointing out Sister's logical fallacy when he heeded a warning look from Liz. Freedom of discussion was not one of the guiding principles of the Christ Commune. You could express any thought you wanted, so long as it was "correct." Alas, poor Hugh was almost always "incorrect."

What if there were to be a change in the vow of celibacy? he thought during a reverie in his cubicle. Had he been wrong all along? Had he sacrificed marriage for a historical mistake? If there was a change in the next ten years—and everyone in the Christ Commune was confident there would be—would it be too late for him?

To the world, Hugh was the sensible, loyal priest who kept his head in the midst of chaos, so sensible that he was able to resist the fads and fashions of the moment. He didn't even sign a petition to the Pope demanding reconsideration of the birth-control decision, although Liz refused to talk to him for a week.

He was much less obsessed by the Church than were the Christ Commune members. Although the disgrace and defeat at St. Jarlath's still rankled, he had learned that injustice and stupidity were as prevalent in the secular world as they were in the Church.

Liz and her Christ Commune colleagues were angry at the Church because it didn't live up to their faith. Hugh's problem was that he wasn't sure any religious faith was valid or necessary.

He spent most of his waking hours with men and women who didn't believe. Yet they were good and generous human beings. Unlike Professor Homans and some of the other exploiters of graduate students, they helped him in his work, were sympathetic to his early confusion, quietly supported him in his battles with Homans. Their questions about his religion were more curious than offensive.

How could such moral and intelligent men and women live without religion? Could a faith possibly be true that responded to none of their needs?

Having been raised in an environment in which faith was taken for granted, Hugh could not comprehend an environment in which nonbelieving was equally assumed. If he was right, then all these people were mistaken. But if they were right?

"You're a Catholic because you were raised a Catholic," Duncan Leo had said to him once, not as an objection but as a statement of fact. "I was raised a Unitarian. If I'd been raised a Catholic, I'd be like you."

The religion Hugh had inherited was as unconsidered as the language he used. He'd never examined his faith because it had never seemed to require examination.

Sometime he would have to resolve the God question, just as he would have to take a vacation, catch up on his theological and spiritual reading, and devote more time to prayer. But for the moment he had to concentrate on revising his dissertation and deciding whether to take the appointment at Michigan or to work for the cardinal.

"Is the world's best demographer still slaving away?"

It was Liz at the door, slim and lovely in a cloth coat, red scarf, and matching mittens; Liz, about whom he had erotic fantasies at night and whom he chastely admired when he was with her.

"The best has gone to Indonesia." He stood up and kissed her lightly on the cheek. "The second best has papers to correct."

"I thought you might walk home with me," she said, pretending to pout.

"I promised Jack and Pat I'd go to the *Messiah* with them tonight."

"The concert is Sunday." For Liz, the whole world was the university.

"At the University Chapel. We're going to Orchestra Hall for the Apollo Music Club."

She was lovely even when she pouted. How had he survived the last two years without her? Third way or not, it felt good to be important to a woman, especially one as gravely beautiful as Liz.

"So I'll take you on Sunday. No harm in hearing it twice."

"I'm not sure I'll be back by then. Mother wants to see me on Saturday. I'll have to drive all the way to Wisconsin." The pretended pout turned to a worried frown.

"Anything wrong?" Anxiety clutched at his throat too. "They promised you could finish your graduate work this time."

"Mother was very friendly and said she had good news to report." Her lip began to tremble. "Only I'm not sure we have the same definition of good news."

"I'll have lunch with you tomorrow." Hugh tried to reassure her. "I won't let her change her mind."

She rushed to him in gratitude. "Oh, Hugh. What a saint you are." She touched his cheek, then ardently embraced him.

He drew back, then drew her closer, impelled, despite himself, by a fundamental need to help.

Liz went limp in his arms, then pressed hard against him. Need, hunger, fear, combined into a desperate longing.

Their kisses were intimate, skillful, tender. They communicated their passion in the precise amounts needed by the other. Liz suddenly stiffened.

"What's wrong?"

A fantasy of the kind he didn't acknowledge raced through his fevered brain.

She relaxed and slipped away. "Worried about the trip to the motherhouse? Don't." She kissed him on the mouth. "See you tomorrow at noon."

Jack Howard and Pat Cleary were waiting for him in Orchestra Hall. As usual, Jack had obtained center-aisle seats.

"You look like hell, Hugh," he said. "Are you getting away at Christmas?"

"I don't think so. I've got to see Himself, a decision about next year."

Hugh told them about the Michigan job. They offered perfunctory congratulations.

"I can tell from your overjoyed expressions that you're dying for me to take it."

"There's room for you here in the archdiocese," Jack said mildly.

"At St. Jarlath's with Monsignor Sullivan?" Hugh was unable to hide his bitterness.

"That's not fair, Hugh," Jack remonstrated. "Gus is in retirement and so are all the other brats. Eammon's running a fine archdiocese. There's plenty of room for talented people here now."

The music began and hundreds of voices filled the red and ivory hall with joyous cadences celebrating the victory of the King of Kings over the forces of darkness.

It isn't that easy, Hugh thought. Too hard these days to tell what's light and what's darkness.

At intermission Hugh and Pat went to the lobby while Jack crossed the auditorium to speak to friends.

Still transported by the music, they watched the snowflakes falling lazily in the beams of the headlights on Michigan Avenue. Hugh felt a light kiss on his cheek.

"If it wasn't for that second glass of wine at dinner, I'd never have dared. Hugh, you know the commander. He's a full three-stripe commander now."

"Maria . . ."

"Don't look so astonished. I'm a big girl now. Home for the holidays"—she looked at her husband—"and maybe a little longer. . . . You look older, Hugh, but still as handsome as ever."

She turned to Pat. "I'm Maria McLain, Father. My old swain is too appalled by the deterioration of my appearance to observe the social amenities. This is my husband, Steven."

The commander shook hands with both of them, clearly delighted by his wife's social ease. "We've been at Glenview for a year and now I'm going back overseas," he said.

"You've been at Glenview, darling," Maria corrected. "I've been raising two hellions and getting an accounting degree." She turned to Hugh. "Is it celibacy or demography that's wearing you out? Don't answer me," she said without missing a beat. "How's the family?"

"They're fine," Hugh said shyly.

"How many kids?"

"Marge has two—two little daughters—and Tim has three. Mom and Dad are getting older but they seem to be all right."

Maria's face turned almost melancholy, transiently close to tears. "It's good to see you again, Hugh." The tears disappeared. "You see, there really is a Father Hugh Donlon. I tell my kids I knew this man who became a priest and they don't believe me. The young one says he wants to be a priest. Fortunately he hasn't reached the age of reason yet. . . ."

And so it went. A few bits of news exchanged, a few vain promises made to stay in touch, a lot of old memories inflamed and quickly extinguished, a couple of difficult, searing, bittersweet, wonderful moments. Another firm handshake and auld lang syne kiss. And she and her husband were lost in the crowd.

"My God," breathed Pat Cleary. "Who was that?"

"That was Maria, someone out of my past. . . ."

Maria of his dreams, countess, comic, clear-eyed waif, and now woman banker, alive and bigger than life, bigger even than his dreams. At the height of her physical attractiveness, somewhat more smoothly rounded and infinitely more sensual.

Oh, my lovely Maria, why did I ever lose you?

It was a foolish, romantic question, yet not even the soaring sopranos of George F. Handel could drive it out of his mind.

Maria's face was still warm and her heart was pounding when she and Steven returned to their seats. Hugh Donlon could still turn her into melting butter. She held her husband's hand. No point in trying to fool old Commander Steven.

He smiled at her and winked.

Chapter Eighteen
1968

ON SATURDAY AFTERNOON Hugh was scheduled to say Mass at the Christ Commune. A wan and red-eyed Liz kissed him quickly on the cheek when he came in. "Let's walk after dinner. It was terrible, simply terrible."

Her anguish distracted him from the holiday festivities at Mass. The reader wore a Santa Claus costume and the director of song a south-sea sarong, for which she lacked the figure. The bread of the Eucharist was brandied plum pudding and the wine was steaming wassail. Both were carried to the altar by priests wearing white placards around their necks, one reading, "Joseph, killed by American bombs," the other, "Mary, burned by American napalm." They offered prayers asking God to rain destruction on the Dow Chemical Company and urging the American people to overthrow Richard Nixon.

Hugh preached a sermon about the silent peace of the heart, the secret of the love in the cave at Bethlehem. "Only those who are at peace in their hearts," he told the Commune, "can bring peace to other hearts."

They'll climb all over me at dinner, he thought.

During the offertory there was a modern dance by women in leotards and men in swimming trunks. Hugh couldn't figure it out, save that it was about sex and Christmas.

Dinner was a vegetarian meal, in deference to the poor of the world. Bread and wine, banished from the altar, were served at the dinner table, along with fruit, a hot vegetable compote, and salad, the lettuce for which, having come from union fields, was not subject to the current boycott.

Jackie recited a long grace, reminding all present that Christianity embodied not peace but the sword.

Hugh didn't argue. He wanted to finish the meal as quickly as possible so that he and Liz could escape.

Finally they did.

Liz was crying as soon as they reached the foot of the stairs in the apartment building. Hugh let her cry as they walked down the snow-covered sidewalk in the brisk starlit winter night.

Where's Bethlehem now?

The tears slowly turned into spasms of sniffles.

"Bad?" They both walked on silently, feet crunching the newly fallen snow.

"It's all over. Mother is calling me home to be president of the college. I can do the dissertation in my spare time. Even come back for summer school. She has assigned me for the next six years. And no guarantee of anything after that. Hates to do it. For the good of the Order. The good of the Church. That kind of shit."

"I'm sorry," Hugh stammered.

"I don't want to spend the rest of my life playing nursemaid to late-adolescent females and creepy old nuns."

Then she clung to him and sobbed.

When the second onset of tears was over, she still held on to him, as if her existence depended on his support.

Then she pulled herself together, wiped the tears from her eyes, and leaned against him. "It was all so ruthless. I was just a thing to be used. None of them—

the whole council was there with Mother—gave a damn about my wishes. I felt just exactly the way I did when those brutes dragged me from the altar at St. Jarlath's.''

"Miserable bitches," Hugh muttered into her long soft hair.

The Church destroys its own.

Tim Donlon spent Christmas Eve in a cocktail lounge on Rush Street, sipping gin and getting quietly drunk.

He was more alone than ever.

The marriage wasn't working. Estelle was an old-fashioned Catholic who didn't believe in birth control. So after three children in four years, she'd ordered him out of her bed. And he'd gone, more or less quietly.

He had worked at the marriage, more than he thought he would. He didn't love Estelle, but he enjoyed the kids and it seemed worthwhile to him to try to hold the family together.

There would be more battles and more reconciliations. Estelle didn't believe in divorce either.

Not that divorce would help him.

The doctor said that character disorders like his could be controlled. A lot the doctor knew.

God knows he'd tried. He'd played it straight at the Exchange for two years and made a fortune. Then he'd grown bored and taken a few chances. He'd lost most of the money and was suspended again. Estelle had to use her own money to buy the kids Christmas presents.

And she absolutely refused to visit the Donlon house on Christmas Day.

"Creepy," she said. "No booze and that fat mother of yours looks down her nose at me like a dowager Chinese empress. We'll go to our house"—meaning her parents' house in Oak Brook, a grotesque Gothic pile she'd designed—"and that's that. You can stop by that old dump but I absolutely forbid you to take the kids."

Peggy was not fat. Indeed, Estelle outweighed her by twenty pounds and was jealous of her good looks.

Tim signaled for another drink. The fun had all run out.

And there weren't any hookers around on Christmas Eve.

Liz called Hugh at St. Medard's during the supper hour on Christmas Eve, between afternoon and evening confessions. "I'll be at the Midnight Mass. Most of the Commune has left already. Then I'm going up to St. Jarlath's for Christmas. That's right, darling. Only for the day though." She hesitated. "Could you come over here for breakfast after the Mass, just for an hour or so? It will be the only chance we'll have to celebrate Christmas."

"Sure."

The St. Medard's liturgy was excellent, well-prepared congregational singing and well-directed choir. The festive midnight service moved along with spirit and pomp. The gold vestments, the smell of evergreens, the banks of red poinsettia, stirring carols echoing in the heavy stone Romanesque vault—all brought back to Hugh memories of Christmases at St. Ursula's.

His sermon was strong and moving. "Bethlehem is light in darkness, love in hate, life in death, good in evil. Just as darkness will never put out the light of

Bethlehem, so hate will never obliterate love, death will never destroy life, evil will never triumph over good.

"The light of Bethlehem has survived two thousand years of darkness. Nothing will ever put it out in the world. Only our own fears can extinguish it inside ourselves."

It was not enough, he said, to exult in the light of Bethlehem. We must make that light shine more brightly in the world. Bethlehem's was renewed by the light of patient and self-sacrificing love in all our lives. Therefore we must strive to love as fully every day as we do on Christmas Day. "Then the family of Bethlehem will be with us always."

After Mass there were more rituals, again evoking bittersweet memories of St. Ursula's—more carols, feet stamping on fresh snow, handshaking, and shouts of "Merry Christmas" in back of the church and then a weary, contented return to the rectory.

Hugh drank a Christmas toast with the pastor and shortly excused himself. "A breakfast with some priests from the university," he said.

His heart was beating rapidly as he climbed the steps to the Commune's apartment.

"A beautiful sermon, Hugh." Liz's smile shattered the cold and the darkness and her embrace suffused him with warmth and happiness.

He gave her a pair of jade earrings, which she unwrapped and put on with the delight of a high school girl.

"They're too good for me," she said, suddenly sad. She was especially beautiful that night, dressed in a light gray jersey dress, belted at the waist, that softly outlined her figure, her hair neatly done, face carefully made up, a sprig of holly at the open neck of the dress.

"You look lovely," he said, and he kissed her again, a slow, adoring kiss.

"There's nothing wrong with a feminist looking feminine if she does so to please herself," she said primly.

"It's all right, isn't it, if a man is pleased too?" He released her only slowly.

"I guess." She laughed and touched him on the chin. "So long as he doesn't think her femininity makes her inferior to him."

"God forbid."

Breakfast was elaborate, small steaks, homemade coffee cake, coffee brewed from freshly ground beans.

The vegetarian ideologues of the Christ Commune wouldn't approve at all, but Hugh decided not to mention them.

"Remember our first breakfast together?" she asked gaily as she filled his wineglass with a vintage red Rhône that the communards would not have appreciated either.

"Sure, the week before you were dragged from the altar."

"A lot of things have changed since then," she said softly, lighting her first cigarette of the day.

"Maybe for the better," he said. "Maybe if Michigan turns me down, you can hire me."

Her face fell. "I wish you hadn't said that, Hugh."

"Sorry; it was dumb."

She snubbed out her cigarette, knowing he didn't like her to smoke. "It's okay," she said at length. "I know you didn't mean to make fun of it."

The hours slipped past like minutes. Soon it was four in the morning.

Hugh realized he should be going, but didn't want to leave. Why couldn't it be the two of them, together for the rest of eternity?

He took her chin in his hand. "Very nice breakfast, ma'am."

Her eyes were troubled, her face grave. She was trying to control rough, painful emotions.

Hugh silently reassured himself that nothing was going to happen.

His hands caressed her face, her neck, her throat. They stopped, one hand on either side of her neck, her head drawn close, so he could inspect her face. He saw invitation and acceptance.

Why had he waited so long?

In her bedroom he kissed her and slowly opened the buttons of her dress. His hand slipped to the belt. He kissed her again. Her lips surrendered. She was his for whatever he wanted.

He eased the dress off her shoulders. She held it at her waist. He twisted it out of her hand and dropped it to the floor. Her underwear was delicate pearl-gray lace, matching her dress. Deftly, as if it were not the first time, he opened hooks, stretched elastic, peeled away her modest fingers, and removed the filmy garments.

His heart was pounding, his head giddy. He had not felt so free or so happy since his boyhood sailing on Lake Geneva. He would make her his own, become one with her the way he had once been one with the wind and the waves.

"Hugh, I love you," she breathed. "You're so kind and good."

He quickly pulled off his own clothes. For a moment they stood clinging to each other, two terrified, naked animals, in a ritual older than the race. They knew they would go ahead. But first they would summon all the resources of their love.

Hugh wished he could think of something to say to break the tension. There were no words. His hands began to probe more fiercely.

No, not that way. She required the same delicate, experienced touch as the sails and the tiller of the *Pegeen*.

But his hands were unsteady, his lips uncertain, his movements fumbling and inept. So much beauty, so many places to touch for the first time . . . and no skills at touching them. He didn't know how to love a woman, and had only a few moments to learn.

"I don't want to hurt you," he groaned.

"You won't hurt me," she said. Liz tried to reassure him, though she was as uncertain as he.

The fierce demands of his ardor were too much for him. There was no time left to be tender. He eased her back onto the bed, struggling with all his might not to be abrupt. She sighed and moved awkwardly in his embrace. "Love me Hugh," she pleaded.

Then he could endure no further delay. He parted her legs and, as gently as he could, invaded her, deflowered her, reveled in her flesh, and made her his mate.

Liz's maidenhood did not yield easily and her body did not explode in pleasure, as his did.

Still, she seemed blissfully happy in his arms. She kissed him repeatedly and assured him that it had been the happiest moment in her life, that it was the right, right thing for them, that at last they knew how much they loved.

Abruptly he looked at his watch. It was five o'clock. My God, he thought, I've got to get back.

"Again?" she asked, clinging to him, still naked as he left.

"Of course, again. Over the weekend."

He shouldn't leave her. But he had to. The priests at St. Medard's, the family later in the day. He had obligations. . . .

The *Pegeen* was floating in a soft, warm cloud high above the earth, its sails slack, its crew blissfully lolling in the stern. Maria was naked beside him, her face smeared with raspberry juice. He began to make love to her again.

She fought him. Their struggle tipped the boat to one side. It capsized and plunged out of the cloud and toward the earth, heading straight for the smoke- and fire-belching crater of a volcano.

Hugh struggled to regain control of the boat and still make love to his prisoner. Liz. No, Helen. No, Peggy.

No, it was Maria all along, laughing at him as she fought and changed appearances. He tried to explain about the volcano.

But it was too late.

He woke at eleven o'clock feeling both complacent and guilty.

Still half asleep, he remembered.

He had made love to a woman, he had successfully initiated a virgin. He was pleased and proud of his manhood. He would enjoy her again and again.

Then, as he emerged into full awareness, he felt enormous guilt. Mortal sin, sacrilege, violation of his priestly vows. He was a beast, an animal. "God in heaven, forgive me," he pleaded. "I'll never do it again."

Chapter Nineteen
1968–1969

THE BIG BUNGALOW at the corner of Lemoyne and Mason was beginning to show its age, along with the rest of the St. Ursula's neighboorhood. Many of the parishioners had migrated to River Forest as black families moved into the south end of the parish. The decline of the neighborhood and the deterioration of his family home depressed Hugh. But even with the burden of Liz on his mind, he could hardly wait to be inside.

The Wentworths were already there. They had flown over from Shannon to spend three weeks. Liam was almost as much in love with his in-laws as he was with his wife. The two little girls, Fionna and Graine, aged two and three, were quiet, mysterious little creatures with elfin smiles and lovely eyes, promising the beauty of their mother and grandmother with a dash of the fey added to their personalities.

Tim wasn't there. He and Estelle had begged off again on the grounds they would be so busy with her large family that they "simply could not make it." Hugh discreetly asked no questions. Every year Tim was more of a burden. His drinking, his strange humor, and his scrapes with the Business Practices Committee at the Board of Trade caused constant worry to his mother and father.

But there was nothing anyone could do about poor Tim.

The four adults agreed that Hugh looked fine and fit, better than he had in years.

"Good skin color. Can tell a healthy man by his skin. Time you took it easy. Ireland."

That could mean he should come to Ireland or that was the way they lived there. Judging from what he'd read about Lord Kerry's involvement in oil exploration, Hugh was not sure he took it easy himself.

"The little girls think he's a doll. He looks so relaxed and happy," Marge agreed.

Both girls climbed into his lap and remained there contentedly until Christmas dinner was served.

At dinner Marge talked about her favorite subject, the Church. "Are many priests going to bed with women, Hugh? I think it's disgusting. I like the changes in the Church, but if I have to keep my promises to Liam, I don't see why they don't have to keep their promises to God."

"These are rough and uneven times, Marge. People do odd things before they straighten themselves out. My pastor at St. Jarlath's never laid a hand on a woman. But I don't think he was a very good priest."

"It must be very lonely for some of them, isn't it, Hugh?" Peggy said, pouring herself another drink of the claret Liam had brought with him. It was, she admitted, "rather tasty," appropriate for a holiday.

"Life is lonely for everyone, Mom. I suppose that loneliness is one of the reasons, and curiosity, desire, a willing woman, uncertainty about faith. . ."

"I still think it's a disgrace," Marge insisted.

Disconcerted by Hugh's noncommittal response, they switched the conversation to his offer from Michigan.

"After all," Peggy observed serenely, "Ann Arbor is closer than Killarney."

"Not really, old girl," Lord Wentworth insisted. "Not really. Fly to O'Hare as quickly as you can drive from there. Surely, my dear. Have some more claret."

"Speaking of O'Hare"—Marge helped herself to a second serving of turkey stuffing—"did we tell you we saw Maria and Steve McLain at the airport? They were flying to Charleston to see his family before he goes back to Vietnam."

"Poor Maria," Peggy sympathized. "It's not fair that anyone should have to suffer that twice."

"He's going to command an air group," Judge Donlon said. "A dangerous job."

"I know she's worried sick, but she keeps her spirits up remarkably well." Marge shook her head in wonder. "Same old Maria. She pretended that Liam couldn't speak English and that I had to translate for him . . . said they saw you at the *Messiah* concert, Hugh."

"Same old Maria," he agreed cautiously.

"Hugh dated Maria for a while, Liam," Marge explained.

"Only for two weeks."

"Too long for that gel," Liam said, his eyes wide in appreciation. "One week or life."

They all laughed, even Hugh, whose stomach was knotted in pain, not from Christmas food, but from regret.

In her tiny room at St. Jarlath's convent, Liz tried to cry herself to sleep. The tears came and went but sleep did not follow them.

She was appalled by what they had done, ashamed, humiliated, and outraged. Hugh had deceived her, exploited her, practically raped her, in fact.

How dare he think he could use her in such a way? A receptacle to be enjoyed and thrown away. How dare he behave like such a bestial, such a gluttonous, middle-class pig?

She abruptly relented in a new outburst of tears. It wasn't true. He did care. And had tried to be gentle with her.

She recalled how beautiful he'd looked lying asleep in the bed beside her and how her rage had been transformed into sudden desire, how frightened she'd been, not for herself, but for him.

She loved him passionately, she had no doubt about that. But he had to be taught restraint so he would be able to love her appropriately in return.

Love, she must teach him, was not simply satisfying his sexual cravings.

Tom Donlon usually felt a letdown after festivities, and the more joyous the event, the greater the letdown. Despite Tim's absence, the Christmas dinner had been a great success. So now he was greatly depressed, lamenting the shortness of life, the fragility of its pleasures, the vanity of his hopes and ambitions.

He didn't regret for a moment his decision to decline LBJ's proffer of a Supreme Court seat, not even in light of the fact that Abe Fortas, who was appointed in his place, might be forced to resign, giving President-elect Nixon a chance to fill the vacancy with a Republican.

He belonged here on Mason Avenue, not in Washington.

Yet this Christmas night he viewed his life as a failure.

He wanted to sleep, to shake off the gloom. When would Peggy finish her "quick cleanup" and join him?

At length she came into the bedroom dressed in her dark green Christmas nightgown and carrying a half-empty bottle of claret and two wine goblets.

"I'm tired, Peg; I don't want anything more to drink."

"Nonsense," she said primly. "You've been wanting the chance to make love to a tipsy wife since we were married. Here, drink up." She filled a glass and extended it to him. "Liam says you shouldn't empty the bottle." She considered it thoughtfully. "But then my palate is still untrained. Liam says that too." She giggled.

"Our children seemed well today." He was a little afraid of this wanton stranger.

She kissed him slowly, affectionately, then lasciviously. "Let's not talk about the children. We do that too often."

One of the straps of her gown slipped off her shoulder. Tom Donlon felt like a young man again.

"I suppose that wine makes you see things more clearly. Does it, Tommy? Or am I only imagining I see more clearly? Anyway, what I see tonight is that if I had spent less time worrying about the children and more time loving you, we all would be much happier."

Again her lips brushed his.

God bless Liam Wentworth and his claret.

The cardinal found time to see Hugh the day after Christmas.

"You look well, Father. Have you had some time off?"

Hugh shook his head. "Actually, the worst of the work is almost over. I should have the degree by spring or summer at the latest."

"I'm delighted to hear it. And my colleague in Detroit? Will he have a chance to avail himself of your occasional services?"

"That's why I came, Cardinal. The University of Michigan is making me a fine offer, as you know. I thought I'd tell you that while I must certainly be open to their offers and consider them seriously, I'm fairly certain that I want to stay here. . . . It's home, you see."

"Yes, you Chicagoans do value your city, not without reason, I might say." He touched his glasses, as he often did when hunting for the proper response. "I am not without some interest in your decision, as you may well imagine. And I do appreciate your telling me. Whatever your decision, you can count on my full blessing, for whatever it may be worth."

"Plenty." Hugh grinned.

It was a strange conversation to have right before going to an apartment to make love to a woman. Hugh wanted to explain his trip to Michigan. He also wanted to assure himself that, no matter how strong his doubts and no matter how much he would enjoy the things he was going to do with Liz, and no matter how much he would loathe himself for this lust after he left her, he was still a priest and would remain one.

Liz was still furious at him. Not only did he combine obnoxious masculine ego with clumsy lovemaking; he did not have the common human decency to call her the day after or the next or the next.

She also loved him with every angry cell in her body and wanted him back in her bed.

She had wanted what happened on Christmas, had expected it to happen, had prepared for it, and had dressed for it from the skin out. She would have been crushed and humiliated if he hadn't responded to her. Yet she still resented his imperious masculine triumph.

She was sitting at her typewriter, in jeans and a maroon university sweat shirt, working again on her dissertation when Hugh entered, smiling arrogantly.

"I'm going to make love to you all afternoon," he whispered into her ear.

"You are not," she said with little conviction in her voice.

"Yes, I am." His warm hands were already under her shirt, touching her cold flesh, one holding her so tight, she couldn't move, the other challenging, teasing, comforting. At first he was uncertain and awkward as he had been on Christmas morning; then, as he watched her eager reactions, he became more confident.

She heard, as though from a great distance, a voice inside her head, a voice both past and present. . . . He's seducing you. . . . Damn him he's good at it. . . . You enjoy it, you shameless little slut. . . . Make him stop. . . . Oh, please, don't stop. . . . No, you must stop him. . . . Oh, God, no . . . too much pleasure . . .

He cuddled her, fondled her, rhythmically caressed her, laughing at her insincere protests.

Then her body discovered a rhythm of its own, independent of her wishes and her thoughts, demanding she give up to its movements and energies, insisting she merge with the raw powers and forces churning within her.

Her father's hands pawing her. No, not her father. Someone else.

A slow fuse lighted in her loins, the fire moving through her nervous system, then exploding, a mushroom cloud of pleasure, shudders, twists, contortions, groans of delight, and a writhing body—surely not her own—rose up to meet his, wanting only to become one with him.

A moment of blackness, then floods of peace and joy.

It was dark when he finally left. She lay limp and exhausted on her bed, a rumpled sheet carelessly pulled over her deeply satisfied body, her emotions a jumbled mess.

She was pleased, angry, and terrified. So this was what intimacy was like. Soon he would be able to do with her anything he liked. She was horrified, wanted to run away from him, wanted to run to him, didn't want him ever to touch her again, wanted him there touching her that very moment.

She was outraged. He was damnably pleased with himself. He knew he was a good lover, just as he was a good athlete. She hated his arrogance. She dreaded his dominance. But, above all, she wanted to be one with him.

She fell asleep happy, uncertain, confused. Her anger crept down into the subterranean regions of her soul and waited.

The reaction of the faculty and students at Michigan to Hugh's visit in early January was extremely flattering. Most of the senior faculty came to his lecture on village structure, and a large number of graduate students did too.

At supper with some of the faculty, the conversation ranged far and wide. They were impressed by Hugh's mastery of many of the key issues of international finance and delighted that he had found time to take courses in economics.

"One delicate matter that I suppose we have to raise, Father . . ." said the gray-haired dean. "I will be asked by others—up the line—if you will wear clerical garb in the classroom. You are perfectly within your rights to do so and if—"

"Forget it," Hugh said. "No problem. I don't think it worries anyone these days. They don't even wear clericals in the universities in Rome."

The dean sighed with relief.

"You are going to remain a priest?" asked an assistant professor tentatively.

"Sure," said Hugh. "Why not?"

On his way back to O'Hare from Detroit Metropolitan, he knew that he had impressed and charmed the Michigan faculty. They were a much more civilized and friendly bunch than his professors at the university. The Ann Arbor environment would be a pleasant one in which to work and intellectually exciting and stimulating.

It was tempting, more tempting than he'd expected. There would be time at Michigan to slow down, to read, to pray, to think out his religious problems, and to make the decisions he had to make.

The appointment would also be a natural end to the relationship with Liz, should the relationship last that long.

After his Mass the next morning, Hugh remained in church to pray. He should not be saying Mass without confessing his sins. Yet he'd made love in a different order of reality from that in which he said Mass. The body of Christ was one thing, the body of Sister Elizabeth Ann something else. God would not mind his saying Mass while he tried to straighten out his convictions and emotions.

Dear God, he prayed, I'm a mess. I don't know what I should do or what I want to do. Liz is a wonderful woman and I love her dearly, but neither of us wants marriage. I don't want to give her up, not yet anyway.

I know I should do what is most difficult. I should do what I am required to do, what I ought to do, what it is my obligation to do.

But what are my obligations now? How can I sort them out? What comes first?

It was all so easy when I was young—the seminary or Maria. It's not so easy anymore.

Help me, I pray.

The next day he sat at his desk in the cubbyhole at CRUD, working through the revision of his second chapter. TKH had not returned from Indonesia. Rather, he'd sent a cable: "Returning soon. Orientate students."

That meant "take my classes until I come back and be prepared to give them their final exams at the end of the quarter."

And it was snowing again.

He wanted Liz. The Christ Commune reassembled after the Christmas vacation. They would be tolerant of anything that went on in their circle of "absolute freedom to do your own thing," but they would not be silent about it.

Hugh drummed his pen on the page he was revising and called the hotel in Palm Desert where his parents and the Wentworths were vacationing.

Peggy answered. Wonderfully lovely place. Why hadn't they come every winter of their lives? Liam was a grace from heaven. No, I'm not drinking a lot of wine. Only a glass at meals, well sometimes two. Your father thinks it's funny too. Marge is really quite delightful. I think she still feels a little guilty about all those years. Yes, the heat is on in the house at Lake Geneva. This weekend? I'm so glad you finally are going to take a weekend off and relax. It's time you did.

Self-contempt and lust battled inside him as he hung up the phone. He knew he would hate himself even more after the weekend idyll. Fornication and sacrilege in his family's summer home . . . how low could he get?

He gave Liz five minutes to pack. "You'll only need a few things. The place is filled with clothes. Besides, I don't plan to let you be anything else but naked most of the weekend."

She didn't want to go, to put herself so completely at his disposal. But, afraid of a conflict, she packed a small bag and climbed into the car beside him.

At Lake Geneva, they walked in the snow and on the frozen lake, lay by the blazing fire, drank wine from a bottle, ate roast beef, and talked. Mostly, however, they made love.

She gave up her attempts to isolate herself from her feelings. Instead, for two days she was nothing more than the sharp spasms of pleasure that racked her body and threatened to tear it delightfully apart.

She was viscerally terrified of his sexual dominance. But until Sunday afternoon she willed the terror not to interfere. He was using her as if she were a harem slave, and she was reveling in every minute of it. For this weekend, at least, she intended to live in paradise.

On Sunday afternoon the sky was a hard blue and the sun glared brightly off the ice. The temperature had fallen below zero the night before and a strong north wind was blowing. They paid but slight attention to the weather as, pleasantly exhausted, they lay in front of the fireplace, he with a blanket around his loins, she in one of his robes.

"Ready for some serious talk?" She rubbed his unshaven cheek with her hand.

Not terror, but common sense, she mentally insisted.

"If you say so." He kissed her lips.

"This has been wonderful. I wouldn't have believed such peace and happiness could exist. But, Hugh, these weekends of love can't go on forever. We both have responsibilities. We've committed ourselves to making the world a better place, bringing peace and justice to the oppressed, lifting the burdens of the poor, making the Church relevant again to the people of God. . ."

"No room for us in all those grand designs?"

"Certainly . . . but we're not important, the purposes are."

"I want to be important," he insisted.

"You are important, Hugh. To me . . ."

He rolled over and turned toward the fireplace. She wrapped her arms around him, lightly pressing against his back.

"You're the more realistic of the two of us, Liz; I'd rather not face that."

"We both must realize that this has to stop." Anger, buried through the weekend of delights, crawled up out of its underground cave. God, he was dumb. Did he think she would marry him?

"We both have our work, our obligations, our responsibilties." She kissed his neck. If she could talk about responsibilities, her terror would go away.

"This is the last time?" He rolled over and drew the robe from her shoulders. She removed the blanket from his waist.

"Do we have any choice?" She snuggled close to him, confident now that her protective armor was returning to its place. She need no longer fear his power.

"No, I guess not. . . . All right, it ends tomorrow. But let's enjoy what's left of today."

On February tenth Hugh drafted a letter to the dean at Michigan telling him he regretfully was declining their generous offer. He sealed the letter and placed it on the hard chair at the door of his cubbyhold.

He had gone to confession in the busy marble sacrament factory at St. Peter's in the Loop. The young friar who heard his sins had been gentle and sympathetic.

"You must not be so disgusted with yourself, Father," he whispered softly. "You seem less willing to forgive yourself than God is."

"Thus adding pride to lust," Hugh said bitterly.

"Come, now," the young priest protested. "Some disgust is appropriate. But you have a purpose of amendment, you intend to end the relationship. You would do much better to atone by hard work instead of self-hatred."

Hugh restrained an urge to laugh at his own foolishness. "I'll try, Father."

"Which is all God expects of any of us."

Lifting the telephone receiver on his desk, he called Sean Cronin for an appointment with the cardinal.

As he hung up after the conversation with Cronin, Liz appeared at the door of the cubbyhole, her face stained with tears, handkerchief twisted in her hand. She seemed tired and sick.

She was due to leave for her new assignment at the end of the month. He'd miss her, but it would be the best thing in the world for her. Some administrative responsibility finally. Best thing for him too. He couldn't see her without wanting her.

"What's wrong? Second thoughts about the college? It's the best thing, Liz, it truly is. You'll love it by the end of the first term."

"Hugh," she sniffled, "I think I'm pregnant."

Chapter Twenty
1969

"WELL, MY DEAR, you have created a problem for yourself, haven't you?" Mother Baldwina, a vigorous, athletic nun in her middle fifties, was making a statement, not registering a complaint.

"Yes, Mother." Liz could hardly hear her own voice.

"Surely you must have anticipated this possibility?"

"I . . . I didn't think much about it . . . he should have. . . ."

"Come, now, Sister; we will not blame him here in this room. Doubtless he has his share of responsibility. Feminist ideology wil not help us solve your problem, however."

"But he's so arrogant. . . . All men . . ."

"I will say this candidly, Sister. If you're pregnant the reason is that you wanted to be pregnant. I will not try to analyze what that reason might be. If you want to marry him, then I won't try to talk you out of it, though you do not talk like a woman in love."

"I do love him," she said stubbornly.

"Enough to spend the rest of your life with him? Think about that, Sister. It's a long time."

"I—I don't know. . . ."

"Matters can be arranged. You could take a leave. I will not recommend the cancellation of your appointment as president of our college. I think I can persuade the one or two board members to whom I must speak that the problem should be kept confidential. We are not going to force you out on your own, as we would have done only a few years ago, God forgive us."

Outside, through the Mother's windows, the fresh snow gleamed white and pure on the motherhouse grounds.

"I appreciate that, Mother." She dabbed at her eyes with a tissue. "I don't know what to do."

"Nor will I tell you, Sister." Mother's face was unreadable. "You must think it over yourself. You have some time to do so, not much but enough. I will support you whatever you do."

"Thank you, Mother," Liz said gratefully, barely sensing the rage she'd soon feel toward Mother Baldwina's presumption.

Xav Martin was more upset than Hugh had anticipated.

"Don't marry her, Hugh. I don't know the woman at all, but I know you shouldn't marry her."

"Why?" He leaned forward on the rector's chair—the same one he'd twisted on anxiously when he talked about Maria.

"You don't want to marry her. You've trapped yourself in your irrational sense of obligation. You'll crucify yourself if you marry her."

Hugh sat back in the chair. "I don't understand. . . ."

"You don't love her, Hugh, not one bit."

"I think I do, Xav," he said hotly.

"Then you're kidding yourself. Don't do it, Hugh; it won't be a happy marriage. Then there'll be other women. You won't be able to control yourself once you've gone off the deep end. The demons will drag you down into hell."

"Harsh words, Xav: demons, hell—do you mean them seriously?"

"I'm not talking about everlasting hellfire, Hugh." He waved off the suggestion with his usual quick gesture. "You know that. I'm talking about a man-made hell. Marry that woman and you'll take the first step on your own descent into hell."

"Maybe. . . ."

"Think about it, Hugh. And don't marry her because you feel responsible. There are other appropriate motivations for human behavior."

"Like what?" The words slipped out of Hugh's mouth before he realized how damning they were.

"Like survival."

"Do you want me to get an abortion?" Liz asked resentfully.

"No . . . don't be absurd; an abortion is out of the question."

"Why should it be out of the question? Most moral theologians today don't believe there is a human person for the first two weeks. A month, six weeks, isn't much longer."

"Do you want an abortion?" he asked wearily. It had been a long, convoluted, and acrimonious conversation in the office at St. Medard's, with boxes of collection envelopes piled in the corner and high, dirty walls looming around them in shocked silence, the only place where they could talk privately.

She hesitated before answering. it was a solution, heaven knows, however morally repugnant to them both.

Liz was bitterly angry. Men had the fun and women paid the price. Yes, the doctor was sure she was pregnant. No, of course, she had not done anything to prevent conception. No, she didn't want to marry. Yes, she would go away and have the child. No, she had no intention of staying in the Order.

He asked mildly if she hadn't thought she might conceive if she did nothing to prevent it.

She shouted furiously that he'd done nothing to prevent it either.

He took it for granted, still, that they would marry. It was the only thing for him to do. Liz knew that as well as he did. It was, he suspected, an altogether acceptable solution from her point of view. To be sure, she would need to work through her anger and outrage, draw from it the last measure of satisfaction, and then realistically face the future.

"Maybe an abortion is not a bad idea. It wouldn't be as terrible a sin as your forcing me into a marriage that neither of us wants."

He didn't blame her for bluffing. She was, after all, the victim more than he. Perhaps, nonetheless, it was a bluff that ought to be called.

"That's a decision that is entirely up to you," he said carefully. "I disapprove of it. I'm asking to marry you, I want to marry you, this . . . this event merely forces me to face what I wanted all along. . . ."

Did he? He didn't know. Michigan, a wife, a family . . .

"If you insist on having the child out of wedlock, I'll do whatever is needed. If you want an abortion, I won't cooperate, but I will grant you that it's your body and your choice."

"So I'm stuck with the mortal sin and you're home free?" She jumped up, grabbed her purse and gloves, and dashed from the room.

Hugh realized he must resign himself to not winning in the present crisis. Liz was upset and angry, struggling with her guilt. Her attitude would change.

But what if he were to dig in his heels. What if he took her at her word and refused to marry her? How often had he advised pregnant young women not to marry? Most marriages of that sort, he used to say serenely, were ill-advised. Was this one ill-advised? He knew he would despise himself if he dumped her. But maybe that was the best thing to do.

He dialed his father's private number in chambers. Could they meet tomorrow? No, not for lunch; he would prefer to see him in his office. Something important. Bad news? Not really.

Not much, Hugh thought as he hung up.

A considerable part of his life was being wiped out. There would be heartache and suffering for his family, reproach and recriminations from his friends, some explicit, most of it implied.

So be it.

He'd wasted a lot of time, seven years in the seminary, twelve years in the priesthood. He must begin to make up for lost time.

The judge listened quietly as Hugh talked, his face devoid of expression, his fingers toying with a paper clip. "You will forgive me, Hugh, for being the lawyer and asking a few questions?"

"That's a good way to begin, Dad."

"You're sure this child is yours . . . ?

"Quite sure."

"You are also sure that the young woman would not be better off having the child out of wedlock?"

"She hasn't made up her mind, Dad. I have. I won't let down either her or our child."

"Indeed. Do you want to leave the priesthood?"

"That's the big one. And it's not easy to answer. Would I leave the priesthood now if Liz wasn't pregnant? Probably not. Would I leave eventually? I don't know. If I were a psychiatrist, I'd say that I did what I did because it would force me to leave."

"I see." His father delicately laid aside the paper clip. "Do you think becoming a priest in the first place was a mistake?"

"I wanted to be a priest, Dad. No one sold me on it. It . . . wasn't quite what I expected. I've never put it this way before, not even to myself . . . those years at St. Jarlath's were not very rewarding. If I hadn't had Monsignor Sullivan to fight, I might have been bored stiff."

"You will, I take it, seek a dispensation from your vows?"

"Yes, of course." He had thought that he wouldn't bother. It made no difference to him. But it would be important to his family.

"You wish me to speak to your mother before you do?"

"Whatever you think best."

The paper clip now was suspended between finger and thumb, like a life hesitating on the brink of extinction.

"I'm sure it would be advisable for me to discuss the matter with her. . . . Through the years one learns how to break bad news. As I'm sure you're aware, she will take it to be bad news."

"Yes."

The judge sighed softly. He looked very old. "I hardly need say, Hugh, that you are our son, and that we will stand by you. If you are making this choice, it is the right choice for you. You must be patient with our disappointment. . . . Do not misinterpret it."

The lump in Hugh's throat was so big he could not speak for a few seconds. "I knew I could count on you, Dad."

"Do you intend to continue your academic career? The appointment at Michigan?"

"That seems to be the wisest thing."

"You'll forgive me for raising an objection. If the work of the parish priest was not . . . ah . . . stimulating enough, do you think that college teaching will be?"

Hugh had not thought of that.

A sheepish Liz was waiting for him in his cubbyhole.

"I'm a terrible bitch," she said forlornly.

He touched her cheek. "No, you're not. You're under great strain, and sick every morning besides."

"Do you really want to marry such an awful woman?"

"Yes, certainly I do. There's nothing I want to do more."

She breathed deeply. "Do you think I seduced you so you would be forced to marry me?"

A dangerous mine field. "We've loved each other for a long time, Liz. We wanted to consummate that love. We knew what could happen . . . you no less than I and no more. . . ."

She frowned, puzzling over his response, searching perhaps for something more definitive. "I guess . . . I've tormented myself wondering. I'm not sure. I do love you. I do want to marry you. I know that."

He kissed her forehead. "That's all that matters. Let's not worry about sorting out the blame."

"Would you mind if Theo marries us? At the Commune?"

Yes, he would mind. Mom, Dad, maybe Tim, and Marge.

"I think it would be appropriate if we had something very quiet at the county clerk's office."

She was disappointed. If she insisted, he'd give in.

She didn't insist.

He wrote a new letter to the chairman at Michigan. He tentatively accepted the appointment, pending their formal offer at the end of March. It was not a binding commitment. Negotiation in the academic jungle was delicate and indirect until the ink was on the contract paper.

His father's question worried him. What was there for him to do that might be more exciting?

Chapter Twenty-one
1969

"COME ON IN, Hugh. Sit down." Sean Cronin was in an expansive mood. "Smoke if you want . . . no, that's right, you don't smoke either. How you been?" Cronin put his feet up on the desk. "A strange time to be a priest, Hugh. The best of times, the worst of times. And it's hard to tell which is which. What's new in your life?"

"I'm resigning from the active ministry, Sean." He had been warned that Cronin was uptight on the subject of resignations and was prepared for an explosion.

If he had shoved a knife into the vice-chancellor's stomach, the pain on the man's face could not have been more intense. "Oh, God, Hugh, don't. . . ."

"I'm sorry, Sean."

"It will break the old man's heart. He was so pleased with your work."

"I have to do it."

"A year's leave of absence. . . . Take time off to think about it . . . go to Michigan . . . out West."

"I'm planning to marry, Sean. I've come for the forms for a dispensation."

The other priest nodded grimly, pulled open his desk, and took out a pile of papers. "You'd better be prepared to say that at ordination you were not free to make a fully human choice and that you didn't understand completely what celibacy meant and that your salvation depends on entering a married life. . . . Are you prepared to swear to those things, Father?"

There was heavy irony in Cronin's voice, and bitter wrath.

"If that's what others swear to, then I suppose I can too."

Cronin nodded. "It's a game. I don't know . . . hell, send them in as soon as you can and I'll try to push them through. The Pope is erratic on these things, depending which way his conscience is swinging. When are you planning to be married?"

"In a few weeks."

"In a rush?" One of his eyebrows shot up.

"The young woman is pregnant, Monsignor."

"Yeah, I thought it was something like that." He shoved the papers to Hugh's edge of the desk with unconcealed contempt.

Hugh's anger finally erupted. Cronin was merely the perfect target for his own self-contempt. The vice-chancellor was a cold, ambitious bastard. Hugh grabbed the dispensation forms, tore them into shreds, and threw them at the dazed prelate. "Shove this stuff up your ass," he said.

As he rushed out into the corridor, wanting to get out of the creepy, clammy old building and never return, he heard Cronin's voice calling after him.

"I'll mail the forms to St. Medard's."

He turned. The monsignor was standing in his doorway, leaning against the doorframe, holding the torn documents, his shoulders slumped.

Hugh ran down the stairs and out into the street.

Thank God, he didn't have to see the cardinal.

. . .

In the thirty-six years of their marriage, Judge Tom Donlon and his wife had never quarreled so violently. For almost twenty-four hours, they had not said a word to each other. His confidence that he could handle Peg's passionate emotions was utterly spent.

God knew what would come of this confrontation—no other word was appropriate—with Hugh.

The son had sensed something was wrong the moment he entered the parlor and saw his mother, tight-lipped and white-faced, sitting rigidly upright on her "favorite" couch, the one on which she had repaired so many tattered pairs of socks.

"I'm sorry, Mom," he began miserably.

"You're a fool, Hugh, a terrible fool. Don't marry that woman; you'll regret it the rest of your life. Leave the priesthood if you must, become a professor if that's what you want, find yourself a wife if you will be happier with one, but don't marry that self-righteous little bitch."

Hugh rocked back as if she had hit him with an iron pipe. "I love her, Mom."

"I doubt it. You lusted after her and she led you on. You don't love her."

"I'm sorry you feel that way, Mom. She's going to bear my child."

"So what?" said Peg harshly. "Would she be the first woman to bear a man's child out of wedlock?"

"We owe it to the child to give him . . . or her . . . a chance at a happy life."

"Your father says I should stand behind you. I do. Someone has to tell you the truth. And he won't. You are creating for yourself a life of unending misery."

"Peg," said the judge sharply, "that's enough."

"No, it isn't enough, Tom," she shot back. "I'm finished doing everything you want me to do. However late in the day, I'm declaring my independence. I can't stop you from marrying her, Hugh. If you want to be a martyr to her schemes and your weaknesses, go right ahead. But don't expect me to be at the wedding or treat her like a daughter-in-law. I can't do it. Hugh. I won't do it."

"Peg, I won't tolerate another word." The judge tried to face her down.

"I don't care what you won't tolerate," she cried, and she ran from the room.

"She'll get over it, son. The shock, you know. . . ."

"I don't think she will; she sounds like Xav Martin. . . ." Hugh stood in the middle of the parlor, his hands hanging powerlessly at his sides, looking as if he were a soldier deserted by his last comrade. "I'm sorry to have made trouble between you."

"It'll be all right in a few days," the judge said without much confidence. "You better go now."

Later, he tried to talk to Peg in her studio, where she was viciously dabbing paints on paper.

She refused to listen to him. "Get out and leave me alone."

He left, now angry as well as hurt and humiliated.

That night for the first time since they'd lived in the house, Tom Donlon did not sleep in the same bed as his wife. He moved into what had been Hugh's room, resigning himself regretfully to what might be for all practical purposes the end of their marriage.

And wondering if perhaps Peggy might not be right.

. . .

Hugh Donlon knelt in the darkened nave of St. Medard's Church and prayed as his father had told him he had prayed the night Hugh was born.

The vehemence of his mother's attack had seared him. Disappointment at his leaving the priesthood he had expected, but anger over Liz, especially such biting anger, was beyond his comprehension. She hardly knew the girl. One dinner on a Sunday afternoon was not enough to justify such harsh condemnation.

Dear God, if You are up there listening to me, what am I to do? I love Liz, I want her for my wife. I love my mother, I don't want to hurt her.

The answer was that a man must cleave to his wife.

Liz wasn't his wife yet. Maybe she ought not to be his wife. Maybe now was the time to jump ship while he still could. . . .

For one giddy moment, he made up his mind to follow Peggy's advice.

And experienced joy and relief.

But as he left the church to go to his basement bedroom and the third chapter of his dissertation, he knew that he could never abandon Liz.

"Good God," exclaimed Marge. "Hugh's getting married."

The rain was crashing against the windowpane and the mists were rushing by their house. A soft day in Ireland, indeed.

Liam looked up from his preprandial sherry. "Can't. He's a priest."

"He's marrying some ex-nun he's got pregnant."

"Most astonishing." Liam spilled half his glass of sherry.

"Mom and Dad had a terrible fight. They haven't talked to each other for a week. Can you imagine that, Liam?"

"Bad show."

"The marriage is in the county clerk's office next Monday. Only Dad and Tim and some other ex-nun are going."

Liam watched the mists swirl by, masking almost completely the waters of Dingle Bay and the Purple Mountain in the far distance.

"Is there anything we can do, my darling? Any way we can help? Should we fly over and try to bind up the wounds?"

Marge tapped the letter thoughtfully against her Sheraton desk.

"Right now the only thing for us to do is stay out of it and pray. . . ."

"I daresay you're right. Makes one feel helpless."

She walked over to him and laid her hand on his shoulder.

"I don't know what I would do without you, Liam."

"Too much credit. Bumbling oaf. Like all Anglo-Irish. Daft dolt."

She laughed and she cried and she clung to him as if she would never let go.

Later he called the judge and had a "word or two" with him.

Hugh and Liz fell from grace again, quite consciously and deliberately. He wanted desperately to make love. She was the one to suggest it, however.

"What difference do a few days make? And a legal ceremony?"

They checked into the Blackstone Hotel, a very proper old matron on Michigan Avenue that seemed to be holding up her skirts, lest they be muddied by the crowds of conventioneers down the street. They brought along two pieces of luggage, holding mostly books, and looked so much like a married couple that not an eyebrow was raised at the registration desk.

Their love was gentle, kind, and sweet. Hugh was proud of the speed with which he'd learned the little secrets of making love to Liz, the kisses she most enjoyed, the caresses that brought her the greatest pleasure, the most sensitive areas of her body, the mixture of gentleness and force that seemed to arouse her best, the points at which delay changed from delight to agony and at which sweet agony turned to unbearable need.

They ate supper in the hotel restaurant and returned for another session of tenderness. Then she knelt next to him in their bed, a picture of satisfied lust.

"Promise me one thing, please, my darling." She raised his hand to her lips.

Sleepily Hugh looked up at her.

"Don't let my moods come between us. You know how bad I can be. Don't let them ever keep us from loving each other the way we do tonight." She stroked his face lightly, as though he were a small child who needed the greatest delicacy of touch.

"Your moods aren't all that bad; we won't worry about them," he said.

She lay down beside him and reached across his chest. She pillowed his head against her full young breasts and contentedly he fell asleep.

Soon the difficulties would be behind them, she thought, and a new life would begin, one filled with innocence and promise.

The wedding was a five-minute affair. Liz wore a simple white dress under a cloth coat, and Hugh wore a navy blue suit. The county clerk was correct, too much the politician to hint at what he, a devout Irish Catholic, thought of a marriage between a nun and a priest.

Ex-Sister Jackie kissed everyone delightedly.

Tim was nervous and twitchy, his bloodshot eyes and lined face suggesting he didn't like what has happening. Strange that Tim should care.

The judge put a brave face on it all, congratulating the new Mr. and Mrs. Donlon and insisting the party have lunch with him in a private dining room he'd reserved at the Palmer House.

After the lunch, Hugh and Liz drove out to Lake Geneva for a three-day honeymoon. Both had to return to the university to finish their degrees. Liz's career as a college president had died aborning. She'd written a letter to Mother Baldwina, curtly ending her relationship with the Order.

That was that.

Their days at Lake Geneva were pleasant, despite the gray March weather. However, the blazing passion of the previous interlude there was not repeated. They were settling down into the serious routine of marriage, in which there would be little time or inclination for such luxurious escapades.

One afternoon Hugh walked around the shore of the lake, watching the ice melt. It had been a bitter cold winter and the cover of ice was thick. Even though there was water and slush on the surface, it would take weeks for the sunlight to break through the prison that held the blue waters of his youth.

And by then they'd be gone.

They ate dinner the last night in Geneva town and then walked out to the end of the sad, lonely pier, closed till the coming of summer.

"Strange place." Liz clung to his arm, gazing at the tawdry amusement arcade. "Did you have fun here when you were young?"

"It seemed so then. I was just a kid."

"Must have been a rendezvous for many a cheap encounter."

And one that was not so cheap.

Two weeks later, Liz awoke with a terrible pain in her stomach and blood all over the bed. Hugh rushed her to the emergency room at University Hospital. The young OB resident who was summoned examined her quickly and ordered her to surgery immediately.

Two hours later, he came out of the operating room.

"She's all right, Mr. Donlon," he said cheerfully. "Be sick for a few days and a little weak. Lost a lot of blood. We're giving her some transfusions. Nothing to worry about, though. Frequent enough in a first pregnancy."

"And our child?"

"There wasn't a child."

"No child?"

"No fetus, properly speaking. Just a ring of tissue cells with a hole as big as a pin. Nothing really, not after the first couple of weeks."

BOOK FOUR

"My God, my God, why hast thou forsaken me?"

Chapter Twenty-two
1970

EVERY MORNING AT five thirty Hugh Donlon rose carefully from the bed in his decrepit Hyde Park apartment, tiptoed quietly into the bathroom, so as not to wake Liz, who was pregnant again, and vomited.

He drank two cups of coffee in the dirty kitchen, looked over his records of the previous day's closings, slipped out of the apartment, and walked briskly to the 53rd Street train station to catch the first South Shore train to the Loop. On the brief ride he would glance at the headlines in the *Tribune*—American invasion of Cambodia, more student protests—and then turn to the financial pages.

His stomach was still tied in knots and would be until the end of the trading day. He ate his main meal of the day after two o'clock at one of the small restaurants off LaSalle Street where the runners and messengers and clerks who kept the Board of Trade working ate. He was not ready to join the other traders at such places as Trader's Inn till he won his spurs.

Liz left the apartment at noon for the parish in the south suburbs where she was director of religious education and did not return till eleven at night, long after Hugh had fallen into a deep but restless sleep, a dark and troubled oblivion from which he would often awaken in the morning darkness more exhausted than when he went to bed.

Hugh was a commodities trader instead of a college professor because of a conversation he'd had at the Faculty Club at the university shortly after his marriage.

His father, who'd proposed the lunch, said that Liam had called and that they together were prepared to stake him to a seat on the Chicago Board of Trade.

"Liam and I came to the same conclusion separately," the judge said. "We both think that you might be much happier if you followed Tim onto the CBT."

"Keep an eye on him?"

"Frankly, that would be one concern. Recently there has been a problem in deferred contracts, which fortunately did not lead to formal charges. I do think that your presence there would be helpful for him."

And so duty and family had won again, they and the old football-trained competitive instinct. If he wasn't going to be a priest any longer, he might as well make a splash. Too many years of denying that potential.

Liz had not been pleased with the change in his career plans when he told her about it in their tiny and rather dingy apartment in Hyde Park. She wanted to escape from Chicago and the influence of the Donlon family. She knew nothing of the Board of Trade and was wary of "capitalists." However, she saw the gleam in her husband's eye. She sulked for a day and then told him she felt a commodities trader's life was incompatible with marital happiness.

"I know from St. Jarlath's what kind of lives those men live. It's not healthy. Besides, we're beginning our marriage and you won't have time to work on it with me. A professor has more time for his wife and family than a trader."

"I'd be finished working at one thirty."

Liz sniffed disdainfully. "How many Ben Fowlers come home at one thirty?"

Hugh had been caught in the middle—his family wanted one career, his wife another. For a few moments he'd considered what he wanted and admitted to himself that he did not know.

No matter which choice he made, he would disappoint someone.

The marriage would require considerable effort if it were not to collapse. Liz's depression after her miscarriage had been intense.

She thought it was foolish to give up the $17,500 Michigan salary.

"How much money do these men make?" she asked.

"An experienced and skillful trader can easily clear a half million a year." Liz didn't believe him.

The hours between 6:30 and 8:00 A.M. in the tiny office he shared with Tim were the best in the working day. Cut off from the rest of the world as surely as if he were in a monastery, Hugh prepared for combat, like an ambitious and hungry heavyweight boxer before a fight. Slowly the tension in his body turned from paralysis to creative energy. Like a gladiator readying himself for combat, like a quarterback before a playoff game, he went carefully through a routine of preparation, physical, mental, and moral, for the four and a half hours from eight forty to one twenty.

When the opening gong sounded, he was a new man. The anxiety and tension drained away to be replaced by an enormous surge of energy. He rushed onto the trading floor with the same disciplined enthusiasm that he had used to lead the Fenwick Friars onto the football field.

His colleagues already had him pegged as a "cool" operator who never winced under pressure. They had no notion of the terror with which he woke every morning, knowing that each day he would sink or swim on his own in the world's greatest game.

The Chicago Board of Trade was one of the last of the pure marketplaces in the world. Despite the mild regulation provided by the Commodities Exchange Authority of the Department of Agriculture, the "haggling" between buyers and sellers was more sustained and more frantic than it would have been in an Oriental bazaar where "real" objects were sold. In the trading pits no physical objects changed hands. The traders bought and sold "futures"—consignments of commodities that the traders never saw and never owned.

They spoke their own language, shouting fractions at one another and waving their hands to indicate whether they were selling or buying contracts, aided by hand signals that indicated the fraction of the trading price they were bidding or offering. Dressed in light, colored blazers, they swarmed around their "pit," one of the three-step platforms constructed on the trading floor. They scrawled sales contracts on small sheets of paper, which they dropped on the floor to be snatched by messengers and coordinated later in the day by the "Clearing Corporation," the self-policing and account-balancing organization that prevented the chaos of the trading floor from degenerating into anarchy.

Hugh was trading in silver, the least active of the commodities. New on the Board of Trade, silver contracts for the most part attracted speculators and brokers trying to avoid taxes legally by showing a loss at the end of one year and taking it all back as a capital gain the first week of the next.

He liked the silver pit. It was a place to learn the game in a relatively quiet way; silver, he was convinced, would develop into an attractive commodity as inflation rose and increased demand for the industrial uses of the metal put pressure on the world supply. Moreover, the fluctuations in silver were abrupt and dramatic and the game therefore exciting and demanding.

Exactly the kind of game for which Hugh was looking as a way to begin.

July silver was fluctuating around 160—a dollar sixty cents a troy ounce, or eight thousand dollars for a five-thousand-ounce contract. Because the margin requirement was only five percent, one could buy a silver contract for about four hundred dollars. A five-cent increase in the price would earn someone who had gone long, "bought" July silver the previous day, two hundred and fifty dollars on his investment or a sixty-three percent profit. If silver went up the ten-cent-per-ounce limit established by the Board, the contract purchaser would earn five hundred dollars, or a hundred and twenty-five percent profit.

On the other hand, if the price fell the limit (after which no more decline in price was permitted), the buyer would have his investment wiped out and would owe someone one hundred dollars. Moreover, if the price "locked down" at the opening of the following day and he was unable to sell his contract, he could lose six hundred dollars out of his pocket, in which hopefully there was some money left.

Moreover, in a bear market, the price would go "limit down" at the beginning of each day so that one would be stuck with a losing position for several days, losing more money each day and falling back on more of one's resources to meet the ever-increasing margin requirements.

If, instead of speculating with one contract, he was speculating with, say, one hundred contracts, he could make or lose more than fifty thousand dollars in a day or two. The unwary trader could be wiped out completely almost before he knew what happened. And it was easier to be wiped out than to make a fortune.

Commodities trading was popular with the speculator who liked to make big gains and was willing to run the risk of big losses precisely because of the "leverage" that the low margin requirements made possible. Now that the stock market was closely regulated by the government and dominated by the big institutional investors, such as pension funds, traders on the floor of the CBT were confidently predicting that the 1970s would be their decade.

And, Hugh Donlon told himself, his decade too.

"How's the wife doing?" Benedict Fowler greet him with a broad grin as Hugh walked on the floor a few minutes before the opening gong. Ben traded in soybeans, soybean meal, and soybean oil, usually with a complex spread or "crush" involving all three commodities. He had shown Hugh the ropes in those pits, and occasionally when the silver market was even more quiet than usual, Hugh would join the mania in the soybean pit, just as he would join Tim at the frantic wheat pit. Because he was trading entirely for his own account, and not "with the deck," filling orders from brokers (who shied away from new men), he could go wherever he wanted.

"Pretty good; she's not sick as much as she was last week and the doctor says the danger of miscarriage is over now."

"She still working?"

"She'll finish out the school year," Hugh answered cautiously. He did not know when Liz would quit her job. When he'd asked, she'd refused to answer. It was her decision, she'd insisted, not his.

Ben apparently did not know that Hugh knew he was the one who'd warned Monsignor Sullivan about the parishioners' plot.

Hugh had abandoned his lust for revenge—or told himself he had—but he did not want Ben as a friend. Neither, however, did he want such a powerful trader as an enemy. So he kept up the pretense of camaraderie.

Still, it was none of Ben's business whether they needed Liz's income to live on, which Hugh suspected was the point of the question.

In fact, Hugh had made more than enough in his first year on the floor to survive without his wife's salary—no big killings yet, but no dramatic losses either.

Then the bell rang and Ben was pushing his hands to sell off a half-point from the previous day's closing.

The trading floor reminded Hugh, somewhat irreverently, of a parody of a solemn pontifical Mass. The traders in their multicolored jackets were the celebrants, the messengers and runners were acolytes, the huge windows looking out on LaSalle Street were the rose window, the quotation boards, some marked in chalk, some in computer-fed lights, were the stained-glass windows of the nave, and the choir stalls from which CBT officials, brokers, and commission house representatives watched and sent their messages were the choir lofts. The sometimes hysterical babble of the traders was plainsong rising in respectful worship of July silver and December wheat.

It was time for him to win a big one, to show the skeptics like Ben Fowler that an ex-priest could play the game with the best of them—no, better than the best of them. Hugh gave himself to his new vocation and to the service of his new deity with as much enthusiasm as he had to his old one.

His mother had taught him long ago that if you did something, you must do it well.

For a week silver had been fluctuating up and down with little reason. Something unusual was taking place, and as Hugh opened with a bid to acquire two more contracts, he resolved to be cautious. The Cambodian invasion should force the price of silver up and keep it up for a while. Yet on the last two days after rising the limit it had fallen back sharply to the opening price, the kind of market in which one could be cleaned out in a half minute if one were inattentive.

In the first half hour silver rose four and a half cents, a gain for Hugh of almost twenty-five hundred dollars on his ten-contract purchase.

The action in the silver pit then slowed down as quickly as it had flared. Who was buying all the silver and then selling it? Hugh violated his stern resolve to concentrate on nothing but silver and thought briefly of Liz.

The marriage was going through a period of "adjustment," or so he told himself. There was no reason to expect that he and Liz were immune to the ordinary processes of marital change.

There were moments of ecstatic contentment when they lay in each other's arms, exhausted and happy; or when on Sunday afternoons they sat peacefully next to each other in their apartment, reading and listening to music on the hi-fi and not talking because the emotions of love that bound them together made talking unnecessary.

But there'd been fewer such moments each passing month. Liz was not interested in his work. "I can't understand all that capitalist jargon," she would protest, "and I don't like gambling."

He knew there was no argument, practical or theoretical, against her ideology. After a few attempts to explain the social utility of futures trading he gave up.

He was forced, however, to listen to accounts of her work—the new techniques of religious education and particularly "salvation history," which sounded to him like one more obscure Belgian fad that satisfied the need of priests and nuns for the old certainties.

Children, he was sure, knew very little about history, did not understand the word "salvation," and were not particularly interested in the Old Testament.

He bit his tongue. Nor did he tell her that he was no longer interested in the internal fashions of the Catholic Church.

Liz, he realized, was still a nun, a married nun perhaps, but a nun, nevertheless. She would always be caught up in the clerical culture that he'd abandoned when he left the priesthood. Her friends would always be angry priests and nuns, and angry former priests and former nuns, who could not leave the clerical world behind.

When Hugh resigned from the priesthood, he'd left it; he wanted no part of the organized Church, and attended Mass on Sundays only to keep Liz happy. He did not return phone calls from priests, not even from Jack Howard.

If his wife wanted to continue to be part of the Church, that was her right. But strangely, she was much more angry at Catholicism, and her anger was fanned by the anger of her friends. They couldn't leave the Church and they couldn't stop hating it.

"You think I ought to forget about the Church, don't you, Hugh?" she had inquired one night, lying peacefully in his arms. "You think I'm clinging to the past by associating with those people?"

"You have the right to do whatever you want," he said, and then, because the moments of tenderness were few and far between, he kissed her on the cheek. "I don't know whether all the anger helps, though."

She sighed peacefully. "I suppose a psychologist would say I'm working out anger I feel toward my parents."

"The Church has ruined enough of our lives." He felt a fierce need to defend this tense and haunted woman. He drew her closer, warm skin touching warm skin.

"Maybe I ought to see a shrink and get Catholicism out of my system." She held his head against her chest, as though she were afraid she'd lose him.

"That's up to you, darling."

But she had not seen a shrink, and Hugh suspected that she never would.

Her anger was like a cancer, slowly destroying her appealing sweetness. When talking about the children she was teaching and during their moments of love, she was the gentle sister of the past. Leaving the religious life should have removed her from the causes of much of her anger, but, instead, her break with the Order had made her more angry than ever.

Lately, especially during the sickness of early pregnancy, the anger seemed to be turning on him.

What could he do about that? What should he do?

They were questions he swept under the rug, to await his conquest of the Chicago Board of Trade.

At noon the silver pit came alive again in another buying wave. The price shot up five cents, wavered, and fell three. Hugh jumped in and bought four contracts of his own.

Almost at once there was another flood of purchase orders. The price rose to the limit.

He hesitated. He could pyramid his profits and buy more contracts at the end of the day when the price might fall a few points. Or he could take his eight-thousand-dollar profit and run.

Pigs lose, he told himself, and began to push his hands outward in an offer to sell at a point off the limit. His contracts were quickly snatched up, the price fell a point and a half, then rebounded back to the limit.

Then the price slumped again, down eight cents, back to where it was in early morning, then rallied a cent just as the bell rang.

"You stayed out of the final rush?" asked Ben Fowler.

"Got out at the limit."

"Smart man; you'll put us all out of business yet."

"I didn't sell short on the way down," he replied. "Might have doubled the haul."

"It takes time," said Ben sympathetically.

As Hugh walked off the floor, an elderly trader with white hair and a light blue jacket stopped him.

"Uh, Hugh, I have to catch a plane to Arizona and I'm not going to have time to go over to St. Pete's. Could you hear my confession?"

Hugh did not know how to respond to such a request. "I can do it legitimately only in a case of necessity," he said cautiously.

The other trader smiled. "Come on, Hugh; they can't take the power away from you. Besides, an airplane ride to Phoenix is serious danger as far as I'm concerned."

So in a quiet corner of the trading floor as the last of the traders straggled away to their lunch and their first drink, Hugh shrove the old man of sins of anger, impure thoughts, and drinking "too much, about twenty times."

So far Xav Martin's somber prophecy of "demons from hell" had not come true. He had left the priesthood, but the priesthood would not leave him.

"Saw you talking to Benedict the Manic," Tim said when Hugh joined him in the office. Tim never asked how he had done on the floor.

"Friendly chatter."

"Don't trust him." Tim's small eyes danced. "He's a bit of a fraud, you know, and he doesn't like you either. Ever make it with that gorgeous iceberg he's married to? Ben doesn't use her much; wants her around for show but doesn't want anyone else feeling up the merchandise."

"No, Tim, I haven't gone after Helen." Hugh considered he was telling only a half lie.

Tim shook his head. "Can't figure it, then. Anyway, he's got it in for you. Be careful."

"How do you know?" Hugh peeled off his coat, monsignorial red in color.

Tim stretched lazily. "Takes one to know one, maybe; I can feel it. . . . Anyway, there's a message here from someone named Cronin and Mom called to say that Maria Manfredy's husband—you remember her, don't you?—is missing in action in Nam . . . some kind of fly boy in the Navy.''

"Yes, off a carrier.''

"Well, maybe he's a prisoner." Tim wasn't very interested.

Hugh dialed the chancery office phone, trying for the moment to repress his sorrow for Maria's suffering. She was still working at the bank out on Madison Street. Poor woman.

"Cronin," said the vicar general of the Archdiocese of Chicago.

"Hugh Donlon. You called?"

"I've got good news. Well, I hope it's good news. Up to you, I guess. The dispensation came through. Paul the Sixth's conscience is working again. If you want—and I stress want—you can have a Church marriage. Jack Howard, I presume . . ."

Hugh hesitated. The dispensation meant nothing to him. Liz was his wife, no matter what the Church thought. Yet it would please his parents, and perhaps hers too.

"I'll talk to my wife, Sean," he said cautiously, emphasizing the word *wife*.

"Fine. There's a regulation about a private ceremony. You don't need to pay attention to that, if you don't want to. Family and friends, whoever you want.''

"My wife is pregnant, Monsignor.''

"Congratulations." Cronin was not flustered in the least. "Make a million or two at the Board of Trade, only don't leave it to the Church. Give me a ring.''

Tim smiled beatifically. "Looks like another family crisis shaping up.''

"Not my fault," said Hugh.

"Never mind fault," said Tim. "Sit back and enjoy.''

Tim watched his brother's broad back as Hugh rushed out of the office. Always the boy scout.

Although Tim resented Hugh, he had resolved that the best way to live in his own isolated universe was to be cool, laid back, uninvolved. You seized the excitement when it came near you, but you did not go out of your way to find it.

A conflict with Hugh would require too much effort and there wouldn't be enough payoff. Tim despised the way his father and brother had muscled into the commodities racket with Marge's husband's money. He, God knows, could have found his own capital. Larry Maguire would have put it up and promised not to tell his daughter, Estelle. Now Hugh was the big Donlon on the floor.

Well, Tim would take life as it came. There were still plenty of women who found him attractive and a variety of thrills that did not require the risks of the trading floor. He and Estelle were in one of their reconciliations, seeing a priest counselor every week. Tim had learned from his various shrinks the answers to give, so both Estelle and Father Carmody thought he was making great progress.

Tim sighed and struggled to his feet. Time for the first drink of the afternoon.

Fowler was a barracuda. Hugh ought to be more worried about him. Tim would watch closely. The fight should be an interesting one—a barracuda and a boy scout.

There were some advantages in being alone. That way you could enjoy the battles between the other animals in the jungle without getting killed yourself.

Chapter Twenty-three
1970

Hugh assumed that Liz would not want to be bothered with the Church's blessing on their marriage. He was surprised by her reaction when he told her late that night.

"Of course, we'll do it," she said briskly. "In my role, it's important to be seen as one who is in a sacramental marriage."

"I think our marriage is sacramental enough," he said defensively.

"The waiting was unjust and the requirements are unjust," she said, unbuttoning her plain blouse. "Yet we shouldn't let that interfere with a public celebration of our union with each other in the Lord."

Some new party line among the religious-education crowd, he thought. A year ago, she would have ridiculed the importance of the Church's blessing.

"All right, we'll have a celebration."

"Can we afford thirty or forty guests?"

"Of course, we can. . . ." Thirty or forty—her bearded priest friends and their nun mistresses, and the gays. What would his mother say, if she came this time?

Her skirt joined the blouse on the floor. Liz rarely picked things up. Even in drab white underwear—fancy lingerie was now a symbol of decadence and a concession to male chauvinism—Liz was delectable. Hugh enveloped her in his arms.

"Hugh, I'm so tired," she said weakly.

"So am I."

In a few minutes, however, she was as eager for love as he. Once they began, fatigue no longer seemed to interfere.

"Oh, Hugh," she sighed happily when they were through, "that was wonderful."

"You're what's wonderful," he said.

"Do you think we could make it fifty or sixty guests?" She snuggled closer to him.

"Whatever you want."

Hugh wondered what her thoughts had been when they were making love. Probably searching for an ideological cutting edge for her potential guest list. Women, he supposed, reacted differently.

Liz stayed awake after Hugh fell asleep. He could be quite sweet, she thought, tonight especially. But she was beginning to resent his constant sexual demands, particularly, as was increasingly the case, when she found them perfunctory. Why couldn't he love her for herself and not for her body?

Terror had been exorcised from their marriage, and with it most of the pleasure. She no longer feared his power over her and thus no longer especially felt the pleasure he could give. She was angry at him most of the time. How could anyone not be angry at his chauvinism and his false consciousness and his capitalist ambitions and his stupid family? He meant well, no doubt, but in the present state of the world that was not enough. Having ceased to confront the problems of social and sexual inequality, he was now part of the problem himself.

Their wedding might be a turning point. Liz believed in turning points—
kairoi, as the Greeks called them—times when there were special opportunities.
It had been such a turning point, during the retreat after her senior prom, that had
led her to the religious life. And another, after the loss of their child—which was
Hugh's fault for not listening to her fears about a miscarriage—that had made her
decide to serve God by pursuing a career as a professional religious educator who
would dedicate her life to raising the consciousness of young women.

As she fell asleep, she remembered the priest at the retreat, a wonderful old
man, holy enough to be a saint, she'd thought then. He was the first person she'd
dared tell about the things her father had done to her. He'd suggested the convent
as a way she could find peace and forgiveness. But now she thought he had
probably been a male chauvinist pig too.

"I'm not going to that wedding." Estelle looked up from the floor plans on
which she was working. She was always working on plans. Usually the house
was never built, for which Tim was deeply grateful.

"Suit yourself," he said. "I think it ought to be quite a show—her faggoty
friends with my mom and dad, and Hugh playing Prince Valiant to everyone."

"I'll be visiting my mother in Florida." She returned her attention to the floor
plans.

"First I've heard of it." Tim no longer found the game of bending Estelle to
his wishes fun, save on the rare occasions when he wanted to make clear to
everyone that he had the power to do so.

"She's a whore," Estelle said. "She seduced him."

"Probably did," Tim agreed philosophically. "Got herself pregnant so he had
to marry her."

He watched with considerable pleasure the ring of red rise on the back of her
fat neck.

The silver market continued to move erratically upward and Hugh continued
to make substantial gains by sticking with a decisive choice made shortly after
twelve o'clock. He had figured out the silver pit. If he could master a few other
pits, then he would be ready to open his own firm and trade in his own name for
everything from gold to plywood futures.

In the meantime, he wanted to make enough money to pay off Liam and his
father by Saturday, the "wedding day"—and make a down payment on a decent
house.

"Another great day?" Ben clapped him on the back as they walked off the
trading floor.

"I guess so. I hate to make money on that Kent State shooting." Hugh's
liberal conscience still bothered him.

"Can't be helped. Anyway, time the kids were taught a lesson." He turned
abruptly. "Stay away from the soybean pits till I make enough to retire. . . ."

Liz hardly heard Hugh when he confided to her his desire to buy her a house
for a wedding present.

"Can't that wait till after Saturday, dear?" she pleaded in the saccharine tone of forced affection that he had grown to fear more than her anger. She was clearly living on her nerve ends.

"I thought you'd be happy to hear about it," he said.

"I am," she agreed carelessly, "but we have so much to do. Do you think you could call the caterer and tell him there'll be ten more? Sister Sophie is bringing all the sisters from Vandalia."

"Sister Sophie?"

"You remember her." She looked at him impatiently. "We were novices together."

"But the whole Order?"

"You begrudge me my few friends?" Her eyes were hard and resentful.

"Not at all," he responded easily. "Have as many guests as you want."

The ceremony would be in the combination school hall and church, made of concrete blocks and steel beams, in the South Holland parish where she worked. After Mass the church would be converted back into a hall for the wedding party—and for guests, most of them the clergy and ex-clergy that Liz cultivated and their dates.

Liz was celebrating her transition to the status of a "validly" married nun as if it were a triumph.

"Then please be helpful and make the phone call," she said, distracted by some other unfinished chore. "And after that, I have something else that needs to be done, if I can only remember what it is."

"A year ago you didn't want a Church validation," Hugh said.

"God damn it, Hugh, make the phone call and stop preaching."

She left the room, list in hand, mother superior on a rampage because no one else was as efficient as she.

Hugh made the phone call, as ordered.

Wednesday was a frantic day on the Exchange and Hugh was drawn taut as a high tension wire about to snap. His instincts told him that something was wrong. Someone was manipulating the price of silver, probably someone on the Comex in New York. He was making a large profit from guessing which way the price would bounce, yet he hesitated to risk too much on the wisdom of his guesses. He lacked the experience to understand who was playing with the silver market and why.

He wanted desperately to make a big profit so he could celebrate the Church's blessing of his union with Liz by paying off his debts and telling her they could buy the house.

"You Donlons always end on your feet." Maria considered her guests over the top of her beer mug. "Peggy becomes a painter whose work sells the day she opens her exhibits. And Marge finds a nobleperson who is quite nice even if he can't speak English and carries a pike all the time—and see, Margie, I've got the right weapon now. Irish pirates carry pikes, not halberds. The boys make tons of money in that gamblers den on LaSalle Street . . . and the judge turns down the Supreme Court and is celebrated on the cover of *Time*. Don't tell me it's just Donlon luck."

"You're doing all right yourself," Marge replied.

"Only because I heard about computers at the Pentagon when Steven was there and took a few courses."

She hoped her front wasn't wearing thin. Not a second passed in which she wasn't agonizing about Steven. He was alive—of that she was sure; his wingman had seen the parachute open—but the worry . . . the uncertainty . . . would she ever see him again? Pull yourself together, Maria Angelica. . . .

"They scare me," Peggy admitted. "I'm afraid they'll take over the world."

"Spoken like a true artist, darling. Don't worry. They're only smart adding machines. They're still dumb when they're not adding . . . rigid creatures . . . only cope with a yes or a no. Males, I think."

What did they want? Maria was confounded. Peggy had never once come in the bank, even to cash a check. Now she and Marge show up and are surprised to bump into the local computer whiz in the bank lobby telling off a software con man. Want to see how I'm holding up with Steve MIA? No, the Donlons aren't ghouls.

She'd brought them to Doc's for lunch because that's where she ate every day. Peggy didn't seem to mind the place, especially as they served beer and wine. The world sure was changing.

Marge's skirt was midthigh; the minis were shorter in Britain. Even Peggy had raised her hem to the knee.

I should have legs that good at her age.

At my age.

What's going on here?

"Hugh's being married day after tomorrow," Marge blurted. "I mean a real church wedding, with the Pope's permission."

"We thought you might want to come," Peggy said anxiously. "You were at Marge's wedding. . . ."

Warning lights went off and on in the back of Maria's head, bright red, Sicilian warning lights that said "Beware, Maria Angelica. . . ."

"Married?" she said.

"To the former nun."

"I think I might be out of place. . . ."

"You're a friend of the family," Marge said confidently.

"All the same . . . Oh, hell, darlings, in a way I'd love to. . . . But I don't know. . . ."

"We understand perfectly, my dear," Peg said.

Do you really? No, you don't. How can you when I don't?

In her office after lunch, Maria wished she'd ordered a third glass of beer. Then she cried a little while. Not for herself. Not even for Hugh or his family. Rather, for all the people in the world whose dreams didn't come true.

Peg was wearing a burgundy robe, lacy and low cut. She carried a tray with a bottle of unopened white wine and two glasses. She sat down across the desk. Tom pushed aside the manuscript on which he was working; Niersteiner Eiswein, he noted. Forty dollars a bottle.

He both welcomed and feared the conversation that was about to occur. She'd tried twice before to begin the reconciliation process. Hurt and in the mood to punish himself as well as her, he'd turned her away. Now he desperately wanted his wife back and didn't know how to begin.

She was making the start for him, and that gave her considerable moral superiority, which, to judge by the glint in her eye, she intended to use.

"I'm going to be here every night, Tommy, and in a different expensive gown. I don't think you will be able to resist me indefinitely."

"Oh?"

"It's gone on long enough," she said, ignoring his unpromising answer. "You know it and I know it. There are some things that have to be said first."

"Say them."

She folded her hands on the desk and leaned forward.

"I suppose that I've always done what you have wanted because I was so young when we married and because you are so much smarter than I am." She smiled ruefully. "I acted like a little fool. I'll go to the wedding—or whatever it is—even though I know it cuts off his last chance of escaping from her."

"You admit you were wrong?" He could not believe he was getting off so easily.

"Not for a moment. Hugh will regret the day he set eyes on her." Her own eyes flashed dangerously. "But you were right that I should have gone to that ceremony in City Hall." She paused and began to open the wine bottle. She was quite skillful at opening wine bottles these days. "I've already apologized to Hugh and to her. And I apologize to you."

"But—"

"But"—tears were forming in her eyes—"I'm not stupid and I'm not a little girl anymore. Never, never, Thomas Raymond Donlon, take for granted again that I'll go along with anything you say, simply because you say it."

He reached across the desk and began to caress her throat. She smiled at him the way she had smiled after Mass at Twin Lakes the first time they'd met.

Careful not to disturb the movements of his hand, she uncorked the wine bottle.

On the Thursday before the Church's official blessing of his marriage, Hugh Donlon was not thinking about the commodity market as he rode on the South Shore train from Hyde Park to the Loop. He hardly noticed the serene blue of Lake Michigan and the soft green of Grant Park.

If there was no ceremony on Saturday, his marriage to Liz would not be valid in the eyes of the Church. He was committed to Liz for life, regardless of what the Church said or did. Yet there was a finality, a definitiveness, about the step that unnerved him.

After Saturday there would be no possibility of returning to the priesthood and no other loves in his life. He and Liz would be bound until death.

He wanted no other loves nor did he want to return to the priesthood. But there were too many undiscussed topics, too many subjects ruled off the agenda—the people with whom she associated, her contempt for his work, her refusal to leave the organized Church behind, her strident ideologies and shallow crusades.

The argument earlier in the week—if that's what it was—displayed a facet of her that he usually refused to acknowledge. She was sweet and lovely and often pliant in bed, yes, but she was also an angry and potentially domineering woman.

What was it Jack Howard had said? She needs a strong parent figure to blame for what goes wrong in her life; the Order was the old parent, her husband the new.

Jack was exaggerating, of course. Or was he?

Friday morning started quietly enough. The first contracts sold close to the previous day's closing price. Then, however, there was a brisk interlude of selling. It made no more sense than the locked-up close yesterday. The market stabilized at ten thirty, down five and a quarter cents, then at eleven fifteen it plunged again, limit down.

No sense at all—it's too low now; it's bound to soar.

He hesitated, trying to banish thoughts of Liz from his mind. You had to concentrate in this business, had to listen for every sound around the pit.

Then silver came off the limit, slowly at first, then quickly. By noon the loss was erased. Hugh cursed himself for his hesitancy. If he'd bought in at the low, he would already have the money to pay off Liam and his father.

He bought five hundred contracts, a hundred thousand dollars, almost all his equity. It was the biggest purchase he had ever attempted. The man across the pit was startled by the trade and watched him keenly as he jotted down the transaction on his card and stuffed it into his shirt pocket.

The man's expression turned to amazement and grudging respect as the silver quotations on the rapidly moving yellow band above the floor climbed, for a half point, then a point, then five points. At twelve forty-five, Hugh Donlon had made almost four hundred thousand dollars. He could have made more than that if he'd had the courage of his convictions and jumped in earlier.

Then the slide began, just as the price of silver went up, so it went down. Hugh watched in disbelief as panic selling exploded. The market was congested, investors were suddenly abandoning silver, no one was buying, the bulls were terrified, the bears were having a field day.

Hugh refused to panic. He would hang on, take a small profit, and then reclaim his gains next week.

Silver continued to fall, not pausing at the opening price. It plummeted like a stone thrown over the side of a boat.

Hugh felt as if he were a man frozen at the helm of the boat that was sinking. He ought to sell, quickly, before it was too late.

Yet he did not move. The price continued to fall until the bell rang at one twenty, ending the grain trading. It stirred him out of his reverie. Sell, yes, sell, while you can.

It was too late. The silver market was locked down and no one was buying at that price.

His profits were wiped out and so was his investment equity.

Tomorrow the Church would bless the marriage of a penniless failure.

Tim was waiting for him in the office.

"Looks like you've had a rough day?"

"Cleaned out," Hugh said through clenched teeth. Tim knew; did everyone on the trading floor know too?

"Can you meet a margin call?" Tim stretched. "If not, you'll have to liquidate or the Clearing Corp. will do it for you."

"Just about. I won't have anything left. If we go limit down on Monday and I can't unload, I'll be finished.

"You shouldn't blame yourself. I warned you about Ben; he's been out to get you since you came on the floor. Maybe he'll leave you alone now that he's drawn some blood. Can't tell about Ben; maybe he'll want more blood."

Hugh slumped in his hardback chair. "What does Ben have to do with it?"

"I thought you knew." Tim's thin red eyebrows arched in surprise. "He and a couple of other guys have been buying and selling silver, shooting the market up and down like a roller coaster. They hedge everything in New York, of course; so they don't lose any money. Probably even make a few dollars on the arbitrage between here and Comex. But that wasn't the idea. Ben wanted to jiggle you off the rope. Start real gentlelike and then increase the motion till you were dangling and finally give it one sharp tug. Presto! Hughie falls into space."

"How did you know?"

Tim shrugged. "Heard some guys talking about it in the elevator. Rotten trick, they thought. Figured you'd get even with Ben eventually. I thought you'd caught on."

"I'll get even, all right," Hugh said, surprised at his vehemence. "Ben Fowler will regret the day he came on the trading floor by the time I'm finished with him."

"That's my boy," Tim said appreciatively.

And you better watch out too.

Hugh was only too well aware that he was at the mercy of misfits like his brother and bastards like Ben Fowler. All right, then, he vowed, he'd find power and plenty of it, more than he'd ever need.

And then Ben would pay in spades.

Chapter Twenty-four
1970

JACK HOWARD PRESIDED over the brief wedding ceremony with dignity and taste. His few remarks about God's blessing on this couple who had given so much and who had so much to give set the right tone.

Unfortunately the tone ended as soon as Hugh and Liz turned away from the portable altar on the big, graceless auditorium stage. A group of women—they must have been nuns—whooped enthusiastically, as if their team had just won a basketball game. Liz, now about three months pregnant, had the sense not to wear white but she still acted like a blushing bride, hugging and kissing everyone without the slightest restraint.

Marge escaped with a brief bear hug, but Peggy was clutched for a full half-minute, while Liz assured her that everything would now be fine.

"Your idea, darling," Marge said, alluding to the disagreement they'd had before leaving Ireland. "Thank God Maria had more sense. . . ."

"Tasteless little thing. Her family?"

"Oh, they wouldn't come; sacrilegious union or something like that. We're the ones who have to take the rap."

"Damn shame." That could mean it was a damn shame Liz's family hadn't come, or that they thought the marriage was a sacrilege, or that the marriage was a damn shame.

Or all of the above.

"Too right," she agreed.

The beaded, bearded celebrants were finally persuaded to take their seats at the tables and Tim, reluctant and embarrassed, rose to propose a toast. "To my brother and sister-in-law"—Timmy raised his champagne glass—"may they have a long and happy marriage."

Before Hugh could get to his feet and attempt a reply, one of Liz's Commune brethren dashed to the head table and preempted him.

"I think we need more of a toast than that," he said. "This is an important event in Hugh's and Liz's life and I want to say some words about this event. First of all, we can't celebrate with an easy conscience while American soldiers are murdering innocent Vietnamese. So the first toast I offer is to the victory of the Vietcong and true freedom for all the Vietnamese people."

Cheers and shouts of "Ho, Ho, Ho Chi Minh!"

None of the Donlons drank the toast, not even Hugh. But Liz emptied her entire glass and extended it to the judge, who refilled it with a spasm of distaste.

"Then I want to drink to Father Hugh Donlon and his wife. Hugh is one of the best priests in the archdiocese. He's on a temporary leave of absence until the Church wakes up to the fact that it can no longer impose the archaic law of celibacy on its best priests. Hugh is a pioneer, a man who made a brave sacrifice to teach the Church a lesson; it won't be a useless sacrifice. Hugh, my boy, when enough other priests have the same courage as you do, the Vatican will have to bow to the will of the people and permit priests to marry. So I propose a toast to a married clergy and Hugh's speedy return to the active ministry."

More loud cheers. God, what a vulgar crowd, Marge thought. How many of them are still priests? Impossible to tell. Poor Jack Howard, the only one in a Roman collar.

Hugh sat ashen and silent next to Liz. She nudged him, but he didn't move. She whispered impatiently in his ear.

Slowly he rose to his feet. "Thanks, Tim; thanks, Charley, for the fine toasts. I simply want to drink to my wife."

There was polite applause.

Liz looked sullen and unhappy.

"Bad show," said Liam.

"Decidedly, darling," Marge agreed.

After the tables were cleared a three-piece orchestra arrived and the singing began. "We Shall Overcome" was the overture.

Then suddenly Liam jumped up and, snatching the violin from an astonished concertmaster, shouted at the top of his rich Celtic baritone, and with the brogue laid on thick, "Ah, sure'n I thought we should sing a few Irish tunes. First of all, one in honor of our brothers in Ulster. It's called the 'Old Orange Flute.' Sing along if you know the words."

Marge, who had heard Liam play only Bach partitas and sing in church, was amazed that he could dominate such an unlikely audience with songs in English, Gaelic, and Highland Scotch and wedding stories from all three cultures.

When he was finished the guests were exhausted and their voices hoarse. Quietly they straggled out. Only the Donlons and Jack Howard remained.

"Darling, I still don't believe it." Laughing, Marge kissed Liam on the cheek.

"Remarkable," said Jack Howard.

"Thank you very much, your lordship," said Liz, obviously tipsy.

"Cold winter nights in Ireland," said Liam, grinning like a giant leprechaun.

A few minutes later Liam cornered Hugh as he was getting into his Chevy; Liz was already asleep in the front seat.

"Good luck, that sort of thing."

"We're not going on a honeymoon, Liam, only back to the apartment. . . . I appreciate what you did. It saved Mom and Dad a terrible defeat. Liz's . . . our friends mean well. They just don't understand."

"Nothing. Heard about your trouble, the crook on the floor. Tim, you know. Bad show. Here's a loan, usual interest rates, stern accountant here. Pay me back when you can. I insist. That's all."

Hugh was left standing, an envelope in his hand, as Liam shambled across the church parking lot to his waiting wife and their rented Mercedes. I have to take it, don't I? It will save me on Monday. Another chance. God, do I need another chance.

The check was for one hundred thousand dollars.

"God bless you, Liam," Hugh mumbled through savagely clenched teeth. Damn right I'll pay it back. And I'll have so much power by then that I'll never have to depend on your charity again.

Nor anyone else's.

On Monday morning, Hugh was able to sell his silver contracts as soon as the market opened. The price was a cent and a half an ounce above Friday's close. He recovered some of his own money.

None of the money was his yet; he still had to prove himself, then to amass the power that would win him freedom from other people's help. It would be a long summer.

On a Sunday in July Ben Fowler invited Hugh and Liz to a lawn party at the Fowler beach house in Michigan. At first, Hugh decided not to attend, then he changed his mind. Let Ben think that he suspected nothing.

Liz agreed to accompany him, much to his surprise; she looked quite attractive in a maternity sundress and was charming through the afternoon. "Such an advantage for their children to have a place like this," she whispered to him, quite forgetting that it had been purchased by capitalist money.

"A swimming pool on the shore of the lake is a special advantage," he replied.

She missed his irony. "His wife certainly is lovely for a woman of her age, isn't she?"

Helen was climbing out of the pool, taut, solid, and sexy in a skintight black one-piece swimsuit. "For a woman of her age, yes."

"And her daughter is lovely; how old is she now?"

Linda was standing next to her mother, taller and more slender but just as sexy—two blond goddesses, on display to impress the world with Ben Fowler's success and power.

"Eighteen or so, I think. I'll get you a drink. Don't stay out in the sun too long."

"I'll go into the parlor; it has such a lovely view of the lake," Liz said wistfully.

"We'll have one of our own someday."

The Fowlers were standing at the informal bar, greeting their guests, Ben in gaudy Hawaiian shirt and swim trunks, sweat pouring down his face, and the two women in transparent cover-ups over their swimsuits.

"You look good, Hugh," Helen said coolly. "You seem a little thinner."

"What should I call you now, anyway?" Linda tossed her head to indicate the question was boring but she knew she had to say something. "Father isn't right anymore, is it?"

"Linda." Helen was stunned. "Please, don't be so bold."

"Hugh's fine," he said easily.

"Your wife is very pretty," Helen volunteered. "I never noticed that when she was a nun. I suppose one wouldn't."

"And she doesn't wear nunny clothes either," Linda agreed. "So many nuns could use a course in a charm school after they leave the convent."

"Liz is very happy these days."

"How are you, pal?" Ben's big fleshy hand grabbed Hugh's shoulder. "Glad you could make it. The little woman looks fine, though she won't be little much longer, huh? Great, great . . . and with your profits it won't be long before you have a house like this."

"Next year," Hugh said. He picked up his drink and walked away, feeling quite ashamed of himself. Were his preposterous fantasies about Helen and Linda the beginning of Xav Martin's descent into hell?

"Thought you'd never come, we're both dying of thirst," Liz said when he entered the parlor with her gin and tonic.

"Sorry, I was distracted."

"No problem; I was enjoying the view of the lake." Since the wedding ceremony debacle, Liz had been on her best behavior. She'd stopped working and was attending the Pastoral Institute at Loyola only two mornings a week.

Hugh crossed Helen's path once more during the party. She was serving potato salad at the buffet and he was filling plates for himself and Liz. There was a moment when no one was near enough to hear what was said.

"I'm sorry about St. Jarlath's," she said quickly under her breath. "It was my fault. I'm terribly sorry."

"It didn't matter. Don't worry about it," he said, just as quickly, and shifted a plate from one hand to the other.

When he made love to a willing and eager Liz that night, it was Helen's bland face and compact body that invaded his imagination.

The next week there was another attempt to jiggle him off the rope at the Exchange, as if Ben knew of his lustful thoughts. Hugh was ready this time, made his own hedges on the Comex in New York, and cleared a neat profit working the arbitrage between the two exchanges. Ben wasn't so fortunate.

"I hear he got a minor bloody nose on a silver arbitrage thing," said Tim at the end of the trading day.

"Did he really?"

"Maybe the rope jiggling is over."

"I doubt it." Ben wanted him off the floor and would not be content till he was beaten into the ground and forced to give up in disgrace.

"We'll see."
"We sure will, Tim."

That night Henry and Jean Kincaid phoned. One of Henry's clients was involved in complex litigation in Chicago. Jean and Henry came to the city occasionally and took Hugh to supper at the crowded Cape Cod Room at the Drake. Liz had never found the time to join him at these pleasant meals.

Their third child, a five-year-old boy, had been injured by a hit and run driver. He was in a coma. The doctors were not too hopeful.

"We called for your prayers," Jean said.

"I'm not a priest anymore," he replied ruefully.

"Of course, you are, Father Hugh," Henry insisted.

"You always will be for us," Jean said. "You know that, Hugh. . . . Laura wants to say hello."

"When are you going to come see us, Uncle Hugh?"

How old was Laura? Twelve? Thirteen?

"I won't recognize a grown-up thirteen-year-old."

"Fourteen," she corrected him. "Yes, you will. I look just like my mother. . . . Maybe if you come now you could give Johnny a special blessing to make him well again."

Catholic schooling had prevailed over Lutheran ancestry. The child believed in blessings, even from renegrade priests.

"I'll say a special prayer for him here, Laura, and I'll see you people by Christmas."

"Anyone I know?" Liz asked as he hung up.

"Old friends, voices from the past." He told her again about the Kincaids, and about the injury to their child.

"How horrible . . . the poor family . . . but, you see, Hugh, once a priest always a priest for those you help."

"Perhaps for others, Liz. Not for me. I've left that role behind."

"Maybe it won't leave you behind."

Two weeks later Hugh shared lunch with Jack Howard at the Sign of the Trader, a crowded noisy restaurant on the first floor of the Exchange.

"You seem to be thriving on the excitement."

"All my life, Jack . . . hey, more roast beef? It's good, isn't it? Nothing elaborate for your wealthy Irish traders, just the best quality meat. Where was I? Oh, yeah, all my life I've made it on someone else's name. Judge Donlon's son, Father Donlon the priest, now I have to make it on my own, build up my own power. I love it."

Jack moved aside his plate. "No, no more wine. I have to drive back to the West Side. These are strange times in the Church, Hugh." His comment did not seem to follow from what Hugh had said. Perhaps it was an attempt to explain why he had not followed Hugh out of the priesthood. "You can accomplish a lot if you know how to work within the system. In St. Mark's, for example, the old monsignor never heard of a budget or a financial plan, never even made an annual report. Now there's a parish finance committee headed by a woman banker and we're the best organized parish in the diocese. It's all on computer tapes and disks and she has the old man eating out of her hand."

Hugh's heart did a little dance. "Oh? What's her name?"

Maria's pilgrimage had brought her to the new, new neighborhood, just as his father had thought it might.

"Maria McLain. Her husband's a Navy pilot missing in Vietnam. A classy, classy woman. Why? Do you know her?"

"Not really. She went to school with Marge." Hugh felt an onrush of pride. "Give her my best and tell her I'm praying for her husband."

Hugh made enough money during the summer to take a vacation the last two weeks of August. He would rather have stayed on the job and continued the slow repair of his fortunes from the havoc that Ben had worked, but he and Liz needed the time together. She'd agreed to the vacation cheerfully and suggested they drive to Iowa to visit her family.

"Maybe next year when we have a grandchild to please them," he'd said. "It might be a little awkward now. Besides, we need some time together."

"We could see them and still have time together."

"It wouldn't work out, Liz."

"All right," she relented. "I suppose you know best."

Their love was renewed on the trip. The future looked hopeful again. Ben Fowler and his family were bad memories from a past that was no longer important.

Liz seemed to agree. She held him close as they watched the sunrise over the Atlantic from a small hotel on the Maine coast, listened to the drum fire of the surf, and breathed the healing salt air.

"Not much sleep."

"I don't see how you can love a woman who's so fat."

"It's easy."

"It certainly seems that way." She coughed.

"Every marriage has its ups and downs," he quoted from his Cana Conference talk. "We must have sense enough in the middle of the downs to know that we should go away together and straighten things out."

"You're so busy with your job and next year we'll both be busy with Brian. . . ."

He patted the forthcoming offspring—around Christmastime it would appear. "My work will ease up in a year or so when I make my big breakthrough on the Board. Then I'll have afternoons free. I'll be home by two thirty, under your feet all the time."

"I'll love that. I should continue my own career, you know."

"That's up to you. I agree with you feminists that a father should know his children." He agreed in theory, at any rate, though he was not sure that a mother was wise to have a career, at least while the children were young.

"Otherwise I'm just a sex object, good only for lovemaking and bearing children."

"You're not an object, Liz, and never will be, whether you have a career or not."

"You don't want me to have a career?" She tightened up in his arms.

"Of course, I do. You know that. But a career won't provide you with any more dignity or worth as a person than you already have, which is plenty."

"I don't like that." She remained tense. "If you must prove yourself at that terrible place, why can't I prove myself?"

"That's different."

"How?" She tried to pull away from him.

He recaptured her gently. "I'm only trying to prove I can do that kind of work. My worth as a man doesn't depend on it."

He didn't quite believe that.

"All right, then." She relaxed. "So long as you see it that way, then I can do my kind of work too."

"I couldn't agree more."

He didn't quite believe that either.

The trip was a success and they returned confident about the future of their marriage. However, Hugh still felt niggling little doubts. Liz wasn't like his mother or Marge or any of the other women he knew. The others he could watch and study and understand. Their reactions were predictable. Even the unpredictable Maria was not mysterious, only illusive.

Liz's reactions depended on her mood, and her moods were erratic and patternless. They seemed to be shaped not by the world outside but rather by her inner world, a world frequently distracted by distant drums.

On the way home, Liz brooded on that conversation. Hugh would never change. It was not even his fault. His mother's false consciousness had been pounded into him at such an early age that he couldn't overcome it. He might make all the right sounds, but he was still an incorrigible chauvinist. He would not help her to raise the children. And he didn't think her career was as important as his—it was a hobby, like collecting stamps or being a candy striper at the hospital.

Liz vowed that she would show him. She would be a successful mother and a successful careerperson. And he would fail as a father and as a trader. Then he would come to her seeking her forgiveness.

That was the only way he would ever learn.

In late November, Jean Kincaid phoned again. Johnny was dead. Could Hugh spend a few days with them in Manhattan Beach? They desperately needed someone to talk to. The new priest in their parish wasn't much help.

Hugh didn't want to leave Chicago. His slow climb back up the ladder to success was progressing. He couldn't afford to miss a day at the Exchange. Besides, he didn't want to be forced back into the priest role he had given up. Moreover, the baby was due in only a month.

But he could not refuse Jean and Henry and grief-stricken Laura. In a way they were all that was left of his parish. And, he realized intuitively, it was only the remnants of his parish that had prevented the descent into hell that Xav Martin had predicted.

"I think it's a terrible imposition." Liz was querulous in the final month of her pregnancy. "You hardly knew the little boy. And what if our baby comes?"

"You're only five minutes from Billings Hospital."

"What if it's the middle of the night?"

"And I'm only five hours from O'Hare. Didn't the doctor say that the baby would be on time or even late?"

"A lot he knows."

"I have to go to them, Liz; it's an obligation from my past."

"And I'm an obligation in the present. Is she better-looking than I am?"

"That has nothing to do with it."

"Oh, all right, go ahead if you have to. But stay in touch."

He promised he would. It was the first separation since their marriage. He looked forward to it eagerly.

Chapter Twenty-five
1970

HUGH FLEW OUT of O'Hare on Friday morning, planning to return on Monday morning, thus missing only two days on the Board. The only plane on which he could find a reservation stopped at Denver. Another hour would have to be wasted.

The weather forecast called for clear, cold weather all the way to the Pacific mountains, then high clouds into Los Angeles. As the DC-8 winged its way westward, he looked down at the brown fields with snow lacing, like frosting on a pound cake. Tim's winter wheat, food for the world, Hugh thought as they turned south for the approach to Denver. Then he saw an ominous line of black hanging across the northwest horizon and inching slowly in their direction.

He watched it with detached interest. It disappeared behind the Rockies as the plane settled onto Stapleton Field.

He decided not to leave the plane. As the baggage trucks pulled up to the plane like eager puppies seeking nourishment from their mother, a vague notion, floating hazily in his mind, began to take shape.

It was supposed to be a bumper crop of winter wheat. Tim insisted that no one in his right mind would buy wheat with a big harvest staring him in the face.

He walked up to the flight deck.

"Bit of weather on the other side of the mountains, Captain?"

The pilot, a grizzled veteran with a dazzling smile, said, "Is there ever. Don't worry, though. We'll be out of here long before it hits. There's going to be a lot of snow from here to Chicago by tomorrow night."

"I imagine. A big one, huh?"

"You bet. Came up all of a sudden. The weather people haven't caught on to it yet. It'll take them another hour."

Calmly Hugh strolled off the plane, walked through the jetway, and went out to the lobby. He found only one unoccupied phone booth. The phone in it was not working. Patiently, he waited, watching the Denver passengers checking in for his flight.

Finally, an elderly woman tottered away from one of the booths.

The phone at the office was busy.

He cursed mildly and called again.

Still busy.

Boarding for his flight was announced. He phoned once more.

Tim answered. "Tim Donlon."

"Hugh . . ."

"Hi . . . nothing in the market; silver is down a few cents."

"What's the weather like?" He tried to restrain his excitement.

"Cold but sunny, supposed to warm up over the weekend. Why?"

"I want to buy two million bushels of December wheat at the market."

"You're crazy . . . that's all the money you have."

"I have to catch a plane." He would not tell Tim about the storm; the news would spread all over the floor in a half hour if he did. "Do it, Tim, and if you're smart, buy some yourself."

"What stop loss?"

"There isn't going to be any loss. We'll let it ride till Tuesday when I come back. I have to run."

As the plane lifted out of Stapleton, Hugh was reassured by the weather front. It was much closer now and darkly evil, like a deadly infection sweeping toward the wheat fields.

Tim was the bear of the family, selling short and profiting from bad news. No one really liked a bear. A bull went long, investing in good news. Or so they told themselves.

The snowstorm was good news for the market. December wheat would run sky high. It would lock up for three days, making Hugh almost a millionaire.

Yet it was bad news for the farmers and the hungry of the world. He would become rich because of a natural disaster.

Yet if it were not for the commodity exchanges, the disaster would be even worse. The loss for the farmers had already been absorbed by the speculators, who, in the tried and true apologia for the Board, were said to take the risk out of farming as a price they paid for the opportunity to speculate.

The speculators would pay for the storm. They would be the losers. Other speculators, that is. Hugh Donlon would be the winner because he had seen the meaning in a huge low-pressure ridge over the Rockies.

And with victory would come power and freedom.

He hoped that Ben Fowler was short December wheat.

Hugh made another phone call as soon as they touched down in Los Angeles.

"I did it," Tim said. "I even bought some myself. Both at the low. I wouldn't be surprised if it locks down on Monday. You could lose your shirt."

"Not on your life. There's a granddaddy of a winter storm on its way."

"No trace of it on LaSalle Street. Let me look out the window. . . . My God." His voice was suddenly as hushed as if he were praying. "The sky outside is dark gray. I should have bought more for myself."

"You haven't seen anything yet."

The Kincaids were badly shaken, mother, father, two teenage children—Laura and her brother Pete—and a sweet little blond three-year-old named Tillie, short for Mathilda.

Laura, a tall slender blonde plainswoman like her mother, was the hardest hit by her brother's death. "If only I'd watched for the traffic," she said softly and solemnly.

"Stop that, Laura," Hugh ordered sharply, the automatic response of a priest to a potentially hysterical adolescent. "God wanted Johnny home. It's not your fault."

"I know, Uncle Hugh. But I miss him so much. Would you say Mass for us? It was so terrible at the church."

"A birth control sermon," said Jean, who was even more handsome than Hugh had remembered her from the last dinner at the Cape Cod Room. "The new pastor is an Old Country Irishman without much feeling for anyone. Trust in God. Sure we trust in God, but that doesn't mean we don't hurt.''

"Do say Mass for us," Henry pleaded. "Laura borrowed the vestments from her high school. We need to have a funeral ceremony at which we can grieve.''

"I'm not supposed to say Mass anymore," Hugh objected.

"Please, Uncle Hugh," Laura implored.

So with his congregation gathered around the table in the kitchen overlooking the Pacific, Hugh Donlon said Mass for the first time since he'd resigned from the active ministry, with the surging blue waves of the ocean, framed in a picture window, serving as the altar-piece. He preached feelingly of Johnny Kincaid, now a spiritual and human giant in the life that awaits us all. He wasn't sure he believed any of it, but his congregation believed, and that perhaps was enough.

All the Kincaids wept.

At supper, however, their vitality returned. Even the lovely Laura laughed.

Later in the evening, Hugh phoned Liz, guilty that he had not called before.

"I thought you'd never call," she complained.

"Weather delay," he excused himself. "What's it like there?''

"It's snowing, an inch on the ground already. Hugh, what if the baby comes tonight? You won't be able to get home.''

"Planes fly in snowstorms. Why? Any signs?''

"No," she admitted reluctantly. "And I don't want you flying in a snow-storm. What would we do without you?''

"Nothing will happen, Liz. Don't worry. I'll call you first thing in the morning.''

Hugh lay awake in his bed in the guest room for hours, listening to the Pacific surf and brooding on the terrible misfortune that had befallen his friends. He had wanted to use his life to bring happiness and comfort to others. But somehow it hadn't worked out that way. The passionate love that periodically surged within him was dammed up like a raw mountain stream, which, because of ingenious human intervention, could not rush madly to the sea. The priesthood hadn't freed him to love. Neither had marriage. So he would make a fortune on a tragic winter storm.

Something had gone wrong with his ability to love, to bring others happiness and himself joy. The pounding surf of his emotions had been reduced to a quiet murmur—or sometimes a nasty whine.

The plane was vectored to the north of O'Hare on Monday afternoon. Hugh caught a quick glimpse of the red brick buildings of the seminary. I'm a rich and powerful man now, Monsignor Xav, he said to himself. We'll see whether anyone dares to try to drag me down into hell.

The snow was plowed into enormous piles on the side of the runways, the sky was clear and hard and the sun bright, but there was no water on the runway to indicate that melting had begun.

He phoned the office.

"Locked up," said Tim without waiting to hear who it was.

"Only the beginning. I hope Ben was short.''

"Like everyone else.''

Good. He would pay off his father and Liam, and buy a new house for his wife and son.

And then he'd settle with Benedict Fowler.

Now he was one of the big guys.

And on his way to being the biggest.

Chapter Twenty-six
1972

"MAY I SEE you after the session, Mr. Donlon?" It was one of the runners. Her pretty gray eyes were worried. "It's a . . . uh . . . something private."

Hugh didn't have time for her.

He'd abandoned his heavy investment in silver at the end of 1971, at the time his daughter Lise was born; he was convinced that the 1970s silver boom would not start till after the presidential election and after the conclusion of some kind of peace in Vietnam.

To his surprise, silver had shot up in January and was now selling at two dollars and sixty-eight cents an ounce, almost a dollar higher than when he and his Managed Accounts pulled out. Some of his select group of clients for whom he had recently begun to work were muttering unhappily.

It was a mistake, one of a large number in the past three years. Now he was successful enough and powerful enough to admit that mistakes were part of the game, even big ones.

By the end of March, he suspected, silver would fall below two dollars and twenty cents. Then he would jump in and bring his clients with him. The roller coaster would ride up to almost three dollars by the end of May and then he would slip out and wait for the next upswing.

He had no time to play priest counselor to a pregnant teen-ager, and he had seen the worried eyes often enough to know what the problem was. She probably wanted a priest, even an unfrocked priest, to approve of an abortion.

"Of course, Kathy; my office after the gong?"

Why had he said that? Still the superstition that the tattered remains of the priesthood would protect him from Xav Martin's prediction, a prophecy that he now thought of as a curse?

The girl had nodded solemnly. "Thank you very much, Mr. Donlon."

What was her last name? Something Polish? Clear fresh face, native intelligence, lots of self-possession. Probably would survive. Damn, he should remember her last name. He prided himself on knowing the last names of all the kids on the floor, as he had in the days when he was running the High Club.

Now he'd be late for his date with Helen at the harbor. She'd wait. She always did.

Tim drifted by the silver pit after the one-fifteen bell ended the grain markets.

"Still sitting tight? My brother the bull acting like a bear? I thought the unsettled world economy made metals the real thing? What about the Russian winter wheat fiasco?"

"Just wait."

Hugh Donlon was now a successful man with a large home in Kenilworth, a number of wealthy private accounts, and the respect due a trader with uncanny instincts and iron nerve.

He was not, however, satisfied. He was weary of the narrowness of floor trading. He still reveled in the intense thrills of a turbulent market; but he wanted something more, grander thrills and more challenging excitement.

He had become a thrill addict like Tim. Maybe worse than Tim.

That was probably part of Xav Martin's hell.

Why couldn't he drive Xav's warning from his mind?

Anyway, he wanted his own commission house and the opportunity to manage other people's money as well as his own, to throw the dice for others as well as himself and to throw them in many different games simultaneously.

But in the meantime there was Kathy and her abortion.

"Well, Kath?" He put on his kindliest face as his imagination routinely peeled off her clothes. Nice young body. Cute breasts, trim thighs.

Women are easier to dominate when you strip them, even mentally. They sense that you've done it and that they've lost a little of their independence.

She sat on the edge of the chair, a sixth-grader called to the principal's office for throwing snowballs.

"I'm pregnant, Mr. Donlon." The words and the tears came in torrents. "My parents want me to go away to have the baby. Joe and I want to get married; Joe, he's my boyfriend, doesn't have a job; he's still in school; and he came back from the service at Christmastime; and his family is against the marriage too. And you're so kind and friendly I thought you might advise us what to do."

"You're not thinking of an abortion?" The priest replaced the collector of women. His imagination respectfully put her clothes back on.

"Oh, no." Her eyes were wide in horror. "I mean, you always think of something like that, but I couldn't do it. I have to give the little thing a chance to live. I love Joe; we've been best friends since grammar school; and we were planning to be married in three years when he graduates."

The automatic calculus a priest makes in such a case changed. The indicators were positive—they'd known each other a long time, same religious and cultural background, eventual plans to marry. . . . Nowak, that was her last name, probably short for Nowakowski.

"Eighteen is too young to marry. . . ." What would Peggy say about that.

"I know, Mr. Donlon. . . ."

"Age is important, but it doesn't guarantee maturity necessarily. Would Joe come and see me with you?"

"Oh, yes. Our parish priest is old-fashioned. He yells at us and won't listen. Says we're terrible sinners. We know that, Mr. Donlon. We don't want to sin anymore."

"We're all terrible sinners, Kathy. But God must like us because he made so many of us."

A minute later Hugh left a grateful and happy Kathy Nowak and walked under the implacable sun across the Loop and through the crowded park to Burnham Harbor and his own sin, an offense for which he felt no guilt at all, nor fear of the wrath of a problematic God.

Financial success had created an overpowering sexual hunger in him, as if the pressures of lust that had built up through the years of celibacy had finally broken through the red line on the safety gauge and exploded. In the morning he reveled in the thrill of conquest on the trading floor and in the afternoon, as often as possible, he luxuriated in the embrace of a woman.

His marriage was floundering. Liz had become pregnant again within three months after the birth of Brian—her choice, not his—and was now totally preoccupied with her two children.

She was obsessed by an obligation to care for the children even when they didn't need care. The two babies, nervous kids to begin with, it seemed, had reacted anxiously to their mother's anxieties and quickly learned to manipulate her. Liz smothered them with attention.

They were raising two little monsters—spoiled, neurotic children. His dutiful attempts to come home early to assist Liz were swept aside with ridicule; Lise was forcibly pulled from his arms and he was told that he was spoiling the child by giving her too much affection and holding her the wrong way besides.

He gave up, hoping that at a later stage in their life he might have a chance to reclaim them.

Even before Lise's birth, Liz's interest in sex had fallen "limit down" to zero. His amorous advances were rejected with "how dare you?" anger or "how could you?" tears.

At the same time, he'd become a skilled and sensitive connoisseur of women, like the collectors of vintage French wines. A woman was a puzzle to be solved, a mystery to be explored, a prize to be won. You explored a woman's whims and weaknesses, you studied her reactions, you flattered her vanities, you deluged her with gifts, eventually you explored her body, discovering its pleasure points and its pain points. You rewarded her, you punished her, you pleasured her, plundered her, you delighted her, and you teased and caressed her.

You understood that the best way to keep her under your control until the next time you wanted her was to make the last experience as rewarding as possible for her.

And when all else failed, you took possesion of her by winning her sympathy.

Not that women were merely bodies to be enjoyed. They were endlessly intriguing subjects for investigation and understanding, so like you and so different. Even a Helen Fowler, who seemed at first to be bland and uninteresting, could be forced to reveal herself and emerge as a complex, indeed fascinating, human being.

A woman's psychological self-revelation was pure delight, far more enjoyable than her physical undressing. Self-disclosure bound her closely to you, as long as you wanted her to be bound. She became a more valuable trophy in your collection after you had invaded her deepest secrets.

As a collector's item, a woman existed for you.

Judge Donlon spotted Maria at the beginning of his lecture. The Chicago Association of Financial Planners had grown sufficiently liberal in the last few years to admit a few women members and even to allow them to attend meetings in the prestigious, if somewhat dull, oak-paneled University Club. The women bankers, however, were not usually strikingly attractive blondes. Nor did the typical woman member wear a red dress that skated close to the boundary of sexiness and then skated triumphantly away.

"It is not for a judge to say, of course, since, despite the propensity of some of my colleagues to be instant experts on all subjects, the law will be of little direct, positive help to planners. Yet the law came from small communities and perhaps in reflecting on the origins of the law in such communities you may discover insights that will be useful in your work.''

Maria's expressive face said, ''Come on, Your Honor, don't be humble; you know what we drones should be doing.''

Ah, Maria, how could we have lost you?

''Great talk, Your Honor.'' She kissed him generously, despite a few raised eyebrows from her stuffy male colleagues.

''Your husband?'' he asked gently.

''We saw a picture of him on TV with that bitch Jane Fonda. So he's alive.'' Maria was in command of her grief, neither hiding it nor giving in to it. ''The McLains are old hands at POW camps. Great-Great-Granddaddy Alexander Bonaparte McLain was in Andersonville during the War Between the States.''

''Andersonville was a Confederate prison, my dear.''

''I know; the McLains are from South Carolina but one line of the family supported the Union. You should hear them talk about Mr. Lincoln. You expect this guy with a beard to come around the corner. . . . My man will get out alive and well and cultivated and charming. . . . And how's your family? Herself rejoicing in the grandkids?''

''The Wentworths are pure joy, if I may say so. We don't see them as often as we'd like.''

''And Tim?''

''It is no secret that we are not close to Tim's family. His wife and Mrs. Donlon will never get along.''

''She designs weird homes. I'd like one of her summer palaces for the fun of it. . . .'' There was a slight pause. ''And Hugh?''

''I candidly do not know, my dear; he's successful. It seems to me that he has yet to find the happiness he's seeking.''

''He will someday, Judge Donlon; don't doubt that for a moment.''

''I hope you're right, my dear. I truly hope you're right.''

She kissed him again. ''That's for Peggy. Tell her to keep painting up a storm. I loved her last exhibition.''

Joe Marshal was at the most an inch taller than Kathy and looked even younger than she, a very polite and very worried choir boy. If only one could take charge of their marriage—for they would surely marry if he did not tell them not to— and protect them from all the mistakes.

''You were in computer work for the Army, Joe?''

''Yes, sir. Never got out of Washington for the whole first year. Simulations mostly. Lot of graph and chart work.''

''Oh?'' Hugh picked up the latest copy of *Commodity Perspectives*. ''What would you make of this chart?''

Joe glanced at it quickly. ''I'd say that you should always sell May wheat by February.''

''You never heard that before?''

''No, sir. Kathy and I haven't had time to talk about her work. It seems interesting though.''

Hugh rapidly flipped the pages. Joe's comments on soybeans, pork bellies, and plywood were as quick, as definitive, and as correct as his comments on wheat.

''Why do you folks only have two-dimensional charts, Mr. Donlon?'' He frowned, trying to puzzle it out. "You could learn a lot more from three dimensions, build weather in, for example. I don't know anything about it, of course. . . ."

Hugh realized that he had stumbled onto someone who was likely to be a charting genius, and indispensable to the firm he hoped to start.

"Kathy?" He spoke slowly. "Would you mind if your husband went to work making charts for me part-time while he finishes school?"

"Mr. Donlon, you're wonderful!"

"If our baby is a boy, we'll call him Hugh," Joe declared, dazed by relief and happiness.

"Don't you dare," Hugh laughed.

The two happy young people left his office hand in hand, as though they were leaving a rectory.

And Hugh sat slumped at his desk for a long time.

Chapter Twenty-seven
.... *1972* ....

IN APRIL SILVER fell back to its 1971 levels and speculators lost interest. Hugh learned from a phone call to Zurich that Europeans were buying silver in New York and shipping it across the Atlantic. However, the purchases were not being made on the Exchanges. Hence the low rate of activity and the sideways movement of silver prices in the market.

It was still a potential bull market, waiting for momentum. His instincts about the upswing in silver as a hedge against inflation were correct. He'd missed the last surge because he had mistaken the timing, not the basic trend.

Still, he did not jump back into the market. He would wait patiently until the time seemed right. It was impatience that had hurt him the last time around.

Silver hung for three weeks, till late April, hesitating between two dollars and ten cents and two dollars and twenty cents.

At the end of the third week, with the price at two dollars and eight cents, Hugh bought a hundred contracts for himself and his clients, a lot of money for all concerned. However, if he was right and there was a quick run-up and they could sell off at the top, his reputation as a sage would be made and the Donlon company would be on its way.

"Did you jump in today?" asked Tim in the office, now a bigger and more plush suite with separate rooms for each of the brothers and their private secretaries and a cubbyhole for Joe Marshal.

"Finally."

"Thought you would. It's going to be a quiet summer in everything else. The Russian grain projections are optimistic. No fortunes this year."

"Don't count on it."

Tim shrugged cheerfully. "I know better now than to argue with your instincts. . . . Hey, you know we have to do something about this Ben Fowler one of these days. He's never going to let up on us unless we do."

"What now?" Tim might be telling the truth and, then again, he might not.

"He's trying to block our membership in the Clearing Corp., although everyone knows we have enough money to get in. And he's after me about playing some games with deferred contracts, as though that's the kind of thing I'm into."

If the new firm was to be successful, its reputation must be above reproach. That might be difficult with Tim aboard.

"Can he make any of it stick?"

"I don't think so." Tim slyly ducked the question and glanced at Joe Marshal's work sheets. "Hey, that looks pretty; next thing you'll be moving a computer into the office here."

Joe had created a three-dimensional chart that looked like a mountain range. "Soybeans with a month of bad weather," he observed. "Look, Mr. Donlon, if you have a month of rain, soybeans sell at thirteen dollars."

"Never happen," Tim said flatly.

"We'll have to wait for the month of rain." Hugh looked at the chart. "Sure would be a disaster for Benedict the Badman, wouldn't it?"

Tim considered the chart more carefully. "I may hire me some Sioux to do a rain dance."

Hugh smiled shrewdly.

May was a fantastic month for silver. The price soared from two dollars and eight cents to two dollars and sixty-five cents. On the Friday before the Memorial Day weekend, Hugh decided that it was time for him and his clients to get out. They had made the money that his bad timing had prevented them from making earlier in the year. His mistake was canceled. He had won again and won big.

At home Liz was withdrawn and fretful. Lise, usually a healthy little girl despite her mother's excessive care, was running a slight temperature. Liz was worried that there might be no pediatrician available over the long weekend.

So she listened with little interest as he recapped the day's trading in silver.

"I don't know what you're going to do with all that money," she said. She cradled the unhappy child in her arms while her son tugged at her skirt for his rightful share of attention.

"We could use some of it to make a down payment on that house at the Lake Shore you've been wanting." It was the grand surprise he had been hoarding in hopes that it would make her smile again and give him a chance to break through the wall between them.

"I never said I wanted such a house. I don't know where you come up with such absurd ideas, Hugh. You know very well how dangerous beach houses are for children. Just the other day two children drowned on the Jersey coast."

"We would be very careful."

"How could I keep up a house over there and this terrible big place too and go to the Pastoral Institute during the summer?"

"I didn't know you were planning to go to the Institute." It was the first he had heard of it.

"Of course, I am. Or don't you want me to take interest in my own professional development? You want me to spend all my time around here with these children?"

She rocked Lise too brusquely and the child wailed again.

He clenched his hands. My God, he thought, is there nothing I can do right?

"I want you to do whatever you want to do." He tried to keep his voice even. "Certainly you can go to the Pastoral Institute. I thought you had your heart set on a place across the lake near the Fowlers'."

"Certainly not . . . Now, Brian, can't you see I'm taking care of Lise? You've had your share of time."

Hugh tried to take Brian into his own arms, but the youngster was having no part of it. He wailed for his mother as soon as Hugh picked him up.

"How many times do I have to tell you not to give in to the child that way? Put him down. I'll take care of him."

Brian rushed to his mother's arms and sniffled into silence.

"If Lise is better, might we go house hunting tomorrow morning, nothing definite . . . just look around?"

Liz was horrified. "In Memorial Day traffic? Do you want us all killed?"

"I meant in midmorning when the traffic is light."

"You can go if you want," she said in a martyr's voice. "I'll stay home with the children."

He would accept her last clear and positive signals and look for a home on the Michigan shore.

Liz was thirty-one and, despite her current slovenliness, a beautiful and gifted woman still, with a long and productive life ahead of her—if she could break out of her present malaise.

Was there anything he could do to salvage their marriage? He longed for the sweet and vulnerable young woman to whom he'd first made love in the Hyde Park apartment only a few years before.

Perhaps she was descending into a hell of her own, in a solitary confinement in which there was no room for him or anyone else.

A hell like his.

Liz was upset with herself after Hugh left. Yes, of course, she wanted the house at the lake. Then why hadn't she said yes?

Because Hugh so infuriated her with his money and success and the arrogance that money and success had given him that she couldn't resist the opportunity to put him down.

That was wrong. Their relationship was not properly synchronized. When she wanted to be friend and lover he was not home. And when he tried to pull the marriage together she was not in the mood to humor him.

Partly because he was so insufferably superior and condescending.

And mostly because when they were synchronized, her fears of his power over her returned to threaten her with the loss of her personhood if she lowered all her defenses.

She should have known it would be this way. She could have been a college president probably and a nationally known leader of the movement if he had not seduced her out of the religious life.

If only she'd understood what men were like then.

Not all men were as bad as Hugh. His brother, Tim, for example, was sensitive and sympathetic. And married to that terribly fat woman. Tim knew how to make a woman happy.

She tingled at the memory. Nothing shameful had happened. It was merely an affectionate exchange on a warm April evening. Tim wasn't a beast. Sex was not what he wanted. Merely friendship and understanding.

And none of the other Donlons would give it to him.

There were several superb lakeside homes for sale. Hugh hesitated about his decision. His sentimental memories of Lake Geneva were powerful. Yet Lake Geneva was too crowded. Maybe it was part of the past, just as was the house on Mason Avenue, now that his parents had sold it and moved into a lakefront condominium.

The old new neighborhood was no more. His parents were virtually the last to leave St. Ursula.

He would make an offer on a house next week. It would be a good investment no matter who won the presidential election—Nixon or McGovern—or what happened to the silver market.

When he drove past the Fowler place, he saw a silver Porsche parked in the driveway. Linda was there.

He parked his Mercedes behind the Porsche and rang the bell.

Linda was struggling unsuccessfuly into the halter of a bikini as she opened the door. "Oh, hi, Hugh. The folks are in Naples . . . hey, can you tie this for me? I came running . . . thanks . . . Naples, Florida, that is. Come on in. I'll make you a drink."

She was a tall girl with blond hair that fell to her incredibly narrow waist. Her face was the same model's mask that her mother wore. Although she had lost the bored sultriness of her early teens, there was still an invitation in her provocative posture, somehow a wholesome invitation.

He stepped inside.

"No, don't bother with the drink. I thought I'd take a chance . . ."

"Really, come on and stay a few minutes anyway. I'm not doing anything but catching rays. What will it be? Gin and tonic? Scotch?"

It was early afternoon but he asked for a Scotch. She smelled of suntan oil and sweat.

He drank two Scotches and she matched him. They talked of her problems at school and of her plans to study modern dance after graduation. She was an intelligent young woman, and very much interested in his opinion. She even took notes about books he recommended, after searching fretfully in the parlor for pencil and paper.

"I really should be going. . . ." He rose to leave.

"A last one for the road," she pleaded. "I'll make some coffee and sandwiches too. It's creepy here all alone."

He followed her into the kitchen, where the remains of her breakfast were scattered in the sink.

He stood behind her, put his arms around her waist, and began to kiss her back. It tasted of suntan oil. She was passive, neither resisting nor cooperating, as though she were trying to make up her mind.

He recalled the priestly love he'd once felt for her, his concern to protect her from suffering. He forced himself to release her, freeing her rapidly moving rib cage from his embrace.

She took his hands and pressed them to her firm flesh. "I really want you. I really like you."

After Mass the next morning, on the way out of church, he and Liz met Pat Cleary, assigned to the parish in the new transfers. Pat greeted them warmly. He had finished his Ph.D. in psychology and his twinkling brown eyes and friendly freckled Irish face radiated even more sympathy and understanding than in the seminary, when he had been considered the class "Going My Way" priest.

"I'll be looking forward to working with you both." He looked at Hugh. "It will be like old times."

"That will be exciting, Pat; it really will. Of course, I've got a lot of commitments and responsibilities just now. . . ."

Chapter Twenty-eight
1972

THE FALL AND winter of 1972 were so hectic on the Board of Trade that Hugh barely noticed Richard Nixon's re-election and the beginning of the Watergate investigation. The soybean crop was the largest on record and the wise traders went short, expecting prices to plummet. Then Joe Marshal's three-dimensional model became prophetic: It rained every day in September. Soybeans rotted in the fields.

The Humboldt current then changed its course, imperceptibly, carrying the anchovy schools away from the coasts where they were harvested.

The result of these two quirks of nature was a worldwide shortage of cooking oil. The prices of all three commodities took off.

There was also a worldwide shortage of wheat. The Russian harvest had been a disaster, and Russia moved quickly to purchase American wheat before the news was out. Shrewd traders, the Russians visited the various American grain export firms—Continental, Bunge, Cargill—and bought them out at basement prices, keeping secret each purchase while negotiating for the others.

The Nixon administration, pathetically eager for farm votes, quietly accepted these deals, which in effect forced American consumers to subsidize the mistakes of socialist agriculture.

At the same time, the price of silver took off, its erratic ascent made even more unstable by the volatility of the grain markets.

Seats on the Board of Trade, which had sold for thirty-five thousand dollars only a few years earlier now cost more than a hundred thousand dollars. Wealthy families, perceiving that commodities trading had become a rich man's game, bought them for troublesome sons; the old apprenticeship relations between traders and clerks and runners broke down. Marijuana and cocaine were added to the commodities that could be bought in the building, although no one suggested a futures market in them.

Hugh Donlon was a tower of strength in the days and weeks of panic in September. The more turbulent the market and the more money at stake, the more relaxed he became.

He'd studied Joe's chart carefully, and after the first three days of rain in September, he'd bought one million bushels of soybeans.

"Your friend Ben Fowler finally liquidated his soybean position," Tim said on an afternoon late in September when the rain was still falling. "Do you think Joe's charts are like voodoo dolls? What if we hint to Ben that we put a curse on him?"

"What did he quit at?" Now was the time to finish off Ben Fowler, make him a lesson to anyone who would dare cross Hugh Donlon.

"Three dollars and ninety-five cents." Tim sounded as if he were personally responsible for the rain that had caused the run-up. "He went short at three forty."

Hugh made a note on his chart and glanced at his watch. "Two million bushels . . . one million-dollar loss. Even for Ben that'll be a lot."

Tim uncrossed his legs and crossed them again. His tiny, hard eyes were bloodshot. "A lot more than that; I suspect that like many of the other old timers, he had a couple of accounts in other people's names. He could go down six mil."

Hugh tapped his ballpoint pen thoughtfully. "Can Ben take that?"

"Not for long; he's probably hoping to bounce back, but if this rain keeps up . . ." He looked out the window. The curtains of water, opaque drapes shutting out the light, were so thick you could barely see LaSalle Street. ". . . and it looks like it will, he won't do it in soybeans."

"How will he meet his calls . . . ?" Hugh clenched his fists. "Will he start dipping?"

"Into client funds? Probably. He's done it before and got away with it. A few others have too, although it's a dangerous business. What if the CEA should come in with a random audit?" Tim was watching Hugh narrowly, as he often did these days, afraid of his brother's rampaging hunger to destroy Ben Fowler.

"Not segregating client funds is the mortal sin here."

"If you're caught," Tim said. "No way of knowing for sure whether he's doing it."

"I bet I can find out."

Sex had been unimportant to Helen Fowler at the beginning of her affair with Hugh; her years in the orphanage had taught her to contain her emotions lest she get hurt. She had faked pleasure with him as she had with Ben and for the same reason—in her affection-starved life physical contact with a man was more important than pleasure.

Then Hugh had invaded the inner citadels of her body and soul and captured her completely. There were no secrets there, no place to hide, no last barrier to throw up to protect herself. With Hugh, she was thereafter always naked, always open to pain.

And unspeakably happy.

Their love affair would end someday, she knew, and life would go on to something else. Even now she saw him less often than she had in the past. Still, she would enjoy the romance for as long as it lasted and remember the sweet paralysis that possessed her whenever she heard his voice or saw his face or felt the touch of his hand.

She continued to love her husband as she always had, a quiet, passive love with little conflict and only occasional passion. Ben entered her body as if he were performing a duty, not so much to her as to his own image, the same way he entered a golf club a few Saturdays during the summer months, even though he no longer enjoyed the game and played badly.

In bed and out, he'd been a more gentle husband since his outburst at the time of the St. Jarlath's battle. He hadn't apologized for the beatings, but he hadn't repeated them either. Lavish care and generosity were Ben's rhetoric of apology and he inundated her with gifts as if he were courting her all over again.

She forgave him, telling herself that perhaps she deserved her punishment. They were fond of each other in a desultory way, like colleagues in a law office who worked at opposite desks on different legal matters. It wasn't Ben's fault that sex was a low priority in his life. So it once had been in hers and so it would surely be again. Conjugal affection with one man, passion with another—so, she supposed, did every adulteress justify her sin.

She was lying in Hugh's arms in the apartment he had rented for their meetings on the near North Side, the second floor of an elegant old two-story flat with high ceilings and long corridors. It was furnished with late-nineteenth-century antiques to match the style of the building itself—Hugh was obsessed with furniture and his impossible wife refused to share his interest. Outside the rain was still beating against the windows. Helen was exhausted and content.

"Do you have any positions in the soybean market?" he asked as they lay contentedly together.

"Not real ones; Ben has some in my name, of course; he always does that. It's his money, though."

"A lot . . . ?"

"Two million . . . two million something . . . I don't know. . . ."

"Is he worried like the rest of us?"

"Who . . . do you mean Ben? I don't think so. He says he may have to dip . . . whatever that means. It's done all the time, though, so there's nothing to worry about."

Then he loved her again, overwhelming her with sweetness.

After Helen left, Hugh changed the sheets on the bed and remade it the way he was taught to make a bed in the seminary. He waited in the apartment for two hours, reading *The Wall Street Journal* and *The New York Times* from the past several days. Then a key turned in the door.

It was Linda, wet from the rain and glorious in her excitement over the literature courses she was taking at Hugh's suggestion. He was father, mentor, confidant, and lover to this superb young woman, who idolized and adored him.

Whereas her mother was a passive lover, Linda was athletic and aggressive, not exactly the challenge Hugh needed after an hour of love earlier in the afternoon.

The rain had stopped when Hugh entered his home in Kenilworth. Liz was reading a religious book by someone named Henry Nouwen.

She seemed uninterested in both the fact and the time of his return.

"Good book?"

"Hmm . . ."

"It was another humdinger at the Board today."

"Was it?" She flipped a page.

"Ben Fowler is in deep trouble."

"Serves him right. He's a capitalist pig." All conversational subjects now seemed to demand quick and decisive moral judgments from Liz.

"He might be indicted."

She looked up for the first time from her book. "Hugh," she said, "I've told you that this is the only time I have during the day to myself. Can't you grant me a little privacy and peace?"

"Sure," he said contritely. "Sorry to interrupt."

"He's dipping all right," said Hugh Donlon, "and don't ask me how I know. I know, that's all."

"I won't ask," Tim replied. Either the wife or the daughter or both. You scare the hell out of me, brother dear. Most of the animals in our jungle don't have to hate the way you do.

They were in the office suite before the beginning of the trading day. Outside, light, perhaps even sunlight, threatened to break through the rain clouds that hovered over LaSalle Street.

"How do we do it?" Hugh was frowning.

"Simple. I make a phone call to a friend over at the CEA and drop a hint in the course of conversation . . . subtle enough so they have to think about it and not so subtle that they miss the point. They'll ruminate through the day and probably tomorrow morning show up in Fowler and Company offices with their adding machines. Tomorrow afternoon you'll receive an urgent call from the Business Practices Committee to attend a confidential meeting."

"Brutal."

"That's what we want, isn't it?"

"That's what we want."

Hugh picked up the cards with his own positions on them, shoved them into his shirt pocket, and strode from the office.

"You'd do the same thing to me if I got in the way, wouldn't you?" Tim said to the empty room.

The elderly trader squirmed uncomfortably, adjusting his yellow trading jacket. "It isn't as if Ben's the first one to do it. He's been with us a long time. He may be able to straighten himself out. Hell, which of us wouldn't be grateful for a second chance someday?"

The Business Practices Committee was meeting informally in a windowless room just off the Board of Trade Library. All they knew officially was that there was an audit underway of Fowler and Company. Unofficially they knew the whole story and were preparing a reaction for press and public.

"Sure, Mike," said a younger trader. "We all like second chances. But not when the public is watching the Board as closely as it is now. We're making a lot of money here—well, some of us are"—he corrected himself with a grin; a couple of members of the committee were disastrously short in wheat or soybeans—"and the public and the press are sniffing for scandal. Congress doesn't think the CEA is up to policing us as it is."

Hugh had remained silent till this point in the discussion.

"We don't have any choice. A year's suspension is the least we can do. I don't think we should destroy him though."

"He'll have to liquidate his company to pay off the clients. How will the man live for a year?'' protested the elderly trader. ''My God, he has a wife and a family.''

''Maybe someone can buy out the company and keep Ben on as a junior partner,'' suggested the younger trader, scratching his head thoughtfully. ''Save face for everyone, and leave Ben a little capital and a chance to trade through the firm.''

''Who'd do that?'' snorted the old man. ''Someone would have to love the exchange a hell of a lot to take on Ben.''

''There's basically nothing wrong with Ben's organization, a little old-fashioned, not up to computer technology and that sort of thing. Yet it's a good base, especially with a new and energetic management. . . . Hugh, stop me if I'm out of order. . . . I've been hearing that you and Tim might want to open a medium-size commission house. Would his kind of deal appeal to you?''

Hugh hesitated. He didn't want to seem too eager. ''I'd have to think about that. It's a funny thing, you know. Ben's firm is about the right size . . . this is not the ideal time . . . still, if there's no other way and Ben is willing . . . I'd not want to let anyone down. The Board has been very good to me in the last three years.''

It was just the right note: aware of the possibilities, not eager to sacrifice, and willing to take the chances for the common good.

The meeting broke up with everyone feeling that it had found a solution to the Ben Fowler problem.

''Tell Ben to see me'' were Hugh's last words.

He hoped the other members of the committee hadn't seen him licking his lips.

''You hinted you'd buy the SOB out?'' Tim asked his brother in disbelief the next morning. ''That's wild, Hugh, wild! I wouldn't have come up with anything that good, myself.''

''It solves a lot of problems, Tim.''

''Fowler and Donlon.'' Tim savored the name on his lips.

''Donlon, Fowler, and Donlon,'' Hugh corrected with a broad grin.

''Which Donlon is first?'' Tim asked curiously, wondering how Hugh would handle that.

''Whichever one happens to be talking.''

''Hot shit,'' said Tim. ''We're going to have one hell of a good time.''

The two Donlons went to Ben's office to settle the details. Tim assumed that his brother would be gracious and sympathetic. That's the way things were done in the club. You didn't kick a man when he was down.

''I'm not sure we can do it, Ben,'' Hugh began unceremoniously.

A muscle under Ben's eye twitched. His face was the color of his green trader's jacket. ''My God, Hugh, you must be able to do it . . . I thought we had an agreement. You're the senior partner. . . .''

Hugh shook his head sadly. ''Hard times, Ben, hard times; I can't justify the risk of my capital. You're in deeper than I thought. All those accounts in Helen's name. And Linda's.''

''I'll go under, maybe to jail.'' Ben laid his cold cigar in an ashtray in the shape of a cabin cruiser, his hand trembling so violently that the cigar rolled off like a porpoise thrown back into the ocean. "Think of my family. . . ."

"You should have thought of them when you started dipping."

"Please," Ben slobbered, "I'll do anything. I don't want to go to jail."

"That's not likely to happen; when was the last time they sent a trader to jail?
You should be able to make good on your contracts." Hugh stood up, ready to
leave Ben's opulent suite of offices.

"I can't make good. I'm finished. God in heaven, Hugh. Don't do this to
me."

Tears were running down his ugly face.

Hugh shrugged. "Make me an offer."

Ben coughed. "Why don't I—" Then a spasm of coughing.

"I don't have all day." Hugh moved toward the door.

"Full control . . ." Ben choked out the words.

"All right. You've got yourself a deal. Work out the details with our lawyers.
Today."

"What was the name of that priest at St. Jarlath's?" Tim asked as they rode
down the elevator to their own offices.

"Gus Sullivan. Why?"

"Are you going after him now?"

There was an odd light in Hugh's eyes. Disappointment.

"I can't. He's dead."

Chapter Twenty-nine
···································· *1973* ····································

ON A SUNDAY evening in January Hugh and Liz were watching the late TV
news. The children were in bed and Liz was trying to read the new Hans Küng
book on papal infallibility, a subject that seemed to Hugh to be as remote from
his world as a planet in another galaxy.

Suddenly Maria was on the screen.

"What is the first thing you are going to do when Captain McLain comes
home, Mrs. McLain?" asked the reporter.

Maria, trim and happy in a blue knit dress that matched her eyes, was standing
between two neat and handsome kids in their early teens, with a three-year-old
child in her arms.

"First thing I'll make my own original lasagna recipe and then I'll eat at least
half of it."

"Is that the captain's favorite dish, Mrs. McLain?"

Mock surprise. "Gosh, I don't know. It's my favorite dish, though, and I'm
going to celebrate. Right, guys?"

"Right!" shouted the teen-agers, obviously enjoying the limelight as much as
their mother.

"That woman ought to be ashamed," snapped Liz, "making an exhibition of
herself and her family over a war criminal. She should be confessing her family's
guilt instead of planning a celebration."

"Maybe she doesn't think he's a war criminal."

"Of course, he's a war criminal. He's killed innocent children. Doesn't that
make him a criminal?"

Hugh thought of the tall, gentle naval officer he had met many years before.

"Maybe he thinks he was protecting innocent children from the Vietcong."

"Romantic sentimentalism. The Vietcong are the People. They don't kill innocent women and children but only enemies of the People and then only when they have to."

Hugh gave up the argument.

Tom and Peg Donlon saw the news program about the POWs' families.

"Don't think about it, Peggy," he said firmly. "It was not God's will."

"Can you imagine Hugh living such a frantic, pointless life with Maria his wife instead of Liz?"

"No," he said, "I can't." There wouldn't be any love affairs with a wife like Maria.

Not twice at any rate.

"It was not to be, I suppose. I don't enjoy the thought of explaining to God my part in it. I was so convinced he had a vocation . . . what a fool. . . ."

"Don't be harsh on yourself, Peg. Maybe he did have a vocation. Maybe he did all the good God wanted as a priest and is now doing good at the Board of Trade."

Peggy did not reply.

Hugh celebrated his fortieth birthday by taking his father to lunch at the Trader's Inn, across from the Board of Trade. The formal party would be at his parents' condo on Sunday.

"Liz will be able to come?" his father asked anxiously. "The Wentworths are flying in from Ireland the night before."

Like everyone else, the judge was in awe of Hugh. He chose his words very carefully, so as not to touch his son's hairtrigger temper.

"Yes, Mom said they were. It'll be great to see them again. I imagine I won't recognize the kids. Marge sure lucked out, didn't she?"

I wanted my *enemies* to be afraid of me, not my family.

"Oh, yes." His father wiped his lips discreetly with a napkin. "And Liz will be at the party Sunday?"

"I think so, if Brian and Lise are all right. We've had a bad winter of colds and flu. You know how seriously she takes her responsibilities as a mother."

There was a pause. His father cleared his throat as if he were preparing to deliver an opinion from the bench.

"I was daydreaming as I came down here in the cab. You were born on Good Friday in 1933; the banks were beginning to reopen; we were singing 'Happy Days Are Here Again,' though to be more precise we were really whistling it in the dark. Roosevelt's voice was magic on the radio. Hitler had come to power in Germany. If anyone had told me that day, when my only concerns were your health and your mother's survival, the events that would transpire in these four decades, I would have thought them mad."

"Did you have any plans for me that first day? I mean after you knew that Mom would be all right?"

His father hesitated ever so slightly. "No . . . none at all."
So I was programmed for the priesthood from the start.

After lunch they rode up to the coolly modern new offices of Donlon, Fowler, and Donlon.

A surprise party was awaiting him. The judge had distracted him at lunch while his mother arranged the cake and champagne and supervised the hanging of the bunting and the balloons in their new offices.

Hugh's new employees, friends from the floor, a few relatives, and a lot of the runners and clerks sang a lusty "Happy Birthday" when he and the judge walked in.

His mother stood next to Kathy Marshal while he cut the cake. Kathy was slim and starry-eyed, and glowing after the birth of little Joseph Hugh.

Liz was not present. She had been invited, but of course, Hugh told himself, she'd turned it down, damning the whole enterprise as "irrelevant."

Poor old Ben wandered around like a lost sheep, out of place now in what until only a few days before had been his suite. It wouldn't be long before he went to Florida to stay, it appeared.

Ben Fowler's head on a platter—that's my fortieth birthday present, Hugh mused. And Ben Fowler's wife on a king-size bed. He looked at Helen and then at her daughter. You had to admit it, he thought—they both had class.

After Hugh's family and friends had gone, one of the younger traders offered Hugh a sniff of coke.

He left for the apartment and his rendezvous with Helen in a glorious daze.

Her cry of pain shocked him out of his daze. He pulled away from her, his potency gone, his whole body quaking as though he had been seized by sudden high fever.

"I'm sorry, Helen, my God, I'm sorry . . . the damn cocaine . . ." he moaned, horrified at the rivulet of blood running down her breast. "I didn't mean to hurt you."

Helen put her arm around his waist and caressed him maternally. "You're a violent man, Hugh," she said sadly. "A woman who loves you knows she runs the risk. . . ."

"Forgive me," he pleaded.

She laughed cheerfully. "Of course, I forgive you."

For forty years he had believed that men should protect women, the way his father had protected Peggy. And now he had celebrated his fortieth birthday by inflicting pain on a woman. And for all his shock and dismay, he'd enjoyed it.

Gently and carefully she reawakened his passion and they made tender, affectionate love. He caressed and soothed her, assuring her that he never would hurt her again. Then he covered her violated body with kisses as she purred complacently.

Yet as he rode home on the train that evening he knew that Monsignor Martin's demons must be celebrating.

Exultation in his power to hurt her and heal her tasted like rare white wine. Some of the items in his collection were designed to be hurt and then to be healed so they could be hurt again.

He shivered.

Like silver on a day of the bears, he was locked down.
At the bottom of the pit.

When the housekeeper brought word to the supper table that the visitor was Hugh Donlon, Pat Cleary left the table and went to the rectory parlor.
Hugh poured out his story.
"You always were one for the spectacular, weren't you, Hugh?" Pat said when Hugh had finished the long story of the love affairs of the last two years.
"Or the grotesque."
Pat sighed. "What do you think would happen to the adultery rate if the Church announced that it was only a venial sin?"
Hugh was startled. "I imagine it would hardly change at all."
"Right, sin morality doesn't work. I'm not saying you haven't sinned. You'll understand, however, only when you find what you're looking for."
"Which is . . . ?" he asked.
Pat Cleary seemed surprised. "God . . . what else?"

Chapter Thirty
1973

FROM JUNE TO August of 1973 the price of silver was frozen by government edict. Hugh was restless and bored. The exquisite joy of revenge had faded quickly. Ben Fowler was an unimportant nuisance, hardly worth the trouble. And there were no new enemies to humiliate.

He lost Linda, who told him bluntly, "I like you a lot, Hugh, but I have a boyfriend at school who wants to marry me and he's old-fashioned. He says we should try to be chaste till we're married. If I can't sleep with him, I shouldn't sleep with you."

She called him several times a month to ask advice on courses and papers and to share her excited and sometimes intelligent literary insights. He was no longer a lover to his enemy's daughter; only a mentor, a tamed dirty old man.

So old in fact that his memories of what she was like in bed were quickly reduced to a single word—exhausting.

Exhibit closed because of costly upkeep.

He dreamed often that he was trading in a new pit, not in silver or soybeans, but in ice, something very Dante's seventh circle—a pit formed by loneliness and fear and hatred.

He wanted to escape from the pit before he was frozen into it—ascend back through hell. But he was not yet ready to pay the price.

He came home early one evening to find a forceful Polish-American matron who would not admit him to the house. She was the baby-sitter, hired for two evenings and three days a week. "Missus" said nothing about anyone coming home. His children confirmed his identity, somewhat reluctantly, before she called the police.

"Missus" had joined a Winnetka consciousness-raising group. "I'm sick of being an unpaid day-care center for you. I'm not going to do it anymore."

With a severe short haircut and a trim brown very businesslike suit, Liz looked like a double agent of the KGB.

"I'm delighted that you've found interests outside the house, Liz," Hugh said. "We have the money for all the help you need. I hope the group works out for you."

"Men think we're supposed to spend our lives with diapers, fevers, running noses, and temper tantrums. It's time we confronted them with their own obligations to child rearing."

Impulsively Hugh tried an idea he'd been mulling over a long time. "Do you think we might also go into family therapy? There are some things in our own relationship that we might be able to straighten out."

She blew up. "I show the first signs of independence since we've been married and you want to drag me off to a shrink to force me back into line."

She stormed out of the parlor, leaving Hugh to drive the baby-sitter to her bus.

Despite the hectic pace of the market, Hugh would sneak home early several afternoons a week to play with his children while they were in charge of the baby-sitter. Mostly he told them stories like the ones he told the kids at St. Jarlath's. Maxie the Mad Monk and his friends Erik the Anchorite, Warren the Weird War Lord, and Winnie the Wicked Witch, were reborn. Brian loved the stories and so did Lise when Hugh learned how to adjust them to her age.

Liz caught him one afternoon and exploded that he was interfering with their naps. The baby-sitter was fired and replaced by a new one who made sure the children were protected from their father.

Hugh felt guilty. Maybe he was keeping them from their needed rest. And maybe Liz was right that the stories were scaring them.

So he withdrew, somewhat shamefaced, from one more failure with his children.

Liz was afraid of Hugh that summer, not of the power over her that pleasure and intimacy might give him, but of the unsuppressed rage hiding behind his phony protests of concern and support. Instead of his usual clumsy and hypocritical attempts to take the kids away from her, he now frightened Brian with ridiculous and terrifying stories. Brian and Lise not only disliked him, which made sense; they were afraid of him too.

He's losing his mind, she thought. How else to explain his crazy notion that we need marriage counseling.

There's nothing wrong with me. He knows that. He's the one who needs help. He should see the shrink.

The consciousness-raising group and her new career at St. Rock's were an escape from his anger. In a year or two, when she was in full possession of her own self, there would still be time for her to save him.

Hugh went to dinner at the Marshals' new home. Liz had declined to accompany him because the invitation was "trivial."

Joe and Kathy lived in the small upper story of a brick two-flat a block off Milwaukee Avenue in Jefferson Park, impeccably neat and spotlessly clean, if already overcrowded with furniture.

The sleeping baby was proudly presented, a pleasant-faced replica of his father. He nestled quietly in Hugh's arms, more at ease there than were his own children.

"Nothing wakes him up, Mr. Donlon," Joe said. "You don't have to whisper. I think he has the nerves of a trader."

"We want you to baptize Joe Hughie, Mr. Donlon," Kathy said as she put his coffee cup in front of him after dinner. "You're our priest and we want you to be his priest."

There was a sharp and determined tilt to her ample jaw and an appealing plea in her gray eyes.

"Please. . . ."

"I can't do it, Kathy. I'm not an active priest anymore."

"Kathyrn," her husband said gently, "we ought to respect Mr. Donlon's feelings."

"Of course. . . . I'm sorry. I'm being selfish."

The next day at the end of the trading session, Hugh's secretary said that a Monsignor Martin wanted to see him.

Monsignor Martin was the last man in the world he wanted to see.

Looking out the wndows of the boardroom, he saw Xav Martin, white-haired and dapper, the perfect, neatly groomed, collegial postconciliar pastor. After serving as a wise and flexible rector at Mundelein through a tumultuous transition to the new Order, Xav had been recently rewarded with the pastorate of St. Mark's. He was Jack Howard's new boss.

"Happy, Hugh?"

"Happy enough." He was also the pastor of Maria's parish. Would he remember her from the movie at Lake Geneva a decade and a half and more ago? Would he say anything about her?

"Certainly successful enough. More challenge here than in the priesthood?"

Should he tell Xav that his prophecy had come true? Perhaps now was the time to begin his climb out of hell.

"A certain kind of challenge. You never will be able to accept any of your students' leaving the priesthood, will you, Xav?"

The handsome priest sighed. "I know it's old-fashioned of me, but no, not really. If you did it, Hugh, it was the right thing for you, I don't question that. Yet . . . somehow . . . it's not . . . it's odd your not being in the active ministry. I can't quite adjust to you trading in pork bellies and T bills."

Xav apparently didn't remember his prediction. He too was uneasy in the presence of the great man. My God, what have I done?

"And silver, don't forget the silver. . . ."

"I don't."

"More change than you ever expected when you smuggled in the uncut paperbound books of the French theologians in the old days?" Hugh tried to conjure up nostalgic memories.

The monsignor wanted no part of nostalgia.

"Maybe . . . well, that's not why I barged in here without an appointment. The word is that you don't answer phone calls from priests, so Sean told me to turn up on your doorstep without a warning."

"Sean? What does our new auxiliary bishop want of me?"

Xav Martin turned nervously in his chair, crossing and uncrossing carefully creased tailor-made legs. "He's setting up a board of financial advisers to make recommendations about diocesan investment. He wants to know if you'd accept an appointment on that board.''

Would Maria be on such a board? Would she be afraid of him too? No, of course, she wouldn't be on it; she would have left the bank and moved away to be with her husband again.

"An ex-priest? What's the matter with Cronin?"

"He says you're the best commodity man of your generation. The silver king."

"Tell him thanks but no thanks. I have not forgiven the Catholic Church for St. Jarlath's and I never will."

Xav Martin was obviously relieved to be off the hook. "May I tell him that you'll consider the request again in a few years?"

"Fine, if that satisfies him."

There was sadness in Monsignor Martin's black eyes as he said good-bye. Perhaps he and the bishop and Jack Howard had huddled about the Donlon problem. They wanted to help.

But Hugh was not ready to accept help.

From the Church or anyone else.

Chapter Thirty-one
1973

ON THE FEAST of Yom Kippur Anwar Sadat's armies poured across the Suez Canal without warning. The unprepared Israeli defenders were overwhelmed. Simultaneously, Syrian tanks pushed almost to the rim of the Golan and threatened for thirty-six hours to swarm down into the plains of Galilee. Israel rallied and pushed her enemies back. The Syrian tanks were smashed and an Egyptian army was trapped in the Sinai.

Sadat was able to claim victory, and the Arab oil-producing states imposed an embargo on the United States. OPEC, a Venezuelan cabinet minister's pipedream, suddenly emerged as the most dangerous cartel in human history and the price of petroleum soared.

President Nixon was ill-equipped to deal with these national and international crises because the net of the various Watergate investigations was slowly tightening around his presidency.

On the Board of Trade the Yom Kippur War, the oil embargo, and the long lines at the gas stations created a sensation almost as dramatic as did the soybean crises of the previous year.

Silver began a rise that was to peak at six dollars by the end of the year; gold, grain, government paper all became hot items. As usual, bad news for others meant good news on the exchange. Fortunes were made, unmade, and then made again in the space of a few riotous weeks.

Hugh Donlon amassed more money than he would have dreamed possible. There were no other goals in his life. He gave up his collection of women. He cut himself off from family and friends as best he could.

He enjoyed feeling sorry for himself in his aloneness.

By the end of October he had more client accounts than he wanted. Ben Fowler, restless and unhappy because he was barred from the floor, continued to pace the boardroom of Donlon et al—as the firm was now called—like a father awaiting the birth of a child, his face now permanently gray, his green jacket now permanently dirty, and his cough sounding like a ruler rasping against a blackboard.

One day at the end of October, Hugh was to have lunch with his mother and inspect the watercolors she'd done during her two-month stay with Marge and Liam in the west of Ireland.

Hugh suggested Crickets in the refurbished Tremont Hotel on Chestnut Street. Although it was an insufferably pretentious place, it was far from the bustle of LaSalle Street, which overwhelmed her, and fairly convenient to the new condo on the lake.

Lunch with Peggy, glowing and happy after her trip to Ireland, was blessedly cheerful. There was at least one woman left in the world with whom he could relax.

Her watercolors were a misty green, the Ireland of dreams and visions and gentle ghosts.

Yet Peggy would not have been Peggy if she hadn't provided one short interlude of worry. Hugh explained to her how he had made more money in the previous three weeks than his father, who was reasonably well paid, would make in ten years.

"Do you do anything dishonest, Hugh?" she asked when he was finished.

"No," he said promptly. "Some traders come close to the edge of the law and a few wander over the edge. I don't even come close; I was raised by a strict judge and a conscientious Irish mother . . ."

Peg knew something was wrong and wanted to help. How could he explain that his problem did not fit into her clear-cut moral categories.

". . . who worries too much?" She leaned across the table and kissed him.

"I'm okay, Mom. I'm not breaking any commandments on the trading floor."

"A good Irish mother always worries." Peggy winked at him, something she'd never done before, and toasted him with the expensive Burgundy he'd bought at her suggestion.

Hugh had kept his resolution to avoid Helen until Christmastime, shaken as he was by Pat Cleary's suggestion that his urge to hurt her might be in some way connected with unacknowledged anger toward his mother, of whom Helen reminded him physically.

On Christmas Eve in early afternoon, she phoned him at home, for the first time. "Ben's at Old Orchard doing some last-minute shopping. Could you come over for an hour or so?" No mention of the weeks during which he had not said a word to her.

He told Liz, who was correcting papers, that he'd be out doing some last-minute shopping.

"Suit yourself," she said indifferently.

He parked the car two blocks away from the house and walked the remaining distance, his feet crunching on the newly fallen snow, his face stinging from the winter wind blowing off the lake, his heart beating rapidly.

Helen was clad in jeans and a sweat shirt, her hair was disordered and she wore no makeup. Her forty-four years showed, but they made her somehow even more desirable. Her lips were warm and soft.

"You're a disease, Hugh," she said. His hands slipped underneath her shirt, touching her breasts lightly. She winced with pleasure. "I don't ever want to be cured. . . . Not here: Ben or Linda might come. There's a room in the basement."

She led the way to the basement. The pine-paneled bedroom was steeped in a pungent North Woods smell. It was next to their elaborate recreation room filled with pinball machines and a pool table. Next to the furnace as well, the room was as hot as a summer beach.

Soon both their bodies were covered with sweat.

Hugh loved her slowly, in a mood of half-sad, half-sweet nostalgia, a mood that seemed to match her own. Their slippery bodies combined easily and naturally and remained joined, as though glued, long after their passions were spent.

When they were finished, Helen curled up at the end of the bed, her sweat shirt protectively at her loins, and lit a cigarette.

"That was different, Hugh," she said thoughtfully, her eyes examining his face in a mixture of curiosity and bewilderment.

"Was it?"

She exhaled smoke. "Christmas spirit?"

"Would you believe me if I said love?"

She smiled affectionately, a mother who has caught her son in a harmless lie. She touched his chest gently. "You're terribly vulnerable, Hugh." She leaned toward him, her breasts brushing his chest. "But you don't love me enough to let me live with you where you hurt."

A moment of delicious fear; a woman living with you where you hurt.

"Ben will be home soon," he said wearily.

Reluctantly she snubbed out her cigarette, dried herself with her sweat shirt, and pulled on her panties and slacks, routine movements of such natural and unself-conscious grace that he was almost hypnotized by their rhythm.

"Something wrong?" she asked lightly as she fastened her black bra.

"You still wouldn't believe me," he said sadly. "I don't blame you."

She kissed him briefly. "But it's nice of you to say it. . . . Come on, get dressed. I have some presents to wrap."

He pulled himself together for a return to the surface and followed her as she led the way up the stairs, sweat shirt folded over her arm.

At the top of the stairs she pulled the sweat shirt over her head and pushed the door open.

Hugh would later tell himself that a sweat shirt donned a moment too late and a hint of black lace caused the tragedy, but he knew better.

She screamed as if she'd been stabbed.

Ben Fowler stood next to the Christmas tree, cigar in hand, his face a purple mask of triumph. He raised the cigar hand to identify the adulterers to the world, his lips moving as the accusing words jammed his mouth.

But no words came out. A spasm of coughing, accompanied by an ugly retching rumble, seized him and twisted his body into a parody of orgasmic delight. The mask on his face turned dull white and then darker purple.

He stumbled forward, swayed to regain his balance, then toppled sideways to the floor, knocking down the Christmas tree as he fell.

Hugh pushed around her. Fowler's body was spread-eagled under the tree and surrounded by Christmas gifts. His face was decorated with evergreen and tinsel and his accusing right hand, still brandishing the cigar, had scattered the pieces of the Christmas crèche and smashed to bits the manger and the little figure within it.

Ben Fowler hung between life and death in the Intensive Care Unit of Evanston Hospital till the first week of January and then slowly returned to the ranks of the living.

The doctor said that if Helen had not come downstairs to answer the door when Hugh Donlon rang to leave Christmas presents, Fowler would surely have died.

"You've taken everything away from him, haven't you, Hugh?" Helen said to him as they waited in the hospital corridor on New Year's Day. "His wife, his daughter, his business, maybe even his life? You play for keeps, don't you?"

She looked haggard, old. Her shoulders were slumped despondently and her voice wavered near hysteria.

"Oh, yes, I know about Linda. She told me on Christmas Day. She doesn't know about me. You made your Playboy fantasy come true, didn't you? Was it good?"

"That's not altogether fair," he pleaded.

"When have you been fair?" she fired back at him. "You never gave a damn about me. I was a means of wreaking your terrible revenge."

The look of death on Ben Fowler's face and the trail of spittle on his chin were scorched into Hugh's brain, a fierce warning of his own mortality. He hadn't thought to give Ben absolution. He wasn't a priest at the side of a sick man. Rather, he was just a guilty lover who had escaped again.

"You wouldn't hurt her physically again, but you didn't mind hurting her psychologically?" Pat Cleary said, once more dragged away from his supper table.

"Neither one of us had any illusions."

"Bologna, not to use more scatological language. . . . Tell me, Hugh, have there been any times in your life when you felt free of all these burdens you carry around and that force you into behavior that hurts you and others?"

"Burdens?"

"You know what I mean," Pat said imperiously.

"Well, when I used to sail on the *Pegeen* at Lake Geneva . . . Sometimes it was almost like a religious experience."

"And you sold the boat? Typical. Any memories of it?"

"Some dreams occasionally," he said cautiously, thinking that he had never before been fully aware of the *Pegeen* dreams in his waking hours. "They're good some of the time; nightmares other times. . . ."

"Always had those moments of peace when you were sailing along?"

The tone of Pat's voice said that he assumed the answer would be yes. Hugh would prove him wrong.

"A couple of times with Maria."

Pat jumped from his chair. "That woman we met at the concert? Were you in love with her too?"

"Summer infatuation," he murmured, wishing he hadn't mentioned her . . . and that Pat hadn't remembered the meeting.

"And she loved you too. Why?"

"I don't know." He was lying. He remembered her saying that he was beautiful as if the words had been spoken only yesterday.

"You're a lousy liar. Why did you give her up?"

"Because I had a vocation . . . thought I had a vocation."

Cleary leaned over the desk till his face was only a few inches away. "Even if you hadn't been in the seminary, you'd have run from that one. She was a threat to everything you think you are. . . ."

He saw or felt the sweet, scary light that sometimes was associated with memories of Maria.

"You're wrong, Pat," he insisted, slamming a door shut again.

Pat slumped back into his chair. "You're full of shit, Hugh."

"I'm sorry," he sighed.

"Tell that to the Old Fella," Pat said, apparently in no mood to continue.

"He's not listening to me . . . maybe not to anyone."

"I'm not interested in your theological problems, Hugh. My guess is that you're finished with your era of keeping women at bay by killing them with kindness and pleasure."

"I hope so," he said fervently.

"Maybe, but women are only human. In the next phase, I think you're going to cut yourself off from everyone, man, woman, and child—everyone."

"Why would I do that?" Hugh felt his stomach lurch.

"Because you're still running," Cleary said, shaking his head. "Down the nights and down the years."

Chapter Thirty-two
1974

"YOU AND LIZ," Pat Cleary said as he sank his putt on the fourteenth green, "should go away on a long vacation. Someplace in the South Pacific . . . and start over again."

"It won't help the basic problems." Hugh missed his putt by an inch. Damn, he was out of condition.

His sins had stopped. The monster within was tamed, temporarily. He was faithful to his wife, forgiving of his enemies, considerate to his friends, devoted to his parents.

He was trying to spend more time with his children, though Liz insisted that he made them nervous.

"Who's talking about basic problems?" Pat removed his orange golf hat, wiped his brown hair, and put the hat back on. "It'll give you a new lease on life, away from the kids, the firm, the family, the memories of the past. Isn't that enough?"

Hugh realized that there were two ways of looking at his life and it all depended on the point of view.

To an outsider it would seem that Hugh had every reason to be happy. The new firm was a huge success. Hugh and Les Rosenthal, cautious allies because they were too smart to be enemies, were the most powerful men at the exchange. And Hugh was now nationally famous as well. As a highly respected member of the Trilateral Commission, he'd been asked by the State Department to represent the United States at a GATT meeting in Bangkok, and was often in Washington on consultation. In short, he'd achieved everything he wanted when he first rode on the South Shore Railroad with a knot in his stomach and lust in his heart to do battle with the trading floor.

His wife was attractive-looking and his children seemingly well-behaved. What more could a man want out of life?

But it was all a sham.

The marriage had settled down into a grim containment. The anger was over and so was the hope. Liz's contract at St. Rock's was not renewed, because of conflicts with both the pastor and the parents. She dropped out of the consciousness group. The army of mothers' helpers and baby-sitters remained, although the personnel constantly changed because Liz fought with them so frequently—which, he supposed, was much better than her fighting with him.

Hugh no longer knew what she did during the day, except that in the summer she went with the children to the Lake Shore house. Ironically, she and Helen had become fast friends, part of a group of matrons who sipped more than enough martinis in late afternoon and early evening on the lakeside verandas of their homes.

He and Liz made love occasionally, sometimes at her behest. At those times, he tried to make the union of bodies memorable, faintly hoping that some new flame might be kindled.

But his skills as a lover had deserted him. The results were mildly satisfying for both of them, but did not begin to approach the ecstasy out of which a new love might emerge. Like everything else in their marriage, their sex life had settled into a routine of modest expectations and modest involvements.

"You think that if Liz and I go away together we will fall in love again? We might just as well fight."

"Either would be an improvement."

"We need family therapy, not a vacation." He dubbed his drive.

"A vacation could be a first step." Pat's drive was perfect, 250 yards right down the center of the fairway.

"Liz won't be interested."

After the golf game Hugh found Liz and Helen, both slightly tipsy from the martini pitcher on the table in front of them, lolling on the porch of the Donlon house overlooking Lake Michigan. Helen's greeting kiss was light and sisterly, as though there was no history of passion between them.

Her mouth smelled faintly of vermouth. "Looks like you lost again," she said, faintly amused. "I was just showing Liz the pictures of Linda's baby. Looks like her father, I think."

Hugh agreed as he kissed his wife. No difference at all between the two kisses. Hesitantly, he offered Pat's suggestion about the need for a long vacation from his job.

"Wonderful idea." Liz was ecstatic. "I was telling Helen this afternoon— wasn't I, darling?—that I need to get away from everything. I know just the place—Corfu. The books say that late September is the best time of the year to go to Greece."

She'd been reading books about a vacation.

So Hugh found that he was going to Corfu, after a stop in London, and that once more he had misunderstood his wife's moods.

They spent a week in New York before flying to London. It was the best week of their marriage since their summer trip to New England years before. Liz was Elizabeth Ann again, happy, wide-eyed, enthusiastic, affectionate. The skyline of the Big Apple blotted out all the anger of the years. Pat Cleary was right. You could begin again.

They were walking down Fifth Avenue after lunch at the Four Seasons. Hugh stopped, took Liz's arms in his hands, and said, "You don't mind a profession of love on Fifth Avenue, do you?"

Her pretty blue eyes sparkled. "I'd enjoy every second of it."

"There've been good times and bad times, Liz; a week like this cancels out a lot of bad times."

He realized he'd said the same thing in Maine. Déjà vu?

"Let's say a prayer in St. Patrick's," Liz said. "God won't mind our hugging in there."

So they climbed the steps to the great gray Gothic monument. Inside, Liz was a demure, mystical nun again, kneeling erectly with head bowed, in deep communion with the Deity.

God was out to lunch for Hugh. After Ben's heart attack, he'd tried to pray. The words came easily enough, but no one seemed to be listening. It was as if God had tired of waiting for Hugh Donlon to rediscover Him and was busy on other matters when the affluent Mr. Donlon came to call.

So it was in St. Patrick's too.

"Help me, help her, please, dear God, help us. Forgive me for running out on You in the priesthood. I tried. I'm still trying. So far, my best hasn't been good enough. Give me the strength and the courage to do better."

That night after the theater, Liz insisted they call his parents to tell them how well the vacation was going.

"If the rest of the trip is like New York," Liz bubbled to an astonished Peggy, "we might stay away for a year."

The rest of the trip was not like New York. Their reborn and revitalized marriage was done in by the jet lag. As soon as they checked into the Grosvenor House, Liz collapsed into bed with a migraine and announced that she was tired of traveling.

Hugh pleaded for a few days grace to give the lag time to work out of her system. Liz replied that she didn't like the London rain, the way the English talked, or the condescension of the hotel help, and that the sooner they escaped from London the better.

Marge and Liam flew over from Shannon for dinner in the gracious old dining room of the Connaught. Liz refused to stir from her bed.

"Too bad the gel is under the weather," Liam clucked sympathetically as he destroyed a large hunk of Yorkshire pudding. "Fine food at this place."

"When are you going to live for yourself and not for others?" Marge demanded.

"We all should live for others, unless we want to have selfish and narrow lives," Hugh replied, conscious that Marge seemed to draw from him the same pious clichés that grated at Lake Geneva when she was chasing Joe Delaney.

"You became a priest for Mom, so you could take care of God, and a trader for Dad, so you could take care of Tim, and a husband for Liz, so you could take care of her baby. I don't think you wanted to do any of those things."

"Strong words." Liam drained his glass of claret. "It's Hugh's life."

"I know it's his life, darling; that's my point. Hugh's living other people's commitments, not his own. And besides"—she turned to her brother—"you once promised me, Hugh, that you would never forget how to laugh at yourself. When was the last time you did that?"

Hugh couldn't remember.

The next day he visited the London Metals Exchange. Dressed in bowlers and morning suits, LME traders worked for only five-minute "rings," or "fixings," each morning and afternoon. Not unreasonably, they assumed they could do what Americans did in the final minute of a session without the rest of the session. They also were burdened with much less exchange regulation. There were no limits to the positions a trader might take and no limits to the rise and fall of daily prices.

"Why are you so relaxed about regulations?" Hugh asked one trader.

"Actually, old chap, we think you Americans are rather uptight about limits and that sort of thing. Do you think it might be your puritanism?"

"Not among the Irish. They've never been puritanical about money, only sex."

"I shouldn't have thought the Irish would have the temperament for successful trading."

"There's one man from a family of Irish policemen who made more than twenty million dollars in a month."

"Really? I shouldn't imagine that he managed to save much of it."

"Practically all of it," Hugh said. "Invested it in natural gas reserves."

They attended a black-tie dinner in Hugh's honor at the Grosvenor House that night. Liz, in an off-the-shoulder blue net gown, was convincingly beautiful. Her jet lag forgotten, she was the center of attention and appeared to delight in it. She made small talk with the traders and their wives, and many of the men frankly admitted they envied Hugh such a lovely and intelligent wife.

When it came to commodities, however, the London men were given to understatement in the same way that Chicago traders were given to overstatement. Their opinion seemed to be that the metal markets would go up if they didn't go down. Or possibly the other way around.

They didn't know any more about it than Hugh did, even though they sounded far more sophisticated and experienced. The tones of bullshit were different around the world, but the message was the same. We Chicago Irish are better at it than anyone else, Hugh thought, because we can do it in any language.

"I don't see how you can stand conversation as dull as that," Liz complained as she sank into bed. "Can there be any subject more boring than precious metals?"

"It's a matter of perspective, Liz; they'd find religious education dull."

"I don't make you go to religious education meetings," she sniffed.

He'd wanted to embrace her and recapture the magic of the Big Apple. But tonight, clearly, was not the night to try.

Corfu might be his last chance.

Chapter Thirty-three
1974

CORFU WAS THE subtropical paradise Liz had promised it would be, an island covered with silvery olive trees, stately cypresses, and sturdy evergreens. Multicolored pastel mountain towns perched precariously on verdant hillsides; steep cliffs, crystal-clear blue lagoons, the glass-smooth waters of the Ionian Sea, and the gentle surf of the Adriatic made Corfu seem precisely the right place for Ulysses to wash ashore as, according to local legend, he did, for his rendezvous with the white-armed (as she called herself) Nausikaa.

The Corfu Hilton was in the hamlet of Kanoni, a few miles south of Corfu town on a peninsula overlooking one shining white Greek Orthodox monastery at its end and another on an island in the sea beyond. The sun rose over the mountains of Albania in the morning, hovered over the placid Ionian during the day, and sank contentedly behind the mountains of the island in the evening, changing the olive trees from silver to gold. Hugh felt as if he were in paradise.

Liz, on the other hand, complained bitterly about the noise from the nearby airport and about the slovenly service of the Corfiote staff at the hotel, who were very pleasant but somewhat indifferent to the demands of their mostly American and German patrons.

Hugh reveled in the warm waters of the Ionian and marveled at the caïques with their high stern rudders that lazily sliced the waves off their beach.

Liz complained about the uncomfortable beds and the pebbles and rocks on the beach.

Yet the soothing charms of this magic island were not entirely lost on her either. One day they drove across the island to Paleokastritsa, the seven lagoons of which the nineteenth-century British governor was so fond that he built the best highway on the island in order that he and his native wife could ride there frequently. Liz was enthralled by the beauty and mystery of the Adriatic, as precious and timeless, it seemed to her, as a piece of ancient Egyptian lapis lazuli. "I wish I could stay there till the end of time,"she said.

Indeed, Corfu brought out to the point of caricature the ambiguities in her tormented soul. One moment she was sweet, affectionate, and wide-eyed with wonder, and the next the inflexible ideologue, ethnocentric and judgmental, contemptuous of the slovenliness of the Corfiote people and the squalor of their cheap concrete tourist hotels.

Hugh wanted to help her. Yet, unable to help himself, he did not know how to help his wife, save with the mixture of patience and kindness, duty and responsibility, that had characterized their whole marriage and that patently did not work.

The morning after their trip across the island, Hugh awoke as the sky was turning gray. Liz, in a thin nightgown, stood in the open door to their balcony, watching the quiet Ionian.

He slipped out of bed and put his arm around her. Her upper arms and shoulders were covered with goose bumps, though it was not cold.

"Do you want a robe?" he asked softly.

She shook her head in a negative response. Then he saw the tears falling softly down her face.

"I don't know what demons are fighting inside of you," he said cautiously. "I want to help if I can."

She leaned her head against his shoulder. "If only you could."

"Can you give them a name?"

Again the negative shake of the head and now silent sobs.

"Can I do anything?"

No response.

"Will you come back to bed and let me keep you warm?"

She nodded agreement and leaned on him for support as she walked back toward the bed.

"Do you want me to make love to you or just hold you tight?"

"Just hold me."

After Hugh slipped out of the room to take the bus into town to shop for souvenirs and gifts for the children, Liz showered, put on her bathrobe, and ordered breakfast on the balcony. As she peeled an orange and watched the water skiers cavort on the Ionian Sea, she resolved again to organize her life. Hugh was trying hard to save the trip. But, finally, he could not give up his male chauvinism. She and the children were not human beings; they were burdens, responsibilities, obligations. Whatever he did for them was what he was obliged to do. Even the trip had been an obligation, a responsibility imposed by a well-meaning Pat Cleary.

That was the way Hugh was. If something wasn't an obligation, he couldn't do it.

Instead of a personality, he was a collection of obligations.

He needed her help more than she needed his.

What good did it do for a woman to be on the receiving end of tenderness when she realized that the tenderness was someone's fulfillment of a rule?

Maybe he got some points for trying. But not for realism. She was the more realistic of the two.

She knew that their efforts would always be a waste of time.

With a guilty conscience and a sense of his own incompetency, Hugh rode into Corfu town on the public bus, which lurched from Kanoni to the esplanade at the edge of the harbor every half hour.

Cream-colored buildings, tiny domed churches, arched balconies, narrow streets, stairway sidewalks, pushing crowds, noisy tourists, handsome men, and not-so-handsome women—Corfu town was part Greek and part Italian, revealing both its Greek ethnic origins and its Venetian history. Hugh walked up and down the side streets, dodging three-wheeled vans and small cars and absorbing, as though he were a native sponge, the color and the noise and the intensity of the people and their community. As the lagoons and hills of the Adriatic side were heaven for his wife, the crowds of Corfu town were Elysium for him.

Then he saw a woman examining a Corfu T-shirt on a stand at the entrance to a souvenir shop—red outline of the island with "CORFU" emblazoned in half-foot-high letters. She tossed it aside, obviously perceiving that it wouldn't last one cycle in the automatic washer.

She was dressed in black jeans and a black T-shirt with white trim on the sleeves. Her blond hair was tied in a careless knot on the top of her head.

He followed her down the street as, with a subtle mixture of rowdiness and grace, she slipped through the crowds of Corfu town.

He approached her from behind and looked over her shoulder.

"Maria," he said in disbelief.

"I wondered how long you were going to follow me before you made up your mind whether to run or talk." She turned around and embraced him. "I'm glad you didn't run. Now, to answer your questions in order of importance, Steven and I are staying at the Agios Gordis on the other side of the island, he has a meeting at the embassy in Athens day after tomorrow and, yes, we will be delighted to have dinner with you and your wife—Liz, isn't it?—tonight at the Corfu Palace."

"Would you have let me run?" Reluctantly he let her slip from his arms.

"You saw me first and followed me," she said, directing him with a shove toward the esplanade, which loomed invitingly at the end of the street. "Then you stood behind me and debated, as if I were blind and couldn't see your reflection in the shop window. Anyway, I'll buy you lunch . . . what have you been doing lately . . . since Walworth, Wisconsin, I mean? And don't tell me about making money . . . I know about *that,* though I must say I never quite pictured you in the silver pit."

"Are you as nervous as I am?" he asked.

"Aha, an interesting way to cover up awkwardness. No, I'm not nervous at all. My purse turns wet in my hand this way whenever handsome men follow me down the streets of Levantine towns . . . you like that? Levantine . . . not bad for an illiterate accountant?" She pulled Hugh into a chair at one of the sidewalk restaurants facing the water and deftly summoned a waiter.

"Lunch is on me," she said. "I'm a full-fledged fighting feminist and a bank vice-president on leave but you can pick up the tab for dinner. Now, seriously, without self-pity and undue modesty, tell me what you've been doing since 1954."

So he and Maria sparred and laughed and talked and reminisced and forgave but did not forget for a lunch that lasted two hours.

As they were about to rise from the table, Maria touched his hand. "I've had some pain and a lot of happiness since Lake Geneva. I hope you've been happy too."

"And happy to see you again," he said gallantly.

On the way back to Kanoni, his heart sang. The past had returned to the present, an old friendship was reborn, and some ghosts were exorcised.

Liz didn't seem to mind meeting strangers for dinner. "It will be nice to talk to another American couple. Who is this woman? I never heard you mention her."

"A classmate of Marge's. From the old neighborhood."

Which was true, though hardly the whole truth.

Liz dressed for dinner in a green chiffon evening dress. As always, Hugh was astonished by how quickly she could change from dowdy to chic when the will to impress was upon her.

She was so striking that Maria, herself more than presentable in a white cotton dress and carrying a matching jacket, nodded approval when they were introduced.

Captain McLain's hair was as white as Maria's dress and his eyes were tense. He was, however, as quietly charming as ever.

"Do you like it on the other side of the island?" Hugh asked as they were seated at table on the terrace of the Corfu Palace overlooking the harbor and its glittering lights.

"My husband says it reminds him of the sea islands off South Carolina, which is the highest compliment a McLain can pay. But isn't this nice?"

"The sand is lovely and the surf's mesmerizing," Steve said softly. "Not much for water skiing, though, I'm afraid."

"Not like the other side, I'll tell you." Maria was running on as she did when she was nervous. "A block away from our hotel the women go topless . . . they'd be drawn and quartered in Spain. Not here, though. You're overdressed if you wear more than a G-string."

"I'm glad I'm over here," Liz said primly as, equally nervous, she took a deep draft of her vodka martini.

Maria tried to put her down gently. "Hugh's father said once that people used to swim naked in the Middle Ages. . . ."

"False consciousness," Liz snapped, emptying her drink.

Maria seemed momentarily confused. "Well, I guess one woman's consciousness is another woman's poison," she said.

Good God, Liz, Hugh thought, you don't have to be afraid of her. She wants to like you. Give it a chance.

Liz wasn't about to give it a chance. She drank another martini and chased it with two quick glasses of Greek wine before the lamb was served.

"Are you going to Vietnam?" she suddenly asked Steven.

"Not exactly," he replied. "I'll be on a helicopter platform ship that's standing by to remove personnel from Saigon if the war turns bad, as it probably will."

"You've been there before?" Liz's fingers tightened on her wineglass.

"Yes, twice."

"What did you do?"

"Flew a Phantom," he replied.

"You're a war criminal, in other words." Liz was clearly drunk.

"Some might think so."

Maria bowed her head—no wisecrack, no anger, no fight. A side of her Hugh had never known.

"You killed innocent women and children."

"I hope not. I did my best not to." Steven remained calm, self-possessed, unthreatened.

"Everyone on our side is a war criminal."

He hesitated. It was an old argument, one he knew he couldn't win.

"The military didn't start the war, ma'am. Liberal political leaders did. We advised against the war and we fought it under the most difficult conditions, so as not to harm innocent people. I'm not sure that it's a just war. I'm not sure that it's an unjust one either. But I am sure of one thing. The Vietcong have not spared anyone—military or civilian—whom they perceived to be an obstacle to their aims."

"American propaganda."

Maria was tracing a line on the tablecloth with the handle of a teaspoon, no sign of emotion on her face.

"I think that's enough, Liz," Hugh said.

"You're just as bad as the rest. A mindless apologist." She grabbed the wine bottle and refilled her glass.

She said no more, however, and the meal wound down in awkward mono-syllables. They managed a friendly parting, but that was all.

"You once loved him very much?" Steven said as he drove the rented car carefully over the mountains to the Adriatic coast.

"Teen-age crush. Threatened?"

He patted her knee and quickly returned his hand to the steering wheel. "Would be kind of silly, wouldn't it, Maria?"

"I suppose." She put her arm around him. "If I met one of *your* teen-age sweethearts, I'd be insanely jealous."

"No," he said calmly. "But you would feel constrained to act as if you were."

Maria laughed. "You know me too well. . . . Poor Liz, I feel as sorry for her as I do for Hugh."

"A very disturbed woman. She was a nun?"

"So I understand. He should never have left the priesthood."

"Maybe he shouldn't have been a priest in the first place."

Steven was so damn fair.

"Then I'd be in the Corfu Hilton tonight." She kissed his neck, confident that a good jet pilot wouldn't be distracted by such minor affection, even on a dark mountain road in Corfu.

Dear God, she prayed, protect my Steven for me.

And while you're at it, if you have time, protect poor Hugh too.

Chapter Thirty-four
···*1974*·································

A BOOK CLUTCHED under one arm, a vast beach towel draped around her neck, an outsize purse slung over her shoulder, Maria walked north on the Agios Gordis beach, looking for a secluded dune. She'd wanted to fly to Athens with Steven, but he sensibly had argued that he wouldn't be with her even at night during the two-day gathering at the embassy.

And she would be safer on crime-free Corfu than in Athens.

She found a break between two dunes, spread her towel, and, sitting down, emptied the various suntan lotions from her purse. She stood by her defense of topless beaches, but wanted privacy for her daring nonetheless.

Maria was proud of her durable attractiveness and not at all displeased that men still admired her. If they wanted to look at her bare breasts under the deep blue sky, even that was fine.

But only from a distance, you understand.

She shed her skirt and T-shirt, anointed herself with oil, put her sailor's cap on her head, and curled up with a copy of *Computer Programming for Bankers* to see whether the competition was catching up. As she rested the book on her belly, she wagered with herself that she was the only half-naked woman on the beach reading that book.

She thought about the dinner with the Donlons the previous night. Weird.

The last time she'd seen Hugh had been at Orchestra Hall. He'd still been a priest then, and he'd thrown her for a tailspin in a ten-minute conversation. Same tailspin phenomenon again. Always would love him, she guessed. Too bad polygamy was out of fashion.

She laughed at herself. It was demanding enough being married to one passionate lover without contemplating another.

Her marriage had been transformed since Steven had left for his second tour in Vietnam. During the long months of uncertainty before she knew he was alive and then through the months after that, she'd endured pain she couldn't have imagined before. And she'd kept up her spirits too, not out of virtue, God knew, but out of necessity. Either she smiled or she'd crack.

It was a different Steven who'd come home from the POW camp. The Navy had warned them that they'd find their husbands and sons changed. But she hadn't believed it. Not her Steven.

Her Steven most of all. The patriotic camp leader they'd tortured but couldn't break had returned hoarding all his anger at the enemy and at the American government for getting involved in a stupid war and at the protesters who hadn't understood a thing about it and at the press for turning the men who had to fight into villains and at Maria for not being with him in the POW camp and at his sons for growing up while he was gone.

She didn't know what to do. Her man's simple depths had been twisted and bent. How could she remake him?

Only two gifts could she offer—laughter and love. No anger in return, no long discussion, no self-defense. She wouldn't fight with him. She wouldn't let him fight with her. She simply laughed and sang and tried to find him again.

And she didn't quit, even though the first six months were even worse than the time he'd been MIA. Then one day she came back to their apartment in Alexandria to find a long letter of apology: He had been heartless and cruel, punishing her and the children because of what the Vietnamese had done to him. He was a monster, permanently damaged goods, not to be endured. Surely the Church would grant her an annulment. He would be at the Mayflower until he could move into BOQ.

She drove into Washington against the flow of the rush-hour traffic, stormed up to his room, dragged, pushed, and kicked him out the door and down the hall and into the elevator to the station wagon, which she had abandoned, engine running, in the charge of the doorman. If he ever did anything like that again, she would personally break his neck. Now, drive this around the block while I go back and pay the bill.

It was the turning point, as Steven, poor man, probably sensed it would be. He laughed on the ride home and laughed again when they made love, after she'd disposed of the baby-sitter. The worst was over. Maria's act still worked.

She thereby became the moral leader in the marriage. He refused to reassume the role, preferring to bask in the glow of her tough grace. The family was cemented together by Kenny, the dream child of their reunion, a little doll for an aging mom to play with, a wonder for his father to watch with fascination for hours and a punk for Fast Eddie to protect fiercely.

Their marriage became both deeper and more relaxed. The ups and downs were less dramatic and the course more smooth. She would never be as good a person as Steven, but now that was all right. She didn't have to be.

Now he was returning to Vietnam for the third time. He could have asked for a different assignment and no one would have complained. He didn't plan to stay in the Navy indefinitely. After he made admiral, he'd retire. And he didn't have to do a third tour to make admiral.

This time, her superstitious Sicilian fatalism told her, you will say good-bye to him and never see him again on earth.

She found a tissue in her purse and dried her eyes. Her heart was breaking and she couldn't even share the pain.

Why did their love have to be tested again?

Angry at herself now, she brushed her anxiety aside and focused her attention on her book again.

The surf washed up in gentle rollers, staining the beach each time it came. A pleasant breeze stirred the blue air. The tart smell of brine teased her nostrils and made her sleepy. She dozed off a couple of times.

"Good book?" she heard Hugh say.

Her half-sleep ended abruptly. What a fool she'd been not to have expected him. You're in trouble, Maria Angelica. She pulled on the T-shirt and sat up. "Just happened by, huh?"

"I walked away from your hotel, not toward it; actually, we'd both planned to come over here today. But Liz is under the weather . . . and I thought the rule here was anything goes."

"Not with people from the old neighborhood."

"May I sit down?"

"I don't own the beach."

"I want to apologize."

"Not your fault." Oh God, what a mess.

"Accept my apology anyway. Last night was an off night. It's not always that way. Forgive?"

"Of course. Now, if you give me five minutes to finish this chapter, you can buy me lunch at that pink restaurant down the beach."

"You'll have to pay. I left my wallet in the car. I told you I wasn't looking for you. I'll owe you two when we get back to Chicago."

"We won't be lunching together in Chicago, Hugh, and you know that as well as I do."

Firm, self-disciplined, realistic; that's our Maria Angelica.

"You're right, I suppose."

She pretended to plow through the program designs at the end of Chapter Three, knowing she would have to go over them all again.

"Okay, I have the answer to our problem of cashing bad checks . . . don't take them in the first place. Here, you can carry the book and the towel. I'll handle the luggage."

Lunch was fun at first. The roast lamb was no tougher than usual and the vegetables were spicy and mysterious. And Hugh told scandalous stories about the commodities business while she laughed and mostly forgot the tired lines in his face and the sadness in his eyes.

"I try, Maria." He rested his head in his hands. "God knows, if there is a God, I've tried everything. There's nothing that seems to work. . . ."

She refilled his glass with wine.

"And the kids?" Maria didn't want to know more about Hugh Donlon's suffering. Yet she couldn't stop her catechism.

Hugh shifted guiltily on his chair, playing with a tiny piece of driftwood, unable to look her in the eye. "They're her children, Maria; she's cut them off from me. They don't like me and I can't get through to them."

"That's nonsense, Hugh," she said briskly. "You're their father. Of course, you can get through to them—if you want to."

He clenched his fist. "From the very beginning, Maria, I've done everything I could, absolutely everything. I don't know what more I can do."

Maria exploded. "How like a Donlon! Do! Do! Do! Why not just try *being* for a change!"

"I don't know what you're talking about." He sounded angry. Too bad for him.

"I don't think you love her, Hugh. I don't think you ever loved her. You married her because it was the right thing to do. You go through the motions of loving her because that's what you should do. You try to be close to the kids because that's what a father is expected to do—like the judge did with you. Maybe it wouldn't have worked anyway. But you didn't give it a chance. You were too busy keeping all your goddamn rules ever to *be* anything for her or the kids, much less to be a lover for her. Don't come crying to me. . . ."

"I'm not crying to you," he said hotly.

She touched his hand. "I'm sorry. I didn't mean to shout. Here, have some more wine; it substitutes for purgatory. But, Hugh, my wonderful teen-age dreamboat, why don't you forget all your obligations to them, especially the kids, and try to just plain love them?"

Maria signaled the waiter for another bottle of wine. Careful, Maria Angelica, it may taste terrible but it contains as much alcohol as good wine.

"Maybe you're right."

But he didn't understand. Maybe he never would. She'd preached the same sermon on an old sailing dory twenty years ago. He hadn't understood it then and he doesn't understand it now.

They walked back to her dune, peace and quiet restored.

Hugh closed his eyes and stretched out in the sun.

"I've made pretty much a mess of my life," he said.

Maria hugged her book under her chin, as if to protect herself from his sadness.

"Should you have stayed in the priesthood?"

"I don't know. I wasn't happy as a priest. Then I tried marriage and fatherhood, money and power. They didn't help much either. Neither did some intense sexual experiences."

"I heard about them," Maria said indignantly.

He looked up at her and smiled ruefully. "I can't tell you how much I regret them. I don't know whether I still believe in sin, but I'm sorrier for them than for anything else, except letting the kids down, I guess."

His voice broke.

"The problem isn't sex, is it, Hugh? Not with Liz and not with the others either. . . ."

"No," he agreed sadly, "not really. Power, fear, male ego, you name it. . . ."

The surf lapped at the edge of the beach. Two half-naked girls ran out of the water. Hugh didn't even notice them.

There wasn't a damn thing Maria could do; and she shouldn't try or she'd be in as much trouble as he.

Still, the wine and the sun and the excitement of being with Hugh made her light-headed and reckless.

"Want to swim before you go back?" She pulled off the T-shirt. Wet T-shirts were worse than nothing at all, she reasoned, and, besides, he'd seen her before. She laughed as she rushed into the surf.

He charged into the water behind her. They dove into a wave, rode it to the beach, and then dove again. Wind and water seemed to clear the wine from her brain. She felt free and relaxed. There was, after all, nothing to worry about. They were merely old friends frolicking together on a gorgeous Mediterranean beach.

Says you, Maria Angelica.

A big roller knocked her over and the undertow, gentle and safe, tugged her after it. Hugh helped her to her feet.

"Look at the caïque . . . isn't that a beautiful sail?"

Hugh forced his eyes away from her to the boat. "Lovely. . . ."

"It reminds me of the *Pegeen*." Then an arm around him, her face against his chest. "Oh, God, Hugh, I have to say it. Despite the bad things that have happened and the ugly chains you've tied around yourself, there's as much beauty in you as there was that day. You can still be happy. . . ."

He touched her face, and then her throat, as he'd done so long ago. "Thank you, Maria," he said, repeating the words from the past.

"A glass of lemonade again, Hugh. We've been here before."

"A much more attractive glass now, if I may say so."

"You'd better say so, even if it isn't true. . . . Enough water for one day?" She slipped away from him, alarmed by the ease with which she'd precipitated such tense emotion. A quip, a laugh, and then you walk back to the dune, as steadily as you can.

In the lee of the dune, she reclined on the towel and reached for her T-shirt. He took it out of her hand and touched her hair lightly with his fingers.

Too early with the compliments, Maria Angelica, now you have big problems.

The other hand on her stomach, so tender and gentle; their lips moving toward each other, hers as eagerly as his; then their bodies pressing together, her nipples hard against his chest; his hand moving down her flank to her thigh, her body busy preparing itself.

Dear God, help.

Sweet-tasting fire.

It's my turn to end it.

She wrenched away from him and leaned on the sand, her back to him as his was once to her.

"Go away, Hugh," she said in a low voice. "I never want to see you again."

She heard his soft footsteps vanish down the beach.

She pounded the sand.

Then the tears came.

Liz was waiting for him on the balcony of their suite at the Hilton, two empty Pepsi cans and an ashtray full of cigarette butts beside her.

She reached out a hand to take his as he sat opposite her. The sleeve of her nylon robe slipped back. Did she want him to reassure her with lovemaking? There was no desire left in him, nor would there be for a long time.

So this is what despair is like, he thought.

BOOK FIVE

"It is finished."

Chapter Thirty-five
············· *1979* ·············

A CALL TO prayer floated above the morning mist rising from the majestically moving river. On the balcony of the ambassador's house, it was still pleasantly cool. In a few hours heat would prostrate the entire city.

For the moment, Hugh Donlon, the Ambassador of the United States of America to the People's Democratic Republic of the Upper River, ignored the smells and imagined that the minarets and the gleaming buildings, the river and the jungle on the other side, the slowly moving dugouts and the graceful people in them, were all parts of a romance from the Arabian nights.

In such, however, there would have been no trucks with Uzi-brandishing national police, no rotting concrete soccer stadium, no KGB antennae monitoring his pillow talk with his wife—such as it was—and, of course, no United States Embassy.

He pulled his thin kimono tighter, if only so the KGB binoculars wouldn't discover that he was fifteen pounds overweight. Being an ambassador was very much like being an associate pastor: your freedom of action was strictly limited and both your enemies and your friends spied on you. Royce, his first secretary, a career foreign service officer who had hoped to be named ambassador himself, was just as surely reporting on him to the State Department as was the KGB resident down the street reporting on him to the Kremlin.

Hugh had accepted President Carter's appointment because he thought a term of public service, motivated by generosity if not idealism, might be a way of atoning for his greed. While he shared none of the illusions of his wife and her radical Catholic friends about the Third World, he did hope that he could contribute in some way to preserving order in East Africa while facilitating moderate change.

His training as a demographer, his doctoral dissertation, and the investments he'd made during the Russian wheat run-up had turned him into an acknowledged expert on certain aspects of international agriculture. To be sure, the universities were filled with men who knew more, but they didn't have his money or his power in the business community.

He was one of the first Americans to speak out against rapid modernization and in favor of labor-intensive agriculture for the developing nations. This was a country where labor-intensive agriculture had worked for centuries. Perhaps such a successful economy could be sustained instead of being modernized out of existence.

He would do what he could, for the good of both nations. He would expiate.

But expiation, like contrition, does not set one free. He was still frozen in the pit that Dante described as the seventh circle of hell.

The prayer call lingered in his ear as he walked back into his bedroom. How long since he'd prayed? How long since he'd been to church? Was he restless because he still hungered for God, as Pat Cleary would say? Probably.

Maybe there would be some forgiveness for him, if he could persuade the American government that the secret of aiding a lesser developed country was to strengthen the village structure that was the core of the native culture.

The Principal Leader, himself the product of an up-country village, was terrified of the village people. Should they ever lose their superstitious fear of him as a magically powerful chief, he would end up floating in the river, his body horribly mutilated, as had his four predecessors.

Liz was still asleep, her face relaxed and attractive. Hugh thought reflexively of sex and then abandoned the idea. It wasn't important anymore. Liz could be constrained to make love when his needs were compelling; indeed, as he had slowly discovered, she enjoyed being forced into it. But neither any longer cherished the other.

Liz could have been a good ambassador's wife, he thought. But in the event she'd been a failure. Ideology had stood between her and any slightest sympathy for either nation and her demoralization had begun to show in her clothes and appearance.

She had formed a close relationship with the Papal Nuncio, a fat Italian who loved to expostulate on papal politics. The Nuncio apparently was not enamored of John Paul, an opinion shared by Liz, who thought the Pope was a reactionary and a chauvinist. The Nuncio's objections came from the right, not the left, but as long as Liz could keep informed about Episcopal appointments in the States—all of which displeased her—she felt she was still in touch with "the life of the Church," as she called it.

Her complaints were increasingly shrill. In America she had sung the praises of the Third World. Here, she ridiculed the inefficiency of the local people. She was appalled at the plight of women in the country, but treated the embassy servants with utter disdain. She denounced racism on the one hand and deplored the toilet habits of the natives on the other.

She should have complained just as bitterly if he'd turned down the ambassadorial appointment, or if he'd tried to leave her and the children at home. It was in Liz's nature to complain, it had now become clear. And so, it seemed, was it in the nature of her children, who were, even at eight and seven, chronic malcontents. Hugh remembered how close he'd been to his father when he was their age. He felt guilty that he did not have the same kind of relationship with Brian. Yet it was quite impossible to be close to a child whom Liz had already made an inveterate whiner.

So he dealt with his family the only way he could—with a mixture of tolerance and authoritarianism. It worked, or it worked well enough. No joy, but only occasional pain.

One of the most painful incidents of the last several years had occurred when he took Brian and Lise and the three Wentworth children to the circus, haunted by Maria's charge that he would be close to the children if he wanted to be close to them. The three little micks were wide-eyed and well-behaved. His own two were restless and unpleasant, complaining about the uncomfortable benches in the tattered old International Amphitheater, fighting with one another, stuffing themselves with food and drink and then complaining of stomachaches and refusing to enjoy the fun of the circus.

Liz, he reflected, was no longer the obstacle. Her protection and his indifference in the early years had built walls that would never break. Maria was right that he might have done better when the children were small. She did not realize, however, that once you were frozen into your mistakes, there was no way out of them.

Brian wanted to see the tigers up close. The little girls were not interested. Seamus Wentworth—the husky, green-eyed Wentworth heir—was game for anything. So he left Fionna in charge of the younger girls during the intermission and led the two boys behind the stands to the tiger cage.

The smell of the animals, the taste of cotton candy, and the feel of the sawdust under his feet reminded him of his own childhood circus adventures.

The two boys watched the sleek and sleepy striped animals with awe.

"Big bugger," murmured Seamus.

As though she were offended, a female tiger snarled in protest and leaped at the side of her cage.

Both boys jumped, badly frightened.

Seamus grabbed Hugh's arm in pure terror. Hugh put his hand on Brian's shoulder to reassure him.

Brian twisted away. "I don't need your help," he said.

They walked back to their seats. Fionna, black eyes dancing, had to tell about what the clown said about her Irish brogue.

Hugh barely heard her.

Oddly he was still a priest to many of his embassy colleagues; a Marine guard asked him to hear his confession the day before yesterday, and a young woman foreign service officer—much more able than most—who was deeply involved with a local intellectual, sought his advice a week before. She would get over her dark-skinned lover, hopefully before he ended up in one of the Principal Leader's jails.

All very middle-aged, gray, and gloomy. But he could still enjoy the embassy Cadillac and the salute of the Marine guards and an occasional trip upriver as temporary respites from what Fred Allen, his father's favorite comedian in the old days of radio, called the treadmill to oblivion.

His business was another thing; there, he had no control at all.

Moreover, the latest commodity news from America was disturbing. Bunker Hunt and his family and Arab friends were playing games with silver. Fifteen dollars a troy ounce was too high a price for silver, yet if Bunker and his associates were really building a corner, the price could run up much higher. Hugh felt a faint stir of excitement.

Tim was probably making the most of it, overreaching himself with some kinky scheme that was seventy-five percent sensible and twenty-five percent mindless. In the last letter Hugh received from his mother, she told him about the monstrosity of a house Tim was building in Oakland Beach. He was even planning to build an indoor swimming pool. Since the funds came from his silver speculation, Tim dubbed it his "silver-plated pool." Peggy called it "Tim's folly." So it would always be with Tim.

Hugh had stopped trading before testifying at his Senate confirmation hearing and had liquidated all his positions and turned over his assets to a blind trust. So Tim's bizarre schemes wouldn't cost him a penny, though they might ruin the firm.

Well, he would not intervene. It wouldn't be ethical and no good ever came of his intervening with Tim anyway.

"Why didn't you close the door?" Liz opened her eyes. "You know what it's like trying to cool this place off once it gets hot. I don't know why the government can't provide embassies with air conditioning that works."

Chapter Thirty-six
1979

MARIA McLAIN STRODE briskly down LaSalle Street, enjoying both the crisp October air and the admiring glances of the men who passed her. Her expensive clothes and confident walk said that she was a stunning woman who was a success in the business world.

She put enough time and work into her face, body, and clothes to justify a little vanity, one of the simple joys in life in which you ought to take pleasure as long as you could, she thought.

The visit to her lawyer's office had been a dreary affair, a tryst with mortality in which she'd worked out the provisions of her will to take care of her sons should anything happen to her while they were still young.

"Since you've become a bank president are you too good to notice a hack commodities trader?"

She squinted at the man. "Too vain to wear my glasses, Timmy Donlon." She laughed at herself. "It's great to see you. How's the family? How's the silver market these exciting days? And how's the ambassador?"

"Family's fine. Folks are in Ireland. Silver is more fun than popcorn and from the ambassador I don't hear. How does it feel to be the youngest woman bank president in Cook County?"

She and Tim had met occasionally at meetings and financial community parties. She still enjoyed his wit, though his bloodshot eyes and disheveled clothes and the stories of his marital troubles that everyone in town had heard made her feel bad.

"It feels good, Tim, to tell you the truth. Tell me about Bunker Hunt's silver."

A slow, dark gleam appeared in Tim's bloodshot eyes.

"The Hunts are smart people. They've sewed up Bache and have the Jarecki brothers worried sick. They bought themselves twelve thousand contracts without pushing the price up beyond twelve dollars. They used just about every commission house in the world, ours included, and kept the secret. Now they're going to sit back and watch the price double, maybe triple before they get out."

"Seven or eight billion dollars?"

"Right. You want in?"

"My bank isn't going to play with the Hunts. They're clever, Tim, but from what I hear they're not too bright. They should sell at twenty-five an ounce. You watch, though. They'll hold on. Bears and bulls don't lose; pigs do."

Tim shoved his hands into the pockets of his suit. He probably hadn't been home last night.

"They'll change their position at thirty. So the smart traders will sell short when the price hits twenty-two or so. By March it will be down to ten, where it belongs. The bears will make a killing.''

Most investors, even the shrewd traders on the floor of the CBT, Maria knew, were bulls. They loved a bull market and hated a bear market even when they made money on it. They went short with guilty consciences, as though it were somehow un-American to profit from an economic decline, particularly a spectacular one. Hugh Donlon, from what she'd heard, was a classic bull, though one who knew when to quit.

His brother was just the opposite. Tim loved the dark thrill of profiting from bad news. Temperamentally, he was the ideal bear, but probably too greedy to make as much from his temperamental skills as he should.

''What if they hang on after that? People don't become billionaires by quitting early.''

Tim winked. ''That's not what Hugh says. Anyway, the CBT and the Comex won't let them do it. They'll push the margin rates up so high the Hunt crowd will have to sell before thirty-five dollars an ounce. Want just one contract, I mean personally?''

Maria shook her head. ''I put my cash, such as it is, in money market notes. Got a couple of kids to educate.''

''The oldest boy's at the Citadel, I understand. That's nice. Like his father.''

Maria winced, as she almost always did whenever Steven was mentioned. It had been five years since the helicopter had disappeared in a ball of flame during the evacuation of Saigon, but Maria still had nightmares about the crash she'd seen on the TV screen the next night.

''That's right. He likes it there, just as his father did. And, Tim, promise me that if you're into this silver thing, you've got a hedge.''

Tim's grin broadened. ''I always have a hedge, Maria, always. I wouldn't make a big investment unless I had something stored away to protect me if the market goes the other way. You know that.''

Maria was chilled despite the October sunshine. Tim Donlon had been a little kooky all his life. Now the dark light in his eyes as he discussed the silver market was the glow of a lunatic wizard on the edge of being consumed by his own mad magic.

''Don't get hurt,'' she said lightly.

''When have I been hurt?'' he responded just as lightly.

''And Hugh?'' she asked.

''Oh, he's not in it at all. He put everything in blind trust. No conflict of interest. Probably didn't have to do that. You know Hugh, though. Keep all the rules. And then break them all. I know you like him, Maria, but Hugh is nothing but rules. Some kept and some broken.''

Maria finished her day in the Loop with a visit to the woman's athletic club, which was, as she put it, her downtown swimming hole. She thought about the will and about Steven as she put on her tank suit and dove into the pool. Then with the strong discipline that she had developed over her emotional life since Steven's death, she chased such morbid imaginings away; life now was for her children. Another husband? Maybe. So far no one compared to Steven, who had been the rising and setting sun of her life for a decade and a half.

Tim was a little shark swimming in a sea of big sharks. The Hunt clan were outsiders, rich bumpkins from Texas who wore readymade suits, took taxis instead of limousines, and stayed at the Palmer House when they were in Chicago instead of the Whitehall. They were, nonetheless, the biggest commodities speculators in America.

She switched from the crawl to a backstroke that was supposed to be good for stomach muscles.

She was savvy enough in the ways of the world to imagine the rest of the silver scenario. The Hunts wanted a corner; they didn't figure to own all the silver in the world, but they might control two thirds of it. Then those who sold short, like the powerful Moccata Metals and Englehart Metals companies would be forced to buy silver from the Hunts at enormous losses.

If they were smart, the Hunts would bail out long before that, but while they were rich and determined and even smart in a single-minded fashion, they weren't sophisticated enough to know that the financial powers-that-be wouldn't let them get away with it. The exchanges would force up the margin requirements, the Hunts would suddenly need a lot of money, the silver market would fall, and the government would have to step in to constrain some banks to bail the Hunts out, with big loans probably to their oil company. The establishment would first punish the Hunts, then save them. Salvation would come not because of love, but out of fear that a silver panic might spread to the other commodities and then to the stock market and then to the whole elaborate and shaky financial structure of the country.

Tim was counting on the Hunts to take the money and run, as he would, as any sophisticated speculator would.

The powers would protect the big sharks because they belonged to the club. They wouldn't salvage a small shark like Tim, who didn't belong to the club.

She climbed out of the pool, her fifty laps finished, and shivered under a towel. The Hunts were rogue sharks, the big-time sharks who were part of the pack. Tim was a small and unimportant shark. Guess who would be eaten alive.

She shivered again, though the shower was steaming hot. Then there was Corfu.

She had made a terrible fool out of herself.

No sense, Maria Angelica, in dwelling on the fact that you're a fool where Hugh Donlon's concerned. You've known that since you were sixteen.

Mary, Mother of God—she turned to prayer as she often did under a shower—don't let any of the Donlons be caught among the sharks.

Judge Donlon put aside the galleys of his manuscript on mysticism and law in the Middle Ages. The proofreader from Cornell University Press had missed three typos in the first hundred pages. Before he became a senior judge—semiretired but still serving on an occasional panel—he'd paid little attention to the typing mistakes of secretaries. Now that he was working on his pride and joy, however, he demanded perfection. Foolish old man.

Peggy was discussing her next exhibit with Father Waldek Bronowski, the young art expert of the archdiocese.

"They're wonderful watercolors, Mrs. Donlon," said the round-faced, pudgy priest, "exuding vitality and erotic tension—beautiful bodies elegantly constrained—and your paradoxical soft pastel colors add to the grace of the scenes."

"I only hope they're not sinful, Waldek," she murmured as she filled his sherry glass again. Peg served sherry in her house now, and called young priests by their first names.

The priest laughed softly—everything he did was soft and civilized. "Those who wish to see obscenity can buy *Playboy* or *Penthouse*. Those who come to admire your work will be impressed rather with the purity of the human form."

"I don't know where those pictures come from." Peg put on her glasses to consider them more carefully and more skeptically.

Waldek waved his hands as if he were bestowing a papal blessing. "They come from your own grace-filled and God-filled experience of flesh, Mrs. Donlon. Where does any artist's vision of the body come from? These do you great honor."

Tom Donlon kept a straight face with considerable difficulty. The young priest was confirming Peg's worst fears, telling her that her own sexuality was unveiled in the tense and ecstatic colors and then adding that they revealed high virtue. Finally she had found a priest who answered her anxious questions, and he didn't even know that she was asking them.

At sixty-four, Peg was so handsome that when she entered a dining room men and women turned to admire her. Tom loved her as much as ever, maybe more. And their sex life, openly celebrated now in her paintings, was more pleasurable than it had ever been.

Peggy had stood the test of time and change, heartbreak, and a revolutionary Church better than most people in her generation. She still carried the pearl rosaries, but she also distributed Holy Communion at Mass.

The terrible wrenching pain she and Tom had inflicted on each other at the time of Hugh's wedding was not forgotten, but it was not mentioned either. Never once did Peg hint at "I told you so" on the subject of Liz.

Peggy would always feel that the hostility of her two daughters-in-law and the absence of affection from her sons' children was a punishment from God. "Punishment theology is hard to give up; it seems so accurate," Waldek had said earlier. The Wentworth children, on the other hand, adored her and visited often, but it was a long way from Killarney to Chicago. Even that physical distance seemed sometimes a punishment.

Nevertheless, Peggy was willing to exhibit the misty thighs and buttocks, arms and legs, breasts and throats, that populated her watercolors. God might still punish her, but He might be even more angry if she continued to hide them. He would object, as Father Waldek had once delicately hinted, to her concealing the talents He had given her.

". . . so I cannot speak for the cardinal's schedule." The priest smiled faintly. "Not even his appointment secretary can do that. But you may be sure that he will visit the gallery and if it is possible he will attend the opening."

"The poor, dear man; he has such a busy schedule," Peg protested.

"He likes you, Mrs. Donlon," the priest said dryly.

"I can't imagine why," the judge said, no longer able to contain his laughter.

"I really can't either," Peg agreed, laughing and blushing together.

"Three more years to our golden wedding anniversary, Father," the judge said, not all that irrelevantly, as the priest was leaving.

Peggy put her arms around him and pressed against him a moment later. The feel of her pleased him as much now as when he'd held her first in back of the Red Barn at Twin Lakes.

"We don't deserve such happiness," she said through her tears.

"Let's enjoy it just the same."

She quivered in his embrace. "Oh, Tommy, I have the most terrible feeling. . . ."

"What?" He buried his face in her hair, hardly listening.

"I've felt for days that something terrible is about to happen."

"Nothing terrible is going to happen, Peg, not as long as we have each other."
In the darkest corner of his soul, however, Tom Donlon was afraid she was right.

Chapter Thirty-seven
······································· *1979* **·······································**

"SO YOU'RE GOING short in silver? Risky. Does Hugh know?" Benedict Fowler
frowned unpleasantly.

"Suppose I give you an answer to that question? Suppose I say that, yes, he's
on the phone every day? Suppose I say that I'm really investing his money
because he can't do it himself while he's working for the government?"

Ben pondered the flashing lights of the quotation board outside Tim's office.
"You're not serious, of course." His skin was brown but he didn't look healthy.
Suntan couldn't hide his pallor any more than makeup hid the whiteness of a
corpse.

Tim waved his hand negligently. Silver was up another half-dollar an ounce.
The boardroom outside his office was humming with frantic activity. "Not
much," he said.

Fowler nodded heavily. "I see."

The Principal Leader reminded Hugh of his brother. Same small, skinny body,
same fixed grin, same squinting eyes, same love of the tricky and the risky.
Crazier than Tim, surely, and infinitely more dangerous, but basically the same
kind of person.

The black man fondled the machete with which he was reputed to mutilate his
enemies. "It is most regrettable that the local police force has found reason to
establish roadblocks near the village of mir Hassun," he said, his eyes dreamy.
Was he on drugs too? Probably. From the Russians or the Chinese.

"I'm sure they have their reasons, Exalted One," Hugh said. "Yet we are
interested in that village, as you know. It seemed to be the place where our joint
plan of labor-intensive agriculture was most likely to succeed, an outcome that
would please us all."

The leader waved his knife and smiled. "This year labor-intensive, next year
tractors again. What does it matter, Mr. Ambassador? It is only important that
our peoples resist communism together."

Probably a more realistic view of American foreign policy than I have, Hugh
thought grimly. "We are also concerned about our personnel at mir Hassun. We
haven't been able to communicate with them for a week."

"The lovely Miss Kincaid?" The caresses on the knife became more tender.

Hugh nodded. Laura Kincaid was a Peace Corps volunteer in the country to
which he'd been assigned. The agonized phone call yesterday from Hank and
Jean still haunted him.

"There is nothing to worry about." The Leader laid aside his knife. "Miss
Kincaid is well. This is a civilized country. The police will lift the roadblocks in
a day or two. Then she can return." He rose from his chair, slowly and majes-

tically, like a rich tribal chieftain rising from an ivory throne, to indicate that the audience was over.

Hugh left only slightly reassured. He was learning, as the staff at Tehran had discovered, that serving the United States abroad could be dicey, especially if revolution was in the air. He wished he was back in Chicago, trading in the silver pit again.

Tim leaned back comfortably in his vast chair. The market had paused briefly at twenty-two. Outside the snow was falling. LaSalle Street had assumed its somewhat cynical pre-Christmas glow. Between then and the first of the year, silver would shoot up again, perhaps a dollar a day. Right after the first of the year, the Hunts would unload, and by March or even February the price would be back to less than fifteen dollars. The directors of the Board of Trade were already muttering that the Board was more important than Bunker Hunt and that margin requirements would have to be raised. Les Rosenthal, the chairman of the CBT, was smarter and tougher than the Hunt clan. He'd force them to end the run-up.

So now was the time to make his own move.

He walked out of the office to the desk of Norma Austin, a vice-president of the firm and his principal assistant and occasional mistress.

"Get on the horn to our best floor contact, Norma. For my own personal account . . . a hundred contracts for April silver, spread between twenty-one fifty an ounce and twenty-three fifty."

The tall, stylish brunette gasped. "That's almost four million dollars, Mr. Donlon."

He was Mr. Donlon everywhere but in bed.

Tim smiled happily. "Shoot the works."

"Buy a hundred contracts." She dutifully made a note as Tim turned away.

"No." He smiled beatifically. "Sell!"

Maria McLain walked through the chic Near North Side Gallery on Oak Street just off Rush as if she were in the cathedral at High Mass. Peggy Donlon was a special woman, of that Maria had always been certain; but these paintings were superb.

God, I'm the age she was when I visited them at Lake Geneva, she thought.

Maria usually avoided the elder Donlons even though they moved in the same circles. She saw them occasionally at Butterfield after she finally caved in and bought a membership in the club—mostly to see her parents beam with pleasure when they walked across the dining room like a distinguished duke and duchess entering the new palace of their daughter the empress.

She was still ambivalent about the Donlons, loving their power and charm, and not trusting the chaos she saw in their lives. Moreover, she didn't want to be reminded of Hugh. Maria had loved only two men in her life. One was dead, God rest him, and the other was married to a bitch and a fool.

Her lips tightened in anger and then she laughed at herself. Loneliness often made her think of the two weeks at Lake Geneva, a magic memory in her life, before the world became complicated. Was it possible to recapture any of that youthful joy of first love?

Of course, it wasn't. You're a grown-up, Maria Angelica. She must drive

Hugh Donlon from her bloodstream. It was time for her to marry again. Five years of widowhood were enough. Yet as she'd told her son Eddie when he said the same thing, you marry not because you need a husband, nor even because you want one, but because you can't do without this particular man.

No such man had come along, though there'd been no dearth of contenders. Maybe he never would.

What if Hugh Donlon should seek an annulment of his marriage to Liz? Would she be interested?

Damn right. And you ought not even to think about such things.

She did just the same.

Peggy was talking to a tall, very handsome middle-aged priest, in front of a picture that reminded Maria of herself.

She took Ed's arm and dragged him toward the painting.

Ed pulled on her sleeve as Maria zeroed in on it.

"Mother, I don't think . . ."

"It isn't me, Ed. I never was that good-looking."

"I don't . . ."

"Peggy Curtin Donlon, that picture reminds me of a girl I knew a long time ago. It's sinful and shameful."

Peggy embraced her with grateful tears. "Maria, darling, I'm so glad you could come. We hardly ever see you. The picture isn't anyone. Father Waldek says I paint out of memories. I'm sure I have a memory of you, but I didn't intend . . ."

"I'll buy it," Maria said enthusiastically. "And tell everyone that it's me even if it isn't."

"Perhaps I should draw from live models," Peggy said thoughtfully. "Tommy will tell you that I was the one who wanted to see the Sally Rand show at the World's Fair. . . ."

"I really love it. . . ."

"How wonderful, Maria, but I insist it be a gift."

Maria started to protest and then abandoned the idea. There was no way to get the best of Peggy. "Peg, this is my son, Eddie."

"You look just like your grandfather," Peg said, "and that's a compliment, young man. . . . I suppose you both know Cardinal Cronin?"

"I do," Ed said sheepishly.

Maria felt her face grow warm. "How do you do, Your Eminence? I didn't expect . . ."

Sean Cronin was indeed a charmer. "I do think the picture looks like you, Mrs. McLain. And if you call me Your Eminence again, your son's career in the seminary is finished."

For once, Maria found herself without words.

Chapter Thirty-eight
1980

CHRISTMAS WAS OVER. It was early January and Laura Kincaid's team was still isolated up-country. There'd been one letter just before Christmas, a hasty hand-written note saying they were safe and would be out soon.

At least Henry and Jean knew that their adored Laura was still alive.

The ambassador and his family were eating dinner. Lise was complaining that Brian had hit her, and Brian was complaining that the teacher at the embassy school was mean. And Liz was complaining that the Nuncio would no longer talk to her because of an argument about abortion—he was shocked that a devout Catholic mother would approve of murder.

Royce came into the dining room after his usual discreet knock.

"The Interior Minister called to say that if we send a boat upriver tomorrow we can bring back the team from mir Hassun. It must leave tomorrow morning, however, and you must lead it. Sounds odd to me."

"Royce, we're dealing with a madman; of course, I'll lead it." The people up there were his responsibility. "See that it's organized."

On Friday, January 11, at one thirty-five, April silver closed at thirty-four and a half. In India precious heirlooms were being melted. In New York thieves were bringing their loot directly to silver markets. In Chicago silverware was being sold briskly at second-hand stores. Dentists were even removing silver fillings and replacing them with acrylic.

The greedy Hunts were killing themselves. Unfortunately, Tim thought, they are killing me too.

"You don't have enough of your own funds to cover for the Clearing Corporation on Monday morning." Norma was pale and frightened. Tim was getting tired of her, though now was hardly the time to end the relationship. "At eight thirty tomorrow morning Continental Bank will tell them, and we are in very hot water."

"No problem." There really wasn't a problem because Tim still had plenty of hedges. "Transfer the funds from the segregated accounts."

"Customer money?"

"We'll be all right by this time Monday. But don't tell anyone else."

Norma hesitated and then with a faint shrug turned to her computer terminal to make the transfer.

Tim Donlon was happy that Hugh was in the peaceful tropics.

The jungle smelled of sweet flowers and rotting bodies. Hugh, Liz—who'd insisted on coming along—the third secretary, an innocuous and useless young man from a teachers' college in Arkansas, two drivers, and the five-person team from mir Hassun bumped down rutted tracks toward the relative safety of the river, tracks that once had led to silver mines, long since abandoned, beyond mir Hassun.

The team was battered and nervous after six weeks of isolation and three elaborately staged mock executions. The "rebels' forces" had wiped out their new farms, terrorized the villagers who'd cooperated with them, and kept the team in fear every day of its captivity, without, however, doing it any physical harm. Everson, the team leader, was worn out with fever and Laura Kincaid, the youngest member, was now the de facto leader. Thin and tired, but still beautiful, Laura had greeted the rescue party with the confidence of a warrior queen.

Birds squawked in protest and animals stirred restlessly as they wound their way tortuously toward the river. In another year the forest would obliterate the trail completely. There would be no more village agricultural experiments at mir

Hassun; the message from the Principal Leader was loud and clear.

"Were the rebel soldiers from the Leader's army?" Hugh asked Laura, who sat next to him in the jeep.

"Battle fatigues and a different color beret," she said, shaking her head wearily. "And they had Russian guns. But they were working for him. Otherwise we'd be dead."

Hugh relaxed a little. If the Leader was indulging in a little game with his American allies, then they were safe in the jungle. The group that was playing hide and seek on the track behind them was following them as protection to make sure the drama came to its prescribed end.

After several more turns they finally reached the river, and found their launch still securely tied up at the decaying pier.

Thank God.

As they piled out of their jeeps and hurried toward the launch, an old truck lurched down the track and stopped right behind them. A dozen dark-skinned soldiers armed with rifles and machine pistols poured out of the truck and swarmed all around them.

The Principal Leader had written a different scenario, after all.

One of the troopers jabbed Hugh in the stomach and another hit him over the head with the butt of his rifle. As Hugh staggered backward, he smelled the alcohol. He thought of all the things that had been done to white captives, especially white women captives, in this part of the world by drunken soldiers.

And for the first time in his life he was numb with fear.

First the soldiers beat the men and then they tied them to trees. Then they went after the women, holding both of them at bayonet point against a tree until all the troopers were ready. The noncom in charge then barked an order in a dialect Hugh didn't understand, whereupon several of the men tore off Liz's and Laura's clothes. Fabric that would not tear was cut away with the bayonets. Naked and terrified, the two women were pushed from soldier to soldier, slapped, fondled, pinched, and squeezed. When they tried to resist, they were beaten, but just enough to intimidate them into passivity again. Dark fingers pawed at white flesh, amusing themselves, taking their time, stretching out their own pleasure and the women's pain and humiliation as long as they could. Torture as foreplay, it seemed.

Hugh watched as in a nightmare. So this was Liz's Third World. He hoped she was happy with it.

On January 18, after the silver pit at the CBT had closed, Tim Donlon sat at his desk as if he were frozen there. Silver had closed at forty dollars and fifty cents an ounce, an eighteen dollar run-up since his sale a month ago, an increase of ninety thousand dollars a contract. Those who had bought at that price had made a huge profit; those who had gone short had suffered a gigantic loss.

Tim was one of the losers—more than nine million dollars. There was no money left. The Clearing Corporation would make the call the next morning. He would not be able to meet it. By nine thirty, nervous auditors would be all over them, fearing a scandal that could rock the venerable CBT to its foundations. They would discover that he'd used customers' money to cover almost five million dollars. Before noon they would have a floor broker liquidate his contracts and the firm would be wiped out. Donlon, Fowler, and Donlon would be no more. The clients would have his hide and Hugh would return home to put his personal resources into paying off the debts.

"One more day, just one more day and the market will break," he'd said disconsolately to Norma.

"Can't you get money from your wife?"

"Are you kidding? We've tied up a fortune in the new house. Even the doorknobs are gold-plated—or silver-plated anyway." He laughed to himself as if he'd just said something terribly witty. He was weary of Norma, but he would need her in the days ahead, especially if the Commodity Futures Trading Commission started talking indictment. They usually were satisfied with a suspension if the customers got their money back, but you never could be certain.

Tim was frightened. He'd thought about activating his final hedge, an elegant and ironic protection against this disaster. But there hadn't been enough money in the hedge to cover the margin calls. It would be eaten up in a few days and he would have nothing left.

What if something were to happen to him? Tim considered for a moment. How would Hugh prove his noninvolvement?

He spun to his typewriter and began to put down a statement.

> *I, Timothy Donlon, do hereby attest that my brother, Hugh Donlon, at no time intervened in the activities of our investment firm during his term as ambassador, that he never discussed our silver contacts with me during that time, that it was not his money with which I purchased half of those contracts, and that he never advised me to unsegregate clients' funds to meet our calls at that time. I also attest that I persuaded Benedict Fowler and Norma Austin of precisely the opposite of this. I do not apologize to anyone.*
>
> *Nonetheless, I am writing this affidavit, which Norma Austin will notarize, in case anything should happen to me while investigations are still in progress. I will not disclose here the whereabouts of my final hedge against the current silver market, as I intend to use that for my own honorable retirement.*

The "rebels" enjoyed their game with the two women, a game that by the standards of native soldiery was almost gentle. Liz screamed hysterically as they pawed and jabbed her; Laura gritted her teeth and yelled only when she was being hurt.

The worst of their torments had not begun. And might not. Hugh remained detached and skeptical. The beating administered to the men in the party had been perfunctory. The women were being degraded and humiliated but not seriously injured. Hugh returned to his first explanation: It was a show enacted by the Leader, a disgusting trick.

Or they might die. He did not want to die, although he wasn't quite sure why. His life was such a waste—failed priest, failed husband, failed father, failed human being. Would God forgive him? Was there a God? He'd tried to do his best . . . Maria had faulted him for that. Do, do, do, she'd said. What else was there?

The noncom gave another order.

Hugh searched deep within himself for the courage and the strength to do something. He should be able to react. Passive fatalism, detached despair—that was not Hugh Donlon. He found nothing.

Dear God, save us.

The two women were stretched on the ground, their hands and feet held by troopers, bayonet points at their throats. The noncom swaggered over and stood above them, as if trying to decide which one he would enjoy first.

He pointed at Liz. The soldiers holding her feet jerked them apart. The noncom unfastened his ammunition belt, lowered his pants, and knelt between her legs. Liz screamed and tried to twist away. The bayonet pricked her throat. Blood streaked down her neck.

Another soldier knelt in front of Laura.

"Give me absolution, Hugh, please," she screamed.

An odd time to think about God. God? There was no God. How could there be a God?

"Please," she screamed again.

A soldier hit her breasts with his rifle butt.

Hugh said the words. "I absolve you of your sins, in the name of the Father and of the Son and of the Holy Spirit." Another soldier hit him in the stomach. He vomited.

Then the Principal Leader's gendarmes arrived in a high-powered launch, precisely, Hugh realized, at the prearranged moment.

Hugh was ashamed of his terror and despair. He should have known better.

The smart, handsome young captain of the gendarmes told him that the "rebel" prisoners would be executed. He gestured to his lieutenant, and the bound prisoners were marched away into the jungle, guarded by two powerful gendarmes brandishing deadly Uzis. Laura and Everson and the boy from Arkansas were vomiting. Liz lay unconscious in the embassy launch.

"Let me see them die," Hugh said. "They tortured my wife. I want to see them die."

"We prevented rape," the officer said defensively. "It is not permitted to watch executions of rebels."

As they moved out in the launch, they heard bloodcurdling screams from the jungle and then the light death rattle of the Uzis. Then silence.

"The men who hurt and humiliated you have been hurt in their turn," the captain announced solemnly. "They have died as dogs deserve to die. In the name of the Principal Leader, I apologize to you."

"Bullshit," Hugh said, confident that the rebels were marching back to their homes to playact another day. "Let us see the bodies."

"It is not permitted to see the bodies," said the captain.

A charade, a cunning game arranged by a madman who thought he was God. The Exalted One had arranged a scenario that entertained him, won praises for his police, and sent a powerful message to the American government. There was no reality in the story. It was just a horror film for a few terrified whites.

Chapter Thirty-nine
1980

HAROLD MARKS, THE official who covered Donlon, Fowler, and Donlon for the Commodity Futures Trading Commission, arrived at Tim's office shortly after the auditors. Outside, in the boardroom, panic had not yet begun; the brokers and researchers, the secretaries and the wire room operators, the clerks and messengers, had yet to comprehend what was happening and what it meant to them.

"This is James McConnell of the United States Attorney's office, Mr. Donlon," Marks said with quiet deference, "and these are Special Agents Scott and Harrison of the Federal Bureau of Investigation."

"Come in, gentlemen," Tim said cordially. "Can I get anyone some coffee?"

McConnell was a lean, hard man with thin hair, piercing brown eyes, and a Dakota twang. "You may want to have your attorney present, Mr. Donlon, even at this preliminary stage," he said.

"Mr. Gallagher is on the way over," Tim said cheerfully. "I regret all this, of course, but I can assure you the partnership will make good all client losses promptly."

"Then why wasn't the partnership money used to meet the calls?" sniffed Marks.

"Communication problem," Tim said airily. "As you know, my brother is an ambassador and is no longer active in the firm. He advised me to proceed in this fashion if a serious situation developed and he would cover for it. He preferred to remain in the background with his positions while serving abroad."

"You were trading with your brother's money and acting on his advice?" McConnell's voice was even softer.

Tim was delighted by his power. "I can't comment on that."

"And he agreed to the use of clients' funds to meet the clearing house calls?"

"Or that either," Tim said.

"He called you from the embassy?"

"Of course not," Tim said, as if such a suggestion was an insult to Hugh's intelligence. "I don't know where he called from."

"Very interesting. I suppose there were no witnesses to these arrangements."

"I don't see what difference it makes, do you, Mr. Marks? The money's going to be paid back as soon as we reach my brother. He's up some river in darkest Africa."

"He may also be up a creek," Marks said through tight lips.

"So there were no witnesses?" McConnell probed.

"Well, if it comes to that, sure there were," said Tim, eager to be helpful and cooperative, "though I don't know what's the big deal. Mr. Benedict Fowler, a former partner, attended the luncheon at which he worked out the arrangement before Hugh went abroad. He also talked with him on the phone the last time he was in here. And Mrs. Norma Austin, our vice-president, has participated in most of our phone conversations. I still don't see what's the problem."

"The problem, Mr. Donlon"—McConnell sounded like the sheriff giving orders for a hanging—"is that an employee of the federal government seems to have participated in the theft of five million dollars—at least—of clients' money, in addition to perhaps violating conflict-of-interest laws. Even if the money is returned, the law has been violated. There are silver mines in that country, if I recall correctly. You may not realize it, Mr. Donlon, but the United States government does not approve of the violation of its laws, especially by its own employees.''

Poor Hugh, Tim thought. He would get one with a poker up his ass.

Hugh and Laura were sitting in the ambassador's office. The young woman had recovered from her ordeal with remarkable speed, but Hugh's stomach and shoulder were still sore, reminders that the Principal Leader played hardball when he was in the mood for games.

"We'll miss you here," Hugh said, "but I certainly am thankful you're going. You'll have some time at home to make up your mind whether you want to keep on earning a living in upriver villages."

"I've made up my mind," she said promptly, her unblemished face smiling radiantly.

"A lucky man?" The radiance could only mean love.

"A lucky someone. I pretty much made up my mind two months ago. I decided definitely up in the village when they were holding us prisoner. It's important to me, Hugh, that you understand." She smiled again. "And I want you to know that what happened day before yesterday didn't affect my decision."

"I'm glad I'm important, Laura, but who's the lucky someone?"

"God."

"Who?"

"I'm joining the Poor Clare's. The monastery's in Chicago, so I'll be close to your family. They're more liberal now about visitors. I hope you'll visit me sometimes."

Outside the ambassador's window the mighty river flowed on unastonished.

"Why?" was all he could say.

"Why any love, Hugh? Since I was tiny I've known that someone loved me and wanted me specially. I don't know why He does. I'm perfectly happy in the world. I'm not running, I assure you. He doesn't insist. He doesn't even push. He just waits. He won't love me any less if I say no. Only I don't want to say no." She kissed him on the forehead, the way he'd once kissed her mother.

When she left, he felt very old.

The United States Attorney for the Northern District of Illinois considered James McConnell with distaste that he hoped he didn't conceal.

"I don't see it, Jimmy. We've never pushed one of these CFTC things to a grand jury before. The people over at the Board of Trade have their own rules and their own games. Clients get their money back and the government doesn't waste money on a trial. Maybe there's grounds for civil suits, but I can't see a criminal indictment."

"Five million dollars was stolen, sir. That's not a small matter."

"Was it really stolen, Jimmy? A change in a computer record for a few days with the knowledge that one way or another there was the money to change it back? Only a technicality."

"And a government official?"

"Your two witnesses are not all that reliable. The Austin woman was getting herself banged by that creep Tim Donlon. And I hear Ben Fowler has grudges to settle with Hugh Donlon. A good defense lawyer would tear them apart on the stand.''

''It might not come to that. If there's substance to Fowler's allegations, then Hugh Donlon will have to plea-bargain for probation. We get a conviction without ever worrying about a jury.''

The U.S. Attorney had used the strategy himself on more than one occasion, but never with quite so thin a case. ''A lot of taxpayers' money to improve our record.''

''And to send a warning to those people over at the CBT that they have to respect other people's money, even if their father is a federal judge.''

So that was it. Old Judge Donlon had written a scathing opinion about one of the cases McConnell had messed up. The U.S. Attorney made a mental note to get rid of the man as soon as he could and to make some discreet remarks in the Bar Association dining room.

''We'll see what Washington says.'' He ended the conversation.

Jimmy McConnell didn't give up easily. He called a reporter at the *Star Herald* that afternoon. The next morning Chicago woke to characteristically distorted and dishonest headlines that announced, ''Diplomat Involved in Ten Million Dollar Silver Fraud.''

Royce burst into Hugh's office, unable to conceal his elation. ''The Secretary is on the phone . . . he wants to talk to you at once.''

Hugh was impressed neither by the Secretary's importance nor by his ability. He took his time walking to the phone.

''Donlon,'' he said.

''I want your resignation today,'' the cabinet officer said curtly.

''Any special reason?'' Hugh felt a tug of fear. Something was terribly wrong. A scandal about the upriver mess?

''I think you know already, Ambassador.''

''I don't,'' Hugh said. ''I serve at the pleasure of the President, and am ready to cease serving whenever it's his pleasure; but if you want me out of here, you're going to have to tell me why.''

''Because you've just been accused of stealing ten million dollars, that's why,'' the Secretary said triumphantly.

Chapter Forty
1980

HUGH SAT IN Buck Phelan's inner office, waiting for his lawyer to return from the final conference with the U.S. Attorney, who was clearly embarrassed by the situation one of his assistants and the press had created. If Buck read the signs correctly, then everything would be over in a few days. Hugh could then try to pick up the pieces of his life and career.

Liam Wentworth, who was a mountain of support with money, advice, encouragement, and affection during the crisis, had strongly urged against plea-bargaining. "You'll kill them in court, old chap," he had bellowed. "They don't have a case. Hire yourself another solicitor; Phelan is too slick by half. You deserve to be exonerated for all our sakes."

But the fighting spirit and spontaneous resourcefulness that had appeared in past crises failed to appear this time. Hugh stood paralyzed on the goal line with the football in his hands, able neither to punt nor run.

Mir Hassun again.

So he watched his own downfall as if it were an old black-and-white film on late-night TV. He could not expose his family to the horrors of a trial with Tim testifying against him, and Tim had already accepted a grant of immunity, guessing perhaps that the threat of his testimony would force Hugh to plea-bargain. Tim probably rationalized that in this way no one would be hurt or at least no one would go to jail. Hugh's parents aged before his eyes. The judge immediately resigned from the federal bench, on which he had served with honor and distinction for more than forty years. Peggy put aside her paintbrush and sat by the window of their lakefront condo, staring at the gray waters, searching in the drab mysteries of Lake Michigan for consolation that God could not or would not give.

He would win a trial. But what difference did six months probation make? Like the Principal Leader, McConnell had devised a scenario that pretended to be real but was only dramatic fiction.

Marge agreed with Hugh. "He's right, you know, Liam; the old folks couldn't take a public performance by Tim."

"Time he didn't get away with it."

"Maybe you're right," she said sadly, "but it's too late to change now. We've protected Tim all our lives. This is the last time."

"Damn right," Liam said, wishing perhaps for the old days when traitors were driven out of the hill fort with the wolf hounds howling after them.

Hugh liquidated virtually all of his assets and restored the customers' money. There might be some civil suits about profits lost, but the commodity business was so unpredictable that they could be settled easily out of court. Only the home in Kenilworth was safe; it was registered in Liz's name.

Liz seemed to be considering him much as she would be considering a strange form of insect life she'd found in their room in the embassy. Of all those around him, only Liz might believe Tim's story to be true.

The grand jury believed Tim, however, and returned a quick indictment on fourteen counts of violation of the CFTC act and of fraud. Hugh was arraigned before Judge Arnold Crawford and pleaded not guilty. A further hearing was set for the end of March when the plea might be changed, a light sentence of probation imposed, and the matter forgotten.

He would never forget the shame: His picture on the front page of the paper, a man charged with stealing the money of trusting clients; the reporters and the TV cameras in front of his house every morning; the loud angry questions from the reporters; the suspicious and disdainful expressions on the faces of people on the street. He was an accused criminal and, as far as they were concerned, certainly guilty.

"Ex-Priest Charged in Multi-Million Dollar Theft," said the *National Catholic Reporter*.

Shame was like a virus. Even though it was a foreign substance that invaded your system, it became part of you and aggravated the infection caused by your own guilt and self-hatred. Would to God that he could die before that next courtroom appearance.

Buck Phelan, a slick little man who, despite his success as a political lawyer, reminded Hugh of the kind of attorney who hangs around Traffic Court fixing tickets, rushed into his office, breathless and beaming.

"We cut it, Hughie boy, it's all set. The U.S. Attorney hasn't liked this prosecution from day one. All we need is a nolo contendere plea. They'll settle for a fine and a few months probation. By the first of April you'll be a free man without a care or a worry in the world."

"What about Crawford? He's had a grudge against me for a long time. I pushed his brother around in a schoolyard fight back in the forties. Shouldn't we ask him to disqualify himself? Will he go along?"

"I mentioned that problem to our friend over in the federal building. It's informal, as these things have to be, of course, but Arnie swears that he doesn't even remember the fight and hardly remembers his brother. He says the bargain strikes him as being reasonable and just."

"I guess that's it, then." Hugh was uneasy. It was dishonorable to confess even nolo contendere to something when you were innocent.

"Cheer up, man," said the genial Buck. "Call your family and tell them the good news."

Tim at first had taken refuge with Norma Austin in his grotesque new home at Oakland Beach, complete with sauna bath and indoor swimming pool. But his intuition was to dump Norma and leave Chicago as soon as Hugh's sentence was imposed. Tim had thrown himself on Liz's mercy, easily convincing her that Hugh had been planning to make him take the rap for something Hugh himself had done.

It all seemed altogether plausible to Liz, as Hugh had not made the slightest effort to exonerate himself. A week after they returned to Chicago, she took the children and moved out.

On his way to be sentenced, in a courtroom in the Dirksen Federal Building in which his father had often sat, Hugh walked down Dearborn Street, savoring the beauties of his native city—the Daley Plaza with its Picasso sculpture and a Miro across the street, the Bank Plaza with its Chagall, and the Federal Plaza, just ahead of him now, with his favorite piece of Chicago outdoor art, the red "flamingo" mobile of Alexander Calder. Dearborn Street was the most interesting street in the world. Too bad he'd never found the time to enjoy it. Too busy working LaSalle Street instead.

Judge Arnold Crawford accepted the change of plea to nolo contendere without comment. "Mr. District Attorney, do you have any recommendations about sentencing?"

The U.S. Attorney spoke himself, not trusting McConnell to carry off the deal. "Your Honor, our office feels that there must be a fine as a warning to others who might consider violating the Commodity Futures Trading Act and we also feel that some kind of probationary sentence, six months to a year, would be appropriate. The defendant is not a hardened criminal, the money that was misused has been repaid, his distance from the country in what was actually brave government service at the time of the crime is certainly a mitigating factor. We feel that the disgrace that he has suffered is a sufficient punishment and deterrent to similar crimes.''

Crawford tapped his pen lightly on the bench in front of him. The reporters in the courtroom leaned forward eagerly, the court's dramatic pause giving them hope that there might be more of a story here than the reported plea-bargain deal.

''I normally respect the opinion of the U.S. Attorney's office,'' the judge said sternly, ''but in the present case, I feel I must respectfully disagree.''

''Hugh Thomas Donlon, you are a man of great talents and achievements. You have been well endowed both by nature and by your family background. You have served effectively in several different professions. But I am of the opinion, sir, that you have never learned the meaning of self-restraint or integrity. You have always taken it for granted that you can possess anything or anyone you wanted, by whatever means, legal when convenient, illegal when necessary. To suspend your sentence in a federal correctional institution would be to make a mockery of justice. It would tell the young people of this judicial district that a man from the right family and with the right friends can violate the law with impunity.'' The judge's gray eyes were shining with the triumph of revenge. ''I therefore sentence you to eighteen months in the Federal Correctional Institute at Lexington, Kentucky, and urge you to spend however many of those months you actually serve reflecting on the models of humility that were held up to you for imitation during your years of preparation for the priesthood.''

That day at one thirty, trading in April silver ended at fifteen dollars eighty cents an ounce, and trading in June silver at twenty-two dollars, twenty cents an ounce. The great ''Bunker Hunt'' silver run-up was over.

The next morning the *Tribune* carried a headline on its third page, ''Marxists Take Over African Government.'' The story reported that the mutilated body of the Principal Leader had been found floating in a dugout ten miles downstream from the capital city.

Chapter Forty-one
1980

THE FEDERAL CORRECTIONAL Institution at Lexington, Kentucky, was, as Pete McQueen, Hugh's new lawyer, put it, a jail for those the government knew it ought not to lock away and a place where all the modern penal techniques worked because they were unnecessary.

''The prisoners they send here,'' McQueen told Hugh, ''are guilty of crimes they will never commit again. The place isn't bad enough to deter anyone from committing a similar offense. Society doesn't profit from their being in prison, the taxpayers lose money on it, and certainly the convicts don't benefit. A term here represents the ultimate victory of the prosecuting attorney over the attorney for the defense. It's vengeance, pure and simple. Even if you were guilty, ten months here would not be a constructive way of repaying your debt to society.''

The list of items Hugh could bring revealed the contradictions inherent in the prison—two sports jackets, a tennis racket, a swimming suit, one ring, one watch, two bed sheets, one billfold, two ties . . . not quite the paraphernalia for a country club, but not the sort of things one is usually told to bring to prison.

Yet, even with time off for good behavior, Lexington, a foreboding, red brick former narcotics sanatorium, would be Hugh's home for ten months.

It was, in many ways, not nearly as bad as the Catholic seminary of the 1950s. There was more freedom of movement, less censorship of mail, and no attempt at thought control. Moreover, inmates were rewarded with periodic home leaves for keeping the rules, a reward the seminary had never offered.

Hugh was "processed" through a battery of psychological tests, an interview with a staff psychologist, and an introductory conference with a "social adviser"—the title sounded like that of a dorm mother in a women's college; apparently "social worker" was thought to be an offensive phrase—who monitored his problems much more gently than had Father Meisterhorst.

His "social adviser" was a wispy twenty-five-year-old woman from Georgia named Marilyn Henderson. Her lank blond hair hung around her plain face in shanks.

"I've noticed, Mr. Donlon, that you are working in the laundry. With your skills you could serve on the library staff, or in the computational center, or teach courses. We have a social science program here."

"I like it in the laundry," Hugh replied; it was exhausting work but an excellent substitute for thought, and better than teaching a course on "Coming to Terms with Yourself."

"I've also noticed that you have not asked for another appointment with the psychological staff."

"Is that obligatory? Is it part of the good behavior for which I receive time off?"

"Of course not." She pushed the hair out of her eyes, a useless nervous gesture. "The psychologist reports that, aside from a normal depressive reaction, you are in better mental health than most of the admittees he sees."

"What's normal depression, Ms. Henderson?"

"The sort of depression that men and women who are not institutionalized feel under severe stress."

"I see."

"I've also noticed that you say you expect no visitors. We feel that visitors are an important part of our program. The family is subjected to minimum supervision and there is no harassment or . . . humiliation."

"I think it would be better for me to see my family during the home furlough if I'm granted one. My attorney may come occasionally."

"It's entirely your decision. And you must remember, Mr. Donlon"—she was quoting from a textbook now—"that we on the staff make no judgments about a person's legal or moral standing. Those matters have been decided by other agencies. We are here to help. As you realize, the supervision is minimal. There are no bars. You can even walk out. A minimum security facility such as this is predicated on the assumption that it is to the perceived self-interest of the inmates to monitor their own behavior. Hence, staff members like myself are really here to facilitate your development during the time you are with us. You must think of me as someone who is at your service instead of the other way around."

"I quite understand that, Ms. Henderson."

Hugh didn't feel a victim of the system. Nor did he ever protest his innocence in prison. Nor did he explain why he hadn't contested the indictment in the first place. Before he came to Lexington, he'd depersonalized himself, established a wall between his emotions and the facts of his life.

There was nothing left that merited enthusiasm or commitment, not Church, not government, not business, not even his family. Life in Lexington was only slightly more pointless than life outside.

Yet he was still, oddly, a priest. He gave an occasional absolution to a nervous or scrupulous inmate and counseled several who, like himself, were having severe, if understandable, marital problems. The second week he was in the facility he administered the last rites to a heart attack victim while the chaplain was away on his day off. Ms. Henderson somewhat dubiously found him the key for the sacred oils. The man recovered and the chaplain was anxious lest the ecclesiastical authorities discover that Hugh had dispensed the sacrament. Contemptuously, Hugh cited the relevant canon from the code and offered to write a letter to the archbishop.

Hard work in the laundry, hard exercise in the recreation yard, careful dieting, exhausted sleep at night—these were Hugh's therapies. He lost weight and regained his physical strength. He avoided books and amused himself with summer reruns on TV.

And tried to pretend that the virus of shame was not becoming worse each passing day.

McQueen visited him on a blistering day at the end of August.

"Your mother and father are fine . . . I'm sure you hear from them. The Kerrys or the Wentworths . . . never know what to call them . . . are spending the summer at Lake Geneva with your parents. Hauntingly attractive kids, like characters from an Irish saga. Your parents are holding up well."

Hugh hardly thought of his parents and not at all of Lake Geneva. "I'm glad."

"No luck on the reduction of sentence, I'm afraid. The people at Justice admit there's been a mistake—nice choice of words, huh?—but it has not escaped your attention that Mr. Carter is running for reelection. They don't want it to look like they're taking care of one of their own."

Pete McQueen was a feisty brown-haired young South Side Irishman who looked and acted like a successful lightweight boxer. If he'd been Hugh's attorney at the beginning, Hugh might be at Lake Geneva too. Not that it made much difference.

"Have you heard from your wife?" McQueen acted like a man who'd jumped off a cliff and wondered whether it was a mistake.

"No . . . not a word. Why?"

"She's filing for divorce. Her attorney is one of the toughest divorce lawyers in the city. She wants everything you have, Hugh, and a substantial chunk of the rest of your life."

"Charges?"

"Cruelty, adultery, desertion, the works. It could be messy if we contest it."

"Nolo contendere seems to be my routine plea, doesn't it? She can have everything there is. See that she gets a proportion of my income instead of a dollar figure."

Pete looked up from his notebook, frowning. "Why do that, Hugh? You're going to make a lot of money when you're released. Let her go into court when she wants more."

"Suppose I find a job as a teacher in a junior college somewhere in the sticks, or in the inner city?"

"You wouldn't make such a choice, would you?" His fighter's face showed dismay.

"Do it," Hugh said with more firmness than he'd displayed in months, "and do it all as quietly as possible. I don't want to cause the family any more embarrassment.''

"Do you ever think of yourself, Hugh?" He closed the notebook.

"How else do you think I ended up here?"

"I'm not your priest . . . I'm sorry . . . I forgot . . .''

"No problem.'' It was the first time he'd felt a smile in a long time. "Even priests can have priests.''

Two weeks later Ms. Henderson informed Hugh that there was an "extraordinary visitor'' waiting for him.

Oh, God, he thought to himself, not Liz.

"Do I have to see this person?'' he asked as she led him away from the laundry.

"Not if you don't want to. His name''—she glanced at the file card in her hand—"is Mr. Cronin.''

The cardinal was wearing a white open-neck shirt, gray slacks, and a black Windbreaker—an incognito of tailor-made casuals chosen by a determined sister-in-law who was also a U.S. senator.

With no preliminaries other than a firm handshake, the cardinal began talking about the U.S. senator. "I've asked my sister-in-law Nora to work on the Justice Department. A bunch of phonies. They say there's been an injustice but they can't do anything about it in an election year. You were framed, weren't you?'' The hoods retracted from his probing brown eyes.

"That's what every con says.''

"I'm not interested in every con. I'm interested in one of the priests of my diocese.''

"I'm an ex-priest. I don't have to answer questions from a bishop.''

Sean leaned back in his easy chair and laughed. "Oh, you'll always be a priest, Hugh, till the day you die. Theologically, of course, but personally too. You say Mass here?''

"Lord, no. I administered the last rites when the chaplain was away and he almost had a stroke.''

"I'll have a word with him before I leave. If an inactive priest occasionally says Mass privately, I'm not going to send him off to the dungeons of the Holy Office. Now answer my question.''

"I had no knowledge of anything that was done at Donlon, Fowler, and Donlon during the silver run-up. Tim lied, Fowler lied, Norma Austin lied. Judge Crawford lied when he agreed to a plea-bargain and then used his power to settle an old family feud. I'm guilty of a lot of things in my wasted life, Cardinal, but not of any of the crimes for which I'm here.''

"Sean.'' The cardinal grimaced. "Okay, I wanted to make sure that my judgment was right. Your wife really leaving you?''

"Yes.''

"Bitch.''

"Maybe I've given her reason.''

The cardinal ignored that. "You know about the new annulment rules? We could get you an annulment in short order.''

"I've broken one promise in my life. I don't want to break another.''

"Let God punish you if He wants. Don't punish yourself.''

Hugh understood. "You want me back in the priesthood?''

"You're a priest now, Hugh. Just inactive.''

"After all I've done, you want me back in the active ministry?'' He exhaled a long breath of astonishment.

"As I tell my Polish friend over on the fifth floor of the Vatican, we let the first pope back in, we can let anyone back in . . . and Peter had a wife too."

"Sean, I'm deeply moved. . . ." And he was. For the first time in months genuine emotions tugged at him—humility, gratitude, perhaps even a touch of hope.

"Forget that," the cardinal said as he rose from the chair. "I must be in the big city for a Confirmation at seven thirty. It's an open offer, Hugh. And I'll be back."

Chapter Forty-two
1980

ON A SUNDAY afternoon in the middle of November Marilyn Henderson appeared at the door of the recreation room, where Hugh was agonizing through another disaster by the Chicago Bears. She motioned to him.

It was unusual for her to be working on Sunday and even more unusual for her to be near the rec room.

He followed her into the corridor, noting as he always did how much he expected the smell of disinfectant in what had been a hospital corridor.

"I'm afraid I have bad news, Mr. Donlon. . . ."

Oh, God, not Mom or Dad.

"Your father called from Chicago. There's been an airplane crash in Puerto Rico, a plane flying from St. Maarten to San Juan crashed on landing in a rainstorm. Your brother, Timothy, and his wife and two of their children were on it. I'm afraid we don't know yet which children. You might want to pack some clothes. A furlough authorization will come through shortly."

"Oh," Hugh said dully, realizing how relieved he was that it was Tim and not his parents. Selfish, selfish, selfish. Poor doomed Tim.

"You'll want to go home for the wake and funeral?" she asked uneasily.

Some of his old graciousness toward women returned. Poor kid, she was trying hard. "Certainly, Ms. Henderson, I appreciate your concern very much, particularly on Sunday afternoon, when I'm sure you'd rather be with your family."

His smile had its usual effect on a woman. She blushed and smiled radiantly in return. "My husband is watching the football game, so he didn't mind." When she laughed she was not unattractive. Making life difficult for her was one more sin.

She drove him to the airport in Louisville so he could catch the last Sunday plane to Chicago.

Jack Howard, balding and heavy but with the old infectious grin, was waiting for him at O'Hare.

The grin didn't last long. "Your dad asked me to pick you up, Hugh. They're having a hard time sorting things out. You heard the news?"

"Timmy and Estelle and two of the kids?"

"Then you haven't heard the latest news. . . . I—I guess I have to be the one to tell you." Jack was sweating profusely; he wiped his face with a handkerchief. "Estelle is alive and so are her kids. She's raising hell about the error. . . ."

"But my social adviser . . . said that it was Mr. and Mrs. Timothy Donlon who were missing in the crash. It was Timmy?"

Jack nodded miserably.

"Then who were the woman and children?"

Jack gulped. "Your wife and your two kids."

Maria didn't want to go to the wake, but her two older sons insisted, as did her parents. "The Irish expect it," her father said simply.

The judge and Peggy would be happy to see her. Marge's reaction was hard to predict. She didn't want to think about Hugh.

He was a stranger, a man she never knew, only a faint reflection of a boy she was mad about a quarter of a century ago, a dream stored in the back of her imagination, a fantasy for nights when she was lonely and drank an extra glass of wine.

Still.

Still, what, Maria Angelica?

Still, I'm going to the wake and see what happens.

She almost lost her nerve in the parking lot of the North Shore Funeral Home.

"I'm not going in with all those people," she insisted.

"Well, we're going in, whether you do or not. Right, Steve?" Eddie was as feisty as his mom and as darkly handsome a Taylor Street entrepreneur as his grandfather.

The taller brother, so much like his father, said softly, "No question."

"Stay close to me," Maria entreated.

At the door they met the redoubtable Monsignor Muggsy Brannigan, who bragged that he'd shot his age twice last summer, eighty-two, and broke into the seventies once. "These two galoots yours, Maria? Bet they went to Fenwick."

She introduced her two sons, told Monsignor Muggsy where they were going to college, and added, "And Kenny, the youngest, is in school at St. Mark's. He's the only one in the family who looks like me."

Muggsy's eyes, weak and covered by thick glasses, danced with fun. "She still chew bubble gum, guys?"

Ed pulled a package from his pocket. "Makes me carry it for her."

"Real proud of you, Maria," said the genial old man. "Keep it up . . . and pray for that crowd in there. They need it."

Inside, there were three groups of mourners arrayed in different positions near the four sealed caskets.

On the far right were Liz's family, big, hard-bodied, quiet people from Iowa—old parents, brothers and sisters, nieces and nephews, awkward, silent, grim-faced. There was no line waiting for them and only a few people from the other two lines bothered to speak with them. Neither Chicago nor Irish; they didn't belong. At the center was Estelle, red-faced, fat, bitter, surrounded by her mother and father and children, pointedly ignoring the Donlons and loudly complaining about the funeral arrangements.

Then there were the Donlons on the left—the judge, shaken and bemused; Peggy, pale and drawn; Marge, weeping and lovely; and Hugh, lean now and silver-haired.

"Will they bury them from church?" she whispered to Ed as they waited in line.

"Why not? Oh, you mean the public sin thing? Maybe the local pastor, who's a nerd, will wonder about it. He'll call Sean and get his orders and that will be that."

"Is that what you call the cardinal?" she said disapprovingly.

"Why not? That's his name, isn't it? Everyone calls him Sean—seminarians not quite to his face yet, though he probably couldn't care less. Anyway, if the Apostle John showed up, we wouldn't call him Cardinal Ben Zebedee, would we?"

"I never knew his middle name was Ben."

Peg and Tom barely recognized Maria or the boys. Only when she turned to Marge did Peg realize who they were.

Marge was more forthcoming. "Wonderful of you to come. It's easiest on me; I have Liam and the kids."

Lord Kerry's massive, slow smile made Maria feel warm. The two girls who were with them were fey, lovely creatures who favored her own sons with warm greetings that went beyond courtesy. She would have to warn the boys to avoid Irish colleens.

"Poor Hugh," she said awkwardly. "His whole family. . . ."

Marge sighed. "I think it will be a relief for him to be able to return to the priesthood . . . a blessing in disguise."

Maria had not considered that possibility and she didn't like it a bit.

"Maria . . ." he said, holding her hand. Oh, God, she thought, such pain in those wonderful blue eyes.

"I'm sorry, Hugh."

"It all comes to an end eventually." He seemed spaced out, the smile not empty but otherworldly. What were they doing to him in prison?

There was no Hugh Donlon left, an empty man, hollow, drained of all life and vitality.

More than prison.

He'd been in a prison all his life. The Donlon family prison. A splendid, comfortable, well-intentioned prison. But one that destroyed you just the same. And you couldn't help loving the jailers.

"My son Steve and my son Ed." She introduced the boys.

"You go to the Citadel like your father?" A routine, automatic question. Recited from a memorized script.

"Yes, sir. Family tradition."

"Wonderful, keep it up. And Ed?"

Oh, oh, never thought of that.

"Niles College. I'm going to be a priest."

Hugh was shaken. "Jean and Hank's daughter is becoming a Poor Clare. It all swings around . . . I'm sorry, another family. I'm confused. Good luck to you."

"We'll pray," Maria said helplessly as they edged away.

In the parking lot Maria and her sons met the cardinal, Bishop McGuire, his red-haired, genial second-in-command, the cardinal's tall, striking sister-in-law, Senator Nora Cronin, and her husband, Roy Hurley, the handsome sports announcer. The cardinal performed introductions all around.

The senator knew Steven, who had escorted her daughter Noreen to a number of Washington dances.

"He doesn't tell me about his social life," Maria laughed. "Lucky Steve."

"Lucky Noreen," the senator corrected her.

"Ed, Steve, can you spare me your mother for a moment?" asked the cardinal.

"Sure, Cardinal," the two boys said in unison.

They stepped away from the cardinal's limousine.

"You were once close to him, weren't you, Mrs. McLain?"

"A long time ago, teen-age." Maria was taken aback.

"Forgive me for having asked questions about you and the Donlons. I had a kind of hunch."

"Oh?"

"Maria, I hope you don't mind my using your first name, because I'm going to insist that you call me Sean. Now, shall we leave the future in God's hands and concentrate on getting Hugh out of that hellhole down south? I pried the truth out of him: He didn't know a thing. Tim, God be good to the poor man, lied. Ben Fowler and the Austin woman lied too. So did Judge Crawford, who promised a plea bargain and then reneged."

"I didn't think about any of those things," she admitted. "I knew he hadn't done anything wrong. That was enough."

"Find me the evidence and Nora will take care of the rest." The cardinal's eyes gleamed with a mad light of battle, an Irish freebooter from long ago, one of the wild geese of song.

"Why me?"

Sean Cronin smiled enthusiastically. "I don't know anyone else who cares about him and is smart enough to get him out of jail."

Wearily, as if she had not slept in months, Peg Donlon opened the door of her apartment. She had seen Liz's family off on the plane to Iowa, a dour group departing sullenly, not even pretending to graciousness. Estelle and her family had at least gone through the motions of courtesy, though with enough of an edge to let Peg know they were condescending.

Peg had lost a child too, but that didn't seem important to any of them.

Her stomach was upset—too much hasty eating during the past week. And there was probably not a single Tums in the apartment.

There was a package inside the front door. The people from reception must have brought it up.

She lifted it to the hallway table. Not too heavy but it strained her left shoulder, which had been bothering her for the past few days. Getting old. Sometimes she didn't feel old at all. Now she felt ancient.

She opened the package. How wonderful. The first copies of Tom's book from Cornell. She must try to read it again, though she had no idea what Tom was talking about. She hoped that the academic reviewers would be kind.

What a lovely print of the Chartres rose window on the cover. Maybe after Christmas she and Tom could travel. It would be a cold, lonely Christmas this year.

She laid Tom's book reverently on the coffee table and stood back to admire it.

Then the pain struck, the worst pain she had ever known, an elephant stomping on her chest.

I'm having a heart attack, she thought as she collapsed to the floor. I'm going to die. Poor Tom. I always thought he'd be the first to go. Where is my rosary?

Hugh was poking around his house, preparing to return to Lexington. Marilyn Henderson had offered to extend his furlough, but he'd told her he would prefer time at Christmas.

Actually, he would be happy to be back in Lexington, just as sometimes during the long summer vacations from the seminary he had missed the order and the blessed tedium of its routine. At Lexington there would be no memories.

In the small desk she'd used for her paperwork he found Liz's mementos, a little stack of precious keepsakes that survived after thirty-nine years of life: high school yearbooks, a dry, pressed prom corsage, report cards, love letters from a boy at Iowa State who had manfully accepted her decision to be a "bride of Christ," even congratulations on her marriage.

Vocations, he thought, were different matters these days. Young people like Laura Kincaid had a much clearer idea of what they were doing.

And the young man who was going to be a priest . . . who was he? Hugh had met him at the wake. Ed something or other. Handsome, dark-skinned lad, with a brilliant smile and flashing black eyes.

Ed McLain . . . Maria's son? Maria's son a priest?

He shook his head. Strange.

He went back to Liz's mementos: a prize-winning term paper, seeing signs of grace in Graham Greene, not bad actually; graduation picture; invitation to her profession; picture at her sister's wedding, lovely in the maid of honor's dress; another picture, in a white bridal gown on the day of her own commitment as a bride of Christ—how corny that sounded only a decade and a half later—a letter from the provincial reluctantly approving her plea to attend graduate school. Dispensation from her vows; wedding pictures, baptism pictures of Brian, not of Lise—too busy to take pictures then.

Hugh thought of the early weeks, the first time early Christmas morning, the Sunday afternoon after that, the weekend at Lake Geneva. Bright and promising moments.

How little remains of your hopes and dreams after you are gone, a few perishable records that after ten years would interest no one.

Most poignant of all, Hugh found a first draft of her letter seeking admission to the Order. An eighteen-year-old child who was filled with bright, intelligent youthful ideals—serve God and my fellow human beings with all my heart and to the best of my ability. Dedicate my life to bringing more love and kindness into the world, work for our Lord and his Church. The only way I will ever be happy. Not worthy of a vocation but inspired by the Holy Ghost—he was still a ghost then—to respond to a wonderful gift.

Hugh shoved the papers aside.

How long had she loved Tim? Had she become silent and withdrawn when the scandal broke because she was on Tim's side?

It didn't matter. He'd failed her and their children. Now they were all dead. The grief inside him was so deep he couldn't experience it, face it, discharge it.

He would finish his life frozen and emotionless, like the blue waters of Lake Geneva imprisoned in winter ice.

He picked up from the bed on which he'd been piling the keepsakes the latest school pictures of Brian and Lise—taken at the embassy school by a Marine photographer. Lise would have grown into a beautiful woman. Brian was well-coordinated but not interested in sports. . . .

He wanted with all his soul to grieve for them. Flesh of my flesh, bone of my bone. He remembered the few times that he had played with them. There had been beginnings . . . nothing came of them. His fault . . . ? Liz's? What did it matter?

He remembered other children, the little boy who had committed adultery by saying "shit" to his mother. He had been good with kids in those days.

Brian and Lise would still be dead, even if he had been close to them.

Yet, so much waste. . . .

I do love you, my lost children. Forgive me, you harmless little ones. I failed you. I don't even understand why I failed you, but I did. If there is a place where we can undo our mistakes, I will love you there. Give me another chance.

He sat on the edge of the bed, burying his head in the crook of his arm. Still the tears would not come.

I who was loved so much by my mother and father did not pass love on.

"What's his problem?" Ed McLain asked, watching Hugh Donlon stare grimly at the TV cameras as he walked away from the gravesite of his wife and children.

Maria looked up from her terminal, on which she was pretending to work. What would her sons feel about her having a romance with a man involved in a public scandal? And a former priest? "Same as the whole family. The mother— you met her—wasn't she ravishing?"

"Sure was," Ed said appreciatively, "for a woman her age."

The McLains' living room was furnished with stark modern Scandinavian teak and thick burgundy leather cushions, sufficiently unlikely to boggle most visitors' minds. "Norman background" was her usual explanation.

"We won't discuss women's ages tonight," she warned him. "She's a wonderful woman, full of energy and warmth. The kids all fell in love with her, unsurprisingly enough. But neither she nor the kids ever figured out how to cope with her sex appeal."

Ed was into psychology, so Maria, who'd read a few books herself, tried to speak his language.

"Lingering over rites of passage, such as giving up the nipple?"

"Eddie, that's the dirtiest thing I've ever heard."

"Sorry, Mom." He smiled his Valentino smile. "Call it introjection if you like."

"And that's even worse," she added.

"Are you implying"—he paid no attention to her protest—"that boys who get tied up in intimate relationships with sexy mothers will have troubled lives?"

"If they haven't learned," Maria shot back at him, "that mother's love doesn't have to be earned by pleasing her and if mother isn't up front about her sex appeal, yes."

"You in love with Donlon?" Eddie asked.

So there was the question, out in the open where it belonged. How did a younger son of a widow react when his mother might be falling in love? What did Ed's books tell him about that?

"I was once and I might be again," she said cautiously.

She didn't want to admit to Ed or anyone else that she'd evaluated every man she'd met in the last five years against two models, Steven McLain and Hugh Donlon, and so far no one had passed the test.

"You'll make an impulsive decision, like you always do?"

"Not impulsive, instinctive," Maria said defensively. "And my instincts have served me pretty well all my life. Do you object?"

"Me?" Ed asked in some surprise. "Gosh, no, Mom. I trust your instincts as much as you do. He seems to be a good guy. Tough enough to put up with you when you're in one of your bitchy Sicilian moods."

"Are you sure?"

"Why would I disapprove?" The young man was puzzled. "I don't claim veto rights over your affairs. Anyway, if any woman can straighten him out, it'd be you."

"Oh Eddie." She rolled up her magazine and smacked the palm of her hand. "Say a prayer for a superannuated teen-ager, will you?"

Eddie got up and, crossing the room, lightly kissed her on the forehead. "Sure will," he said.

Hugh began to pack his clothes. Everyone seemed to assume that now that he was free of his family he would return to the priesthood. Marge was explicit about it. "You never would have resigned unless Liz had got herself pregnant. I don't say you shouldn't have left, but now you're free to return. It will make Mom and Dad so happy."

Jack Howard, Bishop Jimmy McGuire, even that strange Polish artist fellow Waldek—all discreetly hinted that Sean would be able to get him back in.

Neither his father nor mother had mentioned it exactly. But they had said, and often if gently during the days of the wake and funeral, that, however terrible the tragedy, he was now able to start his life all over again.

Was that all Liz had been, and Lise and Brian—obstacles to his starting his life again?

And then there had been Maria, slim and aristocratic in a black crepe dress, gold and silver hair falling around her face, her Rembrandt eyes sparkling ice-blue as though in winter, sunlight behind her glasses; Maria, now with a self-possession born of success and tragedy.

His wife buried only a few days, and now he was already thinking about another woman, a woman about whom he knew nothing, really. I love you, Maria. I've never stopped loving you.

He reached for the phone to call her. It rang before he could pick it up.

"Yes, Waldek, I'm sure she's in the apartment. No answer? Yes, I'm concerned too. I'll call my sister, she's staying at the Drake, just a block away. Not at all . . . thanks for calling."

The pain was worse. It was harder to breathe. She didn't have much time. Her life swept by . . . First Communion, Tom's lips and hands at Twin Lakes, the terrible failure of the wedding night, the later delights, Hugh's birth, the paintings, Hugh's first Mass, the terrible quarrel with Tom.

If only I could find my rosary. It's in my purse in the hallway. I'll never touch it again. I'll never touch Tom again. Dear God, one more chance.

There was so much left to do, good-byes to say, love to repeat, pardons to ask.

No time. All right, God, I'm not ready, but You can have me. But please help me to say a last prayer before I leave.

Then one last, desperate word torn from her shattered heart, for Tom and for God and for everyone. . . .

"Love!"

There was light now and someone waiting, then footsteps, and strong arms, and then nothing at all. . . .

Chapter Forty-three
.... *1980–1981* ....

A LETTER FROM Liz was waiting for him when he returned to Lexington. It was postmarked from St. Maarten the day of the crash.

Hugh hesitated before opening it. He didn't want a message from the grave, especially not after his mother's flirtation with death.

Peggy was recovering now. According to the doctors, she was out of danger. Yet who could promise that she wouldn't have another attack tomorrow?

Also, as Marge had bluntly said, it might well be in Hugh's hands whether she lived or not. Marge had wanted a decision about the priesthood before he returned to prison.

And he had all but given it, saying he would write to the cardinal as soon as he got back.

Liam was the one who'd saved Peggy's life. What a scene it must have been, the hulking Irishman in his shirt-sleeves, mother-in-law in his arms, running at full speed down Chestnut Street and across Chicago Avenue in a snowstorm with the wind howling in from the lake.

The doctors in the emergency room at Northwestern Hospital said she would have been dead in a few more minutes. "Not many of us would have had the presence of mind to do what your brother-in-law did," the woman cardiological resident told him.

Hugh opened the letter from Liz.

> *I suppose I must begin this difficult letter at the beginning. I am not going ahead with the divorce unless you want me to. If you would rather be rid of me, then I will go quietly and ask only for enough money to take care of the kids. If you want them—and I can't imagine you will—I won't fight that either.*
>
> *I hope it's not too late for us, but I leave that to you.*
>
> *I have been here in the Caribbean for a week with a lover, the only time I have been unfaithful to you. I wanted to commit adultery many other times, so I am guilty of sin intention anyway. If you are willing to take me back, I'll never do it again.*
>
> *My lover agrees with this decision.*
>
> *The first thing Monday morning I will call a psychiatrist and set up an appointment. You are a good man and a wonderful husband. If I am unhappy in our marriage, it must be my fault. I have never been happy in my life, not in high school, not in the religious life, not in graduate school, not with you, and not now. If*

someone is always unhappy, then the unhappiness is in their own soul. Strange I should use that word out of our past. I'm sick emotionally and sick spiritually.

I am going to try to find health. I hope you will give me a chance.

Love,
Liz

Hugh put the letter aside with trembling fingers. The woman who wrote that letter had always been inside Liz, clear-eyed and brave. But he'd never broken through to her, never tried to see her, never permitted himself to be aware of her existence.

The ice around him grew thicker.

Norma Austin dug into the steak vigorously. "I've had to watch my budget lately; no steaks for an unemployed professional woman."

"And no jobs," Maria said with genuine sympathy.

"Can you blame them? I was mixed up with something pretty shady."

"I'll give it to you straight, Norma. I can find you a job, a pretty good one. Or I can put you in jail for perjury. Which will it be?"

The other woman lost interest in her steak. "You found Tim's affidavit? So you must have found the hedge too. I'm so glad. He wanted it to be found if anything happened to him. You know how he was . . . life was a game."

"We have all we need to obtain a full exoneration for Hugh." Maria was making it up as she went. "Your testimony will be a help, but we can do without it. No one is eager to put you in jail. But if you don't cooperate . . ."

"I'll cooperate," Norma said eagerly. "It's been on my conscience . . . I was so afraid."

"Just trot over to Pete McQueen's office and spill the whole story. And call me tomorrow. I meant it about the job."

Maria Angelica as lady bountiful, she told herself on the way to her swimming pool and essential daily exercise. She would have to cut it short, only twenty-five laps today, because the bank needed her. In love with a bank, of all things.

In the pool she wondered about Tim's affidavit and the "hedge" he'd left with it. Tim had told her about the hedge too. And probably a lot of other people. He was fond of scattering hints. Where and what was it? She'd better try to find out.

Hugh looked out the window on the recreation field, its lifeless brown turf thinly dusted with snow. He saw, however, Twin Lakes in the late nineteen thirties, the lake a sheet of fog-shrouded glass, the lawns wide and green, the pergola a fortress, the clubhouse a feudal castle. He was running down the gravel path toward the lake and his mother, a beautiful young woman waiting for him with open arms. He tripped and fell on the gravel, scraping his knee. His mother picked him up and made the pain go away, pressing him against her and telling him how much she loved him.

When he was not in the chapel praying or, rather, listening, he let his imagination wander through the past, exploring its colors and images. Somehow they seemed to be linked to his still inchoate prayers.

Some of the ice was melting under the hot rays of the happiness that was still locked up inside him. He was beginning to climb out of the pit. But he had a long slow climb back through hell before he could come alive again.

Where could he make that climb better than in the priesthood?

Ronald Harding twisted uneasily in his oversize chair. His handsome face frowned beneath his thatch of white hair.

"I have the information you want, Maria—at least enough of it, I think. However, you won't be able to use it in court."

"I'm not looking for evidence, Ron, just the lay of the land."

They had been almost lovers, for a short time, before Maria had decided the merry-widow game was more trouble than it was worth. Ron was one of the most distinguished lawyers in Chicago, but so uneasy in his distinction that he needed unquestioning adoration. So he didn't need Maria.

"Very well, then. I know I can trust you. The Internal Revenue people are not satisfied that Tim Donlon died penniless. They think Tim embezzled millions of dollars from the firm during the years his brother was away. Typically, Tim left clues and puzzles that others would find virtually impossible to solve."

"Too clever by half."

"Ultimately, yes. And, if I may say so, you are more beautiful than ever."

"Always did have a way with words, Ron." Maria returned the smile. "I hope you and Roberta remember me when you put together the wedding invitation list." Roberta was his twenty-four-year-old mistress soon to become his bride.

"Of course, we will," he said amiably.

"The hell you will, but that's all right," Maria muttered to herself as she escaped from his office, half-angry that she was so skilled at resisting temptation.

Warmth, that's what you want. Warmth.

Hugh's memories brought him to Lake Geneva. He and Maria were sailing in the dinghy. Maria was struggling unsuccessfully with the jib, laughing as the sail flopped against her face. He jibed into the wind, and the boom came about. Maria scurried to shift her position but not fast enough; the boom hit her in the stomach and, still laughing, she was catapulted over the side. For a second he was afraid she was hurt, might even drown. But before he could plunge into the water to save her, she was clinging to the side of the boat, hair pasted to her skull, Fenwick T-shirt soaked, her laughter undiminished.

The colors of his memories were astonishingly vivid, the white of the sail, the blue of the lake, the bronze of Maria's hair, the black of her shirt—all in the bright hues of an early Technicolor movie.

She was so lovely sitting in the boat, shivering in the cool wind, gasping for breath, and laughing.

Why was God sending him images of Maria in this prison chapel?

Maria had always been a distraction to his priesthood. She still was.

Then he realized, as if it were the first time the thought had occurred to him, that there was no obstacle now to him and Maria. He could have her if he wanted. It was Lake Geneva all over again.

The same agonizing choice.

Chapter Forty-four
1981

LIAM WENTWORTH FLEW from London to accompany Maria to Miami, where she spoke with Ben Fowler. He'd made the trip, he admitted, with some hesitation. Marge wanted Hugh to return to the priesthood with all her heart. They all did, as a matter of fact, but Marge particularly.

"It will help his poor mother recover completely if he is back in the priesthood," Liam had explained in one of his rare complete sentences.

"He can't come back with this scandal over his head. Even Sean Cronin couldn't carry that off."

Fowler had refused to return Maria's phone calls; he'd agreed to see them only when some South American friends of Liam Wentworth made certain remarks about finding another Florida financial consultant.

The Fowler house was on a canal in a very expensive new subdivision. Helen answered the door, an unreadable woman who was managing to age gracefully everywhere but in the eyes.

The rumors said she had been Hugh's lover. What could Hugh have seen in her? Maria wondered. Nice figure. . . . Drat it, Maria Angelica, you have no time for jealousy. Stop it.

Ben Fowler, fat and ugly, despite his expensive clothes, was even less friendly, though he was careful not to be disrespectful to the powerful lord.

"There's nothing much I can do to help. I'm sorry that Tim's dead. I'm sorry Hugh's in prison. I stand by my story."

"What if we tell you we have evidence that Hugh was upriver at a place called mir Hassun on the dates of two of those phone calls about which you testified to the grand jury."

"I don't recall any such testimony," Ben said. She'd hit hard with her make-believe evidence, but not hard enough.

"And we have an affidavit from Mrs. Austin denying that Hugh was involved."

"It would be my word against hers, wouldn't it?"

"And we have access to an affidavit from Tim himself charging you with perjury."

Fowler paused thoughtfully. "I'll believe that when I see it."

"You'll see it," Maria exploded.

"Don't want trouble for you. No trial. No public scandal. Just want to clear Hugh." Liam was pulling out all of his own stops. "Quiet word here, quiet word there. No one suffers."

Fowler nodded. "I can understand that. I'm ready to make some discreet representations to the proper authorities when I see that the evidence is leaning toward exoneration. But I'm afraid a document from the Austin woman wouldn't do. She's nothing but a whore."

"Not the only one in the case," snapped Maria, her judgment breaking under the strain.

Liam covered for her. "All will be glad when it's over. Emotions run high. It's time to cool them. We'll be back to you soon."

Helen Fowler showed them to the door. She and Maria stood together for a moment on the canal bank, while Liam searched for their limousine and its driver.

Helen's hands were working nervously. "You won't do anything to Ben, will you?" She watched the placid waters of the canal, not Maria's face.

"Of course not," Maria replied, making a quick and impulsive decision.

"Tim and Liz were here for a day before they left for Saint Maarten. He talked all day about buried treasure."

"Buried treasure?"

"Actually I think he said 'sunken' treasure."

"Thank you," Maria said warmly. "That might be a great help." She didn't know how it would be a great help, but Helen deserved something nice in return for her generosity.

"I would have blown it, Liam, if you hadn't been with me," Maria said wearily as they drove back to the airport. "I don't have the nerves for the private-eye role."

"Rum lot, that chap. Half-victory though. Momentum."

On the long bumpy ride from Miami International to O'Hare, Maria thought about Helen Fowler. No woman, she was sure, would give up High without a great deal of pain.

Well, I'm not giving him up this time.

The U.S. Attorney was gazing out of his window, apparently studying the Calder mobile in the plaza below.

"We'll hang you from that thing," Maria said, "either you or Judge Crawford, take your pick."

"You're bluffing, Mrs. McLain." The stocky, cherubic-faced man turned away from the window and faced her, his eyes less certain than his high-pitched voice.

"You can't afford to take the chance that I am, can you? You're hoping the new crowd will reappoint you, though I don't know why anyone would want your job. If I release a story about how you sent a man against whom you didn't have a case to jail, you're finished."

"It was a plea bargain," he sighed. "Judge Crawford broke his word. I've seen the Austin woman's statement. You bring me one more bit of evidence, especially that document from Tim Donlon that she alleges she witnessed, and I'll take action."

"For what do you pray?" Marilyn Henderson asked. She'd "noticed" that Hugh spent much of his time in chapel. Rather gingerly, she tried to talk to him, and now he wanted someone to talk to.

"Forgiveness," he said promptly. "I don't know whether there is anyone who can forgive or whether He wants to forgive me. I don't deserve it, God knows. But, at least, I want it."

She brushed the hair out of her eyes. "We all want forgiveness. I guess the only religious question that matters is whether someone does forgive." She colored faintly. "If he or she does, it must take a lot of time, there's so much to forgive."

Marilyn was now a kind of Father Meisterhorst, though a much better spiritual director than he. And her husband was a very lucky man. Hugh didn't feel any sexual need for her. But he did note that in her own rather understated way she was very attractive.

Sexual longing was not part of his life anymore. Yet now there was a hint, in his response to Marilyn, that he might not be permanently immune to women.

Fast Eddie put aside Hans Küng's *Does God Exist?*

"Good book?" His mother looked up from the socks she was repairing, compulsive behavior out of her past, at which even Paola laughed. "He sure is a cute-looking fellow."

"Mother," Ed said disapprovingly, "you don't say such things about theologians."

"Only if they are as cute as Hans." The boy was a delight. She looked forward eagerly to his every return from the seminary. What if Hugh had come home from Mundelein that often?

"Stonewalled?" Ed had an uncanny ability to read his mother's mind.

"Absolutely."

"Maybe you're looking at it the wrong way. Maybe you are so in love with Hugh . . ."

"I'm not," she said furiously.

"Okay." He shrugged like an Italian fruit vendor. "Have it your way. Anyway, the point is that Tim had to have been more interested in hedging silver than he was in hiding some document. He put the affidavit with the hedge as an afterthought . . . now what do you hedge a short position—that's the right word isn't it?—what do you hedge a silver short with?"

"A silver long," she said promptly. "But he didn't have any contracts or he would have liquidated them and bailed out."

"How do they store silver?" He leaned forward, putting Hans Küng on the coffee table.

"Normally in thousand-ounce ingots, troy ounces." She punched some numbers into her TI hand calculator. "So that's about seventy-seven pounds; five of them are a normal CBT contract. An ingot would be worth, let me see"—more punches in the calculator, which could also furnish her with cosines if she wanted to build a bridge—"at the present price about ten thousand dollars. Four times that at the top of the run-up. In a few years maybe twenty thousand dollars."

"So you stack two hundred ingots somewhere, that's two million bucks now and a nice investment in the future. Could a man do it? Could he buy something like that and store it away?"

"Sure, he could, in a bank vault somewhere . . . a multimillion-dollar needle in a haystack."

"Not your man Timmy; half the fun of it would be that a person could find it." Ed returned to Hans Küng.

He was only slightly distracted from the great Swiss thinker by his mother's enthusiastic hug.

The Marshals' house in Park Ridge was so neat it made Maria's fastidious housekeeping look sloppy. "We Italians have a hard time keeping things clean," she told the solemn young couple. "All that olive oil coming out of your skin. . . ."

They both smiled self-consciously. It was an awkward conversation. Joseph could not remember any hint in Tim Donlon's conversation about where he might have hid a couple of hundred silver ingots. The three Marshal children watched her with wide, solemn eyes, just like their parents', till they were chased off to bed.

"Will you marry him when he leaves prison?" Kathy asked bluntly.

"Not right after."

Kathy was crying. "He means so much to us. He's our priest, no matter what." She dabbed at her eyes, but the tears didn't stop. "In court he was beaten down, almost dead. You have to bring him back to life."

"Bringing people back from the dead is God's work, hon, not mine."

"If you don't help God bring him back to life, who will?"

"The house at the lake!" Joseph Marshal interjected suddenly. "Mr. Tim talked a blue streak about the house his wife designed in Michigan during the silver run-up. The rate must have risen from two times a month to ten times a week; that figures out to better than one-point-three mentions of the house every day."

Maria hugged them both and raced to the door. "See you at the wedding, kids."

"I think it would be a mistake, Hugh, for you to go back to the priesthood right after you're released." Marilyn Henderson's hair was now tied behind her head in a ponytail, which made her look like a cute teen-ager.

"How else can I obtain forgiveness, unless I rededicate?"

The young woman jumped up from her chair, in an untypical display of passion. "Rededication, bullshit. Rededication is not the answer for you; it's not good psychology and it's not good religion either."

She was disturbingly pretty when she was angry, sexually appealing enough to be classified as a full-fledged temptation. He was half in love with her.

Yet she didn't understand how painful his climb through the upper six circles would have to be.

And no one could climb with him.

Chapter Forty-five
1981

THE HOUSE ESTELLE Donlon had designed at Oakland Beach was a vulgar palace.

"I should have a house with a pool." Maria laughed to herself. She sprawled on one of the enormous couches in the sunken living room.

She had persuaded the real estate agent to give her the keys on the pretext that she was looking for a summer place. She couldn't find a trace of either hedge or affidavit. If there were a couple of hundred silver ingots stored in the house, she had missed them. A good idea, but a wild goose chase.

She was momentarily dazzled by the swimming pool in the basement and its attached sauna and hot tub and beach chairs and sunlamps scattered about in sundry indoor patios. It would have seemed sybaritic—and hence extremely appealing to Maria—had Estelle not entirely covered the pine walls with family pictures. Gross, as the kids would say, but wonderfully convenient, especially if you liked to swim in the nude.

The temperature of the water in the pool was, if the thermometer was to be believed, in the low sixties. That was not exactly the bathtub temperature Maria liked, but tolerable. The agent had told her they had to keep the heat up to avoid freezing and they didn't want to drain the pool while the house was on the market.

Maria was tempted to swim twenty or thirty laps. No exercise for a couple of days.

I can't do that. It would be gross to swim in poor Tim Donlon's pool.

Pool!

Maria sat up in the chair. *Sunken treasure!* Why, sure.

She plunged headlong down the stairs to the terrace surrounding the pool, shedding her suit as she went. She flipped on the floodlights and rushed to the water's edge. The pool was made of tile and plastic, but at the deep end there were painted bricks, either for decoration or to protect the base of the pool from structural stress.

At least, that's what you'd think at first.

She tossed the rest of her clothes on the floor, took a deep breath, and dove in.

My God, it's freezing. Sixty-two degrees is a lie.

She touched bottom, poked at the bricks till her lungs hurt and returned to the surface, gasping for breath.

She thought for a moment, heaved herself out of the pool and, heedless of her shivers, rummaged around the room until she found a tool kit in a narrow closet. Then she dove back in, a screwdriver clenched in her teeth.

Only a few scratches at the paint on the bricks and she saw gleaming metal underneath.

Hanging on the side of the pool again, panting and cold, she considered what to do. At least a hundred and fifty bricks, a million and a half dollars. Whose? Hugh's by right, but he'd have to fight Estelle for it.

She pulled herself out of the pool, hunted for a towel in the cabinets on the wall, wrapped herself in a massive bath sheet, and sat under an unlit sunlamp, shivering and thinking.

Somewhere in this room. . . .

Clutching the towel, she ransacked the cabinets, the tool kits, the books on the tables. Nothing. She searched the sauna room. Nothing there either.

Discouraged and still shivering, she returned to the poolside. Maybe Tim had planted the idea of the affidavit in Norma's head as a final trick. Maybe there wasn't any.

I need my glasses to think properly, she thought. Where's my purse. Damn, I'll buy those contacts next week, the cute soft kind.

Towel tied tightly, she climbed the stairs, ignoring her discarded clothing, and found her purse.

If Hugh is interested in me, I'll definitely invest in contacts.

Maria Angelica, you ought to be ashamed of yourself.

Downstairs again, she put on her glasses, discarded her wet towel, and tugged at the door of a cabinet in search of another.

Her eyes glimpsed the wall next to the cabinet—a picture of the whole Tim Donlon family in swimsuits. Fat wife and fat creepy kids.

I wonder. . . .

She forgot about a dry towel and pulled the back off the frame. Nothing.

On the other wall was a small picture. She rushed across the floor, almost slipping on the tiles. Damn, great place to break your neck.

Sure enough, Lake Geneva, all the Donlons, and a skinny blond girl in a Fenwick T-shirt.

She knew what she would find before she even opened the picture.

The first call was to Cardinal Cronin.

Then to the U.S. Attorney. "It's going to be either your head or Crawford's on a silver platter."

Only then did she notice she'd run upstairs without a stitch. Silly impulsive Sicilian.

"You're joking about the silver platter." He laughed uneasily.

"I've never been more serious in my life."

"Who gave you the right to interfere in our family affairs?" Marge exploded as soon as Maria picked up the phone.

"Huh?" Maria said sleepily.

"Do you want Mom to have another heart attack? What do you think it does to her to have our family secrets in newspaper headlines all over the world . . . *again?*"

"But Hugh is cleared."

"You save him two months or so in jail at the cost of blackening Tim's memory and endangering Mother's health."

"Did Peggy have another attack?" Sleepily she tried to sort out what was happening.

"Not yet, no thanks to you. And it won't do you any good. Hugh's going to be a priest again." Marge hung up.

"Not if I can help it," Maria said.

Judge Donlon was ushered into her office.

"You did hang the picture here," he said tentatively, taking account of Peggy's watercolor on the wall.

Maria was sitting at her desk, poised, erect, competent as well as beautiful, fingers on the keyboard of her computer terminal. Not bad for a hasty pose. "And no one even suggests that it's me. So much for an old woman's vanity."

"I've come to apologize for the call you received from Killarney. Liam told me about it. He was more angry than I would have believed possible."

"No need to apologize." She waved her hand as if in absolution.

"Yes, there is. Marge is a passionate person, like the rest of us. But, unlike the rest of us, she rarely holds her feelings in. Even as a child. . . ."

"I can't hold a grudge, Your Honor. You know that. You're all wonderful people, even Marge, though tell her the next time she wants to shout, please call me in the daytime so I can shout back. Now, give me that copy of your book that you're carrying. I can hardly wait to read it."

Judge Donlon solemnly made the presentation.

Maria responded as though she had been given a rare work of art.

"How's Peggy?" she asked at length, sensing that the visit involved more than the book.

"Fine. Marge exaggerated. My wife had a serious heart attack, but she has recovered quite well. There's no reason to think she won't live for a long time yet. Naturally, it goes without saying that a happy resolution of Hugh's situation would ease her mind. . . ."

So that's it. Well, I love her too. But I'm not about to give up as easily as I did the last time.

"Will she see me . . . ? I mean, I've wanted to visit her, but I didn't know . . ."

"Of course she will."

"Ask her," Maria insisted.

First the cardinal, then Monsignor Martin. Maria was dismayed.

Sean Cronin had pulled no punches.

"He should be a priest, Maria; he did wonderful work under impossible circumstances in Lakeridge. He was a superb priest-scholar. He never should have left us. We need him back."

Maria wished she could see his face. Phone conversations with those in authority unnerved her. Sicilian intuitions didn't take to telephonic vibes.

"I don't think he was ever happy as a priest, Your Eminence—Sean—and don't tell me we're not supposed to be happy. I know we are."

"I think he was happy much of the time. Maybe not. . . . Anyway, all I ask is that you give him a chance to make up his mind. Fight fair."

"You think God is on your side. What if you're wrong?"

The cardinal hesitated. "It won't be the first time, Maria. And maybe God is on your side. Still, I want him back. Give us a chance."

Maria had made no promises, especially not the promise of a fair fight.

They weren't fighting fair. Why should she?

As soon as she left the bank, she went to St. Mark's. Monsignor Martin had said Steven's funeral Mass and sustained her through the years of grief. She had no closer friend in all the world.

And now he was harder on her than the cardinal.

"How can you stand in God's way?" He extended his hands dramatically.

"How can you be sure I'm not God's way? Why is your side automatically right?"

"He was ordained a priest forever, Maria."

At the door, as she was leaving, a final plea: "Will you stop loving me if I win, Monsignor Xav?"

"No, Maria." The pastor shook his head. "But I'll be disappointed in you. Terribly disappointed."

At home she called Ed.

"Xav is partly old school; you have to understand that," he said evasively.

"Will *you* be disappointed in me?" Maria persisted in her search for reassurance.

Ed laughed softly. "No way I'll ever be disappointed in you, Mom."

Peggy looked healthy enough and indeed quite pretty, sitting by the window gazing on the lake and the city, her painting tools in hand.

It was the city, blazing with red, not fire, not blood, some other kind of red.

"Best yet. No more pale pastels?"

"Odd red, isn't it? I think it might be love, but that seems presumptuous."

"I hope you'll forgive me." Bank president or not, Maria had lost her cool with this great lady.

"Nothing to forgive, my dear. I'm the one who should be asking. . . ."

"Maybe we mothers take on too much responsibility for our children. We have them only for a few years, then we give them back to God." It was a sermon she'd heard from Ed; why not use it now. "He forgives our mistakes."

Peggy was silent, watching the real city, not the passion-inflamed one in her watercolor.

"I do hope you're right . . . it would be so much easier."

"Peggy"—Maria was seized by an impulsive notion—"why don't you and I say a decade of the rosary together? On those pearl beads."

"What a wonderful idea, Maria; you always have such wonderful ideas. I keep this rosary close all the time. I didn't have it when I needed it. Of course, God sent Liam anyway, which was interesting, wasn't it? Here, you lead. . . ." She passed the beads to Maria.

On the elevator leaving the building, Maria realized she'd been upstaged. She laughed. Wonderful woman. I may lose to you again, but this time it will be after a fight.

And I won't fight fair.

BOOK SIX

"Into thy hands, I commend my spirit."

Chapter Forty-six
1981

HUGH DONLON LEFT the Federal Correctional Institution at noon on a gray Friday in March. The grass was turning green in Kentucky, although it was only the week before Palm Sunday.

He felt the same fear he had experienced as a young priest leaving the seminary: Institutional life was not pleasant, but it was orderly and predictable. The world outside was risky and uncertain.

He'd been edgy the week before his release. Much of the progress he'd made through prayer and conversation with Marilyn had been undone. The ice sheet around his emotions had thickened. He'd quarreled bitterly with her when she breathlessly congratulated him on his exoneration. Their last interview had been cold and formal.

He'd told his family not to come to meet him at the prison—just send a limo to take him to the airport in Louisville.

A gauntlet of TV cameramen and reporters flanked the walk between him and the shaded windows of the Cadillac. He took a deep breath. The air of freedom didn't smell any different.

A pretty young black woman jabbed a microphone at him. "How does it feel to be out of prison, Mr. Donlon?"

"Better."

"Are you happy that your name has been cleared?"

"I'm sorry my brother's reputation has been clouded." He edged toward the limo.

"Are you going back to the commodity business now that the sanctions have been lifted?"

"No fixed plans. Perhaps I'll teach somewhere."

No questions about the priesthood.

A red-bearded reporter leaned in front of him as he reached the car. "Will you contest your sister-in-law's claim to the silver?"

"What good is the silver?" He opened the door.

He sank into the plush cushion and closed the door. He did not need to see to know who was there, in tinted sunglasses, trim black suit, frilly white blouse, and gold and silver hair.

"While you're in a forgiving mood, do I merit absolution for salvaging your reputation?"

He kissed her lightly on the cheek. "No one can stay angry at you, Maria."

How would he tell her that he was going to return to the priesthood?

"Don't feel you have to talk," Maria said. "I'm in no rush to hear about what it was like. I'll give you five more minutes of morose silence before I start to ask questions. Like my sunglasses? They're called Mafiosa Carissima. . . ."

"Hey, that's the wrong turn."

The limo was going north on I-75 instead of west toward Louisville on I-64.

"We're not going to the airport till Monday morning," Maria said, every inch a bank president who had made up her mind. "This is bluegrass country. There's a resort up in the hills where you're going to be a kept man for the next two and a half days. Can't have you returning to Chicago looking all gray and ex-convictlike. You can call Peg when we get there."

Behind the tinted glasses, she was watching anxiously, a waif lurking behind Her Grace the President.

"Do I get a choice?"

"Nope." She dusted her hands. "No way. You're kidnapped for the weekend."

Gethsemane Abbey the resort was not, as Tim would have said. But it would do—spring flowers, rolling fields, a tumbling stream, neatly cut lawns, and the turf a veritable blue.

"I bet they dye the grass. Don't worry; I've already checked us in."

In their luxurious suite Hugh called his mother. As they talked he watched Maria hustling around the parlor, opening curtains, checking the bottle of champagne in its ice bucket by the sliding glass terrace door, fluffing her hair in the mirror, replacing the sunglasses with oblong-shaped, golden-framed reading glasses.

Beyond the door the sun, which had broken through the clouds, washed the hills and fields and endless white fences.

Not very subtle, Maria.

"I'm fine. I hope you don't mind my taking the weekend off."

The glasses matched her hair. That's not very subtle either, dear.

"Yes, it will be a busy . . . yes, I guess we both have risen from the dead."

Maria made a face.

"You'll live to be a hundred. . . ."

Maria took off her black jacket. The frilly blouse was sheer, as was the bra underneath.

"Yes, it will be wonderful to see Fionna and Graine and little Seamus."

By now totally distracted, Hugh bid his mother good-bye and turned to consider his captor.

"Would you believe that she and I said a decade of the rosary together last week and at my suggestion? Anyway, there are two bedrooms in this suite. On that side, sir, is your room, and over here is mine." She smiled. "Any other arrangements you may choose to make will be a matter of free substitution."

Hugh was saved from finding a response by the arrival of a sumptuous steak dinner, with a 1967 red Bordeaux to follow the champagne.

"How can I tell you . . . ?"

"A toast to freedom!" Maria uncorked the champagne with a single push of the thumb and splashed the frothy elixir into two glasses.

"That. . . ." He sighed, clinking glasses with her. "The past . . ."

"Shh." She cut him off. "For the next sixty hours you're free."

Maria carried the conversational ball as they ate, the stand-up comic doing her desperate routine.

Then, suddenly, she stopped. "It's wonderful to see you laughing again, darling," she said seriously.

The waif lurked behind the clown. Maria was more vulnerable than she appeared. She was risking her life for his with reckless disregard of the near-certainty that she would lose.

"I appreciate what you're doing, Maria." He gripped his dessert spoon bravely.

"You look so lean and silver and distinguished. But you have to get rid of that prison pallor . . . and no more excess pounds. I like men with tight stomach muscles."

With the shock of recognition of her vulnerability came affection, sweet and languid. He didn't deserve her concern but he enjoyed it.

"It wasn't really a prison. I even had a woman social worker, a nice young kid."

"I don't want to hear about her . . . I suppose you had a fight with her before you left."

"How did you know?"

Affection led to tenderness, a longing to protect and care for her.

She waved her hand, dismissing the question as absurd. "That's how you Donlons handle problems with people; you pick a fight so you won't fall in love with them. But, as I said, I don't want to hear about her. . . . How old was she?"

Inevitably, affection and tenderness ignited desire—gasoline on the sparks.

With other women—even with Maria in the hunting cabin and on the beach—Hugh had felt the collapse of ramparts and the fury of a raging torrent pushing him away from his commitments.

But now he felt simply drawn, drifting slowly toward her on a deep and peaceful river, floating to a refuge where he belonged, floating home. What other word could describe this union, but love?

He rose from his chair, took the dessert spoon from her hand, placed it on the table, and lifted her to her feet. "I love you, Maria," he said.

He took her in his arms, bruising her lips with furious kisses. Her lips were as hungry as his.

His trembling fingers were clumsy and the fabric of her blouse became tangled with the chain of her glasses.

"The blouse is designed only for looking, too thin for much else," she apologized, laughing and trembling at the same time. "Mind if I put the glasses away?"

Underneath she was a mass of cream-colored lace, sheer nylon, and elastic. She tried to help him, unbuttoning his shirt at the same time.

Finally she stood before him naked—solemn and clear-eyed—a woman giving herself wholly and without conditions. She unwound her hair and let it fall.

"Your room or mine?" she asked.

"Yours," he replied.

Hugh was grave, but he was not in charge. Maria was a cheerful and light-hearted lover. They would love one another on her terms and that meant laughter. Their union after twenty-seven years was not solemn high liturgy but farce.

When he awoke, lying on her bed, Hugh saw Maria standing before him, hands on her hips, golden and glowing in the late afternoon sun, wearing only her glasses and the plain gold cross at her throat.

"You like?"

She was proud of herself, proud of her smooth, sleek body with its compact, flawlessly shaped breasts, trim waist, and slender haunches. From modest bride to naked countess. . . .

"I like very much." He leaned back on his pillow. "But . . ."

"Now, I hear that you love me, but you still are obliged to go back to the priesthood because you must do penance for your sins and your family expects it and if you don't Peggy will have another heart attack. Go ahead and say it." She folded her arms. "I don't believe a word of it. And neither do you."

"I must seek forgiveness."

"That's nonsense. Remember your sermon at Marge's wedding? Forgiveness is there to begin with. It's given, just as it was given to that poor woman in the Bible they were going to stone to death."

"A naked woman quoting scripture?"

"Why not? It gets attention. Titian—"

"What does he have to do with it?"

"His painting of sacred and profane love. Profane is a stodgy old prude with all her clothes on and Sacred is like me." She raised her arms. "Except she's not wearing glasses."

He circled her waist with his fingers and drew her close. She put her hands on his head, Sacred love offering her benediction. His fingers moved up to her breasts. Holding one in each hand, he kissed them, first one, then the other, with infinite delicacy. She sighed and her eyes dilated with pleasure.

God in heaven, how he loved her. The only one he'd ever loved.

Then he drew back once more.

"Maria . . . I must climb out of hell . . . I can't. . . ."

"No, you don't. You can't escape that way. You should stretch up your hands to God." She recaptured his hands. "And let Him pull you out." She pulled him back to her. "This way."

He wrapped his arms around her.

"Why do you bother with me?" he asked.

Her eyes filled with tears. She leaned her head against his shoulder. "Because I love you, you crazy so and so. I've always loved you and always will, no matter how much you hide from me."

For the first time in four decades, tears spilled out of Hugh Donlon's eyes, tears of agony and pain, of frustration and disappointment, of failure and despair. Maria's arms enveloped him. He buried his head against her chest, his tears washing her breasts, a child in his mother's arms sobbing as though his body would tear itself apart.

When he entered her again, after long and delicate preparation, she said in a voice that was fading into a moan, "If we make a girl baby, we can call her Margaret Mary," and then in a final sigh, "Peggy for short."

And so it was that, close to a monastery named after a garden in which Jesus wept, but not in it, Hugh Donlon forgot about his glacier and experienced peace and happiness.

When Hugh awoke, the sky was turning from black to gray. For a moment he didn't know where he was, only that he had never in his life felt so happy.

Then he remembered.

My God, what have I done? I came out of prison planning to return to the priesthood. And in a couple of hours I'm in bed with a woman.

For a moment he was seized with reflexive guilt. But as quickly the mood passed.

He slipped back into a half sleep, basking in pleasant sensations to which he tried not to give a name. He did not possess; he was possessed. How delicious it was to be possessed. . . .

Another emotion, disturbing but not unpleasant, something to do with being possessed. . . . What was it . . ?

Something like the tiny unease as a sail flaps helplessly against the mast, looking for a freshening breeze . . . what if he should never make it to shore?

Fear.

Could he be afraid of Maria?

He was fully awake again. Yes, indeed; he was in terror of his captor. He must escape from her. He searched for the strength to heave himself out of bed.

The lovely captor was sleeping peacefully beside him, so slender as to seem ethereal, one childlike hand holding a sheet at her waist. I do fear her, but I don't want to escape from her either.

Life had perfected her as a gift, a prize to be given without regard to whether she would suffer or not, a giving mixture of submissiveness and laughter, innocence and hunger. Once more, against his will, he felt a compulsion to protect her. His lips went to her breast again, his teeth gently touching her skin.

She opened her eyes and stretched a hand to the back of his head, holding it in place. Her smile was a smile of complete adoration, a mother nursing a mildly troublesome boy child.

In the sweet taste of her flesh everything else was forgotten and there remained only love and hope.

Hugh had not been convinced, but this time, at least, he did not try to slam shut the door that let in the light.

Hugh took Piedmont 609 from Louisville to Chicago. Maria had business in Louisville, or so she said.

Jack Howard, Marge, Liam, Fionna and Graine and a grinning Seamus met him at O'Hare.

"Am I ever proud of my big brother," Marge gushed as she hugged him. She was an attractive matron now, but no match for her sleek Italian competitor.

"Good show," said Liam. "Jolly good."

"Back in and back in to stay." Jack Howard could hardly contain his happiness.

Both Hugh's nieces called him Father Hugh as they shyly shook hands with him. Seamus called him Uncle.

Maria phoned Kathy Marshal from the airport. As the phone rang she watched the old woman in the glass-covered *U.S. News* ad next to the phone booth. That's me. After seven years of celibacy I forgot what sex could do to you.

In the car on the way to the airport his withdrawn silence, like a teen-age boy who had decided that after all he was not going to the prom, chilled her. She had played for high stakes and lost.

"Operation Resurrection is in trouble, honey. Start spinning the prayer wheels," she said to Kathy.

She should have known better. At her age and with her history, sex couldn't be a casual ploy. Now she was deeply in love, physically a captive if not to Hugh then to her self-constructed need for him.

She recalled their last union in the early hours of the morning. When he was thrusting into her in the final uncontrollable fierceness of his passion, Maria felt like her helpless body was filled with a spring storm—driving rain, rampaging thunder, and jagged bolts of lightning crackling through her body and soul, igniting explosions at every nerve end and in every dark corner of her personality. The unbearable thunderbolts came faster and faster—God how she loved him—and then combined into a single massive outburst of sound and light that momentarily blanked out all sensation and left her floating in a cloud somewhere between heaven and earth, soaked in the storm's cooling rain.

"Maria Angelica"—she shook her head at the woman in the *U.S. News & World Report* ad—"you are about to get yourself badly hurt."

The unspoken assumption that Hugh would, of course, return to the active ministry continued at his parents' condominium. His father's handshake was brisk and businesslike; his mother's tears were brief.

"You look great," Hugh said to her. "Young enough to be my sister."

"Why shouldn't I look great? Just sitting here all day, dabbing with my paints while your poor father waits on me hand and foot? And now those two lovely girls . . . how did we earn such wonderful granddaughters?"

It was all earned, good and bad, Hugh thought.

The judge took her hand. "The doctors are very pleased, Hugh. Your mother will have to slow down a little and avoid big emotional highs and lows, but she'll outlive us all."

The mute appeal in all their faces was unmistakable. Make it be the way it used to be.

As he was leaving for his motel room at the airport—no place else available and he didn't want to stay with them—his father asked tentatively if he had an appointment with the cardinal.

Poor wonderful people, wanting him to be a priest again and wanting him to be free.

"Jack Howard says the boss wants to see me on Friday," he said easily. "Never say no to a cardinal."

Marge was blunter on Tuesday night when he ate dinner with her and Liam at L'Escargot in its new Allerton Hotel location.

"How hard will it be to get back in?"

"If Sean wants me, I can get back in." Hugh didn't want any further controversy. "But I'll probably end up with a long term of penance in a monastery."

"One prison to another, fool Church," Lord Kerry huffed.

"I might like it in a monastery," Hugh said.

"That wouldn't be good at all." Marge dismissed the notion abruptly. "You might have to put up with it for a couple of months, so long as you could come home on weekends. Mom deserves some good news. You know how much your going back to the priesthood means to her and Dad."

"We'll see what the cardinal has to say."

"Jack Howard says the priests are delighted at your coming back. They think it's a major victory for the Church."

"Grand show," said Liam, the friendly local Irish wolfhound.

Had Tim, Liz, Brian, and Lise died simply so that his mother and father might have a happy old age and the Church a great victory?

Monsignor Xav Martin invited Hugh to a late dinner at St. Mark's after the Holy Thursday liturgy. Hugh didn't attend the Mass; the renewal of priestly vows was something he wanted to avoid.

Pat Cleary joined Xav and his associate, Jack Howard, at the dinner table. It was obviously a dinner in Hugh's honor.

"You'll see the boss tomorrow?" Xav asked expansively.

"Before the Good Friday services."

"To celebrate the end of your descent into hell?" Jack asked.

"I'm not sure it's finished. I still have to climb out."

"It will take time," Pat Cleary said, his usual serenity marred by a small frown.

You know too much about me, Pat Cleary.

"It's wonderful to have you back," Xav persisted, "like old times."

"I can't imagine why." Hugh didn't remember the old times.

They recounted them at considerable length, praising his priestly work and his importance to their lives.

"I never realized. . . ." Hugh was touched, in spite of himself.

"You would if you'd listened." Xav lifted a silver eyebrow.

"I suppose." Hugh wanted to be more enthusiastic in his response to their affection.

"Are you going to come back?" Jack finally blurted the blunt question.

Pat Cleary frowned, less enthusiastic than the others, perhaps because he knew the kinks and crannies of Hugh's mind.

"Yes," Hugh said simply, surprised.

His friends cheered and sang the *"Ad Multos Annos"* hymn, wishing him many years in the priesthood. Yet he was not convinced.

On his way to the rectory Hugh was careful to avoid Ashland, the street on which Maria lived, though he had looked up her address in the phone book before going to St. Mark's.

Somehow he was now at the corner of Ashland at the end of Maria's block. A light in a window halfway down the street might be hers.

Maria's house in the new, new neighborhood, he thought. There had been so many houses in his life—the tiny rooms behind her father's store, Mason Avenue, Lake Geneva, the constricted Hyde Park apartment, the richly furnished but empty home in Kenilworth, the den of iniquity off Rush Street, Tim's grotesque Gothic manor with the pool and sauna bath . . .

. . . and now a seemingly ordinary suburban home on an ordinary suburban street. With a light on in the bedroom window. Neat, feminine but not pretentious. Efficient for sleeping and for anything else.

Deceptively, dangerously ordinary.

It was a warm evening for so early in spring; the smell of a coming rainstorm was in the air, humid and fertile.

He must force himself to avoid Maria for now.

He rolled up the car window, started the engine, and turned on the windshield wipers.

For all her chivalrous laughter, Maria was deadly serious about him, grimly determined to remake him in the image of what she thought he ought to be. If he were to be Maria's man, he would have to change—a drastic and painful transformation. And no excuses allowed.

No one in his life, not even his mother, had ever wanted him with such single-minded desire. He was flattered.

And terrified.

The cardinal's secretary enthusiastically welcomed Hugh at the front door and showed him into Sean's study. Hugh waited for a half hour, thinking of Maria and his mother. He loved both of them. How sad that, no matter what he did, he would hurt one.

Sean swept in, eyes glowing, shook Hugh's hand firmly, and tossed his clerical collar and vest on a chair. His white tailor-made shirt contrasted with the sunburst colors of the study.

"Sorry to be late, Hugh. The good old days when a bishop didn't have to listen are no more. Now the bullshit piles up to the top of your mitre in a half hour. Dialogue with nuns is the worst of all. They have read all the right books. . . . But never mind that. You look great. Welcome home."

"It's good to be back."

"Good Friday, so by rights I shouldn't offer you a drink. Why don't we both have a glass of Perrier and pretend we're members of the elite?"

He poured two glasses of sparkling water and then, before Hugh could begin, launched into a monologue.

"I can persuade my Polish friend to take you back. I may have to store you away at the seminary for a few months. He'll give in, though, and say something like 'Cronin, you're too much' and wink a frosty blue eye at me. I can do it, Hugh, and I want to do it. I want you back. I don't like to lose priests from the active ministry and I delight in reclaiming them, especially when they're men like you."

"I understand," Hugh said.

The cardinal held up his hand. "No, you don't, Hugh; no, you don't. I want you back, but I'm not the Holy Spirit. If you want to marry that blond Sicilian tiger, I'll be happy to officiate at the wedding. She claims she's God's will for you and, damn it, she may be right. I can't tell. Only you can. You have a wild card to play, and you'd better play it your way."

He considered Hugh very carefully over the top of his glass.

"No matter what you do, you're a priest of this archdiocese and never forget it."

"It's so hard to know . . ." Hugh stammered. "Should I have been a priest in the first place? Should I have left? Should I return now?"

"Why can't you have a vocation in the active ministry for a while and then a different vocation? I want you back, Hugh, but I want you back only if you're convinced it's the best way for you to go. Either way, you're a priest. The choice is between active ministry and being a priest in some other way no one has yet quite figured out—representing the Church and, yes, ministering for the Church in whatever world you're in.''

"I think I need more time.'' How much he'd sounded like Maria.

"Take it.'' Sean glanced at his watch. "I'd better run.''

"I'll join you in church. I have a lot to think about.''

There was a wild gleam in the cardinal's eyes. "That was the general idea.''

Hugh listened passively to the Good Friday readings, walked forward to kiss the cross, and then later, even though he had not been shriven for the last weekend's activities, returned to the altar to receive Holy Communion.

After the services were over, he retrieved his Hertz car in the parking lot across State Street from the cathedral and drove west on Chicago Avenue through the area where the Gold Coast was reaching for the river, daintily avoiding the monstrosity of the Cabrini-Green housing project, Chicago's latest version of "Little Hell.''

Beyond the river a red light stopped him in the shadow of an old Polish church with a great bulbous green dome. He would drive west another block into the setting sun, then join the light Good Friday rush-hour traffic on the Kennedy back to the O'Hare Marriott.

The melody of the *"Vexilla Regis"* sung in Latin at the cathedral during the veneration of the cross haunted him:

> *Vexilla Regis Prodeunt;*
> *Fulget crucis Mysterium,*
> *Qua vita morten pertulit,*
> *Et morte vitam protulit.*
>
> *muae Vulneratae lanceae*
> *sucrone diro, criminum*
> *Ut nos lavaret sordibus,*
> *Manavit unda, et sanguine.*

Already washed clean? Like Maria's image of God reaching down for outstretched arms and pulling you out of the pit?

The hell of the apostles' creed, the hell of Good Friday, was not the hell of the damned. It was Sheol, where the Patriarchs waited for Jesus to come and collect them. . . .

He was no Patriarch, however.

Only a lost soul.

He remembered a film from childhood, a movie in which Ray Milland played a charming and sinister Satan who led his victims to the island of Almas Perditas— the Isle of Lost Souls. Maybe that's where he belonged.

That was self-pity, he told himself firmly. Salvation was never impossible, no matter how low you sank.

He should drive on to O'Hare. Yet he could still turn left on Milwaukee Avenue, ride by the gigantic heart on the wall of the Polish Roman Catholic Union of America, and then west on Augusta Boulevard through the old Polish neighborhood turned barrio and end up in River Forest.

Maria's sons were in Charleston to spend Easter with their grandmother.

Was it really fornication, this sin he had not confessed? It had not seemed to be. . . . Sacred Love she called herself . . . the first step in a lifelong union?

He hardly knew her—two weeks at Lake Geneva, a few encounters scattered over a quarter-century, a weekend fling. . . . Yet he loved her with the certain knowledge that she was the love of his life. How could he give her up again?

The light changed and he turned north on Milwaukee Avenue. All right, he would enter the Kennedy at Division Street.

Two blocks before Division, however, he turned west on Augusta. The rented Citation bumped through the colorful barrio; the two flat buildings were painted red and yellow and blue and pink, more like Venice than Chicago.

Farther west, he drove through the tired homes of the city's limits, faceless residences lacking both the color of the barrio and calm security of the suburbs; they represented the dull end of the dream of respectability that St. Ursula had offered the Irish in the 1920s and the 1930s, when no one imagined the eventual affluence of Oak Park and River Forest.

He didn't even notice Mason Avenue as he passed it. The old neighborhood where everything started no longer existed. As he crossed Austin Boulevard and entered the gracious, quietly integrated streets of Oak Park, he wished only that he were young again, his life just beginning.

Harlem Avenue was the boundary between Oak Park and River Forest, a very proper street, neatly separating the rich from the richer. He should himself be proper and turn right on Harlem and drive north to O'Hare.

But the Citation stubbornly refused to go along. It went straight on into River Forest.

At Ashland, Maria's street, he stopped the car. This was the point of no return. The bare trees were shining red in the setting sun.

He turned the car around, pointing it toward Harlem.

Halfway down the block to the right he saw two women kneeling on the sidewalk. They were huddled over a small crumpled heap in front of a Dutch Colonial house.

Someone sick? Perhaps they wanted a priest? Let them call St. Mark's. It was only a few minutes away. He turned right into Ashland, not sure exactly what he'd done.

There was Maria, and another woman, apparently comforting a dying old man or woman.

"It's Granny Monaghan," Maria called when she saw him. "She lives right down the street with her great-grandchildren."

Maria was clad in jeans and a silver Fenwick Windbreaker with "Maria!" stitched in black above the pocket. She was chewing bubble gum and wearing her oblong glasses.

The old woman was over eighty, thin, frail, yet with a hint of great beauty and power from long ago.

"It's all right, Granny," Hugh said, rushing to her side, the words coming back with astonishing ease. "I'm a priest. I'm here to help. God loves you, Granny. He's coming to take you home."

"Ah, no, Father"—remnants of a thick Irish brogue—"God will never forgive me; I'm the greatest sinner that ever was. During the Black and Tan Wars and the Troubles, I committed the most terrible sins. I'm an evil old woman; I'm going to hell for certain."

Her eyes closed, her breath stopped for a moment and she seemed to have died, then the poor little chest moved again.

"What's her first name?" Hugh whispered urgently.

"Grace, I think," Maria said.

"You're sorry for all the sins of your life, Grace Monaghan?" He held her hand fiercely; he would not let her die until she was ready.

"I am, Father, I am. It's too late; I'll never be forgiven." She moaned as though she were already among the damned.

"Stop that, woman," Hugh ordered sternly. "I'll not have you talking that way about God, and yourself on your way to join Him. He's forgiven everyone already, and that's a fact. God loves us. . . ."

There was a momentary shrewd gleam in her faded eyes.

"He's a tricky one, isn't He?"

"Lovers are always tricky, Grace, you know that."

"There's truth in that, right enough; quick, now, Father"—her voice was strong and firm—"give me absolution; say the words; He's coming for me; He wants me now; I'll not escape from Him this time."

The old woman tried to sit up, reaching out her arms to embrace an invisible lover.

"I absolve you from all your sins in the name of the Father and of the Son and of the Holy Spirit and by the power granted to me I impart to you the blessing of the Pope and a full pardon for everything you've done wrong in your whole life."

"He's here now, Father, and Himself smiling like a young man in the hedges of Galway." The last rays of the sun caught the old woman's weathered face. For a moment she smiled ecstatically, then slumped forward, unconscious, perhaps dead.

A young priest next to Hugh pushed the oils into his hand. "Go ahead, Father Donlon. You finish."

With a trembling finger, Hugh traced the sign of the cross on her parchment-dry forehead. "Through this most holy anointing and His most tender mercy may God forgive all your sins."

"Jesus, Mary, and Joseph be with me on my last journey," said the young priest.

"Into Thy hands I commend my spirit," repeated the two kneeling women.

"God the Father who made us . . ."

"Into Thy hands I commend my spirit."

"God the Son who saved us . . ."

"Into Thy hands I commend my spirit."

"God the Holy Spirit who loves us . . ."

"Into Thy hands I commend my spirit."

County Galway was long ago and far away. Yet Grace Monaghan had gone home.

As dusk spread, Hugh felt a burst of light and warmth engulf him, drawing him toward the same Love who had crept out of the hedge in front of Maria's house to take Grace Monaghan home.

It was an implacable and impulsive Love, one that forgave without being asked, never turned away from the beloved, and wanted only that the beloved surrender to Love and be happy.

A Love like Maria.

Hugh tried to flee from the Lover's majestic instancy and unperturbed grace, escape from it, hide from it, turn away from it. There was no exit.

"Joe Machowiak, Father. That was beautiful." The young priest extended a beefy paw. The heat and light that had possessed Hugh and drained him momentarily had passed without anyone's noticing.

Someone had come to take Grace Monaghan home and brushed lightly against Hugh as the two of them went by. His life would never be the same.

Maria was watching him. She had never seen him act as a priest for the dying before. Her smile said she was prepared to be a good loser.

Maria.

Her house loomed behind her—trimly painted gables, warm yellow brick, a soft light in the parlor window, the kindly glow of dusk reflected in the other windows. A house he had never entered. Yet he knew it well enough—neat, clean, warm, unconventional furniture, and flamboyant decorations. A pleasant house, inviting, reassuring, comforting. And once you went into its light you never left. Mason Avenue, Lake Geneva, Bethlehem.

The fire department and the doctor arrived, and a granddaughter and her children. The young priest led them in a decade of the rosary. Then it was over, the ambulance with Grace Monaghan's earthly remains departed, everyone else went home, only Hugh and Maria were left standing silently under the streetlight.

"Coming in?"

"If I may."

"Of course, you may. For a visit?"

"To stay, if you'll let me."

"Be my guest." She gestured dubiously toward the doorway, like a motel owner who was not sure whether a potential client was serious. Her Rembrandt eyes, barely visible in the glow of the streetlight, were clouded with tears.

They walked silently to the door, close yet far enough apart so their hands didn't touch. Maria opened the door. Light from the parlor framed her in the doorway, just as she had been framed at Lake Geneva.

"Sure?" she asked hesitantly, holding the door open.

"I'm sure," he said.

He touched her face, tilted her jaw slightly, caressed her cheek with his thumb.

The ancient Greek Easter greeting leaped out of his memory, an explanation for everything.

"Christ is risen, Maria, alleluia."

"Bet you think I don't know the answer to that." The Maria of raspberries and cream had come back. "He is risen indeed, alleluia!"

A PERSONAL AFTERWORD

WHY WOULD A priest write a novel about a man who breaks his vows of celibacy and leaves the active exercise of the priesthood? Am I opposed to celibacy? Do I approve of those who leave the active ministry? Am I trying to justify my own planned departure?

To answer the last three questions in reverse order: I do not intend to resign from the priesthood, nor will I leave even if the powers-that-be try to throw me out. I make no judgments about individuals who leave the active ministry or about those who stay; I can only judge myself. Finally, I am in favor of celibacy, though I also think it might be useful to experiment with limited-term service in the priesthood, a much better strategy, it seems to me, than the abandonment of the celibate tradition.

As to the first question, my story is only secondarily about one man's struggle with a priestly vocation. Like all religious stories this tale is primarily a story of God. The stories of God in the Jewish and Christian scriptures are often both secular and "unedifying." The Joseph and David cycles and the parables of Jesus were stories of God that profoundly scandalized those who heard them. If they don't shock us today, the reason is perhaps that we have heard them too often and do not listen to them.

They are stories of adultery, betrayal, incest, family conflict, rivalry, and envy, of treacherous servants and traitorous brothers, of foolish mothers and indulgent fathers, of unjust judges and incredibly soft-hearted judges, of treasure hunters and crafty merchants, of angry kings and crooked stewards, of impudent workmen and obsessive gardeners, of hardworking housewives and clever investors, of dizzy teen-age girls and angry teen-age boys, of feasts and parties, wars and marriages, life and death.

There is not a character or incident in my story, I think, without a scriptural counterpart and not a story in scripture that would not shock us if we listened to it carefully.

Stories of God are designed to disconcert, to open us up to the power of God's shocking love and to disclose to us new ways of living in the world with the illumination and power that comes from that love.

The parables of Jesus were instruments of controversy. In the parables Jesus tried to persuade the crowds of the attractiveness of his picture of God; he told his stories not to teach doctrinal propositions about the nature of God but to portray, as winningly as he could, how God acts. His are tales not of who God is but how God behaves.

In addition to being both secular and disconcerting, the parables of Jesus are comic; indeed they are comedies of grace. Those who try to deal with God by bargaining, by demanding favor to which they have earned a right through their own good deeds, by winning his mercy and forgiveness through their own efforts—the early Laborers in the Vineyard, the Brother of the Prodigal Son, those who accuse the Woman Taken in Adultery (a story that was probably originally a parable)—are confounded and fall on their faces. While those who have no right to mercy or love—the Laborers of the Eleventh Hour, the helpless robbery victim saved by the Good Samaritan, the Prodigal Son, the Woman Taken in Adultery—are astonished to be swept up in irresistible and overwhelming grace. In the Kingdom of Mercy, there is always comic surprise as Grace has the last laugh on Justice.

And that, says Jesus, is the way God acts.

The doctrinal basis for my story of how God acts is contained in Hugh Donlon's sermon about First Grace (on p. 248) and in the hymn "*Vexilla Regis*," which echoes in Hugh's mind as he drives by the Polish Church on Chicago Avenue; it is documented in the Canon #179 of the Second Council of Orange, which is quoted below.

Although most readers will find it easy to absorb the religious symbols or "sacraments" (realities that reveal the presence of grace, the presence of God in action) that bind this story together, perhaps the images ought to be made explicit for those who are unfamiliar with symbols or stubbornly refuse to see them—most notably Catholic reviewers, who will fail to comprehend the parallel with the Catholic sacraments: water, wind (spirit), breast (food and drink), light, descent and ascent, an open door, house, and woman (especially two lovely women, Peggy and Maria, who represent opposing views of how God acts and for that matter what the Church ought to be).

It also should be noted that Hugh's priesthood is a "sacrament" for him, as well as for others. It reveals to him that the God of grace he preaches to others is not the God of justice who dominates his personal life. The priesthood finally forces him to turn his own word on himself and to realize that the worst sin in his life was to exempt himself from grace.

So, light-years away from them in skill, my comedy of grace seeks to do, however ineptly, what the parables of Jesus did—tell a story of how God acts. Perhaps the reader will be disconcerted by my imagining that God may act like Maria and Maria like God. Comedians both and masters of graceful surprise, God and Maria are, as the theologians would say, "correlates" of one another.

Perhaps the reader who can imagine Maria as a sacrament of God and a revelation of how God works, will then be able to see new ways of living in the light of a story of a God who, like Maria, is illusive, reckless, vulnerable, joyous, unpredictable, irrepressible, unremittingly forgiving, and implacably loving.

THE SECOND COUNCIL OF ORANGE
On the Gratuity of God's Love

IF ANYONE SAYS that mercy is divinely conferred upon us when, without God's grace, we believe, will, desire, strive, labor, pray, keep watch, study, beg, seek, knock for entrance, but does not profess that it is through the interior infusion and inspiration of the Holy Spirit that we believe, will, or are able to do all these things in the way we ought . . . he contradicts the words of the apostle: "What hast thou that thou has not received?" and "By the grace of God I am what I am."

(The Latin text of this canon is contained in Denzinger et al., "Enchiridion Symbolorum" #376. The English translation is from Clarkson et al., "The Church Teaches" #546.)

Lord of
the Dance

For

THE BRENNANS

friends in need

WIPEOUT

Skilled ballerina spinning on the spray
She slices through the wake with disdainful ease
A mature woman, elegant at play
Aloof, discreet in her capacity to please
Then the tizzy teenage trickster topples from her skis
Cartwheels through the air, dancing on her face
A carnival comic choreography
A somersaulting epiphany of grace

Devised by God to guarantee the race
Who gifted them with smiles to incandesce the day
Sculpted summer sunbursts to celebrate in space
And with Technicolor splash our humdrum gray
A designer impeccable in taste
Such sacraments crafted to delight us on our way

The only God worth believing in is a dancing God.

FRIEDRICH NIETZSCHE

Resurrection isn't easy.

NOELE FARRELL

I danced on Friday when the sky turned black
Oh, it's hard to dance with the devil on your back
They buried My body and they thought I'd gone
But I am the dance and the dance goes on
Dance, dance, wherever you may be
I am the Lord of the dance, said He
And I will lead you all wherever you may be
I'll lead you all in the dance, said He.

"Lord of the Dance"
SYDNEY CARTER

There is a universal belief that the dance,
in so far as it is a rhythmic art-form,
is a symbol of the act of creation.

A Dictionary of Symbols,
page 76

Now
there was only the morning
and the dancing man of the broken tomb.
The story says
he dances still.
That is why
down to this day
we lean over the beds of our babies
and in the seconds before sleep
tell the story of the undying dancing man
so the dream of Jesus will carry them to dawn.

"The Storyteller of God"
JOHN SHEA

DISCLAIMER

IT WOULD APPEAR that some readers are the victims of an incurable if not altogether harmless affliction of knowing better than the author who his characters "really" are. Since nothing can dissuade them from this obsession, it is useless for me to try to tell them that the Farrell clan and all the other characters that inhabit this story are totally fictional and products of my own imagination. Nevertheless, I do so assert and warn such readers that a search for resemblances between my characters and actual persons is pursued at the considerable risk of deepening their own obsession.

The portraits in my gallery of minor characters—priests and provosts, politicians and publicists, padrinos and political scientists, punks and prelates, publishers and professors—are drawn from recognizable Chicago types but are based on no one in particular. Nor are the incidents involving the members of the gallery, not all of whom are rogues, by the way, replays of specific incidents or events.

As for the major characters, I know of no priest/TV personality like John Farrell, no professor/politician like Roger Farrell, no naval officer like Daniel Farrell, no secret storyteller like Irene Farrell, no businesswoman like Brigid Farrell. I have known a couple score of young women like Noele Farrell, but she is all of them and none of them.

I do not necessarily approve of the moral behavior of my creatures. Nor do any of the characters speak with my voice, save occasionally Father Ace.

I wish to thank Sydney Carter for writing "Lord of the Dance" and Mary O'Hara for singing it.

FARRELL FAMILY TREE

BRENDAN-Julie Roache

1861–1900   1865–1895

m. 1890

MONICA

1895–1895

WILLIAM-Blanche Hogan

1891–1944   1896–1960

m. 1919

Brigid (Maeve) Flynn-CLARENCE

1922   1919–1963

m. 1939

MARTIN-Florence Carey

1919–1964   1920–1944

m. 1939

Irene Conlon-ROGER

1945   1941

m. 1964

JOHN

1939

Ordained 1963

DANIEL

1949–1964

NOELE MARIE
(MARY NOELE)

1964 (Christmas Day)

M. N. Farrell
Class 3-A
Social Studies

FIRST DANCE

Valse Triste

"Tomorrow shall be my dancing day,
I would my true love did so chance
To see the legend of my play,
To call my true love to my dance
Sing, oh! my love, oh! my love, my love, my love,
This have I done for my true love"

"My Dancing Day"
A Medieval Good Friday Carol

GLOWING IN THE distance, cool, firm, confident, the Himalayas reminded him of Irene. Irish male breast fixation, she would say with an amused little smile. He would reply that a least he had good taste in his fixations. And she would blush with delight, limitless in her capacity to absorb compliments.

He had made the prescribed sweeping turn over the Sinkiang plateau at a point a hundred miles short of the Russian border. At least his sextant, a dubious instrument at best, assured him that Russia was still a hundred miles away.

Halfway home. The sun now at his back. The prevailing winds, too. May the wind be at your back. A long way from the old neighborhood, where that was a wedding toast.

And may you be in heaven a half hour before the devil knows you're dead. . . .

He grinned. No toast yet for him. Jackie would have to give it when he got back. . . . No, not the ruggedly handsome young priest, better the intellectual— Roger. Something more elaborate than an old Irish American cliché. . . . Damn. He missed them both. Too much of their father, Clancy, in them. Still, they were mostly Brigid's kids. . . .

Six more hours. The station chief had told him it was the less important half of the trip, not that you could believe anything they said there. He was stiff and uncomfortable in his pressure suit. This giant blackbird, for all its soaring grace, was more cranky than the others. It needed careful nursing every mile.

You flew over the Himalayas because they were there—and on the way to his destination in northern Thailand. They made him think of Irene again.

Was her ability to forgive as great as her passion? He thought it might be. Lord knows she would have to forgive him for the rest of their lives.

The sun turned the mountains red, reminding him of another haunting image: his uncle Clancy at the foot of the stairs, blood pouring from his head, all that anger snuffed out, looking like a broken Christmas toy.

And then more blood: a young woman's face. Not Irene. Someone else. His mother, probably. She and Irene were often confused in his dreams.

What had really happened to his mother on that day? Did he remember it? Or did he merely remember the stories he had heard when he was older?

A beautiful young face, smashed bloody like Uncle Clancy's. And he was responsible both times.

He would not let it happen to Irene.

Another year and a half on his contract. What could the Chinese be doing down there that was so interesting? In a year they would have spy satellites and they wouldn't need the great blackbirds, half jet and half sailplane.

They would find some use for them, though. And for the kooks who flew them.

They traded the Russians for Gary Powers. No trades with the Chinese.

God, I need Irene. Okay, God, since I brought you up, you know how much I need her.

And she needs me. She'll never survive them without me.

Irene leaning over him on the beach, her long hair touching his motionless body, tantalizing him until he thought he would lose his mind; then the edge of her fingernails . . .

And her blunt warning that he would have to grow up. Their last day together and their last fight.

He hardly noticed the flameout; there was only a change in the sound and an ever so slight downward tilt of the bird. It had happened before. Let her float a few thousand feet and start it over.

He tried at 60,000, 55,000, 50,000. No dice. The Chinese MIGs could make it no higher than 45,000—that's what they told him.

The bird floated lower. 30,000 and still no MIGs. 25,000. Time to jettison, destroy the plane, walk out of Sinkiang.

Where to? Russia?

He pushed the eject button. No reaction. Sixty seconds and the plane would blow up. He pushed the button again. Still no ejection.

Something was beginning to smell. He watched the second hand sweep on his watch: thirty, twenty, ten . . .

Forgive me, I love—

No explosion. Something badly wrong.

Then the MIGs, dancing up to him like angry mosquitoes. The little puffs of light from their tracers. Shoot first, little Chinese friends, ask questions later.

Put the plane into a dive, evade them, try the motor again. It wouldn't start. A MIG following him down. More tracers.

A kaleidoscope of faces. His mother, eyes open and staring; Brigid, her white lace gown torn and covered with blood; Clancy, blood pouring from his head; John, the self-satisfied young priest; Roger, the faintly supercilious intellectual; Irene . . .

Dear God.

Irene.

DANCE TWO

Pavane Pour une Infante Défunte

"A slow, processional type of dance, often combined with a galliard, and later with the saraband and the gigue, and occasionally a hornpipe, into the classical suite."

······················ *John* ······················

"WHAT WAS UNCLE DANNY REALLY like?" Noele Farrell handed her uncle an old newspaper clipping, her green eyes flashing dangerously.

Monsignor John Farrell regretted that he had scheduled this interview with his niece on Saturday morning. Jim Mortimer would be along shortly, and he should be planning a strategy for dealing with the cardinal's emissary instead of dodging questions about the Farrell family past. And there was a month of parish records to catch up on before confessions this afternoon. In the old days curates had done that sort of work.

"He really wasn't your uncle, Noele," he said wearily, "even though he and your father and I were raised together. He was our cousin and not our younger brother."

Noele made an impatient face, a princess displeased. "I know *that*," she said, dismissing his passion for precision. "It's easier for me to think of him as an uncle than as a cousin. Right?" CHICAGO PILOT REPORTED MISSING OVER CHINA, said the black headline from the *Chicago Tribune* of seventeen years ago. John Farrell did not need to reread the story: The Chinese government reported that People's Liberation Army jets had shot down an American spy plane over Sinkiang, the vast and unpopulated steppe in western China, and that a CIA spy, Daniel X. Farrell of Chicago, was killed in the crash. The American government denied any knowledge of the plane or of Daniel X. Farrell. The Farrell family said through a spokesman that Daniel Farrell, a graduate of Annapolis, had left the United States Navy the previous year after three years of active service and was understood to be working in a secret government job. "The son of the late Commander and Mrs. Martin Farrell and the nephew of the late Clarence 'Clancy' Farrell, president of Farrell & Sons Construction Company, Daniel Farrell was

427

a member of one of Chicago's most politically powerful families, a family that has been dogged by tragedy. . . ."

"Why is it necessary to understand Danny?" John asked. "As a matter of fact, why is it necessary to write a term paper about our family history?"

Noele smiled, flashing two rows of flawless white teeth. "It is necessary to do the term paper, Uncle Monsignor, because S'ter Amanda assigned it, and it's necessary to understand Uncle Danny because he is part of my heritage."

"Don't try to glamorize him, Noele." He placed the newspaper clipping on the carefully polished oak of the rectory office desk and straightened the edges of the red leather blotter. "Danny was a charming, witty, gifted child on his way to wasting his life. He was thrown out of the Navy for telling off a commanding officer. Then he took a crazy job with the CIA because he wanted to make a lot of money in a hurry. He thought he was going to be a writer or something of that sort. And he drank too much. If he hadn't died in that plane crash, he would probably be an incurable alcoholic by now. I think God did all of us a favor, including Danny, when he called him home early in life.

"Let the dead bury their dead," he continued heavily. "You're almost seventeen now, Noele. Soon you'll be an adult with adult responsibilities. It's time for you to discover what life is all about, to become serious and mature. . . ."

"Yuksville." Noele's lips dismissed maturity with quick contempt.

Trying to tame Noele, John realized, was like riding a spring storm. Yet she had to be tamed if she was to be prevented from doing herself great harm.

And everyone else in the family too.

"It's true," he continued, trying to sound relentless. "And wasting your time daydreaming about Dan Farrell, dead for all these years, is simply not mature behavior."

A cloud seemed to appear in Noele's glowing green eyes, a cloud, perhaps, of shrewd suspicion. John stirred uneasily and wished the phone at his elbow would ring. One moment she was a giggly, gum-chewing sixteen-year-old, talking the strange teenage version of English, and the next moment an all-knowing, ageless witch.

"You sound like you didn't like him very much, Uncle," she said softly. "And why don't you want me poking around in the family past?"

John tried not to gasp in surprise. Once again Noele, without apparently noticing what she was doing, had responded not to what he'd said but to what he'd thought.

She was not a lush, full-bodied Venus like her mother, but rather a lithe, slender Diana, a dancer and a gymnast with the graceful movements of a ballerina or an Italian policeman directing traffic or a hypnotist conjuring up miracles. You almost did not notice her trim body and finely carved facial features because you were so startled by the colors of her beauty. She was a Celtic goddess in the nineteenth-century illustrations of Irish folklore books, strange, unreal, almost unearthly. Her long, bright red hair, contrasting sharply with her pale, buttermilk skin, swept across the room after her like moving fire. Her green eyes absorbed you as if you were a glass of iced tea on a hot summer evening; they were neither soft green nor cat green, but shamrock green, kelly green. She seemed a pre-Christian deity, a visitor from the many-colored lands of Irish antiquity.

"On the contrary, Noele, I liked him enormously; so did everyone." He hoped he sounded sincere. The words were at least partially true. "Danny was one of the most charming and delightful men I have ever known, with a fantastic sense of humor. . . . You never knew what crazy trick Danny would do next.''

"It must have been hard on you and Dad and Grams when he was killed so soon after Grandpa Clancy died.''

John wet his lips nervously. How much did she know about Clancy's death?

"It was very hard on your grandmother, Noele. She loved Danny like a son. In fact, your father and I, we used to kid her that he was her favorite son.'' They never would have dared say that. Brigid's fury was often much greater than her husband's because she could be angry cold sober. Only Danny dared defy her. John occasionally wondered if Brigid had had a love affair with Martin, her brother-in-law and Danny's father, long ago. She was capable of it, God knows. That might explain her delight in Danny and her grief when Danny died.

Damn him. And damn Brigid, too. A notorious and public sinner.

"And she was only a few years older than your mother is now,'' John continued. "Awfully young to lose a husband. And especially because he was, well, moderately drunk, something that didn't happen to Dad very often. But you know Grams. She pulled herself together and took charge of everything.''

Noele was looking at a photograph of Danny in his white naval aviator's uniform that she had taken from a folder full of clippings, notes, and family pictures. "I wonder what he would have been like if he had lived. Maybe he would have surprised us all. He sure was cute. . . . Is the CIA certain he was killed?''

"The CIA never admitted to us that he was working for them. But Congressman Burns, the father of our present Congressman Burns . . .''

"I know all about the Burns family, Uncle,'' Noele said complacently. "I mean, like totally, right?''

"Oh, yes, I forgot that our next Congressman Burns is a special friend of yours.''

"Jaimie is going to be a senator,'' Noele announced with the timeless confidence of an Irish woman who has planned her man's life for him. "At least if he listens to me he is. ANYWAY, what did his grandfather find out from the CIA?''

"The man who came to visit him in Washington wouldn't admit he was with the CIA but said that the Chinese didn't have the antiaircraft guns to shoot down a U-2. They had learned the plane had crashed because of some mechanical failure, and Danny survived the crash but died later, either because of injuries or because the Chinese executed him. That's all we were told.''

Noele shook her head sadly. "Poor Danny. . . . Well, Uncle Monsignor, you've looked at your watch five times in the last two minutes, so I'd better gather up my notes and go home and start to write the paper—after I watch Jaimie beat Miami on TV.'' Noele bounded up from her chair, scattering the folder of family photographs on the plush carpet of the rectory office. With pantherlike grace she was on the floor scooping them up before John Farrell could move from his custom-made executive's chair.

"Hey, this relative is totally gorgeous. Notre Dame sweat shirt, too; they haven't changed much, have they? Which one is she, Uncle?''

"That's a picture of Flossie Carey, Danny's mother, before she married my Uncle Martin.''

"Did they ever have funny hairstyles in those days.''

Poor Flossie. She had indeed been gorgeous. Should have stayed away from the Farrells.

How many bitter fights with her son, Daniel. And good times, too. Great fun ditching Roger. John had hated Danny Farrell's guts, and at the same time adored him. When he thought he was in love that summer at Grand Beach, it was

Danny who persuaded him to return to the seminary. Said the girl was worthless. Then fell for her himself. . . .

All the Farrells in Noele's dossier are dead. . . .

"I know they're dead," Noele said, responding to his thought again, "but they're part of me. And I have to know who I am."

The rectory door bell chimed as he opened the office door for her, an office carefully designed to create an atmosphere of solid, dark brown warmth. He checked his reflection in a mirror in the hallway to make sure his razorcut, stylishly long hair was properly arranged and his clerical suit as trimly fitting as it ought to be.

The housekeeper, somewhat awed, was admitting Monsignor James Mortimer.

John introduced Noele to Monsignor Mortimer with a touch of pride. Balloonhead would not have a niece like her. She favored the cardinal's errand boy with a smile and her warmest "Hi, Monsignor." Balloonhead hardly acknowleged her existence, save for a vague grimace of disapproval at Noele's green Notre Dame warm-up suit. . . . Emissaries of the cardinal had no time for teenagers, especially when they were dressed inappropriately for a rectory office.

"Thank you, Uncle John. Do you have skeletons in your family closet, Monsignor Mortimer?"

"Only the rich Irish can afford to have skeletons, Miss Farrell," Balloonhead replied solemnly.

"I opened a closet the other day and five skeletons fell on me." Noele pecked at her uncle's cheek and then bounded down the stairs into the golden October sunlight, turning to wave merrily at him just as he closed the rectory door.

She's not going to let go of it, John Farrell decided. When I get rid of Mortimer I will have to call Irene and warn her. There are two many things that could go wrong, especially if her father is dumb enough to decide to run for governor.

"Come on upstairs, Jim," he said to Mortimer. "Mix you a drink?"

Balloonhead blundered up the staircase like a hippo coming out of a tropical river, his idea of the way a man weighed down with the problems of the church would walk. "I never drink before lunch," he announced at the top of his voice.

Even sounded like a bull hippo.

·····*Noele*·····

NOELE WORE HER new green and gold Notre Dame warm-up suit, which matched her eyes, when she went to the rectory neither to impress her uncle nor Father Ace, whom she knew she would see at the Courts after she left the rectory.

Noele wore her warm-up suit and tied a green ribbon around her hair because there might be boys at the Courts. Though she was in love with Jaimie Burns, she was certainly not about to forget her image when there was a possibility that there might be cute boys around.

The trees on the curving streets of the Neighborhood, which Noele thought was the most totally cool place in the world, were turning red, reminding her of the vestments the priests wore at Mass on Pentecost. And the big oaks around the Courts were pure gold, making the sun-drenched asphalt look like a grove. Noele, who loved Latin and was upset that the nuns didn't teach Greek anymore, insisted that the Courts were sacred. They were the center of the parish. When the kids said, "Let's go over to Saint Prax's," they meant not the church but the Courts.

Sacred grove or not, the Courts were devoid not only of cute boys but all boys. Only Father Ace was there, still trying to dunk, and at his age. . . .

He was real old, over forty-five, but definitely kind of cool, with curly brown hair and dancing blue eyes, and a thin, handsome Irish face that was always in motion, usually smiling or laughing—not exactly Paul Newman, but nice just the same. And he could still run on the Courts with any of the boys.

A long time ago, when Moms and Roger and Uncle Monsignor were teenagers, he had been a young priest at St. Praxides. Then he became a marine chaplain and a doctor in psychology and taught at Loyola and came back on weekends, and all the kids liked him, especially since Father Miller wasn't into teenagers, for sure.

Not teenage girls, anyway.

"N.D. going to take the Hurricanes?" he said, bouncing the basketball at her.

"And Jaimie is going to score the winning touchdown on an interception," she blurted as she sank a jump shot and began the inevitable game of horse with Father Ace.

Shit, Noele thought, permitting herself language she never used even mentally except when she was really bummed. Well, I didn't mention that the poor black boy is going to be hurt, though not real bad, thank God.

"So he's going to play?" Father Ace watched her intently just before he missed his jump shot. "They'll let the sleepy-eyed freshman in the game?"

Which is what the newspapers called Jaimie.

"How should I know?" Noele tried to brush it off, realizing that rarely did she fool Father Ace. "And he's not sleepy, either. He just totally looks that way."

Everyone thought that Jaimie was a dreamy young man who did what Noele told him to and then went back to sleep till the next time she gave an order.

But then they had not seen him the night in the bar in South Bend, where they shouldn't have been, when the two flakes had tried to paw her.

Jaimie had flattened them both.

"What was Danny Farrell like, Father Ace?" she asked, trying to sound innocent.

"Still on the term paper?" the priest said, making an expert left-handed hook shot. "And you have to shoot it right-handed."

Noele, who was left-handed, ordinarily would have protested loudly. Now she was more interested in Danny Farrell than in winning the game of horse.

"I mean, you were here when they were young. . . ." She missed the shot.

"I didn't know him very well. He stayed away from the rectory. Nice guy, though afraid to be serious. Was sweet on your mother once—that was after I left the parish. And why are you interested in him?"

Noele held the basketball in her hands and studied the faded label on it, the game forgotten. "I have to know who I am, Father Ace. How can I know what I'm going to do with my life unless I know who I am?"

"I think you have a better idea of what you are than most teenagers do."

"I do not!" she retorted hotly. "I pray and pray and pray." She bounced the basketball fiercely with each *pray*. "And God, like, kind of doesn't say anything much back, and that makes me sooooo bummed."

Father Ace laughed, which he did a lot. "You are someone very special, M.N., you know that."

"Just because I sometimes know what people are thinking before they say it?"

He laughed again. "No, just because you can persuade almost everyone to do what you want them to do and to enjoy it."

"A bossy little bitch," she said disconsolately.

"Only sometimes," he agreed.

"Nerd." She threw the basketball at him.

"But also because you love people so much, and they know you do."

"So I'm president of the High Club and vice president of the student council and captain of the volleyball team and director of the folk music group. . . . I mean, I can't spend the rest of my life doing those things, can I? So I have to figure out who I am. I know there's something I simply have to find out, right?"

"At least you don't deny you're special." He rolled the basketball toward the edge of the court.

"Like Moms did. . . ."

"There you go again." He laughed very loudly this time.

"I'm sorry." She felt her face turn hot. "I can't help it . . . but that's what you were thinking about Moms, wasn't it?"

Father Ace became very serious. "A young priest thinks he can save people from their families. Your mother was bright and happy and graceful. She entertained us all with wonderful stories." He shrugged his shoulders. "I thought if I told her she was special she wouldn't listen to her family. They won."

"And she thinks she let you down," Noele said, reading his thoughts again. "She still writes stories, but she won't show them to anyone, not even me. Well, I won't do that."

"And what will you do, M.N.?" His eyes were not dancing at all now.

"Maybe I should be a nurse or a teacher or even a nun . . . something in which I can help people. Or maybe a politician like Mr. Burns . . . or Roger, if he really runs for governor. Do you think I'd make a good nun, Father Ace?"

"No way I'll answer that, except to say that you should not become anything because you must. Our God doesn't work that way."

"That's why I have to find out . . . I mean, I keep hearing this kind of voice telling me that there's something I have to find out."

"And it has to do with your family?"

She nodded solemnly.

"Is it bad or good?"

"I don't know," she said miserably. "It's just, like, there. All the time. Like somebody or maybe everybody needs my help. I have to find out what it is."

And when you find out, Father Ace thought to himself, you may wish you never knew it.

"I don't care if someday I wish I never knew it," Noele said stubbornly. "If I don't find out, I'll never be anybody."

John

JOHN FARRELL TRIED to calculate how much damage he had done by losing his temper with Monsignor Mortimer. Every rectory in the archdiocese would know about it by tomorrow morning.

The son of two aggressively respectable employees of the Chicago Board of Education—his mother a schoolteacher, his father an engineer—Mortimer had been a few years ahead of John in the seminary, distinguished only by his lack of intelligence and his obvious penchant for cultivating superiors. No one took him seriously in those days. Indeed no one took him seriously after ordination until the cardinal sought a docile errand boy to preside over his expensive and useless television channel, a plaything in which his eminence took great delight. Mortimer promptly adopted a style of speech, dress, and behavior appropriate for a senior offical in the Roman imperium, striving for the impression that he was a confidant of the cardinal, indeed one of his principal policymakers. No one paid much heed to these pretenses. The cardinal had no confidants; he was the sole policymaker in the archdiocese. Nevertheless, Mortimer, bald, overweight, and ponderous of speech, had become something of an important personage, if only because in the group of juvenile delinquents with which the cardinal had surrounded himself, Mortimer looked and acted more like a successful, ecclesiastical bureaucrat than any of the others.

Disregarding the fact that it was half an hour before lunchtime, John Farrell mixed himself another J & B and soda, his imagination drifting to the warm nights at the beach with Irene almost twenty years ago. Mild affection by today's standards. Enough to persuade himself that he didn't have a vocation in those days. He banished the soft and insidious images and willed himself to concentrate on the cardinal's emissary. He stretched out on the luxurious red couch he had inherited from his predecessor. The smooth leather of the couch linked temporarily with the fading memory of the feel of her belly.

"Your health, Jim," John toasted his visitor. "And more success with the television."

· "I notice your ratings are down." Mortimer said somberly. Balloonhead was about as subtle as a 747 landing in the fog.

"Not really," John replied lightly. "A little higher actually than last week and substantially ahead of a year ago last week."

"The cardinal is wondering how long your series will last," Mortimer added, blundering ahead. "You and I know these shows don't run forever."

John Farrell put down his drink, doffed his jacket, and removed his rabat and Roman collar. Noele often needled him for the vanity of his dress. "And a tailor-made shirt with French cuffs. . . . Really, Uncle Monsignor, sometimes you dress like a geek."

"Even Sheen suffered from overexposure," he said cheerfully. "Heaven knows, I'm no Fulton J. But I've just signed a new contract, so I suppose that you can tell the cardinal he can see me on Channel Three once a week for the next twelve months."

"I see," Mortimer said in a tone of voice appropriate for a police captain who had just heard a murder confession. Everyone in Chicago television had heard of the new contract—everyone, that is, but Jim Mortimer.

"I've got to be frank with you," Mortimer continued, his deep voice falling several notes below normal. "The cardinal is embarrassed by the program, John. He goes to meetings around the country and other bishops ask him about the monsignor in his diocese who has a talk show and interviews actresses and feminists and homosexuals and radicals and even heretics like Hans Küng. They wonder why he lets a priest of his own diocese do such harm to the church."

Harm to the church. So that was the new line about his program. ". . . and saints like Mother Teresa.''

"The cardinal thinks Mother Teresa is a faker.''

The issue, John knew, was not Mother Teresa's authenticity. The issue was, rather, whether anyone in the archdiocese would long be tolerated if he seemed to attract more public attention than the cardinal did. For a number of years John had directed the diocese's hand-to-mouth mass-media office, filling up public-service space on Sunday mornings as best he could on a virtually nonexistent budget supplemented by Farrell family money. Then the cardinal purchased his own personal television channel (on which he spoke to ''all the priests and laity'' of the archdiocese for an hour every Monday night, in competition with Howard Cosell) and John's job was abolished. He was rewarded with St. Praxides, his home parish, and, although the cardinal didn't know it, a neighborhood with which he had always been hopelessly in love.

And there he stayed, happily anonymous, until the general manager of Channel 3, more to spite the cardinal for messing in the TV industry than for any other reason, offered John his own half-hour interview program after the news at ten thirty on Saturday night. Astonishingly, the program was a huge success. John's crisp wit, husky black-Irish good looks, and gentle but probing questions won the fancy of Saturday night television viewers. But if *The Monsignor Farrell Show* routed *M*A*S*H* and *Star Trek* replays on the other channels, it also earned for its host the criticism and the envy of many of his fellow priests and the animosity of his cardinal archbishop.

As the pastor of an exciting and prosperous parish, and only a couple of years past his fortieth birthday, John had no desire to break ranks with the ecclesiastical establishment or clerical culture. His identity as a priest who was accepted and respected by his fellow priests was as important to him as a rare painting would be to an art collector. He had ''gone along with the guys'' though all his years in the priesthood and was unnerved by the acid comments that his classmates and friends were making about the diocese's ''TV personality.''

He had enough other problems: an effeminate curate and an angry Mother Superior, racial integration, an unstable parish council, a huge school budget. But even though almost half of his classmates had left the priesthood, John Farrell could not imagine himself forsaking the active priesthood. Yet there was a part of his soul that seemed incurably weary, depressed, and lonely.

And angry. A chain reaction about to start. Damn his temper.

"You know how the guys feel about the program,'' Mortimer said, striking at the weak link in his armor. "A lot of them think you are on an ego trip, John, promoting yourself and not caring about the good of the church. They say you want to be another Sheen.''

"My hair is white at the temples, but it's curly, and Sheen's was straight.''

"That's not the point, John.''

"Well, what is the point?'' John's temper was rising, despite his best efforts to control it. "If the cardinal orders me to give up the program, I will do so. If he doesn't, I will continue for at least another year.''

"The cardinal can't order you to give up the program.'' Mortimer had now adopted a tone he thought smooth and diplomatic. "You know what kind of an outcry there would be in the media if he did that. He's not going to make you a martyr, John.''

There was a model airplane on John's coffee table, a remnant of a boyhood collection he had shared with Danny. He picked it up, trying to restrain the rage building up inside him. "You know this plane, Jim? It's a Mustang, a P-51. A great plane in the Second World War, looked a little bit like a German Messerschmitt. It was good for about a year and a half, and then the war was over and along came the jets. You tell the cardinal that I'm going to be as obsolete as a P-51 in another year or two at the most."

Mortimer relit his cigar as if it were a solemn liturgical function. "It's not good for morale among the guys for one of us to get all that attention," he warned.

A few years ago, even a year ago, such a threat to impose the sanctions of clerical caste would have devastated John Farrell. But that was before he had tasted success in something that did not depend merely on his being a priest.

"God damn the guys!" he shouted, suddenly abandoning his efforts to keep his anger under restraint, and astonishing himself with his own vehemence. "I'm not very good at what I do, but there's nobody else doing anything like it. And if the guys are so small-minded that they can't support one priest on television, then I say screw what they think."

A startled and obsequious Mortimer had left, and now John Farrell wondered uneasily what had happened to him. He was not a fighter, not a hero, surely not somebody who would courageously take on a psychopathic cardinal and an envious presbyterate. Male menopause, he told himself, thinking of the psychologist he had interviewed on his program a few weeks before. And, God, how I love being recognized when I walk down Michigan Avenue or buy something in a shop. Male menopause and vanity.

"I will be right down," he yelled impatiently at the housekeeper, who was ringing the lunch bell for the third time. Jerry Miller, his associate pastor, would not be in until supper. He was attending an interior decorator's convention at the Marriott Hotel. And the Ace would be on the basketball courts, as always. Lunch alone again.

Reviewing his conversation with Mortimer, John realized that he had acted like a damn fool. He ran his fingers through his thick black hair. Maybe I ought to go away for a week's retreat, straighten myself out. I have too much to lose if I leave the priesthood.

But his fight with Mortimer was not the only thing that troubled him. He must call Irene about his interview with Noele. Momentarily he anticipated the pleasure of hearing her voice, pictured in his imagination her spectacular figure, which looked as it always did—as if her clothes had been thrown on hastily and would blow away if you turned your head for a split second.

Desire for Irene lurked in that same secret corner of his soul where lurked the desire to fight the cardinal and all the balloonheads in the archdiocese, a longing that had begun when she had been in eighth grade, a blossoming brown-haired wonder, and he a senior at Quigley, the prep seminary. And thinking he was in love with her that summer in Grand Beach, he had been ready to give up the priesthood, everything, to possess her. It was Danny who had persuaded him to return to the seminary—said that the Conlon girl was worthless, then fell for her himself. . . .

Was that why he had resented Danny all these years? They had been rivals for his mother's love, and for Irene's. And as clever as he was in concealing his emotions, perhaps Noele, with her damned fey sensitivity, had guessed that. But in the end neither he nor Danny had claimed Irene. She belonged to his brother, Roger. Noele was their child. And Danny was dead.

John drummed his fingers on the telephone. What would he say to Irene: that Noele was rattling the skeletons in the family closet and she must be careful what she said to her? Irene was not a Farrell; she had nothing to hide. She knew nothing. . . .

She was a beautiful but rather dull woman. Still, she was an overwhelming physical presence who challenged him to the limits of his manhood. And even if he had built a concrete fortress around his desire for her, inside the bunker it was still fierce, implacable.

Why couldn't he forget her? Why couldn't he erase the memory of Danny from his mind? John Farrell had the common sense, he told himself, to ignore these ghosts of the past. But as he dialed the phone number of his brother's house—on the portable wireless phone that enabled him to answer anywhere on parish property—he thought wistfully that there were many things in life that defied common sense. Vanity, jealousy, lust . . .

Not however, if you were a priest.

Irene

SHE WAS SIPPING a vodka martini in her bathtub when the phone rang. Stumbling out of the tub, she spilled most of the drink, and then slipped on the bathroom floor, barely regaining her balance before she bumped her head on the wash basin. With a towel clutched protectively to her throat, even though there was no one else in the house, and trying not to drip water on the newly shampooed powder blue rug, she rushed to the phone in the bedroom to answer it before the ringing stopped.

Roger would not permit a telephone in the bathroom. "You'd lie in the tub and talk all day," he had insisted, laughing genially when she suggested it.

"Irene, it's John." The usual mysterious enthusiasm was in her brother-in-law's voice, as it always was when he began a conversation with her. It would fade quickly. "I hope I haven't disturbed you."

"Just climbing out of the tub," she lied. "Roger is over at his office at the University, and Noele is off doing research for a term paper. She was interviewing you, wasn't she?"

"That's what I want to talk about. She's working on some family history thing. She was asking a lot of questions about Danny. The skeletons in the Farrell closet ought to stay locked up, Irene, especially now."

One summer, long ago, she had thought John Farrell terribly sweet, and the touch of his strong hands unbearably gentle. She had just graduated from high school and wanted to fall in love. He was supposed to be on leave from the seminary, "trying to make up his mind." She thought he had made it up. Otherwise she would have avoided him. She did not want to fight God.

Their romance had ended as swiftly as it had begun; now he was a self-important ass, charming the women of the parish with his smile and his Irish Republican Army good looks, and winning over the men with brisk, locker-room camaraderie. She supposed that he was a good pastor, although she found his pose as an open-minded, liberal priest unpersuasive. And his success on television made him even more pompous.

How could she, in a stupid teenage crush, have once dreamed of going to bed with him?

The mirrors in the bedroom were beginning to steam from the moisture that had escaped from the bathroom. The fifteen pounds whose loss she was celebrating with the martini clutched in the same hand holding the towel didn't make much difference. Irene turned away from the mirror, embarrassed as she always was by the image of her swelling breasts and full hips.

"Are you still there?" John demanded. "The less said about the past, the better for all of us. . . . You know Noele."

"Yes, I know Noele." Irene was intensely envious of her daughter's confidence, popularity, and grace. She hated herself for her envy, fought against it, and yet could not exorcise it. If only she were sixteen again and had a chance to live her life over.

"I think the child should be steered off the subject." John, like her husband, had a tone of special officiousness when he was giving her orders about Noele, a child they tried to spoil at every opportunity. To Noele's credit, she was immune to their indulgence. Irene supposed that she indulged her too. For in addition to envy, she felt enormous love for her Christmas child—and had no idea how to show it.

"I'll do what I can, although, as you know, she is at a very difficult age." She yearned for the comfort and the warmth of the tub, so like the beach that summer she'd been frightened by *The Birds* and reveled in "Those Lazy, Hazy, Crazy Days of Summer." As she sang for everyone, she was "Irresponsible" eighteen. Her crowd that glorious, wonderful summer thought that John Kennedy on his sailboat was the most handsome man in the world. In a few months he would be dead, and then the next weekend Clancy Farrell would join him in the land of the dead. Her last happy summer. . . .

"You ought to alert Roger, too, don't you think?"

"I'll tell him. He has a much better relationship with Noele than I do."

"Thank you, Irene. Are you going to watch the game this afternoon? It's a big one."

"Wouldn't miss if for the world," she said. The Farrells always watched Notre Dame games when they were on national telelvision, if they were not sitting in the seats the family had owned for thirty years at South Bend.

But in fact, she had no intention of watching the game. She would use the precious moments of Saturday afternoon's peace to draw her stories out of the dark blue Florentine leather file case in which she kept them and continue the delightful task of refining and perfecting them.

"All right," John said. "Give my regards to Roger. I'll see you at Brigid's for dinner tomorrow night."

Irene sighed as she hung up the phone. Second Sunday at Brigid's, as much a part of life as the sun rising in the morning. Part of the comfortable but iron-bound coffin that the Neighborhood had become for her.

She wrapped the towel tightly around herself for the brief journey back to the tub and took a quick gulp from her martini glass. Then, shielded from the bathroom mirror by the heavy humidity radiating from the tub, she folded the towel neatly over the towel bar and slipped back into the water. Her body, a sponge for sensual pleasure, soaked up the reassuring warmth. She had not needed to lose all of the fifteen pounds; her large frame and solid flesh carried weight well. The diet had been for her own morale. It was designed to make her feel less ungainly and assure herself again that she could stop drinking if she wanted to.

Roger had not noticed the weight loss. When he had been informed about it the previous night, after they had made love as routinely as they went to church on Sunday, he said characteristically, "You look fine to me, but then you always look fine. Maybe a little thin now. Why don't you put back about five pounds?"

Everything she did, or was, seemed just a little bit off to Roger. He was almost successful in hiding his embarrassment at faculty parties. His wife led an idle and unproductive existence, mothering their only child, who scarcely needed mothering, and presiding over their elegantly furnished house in the woods at the north end of Jefferson Avenue with the help of two part-time maids. She was an amusement to the older faculty wives and an affront to the younger ones, many of whom tried to raise her consciousness at government department gatherings. But Irene had learned, after making both herself and her husband look ridiculous when they had first returned to Chicago from Berkeley, to remain mysteriously silent at such gatherings. And Roger had paid her the highest compliment of which he was capable when he had said, in his usual half jesting way, that she was at least not an obstacle to his promotion, as were some of the more outspoken faculty wives.

She sank deeper into the waters of the tub and reached for her drink. Unfortunately she had left it on the wash basin, just out of reach, and had to stand halfway up in the tub to claim the glass. It was an act typical of her, she thought—forgetful, awkward, and not very intelligent. At least that was the way everyone saw her—her brother-in-law, her mother-in-law, her husband, even her own parents—and that was the way she sometimes thought of herself.

Noele had a different view: "As a mother, Moms, you can be a trial, but as a woman I think you're, like, kind of interesting. Not just sexy, but sort of deep and knowing and totally awesome. A real woman."

Irene had turned away to hide her pleasure. "You should think of me as your mother and not another woman."

"Mo-*ther,* you should be flattered. Most of the other kids don't have mothers they can think of as women."

So it went with Noele. One never had the last word.

And Roger was fond of her, Irene knew; admired her durable good looks, enjoyed her in their low-key sex life, encouraged her volunteer work, and almost never raised his voice to her. She had learned long ago, when he was a doctoral student at Berkeley and she was typing his papers and working at a stenographic job in the administration building, that Roger was a good and generous man. But in his repertory of emotions sustained passionate love with one woman no longer existed. It wasn't his fault. It was merely the way he was.

He had tried to help her when she strove to finish her undergraduate work after Noele was in school. But his criticisms of her papers, in the form of gentle, lighthearted ridicule, as if she were just a child learning to walk, ended her final academic efforts. And he had encouraged her in creative writing courses she had taken five years ago. He insisted on reading the novella she had written at the end of the program. When he was through rewriting it, correcting her punctuation, grammar, style, and story line (always in the most gentle of words), she had made up her mind never to show him or anyone else any of her other stories.

She was not a child, Irene thought, sinking deeper into the protective waters of the tub. She was almost thirty-seven years old. And she was not dumb. Her

I.Q. when she was in the Academy of Our Lady high school was between 150 and 160, and the stories and poems she had written in the year and a half she was a student at St. Mary's of Notre Dame received virtually automatic A's. She was smarter than most of the faculty wives and probably smarter than many of the faculty members, including her husband. She was not stupid; she was afraid.

Afraid of the Farrells, just as she had been afraid of her own family. Her father, Isaiah Conlon, was hailed as the most honest state's attorney of his generation; and he and his wife, Marybelle, had believed stern discipline essential to raise children to be equally honest. For their daughters that meant strict rules, harsh criticism of even minor "unladylike" behavior, and ridicule of all "pretensions." The harshest sanctions were contained in two questions: "Who do you think you are?" and "What will people say?"

People said that Irene Marie, their youngest daughter, was the loveliest and most vivacious of their children. Isaiah and Marybelle took that acclaim as confirmation of their own darkest fears and began their campaign of ridicule—aided enthusiastically by her brothers and sisters. Irene, even as a little girl, could do nothing right. Her clothes, her hair, her friends, her grades in school, and, as she grew older, her spectacularly blooming body were the targets for their merciless fun.

When she married Roger she moved from a world of nasty ridicule to a world of gentle and amused dismay, a much more pleasant and amiable environment, where John's eyes reduced her to an attractive decoration, Brigid's smile hinted that she was fragile and weak, and Roger's patronizing words suggested that she needed protection like a harmless child.

Of course, she had her own secret, one that she treasured as though it were a priceless jewel, a secret that none of the Farrells would ever be given a chance to profane.

The martini glass was almost empty. Should she turn the hot water on in the tub and mix herself another drink? Or should she open the precious file box and rework the stories that no one would ever read? It was always difficult to begin, like plunging into a cold swimming pool, a scary entrance but then exhilaration the instant after.

It did not finally matter whether she had been born afraid or made fearful through a life of cruel Irish ridicule. The results were the same. Whatever chances she might have had when she was a young woman had been lost long ago. Only with one person had she ever been free, unafraid to be herself.

Irene sighed, drained the martini glass, and then climbed out of the bathtub. In the bedroom she put on her underwear, opened a bedroom window halfway to let in the Indian summer warmth, and reclined on the chaise longue next to her dressing table. Then, picking up the thin leather file case, which she had earlier removed from the secret compartment of the Sheraton desk in her scrupulously neat little office down the hall, she unlocked it and removed a carefully typed manuscript.

> *"I have a confession." He leaned heavily on the windowsill, watching the black sky over the lake turn its first pale gray.*
>
> *"My penances are light," she said sleepily, hoping he would want to make love again.*
>
> *"All I wanted last night was to score. God forgive me for it. I wanted to brag in the locker room at the golf club today that I had made you last night."*

"I know," she said softly.

"I'm really a vicious bastard."

"I know that, too." She laughed.

He turned slowly away from the window. "In God's name, then, why did you let me do it?"

"Because I knew that by this time, the morning after, you would have fallen in love with me."

He came over to the bed, sat down next to her, and removed the sheet that covered her naked body. "You're a scheming little bitch!"

"I know that, too." She jabbed at his stomach, tickling him.

"I'm a victim of witchcraft!" he protested, twisting helplessly at her loving torture.

"Absolutely. And how long do you think I've been casting my spell?"

"Two years?" he said tentatively.

"More like four, darling." She embraced him. "And now that I've got you thoroughly enchanted, I don't propose ever to let you get away."

Yes, it set the right tone for the middle of the story, Irene thought. The first part would be the young man's harsh lust, followed by his guilt and dismay at having ravaged an innocent virgin. In the second part he would discover that the virgin was not all that innocent, and that he was the one who was trapped. Then in the third part, the tragic ending, he would lose her to an accident in the lake, a propeller on a big lake cruiser cutting her in half.

"Hi, Moms," Noele called, exploding into the room. "Still working on those stories of yours? When are you going to let me read one of them?"

Startled, Irene angrily clutched the manila folder against her chest, protecting it as though it were a helpless babe. "How many times do I have to tell you, young woman, you should not come through a closed door without knocking?"

"Mo-*ther,* I know Daddy isn't home, and I know you don't have a lover, and"—she whistled appreciatively—"and you're totally beautiful in that pale gray teddy. Like, I wish I had the figure for things like that. Lucky Roger! Where did you buy it? Bonwit's? I'm really mad that I'm not your size. And you look awesomely cool with all the weight you've lost. You ought to start jogging, too. That'll keep your muscles firm. I want you to be the prettiest mother in the parish!"

It was Noele's firm conviction, Irene knew, that she could convert any situation into one that pleased her if she simply pretended long enough and strongly enough that what she wanted actually existed. In the will of Noele, red-haired, green-eyed, enthusiastic Christmas child that she was, she and her mother were friends, buddies, confidantes; maternal impatience was dismissed as irrelevant, and maternal envy was ignored.

As always, Irene was both flattered and disconcerted by her daughter's frank, almost clinical admiration, linked as it usually was with direct instructions about what she should do to remain attractive. "What if I hadn't been decent?" She sniffed, trying to be indignant.

"Oh, Mo-*ther,* you're always decent. And always pretty, too. As a matter of fact, I'm getting tired of Jaimie Burns staring at you whenever I bring him into the house. I'm afraid we're just going to have to lock you up in a room when the boys come over.''

Irene carefully replaced the manuscript in its leather file and locked it, as though she were storing a priceless pearl necklace. Then she donned a robe that matched the color of her lingerie. ''Which reminds me, young woman, if you want to go out with that Jaimie Burns tonight, your room is going to have to be immaculate by suppertime. As neat as every other room in the house.''

''Uh-huh.'' Noele was unimpressed by the sternness of her mother's command. ''What was Danny Farrell like, anyway?''

Irene felt her throat tighten, her heartbeat increase, her gut wrench. After all these years he can still do that to me.

''He was the sweetest, kindest man who ever lived,'' she blurted without thinking. ''A funny, crazy, Peter Pan kind of man.''

''Oh,'' Noele said, surprised by her mother's intensity.

''You're asking because of the term paper?'' Irene said, trying to recapture her composure.

''Kind of. Did he drink a lot?''

Damn you, John Farrell, for suggesting that.

''Not really. More than Jaimie Burns, I guess. Not as much as a lot of boys then or now.''

The quick little computer underneath Noele's red hair was churning away, trying to reconcile John's picture of Danny with Irene's. ''Was he running away from something, Moms?''

God, yes, child. More than you can imagine.

''I suppose you could say that.'' She paused, wondering how to tell the truth and yet not the whole truth. ''He was really a casualty of the success of the South Side Irish. If we'd still been poor, Danny would never have left us.''

''How come?'' Noele fingered the end of a strand of her bright red hair.

My God, thought Irene, I sound like a social studies teacher.

''We came too far too quickly. We tried to stop being Irish. We gave up poetry, laughter, and dreaming. We held on to our religion and our drink. And we clung to our property as if it were as important as our religion. For people of your grandmother Brigid's generation, property and respectability became a substitute for poetry. They locked themselves in a prison with broken glass and barbed wire on the walls and tried to lock their children up with them. Danny Farrell wanted the poetry—and the laughter, too. But they wouldn't let him have either.''

Noele, sitting now on the edge of the bed, was uncharacteristically puzzled. ''I don't understand, Moms.''

''If he had been a naval aviator like his father or a businessman like his uncle or even a priest like Monsignor John or a teacher like your father, no one would have minded. But he wanted to be a storyteller, a writer, even when he was four or five years younger than you are. The family, especially Grandma Brigid, and everyone else in the Neighborhood said there was no money in that, and he was too gentle a man to fight them. So he acted out some of his stories, used laughter and drink to kill the pain, and died a young man.''

''Was that for the best? That's what Uncle Monsignor said this morning.''

Irene hesitated. God damn John Farrell's arrogant righteousness. ''I don't know, hon; he might have been a great writer or a great drunk. He never had a chance to become either.'' She waited, her head bowed as if she were a prisoner in the dock, for Noele to ask her whether she had loved Daniel Xavier Farrell. How could she answer that question?

Noele did not ask.

"Another way to think about him," Irene rushed on, "is that he was a grown-up teenager. I know that sounds like a contradiction, but when he was twenty-four, right before he died, he hung around with kids my age. If he were alive today, you and your friends Jenny McCabe and Eileen Kelly and Michele Carmody would have a big teenage crush on him."

Noele brightened, "Oh! Now I understand. That makes a lot more sense than what Uncle Monsignor told me."

"We all have to grow up sometime, honey," Irene said, regretting her candor. "And part of growing up and acting like an adult is learning that dreams don't come true. You're almost a grown-up now, Noele, and you have to learn to give up girlish dreams about romantic heroes who died a long time ago. Don't think about Danny too much. Think about the future, not the past."

"Dreams do too come true," Noele said, her pretty little jaw set in a line of grim determination. "If you want them badly enough. And how can I think about the future if I don't know about the past?"

The hard lines of her jaw vanished as quickly as they had appeared, and Noele rose from the edge of the bed to kiss her mother lightly on the forehead. "You smell pretty, too."

Irene felt, as she often did, that she was the child and Noele the mother.

Noele paused at the doorway. "Did Grandpa Clancy drink a lot too?"

"He was a terrible drinker," Irene said without thinking. "That's why he fell down the stairs and killed himself. He was dead drunk that night."

Images of that terrible evening, and Danny's cold fury when Clancy had insulted her and her family, rushed through her mind. Dear God in heaven, I should not have said that to her. I am so stupidly impulsive.

"You should never regret being impulsive, Moms. And you're not stupid, either," Noele said, considering her mother critically, head cocked slightly to one side like a thoughtful robin. "I'll never look good in pale gray because I'll never look regal. You should let your hair grow long."

After Noele had left, Irene returned the file box to the drawer at the bottom of her dressing table, locked it, and put the key in her purse. While Noele was watching the football game, she would work on one of the other stories and then return the file to the desk in her office. Noele had told her not to regret her impulsiveness, as if replying to something Irene had said instead of something she had thought. She and Roger were so used to such fey behavior that they paid little attention to it.

What if Noele heard her thoughts about . . . about . . . the past. Then the Christmas child would no longer pretend that she and her mother were friends. She would hate her mother for the rest of her life.

Irene hesitated. Roger did not like to be bothered at the University. Nevertheless, this was important. He ought to be warned before Noele caught him by surprise.

Then suddenly she was very angry at Roger, angrier than she had been in a long time. Damn him!

A thought to which she'd never had courage to give shape before exploded, jarring her brain as if someone had hit her jaw. She would never be herself as long as she remained married to Roger. He and his brother and his mother would keep her the dull, stupid woman they insisted she was. Other women her age were getting divorces and beginning life again. Why couldn't she?

As she pushed the 753 exchange on her Princess phone she laughed to herself. What a ridiculous idea! How could she possibly survive on her own? And what would happen to Noele.

······*Roger*······

ROGER HAD BECOME bored with the young interviewer even before the telephone rang. Joe Kramer of *The Republic* was tall, thin, blond, apple-cheeked, and painfully uneducated, the kind of naïf who took it for granted that everyone shared his left-wing Catholic ideology and vocabulary. The interview would drag on at least twenty more minutes. There would be no time between Kramer and Martha Clay to open his mail.

"Mr. Farrell," Roger said discreetly to the telephone. At the University faculty members were never doctor or professor.

"I know you don't like to be disturbed, and I wouldn't call unless I thought it might be important." Irene was both anxious and guilty.

"I'm sure it is," he said mildly, hinting faintly at his annoyance.

"It's about Noele. She's doing a term paper in family history and asking questions about Danny. Monsignor John was concerned. You know how Noele is; sometimes she senses and feels things without anyone actually telling her. John is afraid this might be one of those times."

"Couldn't it have waited until I got home?" He raised the pitch of his voice.

"John wanted me to call you," Irene said defensively. "I thought I'd better warn you before Noele corners you."

"I think I know Noele well enough to be able to cope," he said patiently. "You're quite right, however, about her intuition. I appreciate the warning. We don't want her to get hurt. See you tonight."

He hung up before Irene could apologize again for disturbing him.

"Excuse me, Mr. Kramer," Roger said, smiling at the interviewer with the campaign smile he had been practicing. "Sometimes I think it would be easier to have five teenage daughters than just one. Now, we were discussing, let's see, the questions of the relationship between morality and politics?"

"Catholics my age"—Kramer talked with a faint lisp—"find it very hard to understand how you could justify studying a man like Machiavelli."

Oh, God, Roger thought. If I have to be interviewed by idiots like this, I may drop out of the gubernatorial race even before it begins.

"Niccolò Machiavelli was neither a moralist nor an ethicist, Mr. Kramer; he was an empiricist, describing the reality of politics as he knew it. He observed that the Prince—any political leader, really—operated on a set of moral principles that were quite different from the ordinary canons of morality. For the Prince to lie, to steal, to deceive, to cheat, to corrupt, to bribe, was perfectly legitimate so long as the act increased the welfare of the state. Rather like Karl Marx."

"But Marx was correct about morality," protested the young man.

"Let me ask you a question, Mr. Kramer." Roger rested his chin on interlaced fingers, one of his favorite poses in the classroom. "I'm sure that you, as a young journalist, are an admirer of men like Woodward, Bernstein, Hersh, and other investigative reporters, aren't you?''

Kramer nodded earnestly.

"I see. But, of course, they accepted stolen property, they persuaded men to be disloyal and violate their oaths of office, they asked tricky questions and deceived many of the people they interviewed. Are not investigative reporters rather similar to Machiavelli's Prince?''

"They did those things to expose dishonesty in government and to end the war.'' The young man's apple cheeks turned even rosier. "Investigative reporters fight against corruption. They don't engage in it.''

"Well, I certainly don't subscribe to Machiavelli's pragmatism—and would not take him as a model in the event I should ever become governor,'' Roger said smoothly. "I'm sure if Niccolò Machiavelli were here in this room, in fact, he would say if the end justifies the means for somebody, it does for everybody.''

"You wouldn't be a disciple of Machiavelli as governor?'' the young man persisted.

"Of course not,'' Roger said crisply. "Machiavelli is a theorist, someone who helps you to understand the way things are. As governor, I would strive for things to become the way they should be.''

Kramer jotted down the remark vigorously. It would certainly appear in the article.

Finally the young man left, promising that he would be back early the next week to interview students and other faculty members and read the manuscripts of Roger's published articles and books. He wanted to compare the manuscripts with the published works to see how Roger's "creative mind'' worked. All this for a thirty-five-hundred-word article for a college magazine.

There were a few minutes left before Martha would appear, all breathless and glowing and filled with intelligence and sexual energy. Roger opened one letter and then put it aside. He was so eager to possess her that he could not think straight. He had fallen in love with her—the first time that had happened in a career of judicious shopping in the academic slave markets. A sweet high school prom queen, with an overlay of feminist ideology and deep sexual hungers, which he had taught her to acknowledge.

I'm coming apart, he told himself with a sigh. Running for governor is so much fun that my personality is disintegrating. I might as well enjoy it while I can.

He was a fully accepted member of the faculty community, a little too witty and irreverent, but that was excused because he was an Irish Catholic. And a little too modish in his dress, light brown and light blue sport jackets and coordinated slacks—not the dull gray three-piece suits or the jeans and flannel shirts, the alternative-approved uniforms at the University. But that was excused because of his wealth.

He could spend, Roger knew, the next thirty years of his life delivering witty epigrams at the round lunch table in the Faculty Club dining room, and never do another honest day's work. Or he could choose to write an article every year and a slender monograph every two years—any more would be judged excessive by his colleagues and proof that he was not serious. But both choices struck him as profoundly depressing, as did the prospect of more easy conquests in the University's flesh market. The time had come to try the world of active politics, returning, as it were, to the womb, but with a very useful credential taken from the academy.

He would, of course, be known as Dr. Farrell. After all, Henry Kissinger was Dr. Kissinger.

Nonetheless, he should not have permitted himself to fall in love with his doll-like little WASP. Most imprudent.

Not so odd that Clancy and Brigid Farrell should produce two incomplete sons, one a vain realist who was unrealistic about his own vanity and the other an intensely ambitious idealist who spent most of his time pretending to be indifferent to both ideals and success. For a moment Roger considered the elegance of his self-description. It could stand a little polish and did not mention his delight in the female slaves on the trading block. Yet it would do as a single-sentence summary.

He glanced at his watch. The annual woman was a routine part of life for many academics, not all, by any means, but enough so that he was hardly alone in his amusements. Brief amusements. In the long run they became almost as boring as the faculty lunch table. You returned them to the trading block as quickly as possible.

Martha came into his office, eyes glowing with the enthusiastic zeal of a fundamentalist missionary going into the jungles of Latin America to bring salvation to a native tribe. Something remained of her grandparents' years in China, a pious and lovely young Protestant matron rushing to embrace the lions. No, he did not want to return her to the trading block. She was becoming more interesting rather than less. Her toughly worded ideology was only skin-deep. Beneath it she was a mixture of sweetness and passive passion.

"I think I have it this time, Roger," she said cheerfully. "If we look at the strongest relationships these women develop with the important men in their lives, we will find an alienating variable, a contradiction between their own middle-class self-definition and the realities in which they find themselves. This would account for their radicalization."

"Let's see your numbers," Roger said, sounding, he hoped, like a brisk and businesslike political science professional and not like a lecherous pagan hoping to seduce a Salvation Army volunteer.

Numbers were not Roger's thing. But Martha's gibberish was such a mishmash of Marxism and shallow feminism that the only hope for her book was some arresting statistics.

Alas, as he suspected, the statistics were a mishmash too.

Her book was a ponderously dull study of oppression in middle-class family life. It would be published, of course, if he could force her to let go of it and send it off to the press. Anything written about women political activists was published these days, especially when it was submitted to a woman editor at an academic press. Martha's chances of tenure at the University, however, would remain thin. As a rule of thumb a woman scholar must be one and one-half times better than the men with whom she was theoretically competing. Martha was not that much better than her male competition.

A neatly turned out, sweet-faced little honey blonde, she surely had been a sweetheart in high school before being radicalized at Stanford. And if radicalism was supreme in her head, she was still a prom queen in her heart and her body, capitvated by the captain of the basketball team, whom she had married and then divorced after both had been caught up in the turbulence of graduate school in the early seventies.

The dope hadn't known how lucky he was. Probably couldn't cope with her

feminist consciousness and didn't see the possibilities in her delightfully feminine little body.

An assistant professor could either be feminine or a feminist. Unfortunately
Martha was an unstable compound of the two. She was thus an interesting sexual
conquest but an unpromising candidate for a lifetime appointment—and you had
to see the word *lifetime* often when you were probably going to reject a promotion in the social science division of the University.

Roger was committed in principle to her promotion. To reject her and accept
a man not as good as she would be disgraceful. He would vote for her because
she deserved tenure, because he would enjoy his colleagues twisting and turning
as they explained that their decision to reject was really not sexist, and now
because he loved her.

"I'm still troubled by the weakness of some of your correlations," Roger said,
looking up from her manuscript. "They simply are not statistically significant,
you know."

"That's because you're a man," she snapped. Then, changing quickly from
an angry feminist to a helplessly feminine woman, she asked, "Do you think I
ought to rework it again?"

"I don't think so," he said, weighing his words carefully and trying to
concentrate on her text instead of fantasizing about her exquisite legs. "The best
way to cope is to acknowledge candidly in your introduction the weaknesses of
the data and assert that your analytic models are presented for speculative and
illustrative purposes, pending more elaborately designed research. If you do that,
you can fend off both critics and reviewers nicely."

"That's an excellent idea!" she exclaimed, shifting in her chair to a pose not
quite unself-conscious in its sexual appeal. Sometimes Roger thought her recently awakened appetites were more intense than his. She did not want to talk
research this Indian summer Saturday afternoon any more than he did.

"The important thing, Martha, is to send the manuscript off to your publishers. You already have a tentative agreement to publish. We know they have
favorable reports from their readers, and we should be able to say to your review
committee in January that the book has impressed a distinguished academic
publisher."

"How much do you think that's going to help?" Martha's hand darted quickly
to his arm.

I really don't deserve a morsel as tasty and as eager as you. But, since I have
you, I will certainly consume you.

"As I told you before, this case is not going to be decided finally in the
department; it will be a weak vote either way. The decision will be passed on to
the dean and the provost. A book in press will make them think twice about
turning you down." His hand moved to her adorable little ass, so small that he
could cover much of it with his palm and extended fingers. He loved her with the
romantic affection a teenage boy has for his first girl friend—and made love to
her with the exuberant fantasies of an adolescent. Today she would be the
missionary captured by a pagan monarch and introduced to the pleasures of sin
for the first time.

"And maybe win over some votes in the department?" she asked breathlessly,
her hand now moving lightly to his chest.

"It's always difficult to estimate the probability of the reaction of any given
member of our department on any issue, but on the whole," Roger said, trying
to sound like a professor when he was about to be a sexual conqueror, "the

chance of a favorable vote in your case goes up considerably when you have a book in press.''

The critical ploy in edging Martha off the block and out of her clothes was that she must take the initiative herself. Otherwise he might be accused before the high court of ideological feminism of being an exploitive male and she of selling herself to an exploitive male to promote her career.

''Sometimes I wonder whether all the academic politics is worth it,'' she said vaguely as she caressed his cheek, to her a signal of invitation, to him of surrender.

''It's unreal, I admit, and that's what tempts me about the other kind of politics; they're less unreal. Nonetheless, we must not permit academic politics to destroy your career.''

Her fingers, reassured by his hollow piety, traveled from his cheek to his chin and then to his throat. Irene never did anything like that. The trouble with her was that she did not have to be pursued and offered no inducements to the chase. She had long since been conquered and never required taming. She was attractive and mildly diverting, but not nearly so challenging and exciting as this passionate mixture of femininity and feminism he was about to take off the trading block and brand as his own.

Roger's head throbbed with the sweet taste of conquest. You could not stop now, my dear little slave, even if you wanted to. I can do with you what I wish.

Leisurely, as if he were sipping lemonade, he pushed up her sweater and unfastened the front hook on her sheer pink lace bra, a convenient concession to femininity. He squeezed one small breast rather hard. She winced and exclaimed, although they both knew that she wanted to feel the torment of his fingers as much as he wanted to sink them into her flesh.

Then his amusements began in earnest. Soon her delicately lush little body was spread-eagled on his desk, and she was begging him to end the delights of her torment.

An easy conquest, my Salvation Army matron and right here in the corridors of the government department. Then he was flooded with a sweet torrent of affection for her. She was a sister or a daughter, not an amusing little slave girl. He would protect her and take care of her.

For a few moments after they were finished, she nestled naked in his arms, content and happy, sweetly affectionate and submissive. ''I love you, Roger,'' she said simply, cuddling even closer to him.

''And I love you, too,'' he said, realizing that he was swimming in deep waters. And heading away from shore.

Noele

''THEY ARE FOR sure going to lose, M.N.,'' said Eileen Kelly, a tall and pretty blonde from whom the last traces of baby fat had yet to disappear.

In school Noele was known as Mary Noele because the nuns had decided long ago that she needed a Christian name. And to her contemporaries, she was often ''M.N.,'' which she liked even more, but only from teenagers.

''Really,'' she replied, using her generation's favorite all-purpose word. She knew that they were for sure not going to lose. She was not about to repeat her mistake with Father Ace, however.

She could not anticipate what would happen to Notre Dame every Saturday. And sometimes her feelings about the outcome of the weekly battle in defense of Catholicism—as Roger called it with his amused little smile—were wrong. But she was not wrong when Jaimie Burns was involved. He was going to intercept a pass in the last few minutes of the game and run it back for a touchdown.

And that was for sure. Just as her feeling that the first-string free safety would pull a muscle in the second quarter so Jaimie would play the rest of the game and not just on kickoffs had already been confirmed.

"I don't know what's the matter with them," moaned Eileen, Noele's best friend since as long a either could remember, despite theatrical quarrels every couple of weeks. "Like, they score two touchdowns in the first quarter every week and then fall apart. My dad says they used to be unbeaten."

"And the Mass used to be in Latin," said Noele.

"But a real long time ago," Eileen replied. "My Dad says that Notre Dame is the best university in the country."

"Really," Noele said. According to Roger it was a passable undergraduate institution but did not begin to exist as a University. And Roger was an alumnus, just like Doctor Kelly. It ought to be better, Roger would add, given all the money they have taken out of the pockets of rich Catholics.

Noele did not care about such matters. She would go to Notre Dame because her father went there. And because Brigid wanted her to go there. And because Marty Farrell went there.

And because Jaimie Burns went there.

Mostly because of Jaimie Burns.

Besides, if you were a girl, you had to be at the very top of your class to be admitted, and that was the kind of challenge Noele loved.

"Jaimie's playing real good," Eileen said as Congressman Burns's son batted a pass out of the hands of a Hurricane in the end zone.

"Really," Noele replied.

"Are you two coming to the play tomorrow night?" Eileen asked.

"Dinner at Grams's," Noele said. "They won't need the head of crew anyway. We'll make the party afterward."

Miami broke through a collapsing Notre Dame line for another touchdown, going ahead 17–14.

"Really!" the two of them exclaimed together.

Dr. Finnbar Kelly, Eileen's father, was known as the only Democratic surgeon on the South Side. His political principles did not interfere with his life-style, however. The big-screen TV in his gadget-filled family room was as large as Grams's.

All the better to see Jaimie Burns.

He ran the kickoff back to the Miami thirty-five.

"One more block and the sleepy-eyed graduate of Saint Ignatius High School in Chicago," said the announcer, "might have gone all the way."

"Really!" Noele exclaimed, more in anger at the suggestion that Jaimie was sleepy-eyed than at the absence of a block.

"Jaimie Burns go all the way," Eileen repeated, giggling.

"No way, José," Noele said firmly. Like many of her generation, Noele's sexual ethics had more in common with the 1940s than the 1960s. But with Jaimie Burns there was no need to draw any lines.

Notre Dame ran the ball up the middle on the first down, around the end the second down, and, with a third and seven, missed a forward pass by half the state of Indiana.

Suddenly Noele felt uneasy. Something was wrong. Something terrible. Someone was hurting. . . .

Miami ran the short punt back to midfield. Now was the time for the interception. Noele hardly noticed because the vibes of terrible loneliness were getting worse. Her loneliness. She was the one who was hurting. She was in a desert, all by herself. Cut off.

"I'm not lonely," she murmured to herself. "Why should I feel lonely?"

"Huh?" Eileen said.

Before Noele can answer, the poor kid who was the Miami quarterback threw a bomb in the general direction of the Notre Dame end zone.

"He has a receiver open!" screamed the Notre Dame announcer, as though the barbarians were at the gate.

No way, José.

Jaimie appeared out of nowhere, grabbed the ball from the hands of the Miami receiver, and tore down the sidelines.

There was pandemonium in the Orange Bowl—and in Finnbar Kelly's basement. Noele shouted as loudly as Eileen, not because she was surprised, but because she felt she had to cover up her advance knowledge.

But the bad vibes were still there. Total isolation from everyone. Floating on a raft in an empty ocean.

Was Jaimie going to be hurt before the game was over?

No, it was not Jaimie. She was the one who was cut off, completely alone, like some of the older nuns said the people in hell would be.

Slowly the hell feeling faded away.

Notre Dame won. The TV people couldn't find Jaimie after the game for an interview.

Really. By which she meant that of course they couldn't find him.

On her way home in Flame, her red Chevette, Noele gave little thought to the triumph of her Jaimie Burns. Someone needed her help. It was the third time in the last month she had experienced those terrible vibes.

She had to find out why.

Someone buried in loneliness.

And that someone was her.

Roger

LATER THAT AFTERNOON Roger drove home in his Seville—an affront to the University's culture, which virtually demanded that the younger full professor drive a foreign car, preferably Swedish. His wife's Datsun sports car and his own antique Mercedes never appeared in the University parking lots. The Neighborhood, snuggled in the hills and the woods of the Chicago Ridge, once the dunes of an ice-age Lake Michigan but now the southwest fringe of the city, was also an affront to his colleagues. He chose to live there not so much to offend them as to enjoy a peaceful haven from the frantic University environment, intense both in its academic seriousness and in its pursuit of sexual pleasure.

And also because he thought his women were safer there.

Roger was in a thoughtful mood, not about the life that lay ahead of him if he chose to run for governor—surely the most important decision he would ever make—but about the life he would leave behind. After he had been rewarded with his "lifetime appointment," he had casually suggested to a couple of his colleagues that the Slave Market model of the higher academy was as useful to explain the behavior of the professorate as was the Pursuit of Truth model. The campus, he had said, was a sorting mechanism by which the powerful men allotted themselves privileges over the most desirable women—such as these might be. Feminism, he contended, merely changed the rules a bit but also gave the powerful men an ideological support, Sexual Liberation, for asserting their privileges. Horrified, they had begged him not to publish such nonsense.

It was not nonsense. Many, probably most, of the faculty did not engage in the slave trade. And not all the available young women offered themselves on the block. But many came seeking wisdom and sex in equal amounts. And sex as a hidden agenda permeated the dingy gothic corridors of the University buildings like a pervasive if barely visible mist. Martha Clay wanted to become his slave for the current academic year at least as much as he wanted her. She wanted to take off her clothes for him as much as he wanted to strip her.

That they fell in love with each other was pure accident.

And that made him uneasy. It would mean more guilt. And with that thought, as surely as a winter cold comes, even though one pretends that its symptoms are not real, self-revulsion and disgust assaulted him. Why could he never remember before the fact how he would hate himself after the fact?

He pulled his Seville to the curb of a side street next to the Woods, the northern boundary of the Neighborhood, and slumped over the wheel. Dedicated Catholic idealist indeed.

Women were an obsession. Since high school days there had always been a woman to pursue and dominate. He was programmed in his flesh to do so, even though he achieved little permanent satisfaction from his conquests. None of the slim, small-breasted women he had mastered had meant anything to him before Martha. He had never felt as close to any woman as he had to Danny Farrell. Not even to Irene or Martha.

What would Danny have said of Martha Clay's piquant and intense sexual antics this afternoon, of her pleas that he release her from the cliff of sexual frustration on which he had kept her suspended until she cried out in need?

Would Danny have admired his technique?

More likely he would have laughed at the whole absurd business.

The waves of self-contempt ebbed, and he started the car. He had not forgotten Irene's phone call. Nor could he ever forget Danny, and in a way that was just as well. The memories were too sweet to give up. There was, for example, the glorious Holy Thursday evening when they'd been in their early years of high school. In those days Catholics went from church to church praying to the blessed sacrament "exposed" outside of the tabernacle on the altar in preparation for a Good Friday service, which was not, strictly speaking, a Mass. Visiting churches had been a social event—a date for adolescents and young adults, a festive occasion for older men and women, a serious moral, religious, and social responsibility for parents, and a pre-Easter fashion show for upper-middle-class matrons.

St. Praxides had been a much smaller parish then, and the church was in the basement of the school. The pastor, a solemn and pompous personage immensely impressed with his own importance, stood outside the school door in good weather and at the head of the stairs leading to the basement in bad, clad in all the purple his monsignoral dignity could muster, greeting visitors from other parishes and frowning slightly at the occasional Negro Catholic who dared to invade St. Praxides on Holy Thursday.

Stationed at the entrance of the church on a soft spring evening in the 1950s, the monsignor was the last to know that St. Joseph had lost his purple Latin veil and was now dressed in a Notre Dame sweat shirt. And on the other side of the church Blessed Mother had replaced her purple veil with a St. Ignatius High School basketball warm-up jacket. Most of the people in the parish suspected that Danny Farrell was behind the prank, but only Roger, a frightened guard at a distance in the sacristy, knew for certain that his cousin had struck again.

Roger laughed aloud. A damnable shame Danny was dead. Good times died with him—and laughter and hope and a lot of other things.

Noele cornered him in his study as he was watching the news before supper. For a moment she made him think of Martha. No, he would not tolerate those fantasies, no matter how much the heady wine of politcal attention was dissolving his other inhibitions. Roger expected a description in her marvelous teen dialect of the awesome interception by which Jaimie Burns, the prayers of the Catholic nation riding with him, had smashed the last-minute expectations of the Miami Hurricanes.

Instead, she dismissed the victorious Fighting Irish as unimportant. "Roger, can I interview you about the family history I have to do for Sister Kung Fu?"

"That's not her name, Snowflake."

"No, it's Sister Amanda; we, like, kind of call her Sister Kung Fu."

Roger knew better than to seek an explanation for an adolescent nickname. "Interview away."

Noele, in jeans and a Purdue University T-shirt, curled up on the maroon-leather ottoman next to the TV set.

What would I do to a man who made love to her the way I did to Martha Clay, he wondered. The guilt pangs for his conquest that afternoon would last several days. He would pay the full price for his pleasure, and then enjoy his new slave again. That was the way it had to be. Maybe he would fall out of love with her.

Noele flipped open a legal-size notebook. "A lot of sudden deaths in your family, weren't there, Roger?"

For a fraction of a second, Roger Farrell panicked. My God, how much did she know? He had been prepared for a question about Danny X. Farrell, not for . . .

"Whom do you mean?" he asked, hoping his voice did not betray his panic.

"Well, I mean, in 1944 Uncle Danny's father and Great Gramps, who was Danny's grandfather—and Danny's mother, too—all in the same year. And then Danny and Gramps within a few months of each other. Aren't those unusual coincidences?"

Roger marshaled his facts very carefully. "Danny and his father, my uncle Martin, were naval officers, indeed, flyers, at a time when our country was either formally or informally at war. Casualty rates for naval aviators, Snowflake, are high. Danny and his father knew the risks."

Noele said nothing, but she made a couple of quick and decisive notes on her yellow pad.

"And your great-grandfather, William Farrell, was in his early fifties when he died. I know that seems younger now than it did then, but he had a tough life, and everyone in the family knew he worked so hard he would eventually kill himself. The only death that was unusual was that of your grandfather Clancy, as everyone called him. But that was a tragic accident, Snowflake."

"Was he drunk when he fell down the stairs?" Noele said without looking up from her pad.

"Of course not! Who told you that?" Roger shook his head disconsolately. "He simply tripped on the new carpet. I still can't quite get over it. It was so quick and so sudden and so . . . well, unnecessary."

Noele considered her grandfather's death thoughtfully. "You haven't said anything about the death of Danny's mother, Florence Carey. Doesn't she count?"

"That was another tragic accident. The brakes failed on a delivery truck, and it ran her down while she was waiting for a bus. One of those terrible things. . . . The miracle was that Danny wasn't killed, too. She must have seen the truck coming and pushed him out of the way."

"How old was Danny?"

"Let's see, he was born in 1940, so he was four, a very little boy."

"What was he like, Roger? I can't quite get a picture of him."

"If he had become a priest, he would not be a monsignor like your uncle John; he would be a bishop, probably a cardinal. If he had become an academic like me, he would be a university president. Danny Farrell could do anything he wanted and do it spectacularly, even fly a U-2, I suppose. And if his plane crashed in China, you can bet that it wasn't because of pilot error." Roger, despite himself, was moved by his own description of Danny. "Sometimes I dream at night that he's still alive, and then I wake up half persuaded the dream is true, and all the fun, excitement, and all the good times and the craziness is still with us. Even when I was well on my way to being a stuffy academic . . ."

"You're not stuffy, Roger, well, not very often. . . ."

Roger laughed. "Let's hope not too often. Anyway, when Danny found out what I was doing and what I was interested in, he asked me the right questions about Niccolò Machiavelli without ever having read my Florentine friend, and without ever knowing anything of the history of fifteenth-century Italy. He was magic, Snowflake, magic."

"You know, it's a funny thing, Roger: I've talk to you and Moms and Uncle Monsignor today about Danny, and it's almost as if all of you remember three different people."

"That's the way he was, Snowflake."

"And I sort of have the impression that there was something wrong about the way he died. Was there?" Her affectionate green eyes were momentarily as old as sin.

"Something terribly wrong, Snowflake. He shouldn't have died. He shouldn't have been in the CIA flying a U-2 on some crazy mission over China. He shouldn't have gone to Annapolis. He shouldn't have been pushed into being something he wasn't."

"Moms said that too. Who pushed him, anyway?"

"No one was guilty because everyone was guilty, Snowflake, even Danny. But talking about guilt won't bring him back. You're not Dana Andrews, and this is not the late-night movie you like so much. . . ."

"Laura."

"Life is a serious business, Noele. You're at an age when you have to realize that it's not all fun and games. Danny is dead. Don't go falling in love with him."

Noele laughed. "I have enough trouble with Jaimie Burns, Roger, without taking on a ghost." And she bounced out of the room, a vibrant mix of innocent child and glorious woman.

Her father paid no attention to the NBC Saturday night news. Rather, he searched through a cabinet next to his desk and dug out a stack of old pictures, looking for one in particular, Danny at thirteen in Grand Beach in the summertime. They were hiding from John during a Saturday afternoon matinee at the musty little movie theater in Michigan City, closed now because of the big mall on the outskirts of the city. Roger suddenly found himself overwhelmed by an unfamiliar yet irresistible emotion, the same one he had felt that day when he'd reached out in the flickering darkness to touch his cousin. . . .

Danny had calmly repulsed him. It was never mentioned again. Yet . . .

Yes, they were always playing tricks on John, Roger thought. But damn him, Danny cared more for John than for me, even though he was the most important person in my life. John was jealous of him because he resented Brigid's affection for him. I loved him.

Roger put the picture away with a sigh. A foolish adolescent crush. But he felt his eyes sting with tears. He smiled to himself. He was the one who was in love with a ghost, not Noele.

If Noele found out the truth about Danny, it could mean disaster for the whole family, particularly with the election coming up. He hesitated to alarm his mother unnecessarily, but he reached for the telephone. Then he glanced at his wristwatch. Brigid and Burke were having supper at the club. He would have to wait until ten o'clock to call her.

Later that evening Irene came to his study just as he was about to phone the old house on Glenwood Drive. Roger withdrew his hand from the telephone. "Did you talk to Noele?" she asked.

Irene was wearing a silver-gray short gown and matching peignoir. Bonwit's eroticism, he thought contemptuously.

"We had a little talk before supper. But I don't think there's anything to worry about. You know how kids are at her age. They jump from enthusiasm to enthusiasm. Today it's the family history. Tomorrow it'll be the junior play again."

"You know best, I'm sure." Irene leaned over to kiss him good night. Roger felt a faint touch of aversion and something else—terror, perhaps, a not altogether unsweet terror, that contact with his wife sometimes occasioned. Aesthetically, she was doubtless impressive. But by his standards she was too much, a Sears Tower kind of woman for a man who preferred the Prairie School.

"Expensive lingerie," he murmured in faint disapproval.

"Not too expensive," she said defensively.

"You look wonderful," he said soothingly, now that his point had been made. He brushed the back of his hand down her cheek and across her throat with his thumb trailing on her chest. It was a promise of later affection that he would not have to keep. Irene would wait for him for perhaps half an hour and then fall soundly to sleep. Nothing ever interfered with the woman's sleep.

"Don't stay up too late," she said, kissing him again.

Why did she think that if she looked like an over-dressed mannequin in

Bonwit's window she was automatically sexy? What is it about her that repels me? I wonder if Brigid breast-fed us? Might that have something to do . . .

He sighed in dismay at himself—a goddamned academic who had to analyze everything. Then he punched his mother's number on his private telephone with the touch of unease that marked all his dealings with that formidable woman.

Brigid

BRIGID WAS HANGING up her dress when the phone rang. She picked up the brandy snifter on her dressing table as she answered it, noting with approval that the woman in the mirror looked a decade, perhaps a decade and a half, younger than her fifty-nine years, even if tonight she was terribly tired.

It was Roger, sounding like the pompous professor that he was. Both of her sons were a bit of a trial to her, Monsignor John with his paralyzing concern for clerical respectability and Professor Roger with his everlasting pose of effete intellectualism.

Not, mind you, that she wouldn't willingly die for either of them—or tear the eyes out of anyone who dared to criticize them.

"No, Roger, I don't think I'm going to watch John tonight on his program. He's interviewing one of those 'actresses for Christ' people . . . not quite up to that. . . . Oh, dinner at the club is like dinner at the club always is. Too many people getting old there."

Her husband, Burke, entered the bedroom and smiled appreciatively at his half-clothed wife. She winked at him.

"Yes, I had a phone call from Noele this afternoon. I know all about the term paper. What's the problem in that? . . . Asking about Danny?" An ever so slight increase in the beat of her heart. Not really a son, and yet her favorite of the three boys she had raised. "Well, of course she'd ask about Danny. What do you and John expect? . . . Oh, come now. Children Noele's age aren't fey. That's an Irish American myth. I never met a single witch in Ireland. . . . Yes, of course she's quick. . . . Roger, it was seventeen years ago. . . ."

Nervously she put a cigarette in her mouth and tried to light it while holding the phone. Burke flicked the cigarette lighter with a single motion and patted her thick red hair, most of the color of which was still natural.

Burke's hand was smudged, as it always was, with auto grease. His only hobby, other than making love, was fiddling with his collection of four moribund Alfa-Romeos in the vast garage behind their house.

An Alfa is something like a woman, he once remarked.

Brigid had flown at him with mostly mock rage. "And an old Alfa is as good as an old woman."

"I'm well aware," she said impatiently into the phone while deftly dodging Burke's efforts to further undress her, "that we all have much to lose if the closet door is opened and the skeletons come tumbling out. But, Roger, the child is only writing a term paper. . . . Yes, of course I'll be careful. Believe me, nothing will go wrong. . . ." She drew a quick breath as Burke eased off her slip. Then she winked at him again and playfully shoved his hand away from her.

She had to concentrate on poor Roger. It wasn't like him to be so concerned. John was the worrier.

"Well, it's only natural that she should be asking questions about Danny. I'll tell her that your father's death was an accident. I know exactly how to handle the child."

"Damn!" she exploded, hanging up the phone.

"What is it, Bridie?" Burke asked, his haggard, handsome face expressing mild concern, the most he ever displayed.

"Noele is poking around in the past for some term paper about family history. The child has always been too curious for her own good."

She turned to look at herself again in the mirror, mostly undressed now. Would her skin be as smooth if she had stayed in Ireland? Probably not. And she would not have a lover like Burke to caress that skin. Her hair would still be red though, the color of blood. And for an instant she remembered the blood on her hair the night Danny had found her almost unconscious and sworn revenge on her husband.

Roger

ROGER AND HIS brother were the only ones left in the shower room, where Roger felt inferior, as he always did when his body and that of his brother's were naked and inviting comparison.

Both had given up the Chicago Bears game for an Indian summer golf round before dinner at their mother's. They had played in different foursomes, of course; they never played golf together.

"How did you hit them?" asked John, rubbing soap over his firm, masculine body.

"High eighties. I suppose you made your handicap?"

"Two over it," John said, and sighed. "A seventy-eight."

John's strength and good looks had intimidated Roger all his life. John was a better athlete and could consume large amounts of food and drink with no ill effects on his trim waistline and solid stomach. Small wonder that the women of the parish found him attractive.

The physical resemblance between the two men was strong, but Roger was wiry rather than muscular, and he prided himself on having a much better brain. His brother was the blunt-spoken ruggedly handsome Irish countryman, with a big, solid, hairy body, a face that stopped just a little short of being crude, and thick, black curly hair, dusted lightly now with silver, which hung over his forehead in permanently unruly tangles. In an earlier day he would have strode into the field with the men of his parish and swung the hoe with more strength than any of them.

Roger was the local poet or schoolteacher, with a narrow scholar's face, high forehead, inquisitive eyes, and a faint, self-mocking smile always on his thin lips. If women found his slight, smooth body attractive—and there was evidence to believe that they did—it was the intensity of the emotions hiding behind his smile that they admired, and not his physical strength.

I am a feast for a woman of discernment, he thought, quoting some drunken

Irish poet or politician whose name he could not remember. And my brother is a feast for a woman of the land.

Still, he envied John's gruff, forceful manliness almost as much as he'd envied Danny Farrell's explosive speed and coordination. Never satisfied.

Danny, blast him, was a feast for any woman.

Still, Danny was dead, and if John was stronger, Roger was smarter, and that was some consolation. They had chosen not to compete overtly, even as boys, mostly because Brigid would not tolerate either intellectual or athletic competition between them.

For her two natural sons, she was an absolutely fair and dispassionate mother, avoiding at whatever cost a repeat of the devastating sibling rivalry in the previous generation. Unfortunately for her sons, fairness was not a substitute for the affection she felt but would have had a hard time expressing even if she were not obsessed by the duty to be fair.

So the emotional temperature between them was low. They did not fight, but they were not close friends, either. Their only rivalry was over Danny, who soaked up all of Brigid's considerable excess warmth because he needed it, "poor, orphan boy."

And John had won that competition.

But Roger had won Irene, for whatever that was worth.

Did John resent that victory, the way he himself resented John's physical attractiveness and athletic ability?

Sometimes Roger thought that he should have been the priest and John the married man. John was good with women in a casual and superficial way. No woman could fail to find that rock-hard body appealing, even if his facial features were somewhat rougher than Roger's.

Poor Brigid. They were both probably a bit of a disappointment to her. She'd wanted one of them to run the company for her. Roger had turned to the professorate and John, the more manly of the two by a long shot, to the priesthood. Still, Brigid hadn't complained. "God's holy will in a vocation to the priesthood is a great blessing on us," she remarked, "and, sure, aren't the Irish a race of saints and scholars anyway?"

Roger was not altogether certain she believed what she said, but it didn't matter, because she supported both of their vocations with all her very considerable strength. It might have been more generous of the Almighty, nonetheless, to have left John in the lay state. He would have done very well as president of the firm, and if he had married, he undoubtedly would have been faithful to his wife.

Roger was mildly amused by John's fascination with Irene, a fascination that she did not notice and that John thought he hid well. It dated back to that confused summer of 1963 in Grand Beach, when it seemed that the old rector would never be replaced at the seminary and John turned down the subdeaconate and almost abandoned his plans for the priesthood. They would have made an excellent match. Obviously he found her Bonwit's eroticism hard to resist. But there was no need to worry about them.

"Irene told me about your call yesterday," Roger said to his brother, who had just turned off his shower. "I had a talk with the child. I believe it was successful."

John was drying himself briskly with a big towel. "It frightens me every time she seems to be able to read my thoughts. I thought the doctors said it would stop with the advent of puberty."

Roger shrugged as he turned off his own shower. "Irene and I are used to it. As you doubtless remember, I have my doubts about the medical profession. Still, I am not troubled by these, ah, manifestations. It doesn't seem to have had any ill effects on her."

Roger couldn't help himself. With John he always became the dry analytic college professor. Just as John doubtless became the concerned cleric.

John wrapped the wet towel around his waist. "What did you tell her about Danny?"

"I was discreet."

John tried again. "You and Irene should do something to bring the child into line. It's time she started behaving like a mature woman."

"Harness the cyclone?"

"So many of the children in this neighborhood are spoiled."

What a pompous ass you are, dear brother.

"We are not spoiling her, Monsignor," Roger said stiffly. "I don't notice your restraining her power as director of the folk group at the ten o'clock Mass."

John shook his head solemnly. "I'm worried about what the people in the parish think about that. I'm afraid that a lot of the old-timers must think she's dreadfully bold."

"And the pastor's niece, too," Roger commented with heavy irony.

"Precisely." As usual, the pastor did not notice the irony.

The two brothers walked into the locker room together.

"We must all take our chances, I guess," Roger said, and sighed as he turned toward his locker at the other end of the room from John's. "See you later at Mother's."

"Of course. Noele and Irene coming?"

"I assume so."

"Are you really going to get messed up in a race for governor?" John asked, implying that only a fool would do that.

"I might. Are you really going to sign a new contract for that damn fool program, and play the part of a clerical Phil Donahue for another year?"

"I might."

Ah, thought Roger as he dressed, such great brotherly affection.

Ace

CAPTAIN RICHARD McNAMARA, U.S.N. (retired), Ph.D., professor of clinical psychology, was, as one of his friends remarked, crazier than most people thought he was. It was an epigram in which the Ace delighted.

Not very many chaplains would have dared to challenge the Cardinal Archbishop of New York, when that worthy was visiting his base, on the grounds that there had been a ghastly mistake in Rome and that he, rather than the cardinal, should have been presiding over New York.

At first the cardinal had seemed outraged. Then, good County Mayo man that he was, he realized his leg was being pulled and pulled back.

"That's corruption for you, Captain," he had said solemnly.

Then they'd both laughed, the cardinal a bit uneasily.

Nor was the outrageous wit and the merry laughter a mask. McNamara did indeed have leprechaun blood in him.

And his father was reputed to have been the shrewdest police captain on the South Side, a shrewdness Chaplain McNamara had inherited.

So when he saw Noele Farrell flouncing toward the Courts, dressed in her Sunday best, he knew there was trouble.

Of course, he whistled with the other teenagers.

" 'Scuse me, guys," he said in a loud voice. "I have to get my weekly orders from Mother Superior."

"Geeks!" said Noele in mock displeasure.

"You came by to distract us," he said.

How had the Farrells, dull upper crust of the Irish middle class that they were, produced someone like her, a dazzling mixture of fragility and strength, of naiveté and wisdom.

"I came to find out about Danny Farrell and about my grandfather's death." The flattered teenager had instantly become the deadly serious young woman.

Was her intuition a throwback to an earlier phase of the evolutionary process? Or perhaps it was an anticipation of something yet to come, a mixture of shrewd hunches, keen powers of observation, and a remarkable sensitivity to the feelings of others. Whatever it was, she could be hurt so easily.

"I was in chaplain's school learning to be a lean, mean praying machine."

"Keen, too," she said, hearing his unspoken word.

"Anyway . . . anyway, what makes you think he was involved in your grandfather's death?"

"There is something about him, you know, that nobody wants to tell me. They all have different stories about him, okay? Uncle says he was kind of a bum, and Moms says that he was sweet and kind, and Roger says he was brilliant and fun. And they tell me different things about Gramps's death: Uncle says he was a little drunk and Roger says he wasn't. And Moms says he had really, like, bonged a load."

"Bonged a load?" he parried.

"Don't gag me." She would not be put off. "I mean, like, totally soused."

"He did drink a lot."

"See? What did I tell you?"

McNamara flipped the basketball from one hand to the other. The boys waited silently, not daring to risk the redhaired goddess's wrath.

"I really don't know what happened, Noele. I think Clancy simply fell down the stairs, like everyone said he did. Why should you suspect differently?"

You didn't have to be fey to guess that the Farrell clan was loaded with guilty secrets, like a caravan of smugglers crossing the desert at night. If Noele was on to something . . .

"They're hiding the truth, and I'm going to find out what it is."

"Be careful," he said cautiously.

"Yes, sir, Captain, sir." In another dizzy change of mood, she saluted him. "Whatever you say, Captain, sir."

The red car peeled away. Male catcalls followed, and Flame responded with a derisive bleat of its horn.

The captain did not enjoy the rest of the game.

Irene

AFTER SHE HAD dressed for dinner, she watched the leaves falling on Jefferson Avenue, cascading like a multicolored waterfall in the brisk autumn wind. Rain tonight and the end of Indian summer.

Multicolored waterfall . . . not a bad metaphor. She reached in her purse and withdrew a small spiral notebook, in which she made a notation.

One must always record metaphors, even if no one else would ever read them.

Had Roger found a new mistress at the University? Probably. He found one every year. And to protect his ego she had to pretend not to know.

Why did a man with so little passion need a mistress?

She closed her purse thoughtfully.

Probably something to do with his relationship to his mother. That might make an interesting story. . .

She took out her notebook again and made another note. She considered the note thoughtfully and then shrugged.

She closed the notebook, remembered something, and opened it.

Return manuscripts to secret drawer, she wrote.

She had a bad habit of not putting them away after she worked on them. They were still in her vanity.

Maybe she should do it now. No, Roger was waiting for her downstairs, the keys to the Mercedes in hand. After he had chided her mildly for being late, they would drive to Brigid's house over on the drive for second Sunday supper. Solemn high event.

She looked at herself in a mirror. Everything in order. Makeup restrained and skillfully applied. Beige dress not too tight and hanging neatly. A presentably attractive if somewhat full-blown matron.

Noele's teenage entourage, sweaty furniture in the house, covertly ogled her as if she were a naked statue in a museum they were touring under the watchful eyes of a nun. But there was nothing covert in Jaimie Burns's frank admiration. She should be flattered that the eyes of healthy young male animals deemed her worth measuring for a centerfold. Instead she was flustered.

Mysterious and sexy, as Noele claimed? Irene couldn't quite see that.

Her mother-in-law would compliment her on her dress, her hair, or some piece of new jewelry, but behind her soft brogue there would be an edge of ridicule for a woman who had nothing better to do with her time. And if, God help her, she ever ventured an opinion of her own, Brigid would smile condescendingly and change the subject. The unspoken assumption would be, as always, that she had nothing to contribute to the conversation.

And Noele, spunky Christmas child, would drag her into the conversation regardless.

They all underestimated Noele.

Why were they so upset with the child's questions about the past? What were they hiding?

Irene felt guilty. Some secrets belonged only to those who knew them.

Again she was angry at the Farrells, twice now in two days. Perhaps because the autumn leaves made her feel both mortal and cheated. Perhaps she should fight back before it was too late.

Roger

HE SAT IN his study drumming his fingers on the corner of the desk, waiting for his wife. Why did she always take so long to dress? And why, when she finally appeared, did she always look so apprehensive, as if she were wearing someone else's three-hundred-dollar dress? Roger did not particularly enjoy these command performances at his mother's every second Sunday, continuing an alleged custom of Julie Farrell's, an earlier immigrant woman. But he was always amused by the way Brigid's eyes swept quickly and critically over Irene when they arrived. She could never find anything wrong, of course. Irene always looked like a model, if a hesitant and uneasy one.

And then John would follow her every movement, devouring her—stripping her, one might even say—with avid eyes. Small wonder that she often had a bit too much to drink.

Roger took a certain pride in his wife's beauty, if only because other men envied him. Until she opened her mouth, at any rate. But even if he was bored with her, he could not permit himself to be captured by one of his slaves the way some of his colleagues had, some of whom even wrote novels about such reversals. If the slave could dispossess the wife in a process as old as mankind's exploitation of womankind, then the new wife or the new "relevant other" could as easily be dispossessed by one of her successors. . . .

Roger shuddered. As Noele would say, it was gross.

He might have fallen in love with his sweet, sexy little slave creature. He might stay in love with her, although he doubted that. But he would never leave Irene for her or for anyone else.

He believed in marriage commitments as a matter of principle, one of the many convictions from his Catholic Action days that still dominated his life, even though he would admit them only to himself. Moreover, he was quite content with Irene as a wife. Sex with intense, slightly masculine academic women was a pleasant enough obsession despite the self-hatred that came afterward. Living with one of them, however, would be quite impossible. Irene was shy and unobtrusively decorative. She was no particular asset to his academic or political career, but neither was she a liability. She kept the house neat and created for him an ambience of well-ordered tranquility to which he was happy to return. So he remained married for reasons not unlike those which supported his decision to live in the Neighborhood: he preferred the atmosphere of an Irish political and professional neighborhood to that of a mostly Jewish academic neighborhood. And his daughter, as he told one of his colleagues, would not grow up being hassled to sign a petititon every time she went shopping in the co-op.

Moreover, Roger felt genuinely sorry for Irene. She worshiped him and was completely dependent upon him. He had never really loved her; but then he had never really disliked her, either. Her constant need for affection was no more troublesome, really, than that of an affectionate Irish setter.

He would have, in principle, preferred being faithful to her. But fidelity, he had decided regretfully long ago, was quite beyond his powers. So he had remained married to Irene and continued to be a frequent and guilt-ridden sinner.

And, of course, there was Noele. That amazing and miraculous young woman adored her father and bickered with her mother—Irene's envy was all too pathetically open. Noele was, nevertheless, fiercely loyal to her mother. And with a temper as hair-triggered as her grandmother's and her clerical uncle's, she became bitterly angry at Roger whenever he seemed to slight Irene. It would be relatively easy to get along without his wife, but curiously enough, Roger would not want to have to face life without his bright, responsive, witty, faintly mocking daughter.

Noele had left no doubt on the subject of divorce. "Have you ever thought of divorcing Moms?" she had asked him bluntly one night during the summer when he was several hours late in joining them at their summer home in Michiana, accusation and anger darting at him from her dangerous green eyes.

"Of course not, Snowflake," he had said uneasily. "Whatever would make you think that?"

"All teenagers worry about it, and besides, sometimes you don't take Moms very seriously."

"Married people develop codes and protocols."

"Stop talking like a political scientist," she had said. "And just remember, Roger"—she had called him by his first name since she had been a child—"Moms and I may fight a lot, but if you walk out on her, you lose me, too. Is that clear?"

Roger had put up his arms in mock self-defense. "God, I wouldn't want to have you angry at me."

"Really," Noele agreed.

Danny X. Farrell, Roger thought, if you were still alive, you would appreciate Noele; she would probably be the only woman in the neighborhood who would be a match for you.

Noele

"COME ON IN." Grams hugged her vigorously. "I've put on the tea kettle, and we'll brew you a pot of tea. We'll have a wee drop before the others come." They both laughed, because it was Grams's standard greeting. She was self-conscious about her brogue and tried to hide it usually, but not with Noele, because Noele had told her a brogue was cute. " 'Tis a wondrous dress you're wearing there, if an old woman's judgment means anything."

" 'Course it does," Noele said, almost as pleased as she had been by Jaimie's touchdown run.

Noele had figured out long ago the reactions of all her relatives to a red-haired, green-eyed sixteen-year-old. She made Uncle Monsignor nervous and uneasy, as did all teenagers; she enchanted her father with a mixture of wide-eyed adoration and emerging intelligence; she frightened her mother, poor dear, who wanted to be like her and who didn't think much of herself. Noele accepted all of these transparent reactions as a matter of course. That's the way adults acted. It was a shame, maybe, but there was nothing she could do about it.

Grams, on the other hand, was a deep one, sometimes as soft as Irish rain, sometimes as hard as flint; sometimes a gentle angel, and other times, well, a raging devil. Noele often thought that she was more like her grandmother than like anyone else in the family. They both had red hair, though Noele thought that it was ridiculous to say she got her red hair from Grams. It wasn't the same kind of red hair at all.

"Grams's red hair," she had pointed out sadly to Jaimie Burns, "is beautiful; mine is only striking."

Grams warmed the teapot, carefully deposited the tea leaves in it, after measuring them in a teaspoon first, then poured a precise amount of hot water over the leaves.

Unlike others of her age, who were acutely embarrassed at the suggestion of sex between people over thirty, particularly their parents, Noele was fascinated by "old" sex. Probably, she told herself, because she was fascinated by sex. Period.

The coolness between her parents troubled her deeply. And she was delighted and a little frightened by the aura of physical affection between her grandmother and Burke Kennedy. They were like two pirates, saved from ugliness only by their attraction for each other. And the attraction itself, Noele sensed, could be dangerous and deadly.

Small wonder, she decided, that Burke was jazzed by Grams. She was erect and graceful, even though she had never been to modeling school, and had a really excellent build. The lines on her face merely added character. And she smoked too much, and ate and drank as much as she wanted, and it didn't affect her figure at all. Noele was totally bummed. I should be that way when I'm really that old.

"Well, I gather you've been poking around in the family closet looking for skeletons?" said Brigid, lifting the teapot as though to pour it, and then, as part of the ritual, deciding that it needed perhaps another half minute of steeping. "I suppose we will have to put up with that until you are ready to settle down and run the firm for me."

Unlike the other adults of the family Grams did not really expect a reply to her call for maturity and responsibility.

And she totally didn't get one.

"That's what I like about you, Grams. You don't beat around the bush. . . . Hey, look what I've done! I've made a family tree. Isn't it excellent?"

"I never was very good at figuring these things out." Grams tilted the chart in a number of different directions and then put it back on the coffee table. Now the thick, black tea was ready to be poured—the tea before the milk, the Irish way, not the English way of the milk before the tea.

Noele picked up the chart. "First of all, there was Brendan John Farrell, born in Tralee, County Kerry, in 1861. At the age of twenty-nine he married Julie Roache of Castle Island in the same County Kerry, and they emigrated to Chicago, where Brendan John Farrell became a day laborer in the sewers they were constructing on South Parkway—that's Martin Luther King Drive now, Grams."

"I'm not without knowledge of that street name change, young woman."

"Good. Then, in 1891, they had a son who was called William Farrell, and four years later a daughter, Monica Farrell, and both Monica and her mother— the poor thing was only thirty, Grams—died in the cholera epidemic that same year. And Brendan Farrell died five years later in an accident in the sewers—and probably of a broken heart, too, or is that being too romantic?''

"People had broken hearts in 1900, child," Grams said sadly.

"So that left Bill Farrell an orphan at the age of nine. He lived at a place called Feehanville—after some archbishop—which later became St. Mary's Training School and then, even later, Mayville Academy, until he was fifteen, which would be around 1906, I guess. Then he went to work driving a garbage truck, with horses. Can you imagine that, Grams? Horses?''

"Just barely," her grandmother said ironically. "I can just barely imagine a horse-drawn truck."

"Silly. Well, anyway, in 1911, only twenty years old, just three years and a few months older than me, he founded Farrell Construction Company with the money he'd saved from his job. And by 1917 he had enough money to buy an apartment building in Washington Park and to be rich. What was rich then, Grams?''

"About a half-million dollars, I think. But that wasn't all he had, child. Bill Farrell had lots of political clout."

"Doesn't everyone?" asked Noele. "Anyway, he was in the Illinois National Guard, 131st Infantry, and went into the war—that's the First World War, right?—and won a medal in a battle called Belleau Wood, means beautiful place. And then right after the war he married a young woman from Garfield Boulevard named Blanche Hogan. Let me see, she was twenty-three, and he was twenty-eight. Both her parents died in the flu epidemic right after the marriage. I don't remember Great Grams very well. What was she like?''

"Small wonder, child, that you don't remember her well; she was dead eleven years before you were born, as you'd notice if you looked closely at that chart of yours. Blanche Farrell was very pretty, and terribly dependent on her husband, a nervous, flighty little thing, who always got her way by weeping and sniffling. By the time I knew her she was as filled with hate as anyone I've ever known, and all of it hiding behind a sweet smile and a wet handkerchief. Poor woman—went crazy altogether after your great-grandfather died.''

"They had twin sons," Noele continued. "Clarence and Martin, both born at the same time, since they were twins, in 1919. But in 1944, just a month before his son, Lieutenant Martin Farrell, died in the first battle of the Philippine Sea, when his Avenger torpedo bomber ran out of gas, Bill Farrell died of a massive stroke." Noele traced the lines on her neatly drawn chart. "Martin Farrell had married Florence Carey in 1939, a girl from this neighborhood. Gosh, the twins were born in 1919, so that meant that Martin was twenty and his wife was eighteen. That's awfully young to get married!''

"He left Notre Dame after his sophomore year to go into naval fight training," Grams said, her head turned away as if she were trying to remember, or maybe trying to forget. "Those were reckless times, child. People thought very romantic things about not coming back; they didn't seem to realize that would mean they were dead. Your uncle Martin was a very romantic man, as was his wife, poor woman.''

Brigid poured them both a second cup of tea with solemn ceremony, permitting the tea to rise no higher than a half inch from the top of the cup. Noele waited respectfully till the ritual was completed.

"And then Florence was run over by a truck the year her husband's plane crashed. So their son, Daniel Farrell, born in 1944, was the second orphan in the family in this century. Fortunately he had someone to take care of him.''

"Fortunately."

"Because here's where the story gets *really* interesting. Clarence Farrell, Martin's twin brother, had married just a week after Martin a certain Brigid Flynn, an immigrant from Ireland who was—and is—absolutely gorgeous and whose passport said she was eighteen, but she was really just sixteen, no older than me."

" 'Tis the truth, I'm afraid. I wasn't even Brigid. I was baptized Mary Maeve, Maeve for short. My father didn't like me all that much. He said my red hair and freckles were evidence that I was a changeling—a gypsy child. So at the last minute he sent me to the United States to work as a maid and kept my sister, who really was Brigid and was two years older than me, home in Ireland."

"And you've never gone back to see her?"

"You know the story, child, as well as I do. No, I've never sent a word back to them, much less gone to see them. And I never will. It was a cold winter morning with the water frozen. Da woke me up and pulled me out of bed and told me I was going to America instead of Brigid. I wept, I pleaded, I fell on my knees and begged him. All he did was box my ears and order me out of the house."

Deep inside Noele there was a memory of the horrible morning, as though it had happened to her and not Grams, a vague and undefined, but terribly painful, memory, like smoke pouring from a burning room.

"But it was all for the best, wasn't it?" she asked anxiously.

"In a manner of speaking," her grandmother said softly.

Noele rushed on to finish the story, not wanting to expose her grandmother to more pain.

"Well, you and Gramps had two sons: John, who is now a big important monsignor, pastor of this parish, and a famous television personality; and Roger, a college professor and future governor. In 1964 he married Irene Conlon, also from this neighborhood . . . who in turn produced a nosy little girl whose name I don't remember."

"Did she ever!"

"And you and Gramps took over the family business when Bill Farrell died, and Martin Farrell was killed, and Blanche Hogan Farrell went mad. You made heaps of money and bought miles of real estate and gasoline stations and shopping plazas and other neat things. And then, when your poor husband . . ." Noele trailed off.

"When in a fit of anger he slipped and fell down the stairs . . ."

Another explanation, thought Noele, not drunk, but angry.

"How did it happen, Grams?" she asked softly.

"It seemed as natural as though he were sitting down in the TV room after dinner. . . . We'd had drinks here: Father John, as he was then; Roger, home for Christmas from that awful pagan school in Berkeley; Danny, who was about to leave for his new job with the CIA; and your mother, of course. . . ."

"Uh-huh." It was the first she had heard about Moms's presence.

"Well, Danny was in one of his black moods, what with him being thrown out of the Navy and all and sorrowing for President Kennedy, whom he worshiped— God be good to the poor man. And he and Clancy had a fierce argument, nothing that was new; they were fighting all the time. Clancy blamed the Kennedy family for an investigation of the firm. And he said some nasty words about the poor president. That made Danny furious. Then Clancy took out after Irene because her father had dragged him before a grand jury, and that made your mother cry.

She cried too much, if you ask me. Anyway, Danny came as close to striking your grandfather as I'd ever seen him. He didn't, thank God, but he walked out of the club with your mother and took her home. So the party was spoiled. Father John went back to his rectory on the North Side. Your father went down to the basement to play cards. He used to like to play gin rummy at the club in those days—'twas before he became a professor and too great a man to be wasting his time at cards. And your grandfather and I went home. . . .

"We were both tired and went right up the stairs, those stairs over there. Your grandfather was still angry at poor Danny—God be good to him, too. He raved and ranted about what an ungrateful child he was after all we had done for him. I watched him storm up the stairs, cursing and pounding the banister with his fist every step of the way. Then at the head of the stairs, he turned to shout something back at me. Dear God in heaven, he lost his balance, grabbed for the banister, and missed it."

"Oh, Grams," Noele breathed softly, "I didn't mean to . . ."

"That's all right, child. It happened a long time ago, and I can talk about it now. Your grandfather fell all the way down the stairs, and when I rushed to help him, blood was pouring from his head. I looked down at my new white-lace party dress, and it was covered with blood. I didn't know what to do or where the boys were. So I called Burke. He called the police because poor Clancy was dead, even though I didn't want to admit it. He was still crumpled up at the foot of the stairs when the boys got here. Danny was the last to come home. He'd been driving around to cool off after the fight at the club, and you can imagine how he felt when he saw his uncle lying there in a pool of blood."

"How terrible," Noele said softly, wondering how her grandmother could continue to climb those stairs every day.

"That was all there was to it, child. Another inch and he would probably still be alive today."

And where would you and Burkie be then? Noele thought to herself. "God be good to him, too," she said aloud.

"Aye," her grandmother agreed.

"Then," Noele went on quickly, hoping to blot out the memories of that terrible night, "you became the president of the company—I suspect you were running it all along—and made even more tons of money, so that I can drive around in my brand new red Chevette."

"And yourself probably wanting a BMW at that." Brigid lighted a cigarette, even though she knew her granddaughter disapproved.

"Which leads to the second most fascinating person of the Farrell family—after this beautiful granddaughter of yours—Daniel X. Farrell, born in 1940, graduated from Annapolis in 1961, resigned from the United States Navy 1963, missing, presumed dead, in 1964. Is he really dead, Grams?"

"Aye, child, he's really dead. Poor man."

"I know that's what everybody says, but something seems weird about it."

"Weird? He was flying a plane, one of them U-2 things, for the CIA, and it stopped working over China. That's not weird, Noele; it's tragic, but its not mysterious. Besides, if he had lived, they would have released him when Mr. Nixon went to China and all the other prisoners were released."

"Hmmm. . . . What was he like, Grams?"

Brigid's face brightened, and her brogue grew thicker. "Ah, he'd break your heart. He was a rascal, like his father, only worse. Smooth talker, witty, unpredictable—sure you'd think he'd swallowed the whole Blarney stone. But he was smart, God knows. He could have been a great man. But he wanted to be a writer, which was a crazy idea. What kind of good would come from something like that? And he was as lazy as sin. A fast-talking gombeen man who couldn't keep his mouth shut, which is why he got himself thrown out of the Navy, himself defending a lazy black seaman. That was your cousin, Daniel Xavier Farrell.''

"And you loved him a lot?''

"Everyone did.''

"What would he be like today if he had lived?''

"Ah, child, what's the use of asking a question like that. There's no answer to be had at all, at all.''

"Monsignor John said that he would have been an alcoholic, like Great Gramma Blanche. And Moms said that maybe he would have been a great writer. What do you think, Grams?''

Brigid Farrell frowned thoughtfully. "Ah, could have been both of those things and a lot more, too. But we'll never know, will we?''

At that moment Burke Kennedy, who had been watching the Chicago Bears, came into the parlor and asked if he might have a cup of tea.

Noele thought Burkie was cute. And he didn't like to be called Burkie. So naturally she called him Burkie kind of all the time.

She hadn't told either of them that she didn't mind their life-long love affair. They would both be forgiven much because of their devotion to each other.

And, Noele supposed, as cute as they were with each other, there probably was a lot to be forgiven.

She shivered slightly and poured the tea for Burkie with the same elaborate ceremony that Grams used.

"You've been watching another redheaded woman pour tea,'' he said. He smiled, like an old Roman general coming into his wife's villa, but it was an uneasy smile.

"If you're going to do something, you should do it right,'' Noele said, mimicking her grandmother. "Really!''

And you are as nervous about this conversation as she is, Noele thought. Look at the way your fingers are twitching. They're covered with yucky automobile grease, but they're frightened.

I wonder why.

Brigid

THE SECOND SUNDAY dinner was over, a not particularly sparkling event. The child had everyone worried, Brigid thought, as she removed her earrings.

She had cleaned up some of the mess and come upstairs to find Burke waiting for her in his vast shaggy brown robe. He was a big man, and solid, with long white hair and a square red face, and looked like a Celtic warrior preparing to ravage a captive woman. He watched her with obvious admiration as she leaned against the dressing table. Her own body began its subtle cycle of response to both his tough masculine attractiveness and his admiration for her.

Burke Kennedy was a hard, ruthless man. She was a hard, ruthless woman.

That's why they loved each other, though in their love there was breathtaking softness as well as harsh passion.

In 1944, at the time of the deaths of Bill Farrell and his son, Lieutenant Martin Farrell of the United States Navy, Burke Kennedy, who had inherited from his own father responsibility for the Farrell family's complex legal problems, had hinted that some of the legal problems the Farrells faced would be resolved if she would give herself to him. Brigid was flattered and attracted to him, but indignantly refused and reported the proposition to her husband. To her humiliation, Clancy Farrell ordered her to yield.

It was, he argued, essential to keep the firm out of the hands of a court-appointed trustee. If a careful audit was made, he might have to go to jail, though it was his father who had manipulated the funds and bribed the politicians and paid off the racketeers. Besides, they might end up without a penny. Did she want that to happen?

Brigid's feeling of degradation was made worse because she knew that her husband's orders were in fact her mother-in-law's orders. Blanche Hogan Farrell had told her son to give his wife to a man to win a favor for the family, and he had obeyed her.

Brigid had little respect for her husband. A parlor maid in a rich friend's house to whom it was hinted that a much better life was possible if she responded to a young man's interest, she had more or less been purchased by Bill Farrell to assure that there would be grandchildren and heirs if Marty was killed in the war.

Why she had ever interested Clancy was beyond her comprehension. . . .

Brigid had wished that she had been purchased for Martin instead of his twin brother, Clancy. But Marty was quite capable of finding a wife on his own, poor, dear, innocent kid that Flossie was.

The first night with Burke Kennedy began in shame, fury, and terror and ended in mind-numbing pleasure. Both had insisted ever since that the other had been the conqueror.

With Burke's help Brigid had taken de facto control of the firm and made huge profits. Together they carefully covered up Clancy's inept plot to defraud his brother and his brother's son. Together they kept Clancy from doing any more harm to the firm. And together they regularly, if discreetly, made love till Clancy's death. In 1964, with Clancy at last blessedly out of the way, they became, in Father John's lovely phrase, "notorious and public sinners" until Burke's mad wife, Eloise, died of chronic alcoholism and cirrhosis of the liver.

That was six years ago, and Brigid had said, "half fun, in full earnest," that marriage could be a mistake: "Respectability might destroy the excitement."

For thirty years she and Burke had loved each other with a need that grew more demanding each time it was temporarily sated, regardless of what anyone, God himself included, might have thought. She was wary of change, but Burke insisted that it was necessary to marry for the sake of their children, who found their relationship difficult to explain to their friends. Moreover, he said, "I want you as my wife at long last."

Her fears were groundless. She was as good a wife as she had been a mistress. The glow of approval and want in Burke's cynical brown eyes was the same now as on that first emotional, ecstatic night in the Palmer House.

"What can a sixteen-year-old child, admittedly an intelligent and perceptive child, possibly do to cause such concern?" Burke asked.

Brigid ground out her cigarette and leaned against the vanity table. She should brush her hair but was too tired. Instead, she reached for the brandy glass. "The only thing that worries me is that Protestant missionary who claimed he'd been with him in the prison camp."

Burke rose from the bed and placed his hands around Brigid's still presentably slender waist. "Noele is not going to try to interview the director of the Central Intelligence Agency."

She felt the thrill of excitement that always accompanied Burke's touch.

"I'm tired of having to pretend, Burke; all my life . . ." Much to her surprise she was weeping. She leaned her head against her husband's shoulder.

"I wish everybody else knew you, Bridie," he said reassuringly, using the nickname no one else dared to call her as his strong fingers moved up her body, "the way I know you, the frail, immigrant girl, not the tough, successful businesswoman."

The firm, familiar pressure of his fingers made the tears flow more abundantly.

"We're old, Burke," she sobbed. "We don't look as old as our friends at the club, but death is drawing near for us, just as it is for them. And I'm so tired . . ."

Burke encircled her with his arms, soothing and caressing her. The weeping diminished. "I'm an hysterical old woman."

"Merely a tired and beautiful woman," he said. "A woman I love."

Brigid knew she was damned. From the day of her arrival in America in 1934, her life had been nothing but sinful—lust, deceit, adultery, even murder. She was beyond forgiveness. Death would mean an eternity of blackness, not the hell fire of the catechism class of the west of Ireland, nor the hell of frustrated self-fulfillment—about which her son the monsignor was probably talking with the pious young actress on Channel 3 at this very moment—but the hell of black nothingness reserved for those who are so profoundly evil, they can be put nowhere else by divine justice but in a dark and bottomless abyss.

A few more years, and the shadows would close in forever. Please God, though I know you don't listen to me, protect us for those next few years. Don't let the evil come out of the grave to destroy us.

"Love me, Burke," she pleaded.

"I have every intention of doing that, Bridie," he said. "That's why I'm here."

They were elaborately skilled in loving each other, knowing the motions and movements, the touches and the kisses that endeared, tantalized, surprised, and rewarded. As she slipped easily into the never monotonous routine, Brigid remembered the first night in the Palmer House suite, where Burke had been staying for a bar association convention. Tossing aside her clothes, she had stood before him, her face flaming as brightly as her hair, and screamed that she was there on her husband's orders.

Burke was surprised and stunned; he stammered that his proposition was not seriously meant and tried not to look at her.

"It's too late now to pretend that you didn't mean it," she raged. "And God damn you, look at me!"

And it was much too late. They both knew they were trapped. Neither wanted not to be trapped. Their embrace was violent and angry, then somehow—Brigid never understood how—it changed.

They had cheated damnation for thirty years. Time was running out. A few more years and the cheating would be over.

Clancy had beaten her often, though always privately and silently, without visible effects, so that no one would know what he had done—no one but Burke, who was furious at the big bruises on her body. Brigid accepted the beatings as punishment she deserved and forbade Burke to do anything about them.

Burke's body pressed down upon hers the way she liked it to, making her helpless beneath him, able only to respond to his implacable rhythms. She gave herself totally to those rhythms, arching up to meet him and reveling in her total dependence on him. Her world became a single point of pleasure that glowed with a bright red flame, then a fierce white fire that finally exploded and sent her spiraling into space. From a great distance she heard her wild animal cry of pleasure.

Oceans of sweetness washed over her, wiping out the memory of Clancy Farrell's blood turning the new blue carpet crimson.

Dear God, she prayed, as she sailed helplessly through the heavens, give us a little more time.

Burke

STILL BREATHING RAPIDLY, he turned off the dim light by which they made love and with his lips and his hands soothed his wife back to peacefulness.

"We'll civilize you Danes yet," she said sleepily. "Good enough for you."

"Then you'll be the sorry one," he replied.

Preliminaries of sex with Brigid were brisk and businesslike. The actual encounter was normally violent, even savage—the way Burke liked it to be with a woman. But when it was over she was pathetically vulnerable. Even on that first screaming, clawing night in the Palmer House, with the thunderstorm raging outside, he saw when they were finished how fragile this wild, crude, superstitious woman was.

And it was her appealing fragility that bound him to her. Passionate women Burke had known before, but none who were so devastatingly vulnerable.

In a way she had civilized him. After her, there could be no other woman. She was more than enough. And while he had once been one of the most ruthless of the legal powerbrokers—"the smartest crooked lawyer in town," Dick Daley, no admirer of Burke, had once said—he gradually pulled back from the game. He loved it with every fiber of his being, but he loved Brigid more. He could not take the risk of going to jail and leaving her unprotected.

What a shame they did not have children of their own. Her half-made sons had too much of Clancy in them ever to amount to anything. The only one in the family up to her was Noele . . . and she was not really . . .

Burke did not want to think about that ingenious, winning, delightfully impertinent, and possibly very dangerous child.

He felt no guilt about anything he had done. Indeed, for the past six years he had been a model of probity. As for the things before that . . . well, they were over and done with.

The only problem was the dreams.

And he knew that he would have them tonight.

He kissed his love, now sleeping quietly, and prepared to face the terrors of the night.

If anyone threatened Brigid again, he would stop at nothing to protect her. God—if there was one—should expect nothing else from him.

James III

THEY WERE PARKED in Flame, in front of the Farrell house on Jefferson Avenue. Noele nestled close to Jaimie Burns. The same fingers that had stolen the pigskin from the frustrated Hurricanes now stroked the tense muscles in the back of her neck with infinite delicacy. Noele was deeply worried. As she often was.

"What's up, M.N.?" he asked.

"Don't stop," she pleaded.

"I wasn't planning to."

When Jaimie was a little boy, his father had been away in Vietnam—before he ran for Congress—and Jaimie had been very close to his mother. He had learned to be sensitive to women and gentle with them. Most useful skills in dealing with the dazzling, unpredictable, and utterly delightful Mary Noele Farrell. At one moment she was, if not the bossy bitch she frequently called herself, at least very much in charge of everything and everybody. And the next moment she was a terrified affection sponge whom you could not love too much or too tenderly. Jaimie was pleased that he was one of the very few people who had been permitted to be close to the sponge, and indeed to provide vast amounts of affection for her. It beat intercepting passes.

"Do you think Danny Farrell might be still alive?" she asked suddenly.

She could still surprise Jaimie. His fingers stopped dead in their tracks.

"Don't stop," she said, repeating her order.

"He's been dead for eighteen years, Noele. All the prisoners were released when Nixon visited China."

She cuddled closer to him.

"There's something terribly wrong, Jaimie. I just know it. I feel it. They're all lying to me. They tell me different things about Grandpa Clancy's death—he was drunk, he wasn't drunk, he was a little drunk. And different things about Danny, too. He was a genuis, he was a bum, he was Peter Pan, he was a great man. They're afraid of him even though they all say he's dead."

"The world says he's dead too."

She pounded on his chest. "I know, but why do they get so shifty-eyed and dishonest whenever I talk about him?"

Jaimie Burns had as much lust for the bodies of pretty young women as any man his age, maybe a little bit more. And he had been well aware that when Noele was in one of her "collapse" moods—as she was tonight—she was intensely sensual and might possibly be lured off to bed. It was a very attractive possibility, made unattractive by the certainty that the guilt and the anguish of the next day would probably shatter their friendship.

As he said to his father when the congressman worried about the relationship, Noele was a speculation in a future commodity.

"Delayed gratification," he'd told the congressman, who was impressed with the words his son was learning in college.

"A long delay," said James II.

"A gratification worth waiting for," replied James III.

"I think you may love her." His mother laughed, encouraging him, as her laughter always did, because it contained so much respect and affection.

"Tell me about it," her son said.

DANCE THREE

Galliard

*"A gay, rollicking sixteenth-century dance of Italian origin . . .
frequently coupled with a pavane."*

Irene

THERE WAS LAUGHTER coming from Tommy Taylor's room. At last someone
was making the little boy laugh. Her curiosity and her sorrow that she had never
borne a boy child drove Irene to peek in the door of the hospital room.

Her brother-in-law, Monsignor John Farrell, was shadowboxing with the leukemia victim, and pretending to lose.

"Tommy never beat up a monsignor before," John explained, winking at her.

Irene's two volunteer afternoons at the hospital, visiting old people and children, were the high point of her week. With the sick she was, somehow, both
gracious and graceful. But Tommy had always been immune to her laughter and
her stories.

And John had cracked him in five minutes.

He was good with kids, except for teenagers, who were turned over completely to the resilient Father McNamara. Almost every afternoon he could be
seen in the schoolyard, talking and joking with the students as they poured out
of the school—in far more disorderly ranks than would have been tolerated in her
day at St. Praxides.

Tommy hugged John when it was time to leave and then hugged Irene for good
measure.

"I'll be back in a minute, Tommy," she promised.

The litte boy grinned happily. "I'll wait for you."

"What are his chances?" she asked John as they walked down the freshly
scrubbed corridor to the elevator. The hospital smelled of disinfectant, as did all
Catholic hospitals—the price of having floors so clean that one can eat off them.

John threw up his hands in uncertainty. "They think a remission is beginning.
With some luck he could live until they find better cures than they have now. The
parents are the problem."

"They don't come very often. . . ."

He reached into the inside pocket of his carefully fitted jacket and pulled out a stack of the postcards Little Company of Mary Hospital sent to parishes about sick parishioners.

"Crises like a sick kid can tear a marriage apart. Ace—Father McNamara—says that as soon as the diagnosis is made both parents should go into therapy." He shrugged. "I suppose he's right. . . ."

"Could I buy you a cup of coffee?" Irene said, feeling that for once she was on her ground and not Farrell ground.

"I was thinking of making the same offer, but I've got five more patients to visit, two wakes this afternoon, two more this evening, a couple of marriage instructions, and a meeting of the parish school board."

"With a schedule like that, how do you find time for the TV program?"

He laughed, the winning John Farrell laugh that the women of the parish of every age adored. "I wing it, Irene. What else?"

He was, God knows, a hardworking priest, taking up the slack for the two curates the parish used to have—one lost to the priest shortage and the other represented by the usually invisible Father Miller. About his love of his parish and people, there could be no doubt.

"You'll wear yourself out. How long has it been since you've had a vacation?"

"A couple of years now, but I'm going to try to get away for a week after Christmas." He laughed winningly again, but it was wasted on her. "By the way, has Roger said anything more about running for governor? Can't you talk him out of it?"

"Last night we were riding home down the Ryan, coming home from the concert, and he talked about the Taylor homes. We built some of those high-rise public housing slums. Roger feels the need to do something about such problems."

There was no real love between Roger and Irene and not a large amount of affection, either. But sex and a common household made them at least companions, and she was an occasional sounding board for his efforts to recapture the political dedication that had animated him during the 1960s.

"I thought he gave up on politics after 1968," John said. "Kennedy's death, the convention, McCarthy's making a fool of himself. . . . Weren't those too much for my brother's precious idealism?"

How little they understood each other.

"I certainly can't stop him," Irene said, "and Brigid won't. I think she wants a son as governor, even if she won't admit it."

An elevator door opened, but the car was filled with white- and blue-gowned doctors and nurses. John let the door close.

"Governors don't get reelected. . . ." He bit his lip thoughtfully. "Is Noele against the race?"

"She hasn't said. Still has Danny Farrell on her mind, I think."

"That's all we need, isn't it?" He jabbed the elevator button. "She's so young, so naive. . . . Were we ever that young, Irene?"

"I don't think you or Roger were. I might have been for a couple of weeks."

"And Danny?"

"Danny never did grow up," Irene said, instantly regretting her words.

The elevator door opened. John gripped her shoulder and brushed his lips against her cheek, reasonably close to her mouth but not too close—Monsignor John Farrell was with a woman parishioner who was also an in-law.

He was wearing a very pleasant male cologne.

"See you in church, Irene."

And he disappeared behind the quickly closing elevator door.

His rough-hewn masculinity, emphasized by the cologne, stirred an extra heartbeat or two. Sweet-smelling bastard, Irene thought. And then reproved herself. He meant well, and he worked so damn hard.

We were all born middle-aged.

Except Danny.

She hurried back to Tommy's room, hoping that the nun in charge of the floor would not see her tears.

Tommy saw them. "Don't cry, Mrs. Farrell," he said as she hugged him again. "We'll be all right."

She cried a few moments more, nevertheless, for Tommy's hope and for her own despair.

·······*Noele*·······

SHE FELT HER jaw tighten. Ever since he'd been hired, the parish's Director of Music, a thin, waspish, bald man with a slight stutter, had been trying to muscle in on the 9:15 teenage folk Mass, with some help from Father Miller, who vanished whenever Noele was around. Guitar music, the D.O.M. had assured Uncle Monsignor, was no longer sanctioned in the best church-music circles. That meant he had come into a head-on conflict with Noele in her role as vice president of the High Club and principal guitarist of the folk group.

Noele forced her jaw to relax. Jaimie said that she was even more scary than usual when her jaw turned hard. Noele did not want to be a domineering woman— well, not most of the time. And she had to be particularly charming today at lunch with Jaimie's parents, because she had a very big favor to ask Congressman Burns.

Nonetheless, this morning's Mass had to be salvaged. Like her grandmother Brigid, Noele firmly believed that things that were worth doing ought to be done properly, even if it meant that she had to take charge and see that they were done properly. (Keeping one's room neat didn't count, because neatness in the room wasn't important.)

You don't have a proper teenage folk Mass when the D.O.M. and two other retards sing a Mozart trio during Communion. Noele had nothing personal against Mozart, poor man; however, a Mozart trio during Communion wiped out the congregation's enthusiasm for singing, which the folk group had diligently stirred up earlier in the Mass. It was hard enough to get Catholics to sing in church as it was without pouring water on a weak fire with old Wolfgang Amadeus.

Moreover, the final hymn was "Lord of the Dance," Noele's favorite. She couldn't bear to have it sung listlessly.

Father Ace, who said the 9:15 Mass every Sunday, gave the final blessing. As he was urging the congregation to go forth in the peace of Christ, Noele in a vanilla wraparound dress with a green belt that the kids said made her look totally like Jamie Lee Curtis in *Halloween*, slipped up to the microphone on the left-hand side of the sanctuary, beating the slow-moving Director of Music by three feet.

"Our final hymn is 'Lord of the Dance.' " Michele Carmody and the other kids began to hum the familiar melody, which was the same as that of "Simple Gifts." Noele plunged on, like a dolphin that has surfaced and then dives back into the water. "Our lives are a dance, and our friends and families are our dancing partners, and God is the head of the dance. He calls the tunes, and directs the music, and invites us all to dance. Sometimes He even interrupts our normal dances so that He can dance just with us. Let's all sing it like we were dancing so that God will know that we are ready to dance with Him whenever He wants."

Congressman and Mrs. Burns and all the little Burns kids in the second row of the church looked startled. Jaimie rolled his Robert Redford eyes. Father Ace laughed, and behind her the Director of Music coughed as if he were ready to die. Noele didn't budge an inch. Standing at the microphone, strumming vigorously on her guitar, she led the thousand assembled Christians in a rendition of "Lord of the Dance" that made the walls of the long, cool, modern church shake with excitement.

> *I danced in the morning*
> *When the world was begun,*
> *I danced in the moon*
> *And the stars and the sun.*
> *I came down from heaven*
> *And I danced on the earth,*
> *At Bethlehem*
> *I had My birth.*
> *Dance, then,*
> *Wherever you may be,*
> *I am the Lord*
> *Of the Dance, said He.*
> *I'll lead you all*
> *Wherever you may be,*
> *I'll lead you all*
> *In the Dance, said He.*
>
> *I danced for the scribes*
> *And the Pharisees,*
> *But they would not dance,*
> *They wouldn't follow Me.*
> *I danced for the fisherman,*
> *For James and John,*
> *They came with Me*
> *And the dance went on.*
>
> *I danced on a Friday*
> *When the sky turned black,*
> *It's hard to dance*
> *With the devil on your back.*
> *They buried My body*
> *And they thought I'd gone,*
> *But I am the dance*

> *They cut Me down*
> *And I leap up high,*
> *I am the life*
> *That'll never, never die.*
> *I live in you*
> *If you live in Me,*
> *I am the Lord*
> *Of the Dance, said He.*
>
> *Dance, then,*
> *Wherever you may be,*
> *I am the Lord*
> *Of the Dance, said He.*
> *I'll lead you all*
> *Wherever you may be,*
> *I'll lead you all*
> *In the Dance, said He.*

As soon as the song was over Noele slipped away from the folk group, dodging the Director of Music, with whom she did not want to argue, and Father Ace, with whom she did not want to banter. There were more important things to be accomplished this Sunday morning.

Out of the corner of her eye, however, as she made for the Burnses' Lincoln, she saw her uncle surrounded by parishioners who paused to shake his hand before they raced for their cars, newspapers, Sunday breakfast, and the Chicago Bears on TV. They were telling him how much they liked "Lord of the Dance." That would show the nerdy Director of Music.

"Way out, Noele," said Mrs. Burns, who was sooo cool, even though Noele had beaten her in a golf match at Grand Beach last summer.

"You made the church come alive," boomed the congressman. "That was a profound experience."

Always running for office.

Jaimie hugged her and announced, "That's my Noele."

Which really jazzed her.

Jaimie Burns was Noele's first serious boyfriend. He did indeed have Redford eyes and wavy blond hair, and Noele became really fenced when someone suggested that his face was too thin and his body too skinny.

Nor did she like it when they said that she was the boss and he a dreamer who did what she told him. Like, it was Jaimie, not she, who thought of looking up the *New York Times* and *Time* magazine indexes for information about Danny Farrell. He really was totally practical, even if sometimes he acted a little like a space cadet.

What's more, he respected her, which made him really sweet.

At first he had accused her of being a Nancy Drew because of her detective work about the disappearance of Danny Farrell, but nevertheless, he had patiently combed through the *Time* magazine and *New York Times* volumes in the Notre Dame Library seeking information for her. There was very little to be found: A Chinese picture of the plane that might be a U-2, a denial by the American State Department that there were intelligence flights over western China, a denial from the CIA that anyone named Daniel Farrell worked for the agency, a brief editorial in *The New York Times* questioning the advisability of such flights, especially when Chinese assistance might be useful in mitigating the conflict in Vietnam, an article in *Time* about an American missionary who was released from a prison camp in China after Henry Kissinger's first visit with a passing reference to an "American U-2 pilot" whom the missionary had seen briefly in prison. A rundown in the *Times* of Americans who had been held prisoner by the Chinese, concluding that all those who were still alive had been released. Daniel X. Farrell, a Chicagoan who was probably an agent of the CIA, the *Times* said, was presumed to be dead.

Presumed. Noele had snorted when she read the material that Jaimie had delivered. "The last anyone heard of him was through the missionary, and he saw him alive. Who does the presuming?"

"Call the missionary," said Jaimie, his dreamy blue eyes kind of absorbing her.

"Of course I'll call the missionary," Noele had replied crisply, though she would never have thought of it herself.

But the Presbyterian missionary society told her that the Reverend Doctor Cameron had died two years before. Noele wondered why her family had never sought him out. In her bones Noele knew that the two family tragedies, Clancy's death and Danny's disappearance, were connected.

Otherwise why would all the members of her family give different descriptions of Danny Farrell and different accounts of Clancy Farrell's death?

"Aren't you playing with fire, opening Pandora's box, rushing in where angels fear to tread?" asked Jaimie Burns, a long question for him.

Normally Jaimie was content to sit quietly and watch Noele's act with wide-eyed fascination and utter such profundities as "You astonish me," or, when he was really astonished, "You overwhelm me."

He was not much given to pawing, or even to kissing. In fact, Noele usually had to kiss him good night first, though, when he did begin to kiss, Jaimie Burns's lips came alive with breathtaking intensity.

The night she'd wept in his arms after he had decked the two zods in South Bend, Noele realized that she could easily become "way gone" on him . . . and that she might not mind spending the rest of her life in his arms.

But she was not going to make the mistake her mother and grandmother had and get married as a teenager. Not that Jaimie Burns seemed to have either marriage or getting her in bed with him that much on his mind.

"I have to find out, Jaimie," she said.

"Why?"

"What if he's still alive?"

Jaimie answered with another question. "What if he's still alive and comes home and it turns out he killed your grandfather?"

A question that had lurked in the back of her own mind, like a menace in the night, unacknowledged and frightening.

"I don't believe he did that," she said hotly, defending a man she had never met and who was probably dead anyway.

Why do I care?

"But he might have." Jaimie could be very stubborn and tough when he wanted to. The nerd.

"What if he did?" She shifted her tactics, still not knowing why she simply had to defend Danny Farrell. "Wouldn't eighteen years in China be enough punishment?"

Jaimie nodded thoughtfully. "My father might be able to help," he said. "He's on the intelligence subcommittee—"

"Really?" Why hadn't she known that?

"I'll talk to him."

"No, it's my responsibility."

"You overwhelm me," said Jaimie Burns.

He was rewarded with a brief kiss and responded with a much longer one of his own, which Noele would later remark to Eileen Kelly was "really excellent!"

It was a pleasant memory as they drove to the club for breakfast and she prepared her tactics for enlisting Congressman Burns in her campaign to free Danny Farrell.

·······································*Ace*·······································

Dick McNamara hung up his alb with the careful precision he had learned as a chaplain at the San Diego boot camp.

"Yes sir, Captain, sir." He laughed to himself.

The folk Mass had been a show and a half. The best homily likely to be heard in St. Praxides for many a year. And from a kid who was all tied up in emotional knots by a strange, almost spooky, search for her own identity.

If she thinks there's something strange with her identity, there probably is.

"A young woman of some determination," Ace said with a wide grin, greeting the pastor as he strode fretfully into the sacristy.

"I hope she'll grow out of it," John said, and sighed. "Right now, though, she's used to having her own way. Most of the parishioners seem amused, but there will be a lot of raised eyebrows at the breakfast tables all around the Neighborhood. They'll say that if she wasn't my niece, she wouldn't dare be so bold."

You are transparent, Ace thought. I like you, and you're a good priest. But you are so afraid of what people might say, especially parishioners and your fellow priests. Still trying to please Brigid, I suppose.

"I hope she doesn't grow out of it. Most of the Irish women-leader types peak out at sixteen. The world resents so much insight and vitality in someone so young. Like Irene."

Memories of the time when McNamara was the young priest in the neighborhood and John and Irene were kids flickered briefly in Ace's brain. She had done a lot of stupid things to escape her genius. A silly summer fling with a confused and bitter seminarian was one of the silliest.

And for ten years she had avoided him, as though she had let him down. Poor, foolish kid.

What a curious crowd to have produced Noele: Brigid, with her guilt and her superstition; John, with his transparent but harmless vanity; Roger, with his faintly bent idealism; Danny, a doomed genius; Irene, drifting ever more deeply into a dreamworld where she mourned for something she had lost.

So much promise and so much possibility when they were young. And all the opportunites wasted. Happiness offered and rejected. And the damn Neighborhood, with its magic hold on anyone who had experienced it. Yourself included, Richard McNamara.

"I wasn't aware that you had such a high opinion of my sister-in-law," John said stiffly. "And don't think the world will pressure Noele into anything she doesn't want to do."

"It will try," Ace said, but mentally phrased it in the appropriate marine language.

"By the way"—the pastor seemed to be caressing the collection basket, with its mountain of bills and envelopes—"has she been asking you about our family past?"

"Half the kids in the neighborhood are doing the family history term paper. And I happened to be around here when the parents were teenagers."

"What has she told you about us?" John snapped nervously.

Ace hid behind laughter, his favorite mask. "What are you hiding, Monsignor, sir?"

"Sorry, Ace." The pastor quickly recovered himself. "There's been a lot of tragedy in the family. . . ."

"All on the record, as far as I know."

"Sure." John picked up the collection basket to take it to the rectory. "The kid thinks she runs the parish."

"Maybe," said Ace McNamara mysteriously, "she *is* the parish."

················*Noele*················

NOELE LOVED BRUNCH at the Club with the Burns clan—three sons and four daughters—with the hunger of an only child who missed brothers and sisters. But there was too much commotion during the orange juice, bacon and eggs, french toast, pancakes, and strawberries and cream to talk about Daniel Farrell. Constitutents had to shake hands with the congressman, and Notre Dame fans had to congratulate Jaimie on his touchdown interception against Michigan. Mrs. Burns, a pretty woman in her early forties, had to talk to Noele about going away to college, which she would soon be doing. And the congressman was more interested in the Director of Music than in finding out the "something important" that Noele wanted to ask him.

"He seems somewhat, uh, unsympathetic to young people," said Congressman Burns, as massive and as animated a man as his son was slim and mystical.

"Tell me about it," said Noele.

"I'm sure he complained about you to the pastor before the eleven o'clock Mass. He's the kind of fellow, I suspect, who would use your relationship to the monsignor against you. But you have the votes, young woman. Half the adults who come to the nine fifteen Mass do so because they want to see you directing the folk group. If Monsignor gets rid of you, he's going to lose a lot of his constituency."

"Male half, anyway," said Jaimie.

It was only after brunch that Noele was finally able to corner the congressman as they walked through the lobby to the club. Both paused spontaneously to look out over the eighteenth green, bathed in the golden light of the prolonged Indian summer and framed by red, yellow, and purple leaves.

It reminded Noele of the inside of a cathedral late in the afternoon, even though she'd never been in a cathedral late in the afternoon.

"All right, young woman, what's on your mind?" asked the congressman, as if he were dealing with an interesting but faintly troublesome constituent.

"Since you're on the intelligence committee"—Noele took a deep breath—"I want you to find out from the CIA whether Danny Farrell is still alive."

The congressman could not have appeared more astonished if his young constituent had asked for the United States embassy in Katmandu.

"Danny was killed eighteen years ago!"

"Was he?" Noele poured out the story she had pieced together from the Xeroxes his son had provided. "So you see, there was a big change from the time the Presbyterian missionary said he was still alive to the time *The New York Times* said he must be presumed dead. I want to know what happened and why he must be presumed dead."

The congressman's hands were jammed into the pockets of his light brown tailor-made suit and his high forehead wrinkled in skepticism. "You shouldn't play Nancy Drew, young lady."

"The next thing you're going to tell me is that I shouldn't open Pandora's box or rush in where angels fear to tread."

The congressman cocked an appreciative eyebrow. "You're a very interesting girl, Noele."

"Jaimie says I'm overwhelming. But we're not talking about me . . . and there are a lot of other strange things too. His mother's death—"

"Does your family know you're doing this?" the congressman asked suspiciously.

" 'Course they do. I've interviewed all of them. A lot of the kids, like, have to do this term paper. I'm really cranking along on mine."

"You think he's still alive." The congressman was jingling coins in both his pockets.

Noele was enthusiastic. "I think it would be, like, terrible if he were alive and everyone forgot about him. You know?"

"I don't know. . . ." The congressman hesitated.

"It wouldn't do any harm just to kind of nose around, would it, Congressman?" She tried her most appealing smile.

"It might, Noele; it might do a lot of harm to you and to others. But I will kind of nose around about kind of nosing around and see what I can do."

Noele sailed out of the Country Club as if she were Hercule Poirot, Roderick Alleyn, and Lew Archer all rolled into one.

And none of them ever got hurt.

Or if they did, they recovered quickly.

John

JOHN WAS STILL preoccupied with memories of Irene and Danny when they were young when he taped his program later in the week. The guest was a militantly feminist nun who had written a book called *Chauvinism and Peace*. He wondered how it was possible to make something beautiful and attractive like peace seem angry, hateful, and vicious. Yet Celeste had done that easily.

John was certainly sympathetic to the women's movement, and could hold his charming own with virtually every feminist guest he interviewed. Sister Celeste, however, had rolled over him as if she'd been a steam engine.

"I would hardly expect a priest to understand either women or peace. The church will appeal to modern women only if it rids itself of oppressors like you."

John knew he had done badly, though he supposed that his regular viewers would be sympathetic and give him points for patience. That was the danger of involvement in what he called the "television apostolate." You began to worry more about your image and about the audience's reaction to you than you did about the religious purpose that had brought you to television in the first place.

And he did care about what they thought of him. He did care about his image. At first he used no makeup. Now he was fastidious about what kind and how much: "Protect me from the glare," he would lamely rationalize.

Vanity of vanities, he told himself; all is vanity.

He sighed as he parked his Buick Skylark in the rectory garage and pulled down the garage door. A picture of Irene flashed momentarily in his brain, a sharp, vivid, enormously attractive picture. He was *objectifying* her, as Sister Celeste would have said, thinking of her as an attractive object instead of as a person.

It was too late, anyway—too late for all of them. They were all caught living out the results of decisions they and others had made long ago, and he was not sure they'd had the freedom to choose anyway.

His associate pastor, Father Jerry Miller, was sitting at a lunch table in the rectory dining room when John Farrell entered. Jerry was a late 1960s radical, born and ordained out of due season, feminine in his manner, semiliterate in his vocabulary and grammar, and utterly ineffective in the ministry.

The people of St. Praxides, however, were remarkably patient and tolerant of him, arguing that he worked hard (which was not true) and was good at arranging flowers on the altar (which was). The parishioners were charitable, John reasoned. He ought to be charitable too.

"Like, I mean, did you read, you know, Dads Fogarty's article in *Upturn?* Like, I mean, it was really, you know, funny."

In the old days if the pastor didn't like the grammar and vocabulary of a curate, he could simply tell him to shut up.

"I haven't got to the mail yet," John said heavily.

"Like, I mean, you know, it's the most; it's a make-believe interview between Monsignor Harold and an 'actress for Jesus' on TV. Dads has you down perfectly. Like, the phone's been ringing all morning, you know, priests calling up to tell you about it."

John felt slightly sick to his stomach. Dads Fogarty had been a few years ahead of him in the seminary, a pastor who was reported to make the lives of his associates miserable and run his parish with an iron hand. Nonetheless, he had a reputation, undeserved it seemed to John, for being a humorist without equal in the clergy. When he or Terry Quirk, a younger and more vicious, if more gifted, satirist—also with nothing better to do—clobbered you in the newsletter of the Association of Chicago Priests you became the laughingstock of the diocese. Unable to fight their psychopathic leader, the clergy of Chicago stayed alive by eating their own.

"I imagine I will get to read it sometime this afternoon," John said with forced nonchalance.

"You'd better read it soon; I mean, the phone calls are going to start right after lunch."

Indeed, John Farrell did read the article as soon as he went to his study. He was only halfway through it when one of his classmates called. Dads Fogarty's victims never received any sympathy. They were momentarily outside the law, and you could with perfect taste and charity gloat over their predicament.

Which was just what his classmate did. "Boy, does Dads have your mannerisms down perfectly. You'll never dare say 'in the deepest sense of the term' again, will you, John?"

"They tell me three quarters of a million people watch the program," John replied icily. "I don't imagine many of them read *Upturn.*"

His classmate ignored the response. "I'd go easy on the androgyny of God, too, if I were you."

John Farrell sighed. As one of his hilarities, Dads Fogarty had spelled androgyny as though it were andro-*genie*.

"If it's an important theological concept, and I think it is, I'll certainly continue to use it. Now, if you don't mind, I have an appointment . . ."

Screw the bastards, Danny would have said, just as he had when John told him during his seminary days that he was being ridiculed by some of his classmates because of the family's wealth.

He reread the Fogarty article. It was not funny. . . . It did not even begin to measure up as satire. It was simply nasty, vicious, heavy-handed ridicule. Balloonhead Mortimer had been right. The "guys" were closing in. Again John Farrell felt sick to his stomach. He opened the small icebox next to the television set, put three ice cubes in a tumbler, and poured himself one very tall glass of Scotch.

Which was the greater sin, vanity or envy?

He would either cave in to the pressures of the clerical culture—far more of a threat than the cardinal's psychopathic rage—or become a permanent outcast among the men who were the most important people in his life outside of his own family. There wasn't much in the way of an intermediate option.

Damn you, Dan Farrell, why aren't you here when I need you? Why did you have to die on me?

The people of the parish seemed to like his program. In fact, they even seemed a little proud that their pastor was on television.

But from the parishioners, John knew, there would be, and there could be, no consolation and no defense against the animus of his fellow priests.

He opened the rest of the mail but paid little attention to its contents.

He also had to do something about Noele and the folk Mass.

Then he had an idea. His hands began to sweat. Instead of talking to Noele, he would talk to her mother first—not on the telephone, but at home.

Roger

"THIS PLACE KIND of reminds me of the coffee shop at the Tel Aviv Hilton," said Mick Gerety, looking somewhat disdainfully at the oak-paneled, pennant-decorated wall of the Faculty Club.

"It sure isn't the old Morrison Hotel," added Angie Spina. "They all look smart. But I bet not one of them could deliver a precinct if his life depended on it."

"And to make matters worse, a lot of them wouldn't even think delivering a precinct is important."

"You like it here, Rodge?" Spina asked, glancing around the dining room, in which there were two Nobel prize winners, one former cabinet member, and some of the world's most distinguished scholars. "Doesn't it get kind of dull?"

Roger winced at the name Rodge, which always annoyed him. He would have to get used to it if he were going into the rough and tumble of elective politics. "It's like everything else, Angelo. Some good days, some bad days."

"Yeah, well, I think you'll like Springfield better. And between you and me, Rodge, Springfield is only the start. Mick here and I think all you need to run for the roses is a few breaks."

Roger laughed easily. "Let's worry about that bridge when we come to it." It was a bridge that Roger would not have been averse to crossing, however, should they ever come to it.

Gerety and Spina were not organization politicians, although Spina had good connections with the organization, and Gerety good connections with the liberal Independents. Since the death of the Mayor (the only *real* mayor) the organization no longer even appeared to speak with one voice.

In the lacuna after the demise of strong central leadership, powerbrokers like Angie Spina and Mick Gerety dealt with the organization and the other political, social, and civic groups to put together temporary and ad hoc coalitions, either to elect a candidate or accomplish a goal, like planning a World's Fair or scheduling an auto race in Grant Park. Mick was a successful lawyer, Angie the successful president of Atlantic Import Company, and both were involved in politics not for money, and not even for power, but for the sheer love of the game—a fact that made them far more attractive to Roger Farrell than to other politicians, either Regulars or Reformers. The former were interested only in money and power, and the latter were interested only in ideology. Roger had far more respect for gamesmen.

"The point is, Dr. Farrell"—Gerety winked at the formal title—"that there's no end to the possibilities for somebody with your special gifts and background at a time like this. With a few breaks we can win Springfield. And with a few breaks after that . . . well, who knows?"

They were both tall, handsome men, their black hair turning attractively silver, one with dark skin, the other with fair skin. Slick, expensively tailored products of the new Catholic affluent class. They could as easily be, Roger thought to himself, two monsignors on a mission from the Vatican.

"I find the idea of Springfield challenging and the idea of Washington terrifying," Roger said modestly.

"That's all we need, Rodge." Spina waved his hand expressively, flashing some very expensive rings—both the hand and the rings reminders of Taylor Street in a man who had otherwise pretty much left the old neighborhood behind. "We're just exploring possibilities, that's all. Just exploring possibilities."

"People are going to ask"—Gerety's wink was that of the classical Irish pol—"why you're giving up tenure at this place for a job where you'll be lucky if you're reelected once." He shrugged ever so slightly. "What should we tell them?"

Roger hesitated, ordering his thoughts as he did before a classroom lecture for which he had not prepared.

"I'll give as honest an answer as I can, and you'll have to figure out what to do with it. I was deeply involved in the Young Christian Students when I was at

St. Ignatius High School. In those days, back in the late 1950s, we believed that the Catholic layman's mission was to represent the Church in the, uh, temporal order, as we called it then. And we were told we would be most effective in that mission if we were professionally competent. I went into political science at Notre Dame thinking it was the route into politics. I discovered it was the route into graduate school; in those days if you had good marks and could write a decent English sentence—"

"You should have been a lawyer." Gerety laughed.

"I know that's the traditional way in," Roger said, and laughed somewhat uneasily with him. "But if I'd gone to law school, my mother would have wanted me to come into the company and . . . well, I guess I didn't find that very appealing. Too idealistic, I suppose."

Their faces were expressionless.

"If you're running for governor," Spina said tonelessly, "it's just as well that you weren't too closely linked with Burke Kennedy at that time."

"Or the firm, for that matter," Gerety added.

"Not that it's a problem now," Gerety murmured, filling up the awkward pause.

"So I've always had this sense that politics was a form of vocation, a commitment," Roger continued, ignoring their delicate allusion to his stepfather, as he was supposed to ignore it, "that I wanted to make and someday would make."

God, does that sound hypocritical. Yet I meant it . . . or at least I did once. I don't know what I mean anymore.

"That's great public service motive," Angelo said enthusiastically, "but from a professor and not a businessman, so the words are a little different."

They both seemed pleased, neither skeptical about nor impressed by his idealism. They probably did not care whether he was sincere or not.

"Will your wife go along with the campaign, Roger?" Gerety asked cautiously. "I mean, there are demands that will be made of her. She'll lose a lot of her privacy . . . that sort of thing."

"Irene will accept my decision," he said primly. He had never bothered to consider the question of Irene's reaction.

"Will she campaign?" Spina leaned forward. "She's a stunning woman, Rodge; she could be a great asset to the team."

Roger hesitated. "I'm afraid she's not much of a public speaker. She'll be quite visible, of course. I assume that'll be enough?"

"Sure, sure," Spina said easily. "And the kid. What's her name? Noele? No drug problems there or anything like that?"

Roger grinned. "Nothing like that at all. Indeed, Angie, if you even suggested that in her presence, you might be in very serious trouble. You wouldn't want her to campaign, would you? She's been known to give impromptu homilies in church on Sunday."

Gerety laughed uneasily. "Precocious kids can be a problem to a candidate."

"Not Noele."

Not unless someone makes her mad. I'll have to say a word to her.

"There's one thing we've got to be up front about, Roger." Mick Gerety bent over his chocolate ice cream as his waiter—a divinity-school doctoral candidate—filled the coffee cups. "We've got to explore the possibility that you might not be clean. There isn't any nice way to say it, so I'll just say it bluntly."

"Clean?" Roger was amused.

"Yeah, there's no point in the three of us or anybody else getting involved in a campaign when we might find out three, six months down the turnpike that you have some great big scandal in your past."

"That's certainly up front, Mick. What kind of scandal?"

"Well." Gerety shifted in his chair. "It varies. Adlai Stevenson had some trouble back in 1952 because he was divorced. That wouldn't make any difference today. Neither would women, so long as you weren't into kinky things or people with mob connections, like Jack Kennedy. But we could have trouble with fraud, murder, rape, drugs, even psychiatric treatment, like that poor guy Eagleton."

"I see."

"We hate to bring this sort of crap up," Spina said fretfully. "But with the papers being the way they are these days, if you know what I mean . . ."

"Bill Wells and his political people over at the *Star Herald* are almost in our camp," Gerety added, again with the slight, nervous shrug. "But they have to sell newspapers, even if it means doing in someone that Bill personally likes. You know these Chicago circulation wars."

"I understand completely," Roger said suavely. "I'm sure Steve Bilko will have enough fun with my being a professor in politics as it is. Of course, there was my mother and Burke Kennedy. For a long time they were what my brother the priest used to call public and notorious sinners. I don't suppose that matters, since if it did we wouldn't be sitting here."

"Family's all right," Gerety said quickly, "as long as there's nothing really bad. You know what I mean."

"I can't guarantee all my father and grandfather's business practices," Roger said.

"Statute of limitations." Mick Gerety waved an imperious legal hand. "Unless you're talking about murder."

Roger laughed, hoping that he did not sound nervous. "I've probably bored a lot of people to death, comes with being a professor. In fact, though, I have led a pretty dull and blameless life. It's hard to do much else when you're a university faculty member. But it wouldn't hurt to do a little checking on family history."

"We'd appreciate that," Gerety said. "Before we step into public, where the media people will go after us like those man-eating fish in South America."

"The piranha," Roger said, then kicked himself for acting like a know-it-all.

"Yeah, well, Governor, give us a ring in a day or two and let us know for sure."

Both the operators grinned. They were confident that they had a candidate, and that he was a winner.

Governor Farrell. It had a pleasant ring.

And what if the next time they met he told them that there probably had been a murder? It was made to look like an accident. The man who most likely ordered the crime is dead. I had nothing to do with it, though I have suspected the crime for a long time. No proof, but a reporter might dig up some pretty strong suspicions.

"And," he would add hesitantly, "the firm might have been involved."

There would be no wink in Gerety's ice-blue eyes. "It would raise the character issue, like Chappaquiddick: If you knew about it and did not do anything . . ."

No one would call him Governor Farrell again.

In a few days there would be a call saying that they were getting a lot of pressure from some of their friends to go with someone else.

I won't tell them now. I'll think about it. Reread the papers. No reason to make a decision this moment.

Already he was cheating.

Roger Farrell smiled pleasantly as he walked down the broad staircase of the Faculty Club with his two guests. The danger of the horror story—so long as it was an appropriate and modest danger—would make the race for governor even more enjoyable.

Like the enjoyment of being caught with Martha Clay.

···············*Congressman Burns*···············

"CLANCY FARRELL WAS one of the weakest human beings from whom I ever had to take campaign contributions, a jellyfish, oily and greasy and sometimes dangerous," exploded James McDowell Burns, former congressman of the Third District of the Great State of Illinois. "Burke Kennedy may be kinky. But Brigid really improved her situation when she dumped Clancy. Can't blame her in the least. Can't blame Burke, either. Gorgeous woman. Still is, as a matter of fact."

There were three James M. Burnses. The first was the former representative who was always called James, a stalwart seventy-year-old with a big head, on which there had not been much in the way of hair for forty of his seventy years, and a mellow voice, which had marked him, according to those who knew, as the greatest Irish political orator in Illinois in the twentieth century.

When he had stepped down at the age of sixty, after twelve terms in the United States House of Representatives, he was promptly succeeded by his son, James M. Burns, Jr. (called Jimmy by everyone but his wife, who called him Jim, save on those rare occasions when she was angry at him, and then he was Junior), the incumbent congressman, who had no skills at oratory at all, but could read a budget with a colder eye and question a bureaucrat with more devastating precision than almost any member of the House.

James M. Burns III was Jaimie, even when his mother was angry at him, which was practically never, since in her view he was practically perfect. Jaimie was an apparently lackluster young man who displayed no energy whatsoever, save in the presence of either a pigskin or Noele Farrell.

"The daughter-in-law and granddaughter aren't bad either," said Jimmy Burns. "Irene in a spring dress is still one of the greatest distractions to religious devotion in the recent history of St. Praxides. And that young redhead has our Jaimie quite bewitched."

The present and former congressmen were having lunch at the Chicago Athletic Club, on the fifth floor, overlooking a brown but sun-drenched patch of Grant Park and the sparkling blue lake beyond. The House of Representatives had awarded itself a long weekend, and the present congressman was mending fences in his district.

The club was old and conservative and solid, which is to say that it was having a hard time, since the younger generation was flocking to such dubious places as the East Bank Club, where they mixed sex, swimming, and other modernities.

The ex-congressman complained vocally about the mess that "damn fool" had made of the Art Institute. "Same damn fool who built that monstrosity in Colorado Springs."

The incumbent chewed on a celery stalk and remained silent. He rather liked the addition to the Institute. And the artchitect's wife was a sometime political ally. But his constituents did not like it, those who bothered to notice it.

So, as wise politicians do when their friends are on both sides, he said nothing at all.

The heavy maroon curtains that framed the park and the lake ought to have been replaced two years ago. Nonetheless, even though it was in decline, the dining room was a good place to mend fences with a certain generation of South Side Irish business and professional men—a vanishing breed, thought the congressman with a sigh.

He continued on the subject of Noele Farrell.

"That girl is a doll. She reminds me in a way of poor Danny Farrell. The other day she informed us that the solution to all the Jimmys in our family will be for there to be a *Seamus* in the next generation and then announced the name was Norman Irish, a hibernization of *Jacques*." He sighed again. "I don't know what's getting into kids these days. I agree with you about the others, though. I suppose I'd support Roger if he goes for governor, since he's in my district. But I don't like him, and I don't think I trust him. A bit too much of the poseur, if you ask me."

His father's vocal range was in two tones, loud and louder, and it was the latter he used to comment on Roger Farrell as governor. "Goddamned intellectual snob. And not that much to be snobbish about, either. They started in the sewers and never really have been clean since. It was a miracle that old Bill Farrell didn't end up in jail, where he belonged. And Clancy had been a vacillating prick most of the time. He never would have taken over the firm if Martin, who was a decent man, had not been killed in the war. When his mother started whispering in Clancy's ear or he had too much to drink, he thought he was the Lord God Himself and could do anything he pleased. No one was sorry when he died, especially not Brigid, or her boyfriend Burke Kennedy."

"Would Martin have inherited the firm if he had lived?"

"A lot of talk about it in those days. Bill died before Martin, so nothing came of the talk, especially after Martin's wife, Florence, died."

The congressman, having finished his lean hamburger without a bun, relaxed in his chair, fighting off a temptation to order dessert. "They certainly weren't much interested in finding out what happened to Marty's son when he disappeared, were they?"

"Danny?" His father eyed him shrewdly. "What do you mean?"

"Did they push you to find out what happened to him? They were heavy contributors to your campaigns."

James Burns chewed reflectively on his steak. "They went through the motions, nothing more. And heaven knows, that Brigid has never been shy about asking for favors or using her clout. I kind of suspected that they thought he might have defected. Maybe someone from the CIA planted that notion in their heads."

"Why would he defect? The U-2 was not much of a secret even to the Chinese by that time."

"Who knows? He was a crazy kid. Not a sewer type, like the others, but still a little daft. And they tossed him out of the Navy because he intervened to protect a black seaman who was being railroaded into the brig by some redneck C.O. That was back in the days when you could push black sailors around and have the Navy on your side. Or he might have been a CIA double agent, spying on the Chinese for us and then getting himself shot when the Chinese found out.''

"Convenient for the Farrells to have him out of the way, though, wasn't it? No one to challenge our pastor's and our next governor's inheritance?''

"You remember Danny, don't you? Not that kind of person. Why the interest in him, anyway?''

"Noele is writing a term paper.''

"And you're worried about a teenage term paper?'' the retired congressman exploded.

"What do you think it would do to the Democratic party if Roger runs for governor and the papers find out there was something fishy about Danny's disappearance? What if he was a traitor? And what if his family, for reasons we don't know, was glad to be rid of him? As you said, they come from the sewer.''

The ex-congressman scowled. "That all happened a long time ago. How would anybody find out what really went on?''

"All too easily, Dad; a sixteen-year-old girl dug up enough information to make me suspicious, and one question to you here at lunch makes me even more suspicious.''

"You don't think Dan is still alive?''

"Of course not. The issue is not whether he is still alive; the issue is whether his family was glad to have him dead. Or whether maybe he was a defector or a double or triple agent. Can you imagine what that would do to the whole Democratic ticket?''

"We don't need that.'' The former congressman shook his head grimly. "And especially you don't need it.''

"Tell me about it,'' said Jimmy Burns.

Brigid

BRIGID ALMOST NEVER went out to lunch. Instead she would eat a small salad and drink a cup of tea in her cluttered office at Farrell & Sons' headquarters in Blue Island, a suburb south of Chicago. A light lunch and a brisk walk around the perimeters of the firm's vast "yard" were Brigid's only concessions to maintaining her physical health. "I was lucky with my genes," she would explain, "and I'm not going to risk my luck with dangerous things like exercise and diets.''

Sometimes she shared her salad with a staff member with whom she had business. Her companion today was a fellow immigrant from the west of Ireland named Hugh McCauley, a wrinkled little red-faced leprechaun of dubious vintage who was technically an assistant general manager and actually Brigid's political contact and payoff man.

"Business is not good, Biddy.'' Hugh sighed a west-of-Ireland sigh, a sound like the advent of a serious asthma attack. "Not good at all.''

"We've survived bad times before, Hughie,'' she said, taking a cigarette out of her purse and searching for a match.

Hugh had learned long ago that she could never find a match. He flicked his Bic for her, knowing she would grind her cigarette into the ashtray after one or two puffs.

"Ah, we have. But in those days there were ways of dividing up the business and keeping the cut-rate boys out. Now, with the kikes and even the niggers undercutting us and the government watching every move we make, we can't maintain the old standards."

The old standards were a set of arrangements by which the traditional, politically connected construction companies divided the business among themselves by none too gently rigging bids, with, of course, the connivance of the politicians. Everyone had done it and no one minded until the People of the United States, represented by a United States Attorney for the Northern District of Illinois looking for publicity and a career as an elected official, had indicted a score or so of upstanding and civic-minded contractors, all of them Irish, all of them Catholic, and all of them pillars of their party and their parish.

Brigid had evaded indictment and a possible term in jail only because of some devious dealings by Burke. Politicans were still bribed, Democrats and Republicans alike, but the techniques of bribery were much more complex and the competition in the construction marketplace substantially more intense.

"What does the man in DuPage County want?" Brigid came bluntly to the point, not sharing Hughie's Irish love for the indirect and allusive approach.

She ground out her cigarette.

"Your man in DuPage County claims he has a lot of very heavy expenses, campaigns, education for his children, charities . . ."

"How much?" Brigid insisted.

Hughie shrugged. "Half a million dollars in cash, up front, to be deposited in a numbered account in a Swiss bank."

"The holy saints preserve us," Brigid exclaimed prayerfully, "a politician in DuPage County with a numbered account in a Swiss bank. What's the world coming to? No, Hughie, not one penny."

"We need the work, Biddy; with this Reagan budget . . ."

"Damn Reagan and damn his budget and damn DuPage County." Brigid slammed the desk with the palm of her hand. "We'll survive, Hughie. I'm not going to run the risk of a grand jury looking at us and finding something while my boy is running for governor."

"Ah, 'tis true, Biddy." Hugh flipped his head mournfully. "As soon as he announces, I suppose they'll be all over us."

"Well, they can't lay a finger on us, can they?" Brigid said decisively. "And I intend to keep it that way."

After Hugh had left and her young black secretary had taken away the remains of lunch, Brigid returned to her computer output with this month's payroll for the firm. They needed the business even more than Hughie realized. They'd survive, of course, but these were the worst times she had ever seen.

At last, woman, you've been forced to be virtuous, if only to get your son elected governor.

Your sons are not quite what you wanted, but they'll do. Besides, they're yours.

Thanks be to God for the statute of limitations. If they investigated some of the things we did in the 1950s in this office, it would be the end of all of us.

And there's a lot of other things they might look at, too, but reporters are too dumb to think of them. I wish it were as easy to fool God. And again Brigid saw the vast black pit which was certainly waiting for her.

My damn body got me into it. I didn't know what fucking was like until Burke came along. Then I couldn't give it up. Poor Clancy. He was no good at screwing at all. Could hardly get it up unless he beat me.

She remembered the night at the lake, a heavy silent summer night save for the noise of the crickets, when Danny had found her on the floor with her torn nightgown soaked in blood. He had held her in his arms and sworn vengeance against Clancy.

She shook her head in dismay. And, you old whore, you liked being in his arms, just as you liked being in his father's arms the month before he married Flossie. And you're still sorry you didn't let him screw you that night, and yourself knowing all the time how much he loved Floss.

She went back to the payroll, her pencil moving hesitantly down a column of numbers.

Hell is too good for the likes of you.

·······*Roger*·······

JOSEPH KRAMER WAS sitting in Roger's outer office in the new concrete block building in which the University housed its government department. He was taking copious notes on Roger Farrell's doctoral dissertation, comparing the political theories of Niccolò Machiavelli, Vilfredo Pareto, and Benedetto Croce.

"You may be the first person who's read that dissertation since my doctoral committee," Roger said, laughing lightly. "And I'm not sure of *them*."

"I think it's important to understand how a man's ethical thinking has developed." Kramer had the big smile of an intellectually handicapped archangel.

"You certainly are a thorough researcher, especially for a three-thousand-word article."

"A responsible journalist tries to be precise," Kramer said piously.

"I'm sure Mrs. Marshfield will be of every assistance to you in seeing how my manuscripts turn into articles and books." Roger nodded toward his secretary, who was staring vacantly out the window. At the salaries the University paid secretaries, you were lucky if they could speak English, let alone read and write.

"Won't you, Henrietta?"

Henrietta's nod of agreement was something less than enthusiastic.

"Well, then, if you'll excuse me, Mr. Kramer. . . ." Roger opened the lock on his personal file cabinet and withdrew from the second drawer a small metal file box, which was also locked with a padlock and a combination. He closed the drawer of the larger cabinet, locked it, and went into his inner office.

On the whole he felt that his confidential papers were safer at the office with Henrietta than at the house with Irene. While Irene wasn't very intelligent, she might understand some of the contents of the neatly ordered manila folder under *F* inside the safe. There was not the slightest possibility that Henrietta could understand them, even if she were able to read them, which was doubtful.

On his desk were two notes that "Miss Clee" had called. Henrietta was not much at spelling either.

He tore the notes up. I'm a middle-aged professor infatuated with a thirty-two-year-old woman. I must restrain myself for a while. What kind of love . . . To hell with analysis. Enjoy it while you can.

He paused before opening the folder. He had never quite been able to add notes about his father's death to the file. If he were honest with himself and with future generations—Noele's children, perhaps—he ought to complete the story that had begun in 1944 and had its denouement in the autumn of 1963.

He pressed his fingers against his temples and shuddered. His father had begun with an attack on the Kennedys and then turned to the Conlons, making poor Irene weep. Danny had lost his temper, a rare enough event. Then Clancy began to talk about the past. John scoffed in disbelief. Danny listened in stunned silence. And Roger was terrified at the possibility that his father's drunken ravings might be the truth.

A few hours later Roger and John stared at Clancy's dead body, listening to his mother's account of what had happened and Burke's grim plan for coping with it.

What else was there to do?

Then Danny came back to the house, his lips pressed tightly together, his face parchment white. The body was being carried down the steps into the autumn darkness. Captain Nolan and Doctor Keefe had been bribed. The matter was concluded.

Danny said not a single word. Perhaps he thought he was justified in what he had done. And perhaps he was.

He left Chicago the afternoon of the funeral Mass. Roger could not find the courage to talk to him about what had happened. Brigid warned him to stay away from "the poor man."

Roger shook his head, trying to clear the images away.

Keefe and Nolan were the weak links. Yet they would not risk losing their comfortable incomes from Farrell construction—as well as admit to obstruction of justice.

It was not the death of 1963 that might be the problem, but the death of 1944.

He opened the file: the clippings and correspondence he had found among his father's papers, his own notes, further clippings, and the single memo from Burke: "For God's sake, Clancy, forget it!"

His father's picture and Uncle Martin's, identical twins, and yet even as young men the rough black Irish good looks that were part of the family heritage made Martin look strong and Clancy somehow feeble and artificial.

Yet he was not a bad man. It was not his fault that he was ineffectual. He was generous to such liberal politicians as Adlai Stevenson and Paul Douglas, told wonderful stories to his sons, took them to ball games a dozen times every summer, talked sports with them at the supper table every night, did his best to be a friend and companion to them.

He was ineffectual as a father, too, but out of the natural sympathy that children have for the feeble, they pretended that he was a buddy.

No, not a bad man. Yet the conclusion from the file must be that under certain circumstances Clancy could be a monster, especially when his demented mother, Blanche, goaded him into action with the charge that he was not manly. As though she herself were not responsible . . .

Roger shuddered. There was no point living through the horror of such recollections again.

Yet he could not stay away from the folder. Often he would awake in the middle of the night and resolve to finish it. Perhaps there was expiation to be found in truth.

What would the press say if they knew that the father of a reform candidate for governor had been so deeply involved with a cheap crook who had once been the outfit's most feared enforcer?

He thumbed through the clippings and the notes. Marsallo ("The Marshal") had come a long way. From petty torturer to protégé of the Mob's most respected senior leader. Crazy now, they said.

Yet it was all long ago; the connections were thin, and even his own conclusions were speculative. Clancy's outburst the night of his death was the only proof, and even John did not believe it was any more than drunken braggadocio, similar to Clancy's claim to be a war hero who had secretly worked for the OSS.

He closed the folder. . . . No, there was nothing there that was any serious threat. If a reporter were able to put all the pieces together, he might have some kind of story, but a quick and relaxed denial would dispose of it. And no reporter had been in the corner at the Club that dreadful night. . . .

Florence's picture slipped out.

He could hardly bear to look at her. She would be over sixty now, not as well preserved as Brigid, but still probably an attractive woman. The fire that had appealed to Martin and that Dan had kept alive for nineteen years more would still be burning.

She was wearing a formal gown, for a prom or debutante ball, perhaps. So young and so lovely to die.

And such a senseless death. She had only asked a question, not made any threats. . . .

He opened the file again and glanced at the conclusion of his memo to "future Farrells."

"Let me take this opportunity to plead with you, if not for forgiveness, at least for understanding. You will think that my father was a monster. And so it will seem from this story and from other stories I could also tell you. Yet in fact, in everyday life he did not seem evil to his sons. He was generous to us and to the church and to a wide variety of charities. He drank more than was necessary and more than was proper, but I do not think he could have been considered at the time of his death an alcoholic. He was an enthusiastic sports fan and loved to play softball with the two of us, though, in truth, he was not very good in sports. He was weak and ineffectual in most of the things he attempted but well-meaning, save when he felt personally threatened; then he fought like a cornered animal, ruthlessly and viciously, though with neither wisdom nor strength.

"I don't believe that my brother John and I ever loved him. Nonetheless, it is not an exaggeration to say that we genuinely liked him most of the time, save when he was drunk or swept up in the emotions of one of his rare temper tantrums. One could not, finally, love or respect Clancy Farrell as a father, but one could enjoy his company as a child like oneself.

"All of this is by way of trying to persuade you, Farrell descendents of the future, that you must not think my father was thoroughly evil. If, as I believe likely, he was the agent of great harm to others, he was an agent acting with greatly diminished moral responsibility, somewhat more to blame for what happened than would have been a bolt of lightning or a collapsed wall, but substantially less to blame than would have been a free and mature adult."

Roger Farrell hunched over his desk, face in his hands, and sobbed bitterly, as he often did when he thought of the enormous human suffering that had plagued his family. The sordid sins of the past were being expiated by the misery and destruction of the last forty years. Would it ever stop? Was there more suffering ahead of them? Would Noele be harmed? He pounded his desk. God damn it, nothing would touch her—nothing.

Gradually he regained his self-control, placed the folder inside his gray, portable safe, and closed the door, noting absently the words *Confidential. For the Eyes of Roger Farrell Only*, which he had printed in large red letters on the folder.

It's the only scandal that could embarrass us. It will never become public. Yes, I have made up my mind; I am going to have a go at the governorship. That means I will have to lie to Mick and Angie and tell them there is nothing to threaten us from my past. A Young Christian Student from two decades ago, filled with idealism and even a sense of vocation. And you begin your pursuit of political power with a lie.

It probably won't be the last.

His office phone rang. "Mr. Farrell."

"Roger, Martha. I think I've finally reworked the conclusion so it makes sense. I want to put it in the mail tonight. Could you stop over late this afternoon for a drink and reassure me?"

Roger Farrell smiled to himself. It was three thirty. Why waste any time? He had established his virtue by keeping her at bay for two days. "I'll come right over," he said briskly, thinking of himself as an alcoholic who was exulting over the fact that he had stayed out of a tavern for two days.

Today he would be an extraterrestrial who kidnapped a housewife from a supermarket. Just what he needed after coming up out of the family cesspool.

"I don't want to cut short your working day," she protested.

"Who works in this department after three o'clock in the afternoon?"

Two and one-half, perhaps three, hours of amusements with the frightened and then enchanted prisoner, and then push her off his flying saucer, after some brief, justifying remarks on her concluding chapter.

On the way out of his office, already imagining the delightful pleas he would soon compel his earthling captive to breathe, Roger deposited the portable safe, the Florence Farrell folder with its "confidential" label on top, in his personal filing cabinet and closed the door.

Enough of the Farrells for one day.

But not quite enough. Alongside the happily groaning Martha Clay, who was more than content with her brief imprisonment in his space vehicle, he was haunted by the expression on Danny Farrell's face on the cold and rainy day when they returned Clancy's body to the earth from which it had come.

John

JUST AS JOHN was parking his Buick Skylark in front of his brother's house, Irene drove up behind him in her Datsun sports car, a vehicle that made him nervous. Somehow it did not seem proper for the pastor's sister-in-law to drive a high-performance car. She was burdened with several bags of groceries that John courteously offered to help carry into the house. In a beige autumn dress—

Irene preferred dresses to suits—she appeared to John as she always did, a naked woman with a few garments that had been hastily thrown on and that might at any moment drop away.

"You look a little under-the-weather, John," she said. "Let me mix you a drink, and then we can talk about this folk Mass crisis."

His martini was very dry, and very generous, as presumably was her own. Irene's drinking made him nervous. She was, he thought, pre-alcoholic; at least she was a quiet drunk, even quieter than when she was sober.

She sat next to him on the couch in her elaborately antique parlor. "The folk Mass isn't that serious, is it?"

"Oh, no, it's not the folk Mass at all." The hint of sympathy in her liquid brown eyes overwhelmed him. He poured out the whole story: the TV program, the envy of his fellow priests, and the priest association newsletter. In response he expected her to say what any sensible person would say under the circumstances: that it was ridiculous to worry about such things.

But Irene did not dismiss his troubles as foolish. "May I see the newsletter?" she asked quietly.

So eagerly that his hands trembled, he took the paper out of his inside jacket pocket and gave it to her. Irene looked in her purse for reading glasses, and with a martini in one hand she read the newsletter very carefully.

"What an awful man," she said finally. "It isn't funny at all. How can priests think it's funny? It's cruel and sick. I'm so sorry for you. It's not fair. You work very hard on that program. These terrible people should support you and not make fun of you."

"I suppose criticism and envy go with the territory," he said, dissolving in the delightful warmth of her compassion.

"Not in the church, it shouldn't. And you mean to tell me that this nickname, 'Slick,' is sticking to you? You're Slick Farrell?"

"I'm afraid so." He folded the newsletter and put it back into his pocket.

"Another drink?" Not waiting for an answer, Irene took their glasses to the bar, filled them, and returned to the coffee table.

"Are you going to give up the program, John?"

"What do you think?" He was astounded that he would care what his sister-in-law thought.

She pondered his question carefully, holding her drink at her chin as if she wanted to solve the problem before sipping any more vodka.

"I think you ought to tell the whole lot of them to go to hell," she said fiercely. "The people of the archdiocese must like your program or it wouldn't have high ratings. And as long as we like it, why should you care what a bunch of envious priests think?"

An Irene who was thoughtful, intelligent, and spoiling for a fight was not exactly what John had expected. Had she been that way in the summer of 1963? Not that he could recall. Maybe he had been too horny to notice.

"Well, perhaps you're right. Maybe I—at least—ought to finish out the present contract. Now, about the teenage Mass?" he said, changing the subject before he could consider the implications of his change of mind.

Irene drank deeply from her martini glass. "Since I'm being so bold this afternoon—" He glimpsed a breathtaking gleam of white teeth and a spectacular movement of graceful breasts as she spoke "—let me be blunt about that subject, too. Mr. Creepy Crumb—I know that's not his real name, but it's the only one I hear around this house—is trying to manipulate you. He's telling you and others that if Noele weren't your niece, you'd cancel the folk music group. He's playing on your sense of fairness, John; he knows darn well that if she weren't your niece you would tell him to leave that group alone without a moment's hesitation. Teenagers who otherwise might not bother going to church love that Mass, and so do a lot of adults. If you cancel them because he's trying to blackmail you, you may please him, but you are going to offend a lot of other people—and, of course, they'll be like the priests who admire what you do on television, and you'll never hear from them.''

What had happened to Irene this afternoon? ''You're saying that I ought not to discriminate against Noele because she's my niece?''

Irene laughed, another rare event. ''Yes, and I'm also saying, Monsignor John Farrell, that if you want to have a real fight on your hands, try to cancel the folk Mass. Mr. Creepy Crumb is a pushover compared to your niece. And you would be much wiser to fight this awful Dads Fogarty person''—she gestured contemptuously at the newsletter—''than to fight my Christmas child.''

John felt that chains had been torn off his legs. ''You're right, Irene, absolutely right. I ought to sign you up as my spiritual director.''

Irene colored faintly. ''I don't think I'd make much of a spiritual director, John. I'd offer you another drink, but . . .''

''Can't have a pastor driving back to the rectory drunk,'' John said, and rose somewhat shakily to his feet. ''I'd better finish off some work before supper.''

As he stood up to leave, another worry popped into his worry-crammed mind. ''Is Noele finished with her term paper yet?''

''I think so.'' Irene hesitated. ''She hasn't asked me any further questions lately. They bring up painful memories . . . and I wonder if we ought to have told her—''

''About California?'' She had never once mentioned that subject to him. Feeling enormous compassion for her, he stilled the words that almost came to his lips. His hand squeezing her shoulder lightly, he said, ''Don't torment yourself, Renie.''

''Thanks, John.'' She kissed him lightly on the cheek as he was leaving, a routine sign of affection that had occurred many, many times before. As he tottered toward his car in the rapidly falling darkness of an autumn afternoon, John thought that the kiss had meant a little more this time than it ever had before.

Be careful, he told himself. You could fall in love with the woman again.

Noele

NOELE FARRELL PARKED her car, Flame, on Ninety-fifth Street in front of the small, white, brick cottage in which Dr. Michael Keefe had dispensed the wisdom of medical sciences for forty-five years. She had assigned a willing Jaimie to interview his grandfather about Martin and Clancy Farrell when they were young. She would tackle Doctor Keefe about the night of Clancy's death.

It was not fair. James Burns was a cute old man, who told wonderful stories about the past. Doctor Keefe was your all-time classic nerd.

She checked her notes on the legal-size yellow pad. Grams had said that she and her husband had been tired after the fight and had come home from the club immediately after dinner, and that he had gone right up to bed, still complaining about Danny.

That could have been no later than ten thirty.

Yet the time of death on the certificate Jaimie had obtained from the County Recorder's office said one thirty. Doctor Keefe had signed the certificate three hours after Clancy fell down the stairs. All right, suppose that Grams was wrong. Suppose that they came home from the club later. There was no way they wouldn't have been home by eleven thirty. A half hour to call Burke at the most, another half hour to find the doctor who, after all, lived in the parish. . . . Why the extra hour?

And where were John and Roger all that time? If they had known about their father's death, wouldn't they have called another doctor? Come to think of it, why didn't Burke call another doctor? Why have the dead body lying on the floor?

So either he had died much later than seemed possible if Grams was telling the truth, or there had been a long delay. . . . And why would there be such a delay?

To cover up for Danny?

She pounded the steering wheel of Flame in dissatisfaction. I'm obsessive about Danny Farrell, she realized.

Well, after this conversation is over, I'm going to stop.

The terrible feeling of loneliness had returned only once since the Notre Dame–Miami game. Maybe it would never come back.

She slammed the door of Flame in disgust at herself.

She was still disgusted when she entered the cramped waiting room of Dr. Keefe's office. There were two pregnant women, a seventh-grade boy who looked like he had a bad stomachache, and one very old man waiting in the office, leaving a single empty chair for herself. It was that way every time you came to Dr. Keefe's. She was an hour late for her appointment, knowing that the doctor was never punctual and she would still have to wait for another hour. She removed her boring trigonometry homework from her book sack and began to puzzle over sines, cosines, and tangents.

Dr. Keefe was reputed by those over forty in the neighborhood to be a "wonder" and to "have forgotten what those bright young kids out of medical school will never learn." Noele suspected that he had forgotten practically everything about medicine. And she agreed with her mother that Doctor Keefe was a dirty old man.

But it wasn't a matter of health that brought Noele to his office.

Finally, just fiteen minutes before she ought to have been home for supper, she was admitted to the doctor's disorderly office, which smelled of stale disinfectant. He was a wiry little old man with a lean, pale face and several strands of yellow-white hair hanging over his forehead. Noele shuddered.

"Well, young woman," he wheezed, "what brings you to my office on this lovely fall day?"

"I'm not pregnant or anything like that." Noele thought his leer was disgusting. "I'm writing a family history term paper and I am particularly interested in Grandfather Clancy Farrell. I want to do a page or two about his death, and I wonder if you could tell me some of the details."

It was an enormous fib.

The leer disappeared immediately from the old doctor's face and was replaced by an expression of demented cunning.

"Not much to tell. I'm sure your grandma told you about it. Poor man came home from dinner at the club on Sunday evening, climbed up to the top of the steps, tripped, fell down the steps, and landed on his head."

"They left the club early in the evening, Grams said." Noele fiddled with her legal-size pad. "And poor Clancy fell down the stairs about ten thirty."

The doctor's filmy eyes flickered in surprise. "Closer to eleven, as I remember it."

Noele sprang her trap. "Then why does the death certificate say that the time of death was one thirty?"

"Let me see that thing." He grabbed it from her and twisted it in his hands. "Well, that's the time I signed it. . . ." He hesitated. "I was at the hospital delivering a baby. Took them a long time to get to me. . . ."

He was making it up. Grams had not told her the truth about the time of death. It was probably closer to twelve. An hour to get Burke and her sons, a forty-five minute ride for Uncle John from his parish, and the doctor and the police. . . . Why would Grams lie to me?

"Two hours. . . ."

The watery-eyed old goat considered her suspiciously. "What's the point in asking all these questions, young woman? You sound like you're trying to conduct a murder investigation."

Noele laughed disarmingly. "A fine detective I'd make, Dr. Keefe. I don't suspect anything. I'm just trying to figure out how people behave in time of crisis."

"It's easy to see that you are young and inexperienced," the doctor snapped. "Someday a tragedy will occur in your life, and you will realize that people don't always act logically at such times. Your poor grandmother was beside herself with grief. There was her husband at the bottom of the stairs, his eyes wide open, blood pouring out of his head—he'd banged up against the railing at the foot of the steps. She couldn't reach Father John at his rectory, she couldn't get through to your dad at the club because the line was busy, and Danny—that worthless scoundrel—was driving around drunk in somebody's car. She didn't know what to do when I wasn't home, my wife—God have mercy on her"—he crossed himself devoutly—"was away on vacation. I was delivering a baby in Little Company Hospital. It was only when your father finally arrived that Brigid was able to pull herself together. They called me at the hospital, and then Captain Nolan at the Gresham Station, so nobody would be asking the kind of funny questions you're asking, young woman!"

He was a quick and clever liar. But three hours, even two hours, were too much. Were there not neighbors who could have gone over to the club to tell Roger? Were there not other doctors? The neighborhood was filled with doctors, one out of every ten men, according to Uncle Monsignor.

There was either a deliberate delay in calling a doctor or the death had occurred much later. And in that case Grams had lied. Why lie, unless something terrible happened between ten thirty and midnight?

"And it was only when Uncle Monsignor came that they thought about a priest?"

"He got there only half an hour or so before I did. Why should they think about calling a priest from St. Praxides when they have a priest in the family?"

Because if you call another priest, you might give away your cover.

Grams had lied, and Doctor Keefe was trying to protect her lie, even though Noele had surprised him.

What had happened between ten thirty and midnight?

"And his death was an accident?"

"Of course it was an accident," he said impatiently. "Doesn't the death certificate say that?"

But then why would Grams lie to me?

"Okay, Doc." She gave him her very best smile. "I guess that's all I need to know. I'm going home now and finish the term paper tonight after supper."

"I don't know what's happening in Catholic schools these days," the doctor grumbled, and stood halfway up in his chair. Then he added, "I think we'd all be much better off if we left the dead alone."

"So do I," said Noele at the door. "Oh, by the way, was Dan Farrell there when you arrived?"

Again the old doctor hesitated. "He came in just as I was finishing. Looking pale and kind of guilty. He had a big fight with your grandfather earlier in the evening."

"Not drunk anymore?"

"Death sobered him up."

He either thinks that Danny killed Clarence, or he wants me to think that he thinks Danny killed him.

Back in the front seat of Flame she pondered her notes. Clancy Farrell had died sometime between ten o'clock and one o'clock on Sunday night—well, make that sometime between ten thirty and twelve thirty. Dr. Keefe had been summoned from Little Company Hospital between one and one thirty and came to the house almost immediately. Uncle Monsignor had arrived a little bit before that. A forty-five-minute drive from his parish on the North West Side. He must have arrived back at the rectory at a quarter to twelve and picked up the phone then.

Something had happened between a quarter to eleven and a quarter to twelve.

Maybe she should forget the whole thing. The family history term paper had started out as a lark. Then it had become a fascinating mystery, the kind Miss Marple solved in her cute little village of St. Mary Mead. Now it was turning ugly.

There was one very simple explanation. Danny had dropped Moms off, come to the house, and then killed Clancy. Everyone else, including Doctor Keefe, was conspiring to cover up for Danny by pretending that the death had been earlier, when Danny was still with Moms.

Ask Moms about the time she went home? But would she tell me the truth? She loved him, I think, and would still want to protect his reputation. Her parents, who might know what time she really came home, are dead. She could claim that she was with Danny till he showed up after one o'clock. . . .

Something strange had happened that Sunday evening in the late autumn of 1963. Gramps, everyone said, was a nice man until he lost his temper. Maybe he had lost his temper that night and done something that made someone want to kill him—his wife, or his son, or his nephew Danny.

Or Burke. Maybe Burkie was tired of sharing Grams with him. She hesitated. Or maybe even Moms. But Moms couldn't hurt a fly. Brigid could hurt a fly, and so could Roger and so even could Monsignor John, if he were pushed hard enough. Probably Cousin Danny could too. Maybe they were all protecting him. They all loved him. Then he disappeared, and there was no need to protect him anymore. Couldn't blame them for being relieved.

What had he and Clancy fought about earlier? Just the Kennedy family and the federal investigation of the firm? You don't kill people for that sort of an argument.

Even if he'd done it—she was still defending him—he must have had a good reason.

A good reason for murder?

Maybe it was self-defense.

A young pilot defending himself against a weak, middle-aged man?

Or revenge.

Revenge for what?

It had been a long time ago. Dr. Keefe was probably right. The dead should be left alone.

Noele stuffed her yellow pad into her book sack, turned over the ignition to the car, and flipped on the lights. She felt heavy and discouraged. There was a trace of the loneliness teasing at the back of her head. She ought to leave the whole mess alone. She was being a giddy teenager, pretending that real life was like an Agatha Christie mystery story.

If you want me to do it, she informed the One in Charge, you're going to have to send me a sign.

So there.

What kind of sign?

Oh, I don't know, any kind of sign. A rose or something yukky like that.

The light changed to red. Noele was hemmed in by a van.

Geek, she said half aloud.

The light changed and the van moved ahead, its back door flapping in the wind.

They should lock it, she said righteously. Nerds.

A car cut in front of the van, and it slammed to a hasty stop.

Noele screamed as she lunged for her brakes.

Flame rose to the occasion and halted a few inches behind the van. The swinging door hesitated above Flame's hood.

Mount Greenwood Florists.

What you'd expect from yukky Mounties.

The van lurched forward, the door swung drunkenly, and a bundle fell on Flame's waiting hood.

Flakes!

She pulled into a gasoline station and climbed out of the car. It was only when her fingers were about to touch the package that she knew what would be in it.

Totally excessive, she said hotly. I asked only for one, not a bouquet!

Well, I don't have to do it, anyway. She slipped Flame into the flow of the Ninety-fifth Street traffic. She would forget about the whole thing.

After she got a full report from Jaimie.

And talked to Captain Nolan.

DANCE FOUR

Saraband

*"A dance and song, so lascivious in its words,
so ugly in its movements, that it is enough to
inflame even very honest people."*

"Tract Against Public Amusements"
JUAN DE MARIANA

D.C.I.

"MR. RADFORD IS here, sir," said the lean young man who was the administrative assistant to the Director of the Central Intelligence Agency.

"Ask him to come in, please," said the D.C.I. heavily.

A tall, muscular, bearded young man, one of the more recent models of the Harvard graduates who flocked, generation after generation, from Cambridge to Langley, Radford was the D.C.I.'s "man." He was the instrument by which the Director could turn over every stone in the Company's past or present to discover what kind of worms were crawling around under it. Radford's blood was reported to measure only slightly above freezing, and his blue eyes suggested a temperature much below freezing. No one argued with Radford; no one tried to hide anything from him. No one spoke to him when it could possibly be avoided.

In other words, Radford was an absolutely first-rate hatchet man. But the Director, a Wall Street lawyer inexperienced in recent intelligence operations, was as ill at ease with him as anyone else.

"Sit down, Radford," he said. It was possible that Radford had a first name, but the D.C.I. had never been tempted to learn it. "I have a problem out of the past for you to look at."

"Oh?" Radford's voice never betrayed emotion.

The Director knew that he was the most popular and respected man to preside over the Agency in a decade because, as the insiders conceded, he was tougher than any of them. He felt that the reputation was deserved. Wall Street was tougher than the shadow world any day. But if Radford was frightened of him, he did not show it.

"We had operations out of Japan over China until the middle sixties, didn't we?"

"I believe so," Radford agreed cautiously.

He knew damn well there were such operations, that several pilots had been lost in China and that one of them had come back alive. And contemplated running for congress. Wouldn't that be nice. A former employee of the Company sitting on a congressional committee?

"You may remember an incident in 1965, when the Chinese reported shooting down a U-2 over Sinkiang," the Director continued. "We, of course, denied the plane was ours and claimed that we knew nothing about the pilot. Does it ring any bells?"

"Faintly," said Radford.

"So everybody agreed he was dead. The Chinese said he was dead, and I guess we had no reason to think otherwise. Then in 1971, when the Chinese were releasing everybody, a Presbyterian missionary who came home reported seeing the fellow." The Director unnecessarily glanced at the sheet of paper in front of him. "Daniel Farrell . . . in a prison camp in western China. It made one or two of the newspapers, and then apparently was forgotten. If the Company did anything about the missionary's report, it didn't make the papers. The missionary is dead now, of course. He was an old man then."

"Wouldn't the Chinese have released Farrell when they released everyone else?" Radford's eyes remained icy.

"Sure; why not? Only I want to know some more of the details. What we did about the missionary's report. Whether we ever asked the Chinese about this man, Farrell. And if we didn't, why we didn't."

Radford was silent, waiting for an explanation, if one were to be offered.

"You know Congressman Burns, don't you, Radford?"

An ever-so-slight lift of a blond eyebrow. "One of our more intelligent friends on the Hill. Sympathetic, but not a naïf."

"Chicago Irish politicians are never naive, Radford." The Director was proud of himself for scoring one of his occasional points against his young assistant. "Anyway, Jim Burns wants to know if we are sure that Farrell is dead. He also wants to know whether we are certain that there are no worms under that particular rock that might be turned up if somebody took a hard look at it. It seems that Farrell's cousin is probably going to run for governor in Illinois. The congressman is uneasy, by his own admission, that something might turn up on the Farrell affair during the election campaign."

"A reporter could remember the U-2 incident, dig up some facts about the Presbyterian missionary, and maybe smoke out something else even more embarrassing," Radford said tonelessly.

"Precisely. If a reporter shows up here asking about Daniel Farrell, I want to know all there is to know, what I have to tell him, and what I have to try to hide, if anything."

Radford considered silently.

"I don't like it any more than you do," the Director continued. "Something doesn't smell right. Burns thinks the Farrell family was less than diligent in pushing us to find out what happened to this pilot."

For the first time since the D.C.I. had known him, Radford blinked. "There's probably nothing at all under that rock, chief," he said.

It was also the first time the Director had heard him use the word *probably*.

"I tend to agree with you. But we would look awfully silly, Radford, if someone else turns up the rock first and finds there is something under it. Get on it."

"Yes, chief," he said as he slipped out the door.

Despite his height and weight, Radford moved with the speed and grace of a predatory cat. The Director wondered why he thought of a black panther every time his strapping Harvard-trained assistant departed from his office.

Irene

IRENE COULD NOT sleep. She lay next to her husband in bed, craving affectionate contact and wishing that she might at least touch his hand. Roger Farrell did not like physical contact unless they were making love. But Irene's need to touch and be touched was so powerful that she would have been delighted to be held in a man's arms while she was asleep every night, even if there had been no sex between them.

Roger was a skillful enough lover. He knew how to arouse her, to bring her to climax, and to settle and reassure her after lovemaking. But Irene often felt that Roger made love as though he were performing before a group of judges who would hold up cards with numbers on them after he was finished, like the judges at Olympic diving and gymnastic events. And when the applause died down, Irene was left alone, pleasured indeed, but feeling that the depths of her passions had not even been approached.

"It takes me a long time," she had said once to her lover.

"And you're worth waiting for," he'd said tenderly.

But that was long ago, before she had made an irreparable mess of her life.

Roger was less patient. After they made love, physical contact was brought to a decisive end, and she dared not touch him in bed until the next time. While she could not calculate Roger's schedule, she knew that their lovemaking was scheduled according to a formula, as was everything else in his life. And she was reasonably confident that the schedule for her was not correlated—the word he would use—with the schedule for his mistress.

Was that woman unsatisfied too?

Feeling mean, Irene hoped that she was.

There had been a scene at the supper table that evening. Roger had curtly informed his wife and daughter that he intended to run for governor and, in his most professorial tone, had tried to lay down rules for the campaign—how they should dress, what they should say to the papers, how Noele should keep a low profile and Irene a high profile. He was so taken up with his own importance that he did not notice the gathering storm on the Christmas child's face.

"You never asked me whether I wanted you to run for governor, Roger," Irene said mildly.

"You never objected," he replied with some asperity.

"I'm not sure I could get used to being the first lady of Illinois," she replied, knowing she would do whatever he wanted.

"Your friends Angie and Mick sound like total retards to me," Noele shouted. "They're not going to tell me how to be a teenager."

And she soared out of the room, like a comet blazing across the winter sky.

"Have I been pompous?" Roger asked hesitantly.

"Even for you."

"I'd better apologize." He wiped his lips, folded his napkin carefully, and followed Noele out of the room.

He didn't apologize to *me*, Irene thought, but I suppose he'll make love to me tonight. That'll be the only apology I get.

The exchange with John that afternoon had troubled her deeply. He had always seemed a bit of a pompous ass, even as a seminarian with whom she temporarily thought she was in love, mostly because he was a kind of forbidden fruit. Now, as the pastor of St. Praxides, he was someone to whom she was polite and respectful because he was a priest and a brother-in-law, but hardly a man to be considered as a troubled, vulnerable, and attractive male.

Yet that afternoon he had not been nearly as egotistical in his male insecurity as most men. In fact, he'd been rather charming, graceful, and astonishingly honest in his vulnerability. His need for sympathy had won instant response from her. And her response, spontaneous and unconsidered, had triggered an even more disarming self-revelation.

Irene was used to the imaginary undressing men routinely performed on women like her. Sometimes it was flattering, sometimes infuriating, mostly only "boring," as Noele would have said. But the look in John's eyes when she climbed out of the car was quite flattering. Pleased with his admiration, she had been a little more gracious to him than she ordinarily might have been. And thus encouraged, he had spilled his story of unhappiness. Poor man.

I could like him, she thought, shifting uneasily on her side of the bed. I could like him a lot.

I can't let that happen. I've had enough trouble with male members of the Farrell family as it is. I don't need a romance with a Farrell priest.

But if he were in love with me, he would never let me out of his arms. He would apologize if he hurt my feelings.

Like Danny, had he lived.

Roger

ROGER WAS COMPLACENT as he drifted into a pleasant sleep. Normally he would not have made love to his wife the same day he had committed adultery. It was aesthetically unsatisfactory. But sex had been a way to soothe Irene's hurt feelings. He had been a damn fool to behave so insensitively—precisely the sort of behavior he found so offensive in other academics.

He knew, however, that Noele was not so easily appeased. You had to reason with her. And reasoning with a stubborn, willful young woman was not easy. Still, he would have to contain her, no matter how much effort was required.

Curiously, Martha had mentioned Noele that afternoon. She'd been clinging to him after they'd made love, using some new techniques and fantasies he had not tried before, including the idea of Martha as a young man as well as a young woman, a brain-crackling fantasy that increased greatly his affection for her.

"I would like to have a child of yours," she had said, pressing against him as if the oxygen she breathed had to pass through his body first. "Your daughter is so beautiful."

It was the first hint of domesticity in their relationship, and it shocked Roger into momentary speechlessness.

"I thought your principles were against motherhood," he stammered.

"Oh, they are." She kissed his chest. "But because I've chosen not to bring children into this unhappy world doesn't mean that I'm so inhuman as not to have regrets. I wish there was enough justice for women in the world so that it would be possible for me to have a daughter like Nicole."

"Noele," he said mechanically. Would she actually run the risk of pregnancy? Not that there was much chance . . .

"You're not angry with me?" she asked meekly.

"Of course not. In another set of circumstances, I would be happy to father a child of yours."

In a lonely corner of his soul he had to admit that he spoke the truth. Martha was an obsession, a fantasy, an object, and a love—indeed so much of each that he could not pause to figure out what she meant in the other three roles.

And Irene was merely a wife.

At the last moment of wakefulness he perceived a troubling thought lingering at the outer reaches of his consciousness. He struggled to identify it. Something he had overlooked. Something terribly important. . . .

Brigid

"YOU WEAR ME out, woman," Burke murmured contentedly.

"Good enough for you," Brigid said, cuddling even closer to her husband. The forgetfulness, the oblivion of pleasure, passed quickly. "I wish we were young and could fuck twelve times in a night. I heard one of the young women at work claiming that she and her boyfriend had done it twelve times in one night. Do you think that's possible, Burke?"

He laughed. "Possible but remarkable."

Brigid sighed her familiar west-of-Ireland sigh. "The world comes back too quickly."

Burke was always patient with her fears. "Terrible things have happened, Bridie, but I don't think we did anything we didn't have to do. Even loving each other. . . ."

"A fine argument that will be when you plead our case before Himself," Brigid said, and sniffed.

Burke was not altogether sure there was a Himself before whom he would have to plead. Yet with the passage of time even he was beginning to have doubts about his doubts. "I think I can make a damn persuasive case for both of us. Maybe not enough to prevent a guilty verdict, but with mitigating circumstances and time off for good behavior."

"Ah, I hope so. But I doubt it. I think Himself will throw us out of court, and there's no appeal." There was silence for a time, and then Brigid began again. "I'm afraid of what might come out during Roger's election campaign."

Burke was not quite asleep. "Everything's covered, Bridie. The only one who can hurt us is Tim Nolan, and I don't think he's going to risk interfering with his pensions, especially since we've given him a raise. And besides, no one can touch the killer now.''

"Tim was in from the beginning, wasn't he?''

"That's why the greedy SOB receives two pensions from us, one for each cover-up.'' He tightened his arms around her protectively. "We're perfectly safe, Bridie, in this world, and if there is a next one, I think I can make a case there too.''

Poor Burke thought he understood everything, but she hadn't trusted him with the full story. He would never have revealed it, yet it was safer if only two people knew what actually happened.

"I don't like those questions Noele asked Doctor Keefe. She must suspect that Clancy died later than I told her.''

"It doesn't matter, does it? There's no one left to protect.''

Ah, but there was.

The picture was seared in her brain, never to be erased. She was huddled against the wall in the upstairs hallway. Her dress torn away. Clancy's cane flailing at her. The worst beating ever. He was furious because of the romance between Danny and Irene. He's going to kill me this time, she had thought. It would be a welcome relief. Then the cane was snatched from Clancy's hands and was slashing him across the face.

She saw him stumble back against the railing, lose his footing, and then careen head over heels down the steps, his head bouncing off the post at the foot of the staircase with a sickening thud, blood pouring out on the new carpet.

Then more lies. They never seemed to stop. Lies, lies, lies.

She huddled even closer to Burke, who was now sound asleep.

Roger

ROGER RAN HIS finger along the slim curve of Martha's back, his chest moving rapidly up and down in self-satisfied breathlessness. A smooth back, a slim little ass, trim legs. From the rear she could indeed be boy or girl, and she was enjoyable as both. She luxuriated in any sexual innovation he proposed, justifying it by the ideology of sexual freedom and loving it as a passionately aroused woman. She did not have the proportions of a *Playboy* centerfold, but a *Playboy* fantasy she had become. Yet the more he used her as a fantasy object, the more tender and protective he felt toward her during the sweetness of their afterglow affection.

A little bisexuality never hurt anyone, he told himself, knowing full well that he would be assaulted by enormous guilt on the way back to the neighborhood. Martha was a source of greater pleasure than any of the others. And hence a source of greater guilt. And oddly, greater love.

So it must necessarily be in a universe ruled, if not by justice, at least by a rough proportionality.

His campaign for the governorship was beginning to move. He had decided to announce in early December, just before the meeting of the State Democratic Slate-Making Committee; he had been assured privately that all the powerbrokers would support him and that there would be only token opposition in the March Democratic primary.

Even the mayor had sent an ambiguous message of noninterference. The mayor was not to be trusted and might easily turn against him if she thought there was a possibility he could align himself with her political enemy in the next mayoral campaign. But Mick Gerety had assured her in Roger's name that he would take a hands-off position in Chicago politics. Still, as Mick said, "Assurances are not enough for herself. You would have to deposit a gallon of your blood, your right arm, and possibly certain more intimate organs too. But I think she'll stay out of this one. Hell, a primary battle against one of her people would be good for you."

Roger was about to leave on a whirlwind tour of speaking engagements, many of them in sleepy little Downstate towns or in dull industrial cities whose existence he would have preferred not to consider, and he would have to endure a few days without the delights of Martha.

The talks in Chicago had been successful so far. His audiences were warm and responsive. They laughed at his jokes and cheered enthusiastically for his programs—on the whole, a much better reaction than he could have expected from graduate students at the University.

His faculty colleagues had been remarkably tolerant of his descent into the mess of elective politics. It was an amusing quirk in his behavior, they thought, much like his Roman Catholicism. He was, of course, expected to take a leave of absence from the department. And some of his colleagues were doubtless already murmuring behind his back that this "episode" was proof that he was not, after all, a serious scholar. What else can you expect of a Roman Catholic? some of them would say.

But they would not make such comments too loudly, because by voting him a full professor in the political science department, they had by definition decided that he was a serious scholar.

There were some murmurings of protest from other departments, most notably the Committee on Social Theory, that his political speeches had already lowered the standards of the University—a mortal sin in that community. However, others somewhat more pragmatically argued that the University could well use a friend in Springfield.

He was still meeting with his classes, of course; the classroom was never a time-consuming activity for a full professor. One was expected to discuss one's own work and tell anecdotes in lecture courses and, in seminars, to listen without appearing to be bored to student presentations of research they had done for your monographs. His students, in any event, were delighted to learn something about practical politics in a political science course.

During the month of November, he was waging, along with his own campaign, a vigorous battle for the promotion of Martha Clay, a campaign he had raised to a matter of high principle in public discussion of her. Perhaps she was a marginal case for tenure, but so, by the standards of the present, were half the tenured faculty of his department and most of her male peers who were likely to be promoted.

He had been able to swing three votes at the final meeting of the tenured faculty, two abstentions and one positive vote, so that the vote in her favor was seven to four. The opposition came from a peculiar alliance of Marxists and behaviorists, the former because they thought her perspective was "incorrect" and the latter because they thought, quite properly, that her use of empirical data was abominable.

The letter of transmission to the dean was moderately strong. Thus the dean, one of the great memo-initialing clerks of the century, was not being given a clear signal that the department wanted to be overruled. His dilemma, therefore, would be quite difficult, especially since the "standards"-bearing crusaders of the Committee on Social Theory were already mobilizing their considerable resources against Martha, as they did against anyone reputed to be a threat to "standards." Still, now she at least had a chance, which is more than Roger would have given her a couple of months ago. And that chance exorcised much of his continuing guilt over their affair, an affair which, he had begun to realize, was getting out of hand because of the enormous sweetness of his bisexual fantasies.

He would not, he could not, follow the path of other academics who allowed themselves to be captured by their transient mistresses. Noele, the governorship, Irene—all would be lost. Yet he was, he had to admit, utterly and completely besotted with Martha. She was the first woman since the daydreams of his adolescence to preoccupy him during all his waking hours and invade his dreams at night.

She rolled over on her back and looked up at him with soft eyes and a satisfied smile. "Will you always love me, Roger?"

It was a cheerleader/senior prom question. "I can't imagine ever not loving you," he equivocated. Domesticity rears its ugly head again.

"I'm not talking about marriage," she said. "I dread the thought of ever losing you."

"We both believe in total freedom, don't we?" Roger replied, falling back into his usual line of defense.

He would not, he supposed, tire of her for a long time. On the contrary, the curve of satisfaction was going up rather than down. It might, arguably, be very difficult to give her up. Yet a gubernatorial candidate could hardly afford a scandal; and even though he had paid little attention to Irene recently, she was still his wife.

"Certainly." She propped her head up on her elbow. "I'm not making any claim. We're both totally and absolutely free."

Only they were not, Roger realized. The body makes demands of its own, regardless of ideologies. That's why I feel so tender toward her at this moment that I would give up almost anything to make her happy. Fortunately for me— and for her, too—this moment will pass. Separation will be an agonizing problem for me somewhere down the road.

And the thought of walking down the road tickled a spot in the back of his mind, which reminded him intermittently that he had forgotten something terribly important, something potentially very dangerous. What was it?

Noele

IT WAS A really excellent pep rally, Noele told Jaimie Burns, using the favorite superlative of her generation.

Jaimie shrugged indifferently. He was totally unjazzed about football before and after the game. Pep rallies and victory dances were bummers. Only the crunching tackle of a halfback, a ball snatched out of the hands of an unwary wide receiver at the last moment, or best of all, a lazy, spiraling punt arriving in his arm at about the same time tacklers headed for his legs could stir him.

Jaimie had earned a new nickname, which Noele thought was horrid and of which he was inordinately proud, even though Noele insisted that the reporter had mixed his metaphors.

With the unpredictable grace and dazzling speed of a fire racing across the bogs of Ireland, the Fighting Irish's Freshman Free Safety, Jim Burns, raced across the turf here at the Meadowlands this afternoon, said the newspaper story, *sinking the Navy's chances of obtaining a rare victory against their traditional foes from South Bend. Wherever the Middies threw the football, there was Jim Burns, blocking, tackling, and picking off passes, four of them to be exact, not only matching the Notre Dame record, but depriving the Navy of two almost certain T.D's. Asked by someone after final obsequies for the Navy whether his interceptions were "Hail Mary" catches, Burns, the son of a congressman from Chicago, replied with a typically laconic comment, "As my girl friend would say, The Mother of Jesus is on the side of those who practice the longest."*

"I never said it," Noele protested.

"You would have if you'd been there."

"What does *laconic* mean?"

"Totally cas."

So Jaimie was a hero and was now Bogfire Burns and had to stand on the platform during the pep rally.

Noele did not have the heart to tell him that Brigid said bog fires traveled very slowly, "Like molasses in January, child."

After the pep rally they went for a long walk along the shore of the tiny moonlit lake in the center of the Notre Dame campus. She was spending the night before tomorrow's season finale against the Trojans of Southern Cal with friends in one of the women's dorms.

Jaimie recounted, with precise detail, his conversation with his grandfather.

"Why would William Farrell leave his company and all his money to Clancy when he knew that he was such a terrible space cadet?" she asked after Jaimie had described the reputation of the Farrell twins and the rumors of dishonesty and incompetence in the firm's construction of defense plants. "Wouldn't Martin be the one to take over the company when he came back from the war?"

"Granddad said that Martin wasn't especially interested in business. And besides, he was William's favorite son and Clancy was Blanche's, and Blanche always had her way. There were rumors that Bill Farrell was so angry about the government investigation back in 1943 that he was going to change the will, but apparently he never did."

"Hmm. . . . Well, I guess it didn't matter. Martin died, and Clancy would have inherited anyway."

Jaimie thought for a moment. "Not necessarily. Martin was killed in action after his father's death. If the will had been changed . . . let me see . . . yeah, Martin's son would have inherited everything."

"A little boy?"

"That doesn't matter."

"Like, wow! Now we have two motives, one for which he might have killed and another for which he might have been killed."

"No, you don't," he argued. "You have one gratuitous speculation about a will no one says ever existed."

"What's *gratuitous* mean? Oh, never mind. Has your father said anything about the CIA?"

"It means 'way out,' and Dad hasn't said a thing."

"What if he's alive?" Noele said soberly.

"What if he is? And what if he comes back and kills someone else?"

"He'd never do that!" Noele said, flaring instantly. "Anyway, if he's still alive, I'll get him out of China. I suppose you don't think I can do that?"

"I think you can do anything you want to," Jaimie said fervently. "That's why you totally overwhelm me."

So Noele kissed him, which under the circumstances was the only thing to do. Noele noted to herself once again that, like her mother, she was a very sensuous person. More sensuous maybe than Jaimie, who was nonetheless a very good kisser.

Then something melted inside of Noele. She felt herself dissolving into a unity with Jaimie. They were now one person—Noele/Jaimie—and that person was caught in an incandescent electrical current.

She was losing herself to him. And she wanted to.

"Hold me tight, Jaimie . . ." she pleaded.

He did. As if she were a Trojan tight end he was trying to tackle.

". . . forever."

Jaimie laughed, but he hung on.

"I'm afraid, so afraid." The words tumbled out before she knew what they were.

She was fighting to keep away the loneliness that was suddenly all around her, blotting out the lake and the moonlight and the campus and even Jaimie.

"I'll take care of you, Noele, no matter what."

If he wants me this minute, he can have me. . . .

Jaimie ended the embrace, as he usually did. "So you're going to try to interview Captain Nolan?" he asked.

"You know me too well," Noele protested.

He patted her rump with about the same degree of affection he had patted the strong side safety when that young man had blitzed an opposing quarterback. "For sure."

John

THE PARISH COUNCIL was debating whether the lunches and dinners served to members of the parish staff who happened to be in the rectory at mealtime ought to be considered part of their salary and subject to withholding tax. The discussion had deteriorated into an alley fight between Geraldine Leopold, a member of the parish council who worked for the IRS, and Martina O'Rourke, a former nun who was director of the religious education program for students attending non-Catholic schools.

It was the kind of personality fight masquerading as an intellectual argument that made John wonder whether democracy in the church was a good thing. Eddie O'Reilly, a razor-sharp young lawyer, had already provided a solution to the problem. Such meals were professional meetings of the parish staff and could not properly be considered part of their recompense. He was sure if the matter arose—and that was most unlikely—that the IRS would agree. Nonetheless the two angry and frustrated middle-aged women had to be permitted to fight it out to the end, one complaining about "clerical discounts" and the other protesting the "oppression of our capitalist economy." In due course someone would demand the question, and there would be a vote overwhelmingly in favor of O'Reilly's solution. But no one was yet ready to brave the wrath of women by demanding the question.

John had little patience for the debate. He had been denounced in the TV section of the Chicago *Star Herald* that morning, and the phone had been ringing all day with calls from clergymen who, under the pretense of seeking information from him but with every intention of gloating over his plight, asked: "Did you see what the *Star Herald* had to say about you?"

Larry Rieves, the TV columnist, wrote all his columns from a perspective of high moral outrage, a perspective that enabled him to say that a program was popular though its ratings were low, and unpopular though its ratings were high, and then a few weeks later come back and celebrate the accuracy of his self-fulfilling prophecy.

In his latest attack, that morning, Rieves had congratulated himself on the waning popularity of *The Monsignor Farrell Show.* Viewers, he said, were growing tired, just as he had predicted, of Farrell's shallow posturing. Moreover, they were skeptical about whether a priest whose brother was running for governor ought to continue to have access to prime-time television. Finally, many of the Catholics of Chicago, influenced by the insightful criticism of their clergy, were being turned off by Monsignor Farrell, and hence were turning him off.

Much of the remaining two-thirds of the column was devoted to comments from an anonymous but "influential" Chicago priest. John Farrell was "on an ego trip"; he was "hungry for publicity." Everyone knew that he was "just interested in promoting himself and making money" and that he was "neglecting his parish in order to devote his attention to the program."

Monsignor Mortimer, of course.

It was also asserted that John Farrell didn't really care anymore about the people of his parish. He was, in fact, thinking of leaving the priesthood, and had been offered a position as a host of a major New York talk show. (Inconsistent with declining popularity, it would seem, but Rieves was never bothered by consistency.)

Finally, Rieves reported that a committee of St. Praxides parishioners were planning to submit a formal request that Monsignor Farrell choose between the parish and his television program. "We have a good parish here," Rieves wrote, quoting an anonymous member of the community. "Racial integration is working fine. We don't need to have it spoiled by a controversial pastor."

John was numb after he read the column, and then frightened. In the midst of the gloating calls from other priests, there were a few phone calls from anxious parishioners wondering what was going on. And to make matters worse, virtually every member of the parish council, as they came into the rectory for the meeting, asked whether he "saw the job that Rieves did on you this morning."

He did not want to be "controversial." Once that word was applied to a priest, he was finished with his fellow priests and his parishioners. John had been able to survive the trauma of the day only because Irene was the first one on the phone. She told him briskly that his only answer ought to be that his ratings had gone up, not down, and that everything else in the Rieves column was just as untrue as what he had said about the ratings.

It turned out to be a very effective answer, but John realized for the first time in his life that the press could lie about him with impunity. And his clerical adversaries had probably put Rieves up to it. Your enemies might persuade the media to attack your reputation and you would not be able to defend yourself. The media could stamp you with an image totally at odds with what you really were, and you would be stuck with that image for the rest of your life.

He desperately wanted to talk to Irene again, confident that his adolescent lustful fantasies had been wiped out by genuine respect and friendship. A conversation with her over a drink—no, not a drink, she was drinking too much these days—over a cup of coffee after the parish council meeting would relax him and help him to sleep.

He signaled Eddie O'Reilly somewhat impatiently with his eyes, and the young man caught his instruction and moved the question.

John ignored the wrathful looks of Geraldine Leopold and Martina O'Rourke. Would that they were the only ones he had to fear.

·····*D.C.I.*·····

RADFORD WAS IN his office early on the Monday morning after the Thanksgiving weekend, something less than his usual confident self.

"It's bad, chief," he said, using an adjective the Director had never heard before on his lips.

"You'd better tell me the whole thing."

Radford considered the brown Virginia fields outside the windows of the Director's spacious office and then turned and sat in the chair in front of his vast desk. "It was a termination, the sort of thing we used to call termination with extreme prejudice."

"We executed Daniel Farrell?"

"The mechanics, the medics, and the technicians all knew that he was a condemned man, every bit as much as the prison staff does when someone is being electrocuted. His fuel supply was half of what it should have been, the ejection mechanism was fixed so it wouldn't work, all the top-secret material had been taken off the plane, the explosive that would destroy the aircraft was rigged to respond to the ejection trigger. If Farrell tried to eject, the aircraft should have exploded."

"Only it didn't." The Director felt a disturbing sensation in the pit of his stomach.

"Apparently not, if the photographs we have of the wreckage are authentic. Our people tell me they certainly appear to be."

"Why was he terminated? Who ordered it? My predecessor of happy memory?"

"No one ordered it," Radford snapped. "No one here had anything against Farrell. He was a superb pilot, apparently quite trustworthy. The mission security chief claimed to have instructions from us. Indeed, he showed the mission director all the required documentation. It was murder, chief, pure and simple. Cleverly faked orders for termination on the grounds that Farrell was selling secrets to the Soviet Resident in Tokyo."

"And then?"

"Nothing for a year and a half. Then the mission security chief retired early and moved to Mexico with a very large sum of money. One of the technicians on the team—which was disbanded shortly after the crash—smelled a rat and went to the inspector general. There was an investigation."

"And the highest authorities in the Company decided to do nothing about it," said the Director, knowing all too well what was likely to have happened in his office in the late sixties and early seventies.

"That's right. And the last thing we wanted here was some poor old missionary suggesting that Farrell was still alive."

"What a mess. We would be in deep trouble if this story were ever leaked."

Radford spread his massive hands in a gesture of frustration and impotence. "There's worse, chief. Farrell was still alive when the Chinese were releasing all of our prisoners ten years ago. They asked us if we wanted him back, and we told them no."

"In God's name, why?" the Director exploded.

"The members of the team that made the decision are gone now, chief, but I imagine you can guess why. Farrell must have known his plane has been sabotaged. The Company didn't want a U-2 pilot returning after an attempt to terminate him. Much less did we want anyone to open a can of worms about a mission security chief who might be guilty of attempted murder."

"And the mission chief is dead now?" the Director asked, drumming his fingers nervously on his massive oak desk.

"How did you know that?" Radford grinned crookedly. "Natural causes, as far as I know; and incidentally, there is considerable evidence of suspicious links in his past. In fact, he seems to have been one of the unofficial channels of communication the Company used to maintain those links."

"One of those Mafia types that Donovan brought in during the war with the assistance of his friends Cardinal Spellman and Frankie Costello?"

Radford nodded.

"Will we ever get that monkey off our back?" the D.C.I. snapped irritably.

Radford did not comment. Much of his job consisted in taming monkeys out of the past who would not get off the Company's back.

The Director considered the problem carefully. "So the Central Intelligence Agency, acting through its duly appointed and approved mission security chief, carried out a hit contract—for reasons, I suppose, we don't know and can no longer learn?"

"Precisely," Radford agreed somberly.

"And like a lot of our other dirty tricks in those years, we buried it along with Farrell?"

"Exactly."

"Are you sure it's completely buried?"

Radford shrugged imperceptibly. "It would be awfully hard for anyone here to dig it up without your authority. I suppose the syndicate go-betweens know, and whoever ordered the hit, but they're not likely to talk about it."

"Is Farrell still alive?"

"Probably not."

"Probably won't do."

Radford nodded.

Of course it wouldn't do. If Daniel Xavier Farrell were still alive, he might appear at any time, released in some unfathomable Chinese gesture. You could never be quite sure what the Chinese would do. And the longer he was in prison before he was released, the greater the media outrage when he finally did surface.

Radford stirred in his chair. "There's a cocktail party later on this week where I'll bump into the Chinese Resident. We'll exchange information politely and indirectly. Do you want me to ask about Farrell?"

"Is the Resident likely to understand at this point we're only looking for information?"

"Those people"—Radford shrugged—"make the Japanese look transparent. It's anybody's guess, chief."

"You think we ought to leave well enough alone?"

Radford was his old familiar cold-eyed self. "The Company has left well enough alone on the Farrell case for the last sixteen years and got away with it."

"I know," sighed the Director.

Radford waited silently for his chief's decision. The D.C.I. searched for a few words from the ethics class he had attended in a small liberal arts college many years before.

"Talk to the Resident," he said.

Irene

NOELE AND HER mother had a furious fight. Irene became edgy every December. The grayness of winter depressed her. Dresses were replaced by thick skirts or slacks and sweaters, which made men stare at her even more intently. The responsibilities of Christmas shopping, Christmas card lists, and the annual Christmas party that Roger insisted they give for their friends weighed heavily upon her. She told herself that a woman with no job and help in her home every day of the week should be able to cope with the holiday season.

However, her ability to cope diminished with each passing day. She had read an article in the life-style section of the paper the previous year about people who become depressed at Christmastime. It had seemed like a perfect description of herself.

Roger was busy in the campaign, so busy that he hardly seemed aware of her existence, even in bed at night. And Noele was going through a particularly difficult adolescent phase. She snapped Irene's head off every time her mother asked where she was going, where she had been, or why she had been out so late.

"I'm sure that I'm old enough to take care of myself," Noele had ranted after having been mildly castigated for coming home late on a Sunday evening after the last football weekend with Jaimie at Notre Dame. "And I'm sure nobody was asking you those kind of questions when you were my age."

"I'm sure" was a new teenage expression indicating ironic anger. It was also an absolutely certain sign Noele was in one of her bitchy moods. Irene had no idea what was bugging the child. And she did not know how to begin to try to find out.

The battle on this cold Saturday morning in early December as snow flurries pirouetted on Jefferson Avenue was about the condition of Noele's room, a subject about which they engaged in listless combat at least once a week.

Irene had threatened that there would be no Christmas dances or Christmas dates for Noele if she didn't put her room in order. "I simply won't let people come into this house for Daddy's Christmas party and run the risk of their seeing that we have a pigsty on the second floor.''

"I'm sure they'll go up there just to look for my pigsty," Noele fired back.

"Whether they look for it or not, young woman, you're going to clean up your room, and you're going to do it now. I'm really very angry at you.''

"Don't say you're angry," Noele snapped back. "Say you're disappointed in me.''

"I am *not* disappointed. I'm angry," Irene shouted. "What's more, you better shape up and act like a presentable young woman. Your father is going to be running for governor, and he can't have a dork for a daughter." I try to reprimand her, Irene thought, and I use her own ridiculous slang.

"He has a dork for a wife. Why not a dork daughter, too?''

She wanted to hit the little brat.

"You will not go to the Christmas dance, and that's final!''

"I want Roger to be governor." Noele seemed inclined to negotiate, as she often was after an outburst. "But I'm sure a neat room won't elect him.''

"I'll be the judge of that," Irene said, furious at her own impotence.

"And I'm sure you're tough enough to prevent me from going to the Christmas dance, even if I don't clean it up," Noele responded.

"You just try me and find out," Irene shouted furiously.

She knew that if she did work up enough nerve to ban Christmas activities for Noele, Roger would overrule her.

"You're a terrible disciplinarian, Moms," Noele said contemptuously. "You can't make anything stick. I'm sure Roger will let me go to the Christmas dance, particularly the Notre Dame Club of Chicago dance, no matter what you say.''

The child was perfectly right. "Noele Marie Brigid Farrell," Irene ordered, the full name a sign of her anger. "You go to your room this instant. If you act like a nine-year-old, I will treat you like a nine-year-old. This *instant!*''

Surprisingly enough, Noele obeyed, slamming up the stairs like an outraged company of infantry. Irene soon heard the noise of furious movement from her daughter's room. Using all three of her names still worked, Irene mused. I don't quite know why. Maybe it's a signal that I'm still bigger than she is and the time for her to fight back has been temporarily terminated.

Maybe I would have been better off if I'd fought back that way when I was her age.

The door bell rang. John Farrell with new troubles. Irene straightened her dress, fluffed up her hair, inspected her face carefully in the large mirror in the hallway, and opened the door. She kissed John lightly as she admitted him to the house. Externally it was the same sisterly kiss that they had exchanged many times before, but both of them knew it was an expression of affection that was taking on deeper and more dangerous meaning. Irene was thrilled and stimulated by the danger.

"Too early for a drink?" she asked as she ushered John into the parlor.

He hesitated, and then said, "I guess I could do with one, even if it's only eleven thirty.''

John was pale and thin. She wondered how much weight he had lost since the persecution had begun. "Confusion to our enemies," she said, toasting him with what she hoped was something of a crooked grin. Then she sat on the chair next to the couch where he was sitting. Noele was in the house, and they ought not to be too close.

"Their numbers grow," John said. "I suppose this is significant." He gave her a four-color advertising brochure announcing an archdiocesan workshop on communication—two days of seminars, lectures, and discussion of the role of the mass media in the ministry of the church.

Irene glanced over the program and its lists of participants—the director of Vatican Radio and the head of the Papal Office of Social Communication; an anchorman from Washington; a film director from Hollywood, of whom she had never heard, with a long string of film credits; Monsignor Mortimer, director of the Catholic Television Channel; and a number of "Archdiocesan media specialists."

"Someone's missing," she said ruefully.

"I ought not to be surprised." John's eyes were sad, and his face was lined and gaunt, looking the way Irene imagined an ex-convict's would. "I was invited to some of the preparatory meetings last spring, and then didn't hear a word about the project. I figured it had been dropped."

"Is it important to you, John?" She tried to sound warm and sympathetic.

"I suppose it ought not to be." He spread his hands out in a motion of dejection. "The church and the archdiocese have been my life since I first went to the seminary almost thirty years ago. Everything I've done has been directed to the service of the archdiocese. I didn't want to take the damn TV office. The cardinal had to insist. Every priest I know pleaded with me to take the talk show. And now they all think I'm on an ego trip and have begun to pretend I don't exist. . . . I simply don't understand it."

"Envy," Irene said bluntly.

My poor dear, she thought. Your vanity is injured. But vanity is a vice that hurts no one. Envy hurts everyone.

John looked up from his folded hands. "Is that it, Irene? Is it really envy? Or am I really on an ego trip? Sometimes I'm not sure myself. God knows, I don't want to be controversial."

"Don't be ridiculous. Of course you're not on an ego trip. And how can you accomplish anything worthwhile without being controversial?"

Maybe someday I'll tell him the whole truth about himself, but he's not ready for that yet.

"And it keeps up. Read this column by Parson Rails."

Irene had never paid much attention to the *Star Herald*'s religion column, which appeared every Saturday. She could not remember having heard of Parson Rails.

TV PRIESTS WOULD NOT HAVE BEEN ACCEPTED IN THE OLD DAYS DOWNSTATE, the headline read.

Irene glanced through the article. "This is silly, John. Who cares whether the parish priest in the town where he grew up was popular with everyone, even this columnist's Protestant mother, because he fried the chicken himself at the annual chicken roast on Labor Day weekends?"

"Parson Rails is good at nostalgia . . . old-time religion."

"But this is the age of television, and we don't live in small towns Downstate. Parson Rails is as bad as that little toad who does book reviews for the *Star Herald*. What's his name?"

John seemed surprised that she read book reviews. "Manny Sizer? Some people think he's the most mean-spirited, petty, envious critic in America."

"And when he tries to destroy a book, it is a sure sign that it will be an enormous success in Chicago. Why take such vile creatures seriously?"

"I know it's just one more sign of the pressure building up against me. And it's finally got to the parish. You know the Arthur Kellys? They have a different priest at their house once a week for dinner. Well, they've apparently formed a committee of parishioners to request that I either give up the program or resign as pastor." His hands were trembling as he put the brochure for the television workshop and the newspaper clipping back into his coat pocket.

Do you want the cheers of your audience or the support of your people? How unfair it is, poor, simple, innocent man, that you can't have both. Why don't you have an ego implanted in a concrete silo like your brother?

Or like your goddamned cousin Danny?

"You shouldn't pay any attention to them, John. I'm sure they couldn't gather twenty votes against you in the parish."

"I think they could probably get a lot more. Every parish has malcontents, and once they begin to organize, they can make a lot of noise—just as Rieves has been saying in his column."

"John, there will be one hundred parishioners in support of you for every one against you. They can organize too, you know. Eddie O'Reilly would love a good fight."

"I wonder. . . ."

Noele bounced down the stairs dressed in brown corduroy knickers and brown stockings and a light brown shirt with fluffy ruffles. Over an arm was draped the matching corduroy jacket.

"Hi, Uncle Monsignor. Larry Rieves is a creep. And if anybody tries to organize a committee against you, I'll have the High Club picket their homes."

Irene and John laughed spontaneously, both wondering how she knew what they were talking about.

Noele grinned. "It will be really excellent. I'm sure we'll show those yuk-heads who run this parish."

"Mary Noele Brigid Farrell, of course," John said.

"I have an appointment with Father/Captain/Doctor Ace, Mother. I'll finish my room with I come back." Noele hesitated, as if asking for permission.

"Father McNamara merits dress-up clothes and your uncle doesn't?"

"Really, Mo-*ther,* Uncle Monsignor is a relative, and Father/Captain/Doctor Ace isn't."

"Well, you look very pretty, Noele." Her mother gave in. "But I still want that room cleaned."

"As soon as I get back. This is a really important problem I have to solve."

"Thank you for cleaning it," she said.

Noele stopped in midflight and turned to consider her mother carefully. The little computer under her red hair was whirling.

"Anytime, Moms." She threw up her hands in a gesture of mock majesty, like a precinct captain who had done someone a great favor.

From an obnoxious little bitch, to my sweet Christmas child in a few moments, Irene thought. How I wish I were like her.

Noele ran out of the house and into the street, having apparently decided that snow flurries or not, she would walk to the rectory. Of course, she had to show off her new brown corduroy suit.

"Come over to the window, John, and watch her," Irene said.

As Noele moved down the street, trenchcoat open so as to display her new clothes, hands jauntily stuffed into the pockets, an entourage of dogs assembled to follow her. First a languid Irish setter, then a disheartened bloodhound, a happy-go-lucky black Labrador, and finally a yapping schnauzer.

"In order of their appearance, John, the dogs are Melissa, Poindexter, Sebastian, and Heather. She'll probably collect five or six more before she gets to the rectory. Every time the child walks down the street, she's followed by all the dogs and the little children in the neighborhood. See, there's the McCarthy girl, and Josie Holloway's little boy will be right behind her. My Christmas child attracts, among other things, dogs and little children."

"Has she finished the term paper?" John turned away from the street and looked at Irene.

"I think so. She doesn't talk about it anymore. But you never know with that child."

They returned to their pre-luncheon martinis, but this time Irene sat closer to John on the couch, just far enough away so that their knees were not touching.

"Will we ever be able to tell her the truth?" Irene asked sadly.

"I don't see how we can, Irene. Not ever." The lines on John's face seemed to deepen, and his eyes turn hard and distant. "I'm sure it would tear her apart."

"Yet sometimes I wonder if she doesn't already know, deep down inside. Maybe she's already listened in to our thoughts about that terrible day when we . . . when we found her."

"I hope to God she hasn't," John prayed fervently.

They were both silent for a moment, as if on a private visit to the Blessed Sacrament in an empty church.

"You're going to challenge the Kellys head on, aren't you?" she asked, breaking the silence between them. "And do you really want Noele to throw a picket line around their house?"

"No, I won't do that," John said briskly. "But I'm going to ask Eddie O'Reilly to propose a resolution at a special meeting of the parish council, a resolution supporting me and recommending a parishwide petition. That will silence the Kellys in a hurry."

"That's a real Farrell!" Irene hugged him impetuously. He embraced her in return. And then, as if he were terribly weary, he rested his head momentarily on her shoulder.

A delightfully powerless languor crept into Irene's body. She had never committed adultery before. Only two men had ever possessed her. This man could be the third. He needed her. He probably had to have her. And she wanted him.

John Farrell lifted his head as if to pull away from her, but she put her hand on the back of his neck and held his face against her breasts a few moments longer. "Don't worry, John. It's all right. Nothing bad is going to happen."

He sighed softly, as if he would be content to remain in her embrace for the rest of his life.

It all depends, Irene thought to herself, what I mean by *bad*.

Noele

"LIKE MURPHY'S HOBIE Cat the summer before last?"

Noele's face felt very warm. "I was a tomboy then," she said, trying to defend herself.

She and Eileen Kelly had got themselves into a real lot of trouble by kind of borrowing the Murphys' brand-new beach boat and drifting several miles down the shore.

"You're not a tomboy anymore?" Father Ace's eyes were dancing now.

"Only privately," Noele answered and sniffed.

Father Ace laughed the way he always did, joyously enough to make the rectory windowpanes shake. "Come on, M.N.," he said, "what makes you so certain that your grandfather was killed?"

"I know he was. I just absolutely know he was."

"And Danny Farrell killed him?"

"Stop sounding like a district attorney. You're supposed to be the sympathetic counselor." Noele sighed in distress. "No, Father, I don't think so. But he might have . . . Anyway, what did he and Gramps fight about all the time?"

Father McNamara pushed his hands into his Marine Corps fatigue trousers, his standard uniform for when he was talking to teenagers.

"I can't remember that they fought, to tell you the truth. Of course, a lot of things go on in the Neighborhood that we don't hear about in the rectory. And Danny was a comedian, not a fighter. . . ."

"Was it about the firm?"

"Stop peeking in my head." Father Ace was accustomed to Noele's apparent ability to read other people's thoughts. "There *was* a nasty rumor in the parish, amond the old-timers, that Clancy had cheated his brother out of the control of the firm. It doesn't make much sense, though. Martin was killed in the war. Danny might have thought the firm was his by right."

"Wouldn't Brigid have given him the money if he'd asked?"

Father Ace dismissed the dim recollections of the past. "I'm sorry I ever brought it up, Noele. Of course she would have. He would have had no motive at all."

"Except maybe to get even."

"Get even for what?"

"Oh, I don't know, Father. I just know I have to find out."

"Still the Jane Marple of Beverly?"

"Cordelia Gray," Noele said indignantly.

"And you're not going to leave the family skeletons alone until you rattle them all? Even if they fall on you?"

"I guess not," she said slowly. "I have to. I don't know why I have to. . . . It's, like, I'm nobody until I find out."

She could not quite tell him about the horrible feeling of loneliness. He would have wanted to send her to a shrink.

"What happened when you tried to turn the Murphys' boat around?"

"We discovered we couldn't drift back in the direction we came."

"Yeah," said Father Ace.

······················*D.C.I.*·····················

"YOU SAW THE Chinese Resident last night?"

"He was very charming. They're quite charming these days, you know."

"So I gathered," said the Director dryly. "He knew about the Farrell case?"

"If he didn't, he pretended to." A faint frown blemished Radford's handsome face. "Bobbed his head up and down like a marionette and repeated six or seven times, 'Understand, understand,' and didn't lose his painted-on smile."

"A language barrier?" asked the chief.

"He was three years ahead of me at Harvard. He speaks English perfectly."

"So he understands that we're simply making discreet inquiries about the facts of the Farrell situation?"

"I didn't say that, chief." Radford rubbed the arm of his leather chair. "I have no idea whether he's ever heard of Farrell. But I don't think they're going to do anything hasty to embarrass us."

"And how did you leave it at the end of the conversation?"

"He said they would take care of everything."

"That sounds ominous, doesn't it?"

"Not necessarily. At any rate, the Resident said we have nothing to worry about."

The Director had other problems that morning. There were some very strange troop movements going on in southern Africa. Daniel Farrell was only a minor responsibility.

"So we have nothing to worry about? I wonder if Farrell ought to be worrying if he is still alive."

Roger

ON THE WAY home from O'Hare he was finally able to place the gnawing sensation of having overlooked something important.

Maybe he had not locked either his portable safe or his personal file cabinet.

That would have been childishly irresponsible.

He had been in so great a hurry to blot out the memories of the past with the delights of the present. Martha would make him forget Florence Carey.

He smiled to himself, a self-mocking, contemptuous smile. A Freudian would have said that he had done it deliberately to run the risk of exposing the family past so he would not have to run for governor.

He told the cab driver to head for the University instead of the Neighborhood.

Certainly he had locked both the safe and the file.

He had a lecture to the Knights of Columbus Council in the western suburbs that night. Roger hesitated. It could wait till tomorrow.

Nonetheless, it was time to eliminate that nagging peripheral worry definitively.

At the University he told the cabby to wait, and ran across the street to the government department building, leaning into the chilly December west wind.

Mrs. Marshfield was on the telephone when he walked into the outer office. She was always on the telephone. She did not bother to look up or even to acknowledge his presence. One thing he had to say about Mrs. Marshfield: She didn't do any less work in his absence than she did in his presence.

Casually he looked for the key to his personal filing cabinet, opened it, and removed the portable safe.

He had not spun the combination lock.

With trembling fingers, he flipped the top of the lid and thumbed through the files.

The *Farrell, Florence Carey* file was missing. There had to be some mistake. He went through the files again. He found it at the bottom of the filing cabinet drawer, underneath his old tax returns. But he had not put it there. It had been taken out of the safe and then returned to the cabinet drawer.

With quivering fingers he opened the folder. The materials were out of order. His memo was at the end of the clippings, not at the beginning. Someone had been reading them.

"Mrs. Marshfield," he said, his voice quivering. "Has anybody been in this file cabinet?"

"I am on the telephone," she replied haughtily.

Roger leaped across the room, grabbed the telephone out of her hands, and slammed down the receiver. "I don't give a goddamn what you're doing. Answer my question. Has anyone been in my personal filing cabinet?"

"Of course they have," she said, now a wounded martyr. "That boy from the magazine. You told me to cooperate with him. I made copies for him."

"He was to see my manuscripts; I didn't tell you to permit him in my confidential papers!"

"You didn't tell me to keep him out, did you?"

DANCE FIVE

Allemande

*"It is a more heavie daunce than the galliard, fitlie representing
the nature of the people whose name it carieth so that no extraordinary motions are used in the dancing of it."*

*"A Plaine and Easie Introduction to
Practicall Musicke"*
T. MORLEY

Irene

SHE SHOULD NOT have come to the rectory for the meeting of the Spring Luncheon Committee of the Women's Altar Guild. John Farrell was certain to be
there, and he was becoming a delightful obsession. But how could she avoid the
meeting, she asked herself piously. She was the chairman of the committee
because in a weak moment she had acceded to the request of Mrs. Riordan, the
perennial president of the W.A.G., to chair this year's "event."

Spring luncheons were always the same, a search by newly middle-class Irish
housewives for upper-middle-class respectability, a clumsy imitation of the spring
luncheons of Protestant church groups. Even though the Irish in the Neighborhood had long since caught up economically, the older women, like Mrs. Riordan,
were unaware of that fact. They were also unaware that the Protestants were
abandoning spring luncheons, replacing them with matinee concerts at Orchestra
Hall. Mrs. Riordan didn't know that there was an Orchestra Hall, or indeed what
an orchestra hall was.

So there would be a badly prepared meal and a dull fashion show at some
expensive downtown hotel, the Drake or the Ritz-Carlton (the latter if the more
progressive group within the guild won the annual debate about a site for the
"event"), and the women of the parish—such as bothered to come—would
drink too much, flirt with the clergy, and weave their tipsy way home in the early
stages of the rush hour. It was astonishing that none of them had piled up the
family Cadillac after a spring luncheon.

Guardian angels working overtime.

"How do you stand it, John?" Irene asked.

She and John were in the knotty-pine meeting room in the rectory basement, finalizing the plans for the major event of the W.A.G. year. It was customary for the pastor and the chairman to make the final decisions after the women of the committee had consumed most of the pastor's afternoon with foolish and occasionally angry suggestions.

"The argument used to be that these things brought in four or five thousand dollars that we wouldn't get any other way." John leaned back in his chair, strong and handsome—a Roger with broader shoulders and more masculinity. "Now we do it because we've always done it and because old dears like Mrs. Riordan would probably lose their faith if we stopped doing it."

"A High Club for matrons?"

"Something like that." John pushed himself out of his chair. "Goes with the territory. Every Catholic parish has to have one. Come upstairs and have a drink with me. We can't let the afternoon be a complete waste."

Irene knew she should hesitate and then decline. "Wonderful idea!" she said.

All she wanted from John, she had told herself repeatedly, was affection and friendship. The reaction of her body to his presence, the sad eyes, the unruly lock of hair falling over his pale face, the intense line of his mouth, was not to be taken seriously. He was her brother-in-law and a priest, a pompous and stuffy man who had never treated her as anything more than a beautiful object.

Yet, standing now in the pastor's suite in St. Paxides rectory—the holy priest's house of her childhood—she wanted to be naked for him in front of all those popes and cardinals on the wall. Ridiculous horny bitch.

"Any more harassment from the clergy?" she asked as John was preparing the drinks.

"An anonymous letter this time," he called from the other room. "Mailed to every priest in the diocese."

Irene walked into the wet bar, where John was putting the final touches on a large pitcher of martinis. The thrill of their physical closeness triggered with astonishing speed powerful reactions in her body. She bit her lip, trying to assert control of mind over flesh.

"What did it say?"

"I tore it up. I could have sued him if it had been signed. He charged that I was using parish money to pay the expenses of the program and then taking a salary from the program. Also said I was 'carrying on' with the associate producer."

"My God," exclaimed Irene. "What do you do with the money, John?"

"I contribute it to the parish. I don't have to, of course, but the Farrells have more than enough money. Damn fool clergy don't realize how a television station works."

He poured a quarter of the contents of the martini pitcher over the ice in a tumbler marked with the initials J.W.F.

"Are you going to reply?"

"Damned if I do and damned if I don't. If I reply, my priestly brothers will say that because I'm taking the charge seriously, there must be a little bit of fire with all that smoke. And if I don't reply, they'll say the charges have to be true; otherwise I would have replied."

He filled a second glass and, giving her the first one, toasted her silently.

"What are you going to do?"

"I'm going to reply. But I'm not going to tell them either what my salary is on the program—it's only two hundred a week for twenty-six weeks—nor am I going to tell them that I give it to the parish. Jesus did say that the left hand should not know what the right hand is doing.''

"Oh, John," she murmured softly.

She knew as she said it that the tone of sympathy in her voice was provocative for both of them. And she didn't care. He was her brother-in-law, a priest, a man she had often despised, and they were in the pastor's suite in a rectory, but none of that mattered.

They walked back to his parlor in silence and sat next to each other on one of his absurd leather couches. Ecclesiastical pomposity!

She should be on the other side of the room, as far away from him as possible. In a desperate attempt to break the dangerous emotions that had oozed into the room, she changed the subject. "You know about Noele's visit to Doctor Keefe?''

John's face, which had been momentarily soft and childlike as it basked in the warmth of her sympathy, quickly hardened. "Yes, indeed. Brigid called me as soon as she heard from the doctor. My God, Irene, can't you contain the child?''

"You and your brother and your mother have spoiled her rotten all her life, and you expect me to contain her?'' she replied hotly.

John smiled sheepishly. "I'm sorry, Irene."

"You should be sorry. I order her to stop, but she won't obey me because she has always been able to appeal to her father when I give her a command. Roger reasons with her in his ponderous professorial way. She nods solemnly, collects Jaimie Burns, and does what she damn well pleases.''

"We have to stop her." John spread his hands as though in a plea. "Everyone would be hurt.''

"That's all I've heard for weeks," Irene said impatiently. "But no one will tell me why. Or are you trying to hide some family secret that I don't know?''

"You know one secret, isn't that enough?'' John's voice was cruel momentarily, and then it turned gentle again. "Take my word for it, Irene; you're better off not knowing. The Farrells could all be in danger.''

"Most of all my poor Christmas child.''

"All the more reason to stop her.''

Irene nodded sadly. At least she had dissipated the sexual tension between the two of them.

"She thinks Danny is still alive.''

"What?''

Instead of the anger she would have expected, John seemed sad, as though he too wished that Danny were still alive. *After all these years all of us still love him.*

"How do you know she does? Has she told you?''

"No, but I can tell. I *am* her mother, you know.''

"Indeed, I do," he said with some irony.

"She has his old Annapolis graduation picture in a brand new silver frame hanging above her bed, almost as if he were the Sacred Heart. . . .''

"That's spooky, Irene.''

"I know it's spooky. Do you think . . . he might be alive?'' she asked hesitantly, for the first time admitting to herself that the question might be asked.

"Of course not." He waved his hand brusquely.

"But . . . ?''

"But if he were," John said solemnly, "we'd all be in very deep trouble, wouldn't we?"

No one more than I, Irene thought sadly.

Roger

THE OFFICE OF the president of the Catholic college at which Joe Kramer was a student seemed ill-suited to his enormous physical energy, an energy that in Roger's cynical opinion he had increasingly substituted in the last few years for doing his homework. The high ceilings, blue walls, cluttered desk, cramped space and photographs of the president with ecclesiastical and political dignitaries all suggested a more leisurely era when he had not been an international celebrity, characterized by some of his enemies as the Vicar of Bray because of his ability to make friends with every chief executive of the republic for the last two decades.

"We do not tolerate that sort of thing here," said the president decisively.

"I'm glad to hear it," Roger said. "However, Father, I must point out the young man was working on an assignment for your magazine with an expense account provided by the magazine. Thus I would assume the school is legally responsible for what has occurred."

"What really has occurred, Roger? It seems to me that he had permission to go through your files?"

"He asked to see the drafts of my books and articles, to learn how I worked. I did not give him permission to look at, much less make copies of, my personal and confidential notes," Roger said wearily, wondering how often it would be necessary to repeat this fact. "Admittedly, my secretary gave him the key to my personal files. Quite apart from that, however, he surely had no authorization from me or from anyone to remove copies of my personal papers from my office."

"I understand," said the president. "The issue, then, is not so much entering your file as copying the documents and, of course, taking them with him."

"Taking them across state lines, making it a possible federal offense."

"Naturally," the president said smoothly. "Our goal is not to prosecute the young man. Our goal, rather, is to seek the return of the documents and to preserve the good name of the school."

"I have no desire to bring charges," Roger said, sighing. "The documents could be embarrassing for my campaign for governor."

The president held up his hand. "I'm not interested in what is in the documents, Roger; your distinguished academic career speaks for itself. I only seek a happy solution to our problem."

A carefully rehearsed speech, a little too bland, a little too pat.

"Then you'll speak to the young man and have him return the documents?"

"I can make no promises." The president shifted some papers on the blotter in front of him. "I'll tell him that we don't do those sorts of things here and that if he wishes to continue to be a member of the college community, he must return the copies of your papers. But I'll have to be very judicious. I don't want to back the young man into a corner where he may do something desperate."

Roger felt as if he were a criminal pleading to a gentle and sympathetic but faintly supercilious judge.

"I'll leave the tactics to you, Father. Neither the school nor my political career will benefit from the continuation of this situation."

"Yes, of course," said the president, extending his hand cordially. "But the college has survived many terrible crises, as I'm sure you know, Roger."

Noele

MRS. TIMOTHY NOLAN was a tiny woman with snow-white hair, a baby face, and the loud voice of the deaf. She was also a complainer and a fussbudget, though Noele suspected old age had not caused either condition.

On impulse and without telling anyone, not even Jaimie, Noele had ridden her bike up Jefferson Avenue to the Nolan house in the woods, despite the icy north wind that was cutting through the bare trees of the Forest Preserve. A teenager on a bicycle in a *totally* cool white-down jacket, she calculated, would be less of a threat than a teenager in an automobile.

Mrs. Nolan had permitted her into the house with obvious reservations. She offered Noele no pot of tea, seemingly forgetting that the reason for the visit was Noele's wish to talk to her husband "about a term paper I'm writing," and launched immediately into an attack on crazy teenage drivers. Then she switched to the subject of her husband's health—"six heart attacks and two strokes, my dear"—and what a terrible trial "the poor man's health" had been to her.

Almost, Noele thought, as if she'd be happy when he's dead.

Finally Noele was admitted to Captain Nolan's "library." A dark, dingy room smelling of cigar smoke and lined with shelves of books that looked as if they hadn't been moved since they had been placed in their proper positions thirty years before. The captain, a little old man as fragile as a porcelain doll, was sitting in a corner in a deep chair, hiding behind a cloud of cigar smoke and watching a soap opera on a large color-television screen with the sound turned off.

"What do you want, young woman?" he bellowed, doubtless assuming that she was as deaf as his wife. His head reminded Noele of an Easter egg on which the dyes had not worked very well. But his voice was loud and clear, even though it indeed seemed that, as his wife had put it, Timothy Nolan had "one foot in the grave."

"I'm Noele Farrell," she began, determined to be her most charming and innocent teenage self.

"I know who you are," the captain said, considering her carefully, his lecherous old eyes snatching at her sweater and jeans.

"And I'm writing a family-history term paper," she continued, repelled by the way the old gelhead was looking at her.

"No good will come of that," the captain said, smiling affably.

Noele took a very deep breath. "And I wanted to know more about how Clancy Farrell died."

She expected the captain to become very angry. Instead, he continued to puff on his cigar and watch the televison screen with intense concentration.

"Don't know what you're talking about," he said finally. "It was an accidental death, full investigation."

No, there wasn't a full investigation. You're lying. Aloud she said, "How could there have been a full investigation if Doctor Keefe signed the death certificate that night?"

The old man's tiny eyes flickered dangerously. "I did the investigating myself afterward. Informal like, so there would be no police record to embarrass anyone."

"You're afraid of me, aren't you, Captain Nolan?" she said implacably.

"Get out of here, young woman," the old man bellowed. "Margie! God damn the woman; where is she? Get this brat out of here."

Noele stood up. "Really, Captain Nolan, don't be gross. I'm leaving. I don't like to associate with crooked cops any more than I have to, even when they are senile old men."

"Senile, am I?" the captain screamed. "Crooked, am I? The Nolans were always a lot more honest than the Farrells. It's your family that's crooked, kid. Now get out of here."

"At least we didn't violate our oath of office," said Noele haughtily, standing at her chair but not leaving. There had to be more information to pry out of this wicked, angry, frightened old man.

"Oath of office, huh? You'd better be real careful, kid. Another Farrell woman asked too many questions and got herself very dead. Marge! Get this brat out of here!"

Noele's world stood still for a moment. She felt lightheaded and dizzy, as if she had been dieting for days. The smell of Tim Nolan's room made her sick to her stomach.

Captain Nolan was coughing, small wonder with all that cigar smoke. His wife, who had heard none of his shouting, dashed into the room at the first hint of a cough.

"Go away. You Farrells are nothing but trouble, always trouble. Can't you see that the poor man is having another attack!"

"I'm sure I don't want to stay here any longer, Mrs. Nolan," Noele said, rushing out of the room through the parlor into the cold, clear, December sunlight.

Riding home on her bike, Noele wished the family-history term paper had never been assigned.

Someone killed Danny's mother.

My God!

It was half exclamation, half prayer.

She called Jaimie's number at Notre Dame as soon as she had rushed upstairs to her room.

"I need more newspaper clippings, Jaimie. Would you be a dear and check up on the death of Florence Carey Farrell in an auto accident in 1944? And anything else you can find out about who was involved in the accident?"

Jaimie was silent for a moment.

"If you want me to, M.N.," he said finally.

"I do. I think I have a motive for a revenge killing."

Did she want to convict Danny Farrell of avenging his mother's death?

No, of course not.

Then the loneliness came back, as though Florence Farrell's ghost had come into Noele's room.

Was it the loneliness of a restless ghost she felt?

·····Burke·····

THE PHONE WAS clammy from the chill sweat on Burke's hand when he hung up.

She's only a child, he told himself. I can't let anything happen to her. Yet in the jungle in which Burke lived, one chose one's woman over a child if one had to.

He walked to his window and watched the crowds hurrying across the Daley Civic Center plaza. That first word was rarely used in City Hall now. Herself did not like to hear the word *Daley*. She had even moved the official Christmas tree up to the river so there would be no chance that people would associate Daley and Christmas.

Would nothing stop the child?

First there had been Doctor Keefe, who always guessed more than he knew and who knew too much to begin with. Then, dear God, Tim Nolan, of all the dangerous old men in the world. Who else might she have called?

The Marshal? Please, God, not that madman.

The outfit would have to be careful. Her boyfriend's father was a powerful man on the Hill.

Then Burke felt a cold stab of fear. Chairman of the House Intelligence Subcommittee. Had Noele talked to him?

He rushed back to his desk, flipped frantically through his book of confidential phone numbers, and dialed a 202 number.

"Jim? . . . Burke Kennedy here. . . . Yeah, I know. . . . Hope you get home by Christmas. . . . See you at the party for Noele, I suppose. . . . Oh, yeah, great kid . . . kind of hard on her being an only child. . . . Say, did you find out anything from the Company about Dan Farrell? . . . We had to admire her spunk for asking and kind of wondered . . ."

There was dead silence at the other end of the line while the shrewd mind of Jim Burns pondered that bolt from the blue.

And then came the only answer that Burke could have expected, a carefully vague response that told him nothing. "Yeah, I know how the Company is about such things. . . . Sure, he's dead, Jim. . . . You know Bridie . . . Irish mothers never stop hoping. . . ."

Again the fleeting wish that she had borne him a son.

"Well, thanks, Jim. Give my best to Jane. Merry Christmas. . . ."

After he had hung up, Burke Kennedy slumped over his desk, head in hands. There will never be peace. Never.

·····Roger·····

"I REALIZE YOU'RE doing your best, Father," Roger said wearily into the telephone. "But you must understand that I'm under enormous pressure. And the young man's ethical dilemma is very difficult for me to understand."

And now Noele had bearded Tim Nolan in his den. The child has an unerring instinct for stirring up the pot, the cop who . . .

"He claims that the materials are his property," the president said, "now that he has them. He also states that there was no theft because he removed only copies, not the originals."

"How in God's name can he claim that? Not a court in the country would agree that I lose rights to my documents because they have been copied. Don't you teach the Ten Commandments there anymore?"

"I'm only repeating his position." There was reproach in the president's voice. "He feels you relinquished possession of the property when you permitted him to come into your office. He also feels that because you are a major public figure and a success, you are a legitimate target for investigative reporting."

"Which means because I have a few dollars it is moral to steal from me."

Nolan looks like an innocent old man, but he's pure poison. She could get herself killed. And I have to worry about this stupid little prick.

"I'm only trying to explain, Roger. He feels he has a solemn obligation to make these matters public and that if he did not do so he would be violating his professional ethics."

He and Irene had had a flaming row about the Nolan visit. Uncharacteristically she had fought back, telling him that it was his responsibility, not hers.

"Forgive me for being ill-tempered, but as I said, this strain is devastating. I appreciate your efforts very much."

Roger realized that he was a fine one to talk about the Ten Commandments. Another hour—he glanced at his watch—well, another forty-five minutes, he'd violate the sixth commandment, commit adultery once again with Martha Clay.

And in the pleasure of bizarre fantasies he would forget the family past.

But not entirely. When he made love to Martha, he often thought of Dan Farrell, doubtless because Dan used to poke fun at him for his obsession with women, as if he knew that Roger was trying to prove his masculinity.

"If it has skirts on, you'll chase it," Danny would say in his phony Irish brogue. "Though, sure, you don't seem to like women with proper size tits at all, at all."

"I'll leave them all for you," Roger would reply crisply.

He felt guilty about these fantasies, but told himself that as an adulterer, he wasn't adding much to his guilt by permitting himself gay images in the course of lovemaking. In any case, as a trained social scientist he knew that human sexuality was enormously complicated. We're all, he told himself, polymorphously perverse. I might as well enjoy it while I can.

The quarter was over and tomorrow Martha would return to Boston for Christmas with her parents. She would also see her former husband. "You see your wife every day, Roger, and I don't object to that," she had argued persuasively. "Do we have a double standard?"

Martha's promotion was in trouble. The dean had taken him aside at the Faculty Club the day before yesterday to say that he had sent the appointment on to the provost with "the strongest recommendation I could in all conscience give." The dean's "in all conscience" meant a lukewarm recommendation. "Do you think that Mrs. Clay would consider a compromise solution?"

Roger's ears perked up. The University was talking compromise. Then all was not lost.

"You mean a term appointment as associate professor with a review in several years?" In other words, promotion but not tenure.

"Well, obviously I can't speak for the provost," the dean said, "or for the president, but perhaps something along those lines could be worked out if we can find the funds to support such an appointment.''

The University could find funds for anything it really wanted to do, despite its annual poor-mouthing.

"That's a very interesting possibility, Winston. Let me make some discreet inquiries among members of my department.''

But first he would have to consult with Martha, as the dean well knew. She might be offended by the compromise and consider it a degrading, chauvinist insult and reject it out of hand. More likely, she would swallow her principles and accept five more years of employment. She might very well lose in an all-out confrontation, and you don't get paid $28,000 a year for moral victories.

Now unbearably eager to have her again, Roger left his office hastily. How many other faculty members were also departing early to take their pleasure with their current female slaves before the Christmas season would impose a moratorium on such amusements?

He would have to terminate the liaison eventually. If Martha left at the end of the academic year with perhaps a lawsuit against the University, the relationship would end in an easy and natural fashion.

As he walked over to her apartment Roger reflected that it was odd that he would no longer be in trouble with the voters if he was guilty of flagrant adultery. The electorate more or less accepted such aberrations from its political leaders. But he could lose the governorship because a young man had violated all the canons of responsible journalistic ethics and found materials relating to a crime committed in the distant past.

Was there no room left for morality and truth in the world? The full truth could destroy him and his family. It could even threaten his daughter's life.

But who was he to complain?

John

DECEMBER'S SECOND SUNDAY dinner at Brigid's seemed like a century in purgatory. Irene, as she always did at Brigid's, slipped back into her role of passive and insipid housewife. Roger and Brigid patronized her as usual, and John found himself tempted to fit into that routine.

How many times had he insulted her in the last fifteen years? What a pompous, arrogant fool he must have seemed. How could such a lively, sensuous woman have put up with it?

He longed for the warm solid feel of her in his arms. The desire he always felt for her now contained respect and admiration and sympathy, which made her more attractive and even more dangerous. They had come very close in the rectory the other day, too close. He must not permit himself to be alone with her again.

The glum atmosphere around the dinner table was aggravated by the family's unease about Noele. She and Jaimie were at a Christmas dance, and Brigid took the opportunity to interrogate Roger.

"Are you sure we'll have no more of this term paper nonsense from the child?'' she demanded sharply.

"Of course. I had a long talk with her."

"A pity the child's mother can't keep her under control."

The child's mother, treated like a piece of the furniture, acted as if she were just that, speaking not a word in her own defense, hardly seeming to hear the insult.

"Can I have a word with you outside as we leave?" Roger whispered as they adjourned from the supper table.

"Sure," John agreed, expecting to hear more about Noele's escapades.

"We have another problem. A young college reporter has taken some papers from my office that could create a lot of trouble."

"What kind of papers?" John demanded, incensed by his brother's dry academic pose.

"Basically some material I found in Dad's files after the funeral. Documents dealing with the death of Florence Farrell. And some other materials of my own in which I pursued the subject."

John tried to comprehend. "Do you mean Dad was telling the truth that night?"

"Danny believed it, didn't he?" Roger said lightly.

"I don't think I ever did, though, did you? I thought it was more B.S., like the stories about the OSS during the war."

"I take it as almost certain that our beloved father was afraid that Florence might challenge the will. Probably at the urging of our equally beloved grandmother, he made arrangements to have her removed. I wrote this conclusion down in a memo that was part of the material the young man removed from my office."

"My God." John was so horrified that his voice choked.

Roger smiled lightly, as though he were mildly amused by the species Homo Farrellensis.

"Tim Nolan was involved then too. Not only did he protect Danny from the consequences of his action, he also protected Clancy from the consequences of his earlier action. I fear that Noele has guessed some of this. Why else would she go to Nolan?"

John Farrell would not have known how to answer the question of whether he loved his brother, Roger. He was offended by Roger's intellectual posing, and now by his treatment of Irene. Nonetheless, he respected his brother's brilliant intelligence and quick wit.

Love, he would have said to a questioner, didn't matter. You were loyal to your family, especially when they were in trouble, maybe only when they were in trouble, and Roger was in trouble.

"Why the hell did you write that memo?" John asked, masking loyalty, as the Irish often do, with impatience. "That was a damn fool thing to do. Besides, are you sure it was Dad? Arranging a murder. . . ? That's the sort of thing Burke would do."

"What motive?" Roger gestured hopelessly.

"Protecting Mother. What other motive is there in Burke's life?"

"Impossible," said Roger.

You want to believe it was Dad, John thought, but why?

It was cold in front of the old house; the thermometer was well below freezing and heading toward zero. John had not worn a topcoat, preferring the image of the busy parish priest dashing about without a coat.

Now he was shaking, only partly because of the cold winter night.

"I felt that we had to leave some sort of message to those who would come after us," Roger continued. "What if one day someone stumbled on the whole story? A child of Noele's, for example, doing a term paper twenty years in the future."

"The whole world is likely to stumble on it now," John said gruffly.

"I suppose. And to make matters worse, there is an involvement with the Mob. That could be very dangerous."

"What are you doing about it? Can't you find somebody to steal the papers back? Couldn't Burke have some of his friends pay a little visit in this case?"

"Don't think I haven't thought of it. However," he said, laughing, "I am a candidate for governor, you know, and I have to watch myself. Anyway, the president of the college is going to work it out. I just thought I'd alert you."

"Let me know if there is anything I can do to help." John was sympathetic if also helpless.

"If you hear the slightest hint that Noele is still mucking around, let me know. You can imagine how dangerous that would be, especially now."

John nodded his agreement. "I wonder if Dick McNamara might not be a bad influence on her. You know what a romantic he is about youthful enthusiasm."

"Don't we both," said Roger dryly. "Are you going to try to get rid of him?"

"I might . . . though he didn't have much influence on Dan, and Dan didn't want to grow up either."

"When Noele looks at me with those terrible green eyes and asks me what the family acts so guilty about, I'm not sure who's grown-up and who isn't."

Before John could reply to that ominous statement, his mother and Irene appeared in the doorway.

"Monsignor John, get in your car and go home to the rectory," Brigid ordered him as if he were a five-year-old. "You stay out on a night like this without a coat on, and you're likely to get pneumonia."

"Some things don't change." Roger laughed.

"Some of us, I guess, are immune to pneumonia."

"Good night, John," Irene said softly as she joined her husband.

Did Roger realize how fortunate he was? Probably not. None of us ever does until it's too late.

St. Praxides rectory was empty and lonely when he returned to it.

·······················*James III*·······················

NOELE'S PIQUANT, USUALLY mobile face was frozen in an expression of horror, as if she had just seen a child die in an accident. Jaimie touched her chin. Her eyes turned toward him as if he were a stranger. Recognition returned, slowly at first, then with a rush.

"Oh, Jaimie," she said weakly.

The fire was burning in the old-fashioned fireplace of the congressman's study, and the smell of the family Christmas tree drifted in from the next room. The stereo was playing carols, and they were surrounded by the sights, the sounds, the smells, the warmth of Christmas. Noele, in blue sweater and slacks, looked like someone's special Christmas present.

Except for the sadness on her face and the single tear that flowed from each eye.

Jaimie caressed her face with the tips of the fingers of one hand and gathered up the clippings on Rocco "The Marshal" Marsallo from his father's worn brown leather couch with the other.

"He enjoys beating people to death with a baseball bat," she said, still not quite believing what she had read.

"There are people like that," Jaimie said lamely.

"And burning women with cigarette butts—forty burns on that one poor girl."

"He's evil," Jaimie agreed.

He had not wanted to show her his new stack of Xeroxes; a few small clips on the accidental death of Florence Carey, the arrest of the driver of the truck, Rocco Marsallo, and his conviction of a charge of involuntary manslaughter. Nor had he wanted to show her the big collection of articles on the rise of Marsallo in the Mob after his six-month jail term in 1946: enforcer, hit man, torturer, ruler of a prostitution and pornography empire, senior leader in the Mob, and now retired Mob crazy.

There was yet another collection on the dubious police career of Timothy Nolan—charges of Mob links, investigations, threats of indictments, promotions, rumors of bribes. A very bent cop.

But Noele had bugged him for the clippings. And he had finally given in.

"Danny's mother was killed by that man," she said, pulling her face back from his fingertips.

"It might have been an accident. . . ."

"Sure, and Tim Nolan might have accidentally been the cop who arrested him, accidentally said that a Farrell woman had asked two many questions and was killed. Only he didn't say that she was accidentally killed. She asked questions about her son's inheritance and was killed."

"Maybe."

"What else could explain it?" she asked, searching desperately for another explanation.

Jaimie began to stroke her long, soft hair, and she smiled gratefully.

"Suppose the questions about the will would have led to a government investigation and sent Brigid to jail. Wouldn't Burke have a motive for protecting her even then?"

Noele nodded thoughtfully. "They have been sleeping together for a long, long time, and he would do anything to protect her."

"And you don't know that Danny even found out that his mother was killed by a Mob punk."

"Well, then who pushed Clancy down the stairs?" Now she was touching his face, with the respect and reverence due to a sacred vessel.

Jaimie tried to keep his thinking clear and his voice steady. "Maybe he fell, like everyone told you, or . . ."

"Or what?"

"Maybe your grandmother pushed him."

Instantly her hand abandoned his face.

"What a terrible thing to say," she complained. "Why would Grams do that?"

"I didn't want to tell you this, but . . . well, my grandfather said that there were rumors in the old days that Clancy beat her."

"Why?" The deep freeze returned to her face.

"Maybe because he was angry about Burke and . . . well"—he squirmed—"some men only enjoy sex if they . . ."

"S.M.," said Noele promptly.

"Something like that," said Jaimie, embarrassed, as he often was by Noele's sexual knowledge.

"So you think Burke and Brigid were responsible?"

"Not necessarily. I'm only pointing out that you can't prove for certain that there were murders, or, if there were, who were the killers. You can make cases against almost anyone. And it has been such a long time, you can't prove anything. Besides, who else is there to talk to?"

Noele put her arms around him and laid her head on his chest.

"So you want me to forget about it all."

"At least till after Christmas." He held her close, but gently, as though she were a china doll. The most he could expect was an agreement to leave it alone for a time.

"And the CIA hasn't reported to your father?"

"He says they probably won't. And that means they found nothing. That's the way they work."

She kissed him, and he responded. In a moment their lips were working automatically and fervently.

If this keeps up, thought Jaimie, I'm going to want to take off her sweater and kiss her everywhere.

Reluctantly he disentangled himself and pulled her off of the couch.

"Back to decorating the tree," he said.

"Right," she said, none too enthusiastically.

"And no more Farrell family skeletons till after Christmas."

"Right."

Jaimie patted her rump affectionately. "That's my girl."

"Right." She giggled as she jumped to escape a second swat.

And as soon as she got out of this house, Jaimie knew, she'd be right back on the case.

Irene

THE HUM OF the blow dryer down the hallway meant that Irene's privacy was over. Noele was home from school early this afternoon. The gymnastics meet had been canceled, and Noele's fury would be the sole conversational topic at supper, supplanting even Roger's pontifications about his campaign.

God, he was insufferable.

She sighed, sounding to herself a bit like Brigid. The new story she was working on was coming slowly. She was trying to revise the character of Father Tom, the priest who had appeared intermittently in some of her earlier stories—most notably "The Buying of the Baby." He had been a supercilious and insensitive man in the other stories. Now it was necessary to picture him as vulnerable, sensitive, and loving, while maintaining some kind of consistency, a difficult challenge technically, as well as a difficult burden to her personally.

The new story was about a married woman who was strongly attracted to

Father Tom. She was trying to capture on paper her conflicting emotions while recalling how their eyes locked and unlocked across the dining table at Brigid's last Sunday night.

Dressed only in her underwear, she was stretched out on the chaise longue in her bedroom, enjoying the warmth from a furnace that refused to attend to its thermostat. The house was as warm as she liked it, and Roger could not complain about the temperature being over sixty-eight.

Had Father Tom changed? Or had her heroine and alter ego, Lorraine, changed? What was he like in "The Buying of the Baby"?

She took "The Buying of the Baby" out of its folder and reread the ending.

> *Father Tom extended the envelope to the tense young man.*
>
> *He took it quickly, began to look inside as if about to count the bills, and then, shamefaced, stuffed it into the pocket of his old tweed jacket.*
>
> *"Everything will work out for the best," Father Tom said blandly, for the tenth time that day.*
>
> *Lorraine wondered how any man could be so unfeeling. Cash was being exchanged for a beautiful red-haired, green-eyed child. The mother would weep all night, blaming the father for his failure, and he, suffering more acutely, would not be able to weep and would have to blame himself.*
>
> *And Lorraine would hold the crying child in her arms and ask herself once again if they had done the right thing.*

John, Irene now understood, was not the Father Tom of the story. He was hurting that day as much as the rest of us. He has hurt all his life, but he hides his pain under a mask of clerical urbanity. Sometimes so well that he forgets he hurts.

Unfortunately, masks become the person if they are worn often and long enough.

"Hi, Moms." Noele charged into Irene's room clad in a huge, quilted white robe, her long hair still wet and limp. "Wow," she said, and whistled in approval. "You say *my* underwear is what whores wear."

"If you come into my room once more without knocking, young woman," Irene said, acutely embarrassed, "I'll ground you for two months. How many times do I have to tell you—"

"Okay, okay." Noele would humor her mother this afternoon. "Still, I think you look really *excellent*. What are you doing? Writing another story? Can I see it?" She reached for the manuscript.

Irene quickly closed the folder in her lap.

"Can't blame me for trying." Noele grinned. "Someday you're going to break down and let me find out what a really excellent writer you are, right?"

The Christmas child was gone as suddenly as she had appeared, leaving her mother embarrassed, humiliated, and frightened.

She is so innocent and fresh, Irene thought. And how quickly her innocence would be destroyed if she read this story. Everyone seems to be worried that she might be hurt if she continues to ask questions about the past. Who could hurt Noele?

No one—except me.

Rising from the chaise longue, Irene donned a robe and carried the folder with both the stories down the hallway to her office. She would put it in the leather binder with her other stories in the secret compartment of her desk.

She had the usual trouble with the old-fashioned lock of the secret drawer. The key jammed just as the phone rang. Hastily she stuffed the folder into the center drawer of her desk.

It was Mrs. Riordan with a long and complicated question about the spring luncheon.

Roger

AT THE END of the exam period the University had the vitality of a cemetery, especially if, like Roger Farrell, you were waiting anxiously for a telephone call from a college president and wondering whether your suddenly docile daughter had in fact pulled back from the brushfire she had lit.

Roger had been moved by the intensity of his brother's reaction on the previous Sunday evening. John wanted to help. In fact, he wanted desperately, almost pathetically, to help, even if he could express that desire only in hostility over Roger's stupidity at having collected the dangerous documents and written the telltale memo.

We Irish are a strange people, so good at hiding strong affection for one another. Well, there was nothing much John could do.

And what would he think if Roger were to tell him that his predicament might be a punishment for his own sinfulness?

Bless me, brother, for I have sinned. I have committed adultery repeatedly with some special perversity added. Do you want to hear the details of my perversity, brother? I think you would find them rather amusing. I have tried to obtain a tenure appointment for my mistress at the University, one for which she is only marginally qualified. That is why, dear brother, God has sent Joseph Kramer to plague me. I am a man of outstanding public ethical principles and shabby private principles. What is happening to me is something I richly deserve.

The phone rang. A long-distance call, but by the time the operator at the other end got back to her party, the connection was broken.

What would his mother and Burke say if he had to tell them about the memo? They would both be furious, of course. Why did he have to put something that foolish in writing? Damned academic posturing, they would say.

And what if John were right? What if Burke had put out the contract on Florence? It was certainly possible. There was a lot of bullshit in poor Dad. He might have made up the cruel story he shouted at Danny that night because he was so angry at him for consorting with "the little Conlon bitch."

But somehow the thought that Burke had disposed of Florence with Brigid's consent was even more intolerable to Roger than the suspicion that his father had done it. Yet if Brigid were threatened with jail—even remotely threatened— Burke would strike with deadly swiftness.

The phone rang again.

"I think I can promise you a happy Christmas, Roger," said the president of the college. "Mr. Kramer returned the papers to me this afternoon, and I put them in an envelope and sent them to you at your office at the University, special delivery. Our crisis is over."

"Any copies?" Roger asked nervously.

"He assures me that there are no copies," the president said calmly. "We'll have much to give thanks for at the Midnight Mass on Christmas."

Roger felt as if a mountain range had been lifted from him.

"I'm enormously grateful to you, Father. You may be sure I will not forget you or the college."

Well, it was over, thank God. Heaven's punishment for the sins of Roger Farrell had been surprisingly mild.

Even though it was forty-five minutes before quitting time, Mrs. Marshfield had long since left, thoughtfully locking the correspondence that he dictated in her desk so he would not know what, if anything, she had finished.

The phone rang just as he was leaving the office.

"Hello, Roger. This is Lawrence."

The provost at the University referred to himself either as "the provost" or as "Lawrence," the latter a certain signal that you had become part of the University community. Such a favor did not come with tenure, or even with the full professorate. It appeared to Roger that it was bestowed only on those who ate lunch at one of the round tables in the Faculty Club.

"Good afternoon, Lawrence. I hope you're enjoying the weather on St. Maarten."

"It does wonders for Penny's health," the provost replied uneasily. Like other University administrators he justitifed the flight from Chicago cold at the end of the quarter on the grounds of his wife's health. "Actually I'm calling you about the Martha Clay case—in a very informal and confidential manner. I trust you understand."

The provost spoke with a dry little rasp, much as if he expected to die of T.B. before the conversation was over.

Roger understood. The provost will make a compromise offer, and I'll say it won't work. They will turn Martha down, and by spring it will all be over.

All for the best, I guess.

"Of course, Lawrence," he purred in reassurance. He knew there would follow a long and rambling reflection, as though the provost were talking to himself.

"The Mrs. Clay case is a complex one, if I may speak in all candor. This University will not accept the imposition of quotas by outside authority. Neither, however, can we afford to overreact and reject a promising younger scholar merely because we wish to swim against the tide of quotas. Moreover, Mrs. Clay comes to us with a moderately strong endorsement from her own department. On the other hand, some of the most distinguished members of the department are not enthusiastic about the prospects of her future scholarship. And Winston's letter of transmittal was hardly reassuring. You understand my problem, Roger?"

Roger mumbled reassuringly.

"These are difficult times for the University." The times were always difficult. "And the president and I are convinced we do not need another public controversy, especially when the evidence is not clearly weighted against a lifetime appointment. . . ." There was another pause, during which Roger was supposed to admire the provost's wisdom under pressure. "Therefore, I'm inclined now in a tentative sort of way to forward this matter to the president, appending my own cautiously positive recommendation, along with that of the dean. I fear I cannot offer you this as my definitive conclusion on the Mrs. Clay case because, of course, I will have to read the whole dossier.'' The provost, whose publication record in thirty years of academic service was one thin book and two articles, didn't read anything, not even the *Chicago Tribune.*

''Her case is obviously a marginal one,'' the provost rambled on. ''But sometimes the University administration has to go with its instincts and, of course, with the instinct of faculty members whose judgment it trusts.''

''I certainly appreciate your trust in my judgment, Lawrence.'' Roger put his hand over the telephone and muttered ''Stupid cowardly bastard. You're afraid to take on somebody who might be governor.''

''I hardly need to add,'' the provost plodded on, ''that this is all very preliminary, tentative, and confidential. I'm sure that our conversation will be between ourselves and you won't share it with any of our mutual colleagues, even the dean—and especially with Mrs. Clay.''

Don't tell the dean, because he'll have a fit.

''I believe Mrs. Clay has gone to her parents' home in Massachusetts for Christmas,'' Roger said, implying that of course he would not have her phone number, and even if he had, he would not dream of disturbing her Christmas relaxation—quite likely with her former husband, who was some kind of engineer at M.I.T.

''Quite, quite,'' said the provost, with just a faint whiff of his self-image as someone rather like a master in a prestigious college at Cambridge University, a C.P. Snow character who combined both cultures.

I should feel joyous, I've won, Roger told himself, and yet somehow I don't.

The Lord gives and the Lord takes away. In this case it would have been better if he had taken Martha away.

Nonetheless, he permitted himself a vision of the fantasy he would have with her when she returned and he told her the good news.

Brigid

BRIGID LOVED GIMMICKS, whether they were microwave ovens or personal computers. She argued that they made life more convenient. In fact, she loved to play with them, probably because she had had so few toys as a little girl.

Her newest toy was a giant-screen television that enabled her to watch her son interview a bearded peace-activist priest in something larger than life-size. She was dismayed by John's diffidence in dealing with the poor fool, who spoke with much feeling but no intelligence.

''You do look a little vain on the large screen, John,'' she told her absent son. ''And if you were here you probably would be telling me the large screen is a needless luxury, and yourself not knowing what it's like to have to use an outdoor loo for the first fourteen years of your life.''

Burke came in to the TV room, a brandy snifter in either hand, both of them filled almost to the brim. He pushed the button on the television cabinet, instantly extinguishing Monsignor John Farrell. ''I know I'm the one who said we have nothing to worry about, Bridie. But I think we've got troubles.''

She had known there would be troubles eventually. Once more it would be necessary to crush her emotions and respond to the trouble with ruthless cunning. No, it would never stop. "What kind of troubles?"

"Noele." Burke sank wearily into the chair next to her and extended the brandy snifter. "You know that I'm fond of her, Bridie, but right now I have to say she's a nosy little bitch who ought to be spanked."

"Oh, my God, what now?"

"I found out more of the details of her conversation with Tim Nolan. He had a bit too much to drink and called me today to say he thinks Noele smells something about Flossie's death. Tim says he just about had another heart attack."

"I wouldn't mind the son of a bitch having a heart attack," Brigid said fervently.

"Nor I." Burke swallowed a huge gulp of brandy and made a pained face. He thought it was barbaric to drink brandy the way she did, as if it were Pepsi-Cola. "But it's not Nolan I'm worried about. I'm almost certain he called the Marshal. And God knows what that lunatic might do."

"The holy saints preserve us!" Brigid felt dizzy. She put the brandy snifter on the arm of her chair and clamped her hands over her eyes.

"We've got to put a stop to it, Bridie," Burke insisted. "Even if Roger wasn't in a political campaign right now, none of us can afford to have this box of dynamite opened again. You know that."

I know it even better than you do, darling, Brigid thought to herself. "What do you think we ought to do?"

"Someone ought to have a good firm talk with Noele and lay down the law."

"We've tried that." Brigid shook her head. "It works for a while. But Roger isn't tough enough and the woman is worthless. The child is stubborn, more stubborn than anyone in the family, myself included."

Burke swallowed his brandy angrily. "Then what would you suggest?"

"I think we should have a summit meeting between now and Christmas and work out a strategy with everyone."

"What kind of strategy?" Burke squinted suspiciously.

"Make sure that all of us—you and me, John and Roger—agree what our story is and then have someone sit down with her and tell Noele a good deal of the truth."

"The truth?" Burke interrupted in dismay. "How can we tell the truth?"

He looks so old tonight, Brigid thought sadly.

"Admit that Danny Farrell was drunk and that he had a fight with Clancy and pushed him down the stairs. We felt we had to cover it up because it wasn't really murder, only involuntary manslaughter, and the family already had too many scandals."

"That's close enough to the truth," Burke said thoughtfully. "If she'll believe it. The kid is scary. There's something not quite right about her."

"Nonsense," Brigid said briskly. "She's just very smart and very tough." Smarter and tougher than she knows, smarter and tougher than she ought to be for her own good.

"It might work," he admitted grudgingly. "And we keep quiet about the earlier matter?"

"Indeed we do."

She drank the rest of her brandy with a single swallow and coughed as the brandy robbed her of her breath.

"You never were temperate, were you, woman?" Burke permitted himself a grin, which turned into a flattering leer. "And who's going to talk to her?"

"Well," Brigid said after an expressive west-of-Ireland sigh, "certainly not the woman. She's as soft as shit. And to tell you the truth, my son the television interviewer isn't much better. Either me or Roger. Noele respects us both. And I think when she understands what Danny did, she'll lose interest in him—an adolescent love affair, and a sick one at that, if you ask me."

Burke drained his brandy glass and looked at it wistfully. "It's either another glass of brandy tonight or you, my dear."

"Then don't touch the brandy," she said decisively.

Burke put his hand on her shoulder. It was strong, demanding. She felt herself melt.

"Hellish ironies," he said softly.

"And the fires are just getting warm," Brigid agreed.

Irene

THE FIRST DECEMBER cold snap had come—a nasty, snow-coated Canadian thug with a bitter snarl. A strong wind that rattled the windows and crept through every tiny crack in the house. Irene huddled under a thick robe, preferring warm clothes to a hot room during the wintertime. But she hardly noticed the howling wind, because she was so furious about John's pathetic performance. He caved in to every self-righteous, Catholic ideologue who managed to muscle his way onto the program. His ratings would go down after tonight's show. The peace activist was an angry, hate-filled man who would admit no ambiguity, no nuance, no possiblity that anyone who disagreed with his call for immediate, total, and unilateral American disarmament could possibly be in good faith.

"Damn it, John," she said angrily to the television screen, "You know better than that!"

Working on her new short story had exorcised most of the tantalizing heat from Irene's bloodstream. It had been replaced by a numbing chill, much worse than the cold outside her "office" window. The murky half-light in which she had lived so long and in which she had fallen in love with her brother-in-law had been replaced by a cruel, implacable glare, like the harsh lights of a television studio.

At last she saw herself, her husband, and her brother-in-law with brutal clarity. John was a confused, troubled man needing acceptance by his clerical cronies more than he did a woman. If Dads Fogarty wrote something nice about him, he would quickly be cured of his infatuation with her.

Roger was a man of unusual emotional needs married to a woman who did not ignite those emotions. So he found satisfaction with a string of young mistresses. She would probably be a much better sexual match with John than with Roger. But there was no future in such a love affair. Although the experience of sexually initiating a vulnerable and handsome forty-two-year-old male virgin would set Lorraine afire, that character lived in a make-believe world where there were no risks of pain on the morrow.

Irene saw herself with pitiless clarity. She was a stupid fool who had lived her whole life mourning for a dead man. And she had tried to escape and to console herself for her failures by writing stories no one else would read.

Tomorrow she would burn them all.

The interview was coming to an end. John, curly locks slightly askew, leaned toward his guest, his soft blue eyes glittering. Could they be glittering dangerously?

"I'm very grateful to you for appearing with us today, Brother," he began lightly. "And for sharing with us your interesting, challenging, and disturbing point of view. I want to say one thing, however, to you and to the viewers. A great many of us have been concerned about the nuclear arms race for a long time. In fact, I even wrote an article in the *Homiletic and Pastoral Review* seventeen years ago on the subject. In my opinion you have a very naive view of an intricate problem for which there are no clear and easy answers. We have thought about it much longer than you have, prayed over it more than you have, and agonized over it much more intensely than you have.

"Candidly, Brother, I don't need to be told by you that the nuclear arms race is dangerous. Nor do you have any right to assume that your solution is the only one that any decent Christian could possibly advocate. You must forgive me for it, Brother, but I think you an arrogant, self-righteous prig who substitutes enthusiastic dogma for intelligence and understanding."

Irene was as startled as was the speechless peace activist. She flicked off the TV and punched John's personal rectory number on her phone, hoping to talk to him before anyone else was able to reach him.

"You're one tough son of a bitch, John," she said when he answered. "That was awesome."

"You'd better not use that language around your daughter." John laughed, patently delighted by her enthusiasm.

"I know what you should do, John," she said in a rush of confident words: "Challenge Larry Rieves and Parson Rails and Dads Fogarty to come on your program and interview you with all their snide objections. You'd annihilate them."

"Rieves would never do it. He's a stumblebum. He knows he'd lose all his credibility if he went on television, so he resolutely refuses to appear on anyone's program."

"Challenge Rieves first. And, when he won't do it, ask the *Tribune* to send a reporter over who will really give you hell. And then fight back."

There was silence for a moment at the other end of the line. "I really appreciate your confidence in me, Irene," John said, sounding very much like a love-struck teenager, much more infatuated even than poor Jaimie Burns.

"Confidence be damned," Irene replied sharply. "It has nothing to do with confidence. You're good at it, John. Better than you realize, better than the rest of us comprehend. Let yourself get angry. Fight back on your program, and win!"

She leaned forward on the edge of her chair as if she were poised for combat.

"Funny thing, Irene. You're beginning to sound like Danny. Do I get time to think about it?"

She was glad he could not see the heat that flooded into her face. "And even time to ask Father Ace."

I think you cared for Danny in your way as much as I did in mine. Oh, God, how I let him down!

After she had hung up, Roger came into the room with elaborate casualness.

They chatted for a while. And then he began to paw her, his hands creeping beneath her robe. Yes, of course; his mistress was probably away for Christmas break. Well, that's what wives are for, to provide sexual release when the mistress is unavailable.

In their bedroom Irene pretended at first to enjoy the interlude of love. Then Roger's persistent persuasion and her own traitorously sensual body made her response more than pretense. Roger had perhaps learned a few new tricks from his new mistress. But as crushing sweetness leaped up her spine to her brain and then cascaded throughout her body, Irene fantasized that the lover of the night was not her husband, but his brother.

A brother who resembled in mysterious ways his cousin Danny.

·······················*Brigid*·······················

THE FIRST BIG winter storm had swept through Chicago, dropping a foot of wet snow on an unwary city and then, like a drunken Christmas reveler, caroused across the lake to add two more feet on the Michigan shore.

They would shovel out more quickly on the other side, Brigid knew, even if they didn't have mayors to reelect.

There was no hope for their neighborhood. The Nineteenth Ward was on the wrong political side again. Nonetheless, even if it meant that her two sons had to slog through the snow on foot, the meeting would not be postponed.

The martinis and the old fashioneds were mixed and distributed, and her family sat around the comfortable, old-fashioned parlor, the same parlor in which her first husband had died violently. Lord have mercy on him, she thought, mentally crossing herself.

Burke was tired and grim, John preoccupied, and Roger nervous and jittery. A fine crowd to deal with a family crisis.

"We have a serious problem, gentlemen," Brigid began, trying to light a cigarette as she talked and receiving assistance from her husband. "Unless we can resolve it and resolve it soon, we may be in very deep trouble. The name of the problem is Noele. Roger, this family-history project of hers has gotten completely out of hand. You must put a stop to it."

"She's not an easy young woman to stop, Mother," Roger said mildly.

"I'm not unaware of that," Brigid snapped. "Nonetheless, she must be stopped for her own good. She's been asking about Florence's death. And there are no statutes of limitation on murder."

"Then it was murder?" John's face turned pale.

"We suspect so," Burke said gravely. "We've always suspected so, though we have no proof other than your father's terror at the possibility that the will would be challenged."

"And his claim to Danny that night," Roger added softly.

"It will never end. We keep getting in deeper and deeper," John said bluntly, echoing Brigid's own thoughts.

"Rather late in the day for you to think of that, isn't it, old boy?" Roger asked sardonically.

"It'll be the fault of your damn permissive theories of child rearing," John replied sharply. "Sit down and talk it out. You've never been able to give Noele an order and tan her hide when she disobeys."

"You're in no position to tell a married man how to rear his children," Roger flared back, now thoroughly angry.

"His children, indeed," John responded viciously.

"Both of you shut your stupid mouths," Brigid ordered imperiously. "We have to protect the child."

John sighed. "Yes, of course. You must have something in mind, Mother. If you don't, it'll be the first time in your life that you haven't."

Brigid was surprised by the bit of nastiness from her clerical son. The boy would have been much better off if he had been nasty as a child.

"Of course I have something in mind. Someone has to do the thinking in this family. I know there is a difference of opinion among us"—Brigid heard the brogue creeping into her voice, as it did when she was especially tense—"as to whether Noele is fey or just smart. I incline to the latter view. In either case, she will not be easy to fool. Therefore I propose that she be told the truth. Not all the truth, heaven knows."

"We Farrells never tell all the truth," Roger said with a smirk on his lips.

"Roger, do stop sounding like an academic jackass for a few moments, would you please?" Burke said. "This is scarcely a matter for university irony."

"I wasn't aware of being ironic," Roger responded stiffly.

"Will you both be quiet!" Brigid commanded. "And listen to me. Roger, you have to sit down with your daughter in the very near future and tell her that she must stop asking questions about our family history because there are events in our past that could do us enormous harm if they came into the open. Tell her bluntly, since she's already guessed it, that Danny killed Clancy. But tell her that it was a drunken fight, an accident, and that Danny really wasn't responsible." She snubbed out another cigarette, permitting herself only one puff. "So we covered up for him because there were already enough black marks on his record after he was thrown out of the Navy. We all thought that he should have another chance. Dr. Keefe and Captain Nolan cooperated with us because they agreed that Danny wasn't really responsible and that a charge of reckless homicide or involuntary manslaughter would have made too much trouble for everybody—especially Danny. Then God, or the Chinese, or someone intervened, and Danny never got a second chance. Once he was dead, there was no point in reopening the investigation of Clarence's death, and the matter, however tragic for everyone, was over, finished, done."

"That's fundamentally the truth," Burke pointed out.

"Fundamentally." Roger sipped his Scotch and water. "A few points missing that our fey and/or smart little red-head may have already figured out."

"More lies, more lies, more lies." John groaned.

"Neither of you is being very constructive." Brigid was peremptory with them. "We're not exactly lying, John. We're only telling part of the truth."

"And what am I to tell her about Florence?"

"Nothing, unless she asks. If she gives up on Dan, we don't have to worry about what went before."

"And if she does ask?"

"Tell her that we are convinced it was an accident. And that we did not prosecute Rocco Marsallo on a manslaughter charge because we could not afford in those days to offend the Mob."

"Or now, either." Roger smiled thinly.

Brigid ignored him, though she felt a powerful impulse to slap his face, as she had often done when he'd been bold and impudent as a little boy. "Once you tell her what Danny did, that should end her crush on him, and we'll be out of the woods."

"Not nearly enough truth, not nearly enough truth," John said, sighing.

"I do not need, Monsignor," Brigid said ruthlessly, "a sermon from you on religious obligation. I take it we all agree that our responsibility is to protect Noele from her own foolishness. Has anyone a better suggestion?"

"Not I," said Burke, staring moodily at his brandy.

"Under the circumstances, no." Roger shrugged indifferently. "I'll make it a point to talk to her, though she did tell me that she had received an A on the family-history term paper, and that, as far as she was concerned, the project was closed."

"John?" Brigid watched her priest-son carefully.

"I rather think," he spoke softly and very slowly, "that perhaps we ought to tell Noele everything, the entire truth."

"Do you really mean that?" Brigid's eyes locked with his.

"No." John sighed. "You're right, Mother, as always. Telling the whole truth now would do more harm than good—"

"—to everyone." Brigid finished the sentence for him.

"Yes," John agreed. "To everyone."

·····················*John*·····················

JOHN SANK TO his knees on the pre-dieu next to his bed as soon as he returned from the Confirmation service in Evergreen Park. The wood seemed to cut into his knees. He had discarded long ago, in a burst of penitential spirit, the plush purple cushion.

It had been unwise to go to the Confirmation at Holy Savior in Greenwood Park. Indeed, the pastor of the parish seemed quite astonished when John blithely walked into the dining room in the rectory basement. The cardinal shook hands with him in a characteristic show of phony sincerity. "Hello there, John. Good to see you again. Great work you're doing on that television program. We really enjoyed it the other night. You gave that peace fanatic what he deserved. Keep up the good work."

After fifteen years of psychopathic administration in the archdiocese of Chicago, the hypocrisy of the cardinal's compliments was so patent no one bothered to be shocked or upset by it. Nor did John believe for a moment the cardinal had in fact watched the program. Someone else had told him about it, probably Jim Mortimer, whose balloonhead could be seen floating about the other side of the dining room in an aura of self-importance.

Mortimer may also have told the cardinal that the studio had been inundated with phone calls praising Monsignor Farrell's tough honesty. So the cardinal would back off for a bit, only to return later for the kill with the dogged persistence of a grizzly bear stalking its prey.

The brave, honest, and outspoken John Farrell, object of his sister-in-law's confidence and admiration.

Many of the other clergy present at the dinner were less hypocritical than the cardinal. After a sufficient amount of liquor had flowed, they either joshed him, with cruel heavy-handedness, about his "feud" with Larry Rieves, or asked him archly about his slipping ratings (which in fact were fluctuating up and down, but were still considerably ahead of the other three channels at that hour). A few extolled the success of the mass communications workshop and wondered, innocently, if John were to believe them, why he had not been there. As always when the sanctions of clerical culture were being applied, their attitude was a mixture of veiled self-righteousness and patronizing wit. They were like mourners at the wake of a family member who had been killed robbing a bank.

John decided to escape quickly after the dinner and not even lend the dignity of his purple robes to the procession into the church at the beginning of Confirmation. The clergy would not, of course, remain for the ceremony, but would proceed out of the church and back to the rectory for more drinks and bridge or poker and a long night of loud and vulgar masculine conviviality. John wanted no part of it. He packed his cassock into its suitcase, left the rectory, and strode toward his black Buick as if he were running from a house of ill repute.

Henry McKeon, a lean, balding pastor perhaps fifteen years older than John, headed him off in the parking lot. "I think what you're doing on television is fantastic, John," the older man said vigorously. "Don't let the bastards get you down. *Invidia Clericalis* is the devil's own work. Remember there's a lot of us out there in the diocese who are cheering for you, even if most of us are afraid to open our mouths."

With a lump in his throat John thanked McKeon for his kind word. But on his way back to the Neighborhood, while flakes from a light snow flurry assaulted his Buick, he asked himself what good one supporter did when there were so many opponents. Doubtless McKeon was right. There were a lot of other silent allies, men who would come out of the woodwork when he gave up his program and write him letters saying how sorry they were that he had been forced to quit. Not a word of encouragement from any of them, however, when it counted.

Kneeling now at his bedside, John realized that Hank McKeon's reassurance became one more heavy weight in the burden he felt he was carrying. Irene still continued to haunt him. He had been careful not to be alone with her since those deliciously awkward moments in the rectory. Yet her presence at Brigid's at the monthly family dinner had been a torment. She was both inaccessibly distant and immediately available—a haunting, mystical, mysterious presence and a demanding physical challenge.

He tried to persuade himself that the maddening mixture of lust and love he felt for her was diminishing. But then the warmth of her voice on the telephone, the curve of her throat at the dinner table, or merely the imagined click of her heels on the steps to the second floor of the rectory would send a stab of desire racing through his body that paralyzed both his heart and his brain.

His fears for Noele made his need for her mother even more imperious. Someone must protect the two of them. They were both in danger and did not know it. Two innocent, vulnerable women, victims of the Farrell family's lust and greed and of his own cowardly irresponsibility, now possible targets for a man who liked to torture beautiful women.

"Dear God," he begged the figure on the crucifix above, "forgive us, forgive us, forgive us."

Roger

THE FIRST STATEWIDE survey was far more encouraging than Roger had dared hope. The incumbent governor had become unpopular, as all incumbent governors must, because the machinery of state government doesn't work. The pollster, doubly cautious because a professional in political science was to read his rather simpleminded report, said it was altogether possible that Roger could win the election with very little campaigning, so long as he stayed out of trouble and avoided "dangerous" comments to the press.

"Stay out of trouble, ha," Roger said sardonically, tossing the five-page report aside.

He had given his last pre-Christmas address to a group of downtown businessmen who met once a month for an early dinner and even earlier cocktails. Most of them were a little tuned out but were responsive to his vague promise of a "new, creative, and responsible approach to the relationships between federal and state government." They interpreted that to mean less federal and more state regulation of business, not yet comprehending that the state bureaucracy could be and doubtless would be more rigid and mindless in their regulatory requirements than the federal government.

Although he was dead tired when he and Irene finally got home from the Country Club Christmas Dance, long after midnight, he resolved to wait up until Noele returned. It would be reckless in the extreme not to carry out his mother's plan as quickly as possible. He also intended to make love to Irene, after discreetly hinting to her that the dress she had worn at the dance was a bit too revealing. He did not particularly relish watching middle-aged drunks ogle his wife.

Glancing out the window of his study, he saw the lights of an auto reflected on driveway snow and heard a car door slam. He glanced at his watch. One forty-five. Noele was, thank God, not a night owl.

A moment later the lights shifted on the driveway as the car left. Not much prolonged farewell affection between Noele and her lanky, inscrutable boyfriend.

She would come to his study, as she always did at the end of an evening when the lights were still on. But tonight he heard her footsteps in the parlor and then on the staircase. Well, there comes a time, I suppose, when daughters don't kiss their fathers good night. "Did you forget something?" he asked genially.

Halfway up the stairs she glanced over the railing. "Oh, Roger, I didn't know you were still awake."

She backed down the stairs, leaned over the railing, and pecked at his forehead.

She was wearing a dark red dress with a broad white sash, the dress precariously kept in place with thin straps. Everything about her glowed—dress, flaming hair, deep green eyes, fair complexion, neat young shoulders and chest. Her trim, lithe womanliness, fleetingly revealed in the quick movement when she leaped toward him, appealed to Roger far more than his wife's overstated charms.

Despite the vigor of her youthful glow, Noele seemed worried—a mask settled on her face when she wasn't talking.

"Something wrong, Snowflake? Have a fight with Jaimie?"

Noele was astonished. "REALLY, *ROGER*, who could fight with Jaimie Burns?"

He hesitated. The child was not in the mood to talk. A rare enough circumstance. Yet he had to talk to her.

Now.

He did not want to face Brigid's wrath.

"Still working on the family history thing?"

"It's all done. Sister Kung Fu gave me an *A*," she said impatiently, as if he were a very annoying little boy. "I told you that."

"I'm sorry, Snowflake. I forgot. I guess I'm tired too, and I've been doing a lot of speaking. You're going to have to be more patient with me while I work out this governor thing."

She smiled affectionately. "Governor Roger. I think that's totally cool. For sure. Don't worry about me, Governor Roger. I'll be in your camp all the way." She leaned over the railing to kiss him again; then she ran quickly up the stairs, neatly deflecting Roger's scheme to tell her the truth about Danny Farrell.

Irene

IT WAS ALREADY nine thirty, and Irene was still lingering over her breakfast, drinking a third cup of coffee, eating an extra bite of toast, reading the *Star Herald,* and dreading the ten thirty meeting of the hospital volunteers' governing board. She loved visiting the sick, particularly the elderly sick, who had no one else to visit them. Somehow they found her radiant and smiled whenever she came into their rooms. But the governing board, one of the bitchiest groups of women she had ever met, was another matter. In a few moments she would have to go upstairs, put on her dress, and drive over to the hospital to explain to the governing board that no, she didn't want to run for president of the organization, without telling them that the real reason was that she could not stand having to meet with them every month.

She had dreamed of Danny again. The dreams came almost every night now. Before Noele's family-history project, she had never remembered the dreams in the morning. She dreamed of him the way he looked in the old Grand Beach photographs and then later in his ensign's whites. He was such a strange young man, a crazy mixture of deadly serious genius and mad comic. No wonder my parents didn't like him. I would be suspicious of a boy like that who was dating Noele.

If he had lived, he would have blown his life too, just as she had.

Once she'd asked him why he avoided Father McNamara. "You're two of a kind," she argued.

"Aye," he said, escaping into his wonderful fake brogue. "That's why I stay away from the man. He'd read me too well."

"Maybe he could help with your writing. He's been a big help to me."

"Ah, no, I don't want to face him till I have something worthwhile to show him."

"And when will that be?"

He kissed her soundly. "Sooner than you think, and later than you expect."

That's the way he was. . . .

Irene had stayed in bed later than usual that morning. Although she had not touched a drop of liquor at the dance the night before, she still had a headache. She was sick almost every morning lately. For a few days she teased herself with the thought that she might be pregnant.

But that was almost impossible.

Or was it? Maybe Roger's recent randiness was not merely a sign that his mistress was away for the interim at the University. Maybe he had the faint hope that Noele's long demanded little brother would be a campaign bonus.

Bastard.

She was fed up with his endless nagging: she wore the wrong clothes, she drank too much, she said stupid things, nothing she did was right. Everyone else thought she was beautiful at the dance. Some one of these days there would be an explosion.

No, there wouldn't. She had threatened such explosions to herself since the first months of their marriage, and they never occurred.

She turned a page of the newspaper and came to Larry Rieves's column. Oh, no. He's gone after John again.

PRIEST INTERVIEWER IN MORE TROUBLE, the headline read. Rieves had interviewed John's last guest. Brother Shawn Plotke accused Monsignor Farrell of unfairness, insensitivity, lack of moral courage, and indifference to the problems of nuclear destruction. "What else can you expect from a monsignor born with a silver spoon in his mouth?" asked Plotke.

Brother Shawn, however, was the only one of John's critics who did not hide under anonymity. Rieves quoted several more bitter denunciations from participants in the archdiocese's mass communications workshop.

One "highly placed church official" even suggested that if "Monsignor Farrell continues to disgrace the church with his television performance, it may be necessary to take ecclesiastical action against him."

On another page Parson Rails returned again to his Downstate origins to spin a parable about a preacher who became so popular as a guest speaker that he no longer prepared sermons for his own congregation. His contract was finally renewed when he agreed to "stay home and preach to his own people."

"Smug hyppocrite,' Irene snapped, dropping the paper on her breakfast table with shaking fingers, scarcely noticing that she had smeared the sports page with butter.

John had to fight back. Only if he challenged Rieves to come on the program and interview him could he maintain his self-respect and dignity.

Reluctantly Irene shoved the chair away from the breakfast table and glanced at her watch. She usually cleared the table before the cleaning woman came in the morning—she felt guilty if she didn't. Well, today she would live with her guilt. In her bedroom, as she absently unfastened the belt of her robe and let the garment drop to the floor, she looked out the window and shivered at the sight of the sun-sparkled, snow-lined driveway. Bitter cold outside again. Then she saw the squat, black shape of John's Skylark.

Irene removed the skirt of her dress from its coat hanger. Time stood still. Then the despair she had discovered as she wrote her last short story exploded inside her. Her life was an utter waste. The man she loved was dead. She did not and could not love her husband, any more than he could love her. The only good thing she had ever done had turned out to have a bitter taste, through her own fault. No one would miss her when she was gone, and she would leave nothing of importance behind.

She was as damned as Brigid.

She dropped the skirt on her bed and put her robe back on, knotting the belt loosely. She had nothing more to lose. There was an attractive male virgin awaiting the wonders of initiation.

She ran down the stairs to greet him. John's eyes jumped with surprise when she opened the door. He stepped inside and they swayed in each other's arms, body pressing against body in a frantic attempt to become one. Their kisses ignited like tiny fires on a dry prairie, fires that merged and spread as if driven by a high wind. Then they were on the couch, John's face torn with an agony of desire, Irene moaning in anticipation of pleasure. His fingers were underneath her robe, bringing light and peace to her eager body. Despite his intense need, he was gentle and considerate, a naturally skilled lover.

She had not expected that, she told herself, as if observing their desperate embrace from a great distance. I thought you would be a brute, ravishing a woman for the pleasure of triumph. But you are sweet and tender.

Her robe slipped away. Oh, yes, strip me. Take all of me. I want to be yours. Make me come alive with longing and love. You know what I want and need. Just like Danny.

Danny, always Danny.

Reluctantly she pulled away. "We shouldn't, John," she pleaded, hoping that he would not hear.

But he heard.

Only a priest, she thought as they drew apart, would have the self-discipline and the generosity to stop.

I am a tease. And you are a good priest, pompous and vain, but still a good priest. I'm so sorry I have done this to you.

God damn you, Danny Farrell. Won't you ever leave me alone?

Brigid

BURKE AND BRIGID were watching *The Monsignor Farrell Show* on the Saturday before Christmas.

"Some of you may know," John said as he wrapped up the show, "that there's been a bit of criticism of this program by some of my clerical colleagues and by a prominent Chicago TV critic. It seems to me only fair to give them an opportunity to make this criticism on the air. So I'm going to invite Monsignor James Mortimer, the Director of the Chicago Catholic Television Channel, as a representative of the archdiocese, and Mr. Lawrence Rieves, *Star Herald* columnist, to co-host this program next week, as a kind of Christmas present for the viewing audience."

John was smiling cheerfully. "And the guest to be interviewed will be Monsignor John Farrell. Mr. Rieves and Monsignor Mortimer can ask me any question they wish, no holds barred. This may sound like a kind of modern equivalent of the old Irish offer to step out into the alley and settle some matters. And, in fact," he said, grinning, "it is just that. But I can assure the viewers that there will be no physical violence next week, in keeping with the Christmas spirit. There may, however, be lots of good conversation, which is what we try to offer you every Saturday evening.

"I assume that both Monsignor Mortimer and Mr. Rieves will accept my invitation. If they don't, I won't disappoint the viewers who are spoiling for a good old-fashioned alley brawl. I'll find another priest and another journalist who, I guarantee, will give me a harder time than I've ever given any guest on this show. And so, peace on earth, Merry Christmas to all, and to all a good night. I'm John Farrell."

"My God in heaven!" exploded Burke.

"What the hell has happened to the boy?" Brigid asked in total amazement. "He hasn't done anything like that since the days Danny egged him on to devilment."

"If I didn't know him better, I'd think he was getting a good fucking from someone—like the kind you'll be getting in a few minutes if you ask politely enough."

Brigid chuckled. "No fear of that, Burke, no fear of that at all."

Roger

THE CHICAGO PRESS CLUB is shrouded in subterranean darkness. It is made to seem all the more mysterious because its walls are covered with mirrors. One can never really be sure whether one is seeing one's own likeness in the mirror or real people on the other side of the room. The effect created is one of a secret meeting place of a band of Renaissance plotters—poisoners, thieves, and murderers.

In other words the membership of the Chicago Press Club.

Here men decide on the news before it happens, malign the reputations of public personages to curry favor with the arbiters of journalistic taste, assign book reviews to known enemies, cook up schemes of entrapment, abase themselves to visiting firemen from New York, plan sexual seductions of one kind or another, congratulate one another on their knowledge, sophistication, and cynicism, and drown their sorrows in expensive booze.

Anything to escape the cruel fate of going into the winter cold to cover a story.

Roger was lunching there on the day before Christmas Eve with Bill Wells, the editor of the *Star Herald*. The invitation came from Wells, a handsome man whose good looks and liberal ideology made many Chicagoans think of him as a dashing and able young journalist.

It was also alleged that he would like to be a United States senator, even though an endorsement from his paper had been the kiss of death for many a candidate.

"Those people over at the *Star Herald* are important," Mick Gerety had said. "We need their endorsement."

"How many precincts can Wells deliver?" Roger replied with a wink.

Mick winked back. "You're learning, Governor. Real quick. Almost too quick."

The book on Wells was that it took him a long time to get to the subject. He would mumble inaudibly over several drinks before he worked up enough courage to say what was really on his mind.

"Your brother certainly chopped off Larry Rieves's balls the other night, Governor," he said with a faint, carefully practiced smile.

"I didn't even see it. But from the way my wife described it, it hardly sounded like the John Farrell I've known for the last four decades."

Not the total truth. John on occasion displayed considerable fire, although never before such disciplined fire.

"The men and women in the city room have put up posters advertising the Rieves-Farrell fight." Wells stirred his martini thoughtfully.

"Will Rieves really go on?"

Wells laughed. "No more than Jim Mortimer. Your brother would eat them alive, with Parson Rails thrown in for dessert. But I hear he's invited Neal Marlowe of the *Tribune*, one of the most hard-nosed city hall reporters in town, and young Mick Murphy, the president of the Priest Association. Both of them can be counted on to give him a very hard time. It should be the best entertainment of the Christmas season.

"It's a gutsy move," Wells continued. "If he loses, they'll cancel his contract in the next two or three weeks. But if he wins, no one will dare touch him for years. And I'm sure he's smart enough to tell both Marlowe and Murphy to do everything they can to get him fired."

There was an awkward pause. Roger was becoming uneasy. Wells had not invited him to lunch to talk about his brother.

"How's the campaign going, Roger?" He spoke so softly, his eyes on the empty martini glass, that Roger barely heard the words.

"Not all that bad; it's too early to tell, but I think we have a good chance."

Wells did not look up from his martini. "A kid from one of the Catholic colleges came up to see me last week looking for a job. He claimed to have some interesting information about your family that he would give us if we hired him as a full-time reporter. He said that the president of the college would fire him if he knew that we'd got our hands on the papers."

Roger felt the blood draining from his face and his stomach muscles tighten. Was that the way women feel when they are about to be raped for the second time? "Did you look at what he had?"

Wells raised an eyebrow. "Of course, why not?"

"He had no permission to copy that material from my files."

"I didn't know that."

"How in the hell do you think he obtained those papers?" Roger demanded hotly.

"The public has a right to know, Roger," Wells responded soothingly.

"Does your paper routinely review personal documents that are copied from citizens' files?"

"As editor of the paper that will almost certainly endorse you in March and in November, I felt that I would be acting in your name."

"So?"

"So, of course, we didn't see a story in it. Neither did the opposition. On the basis of evidence that seems to us rather thin, you wrote a memo suggesting that your father may have ordered the execution of your aunt almost forty years ago, and that perhaps your mother and stepfather knew of it. That isn't really much of a story, even by contemporary standards."

"And if you had better evidence?"

"That might be another matter, Roger," Wells said lightly, "but I don't see where the evidence could come from. It would be a one-day sensation, though it would sell newspapers that day. . . . Even if we brought in the name of Rocco Marsallo, 'The Marshal,' that would only make it a two-day sensation."

If it was all so minor, why had Wells bothered to invite him to lunch? He felt that he had no choice but to be utterly candid. "Do you think I ought to withdraw from the race, Bill?"

Wells munched thoughtfully on a celery strip.

"If that stuff is floating around out there, somebody will get hold of it. The governor is bound to find out about it, and his people will start snooping. Then all the papers and all the television channels in the state will take a good hard look at your family. Frankly, Roger, there's probably nothing in that file that would generate an indictment if your father was still alive. But with that as a beginning, we would have no choice but to make the Farrell family look like Chicago's Borgias. To tell you the truth, Roger, there have been a lot of rumors about your family for years. Your mother and Burke Kennedy are no worse than a lot of other folks in the construction business, but they have been notably more colorful than the rest of them. Better copy, if you know what I mean."

"None of this, of course, has anything to do either with my own personal life or with my qualifications to be governor?"

"Hell, no!" Wells was now neatly dissecting a carrot stalk. "You're as clean as a whistle, but once the family scandal avalanche begins to bloom, you're going to get swept away too."

For some reason Roger thought of Danny. He'd think of some way to get me out of this scrape, just as he always had when we were kids. He'd know how to protect the women from Rocco Marsallo, too. Damn, why did he have to die on us?

"Can anybody survive this sort of thing?" Roger asked. "Can anyone run for public office if they are subjected to such scrutiny?"

Wells shrugged negligently. "It sells newspapers and improves TV ratings."

A point that Roger told himself that Niccolò Machiavelli would have appreciated. But from a self-professed liberal who demanded the highest standard of ethics from public servants?

"I guess I'll have to think about it very seriously, Bill. I'll let you know."

"Mind you, Roger. You'd make a better governor than anyone who's likely to run. It would be a shame if we had to do you in."

"But you sell newspapers."

"And the public has a right to know," Wells said delicately, breaking a piece of Ry-Krisp in half.

Well, Roger decided, it had been a pleasant campaign while it lasted.

D.C.I.

THE DIRECTOR WAS stuffing documents into his briefcase, determined to leave at three P.M. No matter what peculiar Russian sounds the snoops had picked up, the world would have to survive without him while his family escaped to the Virgin Islands for the Christmas holidays. Radford was standing in the doorway. What did he do at Christmas? Did Radford believe in Christmas? Did Radford have a family? The Director trusted that he would be dispensed from wanting to know the answers to those questions.

"If it's anything serious, Radford, I don't want to hear it."

"I don't think it's serious, sir. I saw our Chinese friend again last night."

"Oh?"

"He told me that the Farrell matter had arranged itself."

"Arranged itself? Does he think we're French?"

"One never knows with those folks."

"All right, Radford, I'm in a hurry. Tell me what you think it means."

"My guess is they misunderstood our message and anticipated our wishes. Farrell, in other words, *was* still alive. And he isn't alive anymore."

"I thought they had given up quick executions."

"Not when one of their loyal allies seems to be requesting such an execution."

"That isn't what we requested."

"No, sir, it was not. But it's what they thought we wanted. It's probably what they would have wanted in our circumstances."

"And you think it's all for the best?"

Radford was his usual icy self. "One could imagine worse outcomes, sir, from the point of view of the Company, of course. Perhaps even from Farrell's point of view. But then we'll never know that, will we, sir?"

Might Radford have requested the Chinese to eliminate the Farrell problem? Not likely. He never exceeded instructions. Not as far as the Director knew, anyway.

"Well, that's that, I suppose," he said somberly. Daniel Farrell's ghost would haunt him through the Christmas vacation. "I'll speak to Jim Burns when Congress comes back next month. Merry Christmas, Radford."

"Merry Christmas, sir."

DANCE SIX

Gigue

"Then on the cross hanged I was
Where a spear to my heart did glance
There issued forth water and blood
to call my true love to the dance."

"My Dancing Day"
A MEDIEVAL GOOD FRIDAY CAROL

John

"YOU HAVE A remarkable appetite this morning," Ace McNamara said, looking up from his copy of *The New York Times*. He had moved into St. Praxides rectory for the Christmas rush. "You have the Christmas spirit a day early? Or is it just the fun of telling off your critics on the program?"

John laughed heartily. "A clear conscience, a happy parish, and a week off after the first of the year. What more does a pastor need at Christmastime?"

He was in love, that's why he felt so good. And even if the love had not been consummated yet, it surely would be soon. Irene loved him as much as he loved her. Only the memory of Danny Farrell stood between them. And if he were kind enough, and considerate enough, and understanding enough, that memory would fade.

Perhaps someday he would confide in the Ace. But right now he felt no guilt, no regret, no sense of sin. Only exuberance. The pastor of St. Praxides would soon have a mistress. So what? He was neither the first nor the last priest in the history of the Catholic Church to stray from the most narrow path of virtue. And in the sweetness of his love for Irene, stolen documents, ancient crimes, lingering guilt, meant nothing.

"So you're going south after the first of the year and leaving the parish in charge of the old Navy chaplain? Dangerous business," said the Ace. "By the time you return, Jerry and I will have moved the rectory across the street."

"I doubt that. You'll be lucky if you see him."

"At least he doesn't work any more when you're around than he does when you're not here."

"Incidentally," John asked, changing a distasteful subject, "are you coming to Noele's birthday party the day after Christmas?"

"Does anyone in this community have a choice? Turning down an invitation to M.N.'s St. Stephen's Day reception is lese majesty, at a minimum."

"I wish you wouldn't encourage her into thinking she's something special," John said with sudden irritability. "She's not special, you know; she's no different from any other dizzy teenage female. And she causes us a considerable amount of trouble. That term paper—"

"A call for you, Father," the housekeeper interrupted him. "Your sister-in-law, I believe."

"I'll take it upstairs, Maeve."

He stood up abruptly from the table. "See you later on in the day."

"Sure," said the Ace. "Say hello to Irene for me. And tell her she's not special either."

As he dashed up the stairs, John wondered if McNamara was baffled by the apparent transformation in him. They had known each other a long time. And the Ace was a very shrewd customer.

Irene

IRENE HUNG UP the phone. Why had she called him? Some stupidity about Noele's party. No, that wasn't the reason at all. She was as much in love as he was.

There had been an article a few months ago in *McCall's* about "romantic love," infatuation, amorous obsession. She had thrown it aside in disgust. That sort of thing happened only to teenagers like Noele and Jaimie. But now it had happened to her. She was more in love with John than Noele was in love with Jaimie.

The article said that the longer the tension of unfulfilled romantic love lasted, the worse the pangs became. And then when the lovers finally possess each other, they quickly fall out of romantic love and either part or settle down to the ordinariness of everyday life.

In her head she knew that she and John did not love each other in any mature and responsible way. They were two lonely, troubled people, conscious of their own mortality, trying to cling to each other for a few moments of warmth on their way to eternal cold. She knew, too, that it was a replay of their adolescent love affair, all the more powerful and demanding because they were older. Nonetheless, after a few romps in bed they would both be cured.

Why not romp in bed then?

Why not find an excuse to go away at Christmas and spend a week in bed together? Get it out of their systems. That's what John wanted. But priest that he was, he was afraid to pressure her.

The damn fool. Why not insist?

He had a reason for not insisting, Irene knew. He had been trained to think about others, even if he often didn't know what that meant.

And why won't I agree to sneak away with him for a week of sex and sun? Because I'm haunted, that's why. I'm haunted by a dead man.

Noele

THE DAY BEFORE Christmas Eve was gross. In the morning there was to be a gymnastics meet at Sacred Heart in Lisle. Then Noele would have to race back for folk music practice in the church at twelve o'clock, then home to wrap her Christmas presents, fix up her bedroom "—spotlessly clean, see, Mo-*ther*—" and finish the decorations for her birthday party the day after Christmas.

And in the middle of all that find time to wash her hair, which was a *mess*.

After all that, she would have to take Jaimie Burns's present (an Aran Isle sweater, specially made in his size) to his house, and then dash over to Grams's for Christmas Eve supper, then back for another practice with the choir, and finally a breakfast after Midnight Mass at the Burnses'. TOO much. And now Flame was on another one of his strikes.

Noele dashed into the house. Roger had gone downtown on the Rock Island for a meeting, so both the Seville and the Datsun were in the garage (and the yukky old Mercedes, which no way would Noele touch). But Moms, typically, was not around when she was needed, and the maid had no idea where she'd gone.

That WOMAN! Noele protested

Well, she kept the spare set of keys for the Seville in the little antique desk in her office. She'd never really told Noele not to take those keys. So, Noele argued to herself, it would be all right to take them. She *had* to drive to the match at Lisle if she was going to be back in time for choir practice.

She bounded up the stairs and down the hallway to Moms's little office, with its cute antique furniture. She opened the desk drawer and snatched up the keys. "If you're angry, Moms, I'll apologize."

There was a small stack of neatly typed pages under the keys. Noele glanced at them. The title in capital letters on the first page read "The Buying of the Baby."

She hesitated. Moms had never shown her one of the stories. They were always locked up carefully. But here was a story that wasn't locked up. Moms had casually left it in a drawer where JUST ANYONE could see it. Then probably she wouldn't mind if someone else read it. AFTER ALL, what kind of a mother wouldn't share at least one of her short stories with her own daughter?

Feeling quite sneaky despite her rationalization, Noele sat on the edge of the little antique desk and began to read the story.

Moms wrote very well. The story of a woman and a priest, Lorraine and Father Tom, going to the town of La Puente outside of Los Angeles to buy a baby, was crisp and sardonic. Father Tom was the brother of Lorraine's husband, Alfred, who refused to participate in the actual purchase of the baby, although he approved of it.

Alfred! Noele felt the blood draining away from her face and her head. Her fingers trembled as she turned the pages. The room became warm, like a sauna someone had turned on without warning.

The description was vivid—the tiny house in which the young couple lived from whom the baby was to be purchased, poor people hemmed in with mortgages and desperately needing the money—scraggly lawn, unpainted walls, cracked window, a car on concrete blocks in the driveway. The woman's name was Marsha and there was anguish in her voice as she said, "If the war gets worse in Vietnam, then there will be more jobs in aerospace, and they'll be hiring engineers at Lockheed again. Then Herbert will have a job, and we can get back on our feet."

Father Tom, a model of ecclesiastical discretion, gave Herbert the crisp, white envelope bulging with hundred-dollar bills "as though they were representatives of the American and Russian government meeting at a bridge between East and West Berlin to exchange prisoners of war."

Nice image, Noele thought mechanically as she turned another page.

The baby was traded for the envelope. Herbert glanced inside, not counting the bills, but estimating them, and Marsha laid the baby gently in Lorraine's arms. She drew the blanket away from the baby's head to make sure that her head was red. Everyone but Father Tom was crying.

"It will all work out for the best," he said unctuously.

Noele sat numbly at the desk, absently rearranging the pages of the story into a neat stack, aligning the edges by tapping the pile on the desk and then sliding it back into the drawer from which she had taken it.

She closed the desk drawer and, keys in hand, ran down the stairs and out into the cheerfully sunny winter day. She drove to Sacred Heart and led her team to victory with her best performance ever on the parallel bars, directed the folk group practice with determined vigor, wrapped all her presents neatly, cleaned up her room, dashed over to the Burnses', kissed Jaimie Burns vigorously when she gave him his sweater, ate supper silently at Grams's house, sang loudly at Midnight Mass, sipped half a glass of champagne at the Burnses' breakfast, and then came back to her own home and in the quiet of her totally neat room sobbed herself hysterically to sleep.

Roger

HIS ARMS LOCKED around his wife, his breath coming in deep and heavy sighs, Roger groped for understanding, feeling that he was an explorer lost in a mysterious jungle.

"Did I hurt you?" he asked tentatively.

"Of course not," she murmured, her fingers sinking more deeply into his buttocks.

It had begun as routine "after Midnight Mass" love. Then they had both become two different persons. His passive, submissive, compliant wife turned into a fiery aggressor who had pushed him to the outer limits of tolerable pleasure. In response, for the first time in their marriage, he gave himself completely and without restraint to her. The paralyzing sweetness of sex with Martha seemed trivial in comparison.

"What happened to us?" he managed to say.

"Politics makes you hungry," she replied.

Perhaps she was right. The heady excitement of the campaign trail might be making him a different person.

He took one of her hands in his own and held it tightly. "I love you, Irene," he said.

How many times had he spoken these words before, not really meaning them. Perhaps he didn't mean them now, either. One wild fling in bed did not transform a lifetime.

But it might be a turning point.

Her other hand began to tease him into arousal. He felt himself respond very quickly.

"More?" he breathed in astonishment, unable to understand either her caresses or his response.

"A lot more," she said fervently.

I will not let them hurt her, he found himself thinking as he pressed her against the mattress, throwing all his physical strength into his new attack.

Loving tenderness seemed to burst his rib cage apart.

Their screams of pleasure exploded at the same time.

"Sleepy?" he asked a few minutes later.

"Uh-huh."

"Can I tell you a story?"

"Of course." This time she sought his hand and held it tightly.

"I may have to give up the campaign."

Irene was instantly awake. "Why?"

"The newspapers have some personal papers of mine, copied without permission in my office. I'm afraid my father hired a young hoodlum to kill Florence and Danny because he was afraid that my grandfather's will would be contested. Mother and Burke may have been involved too."

He had no idea how his wife would respond.

She turned on the light and peered intently at him. She touched his face lightly.

"Dear God," she breathed. "Is that why everyone was so terrified when Noele started asking questions about the past?"

He nodded sadly. "There may be some danger for all of us. The killer is a Mob enforcer."

"Do you want to be governor, Roger?" she asked, tracing the outlines of his face as if to make sure they were real.

"I guess so," he said, chuckling ironically. "As much as I've ever wanted anything, and as you well know, I don't normally want anything very much."

"Then don't quit." She kissed him with slow, loving affection.

At that moment his wife's beautiful breasts, pressed against his chest, did not seem at all excessive.

"What's happening to our family?" Roger asked. "John turns into a fighter, you turn into a wanton—and that's a compliment—and I'm half tempted to turn into a crusader."

"Maybe it's the ghost of Danny Farrell. Maybe Noele has called him back from another world with her term paper."

"You'll stand by me, no matter what happens?" Roger could hardly believe that he had said anything that romantic.

She pulled the sweat-drenched sheet away from him. "Only if you come into the bathroom and take a warm, sudsy shower with me—a long, leisurely one, too."

"At this hour on Christmas morning?" he protested. She had never suggested anything remotely like it before.

"What better time?"

"Sounds," Roger said, astonishing himself again, "like a wonderful idea."

Irene

THERE WAS SOMETHING wrong with Noele. Irene had been so preoccupied with the split of her personality into despair and sensuality that she had hardly noticed her red and green Christmas child.

Irene thought that perhaps she was as guilty of adultery as Roger. One man aroused her, another man made love to her, and a third man's ghost lived in the other two.

But guilt did not seem to stick. She was pleasantly exhausted by her nonstop orgy with Roger. And if he wasn't the only lover in her bed, he was still present. If they continued to enjoy each other as they had the last two nights, the barriers might collapse and they might even become friends.

But Irene was not sure that she wanted such a change.

As she pondered the new mysteries in her life she became vaguely and then sharply aware that the Christmas child was not happy on Christmas day nor on St. Stephen's day, her "official" birthday party day. She seemed to be living on a planet in a different galaxy, perhaps in a different universe. All the motions were there, the winning smiles, the courtesy, the friendliness—she remained very much the reigning monarch of St. Praxides. Yet something was missing. One did not hear "Mo-*ther*" or "Tell me about it," or "Really!" or "I'm sure." The contentious and forceful part of the Christmas child's personality seemed to have dried up, like a Christmas tree deprived of water.

A fight with Jaimie Burns? That did not seem likely. In a room full of guests, he stood at a discreet distance from her, like a modern Lancelot ready to crack the skull of anyone who dared disturb her peace and contentment. Conflict with her friends? Eileen was buzzing around like a vice-regent in the presence of a queen bee. Trouble in school? Noele never had trouble in school.

If there were something truly bothering the new seventeen-year-old, would she confide in her mother? Irene knew with a wrenching pain in her heart that, whatever the pretenses that Noele might attempt, there was no trust between the two of them. Impulsively she sought out the one man in the room who she could be certain would not fall in love with her.

"Hello, Father McNamara," she said to the Ace, who was pontificating to a crowd of Jaimie's friends about boot camp—her first words to him in fifteen years.

The blue eyes had seen terrible pain in Vietnam, but they still danced, and his laugh was as quick as ever.

"Haven't seen you lately, Renie," he said, and grinned. "How was that first semester at St. Mary's?"

"Really yukky."

The boys dissolved into laughter, and then, sensing that they were not needed, disappeared.

"I'm sorry," Irene went on. "I . . . I guess I just blew it."

"What?" He feigned genuine surprise.

"My life."

"Broken old woman." He took a strong drink from his glass of Jameson's. There was an awkward pause as a they both hunted for bland words.

"You look tired," he said tentatively. "Are you going to have some time off after Christmas?"

"The Rafertys have offered us their house in Tucson the week after next. I don't know whether the Governor"—the word came out without any irony—"can get away. But I may go."

"The whole clan will be out of town. The pastor to Puerto Rico, Brigid and Burke to their usual retreat in Acapulco."

"It might improve the parish to be rid of us for a while. Are you going away?"

"I've had enough tropics for one lifetime."

"Can I come see you?" Irene blurted out the frightening words.

"Anytime, Renie."

He didn't even ask why. But perhaps he already knew. He inclined his glass of Jameson's toward the birthday queen. "Something bothering her today, do you think?"

"Do you think so?"

"Watch. Hey, M.N.," he bellowed in his deliberate South Side shanty Irish voice. "When do we get something to eat?"

Noele turned away momentarily from former congressman Burns and smiled sweetly. "In a few minutes, Father McNamara."

"That's not her," Ace said. "No way, José."

"I suppose it's a phase she's going through. They always seem to be in phases."

"Yeah," Ace agreed. "Probably just a phase. But it worries me. Something's wrong."

Brigid

NO MATTER HOW many parties she attended in the Neighborhood, Brigid could never quite get over the feeling that she was an outsider, even at her granddaughter's birthday party: Muggins permitted to peer at the window of the great house and amuse those who really belonged. So she was always irritable at a Neighborhood party, even though she did her best to be charming and fooled everyone but Burke. They should have moved out of the Neighborhood long ago. They had enough money to live in Lake Forest. When the boys left, John to his first assignment on the North Side, Roger to graduate school, Danny—Danny to China—she should have listened to Burke and moved away. But she argued that it was close to the firm. In fact, she wanted to prove to her neighbors that she was something more than an illiterate immigrant girl.

And now most of those she wanted to convince were dead.

As soon she would be.

Noele's young friends, so presentable and grown-up in their good clothes, made her even more uncomfortable. Not so long ago they were infants. And Noele herself, so quiet and subdued—not like her usual self at all. *I never could understand what goes on in that pretty redhead's mind,* she thought; *what does she see with those scary green eyes. She's all that's left now. Everything we've done was done for her. Yet she doesn't seem to care.*

Why must she poke around in the past? Doesn't she realize how easily a young woman can die. Like Florence.

What would be left then for any of us?

Brigid realized that she had been drinking too much. She felt dizzy and slightly sick. The noise of the party made her head ache. Infernal kids. I'll lie down upstairs for a moment, she thought. And then Burke can take me home.

She met the woman in the upstairs hallway, pretty in a pale green dress and still soft as shit.

"Did Roger talk to the child yet?" she said, forgetting in her irritability that Irene did not know about the family meeting.

"I have no idea what you're talking about," Irene replied sharply, trying to walk by Brigid.

"Why aren't you able to control the child? What kind of a mother are you?"

"A mother who can't stop her in-laws from spoiling her daughter," Irene responded tartly.

Ah, a little more fight than normal.

"And a wife who is incapable of giving her husband a good fuck." Brigid wished she could have chopped off her tongue. Why had she said anything that stupid?

"A husband whose mother so dominates his life that he wouldn't know a good fuck if he saw it. And I know what you're trying to hide," Irene shouted. "You and your husband and your lover killed Florence Carey."

"That's a lie." Brigid was insane with rage. "The only killer in our family was Danny. Your previous lover killed my husband."

Irene stared at her in shattered disbelief. "He did not, you evil old bitch."

Then she crumbled like a piece of tissue paper drifting toward the floor. Sobbing, she turned away and rushed down the hallway to her bedroom. She slammed the door shut.

Brigid felt something slam in her heart.

And that, Maeve, she told herself, using her real name, is one of the worst things you've ever done, you goddamned fool.

Ace

THE TEARS POURED down her fresh young cheeks, and though she was not yet hysterical, she was closer to hysteria than Ace had ever expected.

"I know I'm a terrible person for reading the story," Noele said, sobbing.

He chose his words very carefully. He must follow his instincts, as he had in Vietnam—where when someone shouted "Duck!" he ducked without asking why, and was still alive as a result. "The story," he responded, "is not necessarily true, M.N."

"I wanted to find out who I am, and you and Jaimie and everyone else said I should stay away from it. Now I've found out, and I wish I hadn't."

That explained Noele's odd behavior at her birthday party, which had so concerned both Irene and him. Did Renie know she had read the story? Perhaps that's why she had asked to see him.

"Stories are stories, Noele. They may be made up out of real experiences, but they're not necessarily true."

She dried her eyes with a twisted piece of tissue. "You haven't read it."

"Your face is so much like your mother's," he said slowly. "Same bones, same shape, same gorgeous beauty."

She smiled through her tears. "Nerd!"

"I'm serious. You do look your mother's daughter. And I've never seen a father/daughter relationship closer than the one between you and Roger. Anyway, there's nothing wrong with being adopted. You're still you."

"Whoever that is," she said wryly. "Oh, I know, Father Ace, that's what I tell other kids who are totally into a snit because they're adopted. Still . . ."

"Then what are you going to do about it. Ask your parents?"

She shook her head. "I don't know what to do."

He hesitated again. His loyalties were under cross pressures. What the hell! "Why don't you talk to your uncle. . . ."

"Monsignor John?"

"Why not?"

Noele dabbed her eyes with the tissue and smiled. "Why didn't I think about that?"

"What about Danny Farrell?" he asked, wondering if that issue was still alive.

Noele waved the question aside. "Oh, I'm finished with all that, Father Ace. It doesn't, seem, like, important anymore."

"Not convinced he's still alive?"

She considered thoughtfully, her tear-stained face wrinkled in a deep frown. "Not anymore," she said hesitantly. "I did once, kind of. But now . . . Do you think Uncle Monsignor will tell me the truth?"

"Of course."

"Well, I guess I'll have to wait until he comes home from Puerto Rico. Right?"

"Right."

Poor John, thought the Ace. Happy New Year, Monsignor.

Burke

THE FARRELLS SAT around the large-screen television in Brigid's parlor watching with astonishment as John took on two of the toughest interviewers who had ever appeared on Chicago television. Neal Marlowe, a veteran political correspondent, and "Father Micky" Murphy, a tough, red-haired Irish gamecock from Cannaryville, Back of the Yards. They had been told to give Monsignor Farrell a hard time and were enjoying every minute of the combat.

So too, surprisingly, was John.

"Doesn't it all come down, John," said the frowning little red-haired priest, "to a question of whether being a television personality is compatible with being a priest? Don't you think your brother priests are right to be offended at your prostitution of the Roman collar for commercial purposes? Didn't Father Fogarty really speak the truth when he suggested in our newsletter that you're a slick, smooth copout who's using the priesthood as a vehicle for a monumental ego trip?''

"How could anybody be slick and still fight with you, Micky?" John asked with a cheerful laugh. "Actually, I asked Dads Fogarty if he wanted to come on instead of you or along with you. But apparently he only takes on targets who can't fight back. I was raised in an era of the church, Micky, when seminarians were told that priests should strive to be the best in everything they do because Jesus, whom we represent, deserves the best. I feel I represent the catholicity of the church and the priesthood on this program by the questions I ask. My presence here is witness to the church's concern about the mass media and their influence on modern culture. If I didn't think that as a priest I brought a special and unique contribution to the role of talk show host, I'd get off the air tomorrow. I'm disappointed that some of my fellow priests disagree with me, of course. But I still intend to do my best and to follow my own conscience, the way any good priest should.''

All very impressive, thought Burke heavily, but trivial compared to what we're facing. Both of her sons are weaklings, unable to protect her, not even able to comprehend the danger she's in. The kid has more sense than you.

"Yeah, but Father—I mean Monsignor." Marlowe grinned crookedly. Through the whole program he had deliberately confused *Father* and *Monsignor* to see if he could throw John off balance. "Geez, what's a priest doing on television?''

"Hey, Neal," John said, "why don't you call me John and forget about the formal title?" Laughter from the studio audience.

"Okay, Monsignor, I mean, John," Neal Marlowe said ruefully.

Very funny, Burke mumbled to himself—clever, handsome TV priest. Your father was clever and handsome too, but he didn't have any balls either.

"I'm trying to do on television just exactly what Jesus tried to do when he preached in the temple, and what Saint Paul tried to do when he walked up to the statue of the unknown God in the Acropolis and claimed to represent him. I'm nowhere as good at it as Jesus or Saint Paul, but I try. And if Larry Rieves doesn't like it, he's always welcome any week of the year to come on this program and take my place!''

Danny Farrell at least had balls, Burke thought. He was ready to fight for what he believed, poor dumb bastard. Not as slick as you or Roger, but a fighter. I almost wish he were back. We need fighters now. And I'm the only one left.

And I'm old and tired. Too tired maybe.

"I cannot believe my eyes and ears," Brigid said when the program was over. "Something has happened to that boy.''

"I tell you, Bridie," Burke said, repeating his crude joke, "he's screwing somebody.''

Noele, who had been moody and withdrawn all through the program, exploded. "Burkie, that's the most gross thing I've ever heard you say. I'm sure humans don't have to have sex to be passionate.''

"I'm sorry," Burke apologized quickly. "And if I ever needed proof that virginity and fire are not incompatible, you just gave it to me, Noele.''

She was not to be appeased. "I don't want any of your cheap compliments. I demand that you apologize.''

Burke surrendered easily. "All right, Noele, I apologize.''

Noele, quite uncharacteristically, was not gracious in victory. "That's better," she snapped, and then retreated again to her strange, faraway mood.

One fighter I forgot about, Burke thought ruefully.

"What's eating the child?" he asked Brigid as the others were collecting their coats. "Has Roger talked to her? Did he tell her about Flossie?"

"He says he's talked to her, but I'm not sure. I don't think the damn fool is telling the truth."

They stood at the front door watching as Roger caught up with his wife at the door, took her hand, and walked toward the car after their daughter, who had stormed out of the house without saying good-bye either to Brigid or to Burke.

It's all coming apart, Burke thought helplessly. The curtain is rising on the final act.

Noele

THE PHONE RANG. Noele ignored it and continued to type a book report on the new TRS-80 model III that the family had given her for a Christmas present. The phone kept ringing.

"Oh, damn it!" she exploded. "Can't anybody else in the house answer the phone?"

She picked it up and in her most acidly charming voice said, "Farrell residence, Mary Noele speaking." There was a heavy breathing sound on the line.

"Come on, who is it?" Noele demanded impatiently.

The heavy breathing continued. Noele slammed the receiver down.

The phone rang again. She picked it up. "What the hell do you want?"

"You mind your own business, or you'll get your tits cut off," said a muzzled voice. The line clicked.

A gross, obscene phone call. Other girls in the Neighborhood got them too. Scary, but not serious.

Except it was ugly instead of sexy.

Maybe it was a wrong number.

Her hands felt very cold.

Roger

HE LEANED AGAINST the door of Martha Clay's office, a very tiny concrete cubbyhole on the fifth floor of Green Hall. Assistant professors, especially when they were women, were assigned the sort of office space that in the good old days of the late 1960s had been given to junior research assistants. Ah, for the years of the government gravy train.

"Welcome back, Professor Clay. I hope you had a nice vacation."

Martha looked up from the journal she was reading. "A wonderful vacation!" she exclaimed. Then, as though realizing his feelings might be hurt, she quickly added, "But, of course, it's nice to be back."

"And it's nice to have you back." So, another reconciliation with the husband? Well, she would get over that quickly enough. "I'm not supposed to tell you this"—Roger looked discreetly either way down the dimly lit corridor—"but the provost hinted to me—and the phone call was from Saint Maarten, so it must have been important—that they will renew your appointment. Nothing official, of course, but the provost reads the auguries pretty well."

"A five-year term appointment?" she asked expectantly.

So she would have settled for the compromise? "No. They were ready to give in without a fight. The whole works. As they put it, a lifetime appointment in the University."

Martha smiled complacently. "Well, it's certainly nice to win. I suppose we should postpone the formal celebration until the news is official. You never can know with those chauvinists in administration. Somebody might remind them I'm a woman."

"Oh, I think they know that. The provost kept calling you Mrs. Clay. Anyway, I thought we might celebrate informally later on this afternoon, despite the snowstorm."

He let his suggestion for a tryst hang momentarily in the air while Martha glanced out the window at the mantle of new-fallen snow.

Did he want to reassure himself that he could still be dominant in a sexual relationship? Perhaps.

"I'd love to, Roger, but I have a meeting of the faculty women's committee and then a graduate student party—the beginning of a semester, you know. I don't suppose you'll be able to attend."

"No, I guess not. I'm technically on leave of absence already." His wife had been out of town for a week, and Roger was lonely, despite daily phone conversations with her.

"Let's try something tomorrow night or the next night," she said brightly. "Whenever you're free."

"I have a speech in Rock Island tomorrow evening. I could be free late afternoon the next day."

Sex with her would not compare to the ecstasy with Irene at Christmastime, but it was safe. Odd that a wife would be terrifying in bed and a mistress reassuring. He was deeply in love with two women. The thought of losing either hurt like an exposed dental nerve. Yet if he was not very cautious now, he might lose both.

"My apartment about three thirty, then?" She smiled invitingly.

"Woman, you have yourself a deal." Yet as he walked back to his office Roger was worried. There was a false note somewhere in the conversation. Martha was not as enthusiastic as she had been before Christmas. Women's committee meetings would not have been an excuse then. Whether he lost her might not depend completely on his actions. And that somehow did not seem fair.

Back in his office he rolled typing paper into his IBM typewriter. His basic political speech needed some modification. A little more substance, Mick Gerety had said.

If it had not been for Mick's insistence that he couldn't cancel speeches now, even though he was unopposed in the primary, Roger would have escaped to Tucson with Irene. His usually predictable wife had now become wildly unpredictable. Sometimes she was devastatingly affectionate and other times distant, prickly, contentious.

Last night she had been cheerful and seemed genuinely happy to hear from him. The night before she had had no time to talk. He did not need a turbulent relationship with Irene during a campaign that still had eleven months to run.

And he still had not talked to Noele. Brigid saw through his repeated lies and was furious with him.

Roger typed out a paragraph of frightening facts about the deterioration of the Illinois economy vis à vis the Sun Belt states. Irene was in the Sun Belt. What had happened between them? An interlude, a passing phenomenon. It could not survive. She was the devouring mother goddess for a few nights, that was all.

But, dear God in heaven, what magic nights they'd been!

He typed a few more sentences. The Irene who came back would be the old Irene, unappealing and unthreatening.

And the Noele problem was not as serious as Brigid made it out to be. The term paper was over. She had received her *A* in social studies and was now worrying about her PSAT. On the fringes of his consciousness Roger heard a warning that from Noele silence did not mean that a quest was over. Before he could attend to the warning voice, his phone rang.

"A man on the phone says he wants to talk to you," the ineffable Mrs. Marshfield announced, as though she could not believe that the man actually wanted to talk to him.

"Mr. Farrell," he said politely.

"Bill Wells here, Roger. I hadn't heard from you, so I assumed you were going ahead with the race."

"That's right, Bill," Roger said, trying to sound smooth and confident. "I'll have to take my chances on what comes out. If the people don't want me as their governor, the place to indicate that decision is in the ballot booth, not in the editorial columns of newspapers."

Wells was silent for a moment. "That's a pretty hard-nosed stand, Roger."

"I don't think I have much choice, Bill."

"I suppose not. . . . Well, I hear your friend from the magazine was over at the opposition again, looking for a job. They offered him a two-hundred-and-fifty-dollar kill fee for his article, but the kid didn't take it. He still thinks he's a combination Woodward and Bernstein of the 1980s."

"My decision is final, Bill. I'm in this race to the bitter end. Thanks for keeping me informed."

Roger felt ill. It was a dirty, messy world. Maybe he should have been the priest instead of John.

What was he thinking about when the phone rang?

Oh, yes, Noele. And her moods. *Boring* was her latest word. School, the High Club, the folk Mass, ballet lessons, gymnastics—everything was boring. Would she find his story about Danny boring too? No telling how she would react.

He tried to corner her as soon as he came home, but she had to baby-sit at the Foleys'.

Finally, at 11:30, she walked into his study, sat back wearily in the easy chair, and composed herself, as though she were a novice about to hear a sermon from the archbishop.

"All right, what is it you want to talk about?"

Roger wet his lips with his tongue. "It's sort of about that family-history term paper you were doing."

"Oh, that! Roger, I finished that at the beginning of December." She was braiding her long hair, a sure sign that she was *really bored*.

"We've talked about it in the family, Snowflake, and we feel you have the right to know what really happened the night your grandfather died, both because you are a part of the family and because we want you to understand why it's something that we are careful about."

Noele said nothing.

"The truth is . . ." He sighed, again feeling the pain and horror of that terrible night. "Damn it, Noele, this isn't easy to talk about; my father had his faults, heaven knows, and he wasn't very good to your grandmother. But he was my father."

His genuine anguish merited him no sympathy. "I know he wasn't very nice to Grams," Noele said coldly.

"I'll come to the point, then; Danny killed my father. That's the simple and honest truth, Noele."

"I know that," she said impatiently.

"Do you want to know why he did it?"

"If you want to tell me. I don't *have* to know."

"It was a foolish fight. Both of them had too much to drink that night. And when my father was very drunk he became quite . . . well, let's say outspoken. And Danny had a hot temper too. They had had an argument earlier in the evening, and it started up again when they came home, upstairs in the room that's Burke's study now. My father hit Danny with a cane. Danny grabbed the cane away from him and swung it back. My father ran out of the room, tripped at the edge of the stairs, and tumbled down the staircase."

"How horrible," said Noele tonelessly. She wasn't giving much away.

"When the police came, it looked like an accident, and Mom and Father John and I, well . . . we felt sorry for Danny, we knew he was going off on a very dangerous job, and that he would do much more for the country working for the CIA than sitting in the jail down in Joliet. You see, Noele, it wasn't murder, not in the legal sense. They would have called it involuntary manslaughter or something like that, and he would have had a year or two in jail. Danny knew we were protecting him, but he wasn't even able to say thank you. Not even to me, and I was his closest friend."

Roger's voice trembled at the memory of how much Danny's ultimate ingratitude hurt.

"Then he went to the training camp for the CIA out west. And was dead a few months later."

"*If* he's dead," Noele said sullenly.

"Noele," Roger almost screamed, "he *is* dead."

"If you say so, Roger."

There's something else on her mind. What is it? It doesn't matter. I've got to finish this thing. Roger rushed on with the story.

"It would not have brought Dad back to life, but it would have destroyed Dan completely. We thought that, well, maybe if he left the country and worked for the CIA for a couple of years and came back, maybe he would be grown-up and maybe . . . I don't know what, Noele, but do you understand?"

She nodded. "Yes, Roger, I understand."

"So you see why we would rather leave the whole thing just the way it was," he concluded in frustrated desperation. "And why we don't want you to pursue that term paper any further."

"I told you, Roger," she said quietly. "I'm finished with the term paper. It's boring."

Irene

IRENE HUNG UP the phone and rolled over and faced the comforting warmth of the sunlight with her carefully oiled flesh. The Rafertys had been good enough to lend her their house in Tucson, which they hardly ever used anyway. For much of the week she had basked at poolside in the foothills of the Santa Catalina mountains, reveling in the warmth and the peace. Only Roger knew where she was. He called her every day to pour out his dreams of what he would do as governor, idealistic fantasies of the sort that had attracted her when she'd met him at Berkeley, after she had run away from home.

The dreams had been wiped out in the tragedies of 1968—the King and Kennedy murders, the Democratic convention riots, the election of Nixon. He had taken refuge behind the pose of the detached, faintly amused academic.

And now the dreams were back again, and so was something purporting to be love. It would not last; it was merely an episode, albeit a spectacularly passionate one.

Her one extra drink on Christmas Eve had triggered it. She was a sensual mother again, a confidante who could nurse his wounds, a substitute for Brigid, but a passing one.

The same role she played for his brother the priest.

Both furiously passionate men when they were aroused, but lacking the sensitivity that Danny . . .

Always thinking of Danny.

When we began together, Danny knew little more about women's needs than they do now. But he set out to learn and learned very quickly indeed. I was a seminar for him on how to be tender and sweet to a woman, when to be fiercely passionate, and when to be delicately gentle. It was embarrassing—and terribly erotic—the way he watched me and studied me. All the better to hide his real self, of course.

She should not think of Danny. She was here for the peace and the warmth, a naked body on an inflated mattress with a pool into which she could occasionally jump and a full pitcher of martinis.

She did not leave the house except for two trips to a shopping mall for food. No sight-seeing, no shopping, no contact with anyone.

All of her problems would be waiting for her when she returned. But for a few glorious days she could forget about them.

A surprise? Well, not exactly. An interlude rather.

"There are still surprises in life, Renie," Father McNamara had said. "That's what Christmas means."

"Noele was a surprise," she said to him, laughing. "There haven't been any good ones since then."

"None that you've noticed," he said grinning.

It had been a strange conversation. She had not mentioned Brigid's accusation about Danny or her dangerous romance with John or even her hidden stories. Rather, she had begun by apologizing for having let Father McNamara down by her failure to amount to anything.

"And I was so disappointed that I joined the foreign legion."

"Silly, I didn't mean that. But you were counting on us, weren't you?"

"Only to be happy." He laughed again. He laughed all the time, just as he did in the old days. "It was your idea to be a writer, but you had to make it my idea, which turned it into an obligation you had to obey. And then I became your father, and you ran away from me."

"Didn't you want me to write?"

"I didn't even know you could write until you showed me your stories. You were good at it. Probably still are. And writing would make you happy. But that's not the only way. God, unlike the South Side Irish, is a pluralist."

"I suppose."

"You don't want to give up your obligation to please me, do you? Okay, I'll cooperate. I'm a broken man, destroyed because Renie Conlon . . ."

She was laughing as loudly as he. Then she tried to change the subject. "Does Noele feel an obligation to please you?"

"The other way around. And you're trying to change the subject."

She could speak about none of the worries that plagued her, and he did not force her to. A typically Irish plea for help without help being mentioned or any plea made.

But he heard her and told her by his laughter that he was there when she needed him.

Like all the Farrells, she was recklessly running head on for disaster. She would need him all right. And soon.

"You're beautiful."

"John. . . ." He was dimly visible through her sunshades. She should dash for something to cover herself, but lethargy and heat robbed her of her energy. "What are you doing here?"

"I found out where you were. I'm going back to Chicago from the Caribbean via Arizona."

He stood over her, dressed in light blue slacks and a sport jacket, arms folded somberly, like a conquering warrior.

"I want you, Irene."

"I want you, too."

He sat next to her at poolside and began to kiss and caress her. His lips explored her breasts, a child suckling its mother. She drew him close and hugged him with gentle passion.

Yes, yes, yes. Why not? It didn't matter. Nothing mattered anymore.

"Oh, Danny . . ." she murmured.

He drew away from her.

Oh, my God . . .

And he laughed. "You're not ready yet, Irene?"

"I need more time." I must need more time, otherwise why would I make such a terrible mistake. And he's not angry with me. He's patient with me, as he was with poor Tommy Taylor.

"And we both need cooling off."

He rolled her into the pool and dove in after her, clothes and all—and was in those moments even more like Danny.

Later, huddled in a towel and sipping a martini, she told him the truth about himself. "You pretend to be a liberal in the parish, John, but you're really an authoritarian. And you're desperately dependent on the approval of other priests and the people of your parish, so much so that at times you don't have any character at all."

"No clothes left on me," he said lightly, though he was badly hurt.

"Let me finish. And everyone knows those things, and they still love you, because you are kind and good and generous."

"You love me?"

"Of course I do."

He gripped her hand fiercely. "The way everyone else does?"

"No, the way a woman loves a man."

He relaxed his grip. "I can wait, Irene."

"I didn't mean that." What did she mean? Her head was whirling—too much vodka, too much sexual arousal. "Anyone can make love to me. Not anyone can be a priest."

"What's a priest?" he demanded.

"Someone who can love you without having to screw you."

He turned away from her, his eyes scanning the distant mountains bathed in the purple hues of twilight.

Now, why did I say that, Irene thought. I'm drunk. But that doesn't mean I'm wrong. I've only made matters worse. I should have let him make love to me. Then he would get over me quickly. Now . . .

And why did I think he was Danny?

···*Noele*···

JAIMIE BURNS SPENT the first two weeks in January skiing at Steamboat Springs with his roommate, DeWitt Carlisle, and returned with a gorgeous tan.

"Just look at you," Noele complained at Red's hamburger stand after Friday night High Club. "And I look as pale as a ghost."

"A very beautiful ghost," Jaimie assured her.

"You must have done all kinds of bad things in Steamboat Springs to start paying me compliments."

"I didn't do anything bad," Jaimie said cheerfully.

"I'll have a Tab and french fries," she told Red, who always insisted on serving her personally.

"The usual," Red said.

"Tell me about it." Noele smiled at him.

"I'm accused of playing around with coeds in the mountains, and you're flirting with Red."

"Don't be gross. Do you want to hear the end of the Danny Farrell story?"

Jaimie was instantly serious. "You bet I do."

So Noele told him about her conversation with Roger.

"You sound like you don't believe it." Jaimie had been watching her intently.

"I sort of believe it, Jaimie. I mean, I don't think Roger's *totally* lying to me. But there are a lot of things I don't understand." She wasn't going to tell Jaimie yet about the short story "The Buying of the Baby," not yet, maybe not ever.

She had, however, figured out what she would do. As soon as Uncle John came back from Puerto Rico or wherever he was she was going to confront him and demand the whole truth. *Then* she would talk to Father Ace and *maybe* tell Jaimie the whole thing. After that she would have to make lots of decisions.

"Did you ask your father about Florence Farrell's death?"

Noele sighed. "No. He would say it was an accident. And if I pushed him, he'd probably tell me that Clancy arranged it, even if that wasn't true. Clancy is dead and Burkie is alive."

"You think it might have been Burke?"

"Like you said, Burke would do anything to protect Grams . . . anything."

"So, what now?" Jaimie's hand closed on hers.

Gosh, there was a lot of strength in those hands. No wonder he could intercept passes like he was black. She thought she might tell him about the weird phone calls but decided there was no reason to worry him. She could cope by herself.

She was going to have to learn to cope by herself.

"I'm going to think about it a little bit more, then talk to Father Ace, and talk to you again, and then it's all over. . . . Oh, thanks, Red, but that's too many french fries."

Jaimie tilted her chin up so he could look her directly in the eyes.

"There's something I guess I better tell you. Dad called me in Steamboat. The CIA talked to him. Danny is dead. He was a prisoner for a long time, but now he's dead."

"Yes, he's dead," she said slowly. "I guess I've known that for some time now. Maybe I should forget about him."

She felt the same way she had when she'd been a tomboy and was into fence-climbing. She wanted to be free of Danny; she wanted to believe that he was dead so she could forget about him and worry about herself. But she couldn't quite climb to the top of the Danny Farrell fence. She might say she knew he was dead. But she did not fully believe her own words, not quite, not yet.

"Make me a promise?" Jaimie said, his hand even tighter on hers.

"Sure."

"Don't do anything big without talking to me about it first."

"Really!" Noele exclaimed, meaning there was no way she could do anything serious without talking to Jaimie.

Yet she knew that she didn't completely trust anyone anymore, not even Jaimie.

And she was still numb, as numb as she had been on Christmas Eve when she'd read the story.

Nosy little bitch. It serves you right.

She was the only one in the house when Jaimie dropped her off that night. Roger was giving a talk someplace and Moms was still in Arizona. She had pulled the blankets up to her chin when the phone rang. Even before she answered it she knew who it was.

Again the heavy breathing and then the threat. "We'll cut off your tits and then shove them up your cunt."

John

ACE AND JOHN were sitting at the rectory lunch table after the 12:15 P.M. Mass, Ace devouring the "Week in Review" section of the Sunday *New York Times,* John reading the entertainment section of the *Chicago Tribune.*

"Your suntan is a reproach to me for my sinfulness," the Ace said as he peeled an orange—part of a gift package John had brought back from his trip.

"Puerto Rico is a wonderful place; I can recommend it thoroughly."

John decided not to fly from Arizona to Florida and then back to Chicago. Only a few people knew that he was supposed to be in Puerto Rico, and they were not likely to be on the plane from Tucson.

On the crowded DC-10 returning to Chicago, he did not feel the slightest guilt. He was in love. His lover was hesitant. He would be sensitive to her hesitancy as long as was necessary. Then he would have her.

Afterward?

He would worry about that bridge when he came to it. No, he was worrying about it now. Guilt was catching up. He had to talk to someone.

"Dick, would you mind coming upstairs?" he blurted impulsively. "I'd like to talk to you for a few minutes."

"Sure." Ace folded his *New York Times* neatly—the Navy had taught him to do all things neatly—and followed him up the stairs.

John carefully closed the door to his suite and, without asking, mixed two drinks. A vodka martini for himself—one of the many tastes he shared with Irene—and Jameson's neat for Father McNamara.

He put the three bottles on the coffee table.

The two men sat opposite each other on imposing leather armchairs that, John had thought, created the right ambience for a pastor of St. Praxides.

Now the chairs and the couches seemed dull and pompous.

"The guys getting to you?" Ace said sympathetically.

"God, yes," John replied, happy to have a chance to talk about that problem, though it was not what was encroaching upon his sanity.

"You'd better make up your mind, John," the Ace said slowly. "You're at a turning point now. If you go on with your program, particularly if it is syndicated around the country, you'll be a pariah in the priesthood for the rest of your life."

"You too?" John said in surprise.

"I'm not telling you to quit; I'm merely saying what will happen. You'll become the victim of collective envy neurosis. Your motives will be questioned. Your personality and character will be distorted so that you will not recognize yourself. Your friends and your family will be called upon to defend you by almost every priest and nun they encounter. Any attempts you make to reply will be twisted to fit the neurosis. You will become a myth that many of your fellow priests will love to hate. And even those who are free of the neurosis will tell you that you shouldn't expect anything else."

"You'll turn me into a paranoid," John said somberly.

"No, I'm just warning you that a lot of paranoids will be chasing you." McNamara grinned, though not very enthusiastically, at his own joke. "Envy is maybe the third most powerful human motive, after hunger and sex. We have no monopoly on it in the priesthood. Hell, you never hear a word about it in psychology classes because their profession is riddled by it too. It's the fault that even the analysts won't discuss."

"Are we worse?" John asked, seeing with terrible clarity that McNamara was saying nothing but the simple truth.

"Probably. Our reward structure is pretty thin; and we're socialized into it in the seminary because it's a very useful means of imposing control. Ruins talent, of course, but our leaders don't want talent anyway."

"So if I go ahead I better be sure that my friends and family are enough to support me?"

"Don't even count on your friends." The Ace emptied his glass of Jameson's and filled it again. "The negative myth will stick to you for the rest of your life. Some of your friends will secretly envy you and others will succumb to pressure to go along with the myth."

"You too?" John said softly.

The Ace grinned. "Naw, I'm the kind that stays bought. A bottle of Jameson's every weekend and Captain McNamara will go ashore with the first wave of marines."

"I suppose the program's connected with the other thing I want to talk about," John said, trying to muster the courage he needed to talk about Irene. "I'm in love, Dick."

"Huh?" McNamara was obviously utterly surprised.

"I wasn't in the Caribbean all the time. I was somewhere else with a woman. I didn't go to bed with her, not yet. . . ." John saw how petty, almost comic, it all was. How many times must a priest trained in psychology have heard the same words?

"Do you plan to leave the priesthood?" The Ace's eyes were hooded, and his voice neutral.

"I don't know. I . . . I don't think we could ever be married. When I tell you who, you'll understand."

"There's no need for me to know that."

"Yes, there is."

"Oh?"

"Irene."

A flicker in the former chaplain's eyes showed that he was surprised. Or perhaps impressed.

"Maybe you'd better tell me all about it," said Father McNamara.

So John told him everything, all the way back to his grandfather's death and the first battle of the Philippine Sea.

"The priesthood was an escape for me. I felt that by being a good priest I was making up for the bad things that have happened. Even before Irene the priesthood was slipping through my fingers. If I'd stayed off that damn televison program I'd still be an accepted and admired member of the presbyterate. I wouldn't have had to turn to Irene."

"Too simple, John," Ace protested, his usually mobile face grim and somber. "You're at an age when almost anything could push you into a love affair. Don't blame the TV program. And don't blame the family for your vocation. You didn't become a priest to expiate."

"They've made a lot of sacrifices for me. I owe them something." Before Ace could ask what that meant, John's personal phone rang. Reluctantly he answered it.

"Noele." He tried to be bright and cheerful. "Good to talk to you again. Sure, tomorrow night at eight o'clock? Far be it from me to interfere with the gymnastics meet. Everything okay?"

I'm so preoccupied with myself, he thought guiltily as he hung up the phone, *that I forget the danger she could be in if those papers are ever published.*

"Something's bugging her too," he said to Dick McNamara.

"I wouldn't worry all that much about Noele." McNamara smiled for the first time in their conversation. "She may have some hard times ahead, but she can take care of herself."

"And I can't?"

The Ace buried his head in his hands for a moment, searching for a response. "What happens, John, is that either a man leaves the priesthood or he works the woman out of his system."

"What will happen to me?"

"You'll survive; I worry about Irene, a beautiful and gifted woman who probably doesn't love her husband, and almost certainly feels she has wasted her life. Now she's in love with a man who is a surrogate for her dead lover."

"I'm a surrogate for Danny?"

Ace turned in surprise from the bar, where he was pouring himself his third Irish whiskey. "Certainly, John. You mean you haven't figured that out yet?"

Ace

HE LOOKED OUT the window of the tiny guest room in the rectory. The snow was beginning to melt under a quiet winter sun, one of the phony thaws that would tease Chicago for the next two months. The asphalt on the Courts was still covered. No teenagers there today.

Poor John. At a crossroads in the priesthood. Faced by massive rejection from his colleagues and in love at the same time. Randy and romantic, obsessed with a foolish love and unaware that Noele was going to hit him with a massive two-by-four.

John was a survivor. Transparent, vain, generous, pompous, kind—and a survivor.

Again Ace wondered how such a family of self-preoccupied cowards could have produced a Noele.

Genetic mistake? Perhaps not. Danny was a Farrell too. He was not a coward. And not a survivor either. Despite the warmth of his room Ace shivered.

Why did all the Farrells have to turn away stubbornly from the possibilities life offered them and settle on such dull terms of respectability and social approval?

Roger would make the gubernatorial race look like an academic bore, John would turn an important career in mass communications into a fearsome battle with clerical culture, Irene would continue to bury her talent.

And Danny had died young because of some foolish notions of chivalry.

But they had not yet got to Noele.

Not yet, but she was weakening.

What a fool Irene had been to leave that story where Noele could read it. Almost as if she wanted to be caught.

Brigid

IT TOOK SEVERAL days for the warmth of the Mexican sun to melt away her weariness. "We're going to Acapulco," Burke had said to her at supper on January second. It was not an idea for discussion or a suggestion. It was an order. She'd been too tired to argue.

Brigid had never learned to swim, and her fair skin blistered with the first ray of sun. But she loved to look at the sea, lying with Burke in the shade of their patio in a house in the hills overlooking the beach, holding hands like young lovers.

"The woman is not as young as she used to be," she said, and sighed. "It'll take at least another week before I'm ready to go home. I could lie here in the warmth forever."

"Maybe we ought to, Bridie." Burke sat up and leaned against the post supporting the canopy over their heads. "Maybe it's time for you to relax and realize that the world won't rush in and destroy you if you stop working."

"Give up the firm?"

"Retire, relax, and enjoy. For most of your life you've been running—from a cruel father, and a cruel husband, and a cruel foster son who threatened to kill you. Farrell and Sons has never protected you from the demons, has it?"

"No, you're the only protection I have, Burke," she said quickly.

"It's time to stop running, Bridie."

"Is it, now?" she said hotly, her voice tinged with brogue. "Should we stop running and let the truth catch up with us? I don't know about you, but I'm too old to go to jail. How can we relax with all the evil things we've done still on our consciences? I work to forget about them."

"We could try to forget," he said lamely. "Travel . . . get away from Chicago."

"Run out on the firm during a recession? And what about Noele? She's mine, the only grandchild I'll ever have. If the truth catches up—and, God help us, it might—who will protect her if I'm not there?"

"Stop thinking about that," he said impatiently. "The whole matter is closed."

"Maybe it is and maybe it isn't," she said furiously. "All of us are bent on our own destruction. We're going to save the Almighty the task of punishing us by doing it ourselves!"

And then, sorry about her anger, she tried to compromise. "Anyway, will you think this conversation a success if I promise you that I'll think very seriously about it?"

"An enormous success. One that I rarely expect in an initial conversation with you."

She swung at him fiercely. "You're a terrible man, Burke Kennedy."

He grabbed her hand and held it. "And you are a very soft and vulnerable woman, Bridie."

"I know that look in your eye," she said, pretending to escape. "I know what you have on your mind."

He slid the straps of her bathing suit off both her shoulders. "Do you, now?"

The holiday had turned Burke into a young buck. He tugged savagely at her swimsuit.

Brigid was frightened by his hunger—and delighted. It was like the room in the Palmer House once again. A terrible, terrible man, no respect for a decent woman at all, she thought, sighing in abject resignation.

Thank God he still wants me. Dear God, don't take him away from me. Please don't. Not yet.

Not ever.

Despite the banter and the laughter and the pleasure under the cloudless sky,

Brigid was as frightened as she had been on the cold winter morning when her father woke her up to send her away from her home forever.

Roger

THE FIRE IN his study fireplace had died down to embers. There was a black-and-white French Foreign Legion movie on television, to which he was paying no attention, but he was too physically exhausted to turn the set off. A gubernatorial candidate should have a remote control for his TV, he told himself.

Chicago was reeling under ten inches of snow. O'Hare was closed, and Irene's plane had been diverted to Minneapolis and then to Milwaukee. She had phoned from Milwaukee saying that she was boarding a bus that would bring her into the Chicago loop. There were only snow flurries north of the Wisconsin line. "Don't wait up for me," she'd said. "I may not be home until noon tomorrow."

"I'll wait," he said briefly. He was both afraid of her return and eager for it.

"Suit yourself," she had said, every bit as briefly.

It had been a terrible day. The "Farrell for Governor" campaign headquarters had opened for its first full day of work. Channel 6's TV cameras discovered chaos, as its assignment editor knew it would. The telephones were out of order, the duplicating machine broke down, the door to the men's room was jammed shut, several boxes of mailing lists were mysteriously lost, the computerized research system was not functioning, the candidate himself was in everyone's way.

"Not a very good beginning, is it, Dr. Farrell?" asked a tall young blonde with a microphone in her hand.

"Republicans have the smooth beginnings, Ms. Hennessey," he had countered, chuckling, "and Democrats have the strong endings."

"Then you're predicting that you will be the next governor of the state of Illinois?" she demanded, doing her best to sound like a hard-nosed news veteran.

She was a lovely young thing, fair Irish. Politics had its own slave markets. . . .

"Of course." He chuckled again. Have to watch that. Not the same chuckle too many times. "That's why I'm running. Now, if you'll excuse me, Maryjane, I must find out why no one thought of assigning an office to me."

He smiled cheerfully, and he hoped handsomely, at the red light above the lens of the video camera, and waited till the red light flicked off. Then he winked at Maryjane Hennessey and said, "I'm not sure anyone here knows what state this is."

Five minutes later Mick and Angie came into his office, their faces as long as the Mississippi River.

They've found out about Joe Kramer.

"We've been hearing things on the street, Governor," Mick said somberly.

"Why the hell did you let those papers out of your office?" asked Angie.

Roger heard almost none of their arguments. His mind was elsewhere—worrying about Noele and Brigid and Irene. His wife wanted him to stay in the race. She did not know enough about the Marshal to be frightened of him. Perhaps he should withdraw.

Quit.

He hesitated. Prudence dictated that he withdraw. To stay in the race would be like trying to broad-jump the Grand Canyon.

"What is done is done, gentlemen," he said crisply. "I'm in this race to stay, whatever happens to those stolen papers. If someone wants to run as a write-in candidate in the primary, that's up to them. I'll stay in the race. If the governor uses those papers against me in the fall election, I'll stay in the race then, too. Is that clear?"

"It ain't going to help us," said Mick grudgingly.

"I hardly thought it would."

"You're staying in for keeps, no matter what the press says?" Angie asked.

"To the bitter, bitter end, Angelo." It was a decision that he himself was making at that very moment. Damn Irene.

"Got to admire your guts, Governor," Mick said. "Maybe we can keep it out of the paper, and maybe with a few breaks you can turn it around even if it gets in the papers."

Roger smiled benignly. "Michael, it's your job to create the breaks!"

That afternoon he stopped in his office at the University before dropping in at cocktail hour to visit Martha Clay. There was a note on his desk saying that the provost had called. Roger returned the call promptly.

"I'm afraid we've run into a little snag in the case of Mrs. Clay, Roger."

"This has been a day for snags," Roger said easily. "You should have been down at my campaign office, Lawrence."

He heard a dry little rasping laugh. The provost was not ready yet to officially acknowledge that a member of his faculty was actually running for governor.

"Three members of the Committee on Social Theory," he began with the solemnity of one reading a papal encyclical, "have submitted a memo to the dean with copies to me and to the president invoking the Shils report against Mrs. Clay. I won't detain you, Roger, with the contents of the memo, but I'll be happy to send it to you in faculty exchange."

Invoking the Shils report was like quoting scripture before an auto-da-fé.

"Don't bother, Lawrence. I'm sure I know what's in it without reading it. No discussion of Mrs. Clay's work, high praise for the standards set for the University in the past, for the wisdom of the Shils report, and a warning about the too easy gift of lifelong appointments."

Once Roger had asked at the round table whether Shils himself would have measured up to the standards of his sacred writ. There had been no laughter, no smiles, no reaction of any sort.

Blasphemy.

"As you know," Lawrence continued sonorously, "there is a tradition in this University of treating memos from the Committee on Social Theory with great respect."

Respect? More like reverence. The members of the committee rarely published anything. And they rarely met classes. Rather, they existed in a lofty heaven of intellectual abstraction, and accepted as a matter of right the commonly held conviction that their physical presence alone brought the University so much distinction that it was only slightly inferior to Harvard. Their principal activity was meddling in the appointments of other departments in the name of maintaining the same lofty standards of academic productivity and teaching excellence that they maintained themselves.

"How important is this snag going to be?"

The provost hesitated. "The president is quite disturbed by it, as you may imagine. Candidly, Roger, I'm not certain."

Roger decided to play his high card. "Lawrence, I find this outrageous. The government department at this University is distinguished and indeed internationally respected. The majority of the tenured faculty after mature deliberation has made a recommendation. The dean has approved this recommendation. I had an informal communication with you in which you told me you were disposed to transmit our recommendations favorably to the president. Now I'm told another unit of the University, unqualified in any way of which I'm aware to make judgments in the field of political science, has chosen to attempt to override our recommendation. I cannot be responsible, Lawrence, for the consequences of this situation."

A brave idealist as a gubernatorial candidate and a shrewd manipulator working, with dubious motives, for the promotion of his lover. Maybe I would be for her, he told himself, even if I was not obsessed with her. It's a marginal case. There are no strong, positive reasons for expecting that she will be a distinguished or productive member of the University faculty. Yet with a little effort she could easily be as productive as several members of the committee.

"I understand your dismay," said the provost, who had called to see whether Roger proposed to make trouble and learned that he did indeed propose to make trouble. "I assume that you have reason to believe you are not speaking only for yourself?"

Roger laughed bleakly. "You've been at this University for a long time, Lawrence. How the hell do you think government is going to react? Even those of us who had doubts about Mrs. Clay will be furious."

They would be furious only if Roger goaded them to fury, which he was perfectly prepared to do for the love of his mistress.

I am losing control, he told himself. I don't know what I'm doing anymore. I'm like a railroad engine that has jumped the tracks.

"I see," said the provost.

When they met later in the afternoon, the mistress in question seemed both undismayed and unimpressed by Roger's account of the conversation. "More hazing," she said, relaxing comfortably in his embrace.

They had renewed their love affair; yet it was not quite the relationship it used to be. Was it that Martha's abandonment was a little less total? Or was he comparing her unfavorably to his wife?

Afterward they were sipping white wine in her bedroom, partially dressed.

"Have you ever considered the possibility, Roger," she said in her best academic tone, "that you might have bisexual propensities?"

With considerable effort he managed not to choke on the white wine. "I suppose that all of us are bisexual in part," he said. "You'd know more about that because you're more of a Freudian than I am."

It was one thing for him to revel in kinky fantasies, and quite another for the young woman to catch him at it. What the hell kind of game was she playing now?

"Sometimes when you're making love to me"—she was as matter of fact and dispassionate as if they were discussing similarities in Machiavellian and Marxist theory—"I sense you are thinking of me rather more as an attractive boy than as a woman. I'm liberated enough not to mind that; actually, I find it rather stimulating. But it is altogether possible, you know, that it would be healthy for you to seek some sexual release with members of your own sex.''

The rules of intellectualism demanded that he keep the discussion on the same abstract level on which she had placed it. "It's a possibility, of course, and I'll certainly have to take your insight seriously. But I do indeed find you attractive as a woman, Martha. You can take that as a given.''

"Now you're being defensive, Roger. I'm not saying you're gay." She permitted herself a tiny academic smile, rather like the provost's. "I've had more than enough experience to know that you're not—even though, surely, there would be nothing objectionable if you were. I'm merely suggesting that you ought to explore the possibility that some sexual release with men might be morally beneficial for you. I know I'm not gay in any permanent sense of the word. Nonetheless my own lesbian interludes have been very constructive for me.''

Lesbian interludes, he thought derisively. You and someone in your consciousness-raising group played with each other's tits so you both could talk knowingly about "gay sex.''

"I appreciate your candor on the subject, Martha. Let me give it some thought.''

"No need to report back to me.'' Again the tiny, provostlike smile. "More wine?''

The implication was that the homosexual tendency in his personality was so powerful that his mistress could not help but notice it. And if he had yet to experience sexual satisfaction with men, the reason was that he was more repressed and less liberated than she. An infuriating but also frightening suggestion. What if she were right?

And both the fact that she had challenged him and the possibility that the challenge might be valid undercut some of his love for her, as waves undercut a pine-covered bluff. Maybe that was what she intended to happen.

How much time had she spent over Christmas with her ex-husband? Or was he an ex? Was the divorce final?

As he waited for his wife by the light of the dying fire in his study, Roger considered the question of his heterosexuality—objectively, as a good full professor must. He enjoyed the all-male company of the round table of the Faculty Club. And the camaraderie of his golf partners at the Country Club. The only "crush" he could remember in his life was Danny Farrell, and that relationship, while close and intense, had never been overtly physical.

Save in one incident.

And the crush had never ended. Even though Danny was dead.

He had to admit that he did find the physical appearance of handsome young men attractive, although not, on the whole, nearly as attractive as the physical appearance of handsome young women. But maybe he was repressing?

No one could deny that in the Christmas week he had been quite heterosexual with his wife.

But he was ambivalent about continuing such activities.

He groaned aloud. Damn the woman. She'll be able to tell all her feminist bitch friends that I have an interest in young men, which, while not morally objectionable to her, made it very difficult for her to relate to me.

Was she looking for a way out?

And after I went out on a limb with the provost for her.

What a hell of a thing to think. The runaway engine is charging down the embankment.

"Good morning, Governor." He was startled. He had fallen asleep. Irene was leaning provocatively in the doorway of his study in a beige suit that accentuated her glorious suntan.

She peeled off her jacket and flipped it playfully at him. "You look like you want what your mother would delicately call a good fuck."

He was overjoyed at the instant and spontaneous reaction of his body to her suggestion.

·······*John*·······

"SORRY TO KEEP you waiting, Noele," he apologized. "it's been a busy night in the rectory."

"No rush, Uncle Monsignor," Noele said listlessly.

"When I was a young priest, we had orders to close down all rectory offices by ten thirty and be in our rooms by eleven. Nobody would dare to begin a conversation at eleven fifteen."

"Really?" she said, displaying almost no interest.

"And there was a diocesan rule that we were supposed to be in the rectory every night by eleven o'clock. A lot of people didn't keep it, but my first pastor insisted."

Noele was momentarily disconcerted. "Eleven o'clock? You mean you had to be in the rectory every night by eleven o'clock? Were you?"

"I didn't miss a single night in the first four years I was a priest. It had its advantages. I always had an excuse to get out of a boring meeting or party."

Noele seemed very thoughtful.

"I'm sure you didn't come here to talk about old-fashioned clerical rules," he said.

"I want to know who I am," Noele said, her voice a sorrowful whisper.

"I don't understand. You're Noele Marie Farrell, daughter of Roger and Irene Farrell."

"No, I'm not. You and Moms bought me from an out-of-work aerospace engineer in California when I was a baby."

"Did your mother tell you that?" The words burst from John's lips.

"Of course not," his niece replied haughtily. "I *know*, Uncle Monsignor. And don't try to lie to me anymore. I *know*."

"It's not as bad as it seems, Noele." He groped for words of explanation about the past. "And don't judge any of us too harshly."

"Who is my mother? Who is my father?" she demanded.

"Curiously enough, Noele, your mother and father are your mother and father. We did buy you, but we bought you back from a couple who had adopted you. Please give me a chance to explain."

Her swamp-fire eyes were pitiless. "Explain."

"As you probably guessed, your mother was in love with Danny Farrell. Your father was too. Not the same way, of course, but he worshiped the ground that Dan Farrell walked on. And when Danny died, well, your mother and father were drawn to each other. Then Roger went back to graduate school in Berkeley. And Irene simply disappeared. People in the neighborhood thought that she'd had her fill of being ridiculed by her parents and by her brothers and sisters. She was carrying you then, Noele. Roger's child. But she felt that there wasn't any love between her and Roger. She also was afraid of the antagonism between her family and ours. So you were born in California, Noele, the daughter of a mother who could have easily ended your life with an abortion. She was afraid to tell anyone and was convinced that she would fail you as a parent. So you were adopted by a young aerospace engineer and his wife, who'd been told, erroneously, as it turned out, that they would not have any children. Do you understand?''

Noele was as grave as the bishop's master of ceremonies at a solemn pontifical Mass. "So far."

The words were coming quickly and smoothly now. "Your mother and father met again in California. They bumped into each other at a peace rally at Berkeley and discovered that they did indeed love each other after all. It was a quick decision. I went to California to marry them. And then your mother told us about you.''

John rubbed his hand across his forehead. "God in heaven, Noele, the three of us sat there at a cheap little Mexican restaurant in Berkeley and cried about you. We agreed that we had to find some way to get you back.

"I made some inquiries, found out who the family was, and discovered they were under tremendous financial pressure. It was a tough decision for everyone, Noele. What we did may seem terribly cruel to the couple who adopted you. We felt we had to do it.''

The green eyes were now awash with tears, the swamp fire extinguished.

"I didn't mean to make you cry,'' John said wearily. "But didn't it work out for the best? You were reunited with your mother and father who, it turned out, could not have any more children. The people who took care of you for the first ten months of your life later had four children of their own. He is now the president of his own electronics firm. He started the firm with the money—''

"With the money you gave him to buy me?'' Tears were streaming down her face, but she was smiling.

"You are the one who must judge us, Noele. Forgive us if you can.''

"There's nothing for me to forgive.'' She grinned at him, the bumptious director of the folk group again.

Lord, how resilient they are.

"And you're not angry?''

"How could I possibly stay angry at you, Uncle Monsignor?'' She hugged him briskly. And then, almost as an afterthought, she added, "One question though: Do you think Mother married Roger mostly so she could buy me back?''

A bolt of lightning across the night sky after the storm had cleared.

"She married your father, Noele, because she discovered that she had loved him all along. And he discovered the same thing.''

Noele nodded solemnly. "I suppose so.''

A few moments later, on his prie-dieu, the image of the happy youngster bounding down the steps and across the snow-covered street to her red car fresh in his brain, he prayed, "Forgive me. She was sad, and I made her happy, just like we made Brigid happy with the same story. Isn't the truth often what we want it to be?''

SHE SAT AT her desk in a heavy robe staring hypnotically at the chilly winter landscape outside her window. It was fifteen below zero, a bitter cold mid-January day, even though the sky was clear and the sun deceptively bright.

She was still working on her story about the married woman who had an affair with her brother-in-law, who was a priest, a story that subtly explored the possibility that the two lovers reenforced each other, the heroine's passion for the brother igniting a passion her heroine had never felt for her husband.

She opened her secret file and placed the typed pages neatly on her desk. Then she removed an old Cross pen from an austere holder in front of her. She read the first sentence of the manuscript and tried to replace a comma with a semi-colon.

The pen was out of ink. She sighed, resenting as she always did the need to replace the cartridge. She opened the drawer in the center of her desk and then sat up abruptly. Her short story "The Buying of the Baby," was in the drawer, underneath the spare keys to the Seville. It must have been there for weeks.

What a stupid and unthinking thing to do. Suppose Roger had read it. Or Noele. . . . She examined the pages very carefully. They seemed in order and, as well as she could remember them, in the same position in which she had left them in the drawer. But her memory for such things was poor. Anybody might have read the story.

Shivering, she slipped the manuscript into the leather case, restored it to the secret compartment of her desk, and returned uneasily to her story.

She was trying to write an intensely erotic tale without explicit description, all the more powerful in its sexuality, she hoped, precisely because there were no clinical details.

She reread the story with a critical eye, occasionally altering a word or inserting a sentence, until she reached the last page.

> *So she knelt in front of him and teased him lovingly. Numbed by physical exhaustion, guilt, and the worry of flying through a snowstorm, Lorraine was free of all restraint. "I've never loved you as much as I love you tonight." The words tumbled out of her mouth as if spoken by a stranger. Yet at that moment they were the total truth of her life.*

In her small precise hand she wrote a new and final paragraph; she would retype the page later.

> *When they are young, men use love about which they know very little, to obtain sex, about which they know much. Women use sex, about which they know little, to obtain love, about which they know much. And as they mature, if they mature, most men and women are able to share in the perspective of the other. Neither Lorraine nor the two men whose needs she had used to anneal her pain would ever be anything but adolescents.*
>
> *In fleeing from despair to sensuality, Lorraine had become a whore.*

She reread the two paragraphs, pen in hand, and considered adding two final sentences, which were screaming inside her skull.

"Sensuality would depart soon. There would remain only despair."

She scrawled wild circles across the page. A dishonest story. There was no mention of the fourth person in the parallelogram, the man Lorraine loved, the corpse who had her sealed up in his own unmarked tomb.

D.C.I.

A BOTTLE OF beer reassuring his hand, the Director relaxed in front of his television to watch Notre Dame play Georgetown. Beer and basketball—hardly the image he had created for himself at the Company. But he'd played basketball in college and enjoyed the rich, New York accent of Al McGuire as he conducted a coaching seminar illustrating the mistakes of Digger Phelps and John Thompsen.

The red phone next to his chair rang. He sighed and picked it up. What were the Russians doing now?

"Radford, chief. Sorry to interrupt the game."

How did Radford know he was watching the game? "Yes," the Director said crossly.

"I have some rather surprising information for you."

Brigid

THE FAMILY WAS arranged around the dinner table, with the exception of Noele, who had been excused to watch the end of the Notre Dame–Georgetown game and Jaimie's six-foot-eleven-inch black roommate, DeWitt Carlisle. (According to Noele they had stopped counting his I.Q. at 175, and he was totally cute.)

Brigid glanced around the table. The family was off-key again tonight. Irene solemn, John restless and hyperactive, Roger as moody as she had ever seen him, even Burke glum and unreadable.

Perhaps they all realized that they were skating toward the edge of the pit.

After John had led the grace, Brigid, mostly to placate Burke, made the suggestion that she retire from the firm and embark on a "career change," which meant, "if I'm to believe my husband, that I'll make a career of doing practically nothing, but enjoying it all."

"Now that's not fair, Bridie," Burke said stiffly.

"I know it's not fair. But I'll confess to everyone that the prospect of spending another month or two in Mexico is extremely attractive."

"Then what would you do?" John asked. "You're a young woman, Mother, why retire from life?"

"The intention isn't that she retire from life, but merely from the firm. The firm isn't life," Burke insisted.

"A rather shocking view to hear from you, Burke," Roger said. "Do you think Mother is ready to be a grand dame, wandering around on some world tour?''

''I think Burke feels that I'll stay a younger woman longer if I escape some of the madness of the firm.'' Brigid knew that her sons would resist her retirement. ''And you, my dear?'' She nodded at Irene, not altogether sure why, except that the woman had shown some spunk lately.

''Oh, I didn't know that I was supposed to vote. I think you should do exactly what you want to do, Brigid.''

''And what do you think that is?'' she persisted.

''I think you want to do both.'' Irene smiled faintly and then relapsed into the faraway world in which she spent so much of her time.

''A very perceptive answer.'' Brigid looked around the room and prepared to tell her family exactly how she proposed to do both.

Noele entered the dining room. Ah, the child is beautiful, Brigid thought. And the peat shines in her eyes.

But there was something about the glow on her face and the brilliance of the fire in her eyes that stirred fear in the deep substratum of superstition that existed, rock hard, at the core of Brigid's personality.

''The game over?'' Roger asked cheerfully.

''There was a news brief on television after the game ended,'' Noele said, and Brigid heard the sound of fairy dance music in her voice. ''It will probably interest all of you. The American Embassy in Beijing has reported that the last American held prisioner in China has been released. He was an alleged employee of the Central Intelligence Agency, shot down on a U-2 flight in 1964. His name is Daniel Farrell, and his last known address was Chicago, Illinois.''

DANCE SEVEN

Bolero

"Danced by one dancer or a couple, it includes many brilliant and intricate steps, quick movements, and a sudden stop in a characteristic position with one arm held arched over the head."

THE FOLLOWING WEEK, after the Super Bowl game, there was a brief glimpse of Danny Farrell on the NBC Sunday Night News. Dressed in a gray suit, he stood in front of the American Embassy in Beijing, silver-haired, slender, smiling.

"He looks totally like Paul Newman. Look at those awesome eyes!" Noele exclaimed.

"Are you an employee of the Central Intelligence Agency, Mr. Farrell?" asked the journalist who was interviewing him.

The lean, handsome face came alive; the blue eyes glowed. "Of what?"

"The CIA," the reporter insisted.

A wide leprechaunish grin lit Danny's face. "Never heard of the organization. What does it do?"

"I mean, *really,* he has Paul Newman's eyes," Noele insisted. "Don't you think so, Grams?"

"Huh, child," said the weeping Brigid.

"Is it true that you were flying a U-2 over China when you were shot down eighteen years ago?"

"That's what the local authorities say."

"What were you doing in that plane, sir?"

"Taking pictures."

"For whom?"

"For an American news magazine that I hear is dead now."

"Do you feel, sir, like someone who's come back from the dead?"

"Nope, I feel like the rest of the world has come back from the dead. Me, I've been alive all along."

"What have you being doing the past week, Mr. Farrell?"

"Reading back issues of *Time* magazine."

"Are there any changes in American society that disappoint you?"

"Sure are. The miniskirt is gone!"

"What kept you going through the years in Chinese prison?"

The leprechaun grin brightened. "Religious faith."

Jane Pauley was back on the screen. "Farrell will return to the United States in the middle of the week for, as he puts it, conferences with the executives of the news magazine that went out of business a long time ago. Most Washington reporters believe that the conference will occur at the headquarters of the Central Intelligence Agency in Langley, Virginia."

"Same old Danny," John said, as though he could not believe what he had seen and heard.

"Is he?" said Roger thoughtfully. "I wonder."

Brigid was in tears. "Would you look at the color of his hair. Ah, the poor, poor boyo."

"No, not a boy," Burke said solemnly. "Not anymore."

Irene, looking like a widow at a wake, said nothing.

"I still think he looks like Paul Newman," Noele said in a tone that refused to admit the possibility of disagreement. "Really."

···*D.C.I.*···

RADFORD LEANED BACK in his chair, loosened his tie, took out his handkerchief, and wiped his forehead. "Chief, I know damn well you have a bottle of bourbon in that hidden cabinet in your desk," he said. "Pour me a double one. Neat, straight up, and quick."

It was the first time that the Director had seen Radford even slightly rattled.

"Wonderland," Radford said, gulping down half of the tumbler of the Old Fitz the Director had poured for him.

"Certifiably mad?"

Radford leaned forward. "Let me put it this way, chief. If Dan Farrell had come back from that mission and if he'd stayed with the Company, he might have your job now, and all the rest of us might be locked up in an asylum."

"Indeed," said the D.C.I.

"I told him, of course, that we would consider that he has been on the payroll for the last eighteen years with a pay scale commensurate with the usual promotions plus the interest that would have accrued from investments over that period of time."

"That's a big chunk of money," the Director said nervously. "What did he say to that?"

"He said, 'Tom'—he either called me Tom or General all through our conversations— 'Tom, that's not nearly enough to keep me quiet if I want to tell the whole story, and entirely too much if I don't.'"

"Is he going to embarrass us?"

"He claims he won't. He asked who ordered his termination—he'd figured that out—and suggested that if the man was still around he ought to be fired because he'd made a mess of it."

The D.C.I. frowned. "And this novel he's writing? Is it about us?"

"It's about an Irish Catholic family in Chicago. Not his own family, either, or so he says. He claims that he has every word of the novel in his head. That all he has to do is get to a typewriter to put it down. He also says that the Company won't be mentioned once. Then he added, with that funny laugh of his, 'not in this novel, anyway, General.' ''

"What do our shrinks say? Was he brainwashed?"

"He didn't object to our using some hypnotism to probe into his unconscious. Apparently he was subject to no more pressures than anyone else in China during the Great Proletarian Cultural Revolution. The Chinese released him from prison seven years ago and sent him to a commune in Hunan province, where he was an agricultural worker and also a member of the local defense militia. It would seem that he was pretty well integrated into the society. He speaks Chinese fluently and is providing us with some interesting information about how the country works. The shrinks say he was able to make a reasonably satisfactory adjustment to a totally different culture and come out of it suddenly without any immediate or obvious trauma. They tell me that at one level he's a shrewd, flexible guy and that the comedy act is one of the masks he hides behind to survive, a life-long defense mechanism that happened to be very useful for the last eighteen years.''

The Director lifted the bourbon bottle from his desk and filled Radford's glass again. He also filled his own.

"What are the other levels?"

"The first one is the comedian, the stage mick with the phony brogue and the quick wink of the eye. Then there's talent approaching genius, a first-rate flyer, naval officer, and practically anything else he wants to be. But there's anger and fear at the core. It's the personality he went to China with and the one he came out with, and everything is intensified because of the China experience.''

"Anger at whom?"

"Currently at these two people." Radford shuffled through a stack of color photos of the Farrell family. The Director was once again amazed at how the Company could find pictures of people at a minute's notice. "This is Burke Kennedy, his stepfather. Or, rather, his foster stepfather. Married the aunt who raised him. Was her lover for years. A powerful and corrupt political lawyer. One of our shrinks says there's a rivalry there for the foster mother's love. Oedipal thing.''

There was a moment of silence as both of them pondered a possibility they did not want to articulate.

"And the other one?"

"This woman. Irene Conlon Farrell. He apparently loved her very much. She married his foster brother—cousin actually—after Farrell was shot down. The same shrink thinks he resents her betrayal.''

"An incredibly lovely woman. . . . Might he kill her?"

Radford nodded grimly. "Might and then again might not. One of our men says that he is obsessed with vengeance, and the other says Farrell is the kind of person who copes with anger by diffusing it. Typical psychiatric report. They have it both ways. But the hypnotism indicates powerful anger at both of them.''

"We have a potential time bomb on our hands, then?"

"Probably a crisis down the road in a few months."

"That's all we need." The Director thoughtfully considered his glass of bourbon. "What if he explodes on us in six months or a year?"

"And tries to bring us down in the explosion just like we tried to bring him down?''

"Precisely."

"Maybe whoever tried to kill him before will solve our problem for us."

Irene

CHRIS WALLACE WAS interviewing Dan Farrell on the Washington segment of the *Today Show*. Irene watched, her heart beating rapidly, her mind trying unsuccessfully, as it had for the last two weeks, to make sense out of Danny's return and to decide how she should respond to him.

"Now, Mr. Farrell," said the boyishly handsome Wallace, "you were flying a U-2 over Sinkiang when the aircraft malfunctioned. Aren't those aircraft normally operated by the Air Force or Central Intelligence Agency?"

"So they tell me," Danny said brightly.

"And you're sticking to your story that you obtained one of those aircraft to take pictures?"

"That's what the planes are for, Chris."

Oh, God, how many times she'd seen that impish smile. Especially when she tried to break through the protective layers of his personality. Their relationship had been the opposite of the ones she now had with his foster brothers. She listened to them talk about their problems. Danny listened to her, always the sensitive, sympathetic, tender friend. And when she tried to be a friend to him, he would flee, sometimes psychologically, with a wink and a grin, and sometimes physically, by disappearing for days or not writing from the Carrier for weeks. A woman could be his mistress, even his lover, but Danny took flight when she wanted to be his friend.

"And how did you obtain it?"

Danny winked. "That'd be telling."

"So you continue to deny that you were an employee of either the Central Intelligence Agency or the United States Air Force?"

"If I were a CIA employee, do you think I would admit it to you?" Danny asked genially.

When he smiled he looked healthy and happy. When his face was in repose, however, he seemed drawn, weary, distracted.

"Why do Irishmen always answer a question by asking another one?" Wallace asked.

"Do we really?" Danny responded.

"And you say that the novel that you composed in your head in China has nothing to do either with the Chinese prison camp or with the Central Intelligence Agency?"

"Not this novel, anyway."

"Do you have a publisher yet?"

"Not yet. Know any good ones?"

"You've been home from China now for two weeks, more or less out of sight. Where have you been?"

"I was recuperating in a rest home in Virginia."

"Near Langley?"

Danny smiled again. "I think that's what they said the name of the town was."

"And now your plans are to go home to Chicago and finish the novel. Will it be good to go home?"

"It sure will."

"Did you ever come to enjoy it in China, Mr. Farrell?"

There was a long pause. Danny's face filled the whole screen, blank and expressionless.

"Not for one single moment, Chris Wallace."

"I wish you had stayed in China," Irene screamed at the TV screen, and began to sob hysterically.

Brigid

"WE'VE GOT TO give him a chance, Burke. You saw him on television. He doesn't seem angry at all. And you heard him on the telephone today. It's the same old Danny."

"That's exactly what I'm worried about, Bridie," Burke said nervously. "But I'm willing to wait and see. Emotions were running high that night, and it was a long time ago. Nevertheless, I'm going to keep a close eye on him. And I'm not going to let him or anyone else hurt you."

"Promise you won't do anything without discussing it with me first."

Burke hesitated.

"God damn it, Burke, promise me!"

He shrugged in resignation. "All right, Bridie, I promise."

"And"—she held her breath—"promise me you won't even mention Clancy's death to him."

"Why that promise?" He regarded her quizzically. "Oh, all right. In a way, the boy did us a favor. And there never was any point in arguing with you."

She sighed to herself. Now I must make Roger promise the same thing.

I'm so happy he's back that I could die from joy. And so worried that I could die from fear.

John

THE FARRELL BROTHERS stood silently in the pastor's suite watching a snow plow clear the Courts, both of them wondering whether Danny would return to the scene of his former athletic triumphs.

"Will he still play basketball?" Roger asked absently.

"I suppose," John murmured.

His relationship with Irene was certainly finished. Danny would replace him again, damn him.

"I hope he doesn't plan to move back into the neighborhood," Roger said, turning away from the window.

"Don't count on it," John replied gloomily. "You'll talk to him about whether we should meet him at the airport?"

Roger nodded. "I'm getting a lot of free campaign publicity out of it. Angelo Spina says that money couldn't buy it."

John laughed hollowly. "I suppose that you've wished many times, just as I have, that he was still alive."

"And now, just like you, I'm not so sure that it's a good thing."

"Happy to have him back, of course." John sank into one of his horrible, tasteless leather chairs. "Make you a drink?"

"Not now, thanks. Oh, sure, happy to have him back. God knows it will be great to see him." Roger beamed enthusiastically, and then quickly became somber again. "And afraid of the disruption."

"Primal chaos," John agreed. "And we don't know what the new creation will be. If any."

You have a wife to lose. And maybe I . . .

"Irene is taking it well," Roger said thoughtfully.

"Oh?"

"She seems quite self-contained. Doesn't mention him. Noele does all the talking."

"That young woman will bear watching," John warned.

"You're telling me."

Noele

NOELE WAS TOTALLY EDGED.

I mean, I didn't think he'd be short. *Sure he looks like Paul Newman—blue eyes, curly silver hair, cute baby face. But I never expected he'd be, like,* short. *Really!*

Not as short as she was—"almost" five four—but maybe only an inch taller than Moms, who was five eight. She sighed. *And he kind of scrunches down in that grubby old jacket so he looks even shorter. I'll have to do something about his posture.*

Noele decided she would call him Daniel save on those occasions when it was time for him to "act right." Then he would be called Daniel Xavier.

Danny had asked by telephone that his family wait for him at their home rather than meet him at O'Hare. By the time the taxi pulled up in front of the old house, he had shed the mass media.

But Noele watched the reunion with an eye that was as penetrating as the lens of a TV camera.

First Brigid, both of them crying, both of them cooing words of endearment in an Irish brogue. *Daniel Xavier was a bit of a fraud, but he knew how to cope with Grams—lay it on thick, real thick.*

Sometimes his eyes were not Paul Newman's. Nor Robert Redford's, either. Kind of like someone old, the man who was Lawrence of Arabia on the late-night movie.

Then a warm handshake for Burke. "Congratulations to you, Burke. Sorry I couldn't be here for the ceremony, but I had some business out of town."

They didn't like each other very much, Noele decided. And maybe they still don't.

Then an embrace, from a quarterback playing his last game, for Monsignor John. "And, Brigid, now you have a son that's a monsignor and himself a television personality and the pastor of our parish, too. Jackie, it's good to see you again. I hope you'll give me a few weeks before you draft me into service as head usher."

And, of course, you'd be his *head* usher.

"Things have changed in the church, Danny." Uncle Monsignor was not his usual suave self. He stumbled over the words. "You could be head lector at Mass. Or a leader of song, like Noele."

"Not much money in that, is there?"

It was an act, Noele decided, carefully planned, well executed, and not meaning a thing. Underneath all the congeniality and charm there was another Daniel Farrell who had to be watched. He gave himself away when his eyes glowed intermittently, like the brights being clicked on and off by a driver on a country road at night.

He was nervous and frightened and lonely.

And angry too.

He kissed Moms's hand, and she blushed deep red, something she almost never did. "Irene, you're more beautiful than ever. I'll have to confess that coming down in the cab I hoped and prayed that you and herself here would not have grown too old. Now I see that the two of you have both improved with time, like the best of French burgundies."

Oh, *barf!*

"If you think that about me," Moms said, still blushing, half pleased, half angry, "it must be because you haven't seen an American woman in a long, long time."

Daniel laughed enthusiastically. "I sure haven't, but even the ones I have seen don't compare to you, Irene. And Roger"—an embrace for him almost as enthusiastic as for Grams—"the next governor of the state of Illinois. I always knew you'd come to no good—a politician with a Ph.D. I hope you find your old cousin a cushy job where he doesn't have to do an honest day's work for the rest of his life. Hey, I'm not even registered in the state anymore. Can a man come back from the dead and vote in a primary election?"

"I'm sure we can get the board of election commissioners to work something out for you," Roger said. He was the only one in the room who was genuinely happy. He must really have liked Danny when they were kids together.

And now it's my turn. Be cool, Noele, she quoted DeWitt Carlisle's favorite instruction to her.

"I can't really believe that this beautiful queen out of an ancient Irish legend is my niece," Danny began.

"Cousin," Noele corrected him.

He tilted her chin back and brushed his lips against hers. Noele felt very weak in the knees.

"I'm told I owe you a very great debt of gratitude, flame-haired Irish goddess."

For one of the few occasions in her life Noele was speechless.

"How so?" Roger asked him.

"If that Company for which I didn't work is telling the truth, Noele talked to her boyfriend, who talked to his father, who's a congressman, who talked to the president of the Company, who had one of his aides talk to the Chinese. I think I already resent the boyfriend, by the way.''

"I talked to the congressman myself," Noele flared, feeling her face grow very warm.

"You didn't tell us that, honey," Brigid protested.

They were not altogether pleased with her.

"I didn't think it was A.G.B.D.," Noele replied, trying to regain her balance and finding it very difficult as long as he kept his stubborn forefinger gently on her chin and stared admiringly into her eyes.

"A.G.B.D.?" Danny asked, his fingers caressing her chin. "Isn't that the Jesuit motto?"

"No, that's A.M.D.G. A.G.B.D. means 'any great big deal.' " I am, like, totally jazzed, she told herself. Really phased out.

"Of course not. No great big deal. Just get the battered old cousin out of China, a small good deed before suppertime." He winked at her wickedly.

"Really," she stammered.

Noele recovered some of her cool by the time her family gathered around the dinner table and turned the TV camera in her head back on.

Roger was indeed the only one who was completely pleased at Daniel's return. Burke was wary and suspicious. Brigid was uncharacteristically anxious. John's eyes were darting nervously, and Moms was still blushing. You're a strange man, Daniel Xavier Farrell. You've come home and disturbed all of these people's lives. I'm not sure they think I did them a favor at all by talking to Congressman Burns.

"What are you planning to do now that you're back, Danny?" Burke asked.

"Try to stay out of trouble, counselor," Daniel said, and wolfed down the mashed potatoes as if he were trying to make up for the eighteen years of not eating them.

"Don't talk when you have food in your mouth," Noele told him.

He winked mischievously at her, but finished the potatoes.

"Are you going to live in the Neighborhood?" John asked pointedly.

"I've got a room down at the Drake, though I'm told the Mayfair Regent or the Ritz-Carlton are the places to stay. I thought I might rent one of those old houses over on Mandrake Parkway or Dalton Road while I'm working on my novel.''

"Whitehall," Noele said.

"Huh?" Danny's fork was poised over a second helping of potatoes.

"Really cool people stay at the Whitehall."

"See how much I'm learning!" He plunged into the potatoes.

"Do you have a publisher?" Moms asked eagerly.

"Sure." His eyes zoomed quickly around the table as if to drink in her face. "That was the reason for doing the *Today Show*. There was a publisher on the phone by noon; I showed him the first thirty pages that I'd written out, and he gave me a contract and an advance on the spot. I'll finish the book here in the neighborhood and then decide what to make of the rest of my life.''

"Then you probably will move elsewhere?" Uncle Monsignor seemed eager to get rid of Danny.

"You'll have a lot of catching up to do," Grams said.

Daniel put his potato fork down.

"Look, I'm not thinking of trying to catch up, and I'm not thinking of beginning again where I left off eighteen years ago." He was anxiously rubbing his fingers against one another, struggling to keep his tension under control. "It will take time for me to get used to being alive again. All of you go on living your own lives and don't worry about me." He grinned boyishly. "Of course, you can cook me supper occasionally with lots of roast beef and potatoes, Bridie, Irene, and you, too, Noele. You know how to cook?"

"I'm sure, Daniel Xavier."

"*I'm sure*," said Moms, laughing nervously, "is a warning sign. Proceed further at your own risk."

"Mo-*ther*," Noele howled.

"And when you call me Daniel Xavier, does that mean I'm about to get in real trouble?"

"It means," she snapped, "that you'd better start acting right."

Everyone laughed except Noele, who didn't see what was so funny.

"I really mean what I said," Danny went on, waving his hands expansively, like the Pope giving a blessing. Or maybe absolution. "For me it's a completely new life. For you, it's life as usual. And neither should interfere with the other."

Everyone around the table murmured agreement and approval and relief. Everyone, that is, but Noele.

Fat chance, she thought.

He left for his room at the Drake before anyone else was ready to depart. "I have a lot of sleep to catch up on," he explained.

He touched Noele's long red hair at the doorway. "Never in my wildest dreams in China did I expect to come home to find such a gorgeous young woman in the family."

"Really," Noele huffed, but her knees were wobbly again.

And you don't erase the past that easily, Daniel Xavier. No way, José. We're going to see a lot of you.

And there's going to be a lot of trouble.

Ace

HE LEANED ON his broom. "Well, M.N., have you found your identity now that your cousin is home?"

"Geek," she responded. "And stop loafing. I'm not going to do *all* the cleaning up after your teenagers."

As veep of the High Club, Noele was responsible for the clean-up crew that collected the broken Coke bottles and swept up the mess at the end of the evening after the five hundred adolescents deserted the parish hall for Red's and other hot-dog stands around the neighborhood.

In the old days the priest didn't have to work. That was before the Vatican Council and Noele Farrell.

"What's he like?"

"You KNOW."

"Yeah, but I want to hear your opinion. . . . All right, all right, I'm pushing the broom."

"WELL, he's SHORT!"

"You're not exactly a Valkyrie, M.N."

"Be SERIOUS. . . . Anyway, he's also sweet and cute and funny and nice and about as mature as Micky Kelly."

"Eileen's little brother?"

"No, he's even less mature."

"Uh-huh. And how did the rest of the family react?"

"Totally weird. Burkie and Grams are afraid, Moms is embarrassed, John twitches a lot, and Roger acts kind of goofy. I think they all wanted him to be alive and now, like, wish that he had never come back."

"A lot of mystery still?"

"Don't stop sweeping. . . ." They were pushing their two brooms together. "He doesn't know who he is, so how is his coming back going to help me find out who I am?"

"You mean that if you solve the mystery, Danny will grow up and you will know who you are too."

"I mean"—she pounded the broom against the wall—"we'll know why all the Farrells are so geeky."

I'm not sure, Dick McNamara thought, I want to know why.

Brigid

DANNY WAS ON his second helping of watercress soup at the L'Escargot restaurant in the Allerton Hotel. "I can't get over how classy this city has become," he said between gulps of the soup. "I'll have to take your word for it, Burke, that this was an elite French restaurant when it was over on Halsted. My generation didn't go to elite French restaurants on Halsted or anywhere else. We didn't know much about good wine either."

He put down the soup spoon long enough to sip the Chenin Blanc Burke had ordered. "Watercress soup and Chenin Blanc and the Allerton, which used to have a cafeteria in the basement for high school kids. I tell you the city's getting elegant. New buildings, new hotels, new people. . . . It's great to be back!"

L'Escargot was Brigid's choice, even though Danny had requested home-cooked meat and potatoes. She had learned to cultivate a taste for French food, and L'Escargot was her favorite bistro, as she called it. The restaurant's blond wood, the easy friendliness of its staff, and the medium buzz of conversation protected her from the feeling of being intimidated, as she was in other French restaurants.

"Some of them other places," she insisted, "are like high-class funeral homes. You're afraid to talk because you might say something vulgar."

She and Burke were beginning to relax under the glow of Danny's persistent charm. The crisis had not passed yet, but Brigid was hopeful now that it would be manageable.

"And I can't get over the way you look, Bridie. You must have one hell of a sex life; that's the only way I can explain how you're more gorgeous than you were eighteen years ago."

That cracked Burke up. "Ah," he said, faking an Irish brogue, "sure, the woman's a good lay."

Brigid felt her face grow hot. "Shush, now. Both of you. That's locker-room talk and not to be heard in the presence of a decent woman in a public place."

"Go on with you," Danny said. "Decent woman or not, you're pleased as punch to hear two men talking about you that way."

"You shouldn't be so explicit. 'Tis a shocking bad use of language," she persisted.

"It's worked out so far," said Burke. "Of course, you can't tell what the woman will be like a month from now. She works too hard. Maybe you'll join me in trying to persuade her to resign from the firm and live like a person of leisure."

"Ah, I can see her in the Doge's palace or the Uffizi or the Louvre. Of course, you'll have a hard time, Burke, keeping her from eating popcorn."

"Both of you shut your flannel mouths," Brigid ordered, by no means displeased with the flattery.

Burke explained briefly the condition of the firm and the reasons he was urging Brigid to retire and the possible arrangements of administering the firm after her retirement.

"It'll all be yours, Danny, someday. We've taken good care of it," she said, suddenly feeling sad for all the suffering of the years.

He did not respond to what she had said. "Ah, no . . . no more wine. I promised that if I got out of China I'd only drink wine and not much of that."

"And who did you promise?" Brigid asked.

"God, who else?"

Danny walked to Holy Name Cathedral every morning, even in the sub-zero January cold, to go to Mass, behavior she would not have expected from him, not even after eighteen years in China.

"Would you ever be interested in becoming president of the firm?" Burke asked tentatively. "The woman, of course, would have to approve, but it does make sense. It isn't a full-time job, at least not necessarily. You could write your book and still have a bit of an active business life, too."

Danny did not look at either of them directly. "Can I take a rain check for a few months?"

"There's no rush," said Burke soothingly. "Think about it."

"I will, though I have to think about dessert first."

"At least you didn't say no," Brigid observed, watching him closely.

Danny grinned up at her mischievously. "That I didn't, woman; that I didn't."

"Do you trust him now?" she asked Burke anxiously as they drove home in their Mercedes through the quiet and bitterly cold streets of Chicago.

"He was really your favorite, wasn't he?" Burke said. They were silent for a moment; then he continued. "What's done is done, Bridie; we weren't responsible, and there would have been no good of us doing anything after it happened."

"Then why don't you trust him?"

"I'll tell you why. When I was in Sicily before the war, I drove to the foot of Mount Etna. There was a little whiff of smoke curling up from its cone. Peaceful, even charming smoke. How could anything that mild be a threat? Then you realized that at any time, without a bit of warning, that goddamned mountain was going to blow its stack."

Burke

BURKE SEARCHED IN the dark for his sleeping wife's breast, found it, and touched it lightly. She sighed contentedly.

After a certain age, on some nights, even the small pleasures of a woman were almost unbearably sweet.

Slipping under the thin cover of lace, he moved his fingers softly against her flesh, brushing against a nipple, but very gently so as not to wake her. She was so tired.

And for a minute or two there was only peace.

Not enough peace to permit sleep, however. He had forgotten how likable Danny was. There had always been a rivalry between the two of them, lover and favorite son. Yet it had been hard to resent Danny, even in the old days. And now he was a brave man returned from a living hell and still able to laugh.

Yet behind that laugh, underneath Danny's smooth urbanity, Burke was convinced that there was terrible anger, a pent-up rage repressed for almost two decades and about to explode like a boiler whose safety valve was clogged.

Much of that anger, Burke assumed, was directed at him. It could be seen lurking behind those twinkling silver-blue eyes. Yet there were times when he looked away from Brigid, as though he could not stand the sight of her. She trusted him completely and was utterly defenseless against him.

Her nipple was now hard at his fingertip. A little more pressure, and she would awaken, aroused and ready for him. He moved his finger away. Her sleep was more important than his lust.

Love and lust, how they intertwined. Long ago he gave up trying to separate them in his reaction to her.

But he did love her and would destroy anyone who was a threat to her.

I don't trust him. I never will.

He eased her night gown back into place and turned over to face away from her, his imagination filled with a grim vision: two wild beasts pawing in a forest clearing, waiting for the other to attack.

Noele

FLAME DID NOT like cold weather any more than Noele. So he slid and squished in protest down Jefferson Avenue as she tried to combine automobile safety, a subject on which she was obsessive, with the need not to be late for school. Then at Ninety-third Street she saw Danny, in an old Windbreaker and summer jeans, laboring against the wind as he plowed through the partially shoveled sidewalks.

"Daniel Xavier Farrell, what are you doing out there in a morning like this without a hat or a proper coat on?"

"Can I have a ride, Mother?" He grinned wickedly at her.

"You get in Flame this minute," she told him. When he was in the car she demanded, "Don't you have enough money to buy a car or a proper coat?"

"To tell you the truth, pretty cousin, I never want to see a quilted coat again. And as for a car, what do you think I ought to buy?"

"I tell Moms," she said promptly, "that she's silly to be driving a Datsun when she can afford a Porsche. Moms really loves sports cars. Kind of weird. Doesn't fit her personality. Anyway, why don't you buy a Porsche and take her riding with you?"

Out of the corner of her eye she could see that she'd embarrassed Danny. So maybe he was still in love with Moms after all these years. That was yucky.

"I've been so busy pounding away on my book that I haven't had time for the really important things, like buying a car. Will you come with me and help me buy a Porsche?"

"Really!"

"Fine." Danny leaned back in his seat and relaxed. "Driving a Porsche will be almost as much fun as driving a U-2."

"I hope you don't crack the car up too," Noele said, and sniffed like a mother whose son had destroyed a bicycle.

"I didn't really crack it up," he said easily, as though he were totally unfazed by Noele's hunt for information. "The plane flamed out, which means the jet engine stopped working. Then I tried to eject. The ejection mechanism didn't work either. That was the bad news. The good news was that the destruct mechanism, which was supposed to go off sixty seconds after I ejected, also didn't work; and the MIGs that came up after me couldn't shoot straight, so I glided the thing down to land in one of their deserts. It doesn't have wheels you know, it lands on slides."

"Sure, you dropped the wheels after you'd taken off." Noele knew all that there was to know about the U-2. "But it wasn't an accident, then?"

"That's right. The people at the Honorable Company claim that a termination order had been given on me. That means that the mission security chief in Japan, acting on Washington's orders, or so he said, told the technicians that I was no longer a useful employee of the Company. So they sabotaged the plane, and I was supposed to be killed. I think maybe one or two of the technicians had their doubts and gave me a fighting chance."

Noele was outraged. "How dare they give such an order?"

"Oh, they might have done it if they thought I was selling information to somebody who was our enemy then. But the men who run the Company now say that there were never any instructions from Washington to terminate. The mission security chief made up the order on his own. They say he retired a few months later and moved to Mexico, where he lived far beyond any income that the Company knew he had. I kind of think this crowd is telling the truth, though you never can tell about the Honorable Company."

"You mean that somebody paid him to get rid of you?" Noele could scarcely believe her ears.

"It kind of sounds that way." Danny shrugged philosophically, like a man whose horse had quit halfway through the race. You win some and you lose some.

She turned off Glenwood Drive and up Mandrake Parkway, carefully negotiating the slippery street to the top of the hill. She stopped Flame in front of the old stuccco house Danny had rented.

"Don't you realize that whoever tried to kill you once might try again?"

"You're reading too many mystery stories, Noele."

"It was not a fictional killer who paid off the mission security chief."

"I suppose not," Danny Farrell agreed indifferently.

"Daniel Xavier," she said, thumping Flame's steering wheel, "you simply have to grow up. You should buy neat clothes and live a regular life and stand up straight and not feel sorry for yourself and care about whether someone tries to kill you and—"

"Do you order Jaimie Burns around that way?"

"Airhead." She hit his arm, hard. "And anyway, Jaimie doesn't need to be told to act like a grown-up."

"Why do you care about me?" he asked softly, almost as if there were tears in his voice.

"Because you're my cousin, and we thought you were dead but you're not." She was unaccountably running out of breath. "And I want to keep you alive, that's why."

"Angry at me?"

She thumped the steering wheel again. "Tell me about it. You're impossible."

"Your family could have told you that long ago."

He kissed her lightly, slipped out of the car, and shuffled through the snow to his house, head down, shoulders bent.

She was going to be late for school. That didn't matter. *The poor dear man needs me.*

It was several minutes before her face stopped burning and she was able to turn over the ignition key and stir a reluctant Flame back into action.

Roger

"IF YOU WOULD dress up in something besides a Windbreaker and a sweater," Roger said, "I could take you to lunch in one of our more elegant clubs, or a swinging place like the East Bank."

Danny, who as a young man could not walk into a room without attracting attention, had drifted around the Farrell for Governor headquarters without anyone noticing him. The years in China had taught him the art of being invisible. "Let's go somewhere and grab a hamburger," he said. "I'm not up to fancy eating clubs yet."

It was a mid-February false spring day. Temperatures had soared to the fifties. The ice and snow were melting. Secretaries were eating their lunches on the benches in the Dearborn Street plazas. A few musical groups had turned up to provide lunch-hour entertainment and prove that summer could not be all that far away. For once Danny's disreputable Windbreaker suited the weather.

He strolled with Roger along Dearborn, commenting about the transformation of the street since he had seen it last. He chuckled at the Miro and laughed outright at the Picasso across the street in the Daley Civic Center, which in the Byrne administration, Roger explained, was usually called the Chicago Civic Center.

"Himself was taken in on that one," Danny observed. "He fell for Picasso's joke. But then I suppose if you have to fall for somebody's joke, it might as well be Picasso's."

It had been a tense morning at campaign headquarters. Mick Gerety, his face as long as the Tri State Expressway, was waiting for Roger in his office. The "Kramer Papers" had fallen into the hands of one Rodney Weaver, the editor of a small weekly magazine called the *Chicago Informer*. Weaver, a 1960s liberal, was agonizing about whether or not to publish the papers.

"That means he'll wait until after the primary," Mick said gloomily. "And then the rest of the Chicago media, which haven't touched the story so far, will have to report the *Informer* story."

In Roger's opinion the story was going to come out eventually anyway, and it was probably just as well to get it out in the open immediately after the primary instead of right before the November election. By summer the issue would be not his family history but the governor's incompetencies.

Gerety was still grumpy. "There may be some question of the soundness of your judgment in putting that stuff in writing in the first place."

Somewhere deep inside Roger's brain a demon was advising him to get out of the race now and return to the gentle indolence of the round table at the Faculty Club. How in the hell had he gotten mixed up in such a roughhouse?

"We'll just have to fight it out. That's all, Mick. And by the way, how did you like me with Radigan again last night?"

"You were tough, Governor," Gerety admitted grudgingly. "And you're going to have to be tough."

Tim Radigan was a gravel-voiced news commentator on one of the radio stations, a choleric and obtuse shanty Irishman whose sense of fairness had disappeared with the 1933 Century of Progress World's Fair.

How long can I continue to be tough? Roger wondered.

He had thought about confiding in Danny, but that would have meant discussing Danny's mother's death and his own father's death. Roger wanted to touch neither subject.

They walked farther down Dearborn Street. Danny howled with joy at the sight of the great red Calder mobile in the Federal Building Plaza. He left Roger behind and ran over to embrace one of its great scarlet arms.

"She's one of the most beautiful of her species I've ever seen!" he exclaimed, his voice faking religious awe.

"And what species is that?"

Danny turned to him in feigned astonishment. "Why, of course, she's a rare, benign, red tarantula, isn't she?"

"Most Chicagoans think she's a flamingo."

They bought a hamburger at a small shop across from the Dirksen building and then found a bench in the plaza. "What the hell's eating you, Danny?" Roger asked bluntly.

"Fear," Dan mumbled through a mouth filled with hamburger and bun. "I'm scared silly, Roger; haven't you figured that out yet? There hasn't been a night since I left China that I haven't wished that I'd wake up the next day and find myself back in that commune. It wasn't a nice place, but you didn't have to make any decisions. And you didn't have to take care of yourself."

"You give a great imitation of not being afraid," Roger said, squeezing the last bit of catsup out of its little plastic bag and over the remaining half of his hamburger.

"Hey, remember me? Danny Farrell, the inseparable buddy of your youth? Of course I put on a good act. Even eighteen years in China couldn't change that. Just the same, I'm scared shitless. Maybe I shouldn't have come back to the Neighborhood and reopened all the old wounds. I don't know."

He finished his hamburger and wiped his fingers on a paper napkin, which he jammed with the rest of the debris into the pocket of his Windbreaker.

Roger hunted for words and couldn't find them.

"You have nothing to worry about, Roger." Danny hunched over and stared at the plaza concrete. "Brigid and Burke asked me about taking over the firm. But there's not a chance of that. I'd go to pieces the first time I had a tough decision to make. And what you and Renie and Noele have going is too perfect for me to spoil. I'll never mess with that. Or anything else. Maybe I ought to get out of here. My publisher says he can find me an apartment in the Big Apple, as it's called these days."

"An apartment with a built-in woman?" It was the sort of crack Roger would have made twenty years ago.

Danny's laugh this time had a touch of bitterness in it. "I wouldn't know what to do with one, Roger. I got out of the habit. Anyway, remember what I said: I'll never interfere with anything in the family. That's all over and done with."

"As Harry Truman said, Danny, never say never, because never is a long time."

"I guess." He frowned and then dismissed the length of time that never might be with an obvious change of subject. "Hey, what were the 1960s like, I mean, after I left? I keep reading about them, but I can't get a fix. You were an idealist then, and you are one now. You haven't changed."

"I was out of it for a long time, Dan. The disillusionment after 1968 was terrible. We thought then that politics mattered. But when everyone was killed and the war went on anyway, all of us, the radicals and the liberals and even the Catholic moderates like myself bugged out. And now some of us are coming back in, but we're still walking on eggshells."

"Don't bug out this time, Roger. You'll never have peace with yourself if you do."

"And you're the one who uses fear as an excuse," he shot back.

Danny cocked a quizzical eyebrow. "A point for your side, Roger. But don't do as I do; do as I say."

And Roger heard the sound of an escape hatch clanging shut.

He left Danny to return to his office at the University to pick up his mail. There was a note from Lawrence promising a decision in the Mrs. Clay matter any day. Martha Clay was at a woman's social science meeting in Davenport, which seemed to Roger a strange place for radical feminist scholars to assemble. He missed her, even though he was now longing for the end of their relationship. The sting of pressure was too great to give up, yet he longed to be free of it.

Since Danny's return, his relationship with Irene had returned to its old familiar pattern of occasional and restrained passion.

Conversation at the dinner table that night was dominated, as usual, by Noele. And her subject, as usual in recent weeks, was Danny. She approved "totally" of his new Porsche. But his clothes and his posture and his attitude toward life were still "geeky." Roger glanced at Irene occasionally to see how she was reacting to their daughter's fascination with Danny. But Irene did not seem even to notice it.

After dinner Roger worked on a campaign speech for a while and then resolved that this was the time to say the things to Irene that he knew he had to say, no matter how difficult it might be. She was lying in bed reading the latest Book-of-the-Month Club novel when he entered their bedroom. A patronizing comment about her literary taste died on his lips, as patronizing comments had been dying for some time now. And her Bonwit's eroticism had become unbearably appealing.

He sat on the edge of the bed. "Mind a few minutes of serious talk?" he asked tentatively.

She folded the dust jacket into the book, put it aside, and removed her reading glasses. "The BOMC judges left their taste outside the door when they chose this one."

"There's no good way to begin this, Irene. So I'll begin it the only way I know how. Do you want me to move out?"

"Of the house?" She was astonished.

"No, I mean out of our bedroom."

"Oh."

"We should have talked about this before, you know."

"I know, Roger," she sighed. "I admire your courage in bringing it up. But nothing has changed, has it? Danny is confused and frightened and uncertain, and I think not a bit interested in me."

"I suppose not. But I want you to know, Irene, that you are perfectly free to do whatever you want to do."

Irene lay back on the pillows watching him intently. "Do you love Danny so much that you're even willing to give up your wife to him?"

Roger winced, as if someone had plunged a knife into his chest. "I suppose I deserve that, Irene, but it's not altogether fair. I love you so much that I value your freedom more than my own happiness."

She sat up and took his hand. "Forgive me, darling, for being a bitch. I knew that's what you meant."

"I do love you, Irene," he said passionately, the fervor of Christmas Eve returning. "And I'll always regret it took me so many years to find out how much you deserve to be loved."

"That's very beautiful, Roger," she said, tears forming in her eyes. "It took me a long time to discover you, too."

She pressed his hand against her breast and he caressed it gently. For a few seconds the sweetness of their contact was almost unbearable. Then she released his hand, and he withdrew it from her smooth skin.

So quickly did the fires die out.

Could he really give her up?

Would it be up to him to choose?

Irene

SHE ENCOUNTERED DANNY for the first time without other members of the family in the supermarket on Ninety-fifth Street. He wore an obviously new blue and gold Notre Dame Windbreaker.

"I see that Noele at least persuaded you to wear a proper jacket," she said to him as he was trying to make a decision between brands of frozen orange juice. "Don't buy either of those, Danny. It's much better in the bottle."

He smiled shyly. "Maybe I could hire you as a shopping adviser.

"I'm surprised you even have time to shop. You're so involved with your novel that we don't see much more of you than we did when you were in China."

"You can see plenty of me this Saturday night. I let John talk me into appearing on his TV program. What's happened to my two foster brothers, or cousins, or whatever I should call them? Roger's running for public office and turns out to be a fiesty candidate. John is thumbing his nose at church authorities and apparently enjoying it."

"And to make the turn-about complete, you've become a recluse."

Danny terrified her. His eyes dominated her whenever they were together, sometimes undressing and stroking her, other times ripping her to pieces in cold, vengeful fury.

God knows he had reason to hate her.

But worse than the hatred was the mixture of anger and affection. *He cannot make up his mind about me,* Irene thought. *But no matter what he decides, I'm defenseless.*

And she liked the terror of her defenselessness. At least she still mattered to him.

He put his hands in the pockets of his Windbreaker and bowed his head. "What's over is over, Irene," he said softly.

"I understand."

But you don't really mean it, do you, Danny? You may kill me. You may make love to me. You may do both, but it's not over.

"Sometimes I think it would have been better if I'd stayed in China."

"Never!" The word exploded from her lips.

He grinned sheepishly. "You sound like Noele."

"Someday, Danny, you're going to have to write a novel about what it's like to come back from the dead."

"Maybe. Do you still write, Irene?"

"A little bit."

"Can I see it?"

"If I can see your novel."

"I'll think about that. You're not in it, Irene." And there was murderous rage in his eyes.

"I'm disappointed," she said, fighting to keep an answering burst of anger under control.

"Am I in your stories?"

Her anger melted. Make up your mind about me, please, Danny.

"Of course you are."

Roger

"DO YOU WANT to lay down the rules, Maryjane?" Roger ushered Danny and the reporter into a booth in the Riverview Room of the East Bank Club. The frozen North Branch of the Chicago River shone in sub-zero winter sunlight, a rough sheet of uncut crystal.

"Sure, Governor." She ticked off her regulations on her fingers. "Number one, I pay the bill, two, everything is off the record, and three, no passes."

They were her guests for lunch, and after showing them around the club, Maryjane had changed from her East Bank uniform of leotards (white), tights (red), and running trunks (blue) to a loosely fitting heather-green sweater dress with a matching scarf. How to look sexy and at the same time coolly professional on the coldest day of the year.

Folklore reported that women were more likely to stroll around in the buff in their locker room at East Bank than anywhere else in the city. Roger permitted himself to imagine Maryjane that way, a pleasant mixture of boyishness and girlishness, tall, slender, and athletic, a different kind of bisexual fantasy object from Martha, a new interest and challenge.

"Ms. Hennessey doesn't believe in sexual freedom," he explained to Danny.

"Sexual exploitation, both ways," she said brusquely.

"I'm happy to hear that," Danny said genially. "Is that opinion shared by all the lovely women running around this place in varying states of, uh, dishabille?"

"God, you *are* a writer; and no, it isn't. You like the East Bank?"

"A temple to three dramatic changes since I went on my little trip—physical fitness, feminism, and sexual openness, whatever that is."

"That's good. Do you mind if I take notes, just for my own memory?" She pulled out a large spiral ring binder. "Do you approve of those changes? And what did you do for sex in China?"

Roger had forgotten the electricity that so quickly leaped between Danny and a woman. A hint of a smile, a flash of an eye, a courteous attentiveness, and women began to glow.

His magic worked with Maryjane in thirty seconds.

Damn him.

"I don't disapprove," Danny said disarmingly. "And the Chinese control population the way the Irish did in the last century. They abolished sex. After a while you hardly notice. There are more temptations in this Taj Mahal of physical culture in a single day than in a whole year in a Chinese commune."

"Do you plan to marry? What do you think of American women?" Maryjane could hardly contain her questions—and felt no need to link them in any logical order.

Dan laughed. "I have no plans to marry. I think American women are gorgeous, even more so now that they are independent and aggressive. And I'm fascinated by this place: rooms for serious weight lifting, beautiful women in tight clothes, other rooms for medieval torture machines, others where young men and women jump about and sing, tennis courts, beautiful women in loose clothes, handball courts, squash courts, beautiful women in almost no clothes at all, people running around a track with earphones on their heads."

Maryjane grinned sheepishly. She had had a Walkman in her hand as she'd rushed by them on the track.

"You mean exercise classes and exercise machines . . ."

"A swimming pool with the most charmingly indiscreet costumes, a singles bar in the middle of a three-story atrium, marvelous food, politicians and journalists at almost every table. Where else but Chicago could you have so many different purposes served under one roof?"

"You're being satirical. . . ." Her ballpoint pen hesitated, and she cocked an eyebrow in doubt.

"I'm celebrating a monumental plush-carpeted marble mausoleum of cultural diversity," Danny replied. "Why shouldn't one set of walls contain the most advanced methods of both losing weight and putting it on? All the highest virtues and all the most pleasant vices? Seriously, Maryjane, I love it, even if I'm too old and decrepit to fit in."

"You'd fit in fine," she protested hotly.

Oh, God, Danny, you ought to be ashamed of yourself.

"I'm afraid I couldn't compete with all the swingers—that is the word, isn't it?—in their fancy, faded, fanny-hugging jeans."

"Alliteration," Maryjane said. "Let me get that down." She scribbled frantically.

And so it went. Despite her youthful bounce and vitality, Maryjane Hennessey was clear-eyed and clear-headed about the celebrities of the city. Yet Danny dazzled her completely. When she shook hands with him at the end of the lunch, during which Roger said practically nothing, there was hopeless adoration in her lively brown eyes.

She would be much better in bed, Roger decided, than Martha Clay—and was, in all probability, quite unattainable.

"Bastard," he muttered to Danny as they left the humming buzz of forced camaraderie on the main floor of the club and descended to the silent caverns of the parking garage.

"Envious?" Danny asked innocently. "You're not interested in her, are you?"

"Of course not."

"Well, neither am I." Danny was grim. "Or in anyone else, for that matter. It's kind of nice, though, to know I'm not totally a retard, as my lovely cousin says I am."

"Did you mean that about not marrying?" Roger opened the door of the Mercedes.

How could he say to Danny that friendship between men was much more important and much more stable than the endless sexual games men played with women? How hint that he would rather eat lunch with him than with the lovely blond Maryjane?

He could not say it. He would never risk a replay of his humiliation in the movie theater thirty years ago.

"I'd be a bad risk."

The gate opened, and Roger drove up the ramp. Demented cold assaulted the Mercedes and made them both shiver. Roger turned on the heater.

"Don't worry, Roger, You have her. I don't."

"Maryjane?" he said, surprised by the sudden twist of the conversation.

"Of course not."

"We thought you were dead, Dan. Otherwise . . ." His voice trailed off into silence.

"No problem," Danny said, looking away from him and out the window of the car, as if he were studying intently the freezing pedestrians. "No problem at all."

Yes it is, Danny. Yes it is. And it's going to get worse.

Noele

"THIS IS A rather special experience for me tonight," the monsignor said. "My guest is my cousin, Daniel Farrell, who was held prisoner in China for eighteen years due to circumstances that we won't be able to discuss tonight. But everyone in our family, and I suspect a lot of people in your families too, saw him on television last month after the Notre Dame–Georgetown game. And many of us were fascinated to hear Danny say that it was religious faith that kept him going through the seeming hopelessness of the long years as a prisoner. Could you tell us more about that, Danny?"

"I'm sure you, of all people, remember, Monsignor," he replied in mock seriousness, "that I was not exactly a pious youth. There was the time, if you remember, when . . ."

"He isn't going to," Noele said indignantly. Her eyes were glued to the TV screen, absorbing every detail of Danny's appearance.

"Hush," her mother said.

He looked respectable enough. His suit was pressed, and he was sitting up fairly straight. But he wasn't going to tell that *gross* story about putting warm-up jackets on the statues at St. Praxides on Holy Thursday. But that's exactly what he did.

"I think they may want to revoke my ordination after hearing that story," John responded with a chuckle. "But let's get back to your religious faith and China."

Danny spoke slowly, as though choosing his words carefully—even though he had gone over the whole thing with Noele the night before.

"The point of that story was that I wasn't in fact the holiest kid in the neighborhood by a long shot. In fact, I sometimes thought God had dealt me a pretty rotten hand. My father was killed in the Second World War, as you know. And my mother was killed by a runaway truck. But I was raised a Catholic and thought that, on the whole, being a Catholic was a pretty good thing. Then I found out that my Chinese friends weren't going to kill me, and that I might spend a long, long time as a prisoner in a land I didn't know and didn't particularly like. I decided I'd start praying to Whom It May Concern, if to no one else. I sort of got into the habit. A lot of times I thought it was a mistake. Because if I didn't believe in Him—my niece would insist I throw in 'or Her'—I would have certainly killed myself. Sometimes I was very angry He—sorry, Noele, *She*—wouldn't let me die and wouldn't let me give up hope, even when I wanted to. . . ."

"The NERVE of him!" Noele exploded, secretly jazzed to hear her name mentioned on television and eagerly anticipating Jaimie's reaction.

The conversation continued with both of the Farrells saying exactly the right things and making all kinds of points for God and religion and faith and charity. Noele was unimpressed. The two of them talked about God, and they certainly believed in God. But something was missing. They had faith all right, but not enough faith to straighten out the Farrell family puzzles.

She shook her head disapprovingly. Danny was tied in knots despite his glib tongue. And since he'd come back, so was everyone else in the family. Somebody was going to have to untie them. And Noele had not the slightest doubt who that someone would have to be.

After the program Moms and Roger got on the telephone to congratulate the two smooth-talking participants. Noele trudged upstairs, feeling very worried. The phone was ringing as she entered her room, her personal telephone installed two years before so that her calls did not tie up the family phone. She picked up the receiver.

"That's it, kid. I warned you to lay off. You're not sending me to jail after all these years. And that includes your whole fucking family, blabbing the story all over television. You're going to be in the hospital before the next program, you little cunt.''

The line went dead. Noele stood there with the phone in her hand, shaking with a terrible chill. Now she knew who the man was.

·····················*John*·····················

"IF I HADN'T seen it with my own eyes," Danny said, shaking his head in dismay, "I wouldn't have believed it."

"The charismatics have become big since 1965," John said. "I don't especially go for it myself. But it doesn't seem to do anybody any harm, and a lot of people benefit from it."

The two of them were walking back from the parish hall to the rectory. Snowflakes ricocheted off their faces. The false spring had vanished, and winter returned with a vengeance. Danny hung around the rectory now as he never had before, as did young men in their middle twenties occasionally, trying to recapture their teens. In the face of his piquant combination of wit and fragility, John lost all his resentments, indeed, wondered if he had ever truly resented his cousin.

"They call it baptism of the spirit?" Danny asked. "And you mean you let them do that sort of thing around here?"

"You saw it, didn't you? The Dominican brother whips everybody into a frenzy and then one by one they all pass out. All eighty-five of them. One of the things you have to learn about the new church, Danny, is that a pastor lets the people do almost anything they want, short of heresy and public immorality—and it's not altogether clear what those are anymore."

"So they all pass out, but nobody gets banged up when they slide to the floor. My Chinese friends would have understood it very well. . . ."

Rarely did Danny mention China. John did not want to press for an explanation of the similarity between slaying in the spirit and the enthusiastic public demonstrations of the People's Republic. "Come on up to the rectory for a drink?"

"For coffee maybe. My rules say nothing but wine at meals."

John brewed the coffee in his coffee maker.

"What were the reactions to our interview?" Danny asked as he blew on the coffee to cool it.

"The ratings soared, and the general manager of the channel was delighted. But I suppose you saw Larry Rieves this morning, suggesting it was unethical, since my brother was running for governor, to bring on a cousin who was allegedly a hero. Typical Rieves."

"Yeah, I saw it," Danny said grimly. "I'd like to beat the shit out of the son of a bitch."

"My sentiments exactly," John agreed, noting that Danny's flashes of anger were infrequent but frightening.

"And your friends in the church who are giving you a hard time?"

John poured a second cup of coffee, wishing that he could trade it in for a martini. "Edward Keegan was here today. He's the chancellor, the cardinal's number-one man. A big, tall, handsome guy, one of the brightest canon lawyers in the church. He's kept the cardinal in power for the last several years by arguing his case in Rome."

"Sounds like the kind of man who would have done well in China too, especially during the Cultural Revolution."

"The cardinal wants me to stop. In fact, this time it's an order, though not in writing. Too many Farrells in the news, and he thinks that it reflects badly on him."

"On him?" Danny put his coffee cup on the end table next to his chair. "How do the Farrells reflect badly on him?"

"We get public attention, and he doesn't. It was bad enough having to put up with me and Roger. Now that you make it three, he's genuinely threatened. And Keegan knows how to pull out all the stops: the personal wishes of the cardinal, orders from God's representative over me, esteem of my fellow priests—that sort of thing."

"What bullshit!" Danny said contemptuously.

"Is it?" John sighed. "When you've been raised in it, it has a powerful effect on you. Keegan is a sincere and dedicated man, according to his lights. When he tells me that I've lost the most important thing a priest can have, the esteem of his fellow priests, it shakes me. And when he says all my fellow priests think I'm on an ego trip and disgracing the priesthood and the church, I half believe it's true."

"Is it true? Do you have any support at all? Are priests such finks"—Danny spit the word out contemptuously—"that they actually think that way?"

John rubbed his hand across his forehead. "No, not all of them, maybe not even most of them. But it's the ones who think that way who make the noise and call people in the parish to stir up trouble here. The pressure's going to mount again for me either to give up the program or give up the parish."

"Noele told me about the program on which you were the target. Did that help?"

"I didn't hear a single word from any of the priests in the diocese: no letters, no phone calls, no comment from anyone at the funeral for an old priest I attended a week later. It was as though the interview had never happened. So far I haven't heard a word about the program with you, either. The ratings were great, the mail and the phone calls were stupendous, and the priesthood is silent. Those who didn't like it are muttering behind my back and providing the cardinal and Keegan with more ammunition, and those who are on my side are not about to take the chance of speaking out."

"Cowards?"

"No. Just practicing the virtue that I have practiced all my life as a priest up until now—prudence."

"Fuck prudence," Danny exploded. "Roger walks on eggshells in his campaign and you're doing the same thing in the diocese. When are you two going to learn that if you want to do something in this world and you know you can do it well, you've got to fight for it."

He was right, of course. Fuck prudence.

Danny left a few minutes later, walking down the rectory steps, his shoulders hunched over, to his Porsche, the one concession he had made to the fact that he had actually returned from the dead.

Back in his room John mixed himself a double martini and poured it all from the pitcher into a large glass. After Keegan's visit he had called Irene and begged that he might come and see her. Since Danny's return he had avoided her, jamming up his longings and his loneliness by a massive act of will. Keegan had broken not only his self-esteem, but also his willpower.

Irene said no, as he knew she would. But now Danny had fired him up again, just as Irene had done before Christmas. Danny had replaced Irene as his backbone.

A nice irony. All the old envy and jealousy were welling up again. The same emotions he had felt that summer when, after talking him into returning to the seminary, Danny had fallen for Irene himself.

Had he slept with her?

John's fist clenched and unclenched.

John hated Danny because Irene loved him. It was an absurd hatred. But his rage, while silent, was as enormous as Clancy's rage that night.

He emptied the martini glass.

Now the same conflict. And he was doomed to lose again.

Brigid

THEY WERE BIDDING on the construction of a huge office/shopping/condominium plaza on North Michigan Avenue. It was a big job, enough to keep the firm in excellent condition another year, regardless of interest rates. If they won the contract, she would certainly follow Burke's advice and retire. By then they would know what Danny intended to do.

Danny, Danny, how wonderful to have you back, even if you bring so much danger with you.

They had a good shot at the Michigan Avenue project. Only a few firms in the city were big enough to do it right, and Brigid was confident that her stern-eyed costing made Farrell & Sons the most competitive large-scale company in the city. It was not a clout or bribe situation; nothing like the old days, Brigid thought wearily.

She leaned over her desk, ballpoint pen in hand, for one last searching examination, looking for enough fat to knock another million dollars off her bid.

Outside her office window construction vehicles that had not moved in several months were parked in neat rows, like mothballed Navy ships, their green and white paint shining dully in the faint February sunlight.

She had given so much of her time and energy to the firm. In retrospect, it was wasted time. The money she did not need; her sons were not interested in the inheritance. Danny, who had the most right to it, was still confused and, she thought, angry. God knows what would come of that. Burke's Mount Etna was waiting to explode.

She tried to concentrate on the column of figures. They blurred. She closed her eyes and and opened them again. The figures went into focus, then blurred once more. The whole page turned black, and Brigid felt the yawning abyss reaching up, eager to swallow her.

Irene

SHE WAS WORKING part-time in Roger's campaign headquarters at the Midland Hotel, stuffing envelopes, answering phones, typing lists—anything to take her mind off Danny.

She thought she might be invisible in the Midland Hotel offices among all the other volunteers. But she was the candidate's attractive wife and soon very much the center of attention.

Mick Gerety and Angelo Spina were courtly and respectful—and delighted to have her around. Her interviews with the "Life-style" writers from Illinois newspapers were good copy, and pictures of her appeared regularly in the papers.

"You take a great picture, Mrs. Farrell," Angelo said reverently.

"Is it dangerous for a candidate's wife to be too pretty?"

"No way," he said fervently.

She knew that Mick and Angelo and Roger were still worried about the stolen file. And their worried expressions in the campaign office reminded her of what she was trying to forget. It was Danny's mother who had been killed. So long ago. Almost unreal, like an old movie. How would Dan react when the murder, if that's what it was, became public? And Clancy's death? Was that murder, as Brigid had said at Noele's party?

But Danny could not have . . .

She chased those thoughts out of her head. Only a few weeks ago she thought she could love two men. Now she couldn't love either of them. She had failed John. Oh, God, how humiliated he had been when she refused to see him after the chancellor's visit.

We would have made love, John, and I would have pretended you were Danny every minute.

With Roger, most in love with her precisely when he feared that he would lose her, she was able to pretend.

And she no longer cared about his mistress at the University. Or about Maryjane Hennessey, the lovely TV journalist at whom Roger had been gazing hungrily all afternoon.

She is a sexy bitch. I kind of like her.

Maybe you need a couple of women, Roger. Who am I to judge?

And Danny's anger at me is building up. Soon . . . soon . . .

The private line in Roger's office rang. There was no one there to answer it. Irene walked into the office.

"Noele? What? At Little Company? I'll find your father. You and Danny are there already? We'll be right out."

Brigid

DANNY AND NOELE were the first to arrive. Danny sat on the bed next to her, his arm thrown around her shoulders. Noele held her hand as if she were determined never to let it go.

"What sort of nonsense is this now, woman?" Danny said in his fake brogue. "Wasn't it yourself that had a vacation in January, and now you're going to want one in early March, too? We'll have none of this misbehaving from you. Otherwise we'll have to hire a brand-new president for the firm. It won't do to be passing out in the office on winter afternoons."

"I was dead, Danny. And I could feel them reaching up for me to drag me down into the pit."

"I'll have none of that kind of talk," Danny insisted. "The doctors are saying there's nothing wrong with you at all. Your blood pressure is normal, your EKG is fine, you're a fit and healthy woman. You've been working a little bit too hard."

"Maybe they missed me this time. But they'll get me someday, Danny. And they'll drag me down into the pit and keep me there for all eternity."

"Stop that, Grams," Noele said sternly. "When you finally die, which is not going to be for a long time—not until you have great-grandchildren that are teenagers, anyhow—Jesus is going to meet you at the door of his cottage and say, 'Come right on in, Bridie; I've been waiting for you. Sit down, now. I'll make you a pot of tea.' "

Those wonderful, terrifying green eyes were glistening with tears. Brigid embraced both of them. Could Noele be right? Might the terrible things she had done to both of them be forgiven?

Then she looked at Danny.

What had been done to him was beyond forgiveness.

Burke

THE HOUSE WAS hollow without her, a haunted tomb.

I'd always thought I'd die first.

The doctors say it's nothing serious. What do they know?

The hatred in Danny's eyes at her bedside was patent. He's planning something. I know it.

Even Noele had seen it, despite her adolescent crush on the man.

"You look totally unfriendly, Daniel Xavier," she had said to him.

"Just worried about the woman, that's all."

Smooth-talking bastard.

You never wanted me to have her. Well, I've had her for almost forty years. And I'm going to keep her, even if I have to kill you to do it.

Roger

HIS AFFAIR WITH Martha Clay was coming to an end. Yet the closer to its conclusion, the more ecstatic the pleasure. The two of them, knowing the end was near, were trying to drink the last possible ounce of delight from each other, savor the last taste of their fading love. He was harsher and more demanding of her, and the contortions of her marvelous little body in response were like an erotic, superbly choreographed modern dance in which he was a choreographer with total control over her movements. Their cries of pain and pleasure were as shrill and sharp as if they were two beasts locked in combat. And their moments of affection after lovemaking were poignantly bittersweet, a candy bar melting slowly in the mouth.

Roger was no longer worried by his young boy fantasies. They had become an integral part of his enjoyment. For he saw her as a young Danny, a forbidden fantasy that made her even more delicious. Oddly enough, he felt no sexual attraction toward the real Danny. He was merely a somewhat pathetic but always interesting friend.

He had stopped by Danny's house the night before and found his cousin pounding fiercely on a secondhand Smith-Corona typewriter.

"Two hundred and fifty pages," he said, and beamed exuberantly. "When I get to seven hundred and fifty, I'll put an ending on and stop. Save the rest of the ideas for the next one!"

Roger had sunk into the broken sofa, which was the only other furniture in that part of the house besides the typewriter stand and chair. He had finally decided to tell Danny about the cloud that was hanging over his campaign. "There's a nasty aspect of this election campaign that you ought to know about," he began tentatively.

Dan kept his fingers on the typewriter keys. "Fire away."

And so he'd told him a vague story about the copies of the file taken by Joe Kramer from his office—materials about the probate of Bill Farrell's will—and about the phone calls from Rod Weaver threatening to publish the material. He avoided, as he always did, any reference to the death of Danny's mother.

Dan frowned thoughtfully. "I suppose you're warning me because you think when the news breaks the press will be after me for comments. Okay, I'll tell you what I'll say to anyone who asks. 'I don't give a damn what Uncle Clancy did. What is done is done, and he's paid for his sins.' I'm not going to feel guilty about it and neither should you."

The words had begun peacefully enough, but then were spit out in a machine-gun burst of anger. What did Danny mean? Was he saying that he felt no guilt for his own sin?

Roger went home and that night made passionate and violent love to Irene, forcing her out of her dreamy preoccupations. He knew that she would rather have Danny thrusting inside her. And that knowledge made her all the more satisfying.

For one deliriously perfect moment he was fucking both Irene and Danny the boy, the Danny who was forever lost.

Brigid

"I MUST SAY you look the picture of health." Burke deposited his daily dozen roses on the bed stand and kissed her dutifully. "You also smell nice and feel nice, so I suspect you're on the mend."

"Stop the blabbering and tell me whether we've got the contract," Brigid insisted.

"Of course we've got it, Bridie. Even without your shaving that extra million dollars off that put you in the hospital. The announcement will be made tomorrow, but I have my sources. And what do the doctors say about you?"

"They've had the head shrinkers in to talk to me, would you believe? So sure of it now that there's nothing wrong with my poor worn-out old body. And are you certain we've got the contract?"

"Absolutely certain. Have you ever known me to be wrong about these things?"

"No, I haven't," Brigid admitted grudgingly. "Now I suppose you're going to tell me that since we have the contract and since clearly I've been overworking, I should take some time off and then retire."

"I'm a reasonable man, Bridie. I'll give you until Easter, which is only a month away now. The primary election will be over, and you and I are leaving for a long, long time, even if I have to drag you all the way by your gorgeous red hair."

"Sure, I'll come quietly enough. But what about Danny?"

Burke shook his head. "I'll worry less about Danny when I get you away from him. I still don't trust the man. I think he's crazy. That glow in his eyes gets wilder every time I see him."

"Sure, the poor lad is readjusting."

"He's readjusting into an insane asylum if you ask me. Someday he'll explode, and we'll read in the papers he's climbed up on a tower with a high-powered rifle and shot fourteen people."

"Do you think he might really do that, Burke?" She clutched impulsively at his hand.

"Bridie, dearest, I think your nephew and foster son is a ticking time bomb."

Noele

THE SNOW HAD melted off the Courts, and like hibernating animals, the boys of the parish had emerged on Saturday morning to play basketball, including Jaimie, who was old enough to know better. Noele would have driven right by the Courts, greeting the hoopsters with a faint beep from Flame if she hadn't noticed Daniel's silver Porsche parked on Ninety-third Street. She pulled up behind the Porsche, turned off the ignition, and watched. Danny was a little bit out of practice but surprisingly well able to take care of himself with the teenagers.

She got out of the car and sauntered over to the court just as the game ended, with Daniel sinking a twenty-foot jump shot to much applause from the real teenagers. "Is there a new teenager in the Neighborhood, Jaimie Burns?" she asked.

"Uh, a new kid with a pretty good jump shot, though he's kind of out of condition," her lean, dreamy-eyed stalwart replied.

Cousin Daniel was sitting on the court resting his head against the basketball upright and breathing deeply. "The new kid in town needs to get back into condition; that's all, M.N."

"What did you call me?"

He cocked a mischievous eye at her. "M.N. That's your name, isn't it?"

"Only for teenagers."

"Well, you treat me like a retarded teenager. Besides, I think *M.N.* is neat."

"That word went out of style *at least* ten years ago," she said, and sniffed.

One of the boys bounced the basketball toward her. "Can you still shoot, M.N., or have you become too snooty to play with the rest of the guys."

With as much haughty demeanor as she could muster, Noele doffed her white down jacket and sent a jump shot swishing through the rim.

"Let's see you do that, Daniel Xavier."

"You're on, M.N. I'll play you twenty-one!"

Daniel *was* pretty good. He scored his first long shot and a short one after that. Then he hit on three more before it was Noele's turn. She was down thirteen to zip. And the male ruffians were cheering raucously for Daniel.

Noele decided it was time to give them all a lesson. She scored eighteen points in a row before missing a long shot, and then added a short, to be ahead nineteen to thirteen.

"Why don't you play on the varsity?" Daniel demanded as he bounced the ball from the edge of the free-throw circle.

"I find gymnastics a much more civilized sport," she said airily.

The male monsters made their usual animal noises until Noele gave them her "Noele look," which usually reduced male monsters to silence.

Daniel missed his long shot and made the short. Nineteen to fourteen. Noele scored her long and then the short after. Twenty-two to fourteen. "I win!" she exulted. "I beat you, Daniel Xavier! I beat you!"

"No way. You have to win on a long," he insisted.

"That's right, Noele. Fair is fair," Jaimie said.

"Whose side are you on?" Noele demanded.

She missed the shot. Then Danny made two shots and missed the third, leaving the score tied.

He bounced the ball to her. "Next long shot wins, M.N."

Noele walked calmly to the edge of the free-throw circle holding the ball in one hand and smiling her most pleasant smile. Try to edge me before a shot, will he?

"Next long shot wins, Daniel Xavier!"

She swished the shot through without even looking at the basket.

There was more wild cheering from the monsters, a congratulatory hug and kiss from Daniel, and a not enthusiastic enough kiss from Jaimie Burns.

She decided to quit while she was ahead and walked to the car with slightly more exaggerated motions than normal. She assumed that the One who presided over the Courts, having provided her with a lovely ass, would not mind her swinging it when the situation warranted.

As she drove home, her down jacket tossed carelessly in the front seat of Flame, Noele was troubled by two things:

Number one: She was convinced that Daniel was still in love with her mother. She could see it in his eye when he looked at her, an intense hunger that she saw sometimes in Jaimie's eye when they were alone. It was nice to be looked at that way, but when Jaimie wanted her, it was never with the devouring anger with which Daniel wanted Moms.

Number two disturbing thought: Noele realized she was half in love with Daniel.

There were two kinds of love. First of all there was love with boys like Jaimie Burns. You kissed and hugged and caressed and went to dances and parties and bought birthday and Christmas presents for them. And occasionally you were emotionally a Jaimie/Noele person together. Someday she would go to bed with such a boy more or less permanently and have children and grow old together.

The other kind of love was for rock stars and movie actors, basketball players and other distant idols. Daniel Xavier was not a boy like Jaimie.

But he wasn't a rock star, either.

John

HE DRANK THREE martinis before he called the chancellor.

He had not seen Danny in a week. Apparently Danny was wrapped up in his novel. And he did not have the courage to call Irene. His backbone was gone.

And the latest issue of the newsletter of the Priest Association had another satire, this one by Terry Quirk, who, unlike Dads Fogarty, did have a finely honed, if vicious, wit.

Bitter and envious over his own unused talents, Quirk destroyed others. And this time he destroyed both Danny and John, making wild fun of their interview.

He tried to get Danny on the phone to read it to him, but there was no answer.

He did not have the fortitude to keep up his fight. Now was the time to put it all in the past.

"You can tell the cardinal that I'm going to discontinue the series. I'll inform the station when I tape this week's show that the next interview will be the last."

"Your fellow priests will be very proud of you." Keegan said smoothly. "Eventually you will be accepted back into their ranks, just as though nothing ever happened."

"I'm glad to hear that," John said dully.

Irene

NOELE HAD FINALLY talked her into jogging. "The cold weather is no excuse at all, Moms," she'd insisted. "They have running suits that are plenty warm. Besides, it's not that cold these days."

For the first three times Irene ran, her body groaned and complained, muscles resenting the many years of disuse and bones protesting their unaccustomed responsibilities. And then she began to feel more in touch with her body, more in possession of herself.

This morning there was a hint of spring in the air. The temperature was in the high twenties, the sun was bright, and piles of snow along the curbs were melting as she trotted down Ninety-fourth Street.

She was conscious that a car was trailing her but chose to ignore it. It was broad daylight, and there was nothing to fear. She glanced out of the corner of her eye and saw it was a silver Porsche. She kept right on running. The car drew up beside her and the driver rolled down the window. "Good morning," he said politely.

She stopped running and walked over to the car. "You frightened me," she protested.

Her body's instant reactions were not those of fear.

"And you overwhelmed me," he said, his lips slightly parted with a smile.

"I thought you were beyond being affected by women," she said.

"I thought so too."

There was a pause while their eyes found each other's and then locked.

"Come home with me, Irene," he said, half pleading, half ordering.

"I'm all hot and sweaty," she said.

"That doesn't make any difference."

They drove in silence to his house, like mourners on the way to the cemetery after a funeral Mass.

"Are you sure you want to come in?" he asked as he parked in the driveway at the top of the hill. His voice was tense, his fingers white on the wheel of the car.

He can't decide whether to love me or hate me.

"Am I still invited?"

"I'm losing my nerve, I guess."

"You could take me back to my house."

"That would be *gross,* as Noele would say, after waiting all these years."

With some pride he showed her around the house, much more neatly maintained than she expected. Across the street was a small park and beyond that the grounds of a private school that used to be a military academy. From the front windows of the house, perched high on the top of the Ridge, eons ago the dunes on the shore of a prehistoric Lake Michigan, she saw the Sears Tower and the Hancock Center, giant sentinels of the Chicago skyline. On the other side, at the foot of Danny's backyard, I-57 stretched out toward Memphis.

"Highest point in Cook County," he said softly. "Hills, curving streets, trees—hardly Chicago."

His lips were thin, his eyes blank, anger fighting desire.

Irene undid the towel around her neck, took off her knit cap, and unzipped an inch or two of her running jacket while he made them a pot of tea in the kitchen. They sipped the tea quietly, his eyes devouring her and hers smiling back, reveling in his admiration.

"I am very hot and sweaty," she insisted.

"I don't think I'll notice."

"A long time, Danny."

"A long time, and only yesterday."

He put down his teacup, took her hands, and lifted her to her feet. Their lips brushed gently, tentatively, as if exploring an old neighborhood long unvisited.

"I shouldn't be doing this." He tried to pull back, but her hands closed firmly on his.

"You have every right to do it, and so do I."

"You look pretty in red," he said, touching the zipper on her jacket. "You always did."

Hate me, Danny, or love me. I don't care which. But let's end the game.

"Noele picked it out for me. Just like she picked out your Notre Dame Windbreaker."

"Noele takes charge of everything, doesn't she?"

The mention of Noele seemed to change Danny's mood. The tension ebbed from his face and in his eyes there flickered the swiftly moving ghosts of long-forgotten laughter.

Slowly he pulled down the zipper of her jacket. A sweet, passive lethargy oozed through Irene's veins.

I want to be naked for him again.

"That's because she's filled with enough love for the whole world."

Irene had never thought of her persistent daughter quite in those terms.

Danny slid the jacket down her arms.

"Good heavens, woman, what sort of monstrous female garment is this?"

Irene laughed, feeling as if she had been drinking champagne, not tea. "It's a running bra. Noele insisted I wear it. Here, let me get it off. Oh, Danny . . . you haven't forgotten anything, have you?"

His lips were deft and devastating.

"It surprises me how quickly everything comes back."

There is anger in his eyes again. He still has not forgiven me.

He led her to the enclosed front porch, overlooking Mandrake Parkway and the Neighborhood at the foot of the Ridge. A carefully made bed was shoved against the wall. "I like to sleep with windows on three sides," he said, drawing the thin drapes. "Not that there's anyone on Mandrake Parkway to see us."

Leisurely he finished undressing her and then held her arms out, so he could examine her, as though she were a work of art he was appraising. He had only begun the ritual and already she was light-headed with pleasure.

"I'm not graceful anymore, even when I have my clothes off," she said sadly, beginning to feel awkward and shy in her nakedness.

"Quite the contrary, Irene. Now you're graceful all the time."

Their first union was exploratory, a careful revisitation of old neighborhoods. His eyes flashed several times with anger, but he was very gentle with her.

Their timing was off, and their pleasure, at most, only a promise. But so content was Irene that she slept peacefully afterward.

But suddenly her quiet, faceless dream became a nightmare. She was losing her breath. Someone was choking her.

Then she was awake and felt Danny's hand close on her windpipe.

·······Noele·······

IN THICK BLOCK letters she wrote down three words:

Florence

Clancy

Daniel

Three mysteries.

And then, oblivious to Ms. Hounslow's *boring* lecture about the Third World, she thoughtfully added a fourth.

Noele.

Ms. Hounslow was a pretty woman, not too old, maybe twenty-six or so. And she was into feminism and protest and revolution, even though she was too totally ladylike. Noele felt sorry for the people in the Third World, though she couldn't understand Ms. Hounslow's arguments that they were poor because Americans were rich.

After the first name she wrote *Clancy or Burke?*

But she never argued with Ms. Hounslow, because Ms. Hounslow cried when students made fun of her. And then Noele had to force them to apologize.

After the second name she wrote *Daniel?* And then drew an angry line through it, leaving only the question mark.

Noele figured she would probably go into the Peace Corps or something like that after she graduated from college.

After the third name she wrote a large question mark.

Maybe with a husband, if she had one by then.

She crossed out her own name. No one had tried to kill her. The only mystery about her was who she was.

Then shock waves of terror raced through her nervous system, as if she had touched a live electrical wire.

"Is there something wrong, Mary Farrell?" Ms. Hounslow looked scared.

"I'm, like, totally sick," Noele cried, rushing for the door of the classroom.

She ran not to the john but to the chapel.

Brigid

SHE CAME INTO the office after chewing out a crane operator who had damaged an expensive piece of equipment.

Such outbursts made her feel young again, as if she were a girl back in Ireland.

It had been a hard, cruel life, yet somehow she remembered happiness there too.

Burke had not raised the question yet, but she knew it was coming. She must go back to Ireland, become Maeve for a week or so and make peace with the real Brigid and meet her children and grandchildren.

There was no reason to hate her, poor thing. And what would her grandchildren be like? Surely none like Noele.

So quick did forgiveness come.

Life was still hard in Ireland. The make-believe Brigid had had an easier time than the real one.

Life here was gentler, softer. And it so quickly turned sour.

Death—William Farrell, Martin, Florence. Poor, wonderful Florence. How hard it was to hate her, even though she married the man that Brigid wanted.

Then Clancy and Danny.

Only Danny wasn't dead. But there was so much fear around him, lurking like a black halo.

Nothing had worked out right. Except for Noele. And she had been so skeptical about that at first. Noele was the prize that made everything else worthwhile.

Then she was suddenly afraid. Automatically, not understanding why, she reached for her purse and clutched for the old rosary she had brought from

Ireland almost forty-five years ago, her only possession. She did not know for what she was praying. But she prayed harder than she had ever prayed in her life.

················*Irene*················

"I'M SORRY, DANNY." She would not resist her punishment. "I betrayed you."

Her words melted his anger. His grip relaxed, and kisses replaced his fingers on her throat.

"I'm a sick bastard, Renie. Forgive me. It won't happen ever again." He pulled away from her, face twisted by remorse.

"Do whatever you want to me," she said, extending her arm to him in a plea that he return to her.

His body quickly responded to her invitation. And his hands, strong and competent, on her breasts, down her belly, along her thighs, brought healing and grace and benediction. Then his lips on her breasts, drawing sweetness to drown his own pain.

Everything that was fear and terror inside of Irene melted, as if all the snows of winter had thawed at the same instant, and she was swept along by the rushing water, down country streams, into a giant river, over a roaring waterfall, and finally into a peaceful ocean on which she floated for an eternity of happiness.

Afterward she slept again and awakened to see Danny standing above her with a towel around his waist and a stack of typescript in his hand.

"I'll let you read this, if you let me read your stories."

"I'm a lot more naked in my stories than I am here in your bed," she said.

"Then I will really enjoy them," he said, winking like a little boy who had found a copy of *Penthouse*.

He sat down on the bed next to her, placing the neat stack of typescript on the crowded bedstand. His thin shoulders slumped in quick dejection. He seemed so sad and defeated.

"What's the matter, Danny? Are you having second thoughts?"

"And third and fourth and fifth thoughts too. I shouldn't have let it happen, Renie."

"Yes, you should, and I had something to do with it too, you know. I didn't exactly fight you off."

"Ah, you always were a forward one." He smiled wistfully, hiding behind his Irish accent. "But the past can't be recaptured. And I'm terrified of the future."

"Who isn't?" She shifted her position in the bed to see his eyes more clearly. Like the rest of his face, they seemed taut with terror. Unimaginable and undescribed suffering must still be locked up in his head, like pollution in a toxic waste dump. And it had been there even before he was shot down.

"Don't spoil this moment by worrying about the past or the future," she pleaded.

The movement of her body brought something much softer and more tender into his eyes. He bent over her and began to kiss her again with infinite delicacy, as though she were made of fragile tissue paper that might be damaged if handled too roughly.

Later that morning he drove her home and waited in the car. She ran up to her office, took the red leather folder that contained her stories from the secret compartment of her desk, and ran back down the stairs and out to the car to shove the folder into his hands. He smiled, winked, and drove away.

Afterward, in the shower, she realized joyously that having given him the stories, there was nothing left of herself to reveal.

·····*Noele*·····

"YOU LOOK TOTALLY edged, M.N." said Eileen Kelly as Noele joined them at their usual table in the school's noisy, smelly lunchroom. "I looked for you in the john after class."

"I was in chapel," she said, putting her Tab and french fries on the table. "I'm all right now."

The waves of terror had stopped almost as soon as she had fallen to her knees at the altar rail, whether because they were going to stop anyway or because of Noele's prayers, she did not know and did not care.

Daniel. Of course, Daniel.

He was close to terrible evil.

A gross-out. She would tell him what she thought about it.

No, that would not be a wise idea.

It was all right now. For a little while, anyway.

But it might come back, whatever "it" was.

Unless she solved the mysteries on the list she'd made in class.

There were no roses now. Only a heavy weight of obligation.

"I've never seen you look so pale," Eileen Kelly chirped nervously.

"I'm worried about the Third World." She laughed at her friend's concern. Poor Eileen. I'd like to ask her for help.

But I have to do this alone.

·····*Noele*·····

"WERE YOU AS much in love with Moms as Jaimie Burns is in love with me?"

Daniel Xavier made a face, as though she had hit him over the head with a two-by-four. He swallowed his large mouthful of Redburger and came up for air.

"You are certainly candid, M.N.," he said, wiping some of the cole slaw off his lips.

"Which doesn't answer my question," she said briskly. "And PLEASE sit up straight."

He made a mostly unsuccessful effort to obey, but she was distracted by a group of extremely gross freshmen animals who had just come into Red's. Noele gave them her sternest Noele look and that quieted them for a few moments.

"Do you ever lose an argument, M.N.?" he asked, disposing of a trace of mustard from his fingers before she could admonish him to use a napkin.

She considered judiciously. "SOMETIMES Moms thinks she wins, but she really doesn't." She bit into her hamburger. "Mostly in our family I win the arguments."

"I'm sure," he agreed with a wicked grin.

"Airhead," she responded firmly.

She had drafted Danny to act as a chaperone at the High Club Friday night bash and he had, to tell the truth, performed rather well, despite the fact that he admitted that rock music was a change that took "some time to adjust to." He danced with the sophomore girls who asked him to, making Noele insanely jealous, even though she realized that cool chaperones did dance with those silly kids. He shagged away some boys who had too much beer and broke up a couple of fights between gross freshmen animals.

And he was wise enough to dance the last number with Noele. He was a good dancer.

Of course.

Then she spirited him away to Red's and hit him with her two-by-four.

"It was a different relationship. We were older but not so mature. It was an infatuation. You and Jaimie seem . . . well, much more stable than your mother and I."

He smiled his charm smile, which still made Noele's heartbeat do strange things.

"You were going to marry her." Noele jabbed her chili cheese dog at him.

"I . . ." He hesitated. "I don't think that would have happened. It was a summer romance."

"Which ended the night Uncle Clancy was pushed down the steps."

Daniel did not bat an eye.

"Pushed or fell or whatever."

"That had something to do with you falling out of love?"

"Not especially," he replied smoothly. "It was my going off to Asia that cooled things down. . . . Where is all this going, M.N.?"

"I think you ought to get married," she said calmly. "You enjoy women, even those JUVENILE sophomores. You should have, like, a permanent woman."

"Marry your mother?" He choked, even though he didn't have any hamburger in his mouth.

"Don't be gross. She has a husband."

Danny looked relieved. Too relieved, Noele thought.

"You mean any woman? I don't know, M.N. If the right one comes along, maybe. I'm a pretty unstable person, not a good matrimonial risk." He grinned cheerfully. "And I have a lot of things to work out."

"Like growing up," she said. "And sitting up straight."

Guiltily he abandoned his slouch. "Yes, ma'am."

"Airhead." She gave him her most devastating Noele look, a mixture of outrage and disgust.

Danny liked teen talk, was even trying to learn it himself, though he wasn't very good at it. Noele could turn it on and off at will, which was part of the secret.

"I keep trying." He attempted to laugh it off.

"Not hard enough. And you don't care who was responsible for sabotaging your plane. And you don't care whether they might try again. That's obsessively self-destructive."

A potent phrase she'd learned from Jaimie.

Danny bowed his head so that his chin rested on his fingertips.

"I'm a runner, M.N., have been all my life. If you want to play shrink, you could say I'm running from responsibility for my mother's death. I am Joe Hero—that's teen talk from my era—in the short run, but not very good at loving or hating any longer than a week."

Daniel looked so sad and so tired. The lines around his eyes were cool until you realized that they represented an eighteen-year bummer. He was very brave, and he never complained about what had happened to him. He covered it up wonderfully. Only occasionally, as now, did you realize how much unhappiness . . .

Noele's heart did several quick spins.

She reached out and touched his face in a spontaneous gesture of sympathy, the way she would pick up a crying baby.

He kissed her fingers.

"Those freshmen animals will think I'm making a pass." He laughed.

"Barf city," Noele said, trying to regain her composure.

He didn't change his expression when I mentioned Uncle Clancy. And he almost swallowed the whole burger when I asked him about Moms. It's all too totally confusing.

Maybe he did kill Uncle Clancy. And maybe he didn't.

He still loves her, though.

Danny took her home and kissed her at the door.

It wasn't quite like a kiss from Jaimie Burns.

But it was still awesomely sweet.

You're totally falling in love with him, a voice in her brain told her. Really! I don't care, she said, ordering the voice to mind its own business.

····················*Roger*····················

AFTER HE HAD found a parking place on University Avenue, a difficult task even at three o'clock in the afternoon, he strolled briskly down the street and into the concrete catacomb that housed Martha Clay's office. She had been away for the weekend, home for her mother's birthday.

He had good news to share. The administration had managed to mobilize its resources and make its decision. Martha would become an associate professor with tenure, a lifelong appointee at the University.

Almost as good as immortality, he thought ruefully.

It had been another bad day at campaign headquarters. Rod Weaver had come to agonize with them, as though he and Mick Gerety were members of an advisory board whose input would weigh heavily in Weaver's decision to publish his copied files. Rodney was an over-age, overweight swinger with bushy brown hair that did not quite successfully cover a growing bald spot, a bushy brown mustache, and a heavy, pasty face.

Roger had kept his temper carefully under control, much as he would with a highwayman pointing a pistol at him or a mugger with a knife at his throat. He let Rodney do the talking and nodded occasionally in what might have been interpreted as sympathy with the man's ethical agony.

"So you see what the problem is," Rodney said for the fourth time. "If you know what I mean, I have to balance the public's right to know with my obligation not to help a corrupt incompetent be, you know, reelected."

"I think," Roger said, "the governor is in so much trouble, Rod, that you could have evidence that would send me to jail for twenty years and I'd still beat him."

Mick winced.

"Well, you know, there's still the moral problem of winning any extra votes for him."

"You wouldn't look very good, would you, if you published those documents and the governor lost anyway," Mick Gerety suggested.

"The point isn't, you know, what I'd look like." Rodney shook his bushy head. "The problem is, you know, what I ought to do."

He knocked on Martha Clay's office in a rather brisk, businesslike way.

"Come in!"

"Wonderful news, Martha." The words sprang from his lips as he burst into her office. "The dean will notify you officially tomorrow that the president has approved your promotion to associate professor with tenure."

And once more I'll be able to imagine you as Dan Farrell when we make love to celebrate.

Martha's response was underwhelming. "That's very nice, Roger," she said calmly.

Roger felt as if he had been struck with a huge wet blanket. "Only very nice?"

"I certainly appreciate the vote of confidence." She smiled sweetly. "But I'm afraid I'll have to turn it down. You see, I saw Lloyd when I was home this week, and we decided it was time for a reconciliation. I'm returning to Boston next academic year, and the two of us will be commuting back and forth on the weekends the rest of this year. Lloyd is up for tenure at U. Mass. He thinks I can get a part-time teaching job either there or at Boston University or maybe even Boston College with the Jesuits."

Raw animal anger exploded deep within Roger and raced through his body like an electric charge. He grabbed her shoulders in speechless fury and shook her like a rag doll.

"Beat me, if you want," she sobbed as her teeth rattled, her nonchalance shattered by his rage. "I deserve it."

Roger's anger dissipated as quickly as it had erupted, a false alarm from a volcano. He enfolded her in his arms.

"That isn't my favorite feminist talking, is it?" he asked with a laugh.

"I feel so guilty." She spoke through a mixture of laughter and tears. "You taught me how important love is and I realized how much I love Lloyd and how cruel I had been to him. I couldn't believe he'd give me a second chance. But he did."

She wiped her tears away, her tiny round face beaming with joy.

"I'm delighted for both of you," Roger said, feeling as he imagined he would on the day of Noele's engagement.

"I knew you'd understand," she said happily.

Oh, sure, Roger thought ruefully.

. . .

Still in shock, he stood in his bedroom looking slowly and carefully at the familiar objects—the television set on which Irene watched the second half of the *Today Show* while lying in bed, a habit of which he had once severely disapproved, the alarm clock that chimed discreetly to awaken him, an empty vase, the small clutter of tubes and jars on Irene's dressing table.

Who was the fool looking at him from the mirror above that dressing table?

A casual adulterer rejected by a woman he had thought he loved. And an unfaithful husband standing between his wife and the man she loved.

He knew what he had to do, the only thing he could do to restore his self-esteem and his sense of personal integrity. He would give Irene her freedom and perhaps through generosity to her and control of himself, he could recapture a few shreds of dignity.

Typical Catholic idealist doing penance, he thought, and grimaced at his image in the mirror.

But that doesn't mean I'm excused from penance.

He collected an armful of suits and jackets from the closet and carried them down the hall to the guest room. And then returned for toilet articles, shirts, socks, and underwear.

After supper, when Noele had gone up to her own room to do homework, he said to Irene, "I've moved into the guest room for a while. I feel it's the only thing to do until matters are straightened out."

Irene, who seemed especially pretty and especially preoccupied, nodded as if she barely heard him. "I suppose so."

·······································*Noele*································

SHE WAS DRIVING home from school, early in the afternoon for her, and pondering what she would say in a letter she'd write before supper to Jaimie Burns. Notre Dame was only fifty cents a minute away by telephone after five o'clock, but as she told Jaimie, you say a lot of things in love letters that you wouldn't on the telephone.

She also had to do some more systematic thinking about Danny. No one in the family wanted to talk about him. She had the distinct impression they all thought he was a little bit crazy. All but Moms. It was hard to tell what she thought because she never said a word about Danny to anyone.

Was she still in love with him?

Is the Pope Catholic?

And that was bad for everybody, especially if he was still in love with her too. Noele felt a touch of jealousy, for which she severely reprimanded herself.

It was increasingly difficult for Noele to be objective about her cousin. It's a teenage crush, and I know it's a teenage crush. But I'm a teenager and we have crushes. And this is the worst one I've ever had.

She sighed. And what messed it up even more was that Noele knew, as surely as she knew that the sun came up in the morning and set in the evening, that she was the one who was going to have to resolve the Farrell family problem, settle down Daniel Xavier, and get all the Farrells back to the serious business of living their lives.

Including me, she sighed.

Tell me about it, Mary Noele.

She barely saw the van before it hit her. A huge monster, like a giant bull elephant on a rampage, smashed into Flame, turned him over, and extinguished all the lights in Noele's head.

DANCE EIGHT

Ragtime

"Ragtime was an outgrowth of the minstrel show bands and music for dancing at pleasure houses. Ragtime was in great demand around the turn of the century. For many years it was performed in the music departments of the larger ten-cent stores."

Roger

THE PHONE RANG, and Roger, his head slumped into his hands, heaved himself to his feet painfully and walked across the room to answer it. Who would be calling him this time of night? Some fool from the media, no doubt.

There was thick, heavy breathing on the other end of the line.

"Who is this?" Roger barked angrily.

"We warned the little cunt, and still you guys didn't stop. No more snooping, or the next time she's going to get hurt a lot worse." The line clicked.

"Who is this? Who is this?" Roger shouted futilely at the lifeless phone.

He went upstairs to the second floor and down the corridor to Noele's room. She was sitting up in bed, with a bandage on her head and an enormous black eye, engaged in a profoundly serious argument with her mother and Danny.

"Roger, I'm telling Moms that I don't care whether Flame has been totaled. I want him back. Not a new red Chevette, but my old Flame. And I don't care whether it costs every bit as much as buying a new car, I still want him back."

"I think the woman's delirious," Danny said, and winked broadly.

"Daniel Xavier Farrell, I am not delirious. The doctor said I have a bump on my head, a black eye, and some contusions, whatever a contusion is. I don't even have a concussion. I'm not going to let some evil yukhead in a gray van take Flame from me."

There were huge tears in her green eyes at the thought of losing Flame. How readily a seventeen-year-old could become a twelve-year-old, Roger thought. Flame was a four-wheeled doll. Once they're eighteen they no longer can go back to being little girls who play with dolls.

"We'll take good care of Flame, don't worry about that," Roger said. "But now I want to know, young woman, whether anybody's been threatening you lately."

Noele looked anxiously from Roger to Danny to Irene and back. "Well . . ." She dragged out the word.

"In God's name, why didn't you tell us?" he almost screamed at her.

"I didn't want you to worry."

"Snowflake," he said with exaggerated patience, "I'm a candidate for governor. I have, as I'm sure you noticed, a beautiful wife and an equally beautiful daughter, both of whose pictures have been in the papers and on television. That can attract the attention of crazies. Did the man say who he was and what he wanted?"

"He said to stop asking questions about the past," she said glumly.

Roger felt the color drain from his face and his stomach tighten into an anxious knot. "All right, young lady, I'm going to tell Lieutenant McNeally about those phone calls. Promise me that you will tell me if that man calls again. Do you understand?"

"Yes, Roger," she said docilely.

"And that goes for you, too, Irene, and for you, Danny, and anybody else in the family who gets crazy phone calls."

Roger went downstairs to his study, called Lieutenant McNeally, and mixed himself a stiff drink. The policeman, a freckle-faced, sandy-haired young Irishman, was at the door within fifteen minutes.

"It was a professional job, Governor," he said, politely declining the drink Roger offered him. "We have a description of the van from some bystanders and found it abandoned two hours later. It was stolen from an electrical contractor in Oak Lawn. The driver knew exactly how to smash into a car without banging her up too seriously."

"Are you sure of that, Lieutenant?" Roger asked anxiously.

"Maybe it's just a coincidence, but I don't think so. This one has Mob written all over it. Have you done or said anything to offend our friends on the West Side?"

"Not that I know of. Is this the sort of routine warning they send to every candidate?"

"I've never heard of them doing it before."

"How about threatening phone calls? My daughter just told me that she had received several. I answered one myself tonight. The man knew about the accident and said the next time it would be worse."

"That does it, sir. It's the outfit. Someone must have a grudge against your family. We'll step up our protection of your family, Dr. Farrell. But I think I should warn you that if somebody really wants your daughter dead, it will be damn difficult for us to prevent it."

"My God," Roger said in horror. "Are we in a jungle, Lieutenant?"

"We're in America in 1982, sir. Anyone who wants to pay enough can have almost anyone else killed. You can't really protect anybody, not even the President of the United States."

After the policeman left, Roger sank wearily into the easy chair by his fireplace. This was Rocco Marsallo's work. That may have been the Marshal's voice on the phone, worried that a murder committed thirty-eight years before might surface and send him to jail for what little remained of his life.

And it was not Noele's questions that were the threat anymore. The Marshal must know about Weaver's threat to publish the copied documents. It did not matter to him that the Farrells had no control over the *Chicago Informer*. His brain had been damaged by a life of vice. Torturing women amused him. And so he reacted to the threat of exposure the way he reacted to everything at this stage of his physical and mental deterioration—he went after the women of his enemies.

Evil that is irrational, Roger reflected to himself in his best professorial epigrammatic style, is no less dangerous because of its irrationality.

······························*Burke*·······························

FLAME HAD BEEN delivered to him for treatment.

"There's a rattle in one of his rear wheels, Burkie," Noele said. "Could you see if you could fix him, please."

Yes of course he would. Anything to take his mind off the Marshal.

His contacts in the Mob were somber. That boy Rocco is crazy. Out of his mind. But his padrino is very good to him. Owes him for a big favor. A hit man's life would be worth nothing if he accepted a contract. He kills someone, then he's finished. Short of that, the council won't vote against him. Even for a future governor. Yeah, the padrino is that important. You kill him, it's another matter. Even the padrino would approve. But no contracts. Yeah, he probably will slip and kill someone. That's why the council is so patient. They know they'll put him down eventually. All right, but can't you control your own kids? Why is she messing around in Rocco's past?

I'm too old to kill him, Burke thought. So I tinker with cars. He wiped a thick layer of grease off his hands with an old rag. Part of the joy of repairing cars was wiping off the grease.

He had jacked up Flame and removed the left rear wheel. He examined it, and then crawled under the car to inspect the axle. Dangerous. But the jack was firm and the floor of the garage flat. He'd done it a hundred times before.

Lying under the car, he thought about the first Chevy he worked on. A 1934— cost 450 dollars. Probably better built than this one. And much better mileage.

Life looked simple and easy in those days. How had it all gone wrong? Maybe his mother had been right after all. Keep God's laws and you'll stay out of trouble. Burke chuckled somewhat hollowly to himself. He had done neither.

Then he saw the sneakers next to the left rear wheel, a few inches from the jack—Danny's sneakers. A solid kick against the jack and Flame would fall on him, crushing out his life.

Danny was humming "The Whistling Gypsy."

So this is the way it ends. His life rushed before his eyes, as it always did in stories. So many regrets: Mother, father, wife, children. He'd let them all down. Even Bridie.

Damn it, man, get it over with.

One brown and white sneaker was now resting against the jack.

If I had to do it again, I'd still love her. And I'd still kill to protect her, if I could.

Don't prolong it, you bastard. I'm ready.

Danny stopped humming.

Now.

Another song: "Roddy McCorley."

Damn, I wish I had a cigar.

It's fair. I tried to kill you. I'm ready.

Only, dear God, end it.

Dear God. . . .

"Is it yourself under that vehicle?" Danny said.

"It is." His voice was a rasp.

"Ah, 'tis a dangerous place to be, what with it suspended on the jack."

"So I am told." The smell of gasoline was teasing Burke's suddenly sensitive stomach.

"Have you found out what ails himself?"

"Bad axle work."

"Auto repair isn't what it used to be in the old days, is it?"

Damn it, end it.

"It never was very good."

"Sure, then, you should come out from under, so we can put the wheel back on. It's not safe, at all, at all."

Burke eased himself out from under the Chevy and stood up. Every muscle in his body ached from tension.

Danny was leaning nonchalantly against the wall of the garage, needing only a pipe in his mouth to complete his mask as an Irish countryman.

"I think I need a drink," Burke murmured.

"In the middle of the morning?" Danny asked in mock surprise. "That's no way to start the day. Still, I suppose it's all right, just this once. I may have a sip myself."

A reprieve.

But for how long?

Brigid

"I TELL YOU, Bridie, he was going to kill me. His foot was resting on the jack."

They were driving to the Club for Saturday lunch, Burke's hands clutching the wheel of his Alfa, his fingernails still rimmed with traces of grease.

"But he didn't, did he?" she replied.

"You're pretty relaxed about it," he grumbled.

"Well," she said, trying to sound reasonable, "you're still alive, aren't you? I think you're imagining things, what with that terrible man Marsallo on all our minds."

She was deftly asking Burke what he had learned in his muffled phone conversation before they left for the club. She did not like to discuss Burke's connections with the Mob; her superstitions warned her that to mention them made them even more dangerous.

"Some of my friends talked to him. They think he's simmered down for the moment. He's been warned that if there is any more bloodshed his padrino may give up on him."

"But if the papers publish the story?" She found fear clutching at her throat, like a blast of sub-zero cold when you emerge from a warm house on a winter day.

"That may set him off again. He's unpredictable as well as crazy. He could be watching the TV news some night when Roger is on it, think of those damn papers, and decide to do something to someone else who is close to Roger."

"Irene?" Brigid gasped.

Burke drove into the nearly empty parking lot of the club. "Or you."

John

THE FACES IN Kearney's Funeral Parlor rolled up and down, as if they were bobbing in four-foot waves. John blinked several times to clear his vision.

"It is beyond our comprehension why a man so young and with so much promise of happiness ahead of him had to go home in his early forties."

Too much food, too much drink, too much smoking, too many weekends in the office, too much strain.

"We are confident that we will meet him again, but our confidence in the future does not alter our grief in the present. We weep as Jesus did at the death of his friend Lazarus and as Mary did when the lifeless body of her son was placed in her arms. We offer our sympathy as Jesus did to the poor widow of Naim. We reaffirm our faith that Michael Heggarty will rise again, just as the young man did."

There were times when death seemed an easy way out—Noele's life in jeopardy, the family history being passed around among reporters, Danny's return and his suppressed rage, Irene as much in love with him as ever, his own career at the mercy of a psychopathic cardinal.

"And we bow our heads in grief and pray God that time will heal the wounds and give us all the strength to go on."

The widow, looking all of her thirty-nine years, blew her nose and nodded in vigorous agreement. Her oldest daughter, a classmate of Noele's, embraced her mother protectively.

"For we know that, even though we are lost in the fog on the side of a steep mountain, the summit is somewhat above us radiant in the light of everlasting dawn."

John shook hands with the widow, hugged her children, and joined his own family at the back of the red-carpeted funeral parlor.

"I liked the wake service," Danny said. "Chalk up one more for the new Church, and that was a very powerful little talk, Jackie. It meant a lot to the family."

"Maybe you ought to be a priest, Danny," Roger said jovially. "You seem so interested in the church."

Roger had no reason to be grinning. Too many things had gone wrong and worse might still happen.

"The only advantage I can see is the celibacy," Danny replied. "Sure, it would be wonderful to be free from temptations."

"I have them occasionally." John laughed, thinking of how lovely Irene looked in black.

They all laughed, all except Noele, who did not seem amused.

"Uncle Monsignor has his parish to love," she said in her best mother superior tone. "Some people are afraid to love anyone."

"Do you think she means me?" Danny muttered sotto voce.

"Really."Noele sniffed disdainfully. She joined Julie Heggarty and hugged her as the rest of the Farrells walked through the lobby of the funeral parlor toward the snow-packed parking lot. Although it was a "please omit flowers" wake, Kearney's still smelled of mums. The smell was probably sealed into the walls.

As he made his way carefully toward his car, John remembered another wake in an earlier Kearney's. His father was laid out in an open coffin, his head on a satin pillow that concealed the massive wound that had taken his life. Nothing had ever been the same since that night.

He climbed laboriously into his Buick and watched the others stumble across the parking lot, like drunken dancers after an all-night party. A dance of death, John told himself; like the characters at the end of a Bergman film. And if we can't stop that dance, some of us are going to end where Mike Heggarty is tonight.

·····*Roger*·····

MARYJANE LED HIM into Les Nomades and introduced him to Jovan, the proprietor.

"An honor to meet you, Governor," he said, bowing over Roger's hand.

"Old-world charm." Maryjane waved a casual hand. "Bistro atmosphere, Parisian posters, and good food, without worrying about conventioneers."

"My education has been neglected," Roger said mildly.

He was sick with worry. The papers, Noele, Martha, Irene, Danny. He didn't need another love affair. But he was incapable of declining Maryjane's dinner invitation.

"The same rules tonight, Governor, at the risk of repeating myself." The handsome, leggy blonde filled his glass with dry white wine. "First, you're my guest, and I pay the bill. Second, it's deep background, not on the record. Third, no passes."

"I wasn't planning any," he protested, with singular lack of candor.

She raised her hand. "No denials needed. I'm merely setting up the guidelines." She pushed her long hair away from her tiny face. "I happen to believe in marriage, and anyway, I couldn't compete with your resident sex goddess."

"Irene?"

"If I were her and you fooled around, I'd cut off your balls."

He tried to make his laugh disarming. She was serious. Too bad Ireme wasn't that fiercely possessive. Then, in a quick, blinding insight, he realized that he had married Irene as a substitute for Danny.

"Do you object if I say something personal?" Maryjane's conversation seemed to be total free association.

"Not at all," he said, realizing that the explosion of insight had not changed his facial expression in the slightest.

"I meet a lot of politicians in this business." She looked shyly at her wineglass. "And you really are the class of the lot. I've never seen anyone so graceful under pressure."

Roger was dumbfounded. The woman was not trying to seduce him. She meant what she said. He would never have thought of using the word "graceful" of himself. Why would she see grace in him?

"I know what you're going through with that Rod Weaver stuff." A faint flush colored her face. "You're really being quite brave, you know."

No, I'm not. I'm a weakling and a coward. I have been both all my life. And you are a sweet kid, an appealing mixture of toughness and gentleness, of sophistication and naive virtue. You're my Snowflake in a couple of years.

"Did you read the copied documents?" he asked.

"A pile of shit," she said briskly. "Rod wanted me to promise to put him on TV with it. Don't worry, I certainly won't use it. My generation of reporters didn't grow up during Vietnam, so we have some ethical standards."

"You believe in marriage, and you believe in privacy?" Regretfully he removed her from his sex object list. There must have been women like you around when I was younger, women who would have kept me on the path of virtue. His idiot romance with his cousin had blinded him to them.

And he comes back from the dead, and he's not the boy I thought I loved. Probably never was. And despite all my stupidity, I still think I'm qualified to be governor of this state.

"And I don't swear and I don't chase men and I don't drink much and I generally don't talk dirty, and I don't smoke. I only lie a little. But tell me more about Daniel Farrell. He really turned me on. How can anyone spend all that time in jail and still seem perfectly normal?"

"As normal as he ever was." The girl's conversational whirl was making him dizzy. She would be very good in bed, if you could turn off the stream of chatter.

Chauvinist pig.

He saw Martha on his occasional forays back to the University. Crisp and correct in the corridors of the department, she greeted him as she would any other respected senior colleague, save for a glow of starry-eyed admiration in her eyes.

"You're the academic, so you know more about Freud than I do, but what does it mean to a kid to grow up knowing that his mother died to save his life? That's a heavy load to carry around."

Roger never quite thought about it that way.

"Like having a ghost peering over your shoulder," Maryjane said with a sympathetic little frown. "Now, let's talk about state finance, Governor. Order the vegetable soup and the salmon mousse, and remember, it's on me."

Flossie's ghost coming back for vengeance?

Ace

ANOTHER BLIZZARD WAS on the way, so Ace McNamara rode the creaky, cantankerous Rock Island on his weekly pilgimage to St. Prax's, instead of risking his car in the streets of the Nineteenth Ward, a ward that was something less than loyal to the mayor and hence not likely to have a high priority for the city snow plows.

The Rock Island Line, once a proud name, no longer existed; and the Regional Transportation Authority, never a proud name, operated the trains with moderately benign neglect. But it would always be the Rock Island as it wended its weary way through the various Parks until it finally deigned to come down from its elevated roadway and, like a somewhat tipsy dowager, stagger into the Neighborhood.

Ace was not the only naval officer on the train. "Good to have you aboard, sir. Are you having a pleasant trip, sir?"

Ace briskly saluted the man in the N.D. jacket. "Yes, sir."

"At ease, Captain." Dan gave a fair imitation of an admiral.

"Our officers' mess on this ship isn't very good, I'm afraid, sir." Ace saluted again.

Dan stuck out his hand and grinned genially. "Nice to see that one person from the Neighborhood hasn't changed."

"I was about to say the same thing."

They both laughed.

"You were in Nam?" Danny said, now dead serious.

"Three times."

"I think I may have lucked out on that one."

"You'd be dead," Ace said flatly. "You're the kind of flyboy who would have gone back for that last run."

"I guess so."

"How does it feel to be back? Many surprises?"

"There aren't many surprises left when you come out of the fields one evening, dead tired as usual, and there's a geek from the Interior Ministry who says you have to take a plane ride with him. The next morning you're at the U.S. Embassy being interviewed by American television."

"But that's what it's about," Ace said. "Christmas is the surprise of light coming back, Easter the surprise of spring returning. Our faith is the ability to be open to surprises."

"Ah, the poor church has changed so much." Danny fled to the protection of his wonderful brogue. "And here we have a pious and holy priest preaching paganism."

"Catholicism is pagan symbols with a new overlay of meaning—like the blessing of the Easter water with the lighted candle: obviously a pagan intercourse ceremony converted to mean that on Easter Jesus consummated his marriage with his bride, the Church, and that we who are baptized are the fruits of this fertile union."

"Saints protect us and preserve us." Danny made a devout sign of the cross. "Are you after saying that the Holy Easter candle is a phallic symbol?"

"What does it look like? And the water is a womb symbol."

"Ritual intercourse." Danny's eyes opened in mock dismay. "On the main altar during solemn high mass with mother superior watching."

"And the words are 'May this candle fructify these waters.' "

" 'Twas easier in the old days . . . when the clergy didn't go around suggesting that God was horny, Captain, sir." Dan shivered, perhaps from the cold, perhaps from fear of the pursuing, love-crazed deity.

"At least I don't have to interpret the symbolism for the likes of you," Ace said. "It's easy to see where your imagination is."

"Terrible, terrible, terrible. And what comes out of the union," Danny said, changing back to Chicago English, "is a surprise to all concerned."

"As is usually the case."

"It's not easy." Danny shook his head sadly, the comic replaced quickly by the troubled dreamer.

"Order out of disorder, cosmos out of chaos—it's not supposed to be easy," Ace replied. "Creation or re-creation never is."

The Rock Island stopped at Eighty-third Street, blocking traffic as it always did. The stations were designed by a genius who arranged that every stop would block traffic.

Danny was thoughtful. "That's what Noele said the other day when she announced for the millionth time that I am grossly immature: Resurrection is not supposed to be easy."

"Noele said that? Do you think she's right?"

Danny's head sank toward his chest. "If I was certain that she was right, my life might be a lot different in the years ahead."

"You'd keep on taking risks?"

"It was questions like that"—Danny took refuge again in his brogue—"that scared me away from you twenty years ago."

·····················*John*·····················

HE HAD JUST come to his room in the rectory from a Wednesday evening Lenten service in the church. It was the associate's turn to take the service. But Jerry had pleaded in a last-minute phone call, with the noise of barroom conversation in the background, that he had run into a counseling case. So John Farrell took the service—scripture readings, hymn singing, and a homily about the Holy Spirit in the life of the church.

There were thirty or forty pious souls, a couple of devout teenagers, some older people who would have come if it was the rosary or benediction or the stations of the cross, or a sermon in Sanskirt, a few of the prayer group members, and some marriage encounter couples.

Danny, in the inevitable Notre Dame Windbreaker, had made himself at home in the pastor's parlor and was sipping a bottle of Coke the way he used to sip a bottle of beer in years gone by.

John was mildly annoyed. Danny had made the rectory his part-time hang out, wandering in and out almost as if he were a member of the staff. And to tell the truth, he was there more often, it seemed, than the associate pastor.

"Hell of a good sermon tonight, Jackie," Danny said. "Gave me a few ideas for the chapter I'm working on. From what I hear, most priests don't preach as well as you do. Must be the TV experience." He grinned mischievously. "And by the way, I hope you told that guy Keegan to go to hell?"

"No, I told him I would discontinue the program week after next. It made him very happy. He said my fellow priests might eventually restore me to favor and I might be esteemed almost as much as I used to be. Wasn't that nice?"

"And you told them that at the station last week?" Dan's brow furrowed into a deep frown.

"No, I didn't; it was another great program. Two professional football players from the Christian Athletes. The ratings will be sky high. I couldn't spoil their happiness at the station."

"A priest paying attention to ratings and phone calls?" Danny asked, putting the empty Coke bottle on the coffee table.

"You're beginning to sound like Keegan. I'll tell them next week."

The phone rang. It was, bizarrely enough, Ed Keegan. "This is Monsignor Keegan, John," he began formally, as though they had not been contemporaries at the seminary and called each other by first names for most of their lives. "I've heard rumors that you really did not ask to be released from your contract at Channel Three."

John felt irrationally angry. "I'm going to talk about it to them next week."

"The cardinal is most insistent, John. He's the representative of the Pope, the vicar of Christ. I am sure you wouldn't want to slip lower in the esteem of your fellow priests by resisting the cardinal's will any longer."

"I'll talk to them next week."

"Can you go down to see them tomorrow? It would contribute greatly to the cardinal's peace of mind."

So pathetically eager to force the erring cleric back into line. "You don't have to worry, Ed. I'll take care of it. You can assure the cardinal that I intend to be no further threat to his peace of mind."

"I regret very much that I have to say this to you, John, but you give me no choice; if I don't hear within twenty-four hours that you have informed Channel Three you're withdrawing from your television program, then I will at the cardinal's direction institute proceedings to have an administrator appointed in your place. You may continue as pastor and receive the salary of a pastor, so long as you say the required Masses, but your associate will become the de facto pastor of St. Praxides."

If Danny Farrell hadn't been there listening, his blue eyes shining with concern and support, John would have caved in.

"You crazy son of a bitch," he exploded. "Are you so much a creature of the institutional church that you'd turn the best parish in the city over to that creep because the cardinal resents someone else getting publicity? Don't you have any hormones left in your body?"

"The cardinal's will is the will of God," Keegan said righteously.

"Go get him!" Danny whispered, leaping toward the telephone, loving every second of it.

"I know a little bit of canon law too, Ed. You're going to have a hell of a hard time taking this parish away from me. And there are a couple of canon lawyers in the diocese who would dearly love to fight you. We can prolong this case until your psychopathic boss is gone and a new archbishop comes in who thinks it's a good thing to have priests on television. And of course you, you hypocritical bastard, will think the same thing."

"You're defying the will of God, Monsignor?" Keegan said in outraged disbelief.

"Furthermore, you utterly misunderstand the temper of the people of this parish if you think they will accept as acting pastor a man who would rather associate with sixteen-year-old boys than sixteen-year-old girls. Finally, if you lift a finger against me, you or your psychopathic boss, you'll have a thousand angry adolescents around the cardinal's mansion tomorrow morning."

"I'll have to consult his eminence about this," said Keegan stiffly.

"You do that," John said, slamming down the phone.

"Hot shit!" Danny embraced him. "It's like the good old days, only you're crazier now than Roger and I ever were."

"The word will be all over the archdiocese by tomorrow, Danny." He stood up to walk to his liquor cabinet. "And I'll be a pariah in the priesthood for the rest of my life."

"That might just save your soul," Danny said.

·······························*Irene*·······························

SHE AND DANNY sat across from each other at the Country Club, as nervous as two teenagers on their first date. It was an utterly safe place to meet; the eyes of two dozen people were there to watch them. Not that anyone would think it unusual that Danny and his cousin's wife would have an occasional meal together.

"What did you think?" Danny asked anxiously.

She had prepared her reaction very carefully, memorizing it word for word. "I'm prejudiced, Danny, because I've known you for such a long time; but even allowing for that—and I think I'm objective enough to be able to do that—I think it's a great novel. It's got depth, power, and a wonderful story. I'm sure it will be a commercial success. Some of the critics will love it, and some will scream that you're a hack. But they'll all know that there is an important new writer to deal with. The people here at the Club and in the Neighborhood, most of whom won't read it, will wish you'd stayed in China. And those few of us who will read it will celebrate the fact that you came from our parish."

"Well, I guess I can heave my sigh of relief. You're the first one besides my agent and my editor to read it, and I don't trust agents or editors—well, not as much as I trust somebody like you."

"And my stories?"

"I'll give it to you straight, Renie. They're not just very good. They are sensational. You're one of the best there is. They make me hesitate between pride that I know you and envy that I can't write nearly so well. But why have you kept such beautiful work secret for all these years?"

Her hand darted out to touch his fingers and then darted back very quickly. They were, after all, in the dining room of the Country Club.

"And you know what a worthless whore I am?" she said bitterly.

"I know that's the way you see yourself. But that's not the way a reader would see Lorraine. They would view her as a fragile flower at long last ready to bloom."

"That's Lorraine, not me." She felt the sting of tears in the back of her eyes.

"Yes, it is, but I won't argue. You'll find out for yourself in time. Let me send them to my agent. I know he can find a publisher."

"I could never do that."

"And I'm hardly the one to talk about bravery, am I?" he said sadly.

He drove her home after lunch, along streets slick with melting snow drifts.

"Come in," she pleaded.

"I shouldn't."

"Forget *should*s and *shouldn't*s for an hour."

"No."

She kissed him, her tongue jamming into his mouth and demanding his. "Please."

Whatever his hesitancies outside, he was not hesitant after she led him into the first-floor guest room. He undressed her slowly and leisurely, making each zipper and button and strap a delicate ceremony.

"One improvement over 1963 is that a man doesn't have to fight girdles," he said.

"Noele treats them as historical improbabilities, like the Latin Mass."

"Was she really born on Christmas Day?" he asked as he drew her hands to the buttons on his shirt.

"Really born on Christmas day," she replied softly.

"Would she approve of us?" he asked, slipping off her last wisp of clothing.

"I don't know. . . . Oh, Danny."

"I didn't hurt you?"

"You won't leave me anything."

"Clothes?" He was mystified.

"No protection at all." She moaned as her body rebelled against all restraint.

"I've read your stories, Renie." And his fingers and lips were everywhere.

Irene was now only pure sensation, soaring into the skies and dancing on the clouds.

"You're a wonderful lover, Danny," she murmured sleepily afterward as they clung together on the sweaty and rumpled sheets, his head resting on her breasts.

The sun had broken through the clouds, and through the drawn shades bathed the room in soft, approving light when they awoke.

Peaceful and happy, she knelt next to him and he put his hands around her waist, fingers on the small of her back, thumbs on her belly. In this delightful position, she began to talk to him, pouring out everything that had happened since they had been separated. At first the stories were sad, but somehow they became comic and the two of them shook with laughter.

Then she was serious again.

"You've grown, Danny," she said, as her hands touched his face. "You are even more sensitive, more tender, and a better listener than you used to be. You make a woman feel that she is a woman and that she can tell you everything."

"I try," he said, a little puzzled.

"With other men I do the listening. With you I am able to talk."

"And a good talker you are, too." He winked, still mystified.

"But you're still not a friend," she said. "Friends not only listen, they talk. They share their hopes and their fears. You don't."

Danny removed his hands from her body. She put them back.

"I'm getting too close to the real you again, like I did the last time," she said without bitterness. "And you're preparing to escape again."

"I'm no good in the long run." He sighed. "You know that."

She overpowered his lips with her own, holding him motionless with the force of her love. "I won't let you leave me this time."

Noele

THE ONLY AFTEREFFECTS from the automobile accident were an occasional headache and the obligation to call someone every night to find a ride to school while Flame was going through the final phases of rehabilitation at the Chevrolet agency at Ninety-fifth and Kedzie, where Burkie had made ominous complaints.

Only two and a half weeks till Easter. Despite her preoccupation with the Farrell mysteries, Noele had to prepare for the Holy Week Liturgy. She was busy selecting the music the folk group would sing at the end of the interlude between the Vigil services and the Mass on Holy Saturday, an interlude that she managed to pry away from Mr. Creepy Crumb by a combination of charm and stubbornness.

The phone rang. Even though her private number had been changed and there had been no threatening calls since the accident, she knew who it was before she answered. Again the thick, blue voice on the phone. "McNeally and his fink cops aren't going to protect you. You're going to get fucked real good."

Noele slammed down the phone and ran for help.

There was no one in the house.

She threw open the front door and collided with Danny, who was coming in with a stack of pictures of Roger to be hung in neighbors' front windows.

"I'm a precinct captain," he said jovially. "Hey, what's wrong?"

Noele clung to him desperately, sobbing with fear.

He held her tightly, gradually soothing her and exorcising the terror.

It was wonderful to be in his arms.

I love him so much.

John

THE PRIMARY ELECTION in late March was a dry run for Roger's campaign organization. In fact, most of the voters cast ballots for Roger instead of George Washington Lincoln, a perennial Downstate Democratic candidate who wore Davy Crockett clothes, because their local Democratic organizations told them to vote for him, and there were enough organization Democrats in the state to turn out a half-million voters even if Roger had been running against no one. Hence his own personal organization had relatively little to do except admire the skill with which he read the text of his TV advertisements.

The victory celebration was something less than ecstatic in its enthusiasm. The Farrell staff found it hard to rejoice over one more defeat for Georgie Lincoln, especially since there was no evidence from the very modest turnout that Roger had ignited any prairie fire of voter enthusiasm, even though the polls showed him running well ahead of the governor.

But as Angelo Spina had put it, an orangutan would run well ahead of the governor.

The Illinois primary was cruelly early. More than seven months would intervene before the general election in the fall. The candidate and his staff must neither begin too early nor wait too long. In practice this meant no peace for the candidate or his family all summer.

Danny was standing next to Roger at the rear of the modest crowd in the grand ballroom of the Midland Hotel, awaiting the candidate's triumphant appearance. He continued to turn up at odd times and places, seemingly at loose ends save for his novel, which no one, as far as John knew, had ever seen. His dirty jeans, tattered sweat shirt, and the by now badly wrinkled Notre Dame Windbreaker had become part of the scenery. You almost forgot that this was a man who had been in a Chinese prison for eighteen years.

"I suppose the real reason for this celebration," Danny said, "is so the voters of Illinois can get a good look at Irene and Noele and decide if they want those two faces on the front covers of their newspapers for the next four years."

"Very perceptive political observation," John agreed.

There was a burst of applause, not exactly spontaneous, because one of the young staff members was leading it off camera. Mick Gerety appeared at the podium and announced, "And now, ladies and gentlemen, the next governor of the great Prairie State of Illinois!"

The enthusiasm of the group was authentic enough, although perhaps motivated in part by the hope that they would find jobs in the new administration. The victorious candidate appeared with his black-haired wife and his red-haired daughter, both in white dresses that hinted at the coming of spring. There was something wrong between Roger and Irene. But that was not surprising, with Danny on the one hand insisting that he was not interested in turning back the clock, but on the other hand being very much a part of the Farrell family life and thus effectively activating all the old memories.

"This is an important first step," Roger said after the cheers of his supporters died down. "Both of those words are critical. What we have accomplished thus far in our campaign to bring a more compassionate and responsive government to the State of Illinois ought not to be minimized. We have proven that we can organize a mostly volunteer campaign to raise the issues and get out the vote and win decisively. But we have taken only first, cautious steps. While I appreciate the enthusiasm of your applause, I also accept it as your commitment to continue the attempt we have all begun. With God's help, and the help of my wife and daughter"—he smiled and raised his arms in both directions to draw his two women close to him—"we will stay in this fight for the State of Illinois every single day from now until the fourth of November."

"What's the state of your confrontation with the cardinal?" Danny asked as he fumbled with the zipper on his Windbreaker and turned to leave the ballroom.

"He backed down, as I thought he would. He's like running water. He follows the path of least resistance. If you stand up to him, he disappears. And Keegan is left holding the bag, but he's used to that."

His temporary victory had brought back his hunger for Irene. Manhood restored.

"A good week for the Farrells." Danny punched his arm.

"An important first step." John Farrell grinned.

As he turned into the driveway at St. Praxides, John hesitated. The big stained-glass window in the back of the church was not lighted, a stained-glass window depicting St. Praxides marching toward the world with a large farm implement over her shoulder—Prax's ax, the parishioners called it.

John glanced at his watch. The light was turned off by a timer at eleven. It was only 10:45. He backed out of the driveway, and then carefully, because the streets were still slippery with two inches of March snow, drove the fifty yards to the entrance of the church. The massive and beautiful stained-glass windows had been smashed.

John jumped out of the car, opened the back door of the church, and dashed into the darkened nave. In the faint glow of the vestibule light he saw thousands of tiny pieces of colored glass scattered on the pews and a dozen or so large bricks.

In the rectory, even before he called the police, his personal phone rang. An ugly laugh and then a harsh voice. "That's not the only thing that's going to get broken, Monsignor. Unless your brother shuts that punk up."

Irene

SHE ENCOUNTERED DANNY in the lobby of the Midland after the victory celebration.

"Tomorrow morning at my place while you're jogging." His poor face looked so tired, his pale blue eyes so weary.

What did the election victory mean to him? Yet he seemed to be exultant over Roger's victory.

"Of course."

"I can hardly wait."

"Me too."

Brigid

DESPITE BURKE'S WISHES and the doctor's orders, she was the first one to arrive at the plant on the day after the primary. She promised Burke that she would leave before noon, but insisted there were a few "minor matters" about the Streeterville Plaza job to which she must attend. In truth, she wanted to make sure that none of the wrong subcontractors was on the list of bidders.

She paid little attention to the yard as she drove in. It was only as she parked in front of the ramshackle office that she noticed that the cement mixer at the end of the yard was tilted crazily, as though it had been on an all-night binge. She backed up quickly, sliding on the new-fallen snow. The tires of all the construction vehicles had been slashed, and the windows of a dozen or so had been smashed with bricks.

She stumbled into the office and reached for a phone to call Burke. It rang before she could touch it.

"Listen, you sweet-smelling shanty Irish whore," said a deep and menacing voice. "We're going to slash you up like those tires unless your favorite son shuts up that punk kid."

Irene

SHE LEANED OVER him, a sheet clutched at her chest in a senseless gesture of modesty.

He was asleep, his haunted face momentarily at peace. Poor, dear man, he had suffered so much.

Their relationship was changing. He had begun to share himself with her. He was still the competent, demanding lover who could turn her into a mass of seething and uncontrollable reactions, a blob of need and delight. In his arms and at the mercy of his skills, the eighteen years of separation were blotted out. The night at the lake seemed like the day before yesterday.

But then, his conquest complete, his passions spent, he would quickly become the injured little boy, sobbing his hurt against his mother's breasts—unnamed and undescribed, but terrible hurts.

And many of them older than China.

She smoothed his hair and kissed him gently.

A strange mixture of forceful lover and hurt child.

My child.

Oh, Danny, give me a son. Our son. I want to take care of both of you.

Roger

"I WISH I'D known before that we were dealing with the Marshal." McNeally shook his head in discouragement. "That makes it a whole different ball game."

Roger felt he had had no choice but to tell McNeally about the copied documents, documents that might make the demented mobster think he was threatened with jail. The officer's brown eyes had first widened in surprise, then narrowed in shrewd thoughtfulness.

"No wonder Marsallo is so upset. And when he's upset, he turns vicious. A couple of years ago he caught one of his juice men holding back. So he suspended the guy by his feet from pipes in the basement of his mansion in River Forest and beat him in the guts with a baseball bat until his entrails fell out and dangled on the floor. It took a long time for the guy to die."

"And he still roams the streets of Chicago?"

"When he's not playing golf at Far Hills or wandering the streets of River Forest. It's one thing, Governor, to know that he did it, and another to get the evidence that makes it worthwhile even to bring him in. We've never been able to lay a glove on the Marshal."

"A van demolishes my daughter's automobile, a stained-glass window in my brother's church is smashed, vehicles at our family's plant are vandalized, threats are made against the physical safety of my mother and my wife and my daughter, and you tell me you can't lay a hand on Rocco Marsallo?"

"We're doing all we can, Governor. We'll put extra surveillance on your family and its property, and we'll try to keep an eye on the Marshal too. It's a lot harder than it used to be, with all the damn government regulation. I'll be candid, however, Governor. I could assign the whole Chicago police force to your protection, but if the Marshal wants you badly enough, he'll get you.''

"What would you suggest I do, Lieutenant,'' Roger asked stiffly.

"I'd suggest that you persuade Weaver not to publish those papers and to tell everybody he's not going to publish them.'' He tapped the pen on his notebook as he stood at the door of Roger's office at campaign headquarters. "You might make a call to some of your political allies out on the West Side. They don't like the Marshal much. Maybe they can calm him down.''

Half an hour later Roger made a call to the West Side to a contact Angelo Spina suggested. The man was friendly and sympathatic. It was a terrible thing that was happening. A real disgrace to the city, though, thank God, crazy Rocco didn't live in the city but lived in River Forest, which is "a Republican place, Governor.''

"Do you think any of your friends or their friends could put a stop to this?'' Roger asked anxiously.

"That depends.''

"On what?''

"Not on anything you can do, Governor,'' said the West Side politician.

Roger then called Rodney Weaver to plead with him. But Weaver had made up his mind. He was going with the story the week after Easter. He was sorry about the threats and the vandalism but they could not divert him from his commitment to the public's right to know. Indeed, such criminal behavior made it all the more imperative that the whole sorry mess get out into the open. "A free and unfettered public opinion,'' he thundered, "deprives monsters like Marsallo of power.''

"Over the dead bodies of my mother, and my wife, and my daughter?'' Roger asked icily.

"You should have thought about that before your family became involved with a man like Marsallo,'' said Weaver, sounding like an old-fashioned Irish monsignor about to throw a couple out of the rectory as they were embarking on a religiously mixed marriage.

"You know those documents were copied without my permission, Rodney.''

"Frankly, I can live with that,'' he said.

He should have withdrawn from the race as soon as he found his papers were missing. If he withdrew now, Weaver would still publish them and the Marshal might still take his vengeance.

As he was leaving his campaign headquarters there was a call from Angelo's contact on the West Side.

"I had my friends talk to some of their friends, Governor, and they are very sorry. But right now they can't do nothing about that crazy boy Rocco. Maybe later, if you know what I mean. But right now, they feel their hands are tied.''

"What might it take to untie the hands of your friends?''

"Well, Governor, that's a pretty tough question; you see, nobody likes this boy Rocco. They all think he's kind of crazy. You know, he didn't used to be that way; he comes from a very good family, good parents, good wife and kids, though they don't live with him much anymore. He's turned real mean the last few years, and the friends of my friends don't like that at all. Some one of these days he's going to kill somebody that he shouldn't kill. Then they'll have to do something about him.''

It was all quite clear. After somebody was killed, then the outfit would discreetly dispose of Marsallo. His coat still on, Roger sat down at the desk again. Oh, my God, which one will he kill?

A thought that had been lurking in one of the twisted side passages of the cavern of his preconscious finally forced itself to his attention. Suppose that he killed himself, leaving a letter blaming the Mob and in particular the Marshal. The council would have to take action. His death would be the Marshal's death warrant.

Roger had never in his life considered suicide; it was an admission of defeat that he could not tolerate.

Now self-destruction seemed to be a possible path of atonement. He did not drive the possibility out of his mind.

But how does one commit suicide?

Ace

"AND ALL THE time my poor child was in danger, Brigid was being threatened, and Saint Prax's windows broken, the only thing on my mind was screwing."

There was no connection between the events. In or out of Danny's bed, Irene could not have prevented either the vandalism or the threats.

She knew that, of course. But Ace had learned in his years in the priesthood that women handled symbols differently from men. Irene was crying over the contrast between her pleasure and the danger to her family, not assuming responsibility for it.

And the story she had told him was easily the most astonishing tale he had ever heard. What the hell do I say now? I know, I duck.

"I won't touch the moral tangle, Renie; it's too much for me. I'll just say one thing: "Your biggest flaw has always been not placing a high enough value on yourself."

"You mean I give myself away cheaply?"

Her tears stopped.

Irene

ST. PATRICK'S DAY was, as usual, cold, gray, and windy. The festivities of the day were enthusiastic but forced, like a May Day parade in Moscow. The faces of the young people in the park and on the floats were pinched and red. The crowds on the sidewalk spent as much time blowing on their hands as clapping with them. The joviality of the politicians and their wives in the parade and on the reviewing stand was officially enforced, despite the shivering. The celebration no longer basked in the sunlight of Richard J.'s glowing Celtic charm. In the present administration, no one on the reviewing stand could be quite certain whether he was a confidant of the mayor or a member of the "evil Cabal" to which her enemies were assigned with dizzying speed.

Roger, who considered the St. Patrick's Day festivities to be grotesque, had strolled briskly in the first line of the parade along with the mayor, the county board chairman, whom the mayor had just dumped, two Polish congressmen, and one black ward committeeman. When he reached the reviewing stand, the cardinal, looking more than ever like a dissolute Renaissance despot—long white hair and hollow face to match his lean and hollow body—blithely congratulated him on his primary victory and on "the great job your brother's doing on his television program."

Irene would have turned away and refused to speak to the man if Roger had not introduced her before she could escape. Noele, characteristically, was much more candid.

"If my uncle John is so good on television, Cardinal, why is Monsignor Keegan threatening to take the parish away from him unless he gives up the program?"

The cardinal was unperturbed by her assault. "Well, now, young lady, I can't always keep those chancery office people under control. I'll have to have a look-see myself, and if what you say is true, I'll certainly put a stop to it."

"Tell me about it," Noele had said, and sniffed.

Fortunately the cardinal did not understand teenage slang.

Irene shivered on the reviewing stand, smiled, and waved quite spontaneously at the passing marchers. The politicians and their wives on the stand were complaining about the profile of Roger that had appeared that day in *Fort Dearborn* magazine, a slick journal appealing to the limousine liberals of the lakefront Alps and the cocktail-party radicals of the suburbs, who sympathized with the poor and the oppressed so long as they stayed within the city limits. The magazine advertised such left-wing products as fifteen-hundred-dollar stereo sets, twenty-five-thousand-dollar Mercedes automobiles, and half-million-dollar condominiums.

Gery Jensen, the editor, had written the piece without bothering to interview Roger. He quoted one of "Dr. Farrell's distinguished colleagues" from the University as saying that it was "probably a good thing for Roger to be elected to public office. He doesn't have much of a career ahead of him as a scholar. Mind you, he's clever, but not very profound."

And the article observed that "the professor's wife and daughter had faces of pretty, painted plaster of paris—two Barbie dolls, one middle-aged and one pubescent."

"It's not true, Roger," Noele protested. "Moms only uses a little makeup around her eyes, and I don't wear any at all. I mean, my feelings aren't hurt, but why would he lie about us, especially when he hasn't ever seen either of us face to face?'"

"Two answers, my dear," Roger said. "First of all, you have to sell magazines, and second, with his clientele you never lose any circulation by making fun of the Irish. None of us can afford vanity if we're going to be in public life, Snowflake. Besides, we have more serious, more deadly enemies out there than Gery Jensen."

They made the rounds of boisterous cocktail parties and alcoholic receptions after the parade. Each successive appearance exposed the candidate and his family to a higher proportion of drunks, so that by the time they reached the Shamrock Festival, the South Side Irish classic St. Patrick's Day celebration, only a handful of participants were capable of even recognizing the "next governor of the great State of Illinois."

Irene drank a martini at each of the first four stops. A few months ago Roger would have discreetly warned her about that. But now, whatever the changes of chemistry that had occurred between them, he did not say a word. So she stopped after the fourth martini and managed to keep a steady walk and a pleasant face for the rest of the evening.

But at two o'clock in the morning Irene was wide awake. The alcohol had lost its effect in her bloodstream, and her head was clear. Roger was still in his self-imposed exile in the guest room.

Gery Jensen was perfectly correct, she thought. Even if she didn't wear layers of makeup, she was a middle-aged Barbie doll. All her life men had played with her: her father, then Danny, then Roger, and then for a few bittersweet weeks, John.

And now Danny again.

She had always responded, furnishing each of them the pleasures they demanded and enjoying their pleasure as though it were her own. In Danny's case she even provided him with the pleasure of her total candor. Never had she taken charge of herself or her own life. Father Ace was right. She gave herself away cheaply.

She sat up in bed and pounded the pillows angrily. "Noele wouldn't put up with it," she said aloud. "Why should I!"

I am wide awake, I am perfectly sober, I am thinking clearly. I'm angry, angry at all of them and angry at myself. Who the hell is Dan Farrell to think he can keep me dangling on a string until he straightens out his emotional problems?

Feeling that she had crossed a decisive line, Irene bounced out of the bed, threw her mink coat on over her nightgown, shoved her feet into her boots, and rushed out into the hallway. She hesitated for a moment in front of Noele's door. The lights were still on in the Christmas child's room.

She and Noele had been squabbling more than usual lately. Noele surely knew that she and Roger were no longer sleeping together and was angry, not because she didn't understand the situation, but because she thought she did. And, whatever happened, Noele was certain to be affected. Innocently she had brought Danny Farrell back to life and would suffer the consequences like everyone else.

I've sacrificed myself for Noele, more than my Christmas child will ever know. It was time to stop the sacrificing.

She rushed by Noele's door, down the stairs, out of the house, and into the driveway. Chilled by the cold, she jumped into her Datsun and skidded three times on the way to Mandrake Parkway, the third time spinning in a complete circle. She was too angry to be frightened. She pounded the door furiously and leaned on the doorbell for several minutes before Danny, in his shorts and a torn white terrycloth robe appeared to let her in. "Glory be to God, Irene, what are you doing here at this hour of the night?"

She pushed into the house and slammed the door shut.

"I've come to tell you exactly what I think of you, you miserable son of a bitch. I'm sick and tired of being a prize dangling from the wall for men to take when they finally get around to deciding that I'll do until something better comes along. Who do you think you are that you can hide behind your stack of typescript and work through your silly sick psychotic problems while I wait patiently for an answer?"

"You're wonderful," he murmured.

"And when your hormones become active enough that you want a woman, you pick me up off the streets, use me for an hour or so, and then dismiss me like a nice little whore who will keep herself on call in case you get horny again."

"That's not true, but you're glorious."

"And you don't care whether those criminals mutilate all of us—Brigid, Noele, and me."

"That's not fair, Renie. What can I do?" A touch of fear and guilt. "Please—"

"Please what? Take off my coat and go to bed with you because an angry woman turns you on? Then you can pretend that I'm your mother again. I'm not your mother, and I'm not a little girl. I'm an adult woman. Someday you might become an adult man, though I doubt it. But don't expect me to wait around till that happens."

She stormed away from him, out into the cold night, and down the slippery steps to her car, praying to God that she wouldn't fall on her face. And as she pulled away she saw him standing in the panel of light at the door, rubbing his jaw in bemusement.

He's going to run away again. I don't care.

Fuck you, Danny Farrell.

Noele

"WHAT WERE YOU and Maryjane Hennessey talking about yesterday?" Roger asked in his elaborately casual tone as he buttered his toast.

Moms was still in bed, like she always was at this hour, and Noele was trying to catch up on her trig while eating breakfast. She totally did not want to play Roger's inquisitive-father game.

"Colleges. I told her I was thinking of being a journalist."

"You never told me that," he said reproachfully.

"You never asked," she replied, knowing that bitchiness always put him off in the morning.

She had told the truth, but not the whole truth. Maryjane was, like, real cool. And when she assured Noele it was all off the record they had a totally swift talk.

Her idea about Danny was really excellent. Why hadn't she thought of it? Still feeling guilty because he didn't protect his mother.

A totally lame idea, but if a kid grows up being told that his mother died to save his life, it figures that he'll feel guilty. Right?

It all fit in somehow. No wonder Dan was afraid of Moms . . . and of me, too.

But that doesn't tell me who killed Clancy.

And I can't mess with that or those retards will do something worse.

But I still have to find out.

Burke

HIS FRIEND WAS on the phone again.

There had been a meeting of the council, he told Burke. The young men were angry. They didn't need a fight with a candidate for governor. But the padrino insisted that no one was to touch Rocco unless he killed someone. Then the padrino would strangle him with his own hands because he had brought disgrace.

The padrino is a man of honor.

Doubtless. But my family.

If you put him down, it's different. The padrino made that clear.

But I can't hire anyone to do it.

Silence.

And what if he hurts someone in my family, but doesn't kill them?

That would be a real disgrace.

Would the padrino change his mind then?

Too bad you couldn't keep that kid out of things that were not any of her business.

After the call Burke removed his father's gun from the safe. Old Redmond Kennedy had probably used it himself. Burke had hired others to do his killing for him.

His hand trembled as he tried to load the heavy weapon. In frustration he slammed his fist against the safe.

He was useless.

································*John*································

"CAN I COME in?" Ace asked.

"Sure. Pour yourself some Jameson's and sit down."

John was drinking his second martini on the day after the St. Patrick's lunacies, the Friday evening before Passion Sunday.

"I hear your associate has applied to the personnel board for a transfer." The Ace poured himself half a tumbler of Jameson's, considered it critically, and then added several more ounces of the golden fluid.

"I'm not surprised. He and his allies missed their chance to take over here. So they'll probably try a shot at another parish."

"M.N. scared the hell out of the old man at the parade. That young woman wouldn't hesitate to take on the Pope himself. That would be a fun fight to watch." Ace downed a substantial portion of his Irish in pleasant contemplation of the big Pole and the little Irish chewing each other out.

John had so many more serious worries that he had almost forgotten about the cardinal. "Did you know that Danny left town this morning?"

The Ace coughed, wasting some of his precious Jameson's. "He did?"

"He called me from the airport and said he had to go to New York to see his publisher and might stay there, indefinitely. Sounded like something scared the hell out of him."

"Oh." The Ace sucked meditatively on the edge of his tumbler.

"Typical," John muttered. "When things get tough, Danny runs away."

"Do you think he'll be back?"

"Oh, yes. He'll turn up again like a bad penny. He asked me to tell Brigid and Roger. My brother was out campaigning, so I told Irene."

"And she said?"

"Nothing. Just thanked me for calling. She's still in love with him, you know.

Roger was a poor second choice. And as you yourself said, I was a substitute for Danny.''

"Sometimes I think that crazy bastard is a substitute for himself.''

John was astonished by the Ace's vehemence.

"You sound like you're angry at him.''

"I'd like to wring his, you should excuse the expression, fucking neck.''

·····James III·····

"HONESTLY, JAIMIE, I can't imagine anything more gross. Daniel simply went to the airport, got on a plane, and flew to New York without packing any of his clothes and without saying good-bye to anyone but Uncle Monsignor. Isn't that geeky?''

Jaimie was inclined to agree that it was indeed geeky, although he was personally quite happy to have Danny out of town. He liked him but was wary of him as a rival.

He drove slowly, keeping a close eye on the unmarked police car that was following them. He did not know why it was so important but Dr. Farrell said not to get too far ahead of the cops and Jaimie was not about to argue.

He and Noele had driven to Oak Lawn to see a movie called *Cat People,* which Noele wanted to see because she had heard that cat people had green eyes like her own.

It was a weird film—strange, heavy mystical symbolism that Jaimie understood all too well. It frightened and intrigued him.

Noele kept up a running commentary through the film, as she usually did. "Really, I think she looks gross without any clothes on. She looks much better on that poster with a cobra wrapped around her.''

"I think she looks pretty good either way.''

"I'm sure you would,'' she complained.

"Not a bad flick,'' he said tentatively on the way home.

"You like every movie in which the women take off their clothes.''

"It beats studying chemistry,'' he agreed.

"I think the black panthers looked better than she did.''

"You were supposed to see a similarity between the panthers' sleek bodies and hers.''

"Really?'' Noele was surprised. "Gee, I wish I could see the things in flicks that you do.'''

"I thought the redhead was especially sexy, but then I guess I like half-naked redheads.''

"Jaimie Burns! You are the most gross boy I have ever known!''

"Is it *most gross* or *grossest?*'' Jaimie asked.

"Really!''

The signs were there for Jaimie to read. He'd better change the subject. "Why did your cousin go to New York?''

"He said he had to see his publisher, but I think he's afraid of Moms. They were in love once, you know, probably still are. Moms isn't sleeping with Roger these days. Danny left so as not to come between them. Like Enoch Arden.''

"Enoch Arden?"

The police car had not made the stoplight at Western Avenue. Jaimie slowed down, but even after the light changed there was still no police car.

"You remember, it was a novel by Dickens."

"No, I think it was by Tennyson." Jaimie realized that he took a considerable risk correcting Noele, but he was never able to resist the temptation when he caught her in one of her rare mistakes.

"Well, whoever wrote it."

"Actually it was a poem, and Enoch and the girl were married."

"I didn't mean it to be taken literally."

Jaimie never had a chance to pursue his interpretation of the Tennyson poem. As they turned off Ninety-fifth Street into a dark and empty Jefferson Avenue, two cars emerged from driveways, one ahead and one behind them. Jaimie slammed his foot down on his brake as two men jumped out of the car in front and rushed to Jaimie's Chevy, one at either window. Jaimie rolled down the window on his side of the car and only then noticed that they were both wearing ski masks.

The one on his side jammed a gun into Jaimie's throat. "Not a word, punk, or I'll waste you and that slut. Get out of the car real quiet and peaceful." Jaimie opened the door of the car prepared to deck his adversary the same way he would dispose of a wide receiver. He lowered his shoulder and smashed into the man's chin, sending him sprawling across the street.

Then he turned and tried to grab the shotgun away from another man who had appeared out of the darkness. He twisted the gun out of his hands and raised it like a club, swinging it toward the man's skull. But then something slammed against Jaimie's head. He felt himself falling into a deep pit. The last thing he heard as he crashed into the bottom of the pit was Noele's screams.

Later he tried desperately to climb out of the pool of darkness in which he had been struggling. He was in a car bumping down a rough road. His hands were tied, and there was a gag in his mouth. Somewhere in the far distance he heard Noele moaning and groaning. She too was gagged and, through thick and blurry eyes, he saw a man's massive hand poking and jabbing at her bare flesh.

Then they dragged him into a house, either in the country or in a secluded section of the city. It was surrounded by trees, and there were no lights from nearby houses. He was pushed and shoved into the darkened house and then into a brilliantly lighted room.

One of the three men slapped him into consciousness. "We're going to put on a little show for you tonight, punk, and we want you to see the whole thing from beginning to end. It's a preview of what's going to happen unless this slut's family does what we tell them."

Then they made him watch while they tore off Noele's clothes and beat her. Then the three men took turns raping her and sodomizing her.

DANCE NINE

Dance Macabre

"Dance of death . . . depicts Death playing the violin and dancing in the graveyard at midnight. The music includes the Dies Irae from the Requiem Mass."

CONGRESSMAN BURNS WAS screaming like a man being dragged into electroshock therapy. "You're telling me, Lieutenant, that a young couple can be kidnapped and brutalized on the streets of this city and the Chicago police department can't do a thing about it, even when they know who's responsible?"

McNeally had been pushed too far. "God damn it, Congressman, if I had my way we'd go out to River Forest, pick up those bastards, and castrate them. Don't blame us cops for what you congressmen and the Supreme Court have done. You know, I know, we all know, the Marshal is responsible, and that he and his thugs Dubuque Salerno and Little Tony Caputo are the guys who did it. But if I bring them in, their lawyers will have them out in four hours and the newspapers will have the whole story. We don't have a shred of evidence. They wore ski masks. Neither Noele nor your son can identify them."

"Then they're free to do it again, as they threatened?"

"We can lock the girl up in protective custody someplace. We can take her to a new city and give her a new name, or we can send her to Europe. But if the Marshal wants her badly enough, he will still get her."

"What the lieutenant is telling us," Roger said with icy calm, "is that civilization only works when citizens are either committed to stability or afraid of the consequences of instability. Marsallo is a throwback to a pre-civilized era, and those of us who are civilized aren't prepared to respond to him."

The congressman slumped into a chair next to his wife and Irene, who was sitting erect, pale, and silent in the waiting lounge of Little Company of Mary Hospital. "At least I persuaded Jim Wells to kill the newspaper story. I had to threaten the son of a bitch with all kinds of terrible harassment against his goddamned newspaper if he printed it. He kept babbling about the public's right to know!"

"I've heard that line," Roger said ironically. Did the public have the right to know that a gubernatorial candidate now carried with him, wherever he went, a bottle of Valium tablets, obtained on the grounds that he needed to relax after an evening campaign address so that he could sleep, but secreted in his briefcase, in fact, so that the instrument of possible expiating sacrifice was readily available.

"We're putting a twenty-four-hour-a-day guard on both of them," McNeally said, his eyes darting nervously at each of the four parents facing him. "I understand your son will be released from the hospital in the morning, Congressman?"

"About noontime. Bumps and bruises and observation for internal injuries. But I don't think he's in any danger. He wasn't the target. Put the guards on Noele."

The lieutenant nodded. "The Marshal is not likely to do anything in the next few days. He'll know that we have a very close watch on him."

"But there is nothing to prevent him from hiring someone else, is there, Lieutenant?" Irene spoke for the first time since she had emerged from Noele's room shaken and grim.

"I suppose not, but he seems to enjoy participating in these things himself. How's the girl, Mrs. Farrell?"

"Sedated, hysterical, bruised and battered, humiliated, and ravished. How would you expect her to be, Lieutenant?"

"She'll pull through," Roger said, hoping he was right. "She a strong young woman, and she'll bounce back."

"If you were a woman you wouldn't be so confident," Irene said stormily. "She'll never be the same again, and we all know it."

John

HE WAS STILL at his prie-dieu as the early April morning sunlight streaked through the window. The days were getting longer—the triumph of day over night, life over death, Jesus over Satan. In half an hour or so the sun would begin to bathe the place on the Courts where the naked and brutalized body of his niece had been found a few hours before. Score one for darkness over light.

The Farrell family curse? He had never thought of that before. But if it was a curse, three generations of the family had brought it upon themselves. Now the fourth generation was suffering for it, perhaps irreparably. Dear God in heaven, please give her the strength . . . the strength to be herself again. Don't punish her for my sins—or Roger's or Brigid's or Clancy's.

At eight o'clock he would call Ace McNamara at his apartment near the University and tell him what had happened. If anyone could help Noele, it was the Ace.

But who could possibly help an innocent young woman who had been so savagely attacked?

Brigid

RARELY DID BRIGID attend weekday Mass. She was too embarrassed to appear in the church except on Sunday. Himself would think she was turning soft, crawling back to Him in her old age. But this morning she came to St. Praxides for her son's Mass. "Please take me," she begged the deity. "If one of us has to die, let it be me. I'm an old woman, and I'm the one that deserves it. The woman is harmless and the child has never done anything wrong. She didn't deserve to be punished this way. If you want one of us, take me instead. I'm ready to die. I'm even ready to go into the pit, if that's where you want to send me. But let Noele live."

After Mass she joined John in the sacristy, where he was removing the purple chasuble. "We're being punished for our sins," she wailed, nearly hysterical. "That poor child is suffering for all the evil we've done."

"God doesn't work that way, Mother." John tried to be calm, patient, self-contained, though in one corner of his own soul his fears were the same as hers.

"A lot you know about God!" she screamed at him.

John put his arm around her, drawing her close, the way Danny would. She cried herself out of her anger and fear. He had never held her that way, not even the night his father died.

Dear God, why not?

"Have you heard anything from the hospital?" he asked softly.

"The woman called just before I came to church and said Noele was resting comfortably, whatever that means." She wiped her eyes, once again the strong woman who could cope with every terror. "They've probably filled her up with dope. Irene doesn't know when she'll be able to come home. Her problems are likely to be more psychological than physical, and may last a long time. That's what the doctors say, anyway. Though a lot they know. They're all men."

"You sound like you think all men are rapists, Mother."

"Sometimes I think they are. Did you talk to that psychologist priest fellow that she likes so much?"

"I did. He was horrified, of course. But he also said, and I quote, that we were out of our minds if we think Noele isn't going to recover."

"A lot he knows," she sneered.

"A lot he does know, Mother. More than all the rest of us."

Irene

"THAT'S RIGHT. RAPED and sodomized repeatedly by three mobsters. . . . And they made Jaimie watch. . . . Hysterical. What else would you expect? . . And then dumped her on the St. Praxides basketball courts. Phone calls to everyone saying the next time they would do worse to her. . . .

"And the same treatment promised for me and Brigid. . . .

"No, the police can't do anything; they know who the men are, but they can't prove it. . . . They will have round-the-clock guards on her hospital room. But this man Marsallo has lots of money, and he can pay others to do what he wants. . . . I hope you're having a nice time in New York, darling." She slammed the phone down, and huddled over it, wishing she could cry.

···*Noele*···

SHE FELT PAIN and anger and shame and humiliation. She was abused, torn, debased, and discarded. And she was terribly, terribly afraid. They would come back for her again. They would do all those unbearable things to her yet another time—rip off her clothes, torment and torture her, taunt her with their obscene words, and then bury themselves in her body time after time until she thought she would die, wished she would die, begged God to let her die. Then they would kill her, slowly and horribly. No one could stop them. They were demons with unlimited power to hurt and to destroy.

And yet, although she was barely conscious and her mind had been dulled by drugs, Noele was not thinking only of herself.

Something had to be done about Jaimie. He would blame himself for what had happened, and it wasn't his fault at all.

She heard one of the stupid doctors say that there would be so much guilt and anger between her and Jaimie they would never be friends again. But in that small part of her consciousness where Noele was still in charge, she decided they would totally not take Jaimie away from her.

Something had to be done about Moms, too. Noele had pushed her away furiously when she had tried to embrace her, a mean, nasty thing to do—hurt Moms because she had been hurt.

And Roger, frantic, confused, powerless. Trying to explain the reason for what had happened, he had spilled out the story that one of the men had been paid by Clancy to kill Danny's mother. Someone had documents that they'd copied from Roger's office to prove it.

Well, she and Jaimie had suspected that, even though she'd hoped that it had been Burke, because then Danny wouldn't have been the one to kill Clancy.

Noele began to slip into turbulent unconsciousness. She fought the darkness off.

So Danny's mother really had been killed, and that was why he killed Clancy. No, there was something wrong with that. There was too much medicine inside her to think why it was wrong, but it was still wrong. When she was better, she would sort it all out. But now she would give up for a while and let the darkness do what little healing it could.

Later in the day a young shrink came in the room and asked a lot of boring questions. She told him that, really, his questions were boring and she was sure he had better things to do on Saturday afternoon. Besides, she had her own personal psychologist who was coming to see her tomorrow.

"You've been through a very difficult experience, young woman," the shrink said solemnly.

"Tell me about it," Noele replied.

The yukky hospital smell made her want to throw up, hopefully over this geek. The next day she was able to think more clearly and asked herself why someone who seemed so totally not into revenge would have killed even the man who murdered his mother. Daniel Xavier forgave people. And that was good. But he didn't seem to care, and that was bad. He had to learn that you could care and still forgive—like she cared about him and could still forgive him for not being here when she needed him.

Then she slept a little, still not able to separate in her haunted imagination what had happened to her and what had happened to all the others. In her dreams she was Clancy and Brigid, and Moms and Danny, and Roger and John, and Flossie. A lot of the time she was Flossie. Why?

At noon Father Ace looked in the doorway with a quizzical smile on his face. "Ready for your personal psychologist, chaplain, confidant, and Ann Landers?"

She still hurt terribly and was frightened, but she managed to return his smile. "How was the folk group this morning?"

"If that's the only thing on your mind, I suspect you're going to survive." The Ace stood next to her bed, hands in his pockets, his eyes, as always, twinkling.

"Of course I'm going to survive," she said tartly. "There was this *boring* young psychiatrist who wanted me to fall apart yesterday afternoon, and I'm not going to fall apart for anybody. Do you hear that, Father Ace? I'm totally not going to fall apart."

"There are going to be some tough times, M.N.," he said softly.

"That goes with being a woman. We have to learn to live with being raped and things like that."

"This is Passion Sunday, M.N.: suffering goes with being human."

"Will I ever get over it, Father Ace?" She heard her voice catch and was angry at her own weakness. "Will I ever be the little girl I was at the movie with Jaimie?"

"You'll never be the same, M.N.," he said slowly. "What happened will always be part of your life and your memory. Whether you'll come out of this experience a stronger and more mature woman is up to you."

"I never lose fights, Father Ace." She pounded the bed. "Never. And I won't lose this one."

"I'll bet on that, Noele."

"It's all so *boring*." She pounded the bed again.

"We grow up by learning to live with boring things."

"Well, at least I don't have to worry anymore about being a virgin."

"Virginity is not a physical matter, M.N.," he said.

"Yes, it is," she insisted. "Well, partly, anyhow."

"Not mostly," he said, taking her hand in his, a big strong hand, bigger and stronger even than Jaimie's.

"Okay, not mostly. Now I'm going to cry, Father Ace. I'm not going to be hysterical, but I'm going to cry. Can you hold my hand very tightly while I cry and then go take care of Jaimie Burns? It's harder on him than it is on me."

Before he left the room, Father Ace called Uncle Monsignor. "Spread the word around the family. M.N. is okay. How do I know? She said so, that's how I know."

And she and Father Ace laughed, as though they shared a great secret.

That evening she fiddled with her Passion Sunday supper, telling the nurse's aide who'd brought it that the food in the hospital was boring and then said yes, she would like a pill to help her sleep. She watched half an hour of television, called home to tell Moms not to come to the hospital because she wanted to sleep and that she loved her very much, and then closed her eyes.

Her sleep was deep and dark, like swimming in the lake at night with clouds over the moon and stars. But suddenly she was awake, confused, and terrified. Where was she? What had happened? Why was she so tense? Where was Moms? Then it all came back to her, the pain, the horror, the shame, the crude words, the evil, mocking laughter.

Someone was in the room, breathing heavily. Something jammed into her mouth so she couldn't scream. And a cruel hand squeezed her breasts, hurting her again. Something cold and hard against her skin, slicing into it.

"Just a little nick this time, cunt, a hint about what we're going to do to you when we have our next party."

There was more blackness for a moment, and then Noele coughed the gag from her mouth and screamed hysterically. The light went on above her bed and Danny was enveloping her in his arms and swearing that no one would ever hurt her again.

·······*Irene*·······

"PERMISSION TO COME aboard, sir." Father McNamara saluted sharply.

"Permission granted, sir." Dan saluted even more sharply.

"Glad to be aboard, sir." The priest saluted again.

"Glad to have you aboard, Captain, sir." And yet another salute from Dan.

"Glad to be aboard, Commander, sir."

"Idiots." She couldn't help but laugh. They were playing sailor and marine to get a laugh out of her, but also because they were both clowns.

In fact, Dan had been every inch a polished and competent Navy officer all night. He had soothed and reassured Noele even before Irene and Roger came to the hospital. With one of Dan's arms holding her protectively, she was quietly sleeping when they entered her room.

Then he had chewed out the truculent Lieutenant McNeally and called an elite private security firm to arrange for around-the-clock protection.

"To watch the cops," he explained to Irene.

Then he organized a schedule of "our own people" to "watch the cops and the security guards"—Burke, Jaimie, John, Father Ace, the massive and brilliant DeWitt Carlisle.

He was in charge: charming with Brigid, gentle with Noele, reassuring with Roger, brisk and competent with the cops, and funny with her. Somehow he understood that only laughter could temporarily exorcise her demons. Or maybe he remembered that from the past.

Roger was sent on the way to a speech at a luncheon in North Brook. "Don't worry, Governor, she's in good hands, isn't she, Mr. Carlisle, sir? And we must not let them think they have us worried. Give 'em hell in North Brook."

One of the jokes that Danny arranged for her was that a massive young black like DeWitt had better be called "sir." Jaimie's roommate, whose father was a banker, as was his father before him, tried to talk jive with Danny, but he wasn't nearly as good at it. And although he had the disposition of a laid-back cherub, DeWitt did his best to play the part of a "heavy" of whom Danny ought to be afraid.

Danny is so wonderful with young people. What a pity he doesn't have a son of his own. Or a daughter.

Jaimie kissed her on the forehead, a first, when he replaced DeWitt, and the large basketball player looked like he wanted to do the same but was too shy. So Irene, made bold and a little crazy by Danny's contagious wit, kissed him and murmured, "Be cool, DeWitt."

"They blush too," Danny whispered outrageously in her ear. "Would you drive me home for a few hours' sleep? We can leave Jaimie in charge."

Danny Farrell, happy warrior, elegant commanding officer, tender protector of frightened women. How easy it is to love you.

But in the Datsun, he retired into silence.

Irene adjusted the windshield wiper. Rain again.

"That was very impressive, Dan."

"Morale purposes," he said, dismissing his show of competency. "Whistling in the dark."

"We needed it, all of us."

"I'm good in the short run, Renie; you of all people know that. It's the long run that does me in."

She didn't argue.

In front of his house he touched her cheek. "Please, come in with me."

Her longing to do just that burned like an acetylene torch.

"Only on my terms."

Longing turned to pain as he raced through the rain to the door of the house. But she did not cry. She would never again weep for Danny.

Not until tomorrow.

John

DANNY AND JAIMIE stood in front of his desk in the rectory office like two gallowglasses, Irish mercenary soldiers who knew they were doomed to a life that would be short and dangerous, but also grimly determined to give at least as much as they got before they were snuffed out.

"You must be out of your mind," John said. "You'd never get away with something like that."

Danny sat on one of the hard chairs next to John's desk and motioned to Jaimie to do the same. "Let us worry about the prudence of it, John," he said solemnly. "It's theology we want from you. The cops tells us that the Marshal will strike again, and they are powerless to stop him, even if we beg, bribe, or browbeat Rod Weaver into tearing up those papers. It's now become a matter of principle with him. His reputation as a man who can torture anyone he wants is at stake. He might go after Irene or Brigid too."

"I can't believe the police would give up that easily."

"The Marshal's actions are a combination of Mob violence and psychopathic hatred, and no police force in the free world can protect anyone from that." Jaimie spoke with terrifying softness.

The rectory phone rang: "Monsignor Farrell. . . . Oh, yes, hi, Joe. . . . That's right. Our Easter Eve program ought to be special. . . . No, the cardinal turned down our invitation. . . . Anglican bishop? Fine with me. He's a much better television presence than the cardinal anyway . . . A syndication contract? Fifteen markets, including New York and Los Angeles? . . . I'll have to think about that. Although it certainly is good news.''

"Congratulations," Danny said. "You're going to do it, of course." It was an order and not a question. Danny's magic was as tough as Irene's.

"I'll have to decide about that later," John said, dismissing the program as unimportant. "You want to know whether it's permissible to murder Rocco Marsallo?"

"No, Monsignor," Jaimie Burns said quietly. "We want to know about the theology of self-defense. If there were an invading army threatening the lives and the bodies of our women, wouldn't it be permissible to defend ourselves against them? If we were in a jungle and another tribe was attacking our village, if we were in a fort in the West and the Apaches had us surrounded, if the Vikings were storming a castle in medieval Ireland—under all those circumstances, wouldn't we have the right to defend ourselves?"

"Those were uncivilized societies," John argued. "We have police. We have a civil order. This is twentieth-century America, not medieval Ireland."

"Did you notice what happened to your niece in our civilized, ordered, well-policed society?" Danny was dangerously calm. "We're dependent on the Mob to defend us from its own crazies, and the best they can promise is revenge after someone is dead. Is that civilization, John? Hell, it was safer in China."

"He who lives by the sword shall die by the sword," John Farrell said, falling back on his scripture.

"The monks defended the monasteries and the sacred vessels in attacks by the barbarians," Danny countered. "Can we defend Noele?"

"You want revenge?"

"No, we don't, Monsignor," Jaimie insisted. "We want to protect Noele. These men promised they would hurt her again. Neither Mr. Farrell nor I feel we can let them do that."

"I'm not an avenging-angel type," Danny said. "You ought to know that, John."

The attack on Noele had transformed him, John thought, as if he had been driven to pull together the scattered pieces of his personality. He wore a neatly fitting blue suit, had combed his hair, and had polished his shoes. His words were forceful and carefully chosen. He was relaxed and self-possessed. The anger—and the fear—that had lurked in his eyes had disappeared.

"All right." John sighed. "The conditions in moral theology are quite clear. Self-defense of the lives and the physical well-being of one's family is licit when there is no other way to protect legitimate rights—so long as one practices blameless moderation."

"And blameless moderation means?"

"It means you don't go any further than necessary to protect yourself or your family."

"What does that mean concretely?" Danny's fists were clenched, his knuckles white.

"It means you don't use physical violence if moral constraints are enough and, if you do use physical violence, you only use the essential minimum."

"What if the only way to protect your own life and the lives and bodies of your family is to kill?"

John rubbed his hands over his face. The theory was easy, the practice. . .

"Theologians have traditionally said that if someone is in the act of attacking you or those whom you are obliged to defend, and the only way you can defend them is by killing the attacker, then you may do so. This isn't just Catholic theory, Danny, it's traditional Western ethical philosophy."

"You can kill them when you see them coming down the street with guns?"

"It suffices for you to know that they are prepared to strike and will do so shortly. To use your own terms, if you know the Apaches are going to attack you before tomorrow to kill you and carry off your wives and your daughters, you could attack their camp that night. Or you could ram the Viking ship as soon as it entered the estuary and not wait until the Vikings attacked your ring-fort."

"That's all we wanted to know," Dan said. "We'll see you around, John."

He and Jaimie rose and briskly left the office. John followed them quickly. "You can't take the law into your own hands," he said, trying to bar the door of the rectory.

"We're not doing anything with the law," Danny said confidently. "Maybe we won't do anything at all. But I'm not going to let anybody hurt Noele again."

John went back into the office and sat at his desk. He was trembling. He'd given all the right answers, but the solution was wrong.

Or was it?

He should call Joe about the Easter telecast. And the syndication. He'd almost forgotten about it. What difference did it make? Fifteen cities or five hundred— it was all worthless. All sham. To hell with it.

Instead he went over to the church to pray. Like he had never prayed before in his life.

Noele

"AND SO, JAIMIE Burns, don't you dare turn space cadet on me because you feel guilty or because you saw them . . . do what they did. I don't care how many shrinks say we can never be friends again. I will totally not let that happen."

"I promised I'd always protect you, and I didn't," Jaimie said sadly.

She jabbed her finger at him.

"Don't talk like that. I won't stand for it."

"We have to give it time, M.N."

"I know *that*. I'm just telling you what the outcome will be."

Jaimie smiled. "You're still overwhelming."

"Of course," she said, forcing herself to relax on the hospital pillow, and not feeling overwhelming at all.

At the door Jaimie turned and grinned at her.

"It was Tennyson."

"Huh?"

"I was right and you were wrong. Tennyson wrote Enoch Arden, not Dickens."

"Retard." She threw the pillow at him and they both laughed a little.

That's better, she thought after he left. It would be a long time before the Noele/Jaimie person was back. But it would come back.

Maybe.

She thought about asking a nurse for something to help her sleep. But she was afraid of the dreams.

Ace

IRENE WIPED THE tears off her face with a fragile tissue, investing even such a minor action with elegance and grace. Danny was working his magic on her, just as he had done long ago.

"He's the only one who seems to be keeping his head, Father," she said. "Crazy Danny acting like he has common sense."

"You forget that he was a naval officer and probably better than most of them. An honors graduate from Annapolis who stood for racial justice long before it was fashionable. We could have used his intelligence and decisiveness in Nam."

"He was a good officer, Father, because he could be good at anything. But I think he's too gentle for war." A faint flush spread across her cheeks.

Ace wasn't so sure. In war the strong often turn and flee and the gentle fight to the bitter end to protect their own men, and sometimes survive precisely because they were gentle.

"Noele told me yesterday that I was as bad as Danny."

"High praise." Irene laughed. "You two are the only ones who can make her smile. I'm not sure about Jaimie."

"She'll be all right, Renie. . . ."

There was a police car parked outside. The Farrell family was trailed by police now whenever they left their homes.

"I worry a little about Danny. He seems so determined. I hope he doesn't do anything dangerous."

"So the competent, determined Dan Farrell is as dangerous as the runaway Dan Farrell?" He laughed heartily.

She blushed deeply and looked away from him.

"He's acting at the hospital the way he acts in bed."

"And that scares you to the core of your soul?"

"Can fear be sweet?" She looked away.

"You never did get over him, did you, Renie?"

"No," she said, "I never did. And I never will, but I won't sell myself cheap anymore, either. You persuaded me of that."

"Only way to deal with him."

"Right."

But she walked slowly down the stairs of the rectory, like a widow who had just arranged for her husband's funeral.

As he watched her Datsun pull away, followed by the blue and white squad, Ace realized how helpless he too was. The Farrells did not need a psychologist or a Marine Corps chaplain. They needed an archangel.

·······D.C.I.·······

"YOU CAN'T GET away with this sort of blackmail, Farrell," the Director said without much conviction.

"Ah, but I can, Frank," said the grinning leprechaun on the other side of the Director's coffee table, a seating arrangement used only when the Director was faced with a particularly intractable problem.

"I think he can, sir," Radford agreed. "Whatever he wants and as long as he wants it. The proverbial short hairs, if you know what I mean."

"You'll never get away with it," the Director insisted.

"Sure, isn't it a grand plan now?"

The Director was beginning to hate that phony brogue. And, God damn it, Farrell *had* designed an ingenious operation.

"What if you're caught?"

"I assume the Company will be praying that I'm not."

"We would deny any connection."

"Haven't I been through that with you folks once before?" Farrell grinned cheerfully.

"It's only logistical support, sir," Radford said.

"God damn it, Radford, I believe you've been hypnotized by this bastard."

"No, sir," said his aide reproachfully. "I just don't see that we have any alternatives."

Charm, anger, and intelligence—the three layers of Farrell's personality. And the combination was impossible to resist.

"Our shrinks say that if you do this, you'll discharge all your anger from the, ah, China interlude."

"A consummation devoutly to be desired by the Honorable Company, wouldn't you agree, Frank?"

"I think you'll be a millstone around our necks indefinitely."

"Well, I won't run for Congress." Danny smiled beatifically.

"I have no choice but to cooperate," the Director said heavily. "See to it, Radford." And then, because he had daughters himself, he asked about Farrell's niece. "How's the girl doing?"

"Our shrinks think she'll be all right." There was no merriment on his comedian's face when he said it.

"Do you agree?"

"I think she's a very healthy kid, Frank. I intend to keep her that way."

·······Roger·······

"I DON'T THINK this is a very good idea, Danny," he said as his cousin dialed Rocco Marsallo's private phone number.

"Have to do it," said Danny crisply. "It wouldn't be fair not to warn him."

"Warn him of what?"

"Rocco Marsallo?"

"Yeah."

Roger was listening on an extension phone in his study. "You're doing some bad things, Rocco boy."

"Yeah?"

"You lay off those people, or you're going to find yourself dead."

"Yeah?"

The Marshal seemed to think that was an amusing remark.

"A lot of us don't like what you're doing, Rocco Alfredo. Your friends aren't going to be able to keep the lid on us."

"You don't scare me, punk. Me and my boys are just beginning to have fun."

The line went dead.

"Well, he doesn't scare very easily, does he?"

"I don't know why you wanted to do that," Roger said bitterly. "It's like waving a red flag at a bull."

"It may give him something to think about. His padrino must be under a lot of pressure."

"I asked McNeally why he couldn't arrest Marsallo for Florence's murder. He says that there is no evidence that would make a case, only my speculations."

"Did you pass that word on to Rocco Alfredo?" Danny's eyes narrowed.

"Some of my West Side contacts tried to talk to him. He doesn't believe it. We're dealing with a madman."

"And there's nothing we can do?"

"Rodney Weaver has granted us an extension till the day after Easter. That means we still have almost two weeks. Maybe something will work out." Roger was numb with fatigue and worry. Try as he might, he could not find a single ray of light in the darkness. "We're going to send Noele and Irene to Ireland for Easter. The Irish police have promised full cooperation. Marsallo will have a hard time getting at them there."

"And the IRA or some faction wouldn't dream of blowing up two American women in exchange for a couple of million dollars!"

"I know, Dan, I know." Roger noticed that his hands were shaking again, as if he were a man twenty years older. "I keep asking myself whether it would help if I withdrew from the race for personal reasons. Rod Weaver wouldn't attract much attention with his story if I were out of the limelight. He probably wouldn't even get his face on television."

"It wouldn't do any good," Danny said thoughtfully, "would it? By now Weaver is just an excuse for the Marshal. Hang on for another week. Let's see what happens."

"I know what's going to happen," Roger said glumly. "Someone is going to be killed."

"Don't bet on it," Danny said mysteriously.

At the fringes of his consciousness Roger was aware that Danny had been acting strangely for the last day or two. But he was so preoccupied with his own guilt and powerlessness that he had not found the time or energy to reflect on such odd behavior as phoning the Marshal.

Roger walked to the door with his cousin. A pretty black woman patrol officer waited in the parlor; a squad car was parked in the driveway.

"How's the kid?"

"Up and down. Still groggy from sedation, still screaming at night, and still one tough, very self-controlled young woman during the day. The doctors and Father McNamara think that maybe she's too self-controlled."

"The problem with us Farrells," Dan said somberly.

Dan winked at the woman cop, waved at the officers in the squad car parked in the driveway, turned up his raincoat collar, hunched his head between his shoulders, and walked briskly through the early April rainstorm to his Porsche.

Curtains of raindrops danced on the street in the lights of Danny's car. Then the Porsche slipped down the thick avenues of trees, around the corner onto Ninety-first Street, and disappeared in the mists and darkness.

···*Noele*···

"SOME CROSSES DON'T go away when you will them to go away, do they, M.N.?" said Father Ace.

"No, they don't," she admitted ruefully.

Noele was back home in her own room, which she had promptly straightened up so that Moms wouldn't worry about it when visitors came. She had been looking over her family-history notes and charts when Father Ace came to visit her.

She quickly hid her *dossier*—another word she'd learned from Jaimie.

"Some people have to learn you must live with things for a while before they become okay again," Father Ace continued.

"I guess."

"Some people also have to learn that even though they are cute and smart and popular and maybe a little psychic, they please God the most by learning to live with suffering and tragedy."

"I suppose."

"You don't sound enthusiastic about your discovery of limitations, M.N."

She laughed. "Someday I'll understand it all, Father."

"In a little while, M.N., it's going to be mostly all right, and then later on almost completely all right; but it's only going to be perfectly all right, probably, when you have a husband of your own."

Father Ace never gave easy answers.

"How long will it take, Father Ace?" she asked, solemn again and even a little humble.

"The research says six months to six years, if ever."

"You can forget the 'if ever' bit."

"For sure."

"And the six-year bit too."

"For sure."

"Somewhere in between," she said judiciously.

"For sure."

"Tough little bitch, huh?"

"FOR SURE!"

She swung at him and he ducked, but not in time.

"Speaking of such things," she said, brightening a bit, "how's Jaimie Burns? I called him yesterday and pretended to be mad because he hadn't phoned me, and then after a while made him laugh. What do you think?"

"You like Jaimie Burns a lot?"

"Really, Father," she said, and sniffed.

"He's a wonderful young man."

"Tell me about it."

"Wonderful enough to marry?"

"Maybe. Someday."

Father Ace considered her very seriously. "If you want to keep that possibility open, then you'll have to treat him very delicately for a while."

"Which means?"

"Which means . . . well, keep on making him laugh a lot."

"Is *that* all?" Noele felt greatly relieved. "That's no great big deal."

Then Moms came into the room and Father Ace began to kid her about her new short haircut, his usual way of paying women compliments. And, of course, he was trying to cheer her up. Noele realized that Father Ace not only liked Moms—which was easy enough for any man, even a priest, because Moms was so pretty—he also respected her.

"You're not going to Ireland?" he said when he was leaving.

"The decision isn't final," said Moms, sounding very much like a mother.

"Yes, it is," Noele said. "I'm staying right here and learning how to shoot a twenty-two; that's *much* safer than going to Ireland."

"What a bloodthirsty daughter you have, Mrs. Farrell," Father Ace said, kissing her on the forehead. Then he and Moms left her alone.

Noele was still having bad times, especially at night, when in her dreams three ugly demons out of the black pit of hell pursued her with fiery swords and caught her just as she woke up screaming. Each time that happened all the pain, the shame, the anger, and the fear erupted again and made her want to keep screaming.

Her classmates came to see her, having been told that she'd been in another auto accident. She worked in a desultory way at homework, trying to keep pace with what was happening in school. She bickered with Moms and fought with Roger and was moody with Eileen Kelly and Michele Carmody.

Why did it have to take a long time? Why couldn't you suffer all at once and get it over with?

She was still kind of half in love with Daniel and thought he looked especially cute in his neatly fitting suits and gorgeous ties. That would have to wait, however. What would not wait was the Farrell family mystery. Noele knew that she had to solve that one, even if people did laugh at her and call her the Jane Marple of Beverly Hills, because that was the only way any of the Farrells would ever be safe again.

She pulled the dossier out from underneath her pillow. Somewhere in all those notes there had to be an answer.

She looked around her room. Sophomore hop bid, pictures from the grammar school formal, Paul Newman and Robert De Niro, herself and Eileen Kelly on the catamaran. A whole corkboard full of pictures of Jaimie—in white tux, blue graduation hat and gown and, of course, blue and gold football uniform. Teenage room.

She turned on The Who very quietly. So the window didn't shake much.

Typical teenage rape victim. Well, I have better things to do than feel sorry for myself. She started once again to page carefully through her notes.

There were times when she thought she'd seen the solution. In the blink of an eye it was there and then gone. Maybe Daniel did kill Clancy, but there was a stubborn part of her personality that doubted that.

To begin with, there was something funny about Bill Farrell's will. Probably involving Burke and Grams. Was that when they started to love each other? Noele considered it. It was much more fun speculating on that than trying to catch up on the trigonometry lessons.

Yes, that was probably how it started. Someday Grams would have to tell her the whole story, just to get it off her chest.

Anyway, Clancy, who must have been *really* gross, had that terrible Marshal person kill Florence Farrell and tried to kill Danny, even though Grams and Burke did their best to stop them.

When Clancy died, the three boys inherited equal shares in the firm, though Grams controlled the shares as long as she lived. Then Danny died and his part of the firm was split between Roger and Monsignor John. And all of it someday was going to come to her.

Noele was drawing another chart. Funny how all the lines converged on her. Of course, with Danny coming back, some of the money and some of the stock in the firm would go to him.

Well, he ought to have it all. When she finally had her inheritance, she would give it all to him. That would end the trouble. She stared at her chart glumly, and then looked at herself in the mirror over her dressing table.

Really, you do look okay.

Back to the chart. Daniel might have pushed Clancy down the stairs because he was angry about the death of his mother. That was what Roger had told her, and Roger seemed to believe it was true. Brigid might have pushed him down the stairs because she hated him and she wanted to marry Burke—only Burke's wife was still alive and their affair was pretty torrid anyway.

Same thing for Burke. He was a very violent man, Noele thought, beneath his smooth smile and courtly manners. He could have done it in an outburst of temper. Maybe to protect Grams.

Noele jabbed her notes with an angry pen.

Gross city.

Clancy had probably pushed Grams around. And Grams had made Burkie put up with it. But had Roger and John known? That might have a lot to do with what happened. Roger or John might have shoved him down the stairs because he had goaded them to lose their tempers, something he often did when he was drunk, even though he was nice to his boys at other times, taking them to ball games and things like that.

They might have wanted the money too, but she really didn't believe that. Neither her uncle nor her father was very much interested in money, and Brigid was running the firm then, anyway.

Moms? There was something mysterious about Moms. Always had been. And Clancy had torn out after her family at the cocktail party before supper and violently objected to her marrying Danny. Moms wasn't the shoving type. On the other hand, if she were mad enough she might just do it, but Danny would have married her anyway, if he'd come back from China, so she didn't have to kill Clancy. Moms, if she killed anybody, would be much more likely to do it at the end of one of her long, gloomy moods than in an outburst of anger.

Why did Daniel go to China, or Japan, or wherever he'd been, if he loved Moms? Would he have really married her?

For a moment Noele thought she saw the solution; then it slipped away again. She threw her pen on the desk in disgust.

Daniel Xavier Farrell was charming and funny and cool and cute. And scared. Was he that way as a young man?

It certainly seemed like he was the one who killed Clancy, probably not intending it. But it couldn't be that simple. There was still a piece of the puzzle missing.

She shoved aside her notes and her chart, then decided she'd better tear them up into little pieces and throw them down the toilet (not do something *dumb* like Roger). After she disposed of her documents, she came back and glared unhappily at the trig book.

Well, she'd call Jaimie Burns first.

But he wasn't home.

·····*James III*·····

JAIMIE WAS WAITING inside the door of the J. C. Penney store in a shopping plaza in Elmhurst. His own car, a battered old junk Plymouth, was in the shopping plaza across the way, where he'd been instructed to leave it.

Mr. Farrell had called the night before and told him tersely where to be and when. Jaimie felt a little bit the way he did before a football game, maybe because he was leaning lazily against the door of the J. C. Penney the way people said he leaned against the locker-room wall before a game began, a picture of disinterested indifference.

While all the time great fierce fires were burning within him.

He was quite incapable of hating other human beings or wanting revenge. When he decked a wide receiver from another football team, his only goal was to protect the Notre Dame end zone. He had no ill feeling toward the other player, did not try to hurt him, and would have regretted it if he was hurt—though he figured the other player knew the risks he was taking when he went on the football field against the Fighting Irish and ventured into Jaimie's defensive zone.

He felt the same way on this lovely Friday morning in April. There was a job that had to be done, just as the Notre Dame end zone had to be defended. Jaimie had no more thought that they would fail than he ever thought that Notre Dame would lose a football game. Sometimes, however, Notre Dame did lose. And Jaimie Burns felt a touch of fear in the pit of his stomach. Then he thought of Noele and the great fierce bog fires burned again.

At precisely 10:30 a silver gray Citation, indistinguishable from thousands of others in the Chicago area, arrived at the J. C. Penney door. The driver honked three times, briefly, like the call of a wild goose, and stopped a few yards beyond the door. Jaimie pulled his driving gloves out of the pocket of his battered old brown Windbreaker and walked casually around to the driver's door. Mr. Farrell opened the door and then slid into the passenger's seat. He was dressed the same way he had told Jaimie to dress—old jeans, a white T-shirt, Adidas running shoes, and a Windbreaker that looked like every other Windbreaker in the world.

Jaimie drove the car, at Mr. Farrell's instructions, back into Elmhurst and down a side street into a deserted ally behind a supermarket. "You park your car in the shopping center across the street?" Mr. Farrell asked.

"Right."

"We're going to have to change license plates a couple of times. This set first." He handed Jaimie a license plate and a screwdriver.

"I want it done in a quarter of a minute. The screws are loose, and leave them that way."

They scrambled out of the car, Mr. Farrell to the front and Jaimie to the rear, quickly changed the license plates, and jumped back in.

"These license plates we hang on to, because when everything's over, we put them back on, right here."

"When will someone notice this car's missing?" Jaimie asked as they drove out on the state highway and turned south.

"Not till the evening rush hour. And by then the police will have no trouble finding it in the parking lot here. Someday we'll have to thank the owners. I gave them a full tank of gas as rental."

He laughed lightly, as though he were an experienced spy in a le Carré novel.

"Where are we going, sir?" Jaimie asked, pretending for a moment that Mr. Farrell really was George Smiley.

"We're joining our friends for a little game of golf at Far Hills. See the golf bag in the back seat?"

Inside his driving gloves Jaimie's hands were wet, something that had never happened before the kickoff at a Notre Dame game.

They drove on in silence till Mr. Farrell instructed him to turn off the state road into a cross street. "Turn right here, Jaimie," he said at the gates of a large, old Catholic cemetery. "We're going to visit a few graves."

They parked the Citation on one of the back lanes and walked among the tombs to a grave site of a family named Finerty. Both the grandparents had been born in County Kerry in the 1860s and both were dead by 1905. It wasn't an easy life in those days, Jaimie decided.

They walked slowly back to the car while Mr. Farrell glanced at his watch—a bit nervously, Jaimie thought. Then they drove to the far end of the cemetery, out another gate, and down an old asphalt road. They turned off that road into an even smaller gravel lane with trees on either side.

"This is where we hope the rain will wipe away the trails?" Jaimie asked.

"The only part we're leaving to luck and not much luck. The morning weather forecast said eighty percent chance of rain. Even if it doesn't rain, there will be no traces except ordinary Chevy tires, ordinary running shoes, and ordinary men whose appearance you wouldn't remember even if you happened to drive down this road and see them, which isn't very likely. Pull over there, by that big oak tree."

Jaimie did as he was told. As he stopped the car Mr. Farrell reached into the backseat, zipped the cover off the old golf bag, and removed from among the clubs a couple of cylinders that he began to fit together.

"A Russian make, the best rifle in the world. They liked me so much on the commune that they made me one of the leaders in the local civil defense force, which was supposed to hassle the Ruskeys if they came over the border. They were so impressed with what I could do with a rifle that they even let me teach some of the young bucks of the commune how to operate it. If I'd stayed there long enough, I might have put together my own squad and started a revolution."

"Then you haven't fired one in several months?"

Mr. Farrell grinned cheerfully. "You would mention that! Don't worry, it's a good weapon, and I'm only going to be shooting at close range. Take these glasses and see if you can pick out our friends.''

The binoculars were no bigger than opera glasses, but had enormous power. Someone with good technology was assisting Mr. Farrell.

"There are three men teeing off at the seventh hole. Two of them short and stocky. And the third one is tall, with a mustache.''

Mr. Farrell took the glasses. "The beer drinker is Dubuque Salerno. The fat guy in the blue pants is Little Tony Caputo. And the old guy in the white sweater is the Marshal himself. Are they the ones, Jaimie?''

"Not the slightest doubt,'' Jaimie replied firmly.

"Perfect timing. We'll have our little encounter on the eighth green. You see where that is?''

"About a football field and a half away, on a side of a hill, and with no obstructions between us and them.''

"Good boy.'' Fully assembled, the Russian rifle appeared deceptively simple—two rods, a stock, a scope on the top, a clip of ammunition. Mr. Farrell jammed a few more clips into his jacket pocket. "When they tee off up there for the eighth hole, I climb out of the car, hide between the car and the oak tree. When I'm finished, I climb back into the car, and we retrace our way to the cemetery and then back to the state highway into Elmhurst. At the stoplight after the town limits you take a right, then the seventh street to the left, then the third street to the right, then one block, then to the left down the alley. Got it?''

"Got it,'' said Jaimie tersely. "Perhaps I should turn the car around now.''

"Yes, that's a good idea.''

Jaimie backed up the Citation and turned it to face the direction in which they'd come, careful to leave no tracks on the muddy shoulder at either side of the road. The golf course was now on his left, on the driver's side of the car, and the cemetery was on his right. He raised the field glasses again. "They're putting on the seventh green. Then they'll have to climb the hole to the eighth tee.''

"Okay.'' Mr. Farrell fastened another, shorter rod to the barrel of the Russian rifle—a silencer, Jaimie assumed.

If this were in a movie, I'd think it was corny.

"Mr. Farrell, why don't you climb into the backseat of the car, and then get out of the back door on my side? That way no one will see you getting out.''

"Jaimie, there are some people I know in Washington, well, in Virginia, who would like to get to know you. Okay. Here I go over the seat.''

Mr. Farrell placed the Russian rifle in the backseat and then very clumsily climbed over into the back of the auto.

An old car turned down the road from the asphalt street behind the cemetery and raced by them at a high speed.

"Teenagers, probably, Mr. Farrell. Where there's one car, there's likely to be others. Don't take any chances.''

"We'll scrub it if we have to.''

"They're teeing off at eight,'' Jaimie said, watching the golfers with his field glasses.

"It's protection we're looking for, Jaimie, not revenge.''

"Absolutely,'' Jaimie replied. "They're terrible golfers, Mr. Farrell. Each one of them hit the ball into the pond. They're teeing off again.''

Mr. Farrell ducked suddenly into the backseat. "Here comes another one of your teenage friends. You think we've stumbled onto a drag race, Jaimie? Why the hell aren't they in school?''

"Spring vacation, sir."

"Damn. . . . Hey, Jaimie, do me a favor and call me Dan. Our mutual friend will tell you I'm still a teenager at heart."

A second, and then a third, car raced down the road, spitting gravel in either direction. Unless one of these punks was like Jaimie himself, and hence very unusual, he would barely notice the silver-gray Citation at the side of the road next to the big oak tree. And almost certainly nobody would catch its license plate. Moreover, since kids who drove 1975 Dodges did not read the newspapers, they probably would never know what happened in the Far Hills golf course on this Friday morning.

Yet another car raced by, but this one slower and more cautiously. A kid with some sense. And therefore dangerous. "I think that's the last one, Dan."

"Do you think he noticed us?"

"I don't think so. He had his eyes glued on the road, eager to catch up with his buddies but afraid to drive as fast as they do."

"Where are our friends?" Mr. Farrell was a cool, collected Navy officer on the bridge of an aircraft carrier toward which the Zeros were diving.

"They're coming down the hill from the tee and walking around the pond. I think it's time," Jaimie said. A faint breeze touched his face lightly. The smell of the coming rainstorm was already in the air.

Mr. Farrell opened the back door of the car, rolled out, and closed the door, leaving it slightly ajar. Then he worked his way with his elbows and his knees through the dead leaves to the base of the oak tree. There were three rows of trees shielding him from the road, and he was completely invisible from the golf course.

Jaimie glanced quickly to his right. Through the trees to his left were the headstones of the cemetery. No one in sight.

He focused the glasses on the eighth green. The three men were on the fairway, fifty yards off the green, still protected by the trees that encircled them. Each of them dubbed his approach shot.

The last time you over-hit a lousy chip shot, Jaimie thought ironically.

As he watched them climb over the bunker and walk onto the green, Jaimie felt all of his muscles tense, as they did when the kicking team roared down the field, eleven men who wanted in the worst way to nail him to the turf.

Then he heard a click from where Dan Farrell lay on the ground. And one of the men threw his hands up into the air as his face disappeared. That was Dubuque, the man who had shoved the .22 into his throat.

He will never hurt Noele again.

Then another click, and the second man, Little Tony, doubled over, whirled around, and fell to the ground. He tried to stand up again and then, a fraction of a second after another click at the foot of the oak tree, he sprawled on the eighth green, twitched for a few moments, and lay still.

The Marshal was running across the green toward the crest of the hill and safety. There were three rapid clicks from the base of the oak tree, and Rocco Marsallo staggered, his white sweater crimson with blood. Then he crumpled to the earth, rolled down the hill, and crashed into the pin that marked the eighth hole. The pin wavered and fell on top of him, the red of the flag dripping into the red of his blood.

Jaimie lowered the binoculars and watched Mr. Farrell throw aside an ammunition clip. Jaimie almost shouted at him to pick it up, but recollecting what he should be doing, Mr. Farrell salvaged the clip and shoved it into his pocket.

almly and coolly he placed a second clip of ammunition on the top of the Russian rifle. There was another rapid succession of clicks and the three bodies on the green jumped and shook as several more rounds of bullets burrowed into each one of them.

And once each of them had been a little baby, dearly loved by the mother who had suffered to bring him into the world.

Jaimie committed them to God's care, turned over the ignition key of the car, and, hardly noticing that Mr. Farrell had slipped into the backseat and slammed the door shut, drove cautiously down the gravel road, like a sixteen-year-old trying to pass his driver's ed test.

Behind him Mr. Farrell was retching silently.

"Don't worry, Jaimie," he said, "nothing coming up. I haven't eaten for twelve hours."

Jaimie drove through the cemetery and out onto the state highway, observing the speed limit with infinite caution. He followed the signs to Elmhurst and, after making all the turns that Mr. Farrell ordered, he pulled into another deserted alley.

"Here's where we change the license plates, Mr. Farrell," he said tentatively.

"Okay, let's change them, Jaimie, and, God damn it, call me Dan."

The license plates were changed quickly. Mr. Farrell was ashen, but perfectly self-possessed.

Jaimie drove down Washington and turned left into the Forest Preserve.

"No one in the parking lot, Mr. Farrell, I mean Dan. No neckers on Friday morning."

"Do teenagers neck these days?"

"Only when the girl wants to," Jaimie replied.

They laughed louder and at greater length than they normally would have. But the tension eased.

"Some things don't change," Mr. Farrell said. "Well, let's get this phase over with."

They scrambled out of the car. Jaimie jammed the license plates and the spent ammunition clips into the golf bag and threw the superb binoculars in after them. A pity. He zipped the bag up. "You attach license plates number three, Mr. Farrell. No, not number one, number three. I'll throw this into the river. Then we'll drive back to Elmhurst and restore license plates number one."

The Desplanes River was running rapidly, the last of the snow on its banks melting. Jaimie leaned over the Forest Preserve bridge and very carefully dropped the golf bag into the river. It floated for a moment, then changed its color and sank beneath the surface. "Let them figure out how it got there, if they ever find it," he said aloud, and then turned and walked calmly and confidently back to the parking lot, where he found Mr. Farrell had finished changing the license plates.

"Okay, we're on license plates number three," Mr. Farrell said, "which will be connected neither with the car's theft nor with what happened at the golf course. Now we'll ride back to our alley and put on license plates number one, stuff license plates number three under our jackets, park this car in front of J. C. Penney's, walk across the street, get into your car, and go back to the Neighborhood."

They went back to Elmhurst on Lake Street, careful to drive under the speed limit and avoid yellow lights. Then, in Jaimie's Plymouth, they drove down the Eisenhower—or the Congress, as Democrats still called it—to the Ryan and back to the Neighborhood.

The operation had worked perfectly, except for the teenager in the last car. "You must love her very much, Dan," Jaimie said solemnly, at the top of Mandrake Parkway.

"Love who? You mean Noele? Oh, my God, Jaimie, you have it all wrong."

··*Roger*··

HE HAD PLAYED golf at the Club, his first decent exercise since the campaign started. And even though the second nine was rained out, Roger felt better for the exercise. It had cleared his mind and enabled him to make a decision he ought to have made long ago. He'd returned to his home on Jefferson Avenue resolute and determined.

Irene was typing something in her tiny office at the end of the upstairs hallway. He did not disturb her, but went immediately to his own study and began to compose a statement announcing his withdrawal from the gubernatorial race, citing threats on the lives of his family as the reason. That approach might take some of the sting out of Rod Weaver's story, and might even create enough of an uproar to force the Mob to take action against the Marshal.

Maybe I ought to withdraw from life, too.

The thought of self-destruction, a few weeks ago an absurd fantasy, was becoming more attractive every day. What was there left in his life?

Automatically he flipped on the television set to pick up the 4:30 local news, something he had never done before he had become a candidate. Maryjane Hennessey was informing the 4:30 viewers that a sudden rainstorm had ended Chicago's finest Friday since September, that Secretary Haig was in intensive negotiations with Chancellor Schmidt, and that three reputed members of the organized crime underworld had been shot to death at the Far Hills golf course.

It took a few moments for the implications of the third story to penetrate Roger's mind. He turned away from his typewriter and listened impatiently to the stumbling weather announcer and to a faintly bored correspondent trying to make sense of the latest Schmidt-Haig negotiations.

And then Maryjane again, a radiantly lovely combination of beauty, virtue, and competence.

"Three reputed Chicago gangsters were killed by sniper fire at Far Hills Country Club late this morning. The most prominent of the victims was Rocco Marsallo, also known as Robert Marshal and Rocco the Marshal." Maryjane permitted herself only a tiny smile—even mobster's deaths were not supposed to be funny. "Marsallo, sixty-four, was reputed to have been a longtime power in vice and loan-shark activities of organized crime in Chicago. He was also alleged to be an enforcer, or 'hit man,' for organized crime in this area and was reported to be greatly feared because of his cruelty. Even though several brutal gangland slayings were attributed to him, he was never convicted of any of them. The other two victims were associates of Marsallo's known as Dubuque Salerno and Little Tony Caputo.

"The county sheriff's police said that the three men were killed by rifle fire. The weapon may have been of foreign manufacture, possibly Russian. Police sources believe that the killings were a professional gangland-style execution, although they admit that sniper fire is an unusual method for a gangland execution. The investigation continues, but there are no obvious suspects in the crime.''

As she talked, the camera followed three stretchers as they were carried from the rain-soaked golf course clubhouse to the sheriff's police ambulance, and then joined the investigation on the eighth green.

A handsome young county cop in a yellow rain slicker talked to a reporter who was protected by an umbrella. ''The subjects were shot by the alleged perpetrator from a very great distance,'' he said in the computerlike tone cops think is a sign of the professional law enforcement specialist. ''The perpetrator's marksmanship was excellent. Two of the victims died almost instantly, and the third, Rocco Marsallo, alias Robert Marshal, died a few seconds later, while trying to run up the side of the green to safety. The alleged perpetrator fired several more rounds of ammunition into their lifeless bodies, presumably to make sure they were dead.''

''Will the rain hurt your search for clues, Sergeant?''

''All phases of the investigation are continuing,'' said the cop grimly.

Roger turned off the television and ripped the half-typed sheet out of his typewriter, crumpled it, and tossed it in the wastebasket.

It was almost too good to be true. The council must have reversed itself and overruled the Marshal's padrino.

But since when did the outfit use Russian rifles?

·····················*John*·····················

ACE MCNAMARA, BACK from pre-Easter confessions, poked his head into the pastor's study. ''I just heard it on the radio, John. Those three men that attacked Noele have been killed.''

''Are you sure?'' John's hands were trembling.

''There wouldn't be three other guys named the Marshal, Dubuque, and Little Tony, would there?''

''Who did it?''

The Ace unbuttoned his cassock. ''The sheriff's police feel it was a professional, organized-crime hit job. The Lord works in strange ways. Are you coming down for supper?''

''In a few minutes. I have a phone call to make.''

''Monsignor Keegan, please. . . . Ed? John Farrell. I thought you might want to tell the cardinal, before he reads about it in the papers, that Channel Three is going to syndicate my interview program. It will be small at first, only twenty or twenty-five markets. And, Ed, it doesn't take any more work for the program to be on one channel or on fifty, so I'll still be able to handle my obligations here without any difficulty.''

Keegan muttered something about the canonical requirements for permission to engage in public entertainment.

''Anytime you want to make a fight out of it there's a few hundred teenagers dying for a chance to picket the cardinal.''

As he hung up the phone John thought that Irene would be proud of him. And

Danny too. They had both helped him. He was stupid to think of Danny as a rival. Life might begin again now for all of them.

Or maybe it wouldn't.

He was already late for supper. He stood up from the chair, hesitated for a second, then sat down and punched out an Evanston exchange.

"Father Fogarty, please. . . . Dads? This is Slick Farrell. . . . Hard feelings, Dads? Me? . . . Yeah, sure. I know. I'm doing a great job. . . . Well, Dads, when you're thinking of next month's character assassination, you might want to make the point that my ego trip is now going to be syndicated around the country, only thirty markets to begin with, a lot less than Phil Donahue. . . . What cities? Oh, Boston, New York, Los Angeles, San Francisco, Dallas, Houston. Nothing very big, Dads. . . . Sure, I know. Everybody in the diocese will be proud of me. Just like always."

Tonight he had earned his martini.

Noele

PALM SUNDAY WAS a Rembrandt day, with clouds and sunlight, brightness and shadow, racing each other across the sky. Noele struggled out of bed at ten o'clock and turned on the radio to fortify herself with rock music for the rest of the day. The radio announced that there were tornado warnings for the South Side of Chicago.

"Gross."

Even allowing for Father Ace's injunction that some crosses had to be carried slowly, Noele was displeased with herself. She was not shaping up the way she ought to. Not only was she lagging behind in her homework, acting mean to her friends, bickering and bitching all the time with Moms; worst of all, she had abandoned the folk group on Palm Sunday because she was still afraid to go out of the house. She *had* to be better by Holy Thursday.

The dreams were not as bad as last week, and she didn't think that she woke up screaming as often in the middle of the night. But the demons were still after her. Now she was more afraid during the daytime, afraid even to go out of the house.

She turned her hi-fi up full blast and then jumped into the shower, leaving it nice and cold so she would wake up. *Actually* she didn't *look* violated anymore, just a few scratches here and there. It was all in her head now. But then she started to shiver and turned the shower up to warm. She kept shivering. The demons followed her even into the shower. She dressed in her prettiest lace underwear—the kind that Moms said prostitutes used to wear twenty-five years ago—not that Moms didn't wear practically the same thing. Then she put on her best white satin robe, went down to the kitchen, and poured herself a cup of coffee and a glass of grapefruit juice. If she were a real teenager, she'd drink Diet Pepsi instead of coffee.

She took the coffee and juice into the parlor, remembered that she hadn't turned off the stereo upstairs, and decided that it didn't matter anyway. She opened the Sunday newspaper and thumbed through the papers till she found the story she knew would be there, a long feature article about the three "crime syndicate'' hoods who had been shot on Friday morning. She was sorry they were dead, just as she would be sorry anybody was dead. But she was not at all sorry that she didn't have to worry about them anymore. Still, the demons in her head didn't care much whether their real-life counterparts were alive or not.

She read the article through carefully a second time and a paragraph near the end caught her eye. A witness had reported seeing two men parked in a car on a road near the golf course at the time of the killing. But he could not identify the men or the make of the car and did not note the license number. ''For all practical purposes,'' the article said, ''it was one more gangland murder, more spectacular than most, but still destined to be just one of hundreds of unsolved crimes.''

Poor men, they never had much of a chance in life. Well, God would have to take care of them in his own way. Just so long as they weren't in the part of heaven she was in.

Daniel had promised to stop by sometime Sunday morning, and she hoped he would come before her parents got back from Mass. There were a couple of things she had to straighten out with him.

''Well, at least you wear a suit and tie to church on Sunday,'' she greeted him when he came in the door.

''And at least you're out of bed on this Sunday morning.'' He brushed her lips lightly as he always did and fingered her long, red hair. ''Looking quite happy and lovely, too.''

As usual, her knees became very weak. ''I'll bring you a cup of coffee. Do you want some bacon?''

''Yes, please,'' he said humbly. ''Can I help?'' He trailed her into the kitchen.

''Sit in the breakfast room,'' she said, ''and don't distract me. I'll put some cinnamon rolls in the microwave, too.''

''May I read the paper?''

''Really!''

He came back from the living room with the paper and huddled over it.

''Did it feel good to kill those three men?'' she asked as she put a dish with ten strips of bacon in front of him.

Daniel's hand froze in mid-flight toward the bacon strips.

''Don't bother denying it,'' she said as his hand moved back from the bacon. ''When I was doing the term paper that started it all, I looked through your Annapolis yearbook. You were the best rifle shot in your class. And I suppose you learned how to use that Russian thing in China.''

Daniel loosened his tie and shoved the plate of bacon away. Noele filled his coffee cup.

''I was the second-in-command of their local civil defense militia. I taught the others how to operate Russian weapons, old Russian weapons.''

''And what did it feel like to actually kill someone with one of those weapons?''

She had to be pitiless, even though her heart ached for him.

Danny sipped his coffee before he replied. ''Terrible. I haven't been able to sleep a wink since then. Or eat much.''

''I'm sure Jaimie Burns's appetite hasn't been affected at all.''

''Did he tell you?'' Danny rose halfway out of his chair.

''Really. The paper said two men. Who else but you two?''

Danny sank back into his chair and began to absently munch on a strip of bacon. ''We had to do it, Noele. He would have killed you, and maybe your mother and grandmother, too. In my mind I have a clear conscience. But my stomach isn't ready to agree yet.''

"I don't think you did *wrong*.'' She relented a little bit. "I was going to take gun lessons myself.''

"And assertiveness training?'' He grinned crookedly at her.

In spite of herself, Noele laughed, the first good laugh she'd had in a long time.

"And you and Jaimie, er, persuaded Mr. Weaver to return Roger's papers?''

Daniel's eyes flickered with interest and admiration. "You don't miss much, do you, M.N.? Yeah, we made him an offer he couldn't refuse. He was impressed with what happens to people who refuse our offers.''

"And of course, if he had refused, you and Jaimie would have just meekly walked away, but he didn't know you two as well as I do.''

She laughed again. They both laughed together, as though they shared some great comic secret. But she must be serious. Now was her chance to ask the big question.

"Did it feel the way it did when you killed Clancy?''

Daniel was thunderstruck. "Me—kill Clancy?''

"He told you at that cocktail party that he'd ordered the execution of your mother, and you came back and killed him.''

Daniel laughed. "Look, M.N. you didn't know Clancy. No one believed a tenth of what he said, especially when he was drunk.''

"But you had a fight that night. Why?''

"When Clancy was drunk he said and did crazy things. He was terribly mad at me that night because I was interested in your mother, and her father had sought a grand jury indictment against the Farrells. He would have got over that as soon as he sobered up. Her parents would have been more of a problem, but they died right after I flamed out over Sinkiang.''

"And you fought about Moms?''

"He called her some terrible names. Then I lost my temper and called him some even worse ones. Then he said some things about my mother, and I took Irene's hand and ran away from them.''

"So you didn't believe that he was responsible for your mother's death?''

"Would it have brought her back to life?'' he demanded.

"No, but you killed those men to protect me.''

Danny was annoyed with her. "Only because you're still alive. If you were dead, I would have been broken-hearted.'' He smiled quickly, if not very convincingly. "The world wouldn't be the same without you. But what good would it do to kill them? If I could have kept my mother alive by killing Clancy I guess I would have killed him too.''

"You're still angry about her death, I can tell.''

He jammed his hands fiercely into his pockets and began to pace furiously around the kitchen.

"Sure, I am, and guilty about it, too. She died to save my life.''

"Sit down,'' she told him. "You make me nervous pacing around that way.''

He sat down.

"Amd I haven't killed Burke, have I? Even though he deprived me of eighteen years of my life. What else do I have to do to persuade you that I am not into revenge?''

"Burke?'' she whispered.

"Sure, Burke. I guessed that before the plane crashed. I was furious about it till I got back here, and then I figured, why the hell even the score? It wouldn't give me back the eighteen years. Anyway, I suppose he thought he was protecting herself."

"From what?"

Danny began buttering a cinnamon roll.

"Who knows? I never asked him. Why don't you find out? You're the one who asks all the questions."

"Don't talk with food in your mouth," she lectured him, ignoring his sarcasm. She began to nibble on the bacon herself. "Aren't you afraid that he'll do it again?"

Danny waited till the food was out of his mouth. "No way, José. Old Burkie has finally mellowed. He even kind of likes me."

Burke was responsible for Danny's disappearance. Well, that made sense. "He might have killed Clancy, then?"

"Ask him." Danny was impatient again, out of the chair and pacing the breakfast room. "All these questions are crazy, M.N. What does it matter who killed Clancy?"

"Daniel Xavier, can't you see that murder is the key to everything?"

"No, I can't see it, Mary Noele, I can't see it at all. What makes you think it was a murder? Manslaughter at the most, and maybe only an accident. Now, for the love of heaven, M.N., drop it. Will you please?"

"I won't drop it. Here, drink some more coffee. And finish the bacon, too. You look starved. Anyway, I want to know who pushed Clancy down the stairs, and I won't stop until I find out. After that everything will work out. If you don't tell me, I'll find out some other way."

Daniel's Paul Newman eyes glittered sharply. "If I tell you, Noele, you might hate me."

"Tell me anyway."

Danny hesitated, then waved his hands in a gesture of futility. "There's no stopping you. All right, I'll tell you. It was probably Roger."

"Roger! I don't believe it."

He sat down again and nibbled on the one remaining piece of bacon. "See, I told you you wouldn't believe me."

"Oh, I believe you. I mean, I believe you think you're telling the truth. But I'm astonished that you think it was Roger who pushed Clancy down the stairs."

"I can't say for sure. Brigid sort of hinted to me that I shouldn't talk to the poor man—her words—about it. He certainly acted kind of odd toward me the next couple of days."

She almost told him that Roger thought that it was he who had given the fatal shove.

"How can you prove that you didn't give your uncle the final shove?"

"Prove? Final shove? Noele, this isn't an Agatha Christie story."

"I'm sure it isn't."

Daniel forced himself to his feet, like a boxer who had been down for the count of nine and had lost his patience with his persecutor. "Excuse me, M.N., for violating your language rules, but *shit*. I don't want to talk about it anymore. If you need evidence, you can ask your mother. We were together until midnight that night. Then I went home to find Burke, Bridie, Roger, and the body."

"Twelve o'clock!" exclaimed Noele.

"Burke, I suppose, put the fix in with the doctor and the cop so Roger wouldn't have to stand trial for manslaughter. I never could figure out why. No jury would have convicted him of anything. Poor Clancy was beating her with a cane, like he did when he was drunk. Roger pulled him off. They struggled, and that was that. I suppose Brigid wanted to keep it a secret to protect the family name. Ha, that's a joke, isn't it, Noele?''

Poor man, he had every right to be bitter, but Noele could not find a single word to say to him as he stormed out of the house.

Danny was innocent. But who . . . ? The key problem was still what it had been when she'd come out of Dr. Keefe's office. Who was lying about the time of death, Grams, when she said it was early, or the doctor, who said it was late? Or maybe they were both lying.

Noele absently buttered a sweet roll for herself, raisin and cinnamon.

Or maybe they were both telling the truth.

She took a sip of coffee. It was cold and bitter, and then the roll slipped out of her hand.

Of course. Oh, dear God, how horrible for the poor person!

She had seen it all, as if she had been standing in a dark room momentarily illuminated by a flashbulb.

Then the room was dark again, and she had to think about what she had seen.

Roger and Moms came home from Mass, reporting cautiously that the folk group had done only fairly well without her. Absently she hugged Moms and said, ''That's a nice way of putting it.''

Then she hugged Moms again, to make up for some of the mean things she had said and done in the last two weeks.

Roger and Moms had to leave for a political luncheon on the North West Side. She assured them that she wasn't frightened anymore.

She spent most of the afternoon in the parlor, watching the changing lights and shadows as the tornado warnings continued. The wind whipped the still-naked tree branches, and the rain soaked the sidewalks, which dried quickly in the sunlight only to be soaked again.

She went upstairs to dress, put on a spring suit, and picked up her guitar. Too long since she'd used it. She went back to the parlor and strummed it, playing the chords for the Holy Week liturgies and humming the tunes softly.

Poor, silly, stupid people, she thought. None of them evil, except possibly Clancy, and he was crazy some of the time.

Now she had it in her power to free them from the swamp, give them all new lives, painful new lives, but new lives just the same.

Who was she to dare to do a thing like that? I'm only a nosy, bitchy, flaky teenager. What do I know about life? Maybe I ought to forget the whole thing.

Who do you think you are anyway, Mary Noele?

She sighed. It was St. James's epistle, she remembered, that said the truth shall make you free, free to live again, only none of them—not Brigid or Burke or Moms or Roger or Monsignor John or Daniel Xavier—none of them wanted to be free. None of them wanted to live again.

She went back to her room, turned off the stereo, and removed The Who. She replaced them with her favorite singer, Mary O'Hara, the wonderful woman who had been a cloistered nun and came back into the world because she was convinced her vocation was to sing. Noele played the last band on the record— ''Lord of the Dance.''

''I am the dance which will never, never die.'' And Noele could see the little Irish feet as children danced to the song.

Damn right, she murmured to herself, making up her mind.

She lifted the record off the player, fitted it carefully into its jacket, and turned off her stereo. Then she donned a yellow rain slicker and walked down the stairs and out of the house to the squad car in the driveway, where a pretty black patrol officer was reading some geek named Tolstoy.

"Officer Day, could you, like, take me out for a short ride in the patrol car?"

"Sure, honey." She put the paperback book on the seat next to her. "We both need the exercise."

"I want to go to the Courts."

Officer Day hesitated. She knew that Noele had been left at the Courts, tied up and naked.

"No problem," Noele insisted.

"Okay," Officer Day said finally. "If that's what you really want."

"I want," said Noele.

She remembered lying cold and hurt on the asphalt, unable to move or scream for help. But the Courts were still a kind of sacred place. After Easter she would come back and play basketball or volleyball. She would no more give up her Courts than she would give up her Flame or her Jaimie.

The rain had stopped, and the clouds were racing rapidly across the sky, the way humans raced through life. The naked trees seemed to be twisting toward heaven, begging God for the life and the covering and the beauty that spring would give them. And maybe even for the kids on whom the trees had looked down for so many years.

In the story Jesus told, the man who found a treasure buried in the field had to give up everything to buy the field and gain the treasure. He was forced to choose between the old and the new. Some of the members of her family would have to give up everything to choose a second chance. They wouldn't want to do that.

You must lose your life to find it. That's what this next week was about.

That includes you too, Mary Noele.

All right.

Noele Marie Brigid Farrell!

I said all right. All right?

All right.

Stop laughing at me. You're as bad as Moms.

All right.

Well! *You* can laugh at me if you want.

All RIGHT!

Then Noele saw a broad beam of sunlight move lazily down Jefferson Avenue, like a sophomore girl slouching home from the Ninety-fifth Street bus on a warm, Indian summer afternoon, daydreaming about a senior boy to whom she had never spoken a word in her life. Dark clouds moved ahead of the sun as though running from it, and Jefferson Avenue was bright all the way to Ninety-fifth Street.

Noele knew the demons from hell could still touch her, perhaps even hurt her. But they would never prevail against her. She heard in her memory Mary O'Hara's voice and imagined the little Irish kids dancing on the Courts with the Lord of the Dance.

"We can go home now," she told Patrol Officer Day.

DANCE TEN

Boogaloo

"Start with my toes
you old Ghost
Spirit the soles of my shoes
And teach me a Pentecostal
Boogaloo
Sprain my ankles with dancing
Sandal around my feet
to roam with you in the rain
and feel at home in my footprints

Oh! look at me spinning,
Sprinkling, tonguing, teaching
Winsoming wondrous steps
lift me, how?
We'd better quit now,
too all dizzy down giggly
Stop—you're tickling
(My funnybone's fickle for you)
Stop—I'll drop
I'm dying, I'm flying

With your winding my feet and
legs and waist
Lassoed
Stop chasing fool—I'm racing from you

Don't catch me
Do!
I'll drown
Oh, drown me—most
For I love you so
You old Ghost!"

"Poem for Pentecost"
NANCY GALLAGHER MCCREADY

. . .

"Then down to hell I took my way
For my true love's deliverance
And rose again on the third day
Up to my true love and the dance"

"My Dancing Day"
A Medieval Good Friday Carol

Roger

GOOD FRIDAY DINNER was a somber event at Brigid's, another dogged tribute to the family customs begun by the determined Julie Farrell. Always whitefish and light dry white wine, though in Julie's day the Farrells could hardly have afforded Pouilly Fuissé. No potatoes, no dessert, no frivolous conversation.

Are we supposed to be waiting for the Lord's return? Roger wondered. Why would he come back to this crowd?

Brigid and Irene cleared away the fish plates. Noele solemnly poured the tea—no coffee on Good Friday at Brigid's—from the silver service in the middle of the table, and she replaced the teapot as if returning the ciborium to the altar after Communion. Then she seated herself next to Brigid at the head of the table.

"This is a good night to bury the family skeletons," she said, her swamp-fire eyes scorching the room. "If we're going to start living again, everyone has to sacrifice. And tonight truth is the sacrifice. We are all going to tell the truth for a change."

The room was silent, as if someone had just died. It was absurd for a mere child to make such demands, and yet so great was the force of her determination that no one was able to speak or move. Noele had cast a spell that paralyzed them all.

"I have to get back to the rectory to rehearse for tomorrow's liturgy," John said, glancing fretfully at his watch.

"I'm *sure* they need you, Uncle Monsignor. Well, you're not leaving. First of all, Grams, you're going to tell us the truth about Great-Grandfather William Farrell's will."

Brigid was parchment pale.

"And if I don't?"

"Then I will."

"Give me a cigarette, Burke."

He lit it with trembling fingers, and Brigid took one long drag on the cigarette, nervously snuffed it out, and began to speak in a tone of voice appropriate for priests chanting the office of the dead. "It all started when William and Blanche Farrell had twin sons. The second of them, Clarence, was her favorite, supposedly because his birth had been so easy, and Martin's so difficult. I know that sounds crazy, but that's the kind of a woman she was. There had to be a good son and a bad son. Clancy could do no wrong and Marty could do no right. Bill wasn't much interested in raising the boys. He lived for the firm, I guess because it was an excuse to escape from Blanche and her crazy pieties. Oh, yes, she was as pious as they come. . . .

677

"Well, Marty grew up to be one of the finest human beings who ever walked the face of the earth. Everyone loved him—but his mother. And Clancy grew up to be a dull, harmless weakling, poor man—harmless, that is, unless he had a temper tantrum or was drunk or someone suggested that he wasn't much of a man. He flunked out of Loyola—Blanche wouldn't let him go to school away from home. Marty graduated with honors from Notre Dame, where he was in the Navy ROTC, and then went into flight training. He married Flossie, God be good to the poor woman. About the time they were engaged, Bill found me working in a friend's kitchen and liked my spunk. He thought I would put some of it into his Clancy. Blanche hated me from the first day I came into the house.

"William wanted Marty to inherit the firm. But Marty told us all he would have no part of it. He was going to be a career Navy officer. That was one way to escape from Blanche's perpetual bitching. So William drew up a will leaving everything to Clancy. Marty went off to the war, and Clancy took over much of the firm's new work—defense plant construction. Bill insisted that I help because he was afraid Blanche's little boy would make a godawful mess of it.

"Which he did. And then he tried to bribe some government inspectors. I took the money to them, thinking I had to do what my husband told me. Then your father, Irene, got wind of it and would have indicted us if Bill hadn't had a word with Bob Jackson, who was attorney general then.

"Bill was so furious at Clancy that, without telling us, he had Parnell Kennedy, Burke's father, change the will, leaving every last cent to Marty, who was at sea on the *Hornet*. Bill died without warning three months later, the same week as Parnell, and then two months after that Marty died trying to return to the carrier in the battle of the Philippine Sea. Ran out of gas, they said, God rest him. So you see, Danny, every cent the Farrells have is rightfully yours."

Danny's face was an expressionless mask. "My father didn't want it," he said coolly, and "neither do I."

"Bill probably would have calmed down and changed the will again, but he died too soon," Brigid added with a helpless gesture of her hands. "And that started everything."

"When you found the will in your father's files, why did you tear it up, Burkie?" Noele shifted her searing eyes to the grim old man at the other end of the table.

"What right do you have to ask?" he demanded gruffly.

"The right of someone who has benefited from your dishonesty," she replied sharply, a picture of affronted womanly justice as old as the race itself.

Burke shifted his position in the chair and toyed thoughtfully with a spoon. "I agree with Bridie. Bill would have changed his mind if he had lived a little longer and calmed down. He knew that Martin would not touch the company. And while he liked Flossie, he wouldn't have wanted the firm to pass into the hands of the Careys, which is what would have happened. Besides, Noele, the Careys' auditors would have found out how Clancy did business. Conlon was still waiting in the wings with a grand jury. Clancy would have gone to jail. So would your grandmother. I tore up the will to protect her."

"And then, when Danny's mother asked a few innocent questions, Clancy had her killed by that terrible man, Marsallo."

Burke nodded, now no longer a warrior but a shriveled old man. "We tried to stop him. We didn't think he'd do it. I thought I had talked him out of it, but that pious old witch hated Floss even more than she hated Bridie."

"And you were supposed to die too, Daniel, only your mother saved you at the last second, giving her life for yours."

"I don't see what good all of this does, M.N.," Danny said sadly. "We can't change the past."

"We can change the present."

"So Dad was telling the truth that night," Roger interrupted. "My God, Danny. . . ."

"I didn't believe him," Danny said, burying his face in his hands as if he did not want his family to see his pain. "Maybe because I didn't want to believe him. Anyway, what difference does it make?" Danny rose from the table and began to stride back and forth in the dining room. "They're all dead. Drop it, M.N. Let the dead bury their dead."

"I won't let the dead bury the living," she replied tartly. "Go on, Roger, ask Daniel Xavier what you want to ask him."

"But you killed Dad, didn't you, Danny? Didn't you push him down the stairs?" Roger felt like an actor in a play. How did Noele know what his lines would be?

"Certainly not," Danny said impatiently. "Why would I do that? Where did all this nonsense start about my killing Clancy? He wasn't worth killing."

"Are you sure?" said Roger.

"Of course he's sure," Irene said serenely, her face incredibly beautiful. "I could have told you that if you had asked. After the cocktail party he dragged me out of the house and drove to Joliet and back, trying to calm down. I had never seen him so angry."

"Because Clancy claimed to have killed his mother?" Roger asked, still confused.

" 'Course not, Roger." Noele was impatient with his slowness. "Because Grandpa Clancy had said terrible things to Moms. Daniel Xavier protects the living, not the dead."

"This is all crazy." Danny leaned on the table, his eyes beginning to burn with anger. "Why would anyone think I killed Clancy?"

"Because you were supposed to be a hot-tempered, unstable young man. You had been thrown out of the Navy, for defending a black man. Wasn't that enough proof you were unstable? Killing Clancy in a temper tantrum was the kind of thing you might have done."

"No, it wasn't," he insisted. And then, shrugging at the foolishness of trying to convince them, he demanded, "Who says I killed Clancy?"

The room was heavy with silence.

Finally Noele spoke. "Grams," she said softly, "you lied to everybody, didn't you? And to make it believable, you even told Burke that Danny had threatened to come back and kill you, too."

Burke came to life, leaped out of his chair, and hit Brigid in the face twice with the back of his hand. "You murderous, lying whore!" he bellowed, the magnitude of her betrayal made even worse by the power of his wounded love.

Danny jumped across the room, twisting Burke's arm behind his back. "Don't you ever do that again, you son of a bitch," he shouted, "or I'll do to you what I'm supposed to have done to Clancy."

Danny released him. Burke slumped into a chair, his hands quivering like those of a palsy victim as they covered his face.

"So that's why Burke bribed someone to wreck your plane. He wasn't going to let you come back and kill Grams."

"I figured that out in China. Who else would have had the connections? I even guessed that it had something to do with the firm.'' Danny shrugged listlessly. "So what?''

"You should have killed me when you had the chance,'' Burke murmured.

"You *are* worth killing, Burke,'' Danny conceded with a bitter grin. "But I decided it wouldn't give me the eighteen years back.''

"Don't you want to know why Brigid lied?'' Noele sounded like a mother superior in the pre–Vatican Council church reproving a guilty third-grade boy.

"No, not particularly,'' Danny said, his lips pressed tightly together.

"Well, I'm not going to let you run away. Didn't Grams kind of hint to you that Roger might have done it to protect her from another beating by Grandpa Clancy?''

"But, Mother, I couldn't have killed Dad.'' Roger was so astonished, he could not manage to be outraged. "I was playing gin rummy in the Country Club basement.''

"So now we know what actually happened,'' Noele said sternly. "Everyone was told that it was Danny because he was leaving the country and wouldn't be around to defend himself. And Danny was told that it was Roger, because he and Roger were best friends, and he wouldn't do anything to get Roger in trouble. Obviously it had to be somebody else.''

"All right, child, I'll confess,'' Brigid said wearily. "I killed him. I'm glad I did. I should have done it years before.''

"One more lie, Grams. Won't you ever learn to tell the truth? You wouldn't have had to cover up. There were marks on you from the beating. You could have argued self-defense if there'd been a trial. You were not protecting yourself, Grams, you were protecting somebody else, for whom even an involuntary manslaughter charge would have been a disaster, the end of everything important in life.''

"Who would that be?'' Burke asked, sounding like a man who'd just come out of a coma.

"Someone who, when he was a young priest, always returned to the rectory before eleven o'clock at night, but someone Grams couldn't call at the rectory that night until twelve thirty because she knew he wasn't there.''

"I'd do it again, if I had to,'' John said in a barely audible voice. "He was beating Mother with a cane. I pulled him off her. Then he came at me with the cane. I yanked it out of his hands, and he started pounding me with his fists. I put up the cane to defend myself and pushed. He lost his balance. I reached out to grab for him. I think I did, anyway. I wanted to. Maybe I didn't. He fought me off, lost his balance, tipped backward, and then . . . Oh, God, I don't know. . . . I was glad to see him tumble down the stairs. I wanted to sing with joy when I saw his head crack against the floor and the blood come pouring out. I hated the bastard. I wanted him dead.''

The room was as silent as a cemetery.

"No jury would have convicted you,'' Burke said slowly.

"But he would have been finished in the priesthood,'' Brigid said, "sent off to a monastery or exiled to a poor mission country. It wasn't John's fault. I made him lie.''

"No, you didn't,'' John insisted. "I was happy to lie. The priesthood was the only thing that mattered. I was dumb enough to think I could cling to it by lying. I'm sorry, Danny.'' John's hands were clenched on his knees, his head bowed over as if awaiting divine retribution. "It seemed harmless: there wasn't going to be a police investigation. Burke took care of that. You would be away for a couple of years. When you came back we would straighten everything out.''

"Do you think it was, like, a mortal sin?" Noele's voice sliced through the heaviness of the room.

"Mortal sin? Diminished responsibility, self-defense? Telling Roger and Burke that it was Danny was a worse sin.'' John extended his hands as if pleading for absolution he would never receive. "If he'd been lying on the driveway and I hadn't seen him and I'd backed the car out and run over him, it wouldn't have been a mortal sin, and yet I would have been so happy to have killed him. I'm glad he's dead. That's sin enough. There has been no peace since then. Everything else in my life is a sham.''

"But, John.'' Irene spoke for the first time since the beginnning of the conversation. "You weren't responsible. You stopped a man from beating your mother, maybe even from killing her. Of course you're happy he's dead. He was a monster. Just like we're happy those men who might have attacked Brigid and me and Noele again are dead. And if Danny isn't angry, ought you not to forgive yourself?''

"I'm not angry, Jackie,'' Danny said, tears in his eyes for his cousin's pain. "Moms, like, you're the only one in this room who has any common sense.''

"He was my father,'' John sobbed. "He wasn't a monster all the time. I can never forgive myself.''

Brigid's head was buried in her hands, her body erect and frozen, like Lot's wife in the tundra, a shape of suffering woman never to be thawed. "Maybe that's the trouble,'' she said. "We Farrells don't know how to forgive ourselves.''

"Then it's time we started,'' said Irene crisply.

"Really!'' Noele agreed.

I'm a minor character in this drama, Roger thought. I've lost my mistress, I've lost my wife, I've lost the image of the little boy I thought I loved. Maybe I've found myself. And my lost lovers have become my new friends. A little late to grow up, but not too late. Now I'd better make a friend out of my brother.

"It's all over, John.'' Reassuringly, he gripped his brother's shoulder. "We'll work it out. I'll help. It's going to be all right, now. Isn't that, true, Danny? . . . Where's Danny?''

"He ran away a few moments ago, so quietly that no one noticed. Just like he did in 1963.'' Noele sighed. "Well, you can't make a man grow up who doesn't want to. We might as well go home now. I guess that's about everything.''

Not quite, Snowflake, Roger thought, some of his newfound and painfully won maturity slipping away. Not quite.

Burke

IT WAS THE first night since their marriage that they had not slept in the same bed. There was so much anger and hatred between them that they would never sleep in the same bed again.

They were both dead. Only the burial remained.

And yet they ate breakfast together; deprived of speech by their disgust and fury, but at the same table because even horror cannot wipe out the habits of a common life.

She wore a white linen robe, and her red hair hung over it loosely—even this morning a timeless beauty. But Burke no longer desired that beauty. Rather, he was repelled by it. It was her beauty for which he had tried to kill.

Somewhere deep inside him there was sorrow for her pain. She had suffered much and had done her best. But there was no truth in her. No truth and no trust. Not her fault perhaps. It was the way she was made, a greater monster than he was.

Then Danny appeared at the front door, came in the house, and, quite uninvited, sat at the table with them, bright and chipper as the morning sunlight streaming through the breakfast room windows.

"Sure," he said in his fake brogue, "it looks like neither of you had much sleep. Would you toast me some English muffins, woman of the house, and some bacon, too? I have to fly to New York, and I won't be doing it on any empty stomach."

Brigid provided the muffins and the bacon. Burke filled his coffee cup again. Neither of them spoke.

"I'm glad we were after getting the air cleared last night," Danny said cheerfully. "Since I'm about to become a permanent part of the New York literary scene, I'll be at least confident that the firm will be in good hands."

Burke broke his vow of silence. "Is that all you can say?"

"Ah, sure, 'tis yourself that wants some great fucking denunciation, is it now?"

"It would be appropriate," Burke agreed. "We did damn you to almost two decades of prison in China."

Danny dismissed it with a casual wave of his hand. "Best thing in the world for me. Nothing like a stint in a beehive to straighten a man out."

"You're daft," said Brigid.

"That kind of forgiveness isn't possible," Burke said dubiously.

Danny took Burke's hand and Brigid's in his own, and placed them one on top of the other. Burke and Brigid tried to break away, but he stopped them. "You're to make peace, and that's an order. Do you hear me, woman of the house?"

Bridie nodded, tears slipping down her cheeks.

"Good enough for you." Danny kissed her lips tenderly, rose, and walked toward the back door of the house at the end of the breakfast room. "And yourself?" He clasped his hand on the doorknob, his eyes, now ice blue, frozen on Burke.

"I hear." Burke's voice was raw and weary.

Burke broke the silence as Danny was about to walk through the doorway. "Forgiveness cannot be that easy."

Danny turned around, held up a waggish finger, and winked like a mischievous leprechaun. "If it isn't that easy, Burkie, it isn't forgiveness."

He put his head back in the door with a parting shot. "And you remember that, woman, when you go home to see your sister. Next week."

After he had slipped away into the sunlight, Burke and Brigid remained motionless at the table, her hand on his, both of them too shy to face immediately the pain and the delight of beginning again.

IT HAD BEEN a long Good Friday night. She and Roger left the house on Glenwood Drive and drove around for two hours in the Seville, calmly and cordially discussing their problem. Roger was kind, sweet, and generous, making it all the more difficult for her. He knew what had to happen. His only regret was that so many years had been wasted, a waste for which he blamed himself completely, try as Irene might to insist that it was mostly her fault.

Roger was the only innocent. He was a man who had suffered for what others had done, not courageously, perhaps, but at least uncomplainingly. Even to the end he did not complain. And now he was genuinely brave. Irene's regrets were as vast as a mountain range—heavy, implacable, insurmountable.

After her failure later that night to talk Danny out of his plan to flee to New York, Irene drove home at 2:30 in the morning, thinking with considerable irony that she had begun Good Friday with two men—three, counting John—and begun Holy Saturday with none.

The next morning Noele was furiously angry at her.

"Really, Mo-*ther,* I'm sure you and Roger can't continue like this. He is your husband; you're his wife. And it's not good for either of you to be sleeping in different bedrooms."

"Did it ever occur to you, young woman, that my sex life is my business, not yours?" She drew her robe more tightly around her, as if to protect herself from the withering scorn of Noele's eyes.

"I think it's outrageous." Noele was now becoming dramatic, as she often did in her fights with Irene as a prelude to storming out of the room in tears. "Everyone else is ready to forgive and forget and to begin life again. And you're digging in your heels and living stubbornly in the past."

Danny's rejection and Noele's harsh words combined to become a high wind fanning the prairie fire of Irene's anger, made worse by her guilt at not having protected her daughter from rape and not having helped her much after she'd been brutalized. "You think you know so goddamned much, you smart-assed little bitch. Well, let me tell you, you don't understand anything. You have a lot of growing up to do before you give me advice on how to live my life. Now, get out of my room, and leave me alone. I'll work things out with Roger my way."

Noele burst into tears. "You don't have to be vile about it," she sobbed dramatically. "I merely want my mother and father to act like they're husband and wife."

And then the words came, words that she tried to choke back before it was too late. "You stupid little bitch. Roger isn't my husband," she said, spitting out the poisonous words. "And he isn't your father, either."

Noele's tears stopped. She stood, a statue in jeans and a dark blue and red University of Arizona sweat shirt, frozen in the doorway of Irene's office. She watched the facial expressions on the statue begin to change as the little computer beneath the red ponytail worked away. I never should have said it, never, never, never.

She waited patiently, knowing that an outburst of anger and hatred would take place. Will Noele hit me? She had every right to.

I've lost all my men, and now I will lose my Christmas child.

"Shit," said Noele, her own sternly enforced language code collapsing. And then in rapidly ascending tones, "Shit, shit, oh, *shit!*"

"Don't use that kind of language, young woman," Irene said faintly.

Then, astonishingly, Noele was on her lap, her arms wrapped tightly around her neck, her head against her mother's breasts.

"Oh, Moms, poor, poor wonderful Moms, you're the only good person in our whole family. And I bet you did it for me, too."

How little you understand your own children.

"You even are our legitimate daughter, Noele," Irene said absently, as though she were reciting facts from the history of medieval English monarchs to a mildly interested classroom. "We were married the day after Easter, and you were born on Christmas Day, three weeks early."

Noele would never know that they were both drunk and that they'd quarreled, and that that particular night of love had been frustrating for the two of them. She was still a Christmas child, conceived in Easter week.

Noele lifted her head, her eyes round with shock. "Well, *really*, I totally *assumed* that I was legitimate."

Irene knew that she and Noele would continue to fight as mothers and daughters must always fight, but that henceforth they would be friends.

"We were married by a priest in California a week before Daniel left for Japan. Then my father and mother were killed in an auto accident and left all the money to the other kids. When I heard that Danny was dead, too, I went into a depression. I thought I was too young to raise a child and couldn't earn the money to support one, and that I'd ruined my life—and I didn't want to ruin someone else's. It was hard to give you up. You were such a cute red-haired baggage even then." She stroked her daughter's hair. "But I thought they would be able to take care of you and I wouldn't.

"Then I met Roger in Berkeley, where I was typing, and he was kind and sweet. I didn't tell him about you, but I thought that after a while, some way, I might be able to get you back. Then Roger became sick and we couldn't have any children. And the people who were taking care of you had terrible troubles. So we adopted you. Your grandmother thought that you were Roger's child. John didn't know who your father was and never asked, or even suspected."

"You never told any of them that Danny was"—she hesitated—"my father?"

"I didn't know what they would do to you if they knew. And I wanted to keep it my secret, a memory of him. It seemed to be the only thing I had."

"Of *course*, you should have kept it secret." Noele was not prepared to find any fault with her at all. "Poor, dear, wonderful Moms."

"I would have told you this long ago if I'd known that you'd react the way you have."

"I'm so glad that you were able to buy me back. I belong with you and . . ." She straightened up and pondered for a moment. Then with a dramatic sigh, she said, "Well, at least I won't have to choose between Danny and Jaimie. I can love them both."

"I hope so." Irene tried not to laugh at her Christmas child.

"That is a relief," Noele said, the computer in her head whirling again. "And I won't have to worry about names because I call both Danny and Roger by their first names. Poor Roger, of course, he'll get all kinds of sympathy from the voters for making a brave sacrifice because of faith and principles. Besides, he won't have any trouble finding himself another nice wife. Maryjane, maybe. She's cool. I'll have to be very good to him, though, so he knows I still love him." She giggled. "I'm the kind that needs two fathers anyway."

"Noele, do you ever stop worrying about how to take care of other people long enough to worry about who's going to take care of you?"

Her daughter's surprise was genuine. "Of course not, Moms, you'll take care of me. That's what mothers are for. . . . Now, what are we going to do about Daniel?"

"We are not going to do anything about Daniel, young woman. The tissues are over there on the cabinet. Pass me some of them too. Daniel is going to New York to stay. He doesn't believe that the past can be re-created, and he doesn't want to spoil anything for anyone else."

"Well, the nerve of him, how *totally obsessive* of him to do such a geeky thing. You just stop him, that's all."

"I tried, Noele. I tried as hard as I ever did in my life. I threw myself at him the way I did the first time in Michigan, when I was only a year or two older than you. It didn't work. Daniel does not want to be a husband or a father. He does not want a family. He does not even want one child, much less a couple more."

"Did he HUMILIATE you?"

Horrified teenage dramatics. Now I can enjoy them.

"No, darling. He did not humiliate me. Daniel couldn't humilate anybody. He is too afraid of me to humiliate me. He merely wanted to run away from me as quickly as he could."

Noele left her mother's lap and began to pace the floor, just as her father did when he was upset. How much she was like him. "The nerve of him, the absolute nerve of him. You're right, Moms. You shouldn't run after him any-more. The son of a bitch isn't worth it."

"Noele Marie Brigid Farrell, don't use such language!" Somehow Noele's anger was hysterically funny. She bit her lip trying not to laugh.

"If I'd known that he was going to act like such a child," she fumed, "I would have let him rot in China!"

Irene's laughter broke through her clenched teeth. Poor Danny had at last encountered his match.

"Mo-*ther,* it's not funny!"

"No, it's not, but you are!"

"Really!"

"He is your father, and my husband," Irene said, permitting the words finally to cross her lips.

"I know. Is he worth it, Moms?"

"Sure he's worth it," Irene said firmly. "He's still magic, even if immature magic."

"I'll bring him back, but then he's *your* problem."

"As long as either of us lives, Noele, he'll be both our problems."

"Really!" Noele said again, leaving Irene's office in a flurry, pulling off her sweat shirt as she went.

In a moment she was back in again, sweat shirt in hand. "You're not pregnant, are you?"

Irene felt herself turn crimson. "I certainly am not . . . and don't you dare suggest to him . . ."

"Just asking."

THE SUN OF Holy Saturday morning smiled benignly through the great glass window across from the ticket counters at O'Hare International Airport. Danny was bemused by the crowds. A lot of people traveled at Easter. Two decades ago Christmas week was a vacation for many people. Now the Easter break was also time off. Nice work if you can get it.

What a spectacular show it had been last night. Noele by sheer willpower and intelligence and psychic sense had undone fifty years of sickness in the Farrell family, probably not permanently, but still enough to give Bridie and Burke, and Roger and poor John, who would weep himself back into happiness, a second chance on their lives.

He had considered stopping at the rectory, as he had at the house on Glenwood. But the Ace would take care of that. Roger and John needed a psychologist who had been a marine.

Irene?

She was not the woman about whom he had fantasized over Sinkiang just before the jet on the great blackbird had flamed out. She was more self-possessed, more intelligent, more poised, more sophisticated. She had grown up during the last eighteen years, and he had not.

She had become a tiny blur of pain in his memory during the years in prison. Then, as soon as he left for Beijing, he found himself longing for her the way an alcoholic yearns for sparkling champagne while wandering in a desert.

The few times they were together had not slaked his thirst at all.

But the bubbling wine was too rich for him.

She had wept last night, bitterly, angrily. She had accused him of turning his back on her, of walking away from his responsibilities. But leaving her was the best thing he could do—for her and for Roger and, of course, for Noele.

The moment he had set eyes on the Christmas child, he knew who and what she was. For one terrifyingly dizzy moment—like a man at the top of a tall building when the clouds are swept away—he was a little boy again. And the radiant, magic smile was his mother's.

No, it was not Florence Carey Farrell. Not quite, yet almost. He had composed himself quickly and covered up with blarney about Irish mythology.

And was happy and sad and proud and confused.

Irene knew that he knew. And readily admitted that Noele was indeed born on Christmas, conceived on their last night together. And somehow no one else knew, not even Noele.

I hung around the Neighborhood mostly because I wanted to know her better. And at least I saved her life, even if I couldn't save my mother's.

And then suddenly there she was, striding purposefully down the length of the ticket line with the Holy Saturday sunlight burning bright in her long red hair, piled high on her head like a flaming strawberry ice cream cone.

Oh, oh, thought Daniel Farrell. Now I'm in real trouble.

She was dressed not in her usual uniform of jeans and a sweat shirt or blouse, but in a V-neck suit whose color could best be described as apricot, somehow matching the burnished flames of her hair and the crackling glow in her green eyes.

Easter dress.

She won't see me, he prayed.

Who the hell else is wearing a Notre Dame Windbreaker?

This dazzling young woman was, unaccountably, the fruit of his loins, a child of fire and water. As Irene would say, a red and green Christmas child. Part giggly teenager, part sophisticated woman of the world, part ancient Irish witch. And each one of her parts was almost impossible to resist. Noele, his ravaged daughter, now superbly triumphant. Violated and inviolable. Wounded and invulnerable. Battered and resilient, indestructible.

For a moment her hair turned from red to black, and he saw his mother. It was 1944 and he was a little boy.

Then the young woman was Noele again.

She saw him and changed her course like a battle cruiser in the Royal Navy seeking to sink the *Bismarck*. "You are totally not flying to New York, you geek," she announced.

"Airhead," he replied.

"Nerd," she said, continuing the litany.

"Flake."

"Gelhead."

"Retard."

"Hodad."

"That's a new one," he said. "What is it?"

They were both laughing, the way they did on the Courts or at Red's.

"Don't slouch; stand up straight," she demanded, like a schoolteacher warning a little boy to put away his modeling clay.

Automatically he obeyed. "What's a hodad?" he said, repeating his diversionary question.

"A way-out, lame retard, which is exactly what you are. You totally have to come home and provide me with little brothers."

"Plural?"

"Moms has lots of childbearing years left. And besides, there are twins in our family."

"I don't want to mess up anyone's life any more than I already have."

I'm winning, he thought to himself. I'm facing her down. My emotions are still under control.

He barely heard the rest of her words, so fascinated was he by the color of her hair, the dancing fire in her eyes, the glittering white rows of her teeth and her superlative gestures as she pointed first at the floor and then out the windows of O'Hare to the general direction of the city of Chicago as she told what he *had* to do.

"It won't work, M.N." He pleaded his case, gesturing like the merchant who used to sell black-market goods in the commune. "I've been dead too long. I can't come back to life, not that kind of life, anyway. I've tried—I really did try. You and Irene and everybody will be better off if I just slip quietly out of your life."

The green fire in her eyes flared up as if someone had thrown gasoline on it. Her jaw muscles turned as hard as the cement of the airport walls.

She's going to lay down her high card now. What will it be?

He saw it coming. Just as long ago, at the crack of a bat, he had been able to see a line drive headed for deep left center when he was playing the third-base line. He would begin to run as soon as the ball left the bat, knowing that he would not be able to get there in time to catch it.

Oh, yes, he saw it coming and knew that his destiny was written on it.

"Daniel Xavier Farrell," she began solemnly. "Father . . ." Her voice wavered and tears formed in the bog fire. "It's time you grew up and totally acted like an adult. You're magic, just like Moms says. She needs a magic husband and I need a magic . . ." Again the quivering lip and now the first tears spilling out of the swamp. "A magic daddy."

Done. Finished. Forever. The wandering days are over, boyo.

He linked arms with his Easter/Christmas mother/child and began to walk with her to the escalator, which would lead eventually to the parking lot of O'Hare International Airport and the rest of his life.

"Tell me about it."

·······················*Daniel*·······················

DANIEL AND IRENE stood toward the back of St. Praxides church. Monsignor John Farrell had presided over the first half of the Easter Vigil liturgy, lighting the Easter fire, singing of Adam's happy fall, plunging the candle into life-giving water. Now the church was dimly lit, and the smell of extinguished candles and incense teased the nostrils with the memory of the dramatic blessing of the waters and renewal of baptismal promises.

All the Farrells had been reborn, one way or another.

John and Roger would need help. Noele had given him his marching orders on that subject during the drive home from O'Hare in the redoubtable Flame. They would have to wait till tomorrow. There was a greater challenge facing him before then.

He and Irene were still drifting in primal chaos, with little idea what the next step in their lives would be. It had not gone well that afternoon. He'd begun by unwisely saying that he had returned because Noele wanted little brothers.

Irene doubtless wanted little brothers for her too. But that was not a good line with which to start. They replayed their argument from the early morning hours, pouring out the anger and the frustration, the hurt and the pain, the betrayal and the disappointment of the last two decades.

Not even their hands had touched.

And then, exhausted by their fury, they sat silently staring at one another, looking for new ways to misunderstand and injure.

"After three hours of shouting we're still in the same room," he said wearily.

And through the argument his desire for her had increased. Fire yearning for water.

Irene was hunched over, her eyes fixed on the carpet.

She looked up and smiled wanly.

"We'll always be in the same room, Danny. From now on. You know that. . . ." She rose from the couch. "I'll make you a cheese omelet. Then we'd better go to St. Prax's for the Easter Vigil. Noele will be furious if we're not there."

"Woman of the house," he yelled after her, "put some ham in my cheese omelet."

He didn't hear her angry response exactly, since she was already in the kitchen.

But she did serve him a cheese and ham omelet.

I should have asked for mushrooms, too.

In the brief interlude between the Liturgy of the Word (as they called the Mass of the Catechumens these days) and the Liturgy of the Eucharist (né Mass of the Faithful), the folk group materialized quietly in the sanctuary, the young women mature and self-possessed in dresses and high heels, the young men not too awkward in suits and ties.

They were herded on tiptoe to the Easter candle by a dazzling young woman in an apricot suit. The candle, with 1982 and the alpha and omega engraved on it, stood firm and upright, its flame heralding the renewal of life with the coming of spring.

A phallic symbol, if one was to take the Ace seriously.

Sure, what else was it?

I'm the candle and the water is next to me.

Champagne for breakfast every morning. Will I be bored with it?

Not likely.

The folk group was ready, awaiting their leader's signal.

He extended the tips of his fingers, searching for his wife's fingers.

They were waiting for him.

"We're going to sing an Easter hymn about young men and young women," Noele informed the congregation. "It's called *O Filii et Filiae*, which is, like, Latin for teenagers. I'll sing a few of the stanzas in Latin in honor of old priests like the monsignor." She giggled and the congregation laughed. "And then we'll do it in English:

> *O filii et filiae*
> *Rex caelestis rex Gloriae*
> *Morte surrexit hodie*
> *Alleluia!*
>
> *Et mane prima sabbati*
> *Ad ostium monumenti*
> *Accesserunt discipuli*
> *Alleluia!*
>
> *Et Maria Magdalene*
> *Et Jacobii et Salome*
> *Venerunt corpus ungere*
> *Alleluia!*
>
> *In albis sedens Angelus*
> *Praedixit mulieribus*
> *In Galilaea est Dominus*
> *Alleluia!*
>
> *Discipulis astantibus*
> *In medio stet Christus*

> *Dicens pax vobis*
> *omnibus*
> *Alleluia!*

> *In hoc festo sanctissimo*
> *Sic laus et jubilatio*
> *Benedicamus Domino*
> *Alleluia!*

"Now everybody sing it in English," Noele commanded the congregation. Everyone did.

> *"Ye sons and daughters, let us sing!*
> *The King of heaven our glorious King,*
> *From death today rose triumphing.*
> *Alleluia!*

> *That Easter Morn at break of day,*
> *The faithful women went their way*
> *To seek the tomb where Jesus lay*
> *Alleluia!*

> *An Angel clothed in white they see*
> *Which sat and spoke unto the three*
> *Your Lord has gone to Galilee*
> *Alleluia!*

> *That night the apostles met in fear*
> *And Christ in their midst did appear*
> *And said, My peace be with you here*
> *Alleluia!*

> *On this most holy day of days*
> *To God your hearts and voices raise*
> *In laud and jubilee and praise*
> *Alleluia!"*

PERSONAL WORD

I WAS PERSUADED to add to several of my previous novels personal Afterwords in which I explained why a priest would write seemingly worldly stories.

These brief notes were supposed to prevent misinterpretation and distortion of the stories and to provide an answer to the mystified truth seeker who asked, with a puzzled frown, "Why did you write that book?"

The Afterwords, however, turned out to be a waste of time. Those who were determined to misunderstand, misunderstood and misquoted them, just as they misquoted the books. I therefore conclude that those who for reasons of malice and/or ignorance will misinterpret this story will do so no matter how much I try to explain it.

But for those who may still be honestly confused, I suggest rereading Noele's brief homily before she leads the people of St. Praxides in singing "Lord of the Dance" and the conversation between John Farrell and Ace McNamara after the episode and finally the paragraphs at the end of Dance Nine, when Noele, in the sacred grove, sees the sun traveling down the street like a sophomore coming home from school.

If the image of Noele and the Church as correlatives, as sacraments of one another, is incomprehensible or offensive, I figuratively wave my blackthorn stick at the geeks and nerds and gelheads who react that way and say God Bless You!

REALLY!

And TOTALLY!